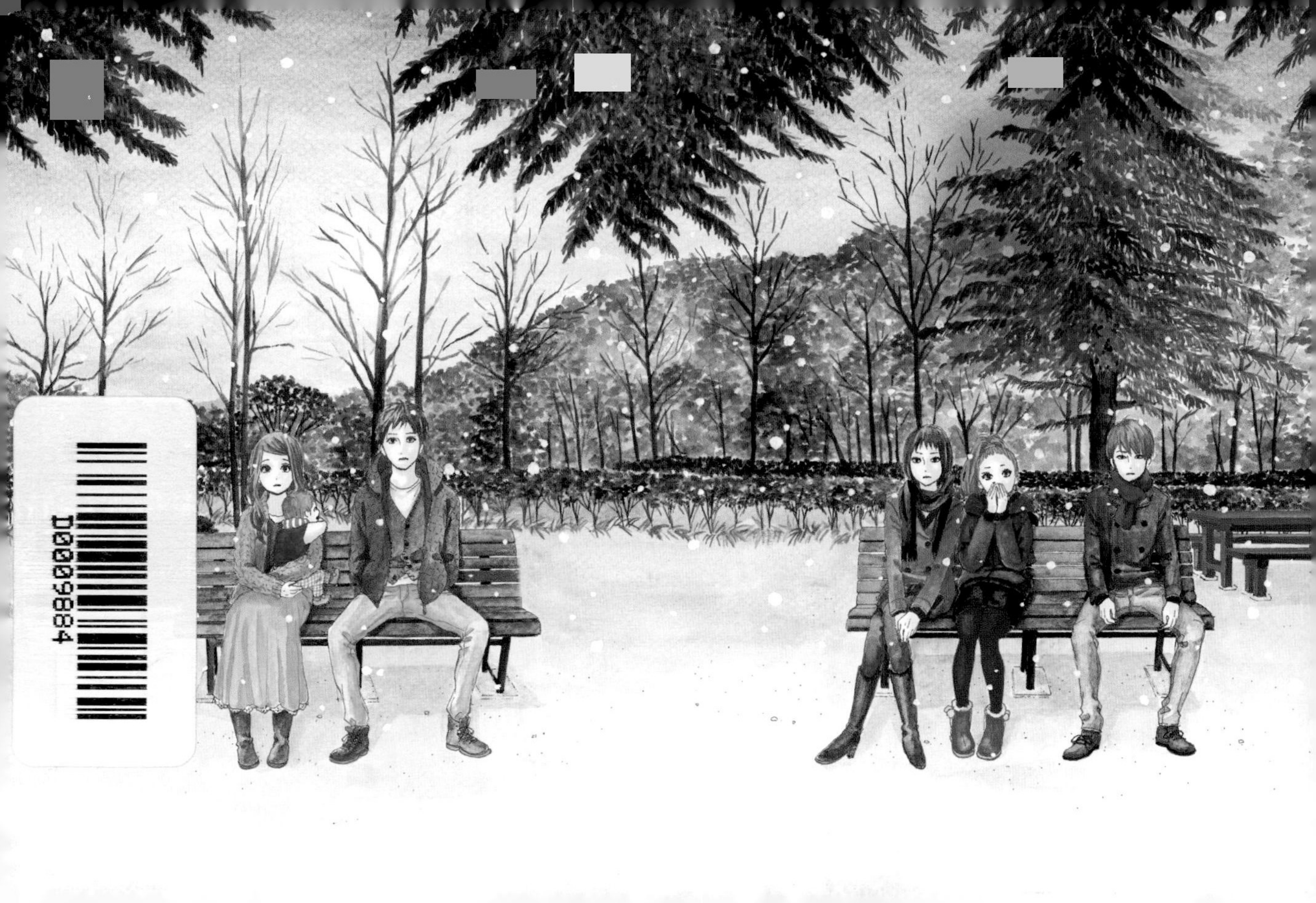

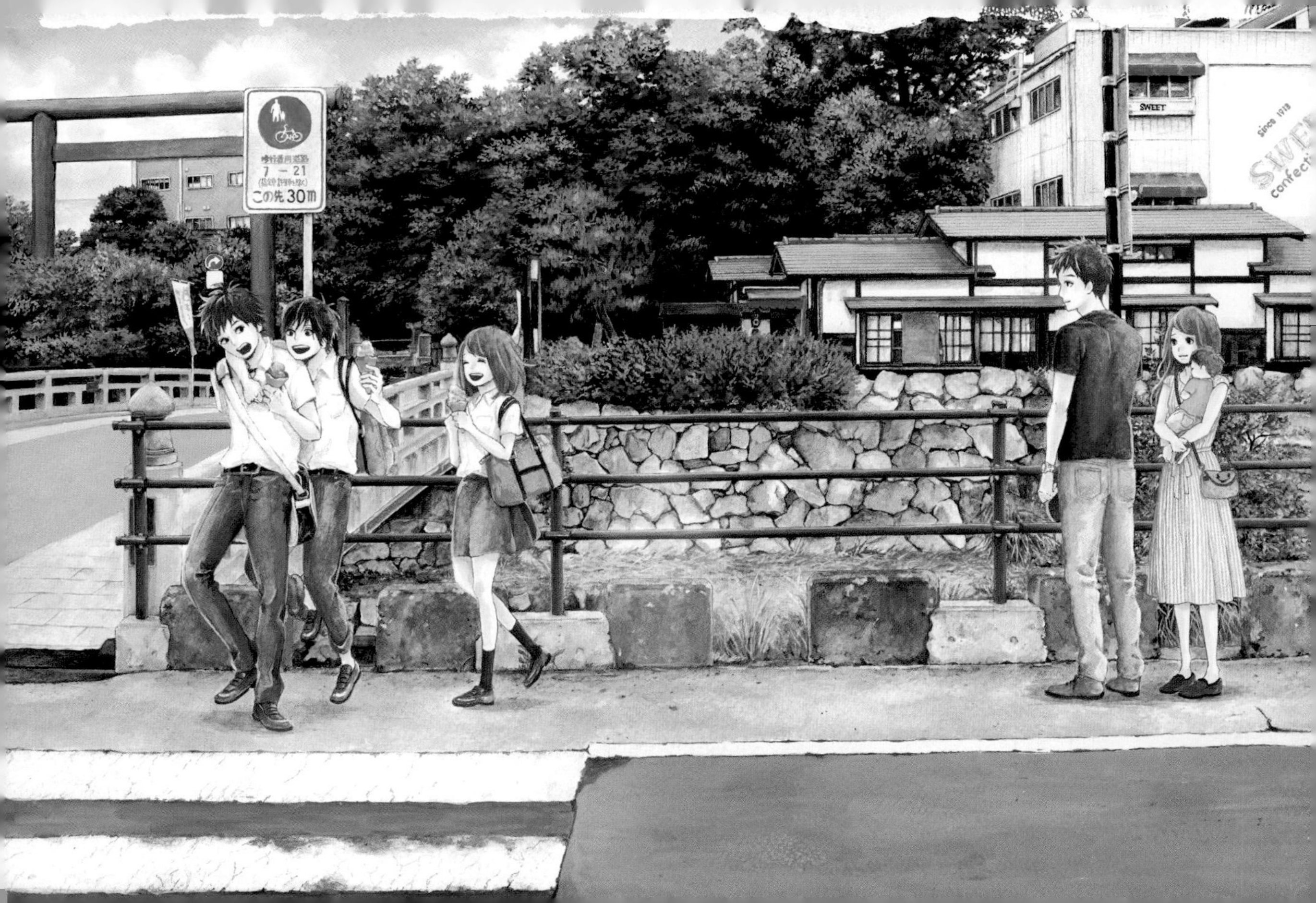
7 − 21
この先30m
SWEET

orange

ICHIGO TAKANO presents

1

the first
volume

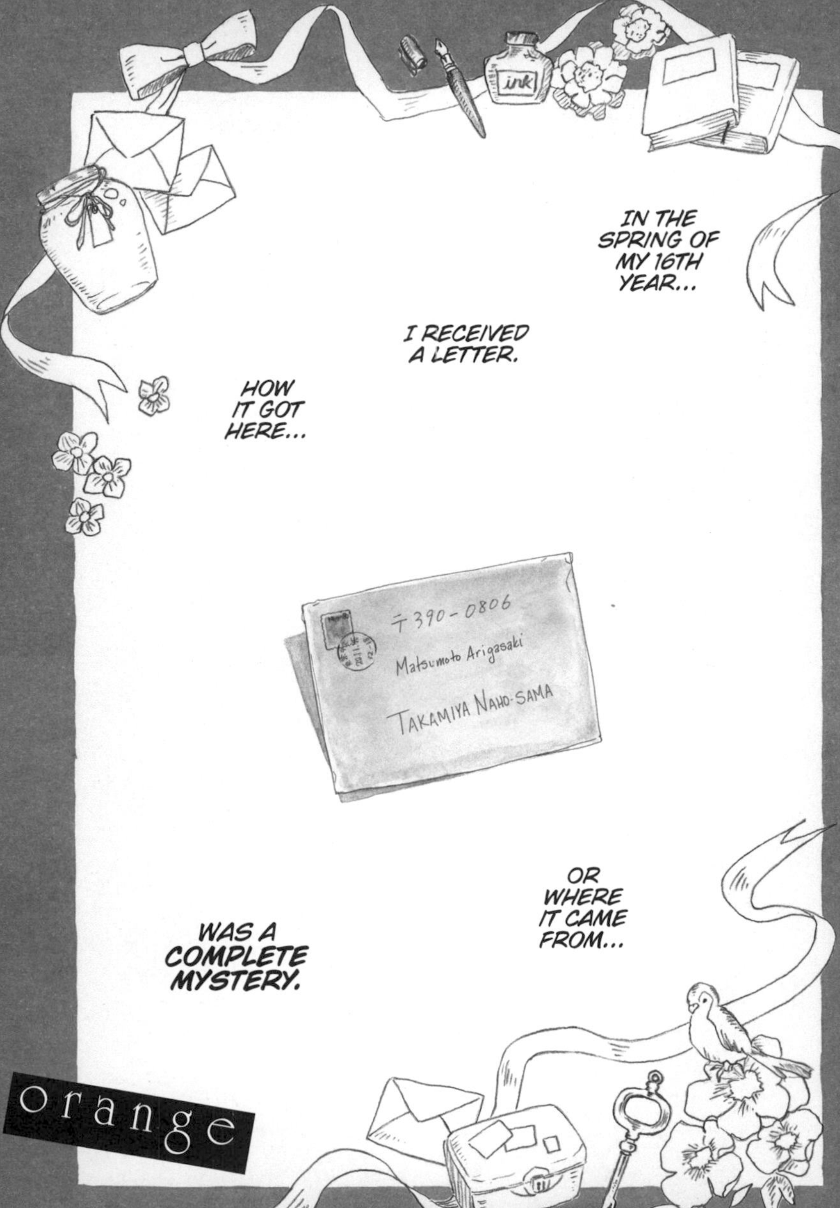
ink
IN THE SPRING OF MY 16TH YEAR...
I RECEIVED A LETTER.
HOW IT GOT HERE...
〒390-0806
Matsumoto Arigasaki
TAKAMIYA NAHO-SAMA
OR WHERE IT CAME FROM...
WAS A COMPLETE MYSTERY.
orange

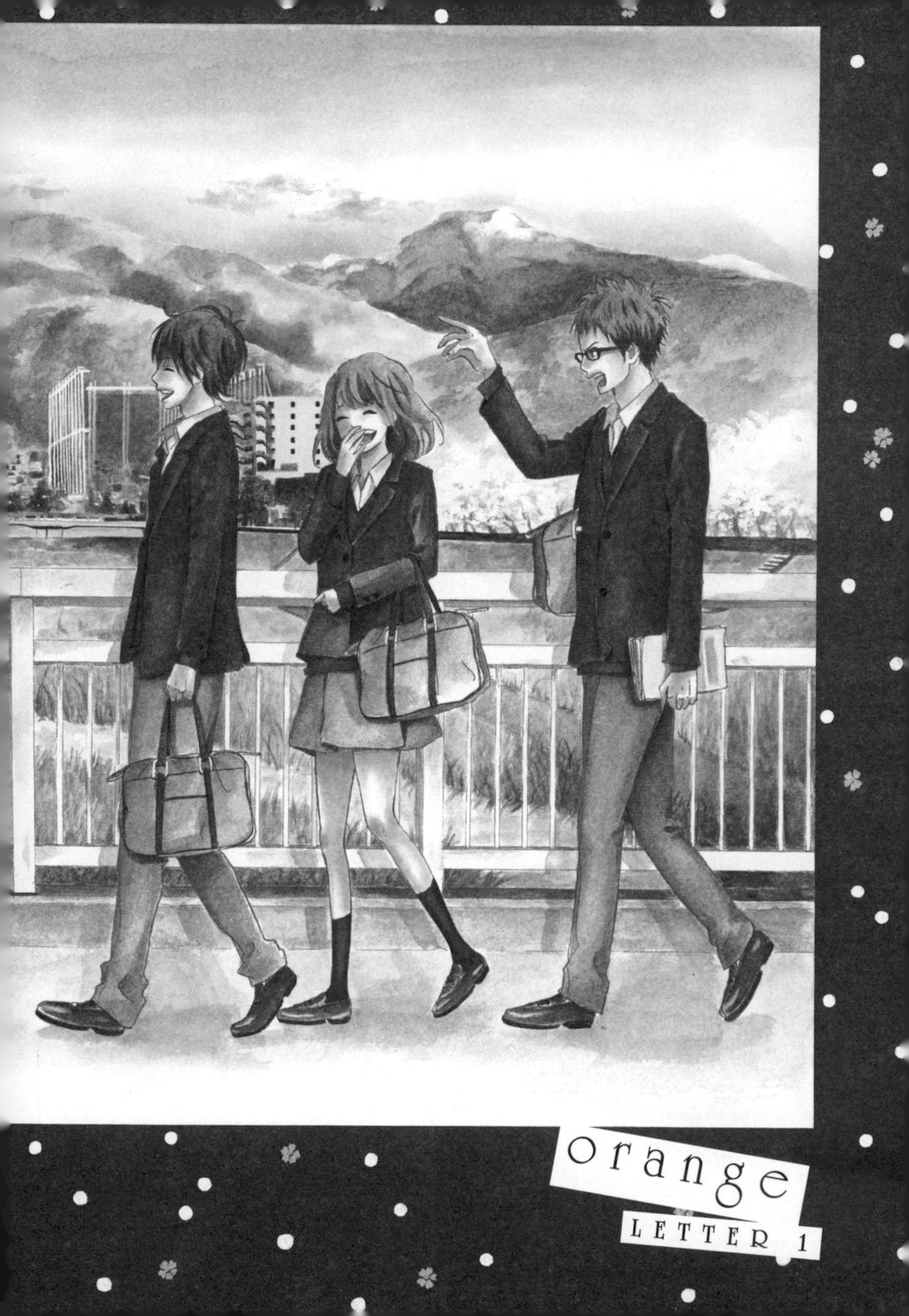
orange
LETTER 1

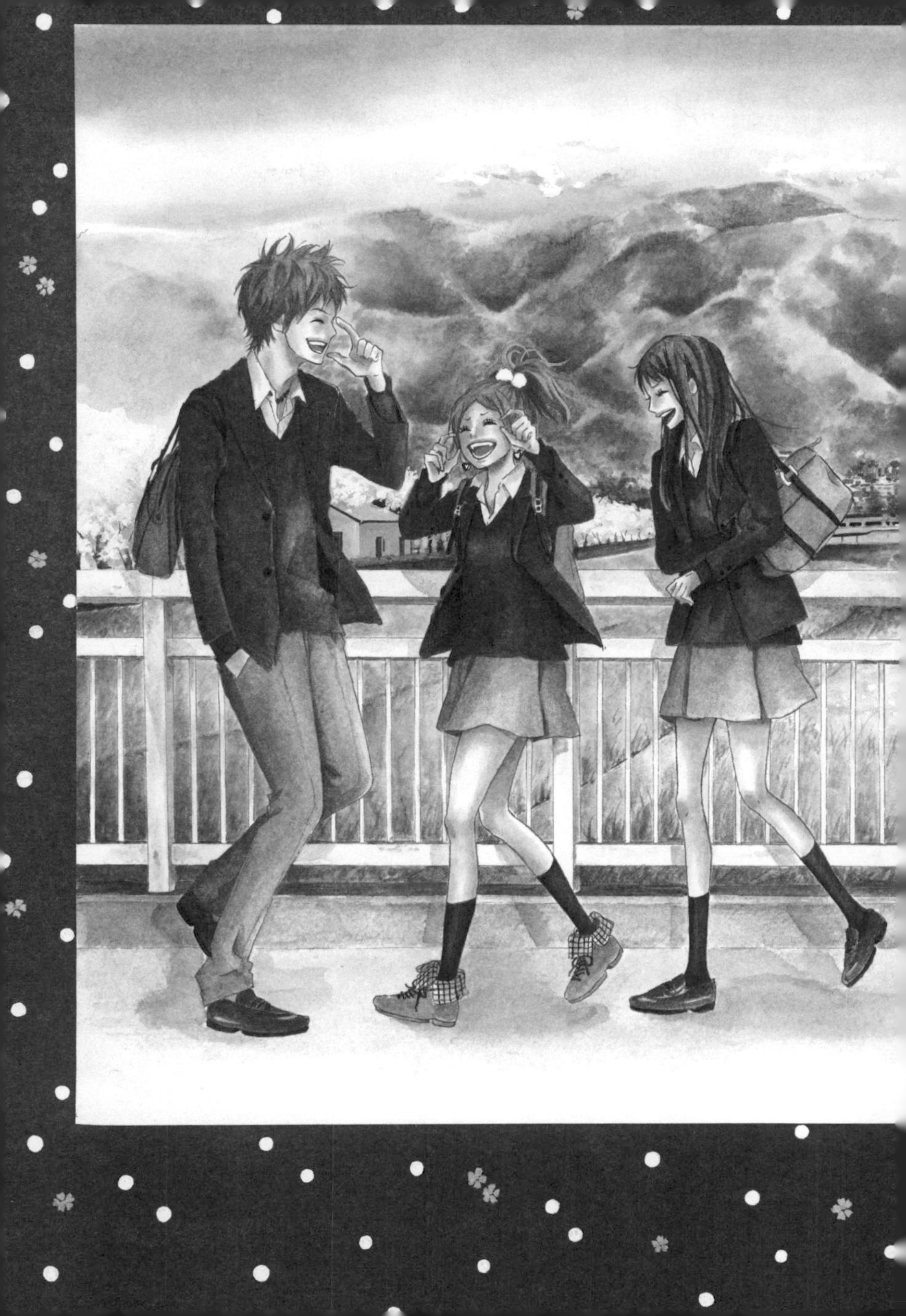

orange

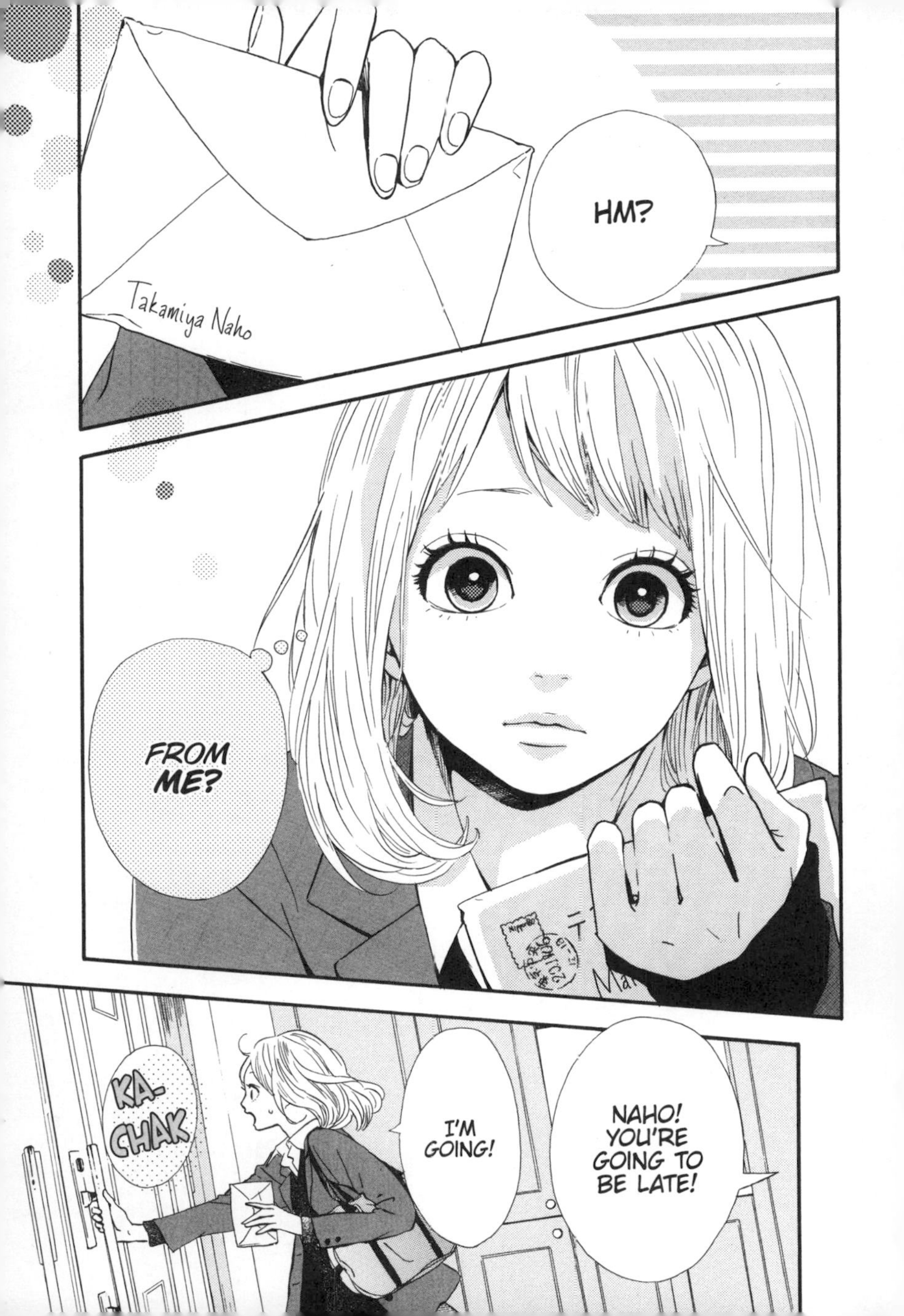
Takamiya Naho
HM?
FROM ME?
NAHO! YOU'RE GOING TO BE LATE!
I'M GOING!
KA-CHAK

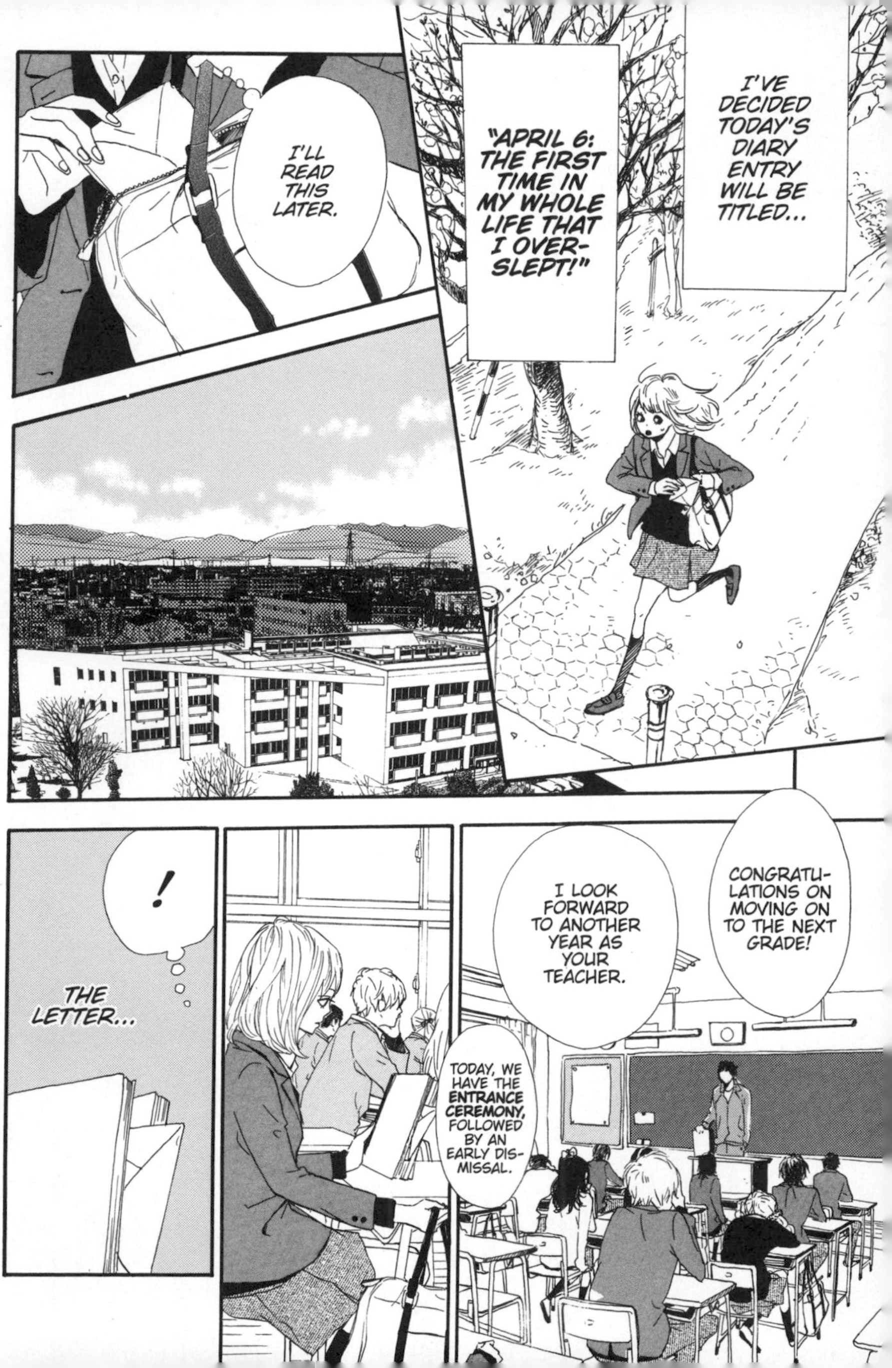
I'VE DECIDED TODAY'S DIARY ENTRY WILL BE TITLED...
"APRIL 6: THE FIRST TIME IN MY WHOLE LIFE THAT I OVER-SLEPT!"
I'LL READ THIS LATER.
CONGRATU-LATIONS ON MOVING ON TO THE NEXT GRADE!
I LOOK FORWARD TO ANOTHER YEAR AS YOUR TEACHER.
TODAY, WE HAVE THE **ENTRANCE CEREMONY**, FOLLOWED BY AN EARLY DIS-MISSAL.
!
THE LETTER...

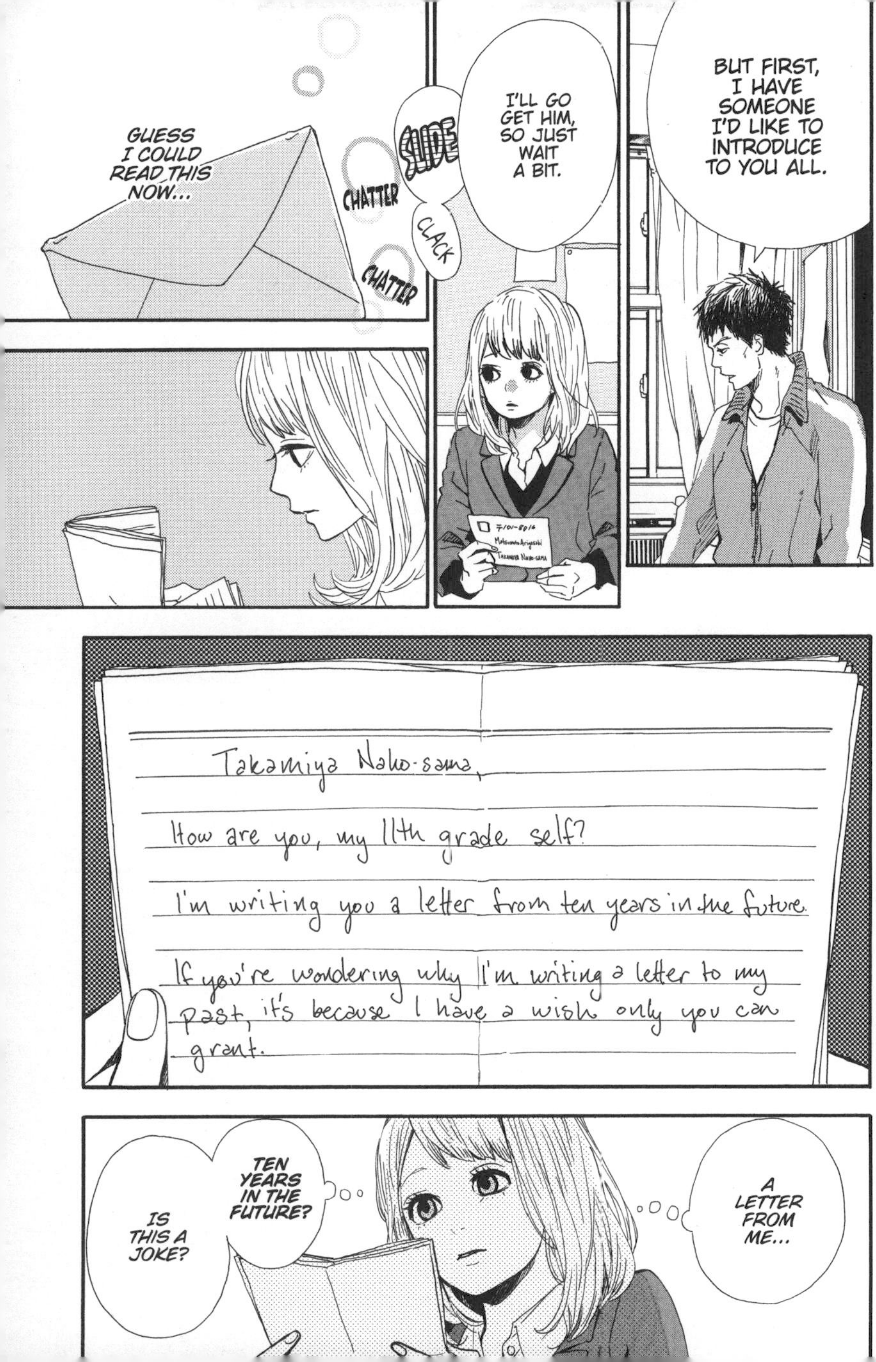
BUT FIRST, I HAVE SOMEONE I'D LIKE TO INTRODUCE TO YOU ALL.
I'LL GO GET HIM, SO JUST WAIT A BIT.
SLIDE
CLACK
CHATTER
CHATTER
GUESS I COULD READ THIS NOW...
Takamiya Naho-sama,
How are you, my 11th grade self?
I'm writing you a letter from ten years in the future.
If you're wondering why I'm writing a letter to my past, it's because I have a wish only you can grant.
A LETTER FROM ME...
TEN YEARS IN THE FUTURE?
IS THIS A JOKE?

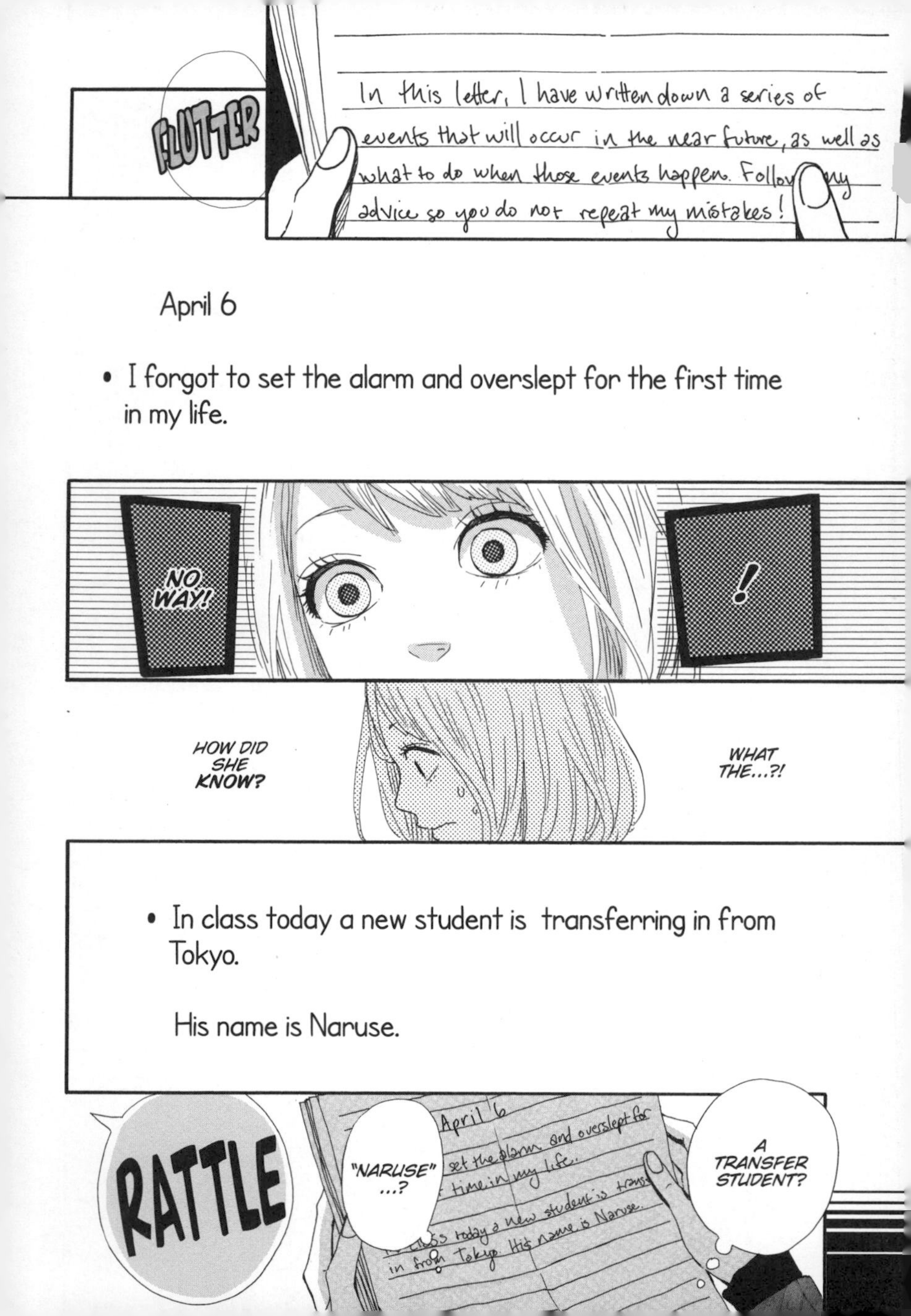
In this letter, I have written down a series of events that will occur in the near future, as well as what to do when those events happen. Follow my advice so you do not repeat my mistakes!
FLUTTER
April 6
• I forgot to set the alarm and overslept for the first time in my life.
!
NO WAY!
WHAT THE...?!
HOW DID SHE KNOW?
• In class today a new student is transferring in from Tokyo.
His name is Naruse.
A TRANSFER STUDENT?
"NARUSE" ...?
RATTLE

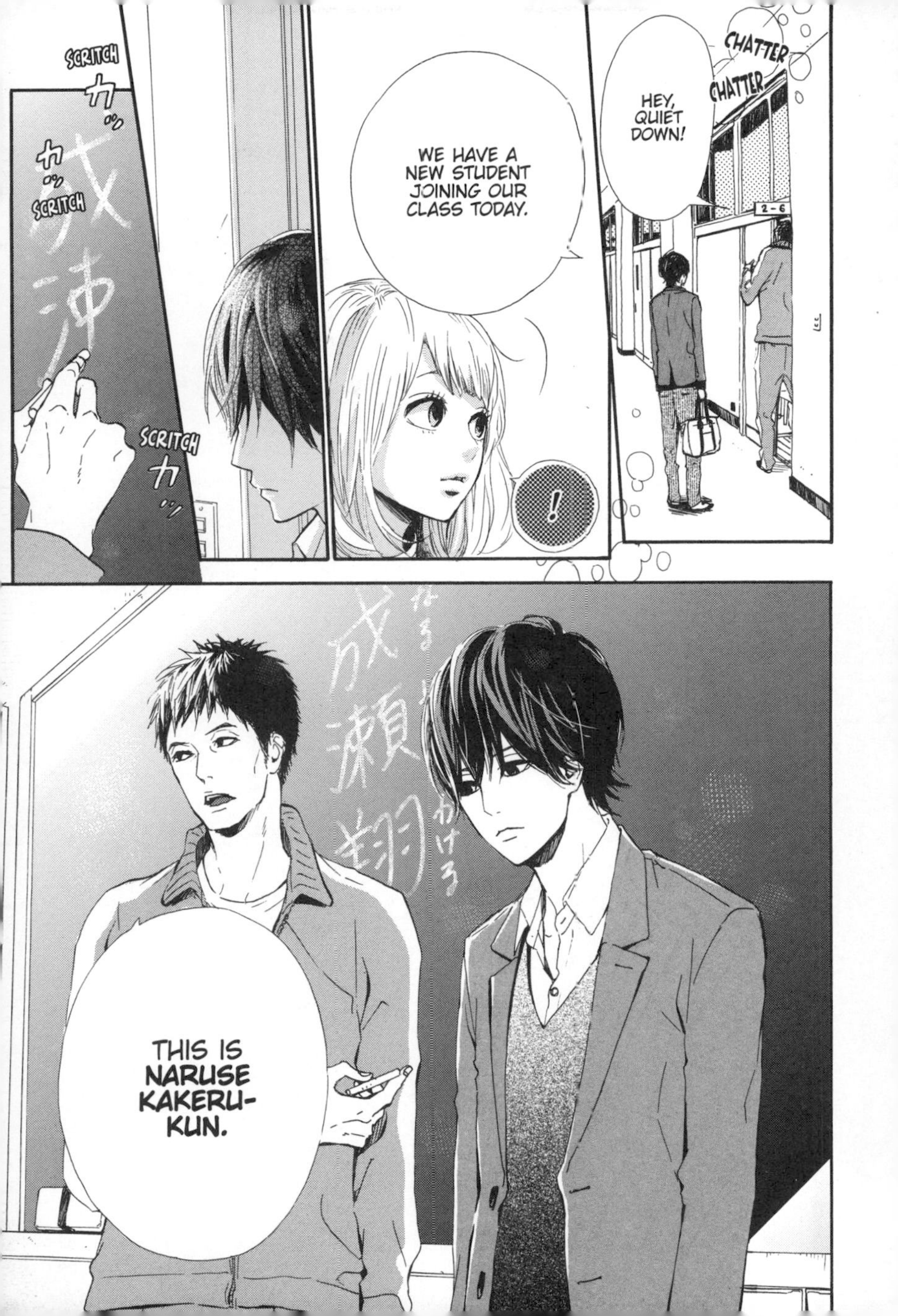
CHATTER
CHATTER
HEY, QUIET DOWN!
WE HAVE A NEW STUDENT JOINING OUR CLASS TODAY.
!
SCRITCH
SCRITCH
SCRITCH
成瀬翔
THIS IS NARUSE KAKERU-KUN.

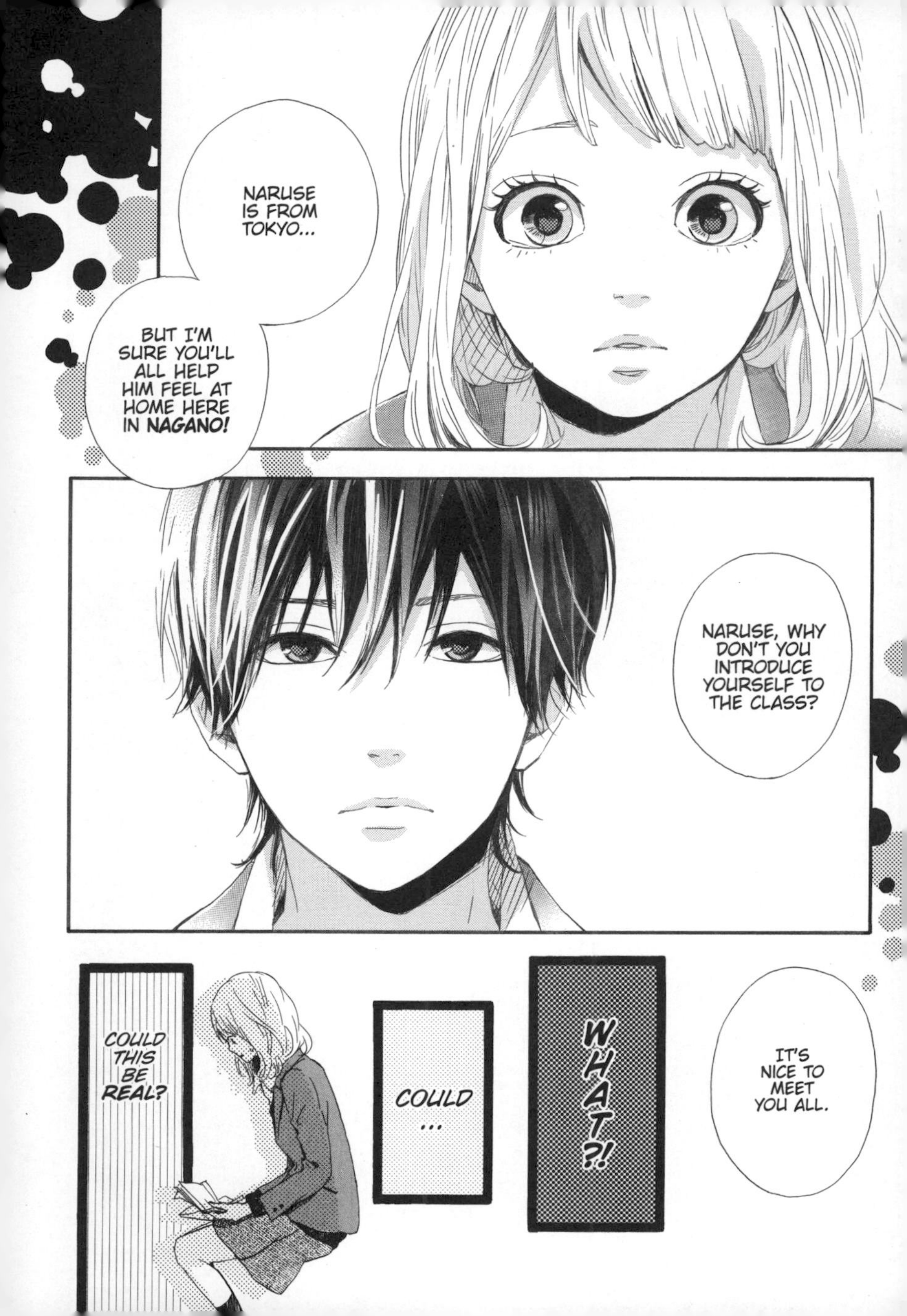
NARUSE IS FROM TOKYO...
BUT I'M SURE YOU'LL ALL HELP HIM FEEL AT HOME HERE IN **NAGANO!**
NARUSE, WHY DON'T YOU INTRODUCE YOURSELF TO THE CLASS?
IT'S NICE TO MEET YOU ALL.
WHAT?!
COULD ...
COULD THIS BE REAL?

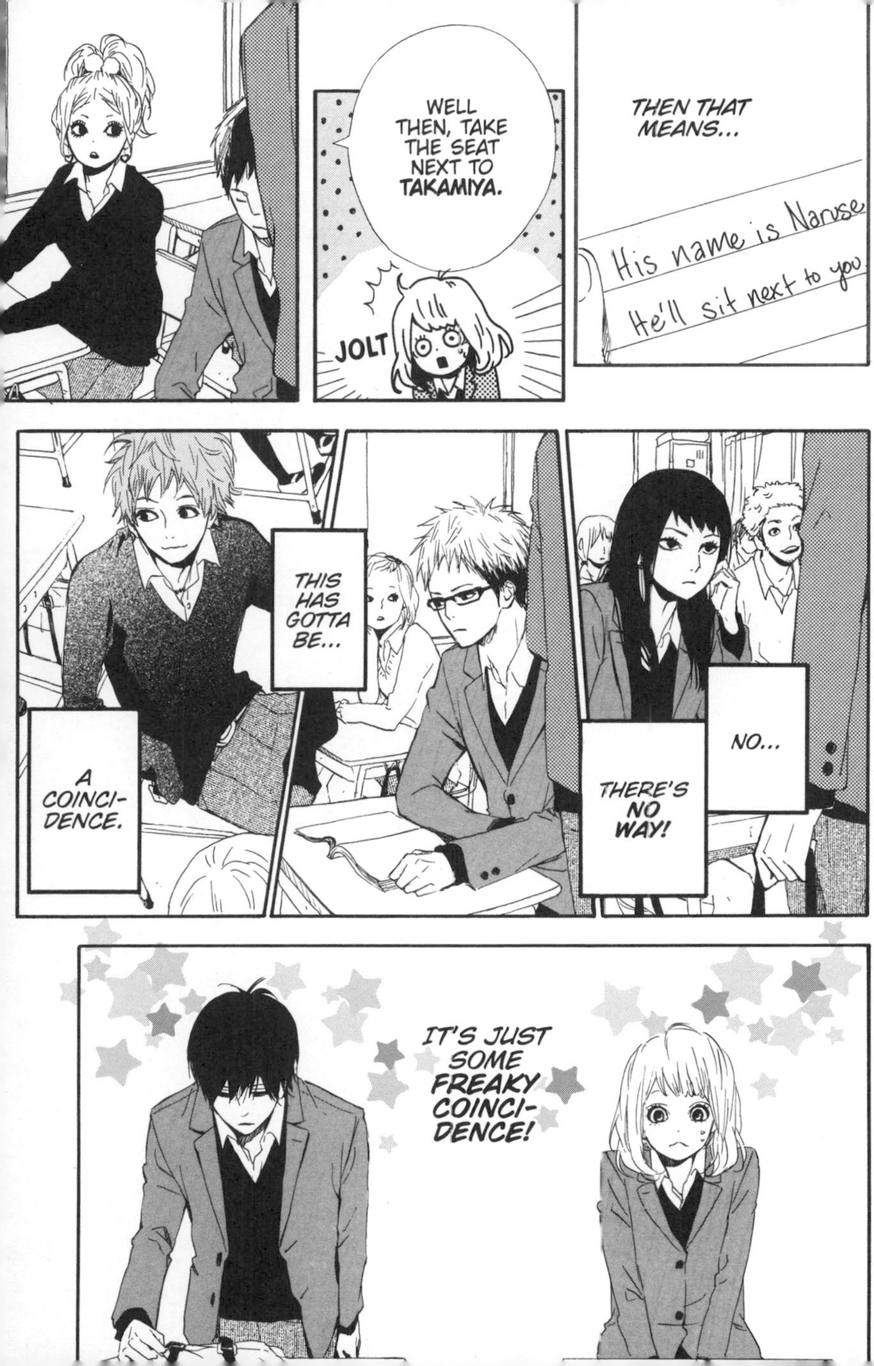
THEN THAT MEANS...
His name is Naruse
He'll sit next to you.
WELL THEN, TAKE THE SEAT NEXT TO TAKAMIYA.
JOLT
NO...
THERE'S NO WAY!
THIS HAS GOTTA BE...
A COINCI-DENCE.
IT'S JUST SOME FREAKY COINCI-DENCE!

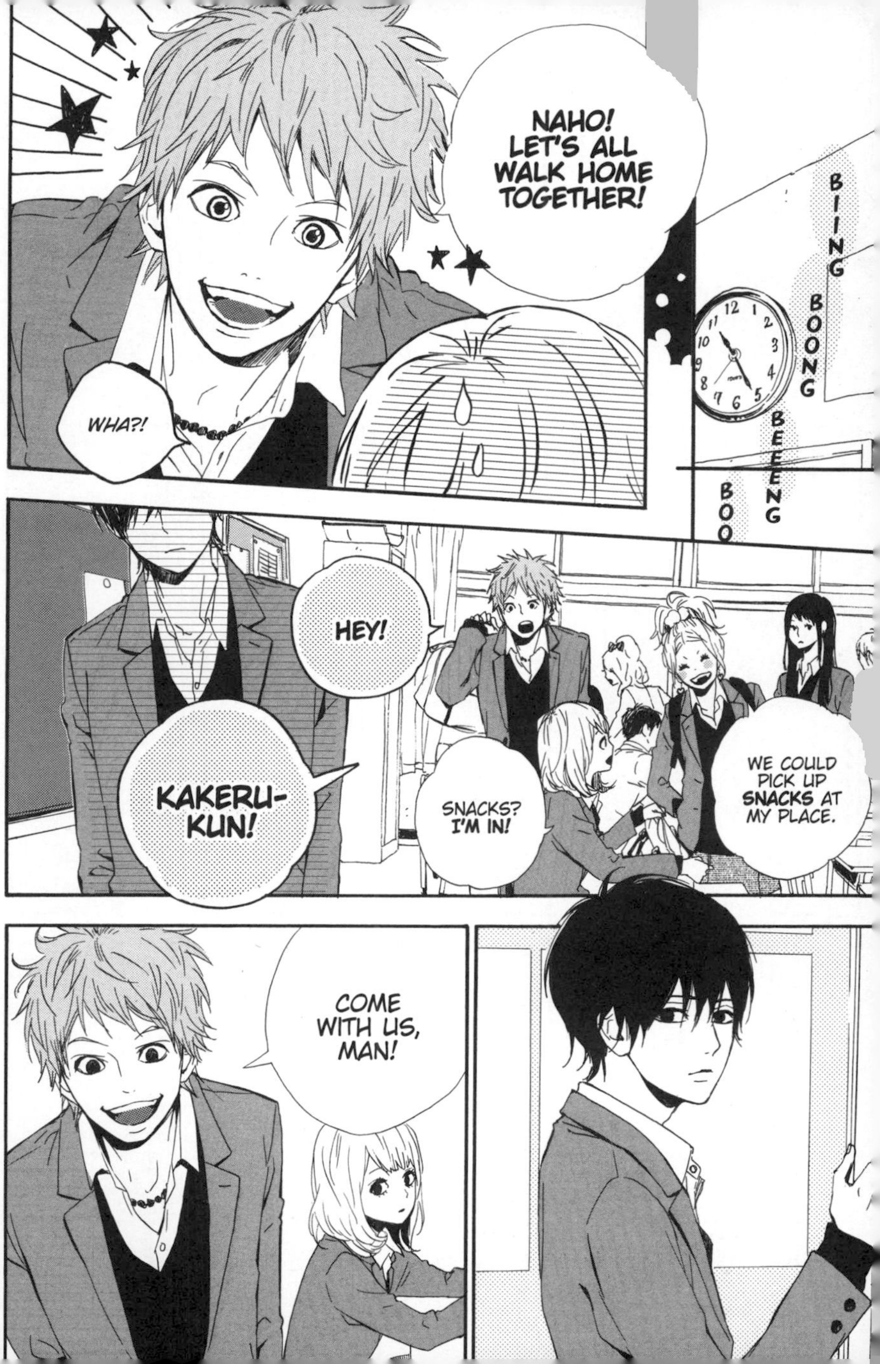
BIING
BOONG
BEEENG
BOO
NAHO! LET'S ALL WALK HOME TOGETHER!
WHA?!
WE COULD PICK UP SNACKS AT MY PLACE.
SNACKS? I'M IN!
HEY!
KAKERU-KUN!
COME WITH US, MAN!

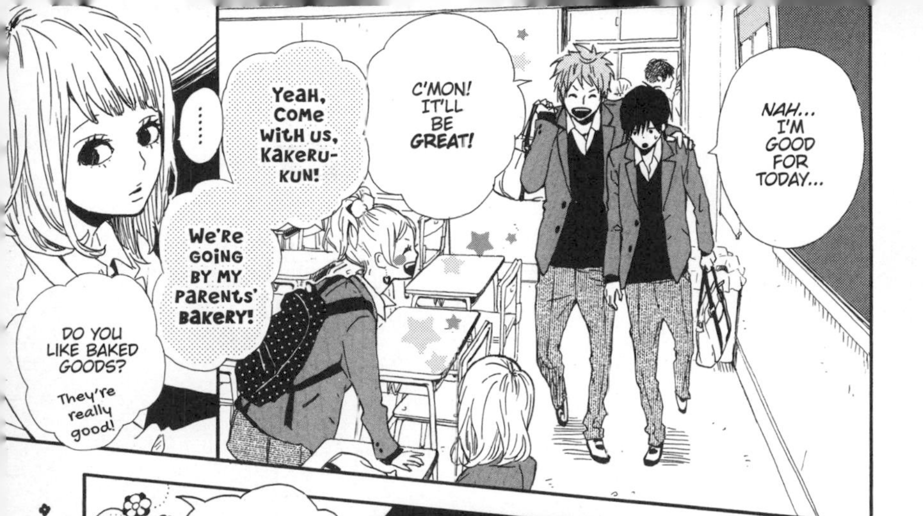
NAH... I'M GOOD FOR TODAY...
C'MON! IT'LL BE GREAT!
Yeah, come with us, Kakeru-kun!
......
We're going by my parents' bakery!
DO YOU LIKE BAKED GOODS?
They're really good!

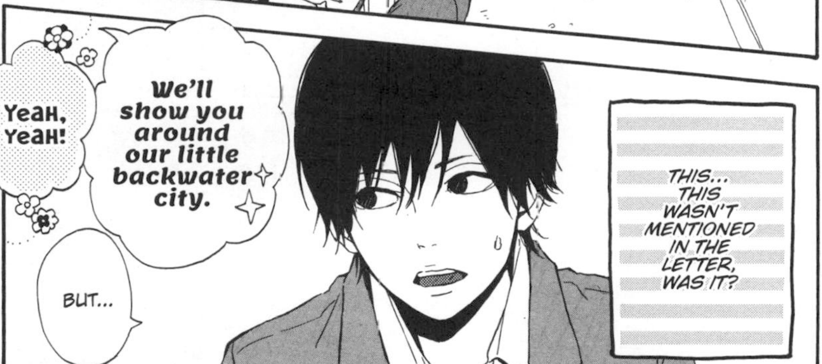
THIS... THIS WASN'T MENTIONED IN THE LETTER, WAS IT?
We'll show you around our little backwater city.
Yeah, yeah!
BUT...

• Kakeru is invited to walk home with the group, but he declines.

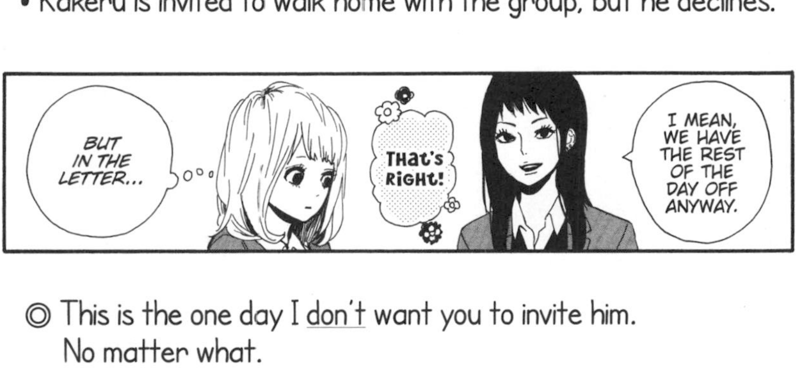
I MEAN, WE HAVE THE REST OF THE DAY OFF ANYWAY.
That's right!
BUT IN THE LETTER...

◎ This is the one day I <u>don't</u> want you to invite him.
No matter what.

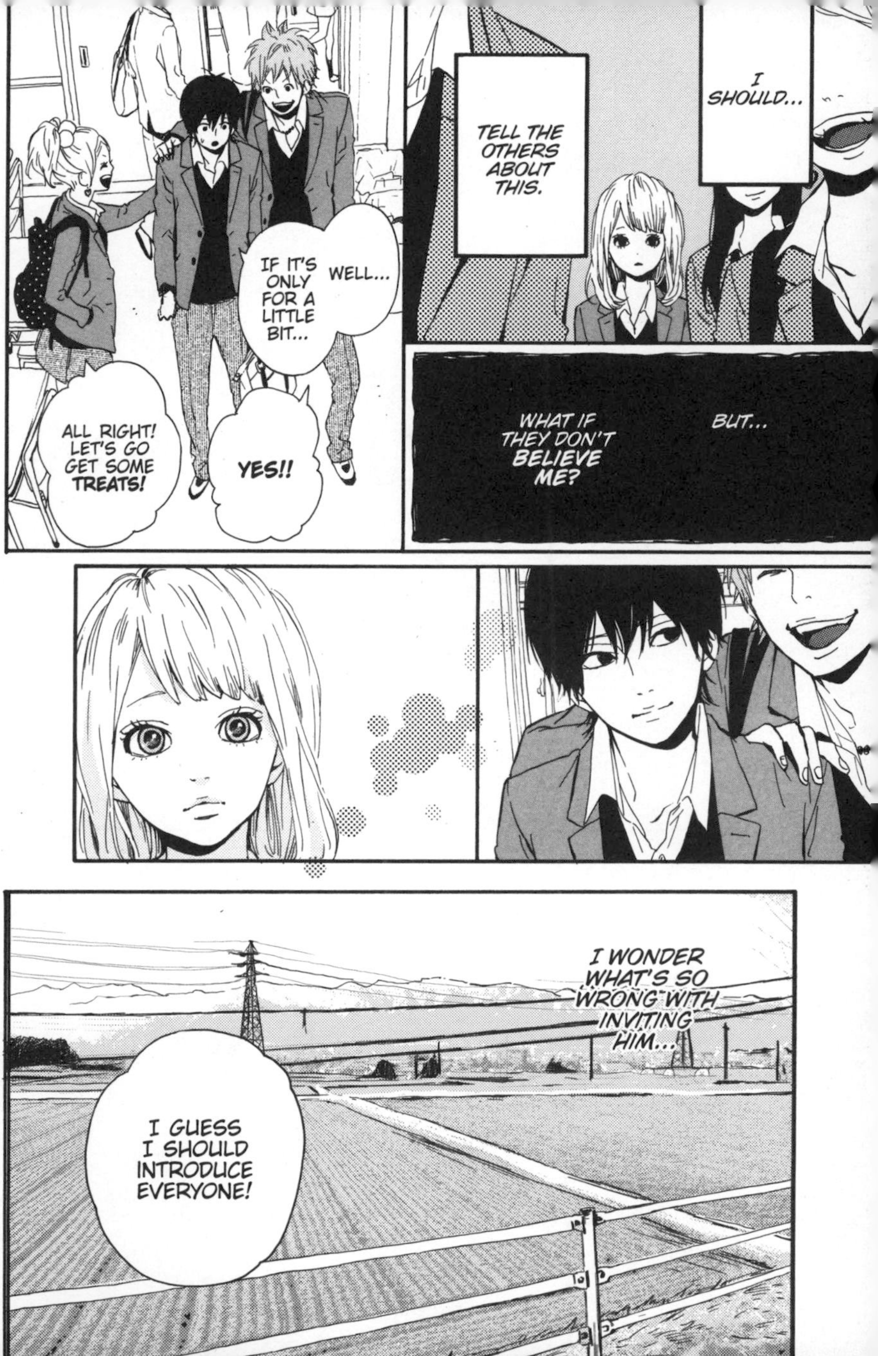
I SHOULD...
TELL THE OTHERS ABOUT THIS.
BUT...
WHAT IF THEY DON'T BELIEVE ME?
WELL...
IF IT'S ONLY FOR A LITTLE BIT...
YES!!
ALL RIGHT! LET'S GO GET SOME TREATS!
I WONDER WHAT'S SO WRONG WITH INVITING HIM...
I GUESS I SHOULD INTRODUCE EVERYONE!

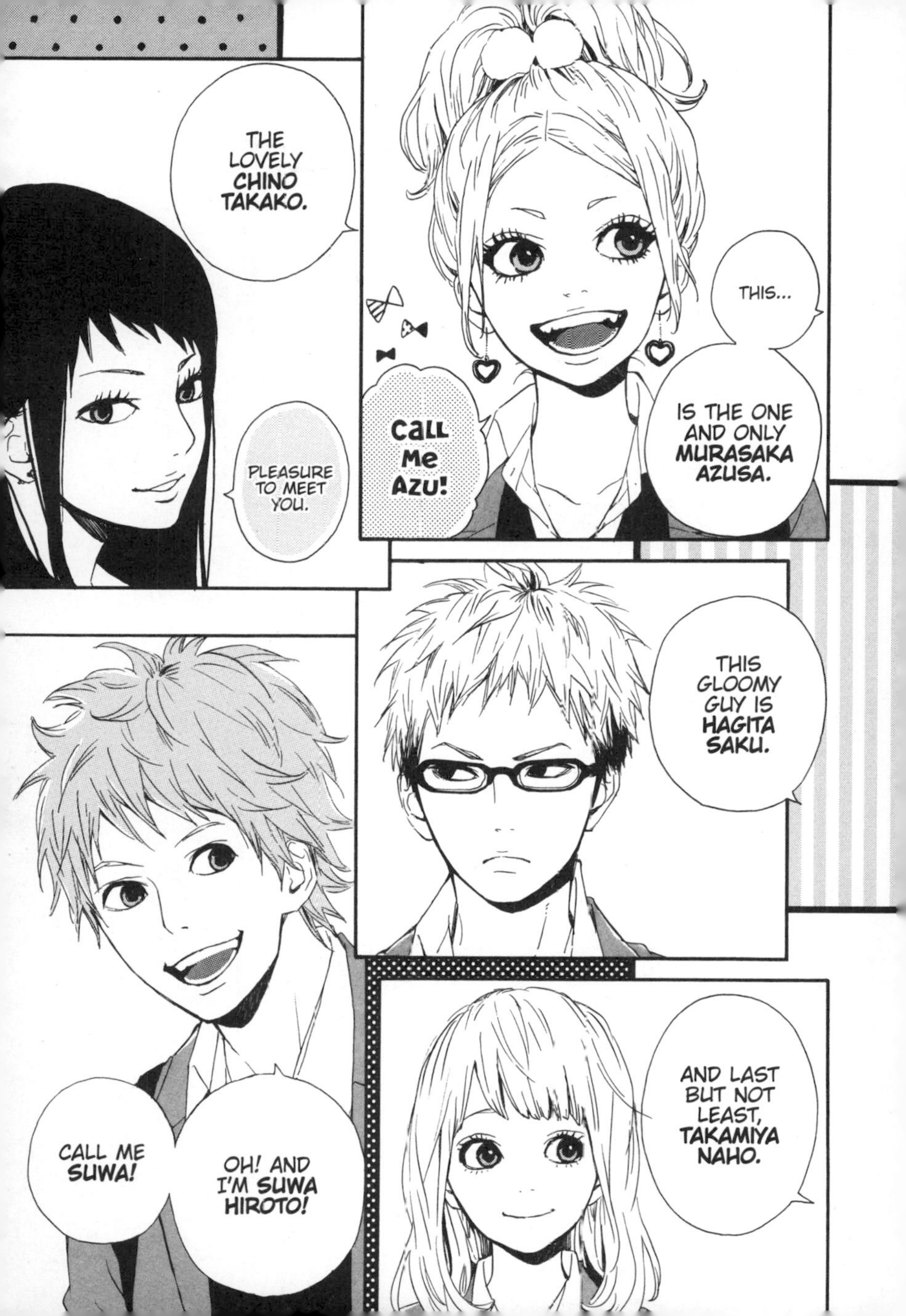
THIS...
IS THE ONE AND ONLY MURASAKA AZUSA.
CALL ME AZU!
THE LOVELY CHINO TAKAKO.
PLEASURE TO MEET YOU.
THIS GLOOMY GUY IS HAGITA SAKU.
AND LAST BUT NOT LEAST, TAKAMIYA NAHO.
OH! AND I'M SUWA HIROTO!
CALL ME SUWA!

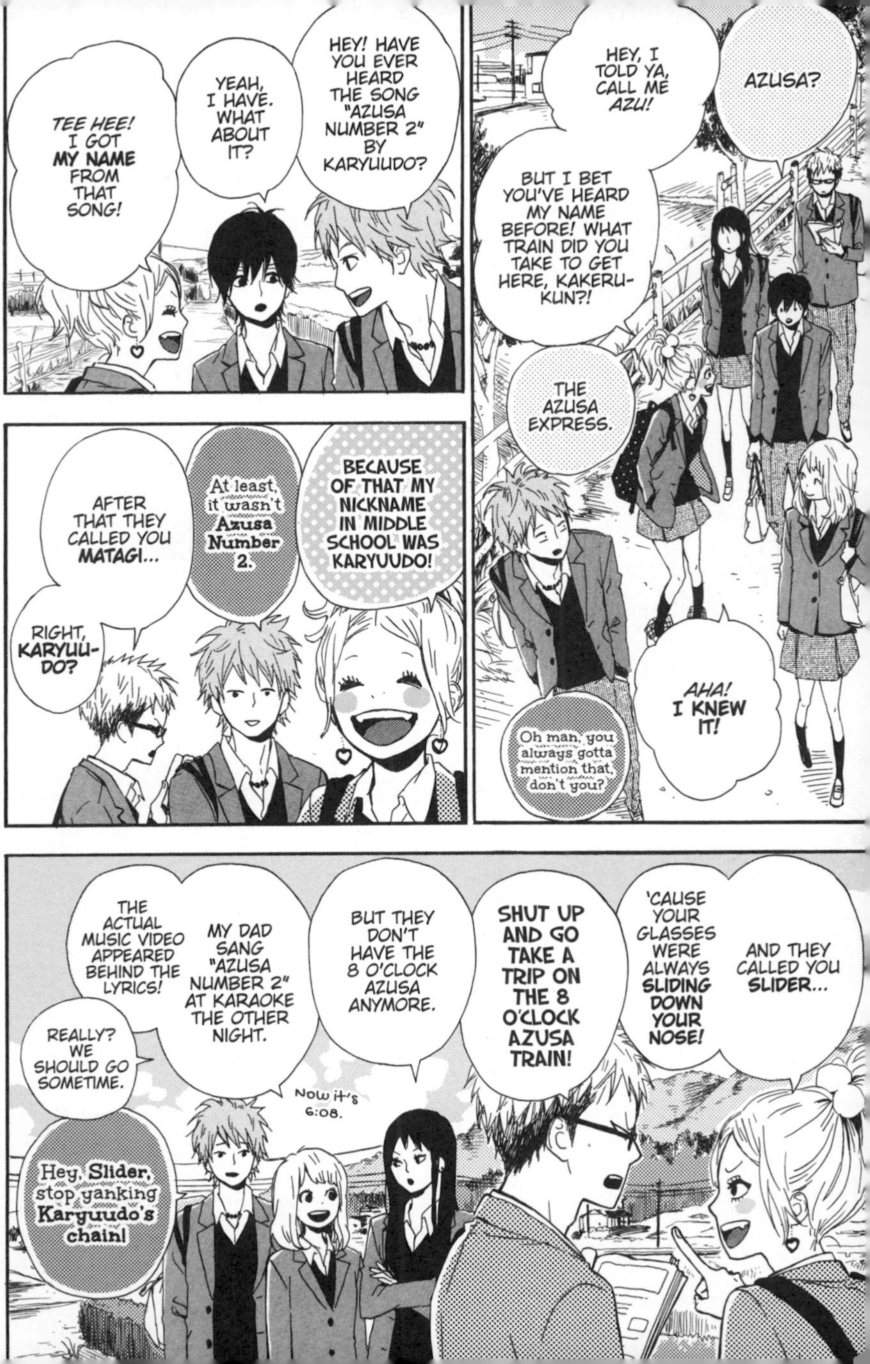
AZUSA?
HEY, I TOLD YA, CALL ME AZU!
BUT I BET YOU'VE HEARD MY NAME BEFORE! WHAT TRAIN DID YOU TAKE TO GET HERE, KAKERU-KUN?!
THE AZUSA EXPRESS.
AHA! I KNEW IT!
Oh man, you always gotta mention that, don't you?
HEY! HAVE YOU EVER HEARD THE SONG "AZUSA NUMBER 2" BY KARYUUDO?
YEAH, I HAVE. WHAT ABOUT IT?
TEE HEE! I GOT MY NAME FROM THAT SONG!
BECAUSE OF THAT MY NICKNAME IN MIDDLE SCHOOL WAS KARYUUDO!
At least, it wasn't Azusa Number 2.
AFTER THAT THEY CALLED YOU MATAGI...
RIGHT, KARYUU-DO?
AND THEY CALLED YOU SLIDER...
'CAUSE YOUR GLASSES WERE ALWAYS SLIDING DOWN YOUR NOSE!
SHUT UP AND GO TAKE A TRIP ON THE 8 O'CLOCK AZUSA TRAIN!
BUT THEY DON'T HAVE THE 8 O'CLOCK AZUSA ANYMORE.
Now it's 6:08.
MY DAD SANG "AZUSA NUMBER 2" AT KARAOKE THE OTHER NIGHT.
THE ACTUAL MUSIC VIDEO APPEARED BEHIND THE LYRICS!
REALLY? WE SHOULD GO SOMETIME.
Hey, Slider, stop yanking Karyuudo's chain!

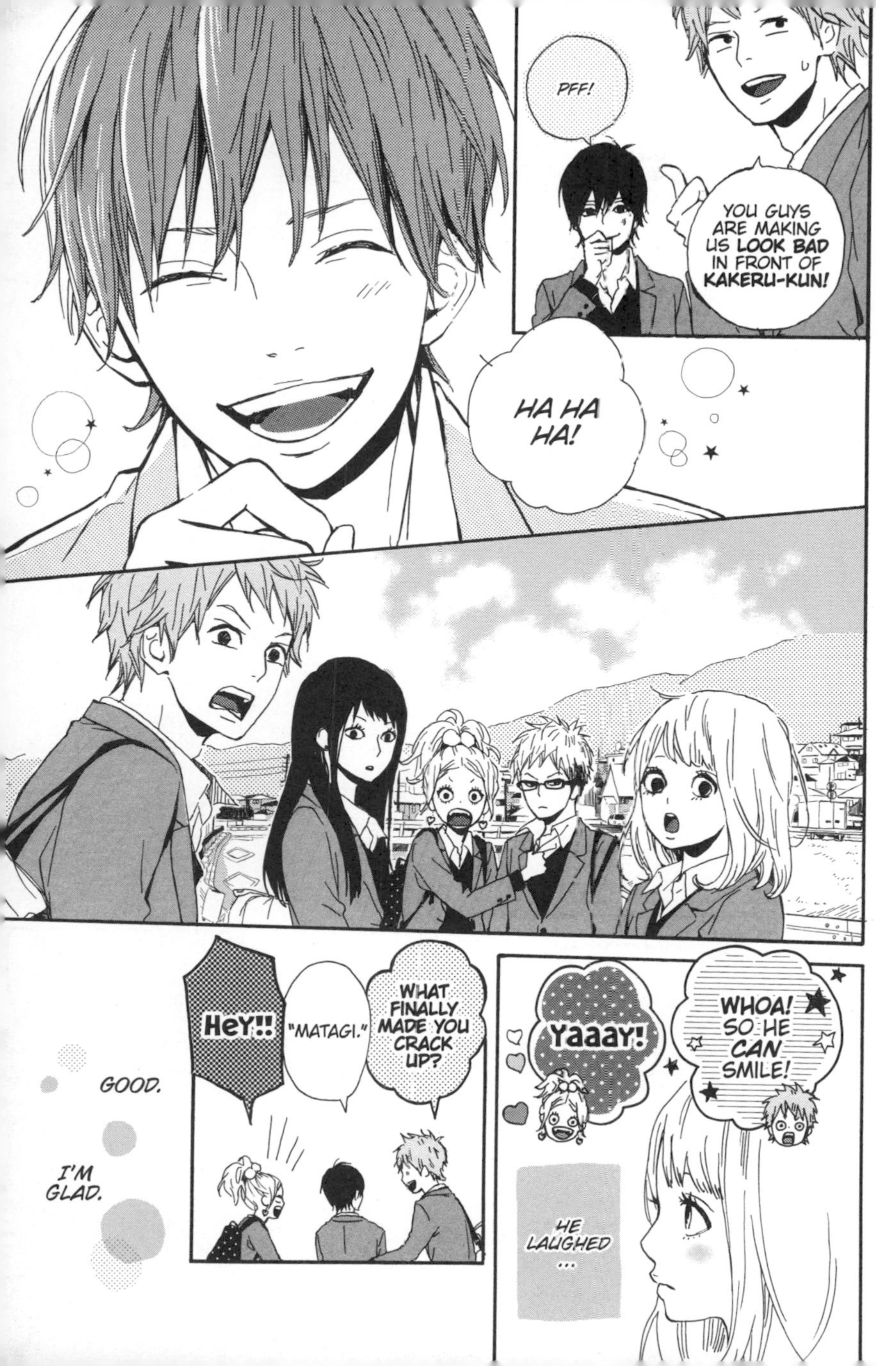
PFF!
YOU GUYS ARE MAKING US LOOK BAD IN FRONT OF KAKERU-KUN!
HA HA HA!
WHOA! SO HE CAN SMILE!
Yaaay!
HE LAUGHED ...
WHAT FINALLY MADE YOU CRACK UP?
"MATAGI."
HeY!!
GOOD.
I'M GLAD.

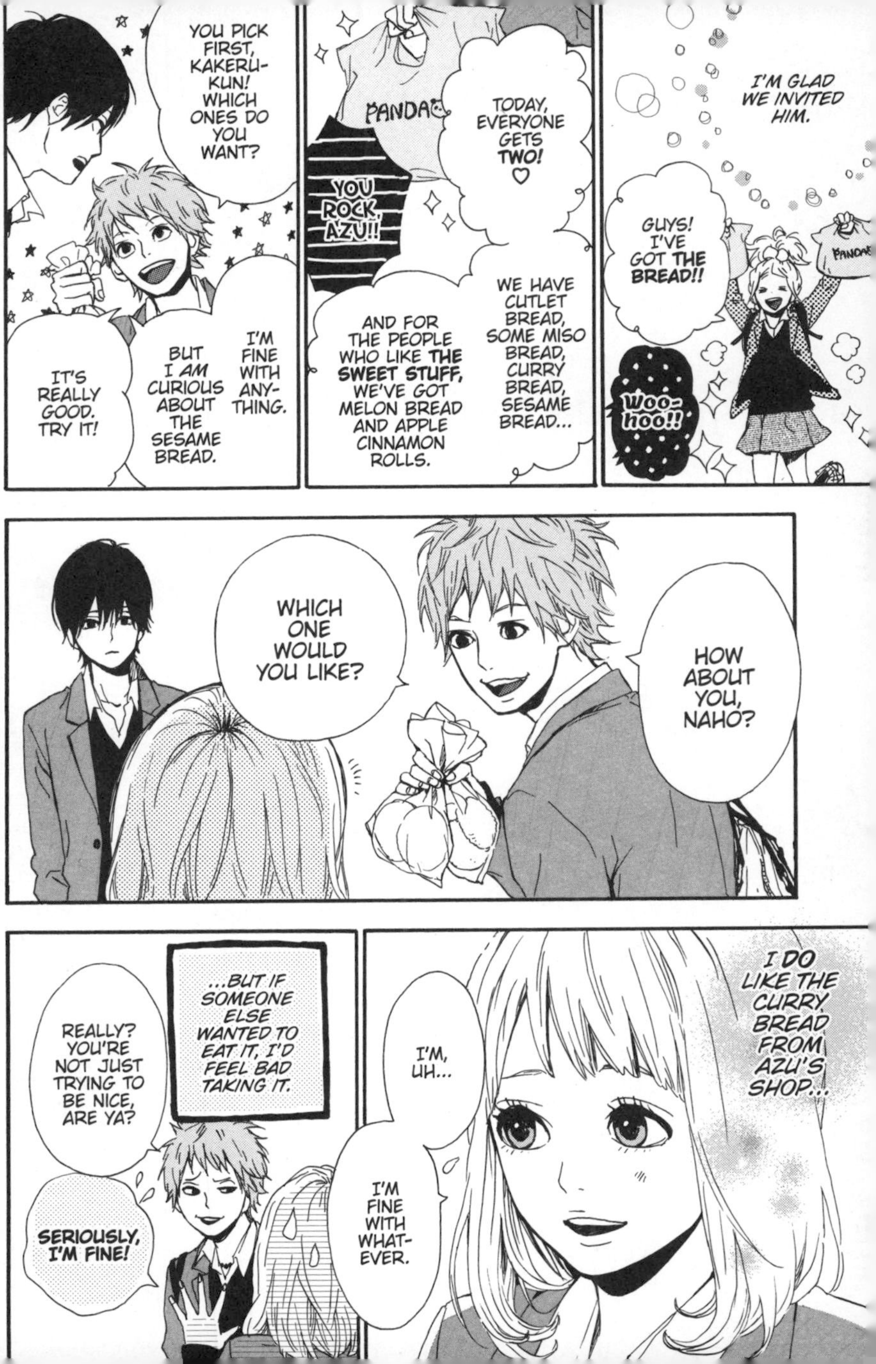
I'M GLAD WE INVITED HIM.
GUYS! I'VE GOT THE BREAD!!
Woo-hoo!!
TODAY, EVERYONE GETS TWO! ♡
YOU ROCK, AZU!!
WE HAVE CUTLET BREAD, SOME MISO BREAD, CURRY BREAD, SESAME BREAD...
AND FOR THE PEOPLE WHO LIKE THE SWEET STUFF, WE'VE GOT MELON BREAD AND APPLE CINNAMON ROLLS.
YOU PICK FIRST, KAKERU-KUN! WHICH ONES DO YOU WANT?
I'M FINE WITH ANYTHING.
BUT I AM CURIOUS ABOUT THE SESAME BREAD.
IT'S REALLY GOOD. TRY IT!
HOW ABOUT YOU, NAHO?
WHICH ONE WOULD YOU LIKE?
I DO LIKE THE CURRY BREAD FROM AZU'S SHOP...
I'M, UH...
I'M FINE WITH WHATEVER.
...BUT IF SOMEONE ELSE WANTED TO EAT IT, I'D FEEL BAD TAKING IT.
REALLY? YOU'RE NOT JUST TRYING TO BE NICE, ARE YA?
SERIOUSLY, I'M FINE!

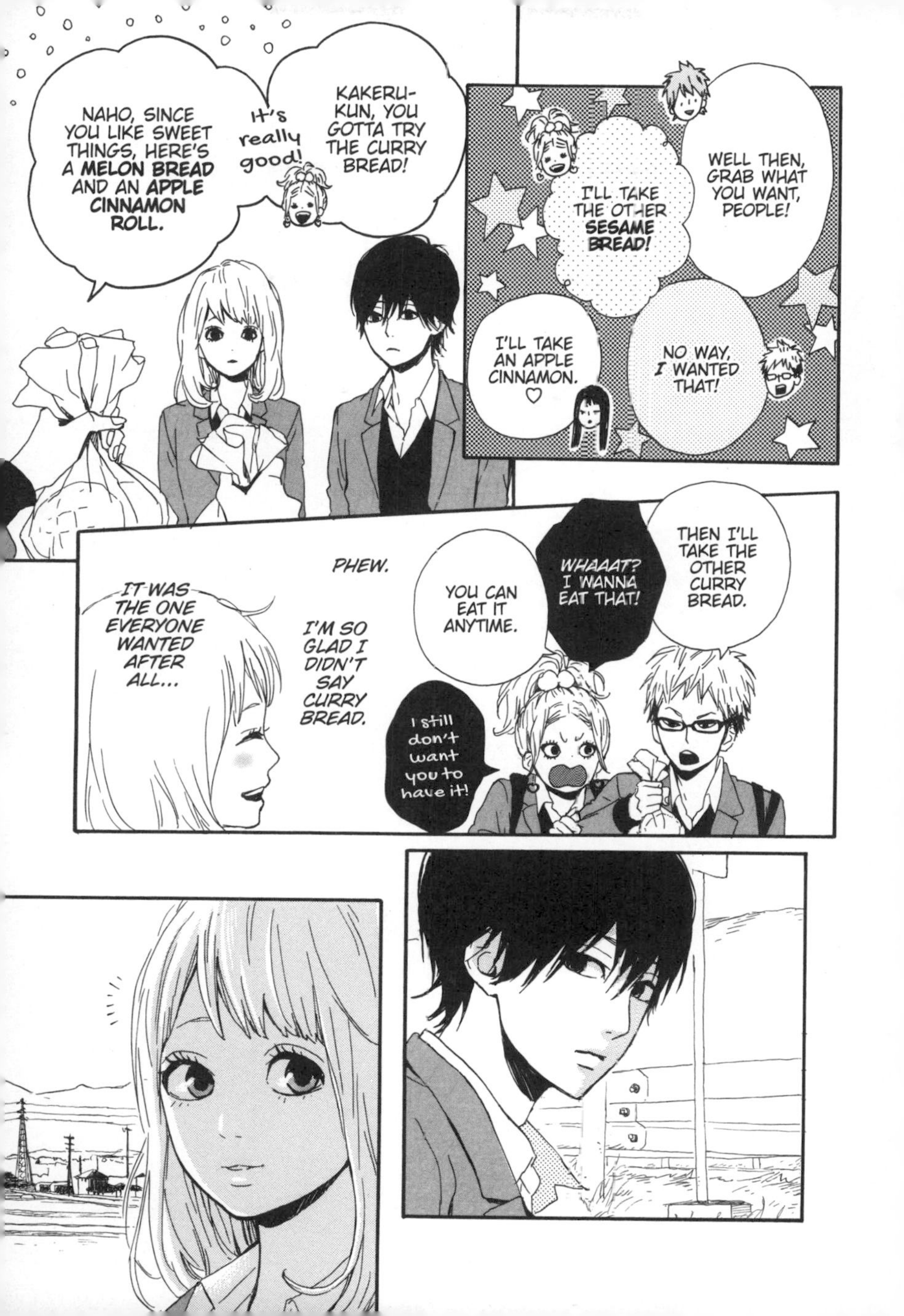
WELL THEN, GRAB WHAT YOU WANT, PEOPLE!
I'LL TAKE THE OTHER SESAME BREAD!
NO WAY, I WANTED THAT!
I'LL TAKE AN APPLE CINNAMON. ♡
KAKERU-KUN, YOU GOTTA TRY THE CURRY BREAD!
It's really good!
NAHO, SINCE YOU LIKE SWEET THINGS, HERE'S A MELON BREAD AND AN APPLE CINNAMON ROLL.
THEN I'LL TAKE THE OTHER CURRY BREAD.
WHAAAT? I WANNA EAT THAT!
YOU CAN EAT IT ANYTIME.
I still don't want you to have it!
PHEW.
I'M SO GLAD I DIDN'T SAY CURRY BREAD.
IT WAS THE ONE EVERYONE WANTED AFTER ALL...

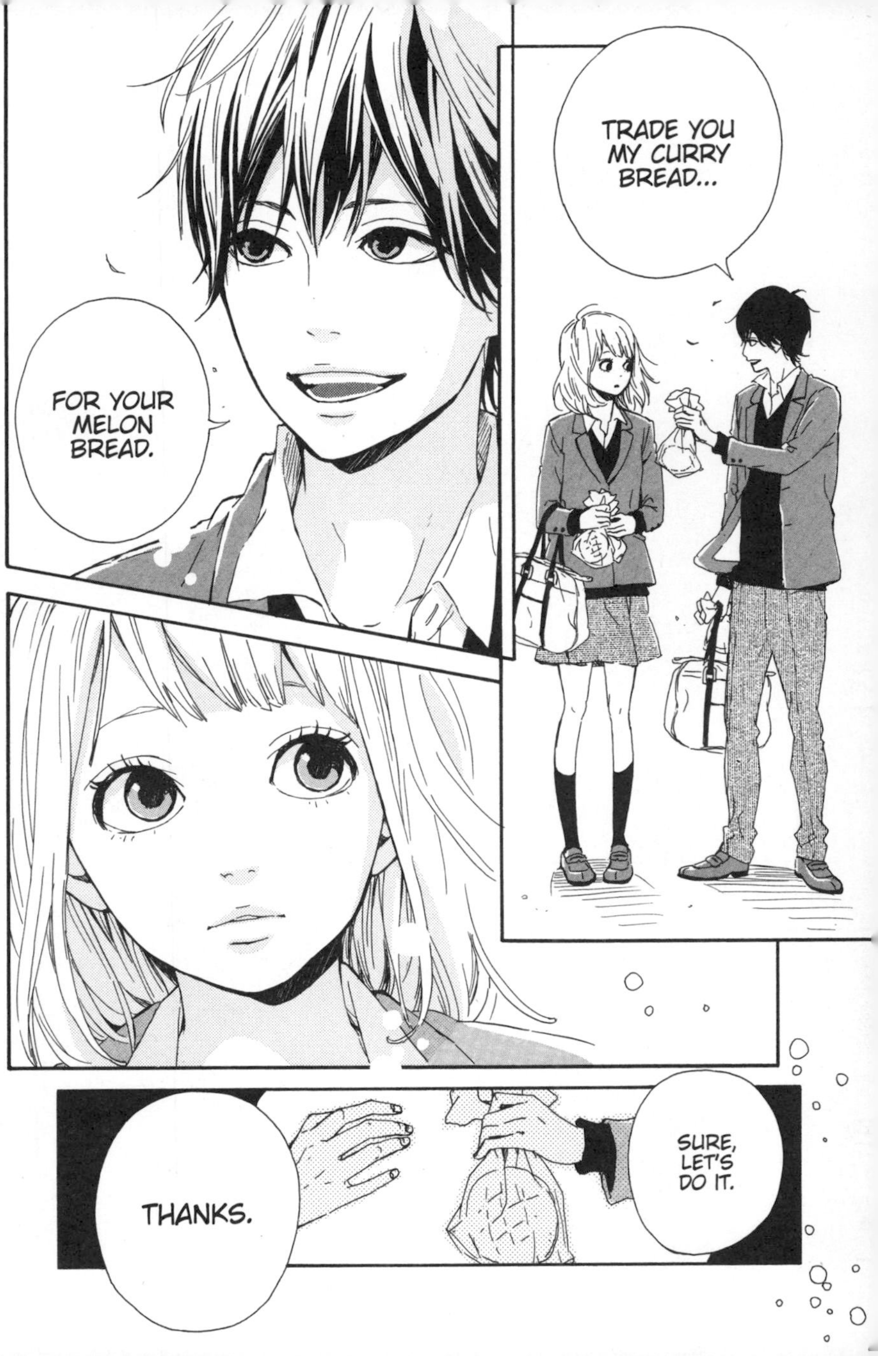
TRADE YOU MY CURRY BREAD...
FOR YOUR MELON BREAD.
SURE, LET'S DO IT.
THANKS.

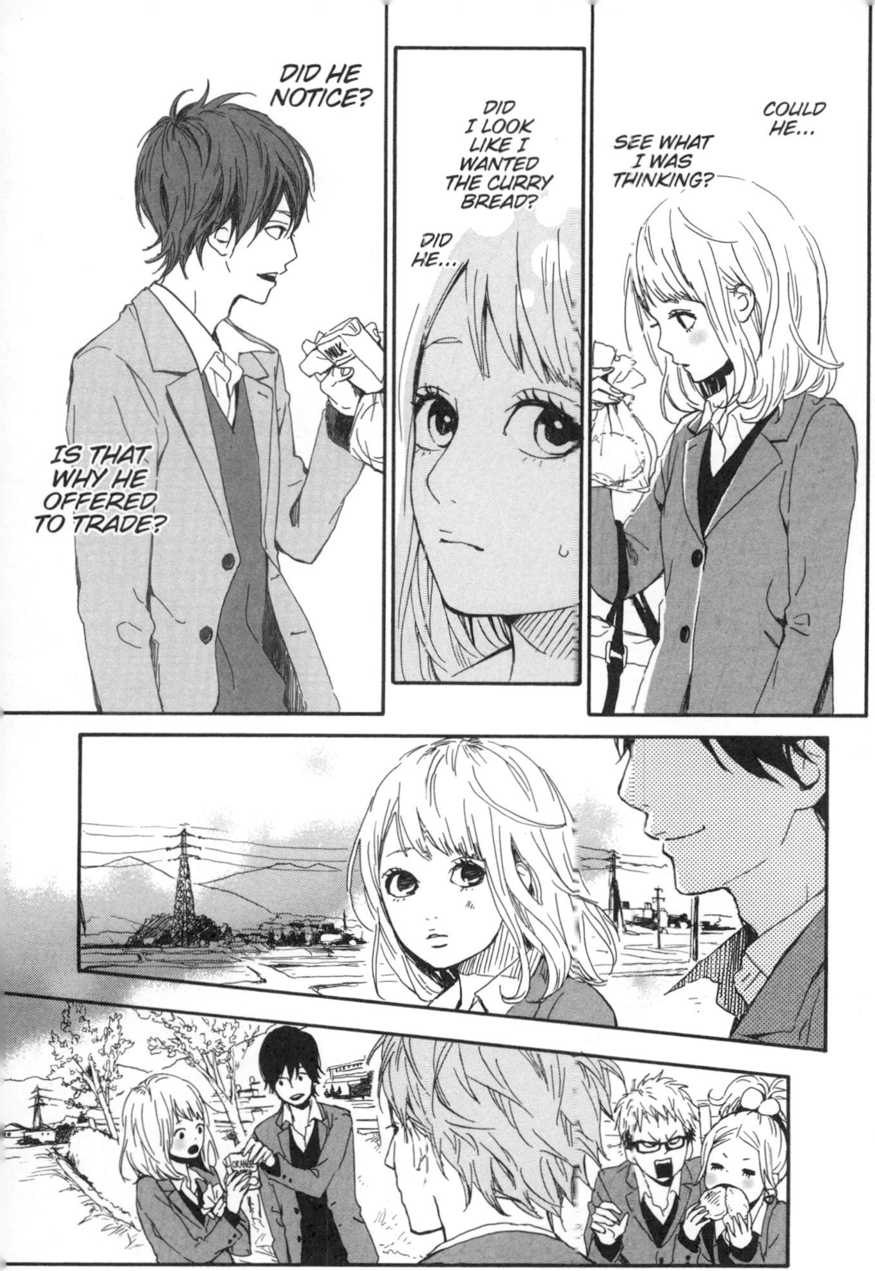
COULD HE...
SEE WHAT I WAS THINKING?
DID I LOOK LIKE I WANTED THE CURRY BREAD?
DID HE...
DID HE NOTICE?
IS THAT WHY HE OFFERED TO TRADE?

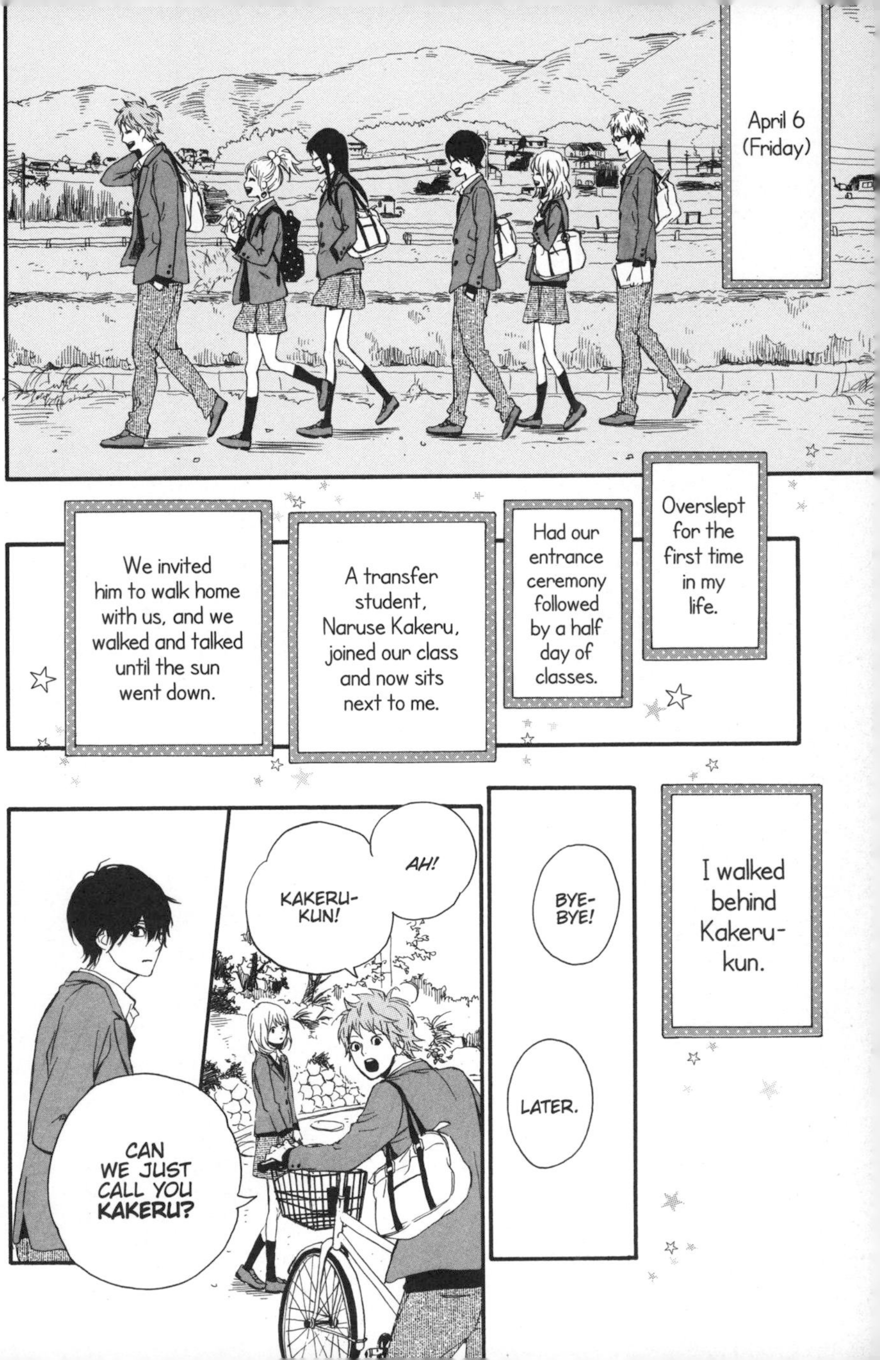
April 6 (Friday)
Overslept for the first time in my life.
Had our entrance ceremony followed by a half day of classes.
A transfer student, Naruse Kakeru, joined our class and now sits next to me.
We invited him to walk home with us, and we walked and talked until the sun went down.
I walked behind Kakeru-kun.
BYE-BYE!
LATER.
AH!
KAKERU-KUN!
CAN WE JUST CALL YOU KAKERU?

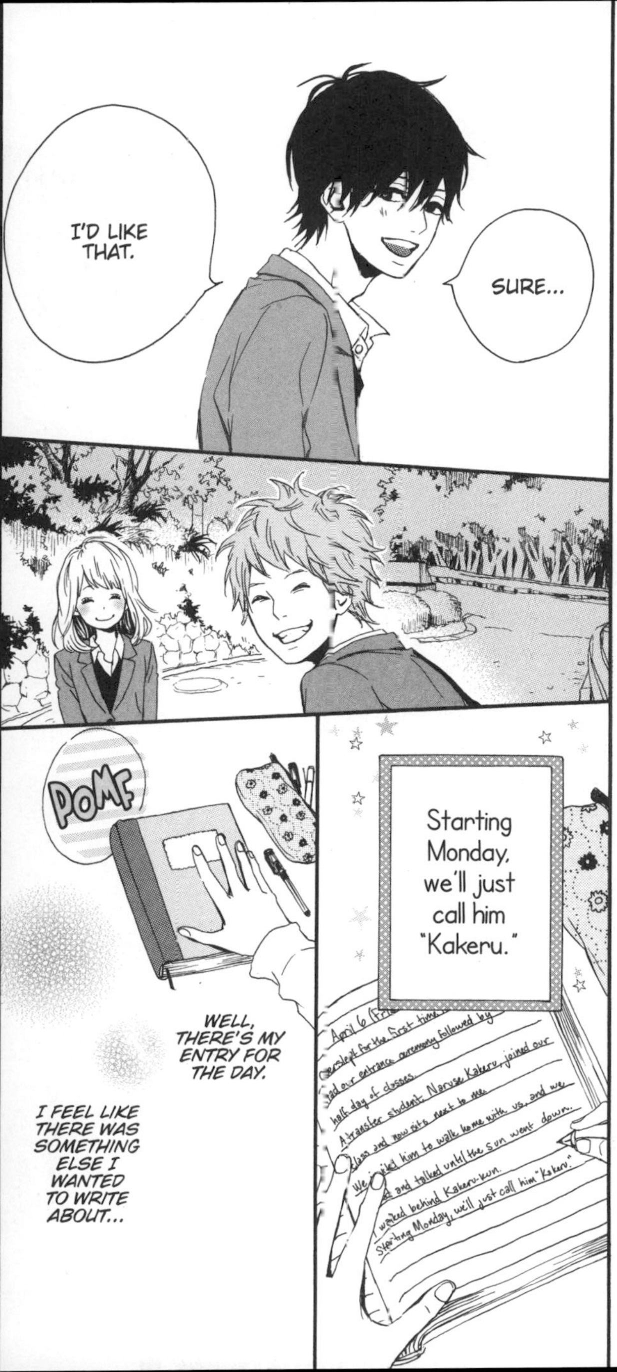
SURE...
I'D LIKE THAT.
Starting Monday, we'll just call him "Kakeru."
April 6
had our entrance ceremony followed by
half day of classes.
A transfer student, Naruse Kakeru, joined our
class and now sits next to me.
him to walk home with us, and we
and talked until the sun went down.
walked behind Kakeru-kun.
Starting Monday, we'll just call him "Kakeru."
POMF
WELL, THERE'S MY ENTRY FOR THE DAY.
I FEEL LIKE THERE WAS SOMETHING ELSE I WANTED TO WRITE ABOUT...

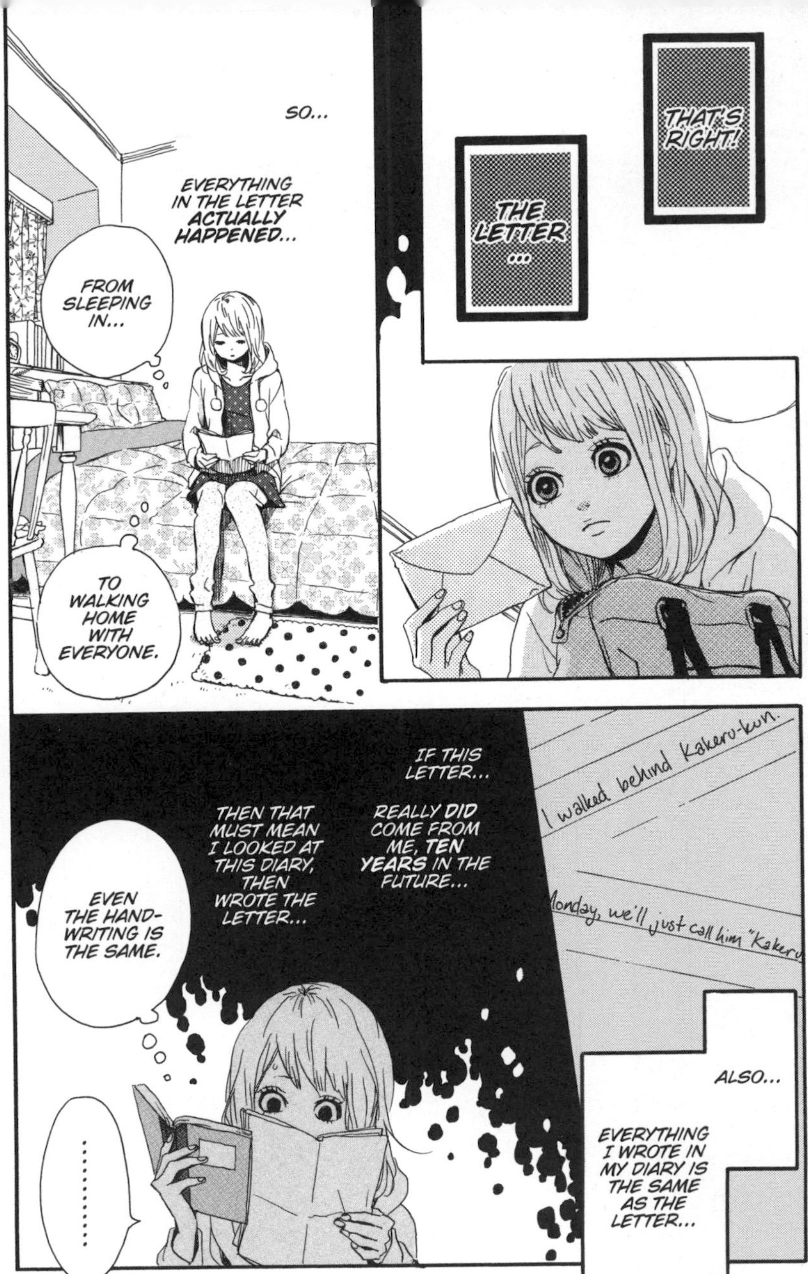
THAT'S RIGHT!
THE LETTER ...
SO...
EVERYTHING IN THE LETTER ACTUALLY HAPPENED...
FROM SLEEPING IN...
TO WALKING HOME WITH EVERYONE.
I walked behind Kakeru-kun.
Monday, we'll just call him "Kakeru
ALSO...
EVERYTHING I WROTE IN MY DIARY IS THE SAME AS THE LETTER...
IF THIS LETTER...
REALLY DID COME FROM ME, TEN YEARS IN THE FUTURE...
THEN THAT MUST MEAN I LOOKED AT THIS DIARY, THEN WROTE THE LETTER...
EVEN THE HAND-WRITING IS THE SAME.
....

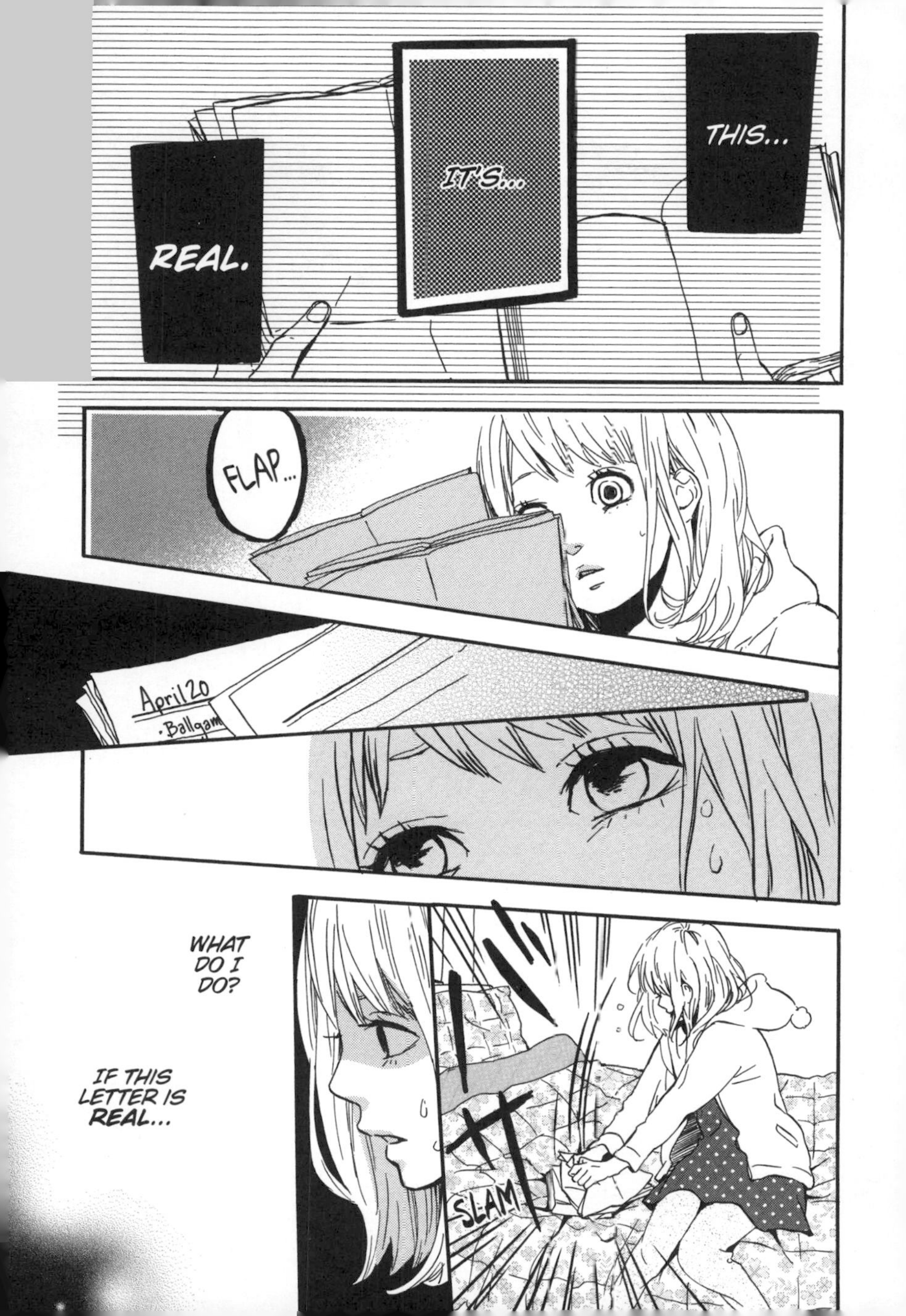
THIS...
IT'S...
REAL.
FLAP...
April20
SLAM
WHAT DO I DO?
IF THIS LETTER IS REAL...

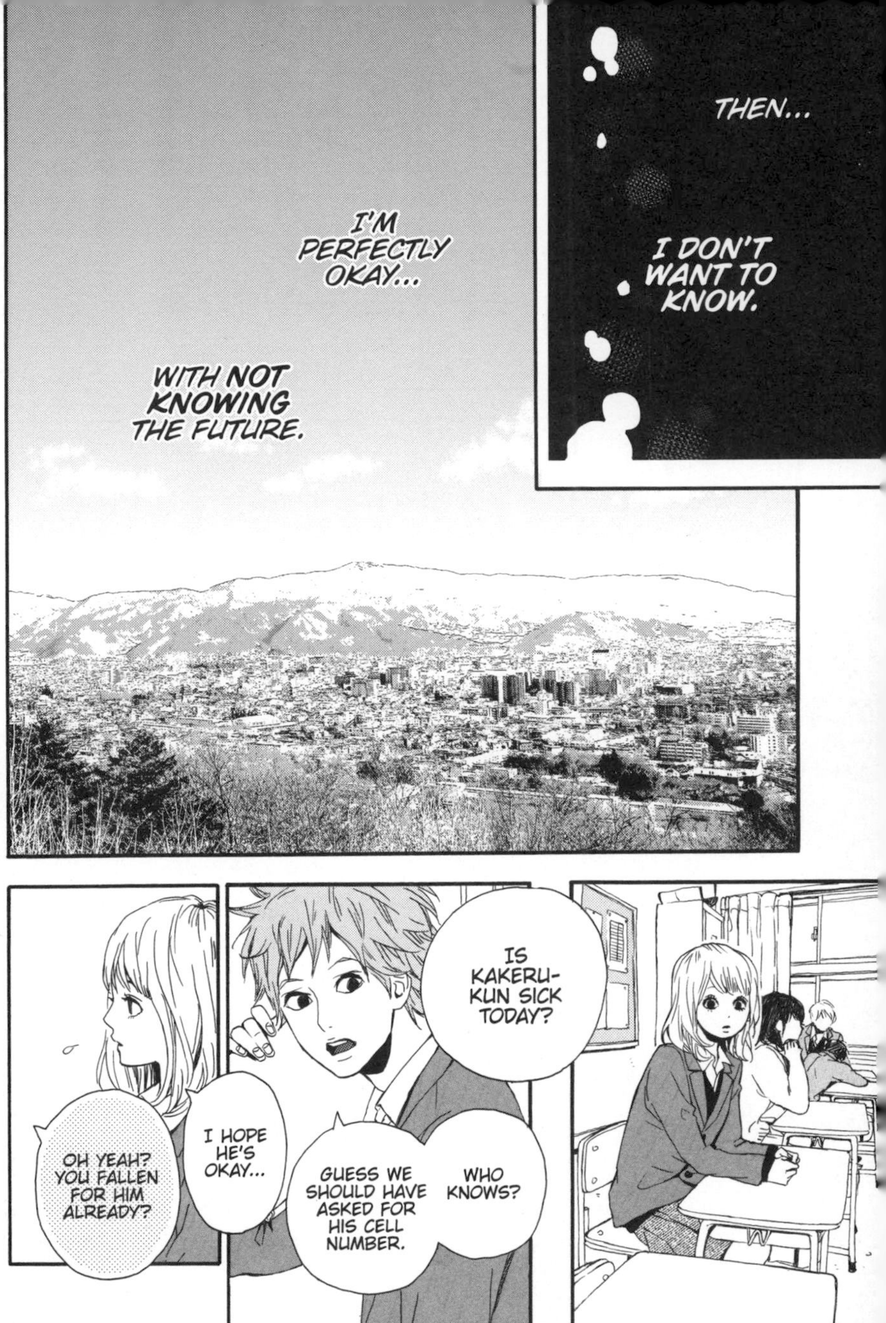
THEN...
I DON'T WANT TO KNOW.
I'M PERFECTLY OKAY...
WITH NOT KNOWING THE FUTURE.
IS KAKERU-KUN SICK TODAY?
WHO KNOWS?
GUESS WE SHOULD HAVE ASKED FOR HIS CELL NUMBER.
I HOPE HE'S OKAY...
OH YEAH? YOU FALLEN FOR HIM ALREADY?

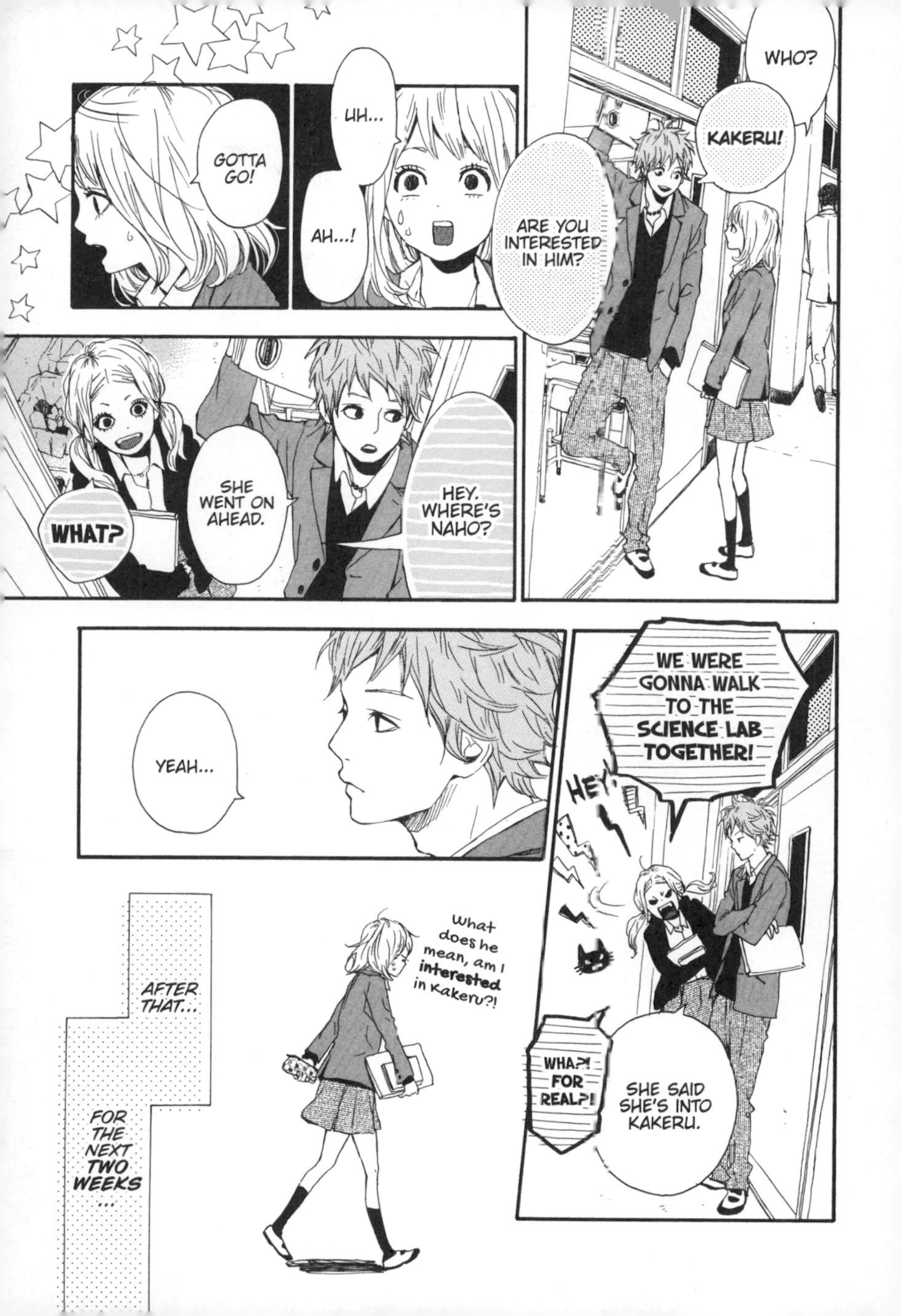
WHO?
KAKERU!
ARE YOU INTERESTED IN HIM?
UH...
AH...!
GOTTA GO!
HEY. WHERE'S NAHO?
SHE WENT ON AHEAD.
WHAT?
WE WERE GONNA WALK TO THE SCIENCE LAB TOGETHER!
HEY!
SHE SAID SHE'S INTO KAKERU.
WHA?! FOR REAL?!
YEAH...
What does he mean, am I interested in Kakeru?!
AFTER THAT...
FOR THE NEXT TWO WEEKS...

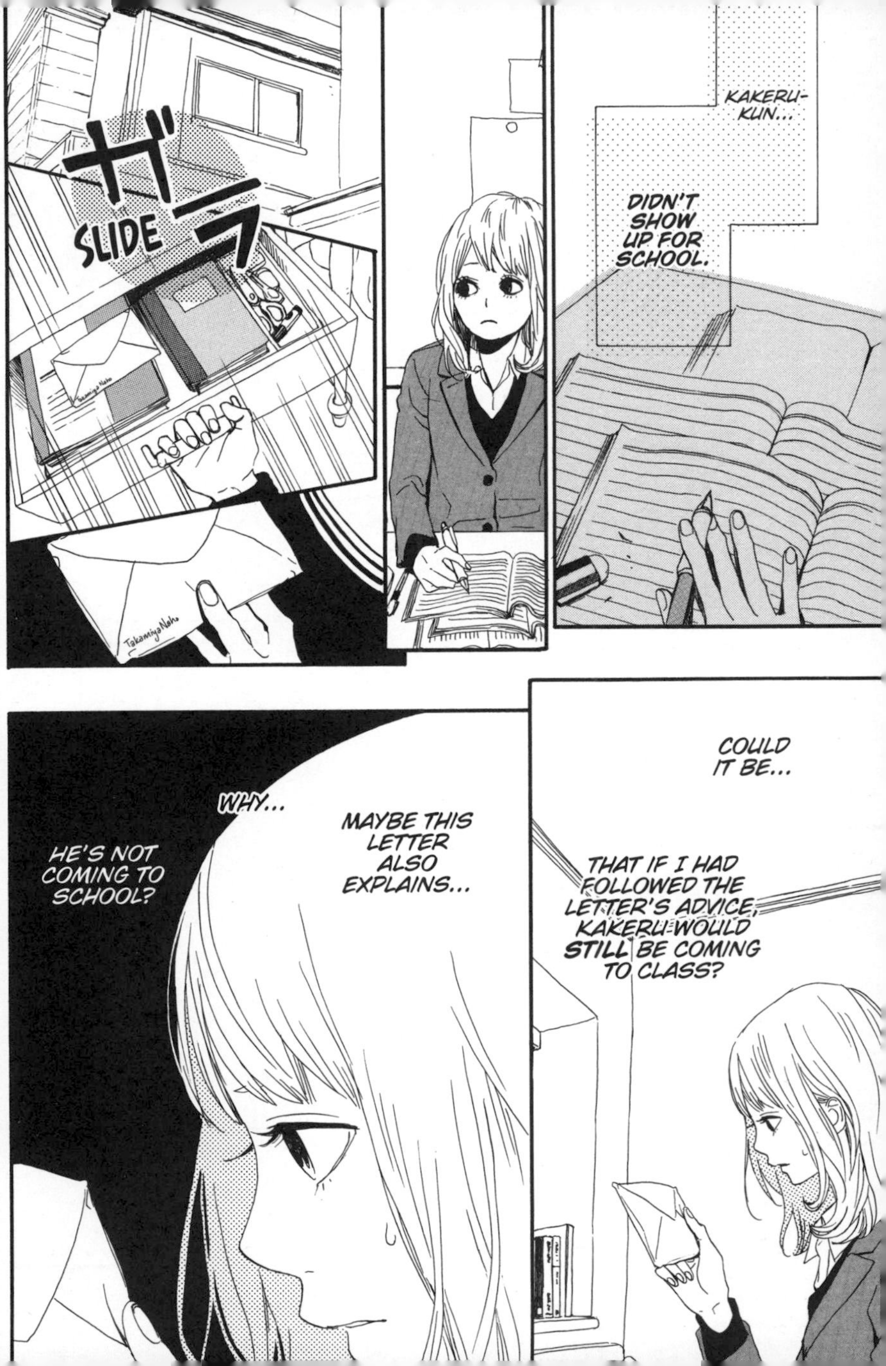
KAKERU-KUN...
DIDN'T SHOW UP FOR SCHOOL.
ガラ
SLIDE
Takamiya Naho
COULD IT BE...
THAT IF I HAD FOLLOWED THE LETTER'S ADVICE, KAKERU WOULD STILL BE COMING TO CLASS?
MAYBE THIS LETTER ALSO EXPLAINS...
WHY...
HE'S NOT COMING TO SCHOOL?

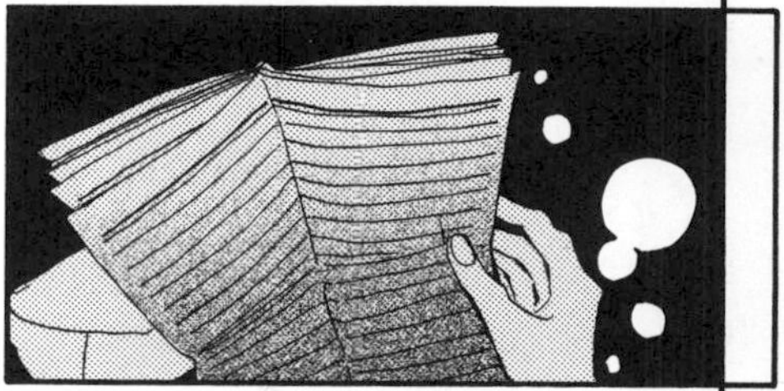

April 20

- Ballgame.
- In the softball match, I was called on to be a pinch hitter.

◎ I regret saying no.
I want you to agree when they ask you to play.

- On this day, I started to like Kakeru.

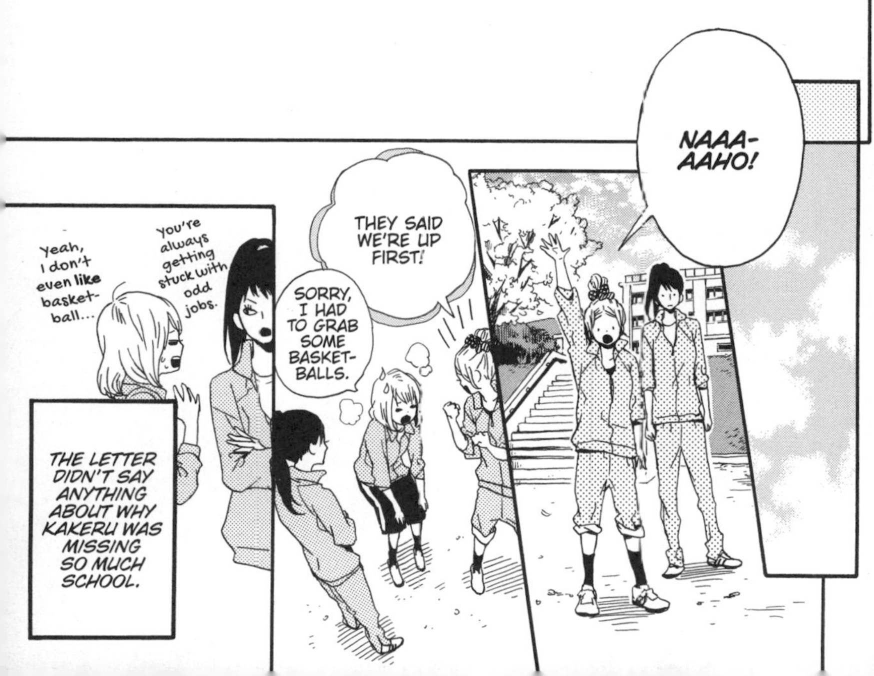
NAAAA-AAHO!
THEY SAID WE'RE UP FIRST!
SORRY, I HAD TO GRAB SOME BASKET-BALLS.
You're always getting stuck with odd jobs.
Yeah, I don't even like basket-ball...
THE LETTER DIDN'T SAY ANYTHING ABOUT WHY KAKERU WAS MISSING SO MUCH SCHOOL.

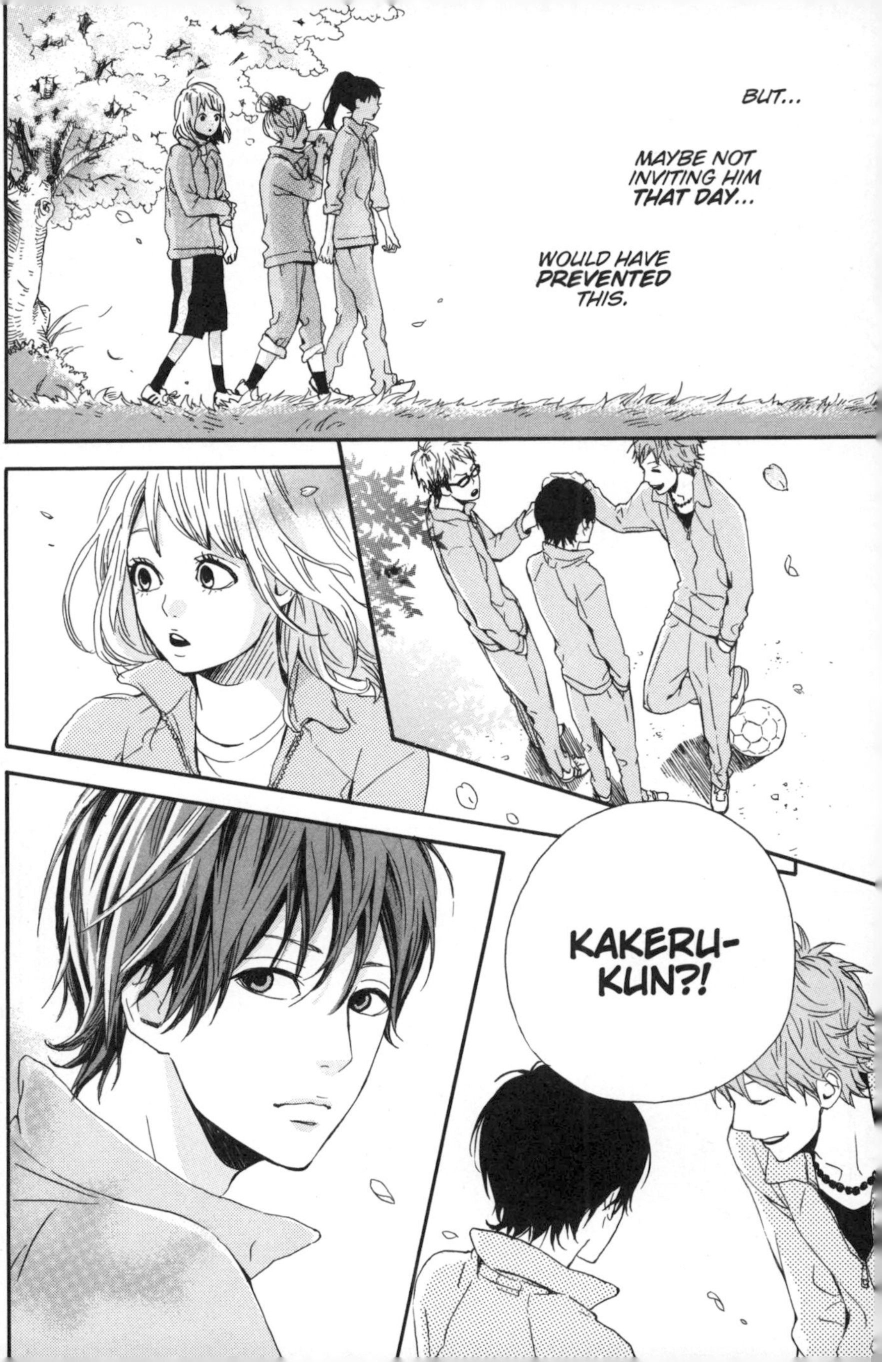
BUT...
MAYBE NOT INVITING HIM THAT DAY...
WOULD HAVE PREVENTED THIS.
KAKERU-KUN?!

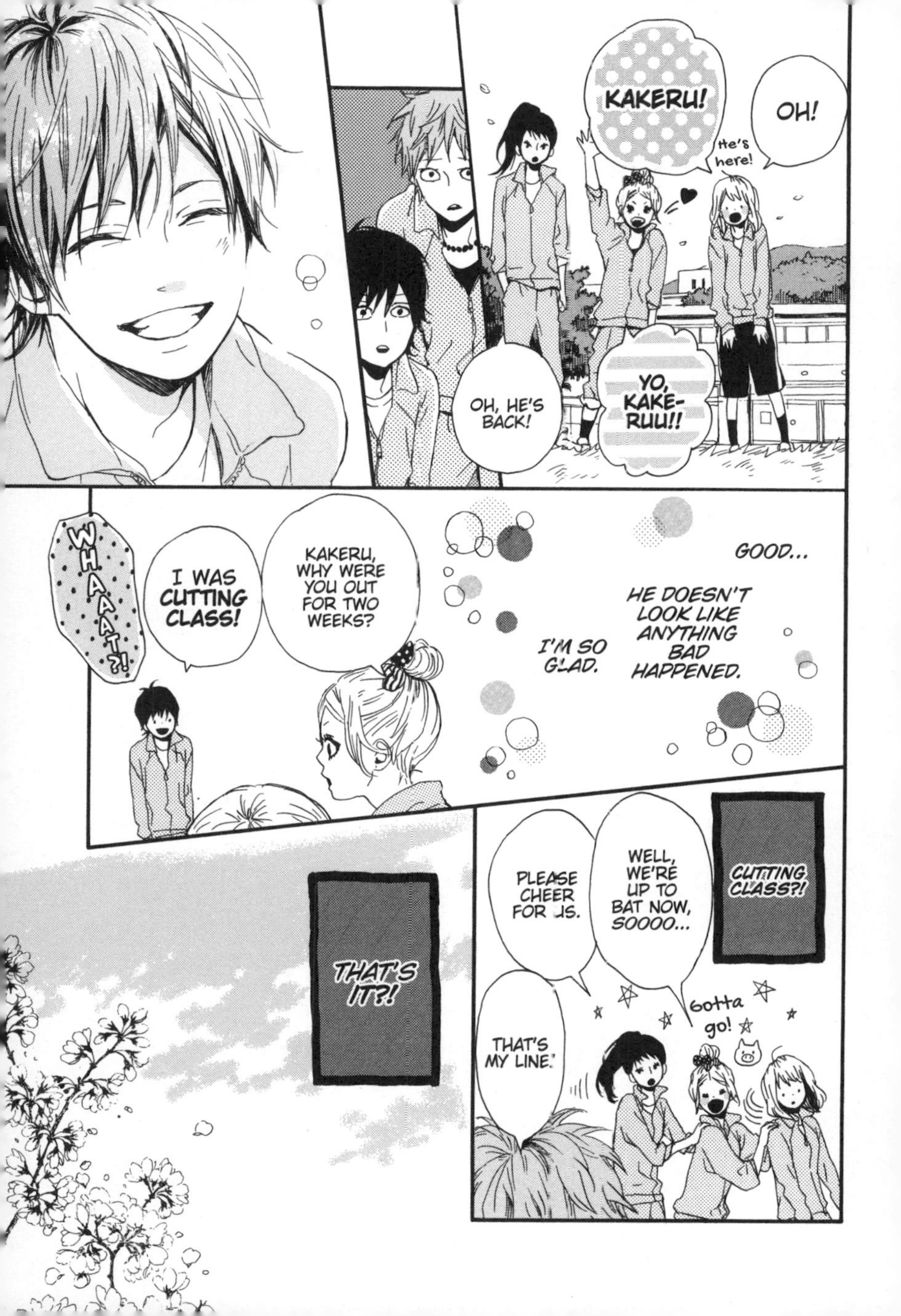
OH!
He's here!
KAKERU!
YO, KAKE-RUU!!
OH, HE'S BACK!
GOOD...
HE DOESN'T LOOK LIKE ANYTHING BAD HAPPENED.
I'M SO GLAD.
KAKERU, WHY WERE YOU OUT FOR TWO WEEKS?
I WAS CUTTING CLASS!
WHAAAT?!
CUTTING CLASS?!
WELL, WE'RE UP TO BAT NOW, SOOOO...
PLEASE CHEER FOR US.
Gotta go!
THAT'S MY LINE.
THAT'S IT?!

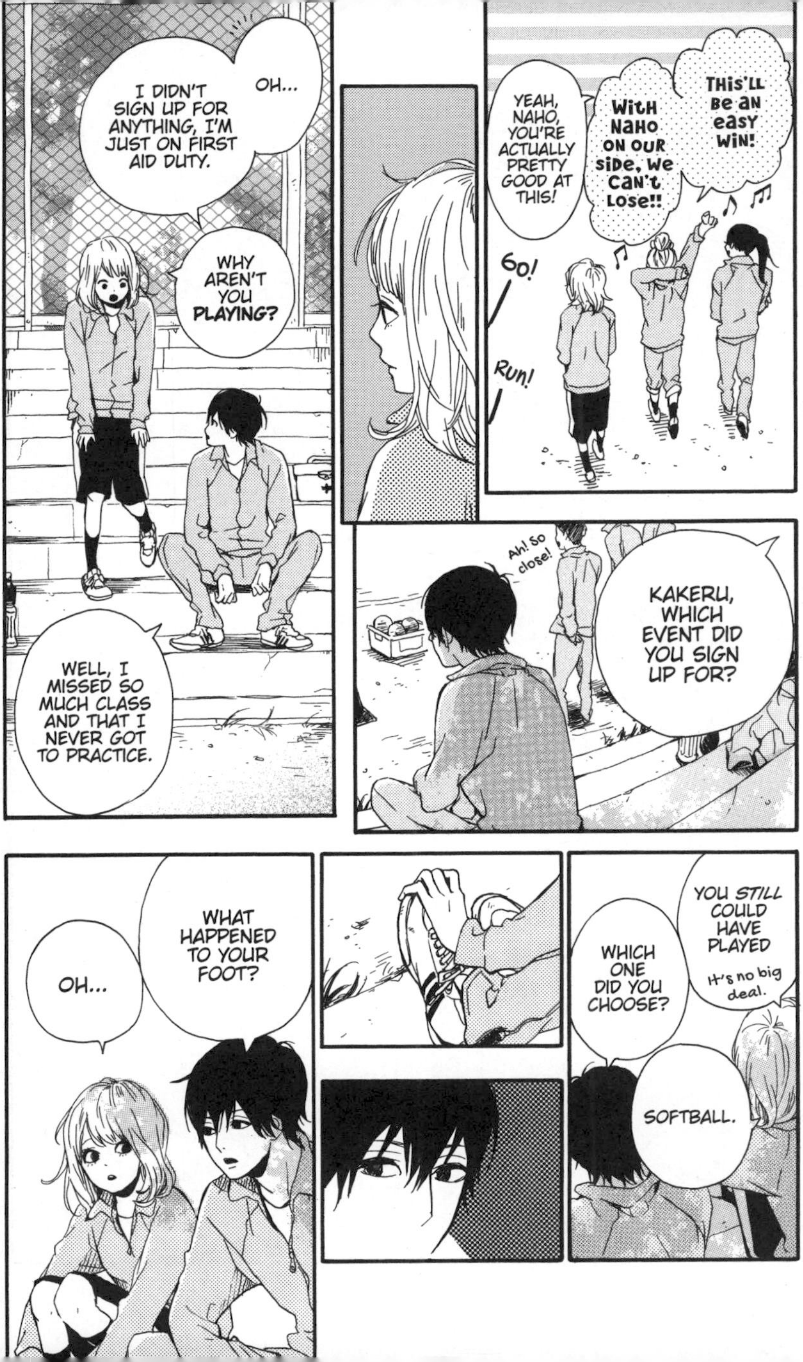
THIS'LL BE AN EASY WIN!
WITH NAHO ON OUR SIDE, WE CAN'T LOSE!!
YEAH, NAHO, YOU'RE ACTUALLY PRETTY GOOD AT THIS!
GO!
RUN!
Ah! So close!
KAKERU, WHICH EVENT DID YOU SIGN UP FOR?
OH...
I DIDN'T SIGN UP FOR ANYTHING, I'M JUST ON FIRST AID DUTY.
WHY AREN'T YOU PLAYING?
WELL, I MISSED SO MUCH CLASS AND THAT I NEVER GOT TO PRACTICE.
YOU STILL COULD HAVE PLAYED
It's no big deal.
WHICH ONE DID YOU CHOOSE?
SOFTBALL.
WHAT HAPPENED TO YOUR FOOT?
OH...

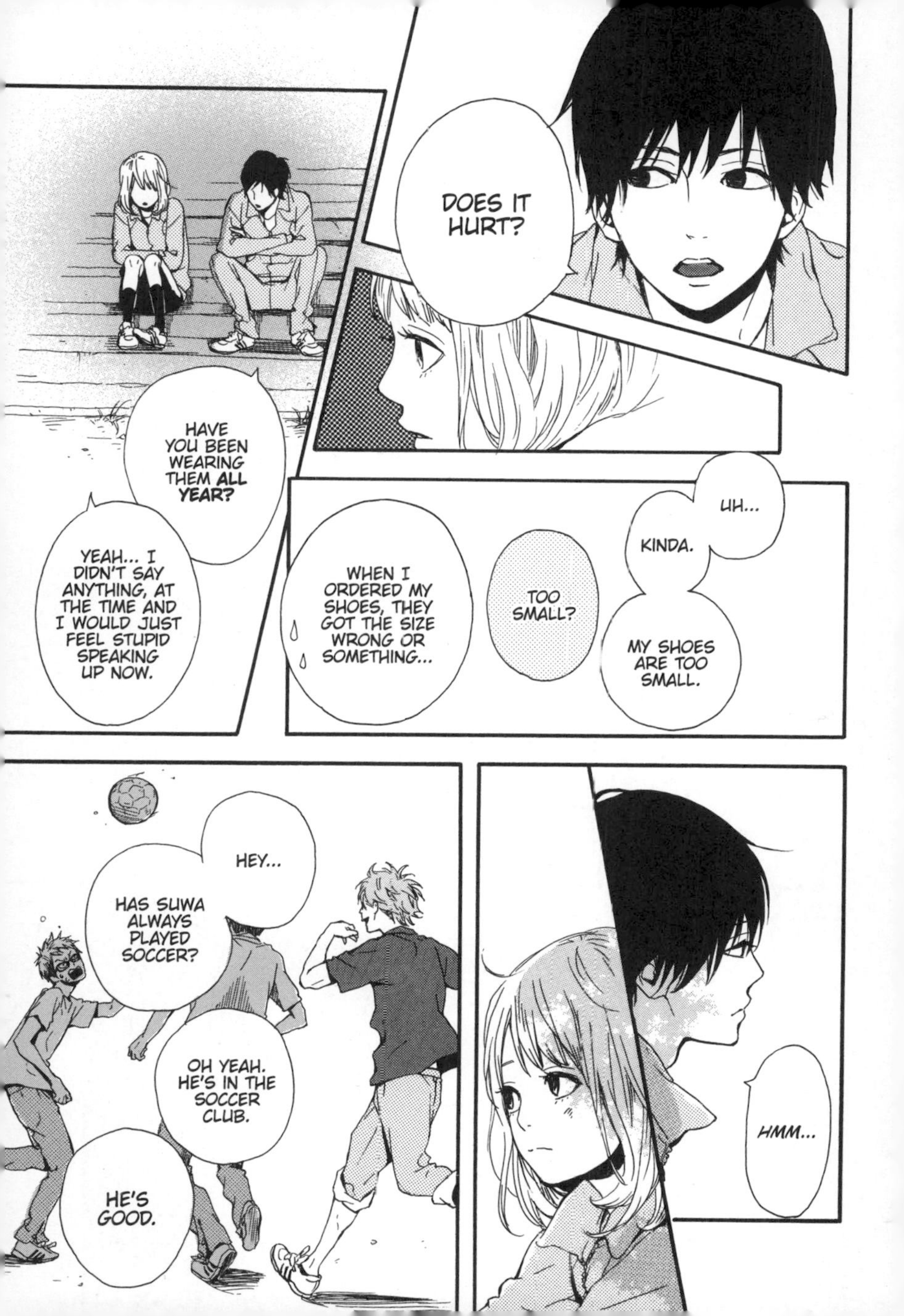
DOES IT HURT?
UH...
KINDA.
MY SHOES ARE TOO SMALL.
TOO SMALL?
WHEN I ORDERED MY SHOES, THEY GOT THE SIZE WRONG OR SOMETHING...
HAVE YOU BEEN WEARING THEM ALL YEAR?
YEAH... I DIDN'T SAY ANYTHING, AT THE TIME AND I WOULD JUST FEEL STUPID SPEAKING UP NOW.
HMM...
HEY...
HAS SUWA ALWAYS PLAYED SOCCER?
OH YEAH. HE'S IN THE SOCCER CLUB.
HE'S GOOD.

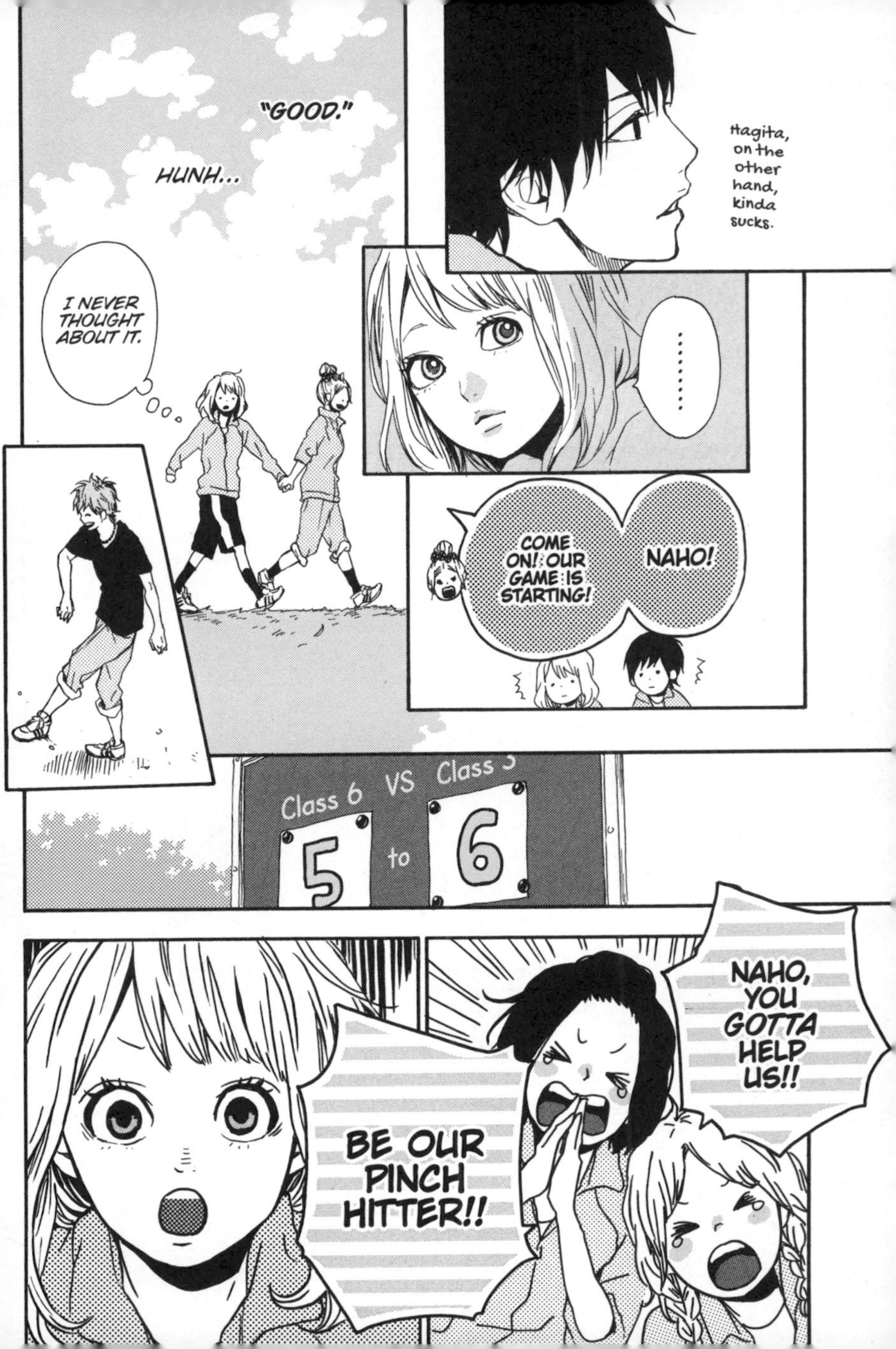
Hagita, on the other hand, kinda sucks.
......
NAHO!
COME ON! OUR GAME IS STARTING!
"GOOD."
HUNH...
I NEVER THOUGHT ABOUT IT.
Class 6 VS Class 3
5 to 6
NAHO, YOU GOTTA HELP US!!
BE OUR PINCH HITTER!!

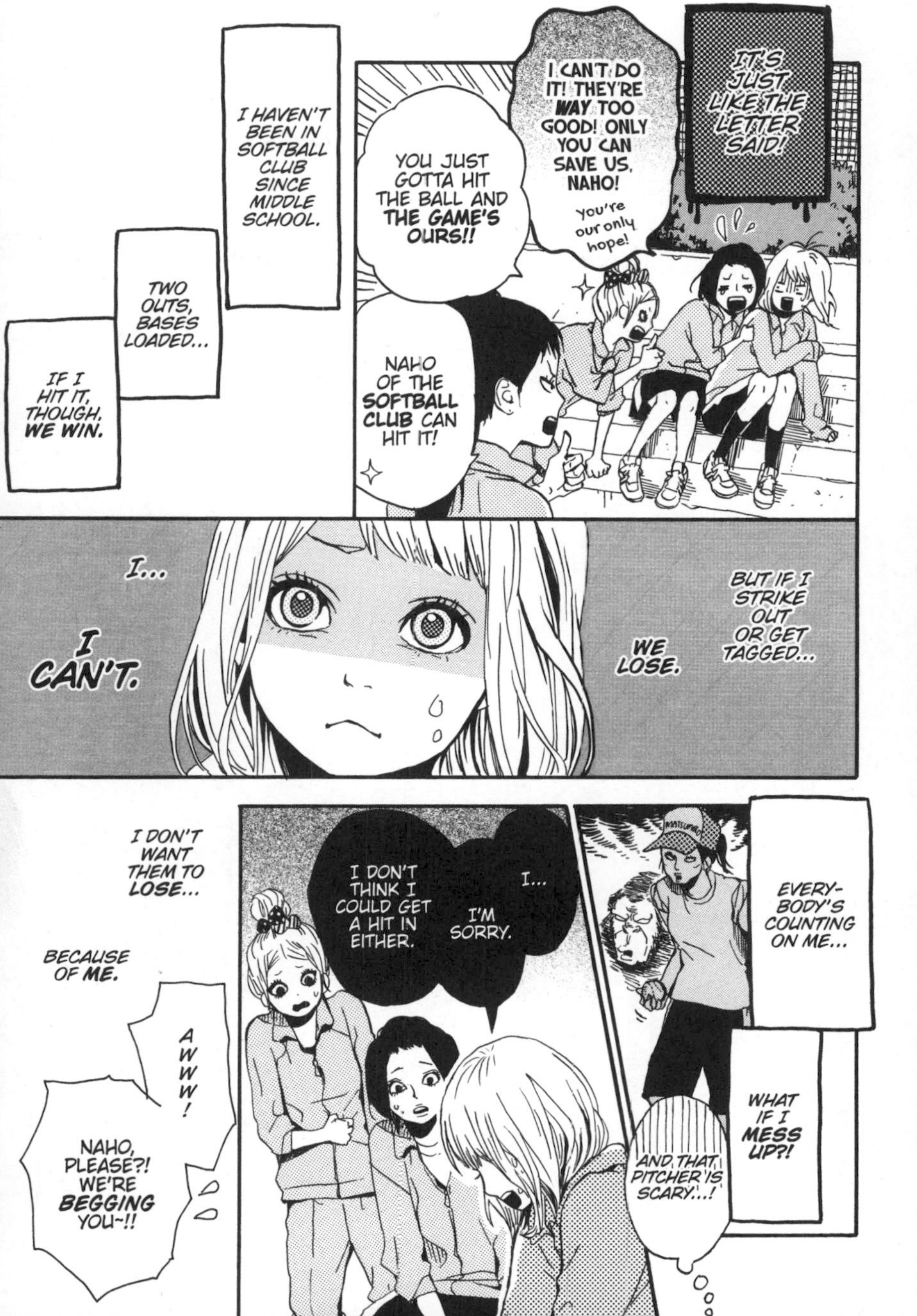
IT'S JUST LIKE THE LETTER SAID!
I CAN'T DO IT! THEY'RE WAY TOO GOOD! ONLY YOU CAN SAVE US, NAHO!
You're our only hope!
YOU JUST GOTTA HIT THE BALL AND THE GAME'S OURS!!
NAHO OF THE SOFTBALL CLUB CAN HIT IT!
I HAVEN'T BEEN IN SOFTBALL CLUB SINCE MIDDLE SCHOOL.
TWO OUTS, BASES LOADED...
IF I HIT IT, THOUGH, WE WIN.
BUT IF I STRIKE OUT OR GET TAGGED...
WE LOSE.
I...
I CAN'T.
EVERY-BODY'S COUNTING ON ME...
WHAT IF I MESS UP?!
AND THAT PITCHER'S SCARY...!
I...
I'M SORRY.
I DON'T THINK I COULD GET A HIT IN EITHER.
AWWW!
NAHO, PLEASE?! WE'RE BEGGING YOU~!!
I DON'T WANT THEM TO LOSE...
BECAUSE OF ME.

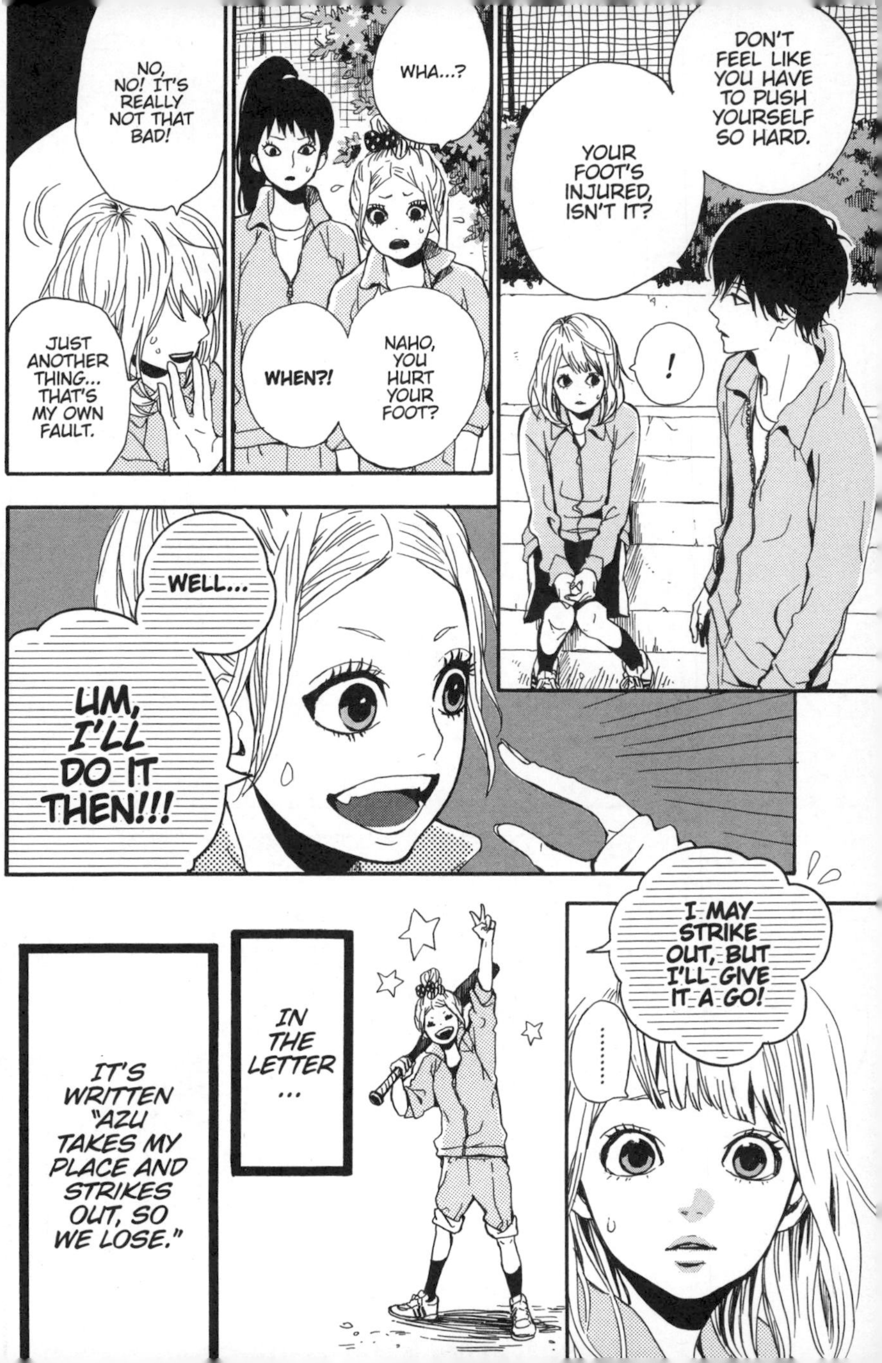
DON'T FEEL LIKE YOU HAVE TO PUSH YOURSELF SO HARD.
YOUR FOOT'S INJURED, ISN'T IT?
!
WHA...?
NAHO, YOU HURT YOUR FOOT?
WHEN?!
NO, NO! IT'S REALLY NOT THAT BAD!
JUST ANOTHER THING... THAT'S MY OWN FAULT.
WELL...
UM, I'LL DO IT THEN!!!
I MAY STRIKE OUT, BUT I'LL GIVE IT A GO!
......
IN THE LETTER...
IT'S WRITTEN "AZU TAKES MY PLACE AND STRIKES OUT, SO WE LOSE."

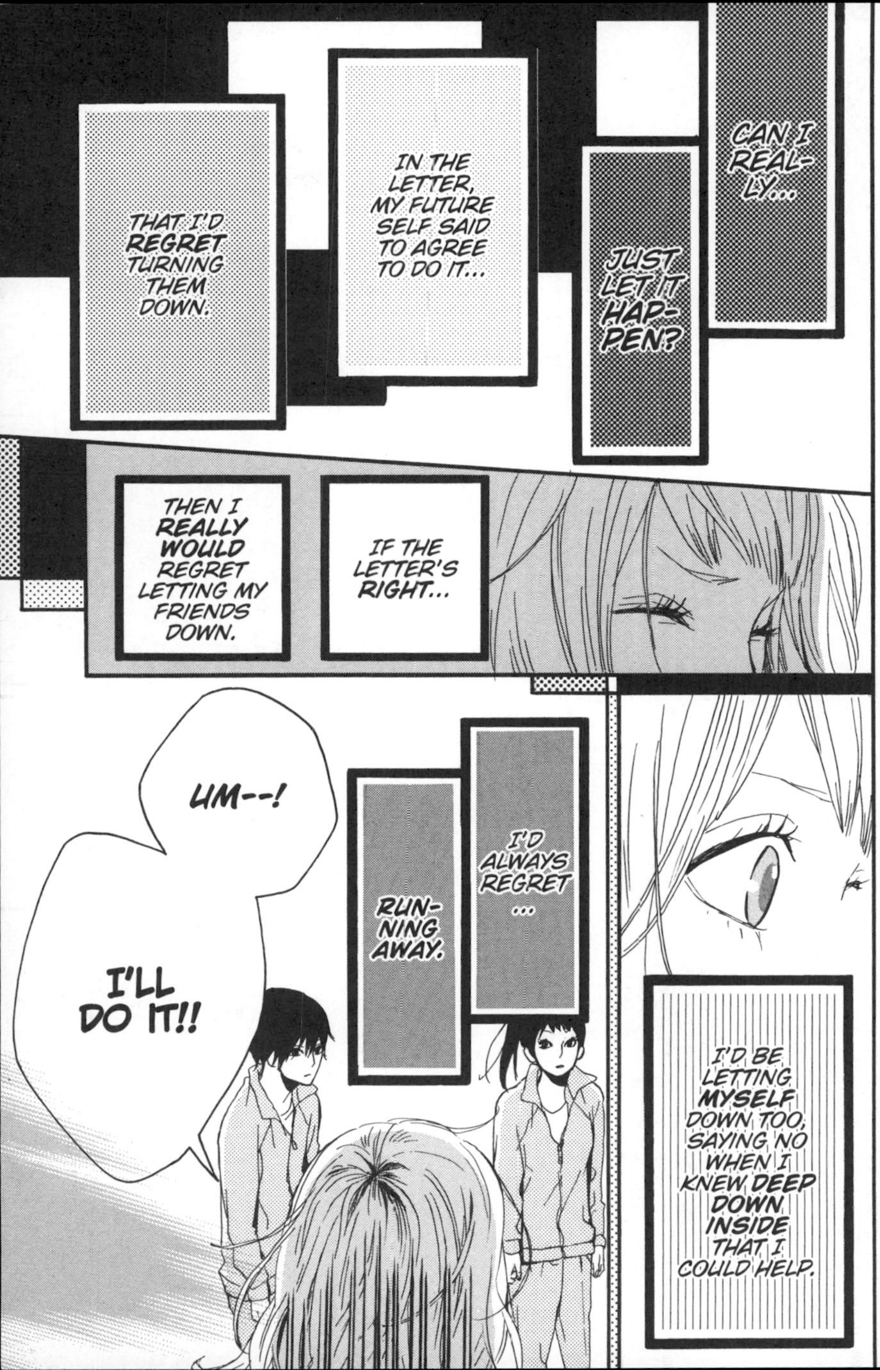
CAN I REALLY...
JUST LET IT HAPPEN?
IN THE LETTER, MY FUTURE SELF SAID TO AGREE TO DO IT...
THAT I'D REGRET TURNING THEM DOWN.
IF THE LETTER'S RIGHT...
THEN I REALLY WOULD REGRET LETTING MY FRIENDS DOWN.
I'D BE LETTING MYSELF DOWN TOO, SAYING NO WHEN I KNEW DEEP DOWN INSIDE THAT I COULD HELP.
I'D ALWAYS REGRET...
RUNNING AWAY.
UM--!
I'LL DO IT!!

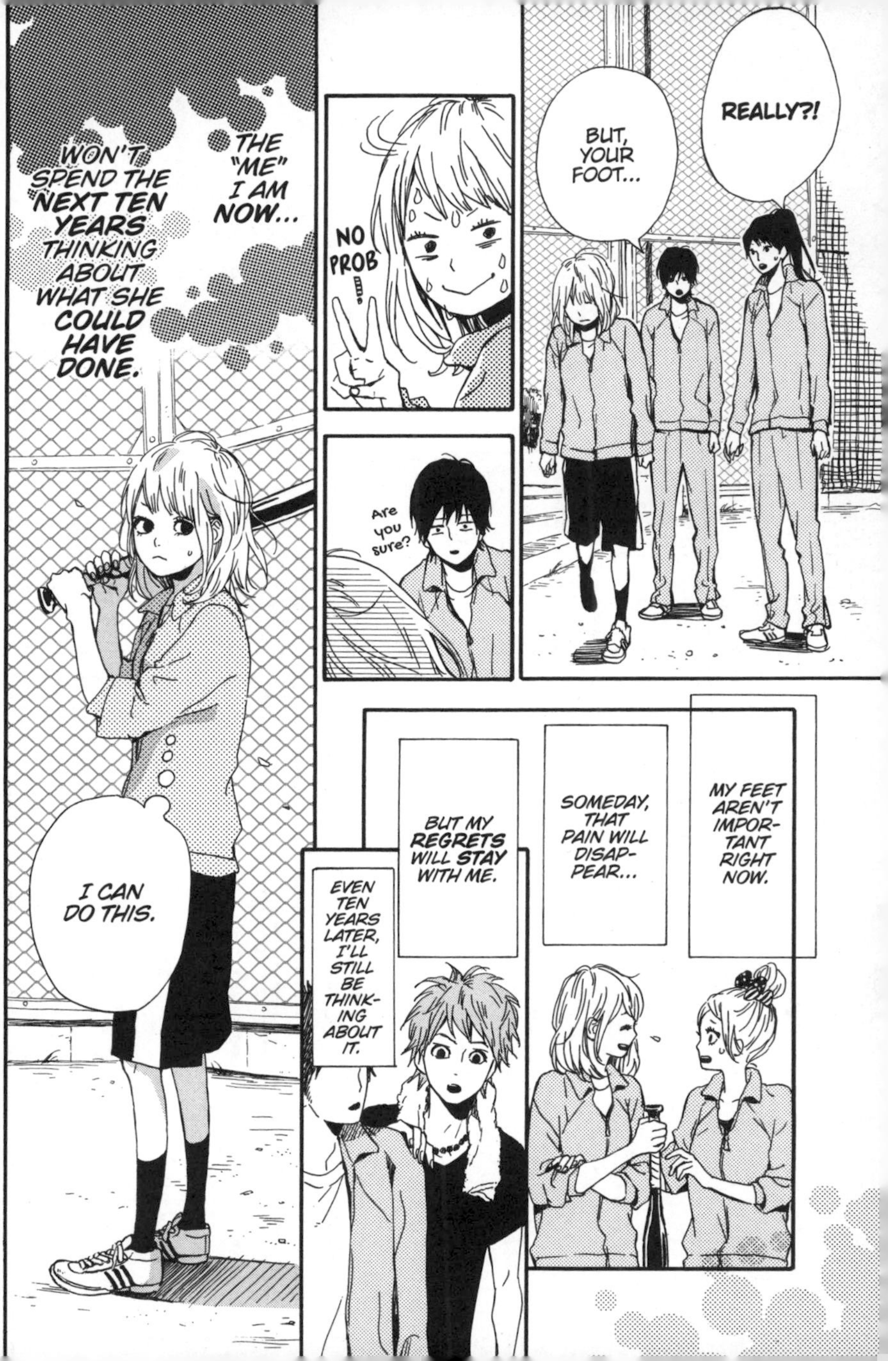
REALLY?!
BUT, YOUR FOOT...
NO PROB...!
Are you sure?
MY FEET AREN'T IMPORTANT RIGHT NOW.
SOMEDAY, THAT PAIN WILL DISAPPEAR...
BUT MY REGRETS WILL STAY WITH ME.
EVEN TEN YEARS LATER, I'LL STILL BE THINKING ABOUT IT.
THE "ME" I AM NOW...
WON'T SPEND THE NEXT TEN YEARS THINKING ABOUT WHAT SHE COULD HAVE DONE.
I CAN DO THIS.

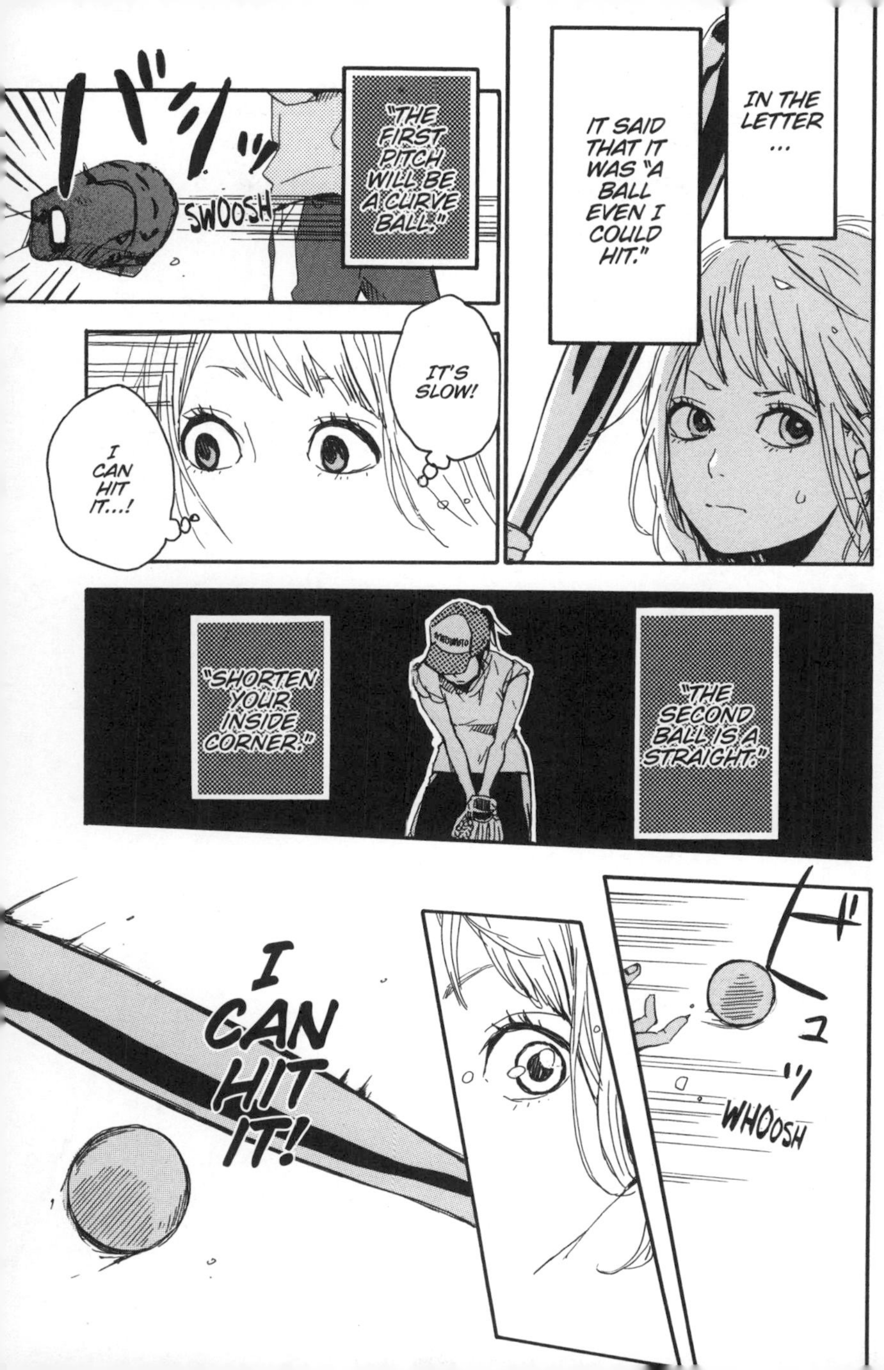
IN THE LETTER ...
IT SAID THAT IT WAS "A BALL EVEN I COULD HIT."
"THE FIRST PITCH WILL BE A CURVE BALL."
SWOOSH
IT'S SLOW!
I CAN HIT IT...!
"THE SECOND BALL IS A STRAIGHT."
"SHORTEN YOUR INSIDE CORNER."
WHOOSH
I CAN HIT IT!

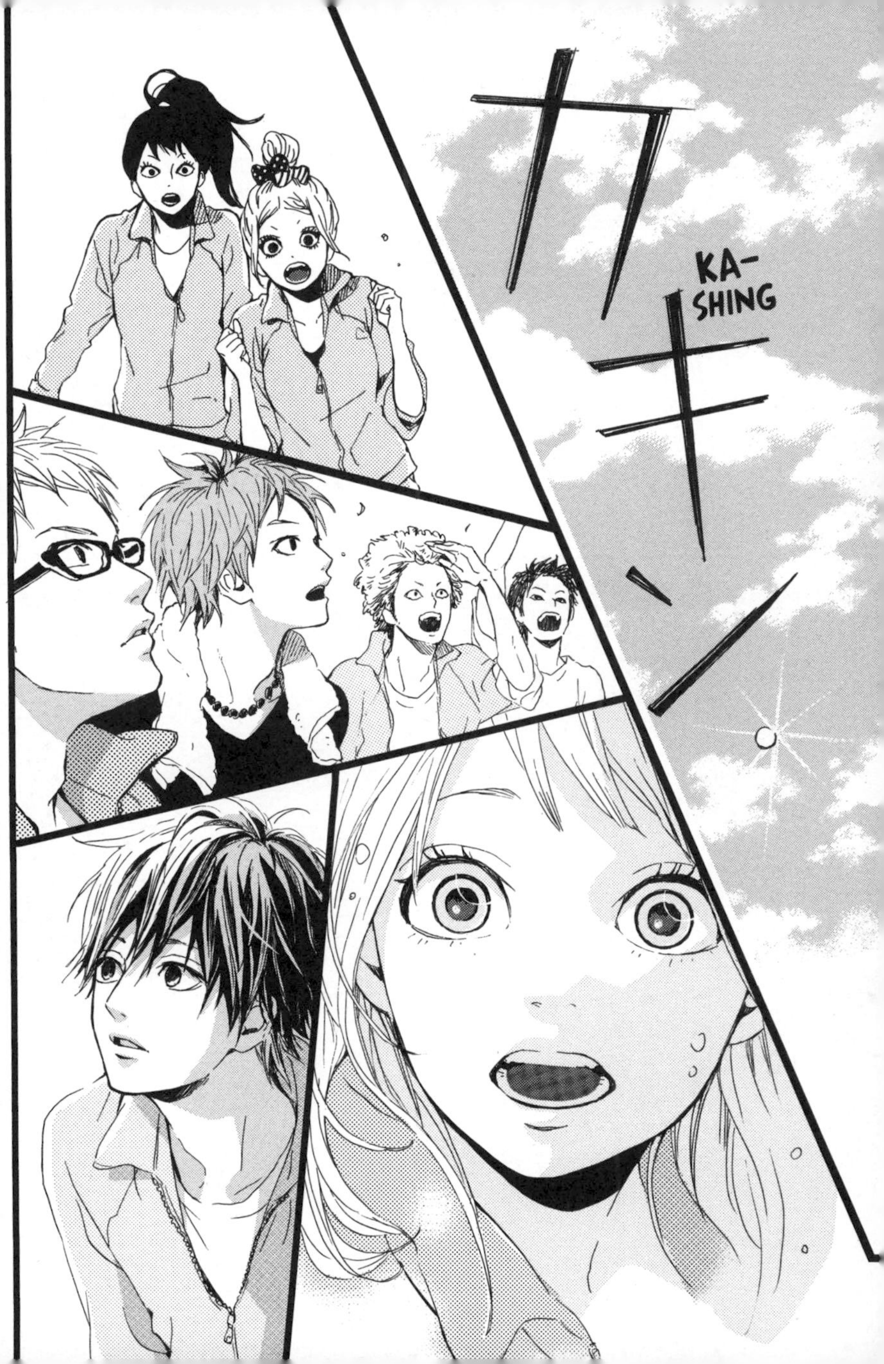
カキン
KA-
SHING

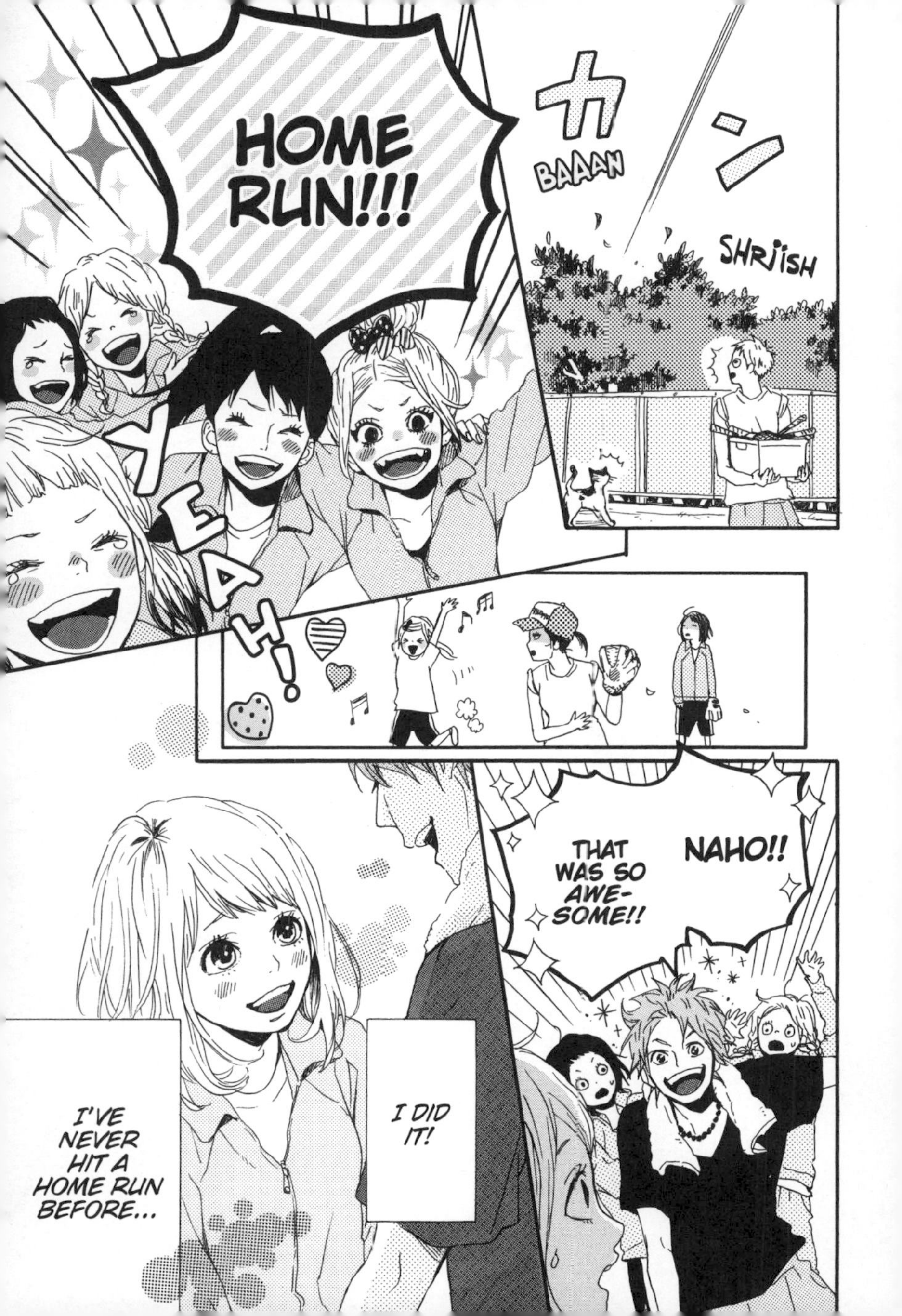
カーン
BAAAN
SHRIISH
HOME RUN!!!
YEAH!
NAHO!!
THAT WAS SO AWESOME!!
I DID IT!
I'VE NEVER HIT A HOME RUN BEFORE...

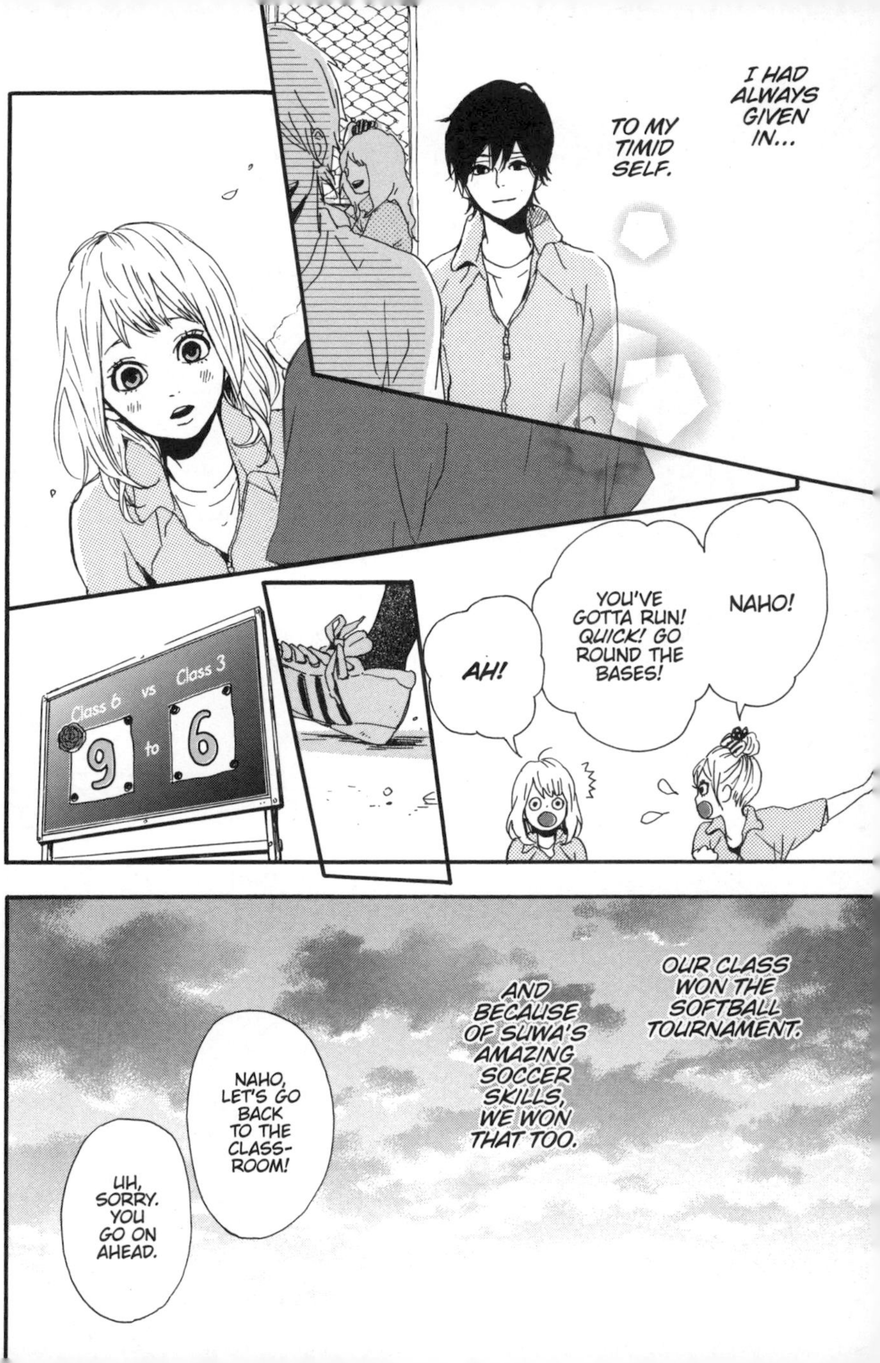
I HAD ALWAYS GIVEN IN...
TO MY TIMID SELF.
NAHO!
YOU'VE GOTTA RUN! QUICK! GO ROUND THE BASES!
AH!
Class 6 vs Class 3
9 to 6
OUR CLASS WON THE SOFTBALL TOURNAMENT.
AND BECAUSE OF SUWA'S AMAZING SOCCER SKILLS, WE WON THAT TOO.
NAHO, LET'S GO BACK TO THE CLASS-ROOM!
UH, SORRY. YOU GO ON AHEAD.

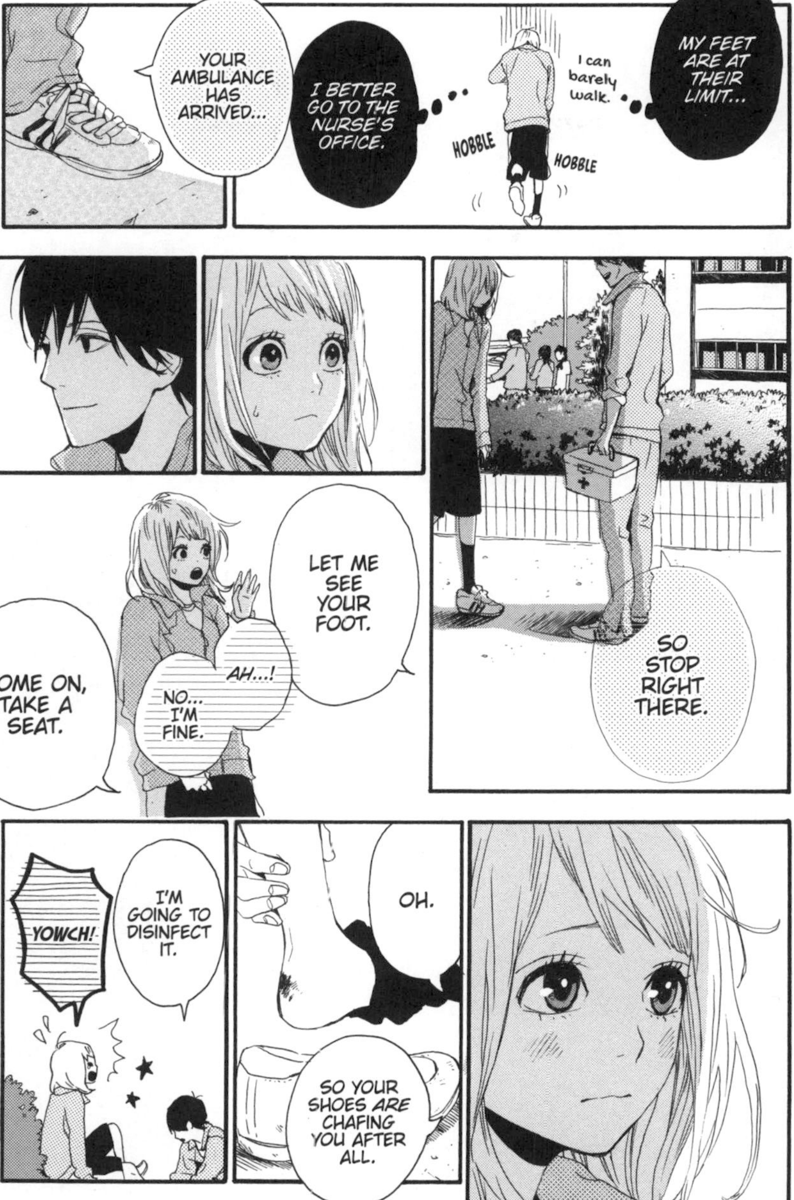
MY FEET ARE AT THEIR LIMIT...
I can barely walk.
I BETTER GO TO THE NURSE'S OFFICE.
HOBBLE
HOBBLE
YOUR AMBULANCE HAS ARRIVED...
SO STOP RIGHT THERE.
LET ME SEE YOUR FOOT.
AH...!
NO... I'M FINE.
COME ON, TAKE A SEAT.
OH.
SO YOUR SHOES ARE CHAFING YOU AFTER ALL.
I'M GOING TO DISINFECT IT.
YOWCH!

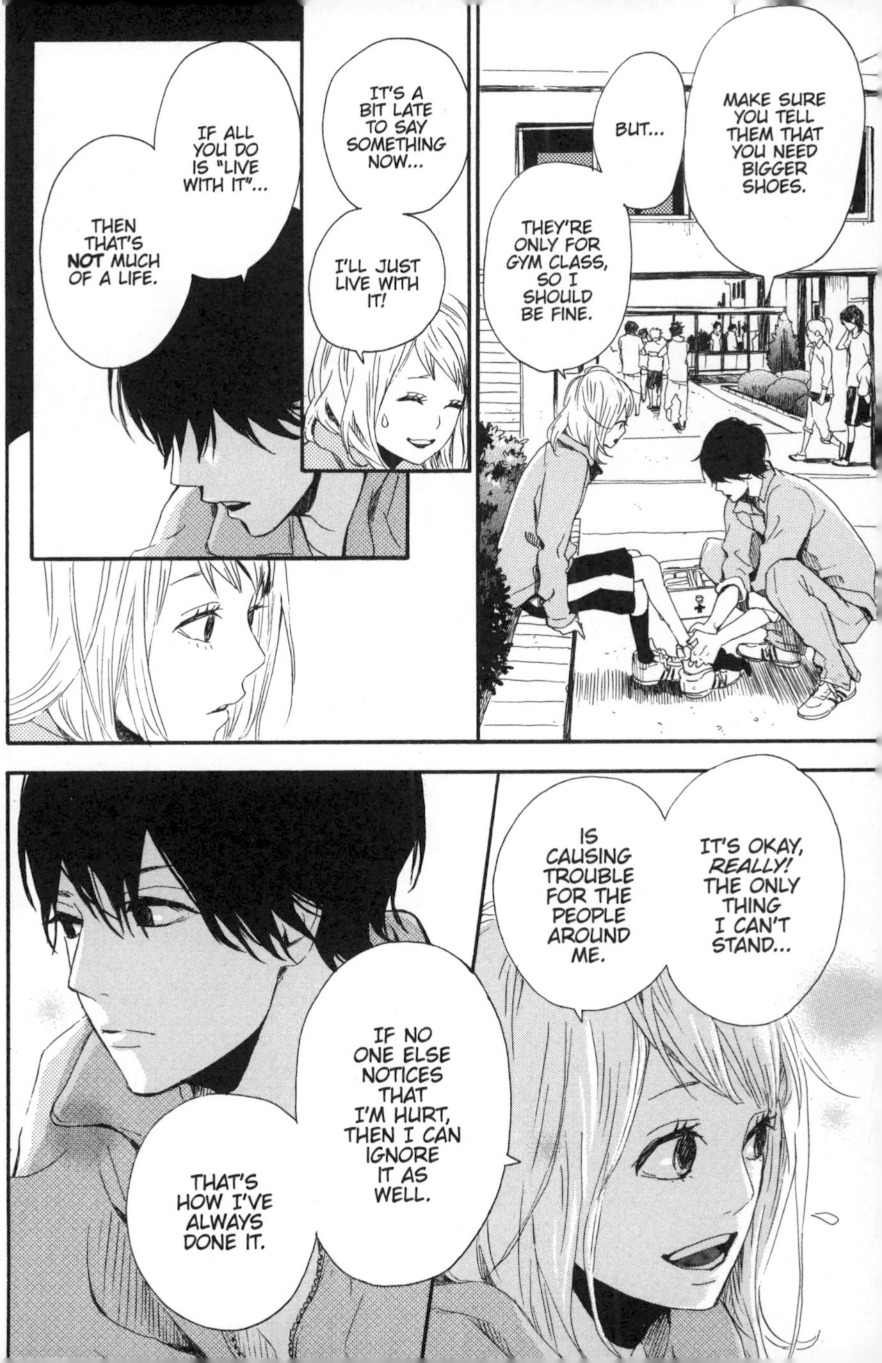
MAKE SURE YOU TELL THEM THAT YOU NEED BIGGER SHOES.
BUT...
THEY'RE ONLY FOR GYM CLASS, SO I SHOULD BE FINE.
IT'S A BIT LATE TO SAY SOMETHING NOW...
I'LL JUST LIVE WITH IT!
IF ALL YOU DO IS "LIVE WITH IT"...
THEN THAT'S **NOT** MUCH OF A LIFE.
IT'S OKAY, *REALLY!* THE ONLY THING I CAN'T STAND...
IS CAUSING TROUBLE FOR THE PEOPLE AROUND ME.
IF NO ONE ELSE NOTICES THAT I'M HURT, THEN I CAN IGNORE IT AS WELL.
THAT'S HOW I'VE ALWAYS DONE IT.

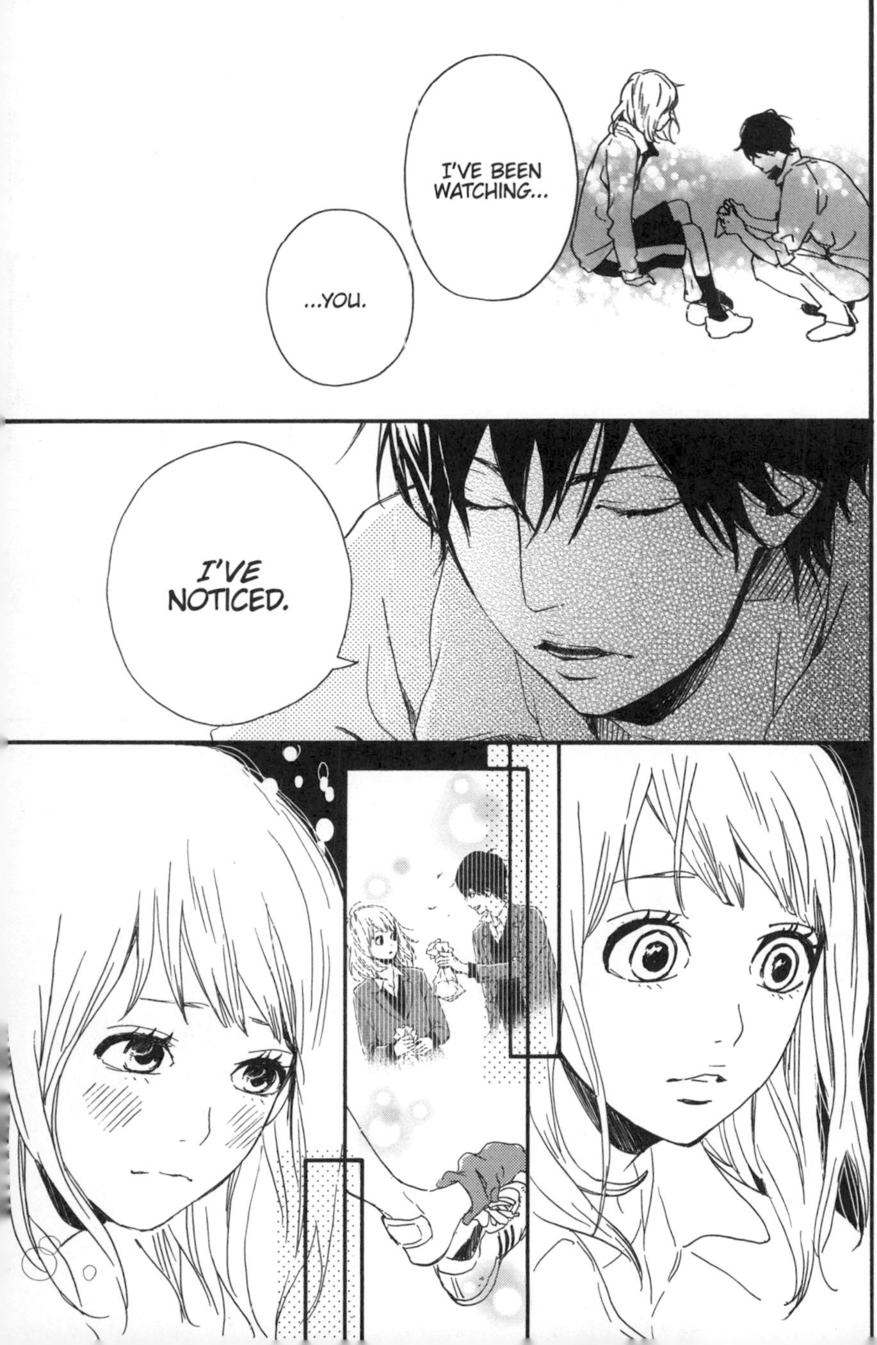
I'VE BEEN WATCHING...
...YOU.
I'VE NOTICED.

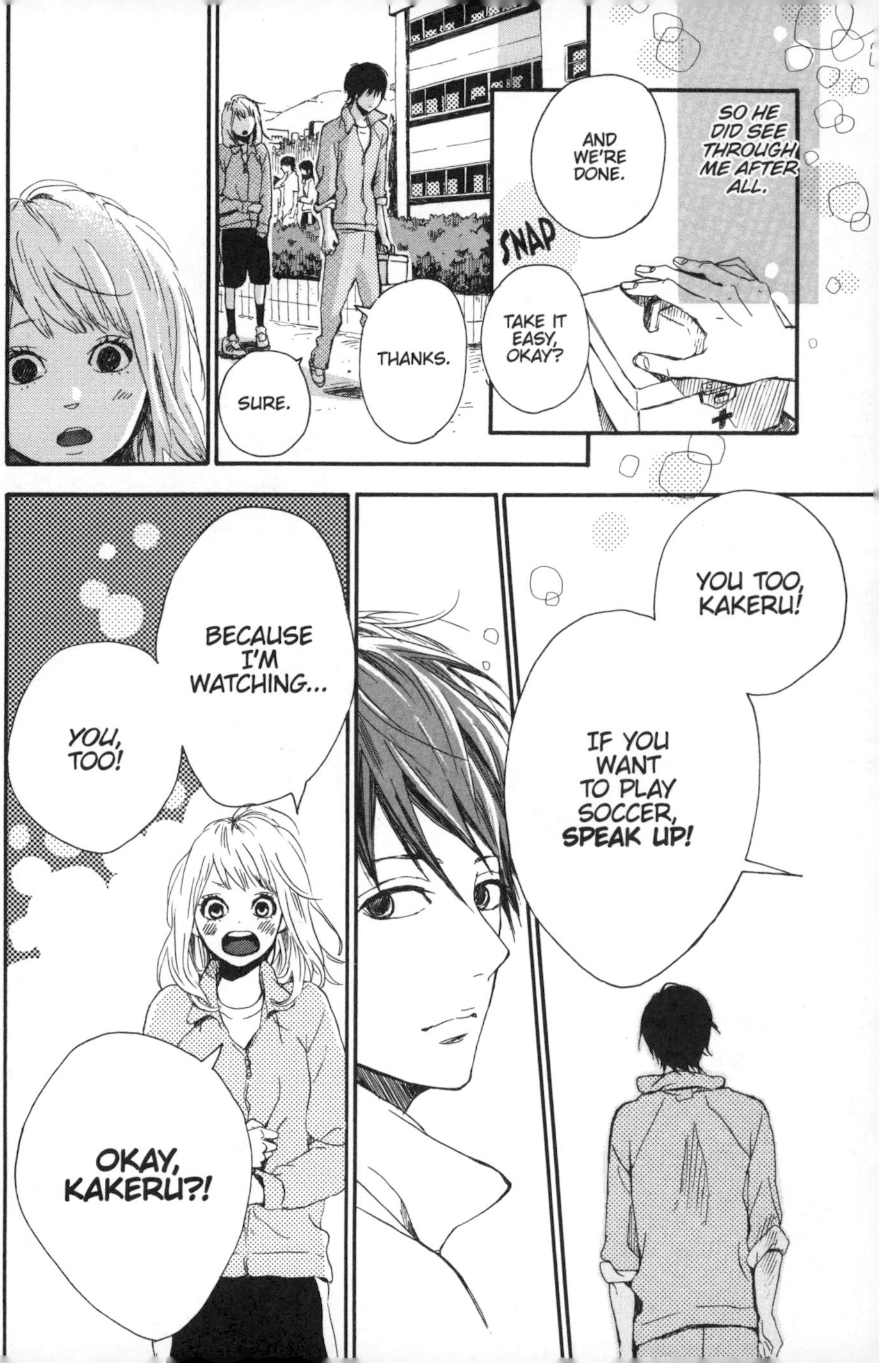

SO HE DID SEE THROUGH ME AFTER ALL.
AND WE'RE DONE.
SNAP
TAKE IT EASY, OKAY?
THANKS.
SURE.
YOU TOO, KAKERU!
IF YOU WANT TO PLAY SOCCER, SPEAK UP!
BECAUSE I'M WATCHING...
YOU, TOO!
OKAY, KAKERU?!

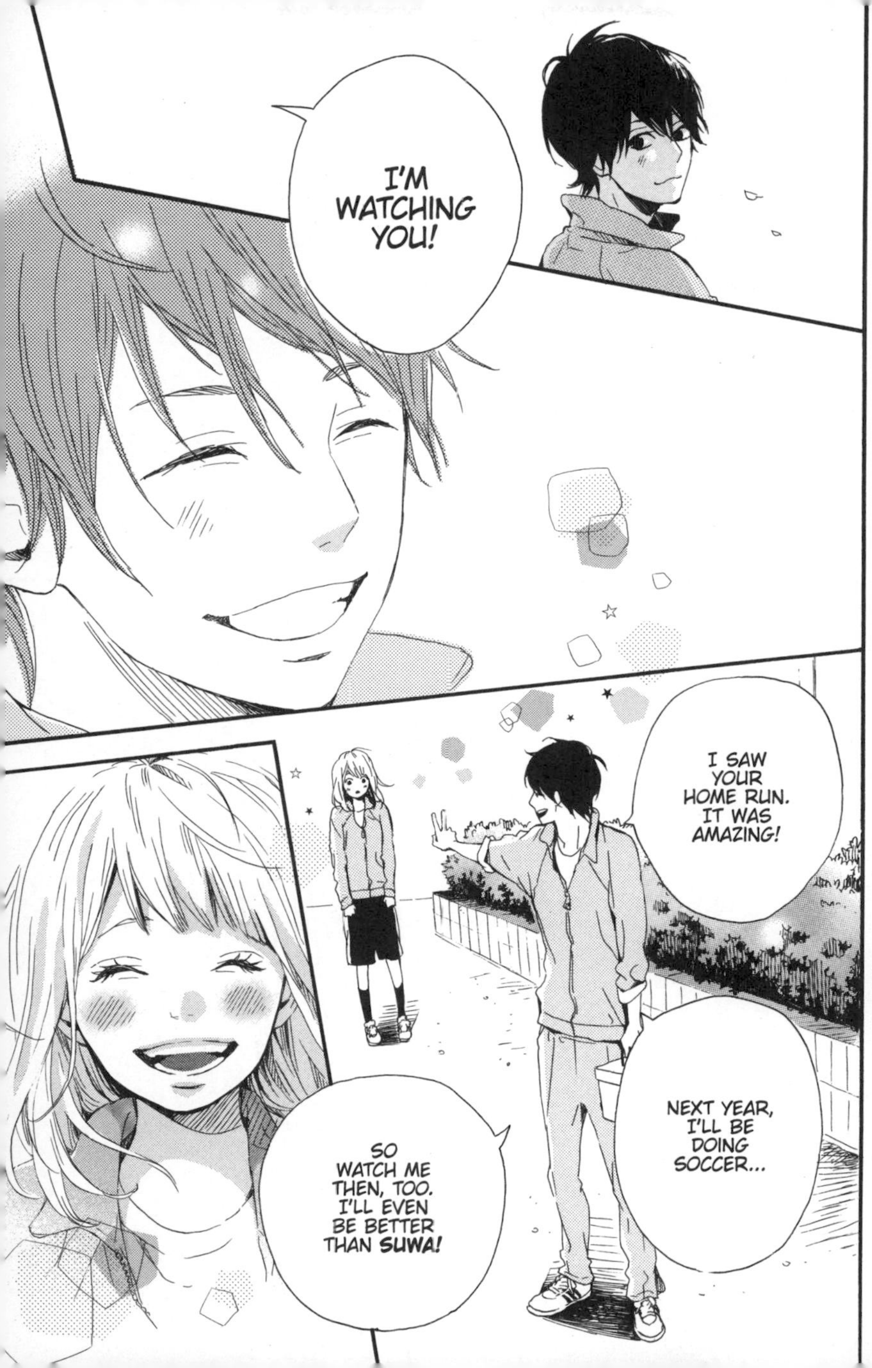
I'M WATCHING YOU!
I SAW YOUR HOME RUN. IT WAS AMAZING!
NEXT YEAR, I'LL BE DOING SOCCER...
SO WATCH ME THEN, TOO. I'LL EVEN BE BETTER THAN **SUWA**!

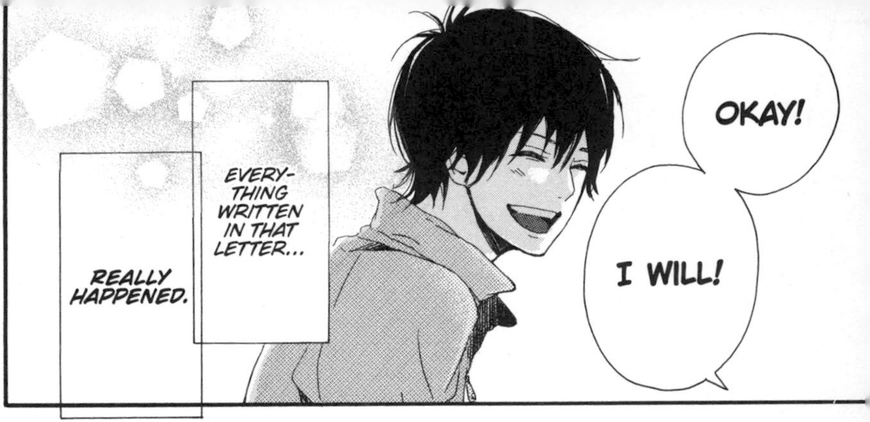
OKAY!
I WILL!
EVERY-THING WRITTEN IN THAT LETTER...
REALLY HAPPENED.

• On this day, I started to like Kakeru.

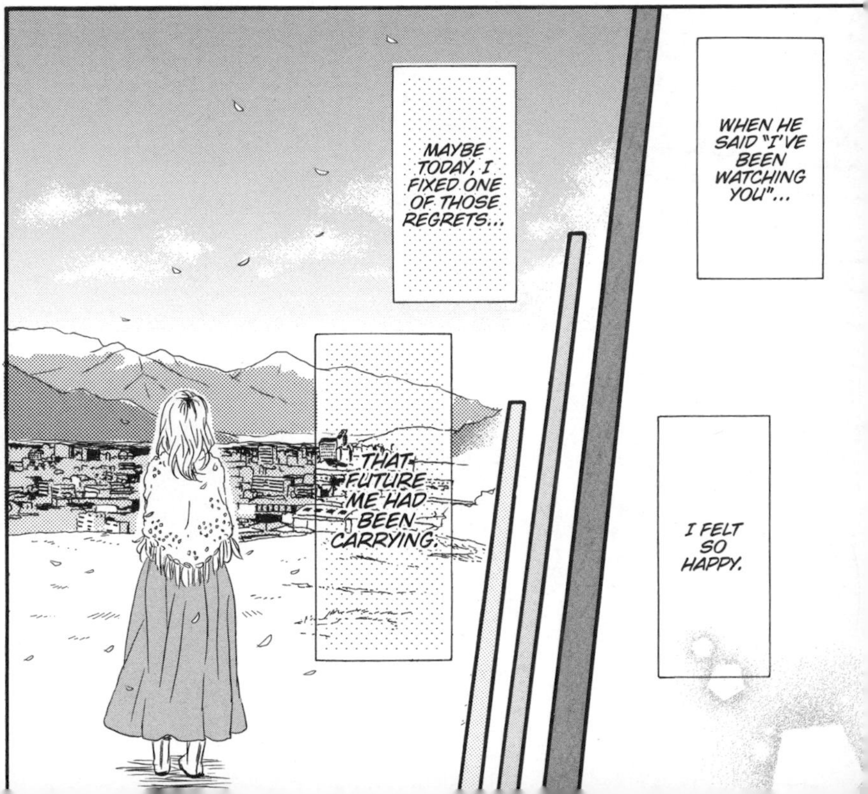
WHEN HE SAID "I'VE BEEN WATCHING YOU"...
I FELT SO HAPPY.
MAYBE TODAY, I FIXED ONE OF THOSE REGRETS...
THAT FUTURE ME HAD BEEN CARRYING.

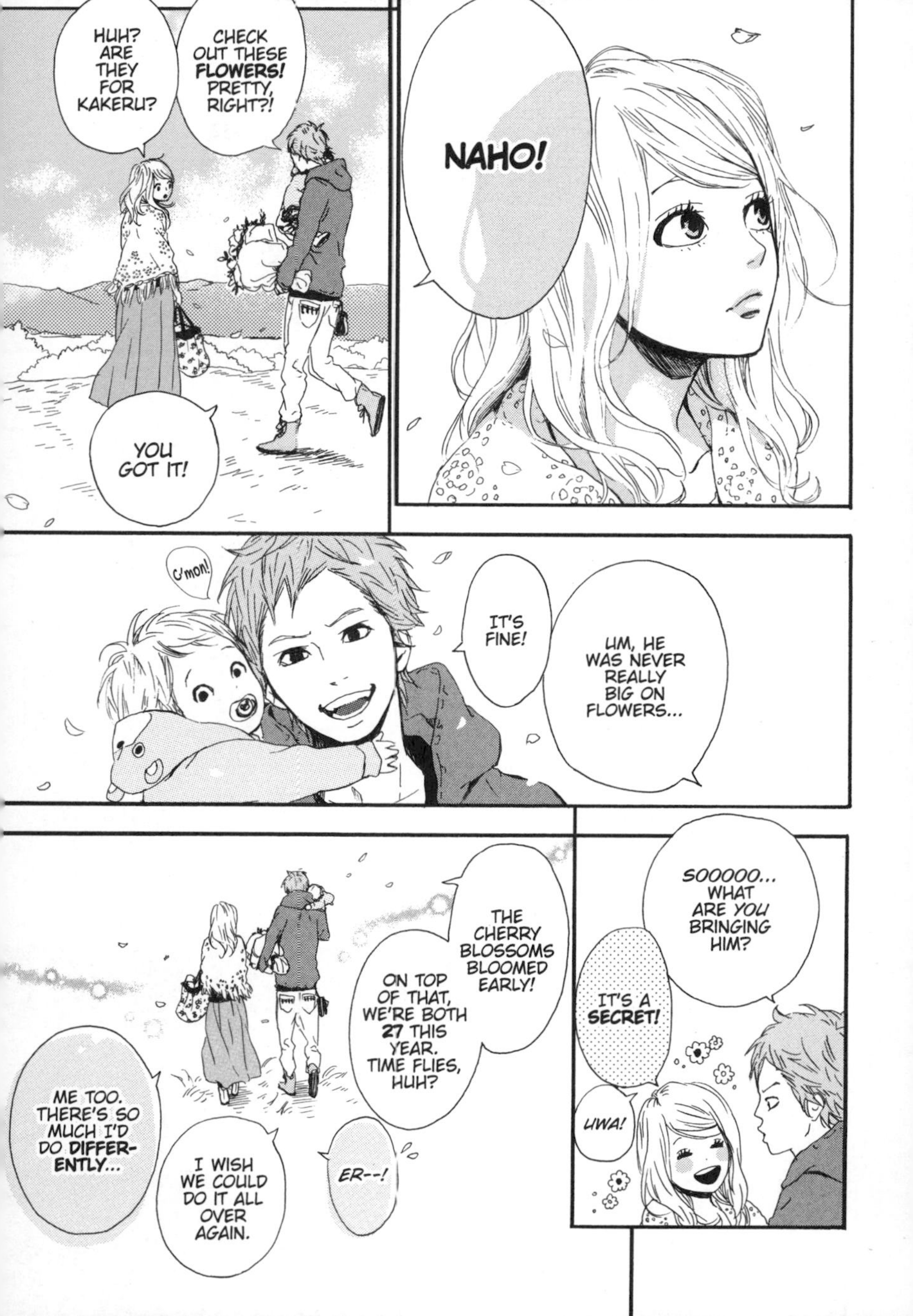
NAHO!
CHECK OUT THESE FLOWERS! PRETTY, RIGHT?!
HUH? ARE THEY FOR KAKERU?
YOU GOT IT!
UM, HE WAS NEVER REALLY BIG ON FLOWERS...
IT'S FINE!
C'mon!
SOOOOO... WHAT ARE YOU BRINGING HIM?
IT'S A SECRET!
UWA!
THE CHERRY BLOSSOMS BLOOMED EARLY!
ON TOP OF THAT, WE'RE BOTH 27 THIS YEAR. TIME FLIES, HUH?
ER--!
I WISH WE COULD DO IT ALL OVER AGAIN.
ME TOO. THERE'S SO MUCH I'D DO DIFFERENTLY...

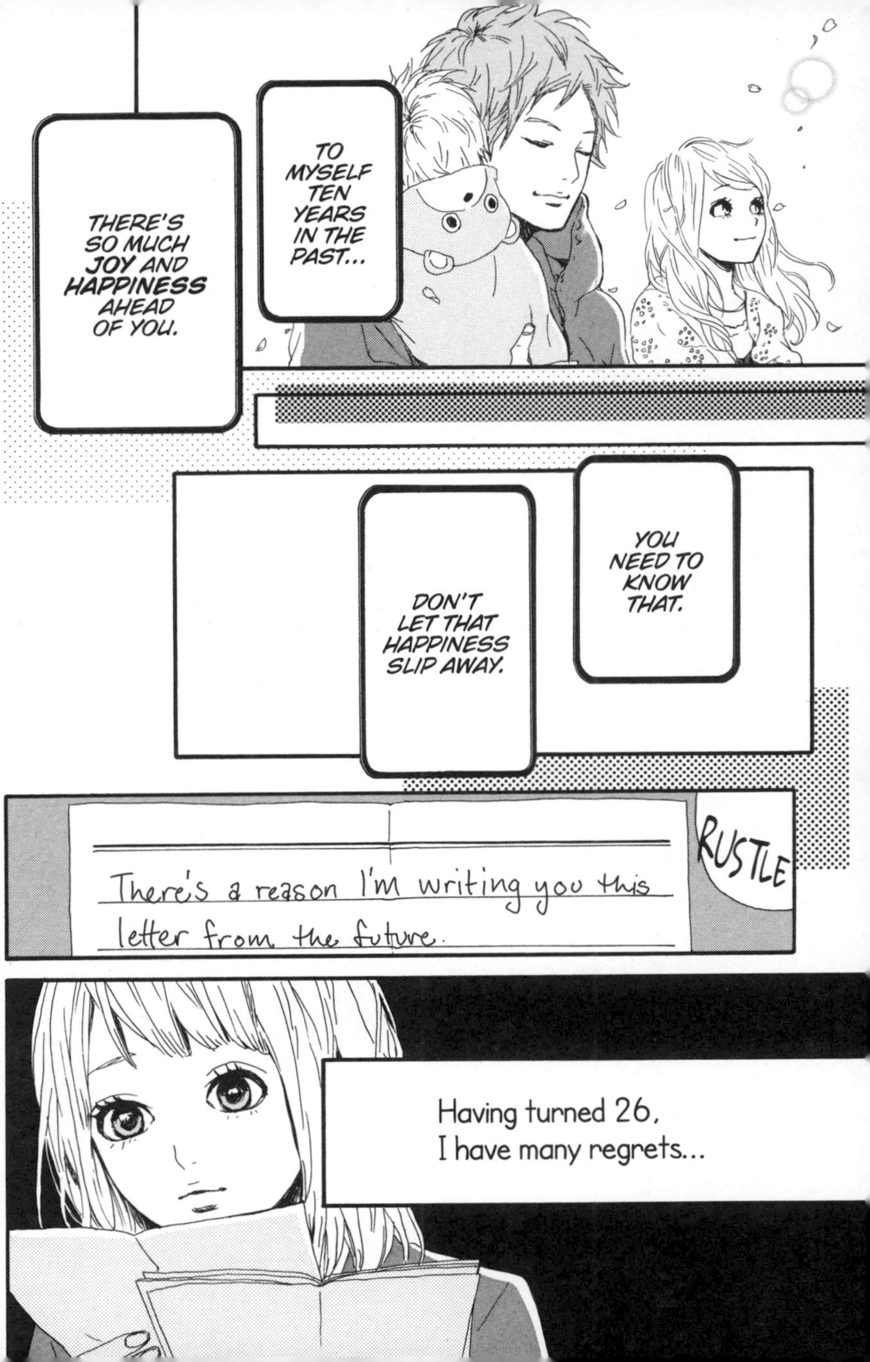
TO MYSELF TEN YEARS IN THE PAST...
THERE'S SO MUCH JOY AND HAPPINESS AHEAD OF YOU.
YOU NEED TO KNOW THAT.
DON'T LET THAT HAPPINESS SLIP AWAY.
RUSTLE
There's a reason I'm writing you this letter from the future.
Having turned 26, I have many regrets...

But there is one **big one** that still haunts me.

Here, ten years in the future,
Kakeru is no longer with us.

Don't lose something so precious.

Watch over Kakeru
with all your heart.

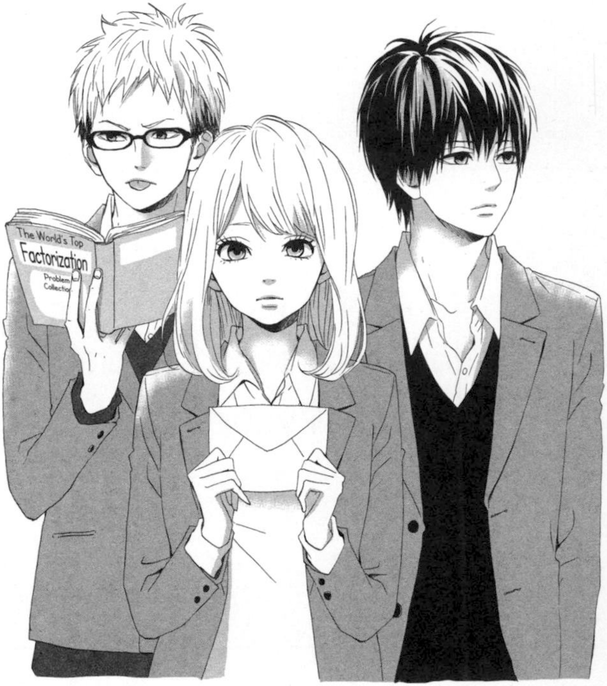
The World's Top
Factorization
Problem
Collectio

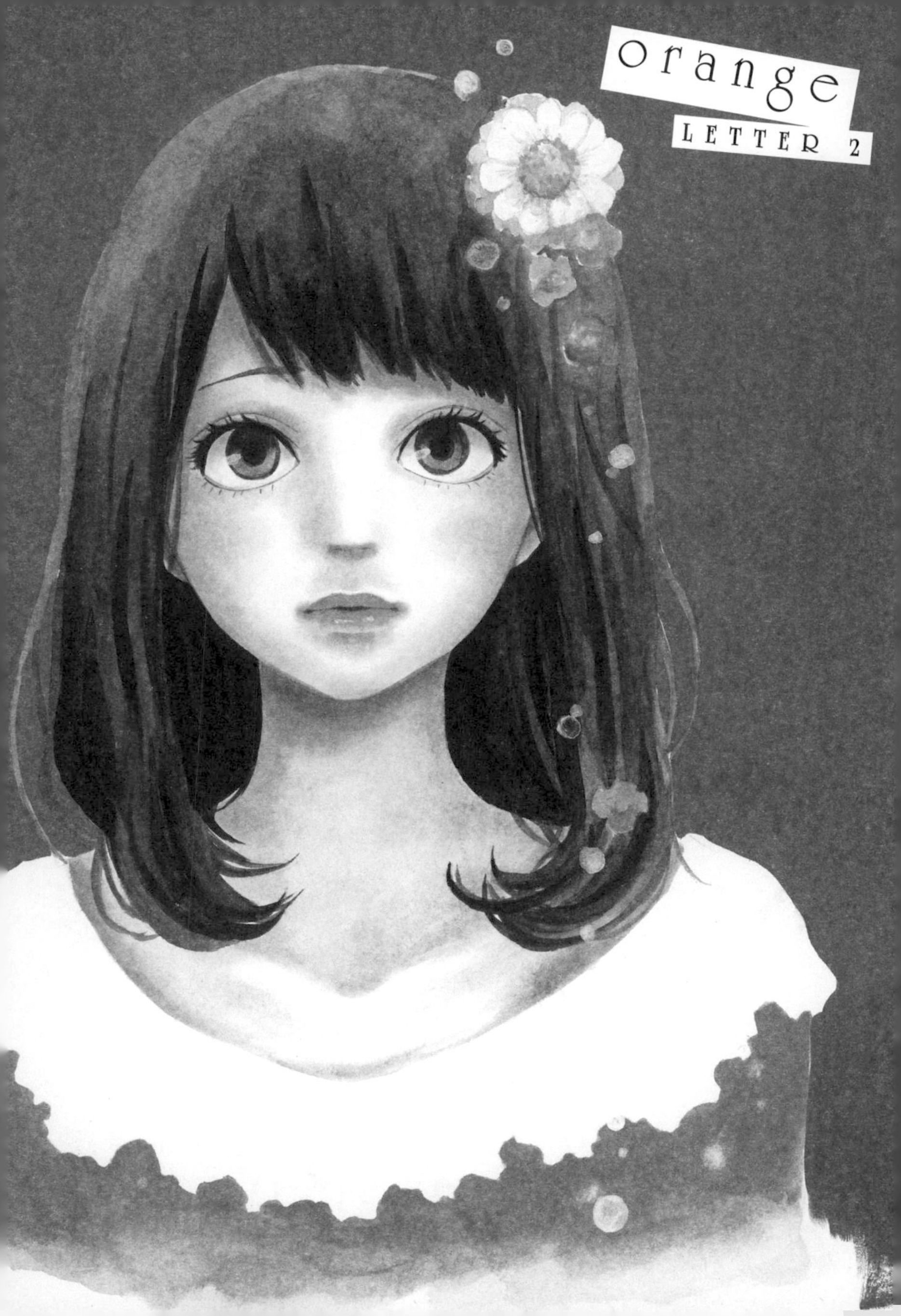
orange
LETTER 2

orange

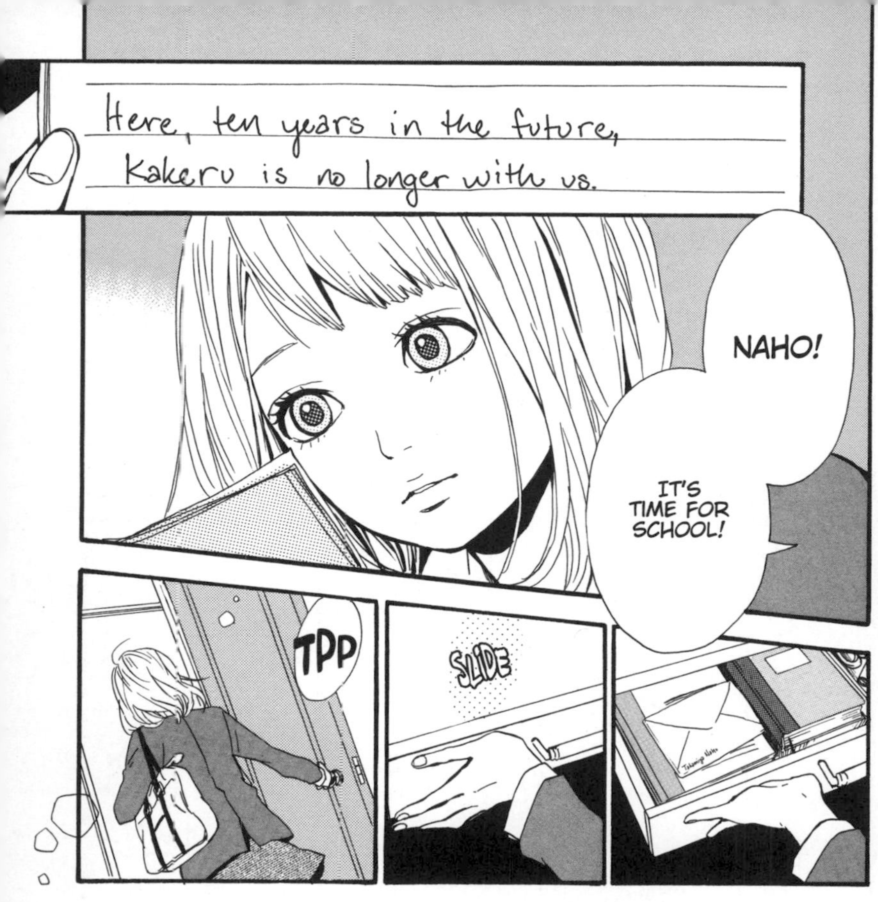
Here, ten years in the future,
Kakeru is no longer with us.
NAHO!
IT'S TIME FOR SCHOOL!
SLIDE
TPP

April 23

- Kakeru joins the soccer team on a trial basis.
- Since Kakeru's mother doesn't make him lunch, I said I would bring a lunch for him tomorrow.

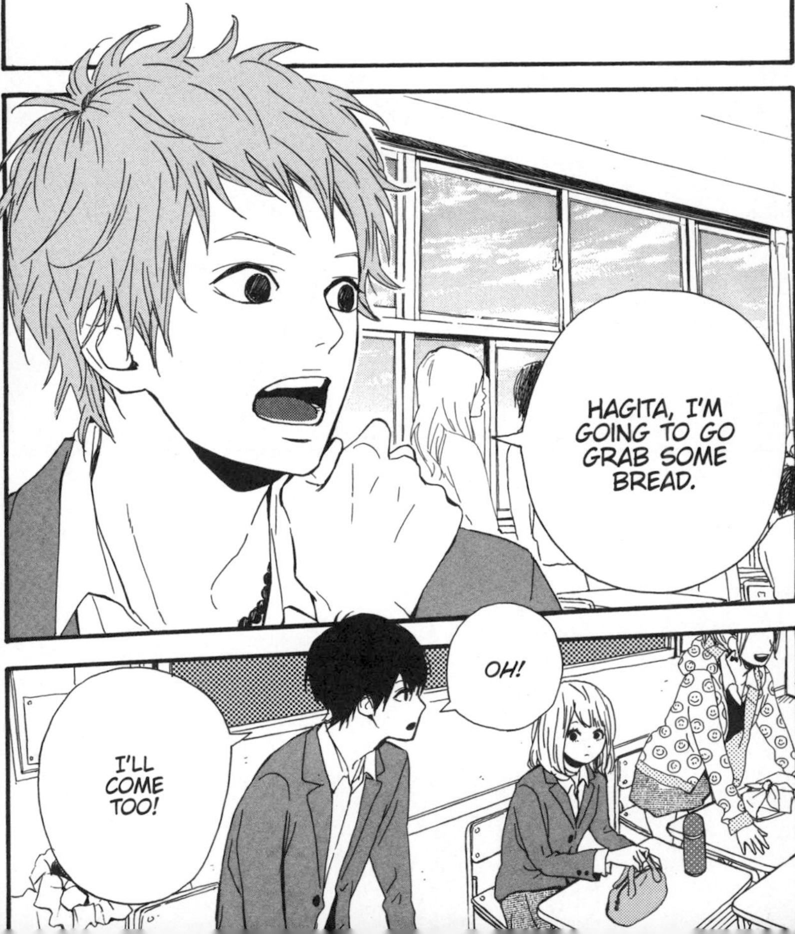
HAGITA, I'M GOING TO GO GRAB SOME BREAD.
OH!
I'LL COME TOO!

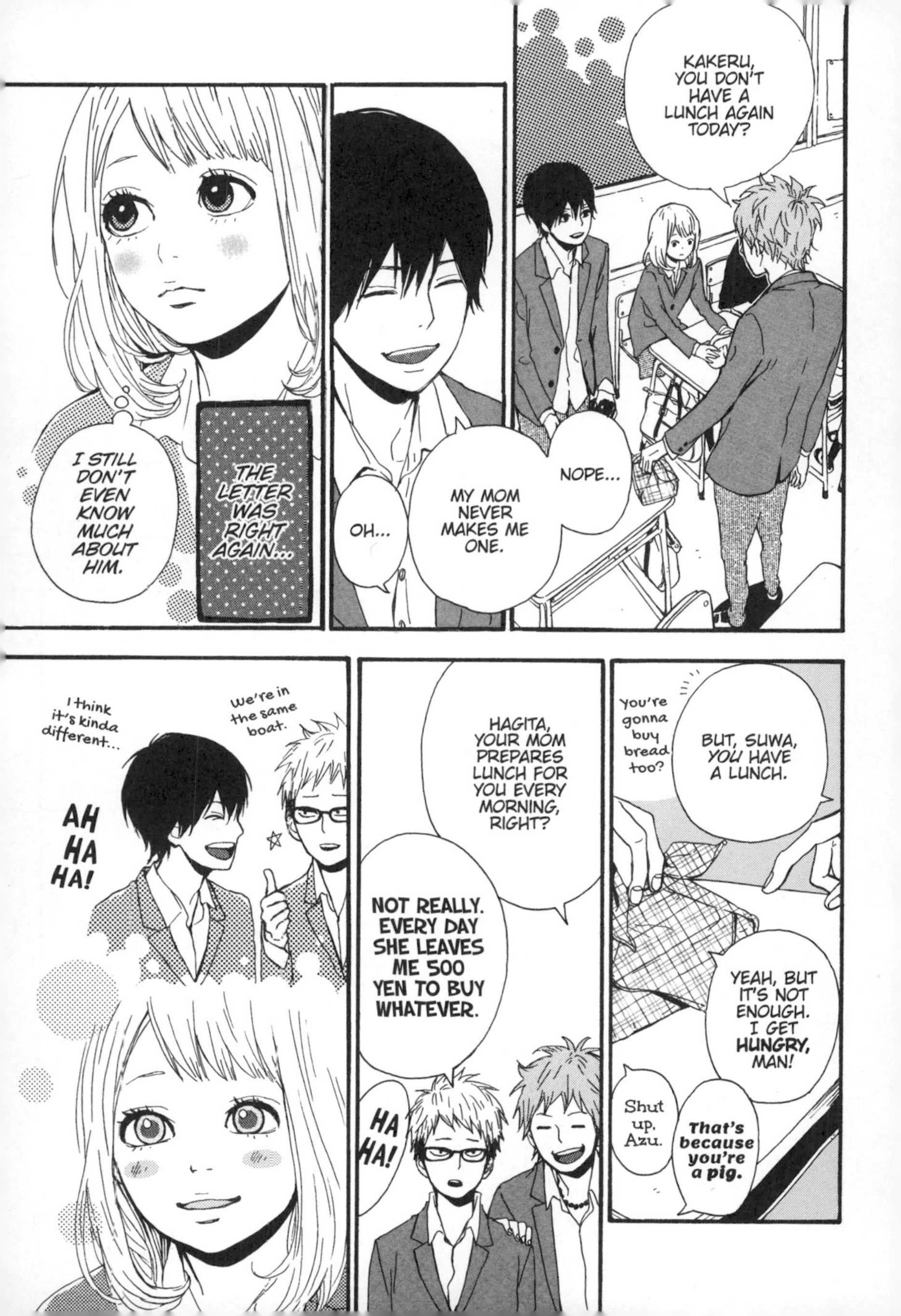
KAKERU, YOU DON'T HAVE A LUNCH AGAIN TODAY?
NOPE...
MY MOM NEVER MAKES ME ONE.
OH...
THE LETTER WAS RIGHT AGAIN...
I STILL DON'T EVEN KNOW MUCH ABOUT HIM.
BUT, SUWA, YOU HAVE A LUNCH.
You're gonna buy bread too?
YEAH, BUT IT'S NOT ENOUGH. I GET HUNGRY, MAN!
That's because you're a pig.
Shut up, Azu.
HAGITA, YOUR MOM PREPARES LUNCH FOR YOU EVERY MORNING, RIGHT?
NOT REALLY. EVERY DAY SHE LEAVES ME 500 YEN TO BUY WHATEVER.
HA HA!
We're in the same boat.
AH HA HA!
I think it's kinda different...

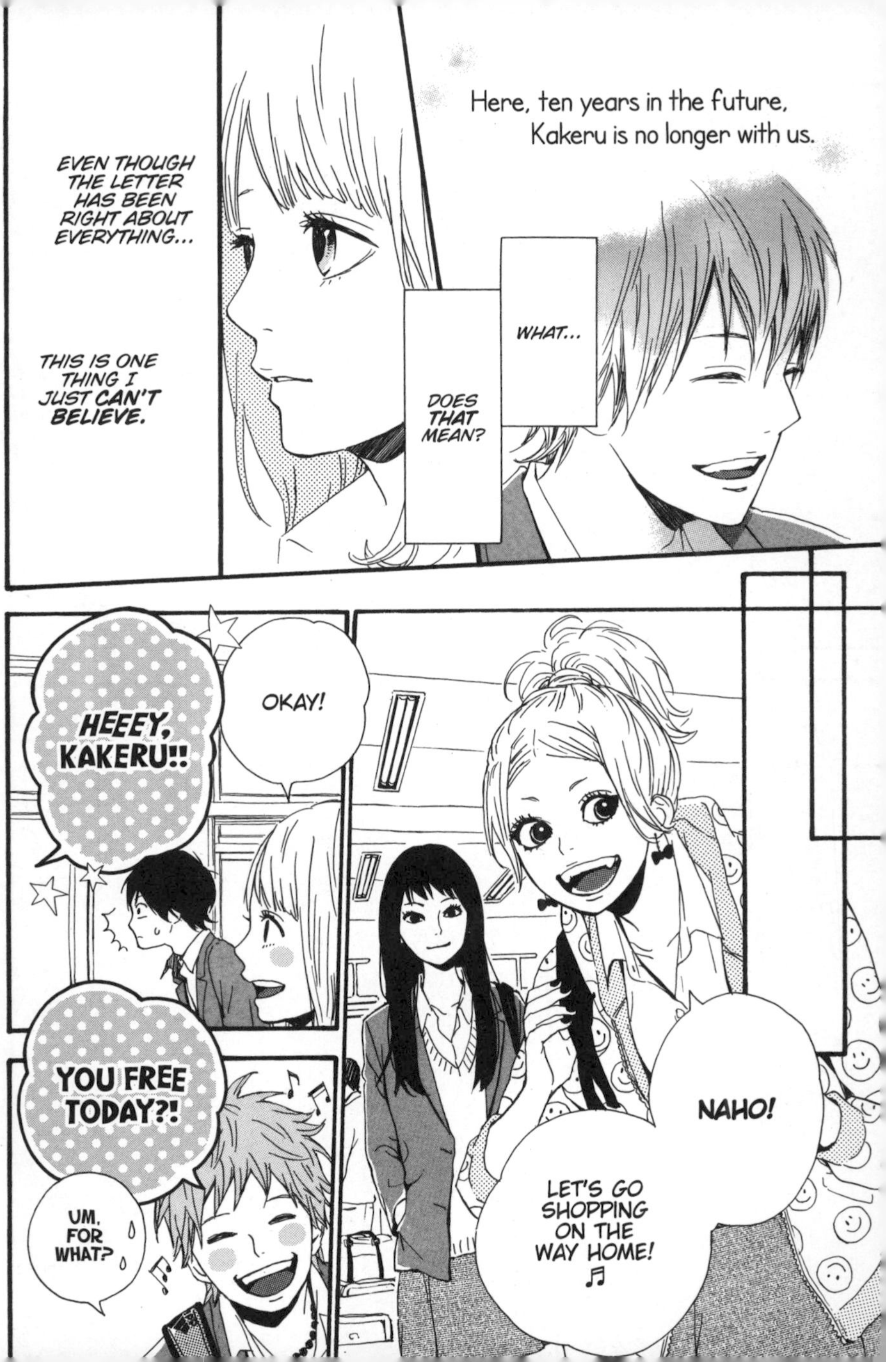
Here, ten years in the future, Kakeru is no longer with us.
WHAT...
DOES THAT MEAN?
EVEN THOUGH THE LETTER HAS BEEN RIGHT ABOUT EVERYTHING...
THIS IS ONE THING I JUST CAN'T BELIEVE.
NAHO!
LET'S GO SHOPPING ON THE WAY HOME! ♫
OKAY!
HEEEY, KAKERU!!
YOU FREE TODAY?!
UM, FOR WHAT?

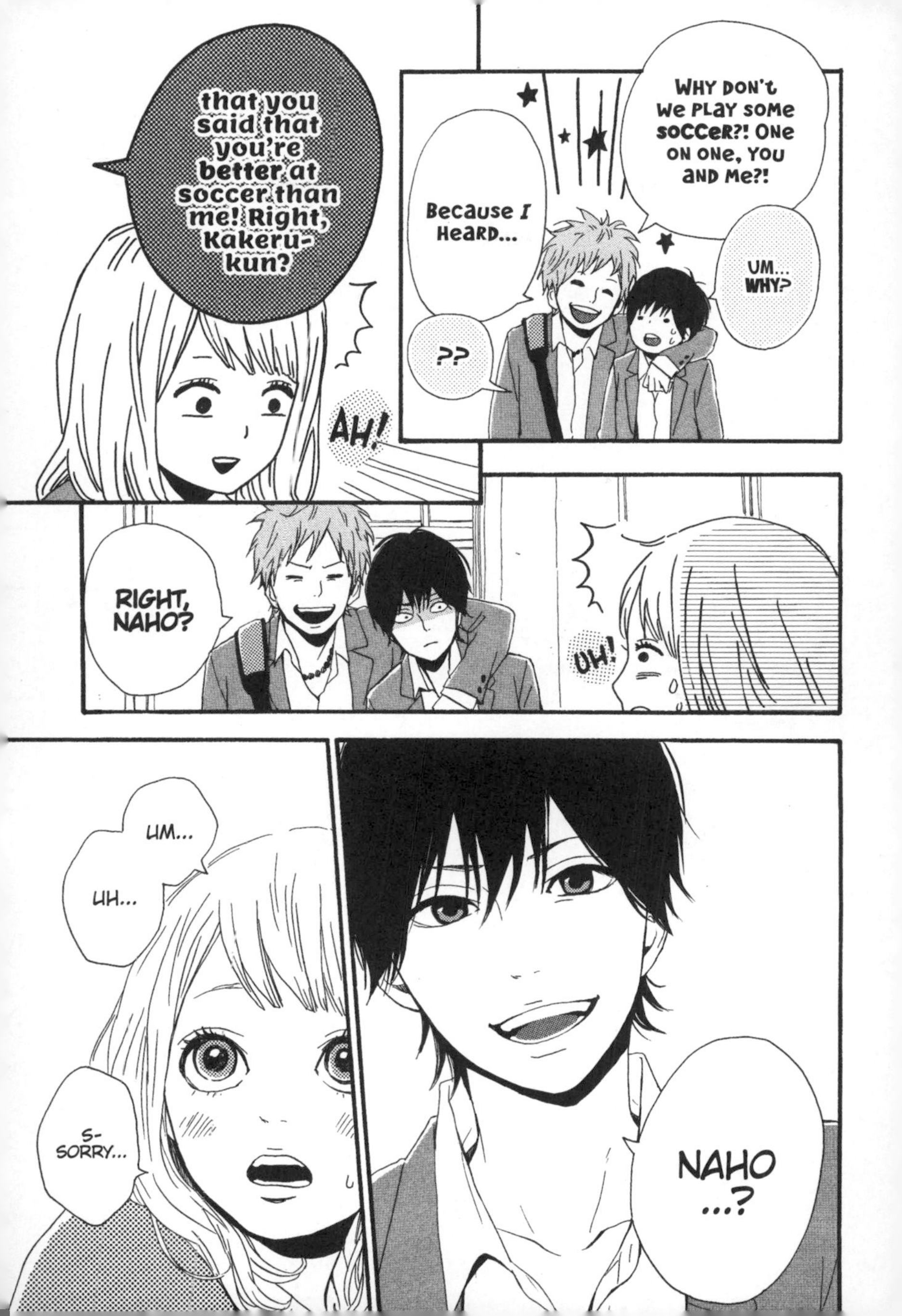
WHY DON'T WE PLAY SOME SOCCER?! ONE ON ONE, YOU AND ME?!
UM... WHY?
Because I HeARD...
??
that you said that you're better at soccer than me! Right, Kakeru-kun?
AH!
UH!
RIGHT, NAHO?
NAHO ...?
UM...
UH...
S-SORRY...

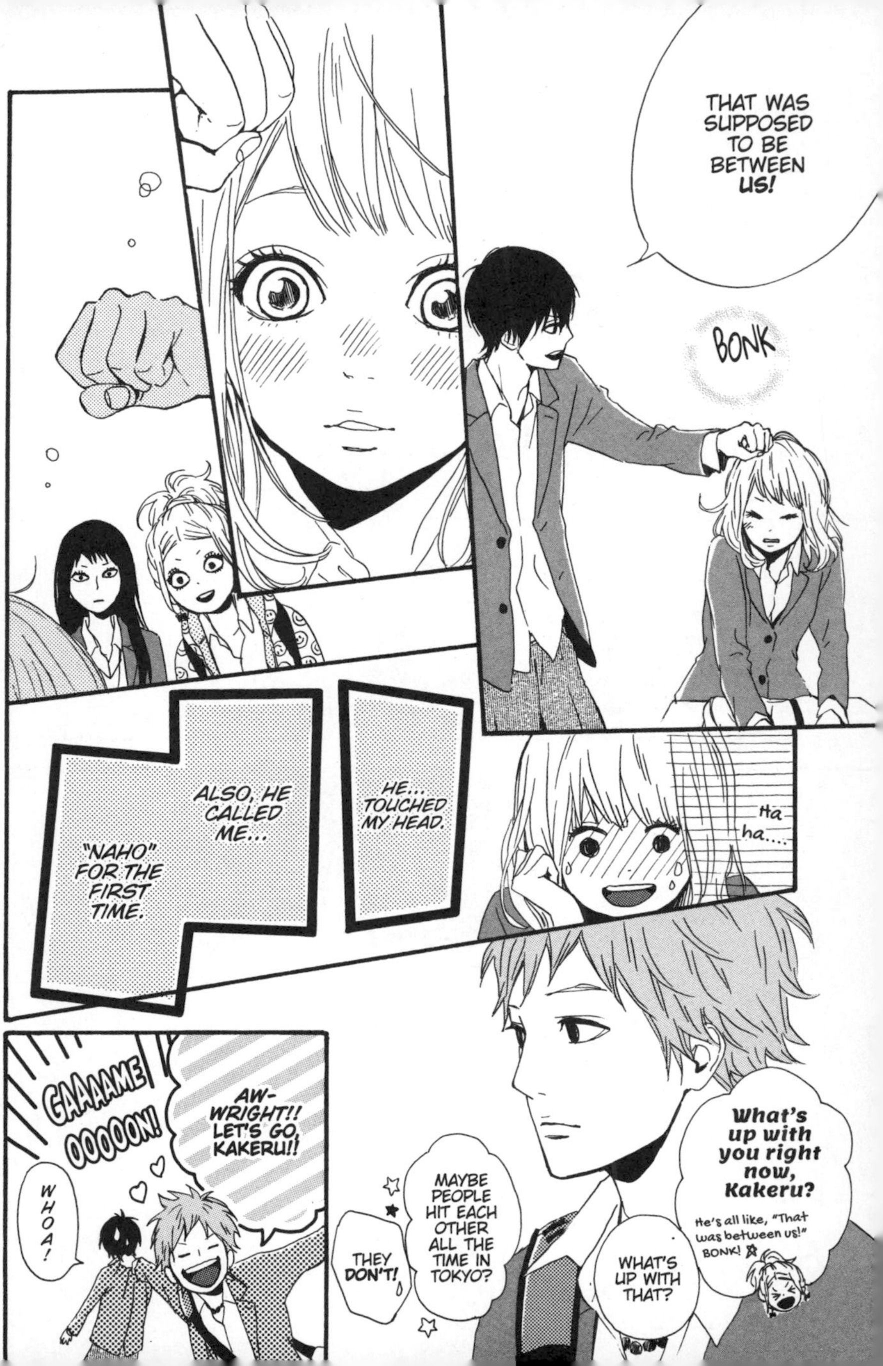
THAT WAS SUPPOSED TO BE BETWEEN **US!**
BONK
Ha ha....
HE... TOUCHED MY HEAD.
ALSO, HE CALLED ME...
"NAHO" FOR THE FIRST TIME.
What's up with you right now, Kakeru?
He's all like, "That was between us!" BONK!
WHAT'S UP WITH THAT?
MAYBE PEOPLE HIT EACH OTHER ALL THE TIME IN TOKYO?
THEY **DON'T!**
AW-WRIGHT!! LET'S GO, KAKERU!!
GAAAAME OOOOON!
WHOA!

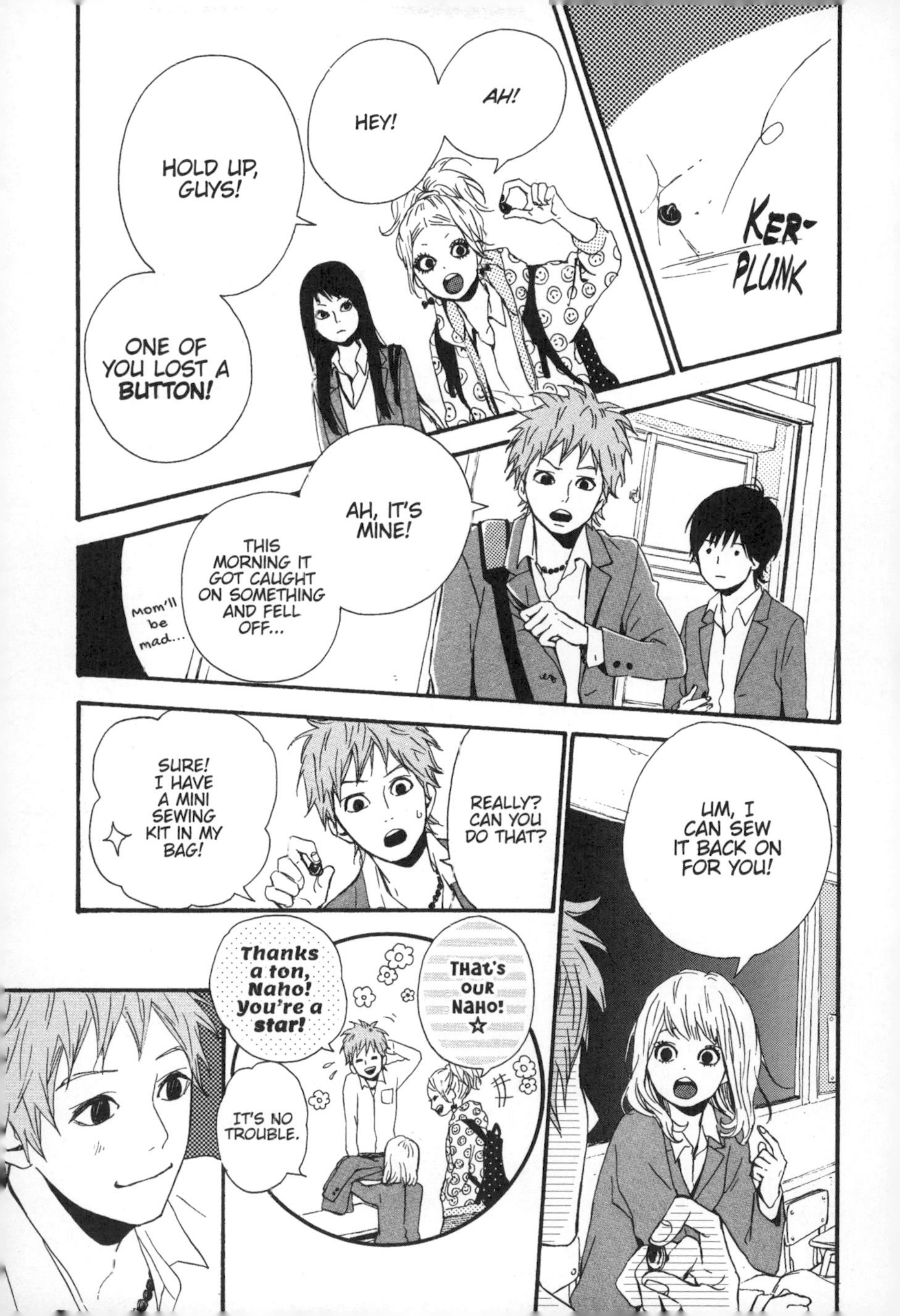
KER-PLUNK
AH!
HEY!
HOLD UP, GUYS!
ONE OF YOU LOST A BUTTON!
AH, IT'S MINE!
THIS MORNING IT GOT CAUGHT ON SOMETHING AND FELL OFF...
Mom'll be mad...
UM, I CAN SEW IT BACK ON FOR YOU!
REALLY? CAN YOU DO THAT?
SURE! I HAVE A MINI SEWING KIT IN MY BAG!
That's our Naho! ☆
Thanks a ton, Naho! You're a star!
IT'S NO TROUBLE.

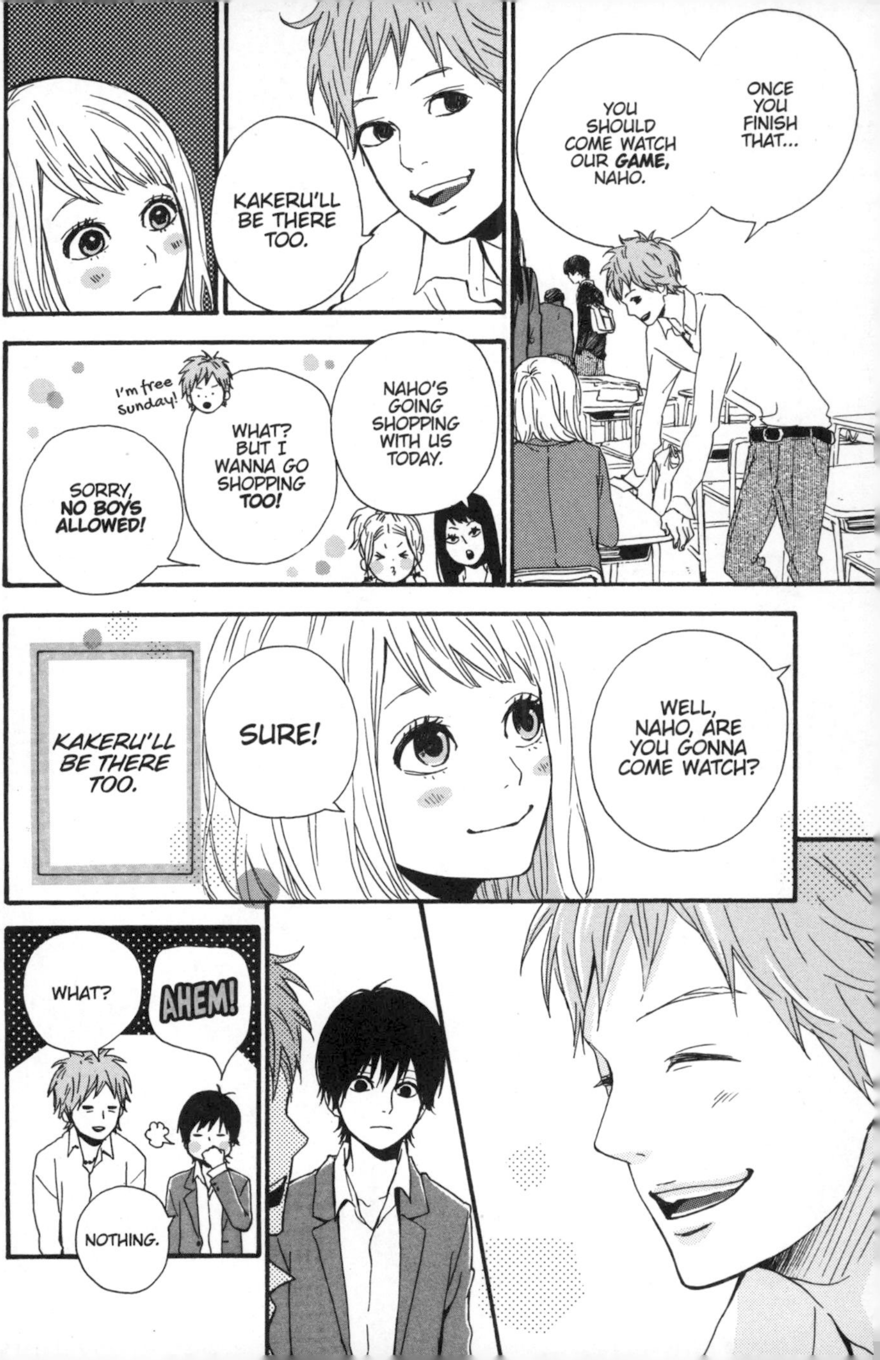
ONCE YOU FINISH THAT...
YOU SHOULD COME WATCH OUR GAME, NAHO.
KAKERU'LL BE THERE TOO.
NAHO'S GOING SHOPPING WITH US TODAY.
WHAT? BUT I WANNA GO SHOPPING TOO!
I'm free sunday!
SORRY, NO BOYS ALLOWED!
WELL, NAHO, ARE YOU GONNA COME WATCH?
SURE!
KAKERU'LL BE THERE TOO.
AHEM!
WHAT?
NOTHING.

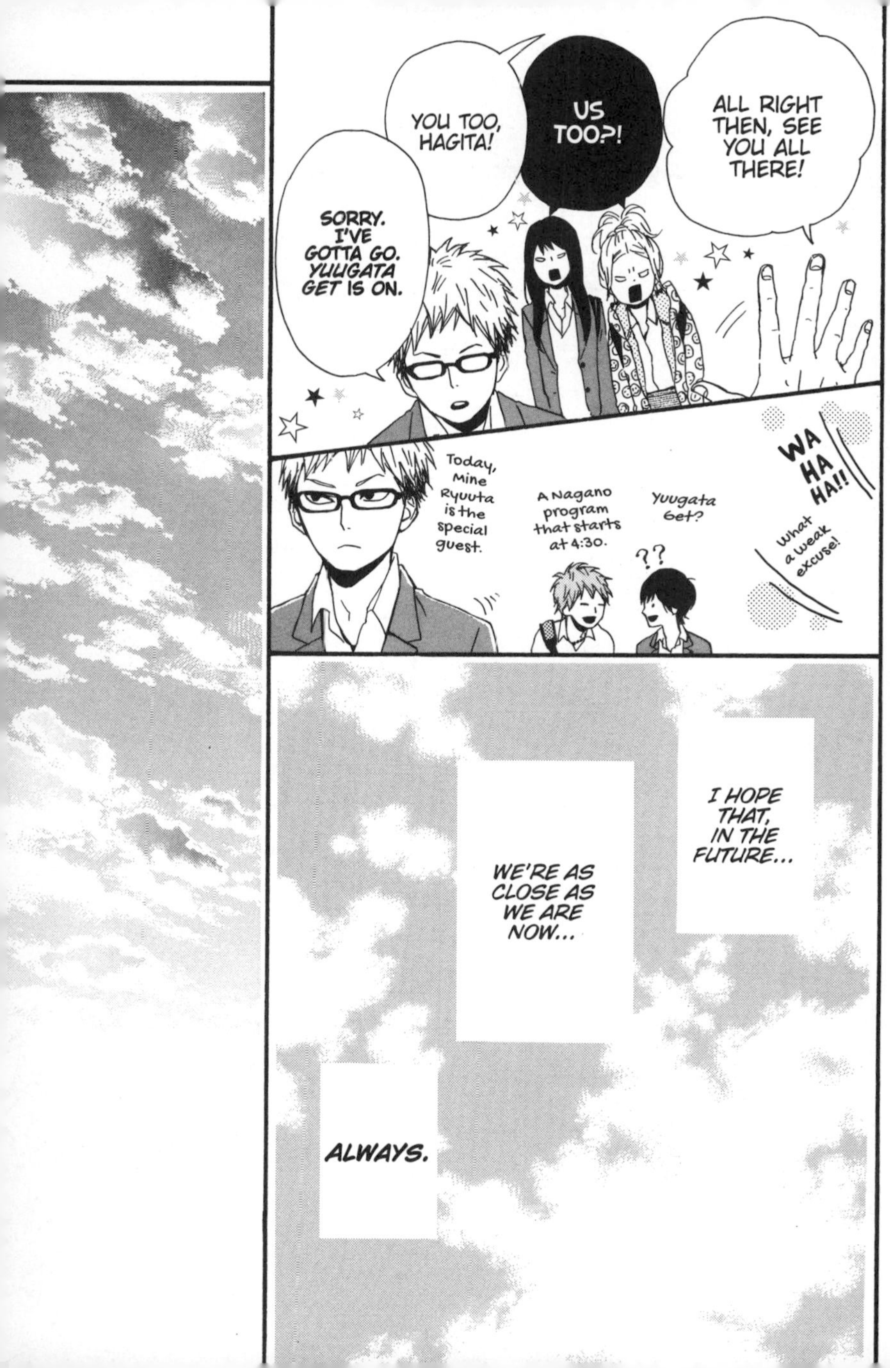
ALL RIGHT THEN, SEE YOU ALL THERE!
US TOO?!
YOU TOO, HAGITA!
SORRY. I'VE GOTTA GO. YUUGATA GET IS ON.
WA HA HA!!
What a weak excuse!
Yuugata Get?
A Nagano program that starts at 4:30.
Today, Mine Ryuuta is the special guest.
I HOPE THAT, IN THE FUTURE...
WE'RE AS CLOSE AS WE ARE NOW...
ALWAYS.

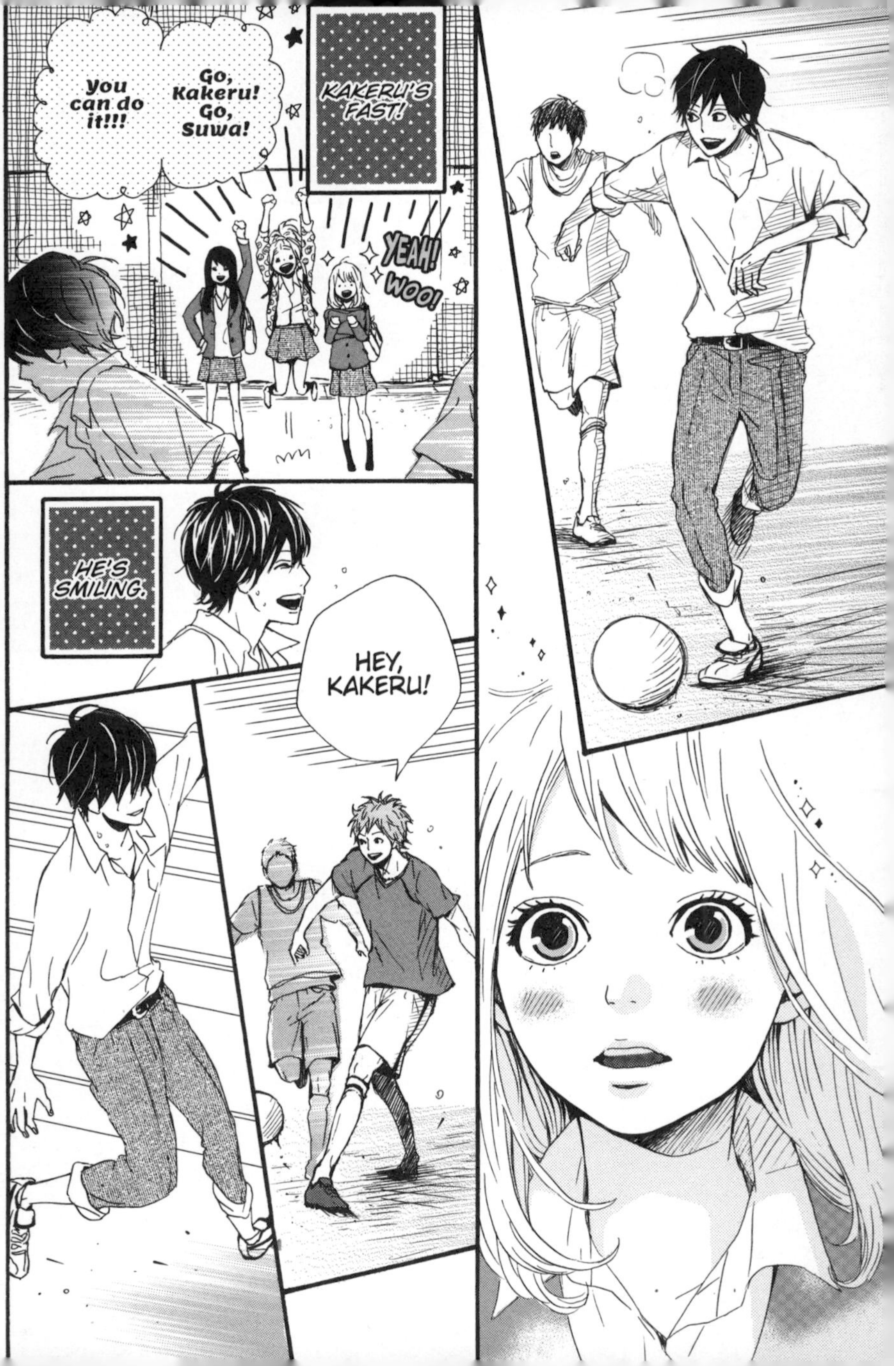
KAKERU'S FAST!
Go, Kakeru! Go, Suwa!
You can do it!!!
YEAH!
WOO!
HE'S SMILING.
HEY, KAKERU!

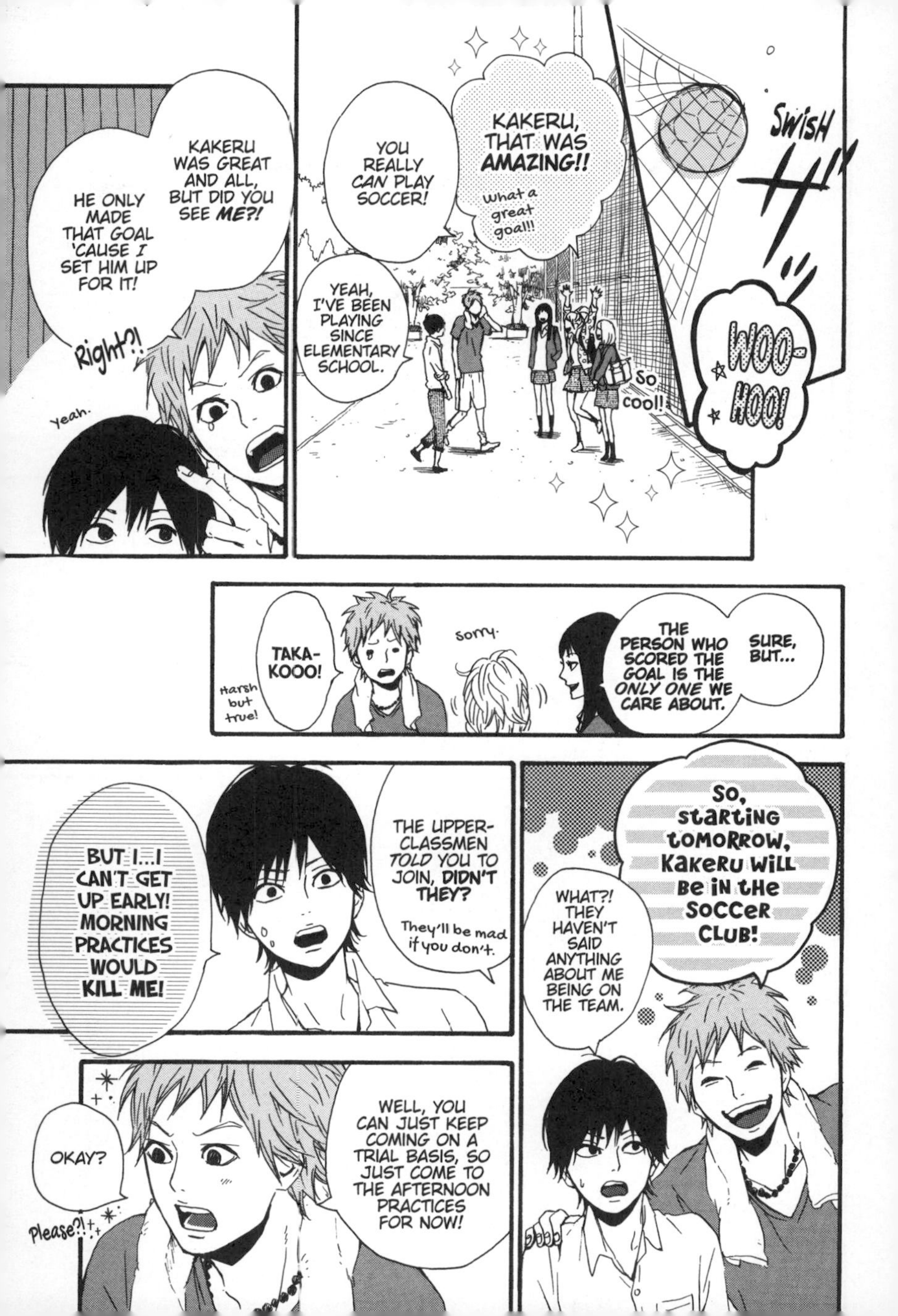
SWISH
WOO-HOO!
So cool!!
KAKERU, THAT WAS AMAZING!!
what a great goal!!
YOU REALLY CAN PLAY SOCCER!
YEAH, I'VE BEEN PLAYING SINCE ELEMENTARY SCHOOL.
KAKERU WAS GREAT AND ALL, BUT DID YOU SEE ME?!
HE ONLY MADE THAT GOAL 'CAUSE I SET HIM UP FOR IT!
Right?!
Yeah.
SURE, BUT...
THE PERSON WHO SCORED THE GOAL IS THE ONLY ONE WE CARE ABOUT.
sorry.
TAKA-KOOO!
Harsh but true!
So, starting tomorrow, Kakeru will be in the soccer club!
WHAT?! THEY HAVEN'T SAID ANYTHING ABOUT ME BEING ON THE TEAM.
THE UPPERCLASSMEN TOLD YOU TO JOIN, DIDN'T THEY?
They'll be mad if you don't.
BUT I...I CAN'T GET UP EARLY! MORNING PRACTICES WOULD KILL ME!
WELL, YOU CAN JUST KEEP COMING ON A TRIAL BASIS, SO JUST COME TO THE AFTERNOON PRACTICES FOR NOW!
OKAY?
Please?!

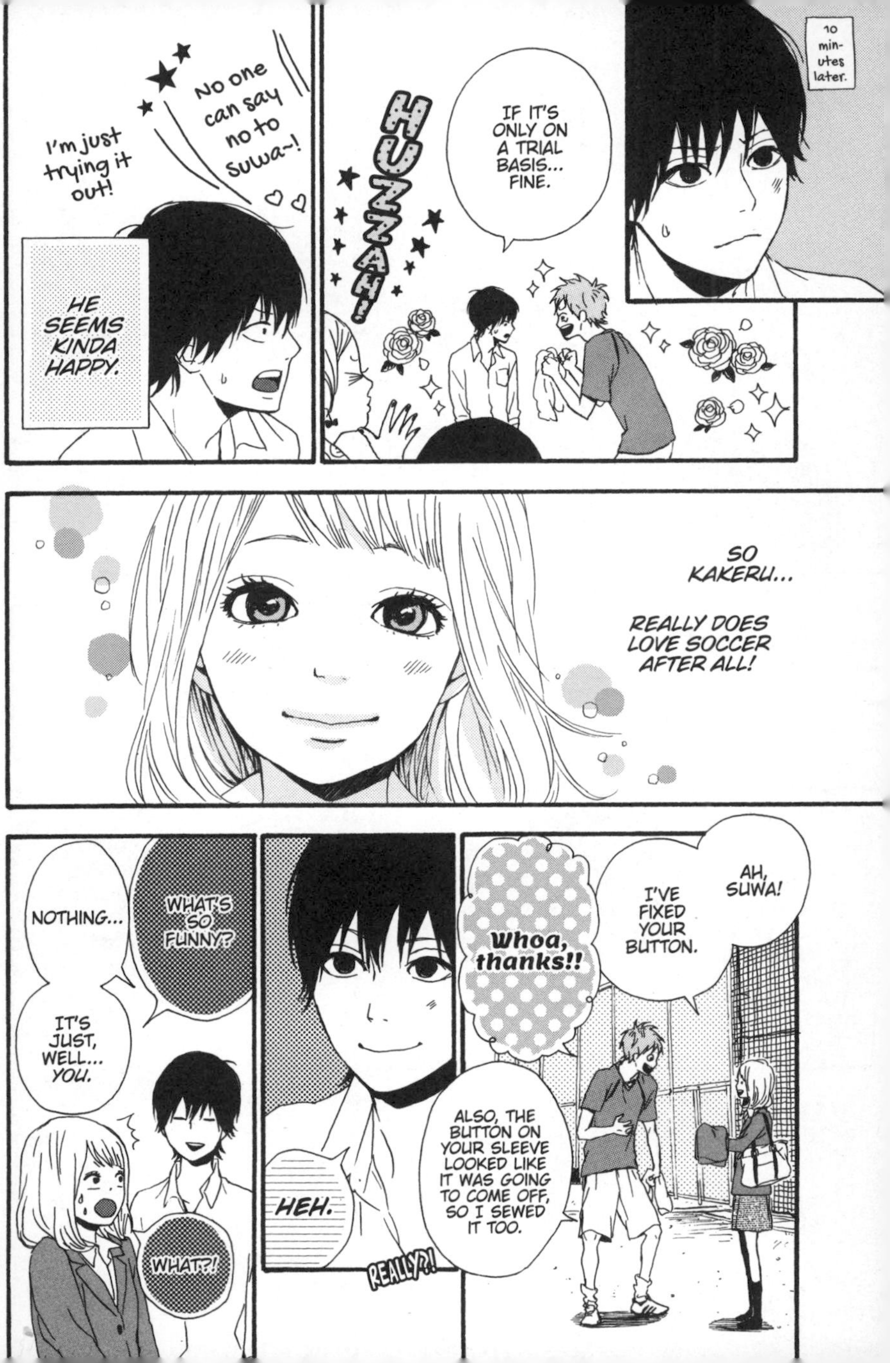
10 minutes later.
IF IT'S ONLY ON A TRIAL BASIS... FINE.
HUZZAH!
No one can say no to Suwa~!
I'm just trying it out!
HE SEEMS KINDA HAPPY.
SO KAKERU...
REALLY DOES LOVE SOCCER AFTER ALL!
AH, SUWA!
I'VE FIXED YOUR BUTTON.
Whoa, thanks!!
ALSO, THE BUTTON ON YOUR SLEEVE LOOKED LIKE IT WAS GOING TO COME OFF, SO I SEWED IT TOO.
REALLY?!
HEH.
WHAT'S SO FUNNY?
NOTHING...
IT'S JUST, WELL... YOU.
WHAT?!

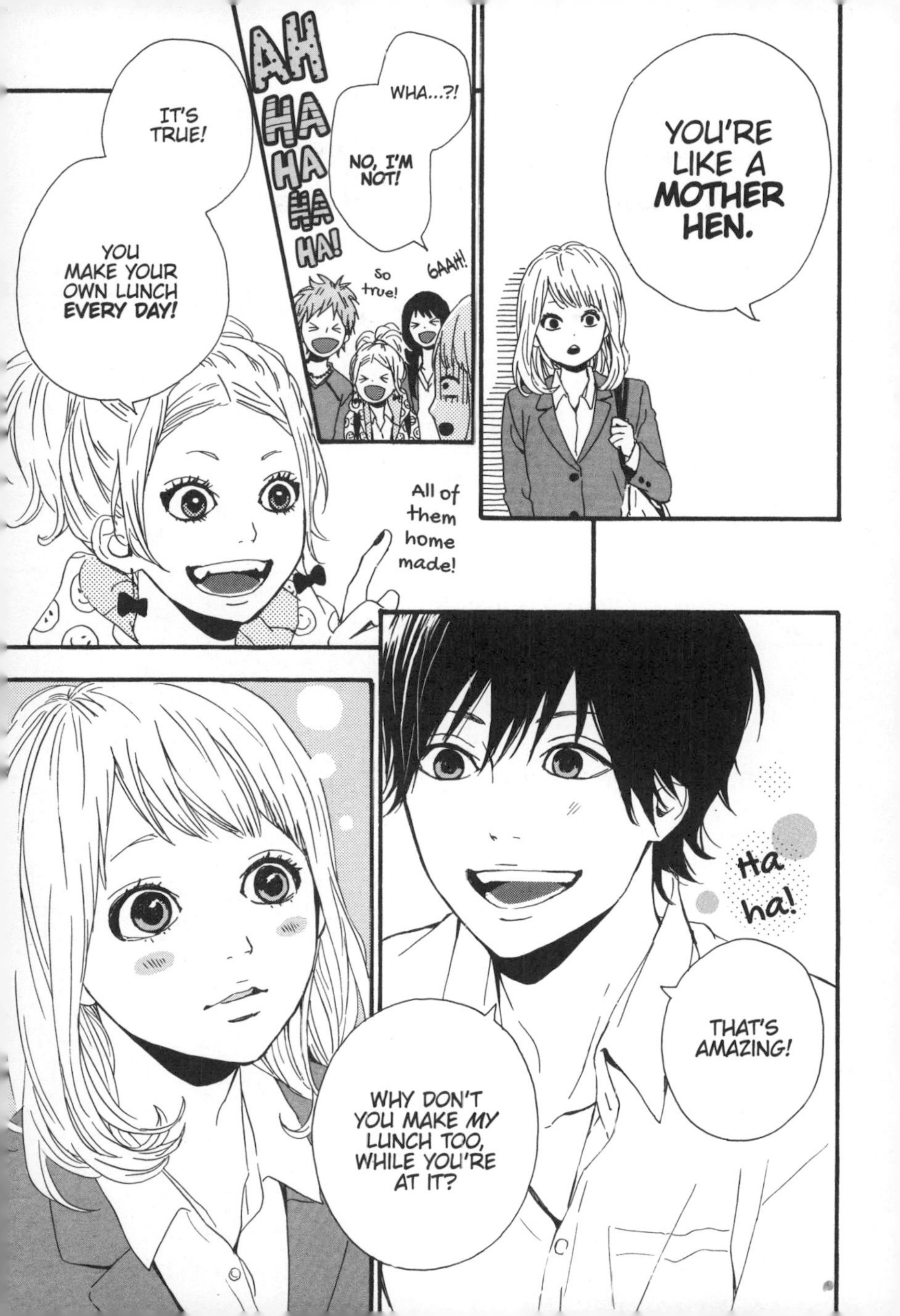
YOU'RE LIKE A MOTHER HEN.
WHA...?!
NO, I'M NOT!
AH HA HA HA HA!
So true!
GAAH!
IT'S TRUE!
YOU MAKE YOUR OWN LUNCH EVERY DAY!
All of them home made!
Ha ha!
THAT'S AMAZING!
WHY DON'T YOU MAKE MY LUNCH TOO, WHILE YOU'RE AT IT?

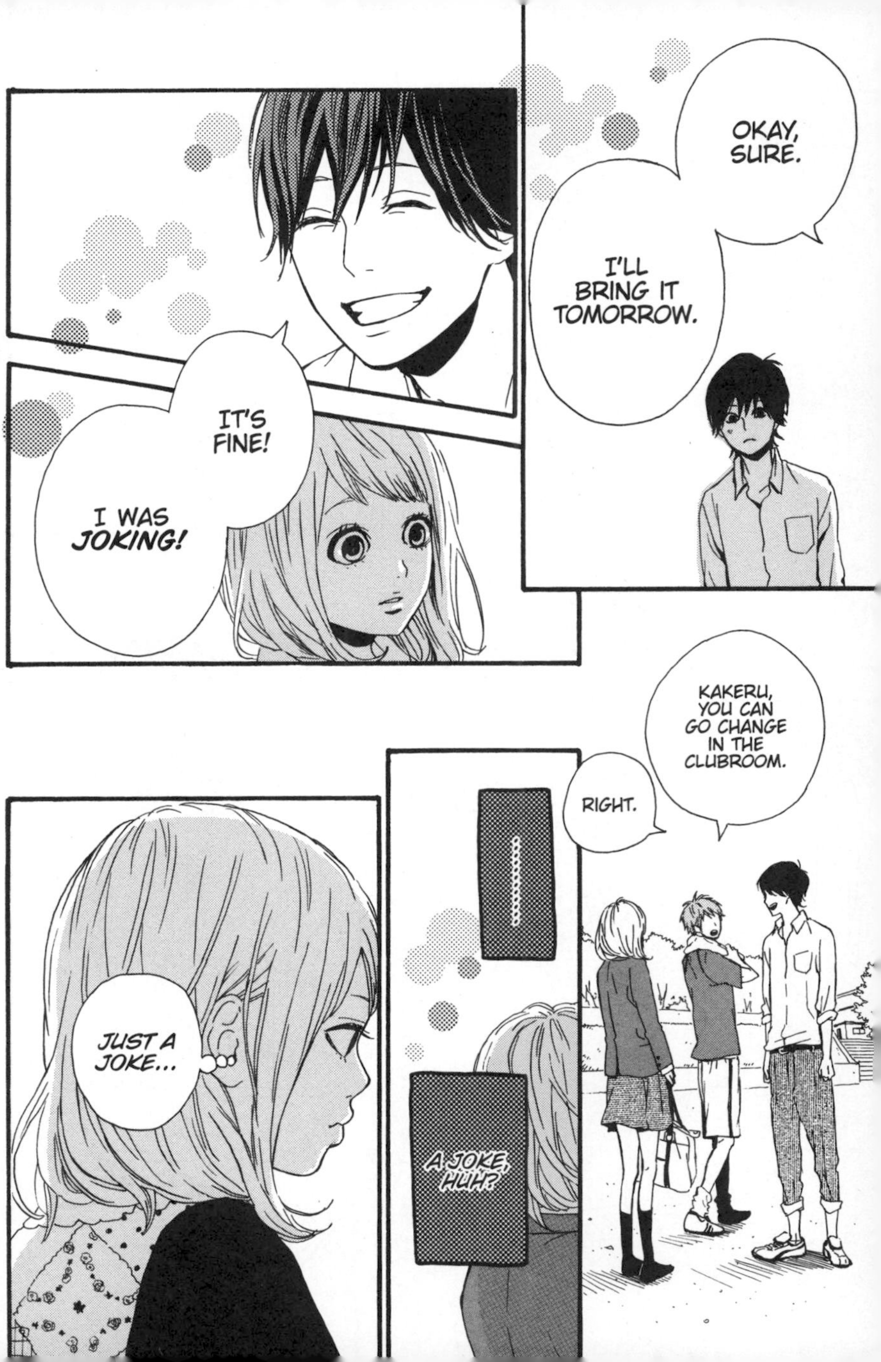
OKAY, SURE.
I'LL BRING IT TOMORROW.
IT'S FINE!
I WAS JOKING!
KAKERU, YOU CAN GO CHANGE IN THE CLUBROOM.
RIGHT.
A JOKE, HUH?
JUST A JOKE...

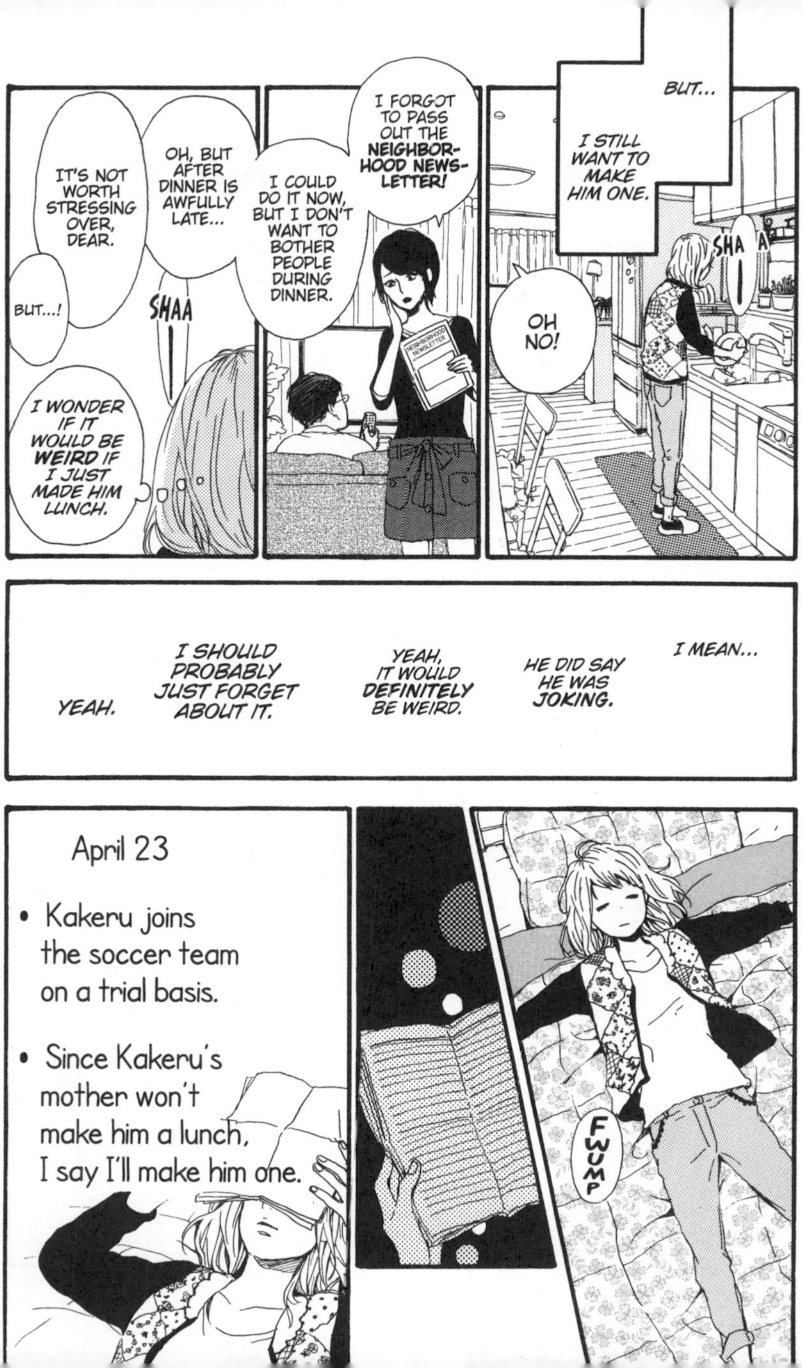
BUT...
I STILL WANT TO MAKE HIM ONE.
SHAA
OH NO!
I FORGOT TO PASS OUT THE NEIGHBORHOOD NEWSLETTER!
I COULD DO IT NOW, BUT I DON'T WANT TO BOTHER PEOPLE DURING DINNER.
NEIGHBORHOOD NEWSLETTER
OH, BUT AFTER DINNER IS AWFULLY LATE...
IT'S NOT WORTH STRESSING OVER, DEAR.
BUT...!
SHAA
I WONDER IF IT WOULD BE WEIRD IF I JUST MADE HIM LUNCH.
I MEAN...
HE DID SAY HE WAS JOKING.
YEAH, IT WOULD DEFINITELY BE WEIRD.
I SHOULD PROBABLY JUST FORGET ABOUT IT.
YEAH.
FWUMP
April 23
• Kakeru joins the soccer team on a trial basis.
• Since Kakeru's mother won't make him a lunch, I say I'll make him one.

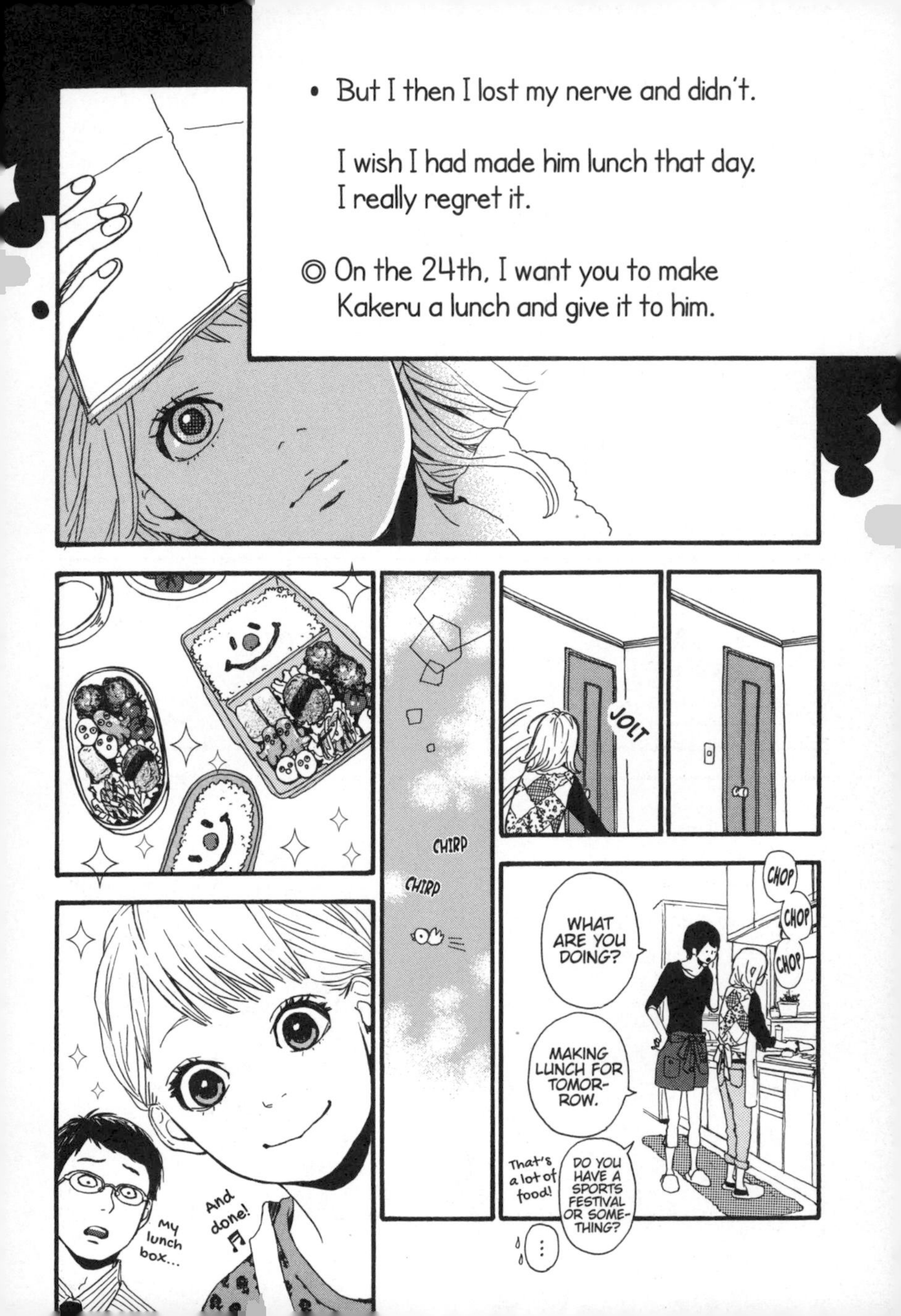

• But I then I lost my nerve and didn't.
I wish I had made him lunch that day.
I really regret it.
◎ On the 24th, I want you to make Kakeru a lunch and give it to him.
JOLT
CHOP
CHOP
CHOP
WHAT ARE YOU DOING?
MAKING LUNCH FOR TOMOR-ROW.
DO YOU HAVE A SPORTS FESTIVAL OR SOME-THING?
That's a lot of food!
...
CHIRP
CHIRP
And done! ♫
My lunch box...

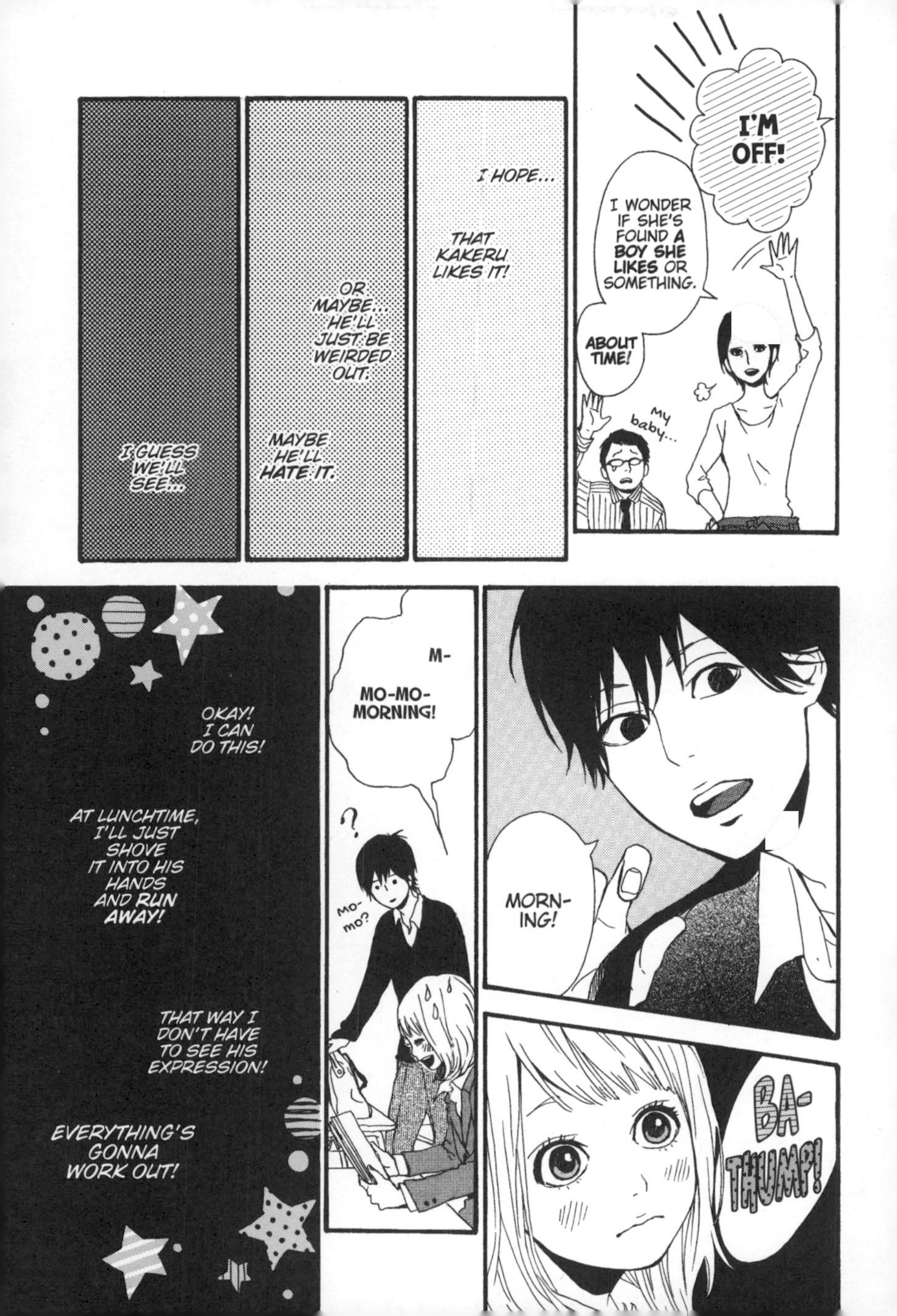
I'M OFF!
I WONDER IF SHE'S FOUND A BOY SHE LIKES OR SOMETHING.
ABOUT TIME!
My baby...
I HOPE...
THAT KAKERU LIKES IT!
MAYBE HE'LL HATE IT.
OR MAYBE... HE'LL JUST BE WEIRDED OUT.
I GUESS WE'LL SEE...
MORN-ING!
BA-THUMP!
M-
MO-MO-MORNING!
Mo-mo?
OKAY! I CAN DO THIS!
AT LUNCHTIME, I'LL JUST SHOVE IT INTO HIS HANDS AND RUN AWAY!
THAT WAY I DON'T HAVE TO SEE HIS EXPRESSION!
EVERYTHING'S GONNA WORK OUT!

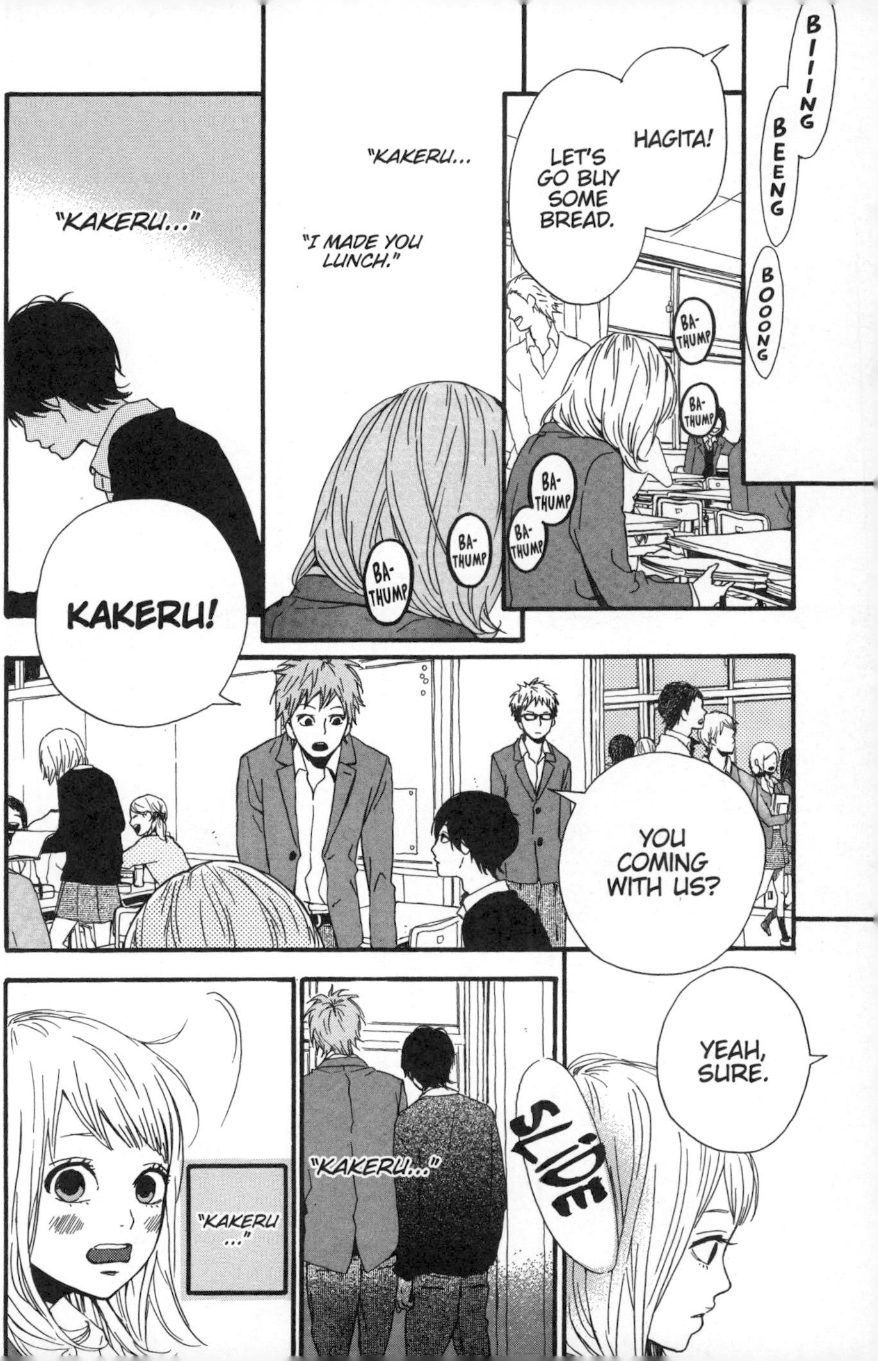
BIIING
BEEENG
BOOOONG
HAGITA!
LET'S GO BUY SOME BREAD.
BA-THUMP
BA-THUMP
BA-THUMP
BA-THUMP
"KAKERU...
"I MADE YOU LUNCH."
BA-THUMP
BA-THUMP
"KAKERU..."
KAKERU!
YOU COMING WITH US?
YEAH, SURE.
SLIDE
"KAKERU..."
"KAKERU ..."

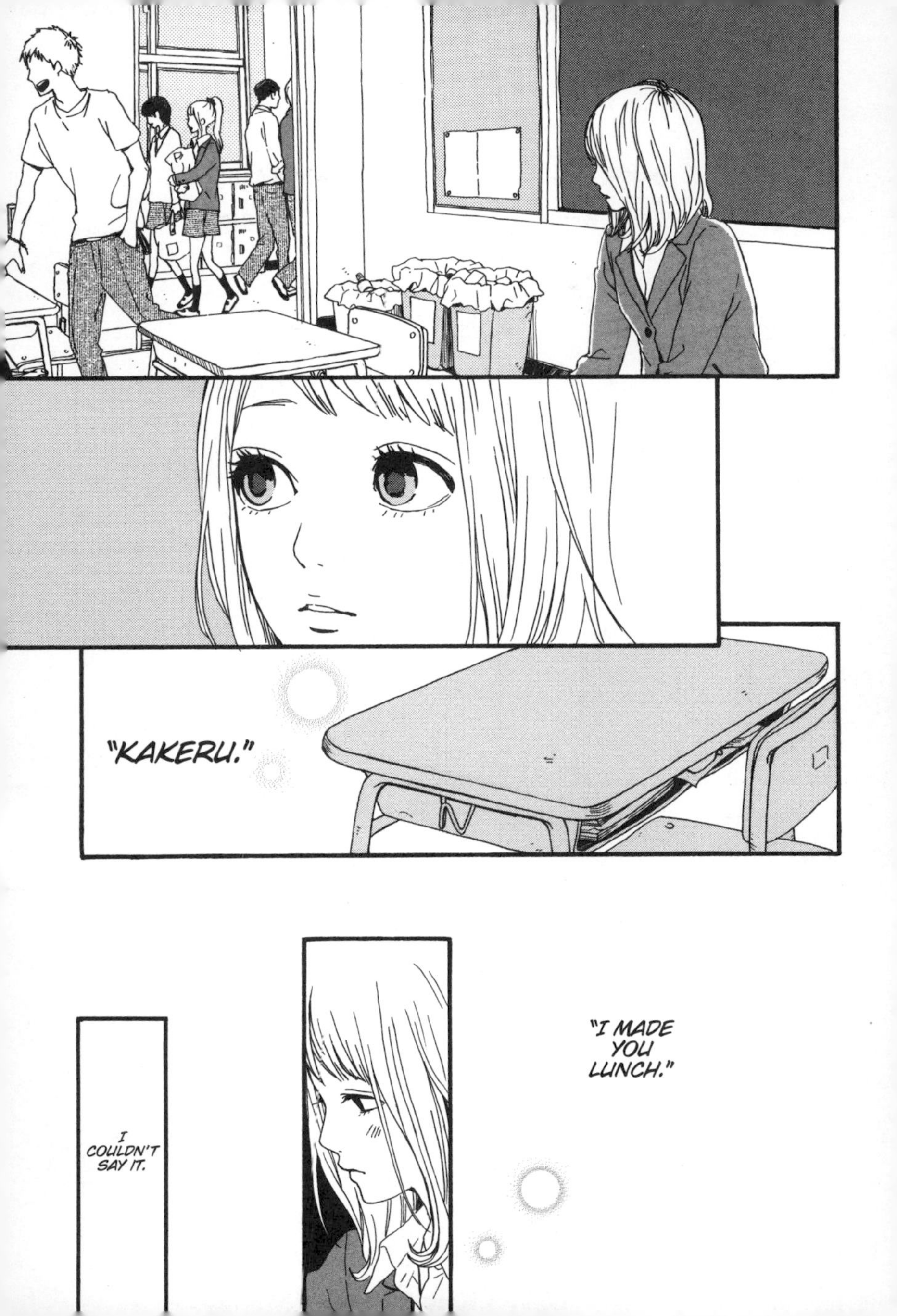
"KAKERU."
"I MADE YOU LUNCH."
I COULDN'T SAY IT.

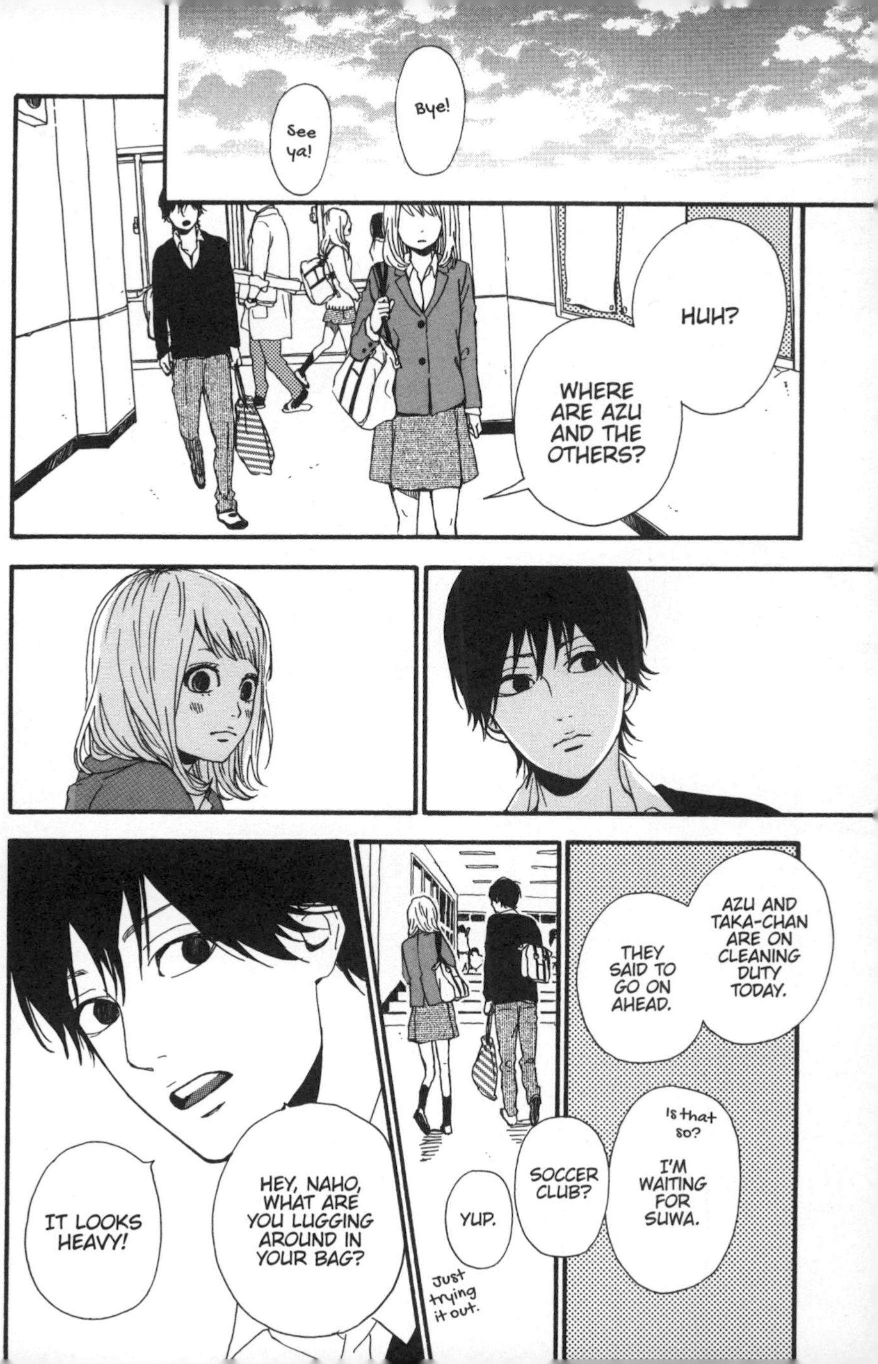
Bye!
See ya!
HUH?
WHERE ARE AZU AND THE OTHERS?
AZU AND TAKA-CHAN ARE ON CLEANING DUTY TODAY.
THEY SAID TO GO ON AHEAD.
Is that so?
I'M WAITING FOR SUWA.
SOCCER CLUB?
YUP.
Just trying it out.
HEY, NAHO, WHAT ARE YOU LUGGING AROUND IN YOUR BAG?
IT LOOKS HEAVY!

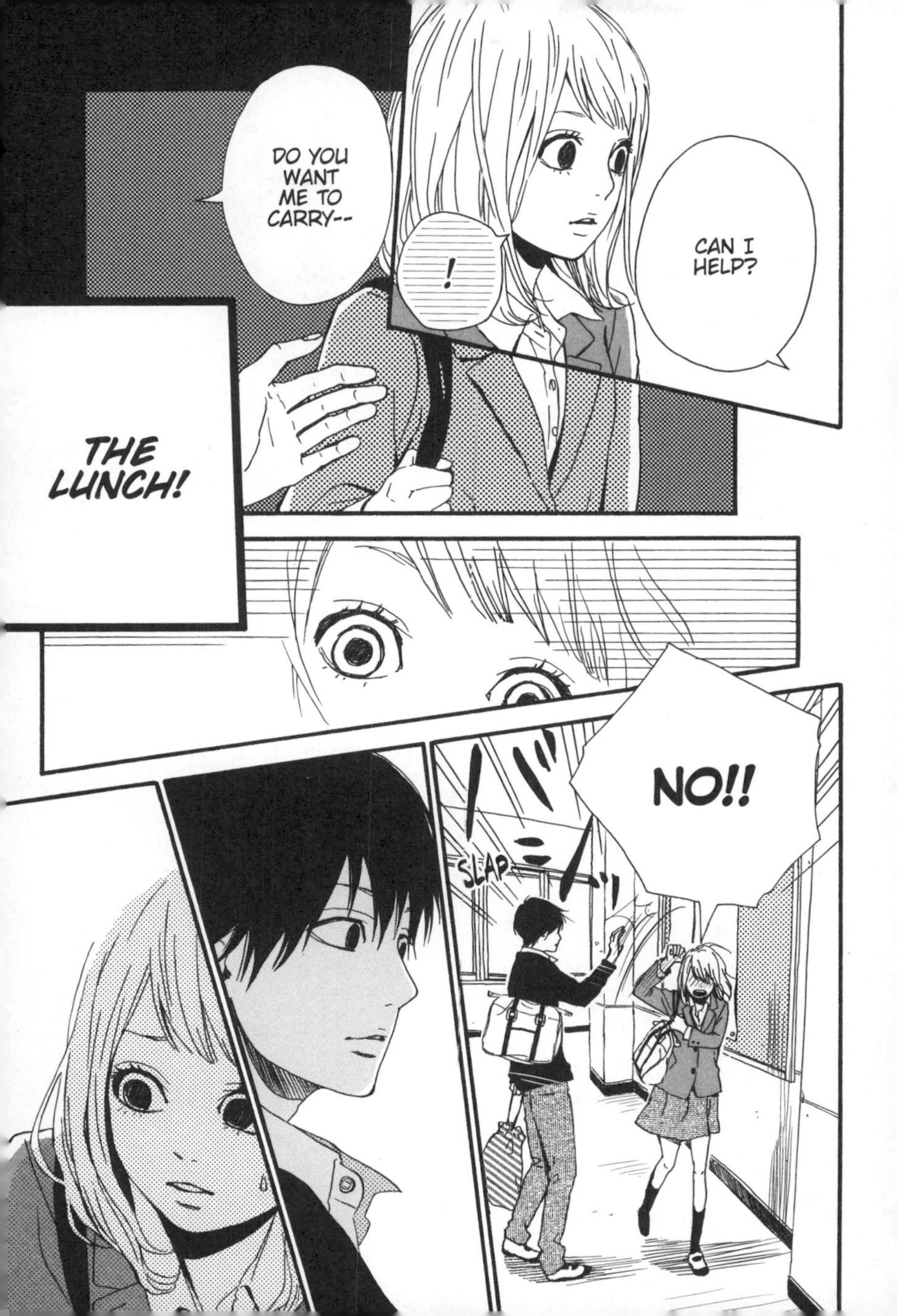
CAN I HELP?
!
DO YOU WANT ME TO CARRY--
THE LUNCH!
NO!!
SLAP

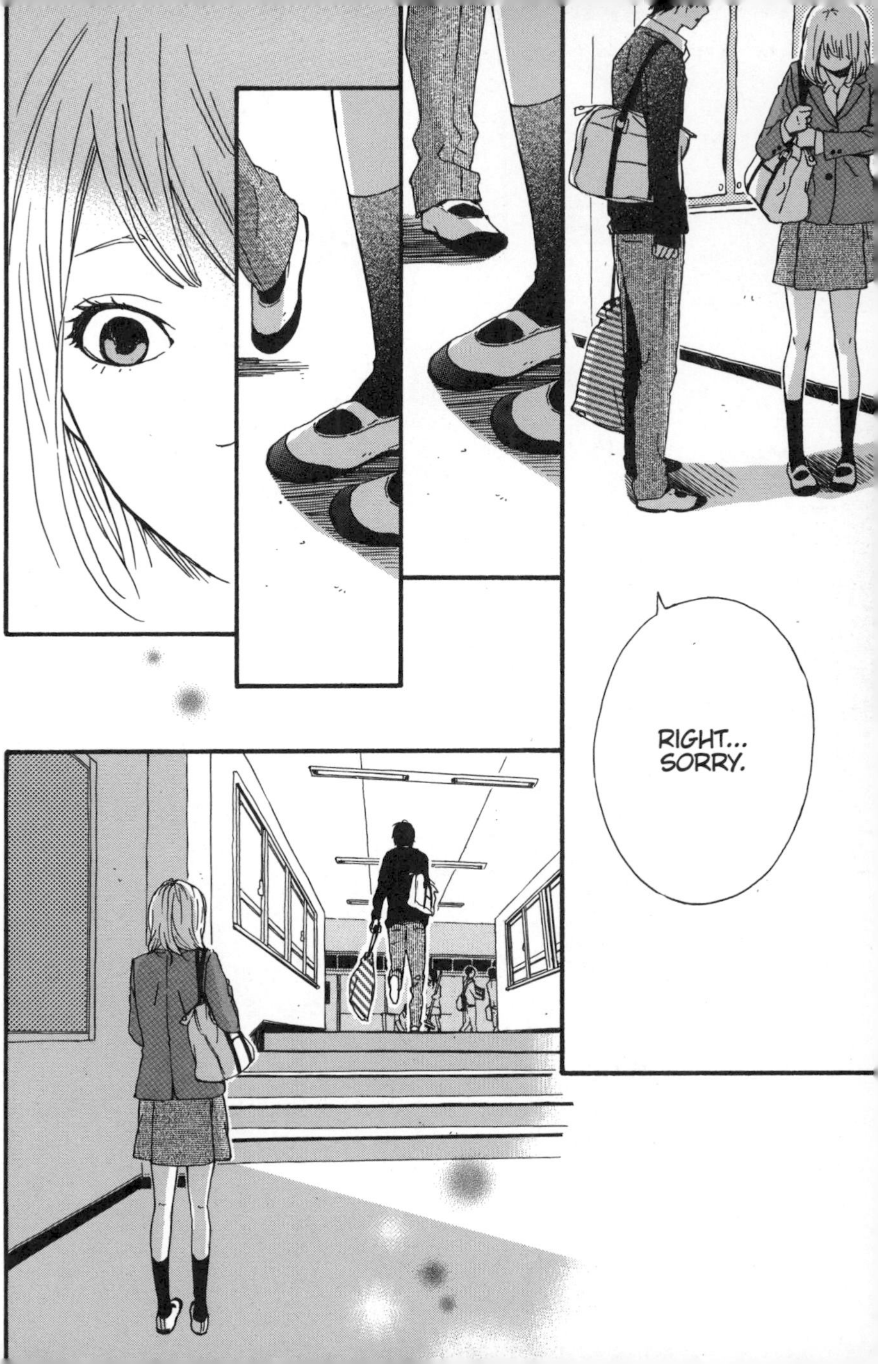
RIGHT... SORRY.

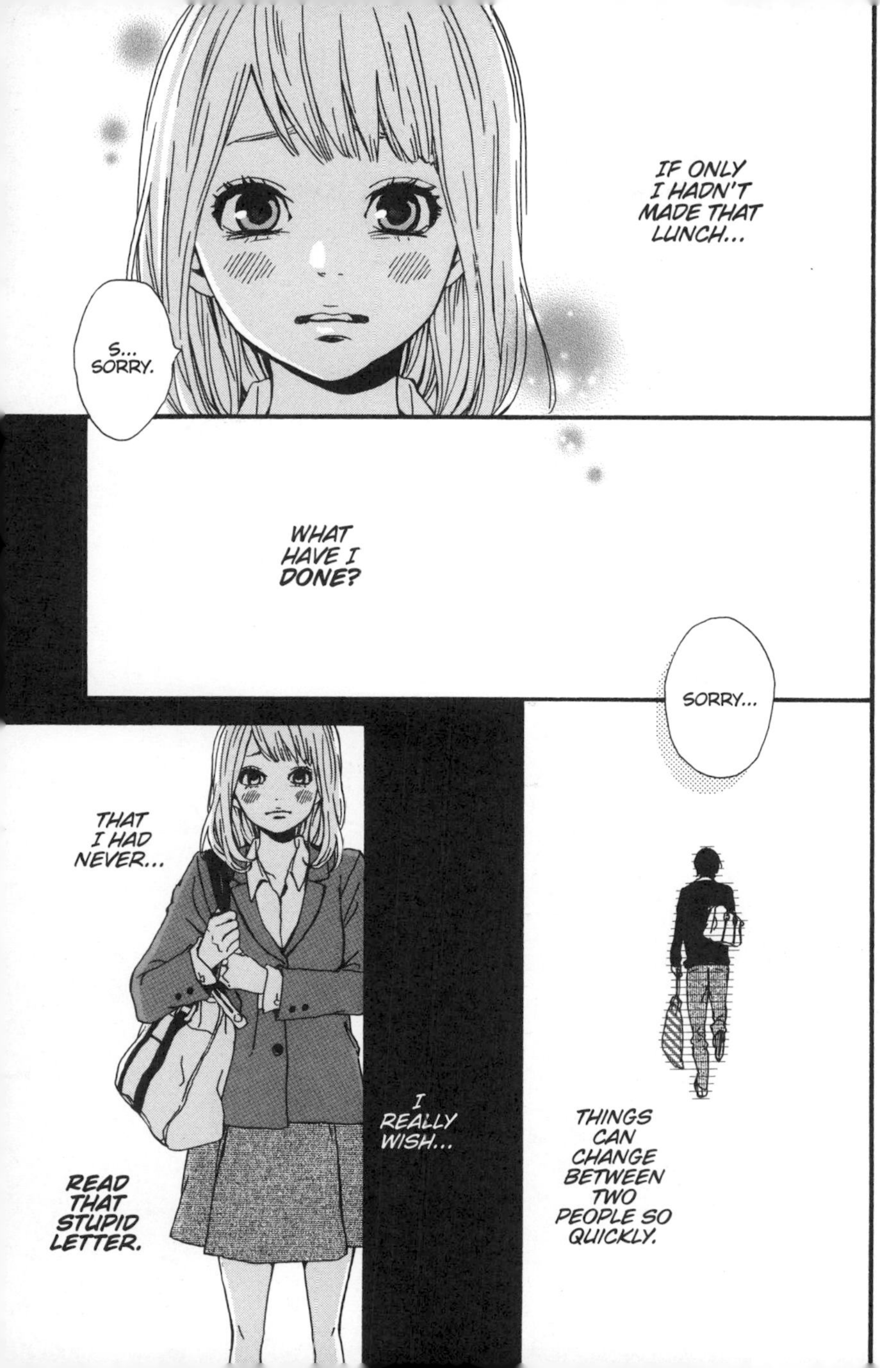
IF ONLY I HADN'T MADE THAT LUNCH...
S... SORRY.
WHAT HAVE I DONE?
SORRY...
THINGS CAN CHANGE BETWEEN TWO PEOPLE SO QUICKLY.
I REALLY WISH...
THAT I HAD NEVER...
READ THAT STUPID LETTER.

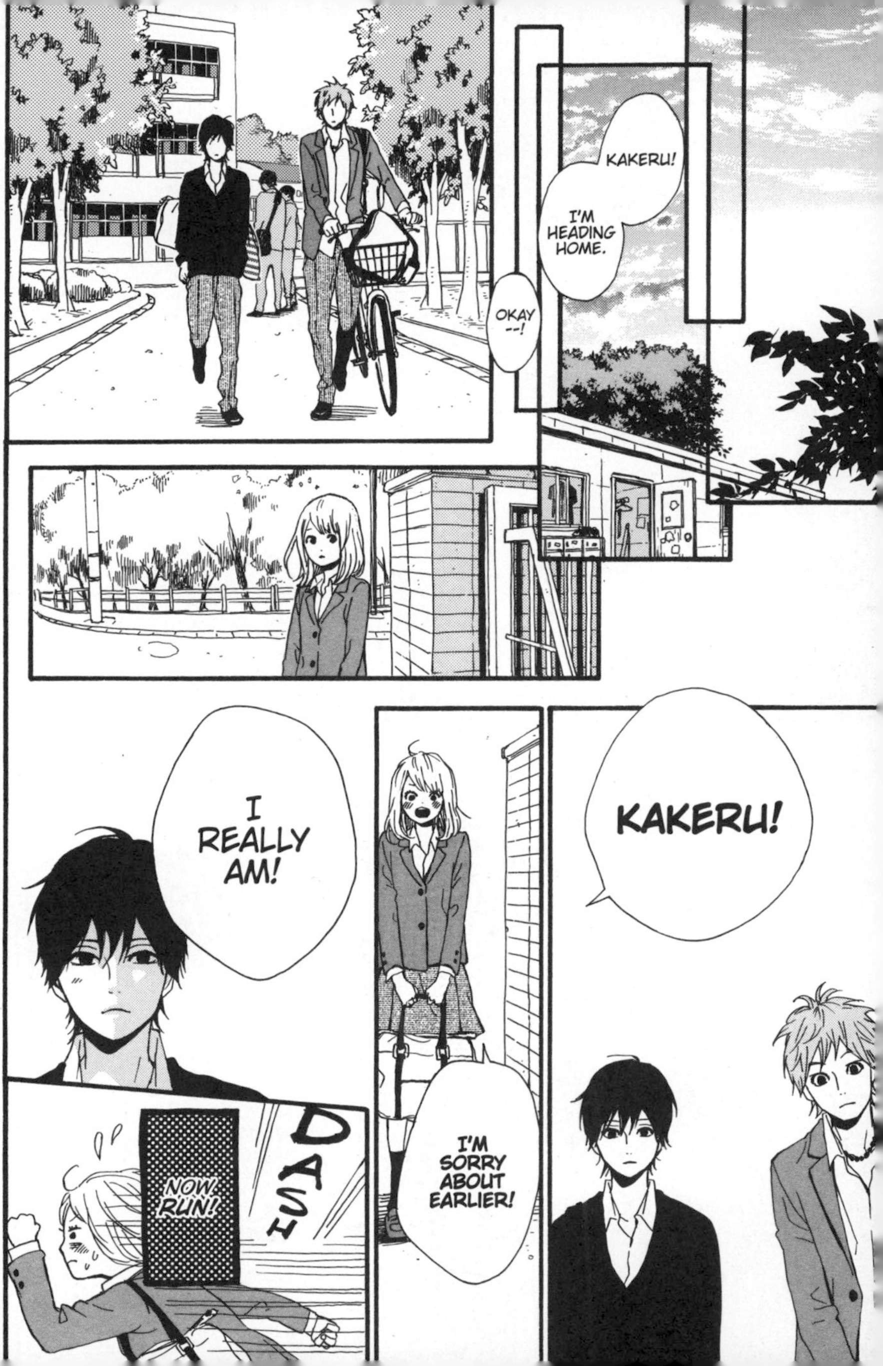
KAKERU!
I'M HEADING HOME.
OKAY --!
KAKERU!
I'M SORRY ABOUT EARLIER!
I REALLY AM!
NOW RUN!
DASH

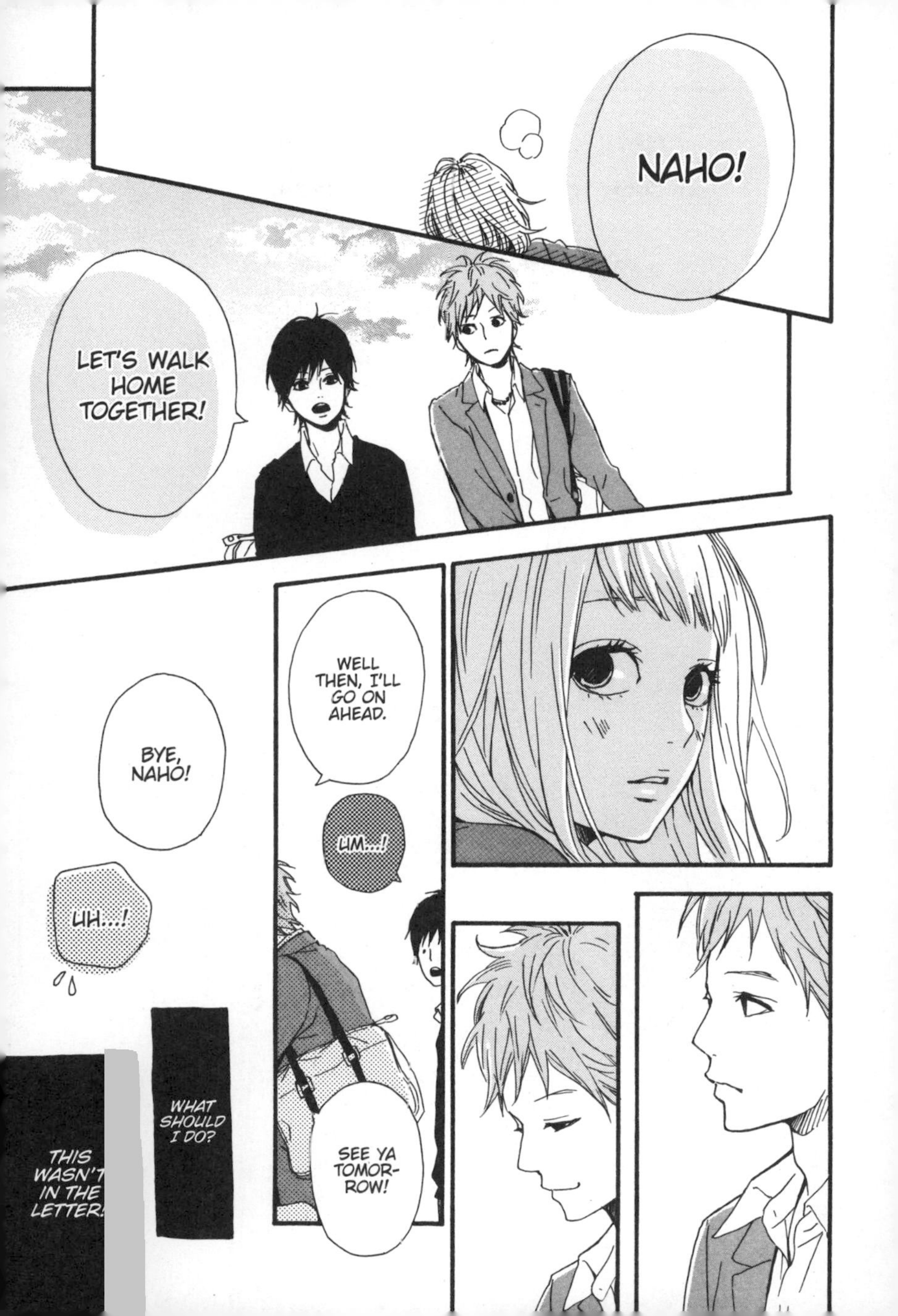
NAHO!
LET'S WALK HOME TOGETHER!
WELL THEN, I'LL GO ON AHEAD.
UM...!
SEE YA TOMORROW!
BYE, NAHO!
UH...!
WHAT SHOULD I DO?
THIS WASN'T IN THE LETTER!

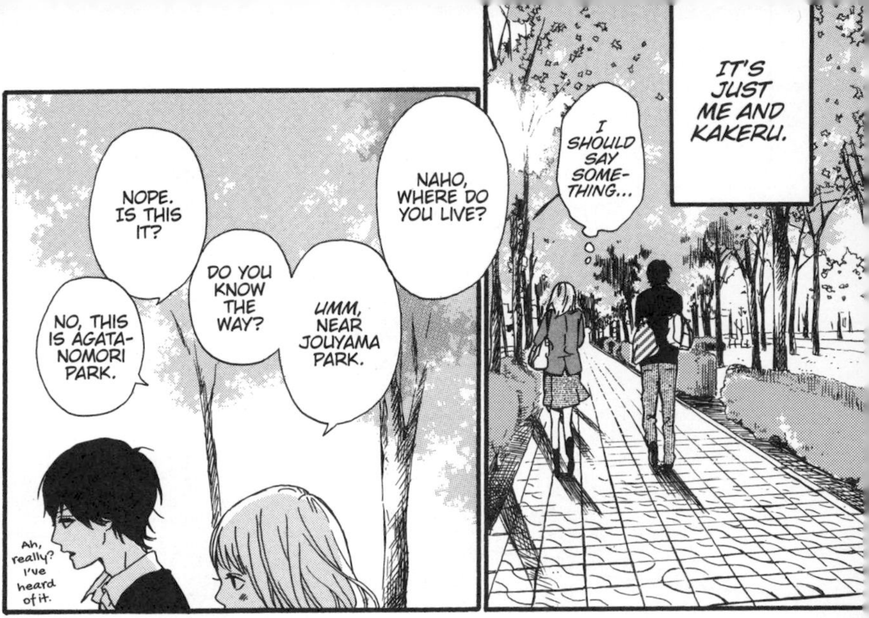
IT'S JUST ME AND KAKERU.
I SHOULD SAY SOME-THING...
NAHO, WHERE DO YOU LIVE?
UMM, NEAR JOUYAMA PARK.
DO YOU KNOW THE WAY?
NOPE. IS THIS IT?
NO, THIS IS AGATA-NOMORI PARK.
Ah, really? I've heard of it.

• If Kakeru looks sad,
I want you to help him.

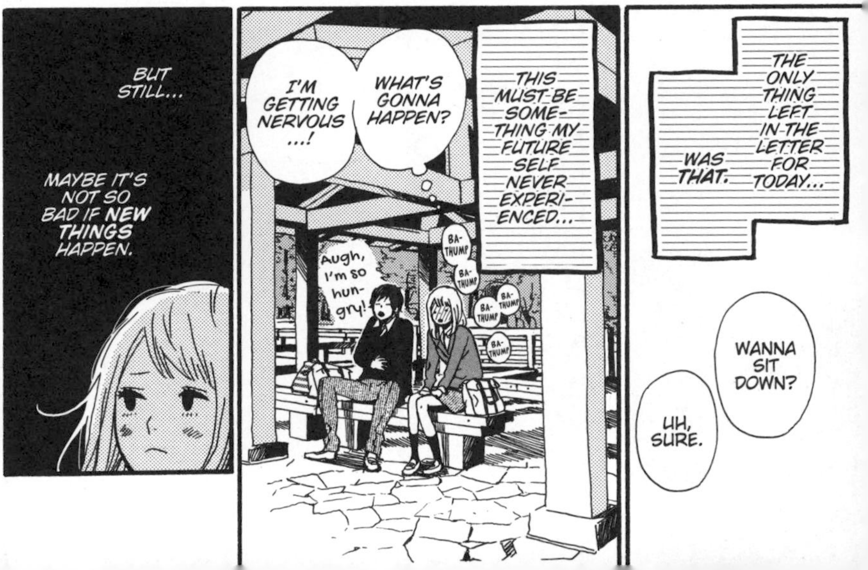
THE ONLY THING LEFT IN THE LETTER FOR TODAY... WAS THAT.
WANNA SIT DOWN?
UH, SURE.
THIS MUST BE SOME-THING MY FUTURE SELF NEVER EXPERI-ENCED...
WHAT'S GONNA HAPPEN?
I'M GETTING NERVOUS ...!
BA-THUMP
BA-THUMP
BA-THUMP
BA-THUMP
BA-THUMP
Augh, I'm so hun-gry!
BUT STILL...
MAYBE IT'S NOT SO BAD IF NEW THINGS HAPPEN.

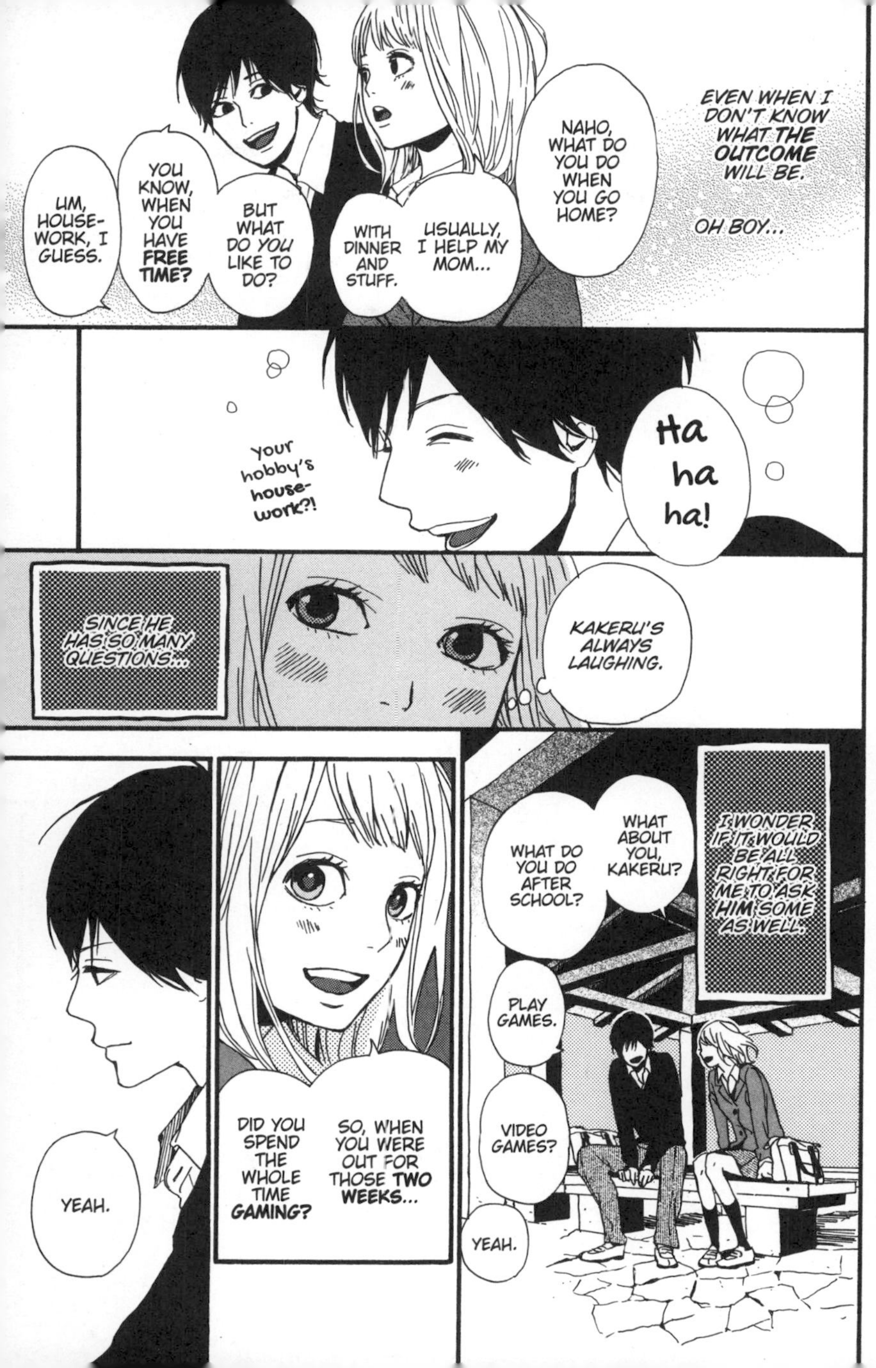
EVEN WHEN I DON'T KNOW WHAT THE OUTCOME WILL BE.
OH BOY...
NAHO, WHAT DO YOU DO WHEN YOU GO HOME?
USUALLY, I HELP MY MOM...
WITH DINNER AND STUFF.
BUT WHAT DO YOU LIKE TO DO?
YOU KNOW, WHEN YOU HAVE FREE TIME?
UM, HOUSE-WORK, I GUESS.
Ha ha ha!
Your hobby's house-work?!
KAKERU'S ALWAYS LAUGHING.
SINCE HE HAS SO MANY QUESTIONS...
I WONDER IF IT WOULD BE ALL RIGHT FOR ME TO ASK HIM SOME AS WELL.
WHAT ABOUT YOU, KAKERU?
WHAT DO YOU DO AFTER SCHOOL?
PLAY GAMES.
VIDEO GAMES?
YEAH.
SO, WHEN YOU WERE OUT FOR THOSE TWO WEEKS...
DID YOU SPEND THE WHOLE TIME GAMING?
YEAH.

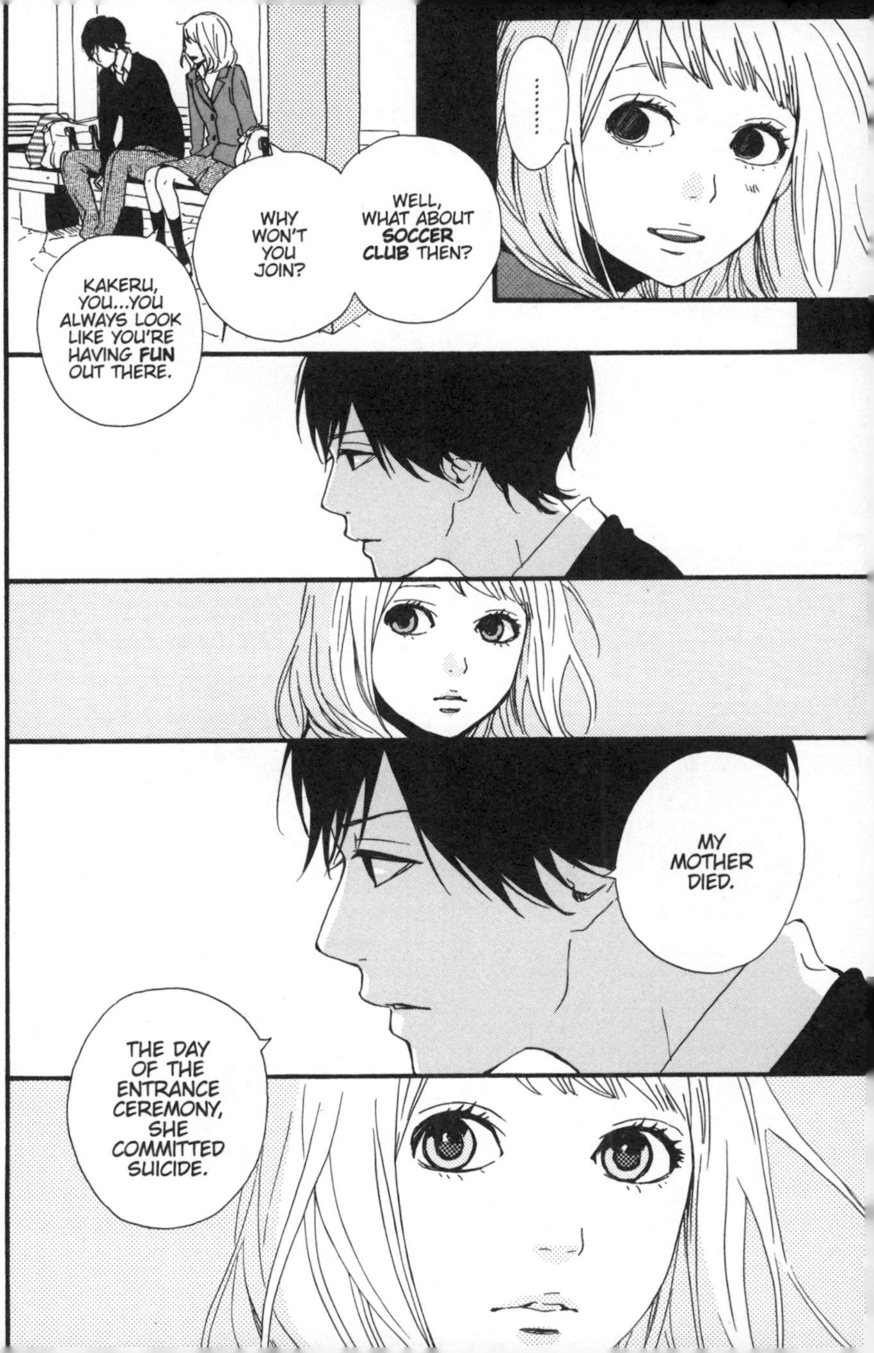
......
WELL, WHAT ABOUT SOCCER CLUB THEN?
WHY WON'T YOU JOIN?
KAKERU, YOU...YOU ALWAYS LOOK LIKE YOU'RE HAVING FUN OUT THERE.
MY MOTHER DIED.
THE DAY OF THE ENTRANCE CEREMONY, SHE COMMITTED SUICIDE.

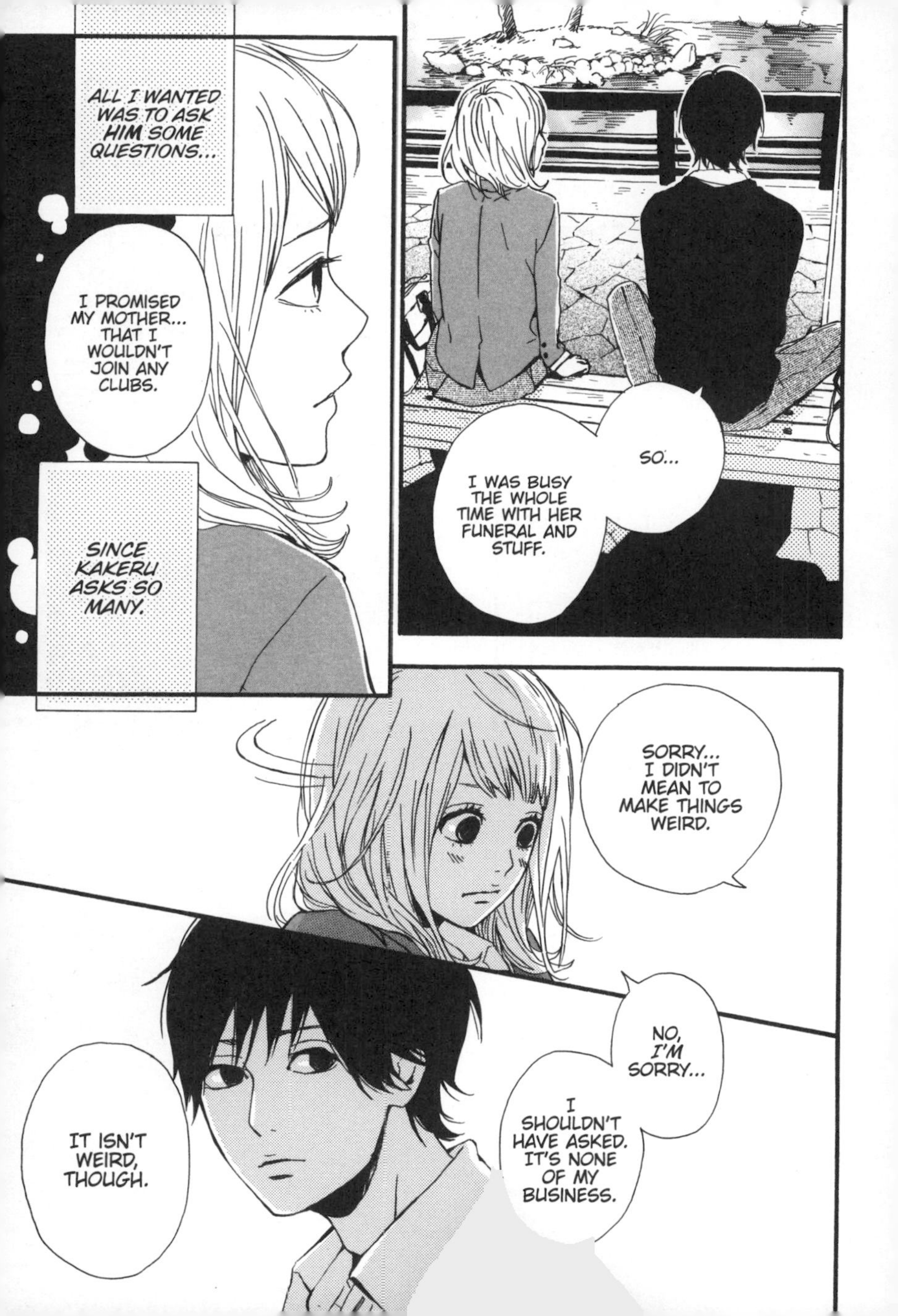
SO...
I WAS BUSY THE WHOLE TIME WITH HER FUNERAL AND STUFF.
ALL I WANTED WAS TO ASK HIM SOME QUESTIONS...
I PROMISED MY MOTHER... THAT I WOULDN'T JOIN ANY CLUBS.
SINCE KAKERU ASKS SO MANY.
SORRY... I DIDN'T MEAN TO MAKE THINGS WEIRD.
NO, I'M SORRY...
I SHOULDN'T HAVE ASKED. IT'S NONE OF MY BUSINESS.
IT ISN'T WEIRD, THOUGH.

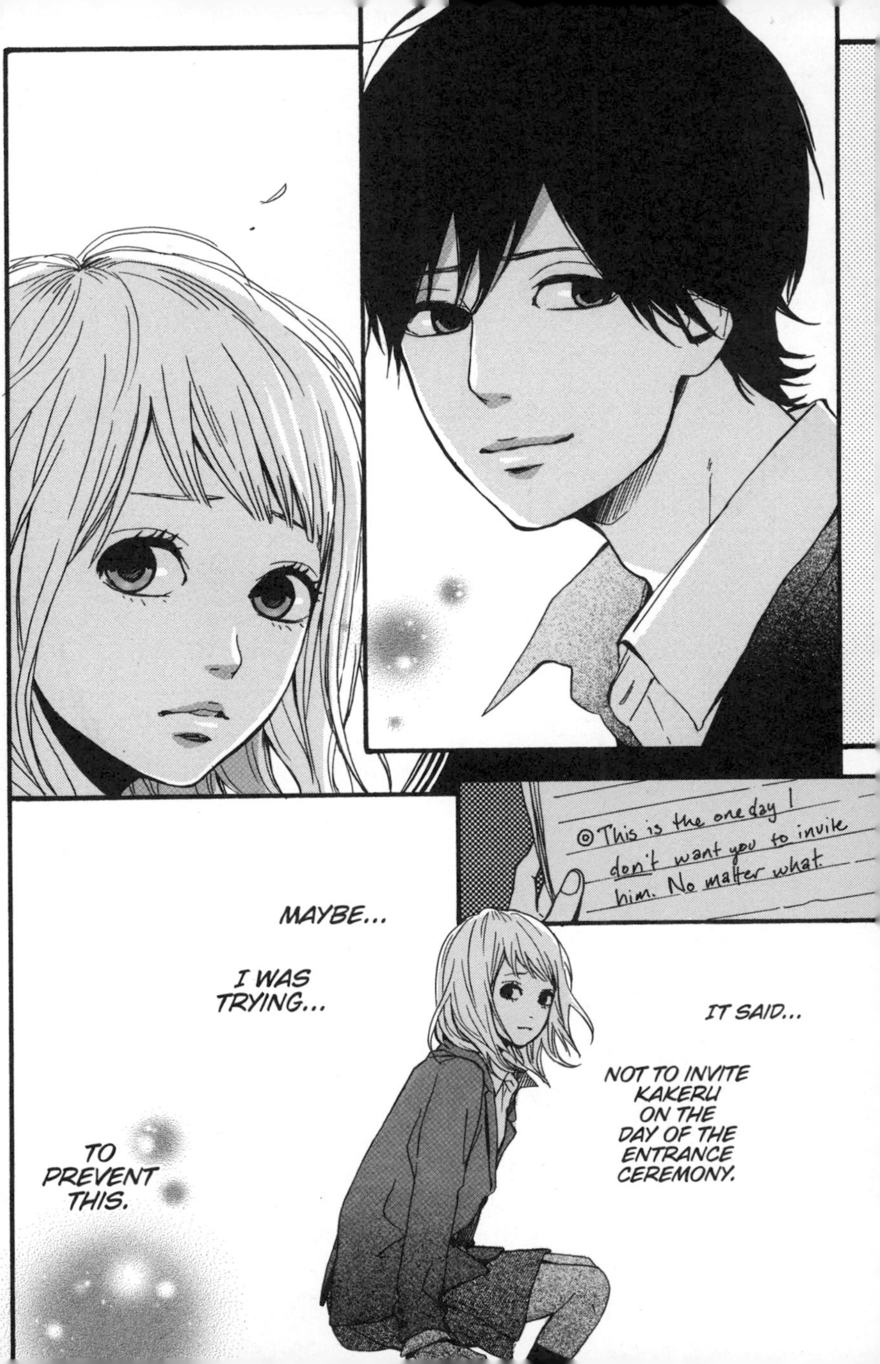
◎ This is the one day I don't want you to invite him. No matter what.
IT SAID...
NOT TO INVITE KAKERU ON THE DAY OF THE ENTRANCE CEREMONY.
MAYBE...
I WAS TRYING...
TO PREVENT THIS.

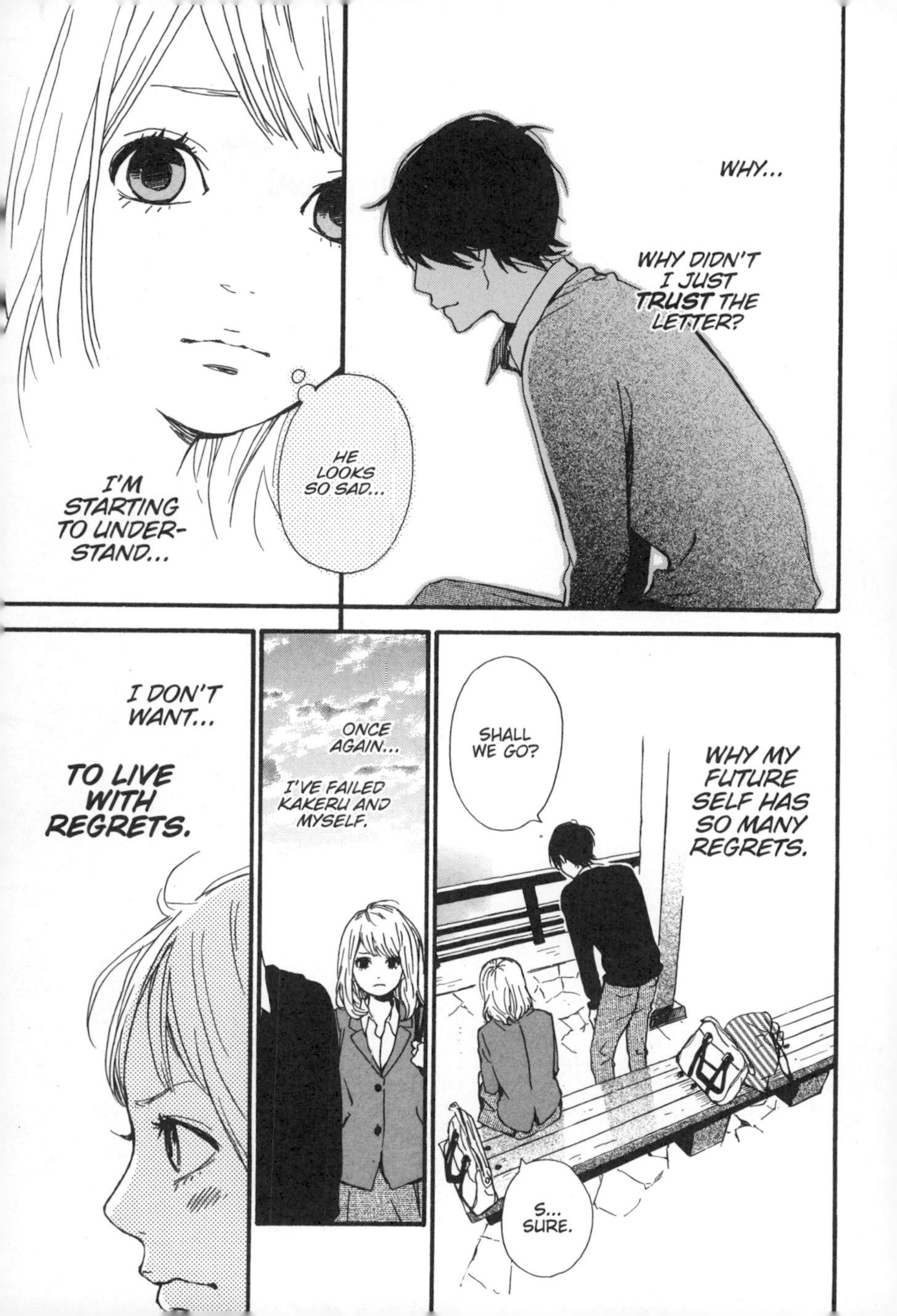
WHY...
WHY DIDN'T I JUST TRUST THE LETTER?
HE LOOKS SO SAD...
I'M STARTING TO UNDER-STAND...
WHY MY FUTURE SELF HAS SO MANY REGRETS.
SHALL WE GO?
S... SURE.
ONCE AGAIN...
I'VE FAILED KAKERU AND MYSELF.
I DON'T WANT...
TO LIVE WITH REGRETS.

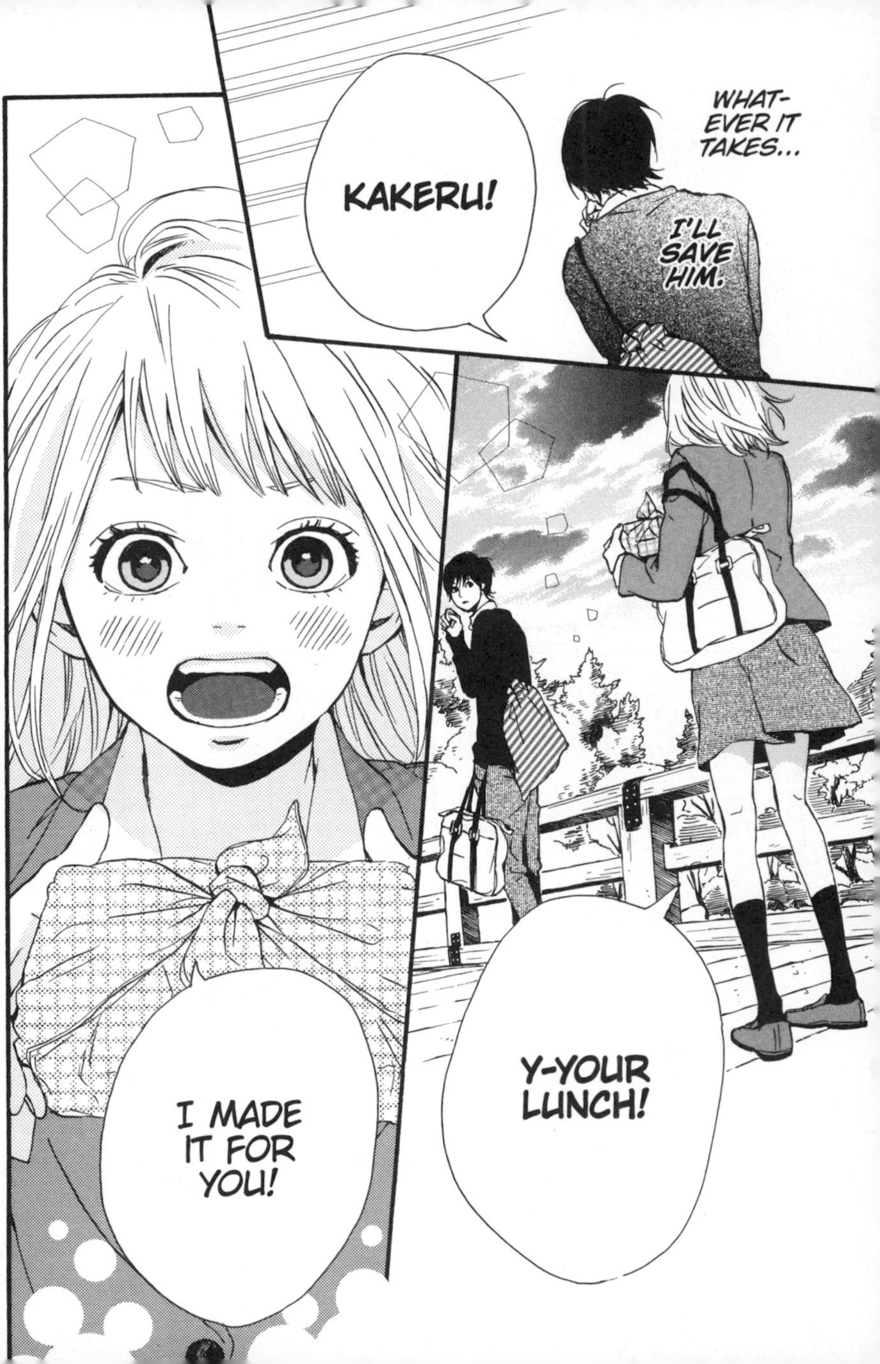
WHATEVER IT TAKES...
I'LL SAVE HIM.
KAKERU!
Y-YOUR LUNCH!
I MADE IT FOR YOU!

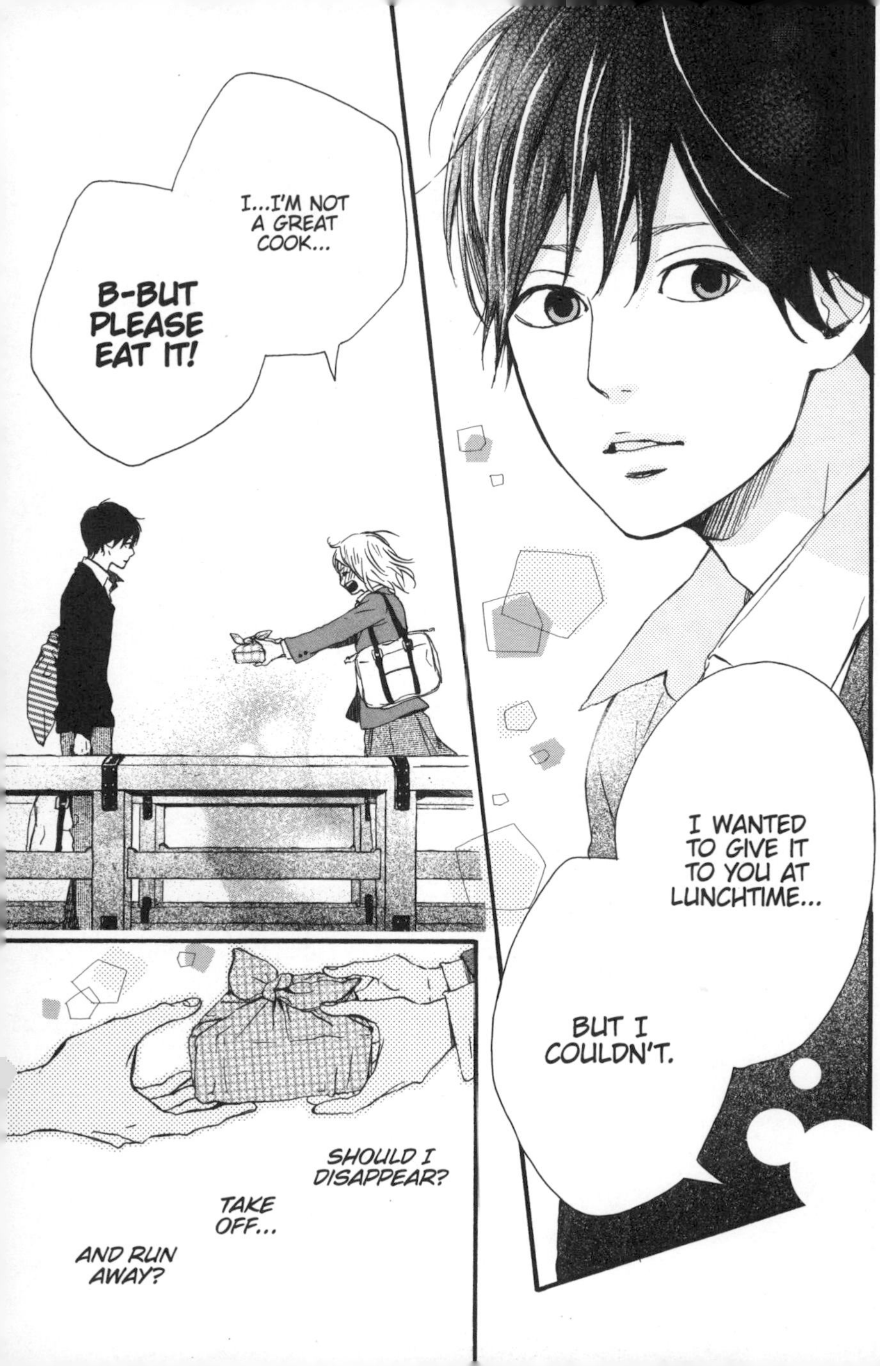
I WANTED TO GIVE IT TO YOU AT LUNCHTIME...
BUT I COULDN'T.
I...I'M NOT A GREAT COOK...
B-BUT PLEASE EAT IT!
SHOULD I DISAPPEAR?
TAKE OFF...
AND RUN AWAY?

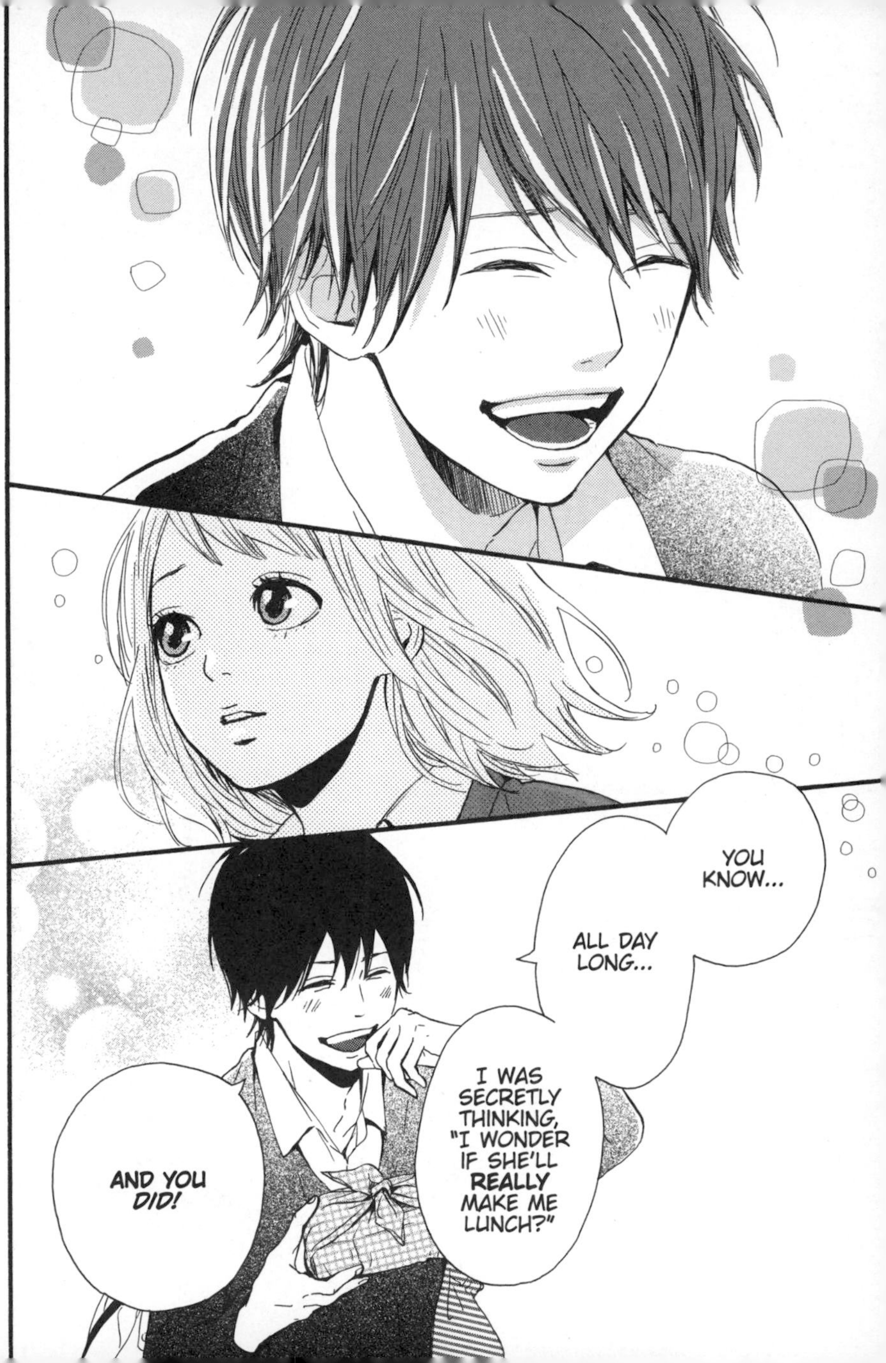
YOU KNOW...
ALL DAY LONG...
I WAS SECRETLY THINKING, "I WONDER IF SHE'LL **REALLY** MAKE ME LUNCH?"
AND YOU *DID!*

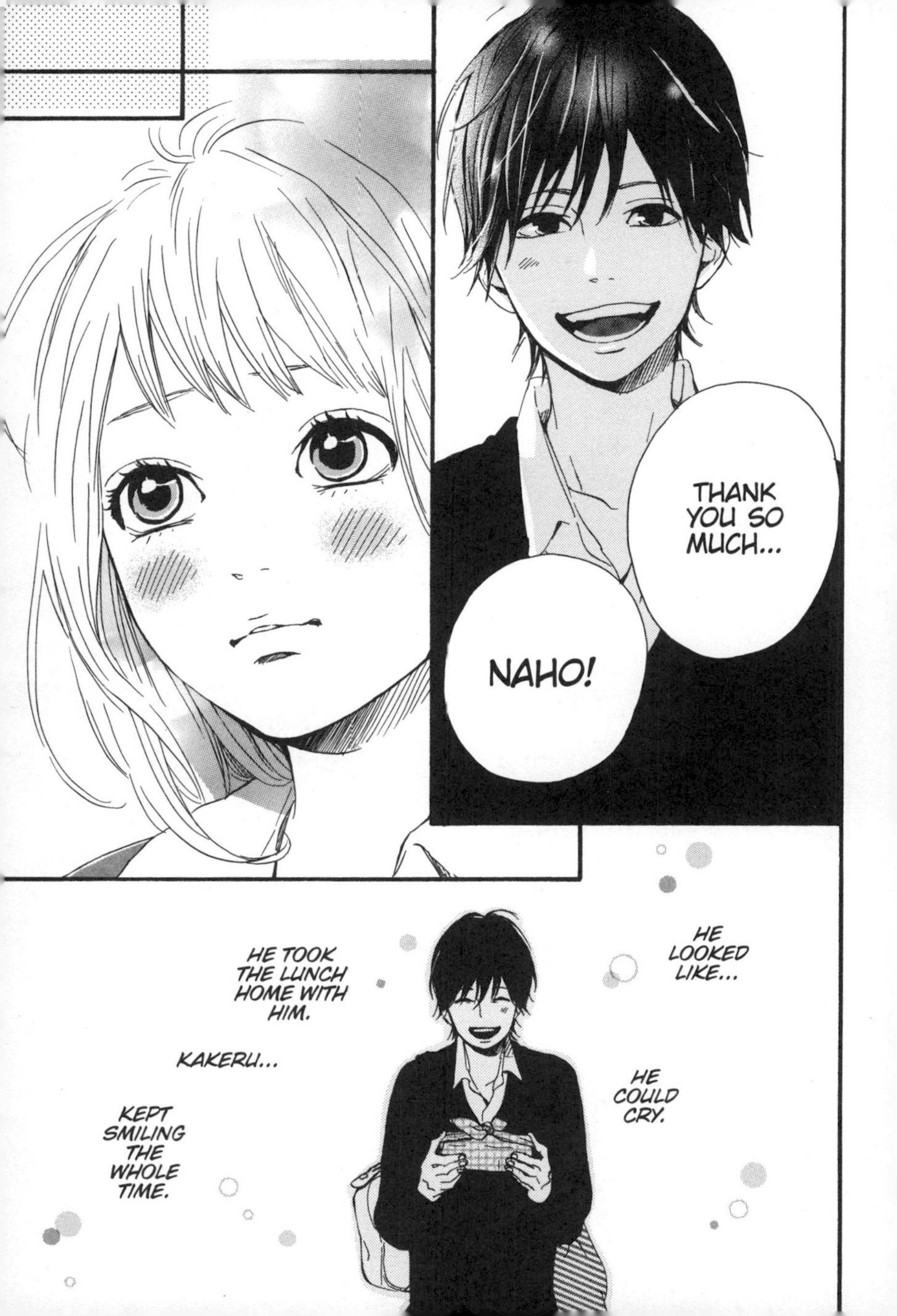
THANK YOU SO MUCH...
NAHO!
HE LOOKED LIKE...
HE COULD CRY.
HE TOOK THE LUNCH HOME WITH HIM.
KAKERU...
KEPT SMILING THE WHOLE TIME.

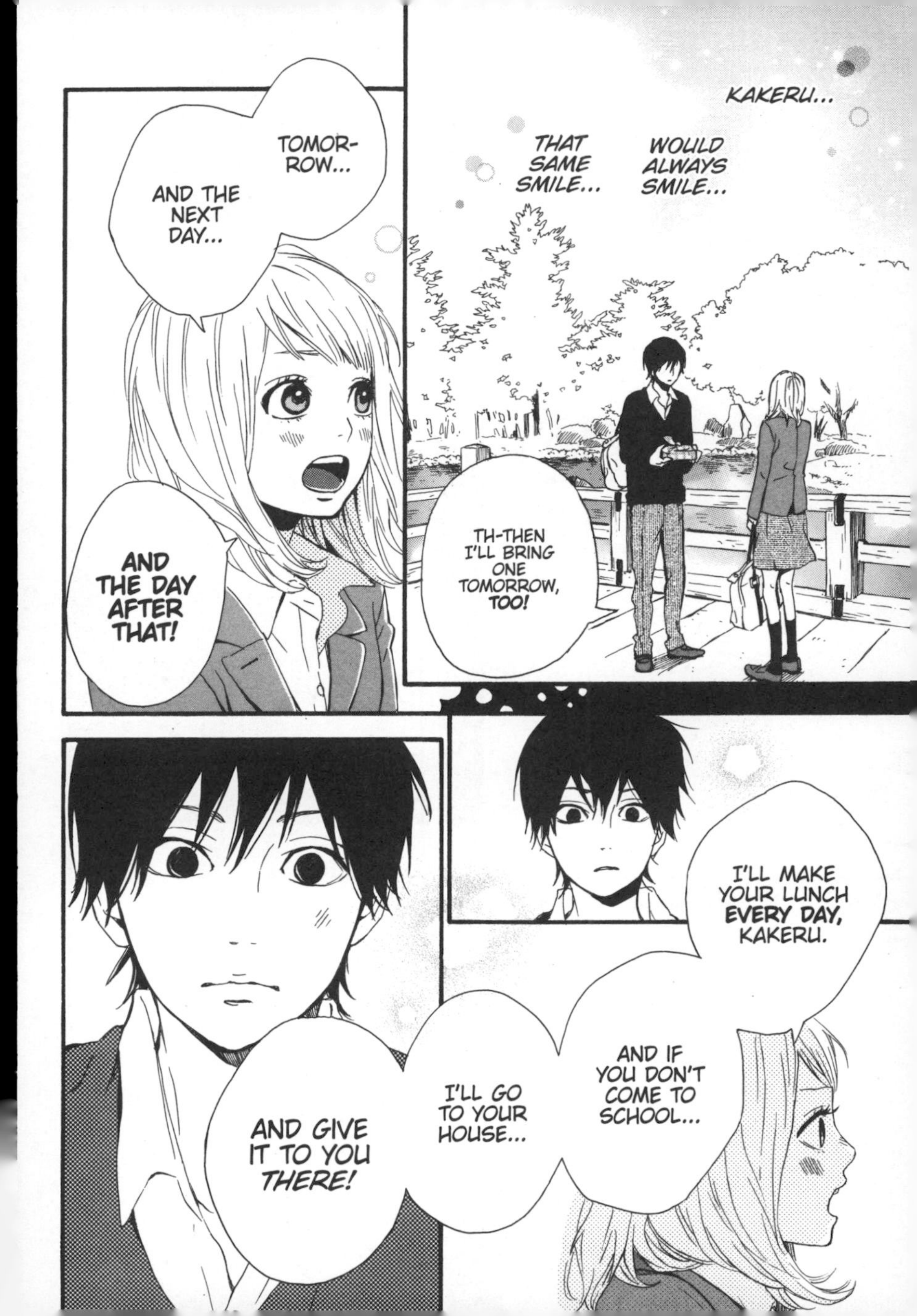
KAKERU...
WOULD ALWAYS SMILE...
THAT SAME SMILE...
TH-THEN I'LL BRING ONE TOMORROW, TOO!
TOMORROW...
AND THE NEXT DAY...
AND THE DAY AFTER THAT!
I'LL MAKE YOUR LUNCH EVERY DAY, KAKERU.
AND IF YOU DON'T COME TO SCHOOL...
I'LL GO TO YOUR HOUSE...
AND GIVE IT TO YOU THERE!

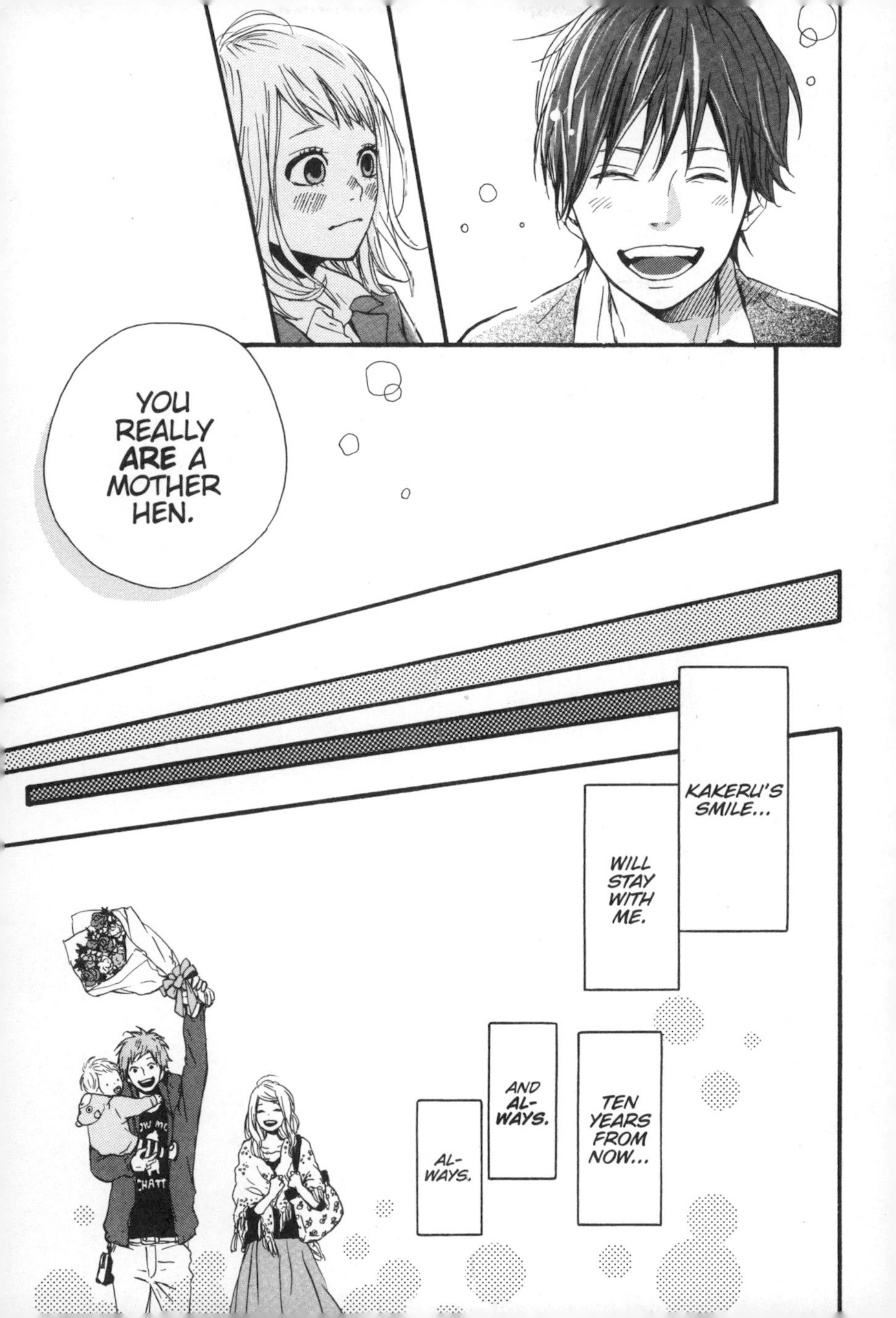
YOU REALLY ARE A MOTHER HEN.
KAKERU'S SMILE...
WILL STAY WITH ME.
TEN YEARS FROM NOW...
AND AL-WAYS.
AL-WAYS.

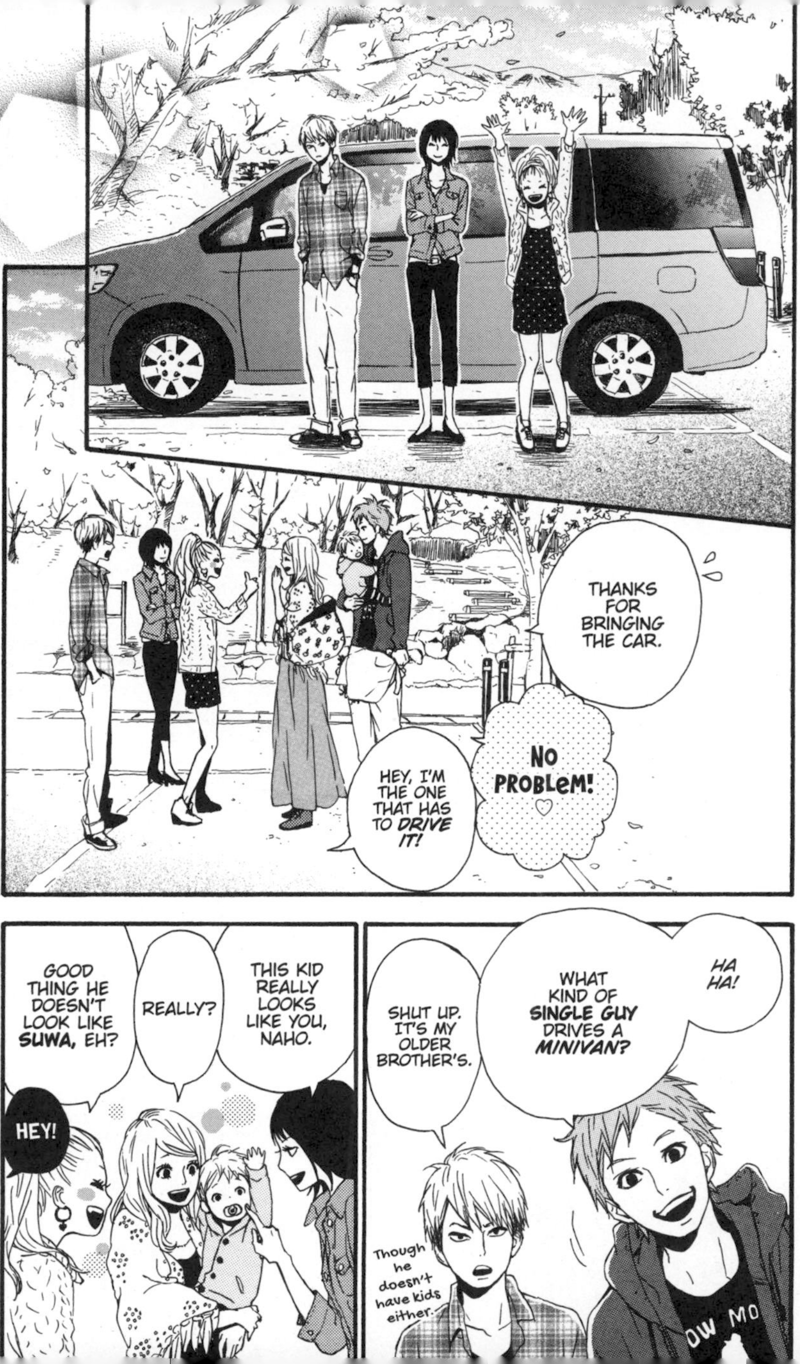
THANKS FOR BRINGING THE CAR.
NO PROBLEM!
HEY, I'M THE ONE THAT HAS TO DRIVE IT!
HA HA!
WHAT KIND OF SINGLE GUY DRIVES A MINIVAN?
SHUT UP. IT'S MY OLDER BROTHER'S.
Though he doesn't have kids either.
THIS KID REALLY LOOKS LIKE YOU, NAHO.
REALLY?
GOOD THING HE DOESN'T LOOK LIKE SUWA, EH?
HEY!

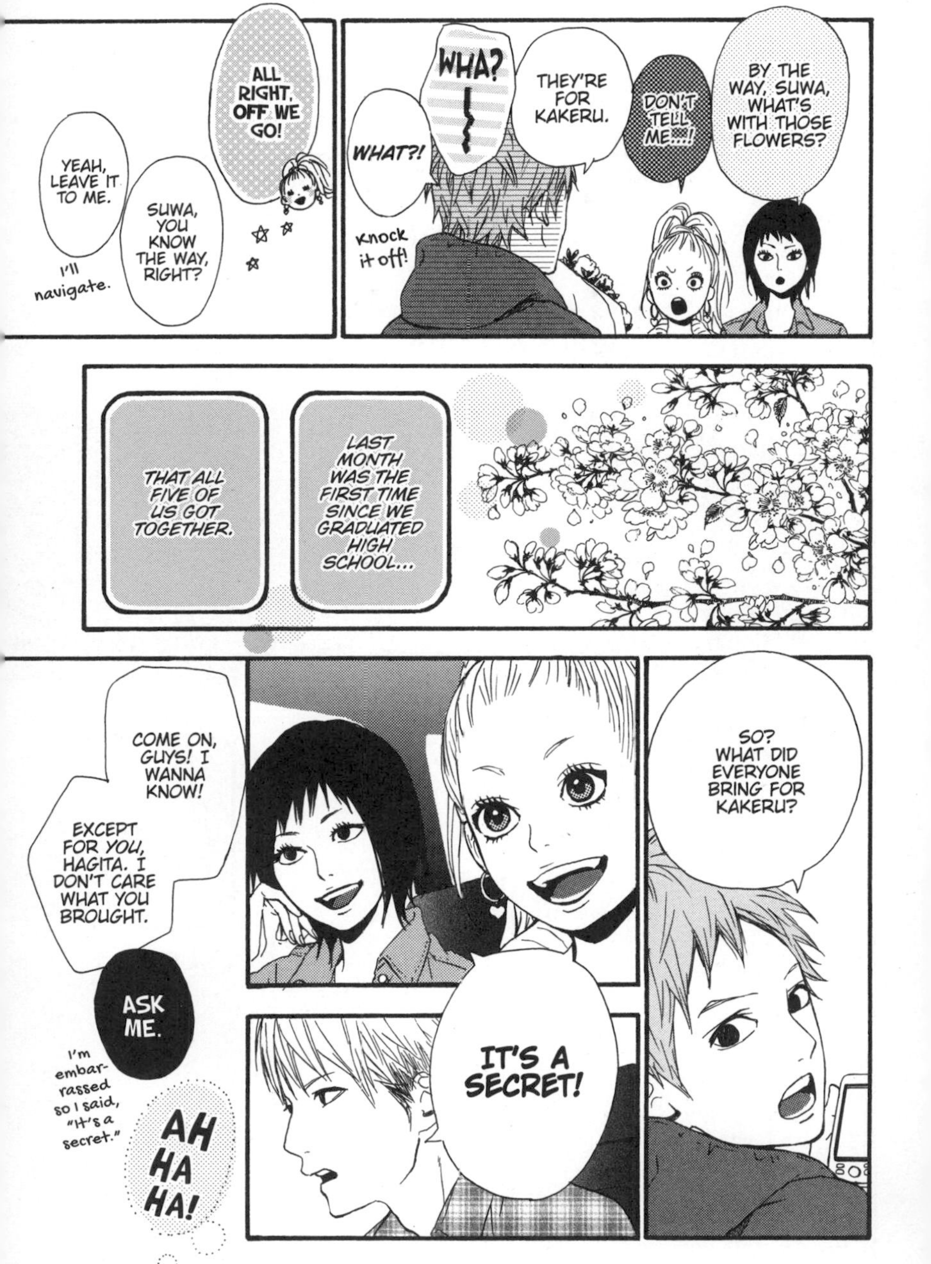
BY THE WAY, SUWA, WHAT'S WITH THOSE FLOWERS?
DON'T TELL ME...!
THEY'RE FOR KAKERU.
WHA?
WHAT?!
Knock it off!
ALL RIGHT, OFF WE GO!
SUWA, YOU KNOW THE WAY, RIGHT?
YEAH, LEAVE IT TO ME.
I'll navigate.
LAST MONTH WAS THE FIRST TIME SINCE WE GRADUATED HIGH SCHOOL...
THAT ALL FIVE OF US GOT TOGETHER.
SO? WHAT DID EVERYONE BRING FOR KAKERU?
COME ON, GUYS! I WANNA KNOW!
EXCEPT FOR YOU, HAGITA. I DON'T CARE WHAT YOU BROUGHT.
IT'S A SECRET!
ASK ME.
I'm embarrassed so I said, "It's a secret."
AH HA HA!

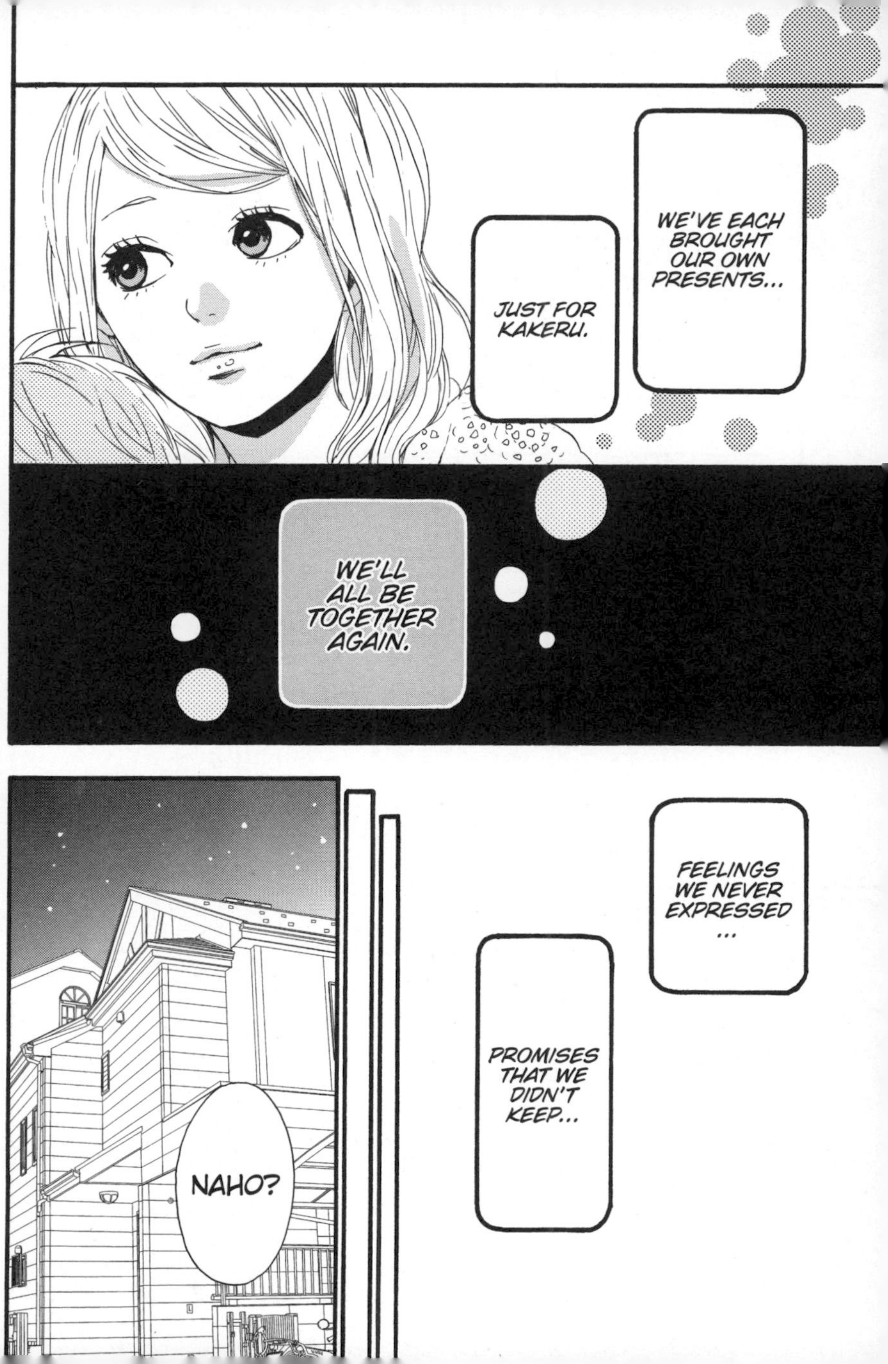
WE'VE EACH BROUGHT OUR OWN PRESENTS...
JUST FOR KAKERU.
WE'LL ALL BE TOGETHER AGAIN.
FEELINGS WE NEVER EXPRESSED ...
PROMISES THAT WE DIDN'T KEEP...
NAHO?

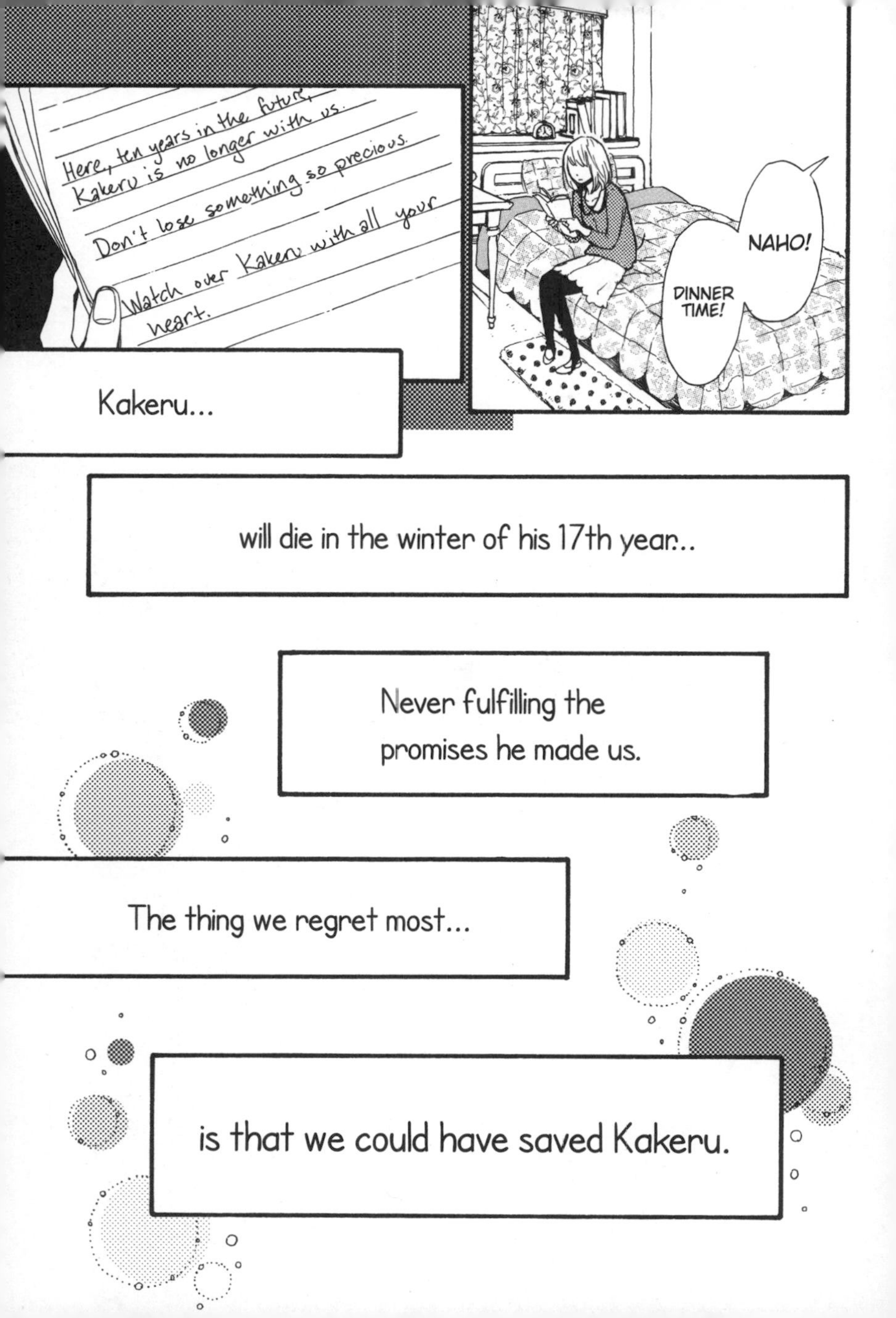
NAHO!
DINNER TIME!
Here, ten years in the future, Kakeru is no longer with us.
Don't lose something so precious.
Watch over Kakeru with all your heart.
Kakeru...
will die in the winter of his 17th year...
Never fulfilling the promises he made us.
The thing we regret most...
is that we could have saved Kakeru.

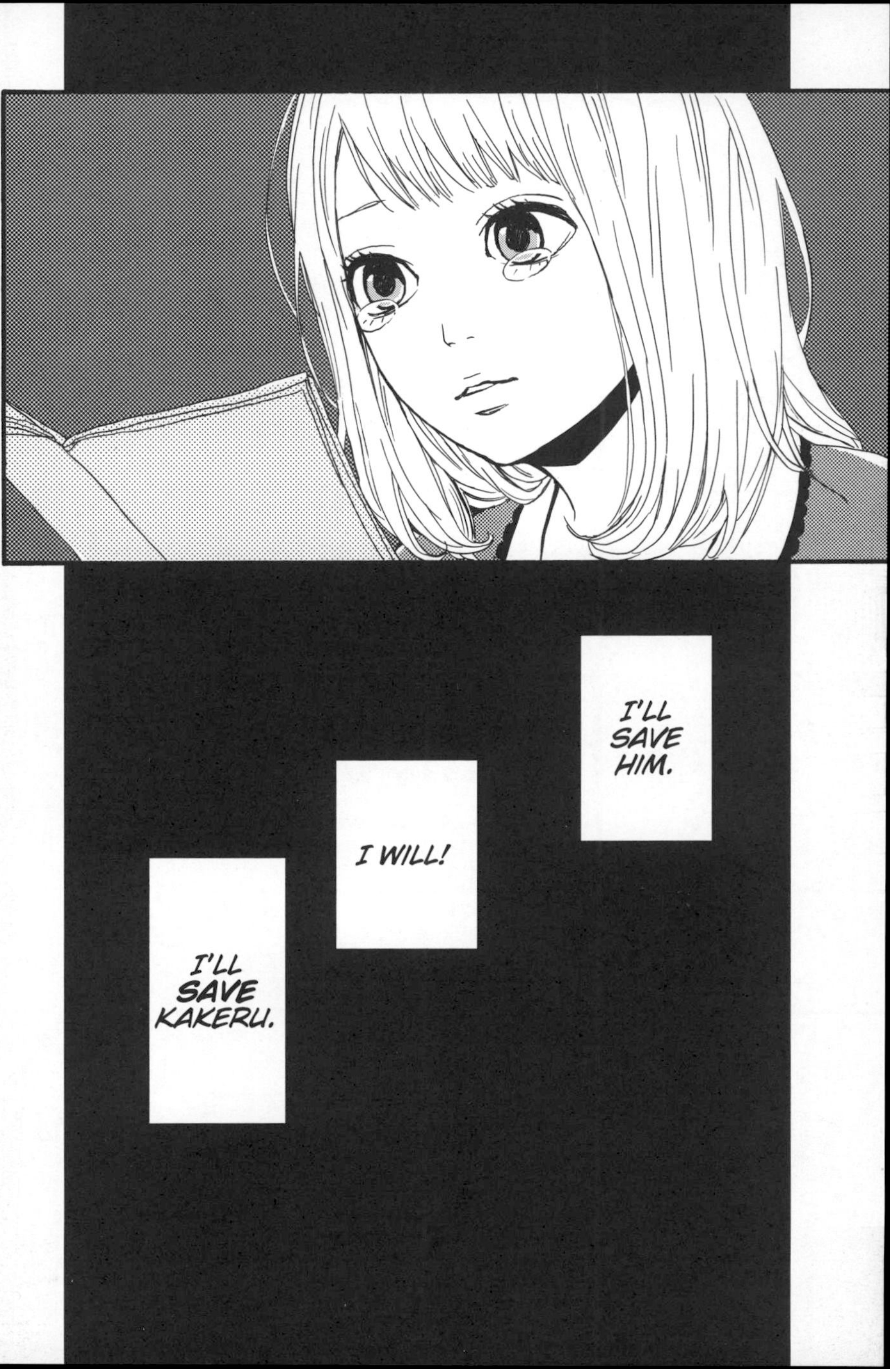
I'LL SAVE HIM.
I WILL!
I'LL SAVE KAKERU.

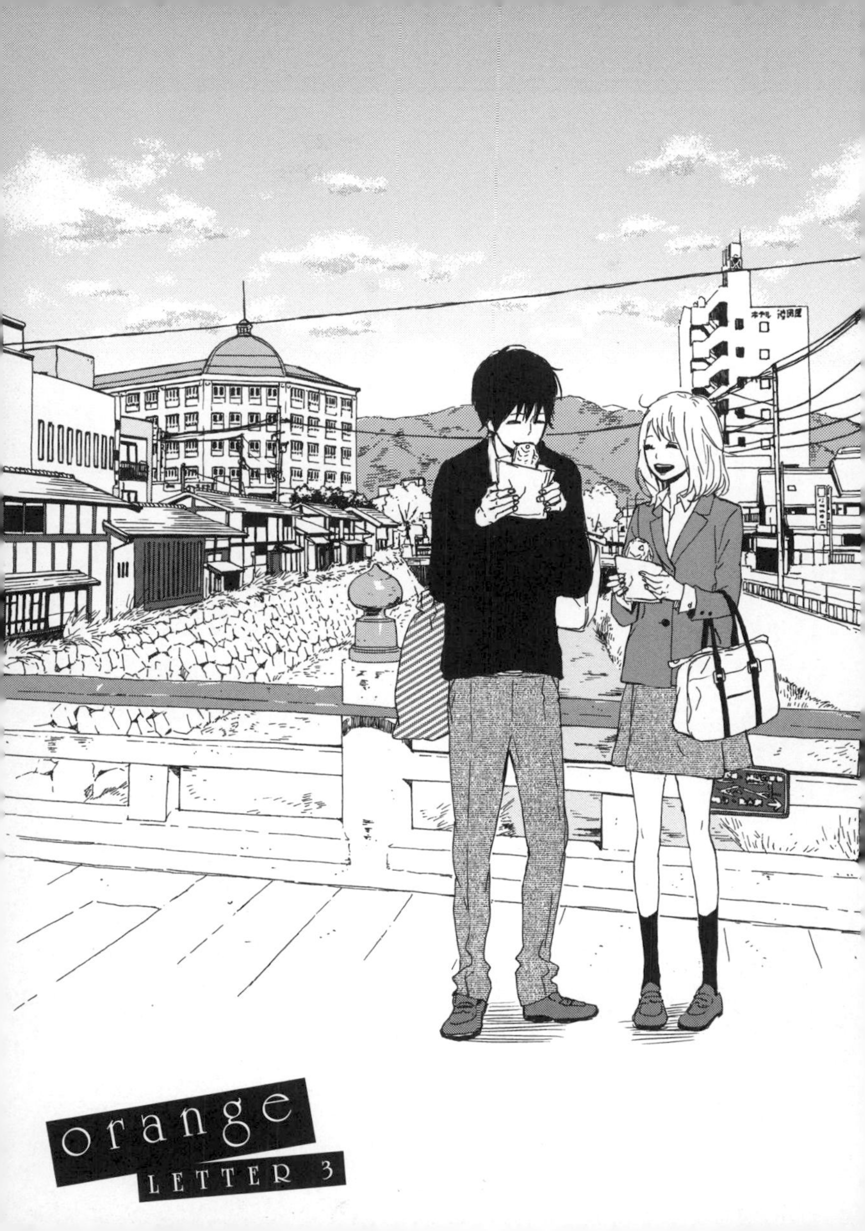
orange
LETTER 3

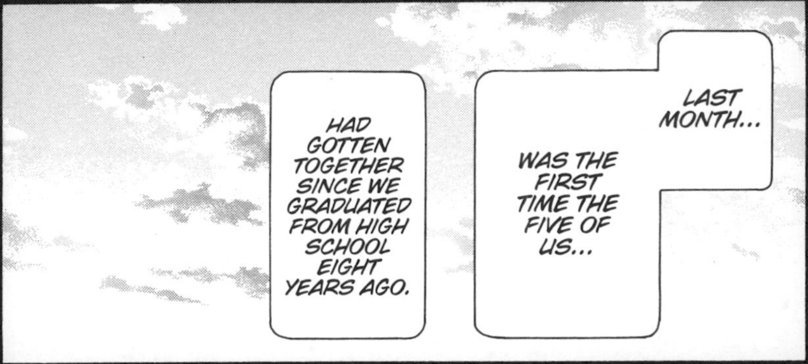
LAST MONTH...
WAS THE FIRST TIME THE FIVE OF US...
HAD GOTTEN TOGETHER SINCE WE GRADUATED FROM HIGH SCHOOL EIGHT YEARS AGO.

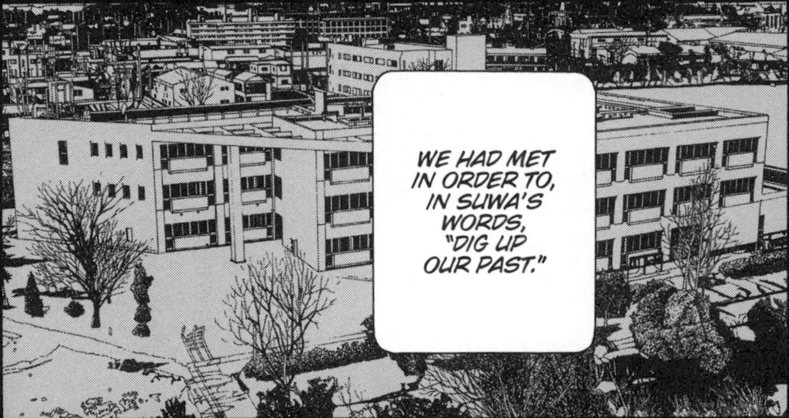
WE HAD MET IN ORDER TO, IN SUWA'S WORDS, "DIG UP OUR PAST."

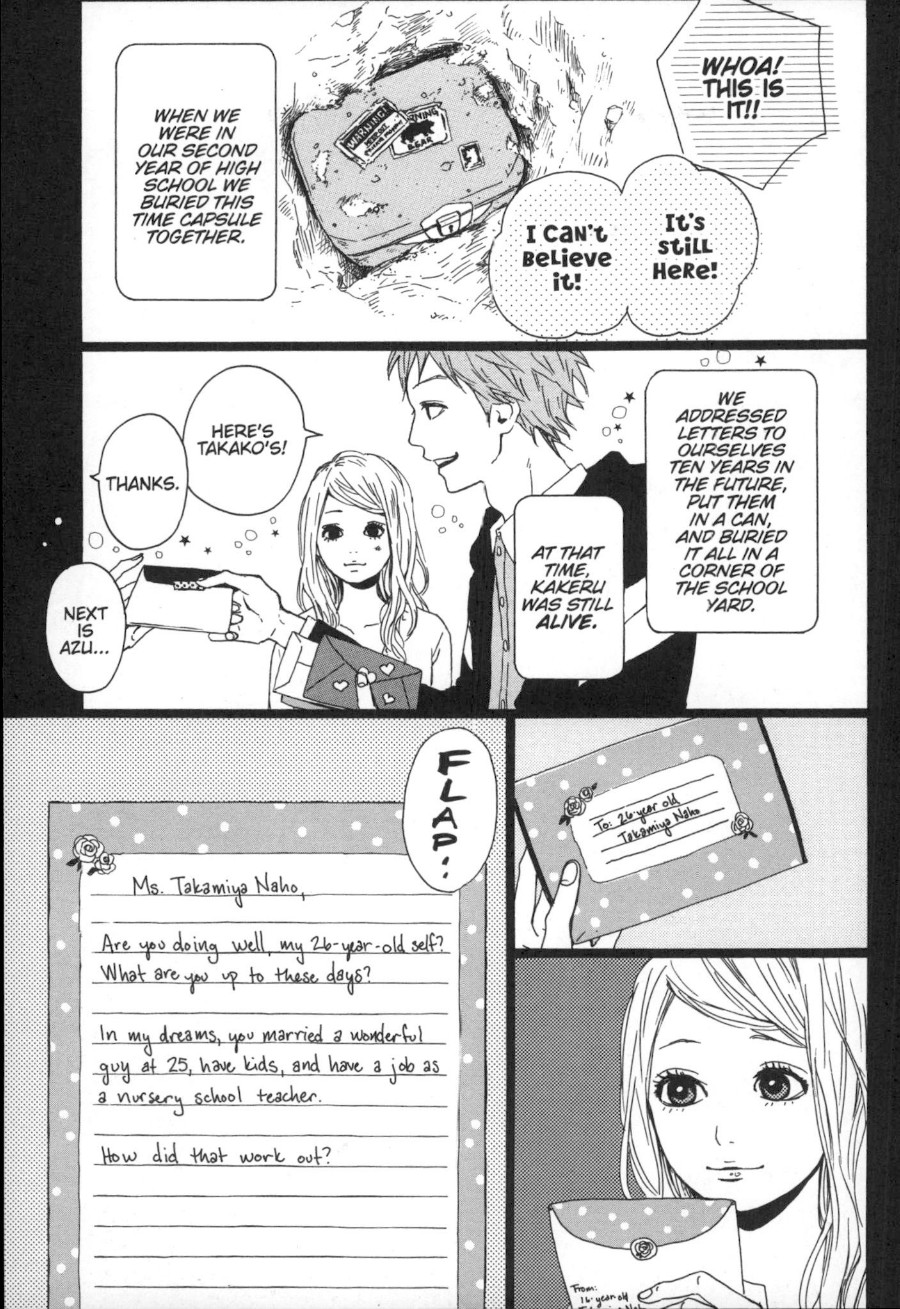
WHEN WE WERE IN OUR SECOND YEAR OF HIGH SCHOOL WE BURIED THIS TIME CAPSULE TOGETHER.
WHOA! THIS IS IT!!
I can't believe it!
It's still here!
HERE'S TAKAKO'S!
THANKS.
NEXT IS AZU...
WE ADDRESSED LETTERS TO OURSELVES TEN YEARS IN THE FUTURE, PUT THEM IN A CAN, AND BURIED IT ALL IN A CORNER OF THE SCHOOL YARD.
AT THAT TIME, KAKERU WAS STILL ALIVE.
FLAP!
To: 26-year old Takamiya Naho
Ms. Takamiya Naho,
Are you doing well, my 26-year-old self?
What are you up to these days?
In my dreams, you married a wonderful guy at 25, have kids, and have a job as a nursery school teacher.
How did that work out?
From:
16-year old

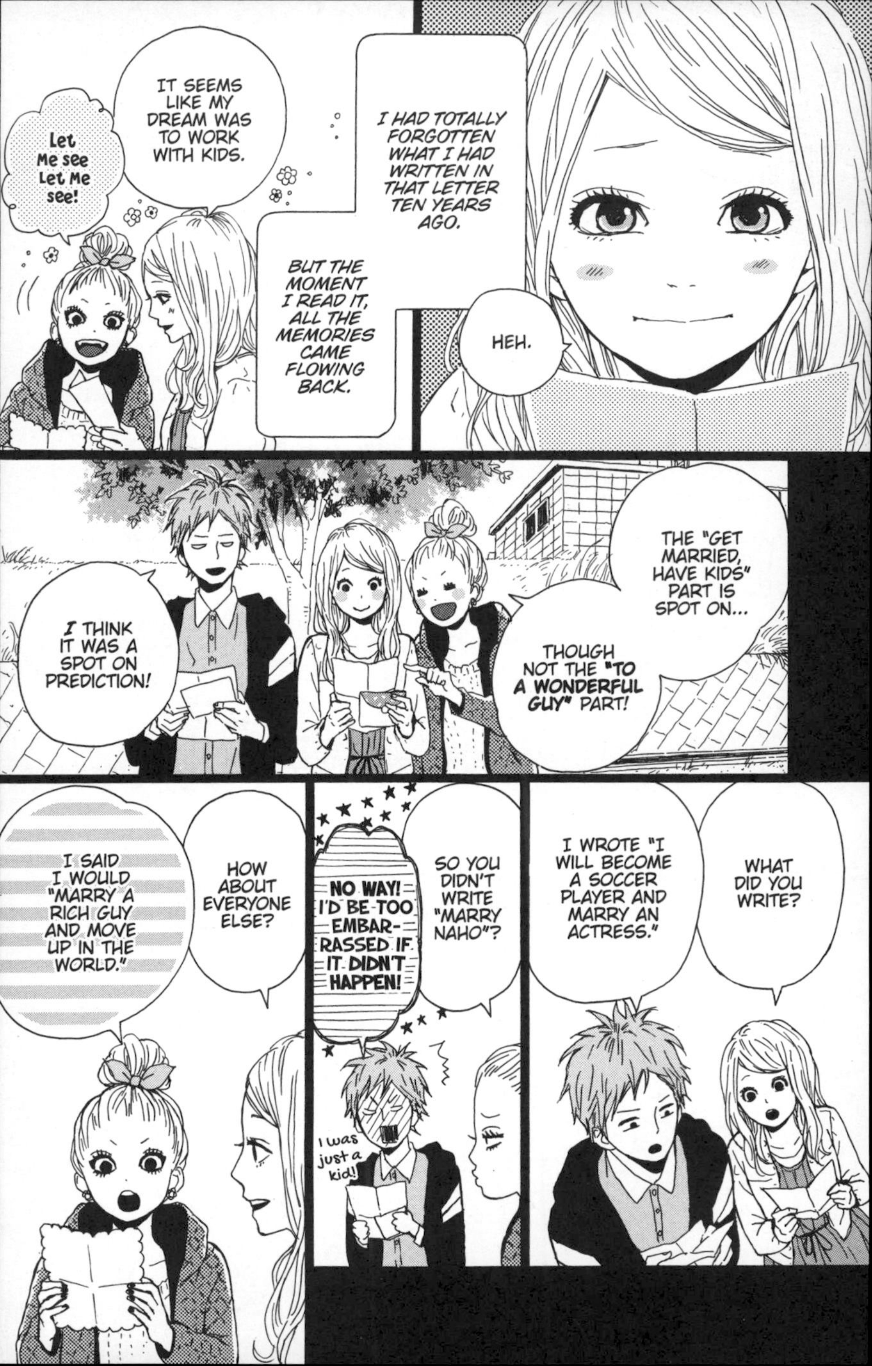
HEH.
I HAD TOTALLY FORGOTTEN WHAT I HAD WRITTEN IN THAT LETTER TEN YEARS AGO.
BUT THE MOMENT I READ IT, ALL THE MEMORIES CAME FLOWING BACK.
IT SEEMS LIKE MY DREAM WAS TO WORK WITH KIDS.
Let Me see Let Me see!
THE "GET MARRIED, HAVE KIDS" PART IS SPOT ON...
THOUGH NOT THE "TO A WONDERFUL GUY" PART!
I THINK IT WAS A SPOT ON PREDICTION!
WHAT DID YOU WRITE?
I WROTE "I WILL BECOME A SOCCER PLAYER AND MARRY AN ACTRESS."
SO YOU DIDN'T WRITE "MARRY NAHO"?
NO WAY! I'D BE TOO EMBARRASSED IF IT DIDN'T HAPPEN!
I was just a kid!
HOW ABOUT EVERYONE ELSE?
I SAID I WOULD "MARRY A RICH GUY AND MOVE UP IN THE WORLD."

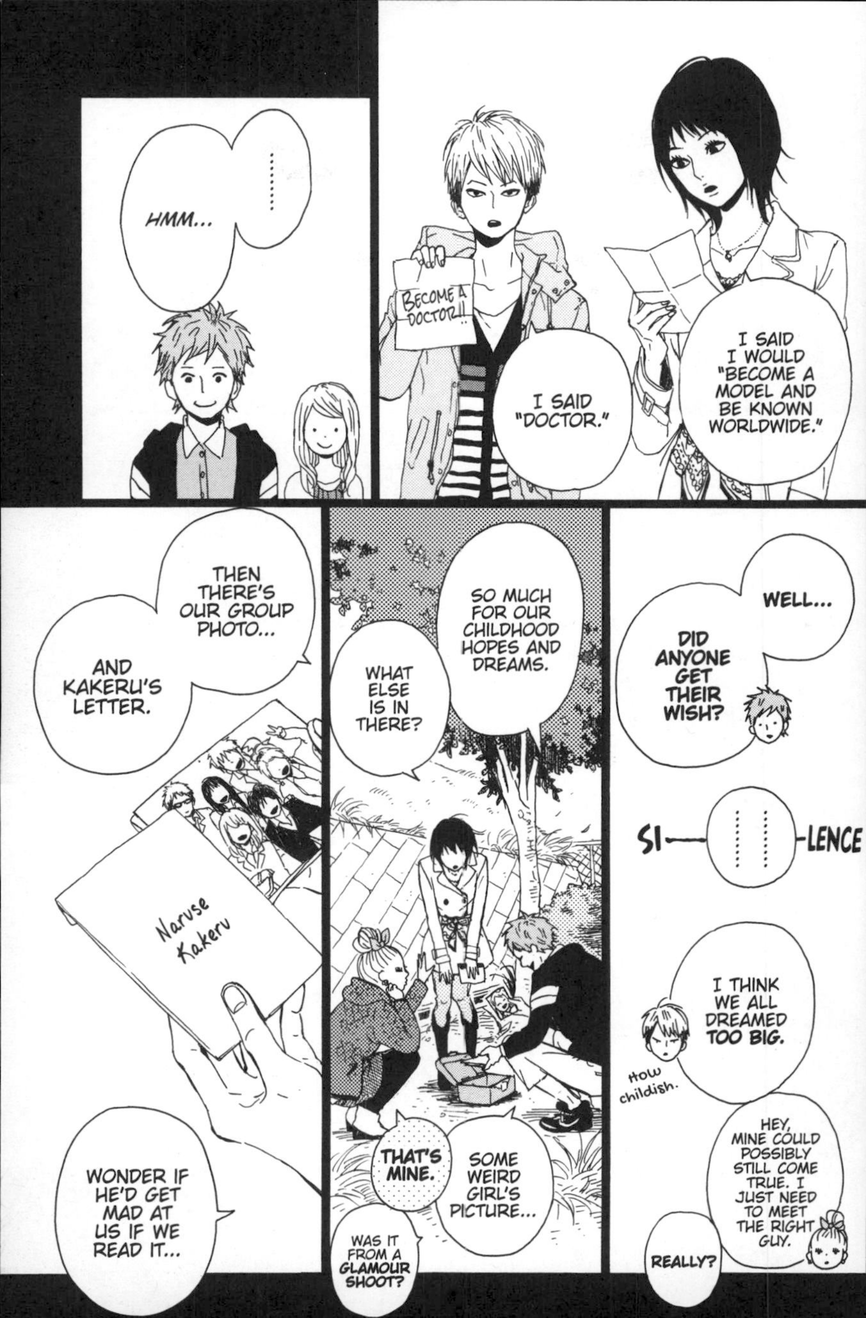
I SAID I WOULD "BECOME A MODEL AND BE KNOWN WORLDWIDE."
BECOME A DOCTOR!!
I SAID "DOCTOR."
……
HMM...
WELL...
DID ANYONE GET THEIR WISH?
SI——……——LENCE
I THINK WE ALL DREAMED TOO BIG.
How childish.
HEY, MINE COULD POSSIBLY STILL COME TRUE. I JUST NEED TO MEET THE RIGHT GUY.
REALLY?
SO MUCH FOR OUR CHILDHOOD HOPES AND DREAMS.
WHAT ELSE IS IN THERE?
SOME WEIRD GIRL'S PICTURE...
THAT'S MINE.
WAS IT FROM A GLAMOUR SHOOT?
THEN THERE'S OUR GROUP PHOTO...
AND KAKERU'S LETTER.
Naruse Kakeru
WONDER IF HE'D GET MAD AT US IF WE READ IT...

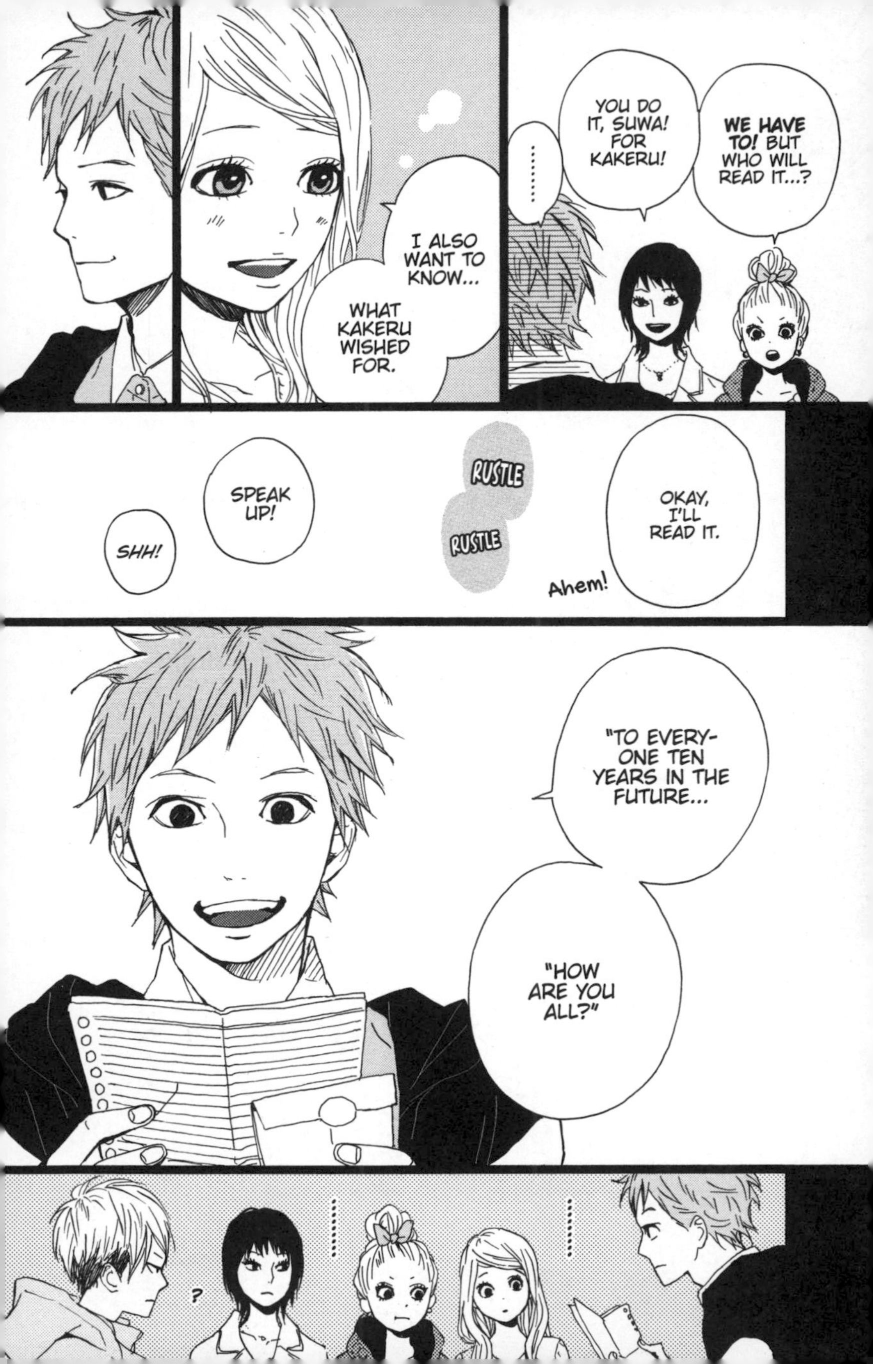
WE HAVE TO! BUT WHO WILL READ IT...?
YOU DO IT, SUWA! FOR KAKERU!
......
I ALSO WANT TO KNOW...
WHAT KAKERU WISHED FOR.
OKAY, I'LL READ IT.
Ahem!
RUSTLE
RUSTLE
SPEAK UP!
SHH!
"TO EVERY-ONE TEN YEARS IN THE FUTURE...
"HOW ARE YOU ALL?"
......
......
?

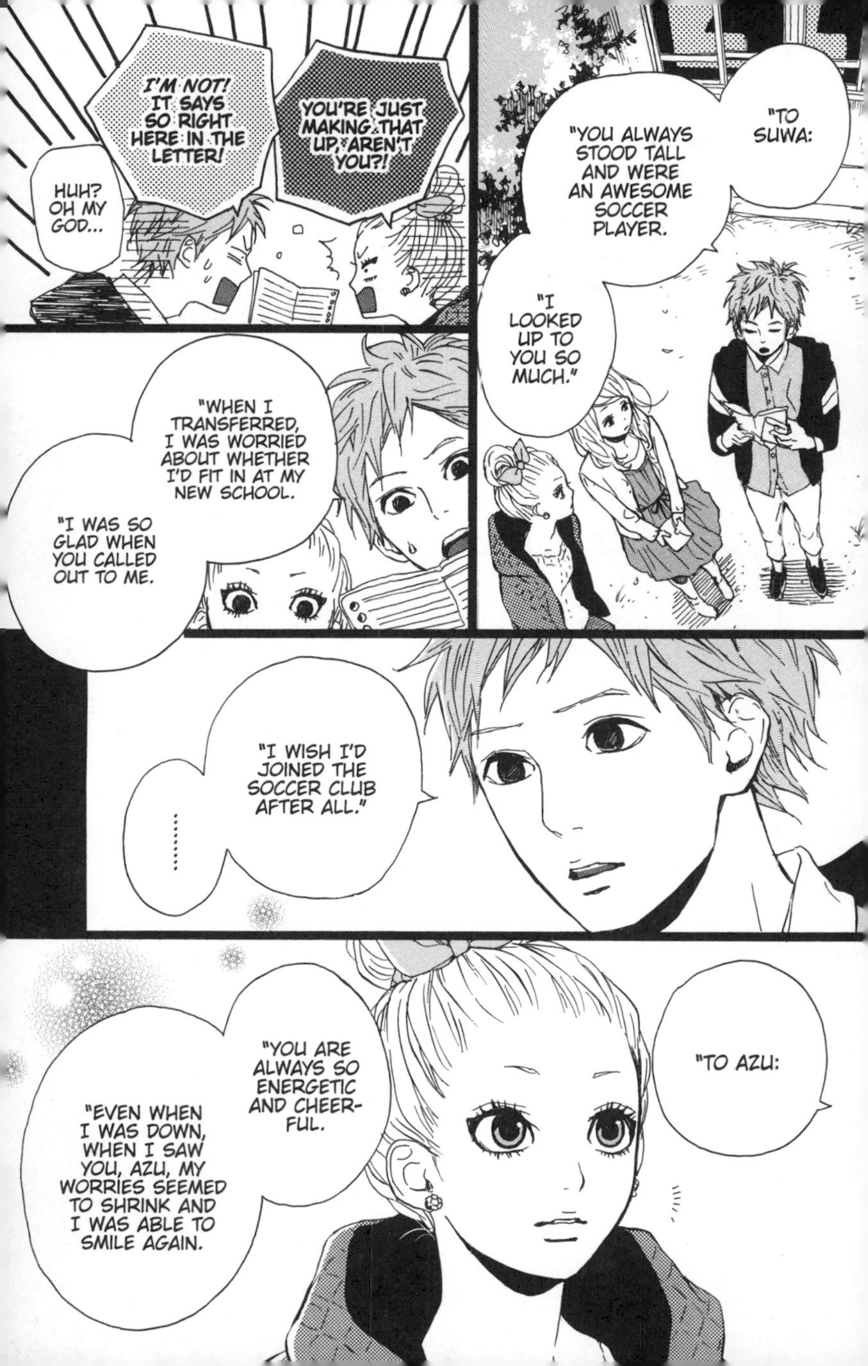
"TO SUWA:
"YOU ALWAYS STOOD TALL AND WERE AN AWESOME SOCCER PLAYER.
"I LOOKED UP TO YOU SO MUCH."
YOU'RE JUST MAKING THAT UP, AREN'T YOU?!
I'M NOT! IT SAYS SO RIGHT HERE IN THE LETTER!
HUH? OH MY GOD...
"WHEN I TRANSFERRED, I WAS WORRIED ABOUT WHETHER I'D FIT IN AT MY NEW SCHOOL.
"I WAS SO GLAD WHEN YOU CALLED OUT TO ME.
"I WISH I'D JOINED THE SOCCER CLUB AFTER ALL."
......
"TO AZU:
"YOU ARE ALWAYS SO ENERGETIC AND CHEER-FUL.
"EVEN WHEN I WAS DOWN, WHEN I SAW YOU, AZU, MY WORRIES SEEMED TO SHRINK AND I WAS ABLE TO SMILE AGAIN.

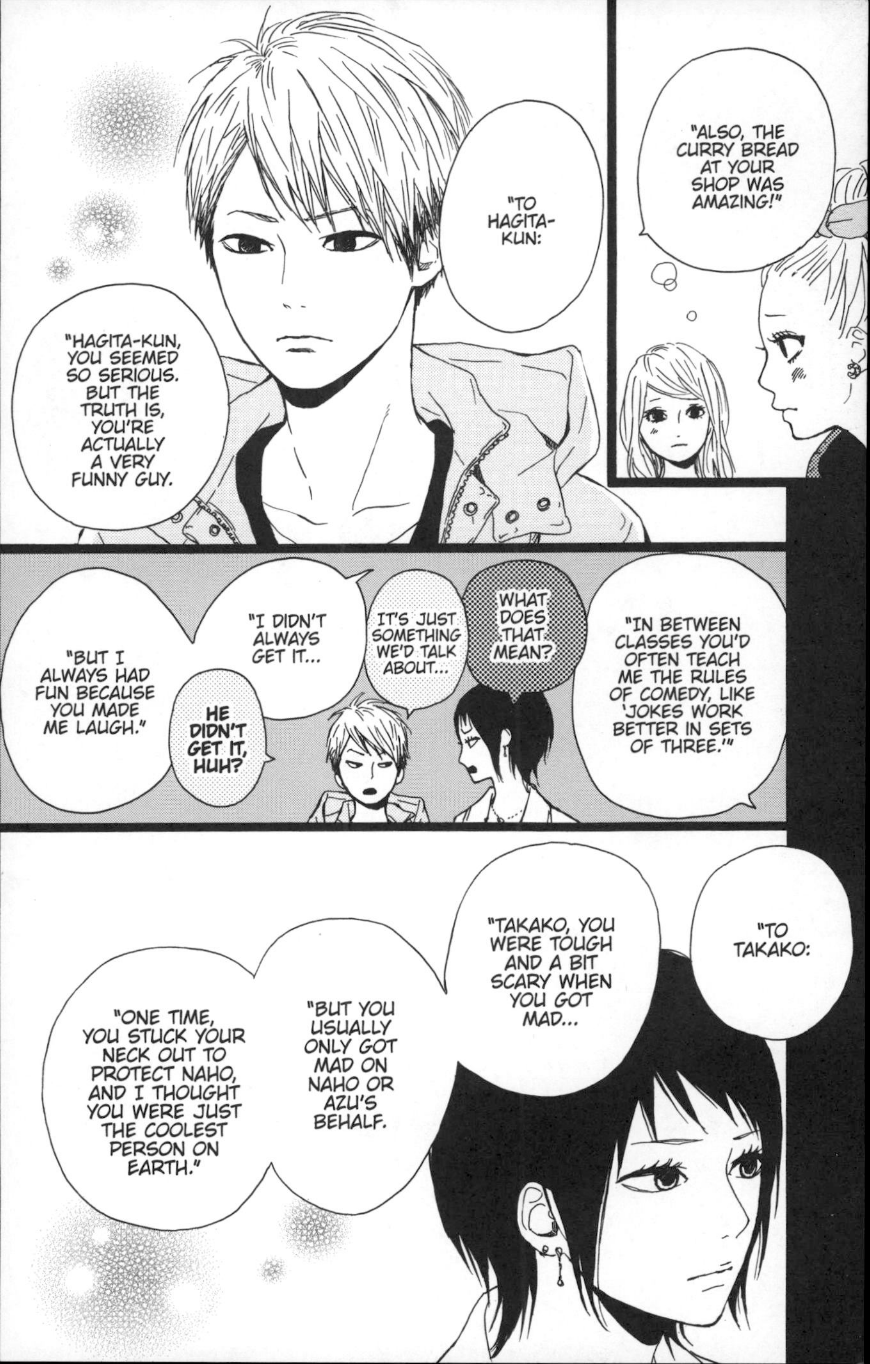
"ALSO, THE CURRY BREAD AT YOUR SHOP WAS AMAZING!"
"TO HAGITA-KUN:
"HAGITA-KUN, YOU SEEMED SO SERIOUS. BUT THE TRUTH IS, YOU'RE ACTUALLY A VERY FUNNY GUY.
"IN BETWEEN CLASSES YOU'D OFTEN TEACH ME THE RULES OF COMEDY, LIKE 'JOKES WORK BETTER IN SETS OF THREE.'"
WHAT DOES THAT MEAN?
IT'S JUST SOMETHING WE'D TALK ABOUT...
"I DIDN'T ALWAYS GET IT...
HE DIDN'T GET IT, HUH?
"BUT I ALWAYS HAD FUN BECAUSE YOU MADE ME LAUGH."
"TO TAKAKO:
"TAKAKO, YOU WERE TOUGH AND A BIT SCARY WHEN YOU GOT MAD...
"BUT YOU USUALLY ONLY GOT MAD ON NAHO OR AZU'S BEHALF.
"ONE TIME, YOU STUCK YOUR NECK OUT TO PROTECT NAHO, AND I THOUGHT YOU WERE JUST THE COOLEST PERSON ON EARTH."

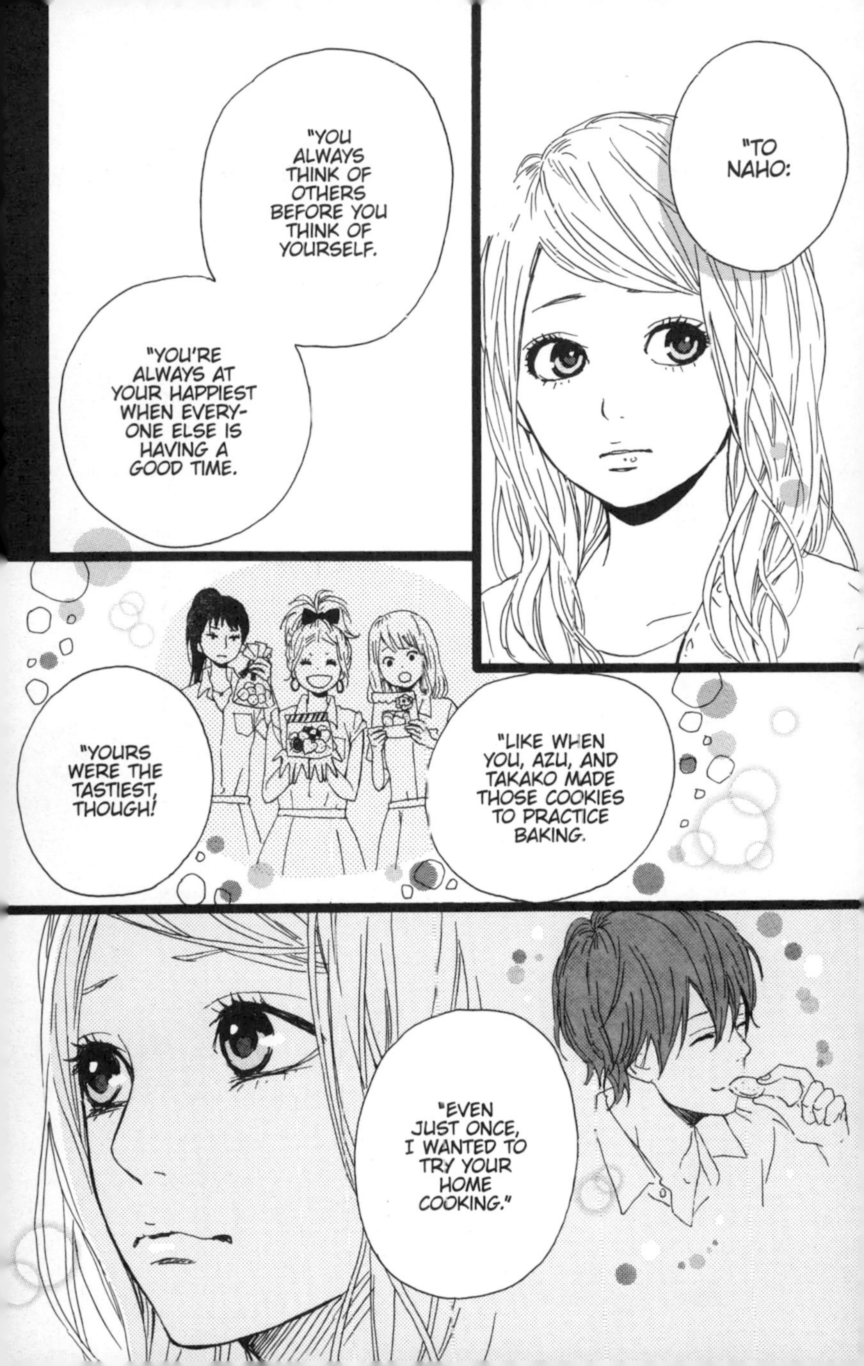
"TO NAHO:
"YOU ALWAYS THINK OF OTHERS BEFORE YOU THINK OF YOURSELF.
"YOU'RE ALWAYS AT YOUR HAPPIEST WHEN EVERY-ONE ELSE IS HAVING A GOOD TIME.
"LIKE WHEN YOU, AZU, AND TAKAKO MADE THOSE COOKIES TO PRACTICE BAKING.
"YOURS WERE THE TASTIEST, THOUGH!
"EVEN JUST ONCE, I WANTED TO TRY YOUR HOME COOKING."

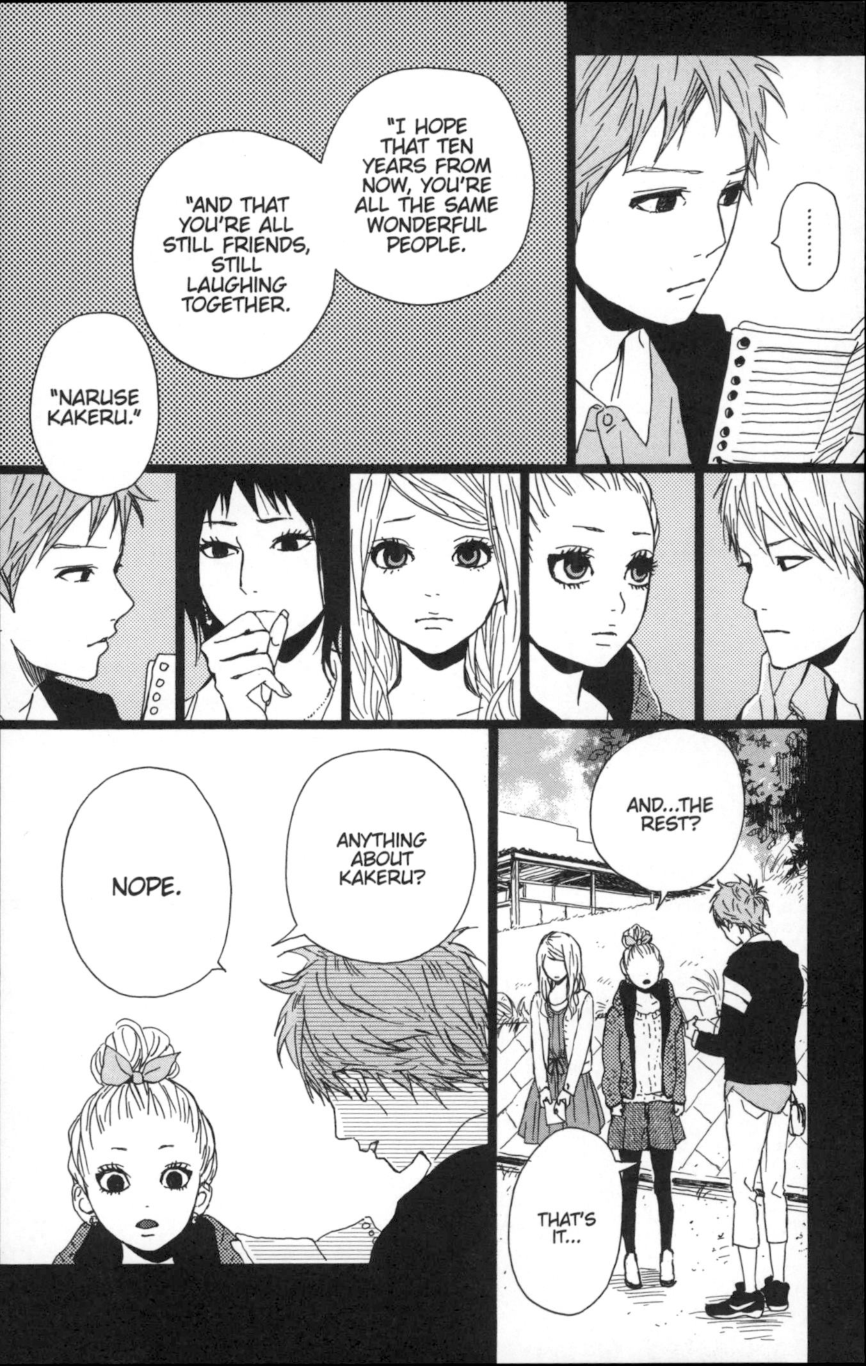
……
"I HOPE THAT TEN YEARS FROM NOW, YOU'RE ALL THE SAME WONDERFUL PEOPLE.
"AND THAT YOU'RE ALL STILL FRIENDS, STILL LAUGHING TOGETHER.
"NARUSE KAKERU."
AND...THE REST?
THAT'S IT...
ANYTHING ABOUT KAKERU?
NOPE.

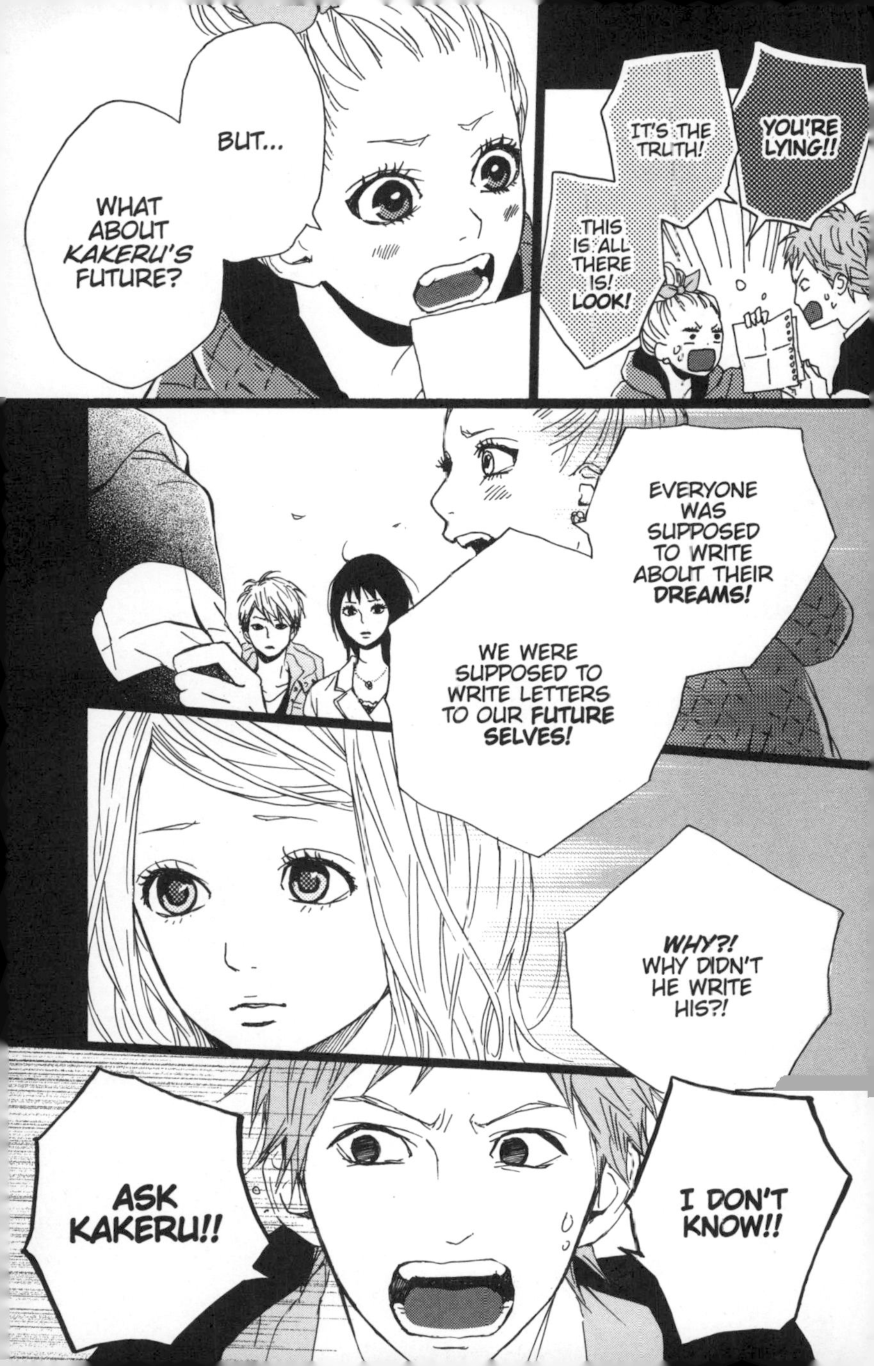
YOU'RE LYING!!
IT'S THE TRUTH!
THIS IS ALL THERE IS! LOOK!
BUT...
WHAT ABOUT KAKERU'S FUTURE?
EVERYONE WAS SUPPOSED TO WRITE ABOUT THEIR DREAMS!
WE WERE SUPPOSED TO WRITE LETTERS TO OUR FUTURE SELVES!
WHY?! WHY DIDN'T HE WRITE HIS?!
I DON'T KNOW!!
ASK KAKERU!!

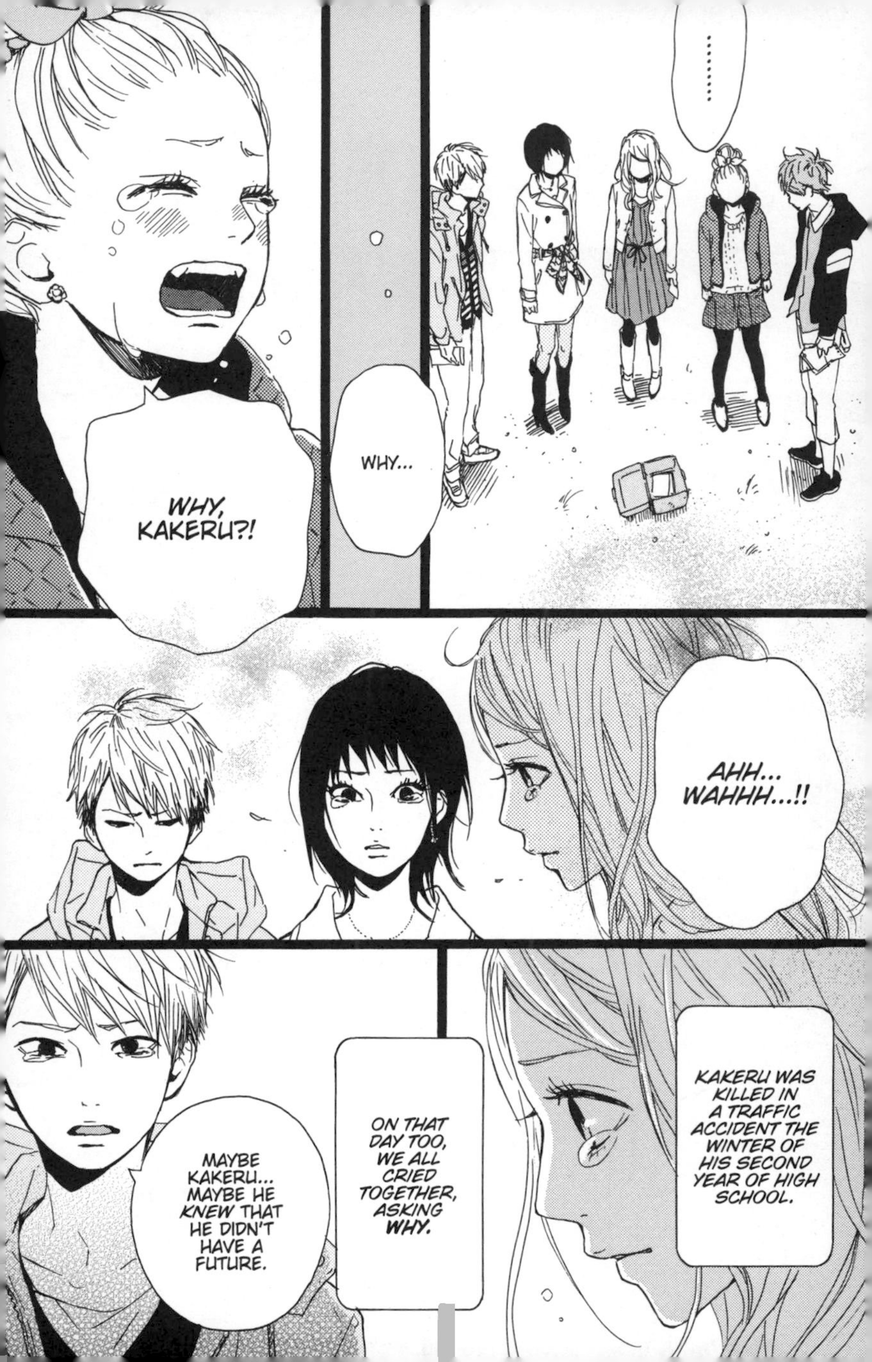
......
WHY...
WHY, KAKERU?!
AHH... WAHHH...!!
KAKERU WAS KILLED IN A TRAFFIC ACCIDENT THE WINTER OF HIS SECOND YEAR OF HIGH SCHOOL.
ON THAT DAY TOO, WE ALL CRIED TOGETHER, ASKING WHY.
MAYBE KAKERU... MAYBE HE KNEW THAT HE DIDN'T HAVE A FUTURE.

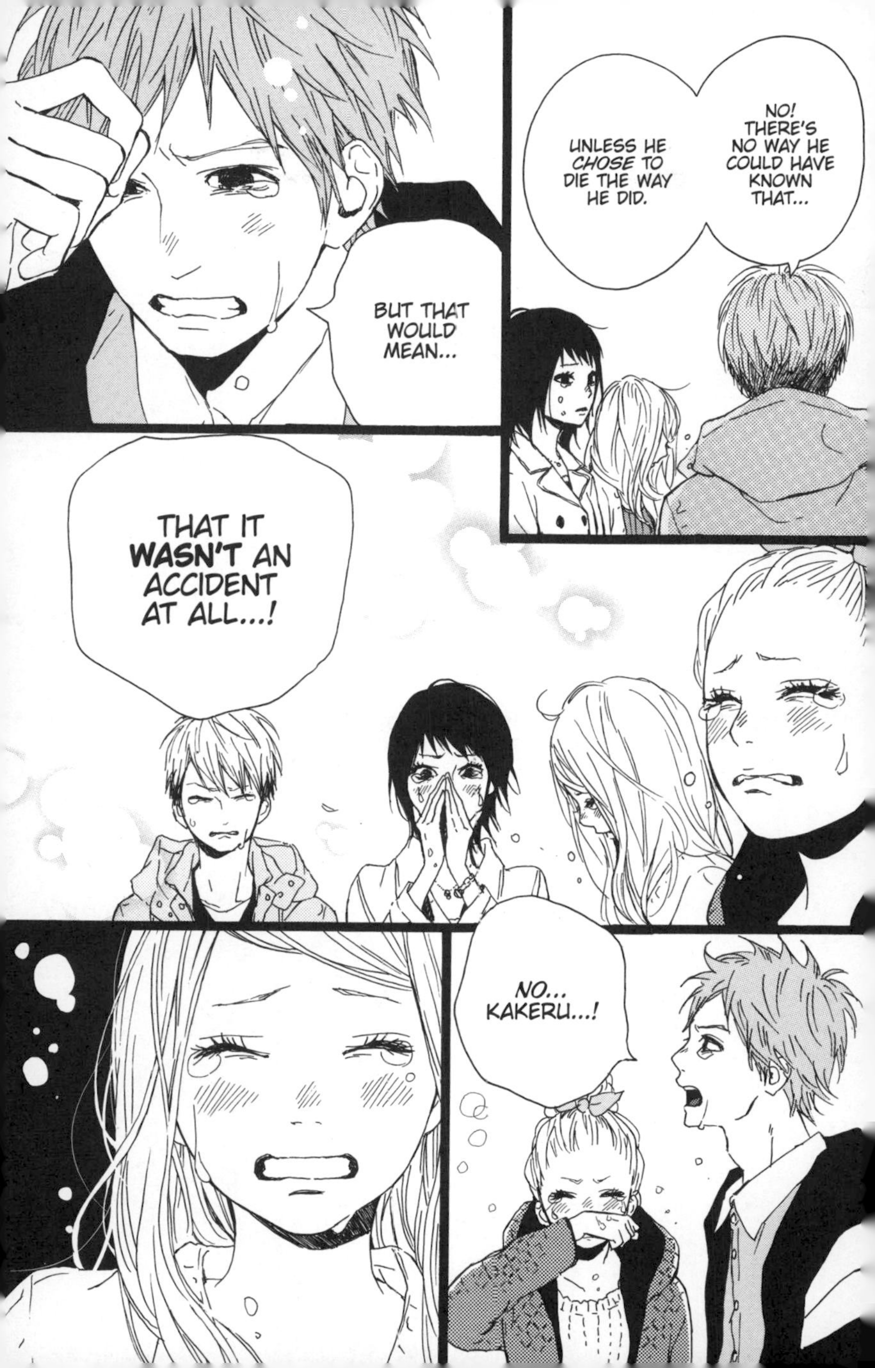
NO! THERE'S NO WAY HE COULD HAVE KNOWN THAT...
UNLESS HE *CHOSE* TO DIE THE WAY HE DID.
BUT THAT WOULD MEAN...
THAT IT **WASN'T** AN ACCIDENT AT ALL...!
NO... KAKERU...!

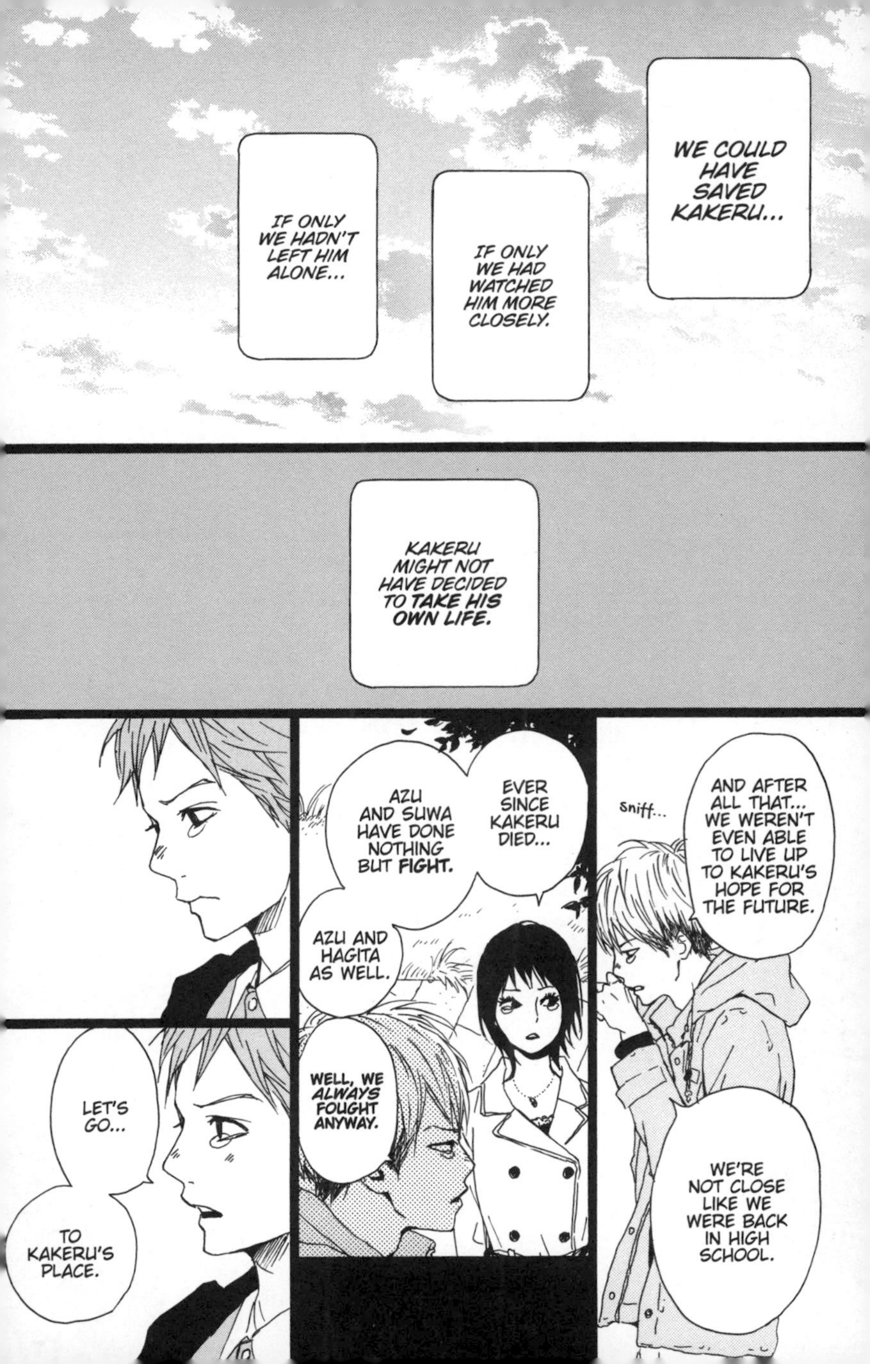
WE COULD HAVE SAVED KAKERU...
IF ONLY WE HAD WATCHED HIM MORE CLOSELY.
IF ONLY WE HADN'T LEFT HIM ALONE...
KAKERU MIGHT NOT HAVE DECIDED TO TAKE HIS OWN LIFE.
AND AFTER ALL THAT... WE WEREN'T EVEN ABLE TO LIVE UP TO KAKERU'S HOPE FOR THE FUTURE.
Sniff...
WE'RE NOT CLOSE LIKE WE WERE BACK IN HIGH SCHOOL.
EVER SINCE KAKERU DIED...
AZU AND SUWA HAVE DONE NOTHING BUT FIGHT.
AZU AND HAGITA AS WELL.
WELL, WE ALWAYS FOUGHT ANYWAY.
LET'S GO...
TO KAKERU'S PLACE.

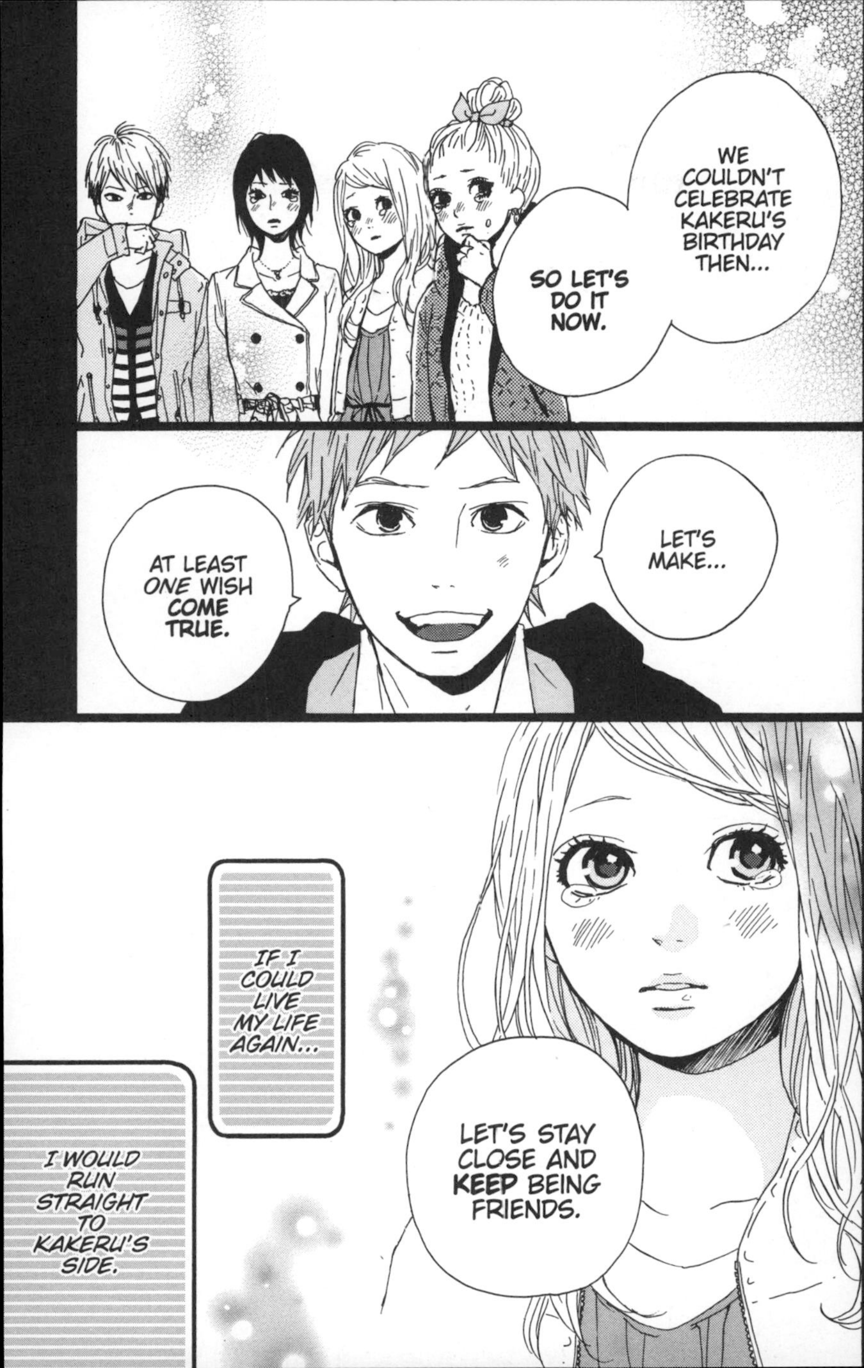
WE COULDN'T CELEBRATE KAKERU'S BIRTHDAY THEN...
SO LET'S DO IT NOW.
LET'S MAKE...
AT LEAST *ONE* WISH COME TRUE.
LET'S STAY CLOSE AND **KEEP** BEING FRIENDS.
IF I COULD LIVE MY LIFE AGAIN...
I WOULD RUN STRAIGHT TO KAKERU'S SIDE.

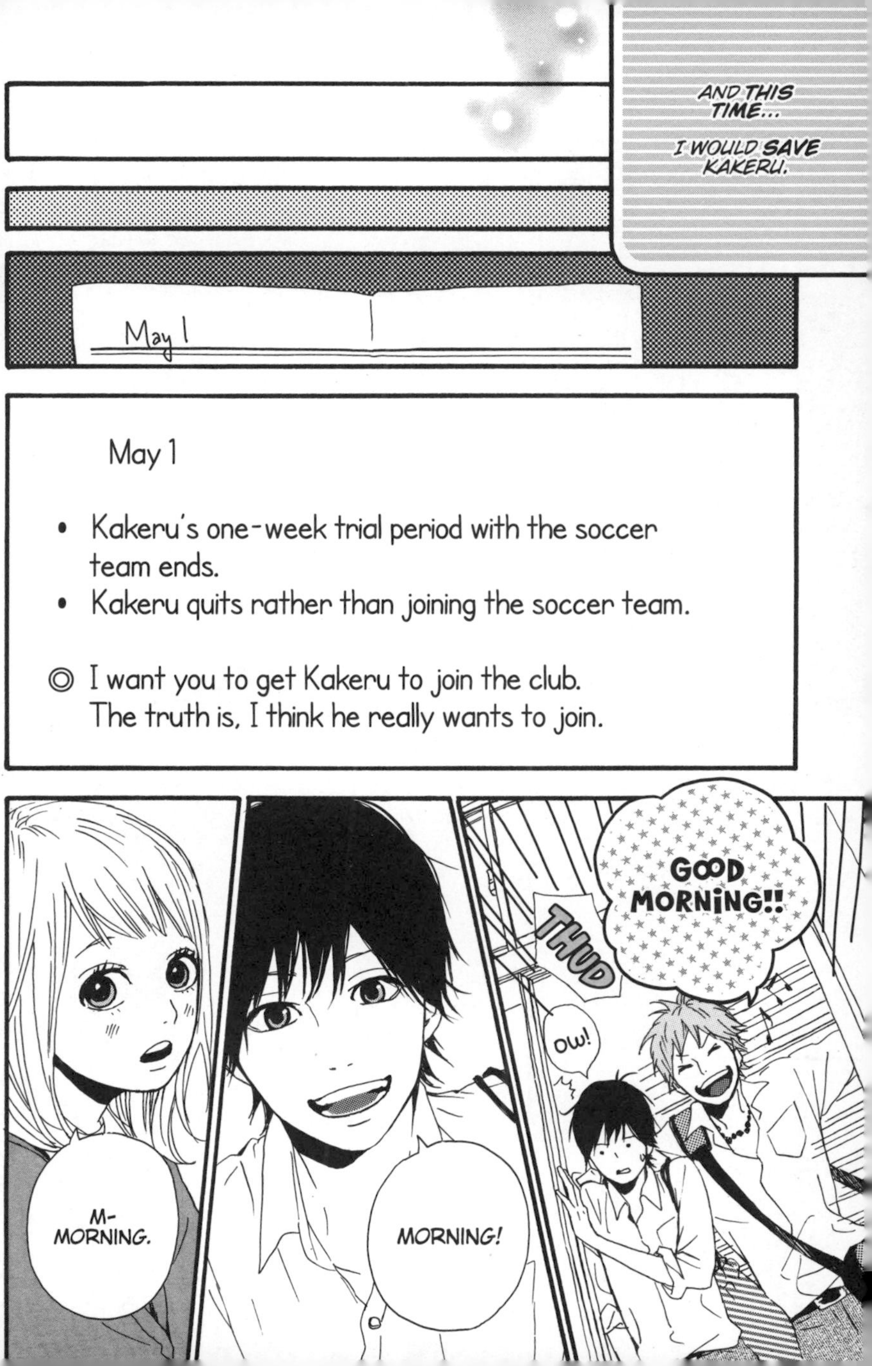
AND THIS TIME...
I WOULD SAVE KAKERU.
May 1
May 1
• Kakeru's one-week trial period with the soccer team ends.
• Kakeru quits rather than joining the soccer team.
◎ I want you to get Kakeru to join the club. The truth is, I think he really wants to join.
GOOD MORNING!!
THUD
OW!
MORNING!
M-MORNING.

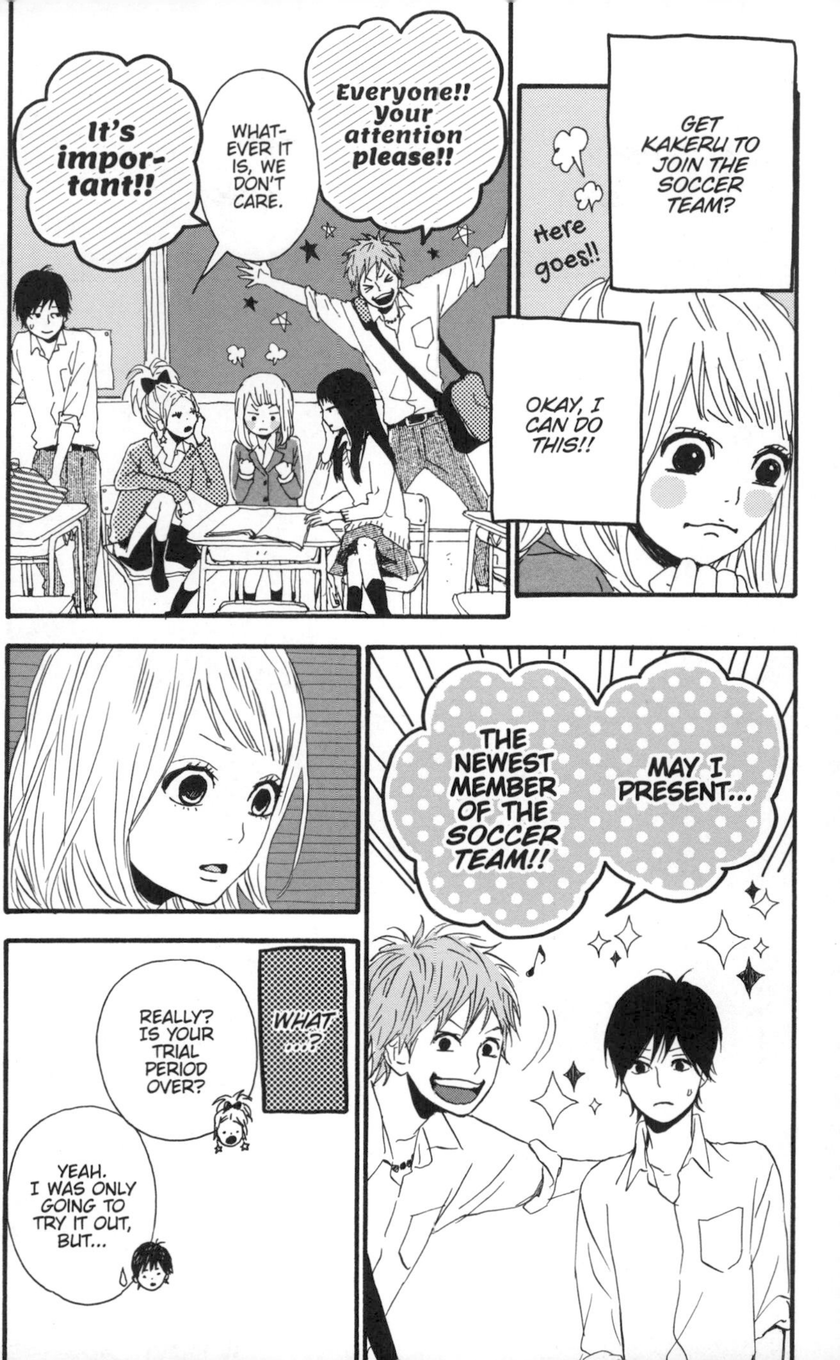
GET KAKERU TO JOIN THE SOCCER TEAM?
Here goes!!
OKAY, I CAN DO THIS!!
Everyone!! Your attention please!!
WHAT-EVER IT IS, WE DON'T CARE.
It's impor-tant!!
MAY I PRESENT...
THE NEWEST MEMBER OF THE SOCCER TEAM!!
WHAT...?
REALLY? IS YOUR TRIAL PERIOD OVER?
YEAH. I WAS ONLY GOING TO TRY IT OUT, BUT...

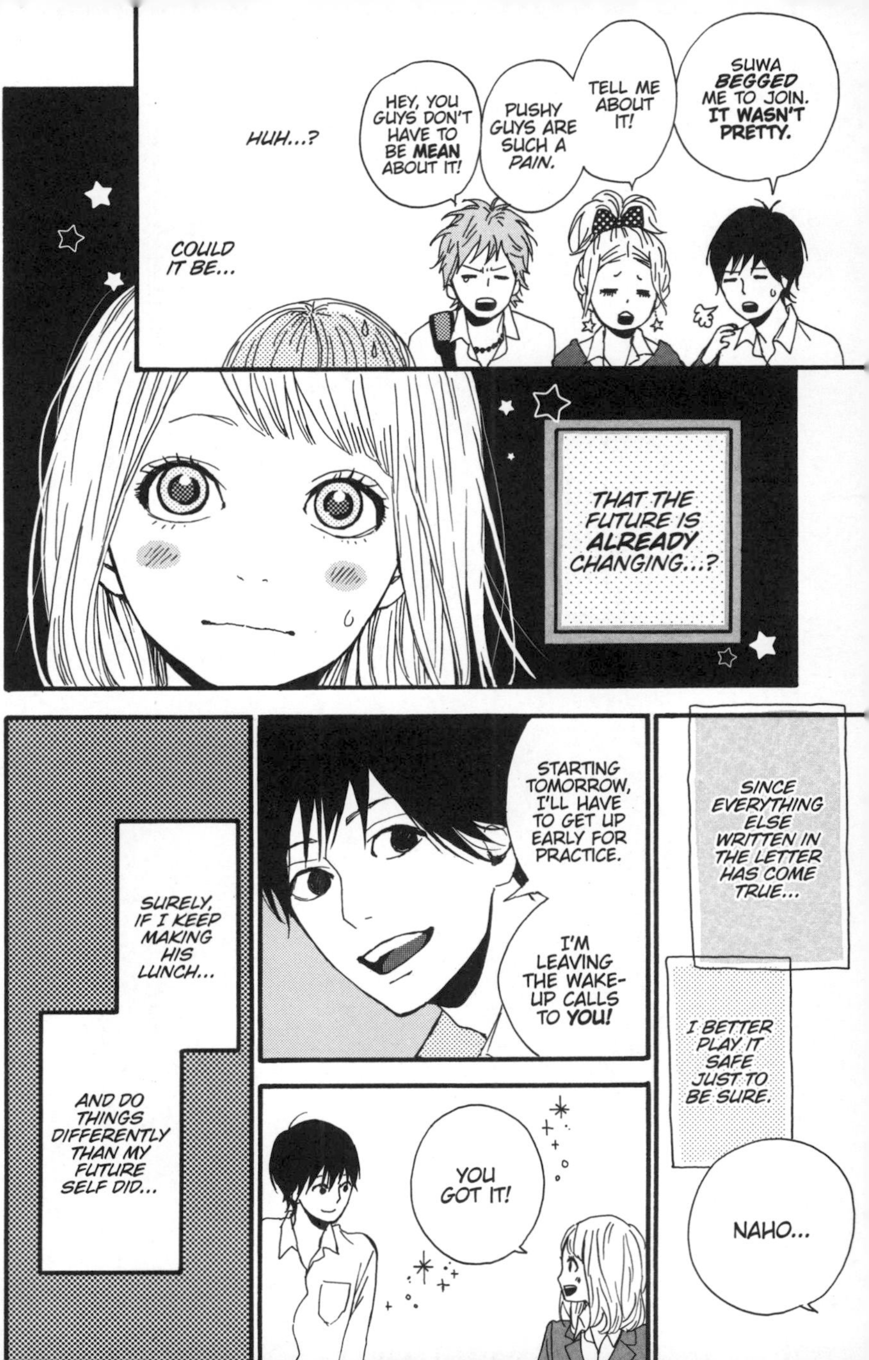
SUWA BEGGED ME TO JOIN. IT WASN'T PRETTY.
TELL ME ABOUT IT!
PUSHY GUYS ARE SUCH A PAIN.
HEY, YOU GUYS DON'T HAVE TO BE MEAN ABOUT IT!
HUH...?
COULD IT BE...
THAT THE FUTURE IS ALREADY CHANGING...?
SINCE EVERYTHING ELSE WRITTEN IN THE LETTER HAS COME TRUE...
I BETTER PLAY IT SAFE JUST TO BE SURE.
NAHO...
STARTING TOMORROW, I'LL HAVE TO GET UP EARLY FOR PRACTICE.
I'M LEAVING THE WAKE-UP CALLS TO YOU!
YOU GOT IT!
SURELY, IF I KEEP MAKING HIS LUNCH...
AND DO THINGS DIFFERENTLY THAN MY FUTURE SELF DID...

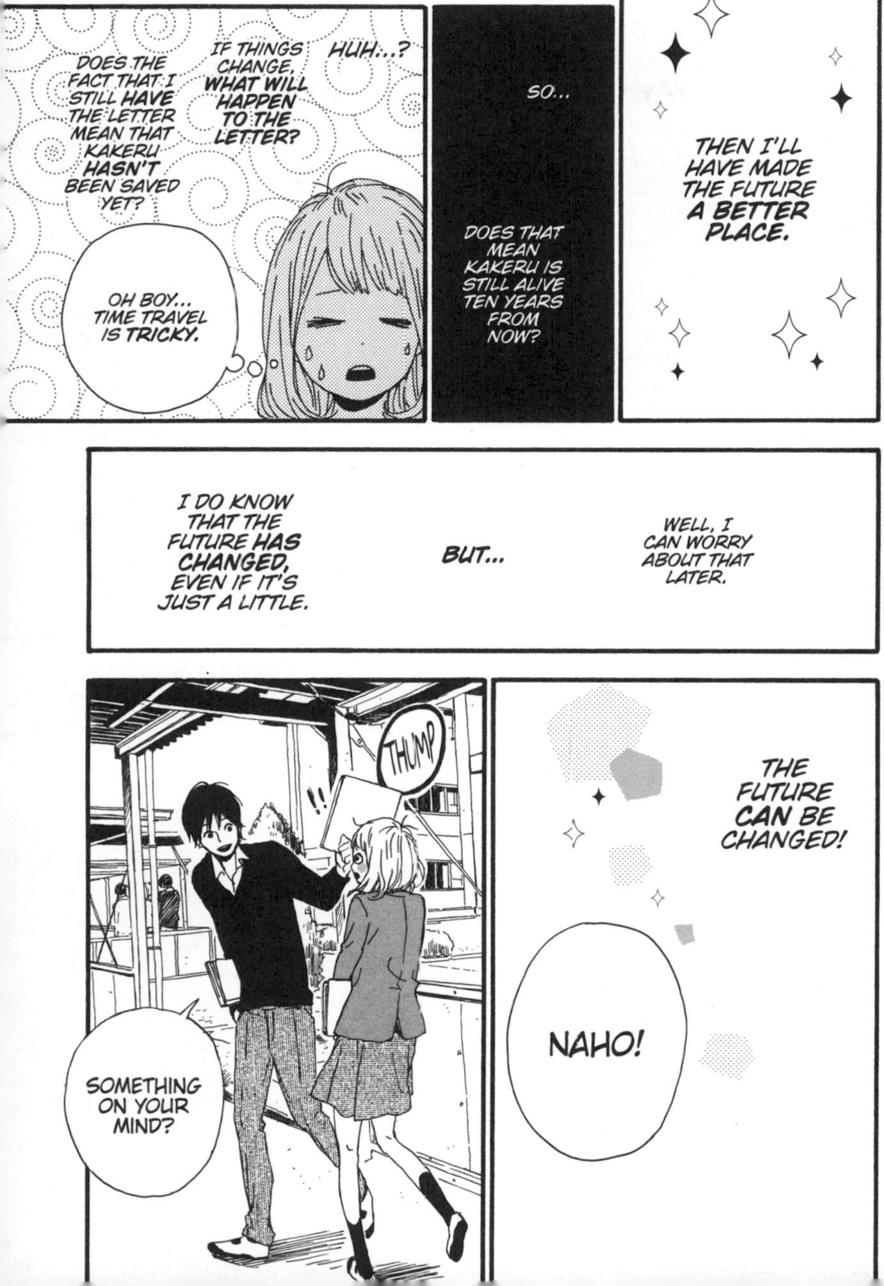
THEN I'LL HAVE MADE THE FUTURE A BETTER PLACE.
SO...
DOES THAT MEAN KAKERU IS STILL ALIVE TEN YEARS FROM NOW?
HUH...?
IF THINGS CHANGE, WHAT WILL HAPPEN TO THE LETTER?
DOES THE FACT THAT I STILL HAVE THE LETTER MEAN THAT KAKERU HASN'T BEEN SAVED YET?
OH BOY... TIME TRAVEL IS TRICKY.
WELL, I CAN WORRY ABOUT THAT LATER.
BUT...
I DO KNOW THAT THE FUTURE HAS CHANGED, EVEN IF IT'S JUST A LITTLE.
THE FUTURE CAN BE CHANGED!
NAHO!
THUMP
!!
SOMETHING ON YOUR MIND?

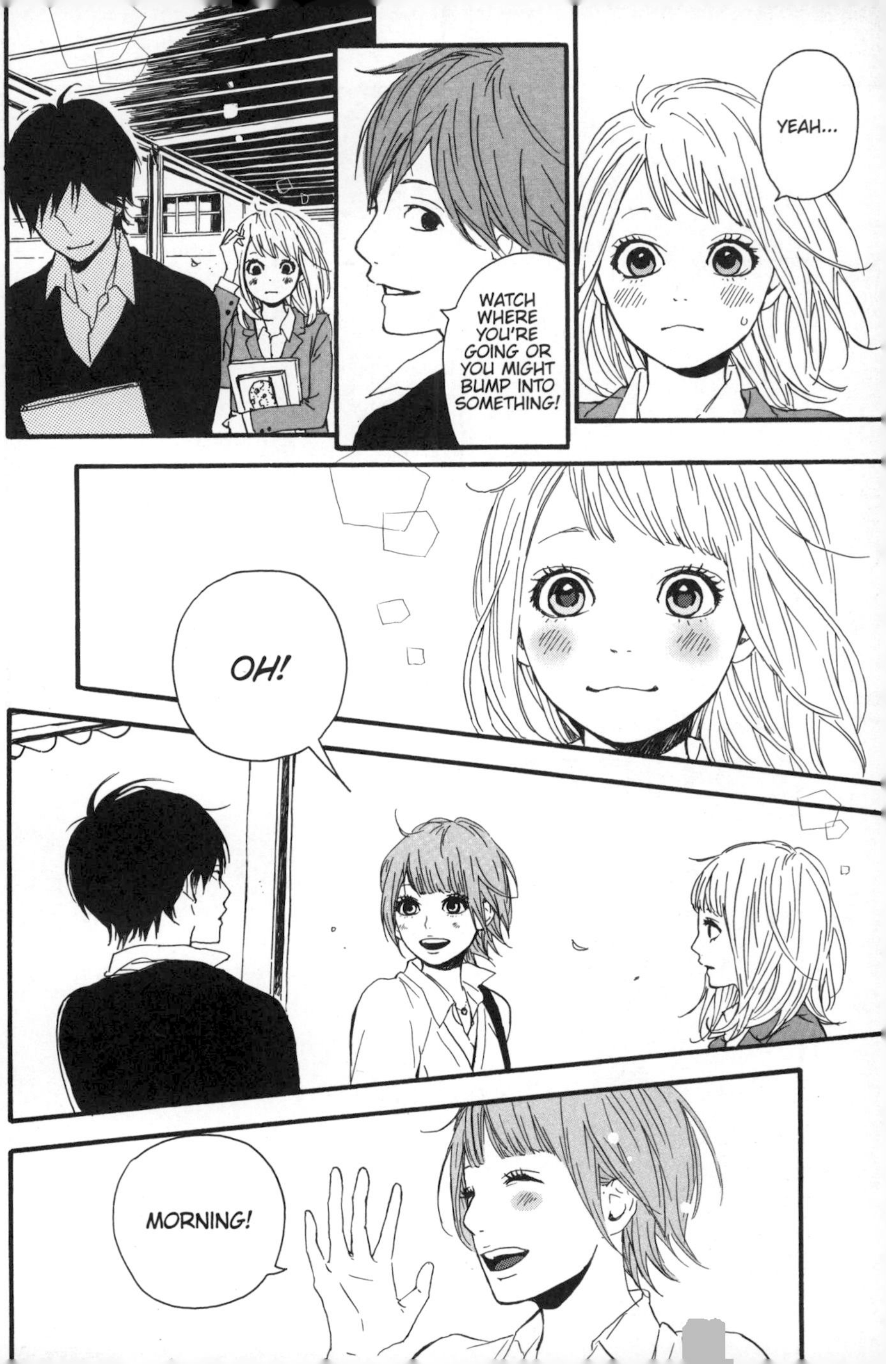
YEAH...
WATCH WHERE YOU'RE GOING OR YOU MIGHT BUMP INTO SOMETHING!
OH!
MORNING!

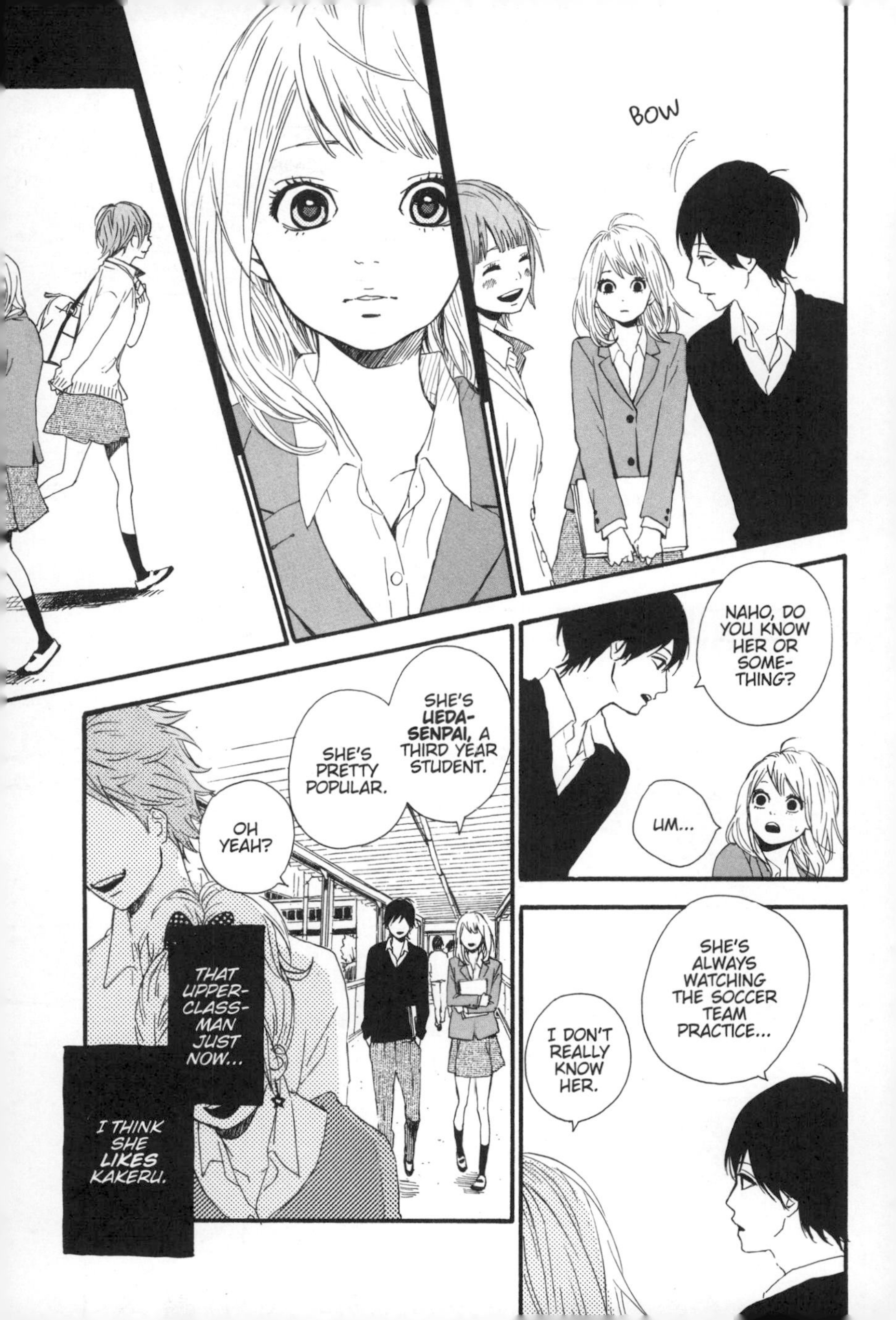
BOW
NAHO, DO YOU KNOW HER OR SOME-THING?
UM...
SHE'S ALWAYS WATCHING THE SOCCER TEAM PRACTICE...
I DON'T REALLY KNOW HER.
SHE'S UEDA-SENPAI, A THIRD YEAR STUDENT.
SHE'S PRETTY POPULAR.
OH YEAH?
THAT UPPER-CLASS-MAN JUST NOW...
I THINK SHE LIKES KAKERU.

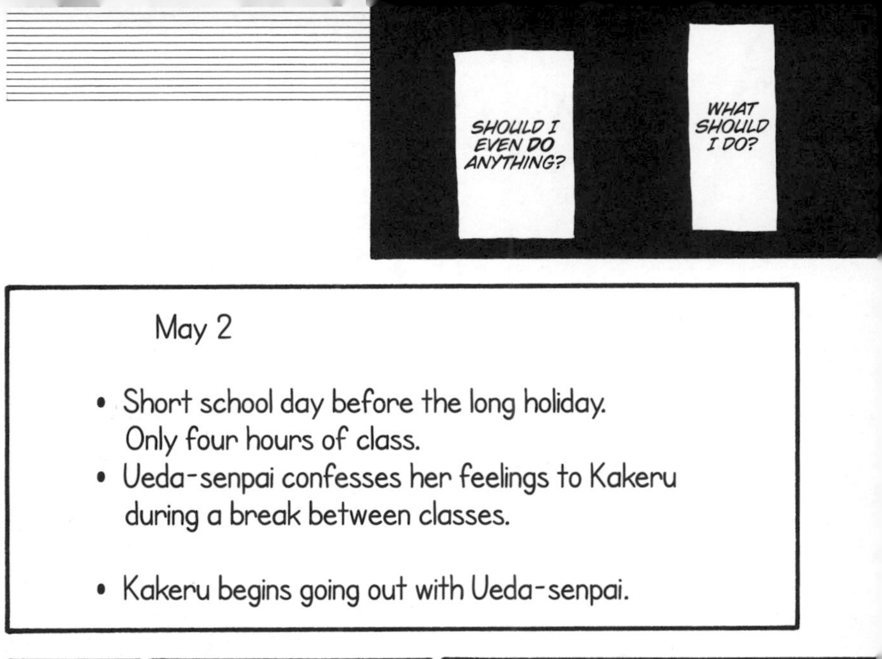
WHAT SHOULD I DO?
SHOULD I EVEN DO ANYTHING?

May 2

- Short school day before the long holiday.
  Only four hours of class.
- Ueda-senpai confesses her feelings to Kakeru during a break between classes.

- Kakeru begins going out with Ueda-senpai.

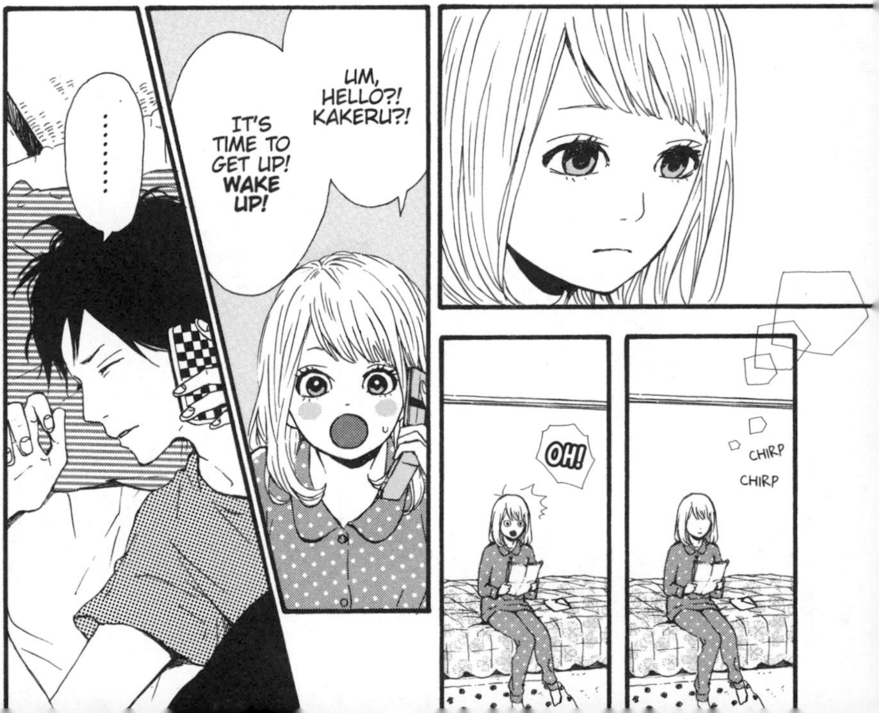
CHIRP
CHIRP
OH!
UM, HELLO?! KAKERU?!
IT'S TIME TO GET UP! WAKE UP!
....

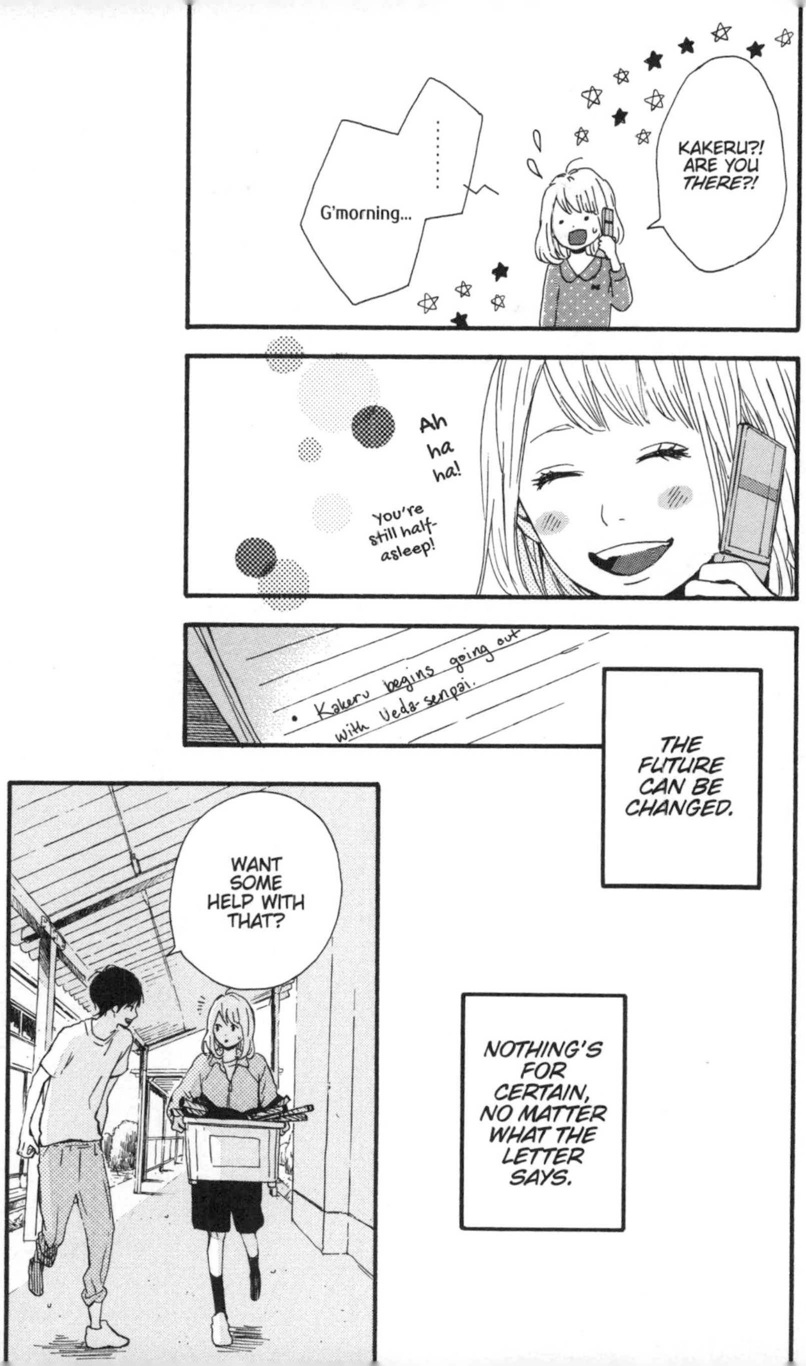
KAKERU?! ARE YOU THERE?!
......
G'morning...
Ah ha ha!
You're still half-asleep!
• Kakeru begins going out with Ueda-senpai.
THE FUTURE CAN BE CHANGED.
NOTHING'S FOR CERTAIN, NO MATTER WHAT THE LETTER SAYS.
WANT SOME HELP WITH THAT?

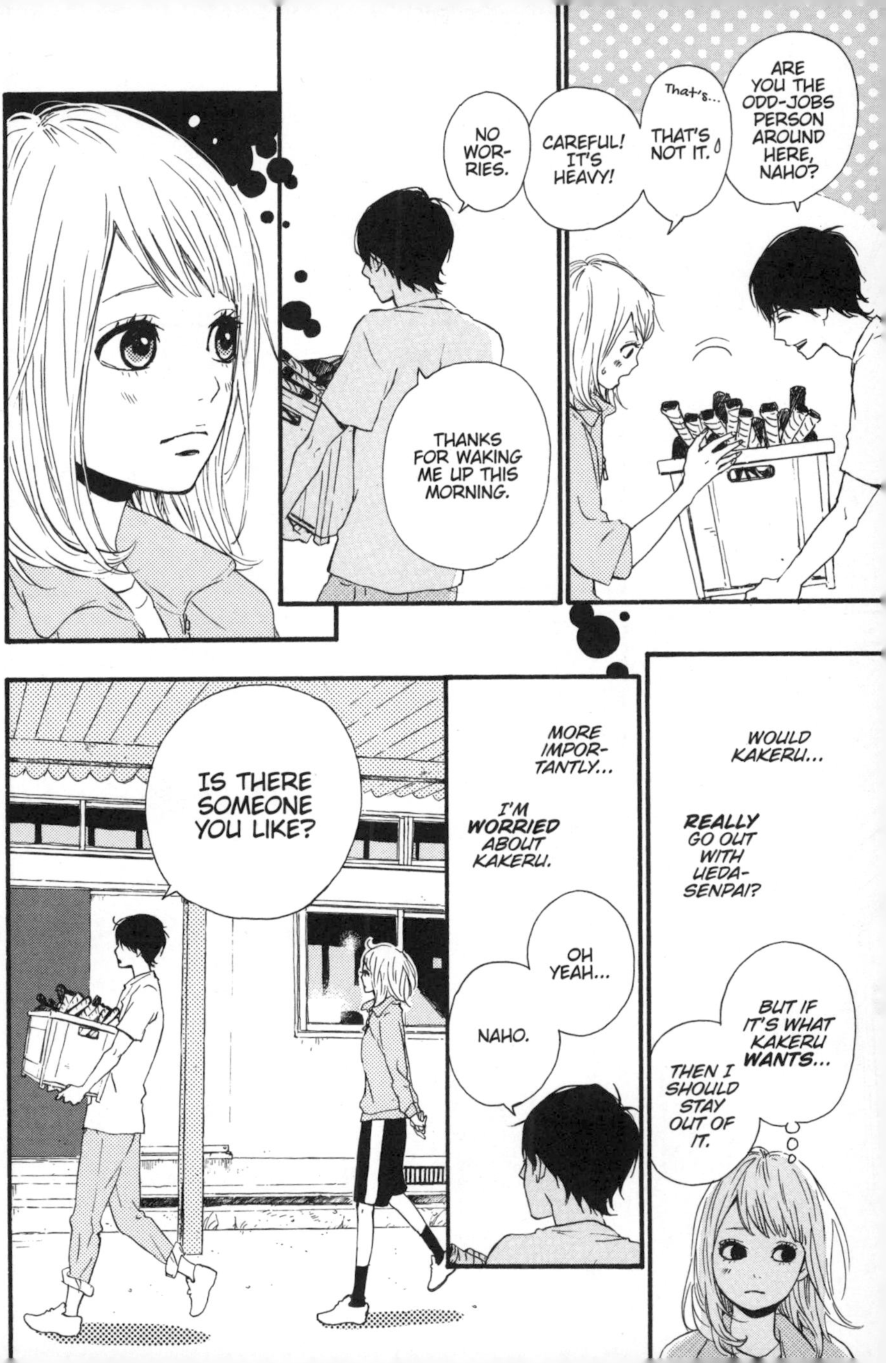

ARE YOU THE ODD-JOBS PERSON AROUND HERE, NAHO?
That's...
THAT'S NOT IT.
CAREFUL! IT'S HEAVY!
NO WOR-RIES.
THANKS FOR WAKING ME UP THIS MORNING.
WOULD KAKERU...
REALLY GO OUT WITH UEDA-SENPAI?
BUT IF IT'S WHAT KAKERU WANTS...
THEN I SHOULD STAY OUT OF IT.
MORE IMPOR-TANTLY...
I'M WORRIED ABOUT KAKERU.
OH YEAH...
NAHO.
IS THERE SOMEONE YOU LIKE?

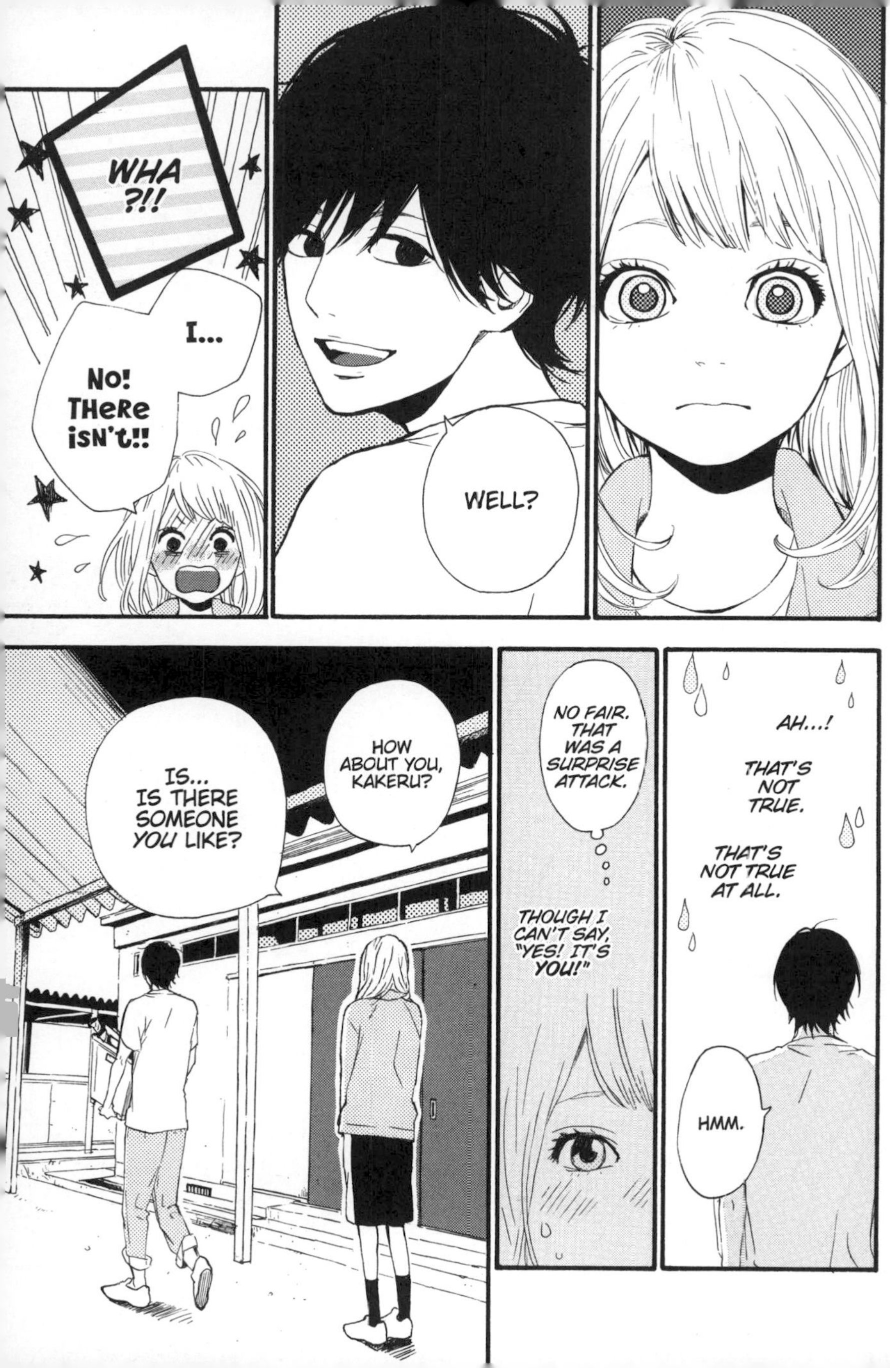
WELL?
WHA ?!!
I...
No! THere isn't!!
AH...!
THAT'S NOT TRUE.
THAT'S NOT TRUE AT ALL.
HMM.
NO FAIR. THAT WAS A SURPRISE ATTACK.
THOUGH I CAN'T SAY, "YES! IT'S YOU!"
HOW ABOUT YOU, KAKERU?
IS... IS THERE SOMEONE YOU LIKE?

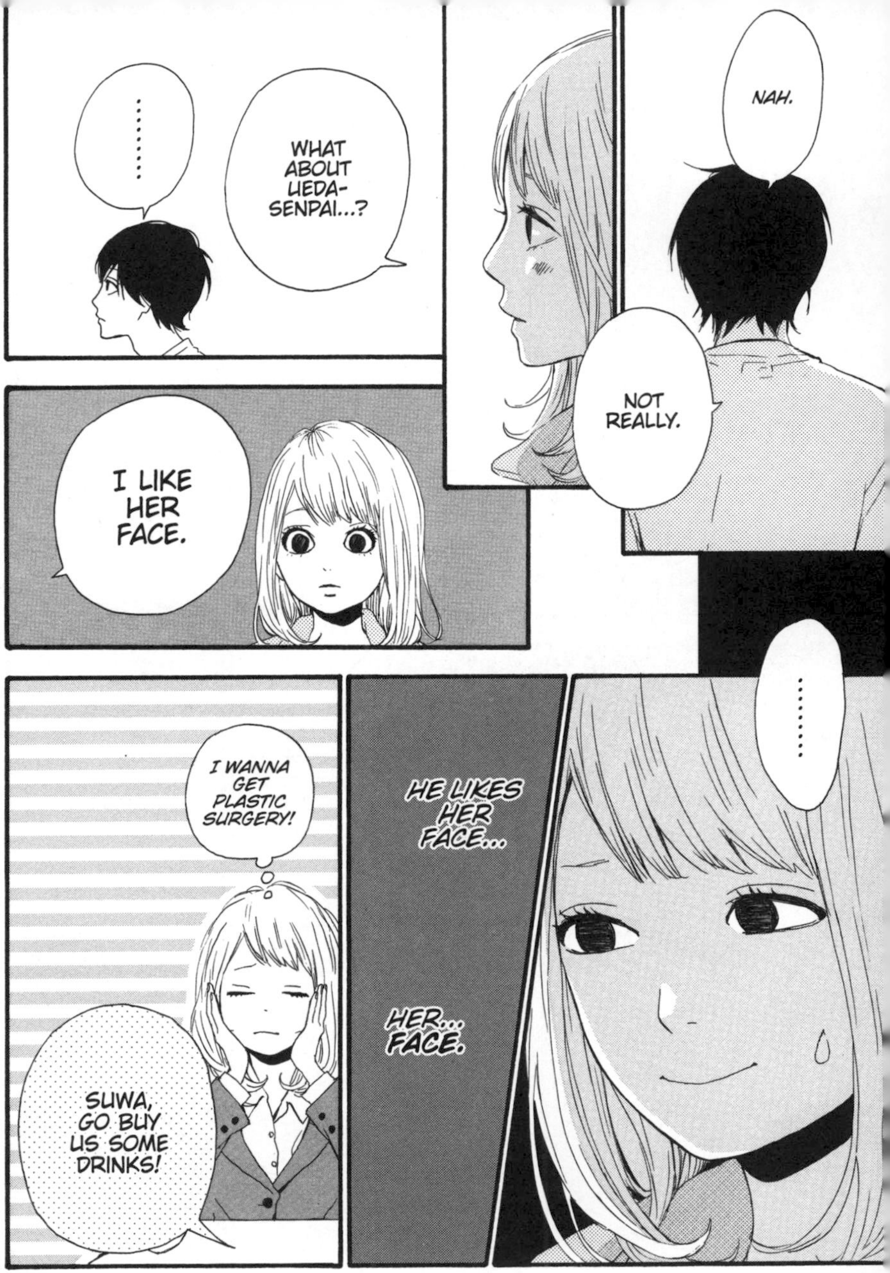
NAH.
NOT REALLY.
WHAT ABOUT UEDA-SENPAI...?
....
I LIKE HER FACE.
....
HE LIKES HER FACE...
HER... FACE.
I WANNA GET PLASTIC SURGERY!
SUWA, GO BUY US SOME DRINKS!

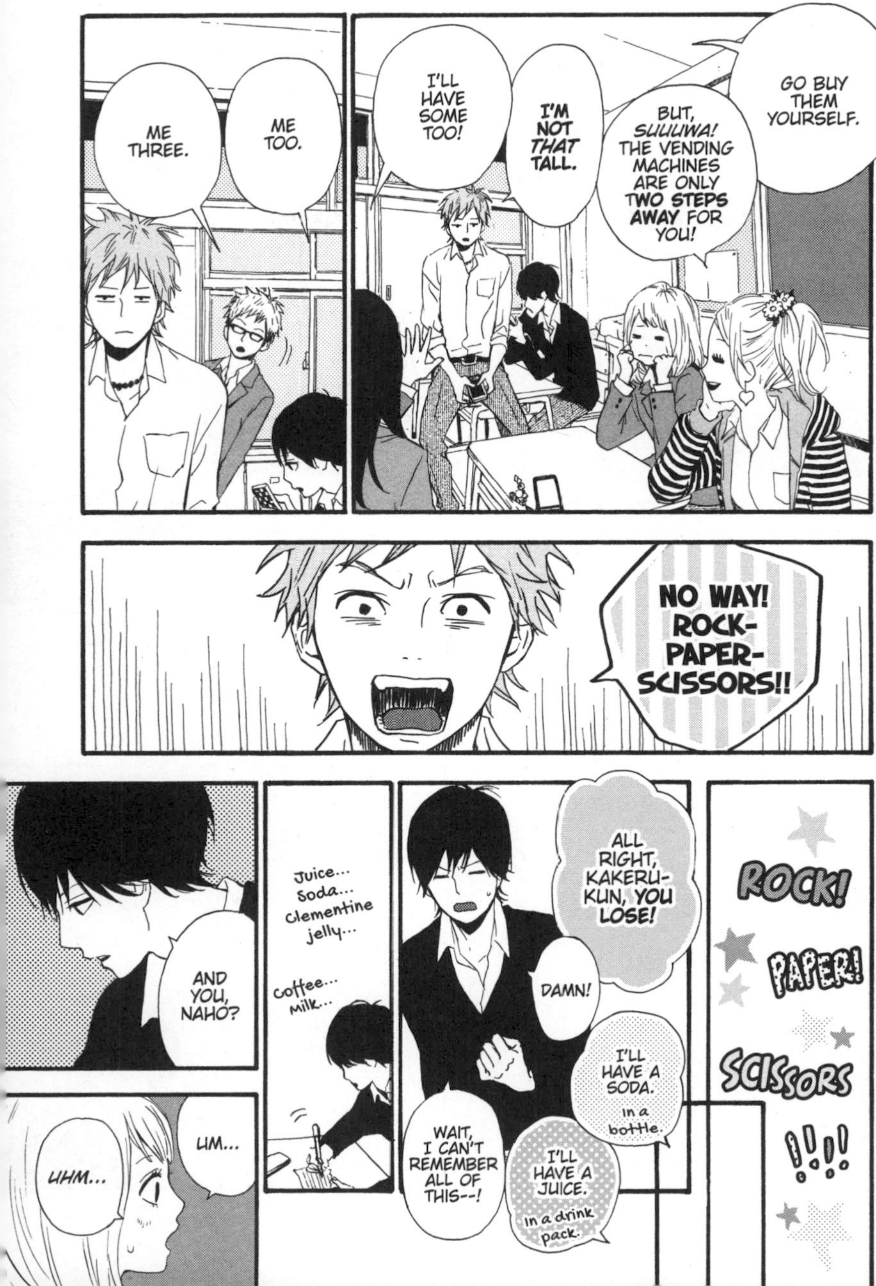
GO BUY THEM YOURSELF.
BUT, SUUUWA! THE VENDING MACHINES ARE ONLY TWO STEPS AWAY FOR YOU!
I'M NOT THAT TALL.
I'LL HAVE SOME TOO!
ME TOO.
ME THREE.
NO WAY! ROCK-PAPER-SCISSORS!!
ROCK!
PAPER!
SCISSORS
!!!!!
ALL RIGHT, KAKERU-KUN, YOU LOSE!
DAMN!
I'LL HAVE A SODA.
In a bottle.
I'LL HAVE A JUICE.
In a drink pack.
WAIT, I CAN'T REMEMBER ALL OF THIS--!
Juice... Soda... Clementine jelly...
coffee... milk...
AND YOU, NAHO?
UM...
UHM...

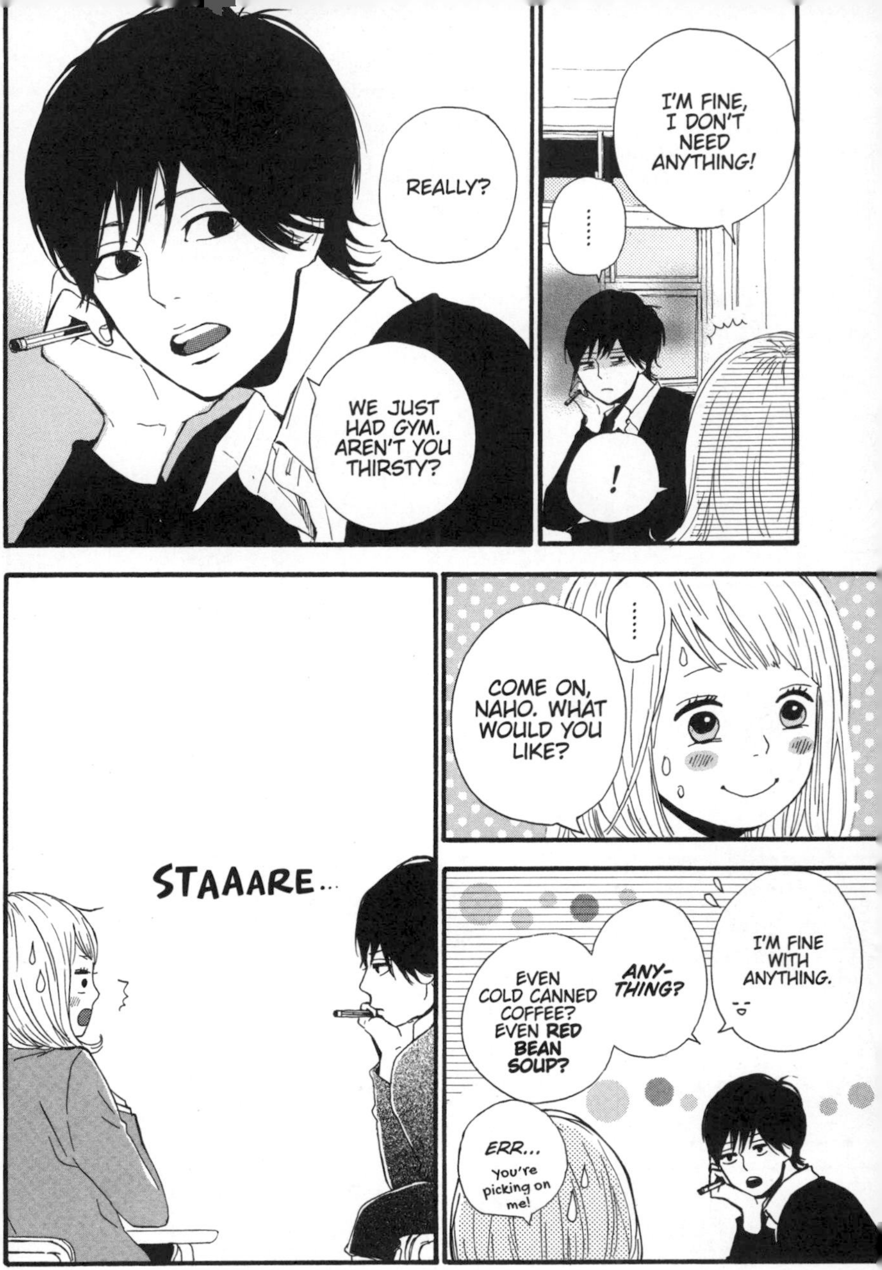
I'M FINE, I DON'T NEED ANYTHING!
......
!
REALLY?
WE JUST HAD GYM. AREN'T YOU THIRSTY?
......
COME ON, NAHO. WHAT WOULD YOU LIKE?
I'M FINE WITH ANYTHING.
ANY-THING?
EVEN COLD CANNED COFFEE? EVEN RED BEAN SOUP?
ERR... you're picking on me!
STAAARE...

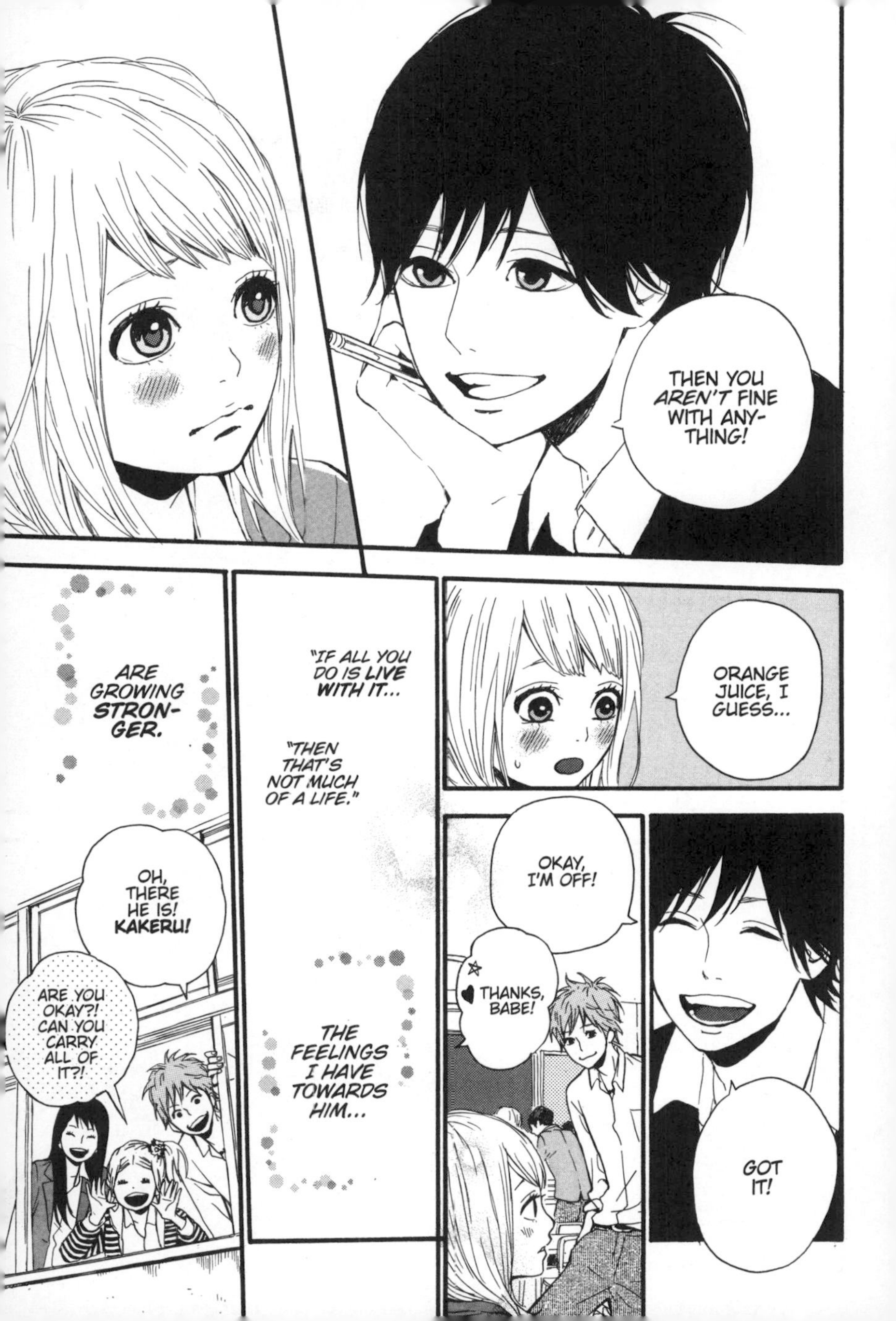
THEN YOU AREN'T FINE WITH ANYTHING!
ORANGE JUICE, I GUESS...
GOT IT!
OKAY, I'M OFF!
THANKS, BABE!
"IF ALL YOU DO IS LIVE WITH IT...
"THEN THAT'S NOT MUCH OF A LIFE."
THE FEELINGS I HAVE TOWARDS HIM...
ARE GROWING STRONGER.
OH, THERE HE IS! KAKERU!
ARE YOU OKAY?! CAN YOU CARRY ALL OF IT?!

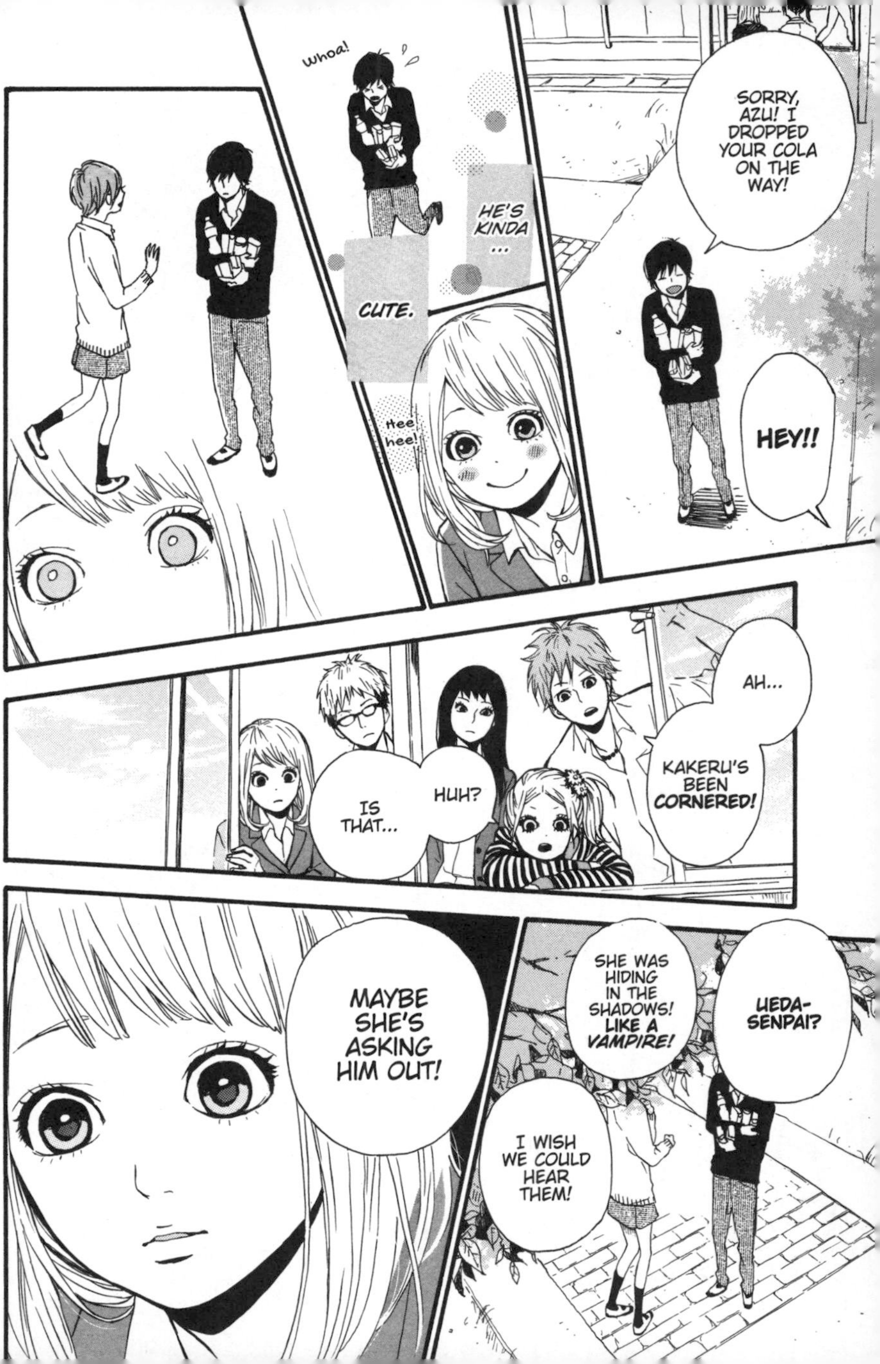
SORRY, AZU! I DROPPED YOUR COLA ON THE WAY!
HEY!!
Whoa!
HE'S KINDA...
CUTE.
Hee hee!
AH...
KAKERU'S BEEN CORNERED!
HUH?
IS THAT...
UEDA-SENPAI?
SHE WAS HIDING IN THE SHADOWS! LIKE A VAMPIRE!
I WISH WE COULD HEAR THEM!
MAYBE SHE'S ASKING HIM OUT!

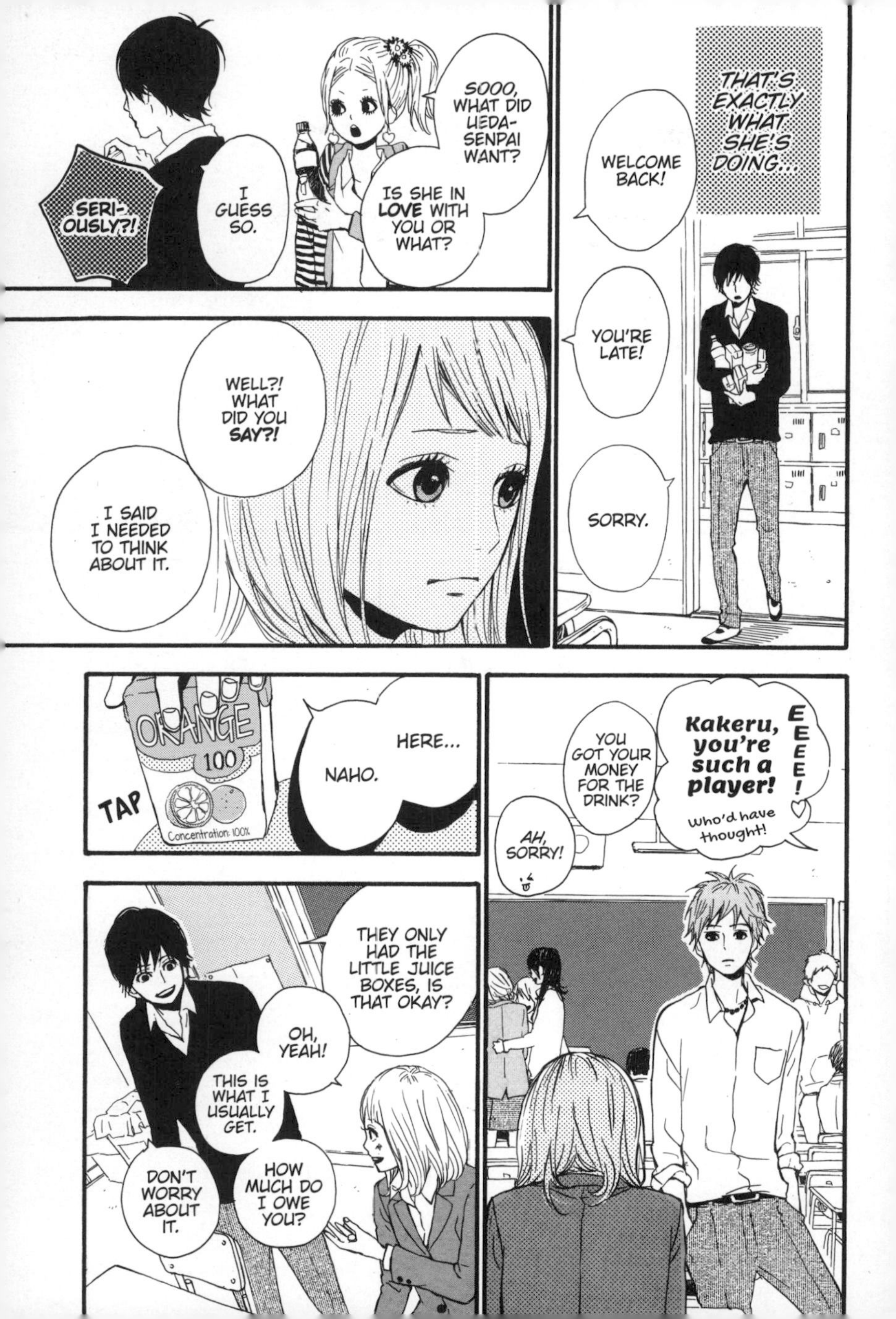
THAT'S EXACTLY WHAT SHE'S DOING...
WELCOME BACK!
YOU'RE LATE!
SORRY.
SOOO, WHAT DID UEDA-SENPAI WANT?
IS SHE IN LOVE WITH YOU OR WHAT?
I GUESS SO.
SERI-OUSLY?!
WELL?! WHAT DID YOU SAY?!
I SAID I NEEDED TO THINK ABOUT IT.
EEEE!
Kakeru, you're such a player!
Who'd have thought!
YOU GOT YOUR MONEY FOR THE DRINK?
AH, SORRY!
HERE...
NAHO.
ORANGE
100
Concentration: 100%
TAP
THEY ONLY HAD THE LITTLE JUICE BOXES, IS THAT OKAY?
OH, YEAH!
THIS IS WHAT I USUALLY GET.
HOW MUCH DO I OWE YOU?
DON'T WORRY ABOUT IT.

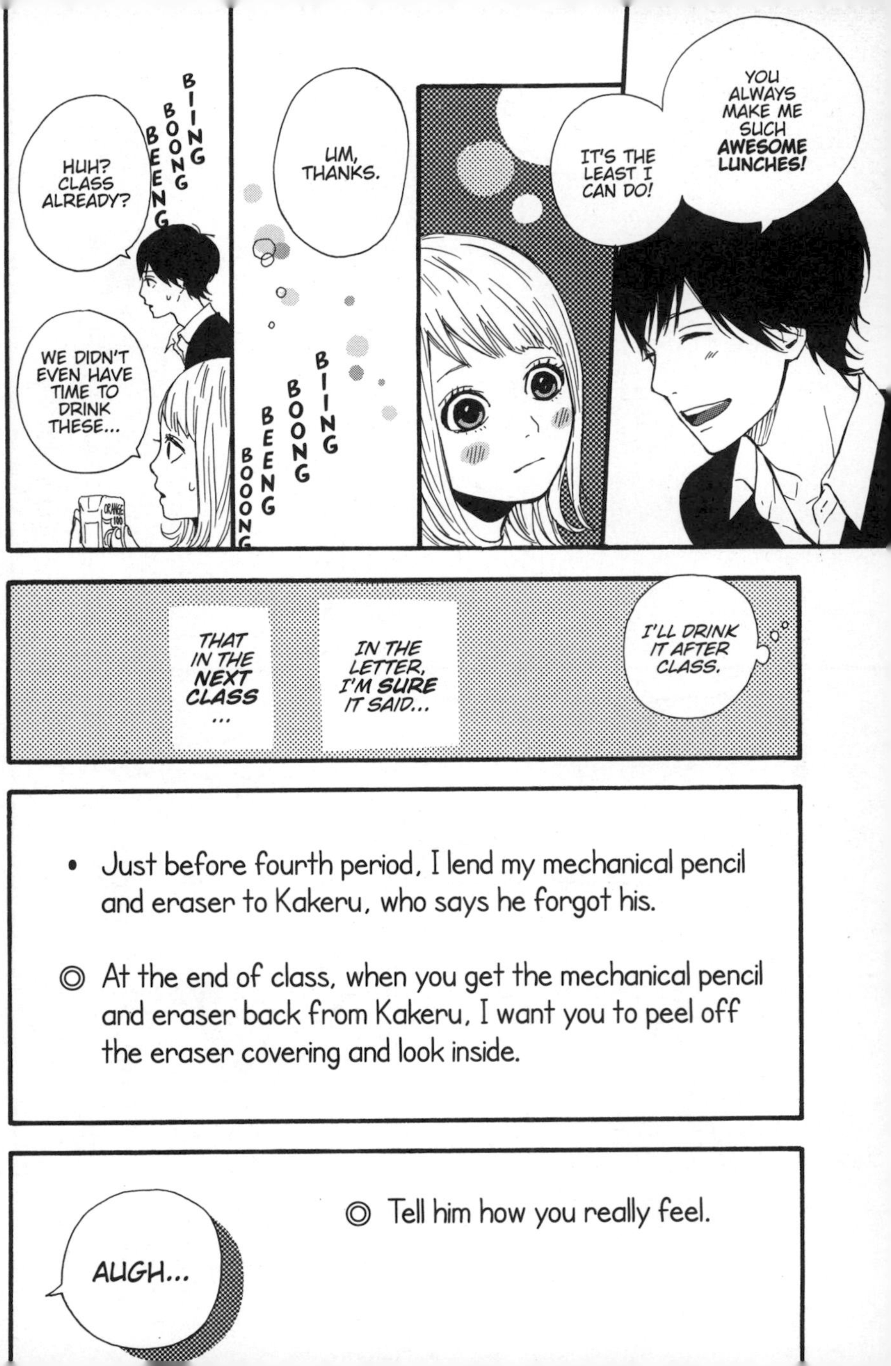
YOU ALWAYS MAKE ME SUCH **AWESOME LUNCHES!**
IT'S THE LEAST I CAN DO!
UM, THANKS.
BIING
BOONG
BEENG
BOOONG
BIING
BOONG
BEENG
HUH? CLASS ALREADY?
WE DIDN'T EVEN HAVE TIME TO DRINK THESE...
ORANGE
I'LL DRINK IT AFTER CLASS.
IN THE LETTER, I'M **SURE** IT SAID...
THAT IN THE **NEXT CLASS** ...
• Just before fourth period, I lend my mechanical pencil and eraser to Kakeru, who says he forgot his.
◎ At the end of class, when you get the mechanical pencil and eraser back from Kakeru, I want you to peel off the eraser covering and look inside.
◎ Tell him how you really feel.
AUGH...

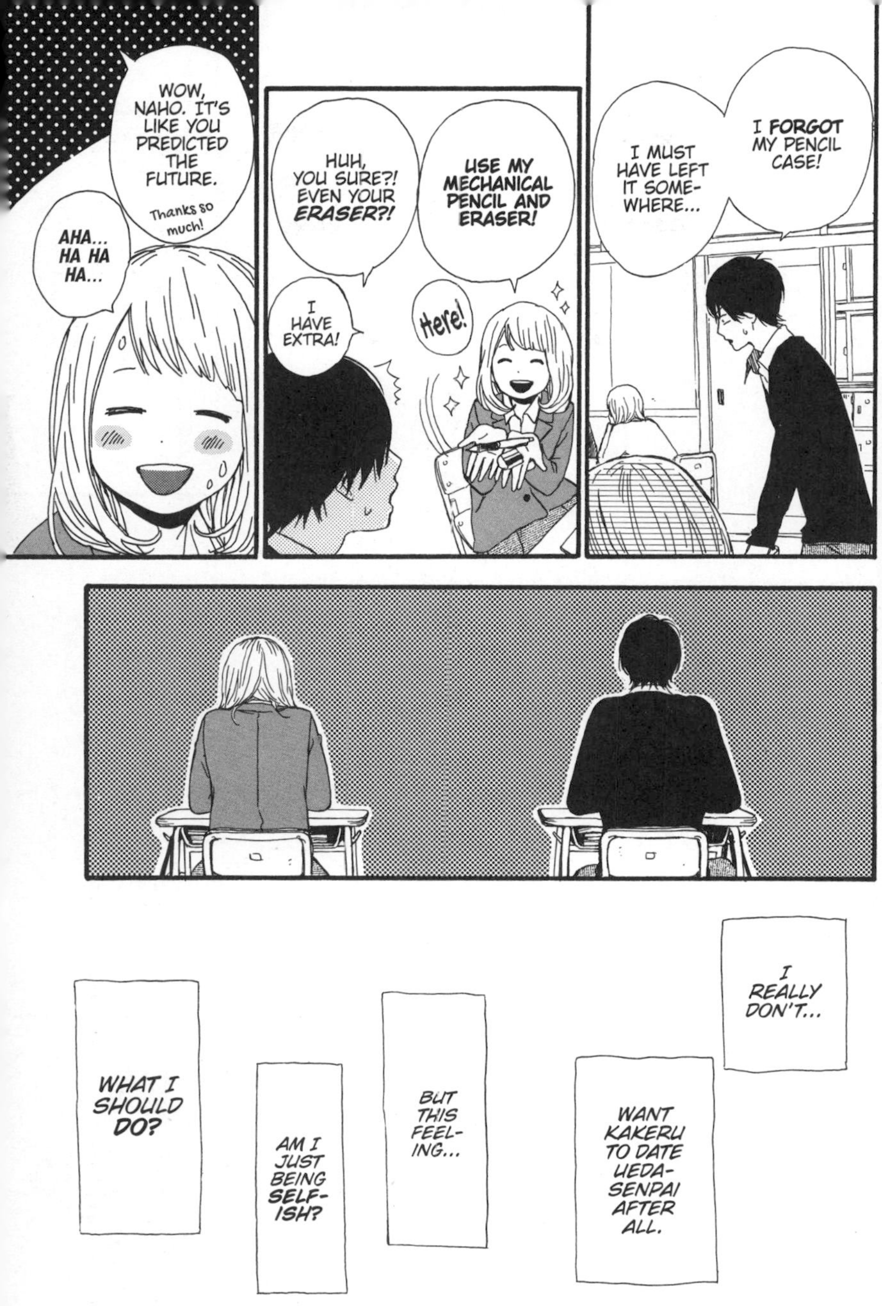
I FORGOT MY PENCIL CASE!
I MUST HAVE LEFT IT SOMEWHERE...
USE MY MECHANICAL PENCIL AND ERASER!
Here!
HUH, YOU SURE?! EVEN YOUR ERASER?!
I HAVE EXTRA!
WOW, NAHO. IT'S LIKE YOU PREDICTED THE FUTURE.
Thanks so much!
AHA... HA HA HA...
I REALLY DON'T...
WANT KAKERU TO DATE UEDA-SENPAI AFTER ALL.
BUT THIS FEELING...
AM I JUST BEING SELFISH?
WHAT I SHOULD DO?

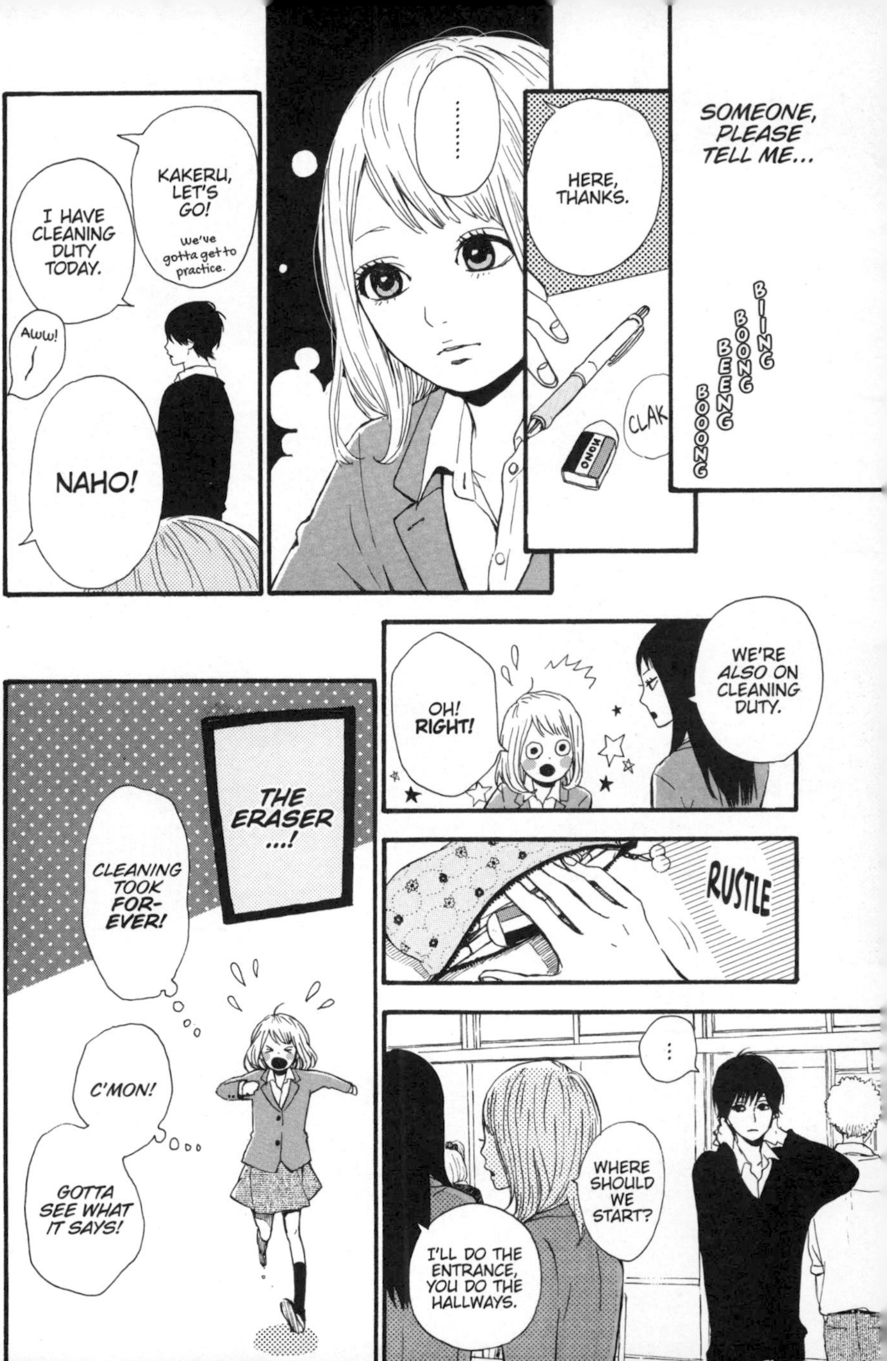
SOMEONE, PLEASE TELL ME...
BIING
BOONG
BEENG
BOOONG
HERE, THANKS.
CLAK
......
KAKERU, LET'S GO! We've gotta get to practice.
I HAVE CLEANING DUTY TODAY.
Aww!
NAHO!
WE'RE ALSO ON CLEANING DUTY.
OH! RIGHT!
RUSTLE
...
WHERE SHOULD WE START?
I'LL DO THE ENTRANCE, YOU DO THE HALLWAYS.
THE ERASER ...!
CLEANING TOOK FOR-EVER!
C'MON!
GOTTA SEE WHAT IT SAYS!

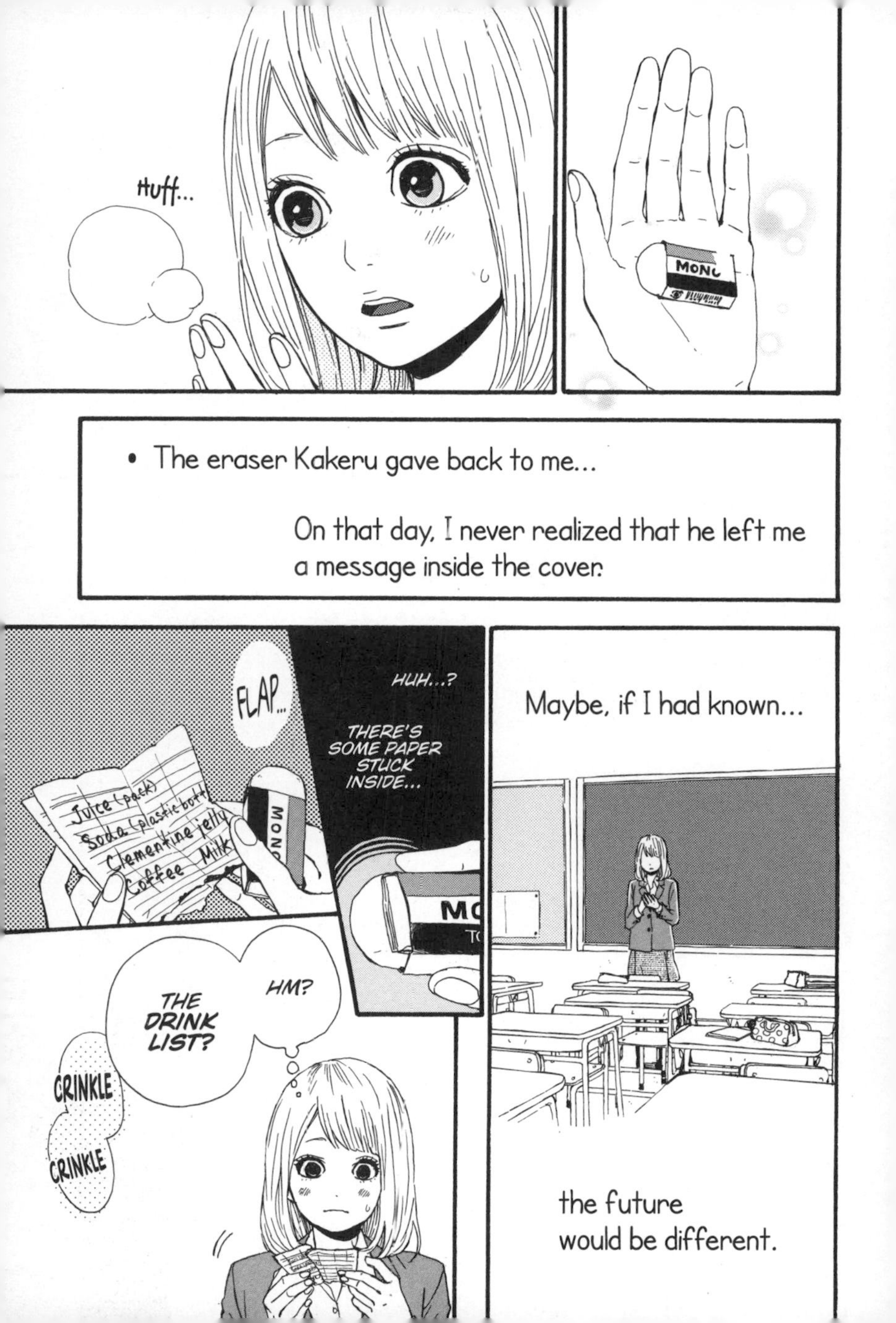
MONO
Huff...
• The eraser Kakeru gave back to me...
On that day, I never realized that he left me a message inside the cover.
Maybe, if I had known...
the future would be different.
HUH...?
THERE'S SOME PAPER STUCK INSIDE...
FLAP...
Juice (pack)
Soda (plastic bott
Clementine jelly
Coffee Milk
HM?
THE DRINK LIST?
CRINKLE
CRINKLE

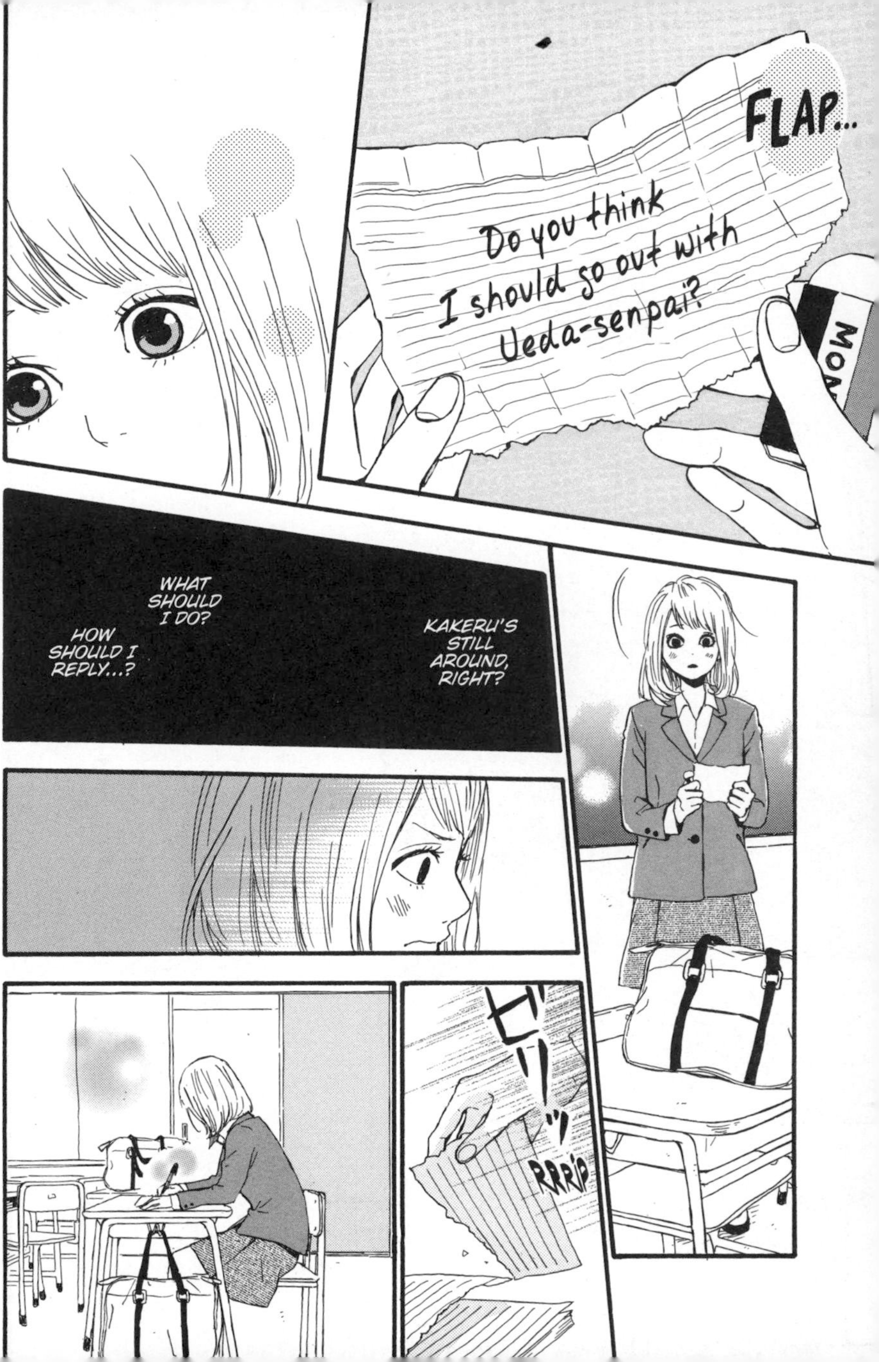
FLAP...
Do you think I should go out with Ueda-senpai?
MOMO
KAKERU'S STILL AROUND, RIGHT?
WHAT SHOULD I DO?
HOW SHOULD I REPLY...?
ビリッ
RRRIP

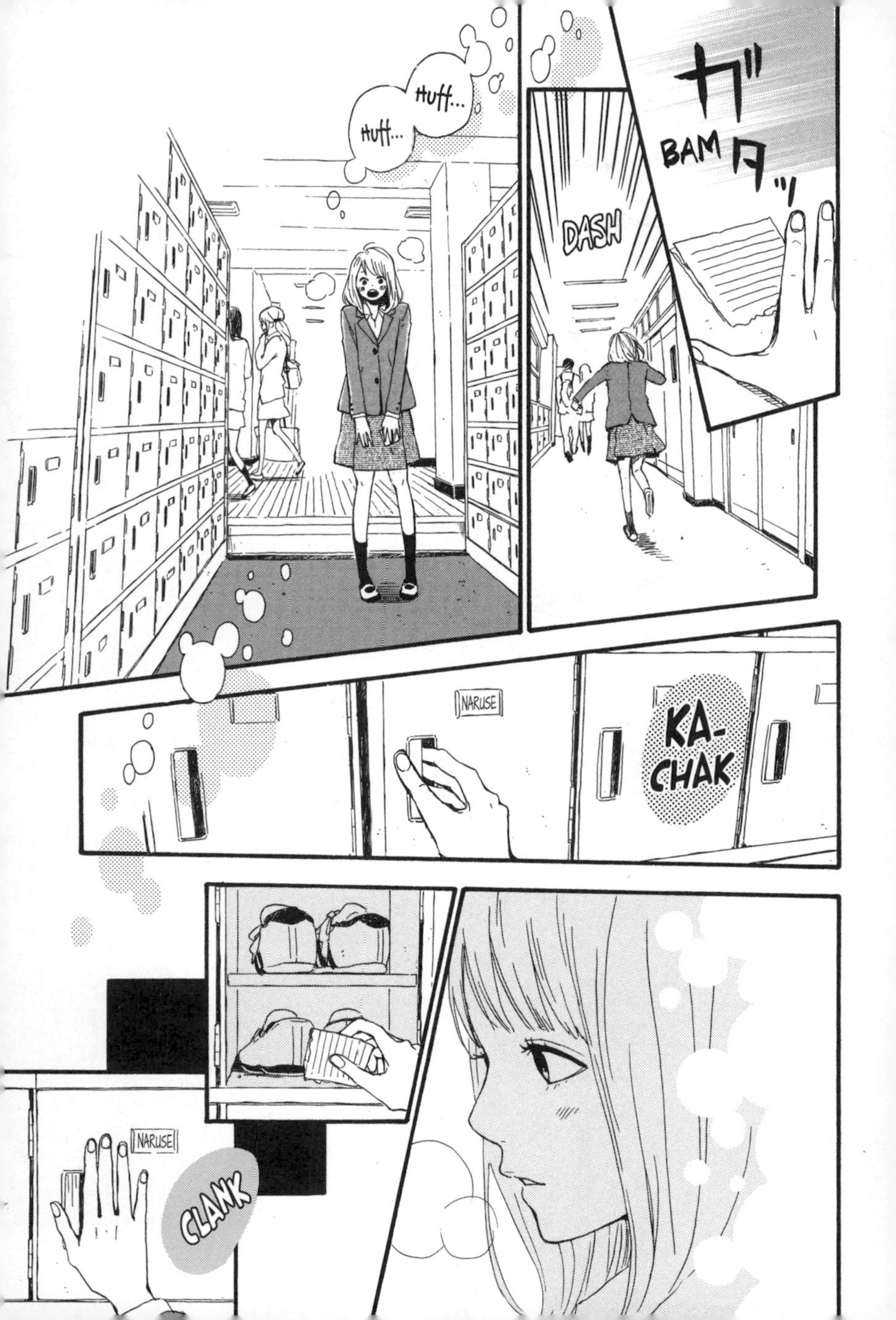
ガタッ
BAM
DASH
Huff...
Huff...
NARUSE
KA-CHAK
NARUSE
CLANK

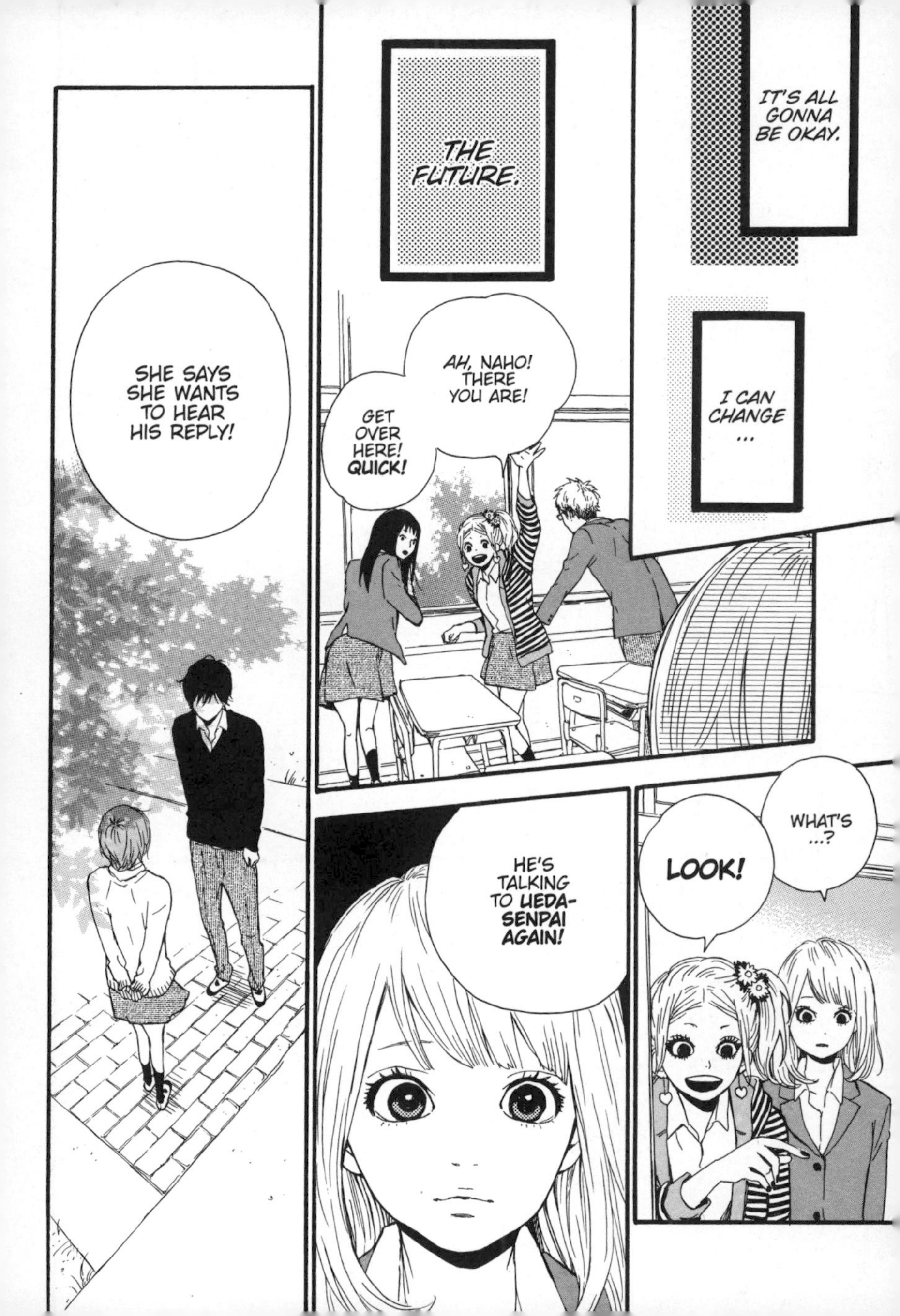

IT'S ALL GONNA BE OKAY.
I CAN CHANGE ...
THE FUTURE.
AH, NAHO! THERE YOU ARE!
GET OVER HERE! **QUICK!**
WHAT'S ...?
LOOK!
HE'S TALKING TO **UEDA-SENPAI AGAIN!**
SHE SAYS SHE WANTS TO HEAR HIS REPLY!

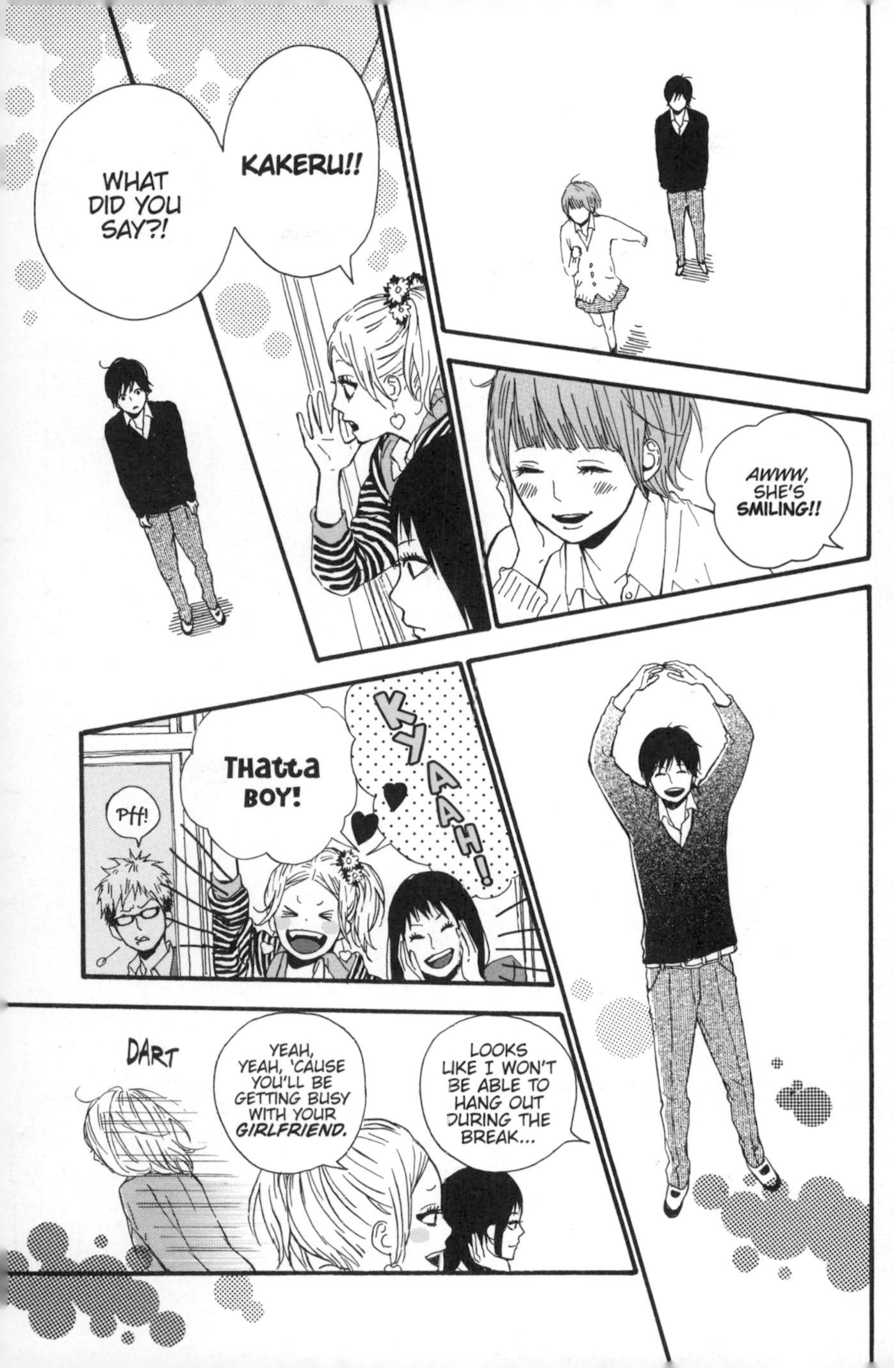
KAKERU!!
WHAT DID YOU SAY?!
AWWW, SHE'S SMILING!!
KYAAAH!
THATTA BOY!
Pff!
LOOKS LIKE I WON'T BE ABLE TO HANG OUT DURING THE BREAK...
YEAH, YEAH, 'CAUSE YOU'LL BE GETTING BUSY WITH YOUR GIRLFRIEND.
DART

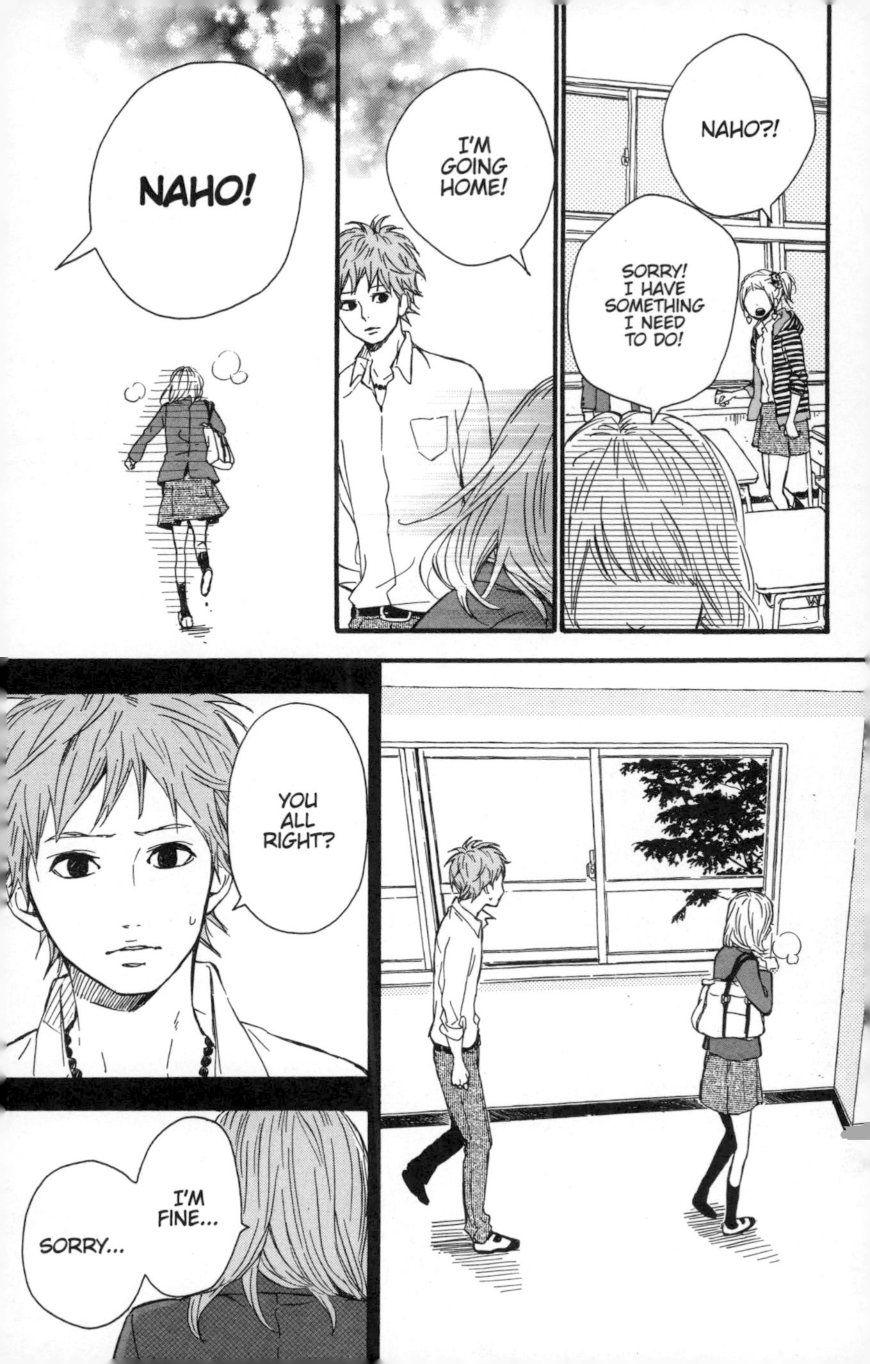
NAHO?!
SORRY! I HAVE SOMETHING I NEED TO DO!
I'M GOING HOME!
NAHO!
YOU ALL RIGHT?
I'M FINE...
SORRY...

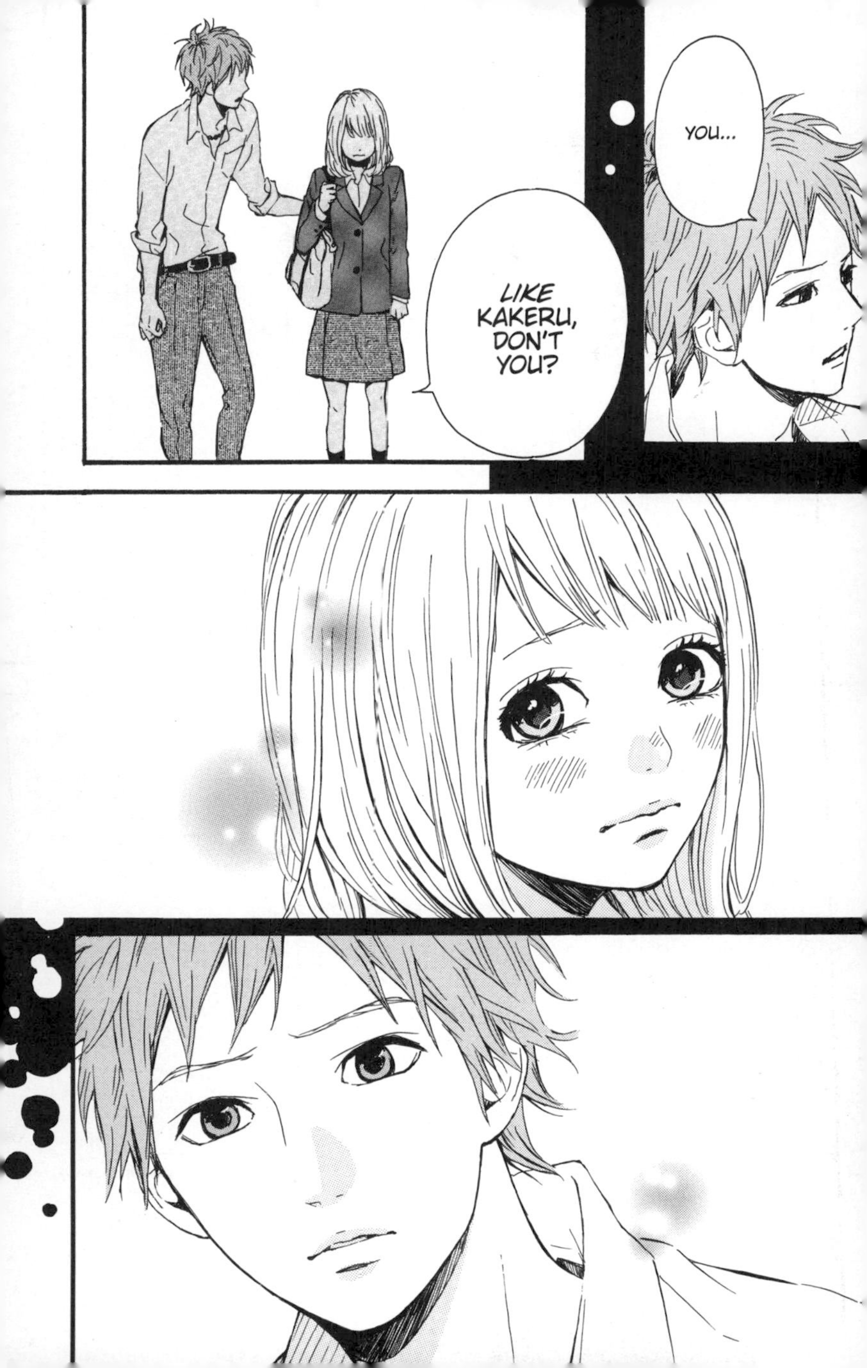
YOU...
LIKE KAKERU, DON'T YOU?

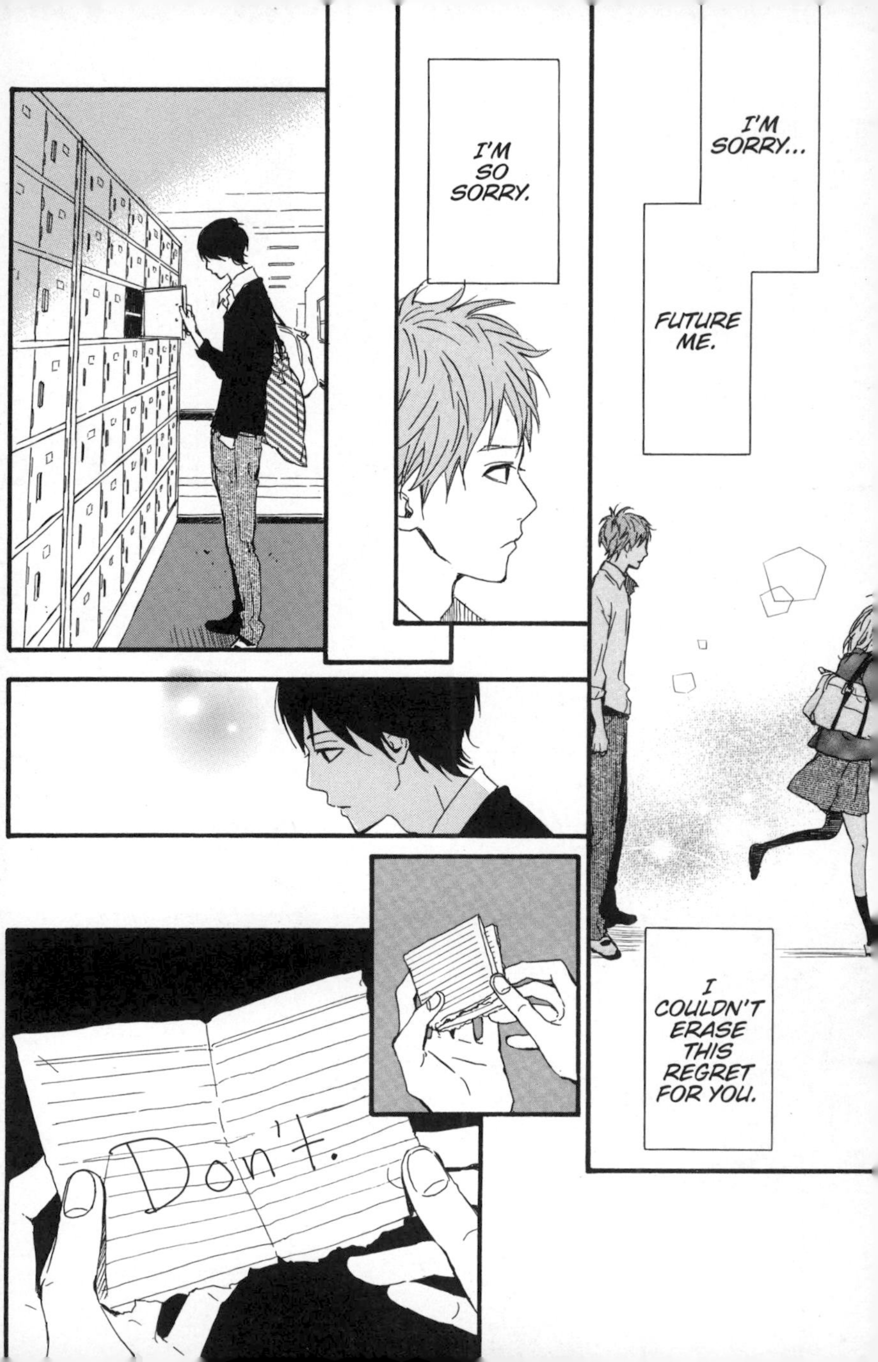
I'M SORRY...
FUTURE ME.
I COULDN'T ERASE THIS REGRET FOR YOU.
I'M SO SORRY.
Don't.

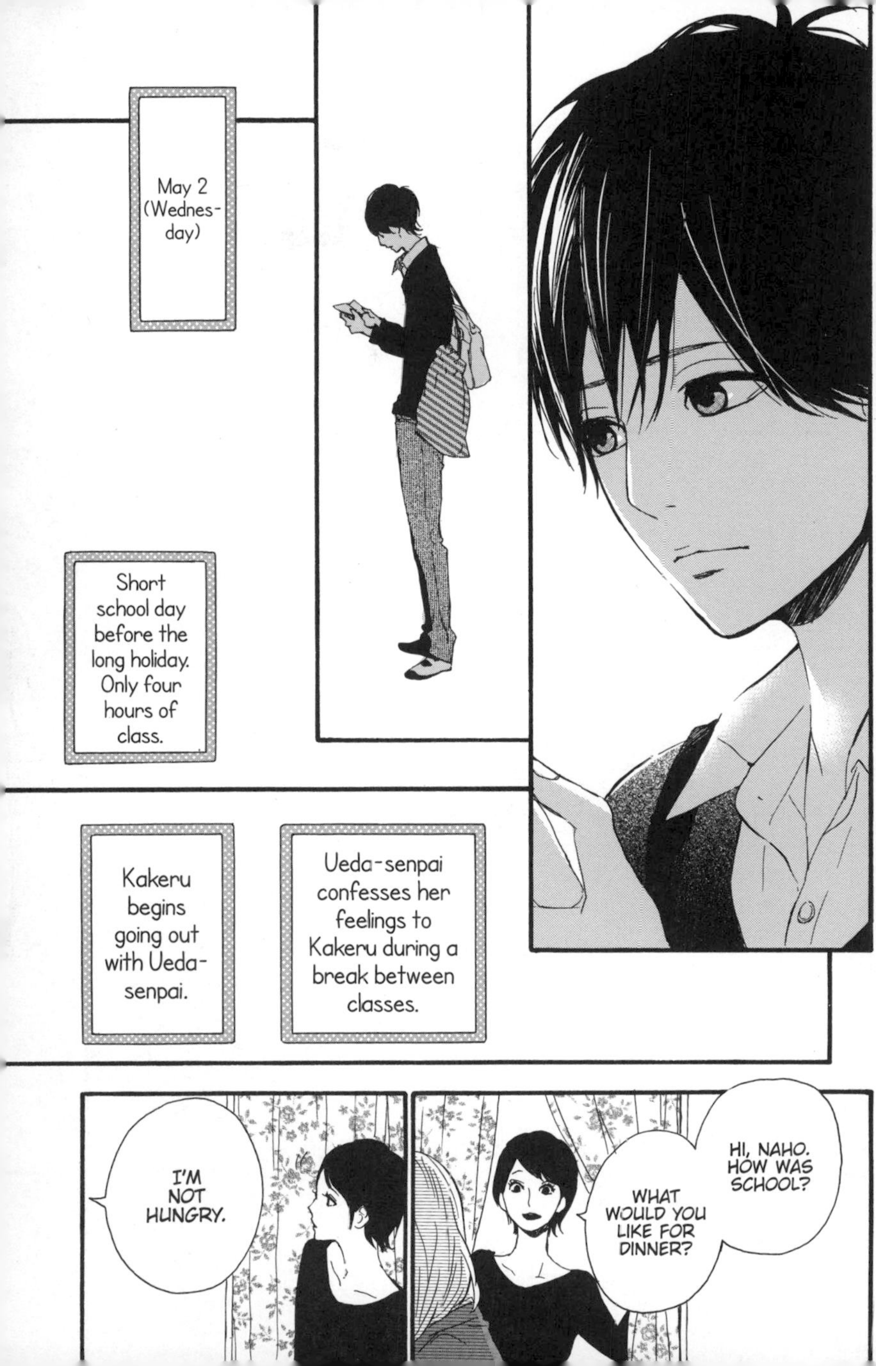
May 2 (Wednes-day)
Short school day before the long holiday. Only four hours of class.
Ueda-senpai confesses her feelings to Kakeru during a break between classes.
Kakeru begins going out with Ueda-senpai.
HI, NAHO. HOW WAS SCHOOL?
WHAT WOULD YOU LIKE FOR DINNER?
I'M NOT HUNGRY.

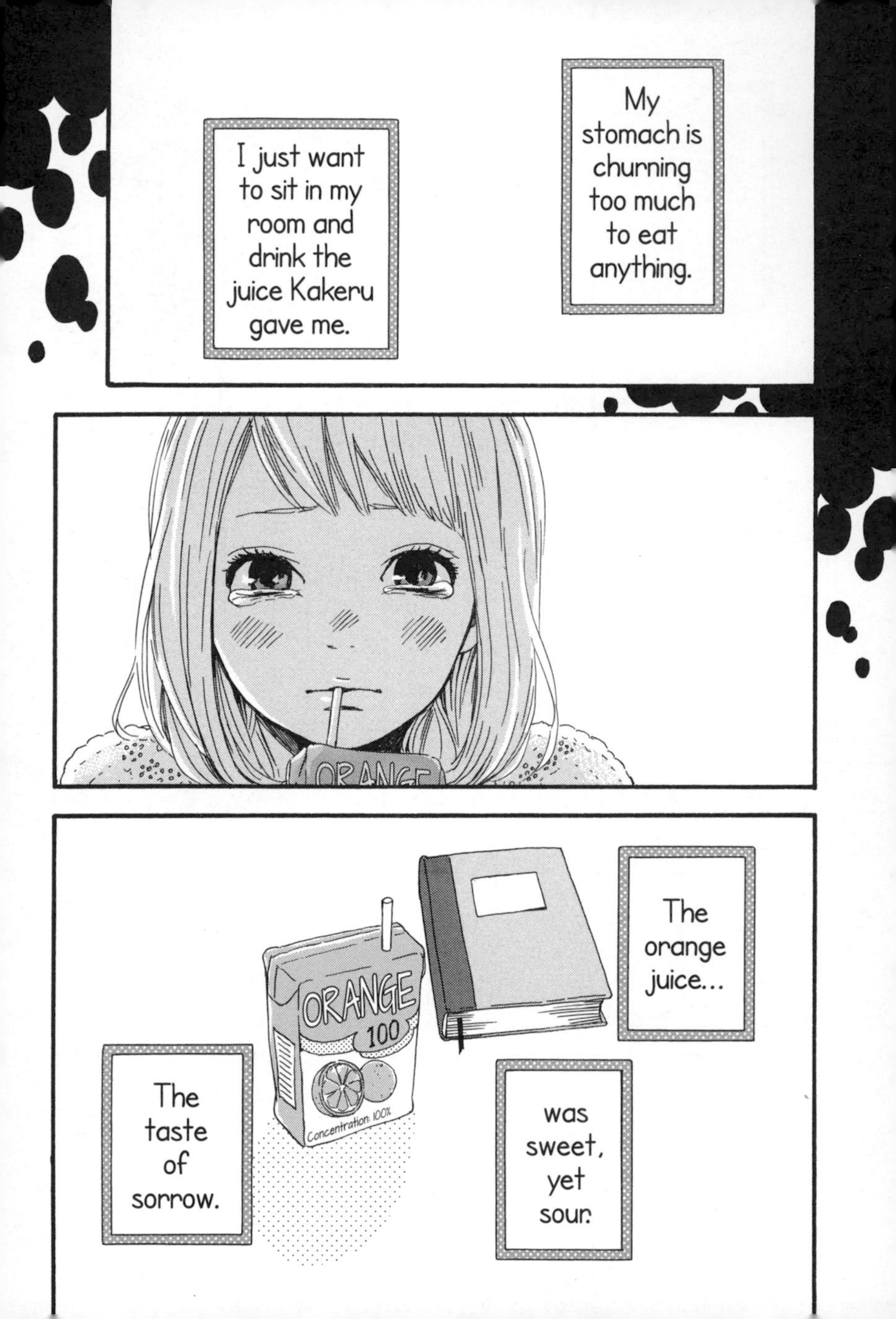
My stomach is churning too much to eat anything.
I just want to sit in my room and drink the juice Kakeru gave me.
The orange juice...
was sweet, yet sour.
ORANGE
100
Concentration: 100%
The taste of sorrow.

orange

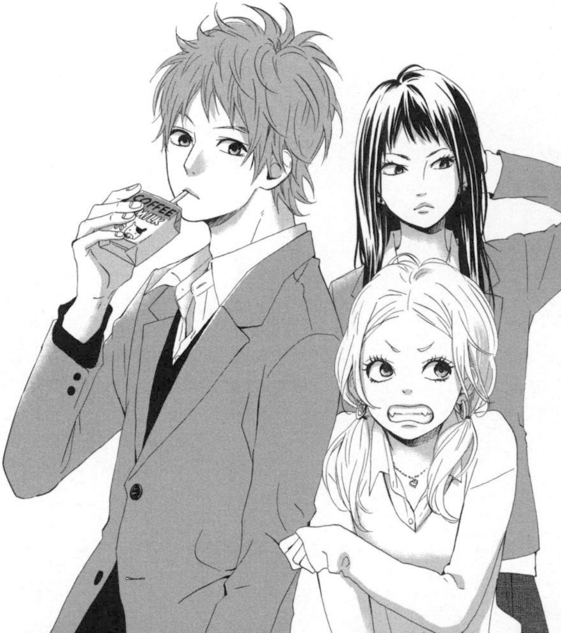
COFFEE

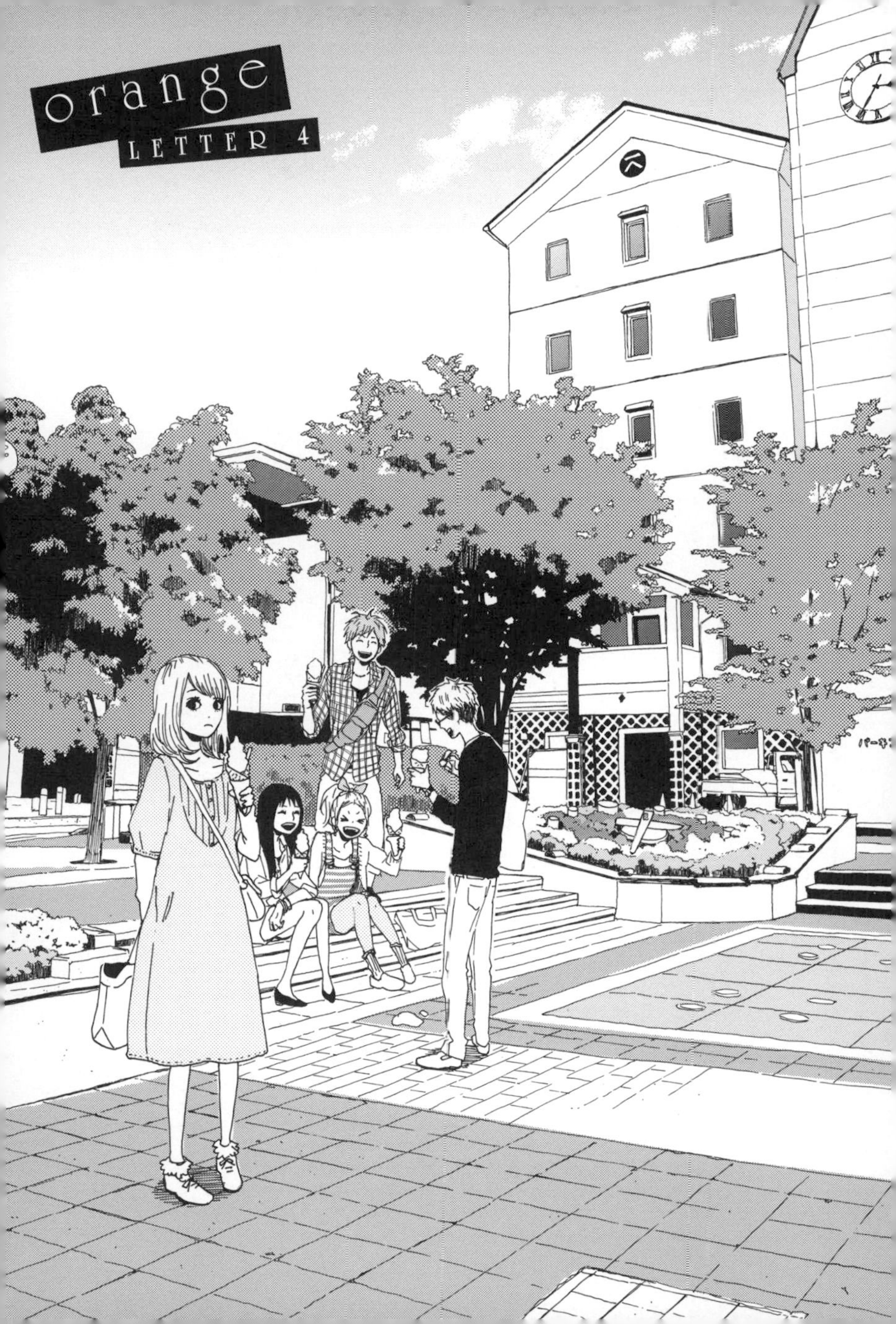
orange
LETTER 4

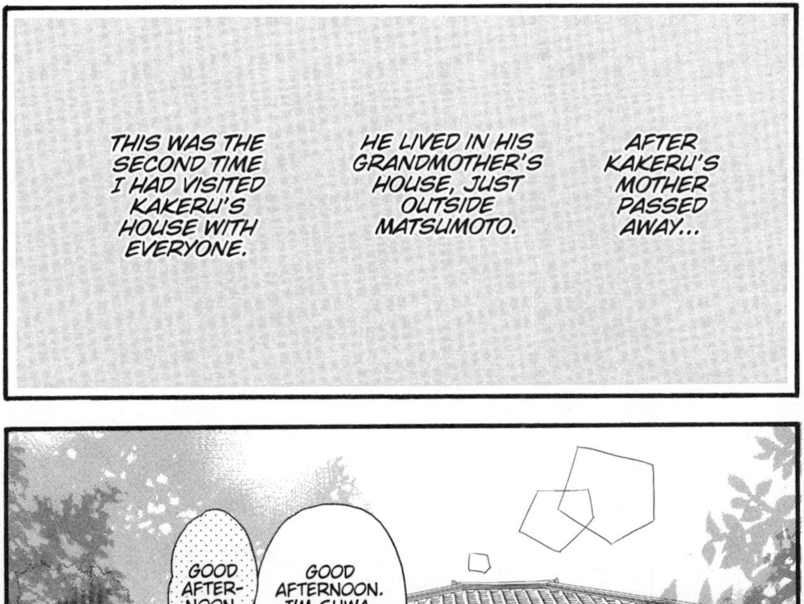
AFTER KAKERU'S MOTHER PASSED AWAY...
HE LIVED IN HIS GRANDMOTHER'S HOUSE, JUST OUTSIDE MATSUMOTO.
THIS WAS THE SECOND TIME I HAD VISITED KAKERU'S HOUSE WITH EVERYONE.
GOOD AFTERNOON. I'M SUWA. WE SPOKE ON THE PHONE THE OTHER DAY.
GOOD AFTER-NOON.
HELLO.

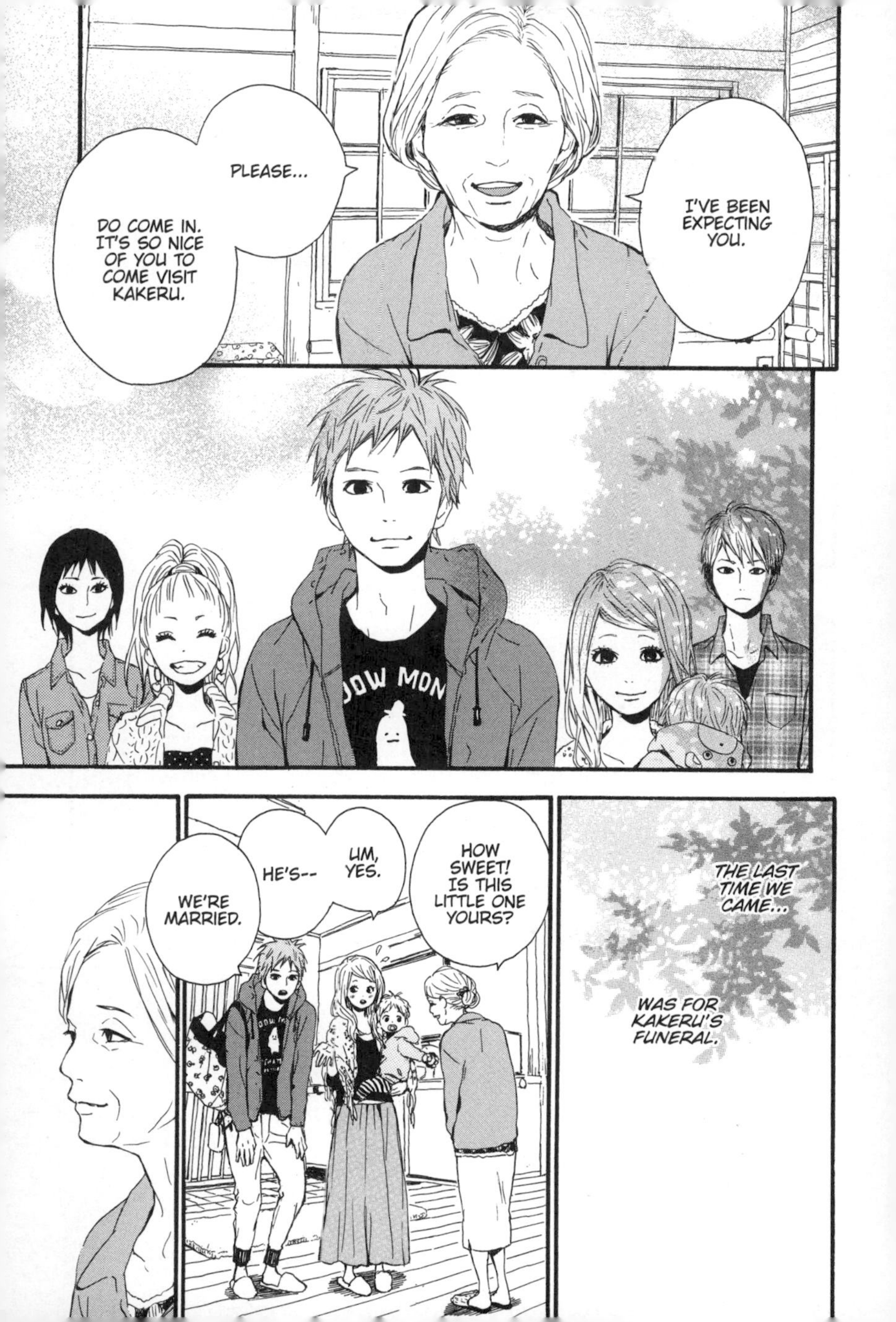
I'VE BEEN EXPECTING YOU.
PLEASE...
DO COME IN. IT'S SO NICE OF YOU TO COME VISIT KAKERU.
THE LAST TIME WE CAME...
WAS FOR KAKERU'S FUNERAL.
HOW SWEET! IS THIS LITTLE ONE YOURS?
UM, YES.
HE'S--
WE'RE MARRIED.

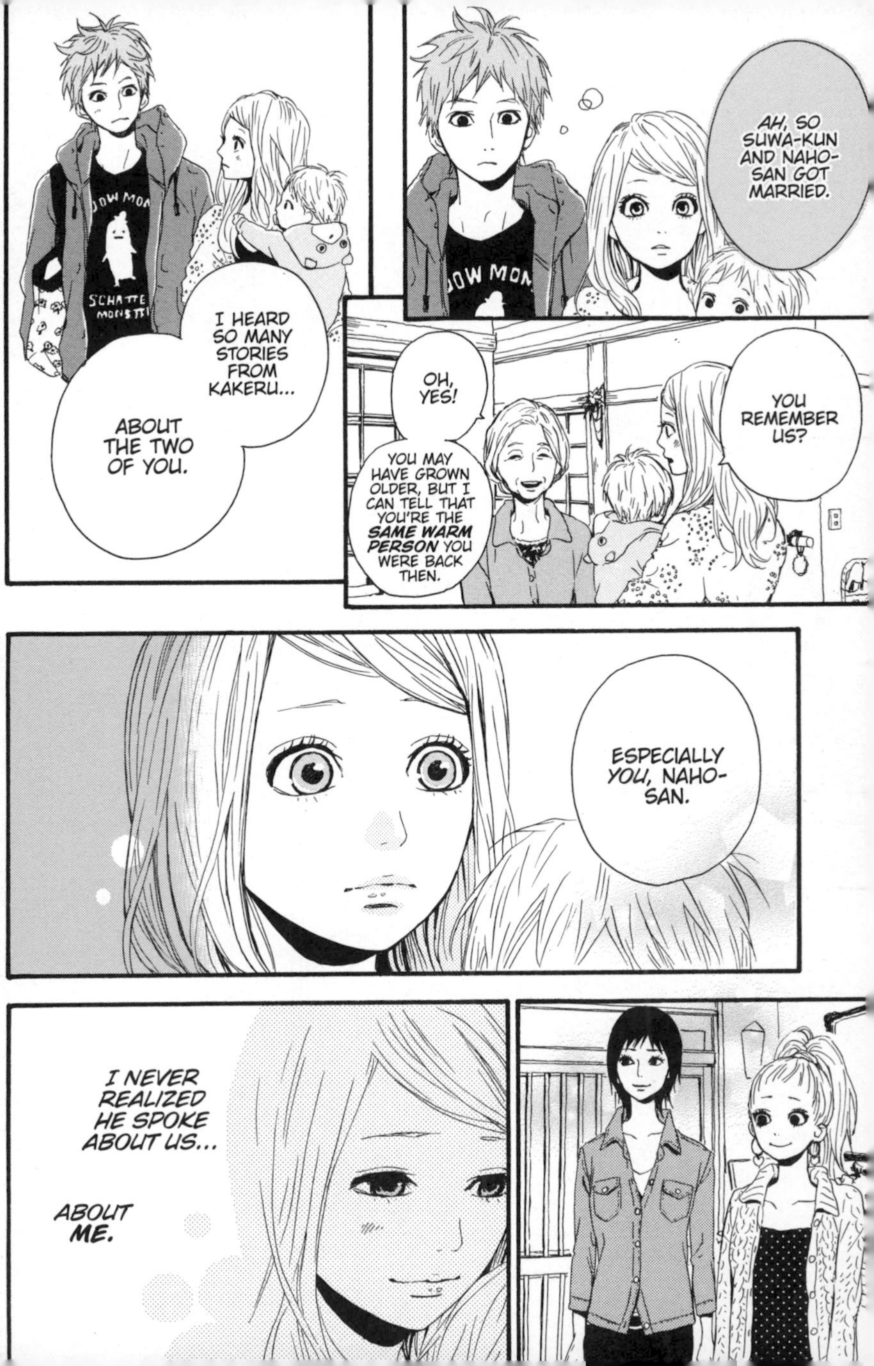
AH, SO SUWA-KUN AND NAHO-SAN GOT MARRIED.
YOU REMEMBER US?
OH, YES!
YOU MAY HAVE GROWN OLDER, BUT I CAN TELL THAT YOU'RE THE **SAME WARM PERSON** YOU WERE BACK THEN.
I HEARD SO MANY STORIES FROM KAKERU...
ABOUT THE TWO OF YOU.
ESPECIALLY *YOU*, NAHO-SAN.
I NEVER REALIZED HE SPOKE ABOUT US...
ABOUT ***ME.***

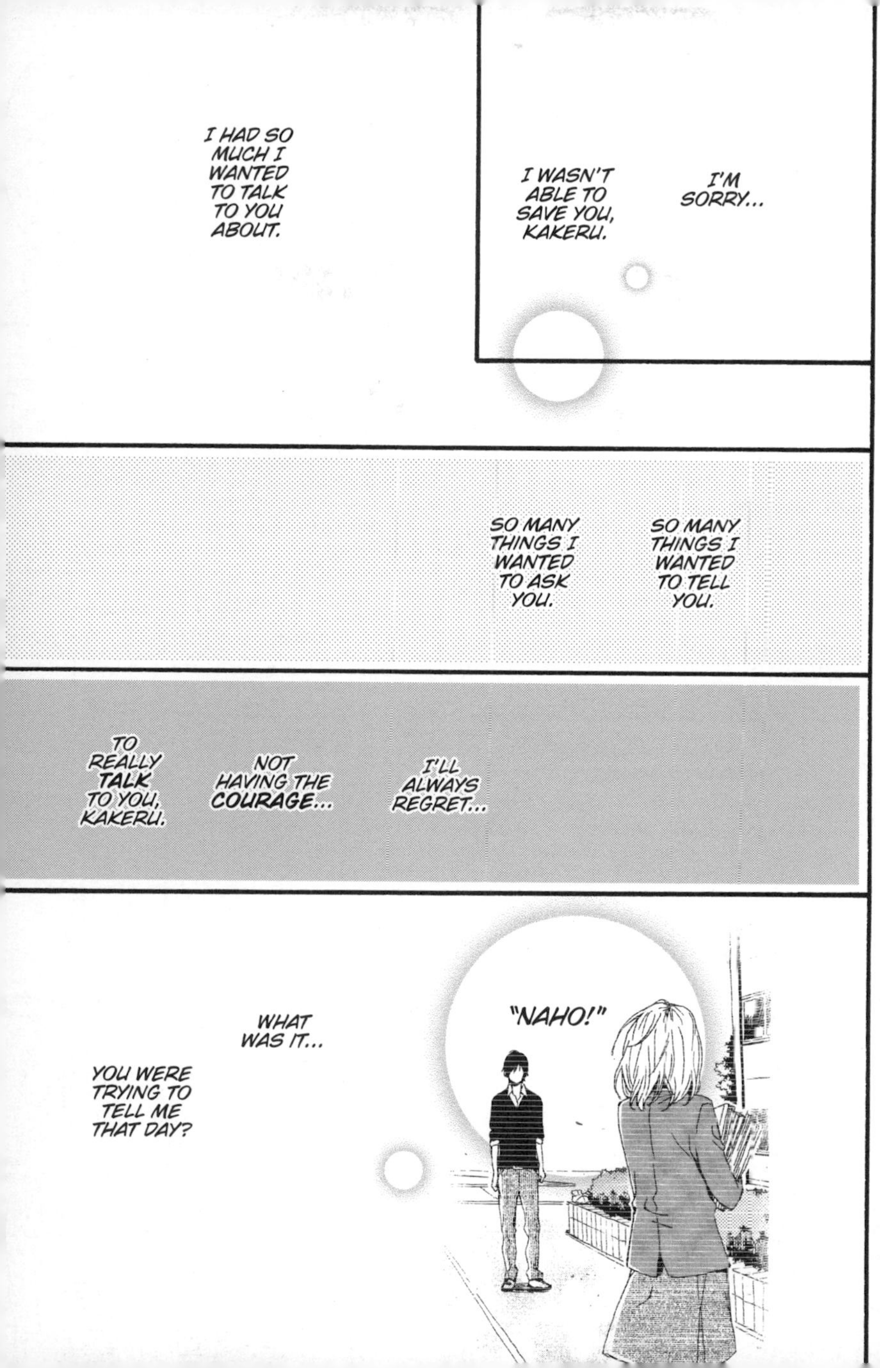
I'M SORRY...
I WASN'T ABLE TO SAVE YOU, KAKERU.
I HAD SO MUCH I WANTED TO TALK TO YOU ABOUT.
SO MANY THINGS I WANTED TO TELL YOU.
SO MANY THINGS I WANTED TO ASK YOU.
I'LL ALWAYS REGRET...
NOT HAVING THE **COURAGE**...
TO REALLY **TALK** TO YOU, KAKERU.
"NAHO!"
WHAT WAS IT...
YOU WERE TRYING TO TELL ME THAT DAY?

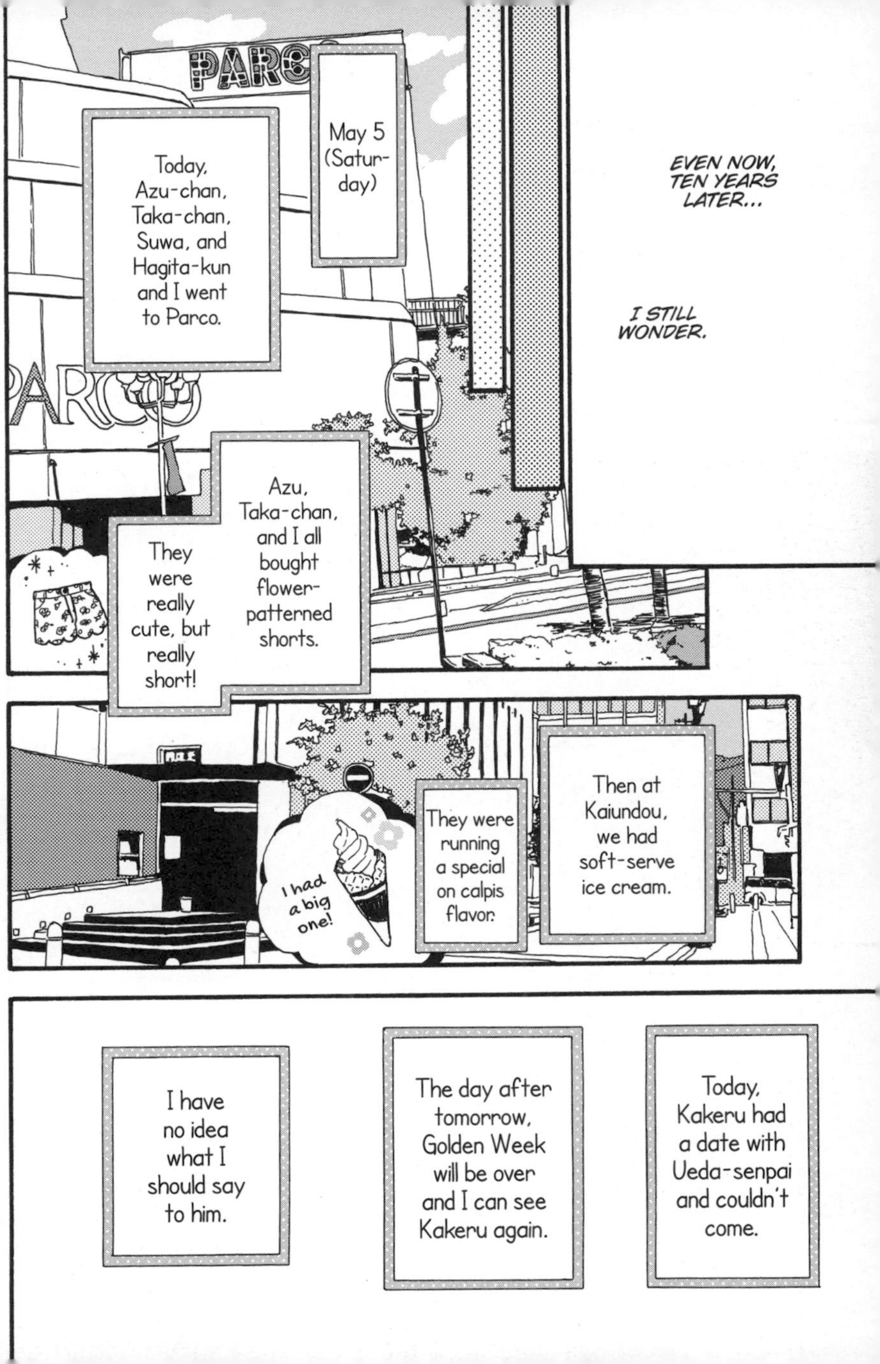
EVEN NOW, TEN YEARS LATER...
I STILL WONDER.
May 5 (Saturday)
Today, Azu-chan, Taka-chan, Suwa, and Hagita-kun and I went to Parco.
Azu, Taka-chan, and I all bought flower-patterned shorts.
They were really cute, but really short!
Then at Kaiundou, we had soft-serve ice cream.
They were running a special on calpis flavor.
I had a big one!
Today, Kakeru had a date with Ueda-senpai and couldn't come.
The day after tomorrow, Golden Week will be over and I can see Kakeru again.
I have no idea what I should say to him.

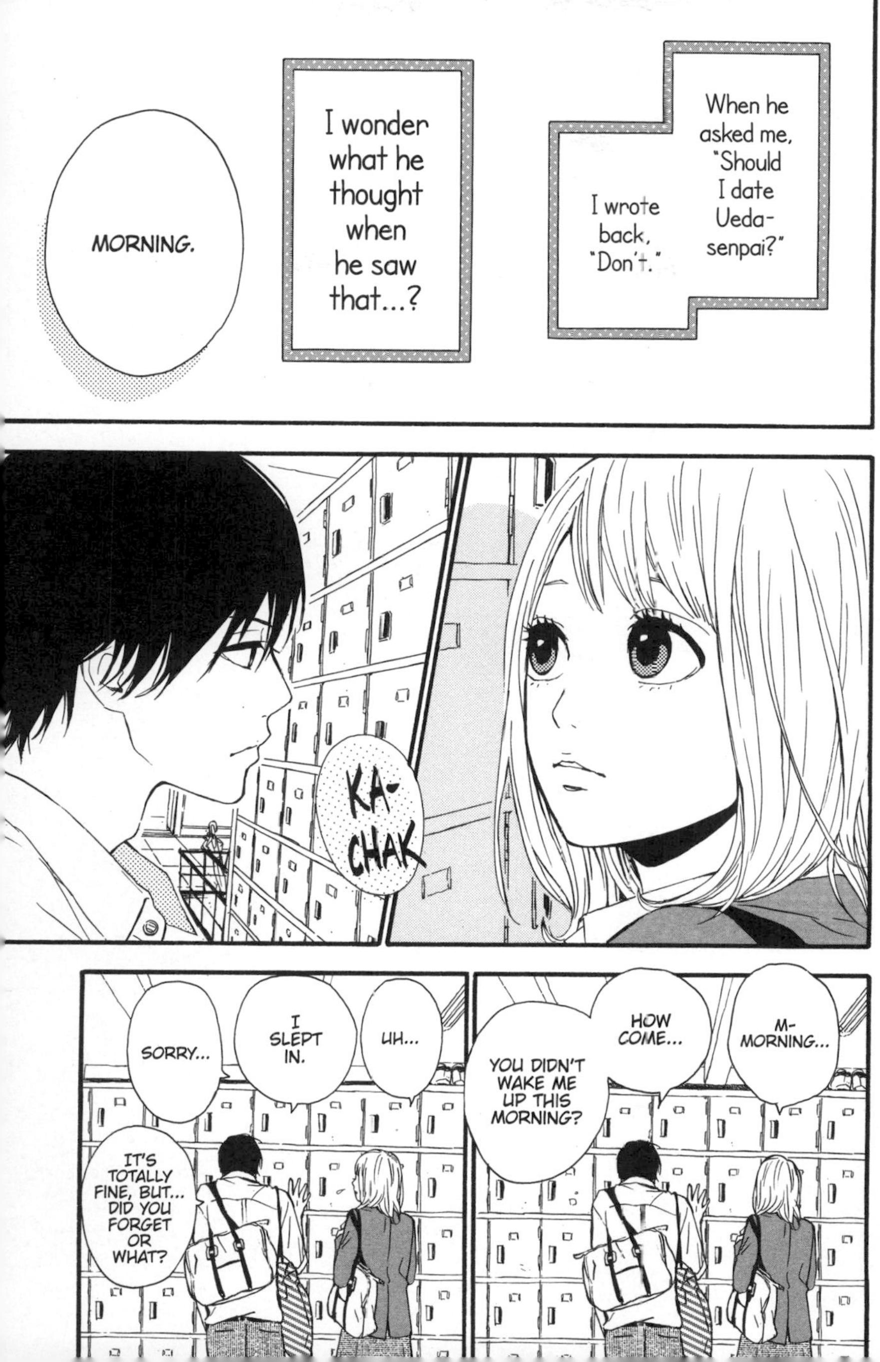
When he asked me, "Should I date Ueda-senpai?"
I wrote back, "Don't."
I wonder what he thought when he saw that...?
MORNING.
KA-CHAK
M-MORNING...
HOW COME...
YOU DIDN'T WAKE ME UP THIS MORNING?
UH...
I SLEPT IN.
SORRY...
IT'S TOTALLY FINE, BUT... DID YOU FORGET OR WHAT?

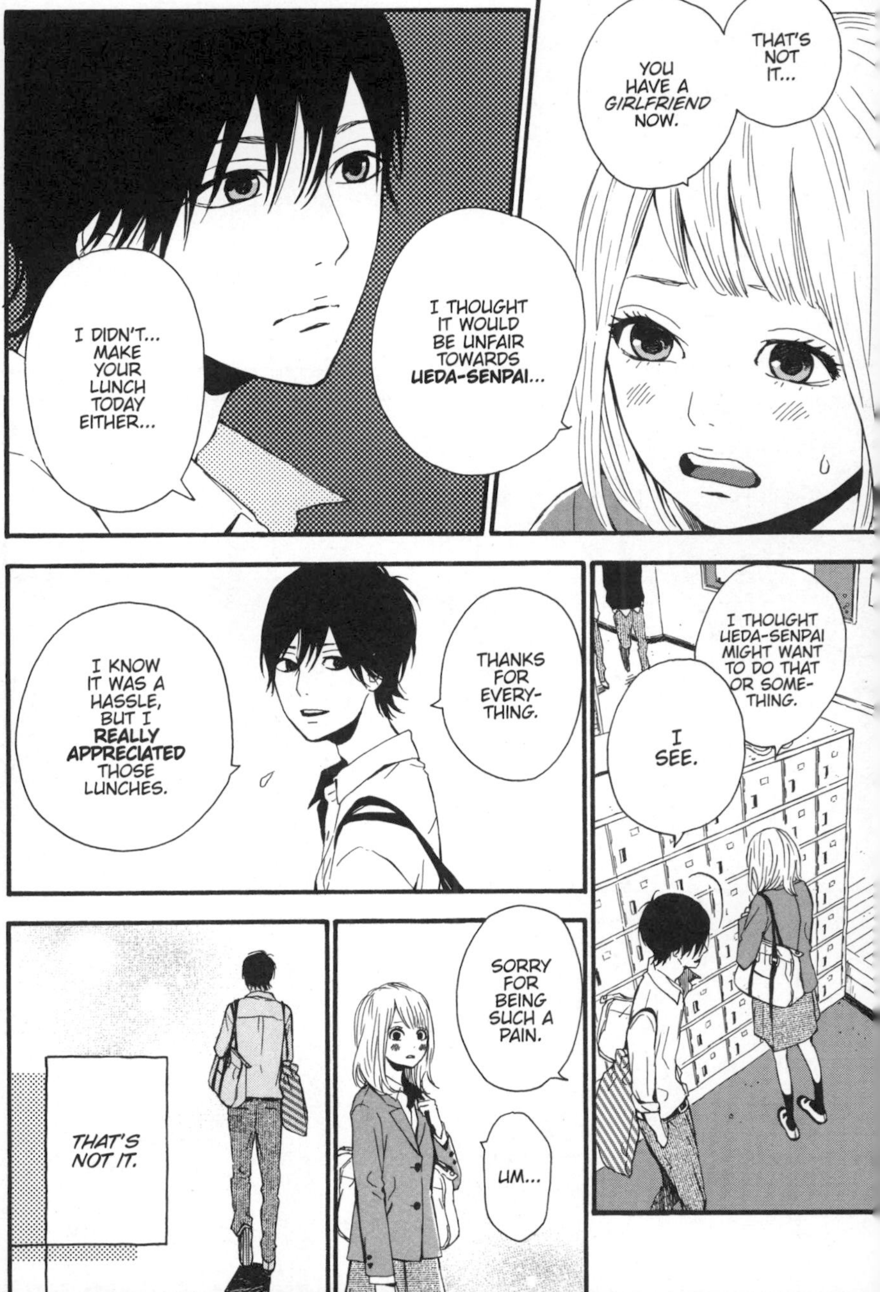
THAT'S NOT IT...
YOU HAVE A GIRLFRIEND NOW.
I THOUGHT IT WOULD BE UNFAIR TOWARDS UEDA-SENPAI...
I DIDN'T... MAKE YOUR LUNCH TODAY EITHER...
I THOUGHT UEDA-SENPAI MIGHT WANT TO DO THAT OR SOME-THING.
I SEE.
THANKS FOR EVERY-THING.
I KNOW IT WAS A HASSLE, BUT I REALLY APPRECIATED THOSE LUNCHES.
SORRY FOR BEING SUCH A PAIN.
UM...
THAT'S NOT IT.

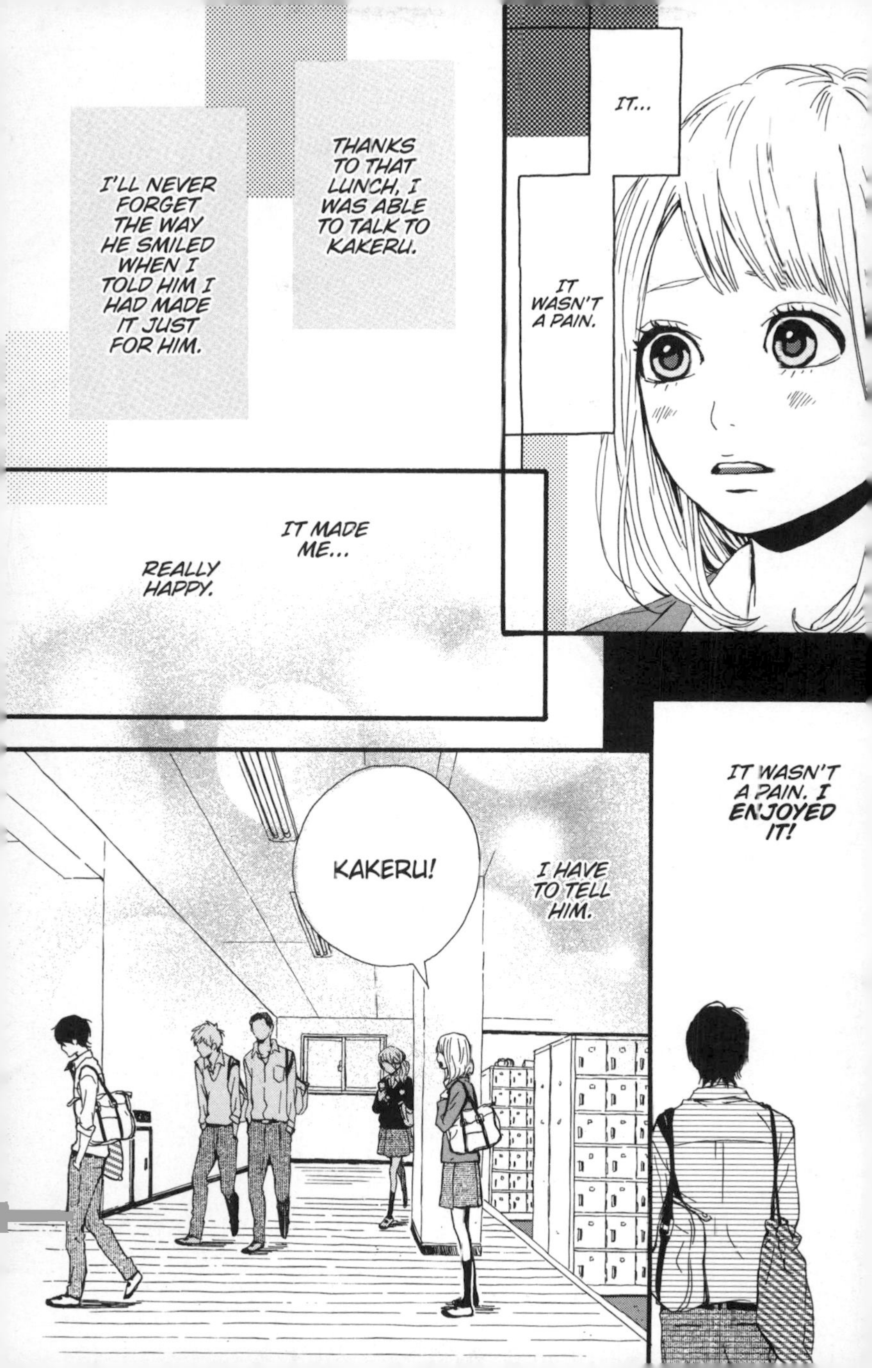
IT...
IT WASN'T A PAIN.
THANKS TO THAT LUNCH, I WAS ABLE TO TALK TO KAKERU.
I'LL NEVER FORGET THE WAY HE SMILED WHEN I TOLD HIM I HAD MADE IT JUST FOR HIM.
IT MADE ME...
REALLY HAPPY.
IT WASN'T A PAIN. I ENJOYED IT!
I HAVE TO TELL HIM.
KAKERU!

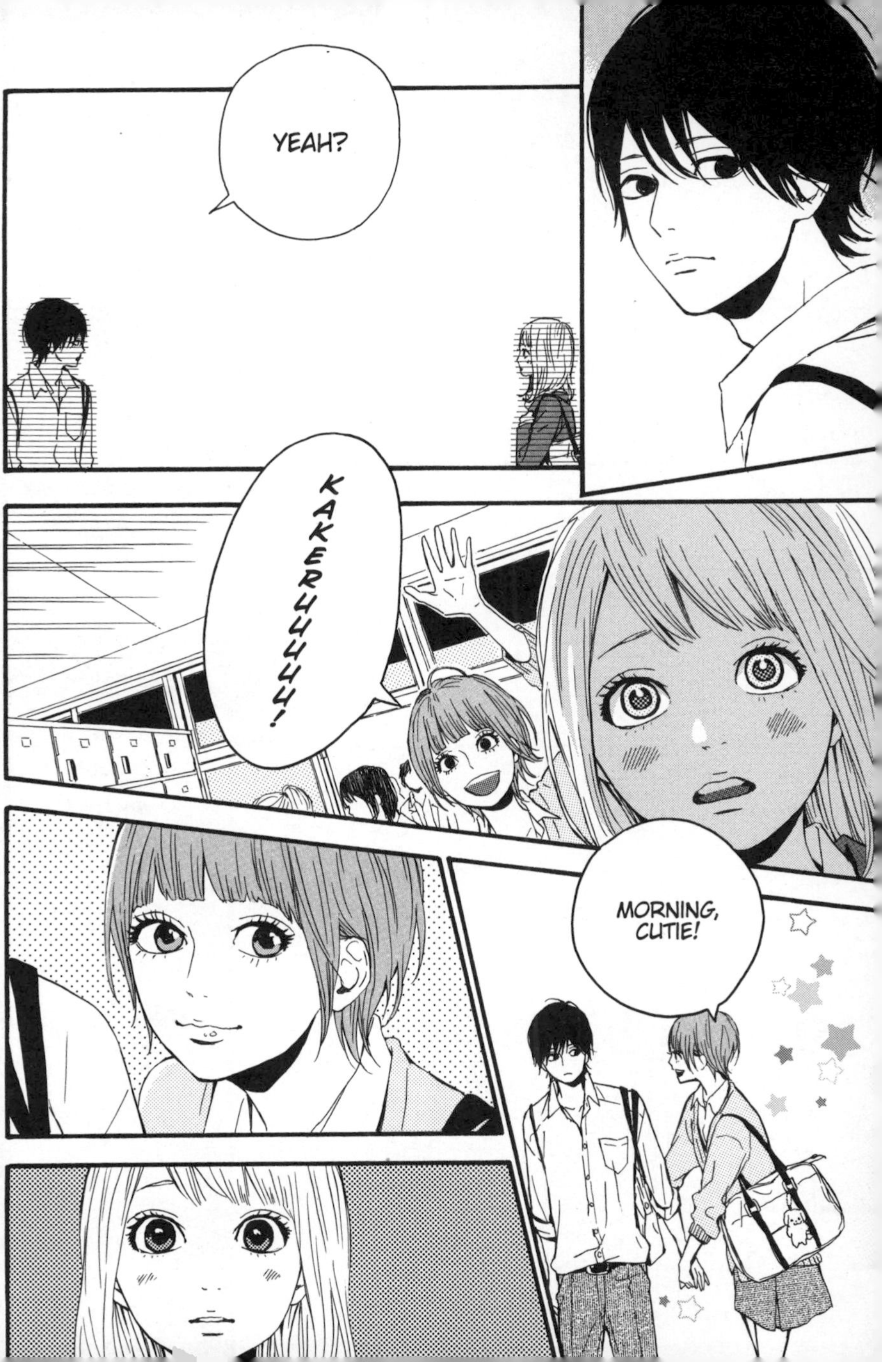
YEAH?
KAKERUUUUU!
MORNING, CUTIE!

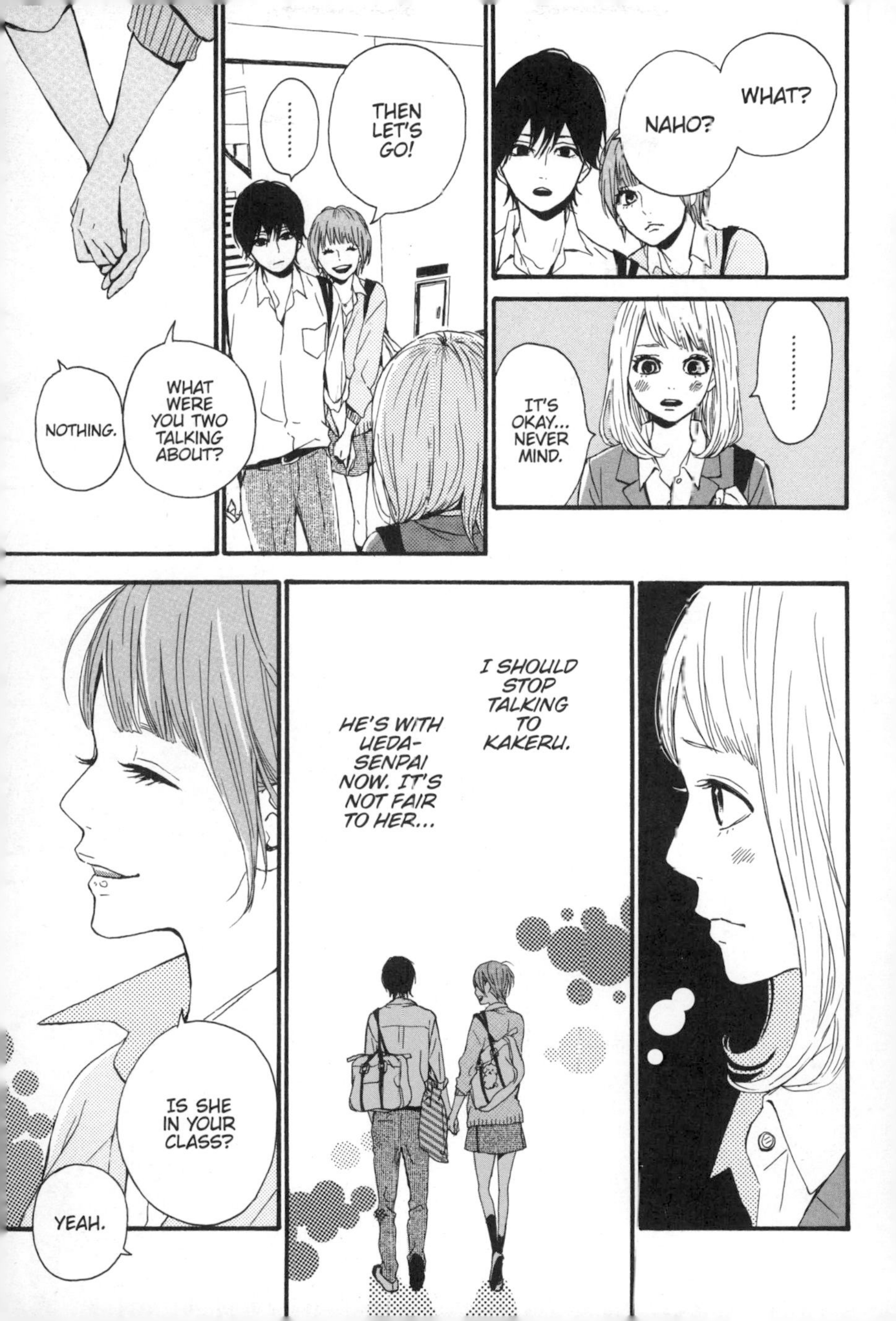
WHAT?
NAHO?
......
IT'S OKAY... NEVER MIND.
THEN LET'S GO!
......
WHAT WERE YOU TWO TALKING ABOUT?
NOTHING.
I SHOULD STOP TALKING TO KAKERU.
HE'S WITH UEDA-SENPAI NOW. IT'S NOT FAIR TO HER...
IS SHE IN YOUR CLASS?
YEAH.

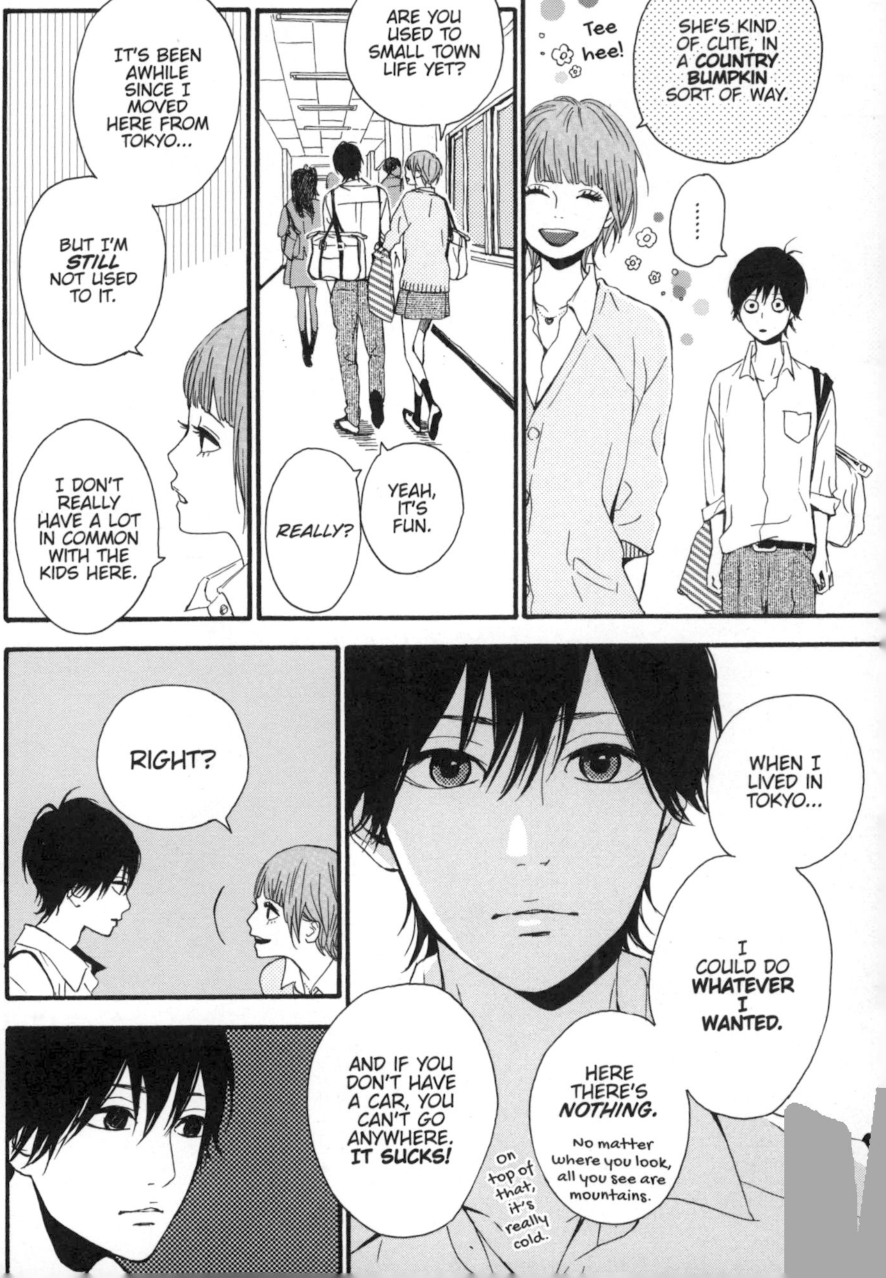
SHE'S KIND OF CUTE, IN A **COUNTRY BUMPKIN** SORT OF WAY.
Tee hee!
......
ARE YOU USED TO SMALL TOWN LIFE YET?
YEAH, IT'S FUN.
REALLY?
IT'S BEEN AWHILE SINCE I MOVED HERE FROM TOKYO...
BUT I'M ***STILL*** NOT USED TO IT.
I DON'T REALLY HAVE A LOT IN COMMON WITH THE KIDS HERE.
WHEN I LIVED IN TOKYO...
I COULD DO **WHATEVER I WANTED.**
HERE THERE'S ***NOTHING.***
No matter where you look, all you see are mountains.
on top of that, it's really cold.
AND IF YOU DON'T HAVE A CAR, YOU CAN'T GO ANYWHERE. **IT SUCKS!**
RIGHT?

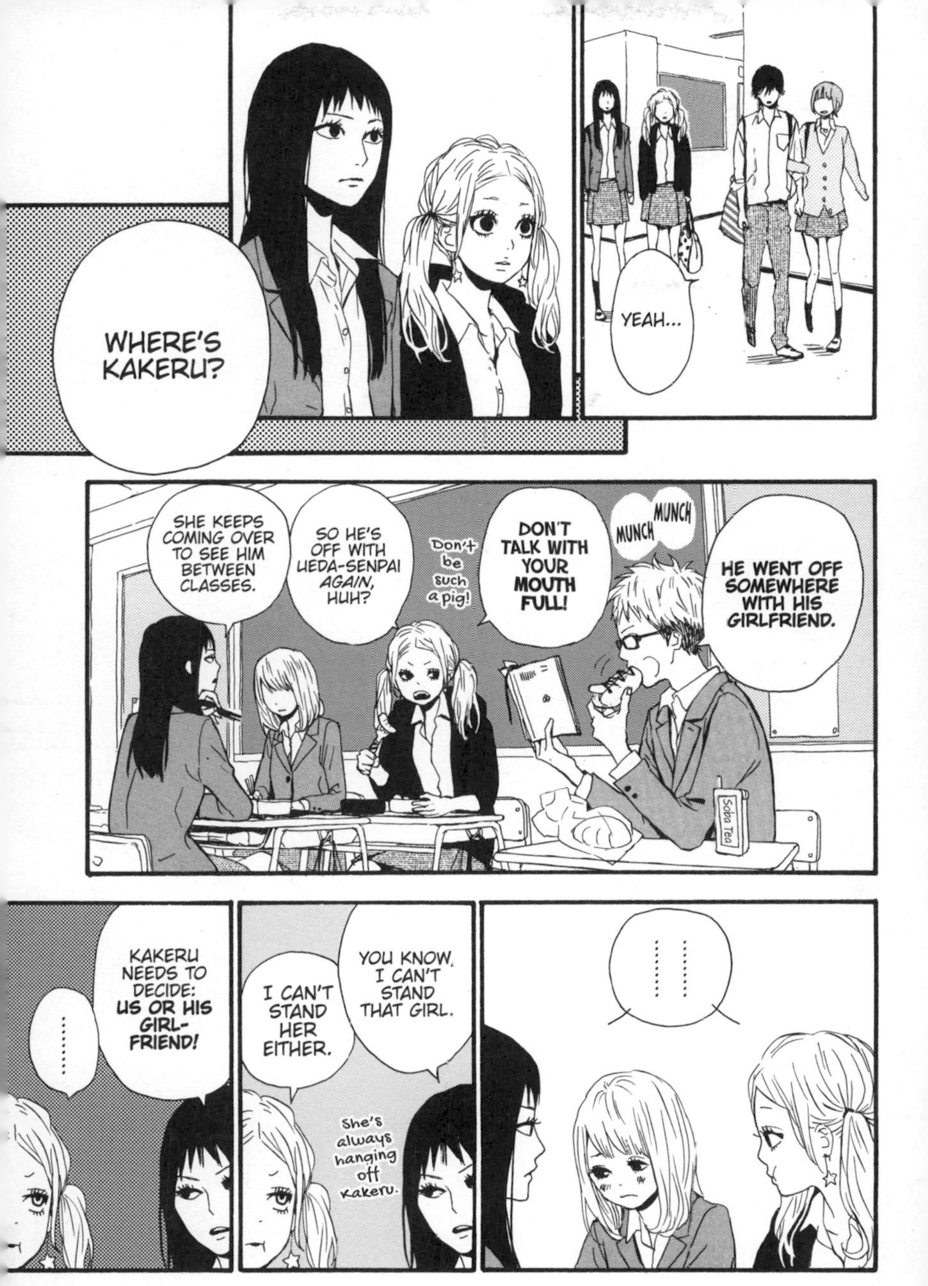
YEAH...
WHERE'S KAKERU?
HE WENT OFF SOMEWHERE WITH HIS GIRLFRIEND.
MUNCH MUNCH
DON'T TALK WITH YOUR MOUTH FULL!
Don't be such a pig!
SO HE'S OFF WITH UEDA-SENPAI AGAIN, HUH?
SHE KEEPS COMING OVER TO SEE HIM BETWEEN CLASSES.
......
YOU KNOW, I CAN'T STAND THAT GIRL.
I CAN'T STAND HER EITHER.
She's always hanging off Kakeru.
KAKERU NEEDS TO DECIDE: US OR HIS GIRLFRIEND!
......

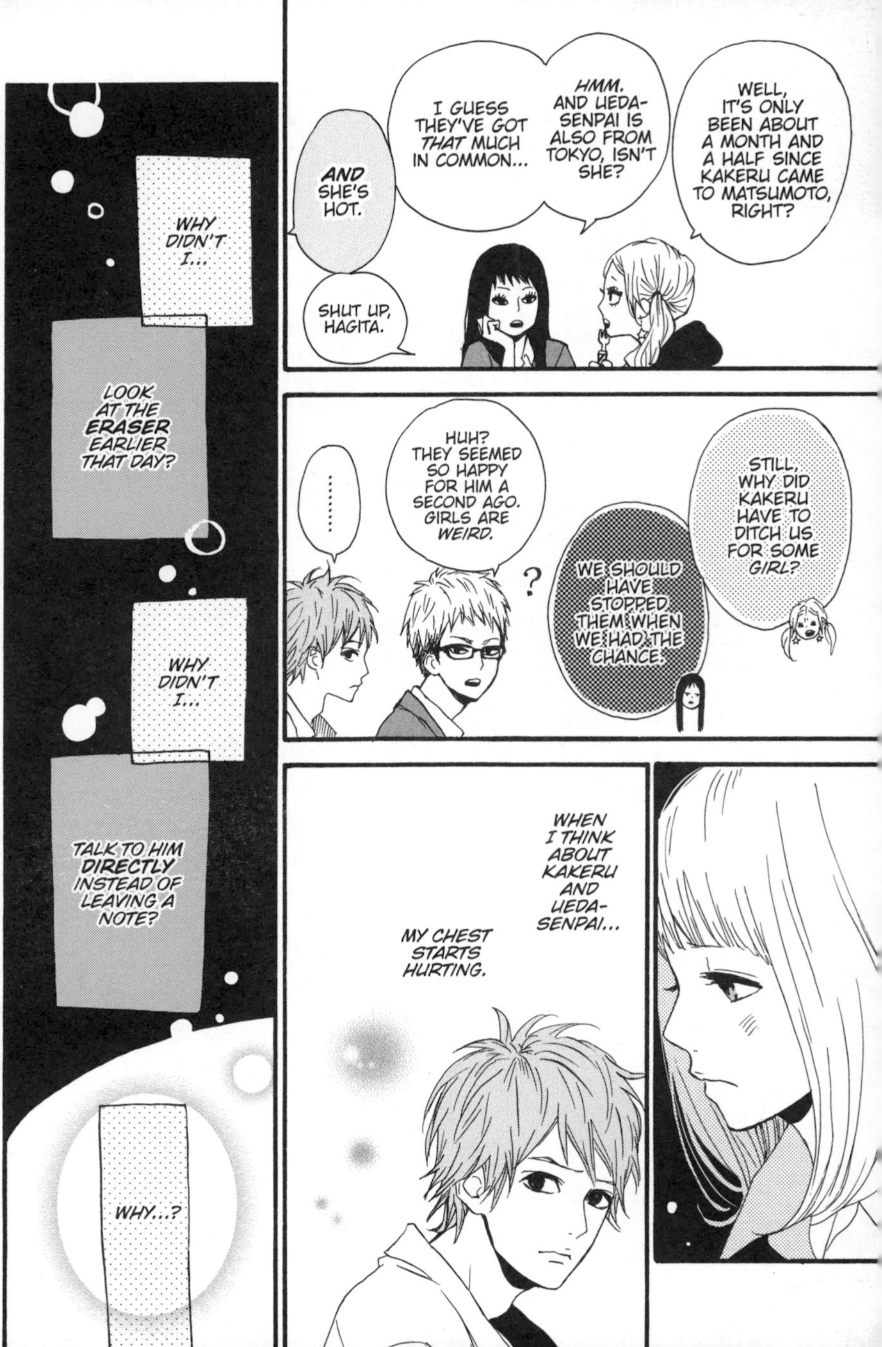
WELL, IT'S ONLY BEEN ABOUT A MONTH AND A HALF SINCE KAKERU CAME TO MATSUMOTO, RIGHT?
HMM. AND UEDA-SENPAI IS ALSO FROM TOKYO, ISN'T SHE?
I GUESS THEY'VE GOT THAT MUCH IN COMMON...
AND SHE'S HOT.
SHUT UP, HAGITA.
STILL, WHY DID KAKERU HAVE TO DITCH US FOR SOME GIRL?
WE SHOULD HAVE STOPPED THEM WHEN WE HAD THE CHANCE.
HUH? THEY SEEMED SO HAPPY FOR HIM A SECOND AGO. GIRLS ARE WEIRD.
?
......
WHEN I THINK ABOUT KAKERU AND UEDA-SENPAI...
MY CHEST STARTS HURTING.
WHY DIDN'T I...
LOOK AT THE ERASER EARLIER THAT DAY?
WHY DIDN'T I...
TALK TO HIM DIRECTLY INSTEAD OF LEAVING A NOTE?
WHY...?

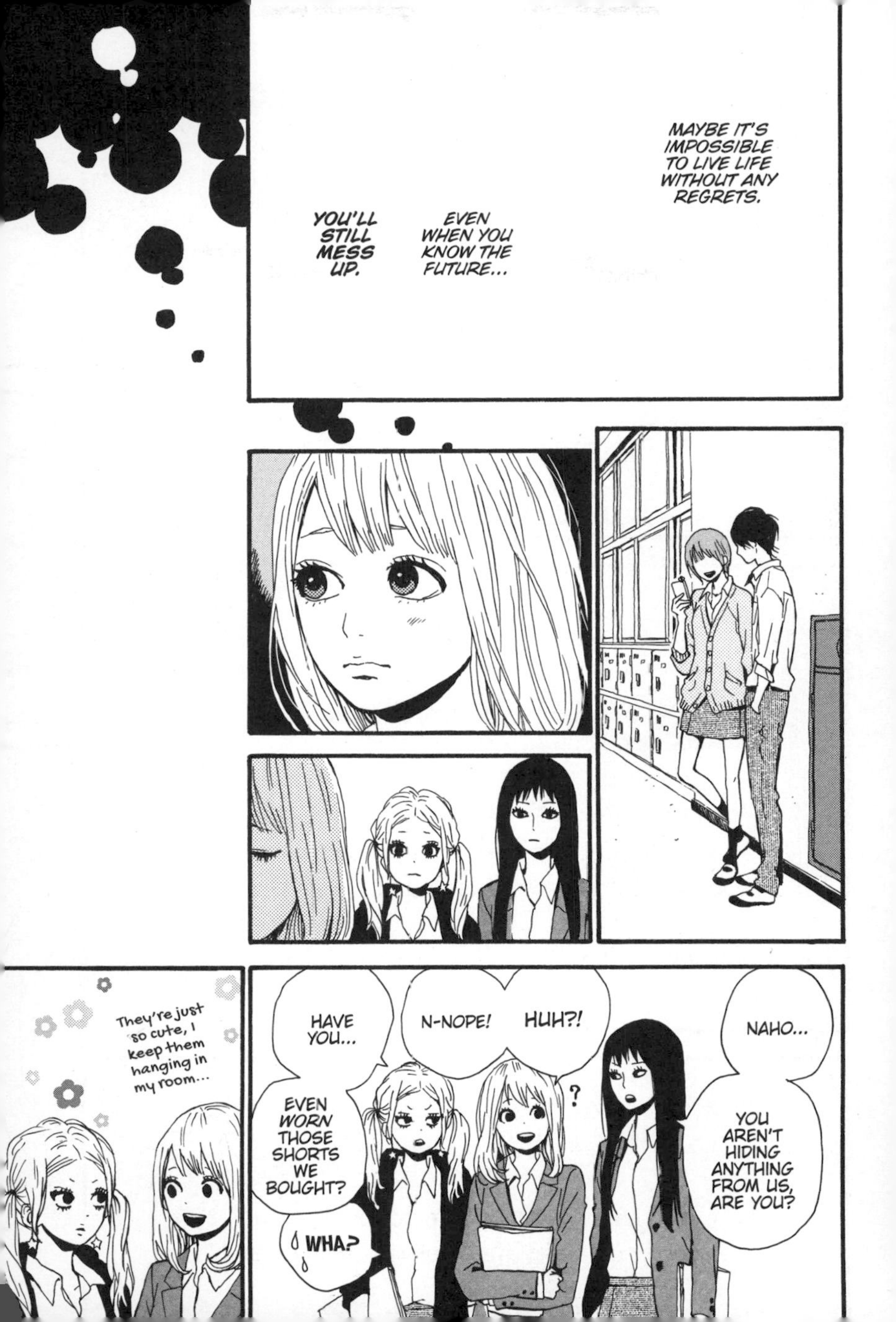
MAYBE IT'S IMPOSSIBLE TO LIVE LIFE WITHOUT ANY REGRETS.
EVEN WHEN YOU KNOW THE FUTURE...
YOU'LL STILL MESS UP.
NAHO...
YOU AREN'T HIDING ANYTHING FROM US, ARE YOU?
HUH?!
N-NOPE!
?
HAVE YOU...
EVEN WORN THOSE SHORTS WE BOUGHT?
WHA?
They're just so cute, I keep them hanging in my room...

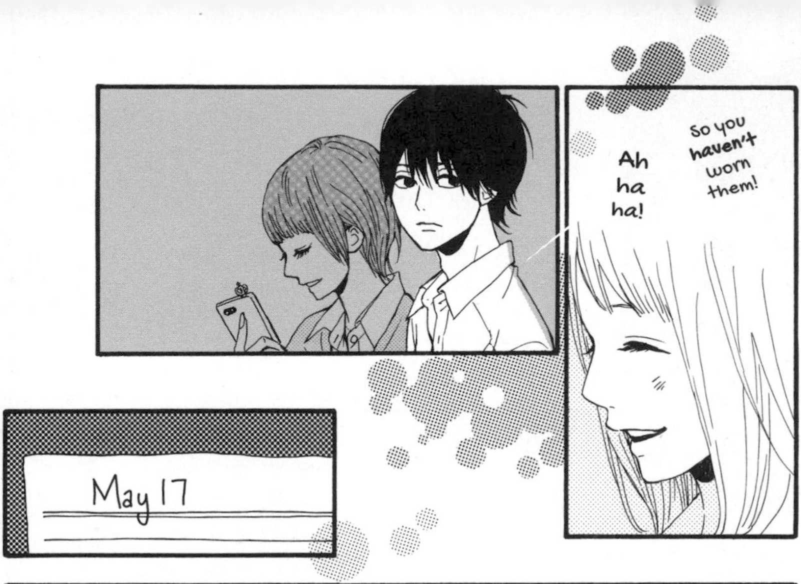
So you haven't worn them!
Ah ha ha!
May 17

May 17

- Since Kakeru and Ueda-senpai began dating, Kakeru and I don't talk as much anymore.
- Today was the first time. Kakeru called out to me at lunch time, but I spotted Ueda-senpai and turned my back to him and pretended I didn't hear him.
- It wouldn't be the last time I ignore Kakeru.

◎ If he calls out to you, I want you to respond, no matter what.

Don't just wait for him to call out to you; I want you to initiate a conversation as well.

I'm sure you'll think of something to say to him.

BUT IT'S HARD TO START A CONVERSATION...

WHEN HE'S ALWAYS WITH UEDA-SENPAI...

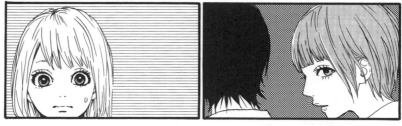

I'M NOT BRAVE ENOUGH TO TALK TO BOTH OF THEM.

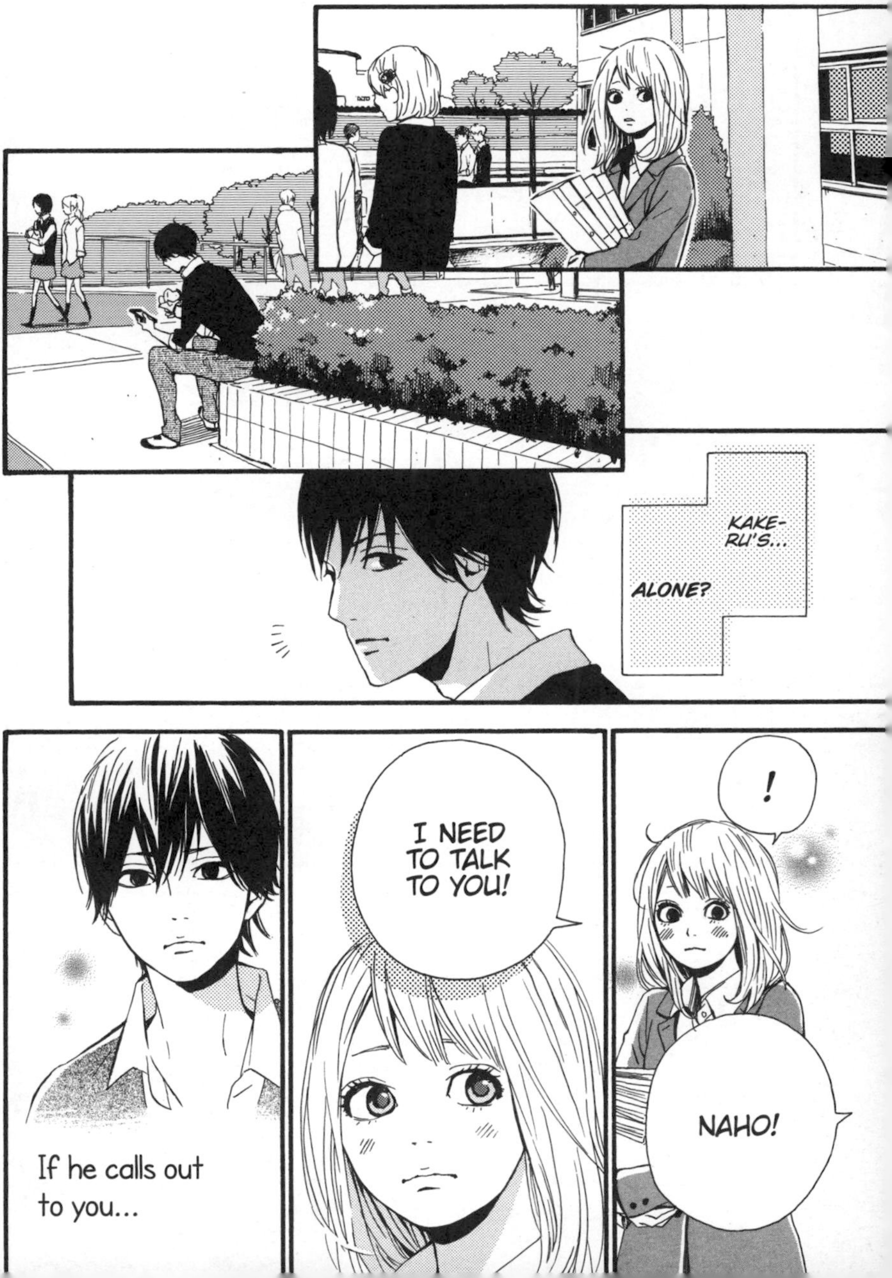
KAKE-RU'S...
ALONE?
!
NAHO!
I NEED TO TALK TO YOU!
If he calls out to you...

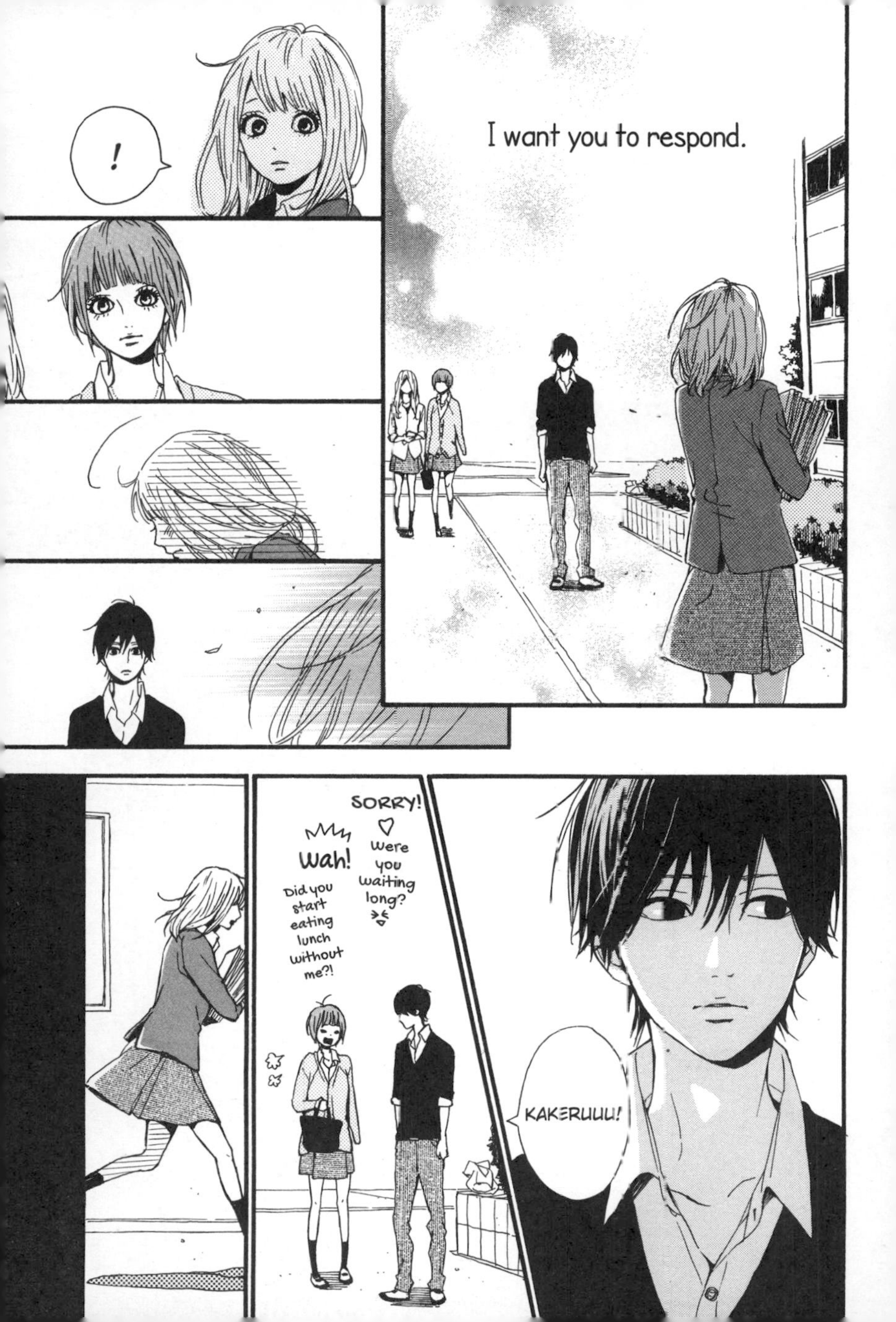
I want you to respond.
!
KAKERUUU!
SORRY!
Were you waiting long?
Wah!
Did you start eating lunch without me?!

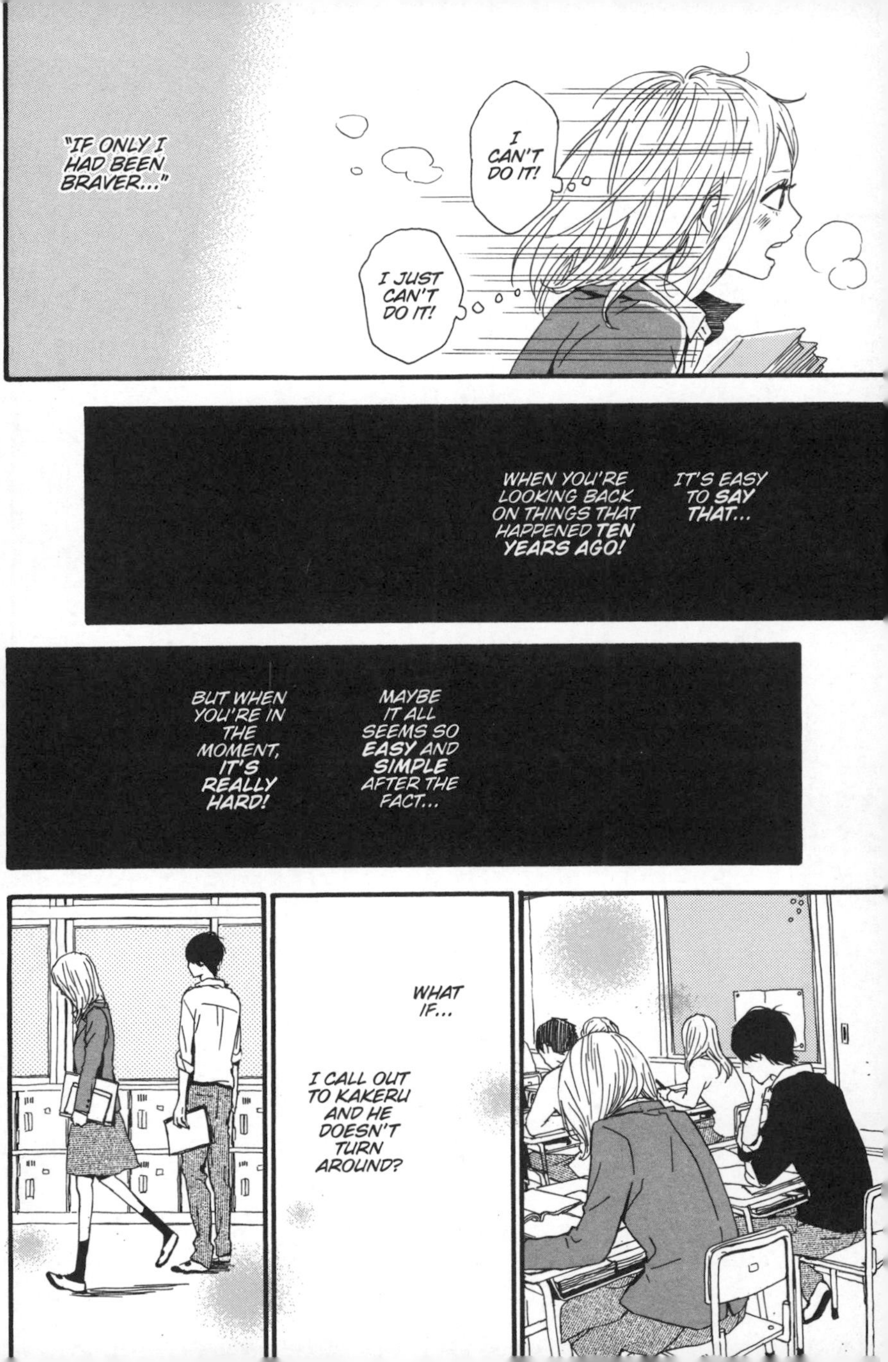
I CAN'T DO IT!
I JUST CAN'T DO IT!
"IF ONLY I HAD BEEN BRAVER..."
IT'S EASY TO SAY THAT...
WHEN YOU'RE LOOKING BACK ON THINGS THAT HAPPENED TEN YEARS AGO!
MAYBE IT ALL SEEMS SO EASY AND SIMPLE AFTER THE FACT...
BUT WHEN YOU'RE IN THE MOMENT, IT'S REALLY HARD!
WHAT IF...
I CALL OUT TO KAKERU AND HE DOESN'T TURN AROUND?

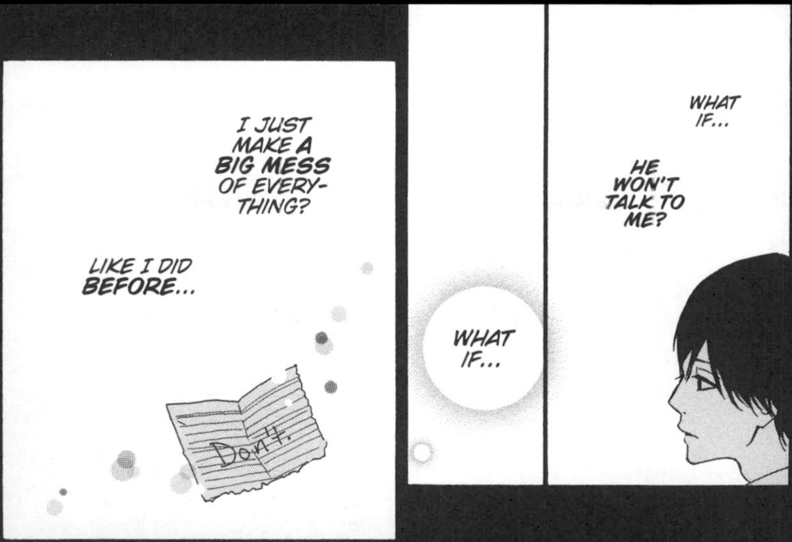
WHAT IF...
HE WON'T TALK TO ME?
WHAT IF...
I JUST MAKE A BIG MESS OF EVERYTHING?
LIKE I DID BEFORE...
Don't.

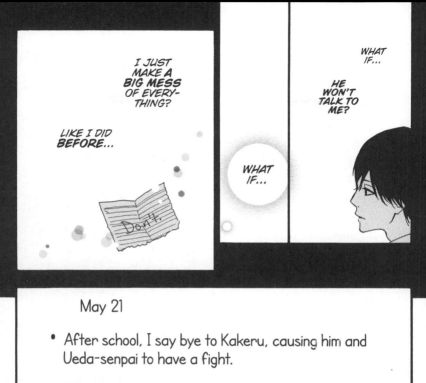

May 21

- After school, I say bye to Kakeru, causing him and Ueda-senpai to have a fight.
- I feel bad about it and I run home without talking to Kakeru.
- Later, I learned that Kakeru was worried about something.

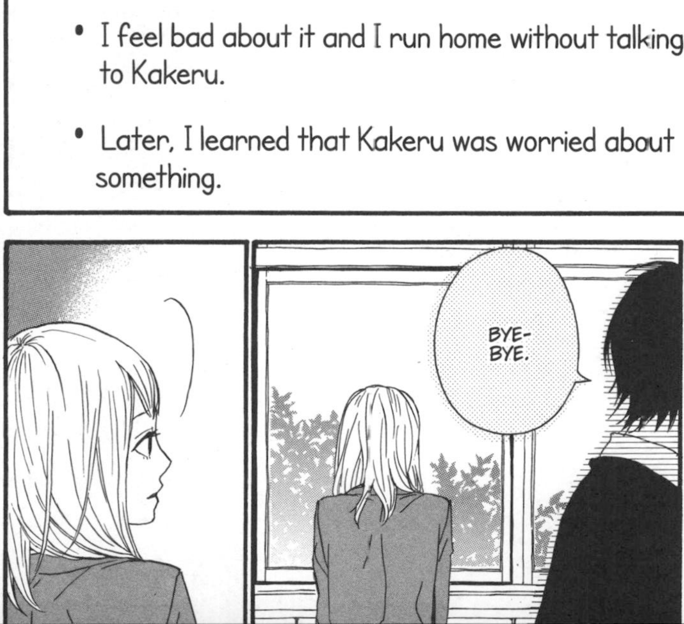
BYE-BYE.

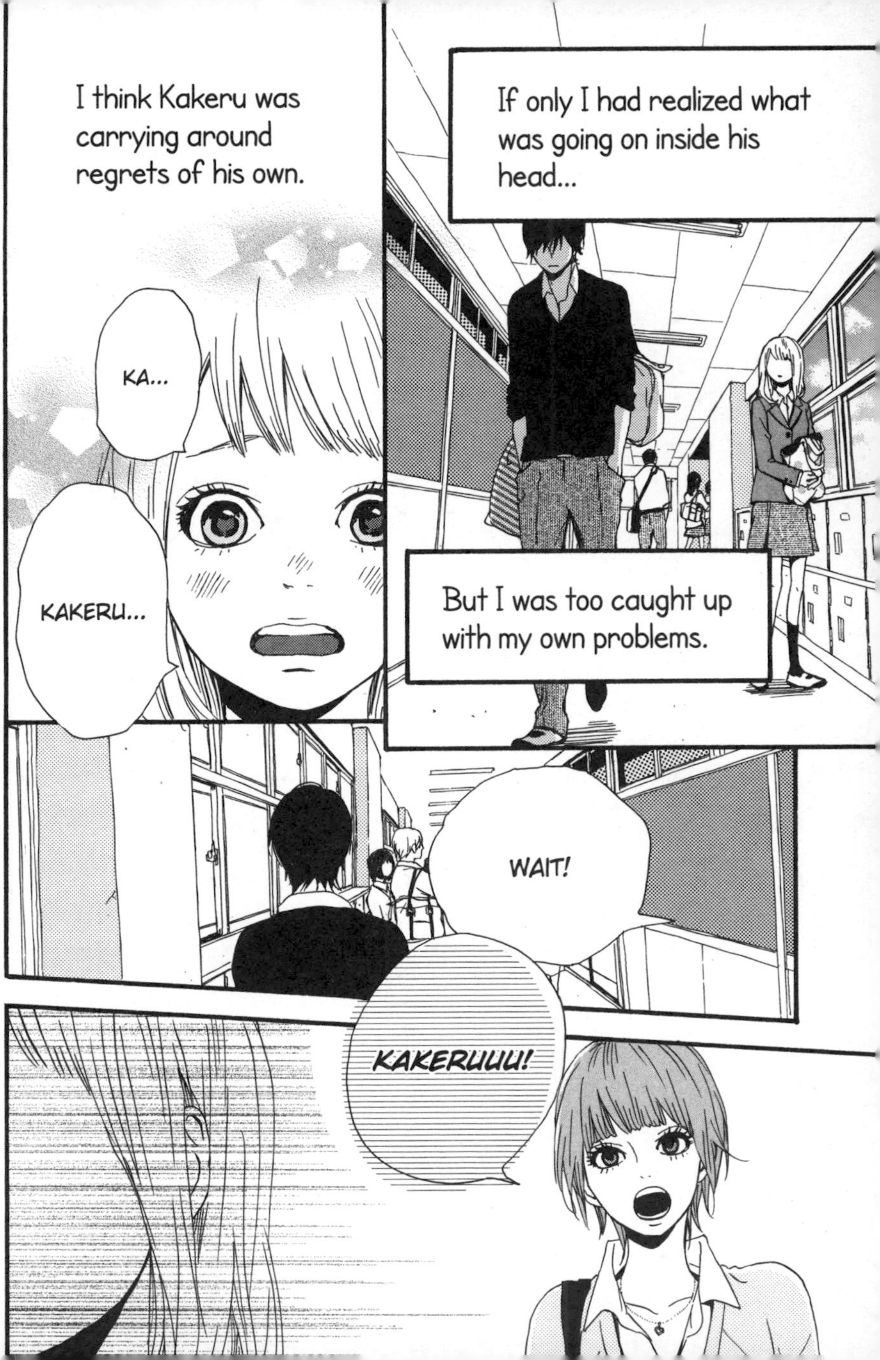
If only I had realized what was going on inside his head...
But I was too caught up with my own problems.
I think Kakeru was carrying around regrets of his own.
KA...
KAKERU...
WAIT!
KAKERUUU!

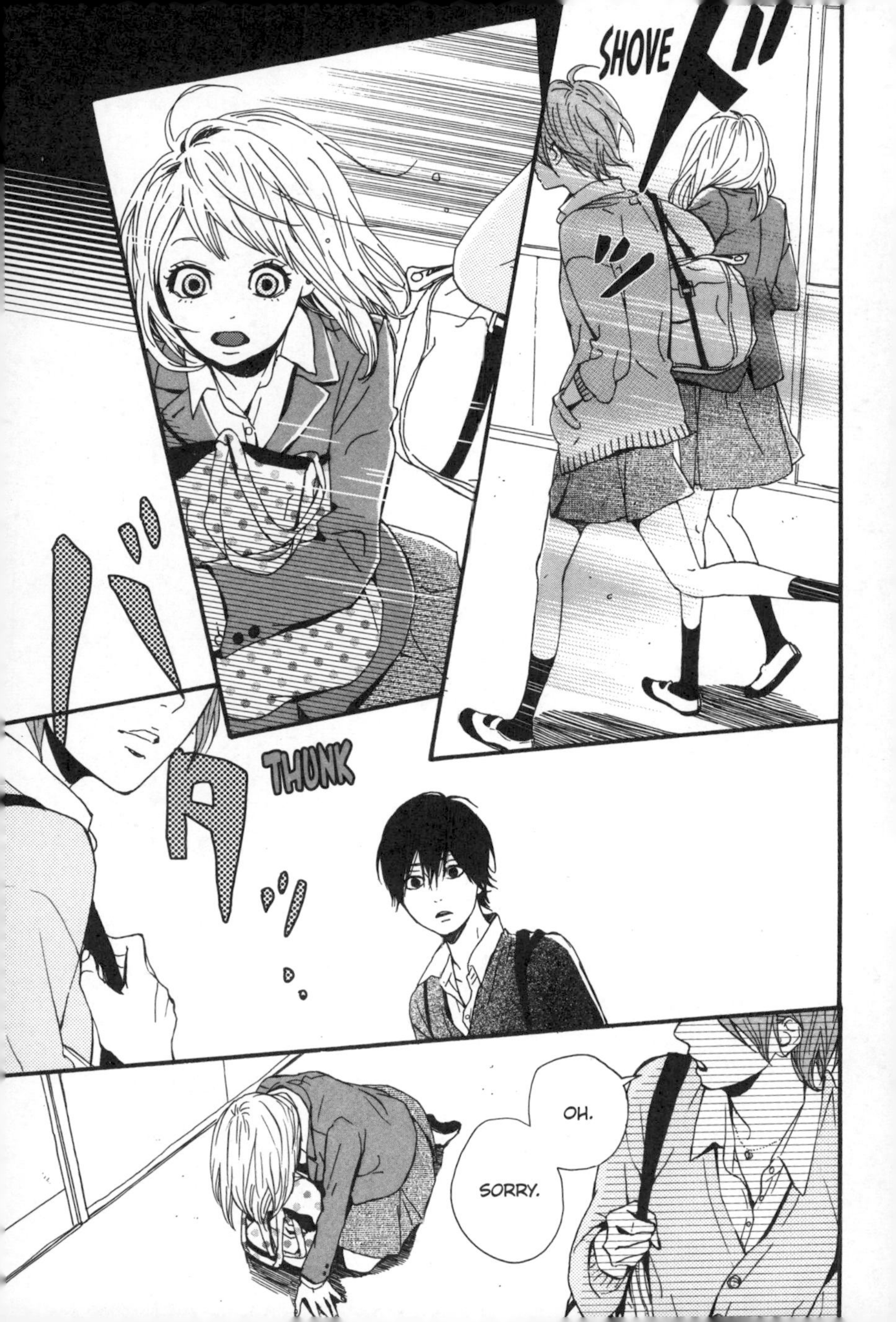
SHOVE
THUNK
OH.
SORRY.

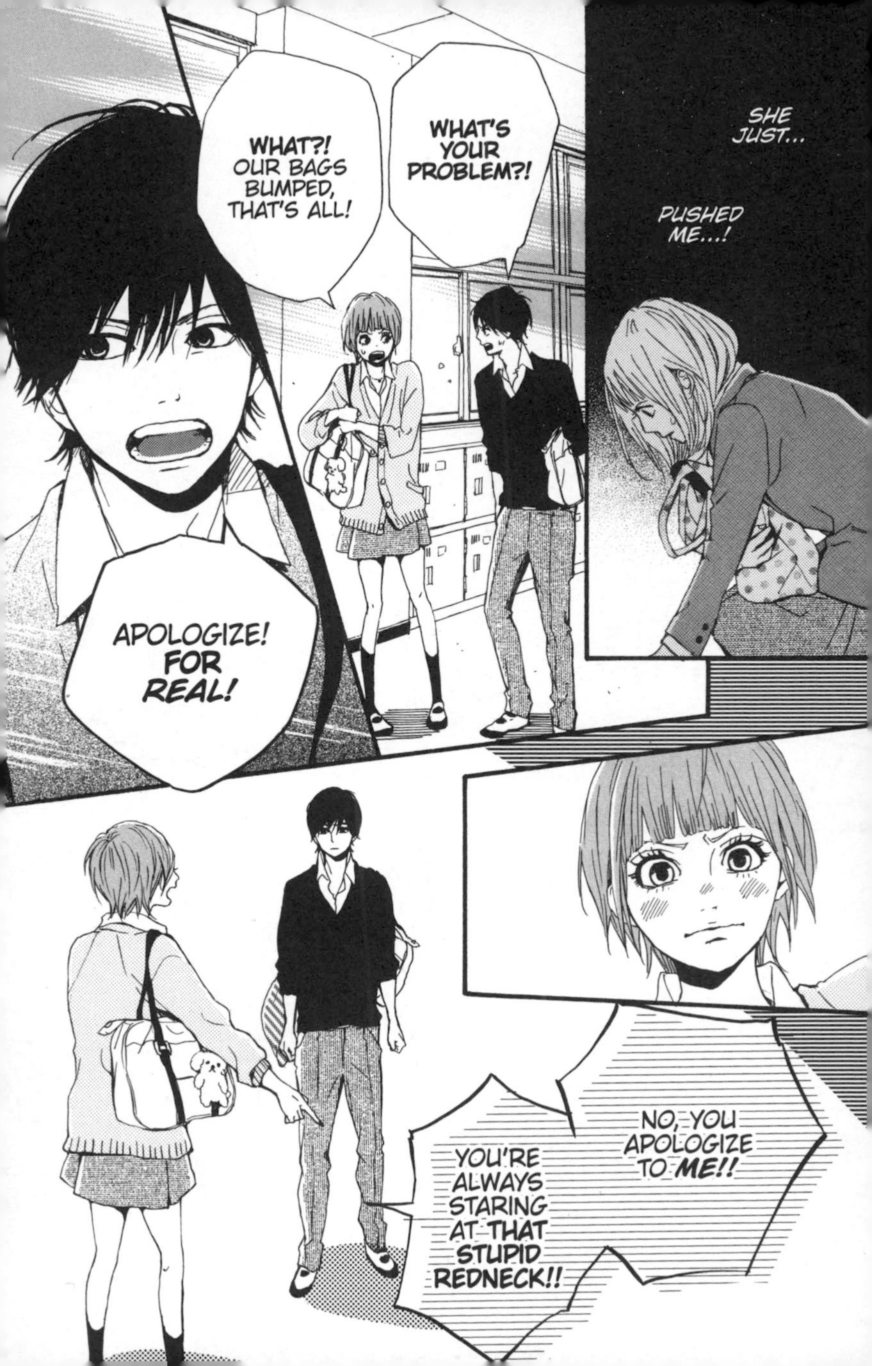
SHE JUST...
PUSHED ME...!
WHAT'S YOUR PROBLEM?!
WHAT?! OUR BAGS BUMPED, THAT'S ALL!
APOLOGIZE! FOR REAL!
NO, YOU APOLOGIZE TO ME!!
YOU'RE ALWAYS STARING AT THAT STUPID REDNECK!!

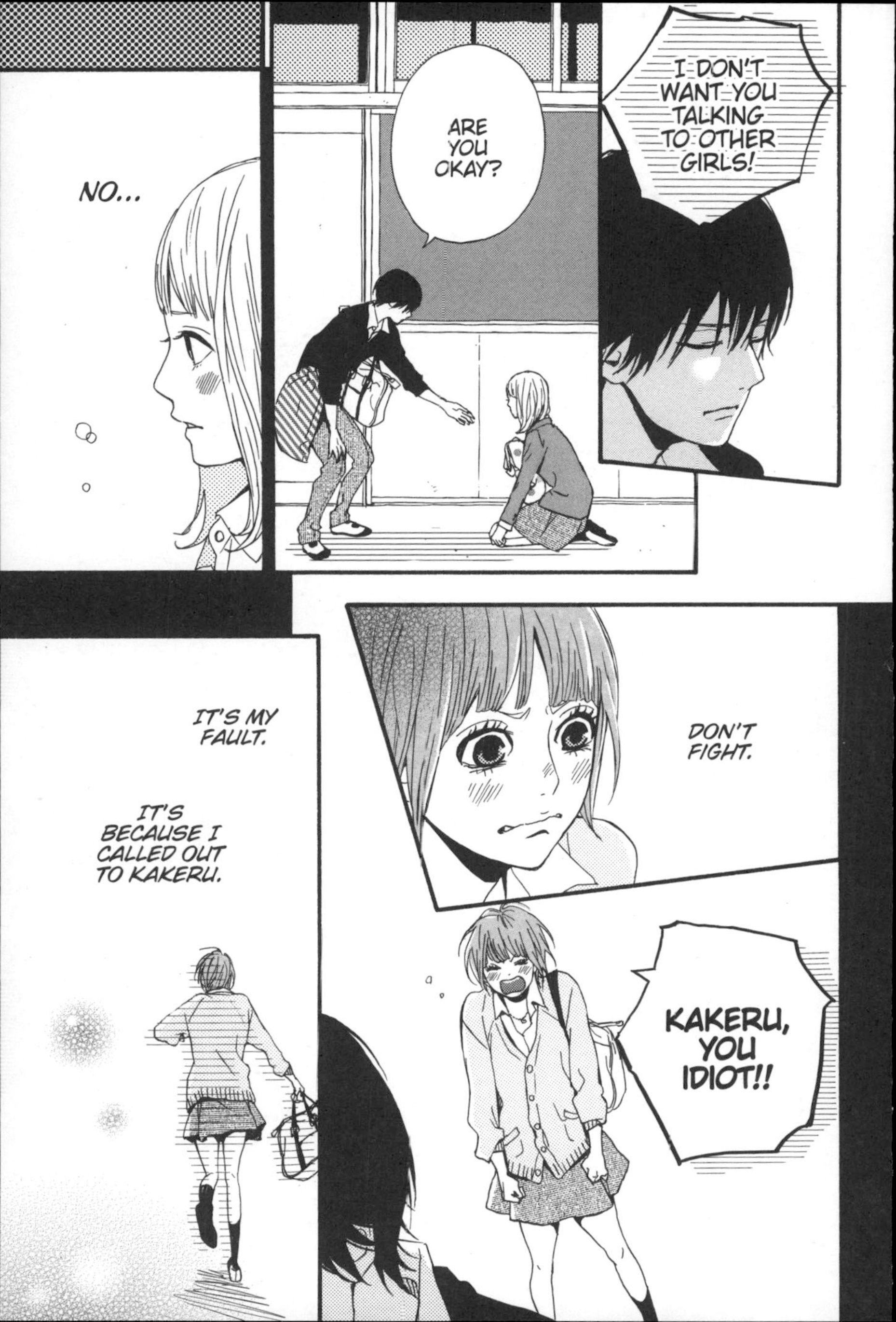

I DON'T WANT YOU TALKING TO OTHER GIRLS!
ARE YOU OKAY?
NO...
DON'T FIGHT.
KAKERU, YOU IDIOT!!
IT'S MY FAULT.
IT'S BECAUSE I CALLED OUT TO KAKERU.

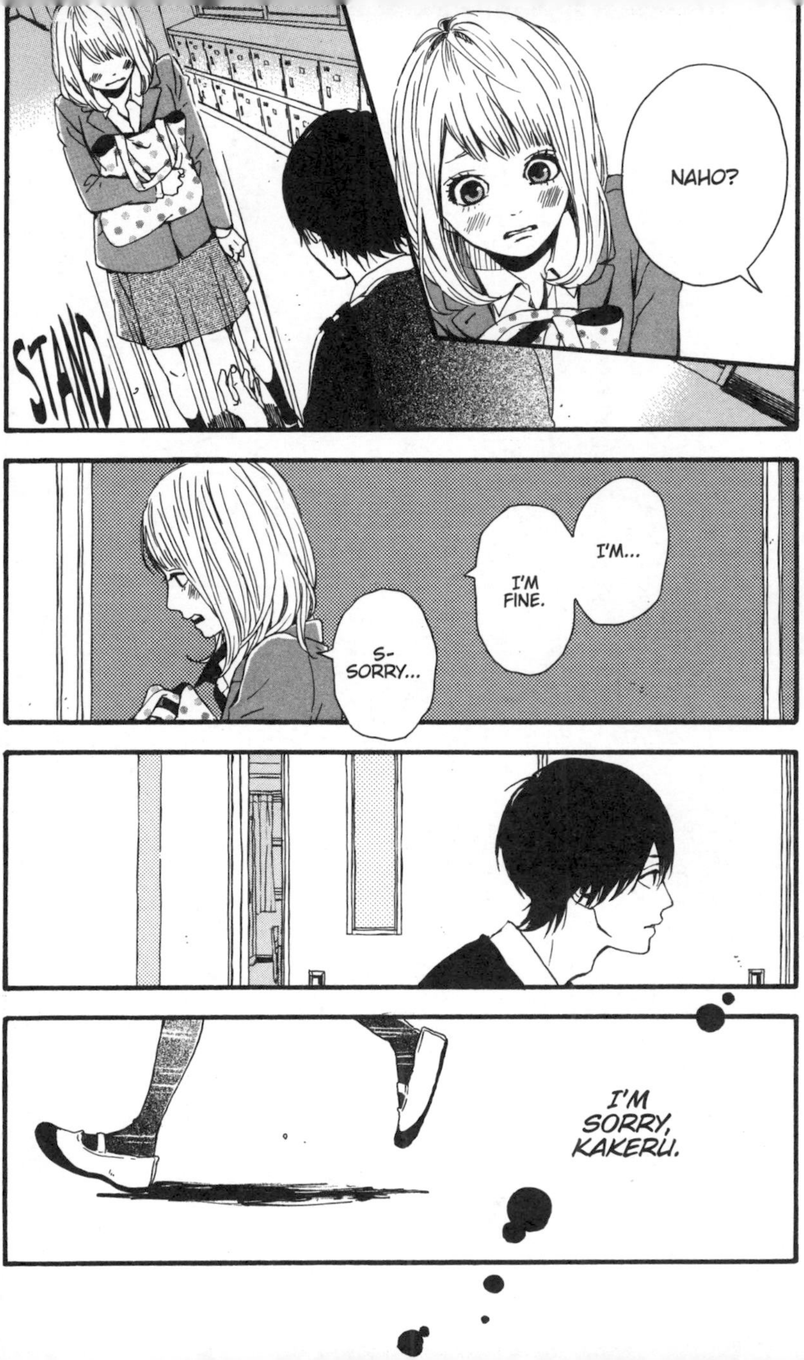
NAHO?
STAND
I'M... I'M FINE.
S- SORRY...
I'M SORRY, KAKERU.

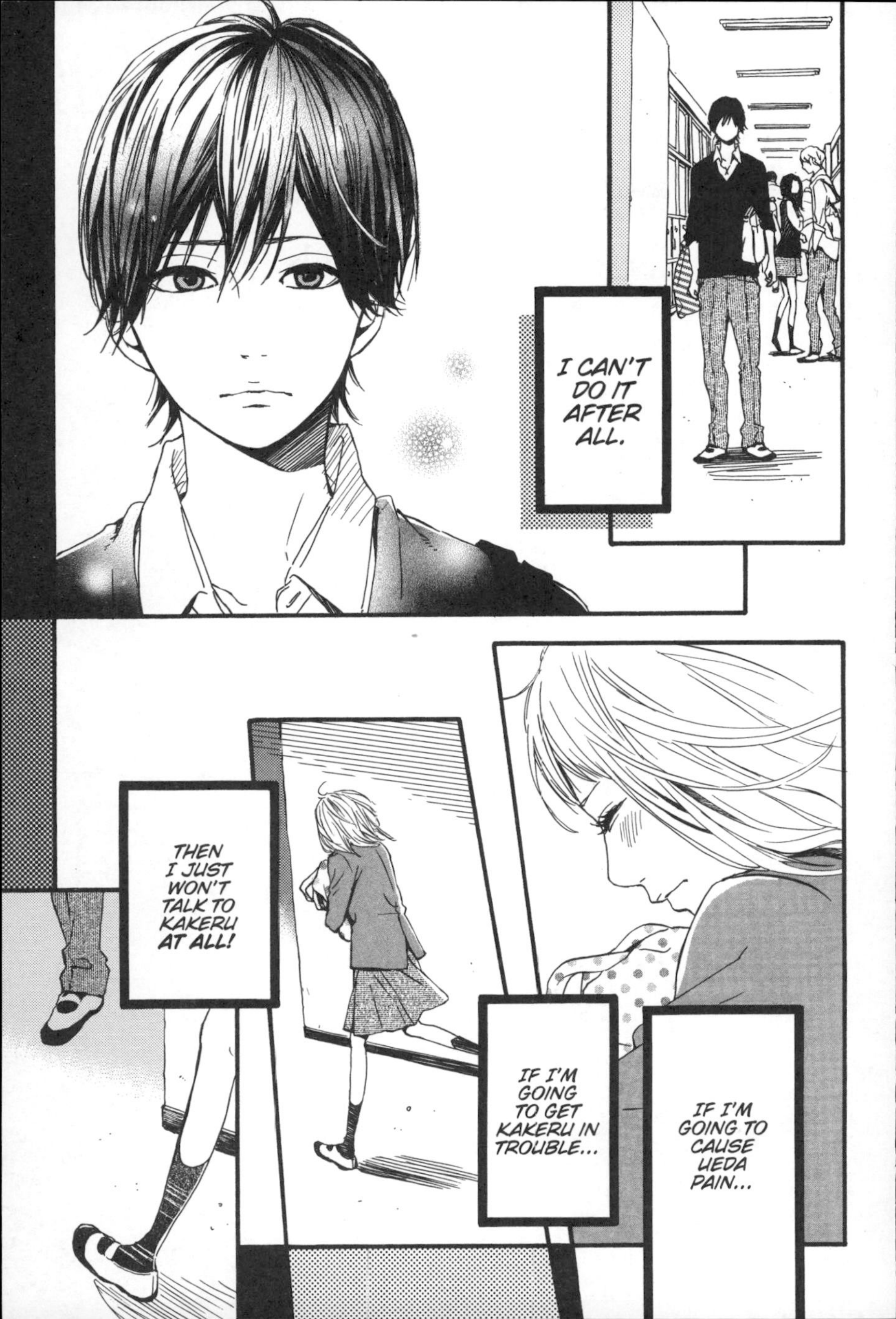
I CAN'T DO IT AFTER ALL.
IF I'M GOING TO CAUSE UEDA PAIN...
IF I'M GOING TO GET KAKERU IN TROUBLE...
THEN I JUST WON'T TALK TO KAKERU AT ALL!

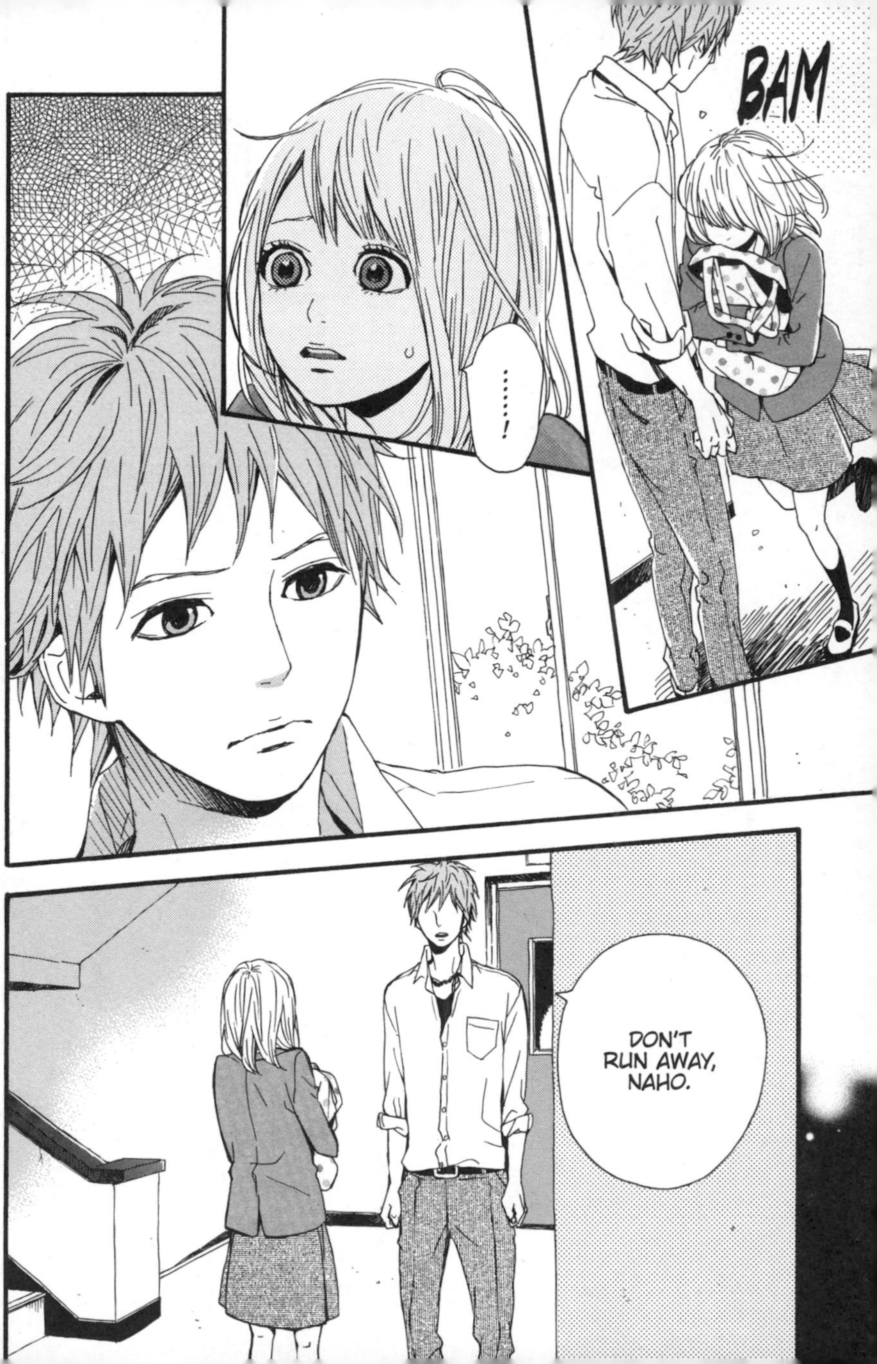
BAM
......!
DON'T RUN AWAY, NAHO.

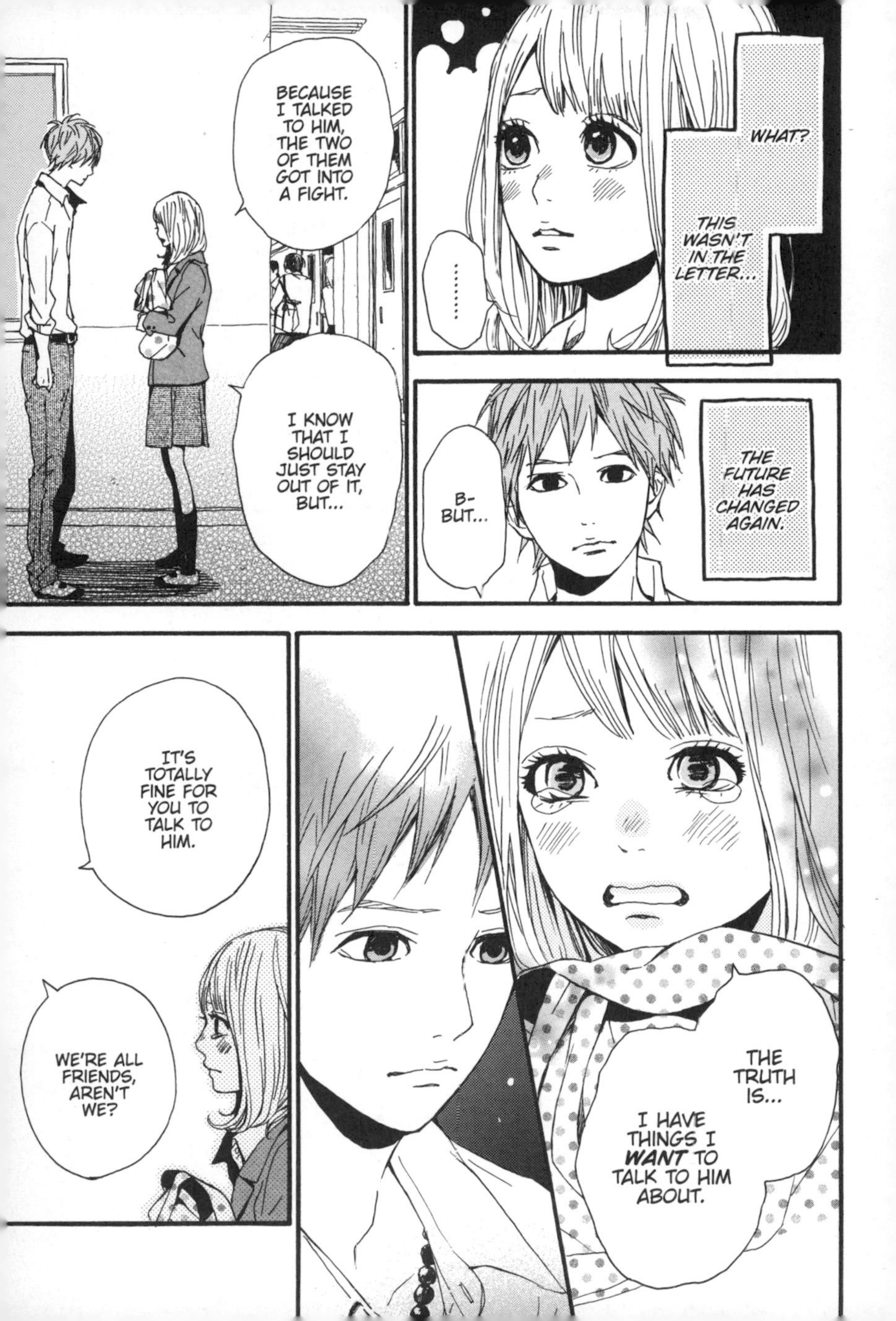
WHAT?
THIS WASN'T IN THE LETTER...
......
THE FUTURE HAS CHANGED AGAIN.
B-BUT...
BECAUSE I TALKED TO HIM, THE TWO OF THEM GOT INTO A FIGHT.
I KNOW THAT I SHOULD JUST STAY OUT OF IT, BUT...
THE TRUTH IS...
I HAVE THINGS I **WANT** TO TALK TO HIM ABOUT.
IT'S TOTALLY FINE FOR YOU TO TALK TO HIM.
WE'RE ALL FRIENDS, AREN'T WE?

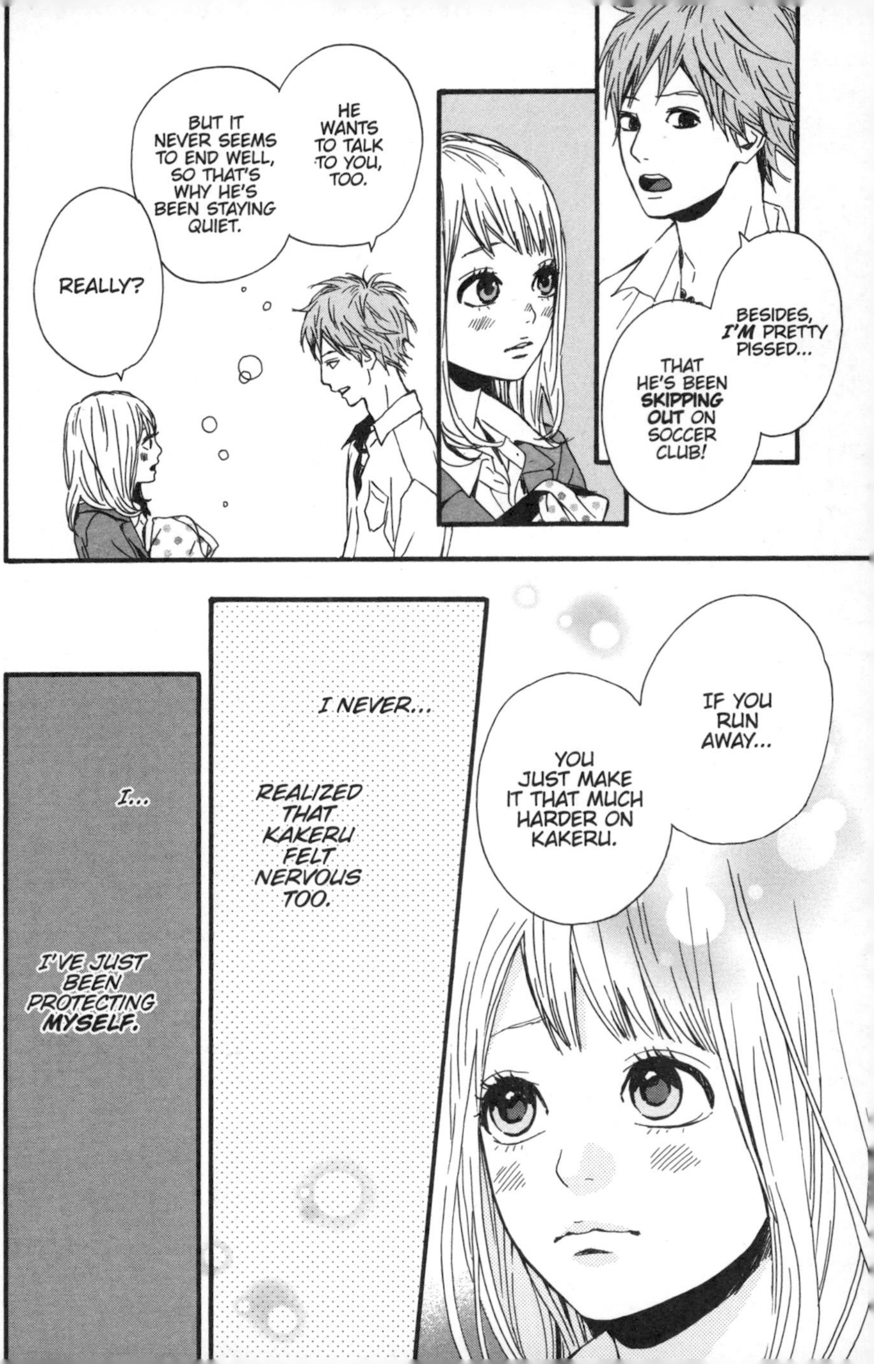
HE WANTS TO TALK TO YOU, TOO.
BUT IT NEVER SEEMS TO END WELL, SO THAT'S WHY HE'S BEEN STAYING QUIET.
REALLY?
BESIDES, *I'M* PRETTY PISSED...
THAT HE'S BEEN **SKIPPING OUT** ON SOCCER CLUB!
IF YOU RUN AWAY...
YOU JUST MAKE IT THAT MUCH HARDER ON KAKERU.
I NEVER...
REALIZED THAT KAKERU FELT NERVOUS TOO.
I...
I'VE JUST BEEN PROTECTING **MYSELF.**

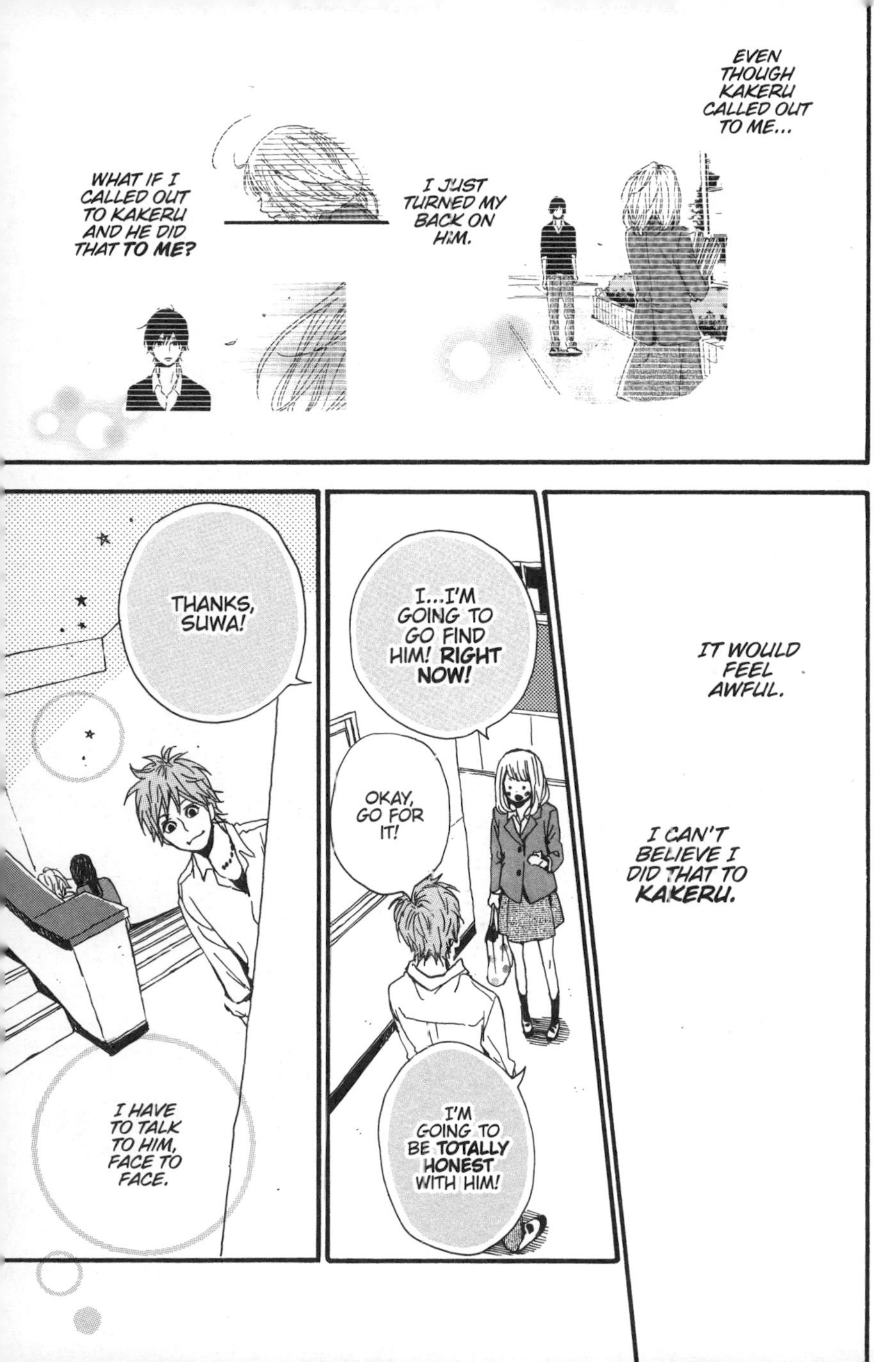
EVEN THOUGH KAKERU CALLED OUT TO ME...
I JUST TURNED MY BACK ON HIM.
WHAT IF I CALLED OUT TO KAKERU AND HE DID THAT TO ME?
IT WOULD FEEL AWFUL.
I CAN'T BELIEVE I DID THAT TO KAKERU.
I...I'M GOING TO GO FIND HIM! RIGHT NOW!
OKAY, GO FOR IT!
I'M GOING TO BE TOTALLY HONEST WITH HIM!
THANKS, SUWA!
I HAVE TO TALK TO HIM, FACE TO FACE.

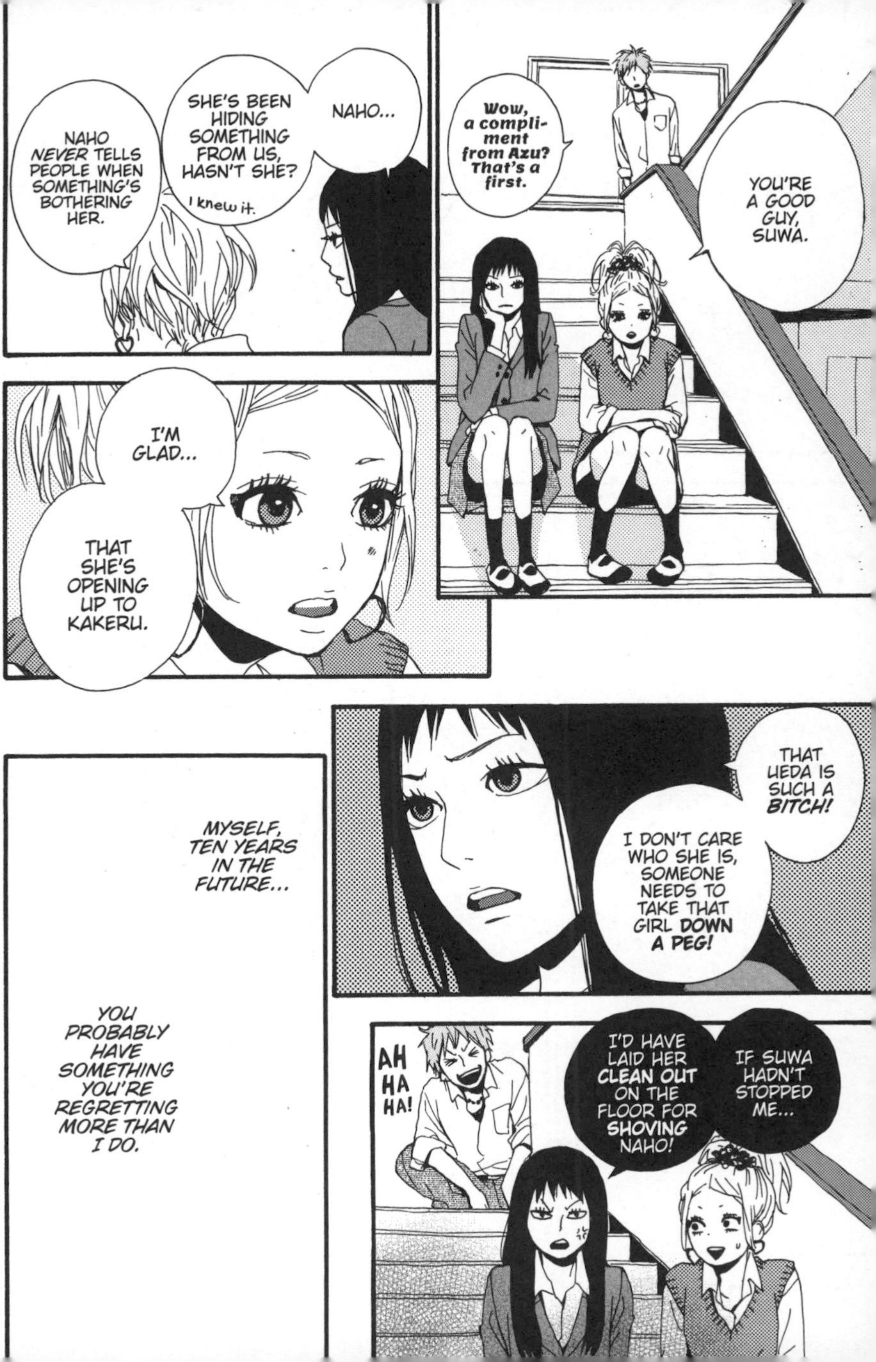
YOU'RE A GOOD GUY, SUWA.
Wow, a compliment from Azu? That's a first.
NAHO...
SHE'S BEEN HIDING SOMETHING FROM US, HASN'T SHE?
I knew it.
NAHO NEVER TELLS PEOPLE WHEN SOMETHING'S BOTHERING HER.
I'M GLAD...
THAT SHE'S OPENING UP TO KAKERU.
THAT UEDA IS SUCH A BITCH!
I DON'T CARE WHO SHE IS, SOMEONE NEEDS TO TAKE THAT GIRL DOWN A PEG!
IF SUWA HADN'T STOPPED ME...
I'D HAVE LAID HER CLEAN OUT ON THE FLOOR FOR SHOVING NAHO!
AH HA HA!
MYSELF, TEN YEARS IN THE FUTURE...
YOU PROBABLY HAVE SOMETHING YOU'RE REGRETTING MORE THAN I DO.

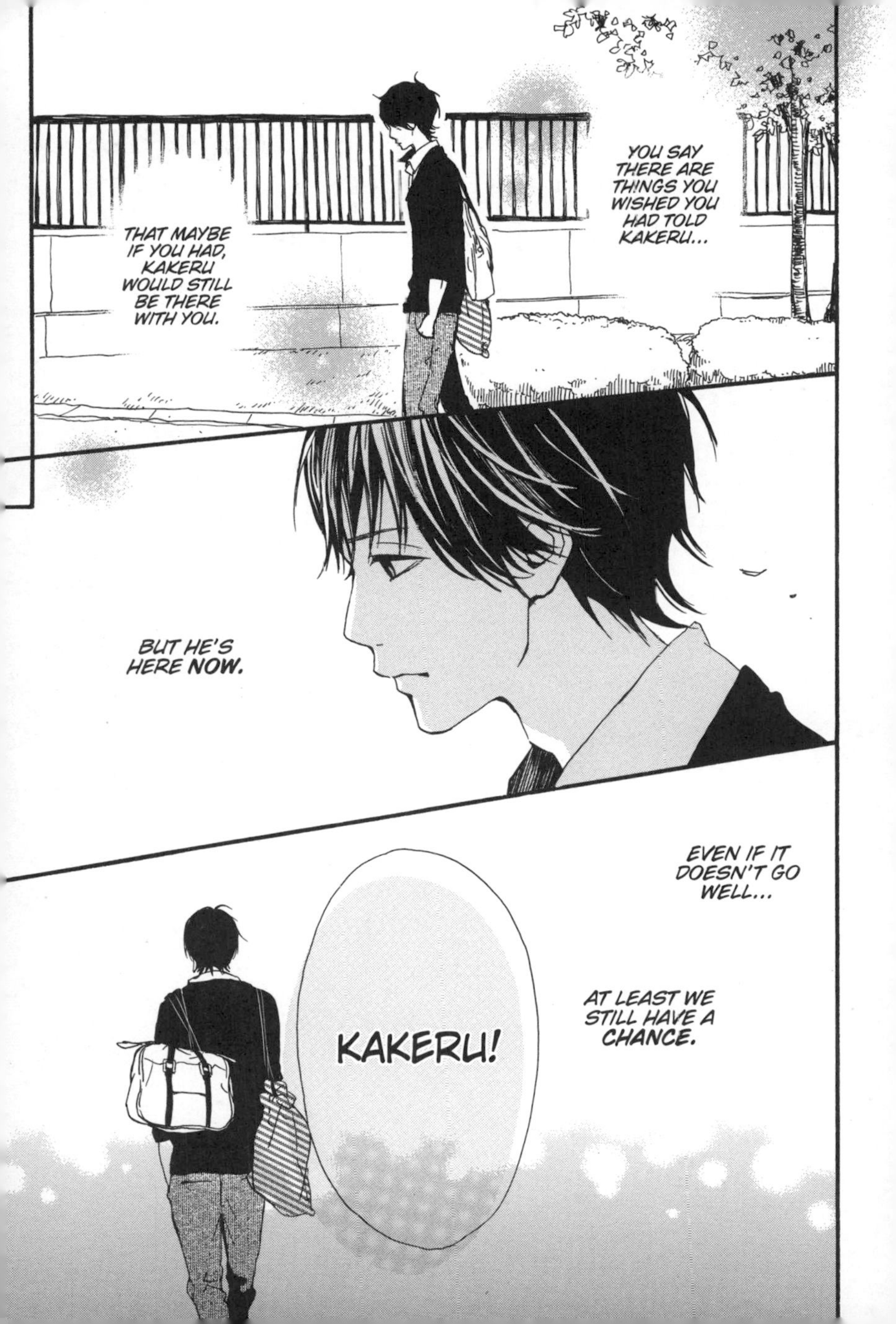
YOU SAY THERE ARE THINGS YOU WISHED YOU HAD TOLD KAKERU...
THAT MAYBE IF YOU HAD, KAKERU WOULD STILL BE THERE WITH YOU.
BUT HE'S HERE NOW.
EVEN IF IT DOESN'T GO WELL...
AT LEAST WE STILL HAVE A CHANCE.
KAKERU!

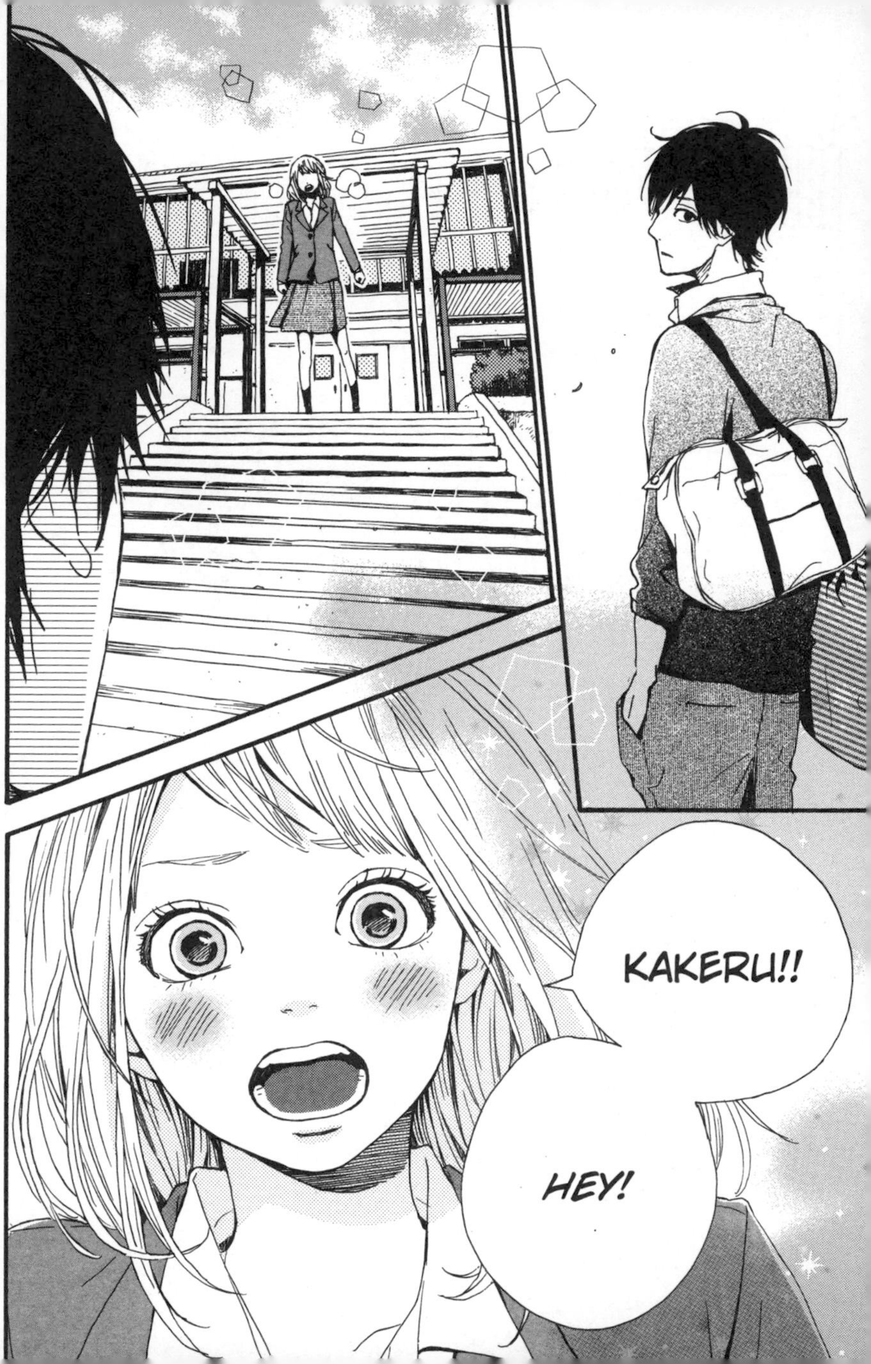
KAKERU!!
HEY!

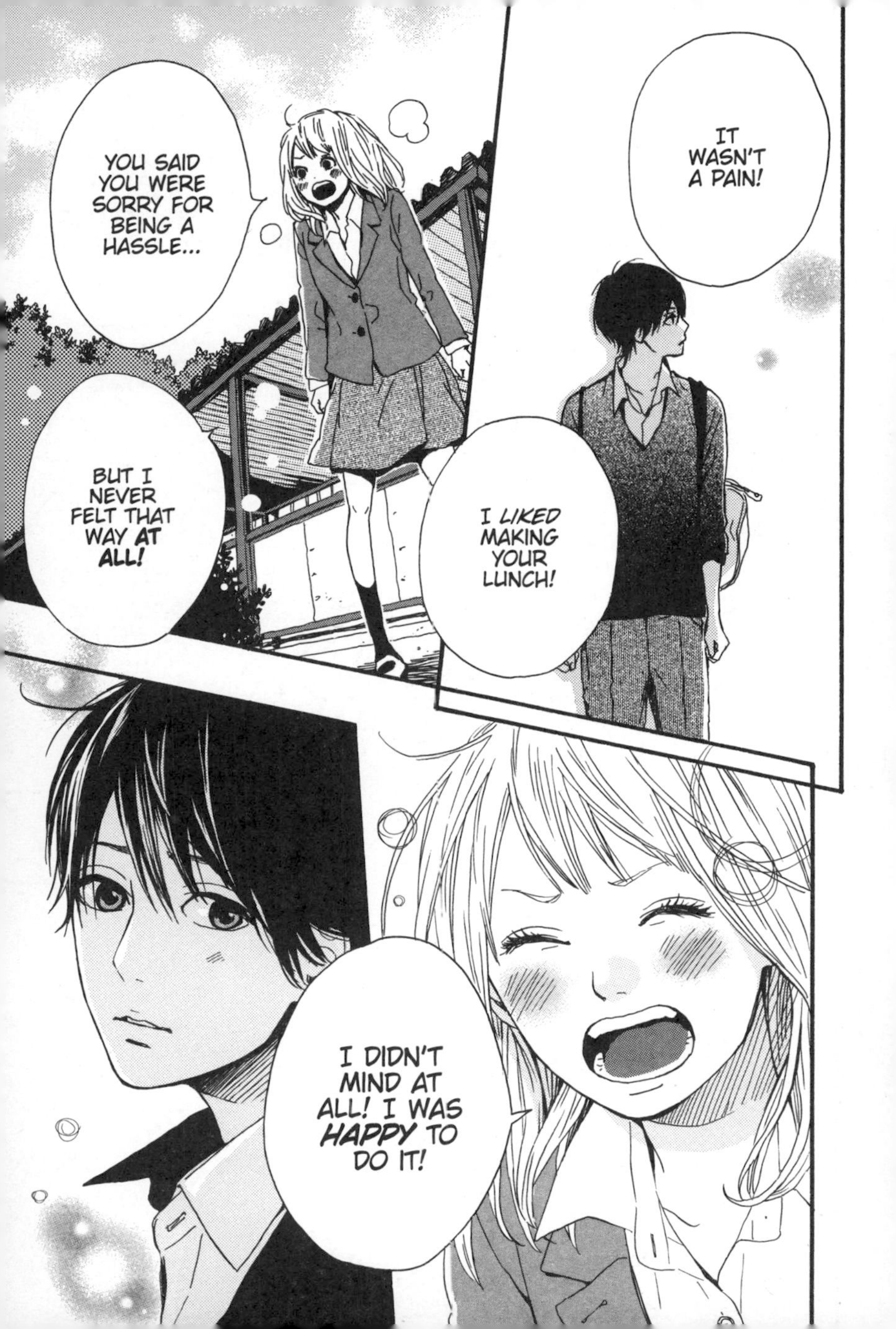
IT WASN'T A PAIN!
I *LIKED* MAKING YOUR LUNCH!
YOU SAID YOU WERE SORRY FOR BEING A HASSLE...
BUT I NEVER FELT THAT WAY **AT ALL!**
I DIDN'T MIND AT ALL! I WAS ***HAPPY*** TO DO IT!

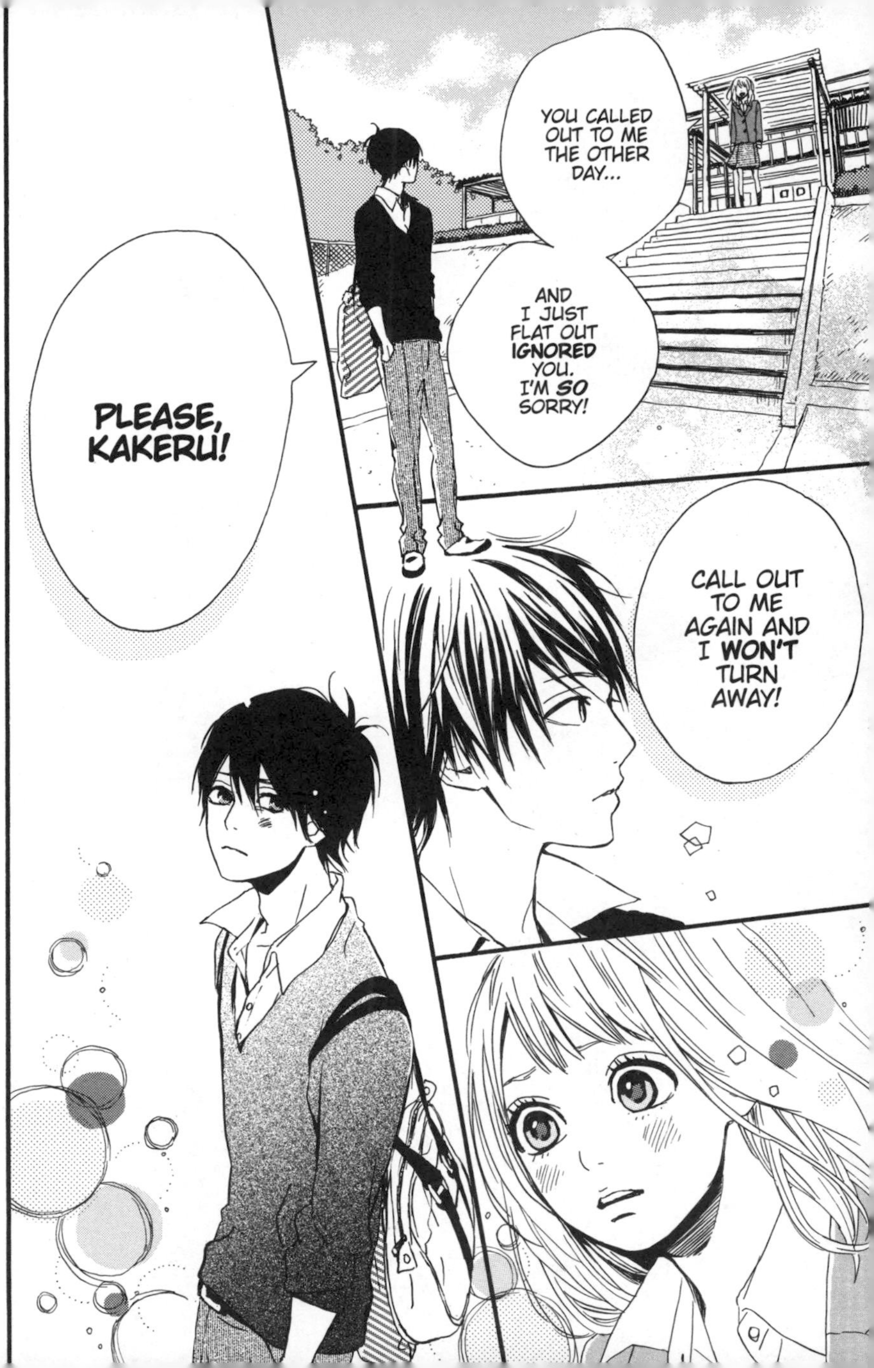
YOU CALLED OUT TO ME THE OTHER DAY...
AND I JUST FLAT OUT **IGNORED** YOU. I'M **SO** SORRY!
CALL OUT TO ME AGAIN AND I **WON'T** TURN AWAY!
PLEASE, KAKERU!

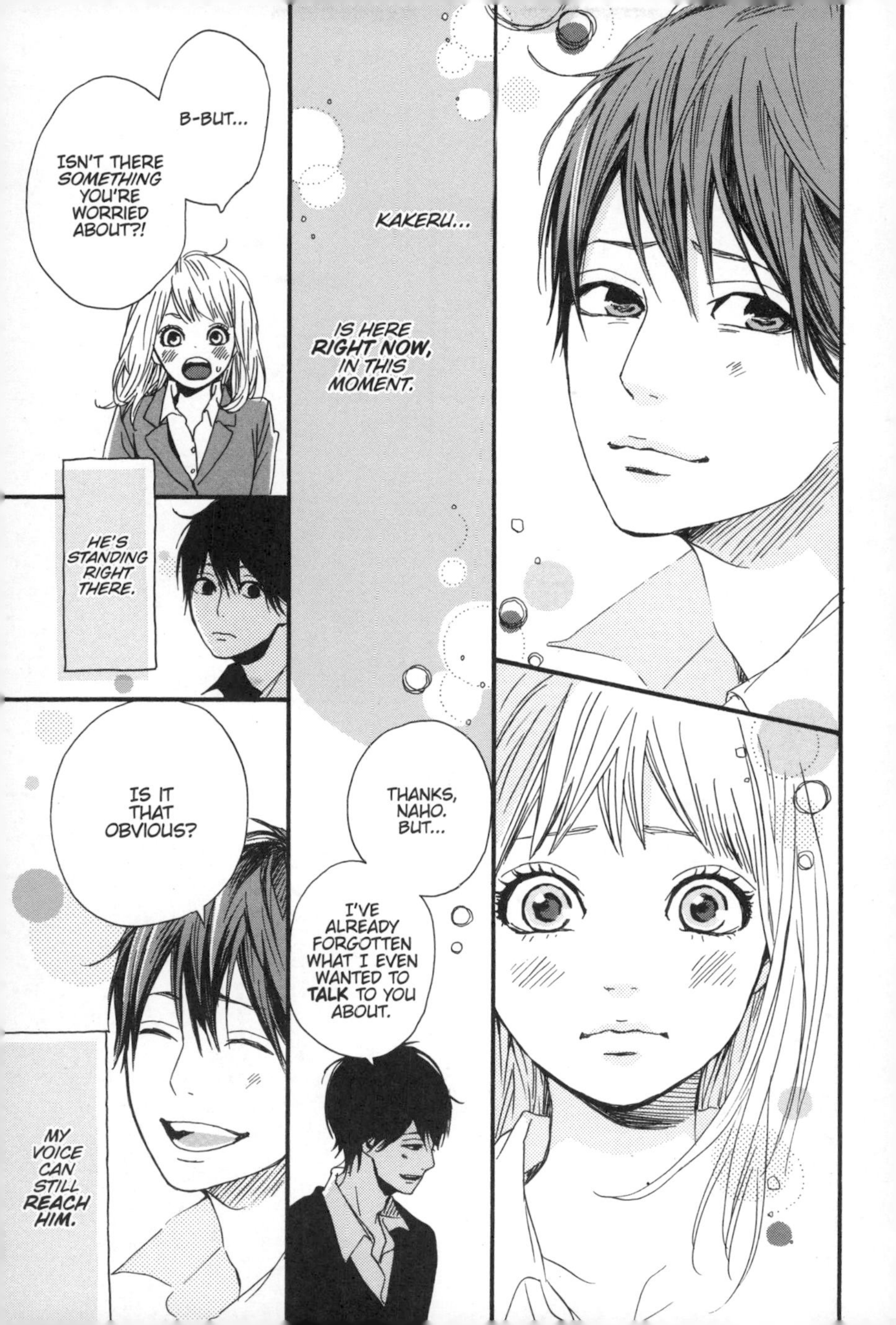
KAKERU...
IS HERE RIGHT NOW, IN THIS MOMENT.
THANKS, NAHO. BUT...
I'VE ALREADY FORGOTTEN WHAT I EVEN WANTED TO TALK TO YOU ABOUT.
B-BUT...
ISN'T THERE SOMETHING YOU'RE WORRIED ABOUT?!
HE'S STANDING RIGHT THERE.
IS IT THAT OBVIOUS?
MY VOICE CAN STILL REACH HIM.

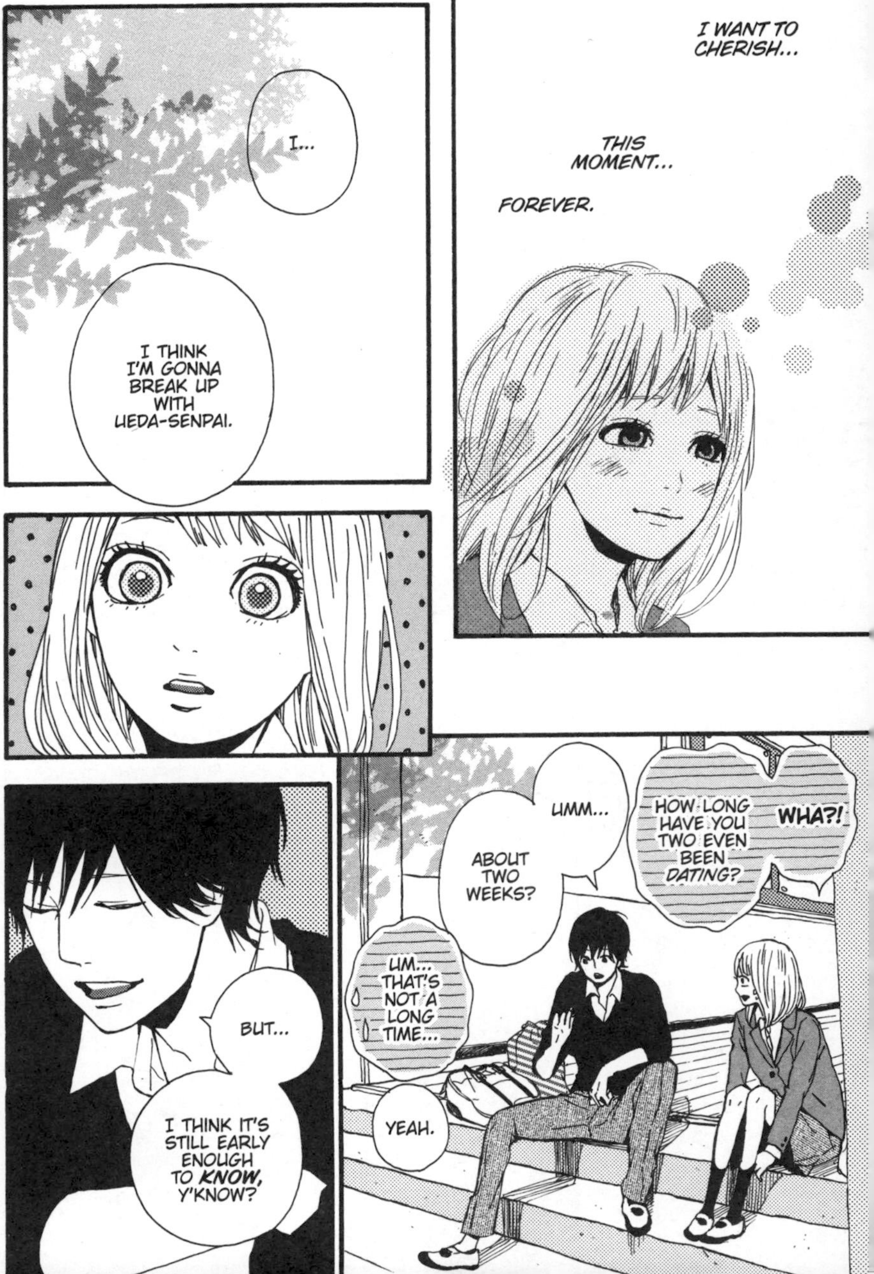
I WANT TO CHERISH...
THIS MOMENT...
FOREVER.
I...
I THINK I'M GONNA BREAK UP WITH UEDA-SENPAI.
WHA?!
HOW LONG HAVE YOU TWO EVEN BEEN DATING?
UMM...
ABOUT TWO WEEKS?
UM... THAT'S NOT A LONG TIME...
YEAH.
BUT...
I THINK IT'S STILL EARLY ENOUGH TO KNOW, Y'KNOW?

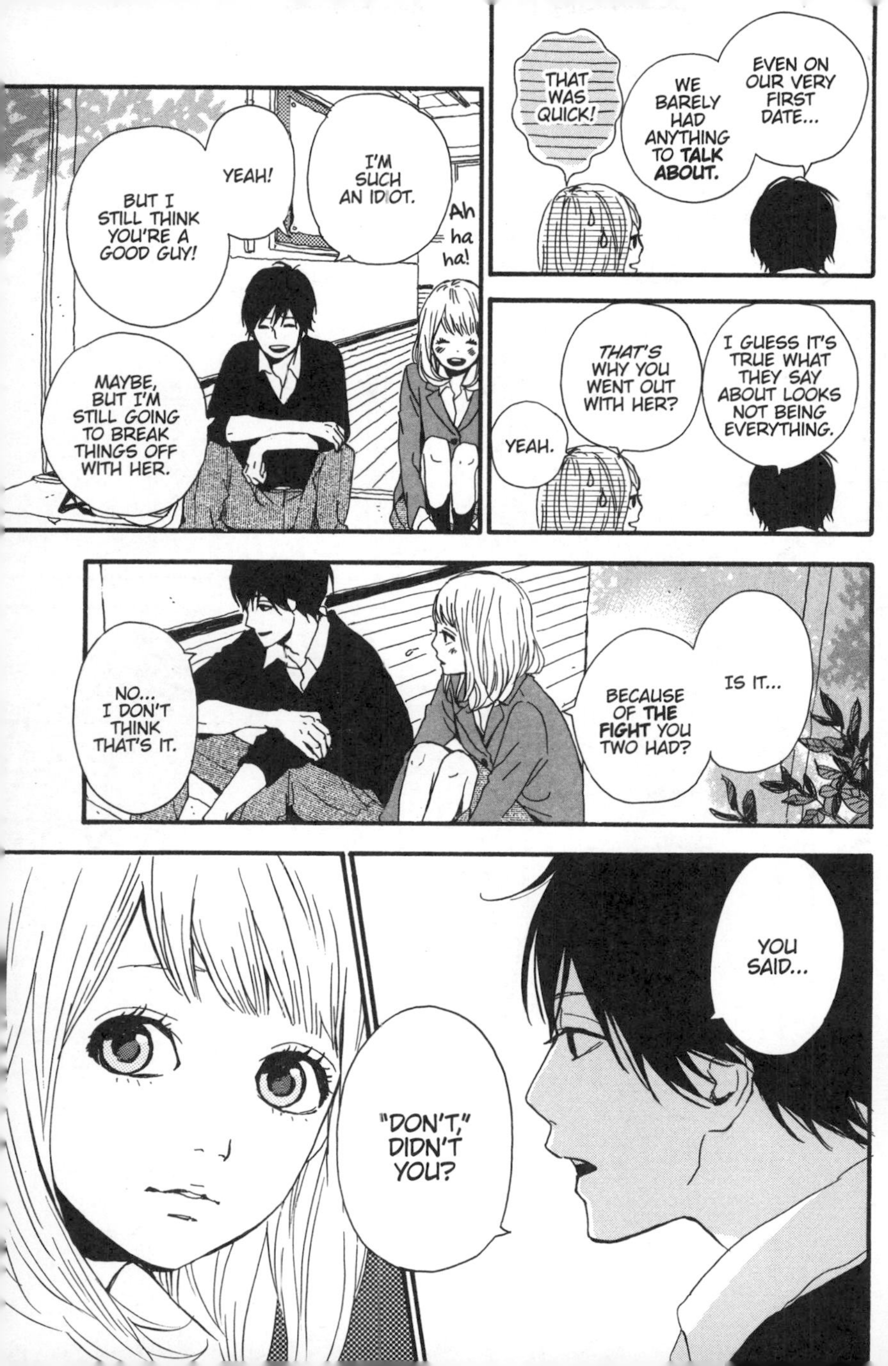
EVEN ON OUR VERY FIRST DATE...
WE BARELY HAD ANYTHING TO TALK ABOUT.
THAT WAS QUICK!
I GUESS IT'S TRUE WHAT THEY SAY ABOUT LOOKS NOT BEING EVERYTHING.
THAT'S WHY YOU WENT OUT WITH HER?
YEAH.
I'M SUCH AN IDIOT.
Ah ha ha!
YEAH!
BUT I STILL THINK YOU'RE A GOOD GUY!
MAYBE, BUT I'M STILL GOING TO BREAK THINGS OFF WITH HER.
IS IT...
BECAUSE OF THE FIGHT YOU TWO HAD?
NO... I DON'T THINK THAT'S IT.
YOU SAID...
"DON'T," DIDN'T YOU?

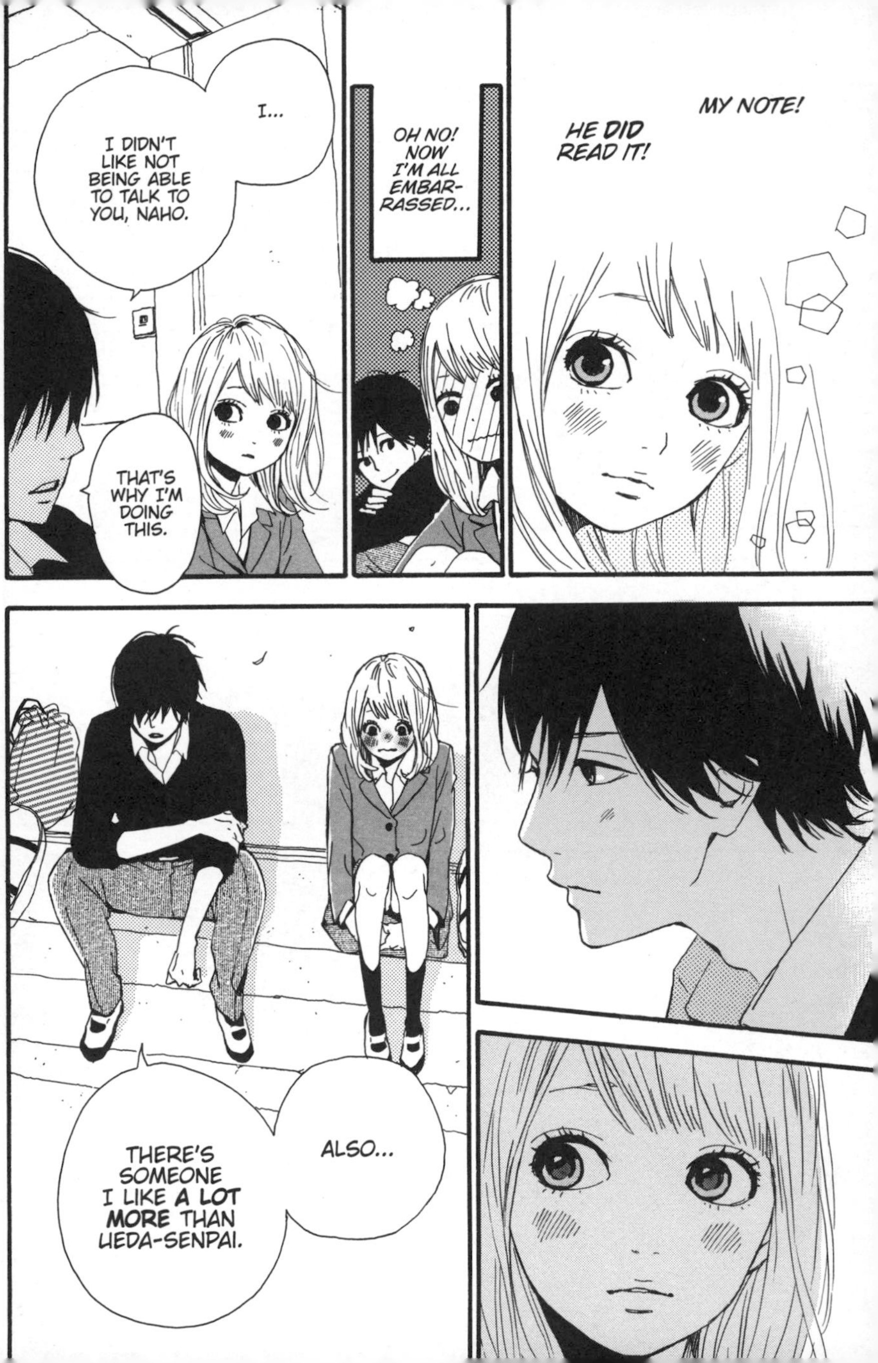
MY NOTE!
HE DID READ IT!
OH NO! NOW I'M ALL EMBAR-RASSED...
I...
I DIDN'T LIKE NOT BEING ABLE TO TALK TO YOU, NAHO.
THAT'S WHY I'M DOING THIS.
ALSO...
THERE'S SOMEONE I LIKE A LOT MORE THAN UEDA-SENPAI.

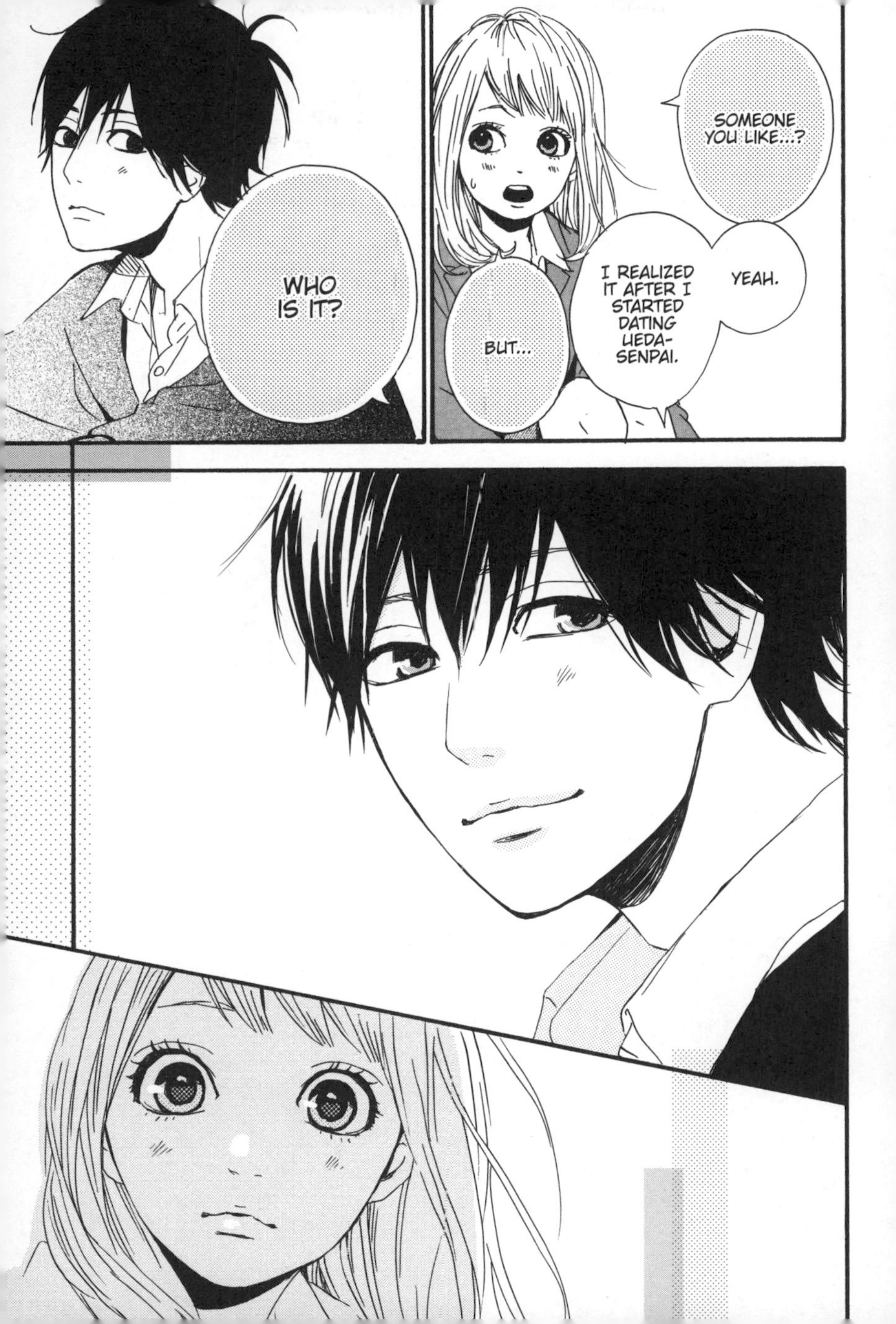
SOMEONE YOU LIKE...?
YEAH.
I REALIZED IT AFTER I STARTED DATING UEDA-SENPAI.
BUT...
WHO IS IT?

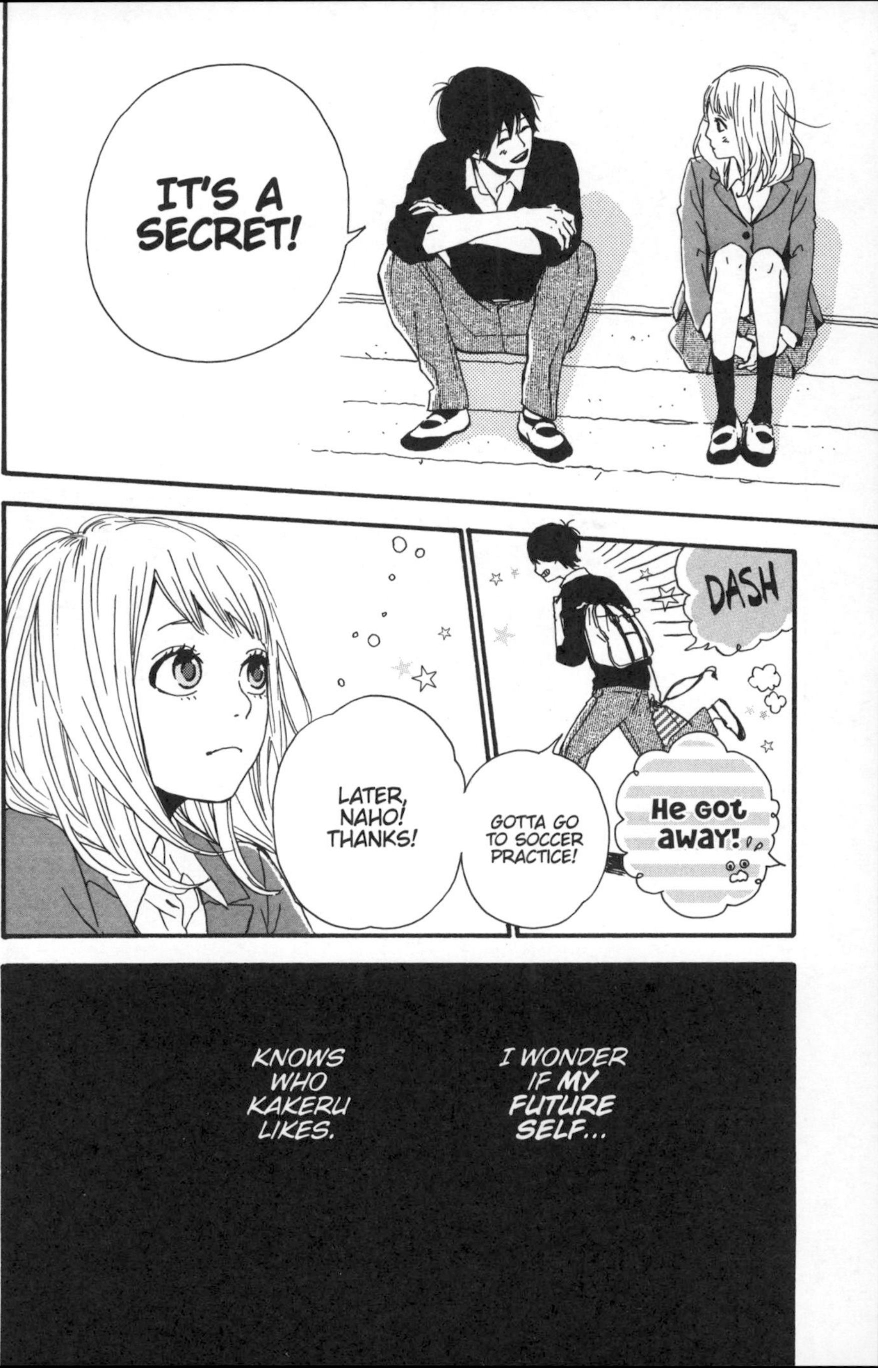
IT'S A SECRET!
DASH
He got away!
GOTTA GO TO SOCCER PRACTICE!
LATER, NAHO! THANKS!
I WONDER IF MY FUTURE SELF...
KNOWS WHO KAKERU LIKES.

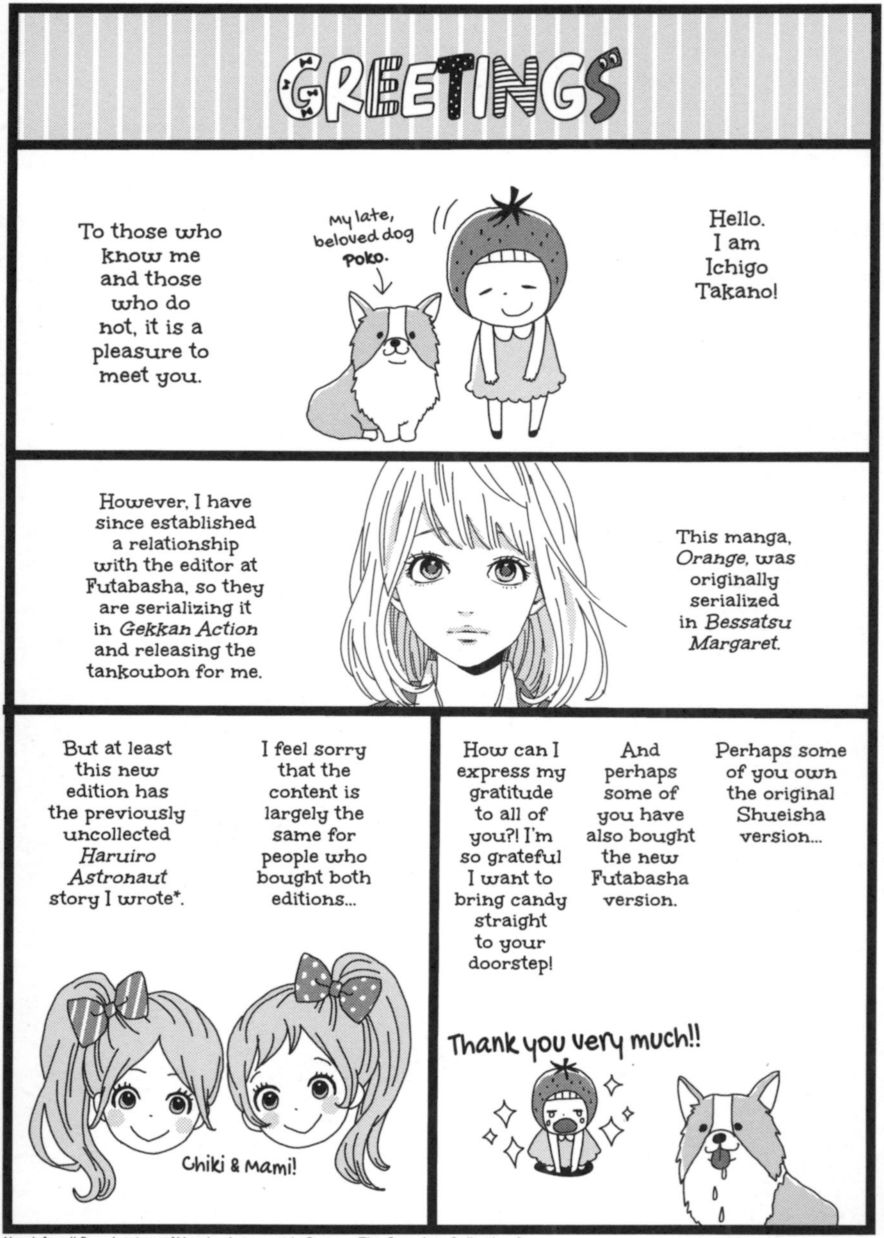
GREETINGS
Hello. I am Ichigo Takano!
My late, beloved dog Poko.
To those who know me and those who do not, it is a pleasure to meet you.
This manga, *Orange*, was originally serialized in *Bessatsu Margaret*.
However, I have since established a relationship with the editor at Futabasha, so they are serializing it in *Gekkan Action* and releasing the tankoubon for me.
Perhaps some of you own the original Shueisha version...
And perhaps some of you have also bought the new Futabasha version.
How can I express my gratitude to all of you?! I'm so grateful I want to bring candy straight to your doorstep!
Thank you very much!!
I feel sorry that the content is largely the same for people who bought both editions...
But at least this new edition has the previously uncollected *Haruiro Astronaut* story I wrote*.
Chiki & Mami!

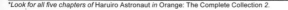

**Look for all five chapters of* Haruiro Astronaut *in* Orange: The Complete Collection *2.*

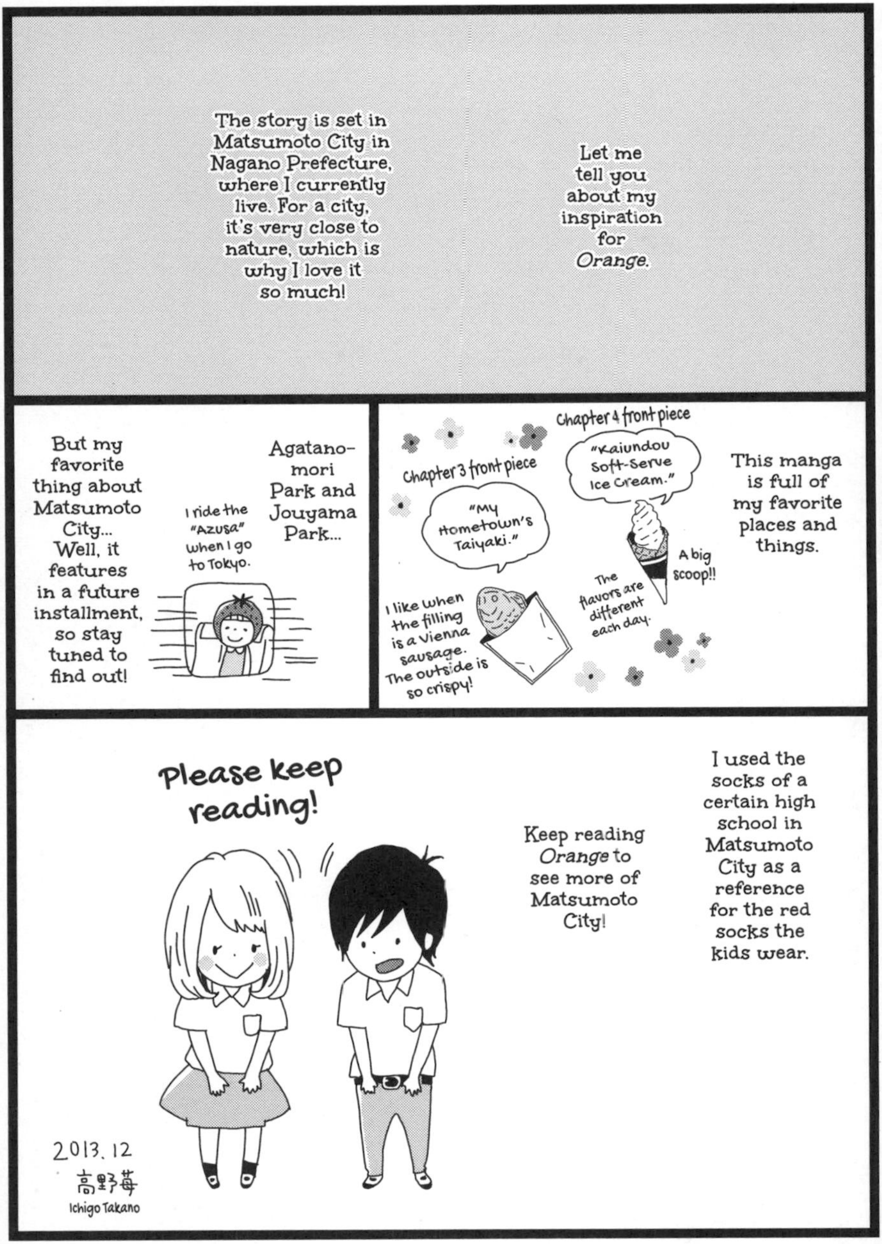
Let me tell you about my inspiration for Orange.
The story is set in Matsumoto City in Nagano Prefecture, where I currently live. For a city, it's very close to nature, which is why I love it so much!
This manga is full of my favorite places and things.
Chapter 4 front piece
"Kaiundou Soft-Serve Ice Cream."
A big scoop!!
The flavors are different each day.
Chapter 3 front piece
"My Hometown's Taiyaki."
I like when the filling is a Vienna sausage. The outside is so crispy!
Agatano-mori Park and Jouyama Park...
I ride the "Azusa" when I go to Tokyo.
But my favorite thing about Matsumoto City... Well, it features in a future installment, so stay tuned to find out!
I used the socks of a certain high school in Matsumoto City as a reference for the red socks the kids wear.
Keep reading Orange to see more of Matsumoto City!
Please keep reading!
2013.12
高野苺
Ichigo Takano

orange

orange

ICHIGO TAKANO presents

2

the second
volume

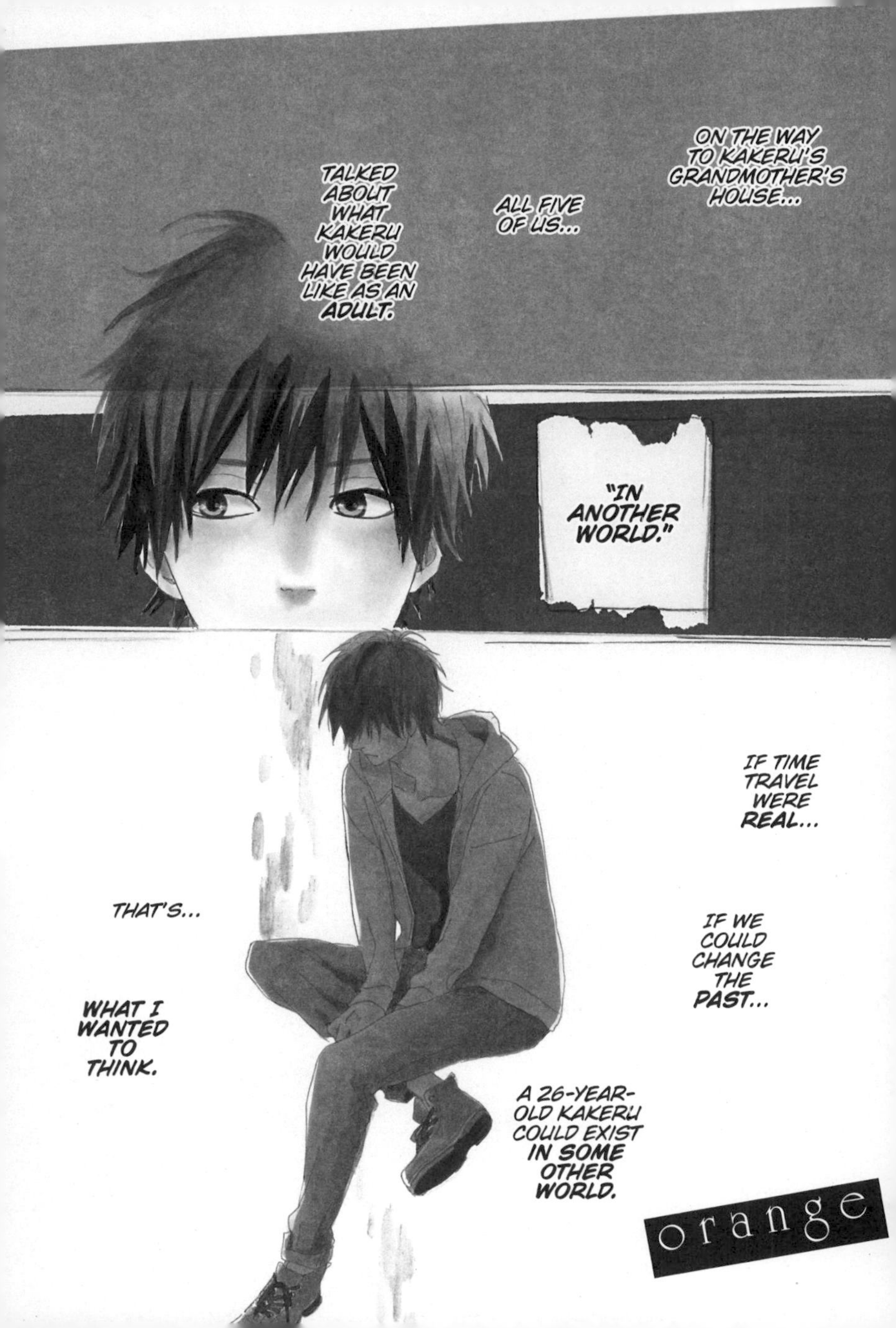
ON THE WAY TO KAKERU'S GRANDMOTHER'S HOUSE...
ALL FIVE OF US...
TALKED ABOUT WHAT KAKERU WOULD HAVE BEEN LIKE AS AN ADULT.
"IN ANOTHER WORLD."
IF TIME TRAVEL WERE REAL...
IF WE COULD CHANGE THE PAST...
A 26-YEAR-OLD KAKERU COULD EXIST IN SOME OTHER WORLD.
THAT'S...
WHAT I WANTED TO THINK.
orange

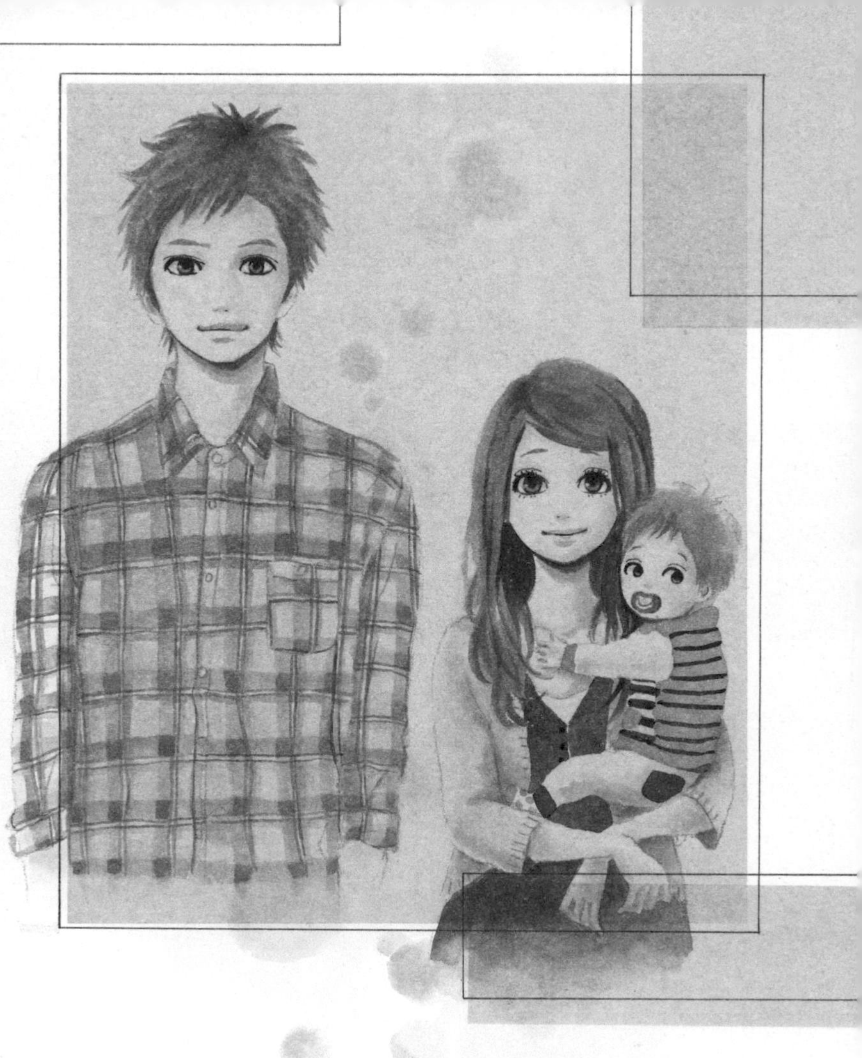

orange
LETTER 5

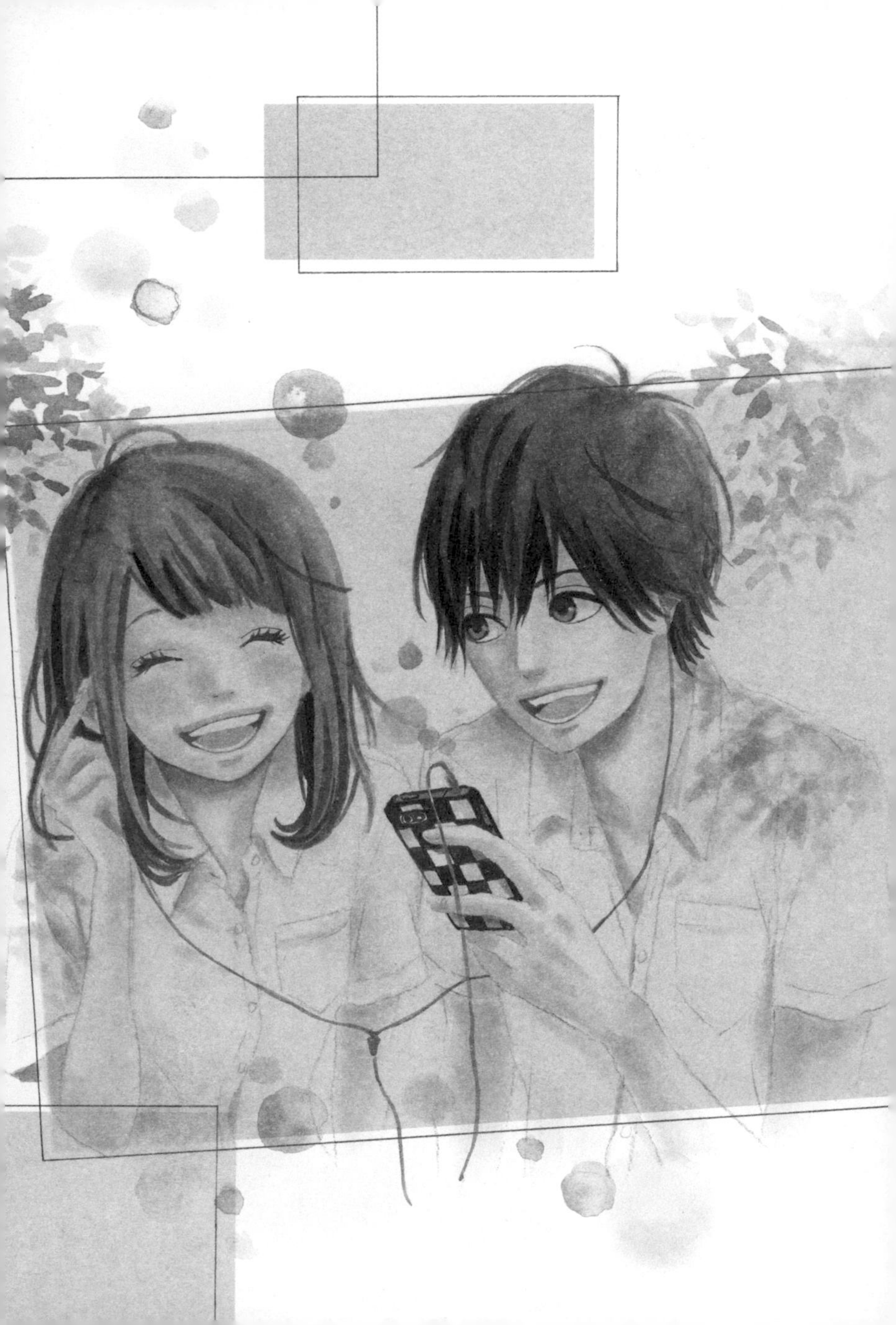

orange

May 24

- Starting today, Kakeru will be absent from school for one week.

- No matter how much I asked what happened, Kakeru wouldn't tell me.

- When I think about it now, it was 49 days since Kakeru's mother passed away, the day when many people perform a final ceremony for the dead.

- After Kakeru passed away...

  I learned that his mother passed away on April 6th, the day of the entrance ceremony.

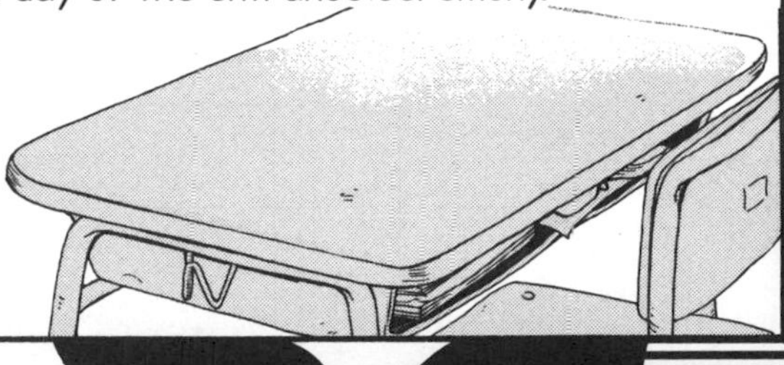

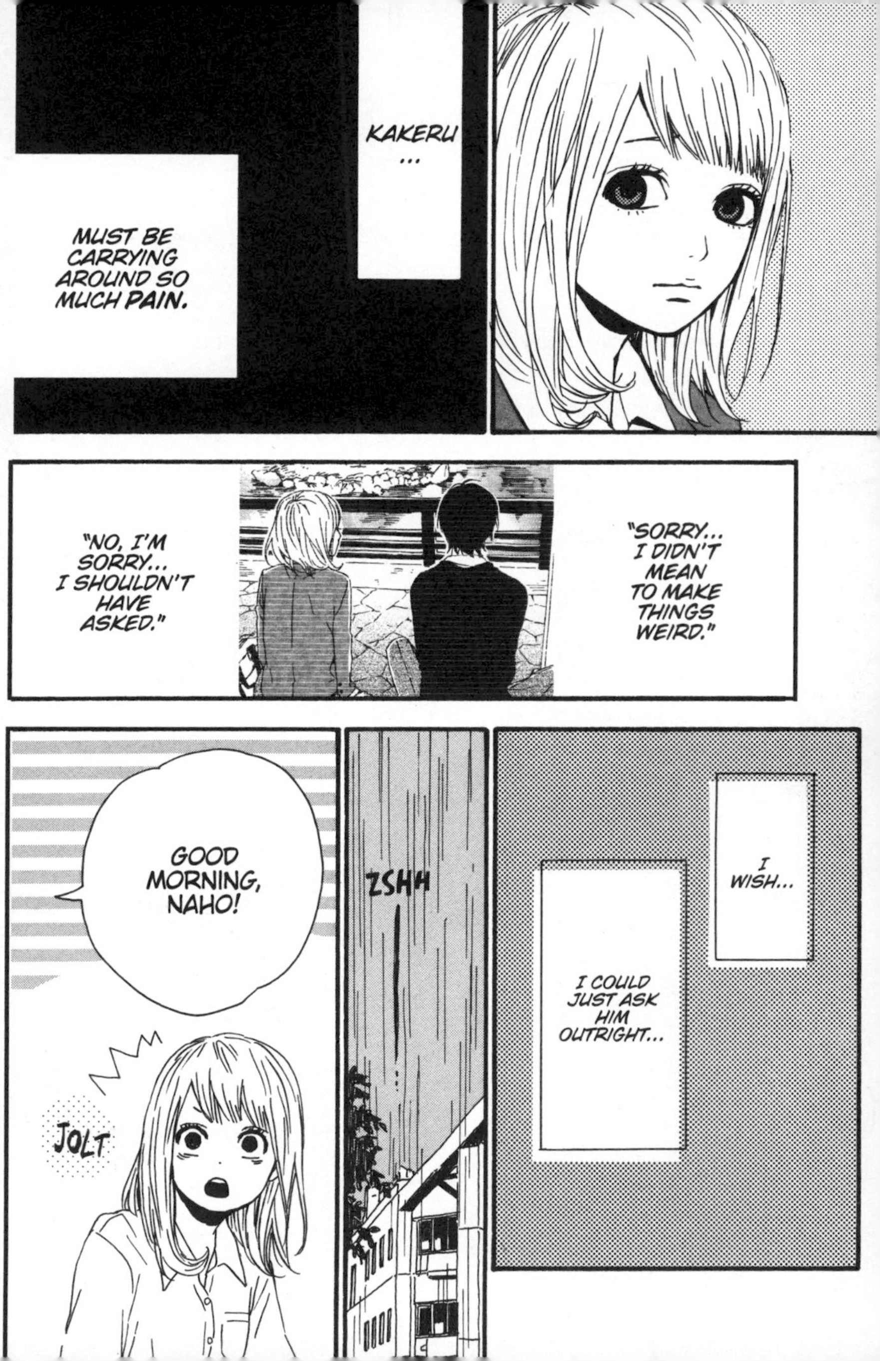
KAKERU ...
MUST BE CARRYING AROUND SO MUCH PAIN.
"SORRY... I DIDN'T MEAN TO MAKE THINGS WEIRD."
"NO, I'M SORRY... I SHOULDN'T HAVE ASKED."
I WISH...
I COULD JUST ASK HIM OUTRIGHT...
ZSHH
GOOD MORNING, NAHO!
JOLT

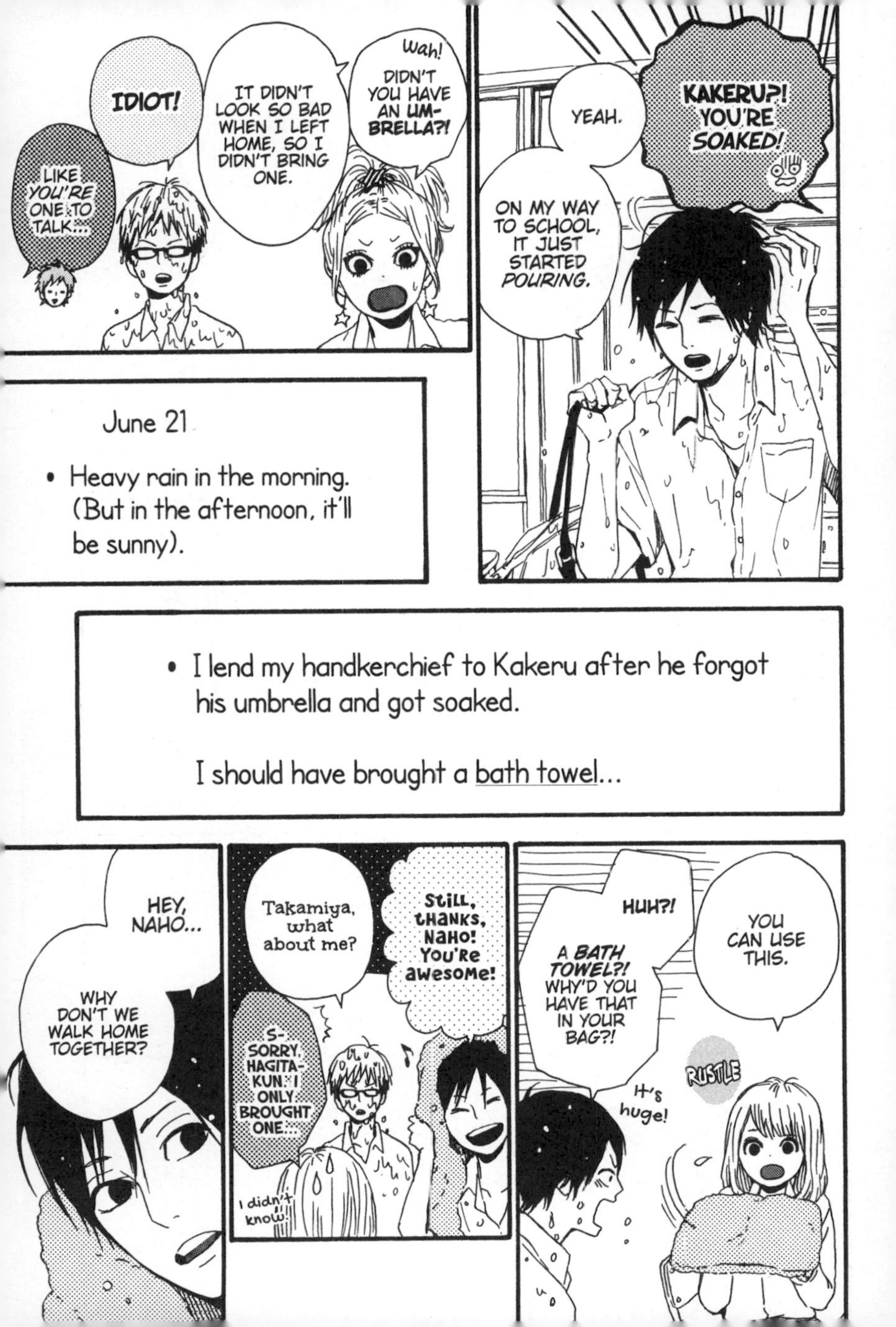
KAKERU?! YOU'RE SOAKED!
YEAH.
ON MY WAY TO SCHOOL, IT JUST STARTED POURING.
Wah!
DIDN'T YOU HAVE AN UMBRELLA?!
IT DIDN'T LOOK SO BAD WHEN I LEFT HOME, SO I DIDN'T BRING ONE.
IDIOT!
LIKE YOU'RE ONE TO TALK...
June 21
• Heavy rain in the morning. (But in the afternoon, it'll be sunny).
• I lend my handkerchief to Kakeru after he forgot his umbrella and got soaked.
I should have brought a bath towel...
YOU CAN USE THIS.
HUH?!
A BATH TOWEL?! WHY'D YOU HAVE THAT IN YOUR BAG?!
RUSTLE
It's huge!
Still, thanks, Naho! You're awesome!
Takamiya, what about me?
S-SORRY, HAGITA-KUN. I ONLY BROUGHT ONE...
I didn't know!
HEY, NAHO...
WHY DON'T WE WALK HOME TOGETHER?

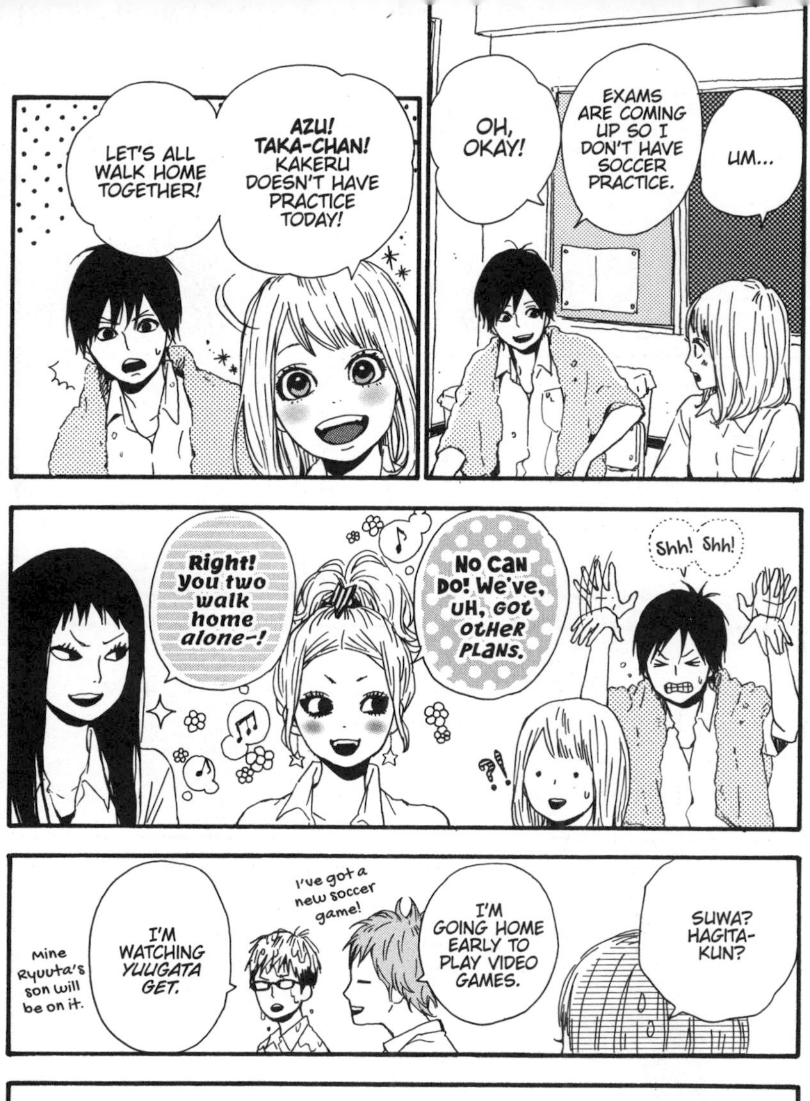
EXAMS ARE COMING UP SO I DON'T HAVE SOCCER PRACTICE.
OH, OKAY!
UM...
AZU! TAKA-CHAN! KAKERU DOESN'T HAVE PRACTICE TODAY!
LET'S ALL WALK HOME TOGETHER!
Shh! Shh!
No can do! We've, uh, got other plans.
Right! You two walk home alone-!
SUWA? HAGITA-KUN?
I'M GOING HOME EARLY TO PLAY VIDEO GAMES.
I've got a new soccer game!
I'M WATCHING YUUGATA GET.
Mine Ryuuta's son will be on it.

- There's no soccer practice because exams are coming up.

All six of us walk home together for the first time in awhile.

After parting with the others, I am invited to "study together over the weekend" by Kakeru.

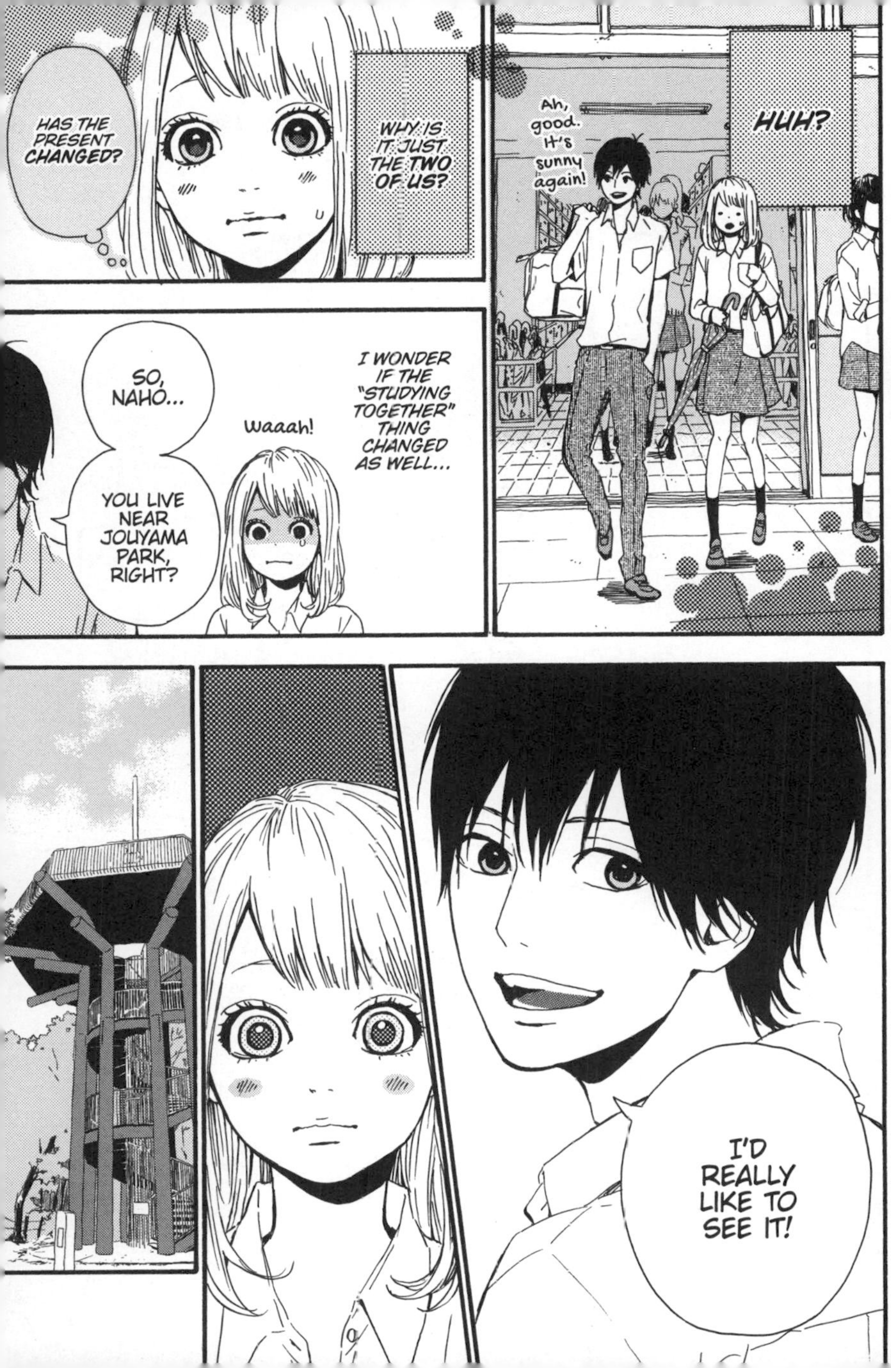
HUH?
Ah, good. It's sunny again!
WHY IS IT JUST THE TWO OF US?
HAS THE PRESENT CHANGED?
I WONDER IF THE "STUDYING TOGETHER" THING CHANGED AS WELL...
Waaah!
SO, NAHO...
YOU LIVE NEAR JOUYAMA PARK, RIGHT?
I'D REALLY LIKE TO SEE IT!

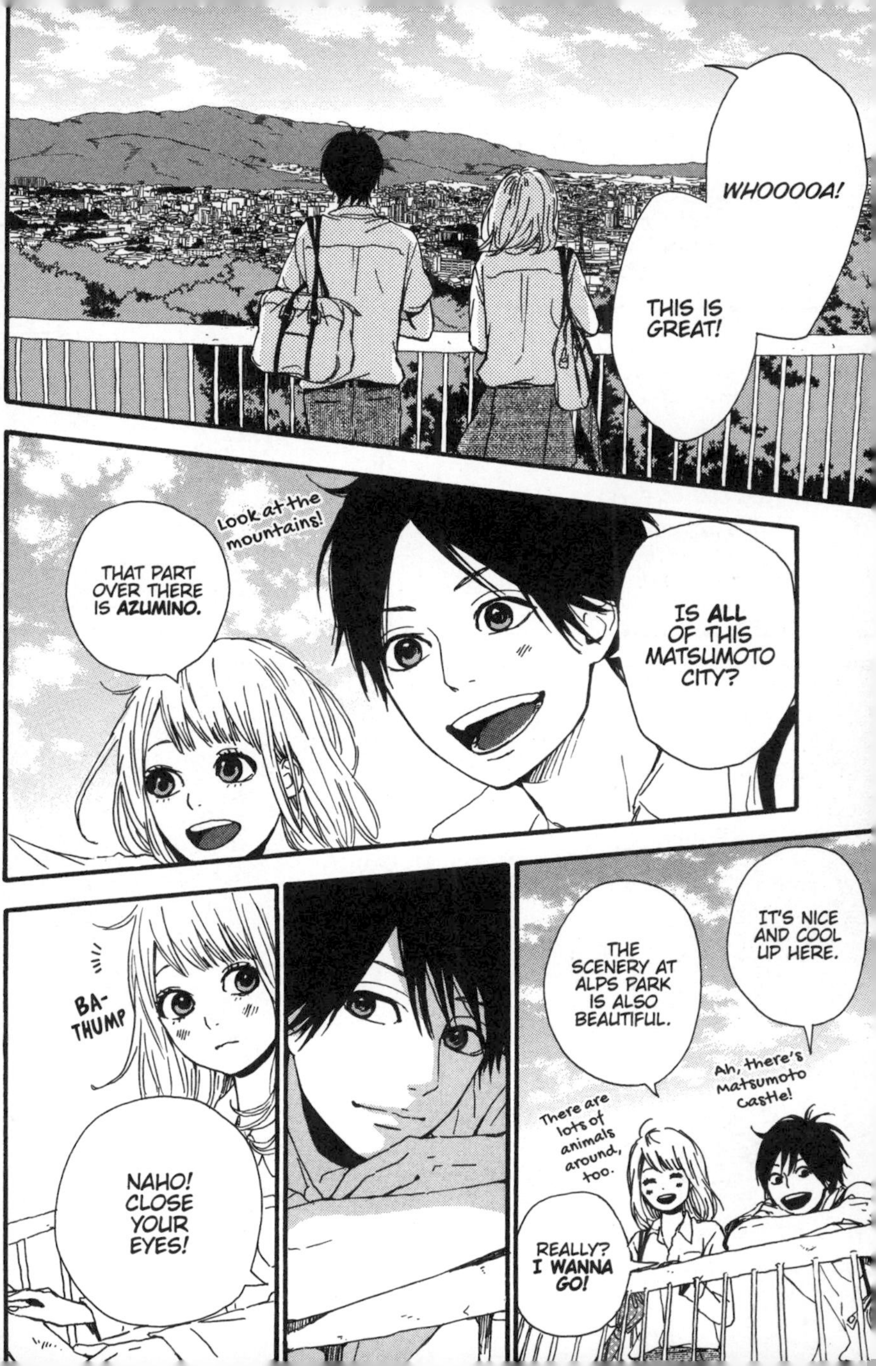
WHOOOOA!
THIS IS GREAT!
IS ALL OF THIS MATSUMOTO CITY?
Look at the mountains!
THAT PART OVER THERE IS AZUMINO.
IT'S NICE AND COOL UP HERE.
THE SCENERY AT ALPS PARK IS ALSO BEAUTIFUL.
Ah, there's Matsumoto Castle!
There are lots of animals around, too.
REALLY? I WANNA GO!
BA-THUMP
NAHO! CLOSE YOUR EYES!

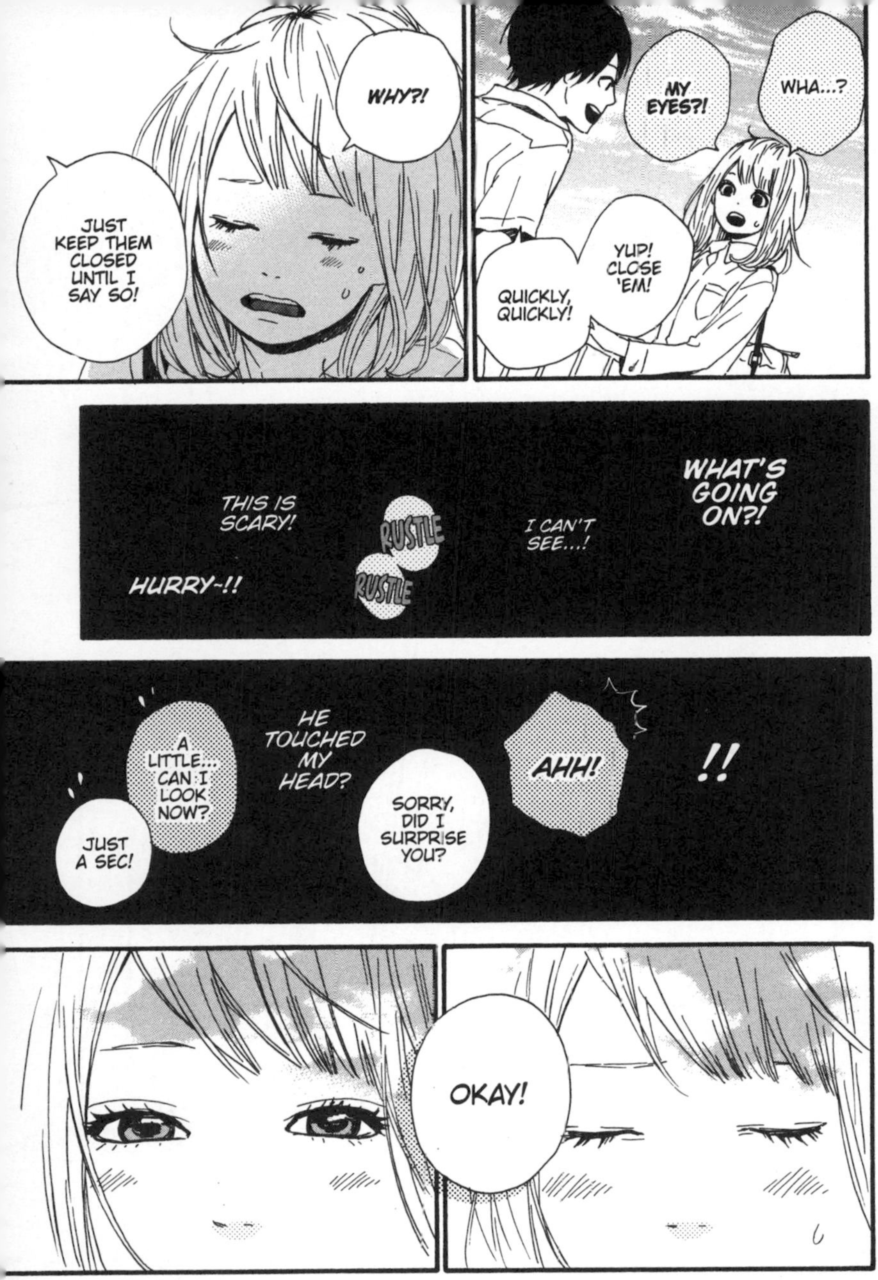
WHA...?
MY EYES?!
YUP! CLOSE 'EM!
QUICKLY, QUICKLY!
WHY?!
JUST KEEP THEM CLOSED UNTIL I SAY SO!
WHAT'S GOING ON?!
I CAN'T SEE...!
RUSTLE
RUSTLE
THIS IS SCARY!
HURRY~!!
!!
AHH!
SORRY, DID I SURPRISE YOU?
HE TOUCHED MY HEAD?
A LITTLE... CAN I LOOK NOW?
JUST A SEC!
OKAY!

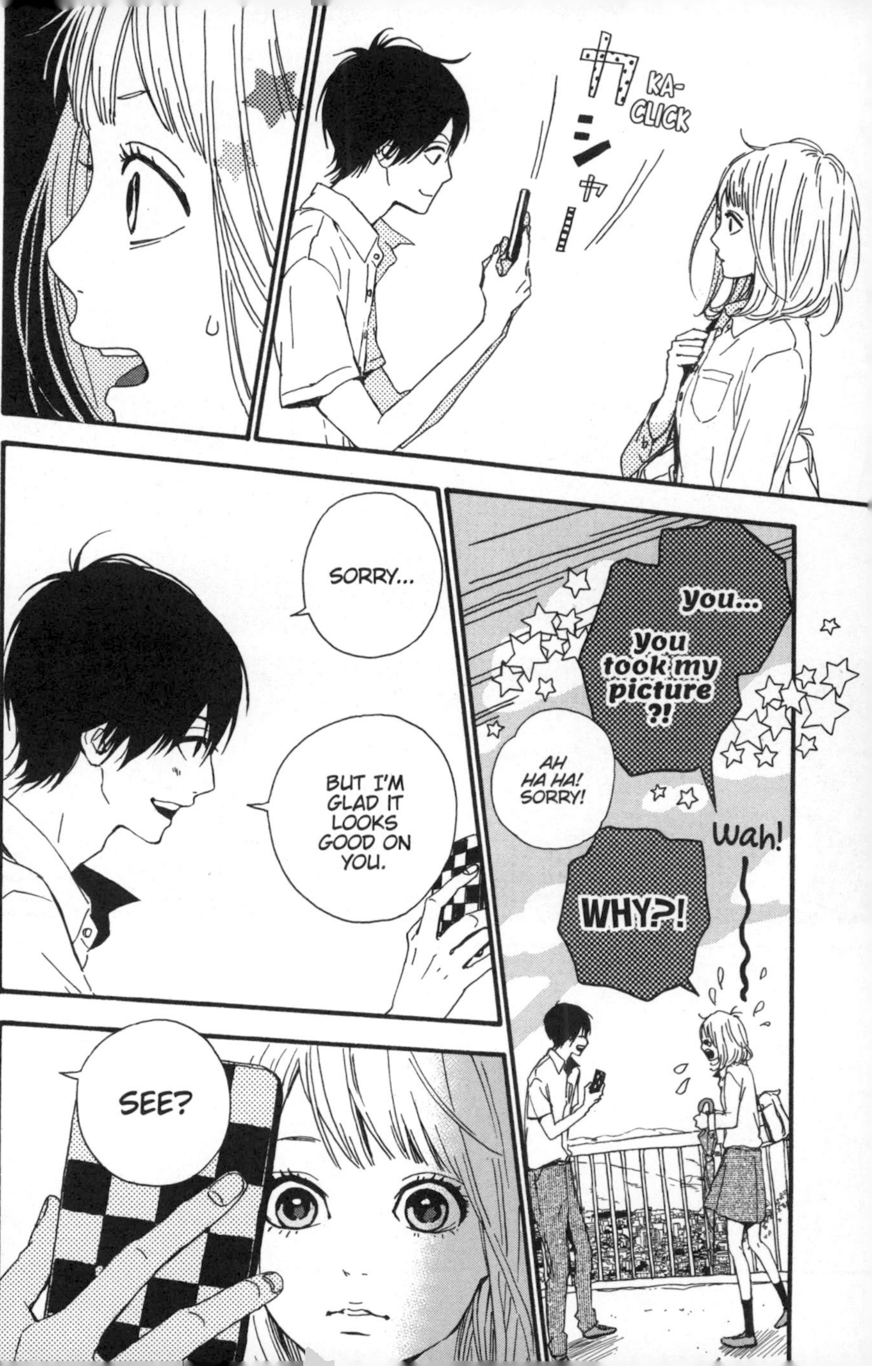
カシャ
KA-CLICK
you... you took my picture?!
AH HA HA! SORRY!
Wah!
WHY?!
SORRY...
BUT I'M GLAD IT LOOKS GOOD ON YOU.
SEE?

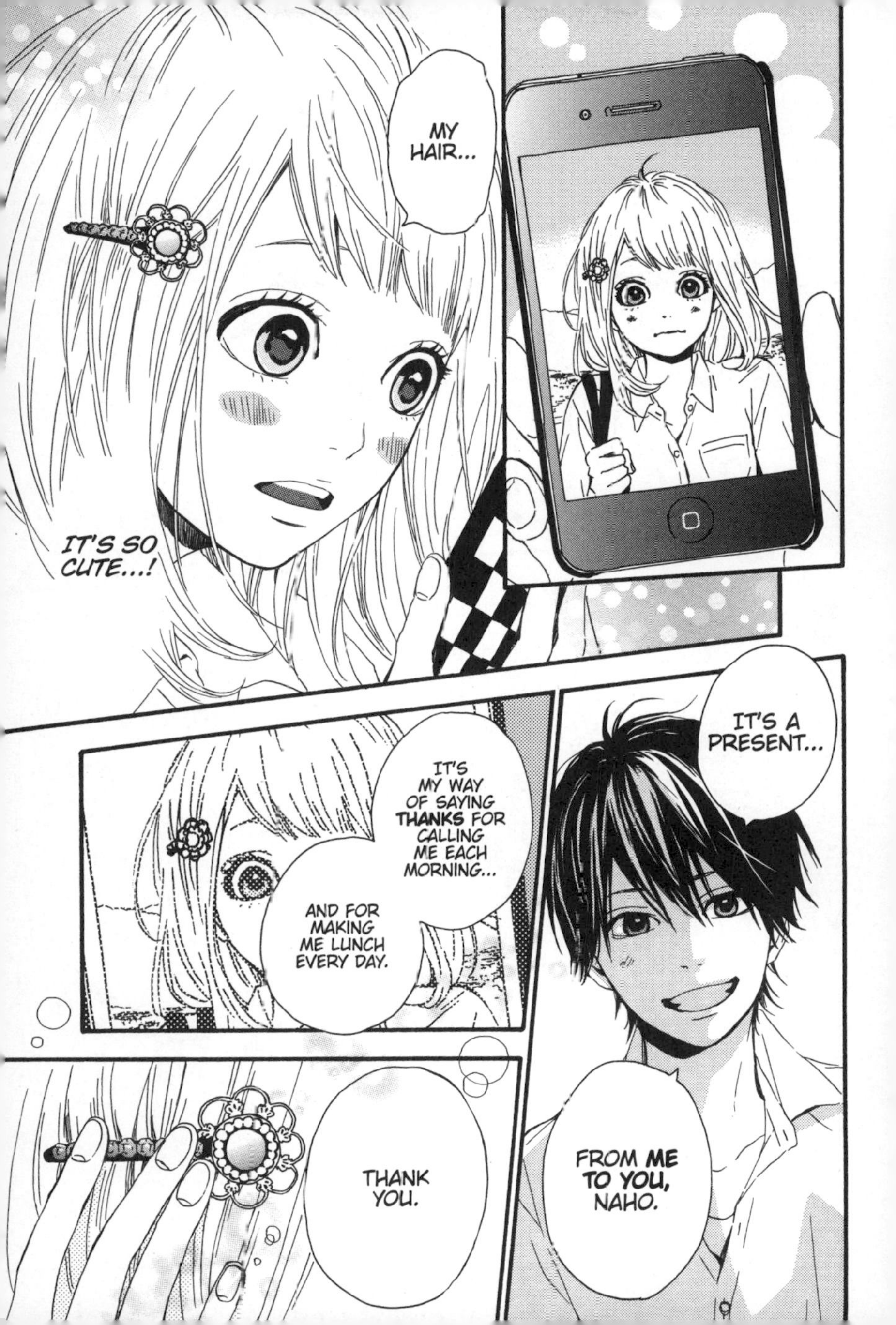
MY HAIR...
IT'S SO CUTE...!
IT'S A PRESENT...
FROM ME TO YOU, NAHO.
IT'S MY WAY OF SAYING THANKS FOR CALLING ME EACH MORNING...
AND FOR MAKING ME LUNCH EVERY DAY.
THANK YOU.

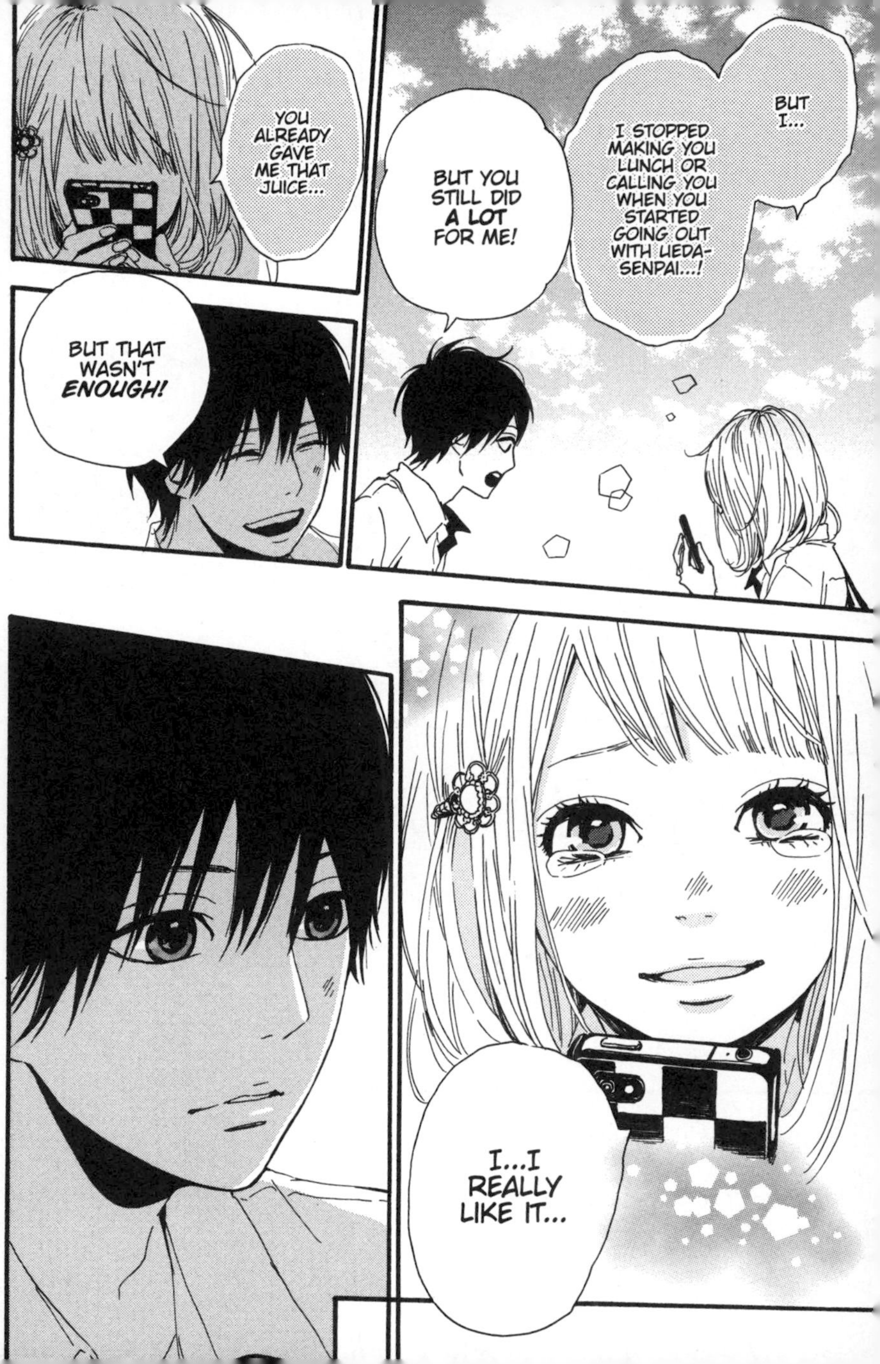
BUT I...
I STOPPED MAKING YOU LUNCH OR CALLING YOU WHEN YOU STARTED GOING OUT WITH UEDA-SENPAI...!
BUT YOU STILL DID A LOT FOR ME!
YOU ALREADY GAVE ME THAT JUICE...
BUT THAT WASN'T ENOUGH!
I...I REALLY LIKE IT...

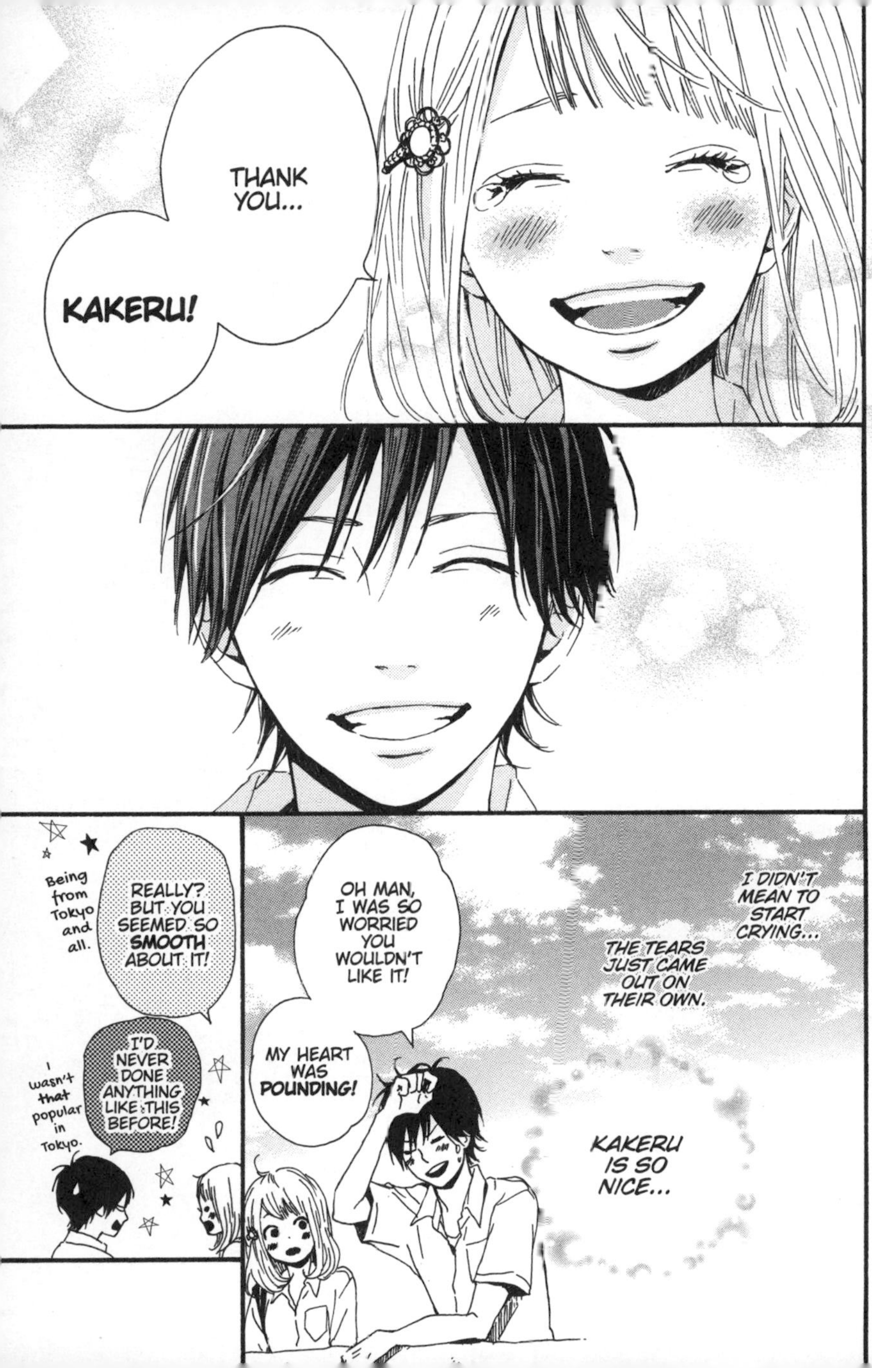
THANK YOU...
KAKERU!
I DIDN'T MEAN TO START CRYING...
THE TEARS JUST CAME OUT ON THEIR OWN.
OH MAN, I WAS SO WORRIED YOU WOULDN'T LIKE IT!
MY HEART WAS POUNDING!
KAKERU IS SO NICE...
REALLY? BUT YOU SEEMED SO SMOOTH ABOUT IT!
Being from Tokyo and all.
I'D NEVER DONE ANYTHING LIKE THIS BEFORE!
I wasn't that popular in Tokyo.

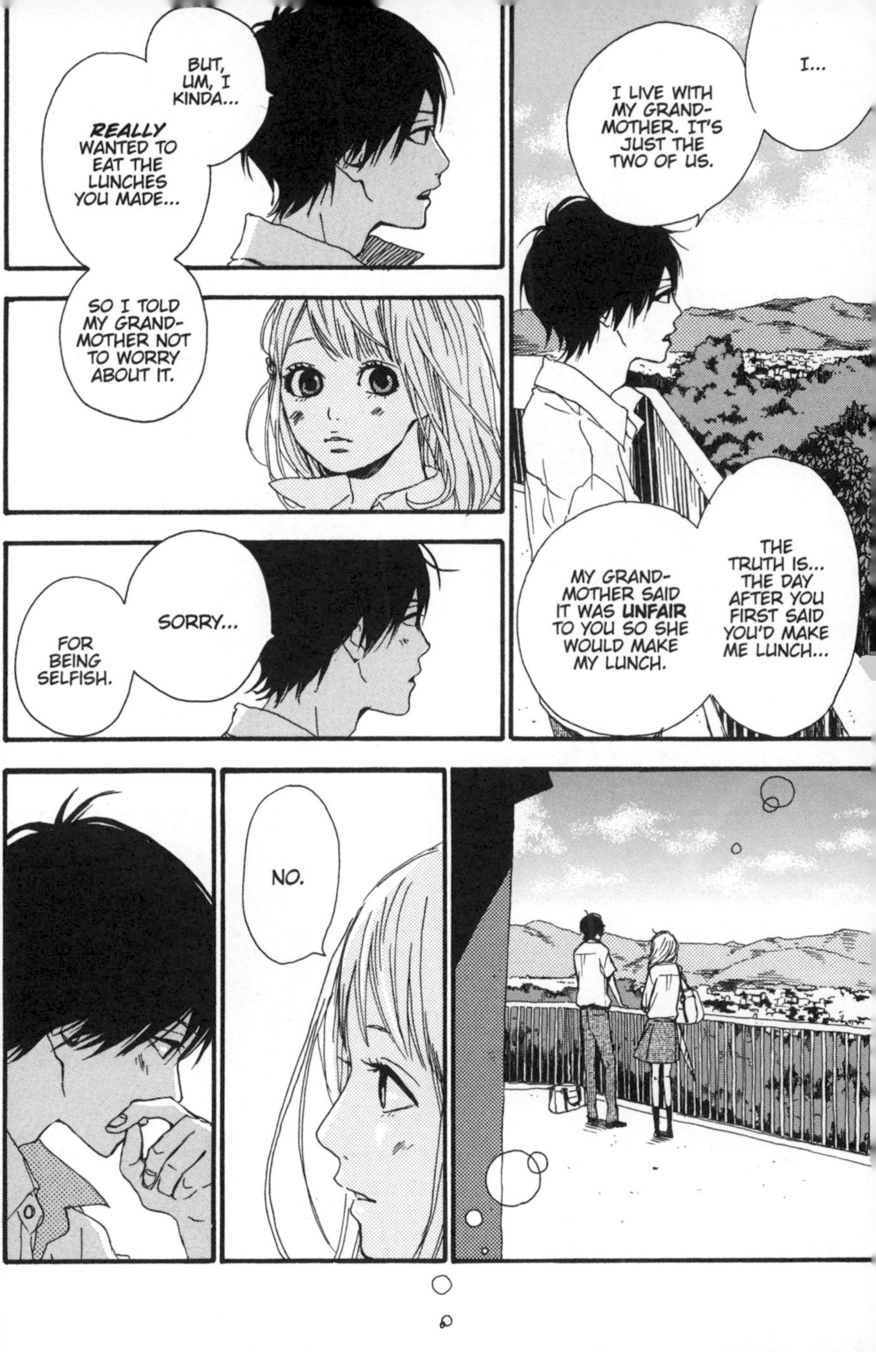
I...
I LIVE WITH MY GRAND-MOTHER. IT'S JUST THE TWO OF US.
THE TRUTH IS... THE DAY AFTER YOU FIRST SAID YOU'D MAKE ME LUNCH...
MY GRAND-MOTHER SAID IT WAS UNFAIR TO YOU SO SHE WOULD MAKE MY LUNCH.
BUT, UM, I KINDA...
REALLY WANTED TO EAT THE LUNCHES YOU MADE...
SO I TOLD MY GRAND-MOTHER NOT TO WORRY ABOUT IT.
SORRY...
FOR BEING SELFISH.
NO.

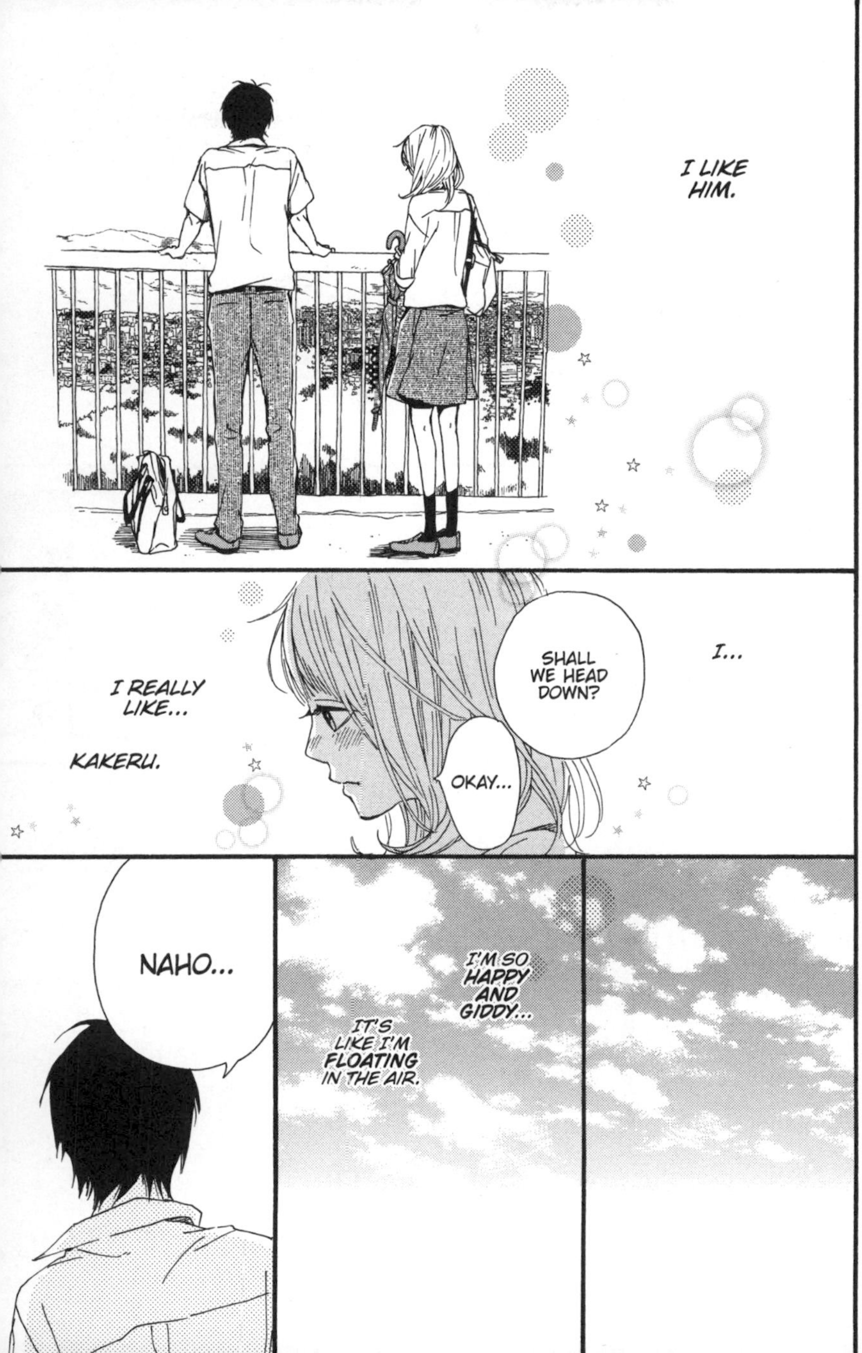
I LIKE HIM.
I...
SHALL WE HEAD DOWN?
OKAY...
I REALLY LIKE...
KAKERU.
I'M SO HAPPY AND GIDDY...
IT'S LIKE I'M FLOATING IN THE AIR.
NAHO...

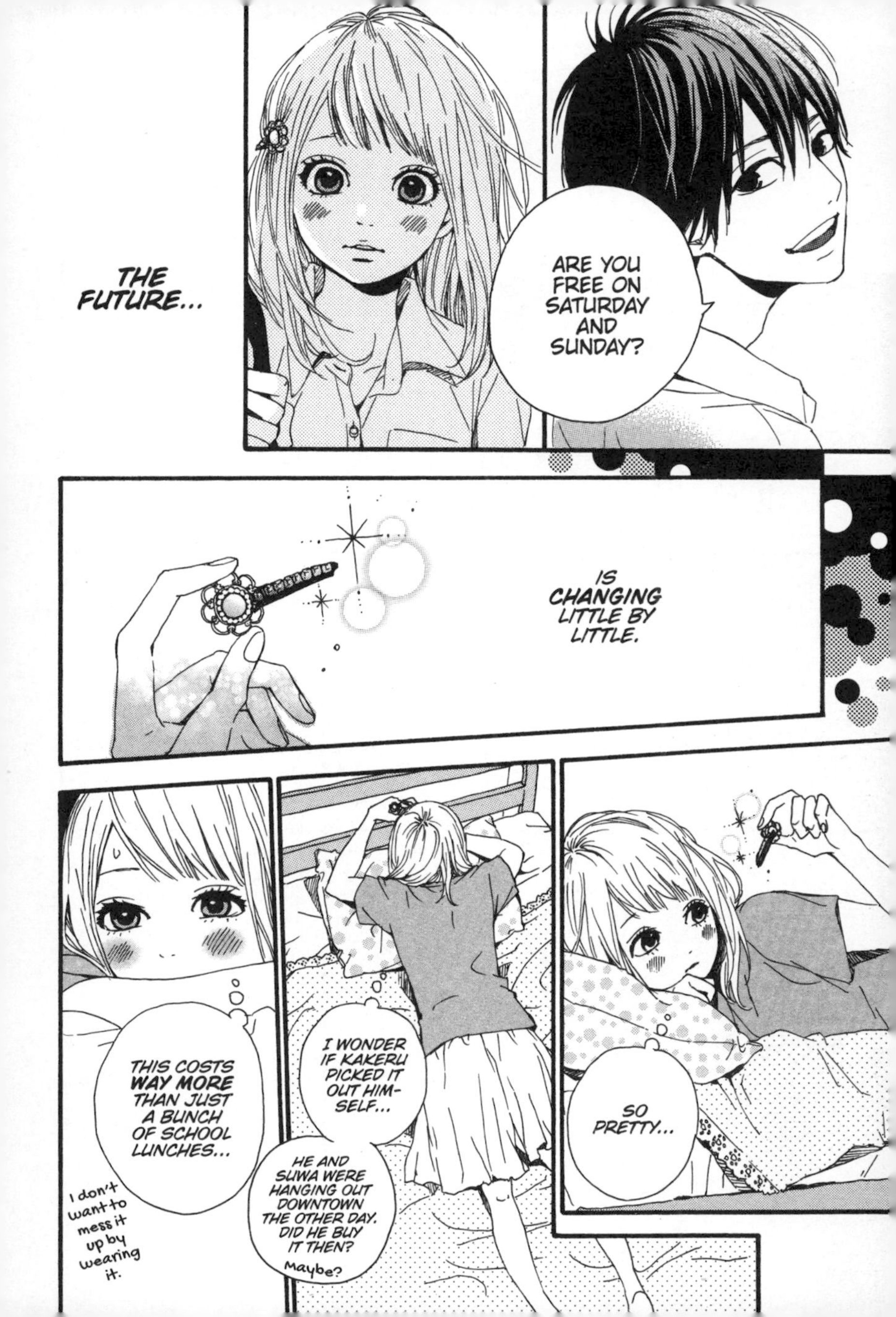
ARE YOU FREE ON SATURDAY AND SUNDAY?
THE FUTURE...
IS CHANGING LITTLE BY LITTLE.
SO PRETTY...
I WONDER IF KAKERU PICKED IT OUT HIM-SELF...
HE AND SUWA WERE HANGING OUT DOWNTOWN THE OTHER DAY. DID HE BUY IT THEN?
Maybe?
THIS COSTS WAY MORE THAN JUST A BUNCH OF SCHOOL LUNCHES...
I don't want to mess it up by wearing it.

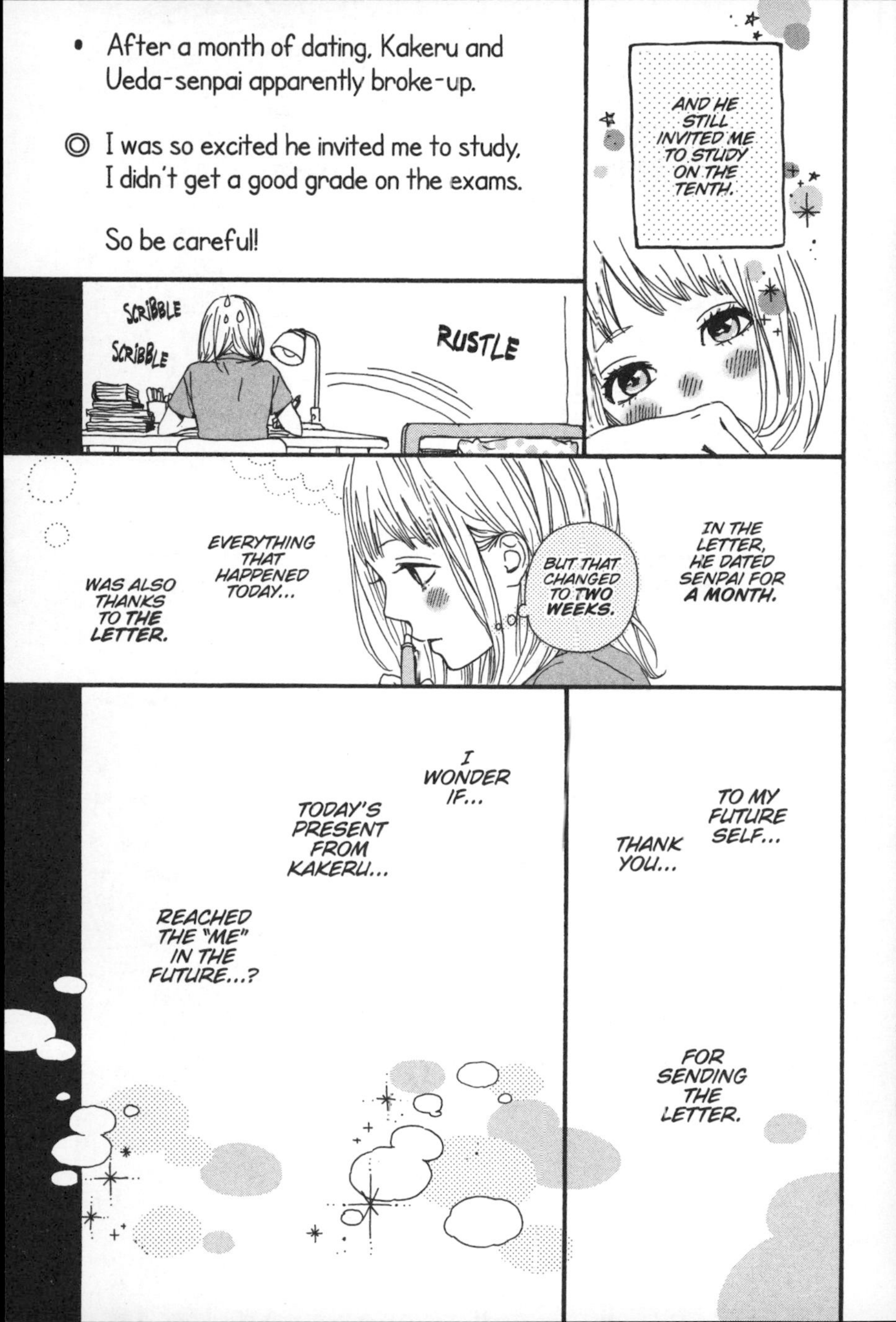
AND HE STILL INVITED ME TO STUDY ON THE TENTH.
• After a month of dating, Kakeru and Ueda-senpai apparently broke-up.
◎ I was so excited he invited me to study, I didn't get a good grade on the exams.
So be careful!
RUSTLE
SCRIBBLE
SCRIBBLE
IN THE LETTER, HE DATED SENPAI FOR A MONTH.
BUT THAT CHANGED TO TWO WEEKS.
EVERYTHING THAT HAPPENED TODAY...
WAS ALSO THANKS TO THE LETTER.
TO MY FUTURE SELF...
THANK YOU...
FOR SENDING THE LETTER.
I WONDER IF...
TODAY'S PRESENT FROM KAKERU...
REACHED THE "ME" IN THE FUTURE...?

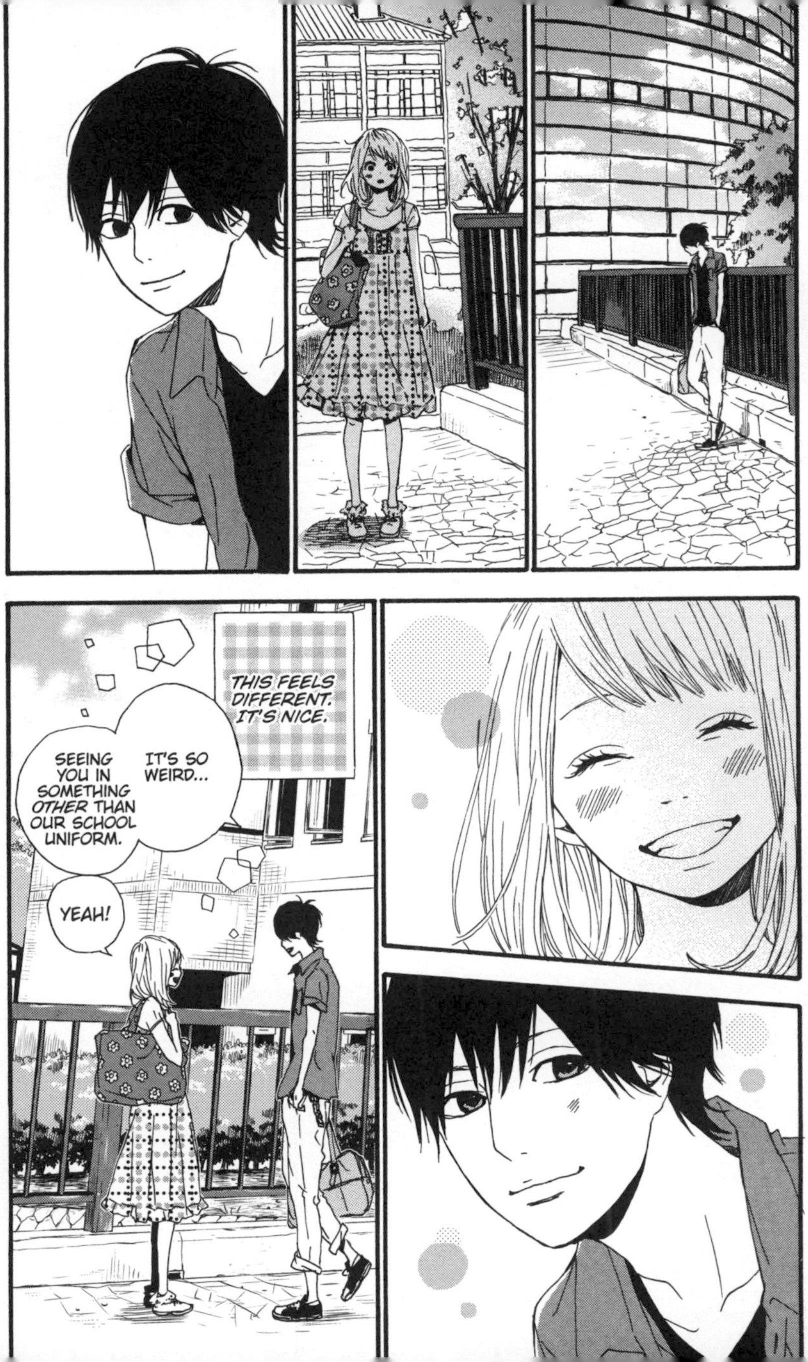
THIS FEELS DIFFERENT. IT'S NICE.
IT'S SO WEIRD... SEEING YOU IN SOMETHING *OTHER* THAN OUR SCHOOL UNIFORM.
YEAH!

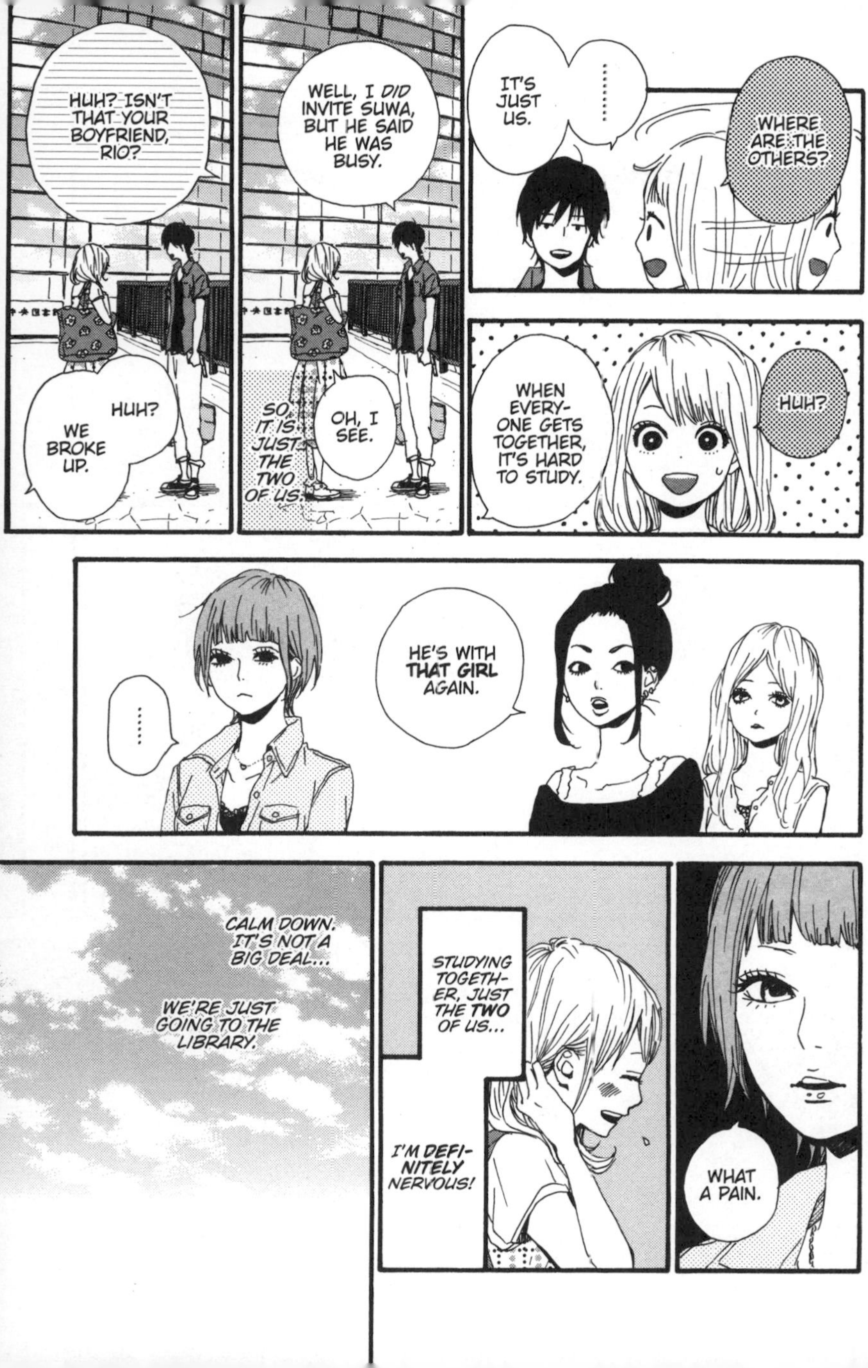
WHERE ARE THE OTHERS?
......
IT'S JUST US.
HUH?
WHEN EVERY-ONE GETS TOGETHER, IT'S HARD TO STUDY.
WELL, I *DID* INVITE SUWA, BUT HE SAID HE WAS BUSY.
OH, I SEE.
SO, IT IS JUST THE TWO OF US.
HUH? ISN'T THAT YOUR BOYFRIEND, RIO?
HUH?
WE BROKE UP.
HE'S WITH **THAT GIRL** AGAIN.
......
WHAT A PAIN.
STUDYING TOGETH-ER, JUST THE **TWO** OF US...
I'M **DEFI-NITELY** NERVOUS!
CALM DOWN. IT'S NOT A BIG DEAL...
WE'RE JUST GOING TO THE LIBRARY.

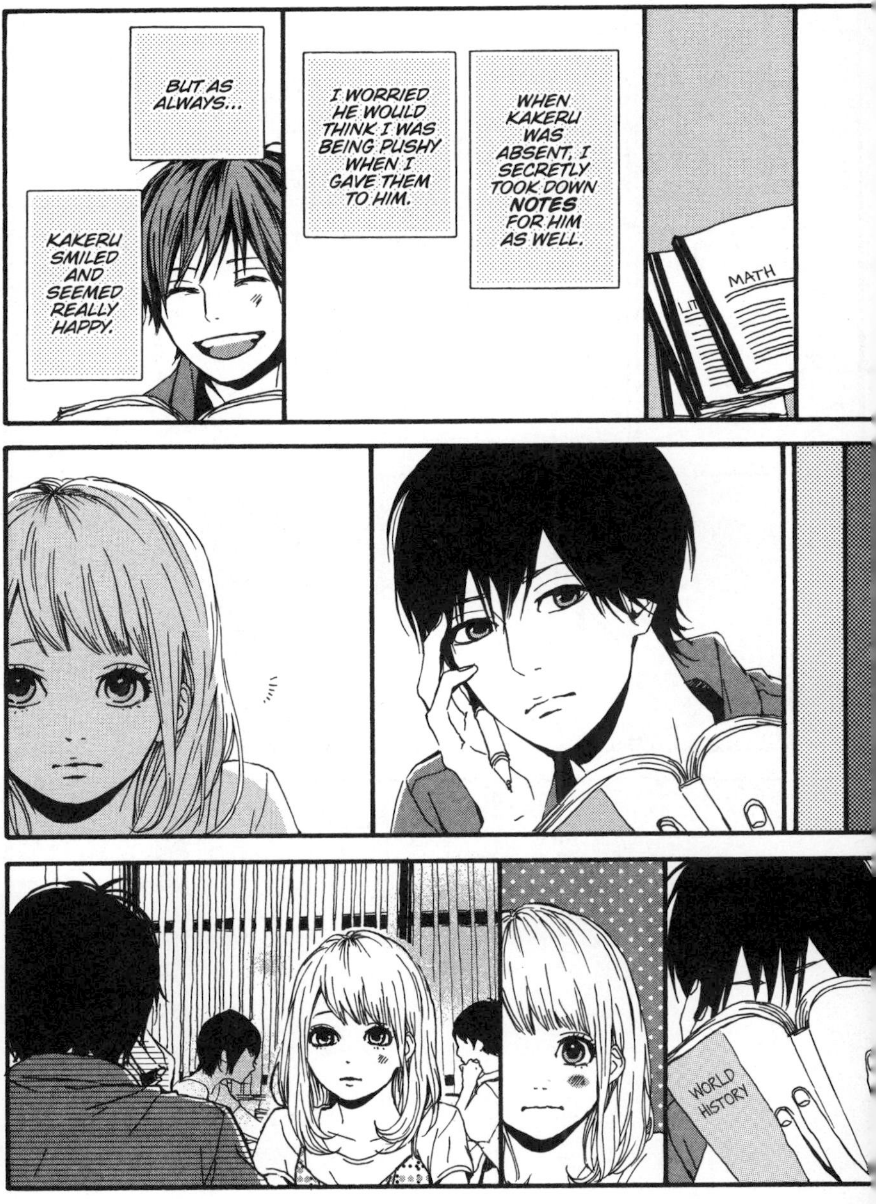
MATH
WHEN KAKERU WAS ABSENT, I SECRETLY TOOK DOWN **NOTES** FOR HIM AS WELL.
I WORRIED HE WOULD THINK I WAS BEING PUSHY WHEN I GAVE THEM TO HIM.
BUT AS ALWAYS...
KAKERU SMILED AND SEEMED REALLY HAPPY.
WORLD HISTORY

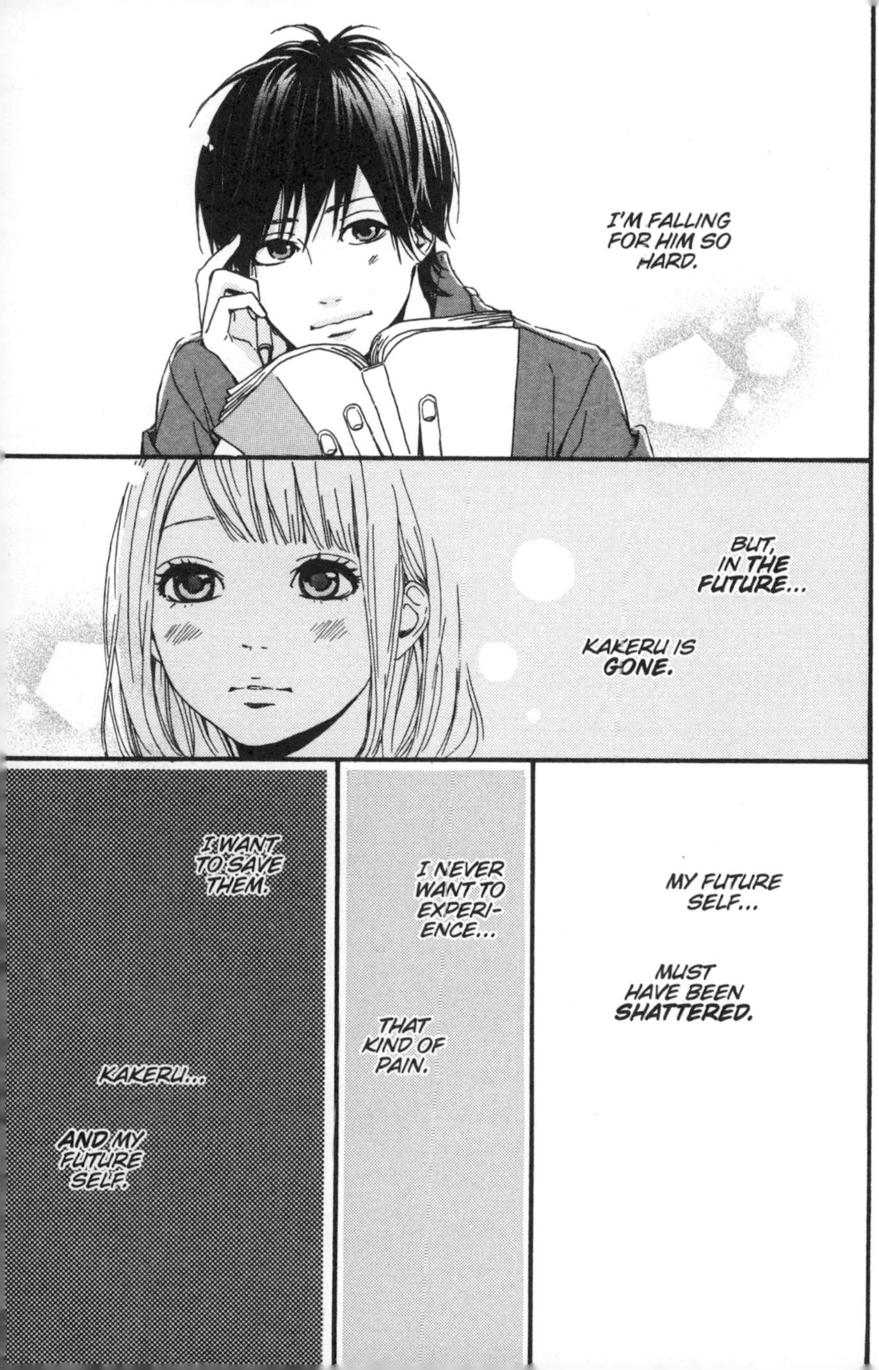

I'M FALLING FOR HIM SO HARD.
BUT, IN THE FUTURE...
KAKERU IS GONE.
MY FUTURE SELF...
MUST HAVE BEEN SHATTERED.
I NEVER WANT TO EXPERI- ENCE...
THAT KIND OF PAIN.
I WANT TO SAVE THEM.
KAKERU...
AND MY FUTURE SELF.

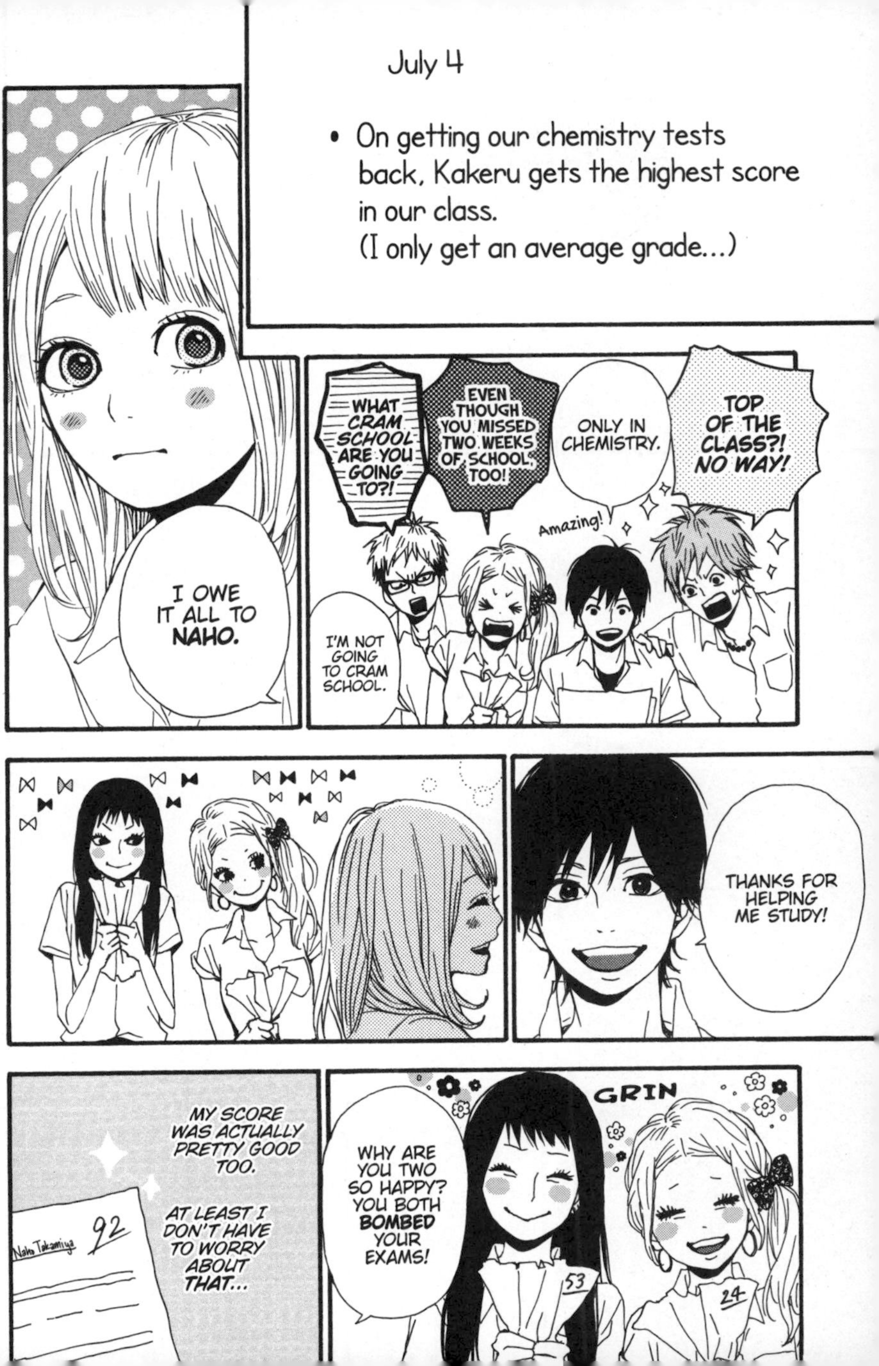
July 4
• On getting our chemistry tests back, Kakeru gets the highest score in our class.
(I only get an average grade...)
TOP OF THE CLASS?! NO WAY!
Amazing!
ONLY IN CHEMISTRY.
EVEN THOUGH YOU MISSED TWO WEEKS OF SCHOOL, TOO!
WHAT CRAM SCHOOL ARE YOU GOING TO?!
I'M NOT GOING TO CRAM SCHOOL.
I OWE IT ALL TO NAHO.
THANKS FOR HELPING ME STUDY!
GRIN
WHY ARE YOU TWO SO HAPPY? YOU BOTH BOMBED YOUR EXAMS!
53
24
MY SCORE WAS ACTUALLY PRETTY GOOD TOO.
AT LEAST I DON'T HAVE TO WORRY ABOUT THAT...
Naho Takamiya
92

• After we get our tests back, there's still time in class, so Nakano-sensei gives a talk.

That talk was so interesting, I remember it even now.

The talk is about **time travel.**

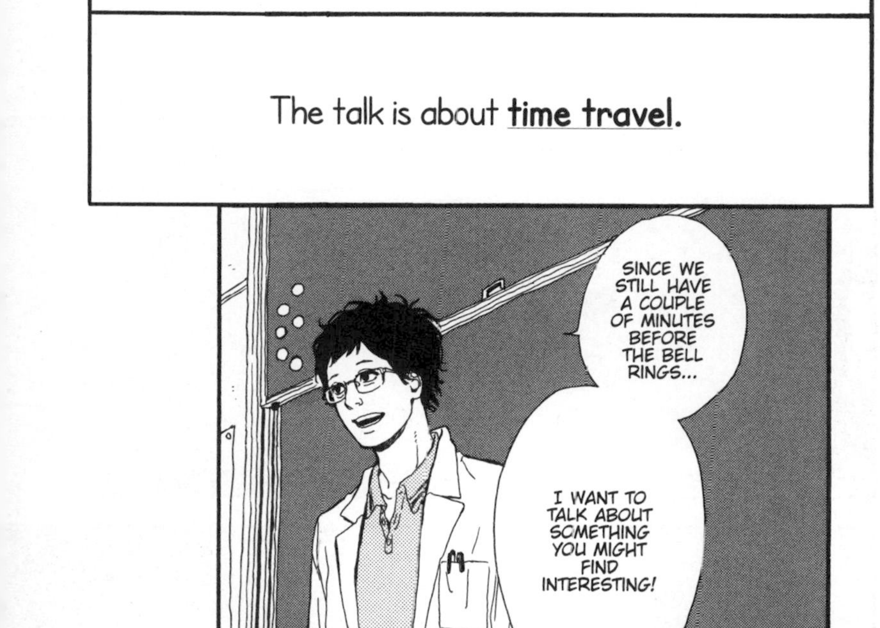
SINCE WE STILL HAVE A COUPLE OF MINUTES BEFORE THE BELL RINGS...
I WANT TO TALK ABOUT SOMETHING YOU MIGHT FIND INTERESTING!

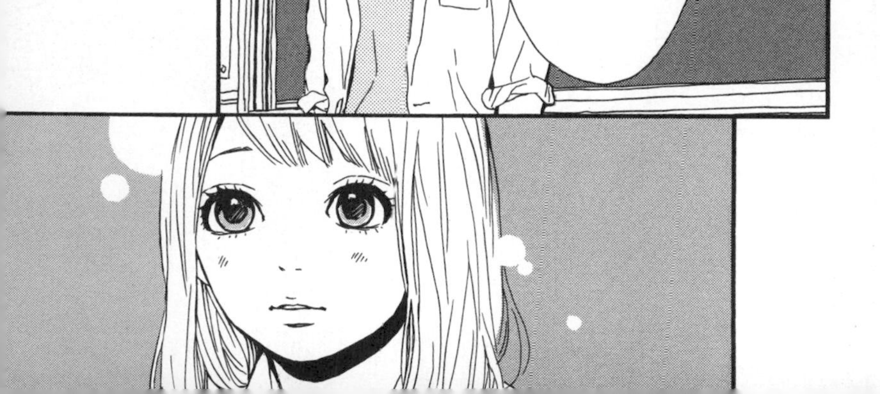

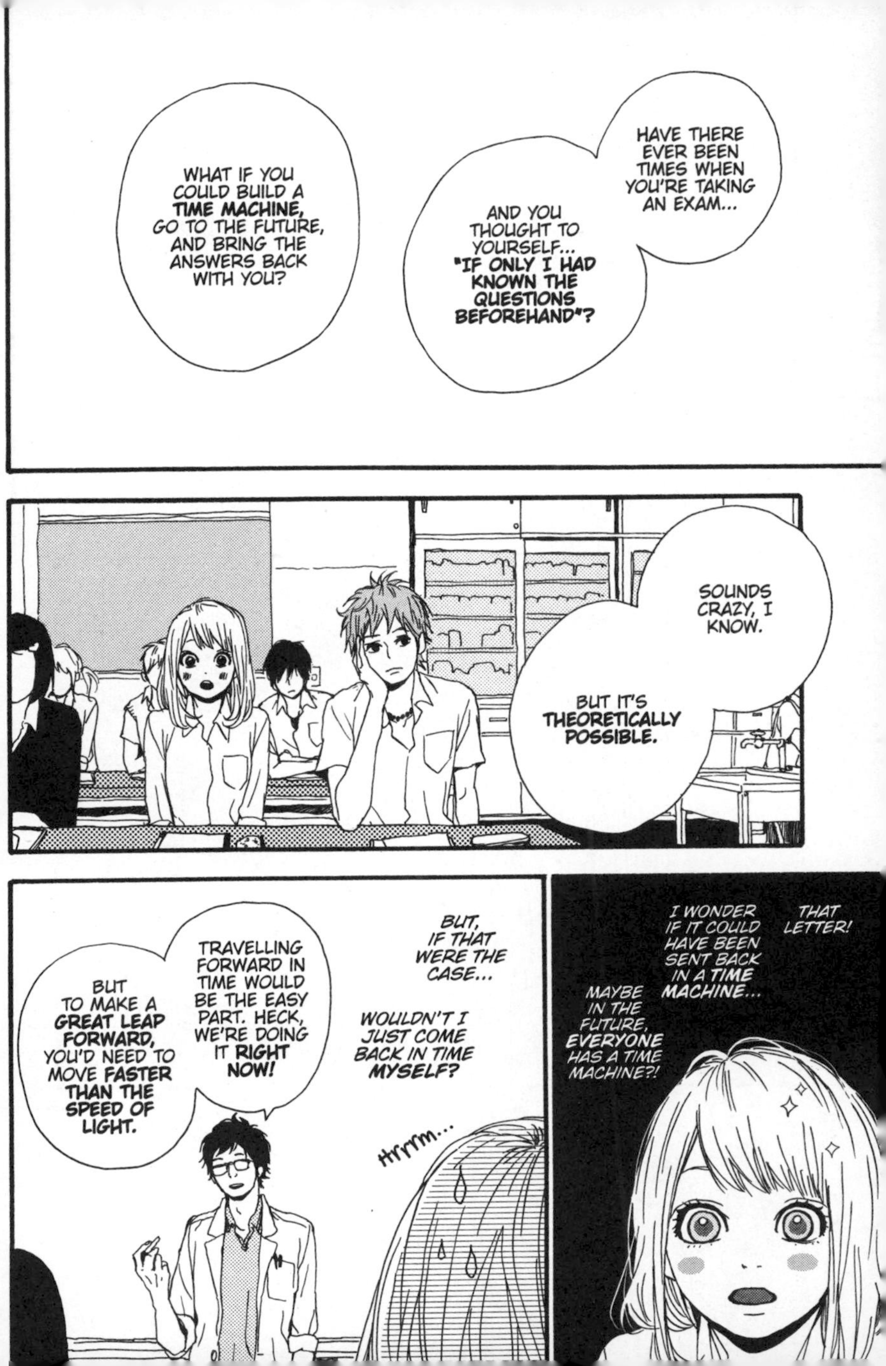
HAVE THERE EVER BEEN TIMES WHEN YOU'RE TAKING AN EXAM...
AND YOU THOUGHT TO YOURSELF... "IF ONLY I HAD KNOWN THE QUESTIONS BEFOREHAND"?
WHAT IF YOU COULD BUILD A TIME MACHINE, GO TO THE FUTURE, AND BRING THE ANSWERS BACK WITH YOU?
SOUNDS CRAZY, I KNOW.
BUT IT'S THEORETICALLY POSSIBLE.
THAT LETTER!
I WONDER IF IT COULD HAVE BEEN SENT BACK IN A TIME MACHINE...
MAYBE IN THE FUTURE, EVERYONE HAS A TIME MACHINE?!
BUT, IF THAT WERE THE CASE...
WOULDN'T I JUST COME BACK IN TIME MYSELF?
Hrrrm...
TRAVELLING FORWARD IN TIME WOULD BE THE EASY PART. HECK, WE'RE DOING IT RIGHT NOW!
BUT TO MAKE A GREAT LEAP FORWARD, YOU'D NEED TO MOVE FASTER THAN THE SPEED OF LIGHT.

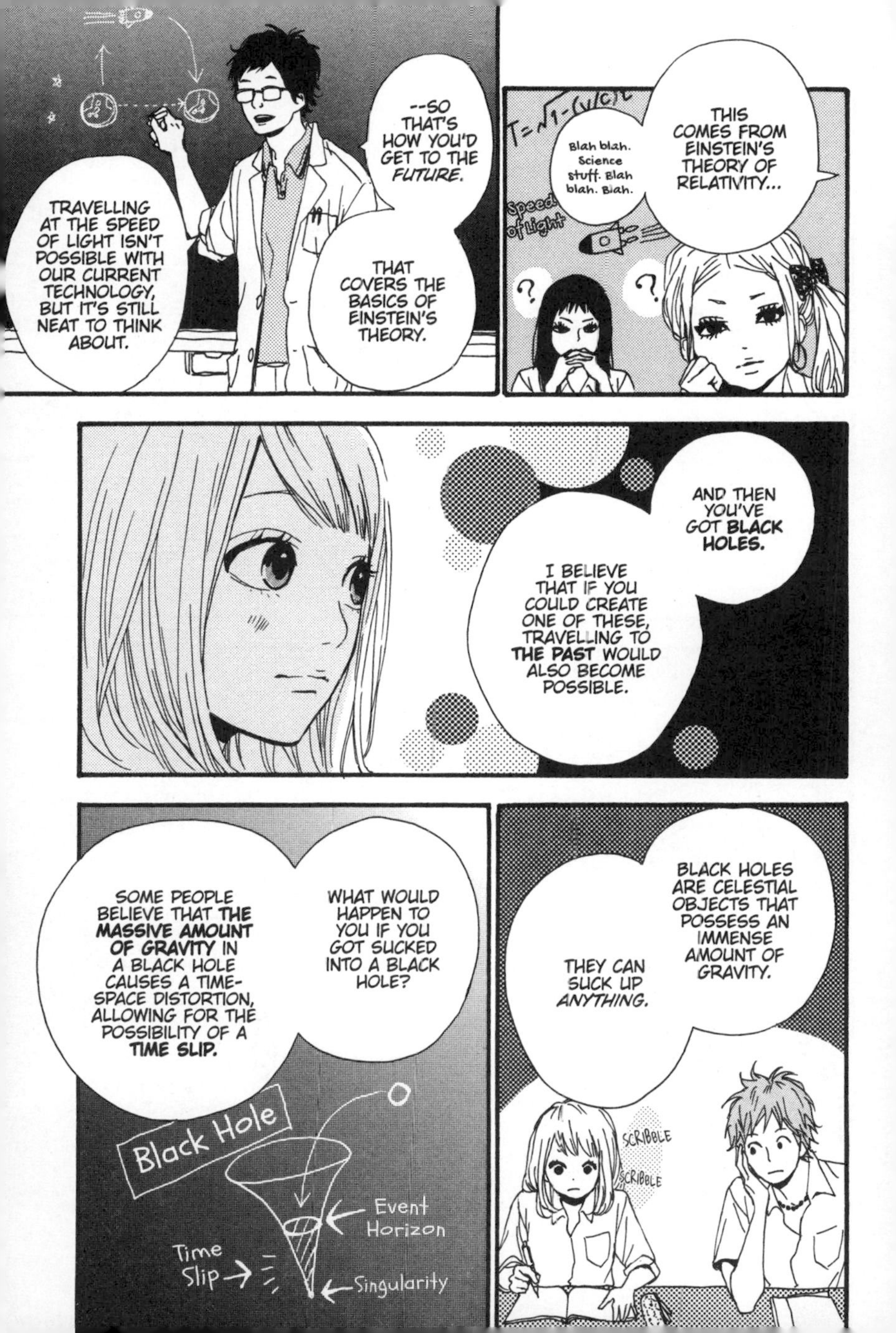
THIS COMES FROM EINSTEIN'S THEORY OF RELATIVITY...
Blah blah. Science stuff. Blah blah. Blah.
Speed of Light
--SO THAT'S HOW YOU'D GET TO THE *FUTURE*.
THAT COVERS THE BASICS OF EINSTEIN'S THEORY.
TRAVELLING AT THE SPEED OF LIGHT ISN'T POSSIBLE WITH OUR CURRENT TECHNOLOGY, BUT IT'S STILL NEAT TO THINK ABOUT.
AND THEN YOU'VE GOT **BLACK HOLES.**
I BELIEVE THAT IF YOU COULD CREATE ONE OF THESE, TRAVELLING TO **THE PAST** WOULD ALSO BECOME POSSIBLE.
BLACK HOLES ARE CELESTIAL OBJECTS THAT POSSESS AN IMMENSE AMOUNT OF GRAVITY.
THEY CAN SUCK UP *ANYTHING*.
SCRIBBLE
SCRIBBLE
WHAT WOULD HAPPEN TO YOU IF YOU GOT SUCKED INTO A BLACK HOLE?
SOME PEOPLE BELIEVE THAT **THE MASSIVE AMOUNT OF GRAVITY** IN A BLACK HOLE CAUSES A TIME-SPACE DISTORTION, ALLOWING FOR THE POSSIBILITY OF A **TIME SLIP.**
Black Hole
Event Horizon
Time Slip
Singularity

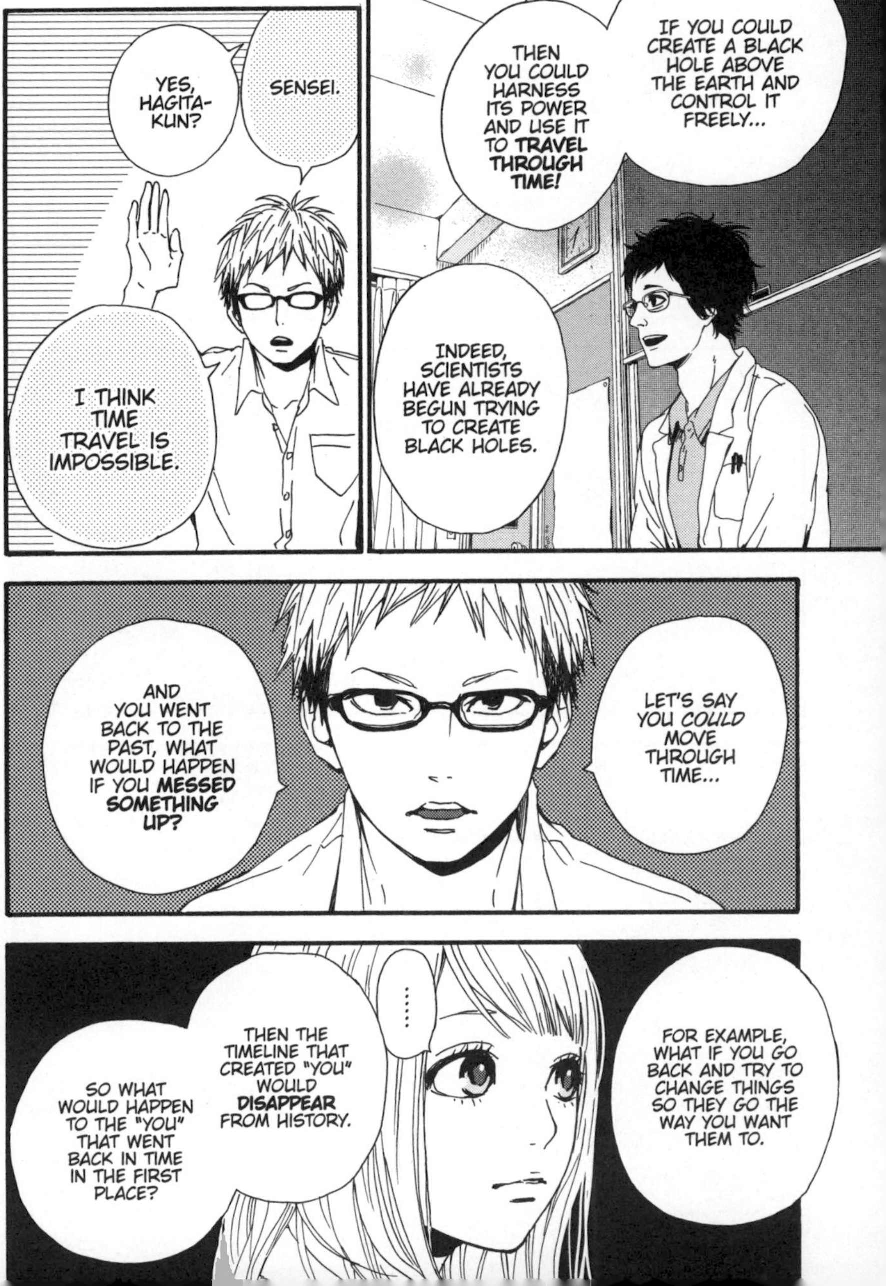
IF YOU COULD CREATE A BLACK HOLE ABOVE THE EARTH AND CONTROL IT FREELY...
THEN YOU COULD HARNESS ITS POWER AND USE IT TO **TRAVEL THROUGH TIME!**
INDEED, SCIENTISTS HAVE ALREADY BEGUN TRYING TO CREATE BLACK HOLES.
SENSEI.
YES, HAGITA-KUN?
I THINK TIME TRAVEL IS IMPOSSIBLE.
LET'S SAY YOU COULD MOVE THROUGH TIME...
AND YOU WENT BACK TO THE PAST, WHAT WOULD HAPPEN IF YOU **MESSED SOMETHING UP?**
FOR EXAMPLE, WHAT IF YOU GO BACK AND TRY TO CHANGE THINGS SO THEY GO THE WAY YOU WANT THEM TO.
......
THEN THE TIMELINE THAT CREATED "YOU" WOULD **DISAPPEAR** FROM HISTORY.
SO WHAT WOULD HAPPEN TO THE "YOU" THAT WENT BACK IN TIME IN THE FIRST PLACE?

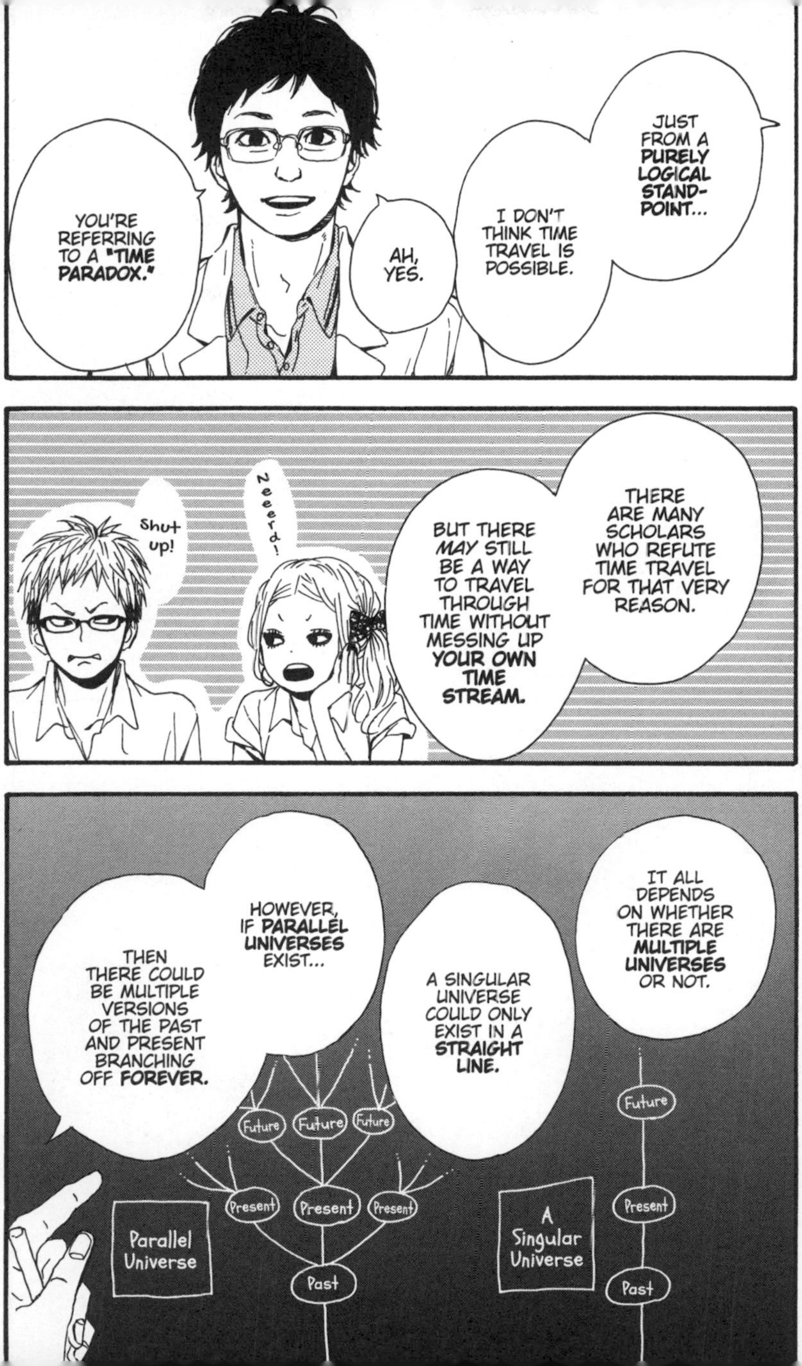
JUST FROM A PURELY LOGICAL STANDPOINT...
I DON'T THINK TIME TRAVEL IS POSSIBLE.
AH, YES.
YOU'RE REFERRING TO A "TIME PARADOX."
THERE ARE MANY SCHOLARS WHO REFUTE TIME TRAVEL FOR THAT VERY REASON.
BUT THERE MAY STILL BE A WAY TO TRAVEL THROUGH TIME WITHOUT MESSING UP YOUR OWN TIME STREAM.
Neeerd!
Shut up!
IT ALL DEPENDS ON WHETHER THERE ARE MULTIPLE UNIVERSES OR NOT.
A SINGULAR UNIVERSE COULD ONLY EXIST IN A STRAIGHT LINE.
HOWEVER, IF PARALLEL UNIVERSES EXIST...
THEN THERE COULD BE MULTIPLE VERSIONS OF THE PAST AND PRESENT BRANCHING OFF FOREVER.
Future
Present
Past
A Singular Universe
Future
Future
Future
Present
Present
Present
Past
Parallel Universe

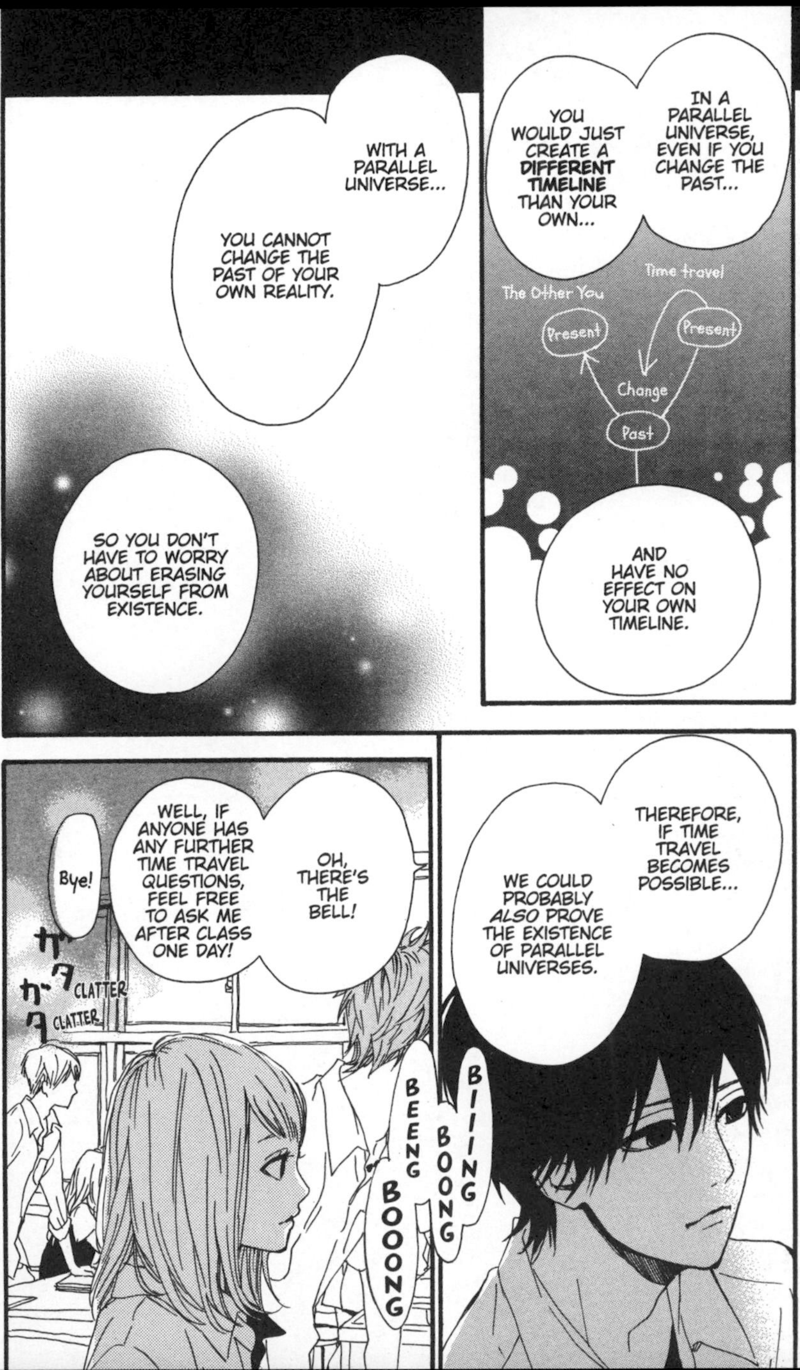
IN A PARALLEL UNIVERSE, EVEN IF YOU CHANGE THE PAST...
YOU WOULD JUST CREATE A **DIFFERENT TIMELINE** THAN YOUR OWN...
Time travel
The Other You
Present
Present
Change
Past
AND HAVE NO EFFECT ON YOUR OWN TIMELINE.
WITH A PARALLEL UNIVERSE...
YOU CANNOT CHANGE THE PAST OF YOUR OWN REALITY.
SO YOU DON'T HAVE TO WORRY ABOUT ERASING YOURSELF FROM EXISTENCE.
THEREFORE, IF TIME TRAVEL BECOMES POSSIBLE...
WE COULD PROBABLY *ALSO* PROVE THE EXISTENCE OF PARALLEL UNIVERSES.
BIIING
BOONG
BEENG
BOOONG
OH, THERE'S THE BELL!
WELL, IF ANYONE HAS ANY FURTHER TIME TRAVEL QUESTIONS, FEEL FREE TO ASK ME AFTER CLASS ONE DAY!
Bye!
ガタ CLATTER
ガタ CLATTER

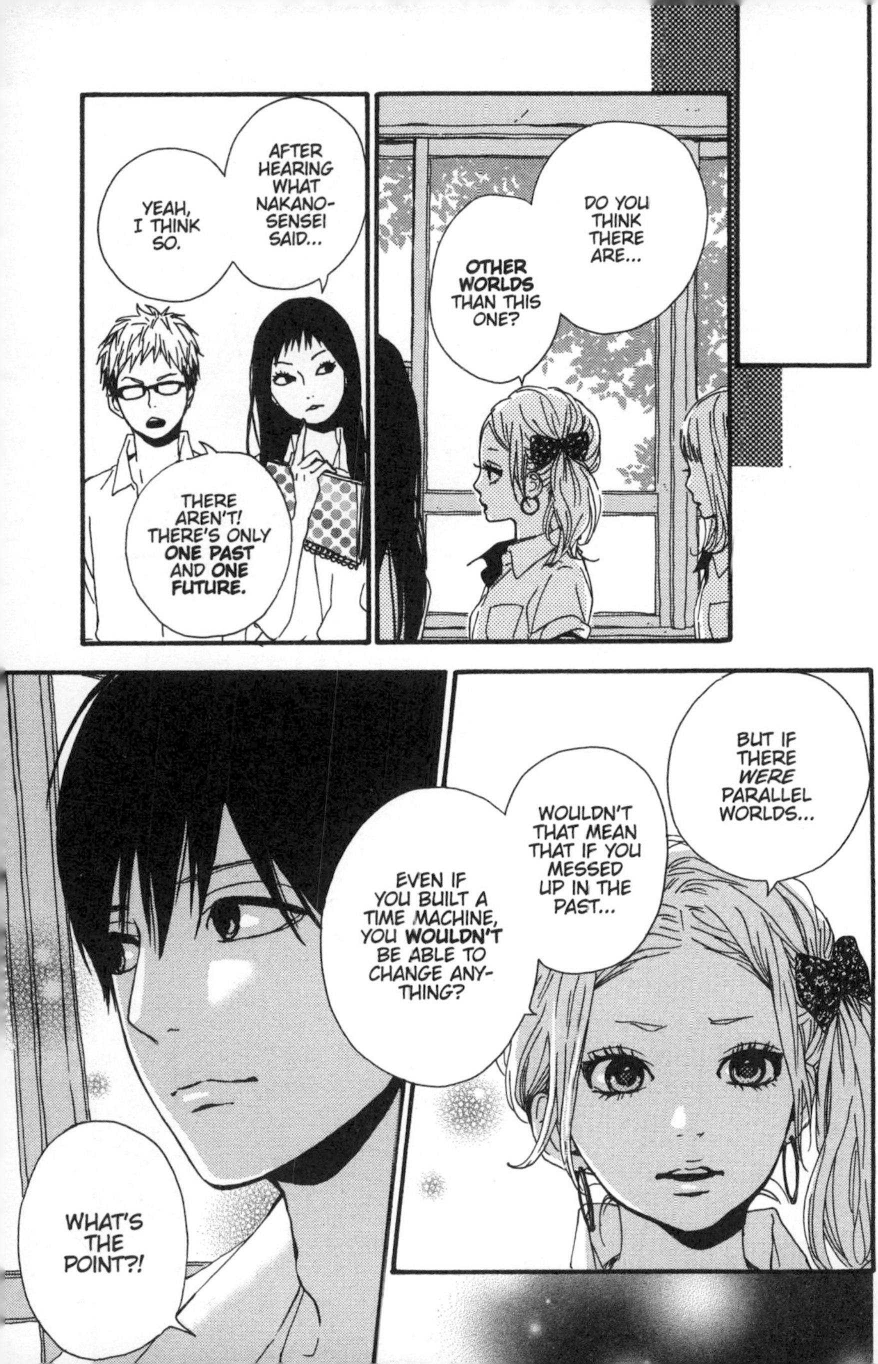
DO YOU THINK THERE ARE...
OTHER WORLDS THAN THIS ONE?
AFTER HEARING WHAT NAKANO-SENSEI SAID...
YEAH, I THINK SO.
THERE AREN'T! THERE'S ONLY ONE PAST AND ONE FUTURE.
BUT IF THERE WERE PARALLEL WORLDS...
WOULDN'T THAT MEAN THAT IF YOU MESSED UP IN THE PAST...
EVEN IF YOU BUILT A TIME MACHINE, YOU WOULDN'T BE ABLE TO CHANGE ANYTHING?
WHAT'S THE POINT?!

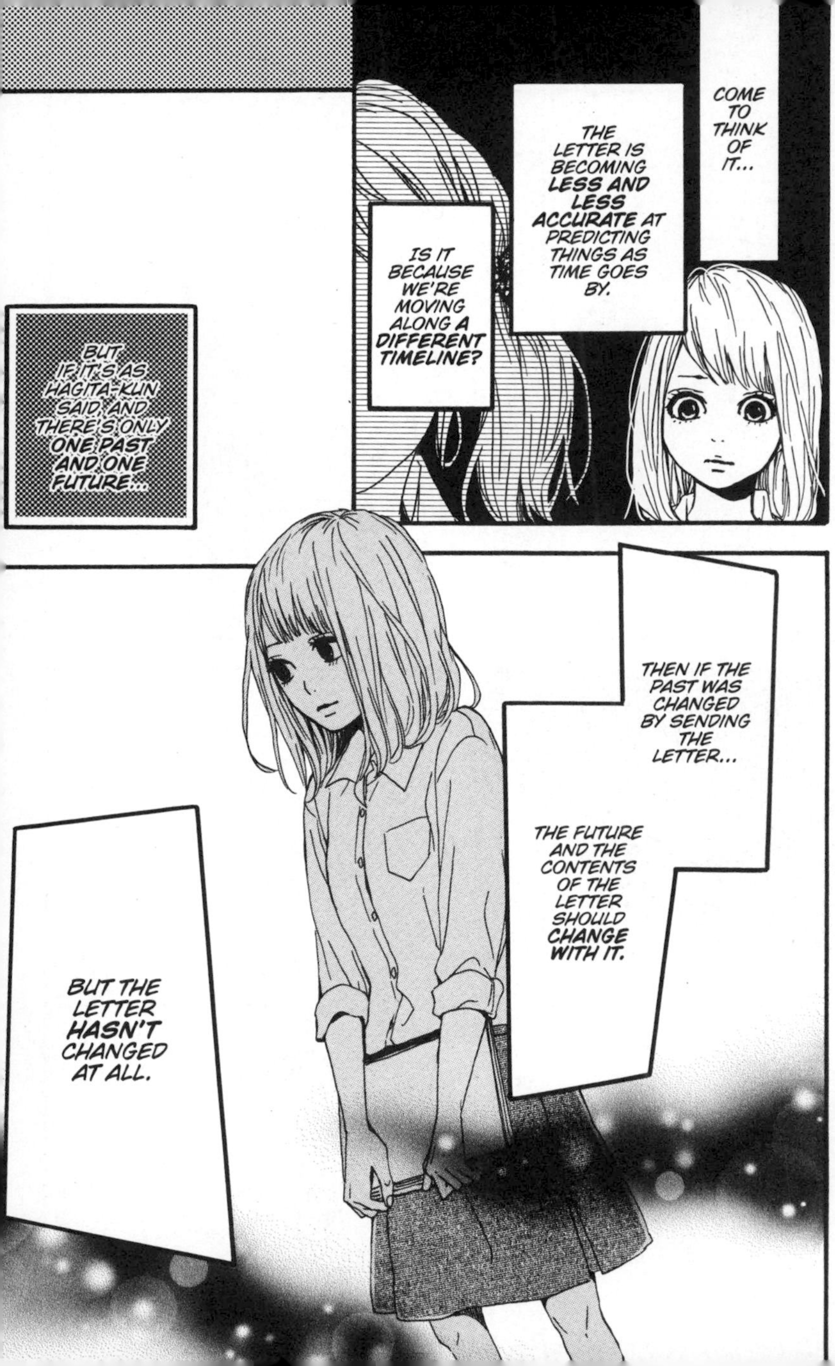
COME TO THINK OF IT...
THE LETTER IS BECOMING LESS AND LESS ACCURATE AT PREDICTING THINGS AS TIME GOES BY.
IS IT BECAUSE WE'RE MOVING ALONG A DIFFERENT TIMELINE?
BUT IF IT'S AS HAGITA-KUN SAID AND THERE'S ONLY ONE PAST AND ONE FUTURE...
THEN IF THE PAST WAS CHANGED BY SENDING THE LETTER...
THE FUTURE AND THE CONTENTS OF THE LETTER SHOULD CHANGE WITH IT.
BUT THE LETTER HASN'T CHANGED AT ALL.

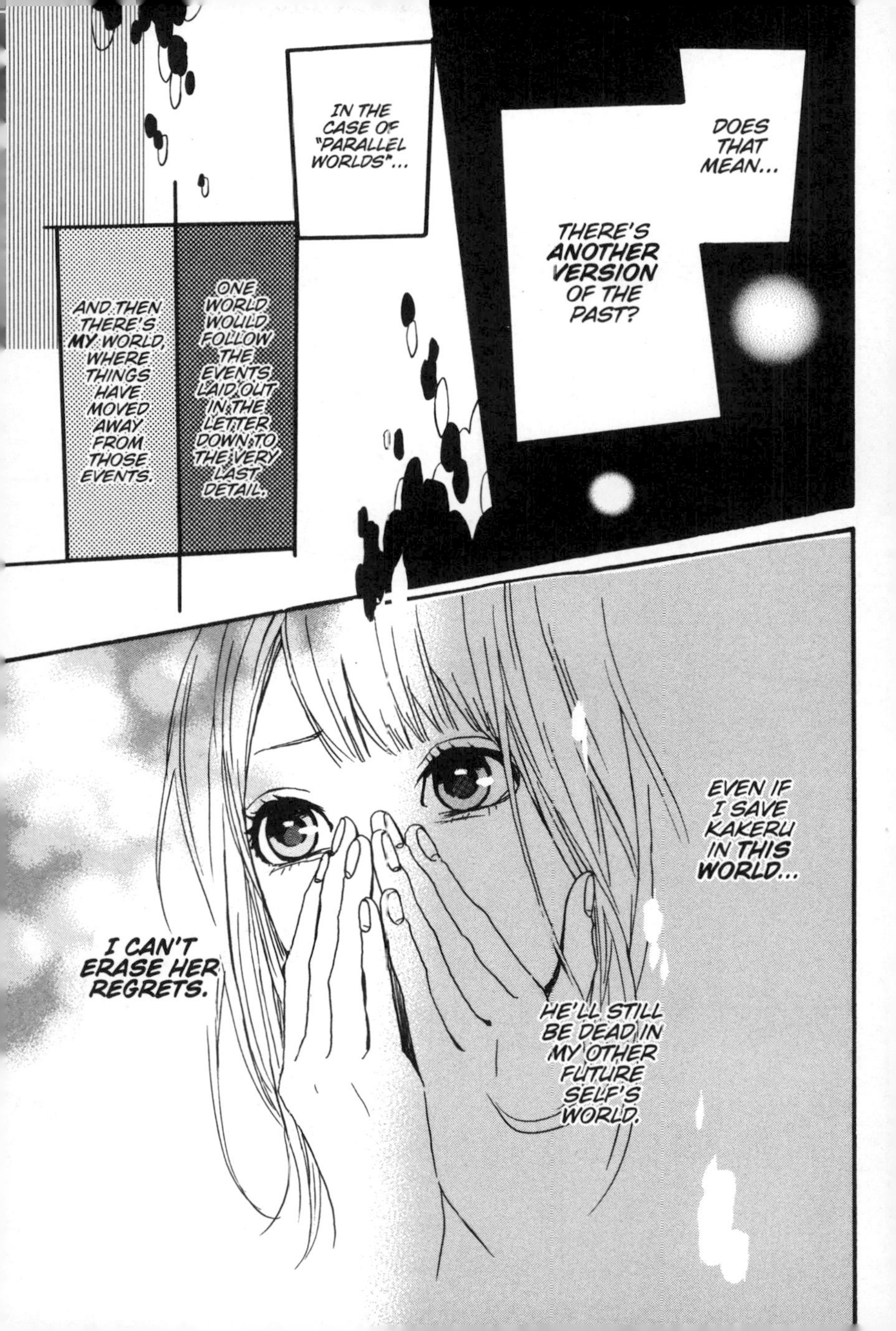

DOES THAT MEAN...
THERE'S ANOTHER VERSION OF THE PAST?
IN THE CASE OF "PARALLEL WORLDS"...
ONE WORLD WOULD FOLLOW THE EVENTS LAID OUT IN THE LETTER DOWN TO THE VERY LAST DETAIL.
AND THEN THERE'S MY WORLD, WHERE THINGS HAVE MOVED AWAY FROM THOSE EVENTS.
EVEN IF I SAVE KAKERU IN THIS WORLD...
HE'LL STILL BE DEAD IN MY OTHER FUTURE SELF'S WORLD.
I CAN'T ERASE HER REGRETS.

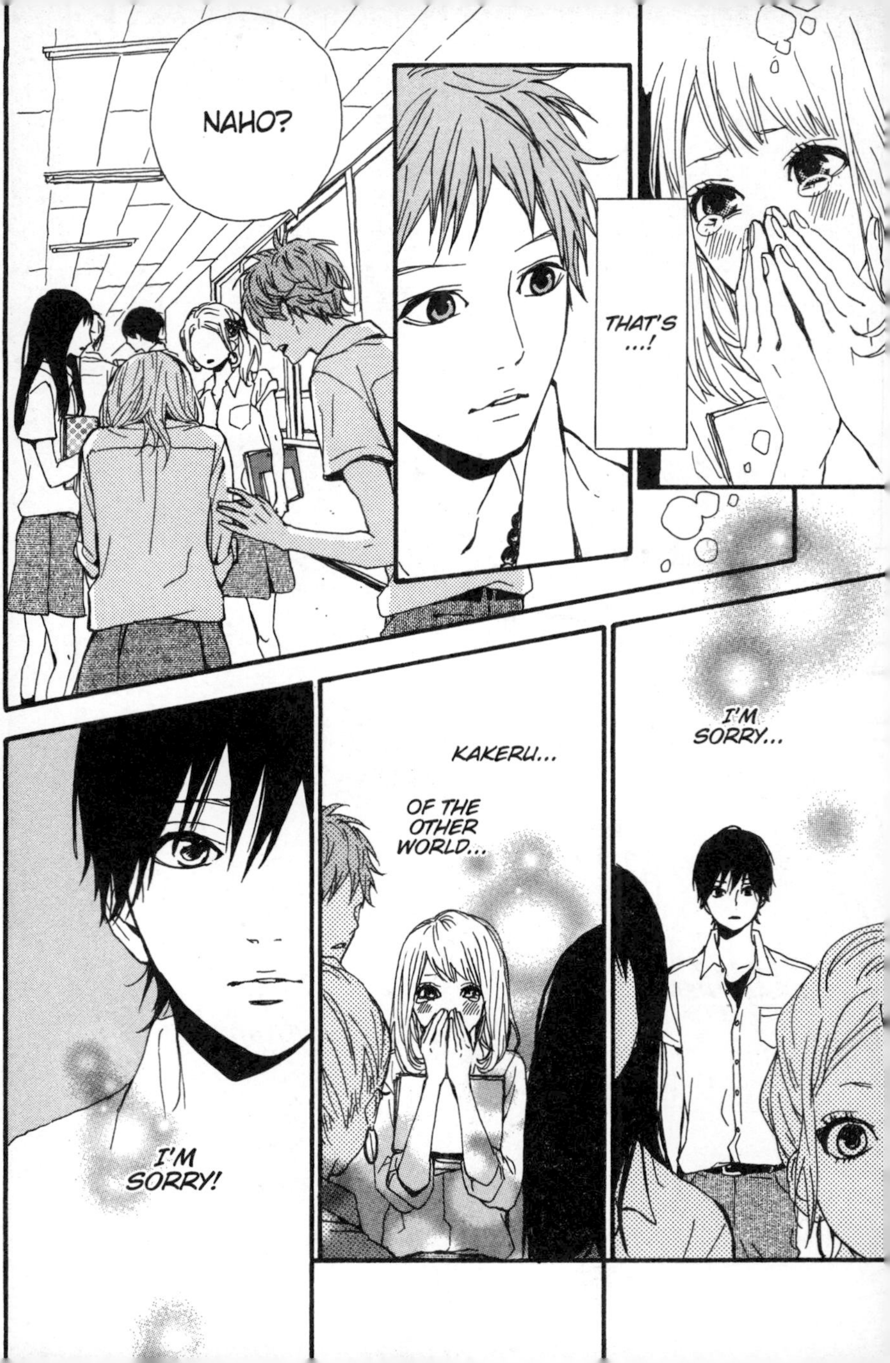
THAT'S ...!
NAHO?
I'M SORRY...
KAKERU...
OF THE OTHER WORLD...
I'M SORRY!

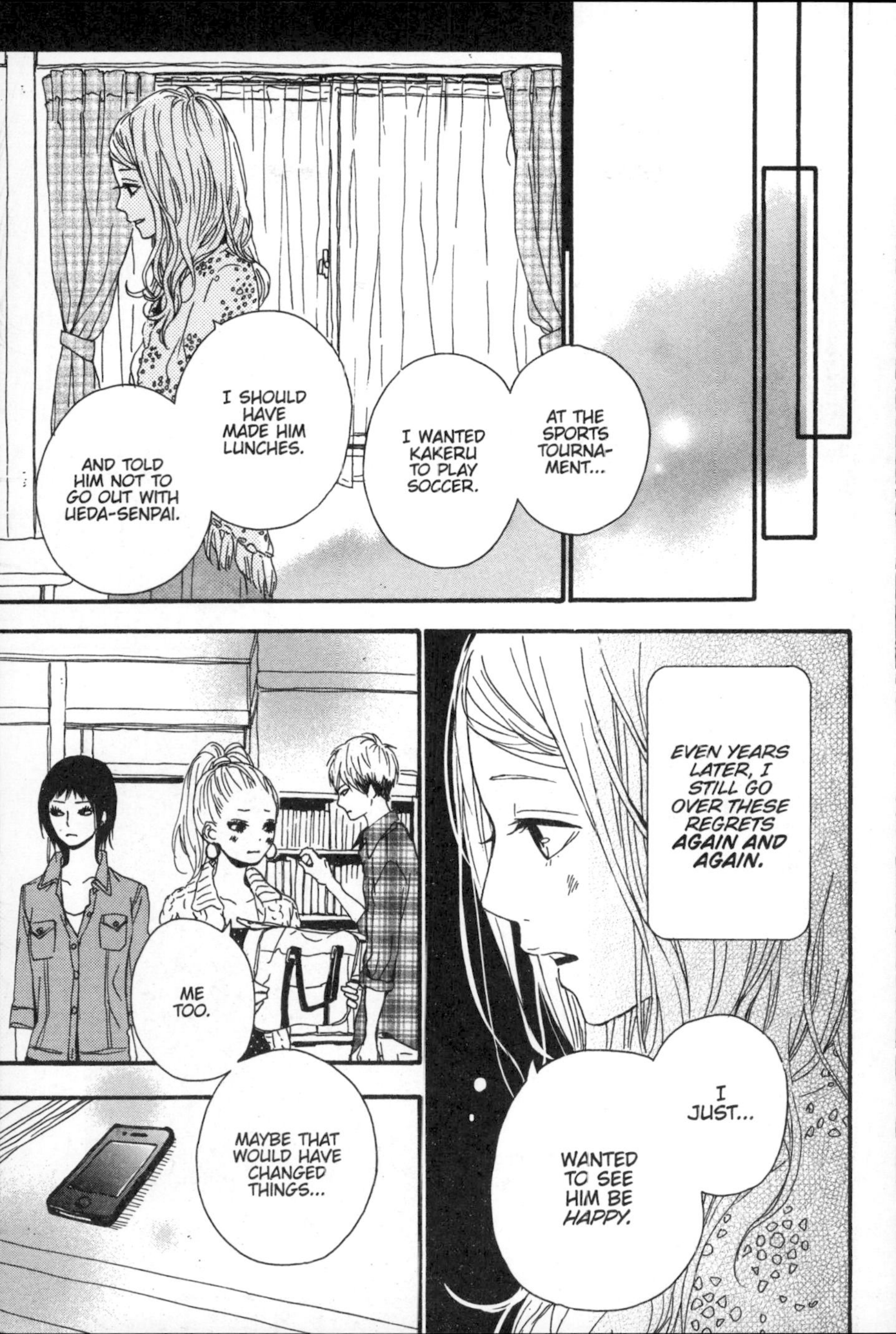
AT THE SPORTS TOURNAMENT...
I WANTED KAKERU TO PLAY SOCCER.
I SHOULD HAVE MADE HIM LUNCHES.
AND TOLD HIM NOT TO GO OUT WITH UEDA-SENPAI.
EVEN YEARS LATER, I STILL GO OVER THESE REGRETS AGAIN AND AGAIN.
I JUST...
WANTED TO SEE HIM BE HAPPY.
ME TOO.
MAYBE THAT WOULD HAVE CHANGED THINGS...

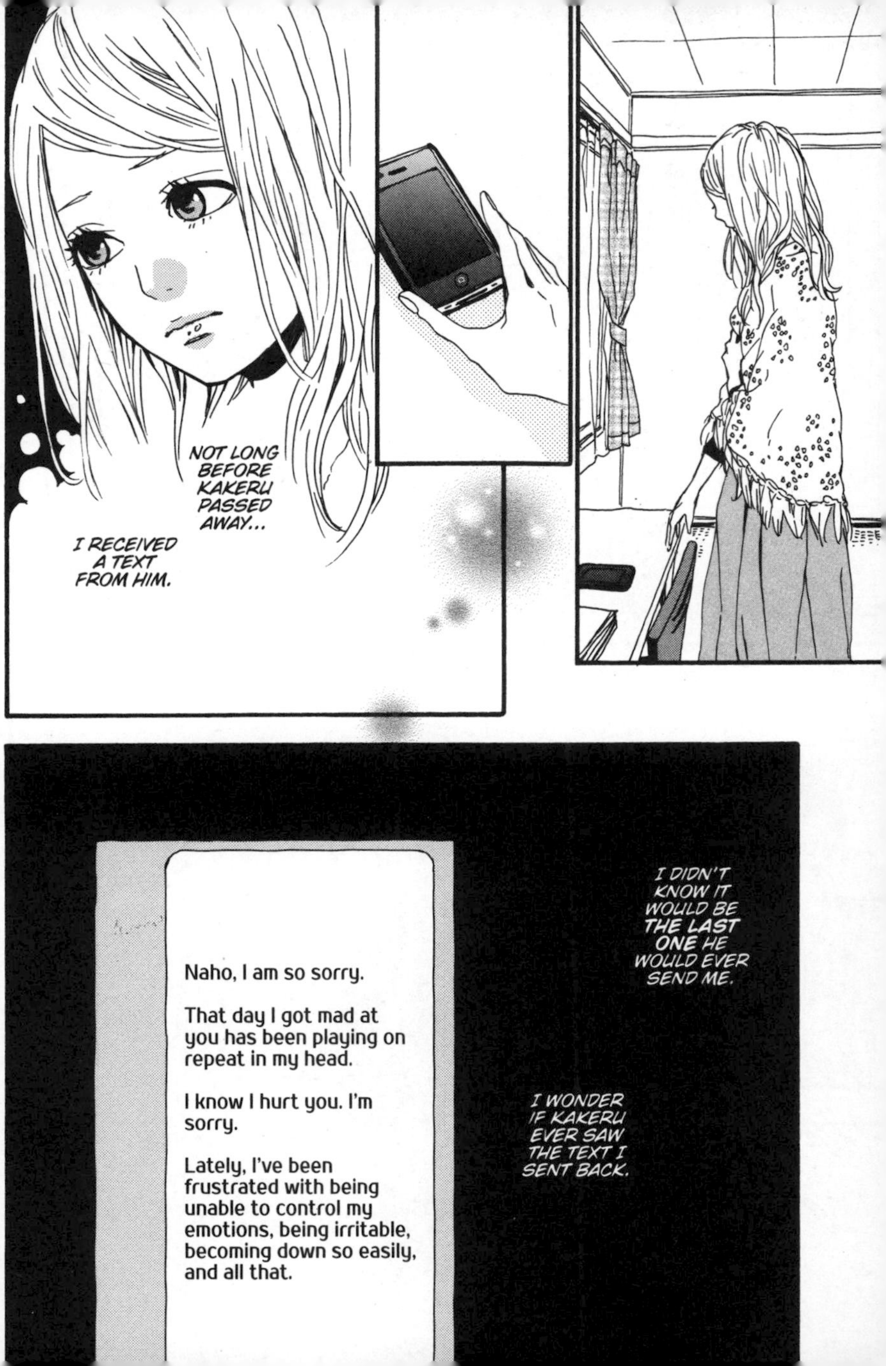
NOT LONG BEFORE KAKERU PASSED AWAY...
I RECEIVED A TEXT FROM HIM.
I DIDN'T KNOW IT WOULD BE THE LAST ONE HE WOULD EVER SEND ME.
I WONDER IF KAKERU EVER SAW THE TEXT I SENT BACK.
Naho, I am so sorry.
That day I got mad at you has been playing on repeat in my head.
I know I hurt you. I'm sorry.
Lately, I've been frustrated with being unable to control my emotions, being irritable, becoming down so easily, and all that.

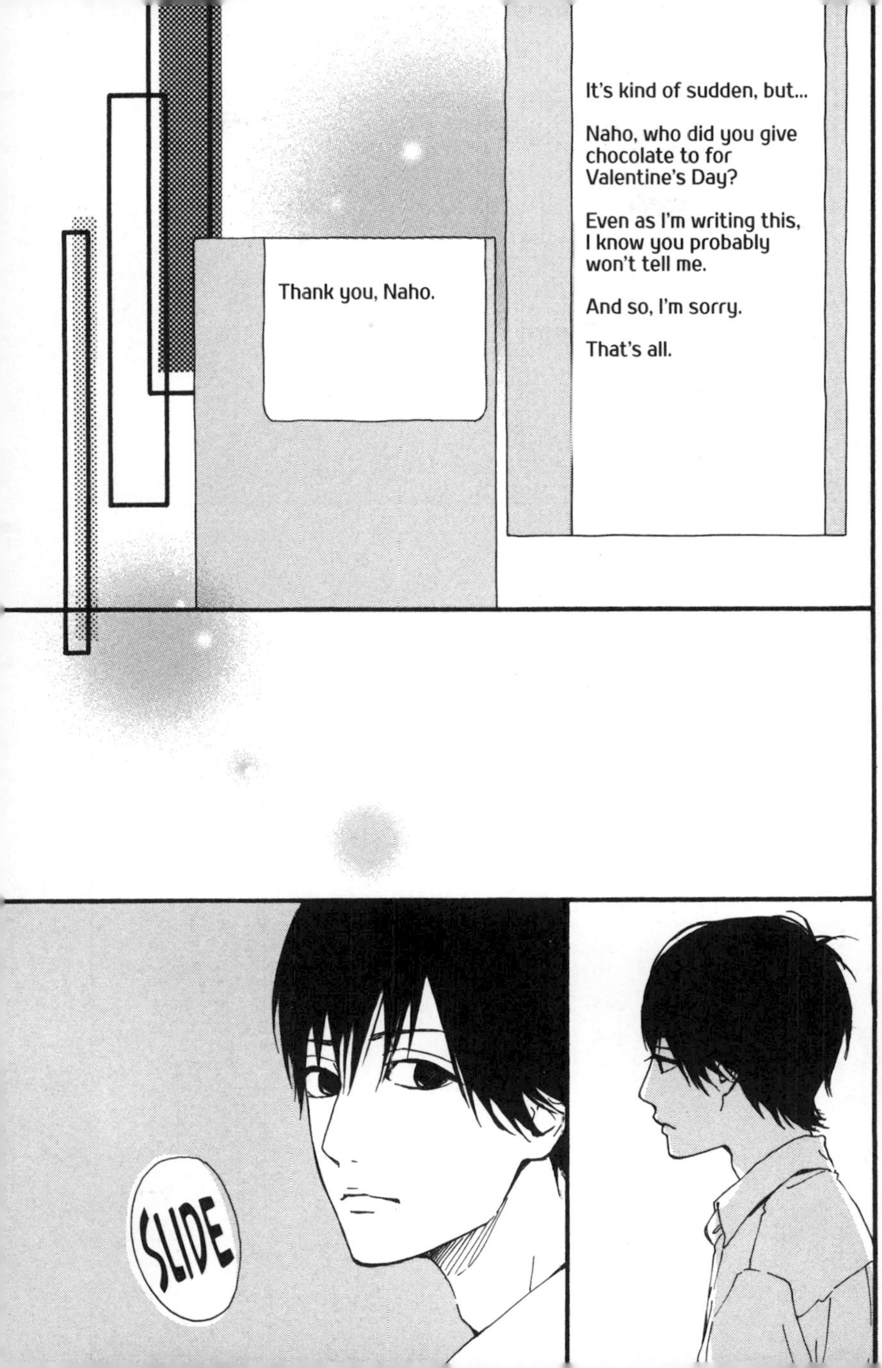
It's kind of sudden, but...
Naho, who did you give chocolate to for Valentine's Day?
Even as I'm writing this, I know you probably won't tell me.
And so, I'm sorry.
That's all.
Thank you, Naho.
SLIDE

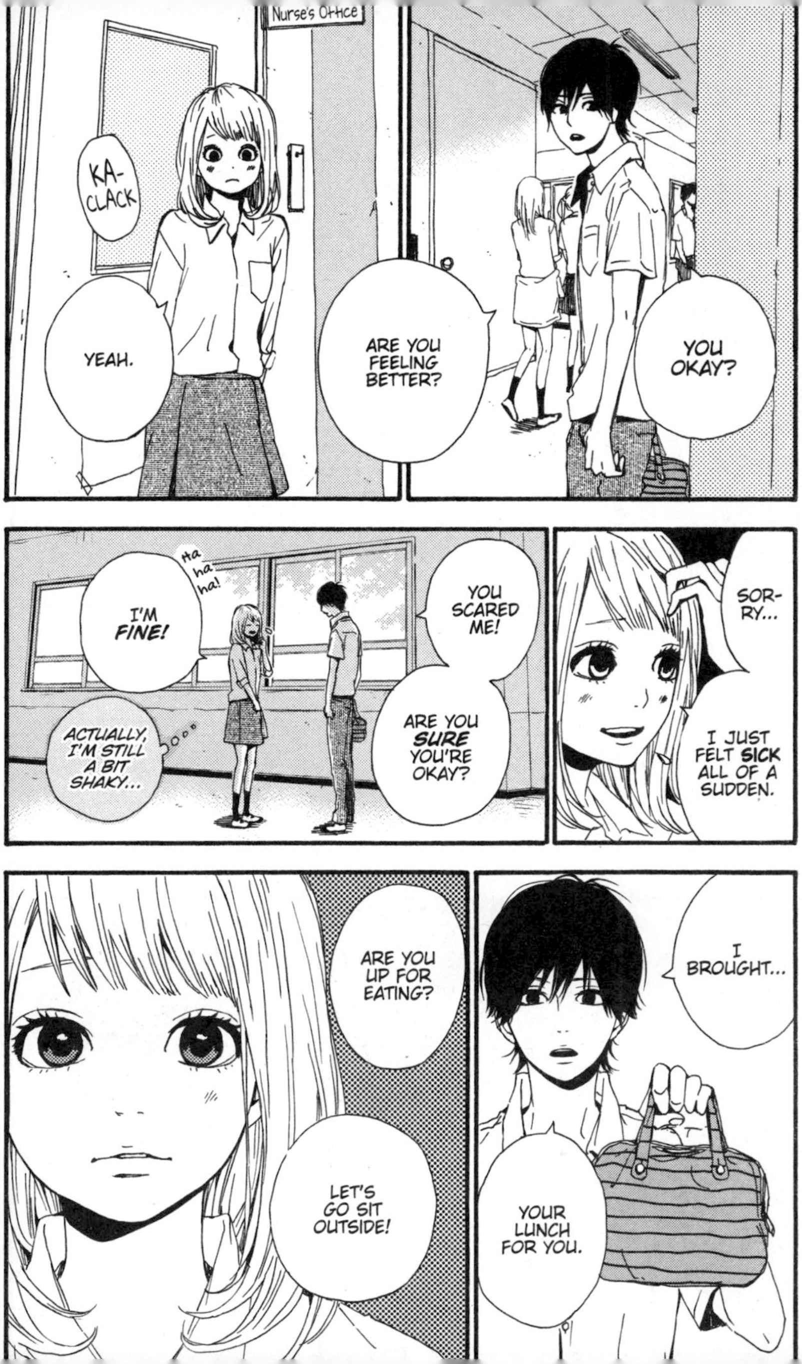
YOU OKAY?
ARE YOU FEELING BETTER?
Nurse's Office
KA-CLACK
YEAH.
SORRY...
I JUST FELT SICK ALL OF A SUDDEN.
YOU SCARED ME!
ARE YOU SURE YOU'RE OKAY?
Ha ha ha!
I'M FINE!
ACTUALLY, I'M STILL A BIT SHAKY...
I BROUGHT...
YOUR LUNCH FOR YOU.
ARE YOU UP FOR EATING?
LET'S GO SIT OUTSIDE!

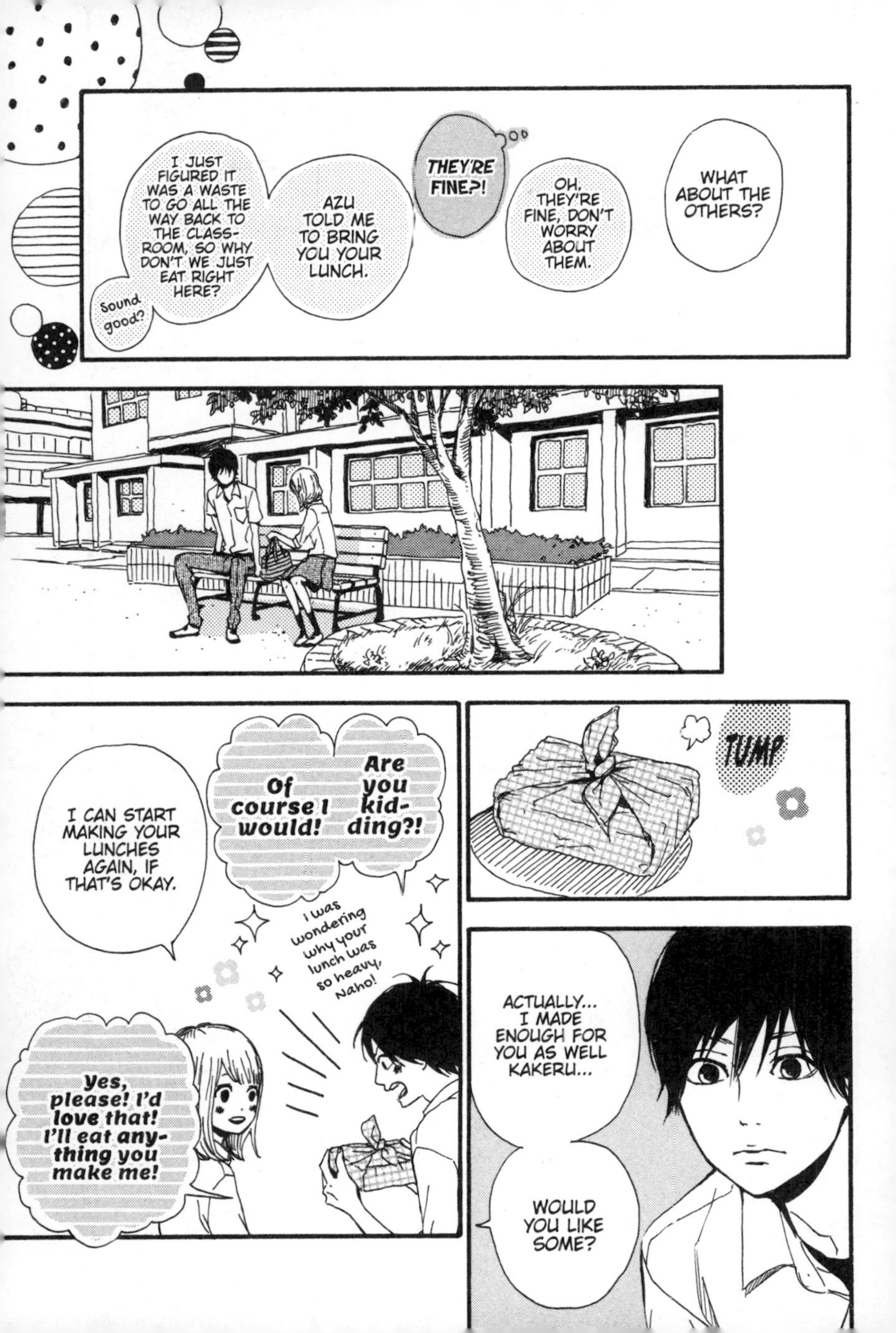
WHAT ABOUT THE OTHERS?
OH, THEY'RE FINE, DON'T WORRY ABOUT THEM.
THEY'RE FINE?!
AZU TOLD ME TO BRING YOU YOUR LUNCH.
I JUST FIGURED IT WAS A WASTE TO GO ALL THE WAY BACK TO THE CLASS-ROOM, SO WHY DON'T WE JUST EAT RIGHT HERE?
Sound good?
TUMP
ACTUALLY... I MADE ENOUGH FOR YOU AS WELL KAKERU...
WOULD YOU LIKE SOME?
Are you kid-ding?!
Of course I would!
I CAN START MAKING YOUR LUNCHES AGAIN, IF THAT'S OKAY.
I was wondering why your lunch was so heavy, Naho!
yes, please! I'd love that! I'll eat any-thing you make me!

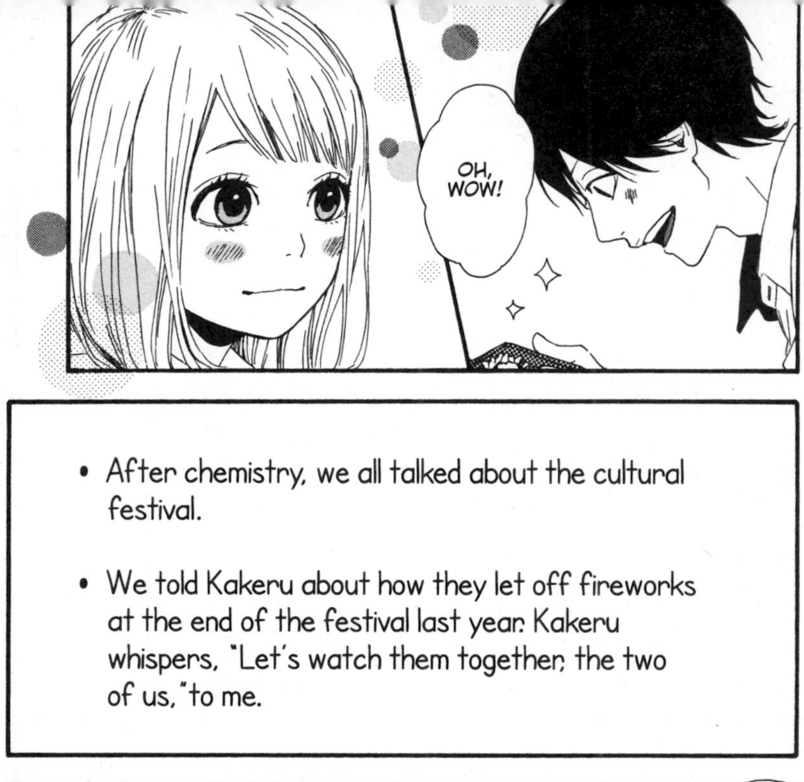
OH, WOW!

- After chemistry, we all talked about the cultural festival.
- We told Kakeru about how they let off fireworks at the end of the festival last year. Kakeru whispers, "Let's watch them together, the two of us," to me.

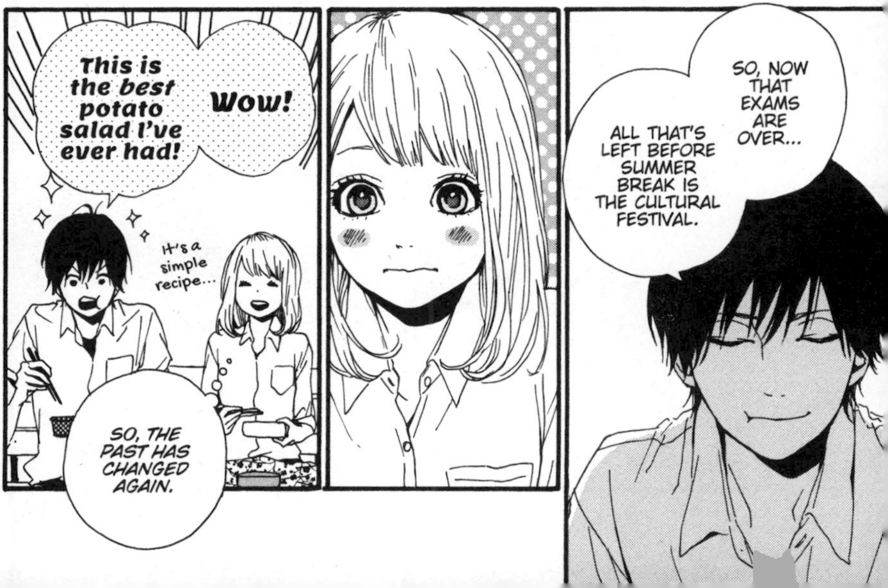
SO, NOW THAT EXAMS ARE OVER...
ALL THAT'S LEFT BEFORE SUMMER BREAK IS THE CULTURAL FESTIVAL.
Wow!
This is the best potato salad I've ever had!
It's a simple recipe...
SO, THE PAST HAS CHANGED AGAIN.

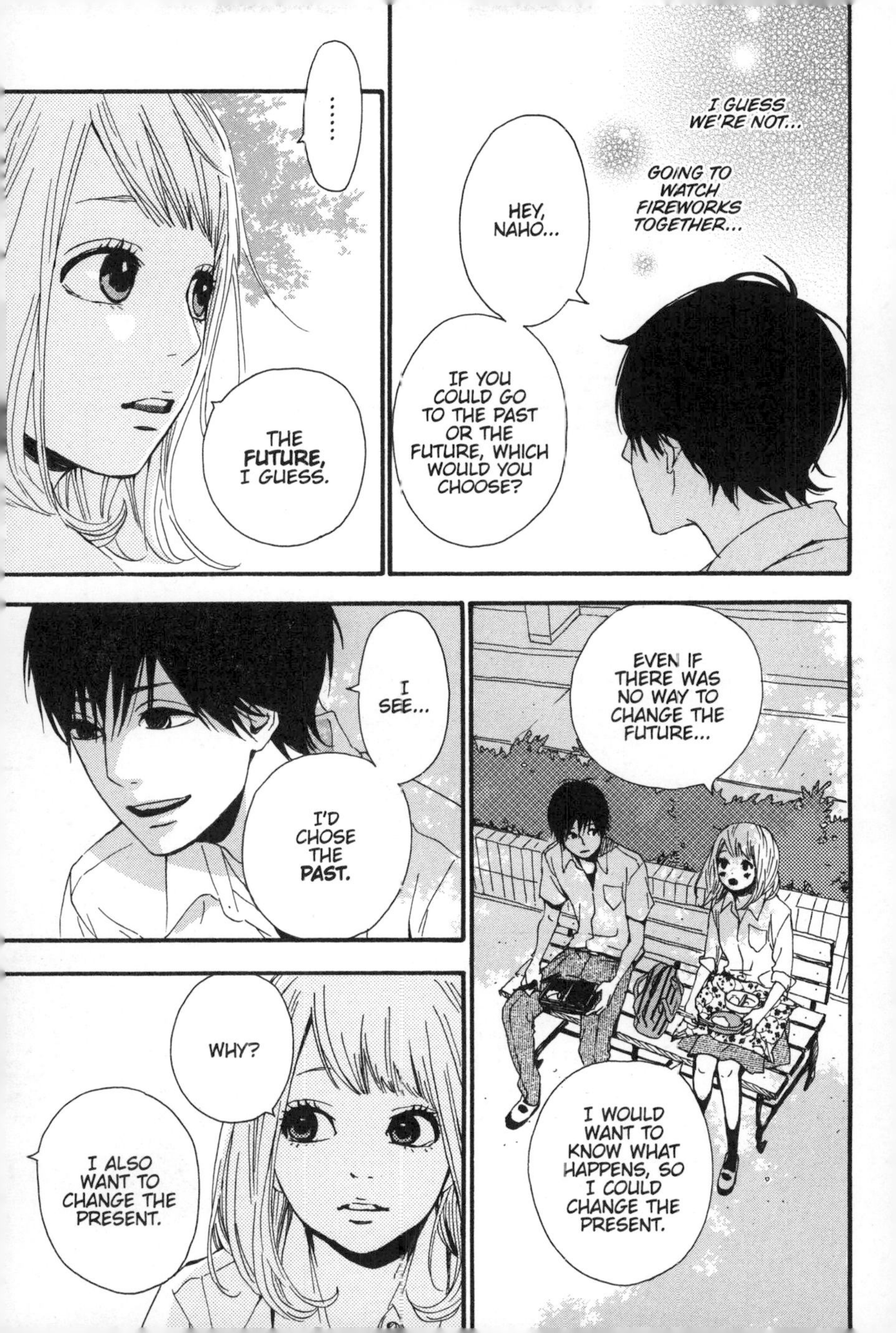
I GUESS WE'RE NOT...
GOING TO WATCH FIREWORKS TOGETHER...
HEY, NAHO...
IF YOU COULD GO TO THE PAST OR THE FUTURE, WHICH WOULD YOU CHOOSE?
......
THE FUTURE, I GUESS.
EVEN IF THERE WAS NO WAY TO CHANGE THE FUTURE...
I WOULD WANT TO KNOW WHAT HAPPENS, SO I COULD CHANGE THE PRESENT.
I SEE...
I'D CHOSE THE PAST.
WHY?
I ALSO WANT TO CHANGE THE PRESENT.

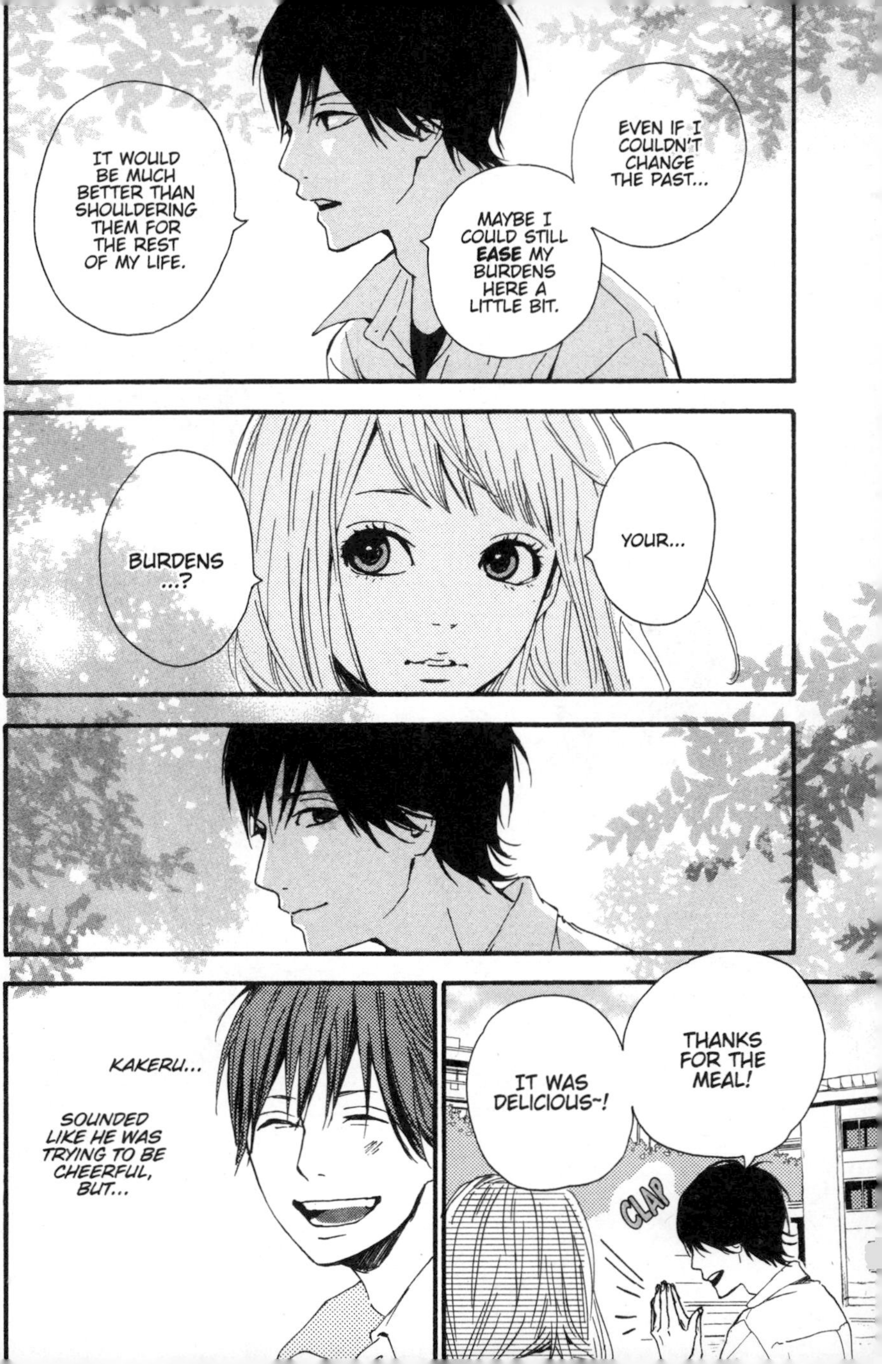
EVEN IF I COULDN'T CHANGE THE PAST...
MAYBE I COULD STILL EASE MY BURDENS HERE A LITTLE BIT.
IT WOULD BE MUCH BETTER THAN SHOULDERING THEM FOR THE REST OF MY LIFE.
YOUR...
BURDENS ...?
THANKS FOR THE MEAL!
IT WAS DELICIOUS~!
CLAP
KAKERU...
SOUNDED LIKE HE WAS TRYING TO BE CHEERFUL, BUT...

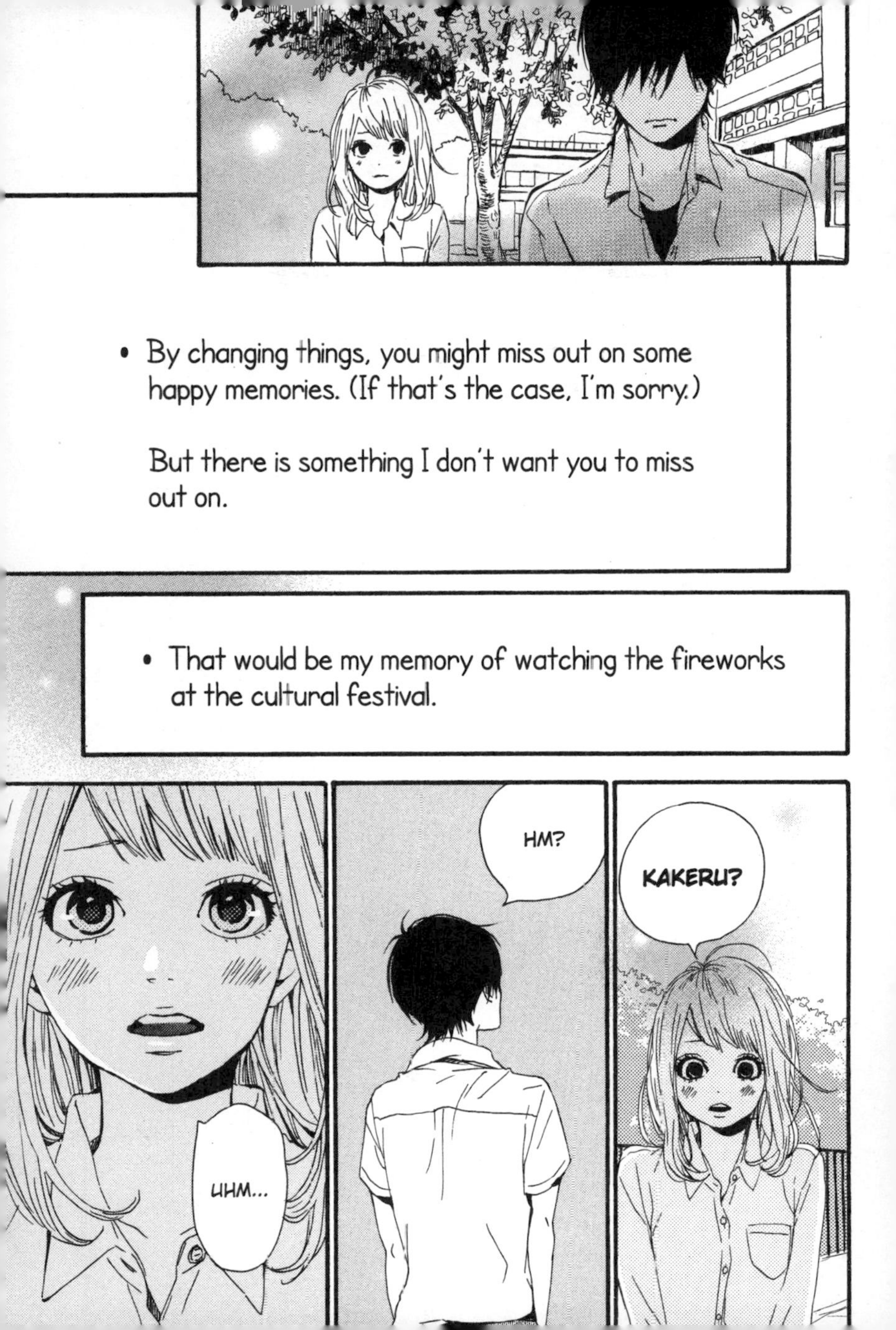
• By changing things, you might miss out on some happy memories. (If that's the case, I'm sorry.)
But there is something I don't want you to miss out on.
• That would be my memory of watching the fireworks at the cultural festival.
KAKERU?
HM?
UHM...

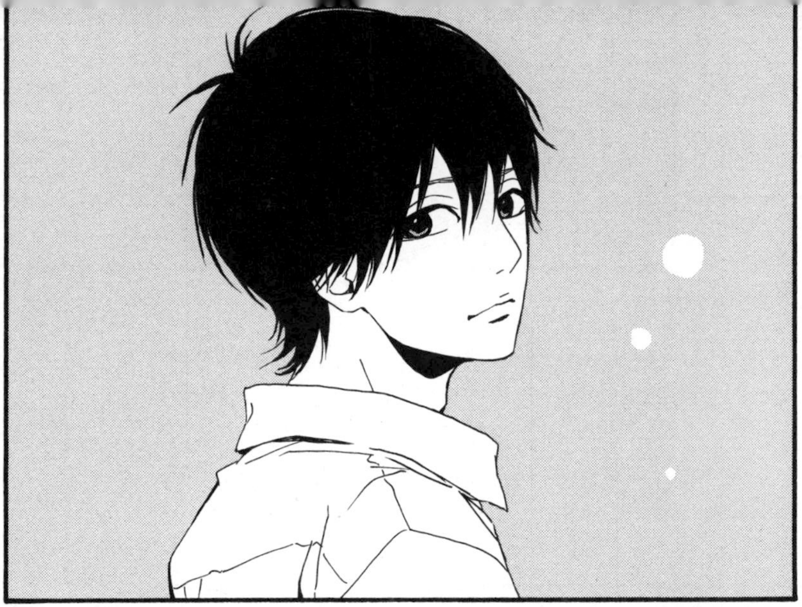

◎ Please don't erase that memory.

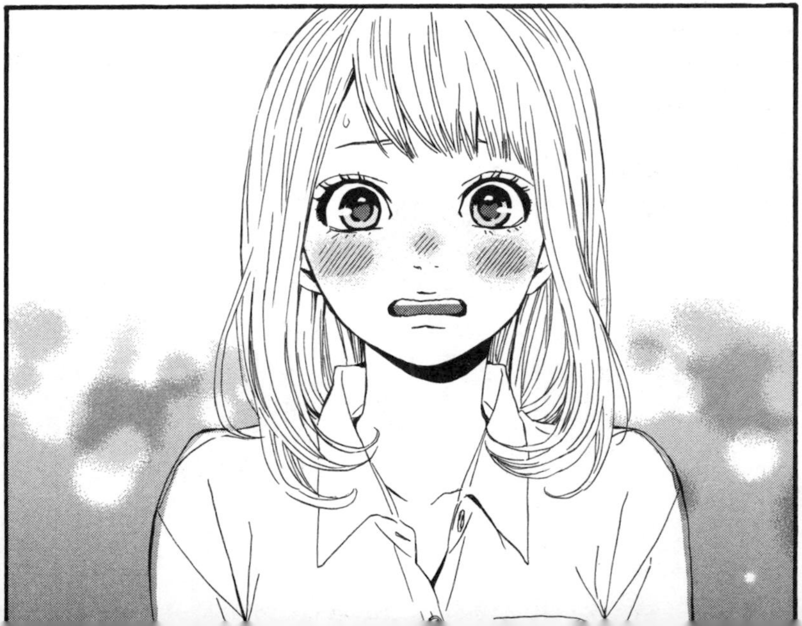

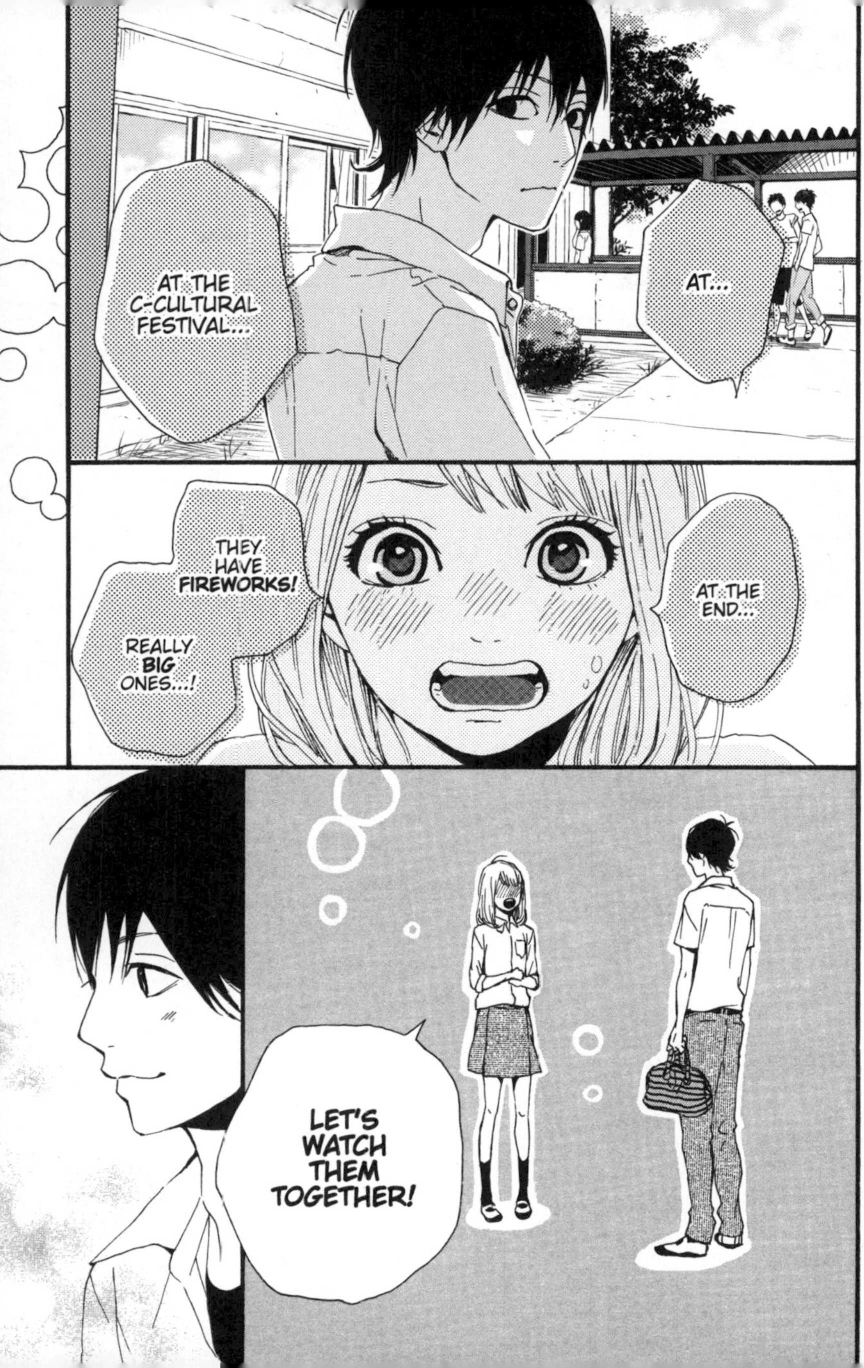
AT...
AT THE C-CULTURAL FESTIVAL...
AT THE END...
THEY HAVE FIREWORKS!
REALLY BIG ONES...!
LET'S WATCH THEM TOGETHER!

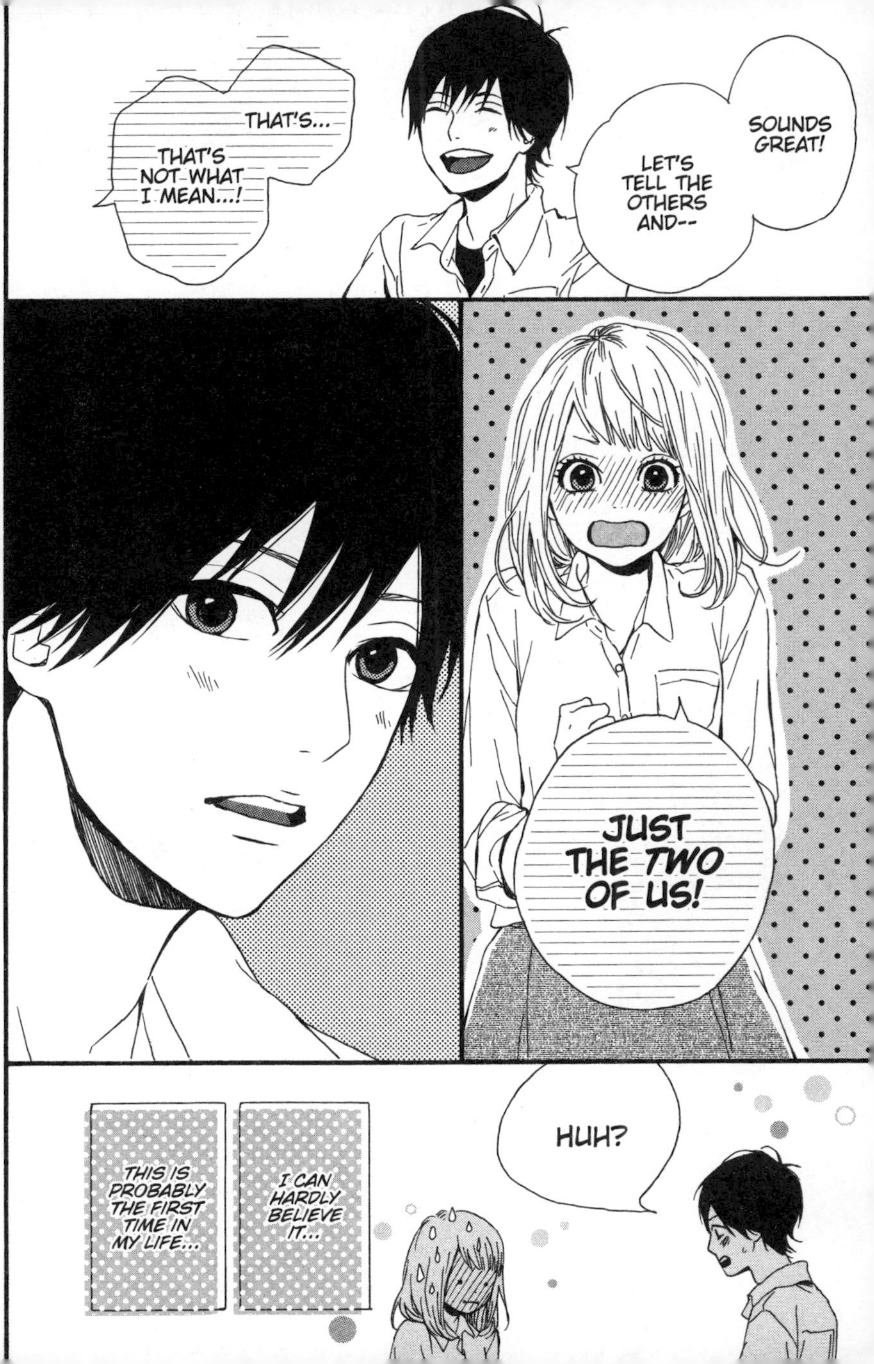
SOUNDS GREAT!
LET'S TELL THE OTHERS AND--
THAT'S...
THAT'S NOT WHAT I MEAN...!
JUST THE TWO OF US!
HUH?
I CAN HARDLY BELIEVE IT...
THIS IS PROBABLY THE FIRST TIME IN MY LIFE...

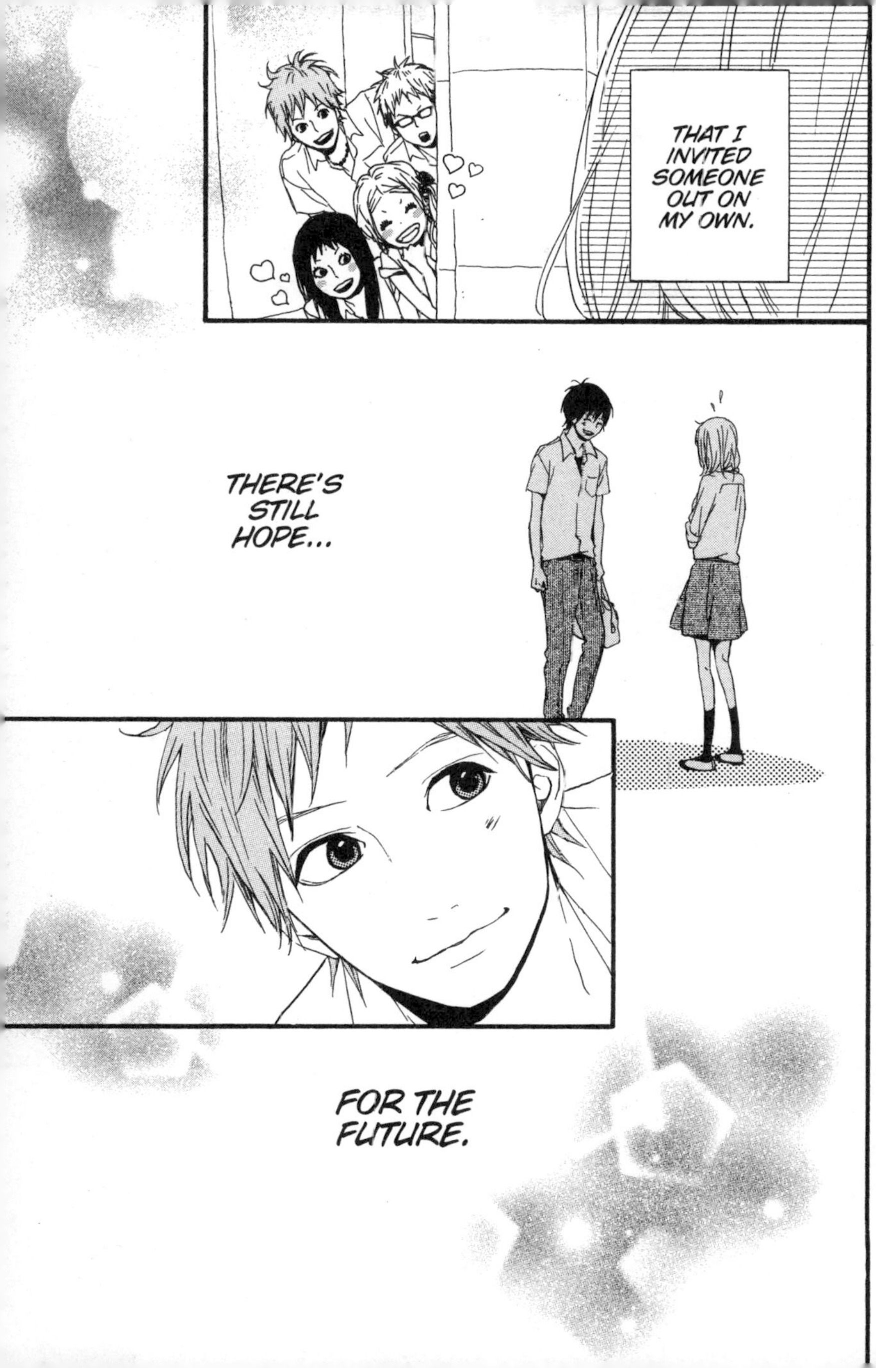
THAT I INVITED SOMEONE OUT ON MY OWN.
THERE'S STILL HOPE...
FOR THE FUTURE.

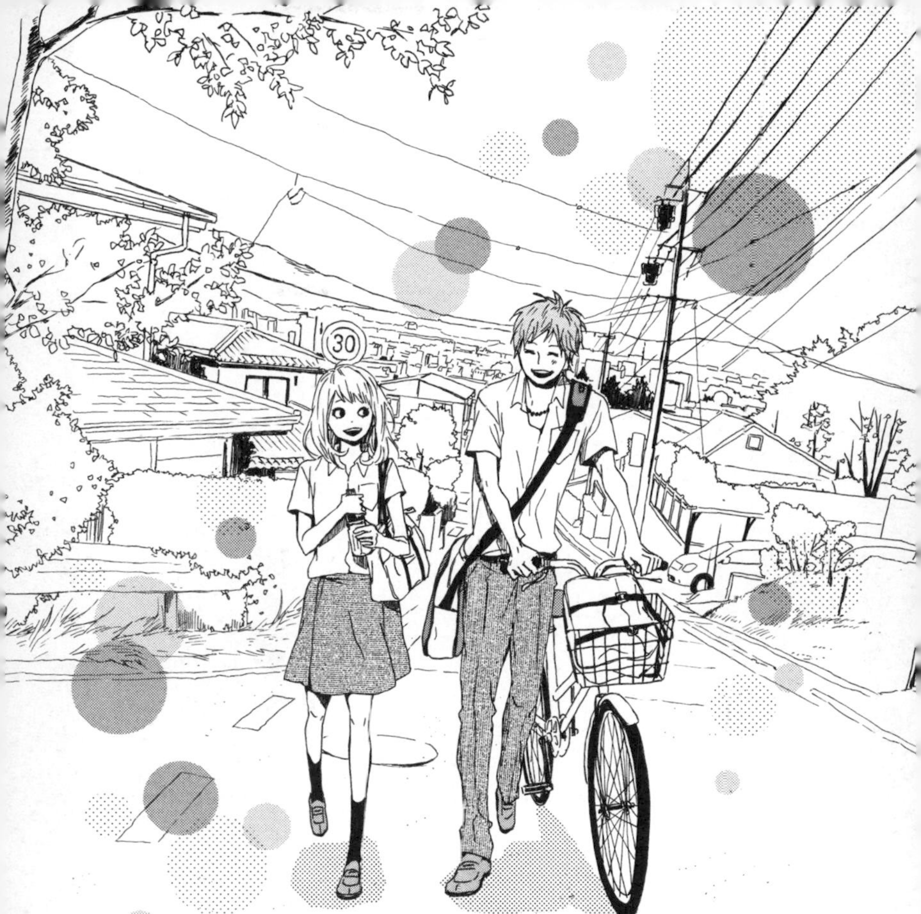
30

orange
LETTER 6

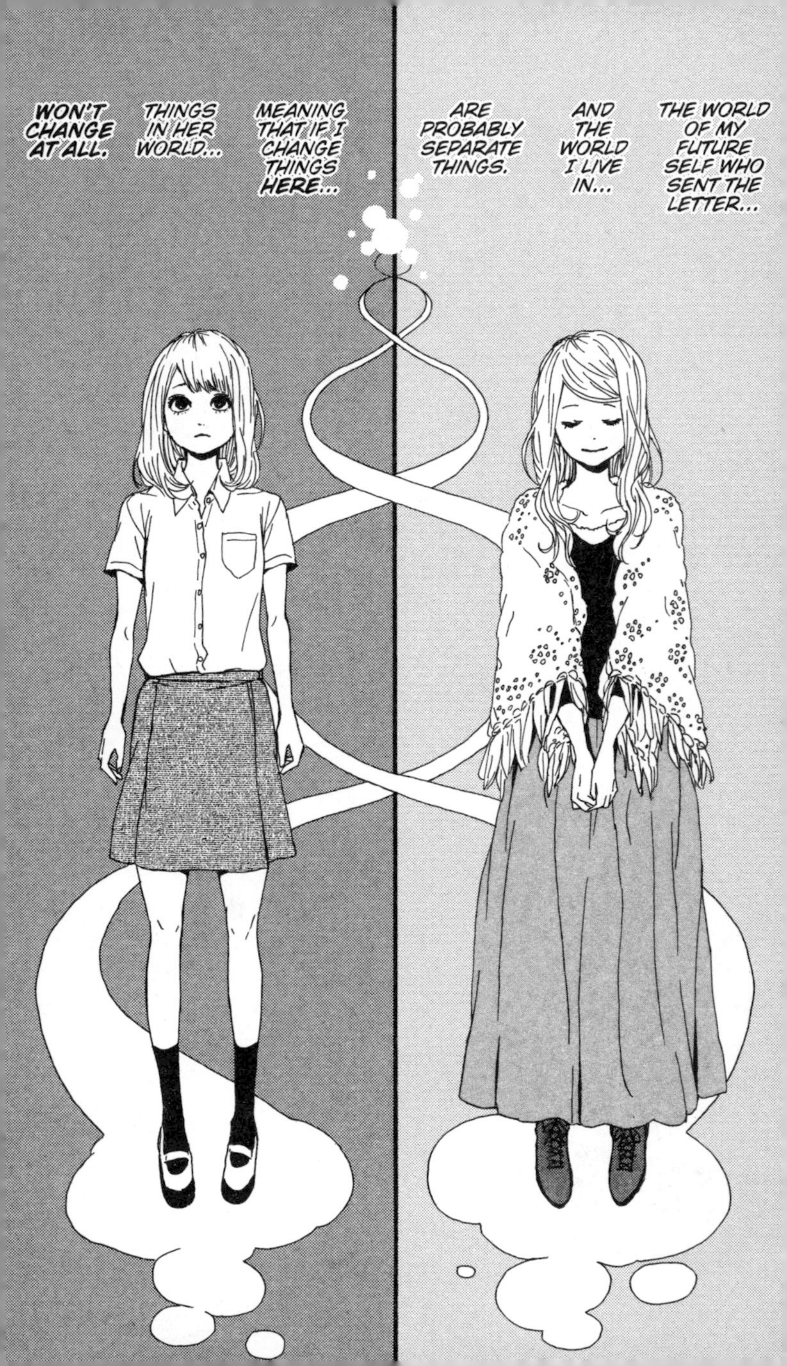
THE WORLD OF MY FUTURE SELF WHO SENT THE LETTER...
AND THE WORLD I LIVE IN...
ARE PROBABLY SEPARATE THINGS.
MEANING THAT IF I CHANGE THINGS HERE...
THINGS IN HER WORLD...
WON'T CHANGE AT ALL.

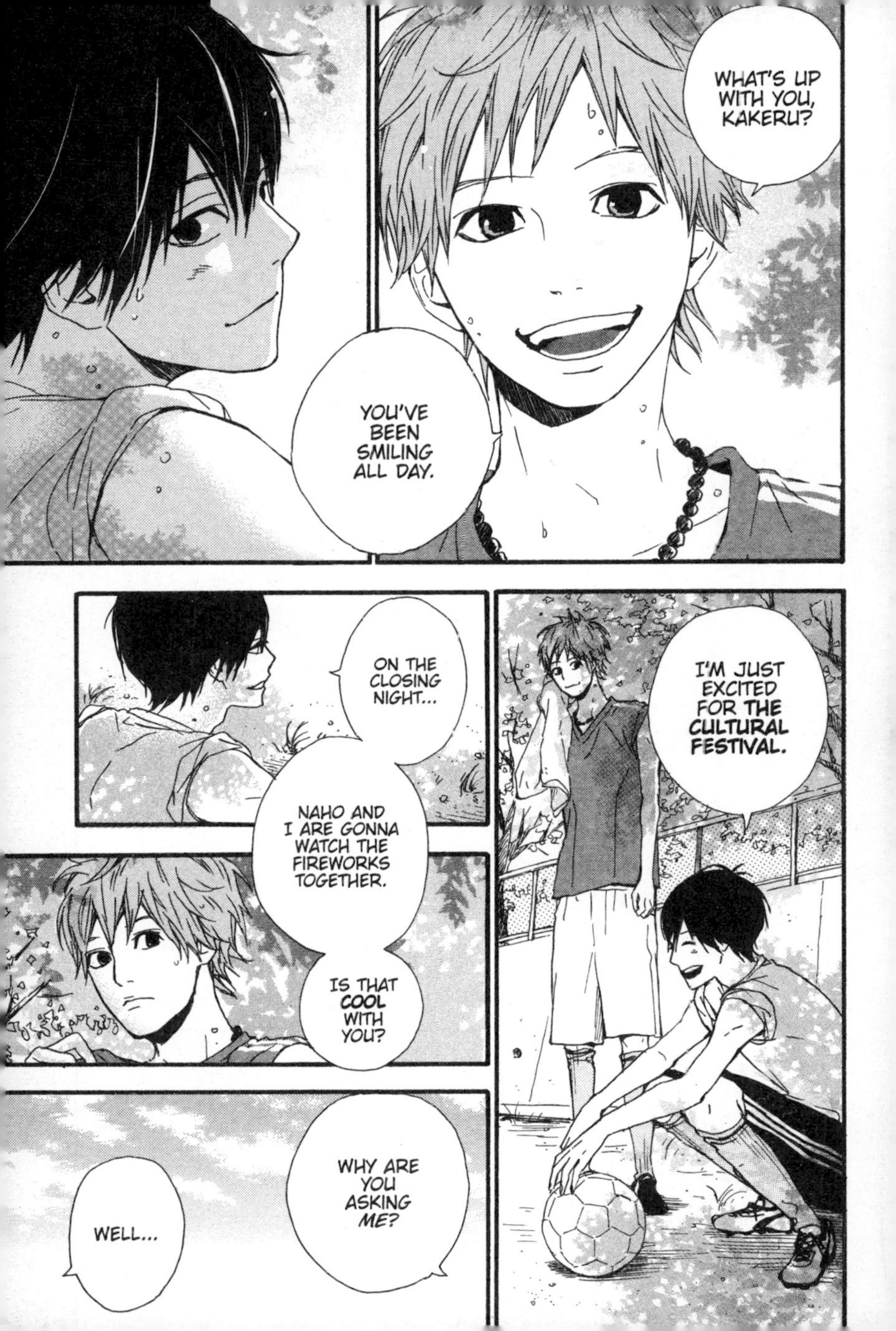
WHAT'S UP WITH YOU, KAKERU?
YOU'VE BEEN SMILING ALL DAY.
I'M JUST EXCITED FOR THE CULTURAL FESTIVAL.
ON THE CLOSING NIGHT...
NAHO AND I ARE GONNA WATCH THE FIREWORKS TOGETHER.
IS THAT COOL WITH YOU?
WHY ARE YOU ASKING ME?
WELL...

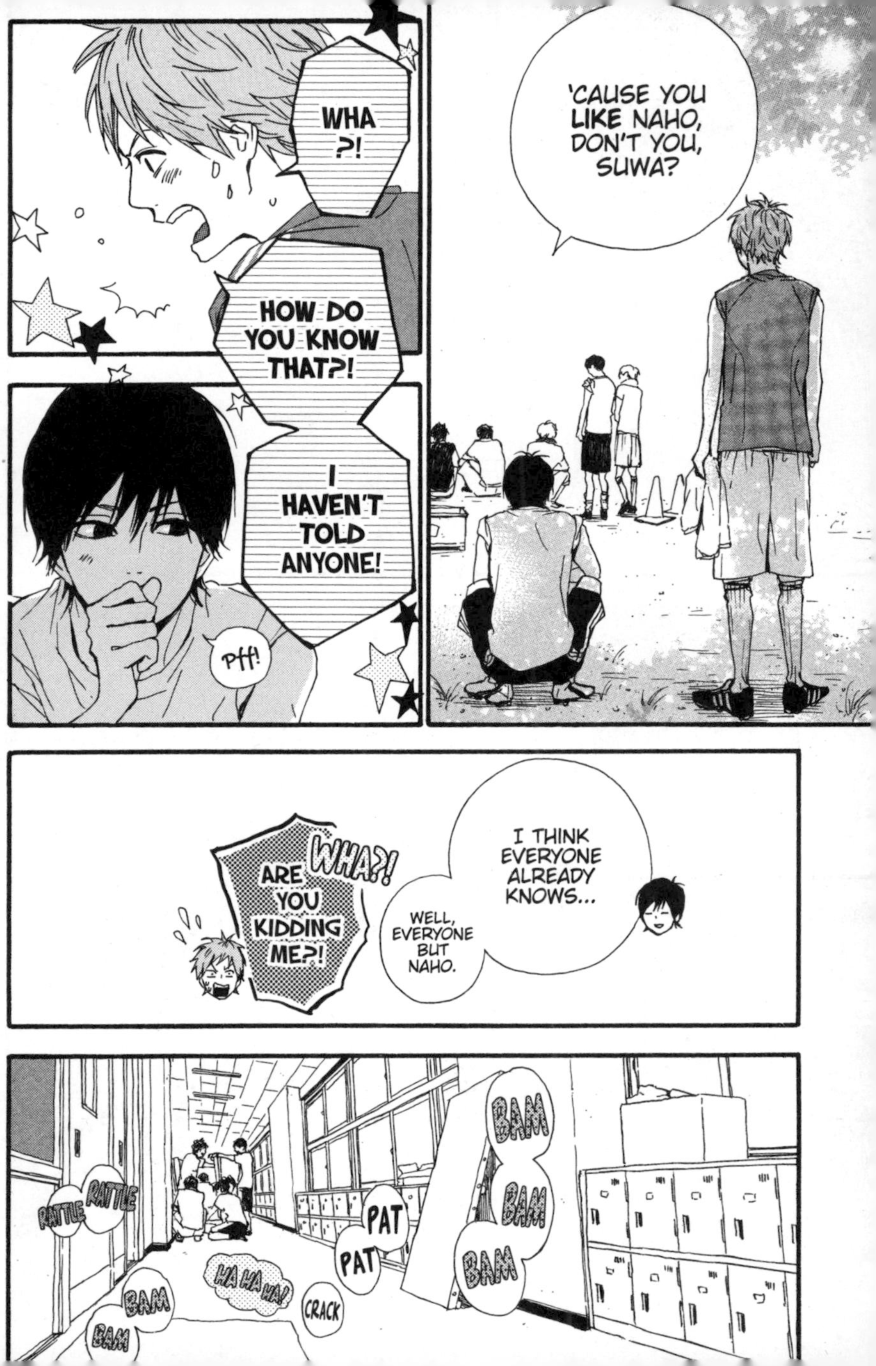
'CAUSE YOU LIKE NAHO, DON'T YOU, SUWA?
WHA ?!
HOW DO YOU KNOW THAT?!
I HAVEN'T TOLD ANYONE!
Pff!
I THINK EVERYONE ALREADY KNOWS...
WELL, EVERYONE BUT NAHO.
WHA?!
ARE YOU KIDDING ME?!
BAM
BAM
BAM
PAT
PAT
CRACK
HA HA HA!
RATTLE RATTLE
BAM
BAM

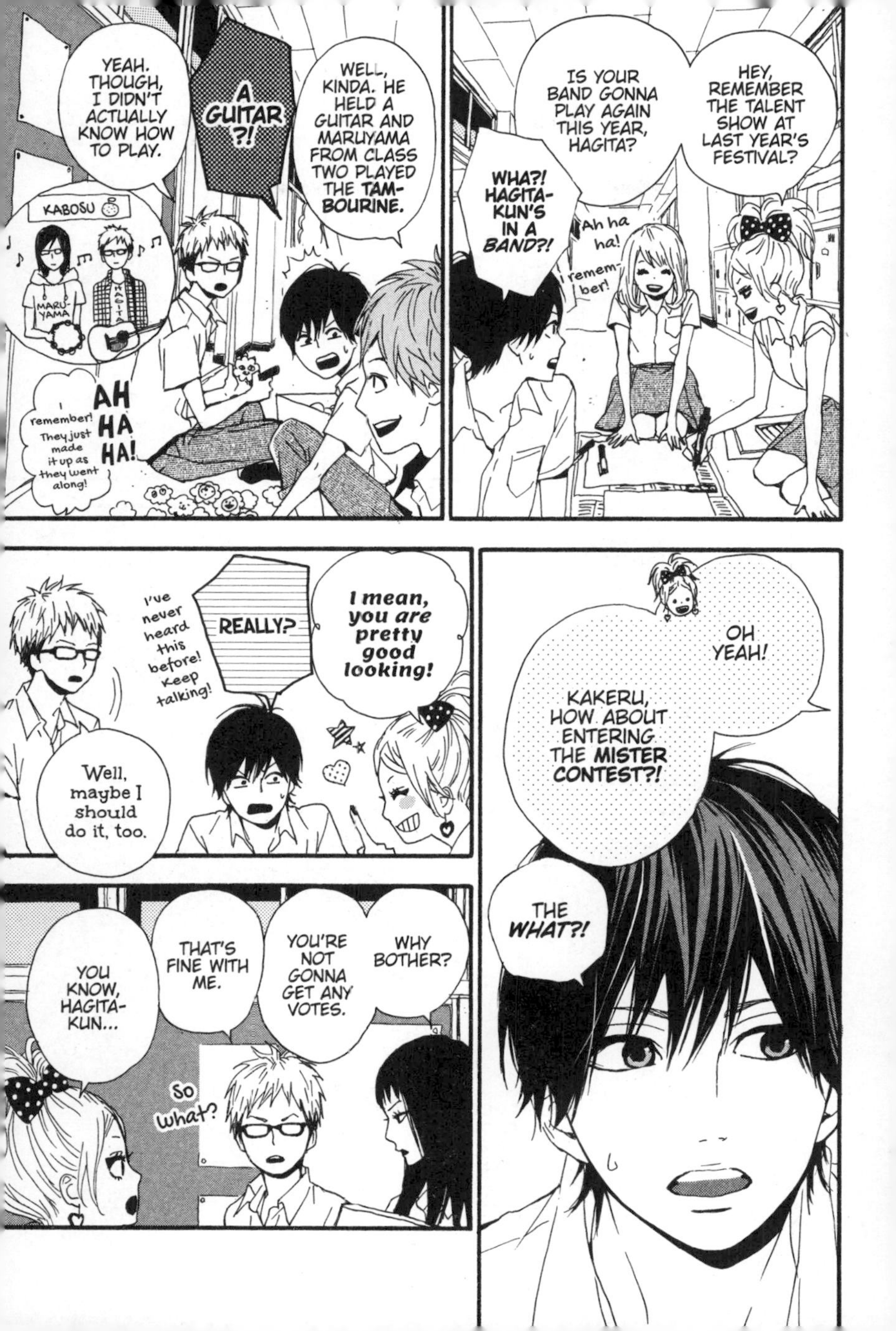
HEY, REMEMBER THE TALENT SHOW AT LAST YEAR'S FESTIVAL?
IS YOUR BAND GONNA PLAY AGAIN THIS YEAR, HAGITA?
Ah ha ha! I remember!
WHA?! HAGITA-KUN'S IN A BAND?!
WELL, KINDA. HE HELD A GUITAR AND MARUYAMA FROM CLASS TWO PLAYED THE TAMBOURINE.
A GUITAR?!
YEAH. THOUGH, I DIDN'T ACTUALLY KNOW HOW TO PLAY.
KABOSU
MARUYAMA
HAGITA
AH HA HA!
I remember! They just made it up as they went along!
OH YEAH!
KAKERU, HOW ABOUT ENTERING THE MISTER CONTEST?!
THE WHAT?!
I mean, you are pretty good looking!
REALLY?
I've never heard this before! Keep talking!
Well, maybe I should do it, too.
WHY BOTHER?
YOU'RE NOT GONNA GET ANY VOTES.
THAT'S FINE WITH ME.
YOU KNOW, HAGITA-KUN...
So what?

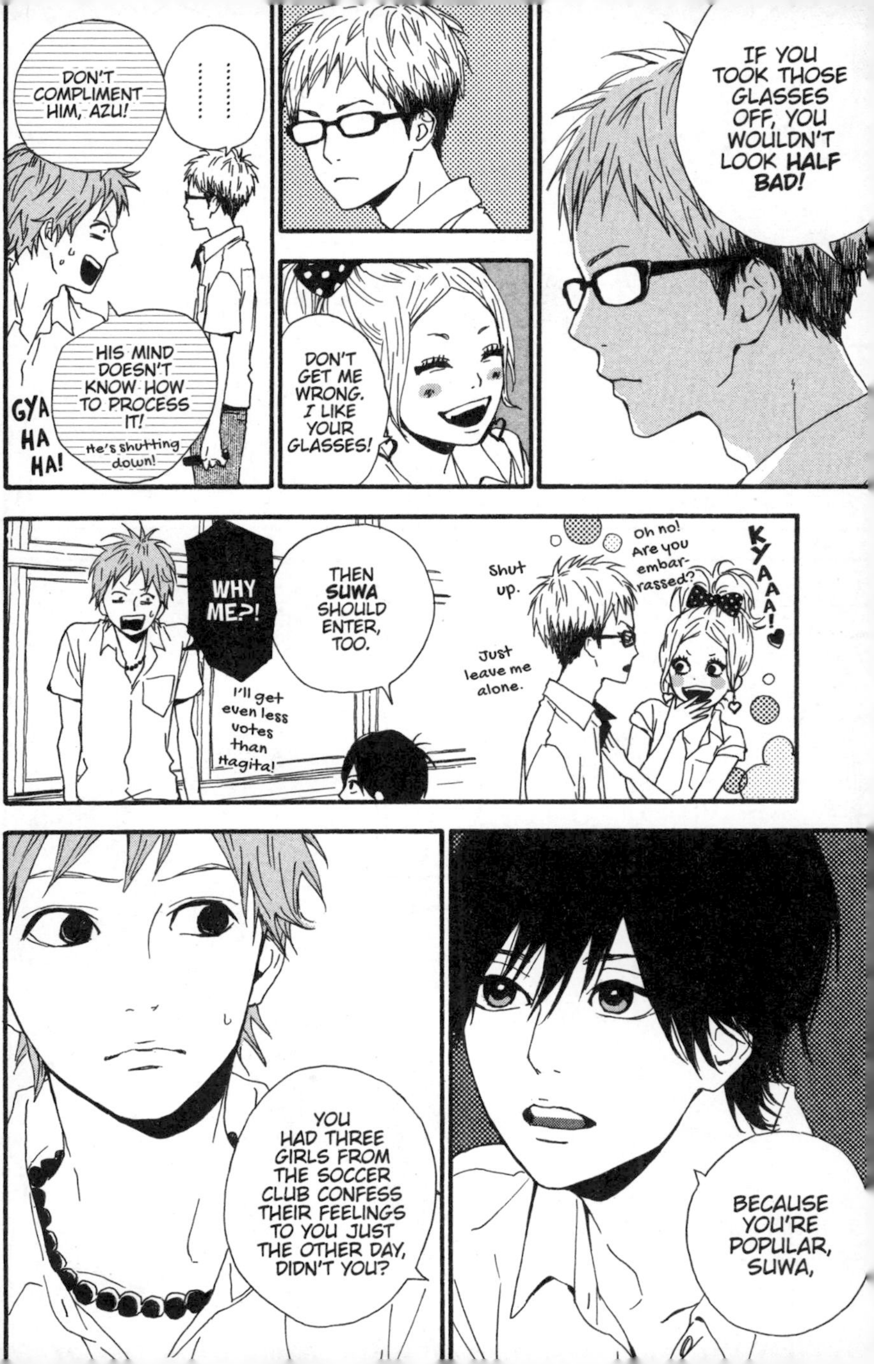
IF YOU TOOK THOSE GLASSES OFF, YOU WOULDN'T LOOK HALF BAD!
DON'T GET ME WRONG. I LIKE YOUR GLASSES!
......
DON'T COMPLIMENT HIM, AZU!
HIS MIND DOESN'T KNOW HOW TO PROCESS IT!
He's shutting down!
GYA HA HA!
KYAAAA!
Oh no! Are you embar-rassed?
Shut up.
Just leave me alone.
THEN SUWA SHOULD ENTER, TOO.
WHY ME?!
I'll get even less votes than Hagita!
BECAUSE YOU'RE POPULAR, SUWA,
YOU HAD THREE GIRLS FROM THE SOCCER CLUB CONFESS THEIR FEELINGS TO YOU JUST THE OTHER DAY, DIDN'T YOU?

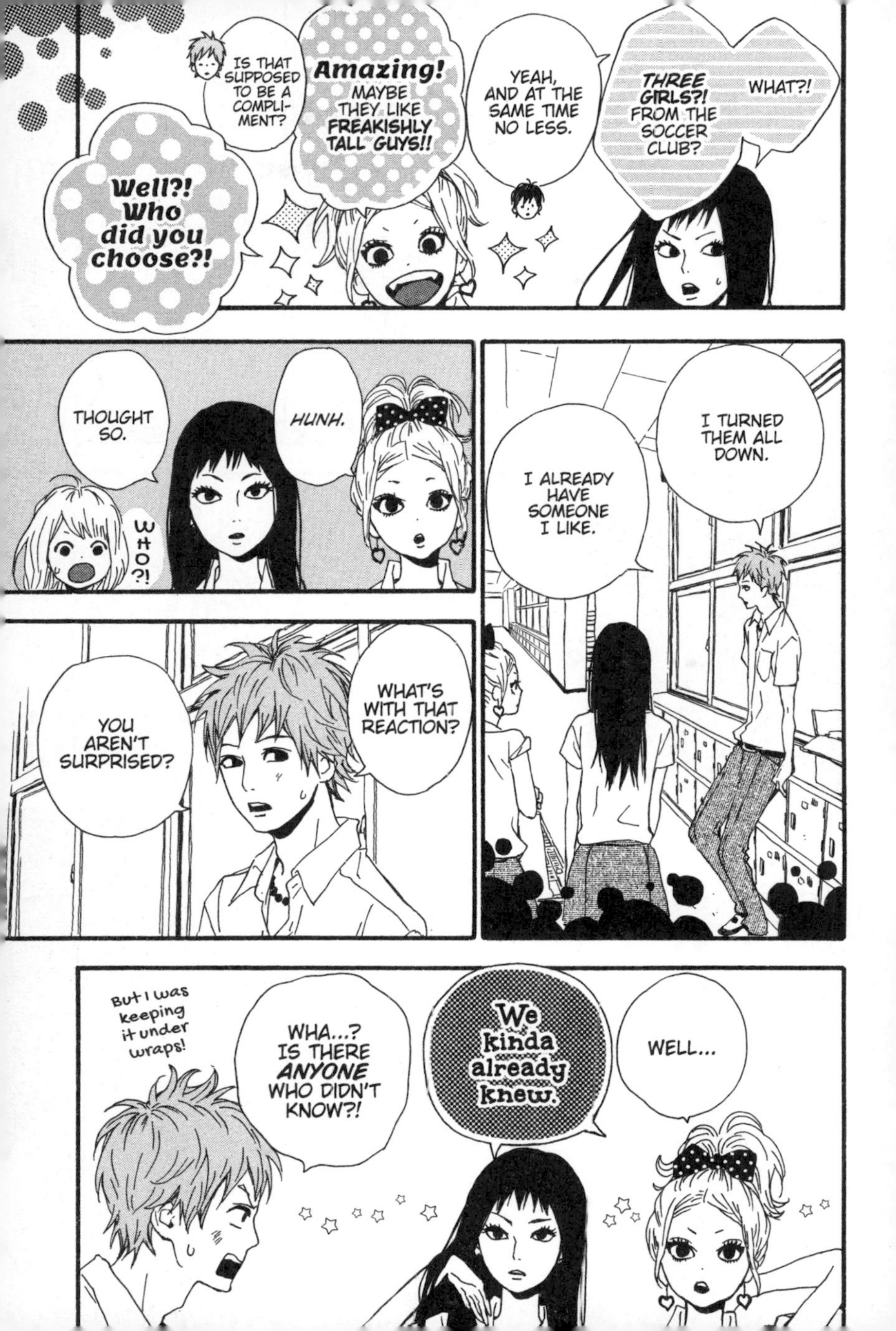
WHAT?!
THREE GIRLS?! FROM THE SOCCER CLUB?
YEAH, AND AT THE SAME TIME NO LESS.
Amazing! MAYBE THEY LIKE FREAKISHLY TALL GUYS!!
IS THAT SUPPOSED TO BE A COMPLIMENT?
Well?! Who did you choose?!
I TURNED THEM ALL DOWN.
I ALREADY HAVE SOMEONE I LIKE.
HUNH.
THOUGHT SO.
WHO?!
WHAT'S WITH THAT REACTION?
YOU AREN'T SURPRISED?
WELL...
We kinda already knew.
WHA...? IS THERE ANYONE WHO DIDN'T KNOW?!
But I was keeping it under wraps!

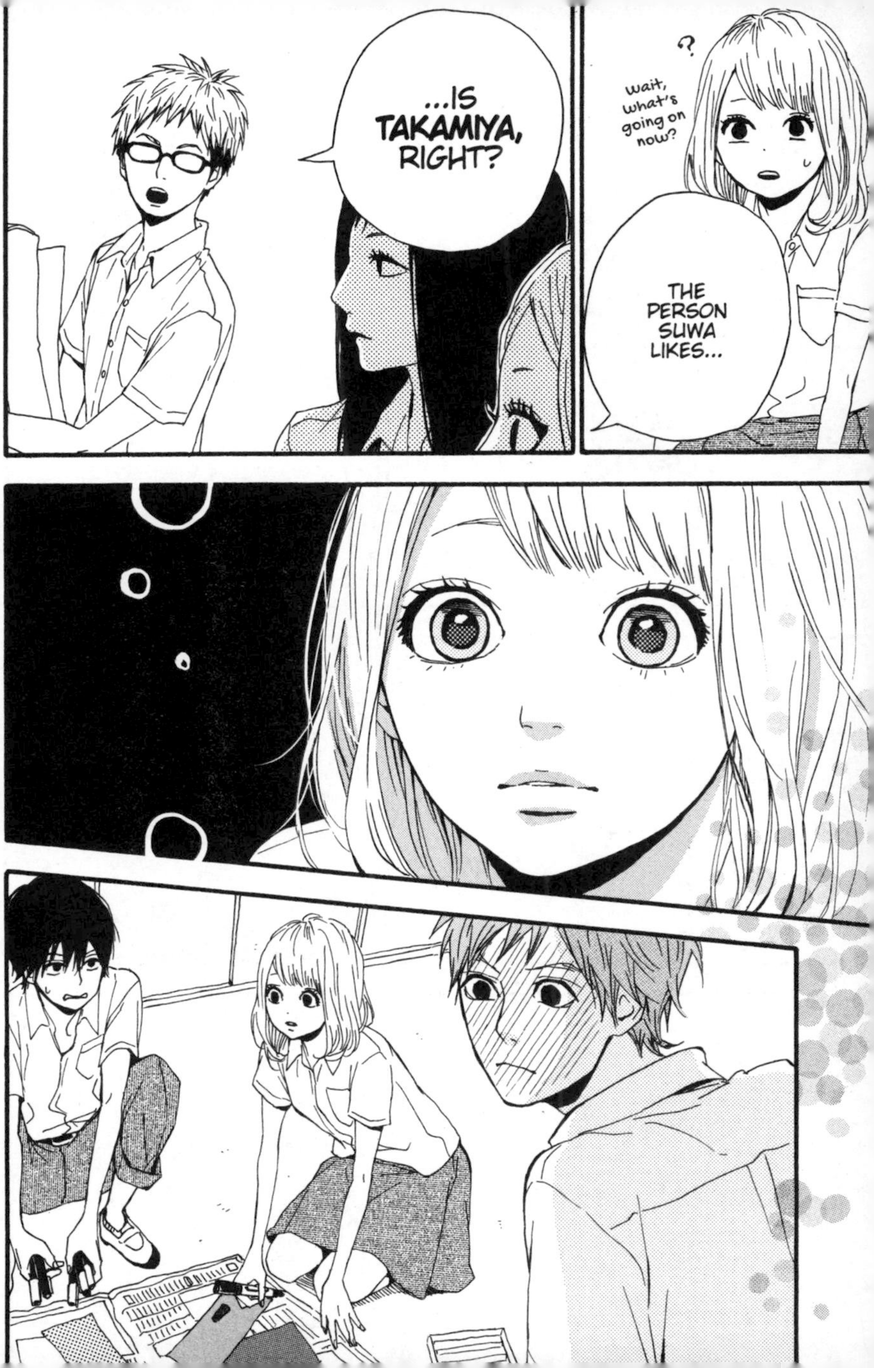
?
wait, what's going on now?
THE PERSON SUWA LIKES...
...IS TAKAMIYA, RIGHT?

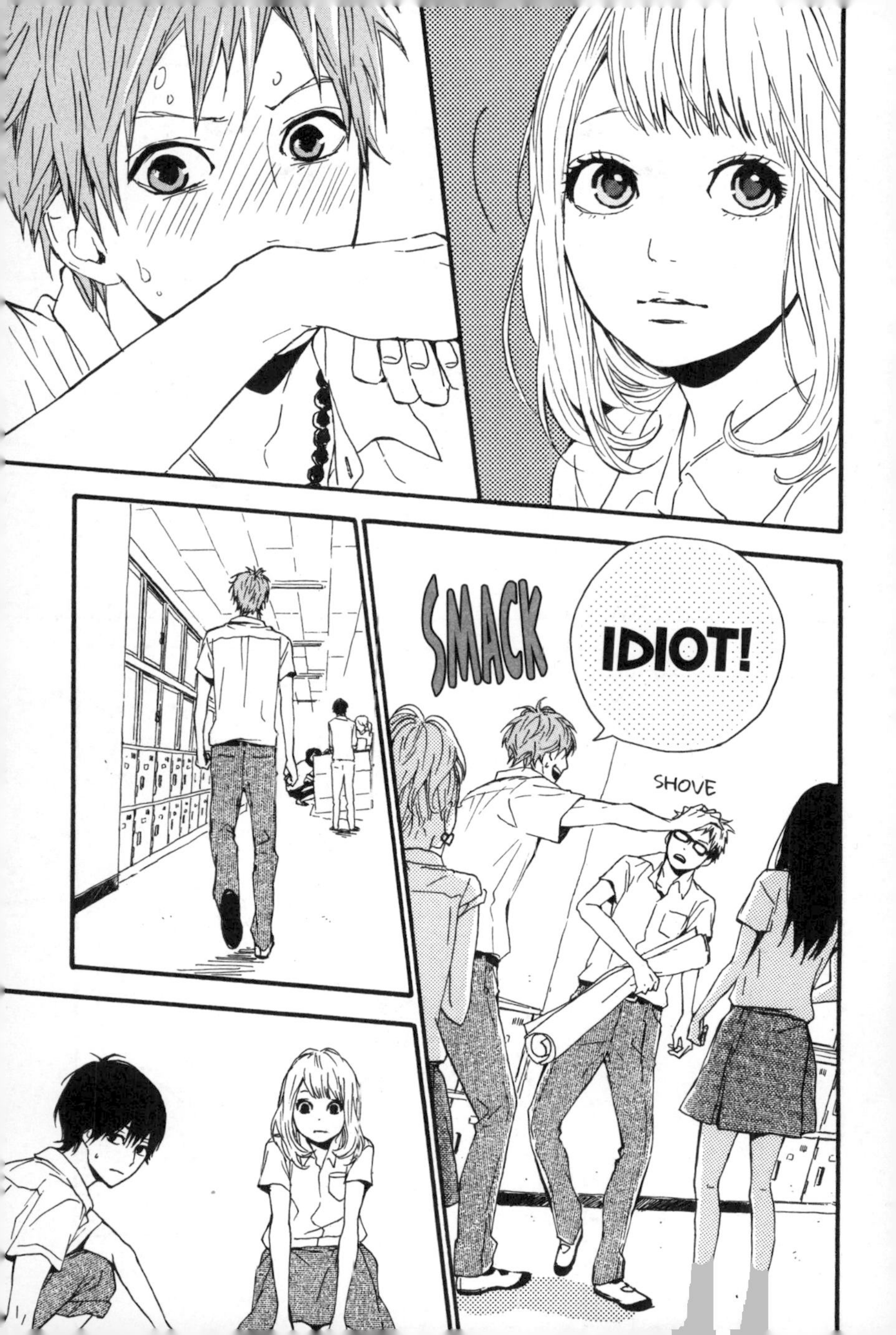
IDIOT!
SMACK
SHOVE

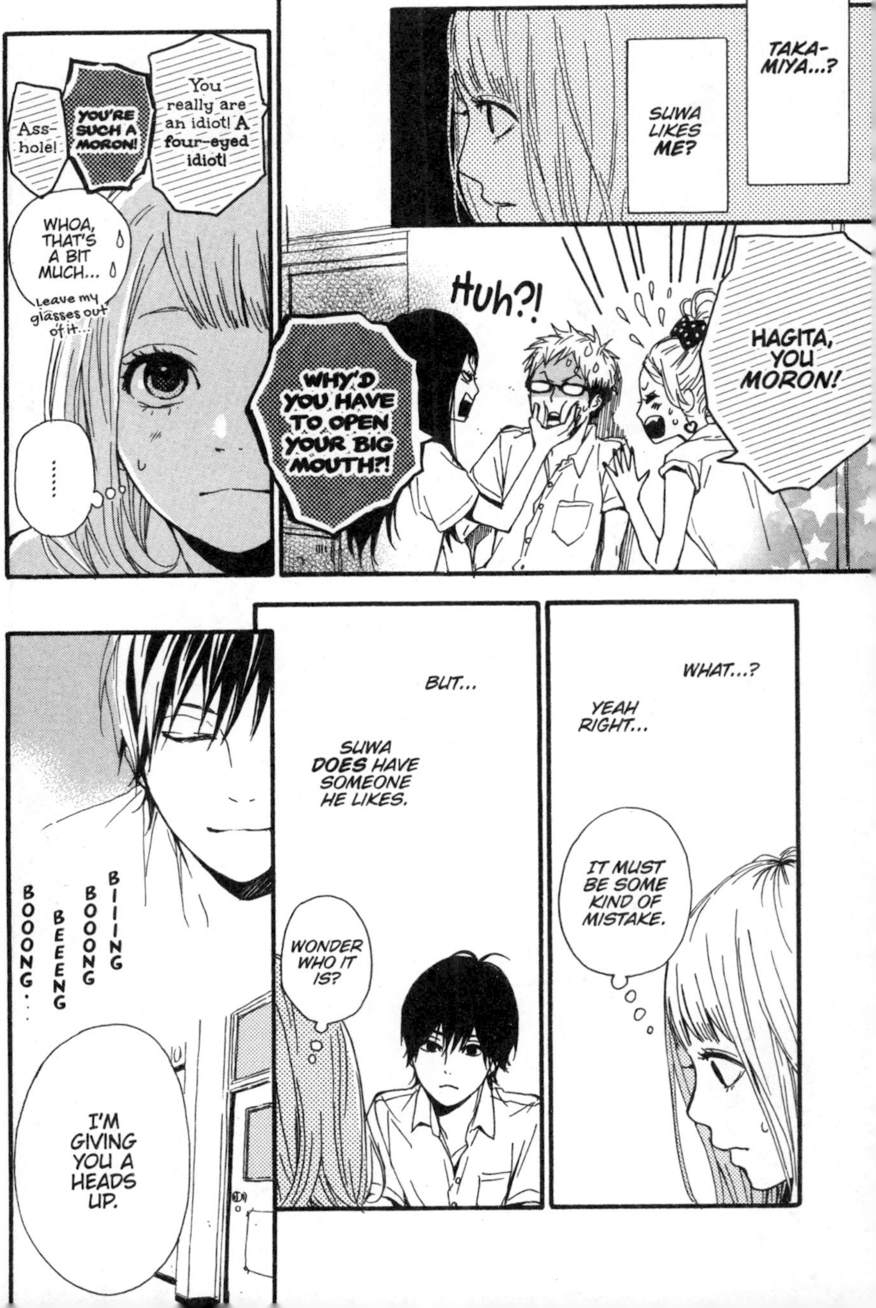
TAKA-MIYA...?
SUWA LIKES ME?
HAGITA, YOU MORON!
Huh?!
WHY'D YOU HAVE TO OPEN YOUR BIG MOUTH?!
You really are an idiot! A four-eyed idiot!
YOU'RE SUCH A MORON!
Ass-hole!
WHOA, THAT'S A BIT MUCH...
Leave my glasses out of it...
......
WHAT...?
YEAH RIGHT...
IT MUST BE SOME KIND OF MISTAKE.
BUT...
SUWA DOES HAVE SOMEONE HE LIKES.
WONDER WHO IT IS?
BIIING
BOOONG
BEEENG
BOOONG...
I'M GIVING YOU A HEADS UP.

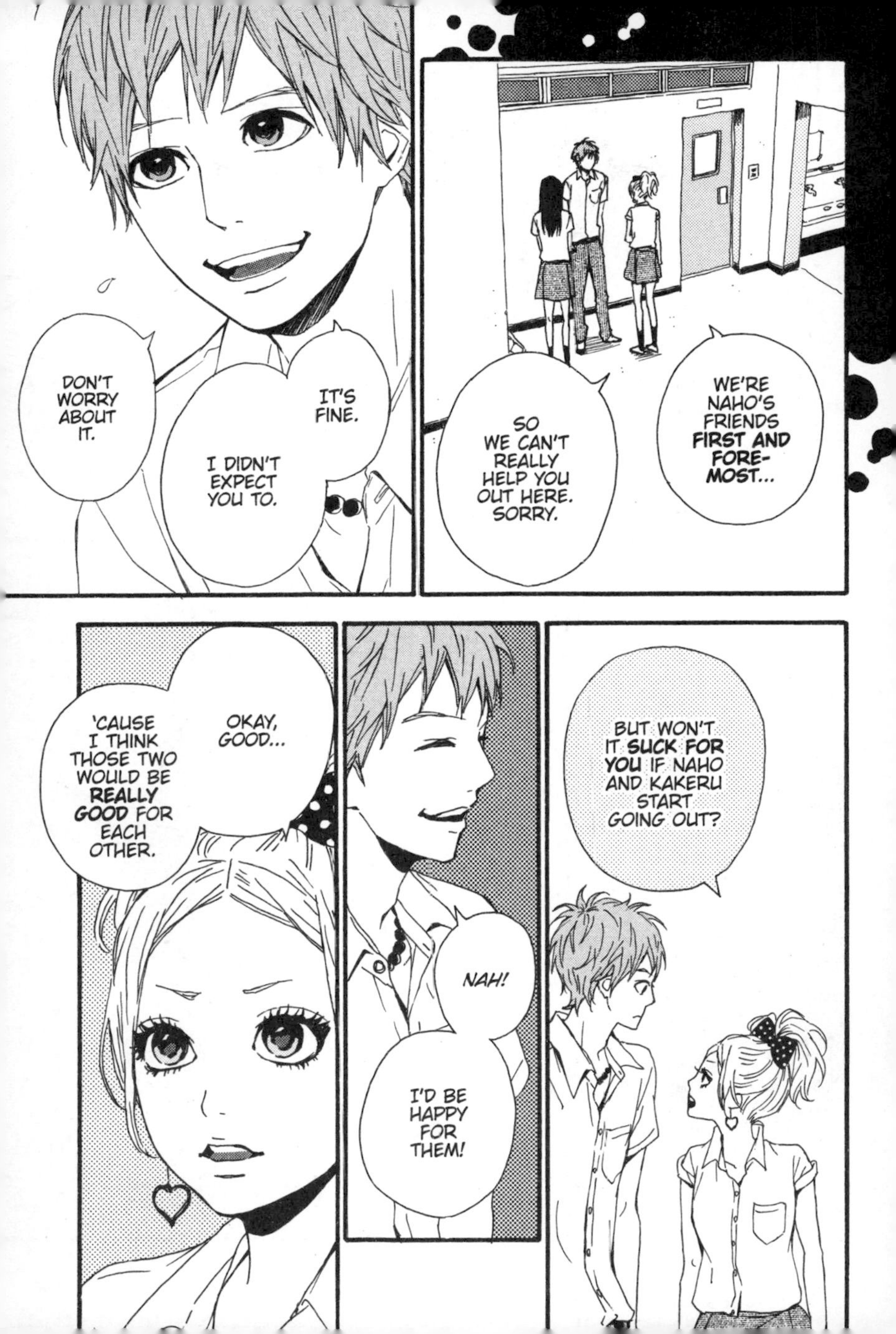
WE'RE NAHO'S FRIENDS FIRST AND FORE-MOST...
SO WE CAN'T REALLY HELP YOU OUT HERE. SORRY.
IT'S FINE.
I DIDN'T EXPECT YOU TO.
DON'T WORRY ABOUT IT.
BUT WON'T IT SUCK FOR YOU IF NAHO AND KAKERU START GOING OUT?
NAH!
I'D BE HAPPY FOR THEM!
OKAY, GOOD...
'CAUSE I THINK THOSE TWO WOULD BE REALLY GOOD FOR EACH OTHER.

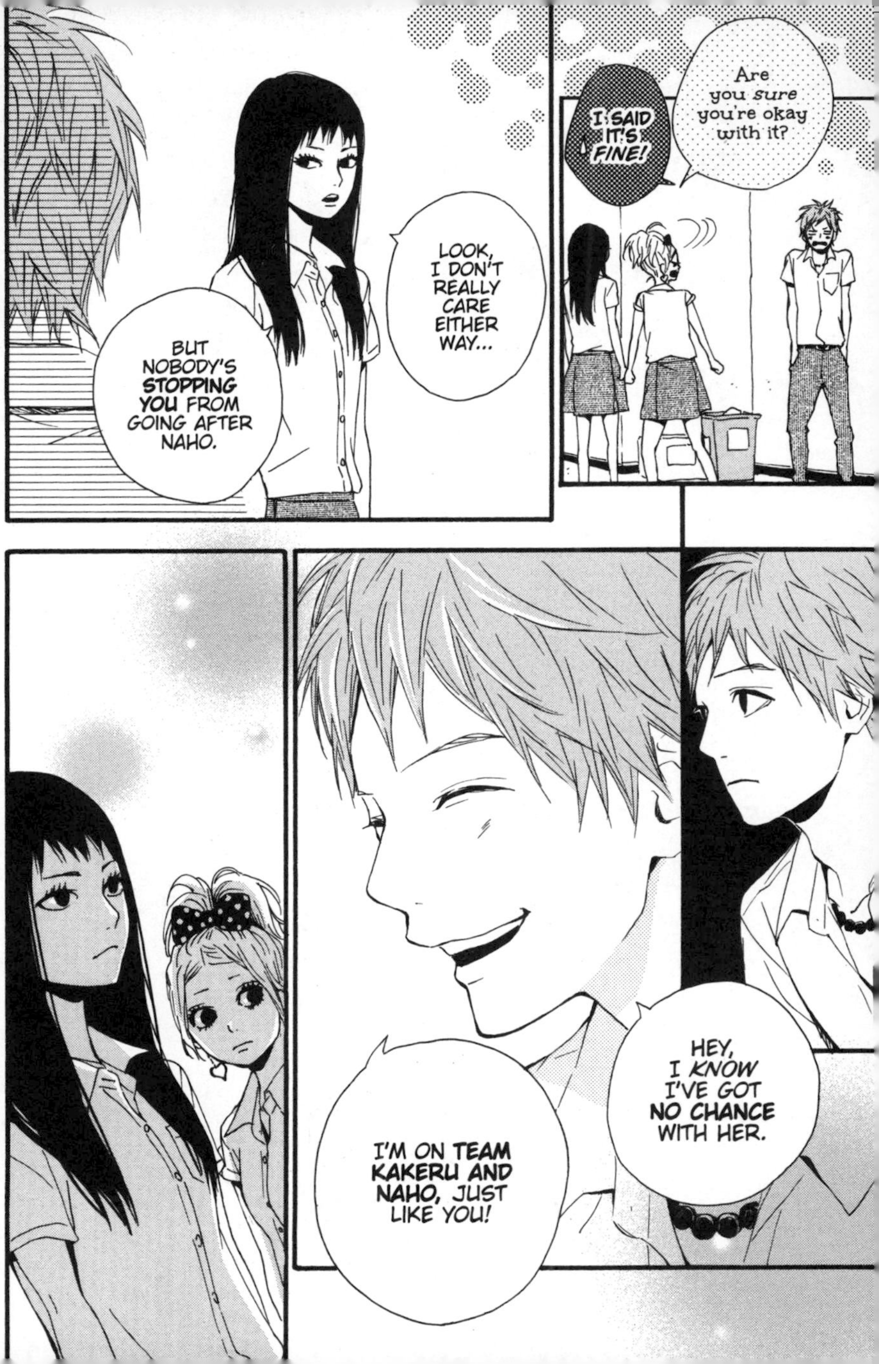
Are you *sure* you're okay with it?
I SAID IT'S *FINE!*
LOOK, I DON'T REALLY CARE EITHER WAY...
BUT NOBODY'S **STOPPING YOU** FROM GOING AFTER NAHO.
HEY, I *KNOW* I'VE GOT **NO CHANCE** WITH HER.
I'M ON **TEAM KAKERU AND NAHO,** JUST LIKE YOU!

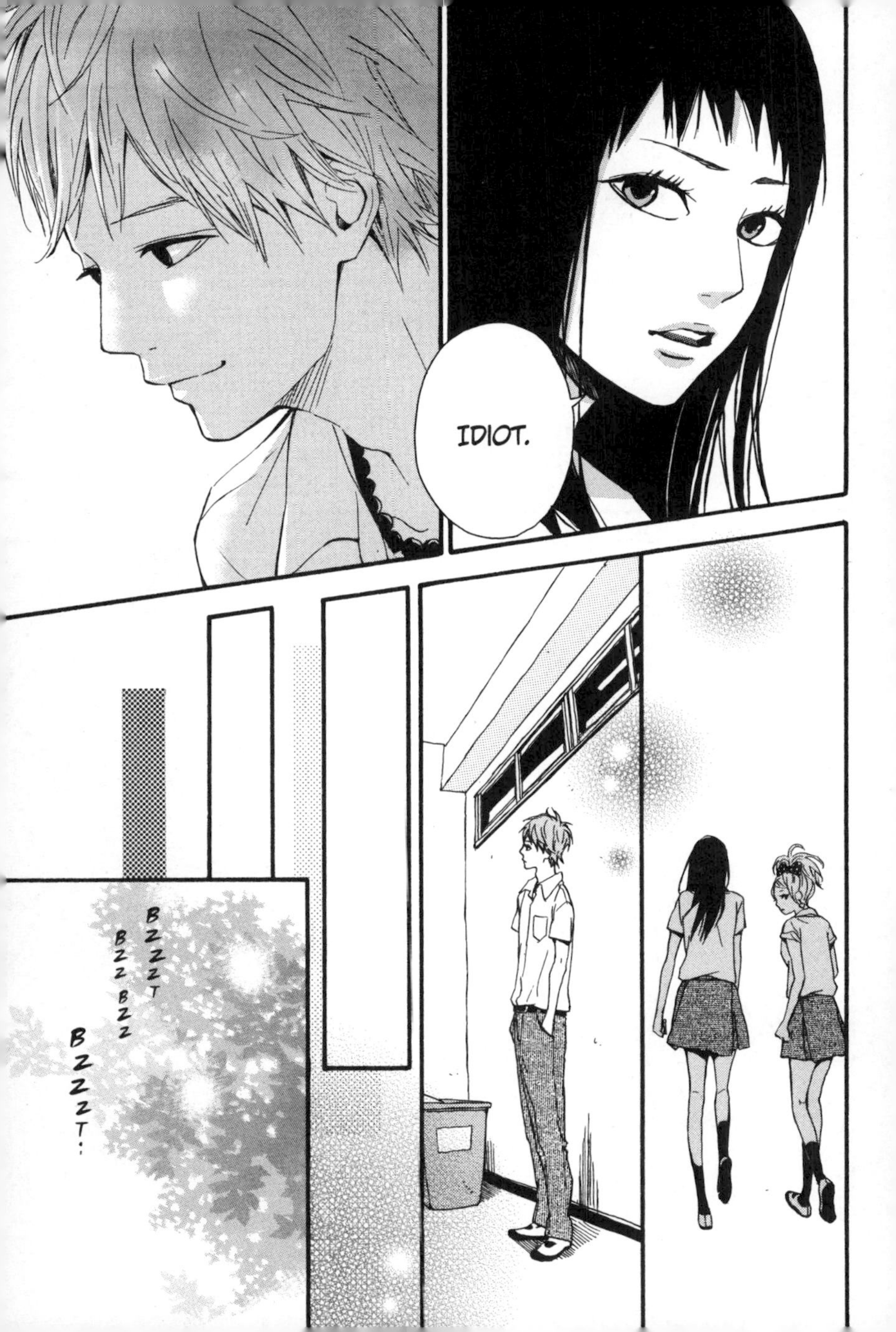
IDIOT.
BZZZT
BZZ BZZ
BZZZT!

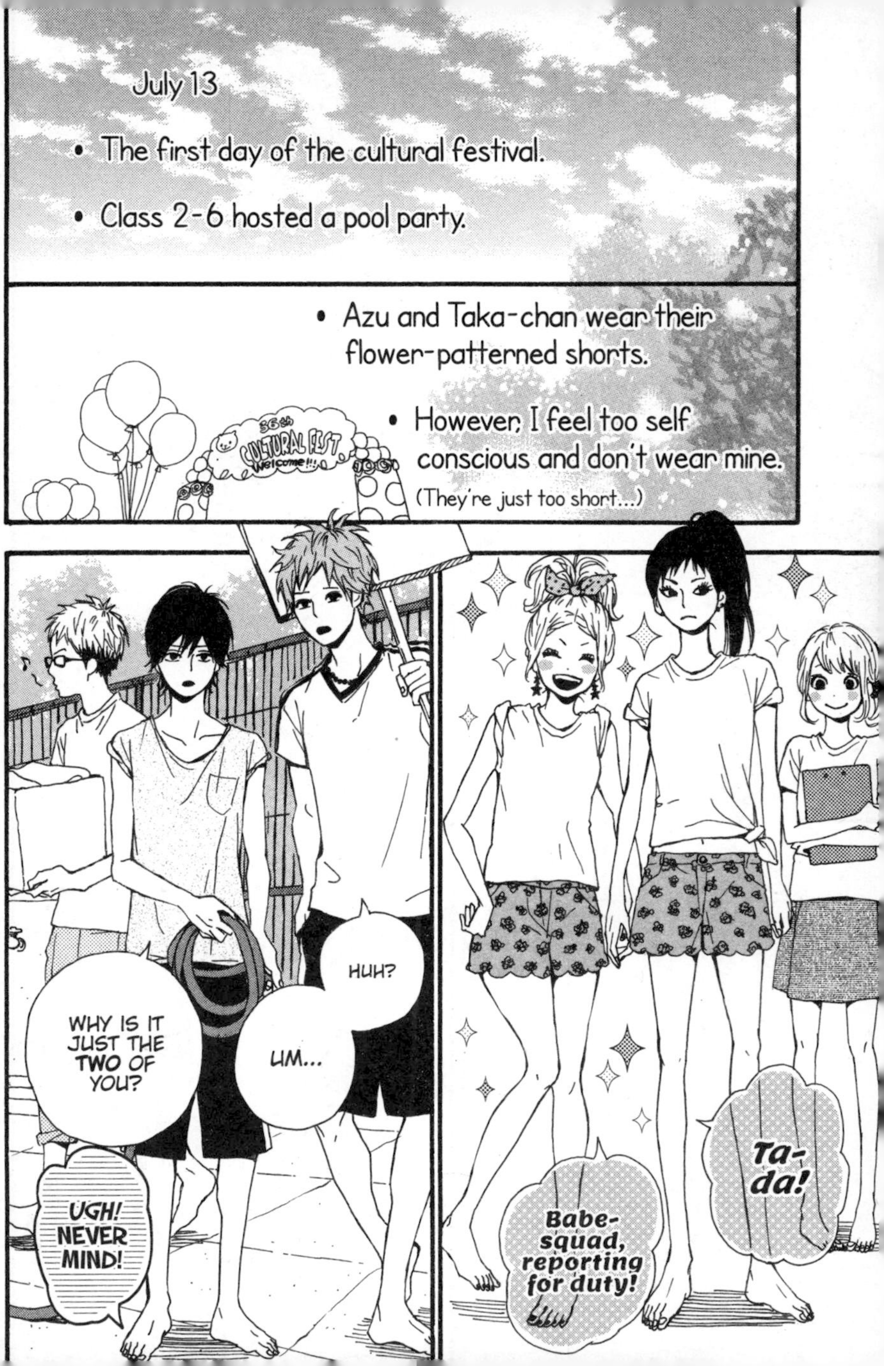

July 13
• The first day of the cultural festival.
• Class 2-6 hosted a pool party.
• Azu and Taka-chan wear their flower-patterned shorts.
• However, I feel too self conscious and don't wear mine.
(They're just too short...)
36th CULTURAL FEST Welcome!!!
Ta-da!
Babe-squad, reporting for duty!
HUH?
UM...
WHY IS IT JUST THE TWO OF YOU?
UGH! NEVER MIND!

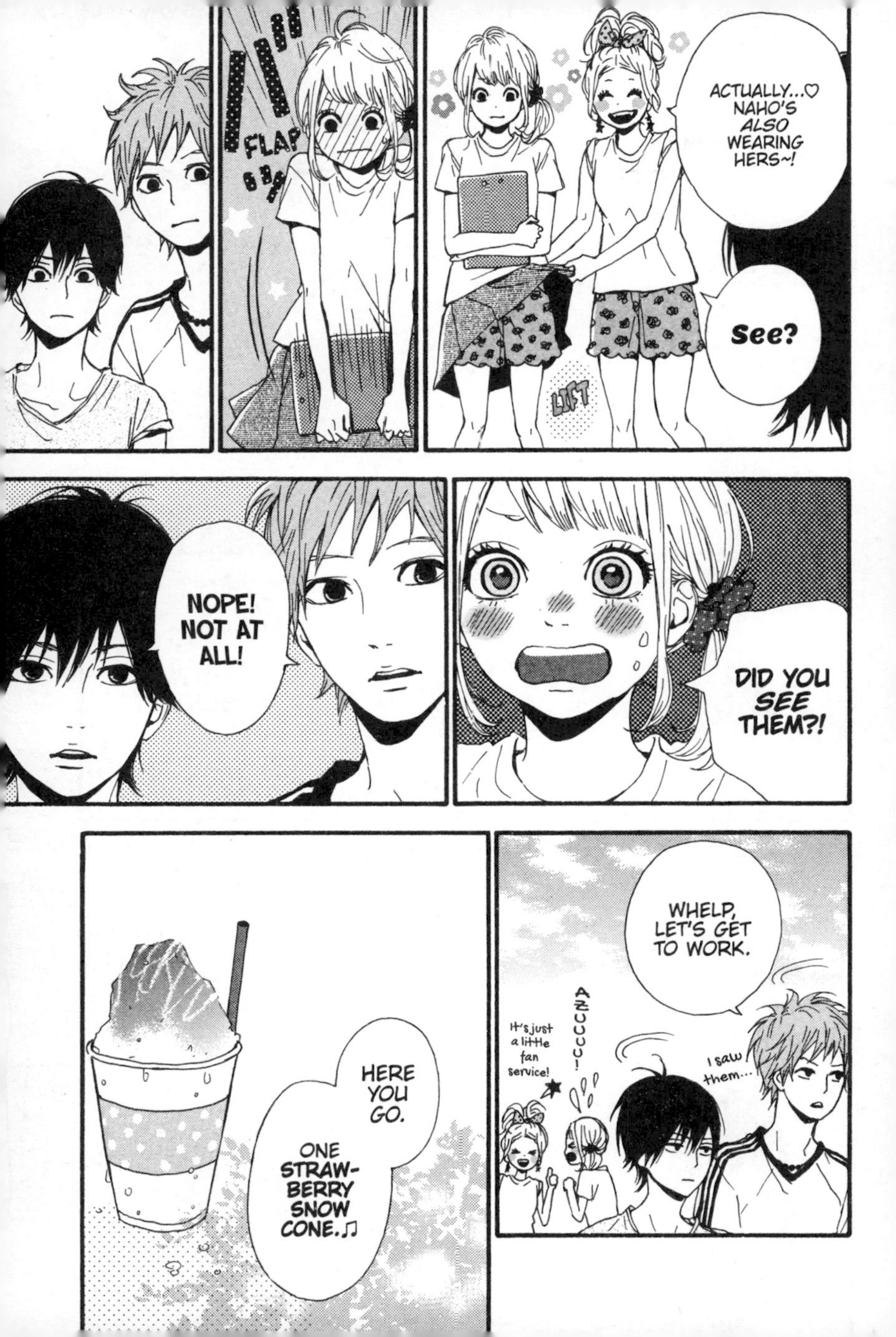
ACTUALLY...♡ NAHO'S ALSO WEARING HERS~!
See?
LIFT
FLAP
DID YOU SEE THEM?!
NOPE! NOT AT ALL!
WHELP, LET'S GET TO WORK.
I saw them...
AZUUUU!
It's just a little fan service!
HERE YOU GO.
ONE STRAW-BERRY SNOW CONE.♫

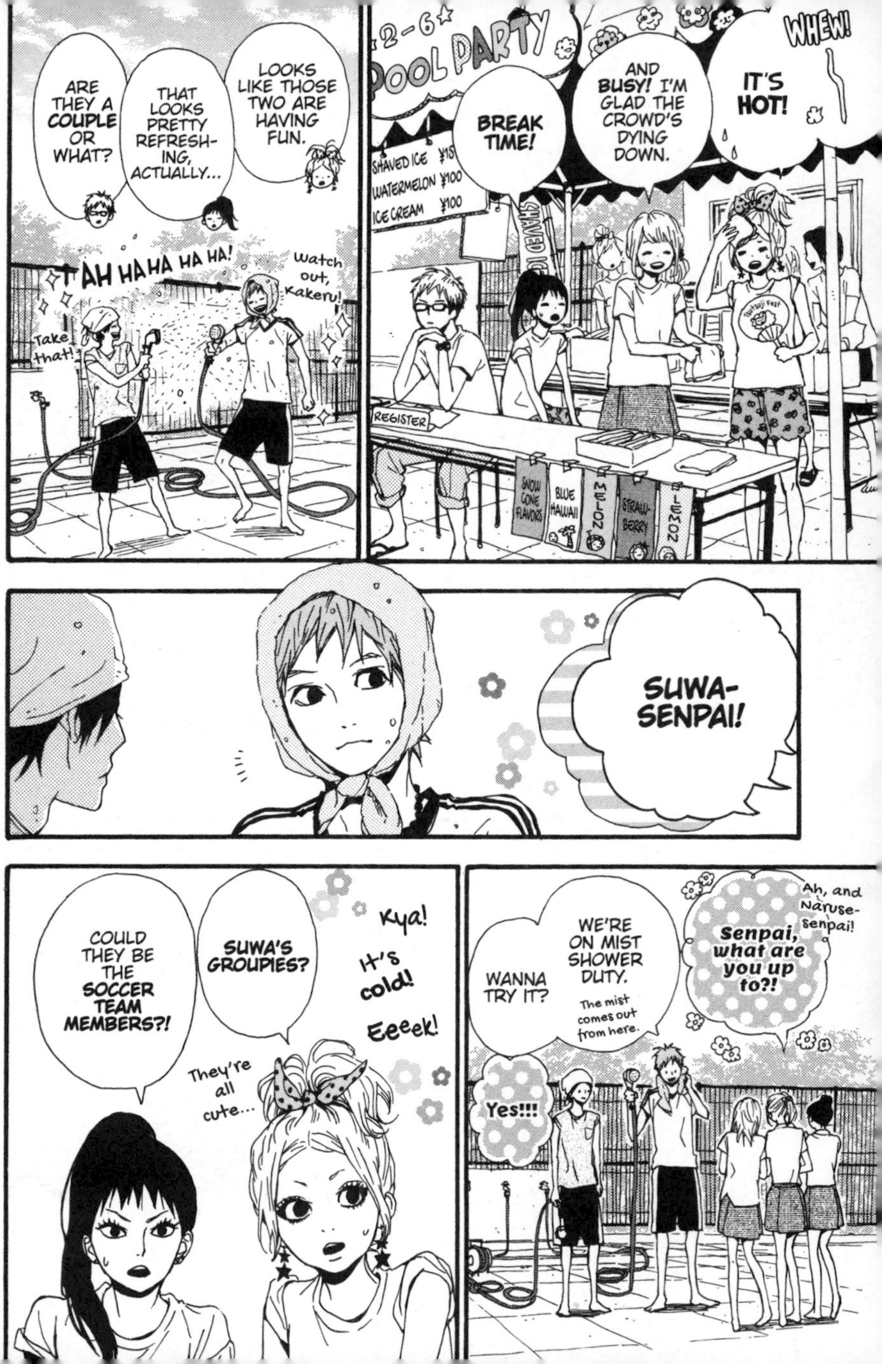
2-6
POOL PARTY
WHEW!
IT'S HOT!
AND BUSY! I'M GLAD THE CROWD'S DYING DOWN.
BREAK TIME!
SHAVED ICE ¥15
WATERMELON ¥100
ICE CREAM ¥100
SHAVED IC
Tsutsuji Fest
REGISTER
SNOW CONE FLAVORS
BLUE HAWAII
MELON
STRAWBERRY
LEMON
LOOKS LIKE THOSE TWO ARE HAVING FUN.
THAT LOOKS PRETTY REFRESHING, ACTUALLY...
ARE THEY A COUPLE OR WHAT?
Watch out, Kakeru!
AH HAHA HA HA!
Take that!
SUWA-SENPAI!
Ah, and Naruse-Senpai!
Senpai, what are you up to?!
WE'RE ON MIST SHOWER DUTY.
The mist comes out from here.
WANNA TRY IT?
Yes!!!
Kya!
It's cold!
Eeeek!
SUWA'S GROUPIES?
COULD THEY BE THE SOCCER TEAM MEMBERS?!
They're all cute...

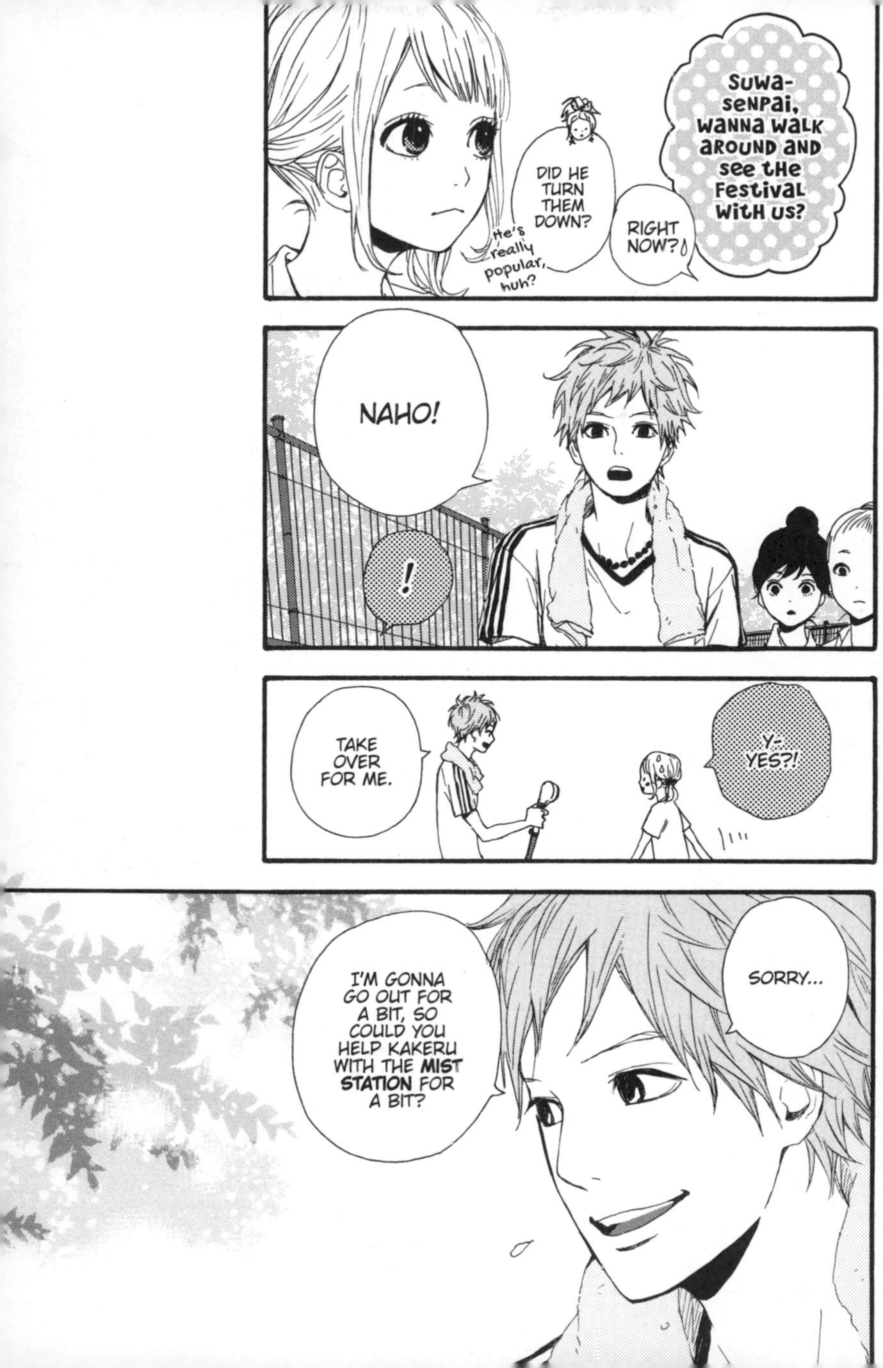
Suwa-senpai, wanna walk around and see the Festival with us?
RIGHT NOW?!
DID HE TURN THEM DOWN?
He's really popular, huh?
NAHO!
!
Y-YES?!
TAKE OVER FOR ME.
SORRY...
I'M GONNA GO OUT FOR A BIT, SO COULD YOU HELP KAKERU WITH THE **MIST STATION** FOR A BIT?

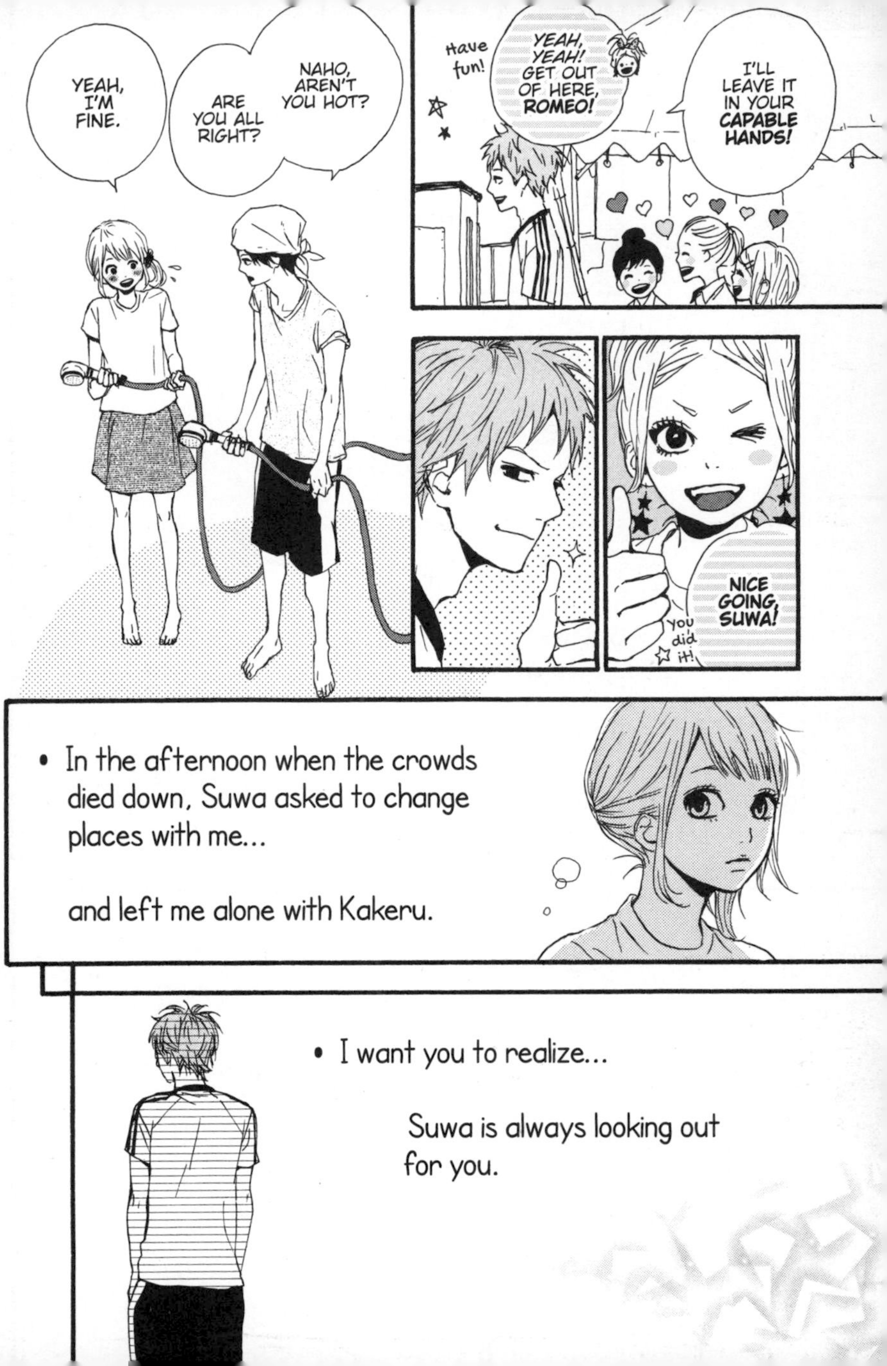
I'LL LEAVE IT IN YOUR CAPABLE HANDS!
YEAH, YEAH! GET OUT OF HERE, ROMEO!
Have fun!
NICE GOING, SUWA!
You did it!
NAHO, AREN'T YOU HOT?
ARE YOU ALL RIGHT?
YEAH, I'M FINE.
• In the afternoon when the crowds died down, Suwa asked to change places with me...
and left me alone with Kakeru.
• I want you to realize...
Suwa is always looking out for you.

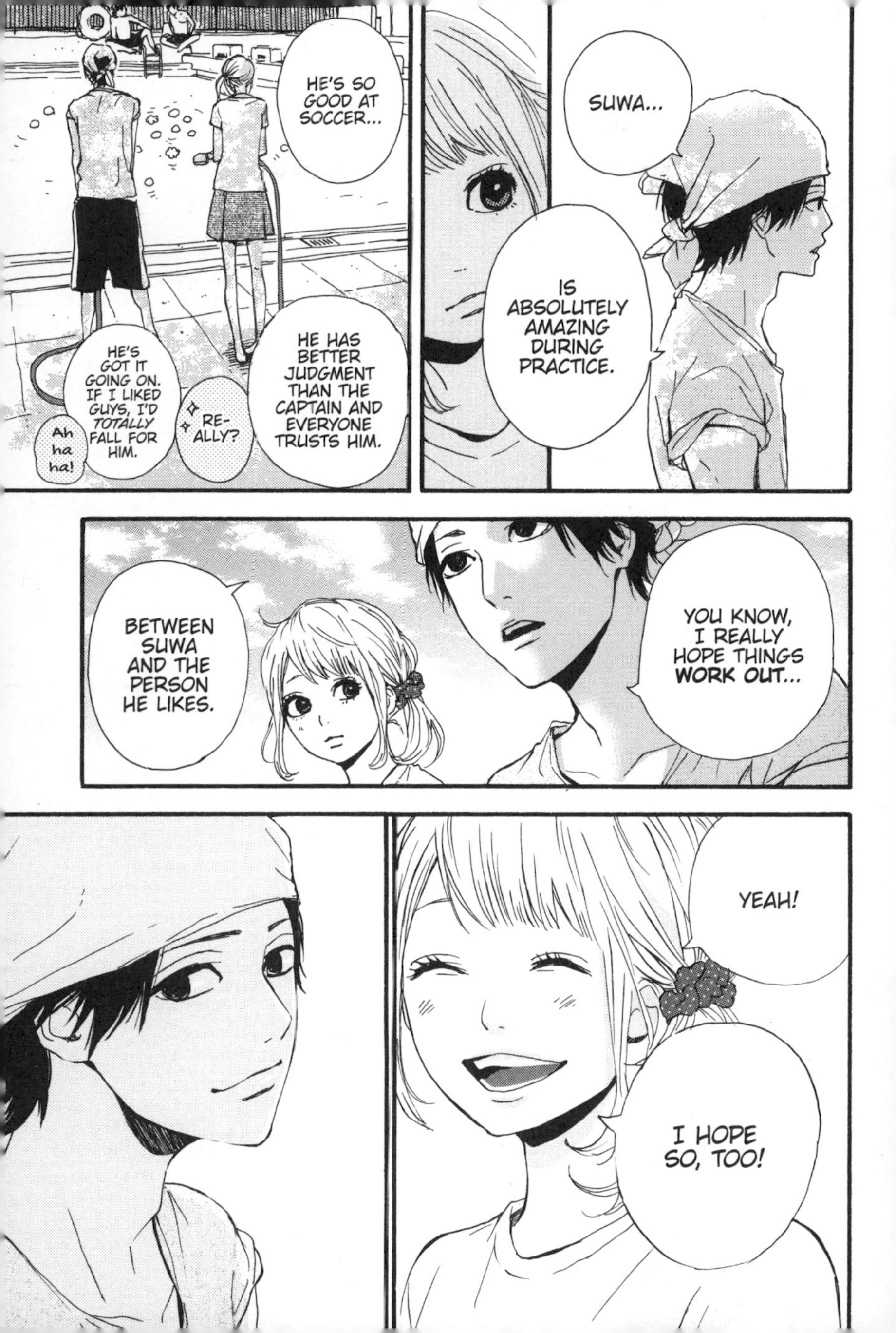
SUWA...
IS ABSOLUTELY AMAZING DURING PRACTICE.
HE'S SO GOOD AT SOCCER...
HE HAS BETTER JUDGMENT THAN THE CAPTAIN AND EVERYONE TRUSTS HIM.
RE-ALLY?
HE'S GOT IT GOING ON. IF I LIKED GUYS, I'D *TOTALLY* FALL FOR HIM.
Ah ha ha!
YOU KNOW, I REALLY HOPE THINGS **WORK OUT**...
BETWEEN SUWA AND THE PERSON HE LIKES.
YEAH!
I HOPE SO, TOO!

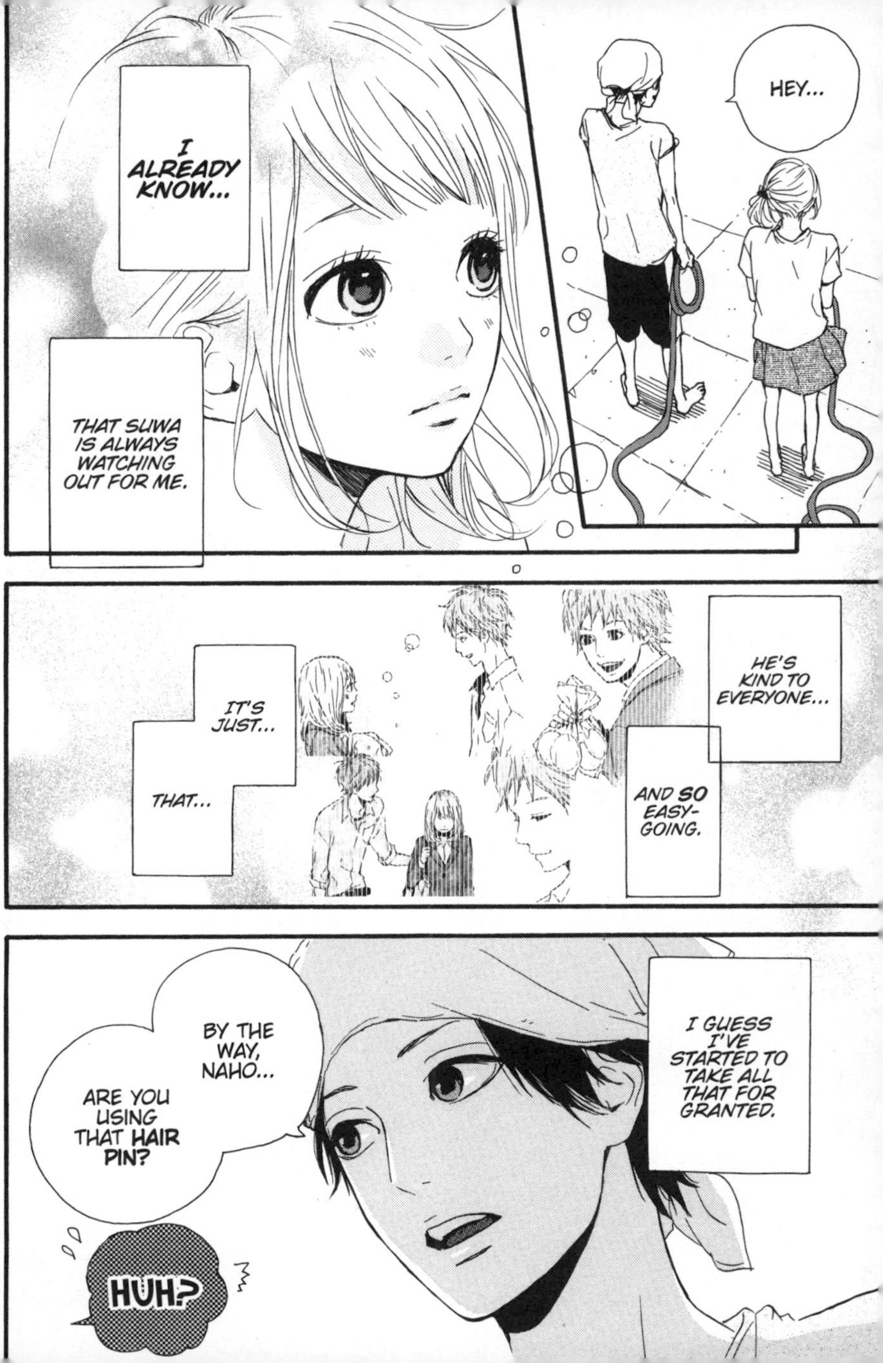
HEY...
I ALREADY KNOW...
THAT SUWA IS ALWAYS WATCHING OUT FOR ME.
HE'S KIND TO EVERYONE...
AND SO EASY-GOING.
IT'S JUST...
THAT...
I GUESS I'VE STARTED TO TAKE ALL THAT FOR GRANTED.
BY THE WAY, NAHO...
ARE YOU USING THAT HAIR PIN?
HUH?

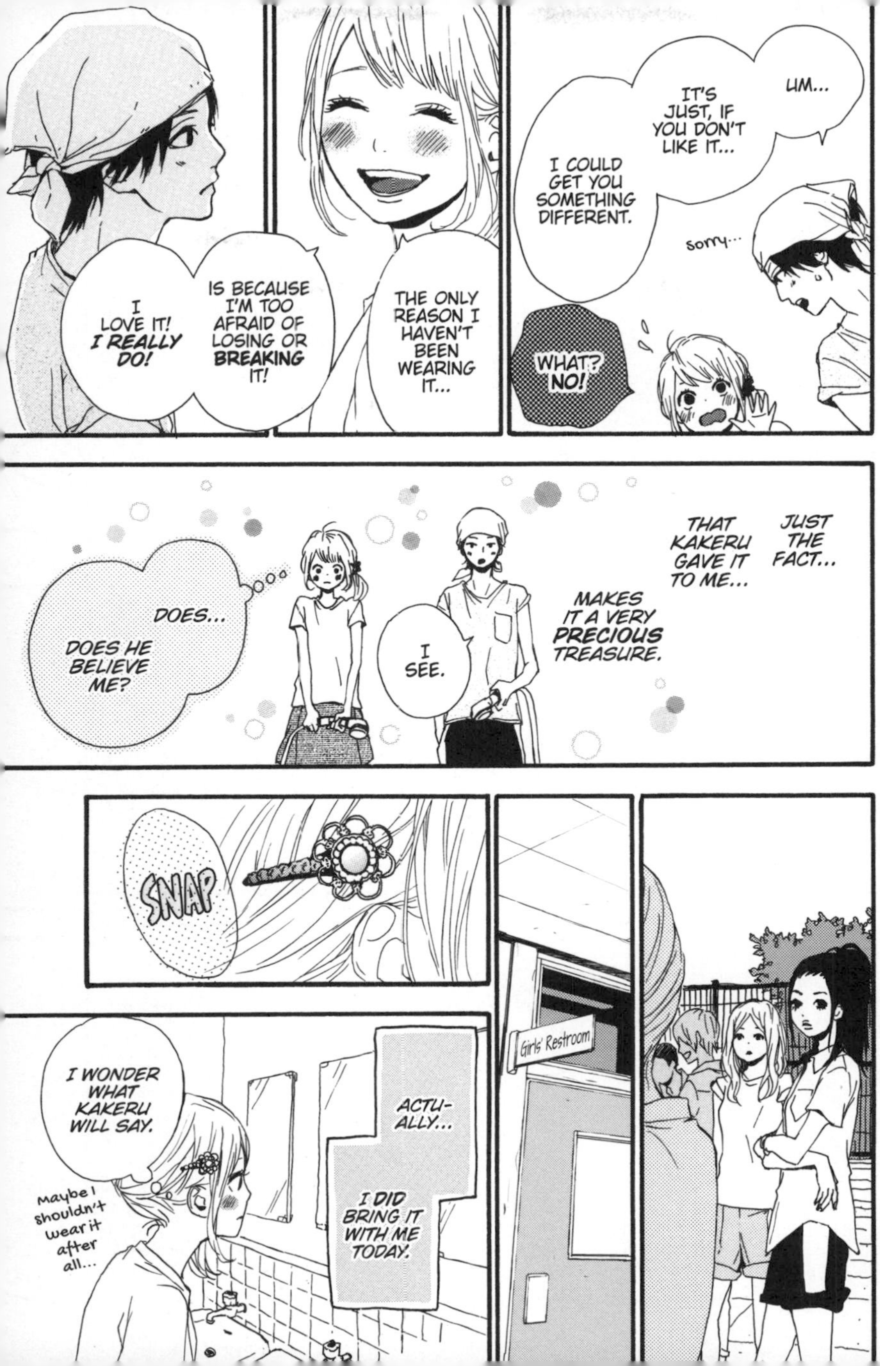
UM...
IT'S JUST, IF YOU DON'T LIKE IT...
I COULD GET YOU SOMETHING DIFFERENT.
sorry...
WHAT? NO!
THE ONLY REASON I HAVEN'T BEEN WEARING IT...
IS BECAUSE I'M TOO AFRAID OF LOSING OR BREAKING IT!
I LOVE IT! I REALLY DO!
JUST THE FACT...
THAT KAKERU GAVE IT TO ME...
MAKES IT A VERY PRECIOUS TREASURE.
I SEE.
DOES...
DOES HE BELIEVE ME?
Girls' Restroom
SNAP
ACTU-ALLY...
I DID BRING IT WITH ME TODAY.
I WONDER WHAT KAKERU WILL SAY.
Maybe I shouldn't wear it after all...

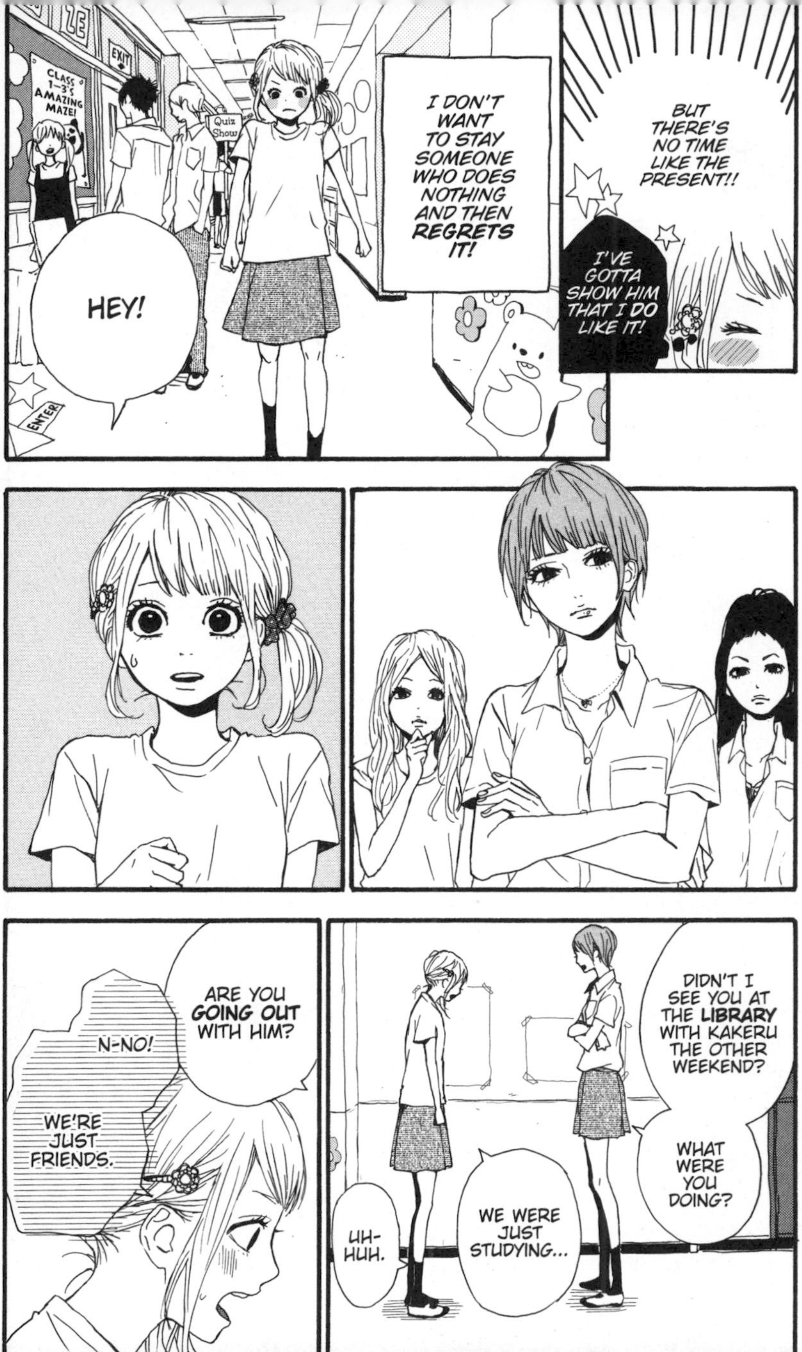

BUT THERE'S NO TIME LIKE THE PRESENT!!
I'VE GOTTA SHOW HIM THAT I DO LIKE IT!
I DON'T WANT TO STAY SOMEONE WHO DOES NOTHING AND THEN REGRETS IT!
EXIT
CLASS 1-3'S AMAZING MAZE!
Quiz Show
HEY!
ENTER
DIDN'T I SEE YOU AT THE LIBRARY WITH KAKERU THE OTHER WEEKEND?
WHAT WERE YOU DOING?
WE WERE JUST STUDYING...
UH-HUH.
ARE YOU GOING OUT WITH HIM?
N-NO!
WE'RE JUST FRIENDS.

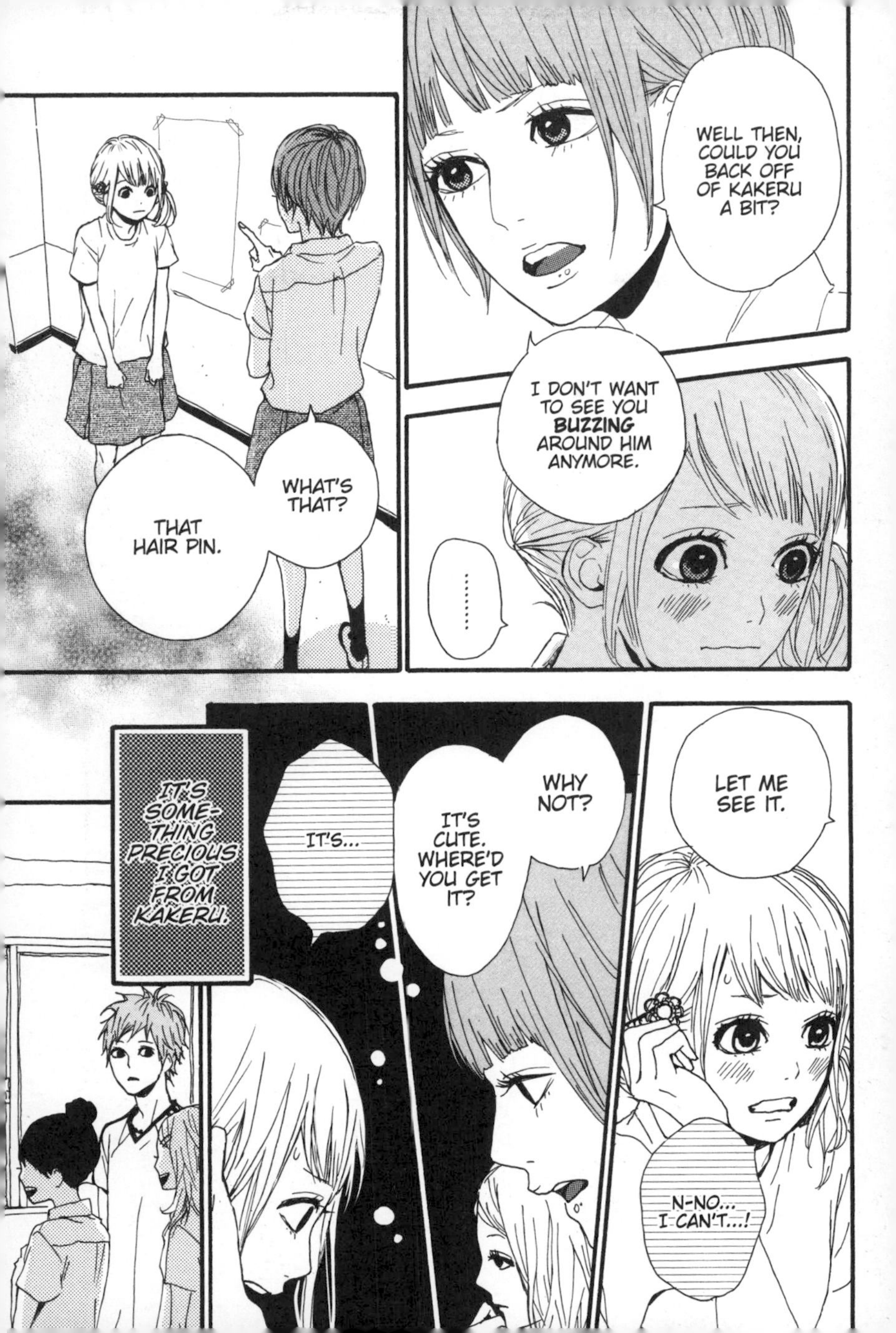
WELL THEN, COULD YOU BACK OFF OF KAKERU A BIT?
I DON'T WANT TO SEE YOU **BUZZING** AROUND HIM ANYMORE.
......
WHAT'S THAT?
THAT HAIR PIN.
LET ME SEE IT.
N-NO... I CAN'T...!
WHY NOT?
IT'S CUTE. WHERE'D YOU GET IT?
IT'S...
IT'S SOMETHING PRECIOUS I GOT FROM KAKERU.

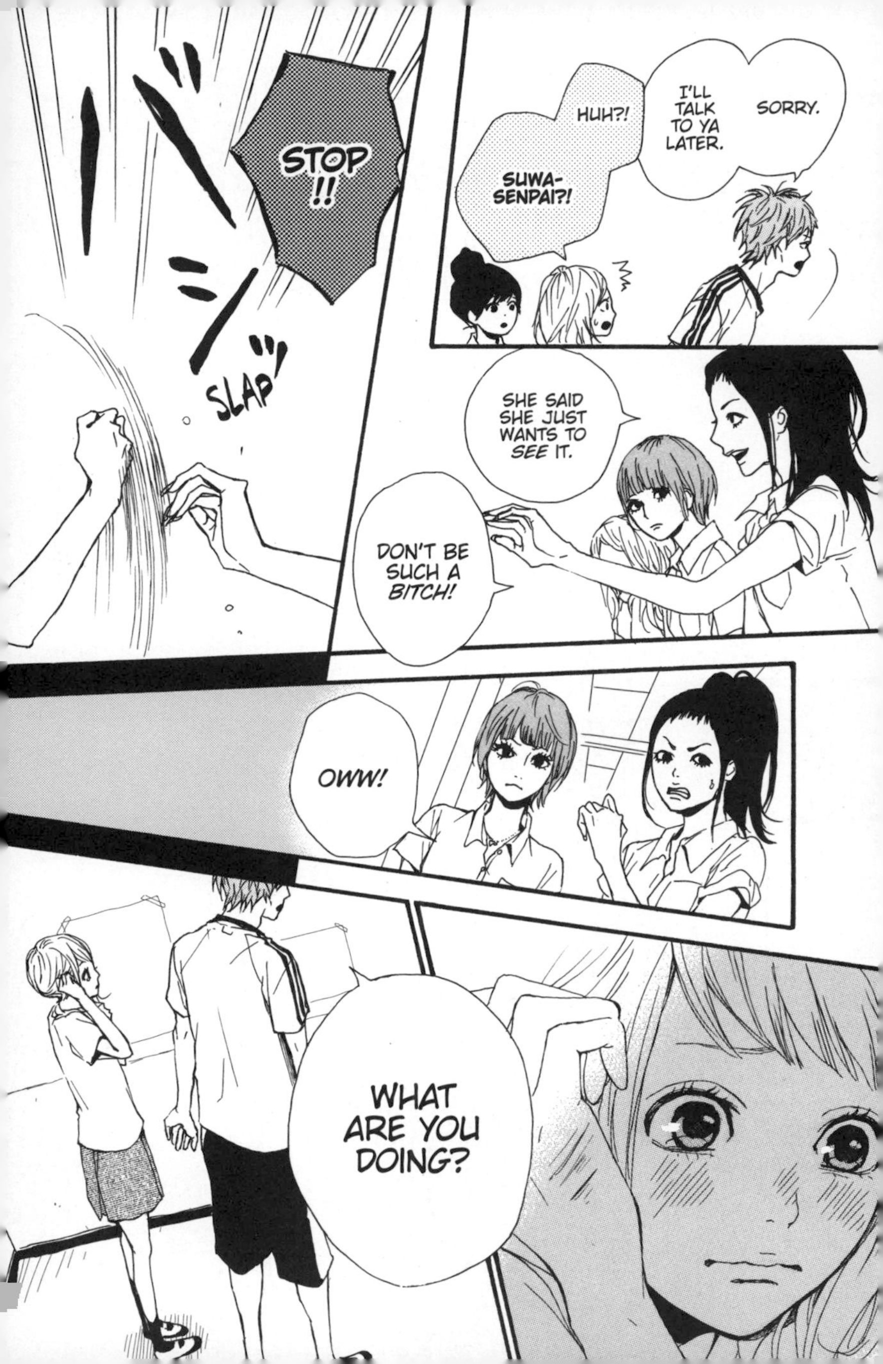
SORRY.
I'LL TALK TO YA LATER.
HUH?!
SUWA-SENPAI?!
SHE SAID SHE JUST WANTS TO SEE IT.
DON'T BE SUCH A BITCH!
STOP!!
SLAP
OWW!
WHAT ARE YOU DOING?

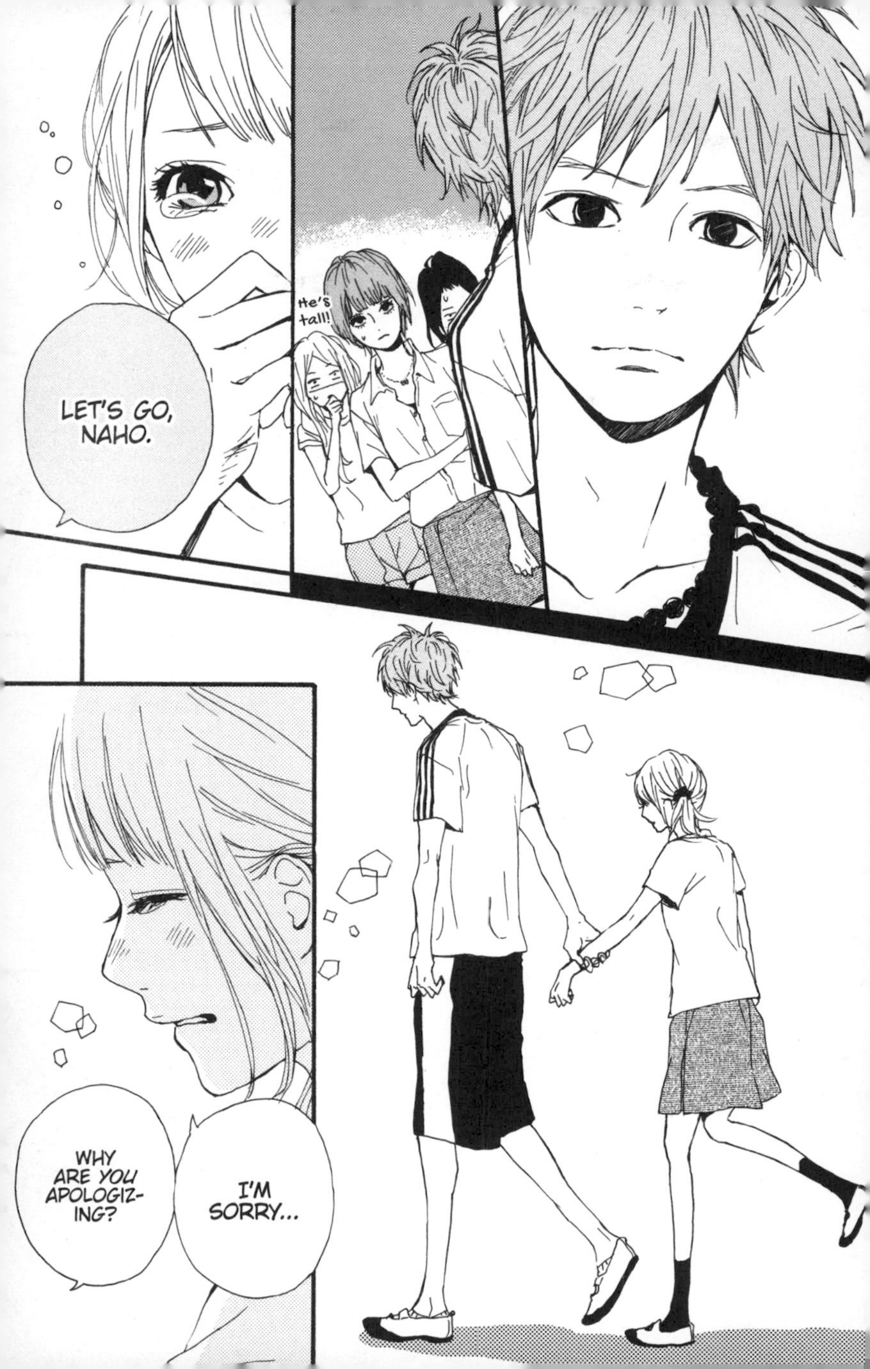
He's tall!
LET'S GO, NAHO.
I'M SORRY...
WHY ARE YOU APOLOGIZ-ING?

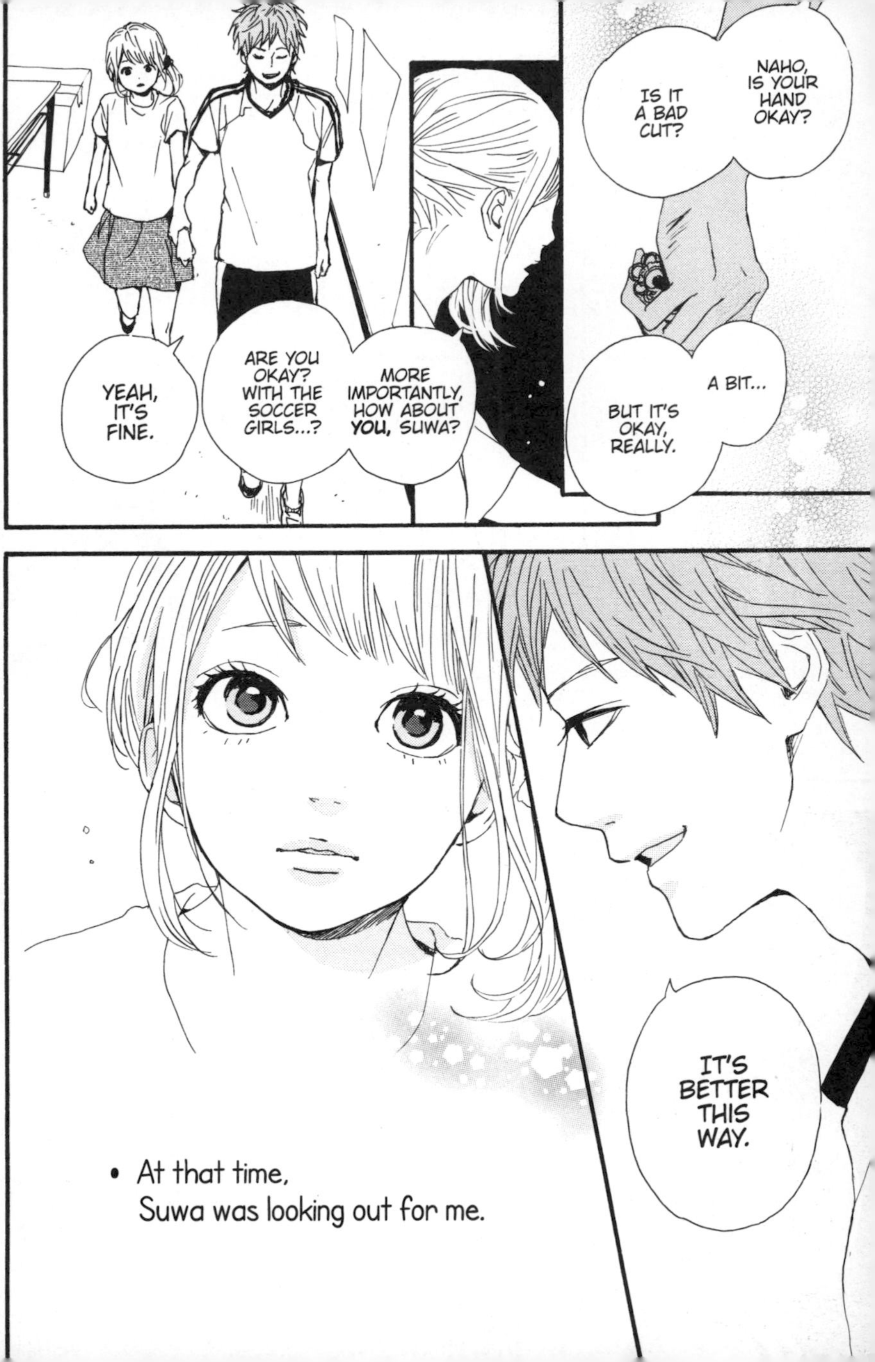
NAHO, IS YOUR HAND OKAY?
IS IT A BAD CUT?
A BIT...
BUT IT'S OKAY, REALLY.
MORE IMPORTANTLY, HOW ABOUT **YOU,** SUWA?
ARE YOU OKAY? WITH THE SOCCER GIRLS...?
YEAH, IT'S FINE.
IT'S BETTER THIS WAY.
• At that time, Suwa was looking out for me.

I wasn't even aware of how much he was doing for me behind the scenes.

So if Suwa does something nice for you, thank him.

I'm sure he'd appreciate it.

SUWA HELD MY HAND...

UNTIL WE REACHED THE POOL.

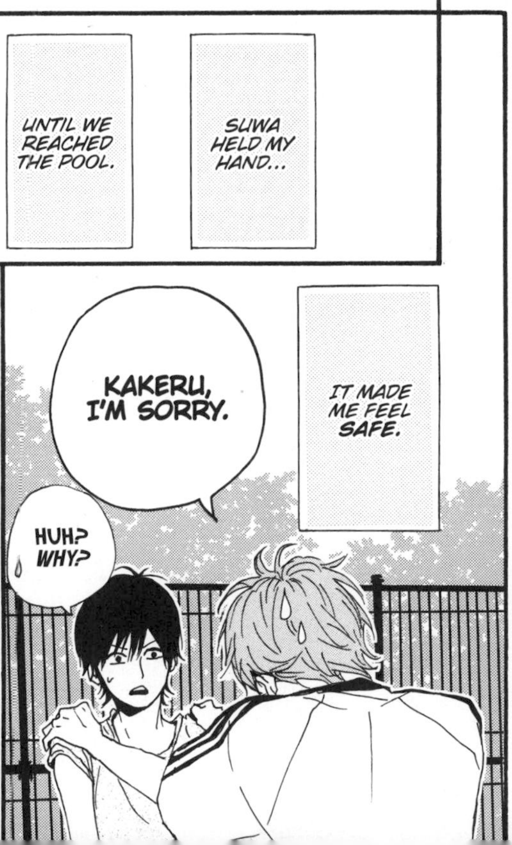
IT MADE ME FEEL SAFE.
KAKERU, I'M SORRY.
HUH? WHY?

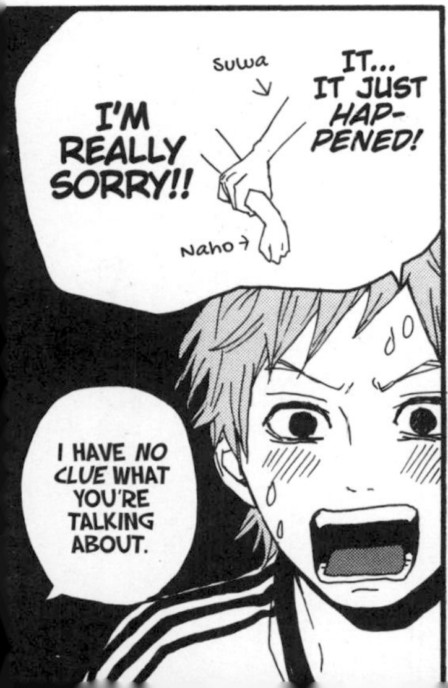
IT... IT JUST HAP-PENED!
I'M REALLY SORRY!!
Suwa
Naho
I HAVE NO CLUE WHAT YOU'RE TALKING ABOUT.

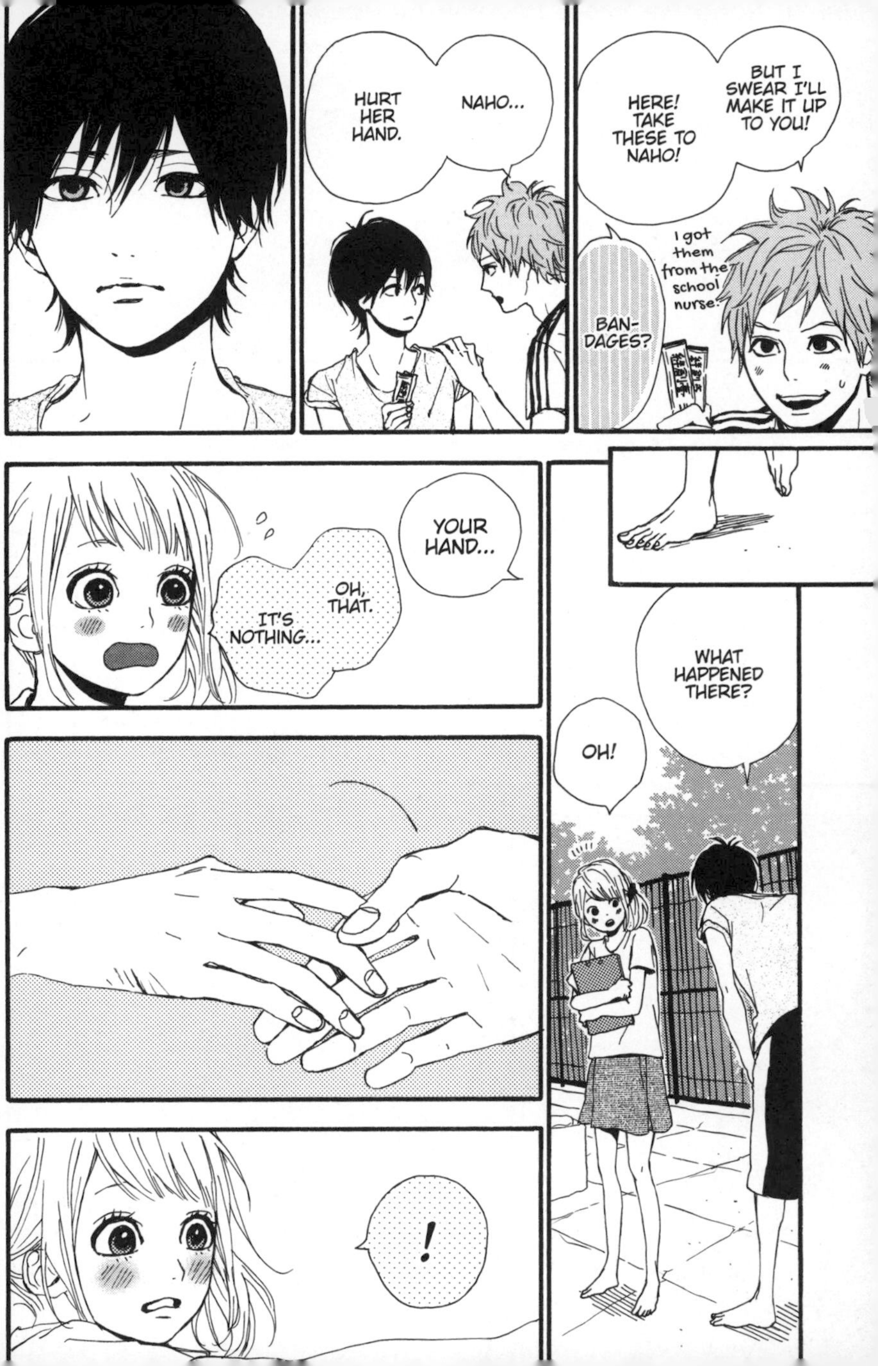
HERE! TAKE THESE TO NAHO!
BUT I SWEAR I'LL MAKE IT UP TO YOU!
I got them from the school nurse.
BAN-DAGES?
NAHO...
HURT HER HAND.
...
WHAT HAPPENED THERE?
OH!
YOUR HAND...
OH, THAT.
IT'S NOTHING...
!

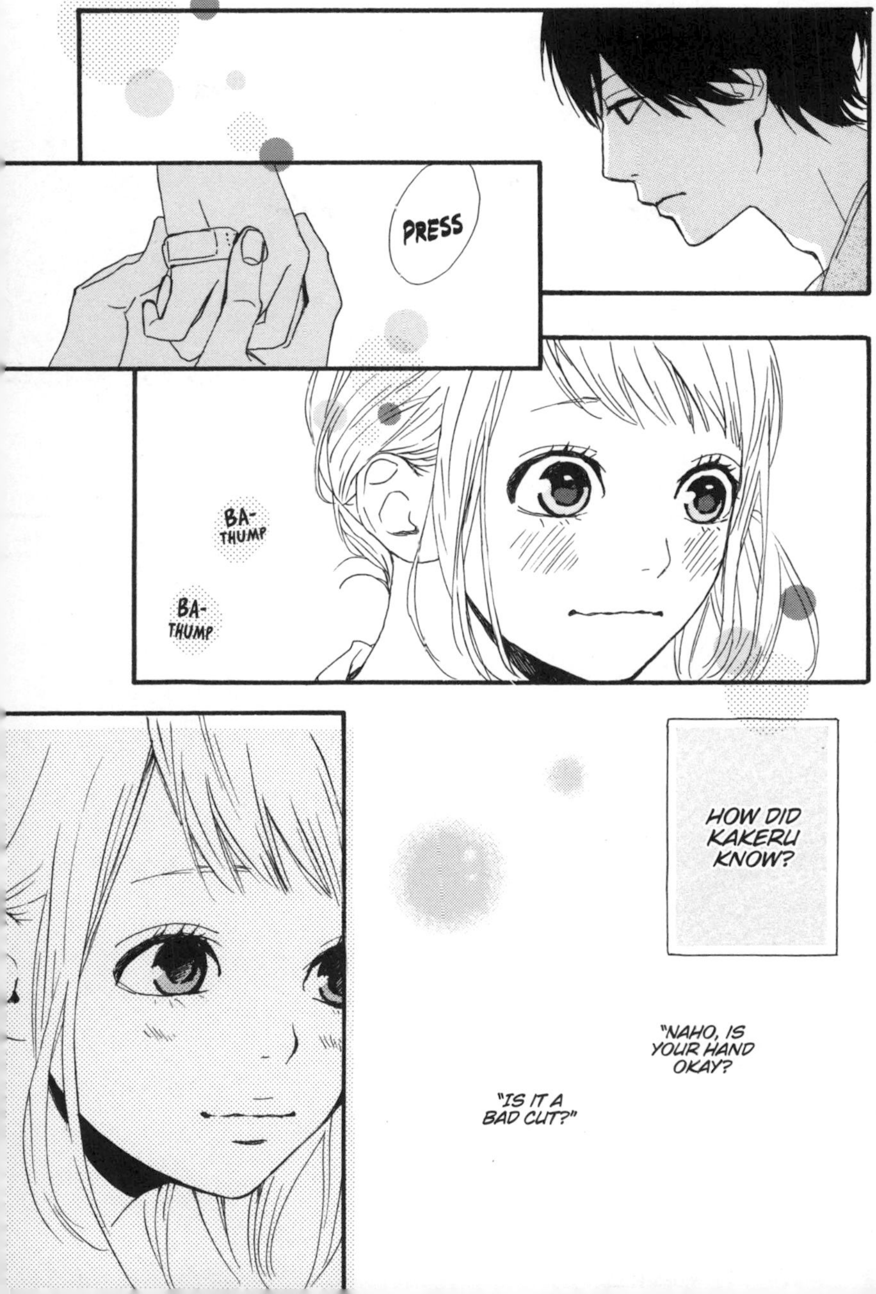
PRESS
BA-THUMP
BA-THUMP
HOW DID KAKERU KNOW?
"NAHO, IS YOUR HAND OKAY?
"IS IT A BAD CUT?"

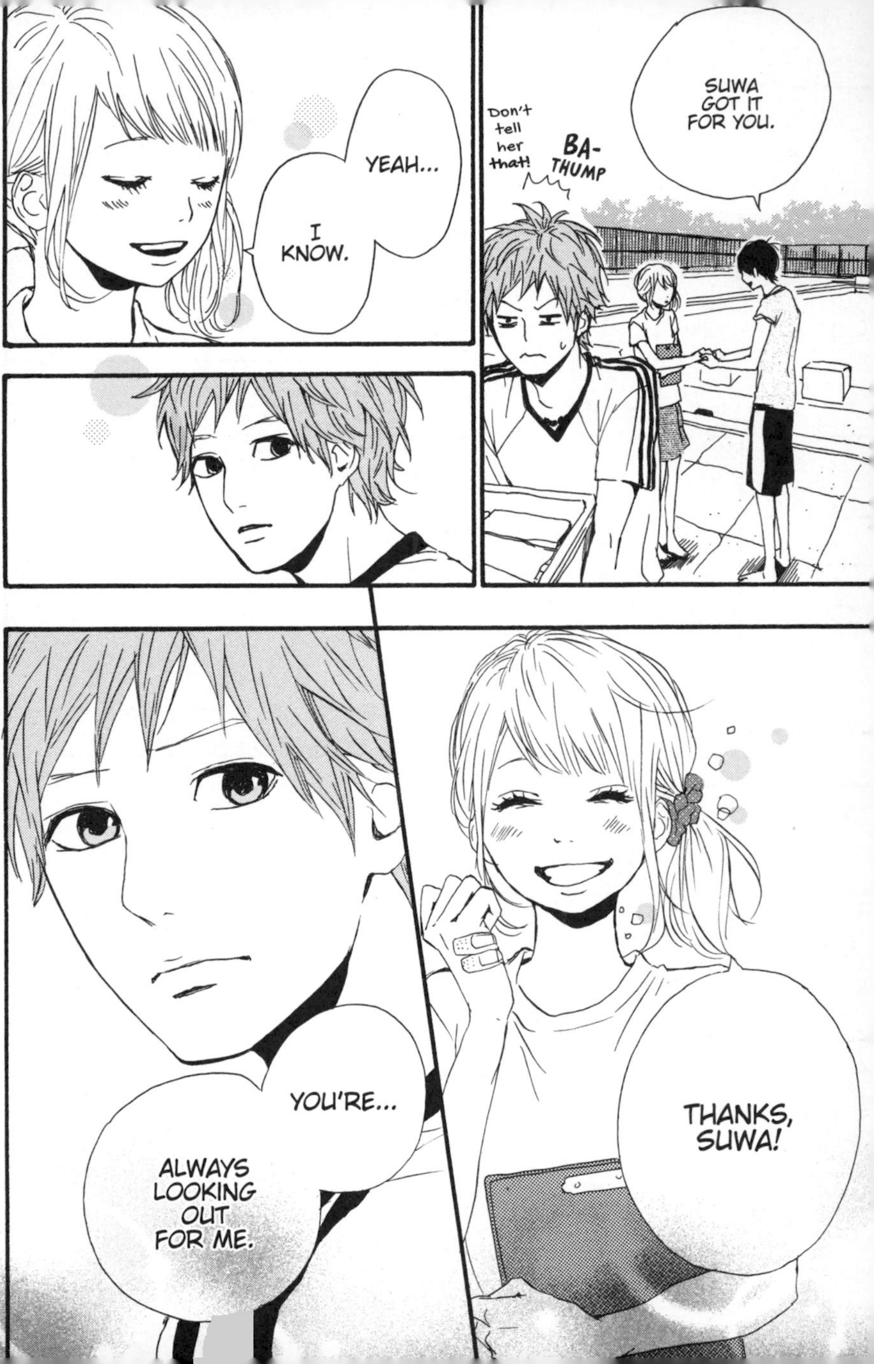
SUWA GOT IT FOR YOU.
BA-THUMP
Don't tell her that!
YEAH...
I KNOW.
THANKS, SUWA!
YOU'RE...
ALWAYS LOOKING OUT FOR ME.

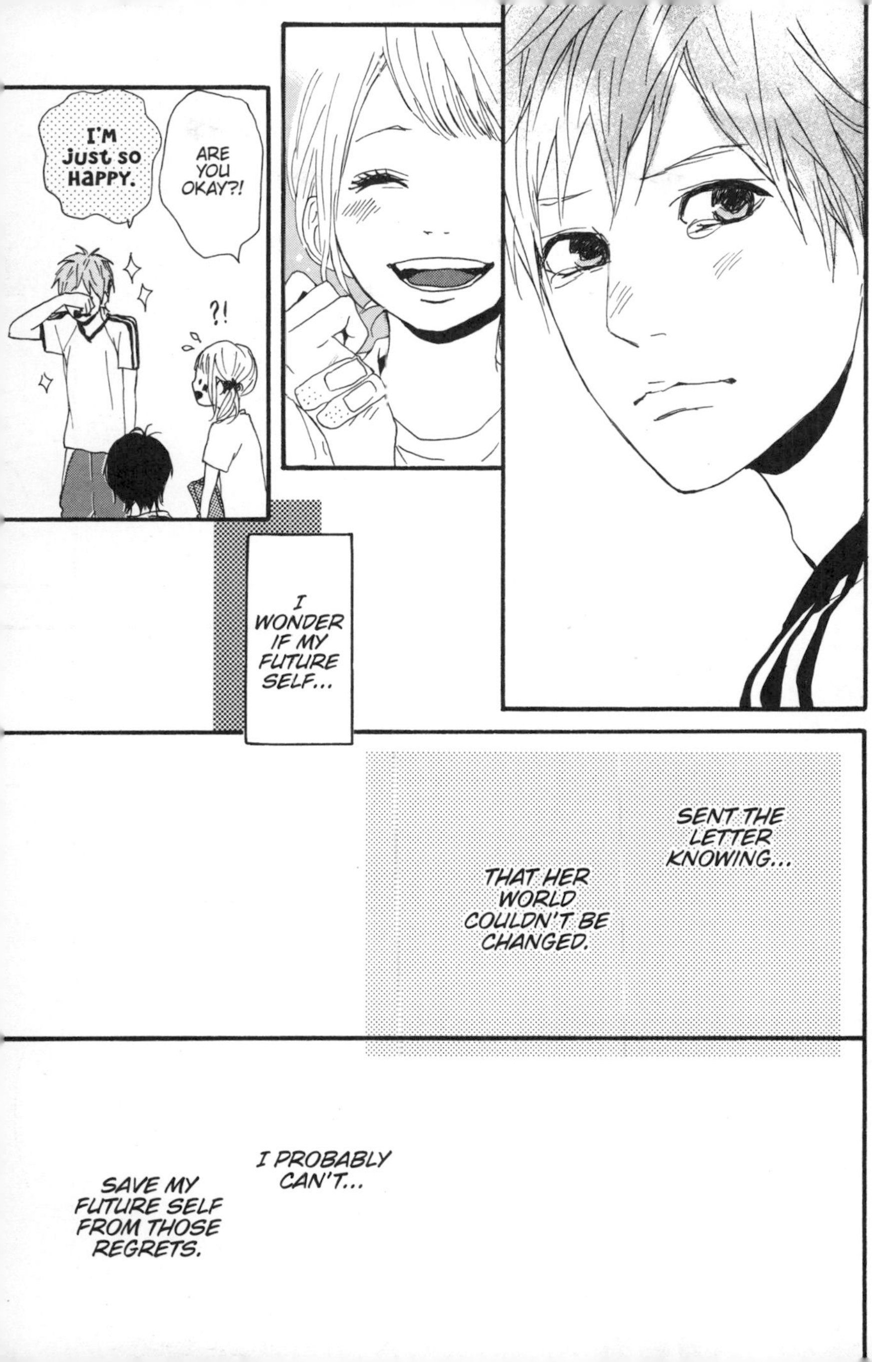
ARE YOU OKAY?!
I'M just so HAPPY.
?!
I WONDER IF MY FUTURE SELF...
SENT THE LETTER KNOWING...
THAT HER WORLD COULDN'T BE CHANGED.
I PROBABLY CAN'T...
SAVE MY FUTURE SELF FROM THOSE REGRETS.

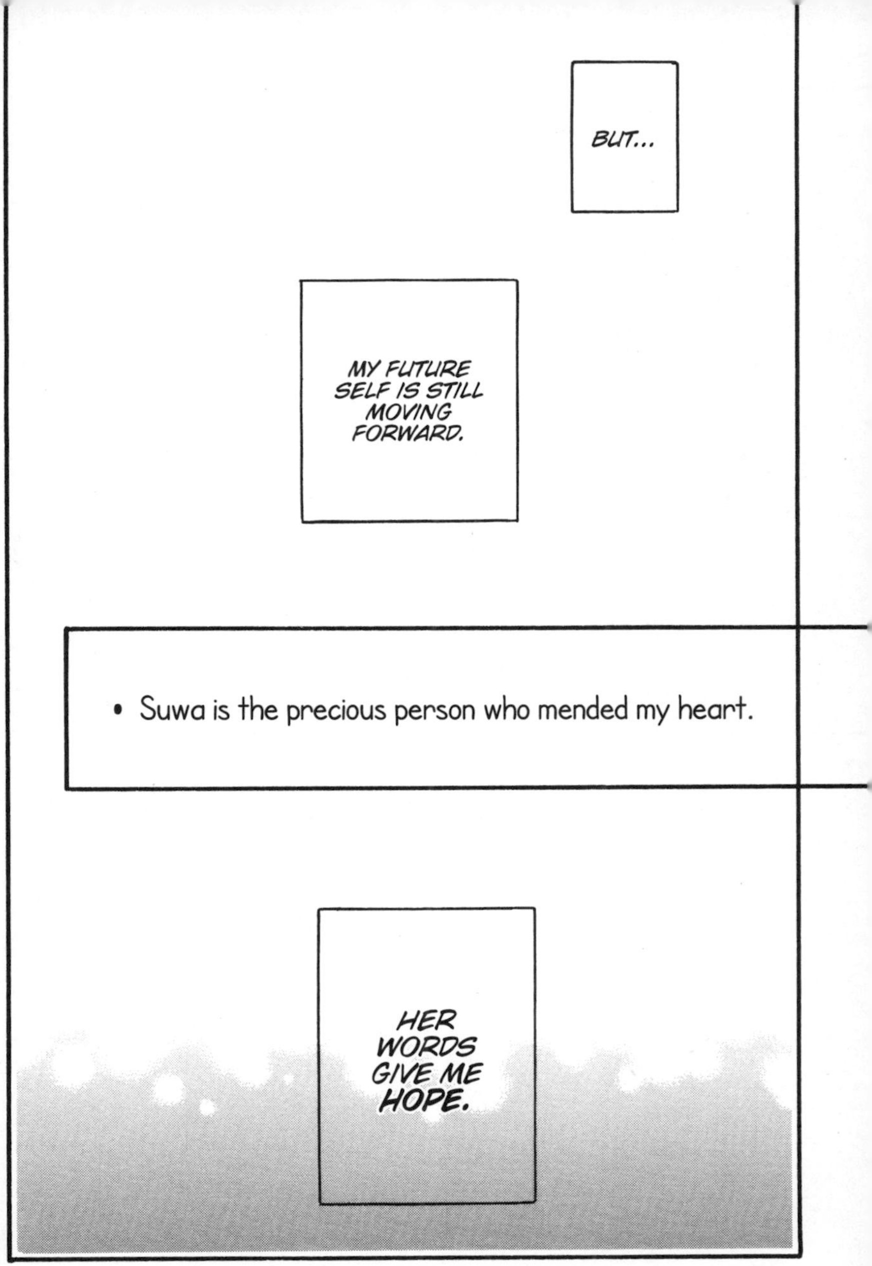
BUT...
MY FUTURE SELF IS STILL MOVING FORWARD.
• Suwa is the precious person who mended my heart.
HER WORDS GIVE ME HOPE.

orange

orange
LETTER 7

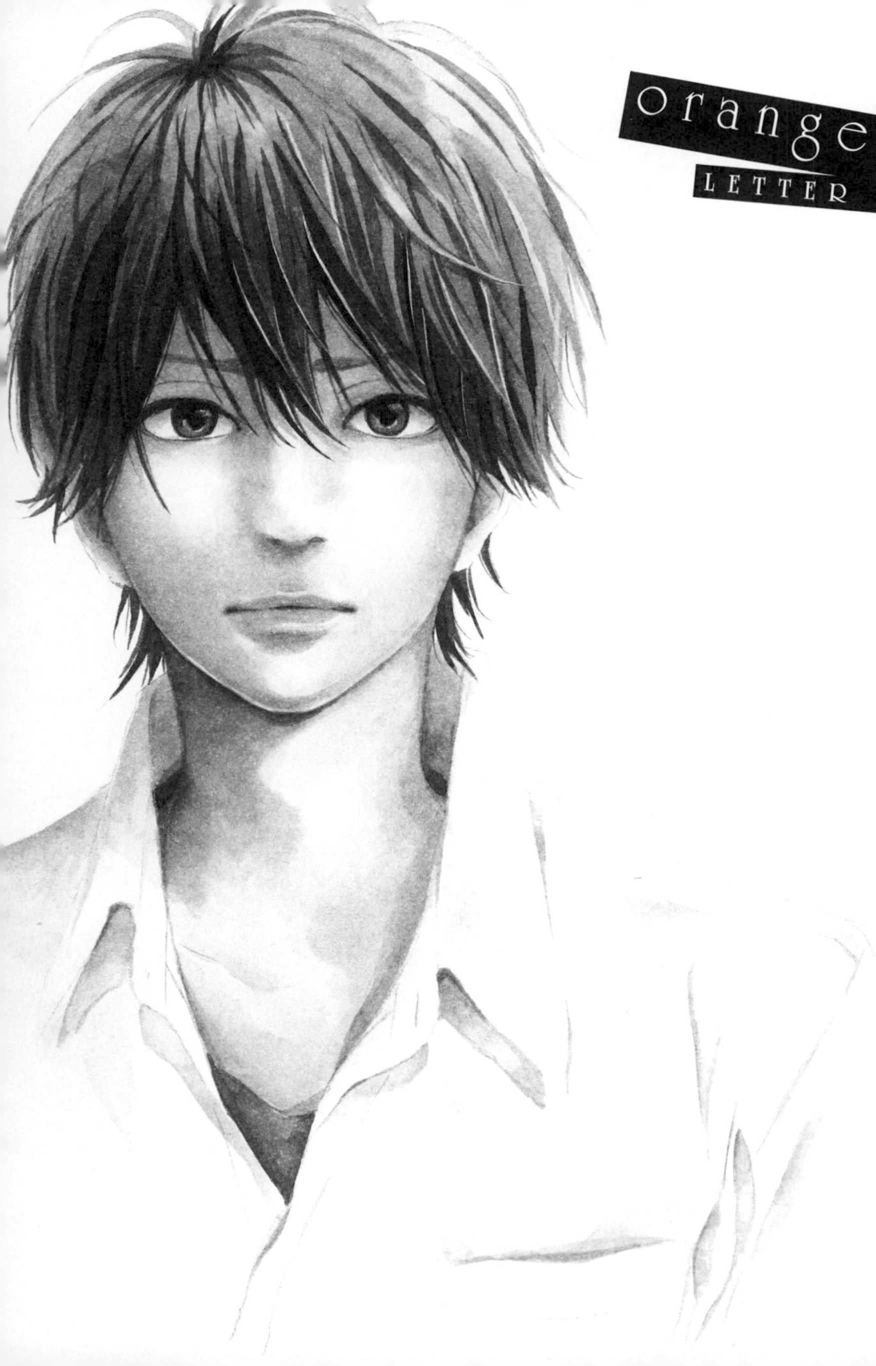

orange

July 15

- The last day of the festival.

- Today, Suwa swapped shifts with me again so I could be with Kakeru.

- When it was just Kakeru and I alone, I was nervous and couldn't really talk to him.

CAN I ASK YOU SOME-THING?

JUST TO KILL THE TIME.

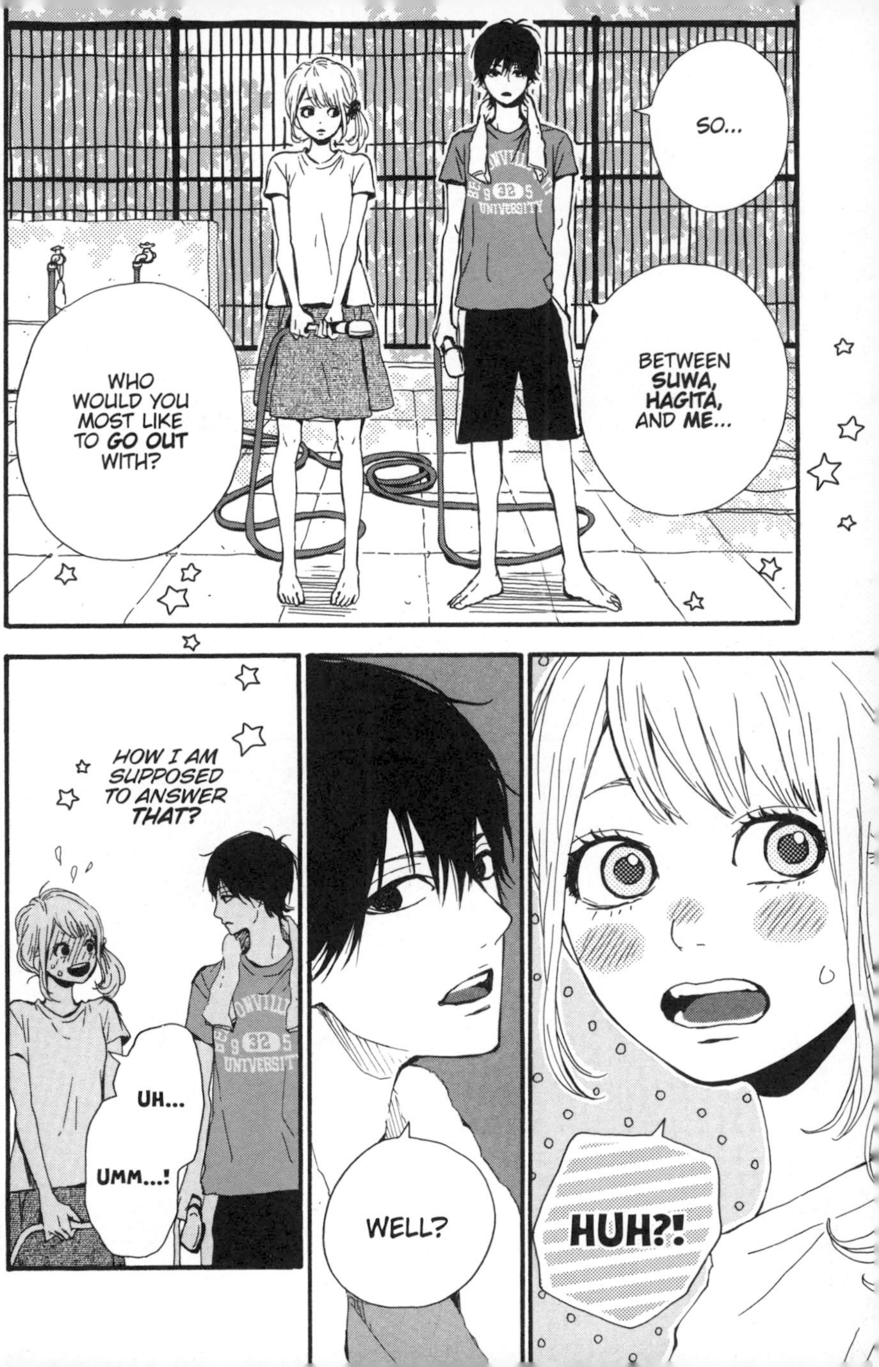
SO...
BETWEEN SUWA, HAGITA, AND ME...
WHO WOULD YOU MOST LIKE TO GO OUT WITH?
HUH?!
WELL?
HOW I AM SUPPOSED TO ANSWER THAT?
UH...
UMM...!

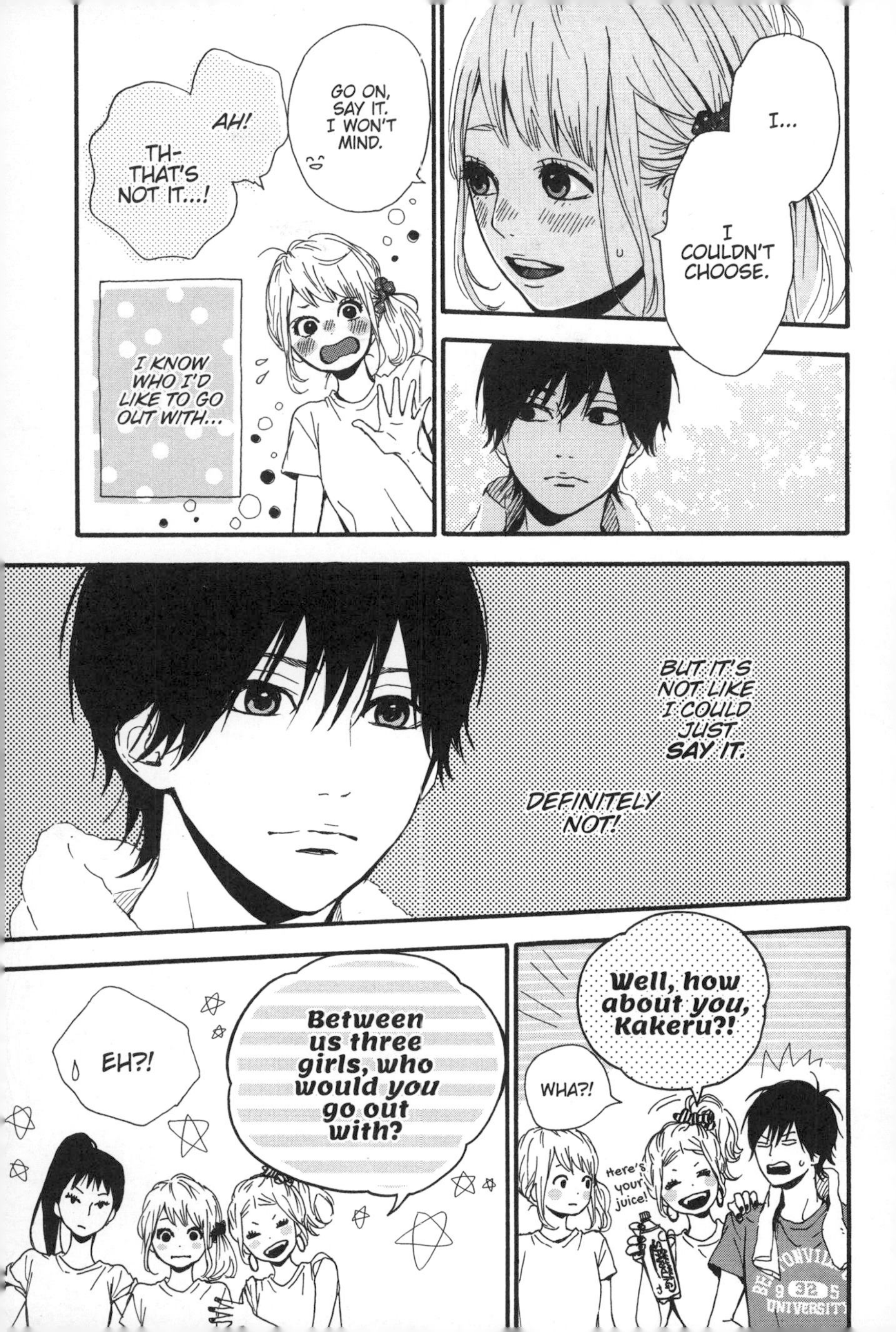
I...
I COULDN'T CHOOSE.
GO ON, SAY IT. I WON'T MIND.
AH!
TH-THAT'S NOT IT...!
I KNOW WHO I'D LIKE TO GO OUT WITH...
BUT IT'S NOT LIKE I COULD JUST SAY IT.
DEFINITELY NOT!
Well, how about you, Kakeru?!
WHA?!
Here's your juice!
Between us three girls, who would you go out with?
EH?!

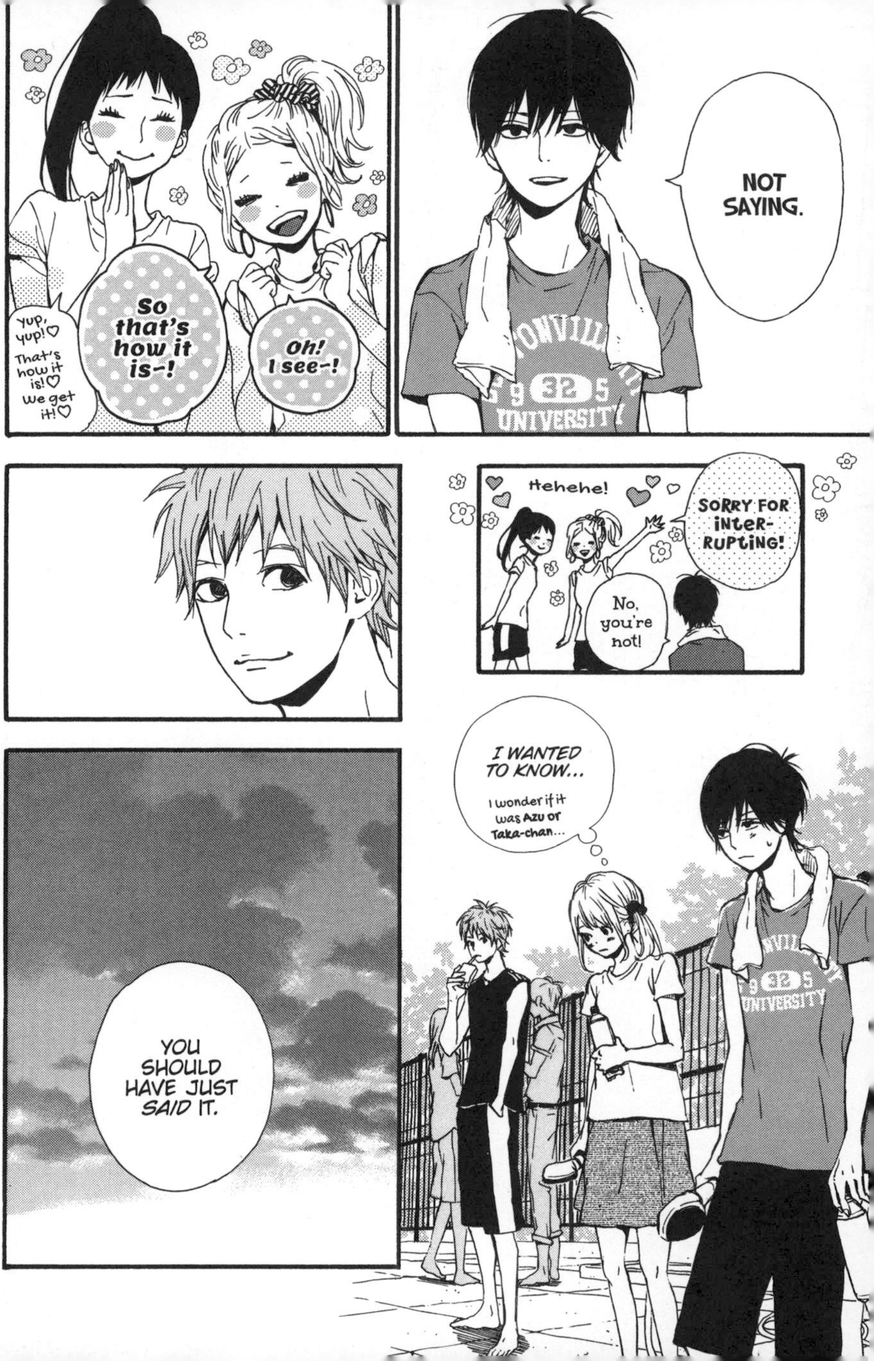
NOT SAYING.
Oh! I see-!
So that's how it is-!
Yup, yup! ♡ That's how it is! ♡ We get it! ♡
Hehehe!
SORRY FOR INTERRUPTING!
No, you're not!
I WANTED TO KNOW...
I wonder if it was Azu or Taka-chan...
YOU SHOULD HAVE JUST SAID IT.

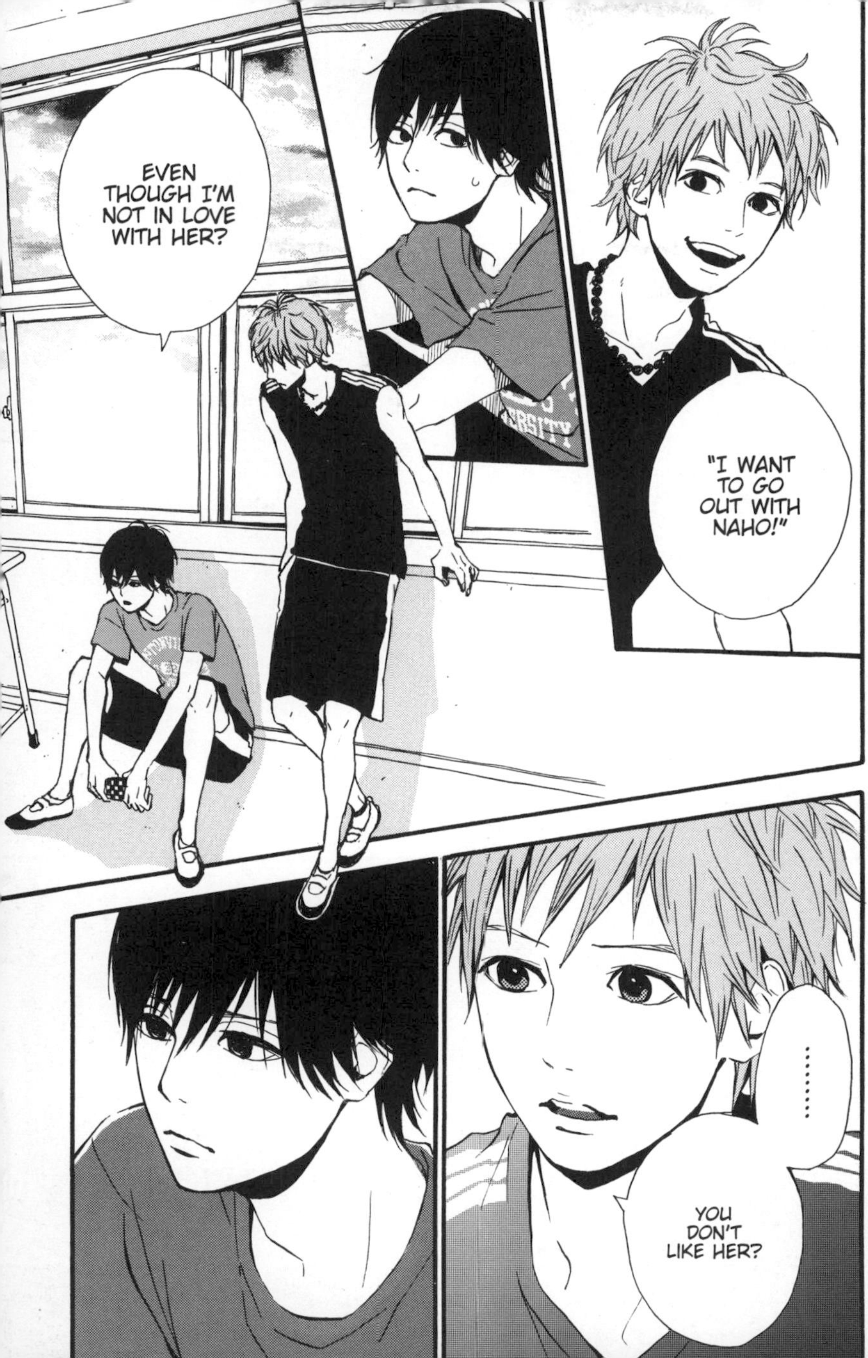
"I WANT TO GO OUT WITH NAHO!"
EVEN THOUGH I'M NOT IN LOVE WITH HER?
......
YOU DON'T LIKE HER?

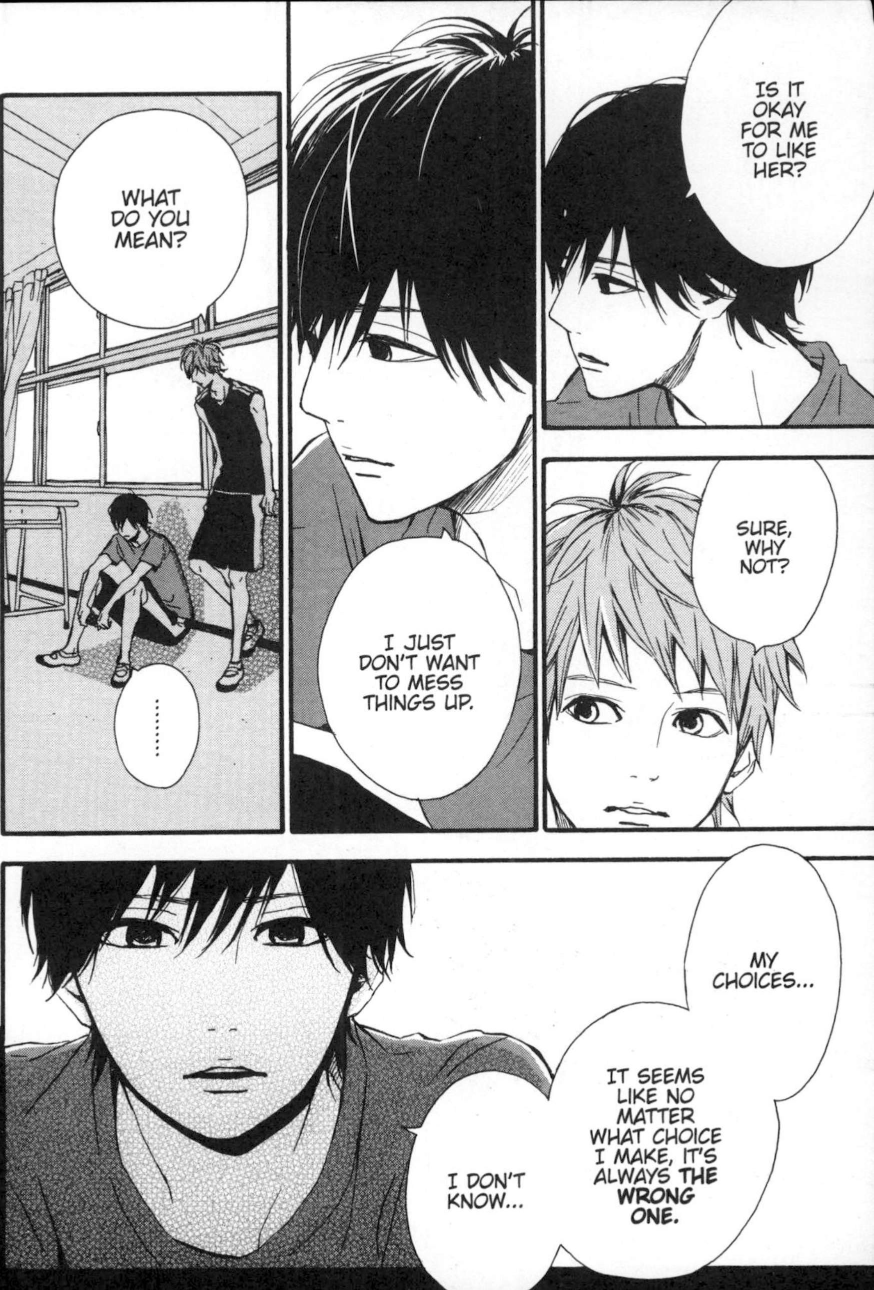
IS IT OKAY FOR ME TO LIKE HER?
SURE, WHY NOT?
I JUST DON'T WANT TO MESS THINGS UP.
WHAT DO YOU MEAN?
......
MY CHOICES...
IT SEEMS LIKE NO MATTER WHAT CHOICE I MAKE, IT'S ALWAYS **THE WRONG ONE.**
I DON'T KNOW...

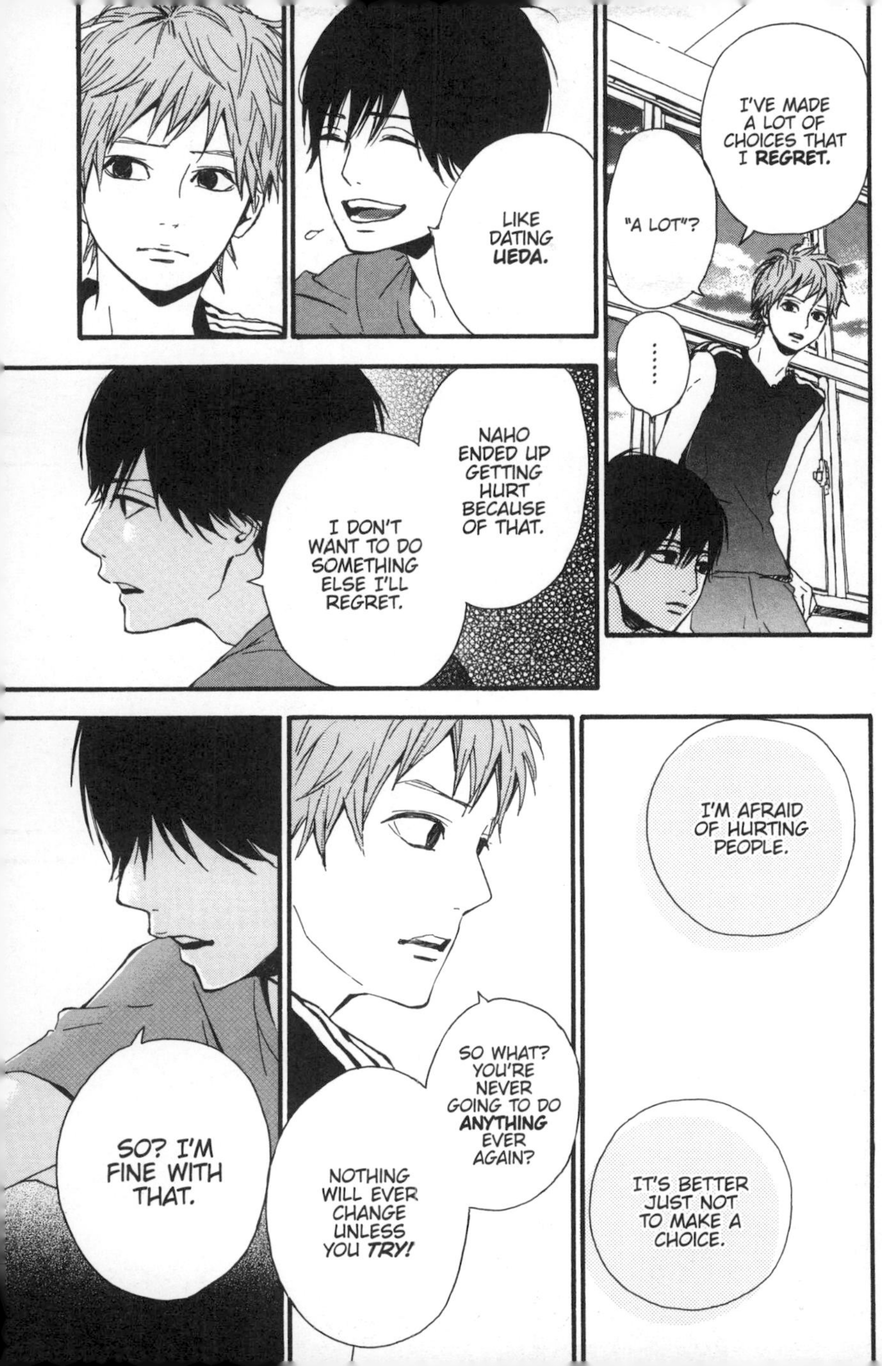
I'VE MADE A LOT OF CHOICES THAT I REGRET.
"A LOT"?
......
LIKE DATING UEDA.
NAHO ENDED UP GETTING HURT BECAUSE OF THAT.
I DON'T WANT TO DO SOMETHING ELSE I'LL REGRET.
I'M AFRAID OF HURTING PEOPLE.
IT'S BETTER JUST NOT TO MAKE A CHOICE.
SO WHAT? YOU'RE NEVER GOING TO DO ANYTHING EVER AGAIN?
NOTHING WILL EVER CHANGE UNLESS YOU TRY!
SO? I'M FINE WITH THAT.

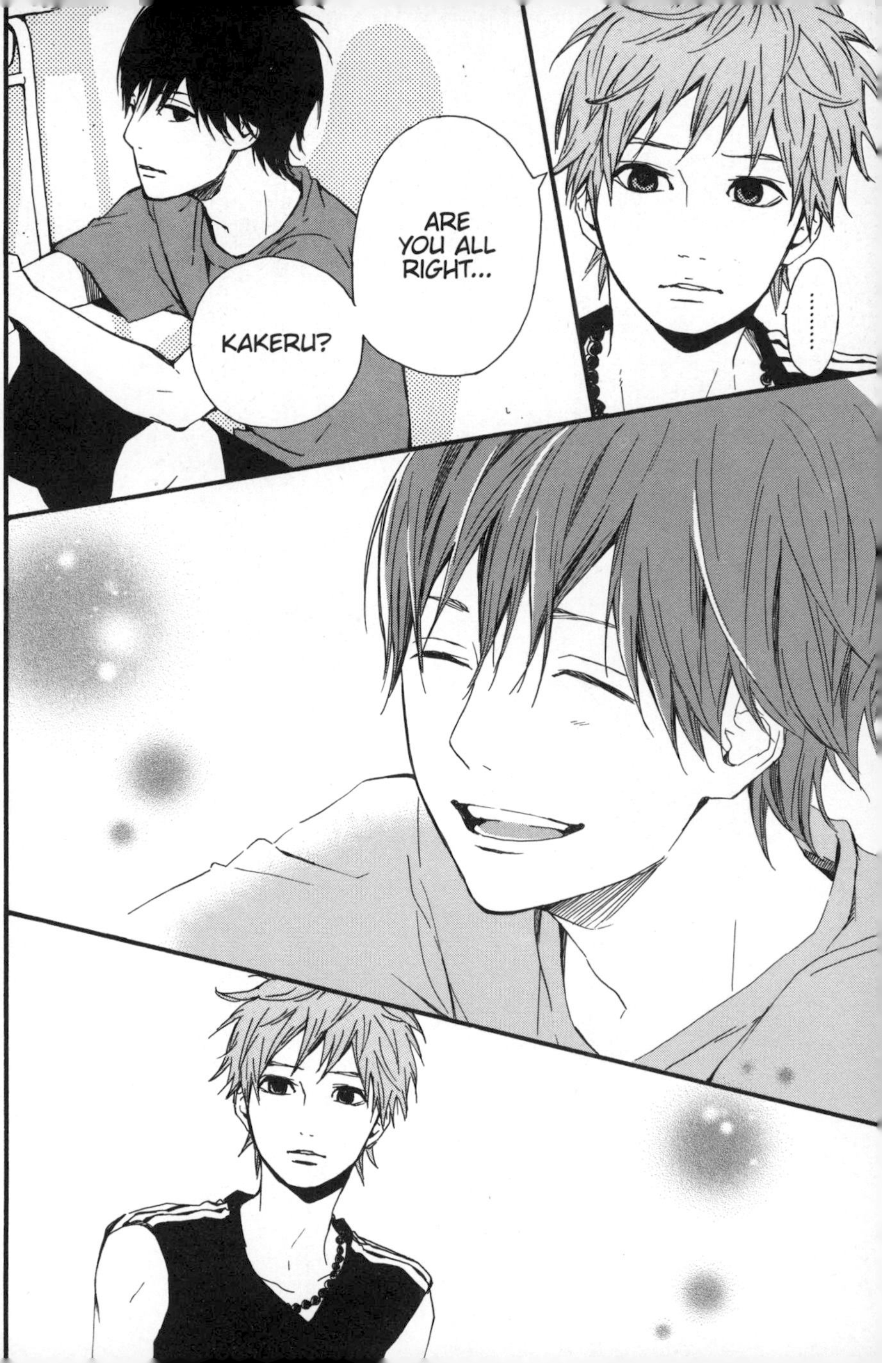
......
ARE YOU ALL RIGHT...
KAKERU?

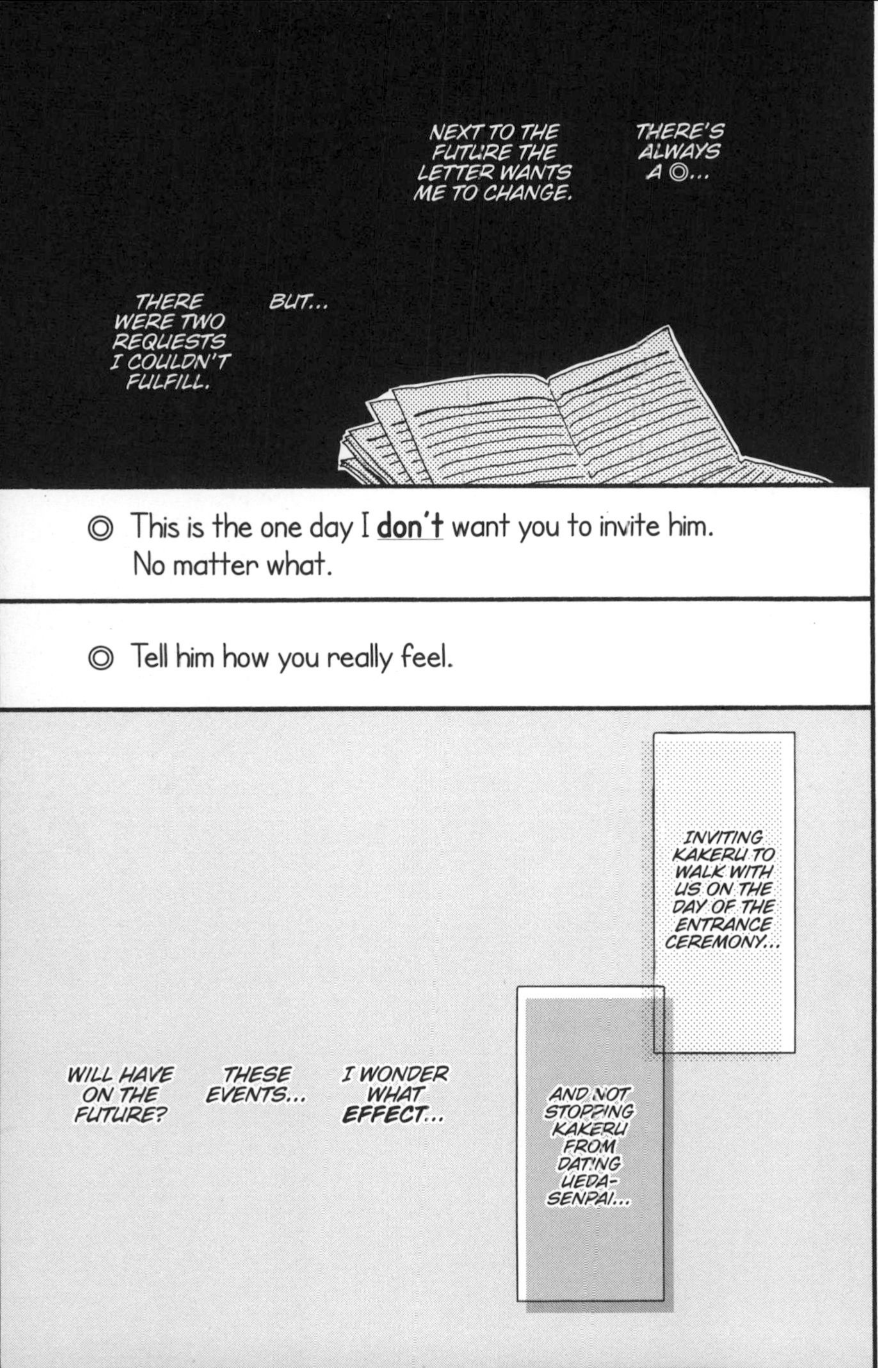
THERE'S ALWAYS A ◎...
NEXT TO THE FUTURE THE LETTER WANTS ME TO CHANGE.
BUT...
THERE WERE TWO REQUESTS I COULDN'T FULFILL.
◎ This is the one day I **don't** want you to invite him. No matter what.
◎ Tell him how you really feel.
INVITING KAKERU TO WALK WITH US ON THE DAY OF THE ENTRANCE CEREMONY...
AND NOT STOPPING KAKERU FROM DATING UEDA-SENPAI...
I WONDER WHAT EFFECT...
THESE EVENTS...
WILL HAVE ON THE FUTURE?

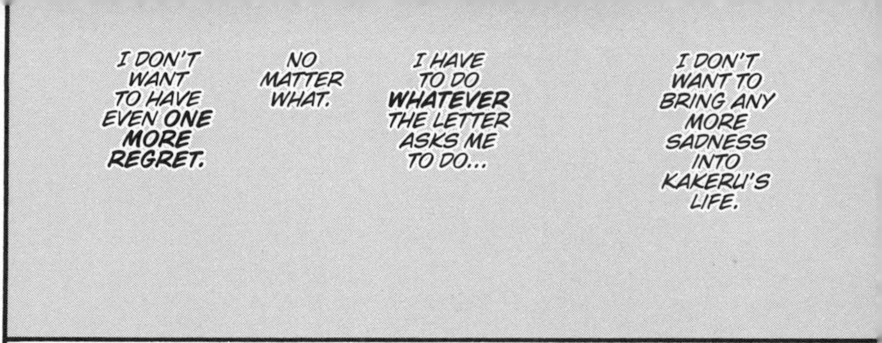
I DON'T WANT TO BRING ANY MORE SADNESS INTO KAKERU'S LIFE.
I HAVE TO DO **WHATEVER** THE LETTER ASKS ME TO DO...
NO MATTER WHAT.
I DON'T WANT TO HAVE EVEN **ONE MORE REGRET.**

◎ At the end of the festival, Kakeru and I watched the fireworks together.

It was nice.

- Today is a day full of wonder. If you just be yourself, you'll be fine.

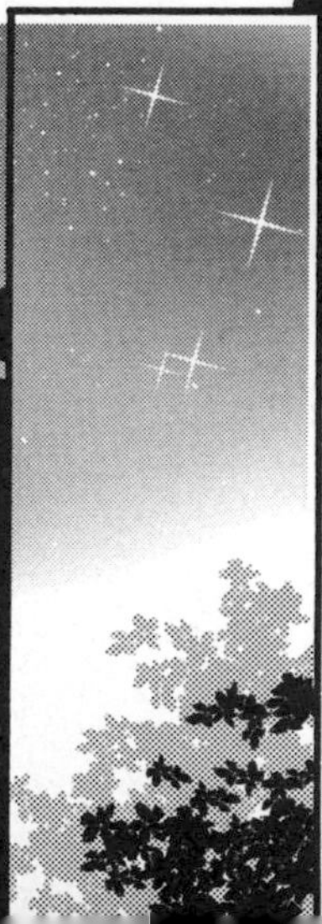

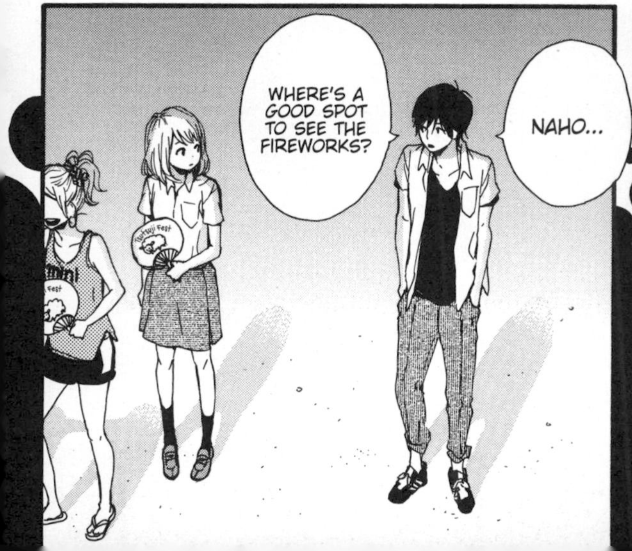
NAHO...
WHERE'S A GOOD SPOT TO SEE THE FIREWORKS?

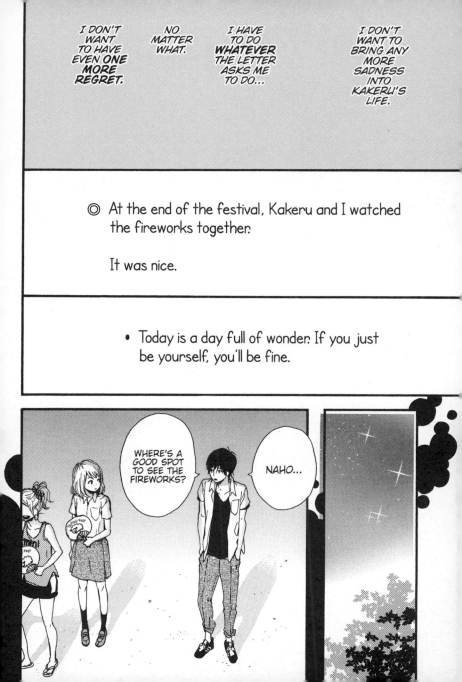

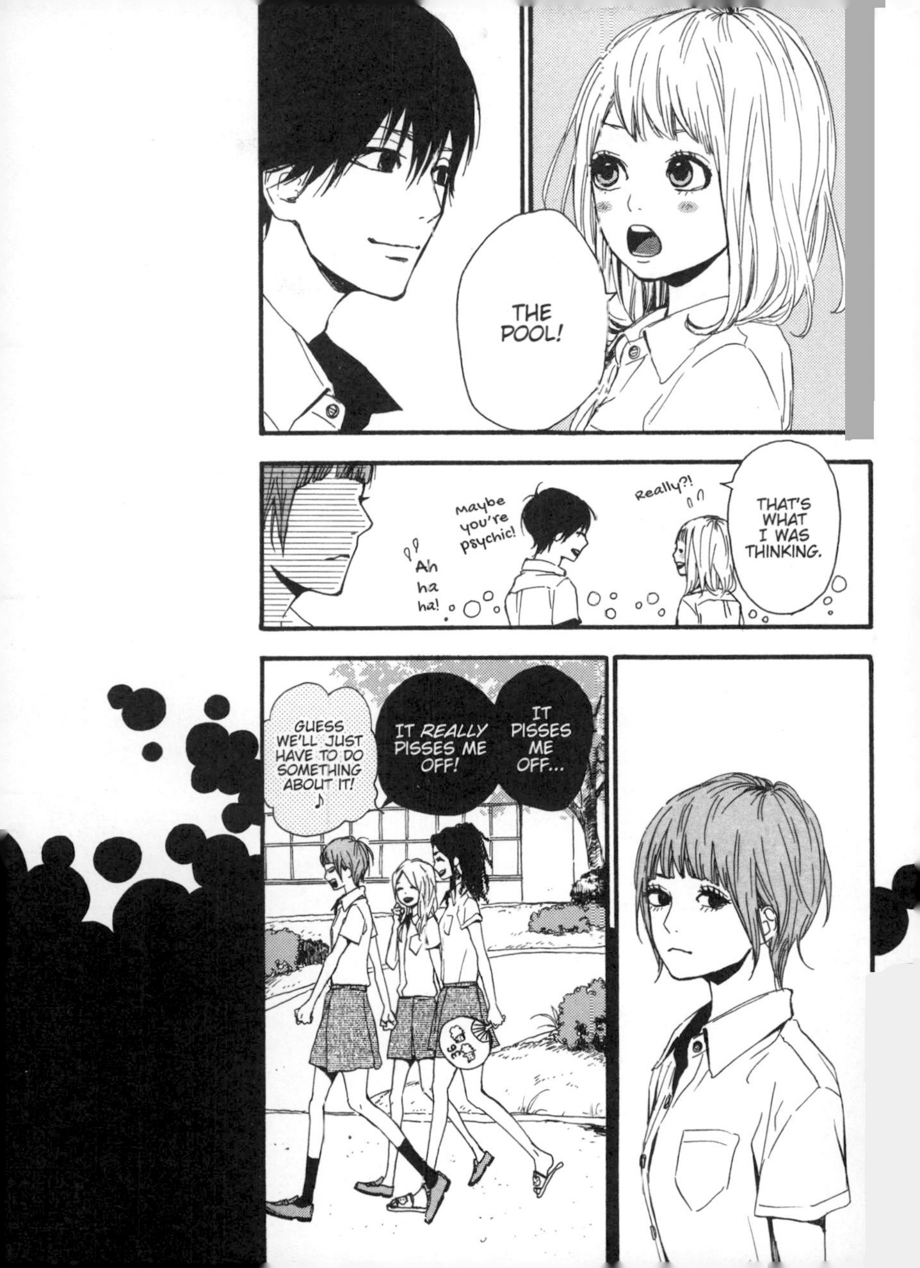
THE POOL!
THAT'S WHAT I WAS THINKING.
Really?!
Maybe you're psychic!
Ah ha ha!
IT PISSES ME OFF...
IT REALLY PISSES ME OFF!
GUESS WE'LL JUST HAVE TO DO SOMETHING ABOUT IT! ♪

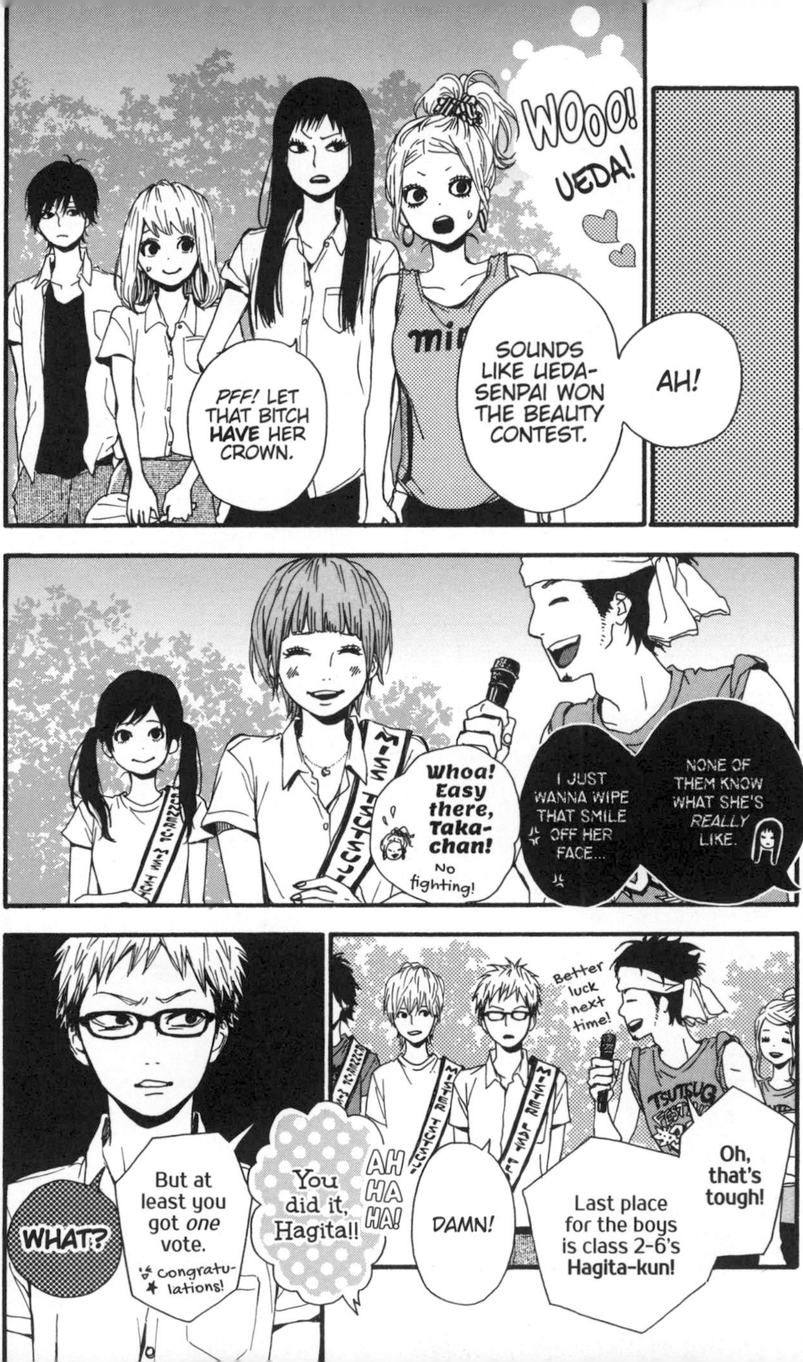
WOOO! UEDA!
AH!
SOUNDS LIKE UEDA-SENPAI WON THE BEAUTY CONTEST.
PFF! LET THAT BITCH HAVE HER CROWN.
NONE OF THEM KNOW WHAT SHE'S REALLY LIKE.
I JUST WANNA WIPE THAT SMILE OFF HER FACE...
Whoa! Easy there, Taka-chan! No fighting!
Oh, that's tough!
Last place for the boys is class 2-6's Hagita-kun!
Better luck next time!
DAMN!
AH HA HA!
You did it, Hagita!!
But at least you got one vote. Congratulations!
WHAT?

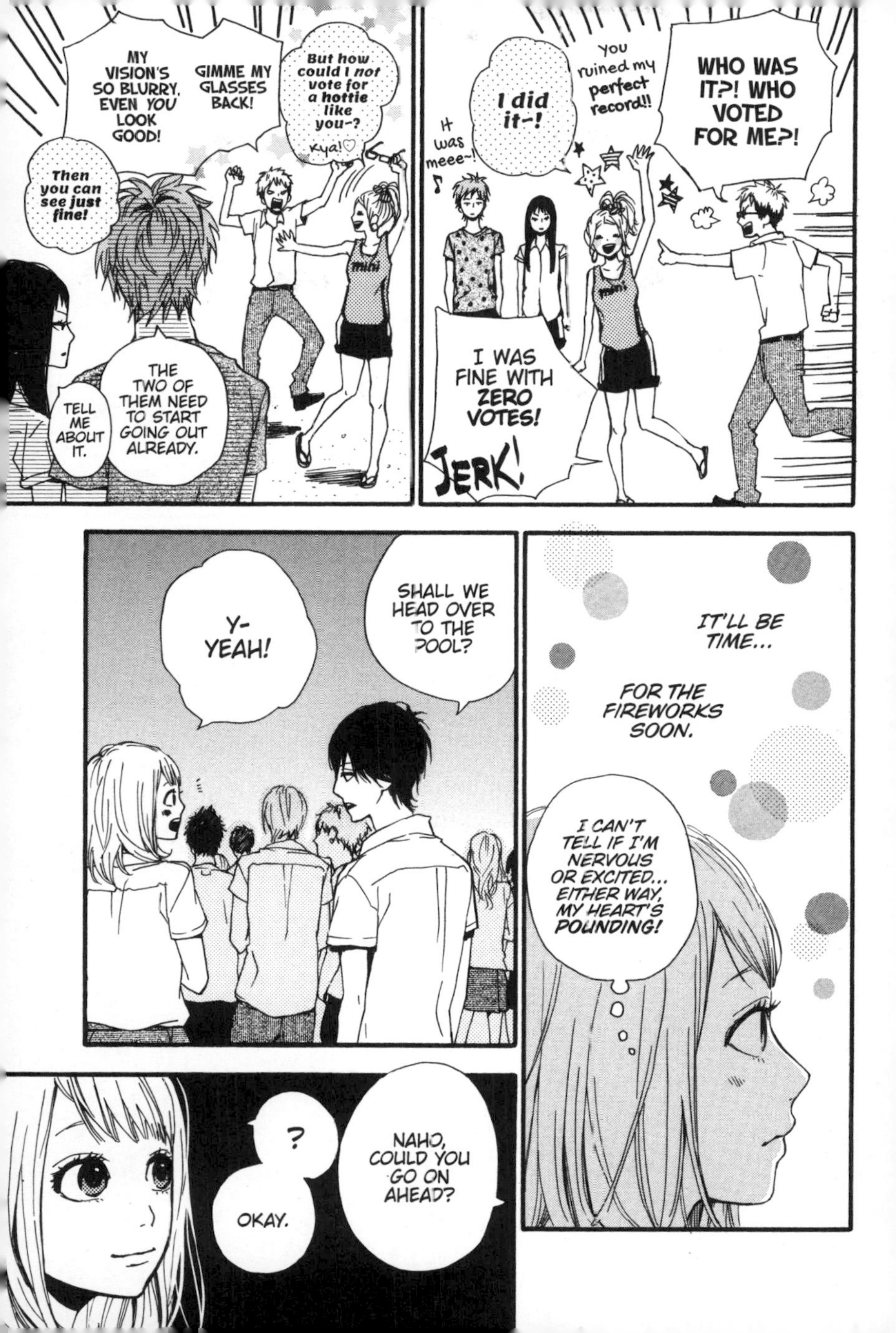
WHO WAS IT?! WHO VOTED FOR ME?!
You ruined my perfect record!!
I did it~!
It was meee~!
I WAS FINE WITH ZERO VOTES!
JERK!
But how could I *not* vote for a hottie like you~?
Kya!♡
GIMME MY GLASSES BACK!
MY VISION'S SO BLURRY, EVEN *YOU* LOOK GOOD!
Then you can see just fine!
THE TWO OF THEM NEED TO START GOING OUT ALREADY.
TELL ME ABOUT IT.
IT'LL BE TIME...
FOR THE FIREWORKS SOON.
I CAN'T TELL IF I'M NERVOUS OR EXCITED... EITHER WAY, MY HEART'S POUNDING!
SHALL WE HEAD OVER TO THE POOL?
Y-YEAH!
NAHO, COULD YOU GO ON AHEAD?
?
OKAY.

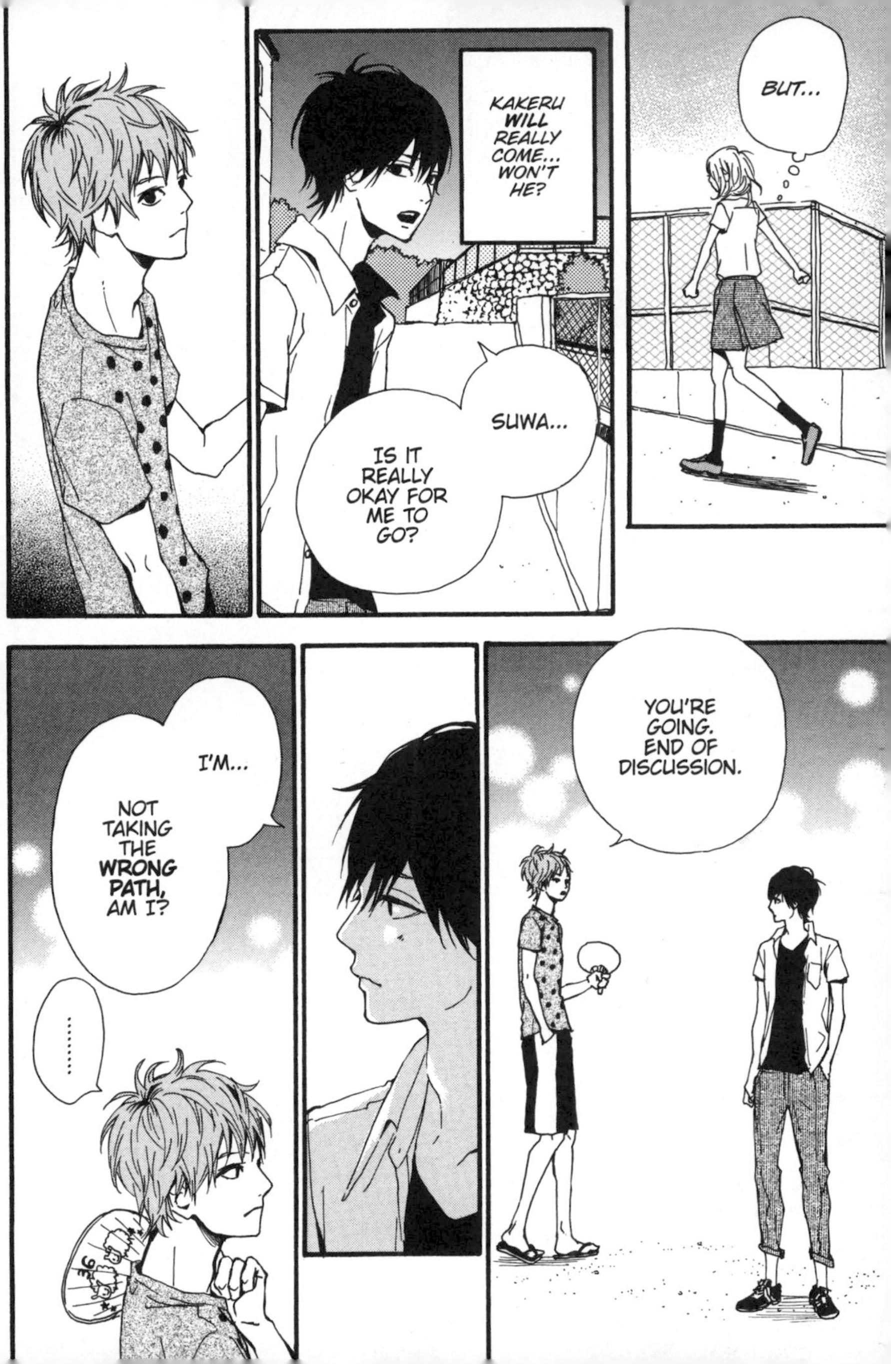
BUT...
KAKERU WILL REALLY COME... WON'T HE?
SUWA...
IS IT REALLY OKAY FOR ME TO GO?
YOU'RE GOING. END OF DISCUSSION.
I'M...
NOT TAKING THE WRONG PATH, AM I?
....

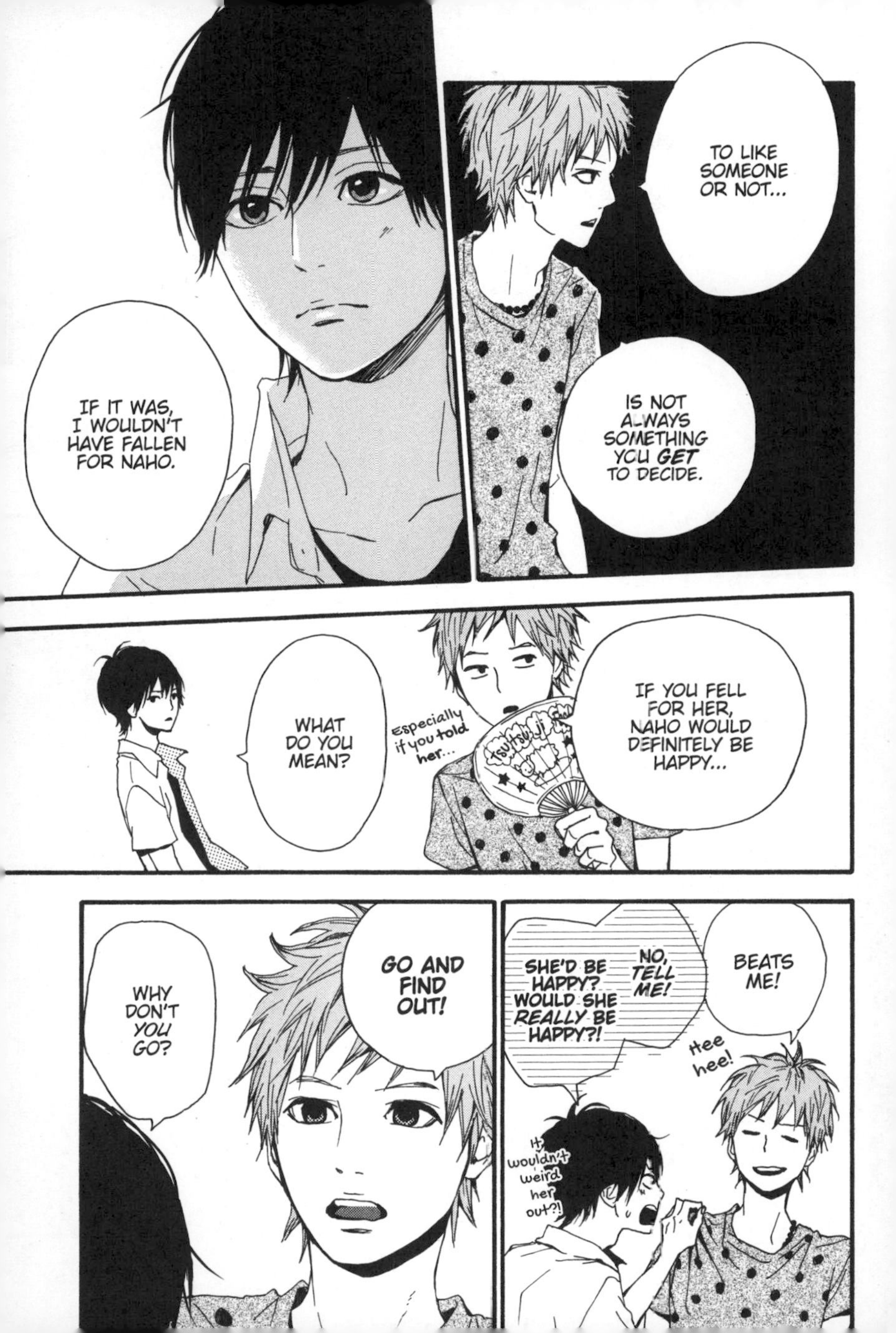
TO LIKE SOMEONE OR NOT...
IS NOT ALWAYS SOMETHING YOU GET TO DECIDE.
IF IT WAS, I WOULDN'T HAVE FALLEN FOR NAHO.
IF YOU FELL FOR HER, NAHO WOULD DEFINITELY BE HAPPY...
Especially if you told her...
WHAT DO YOU MEAN?
BEATS ME!
Hee hee!
NO, TELL ME!
SHE'D BE HAPPY? WOULD SHE REALLY BE HAPPY?!
It wouldn't weird her out?!
GO AND FIND OUT!
WHY DON'T YOU GO?

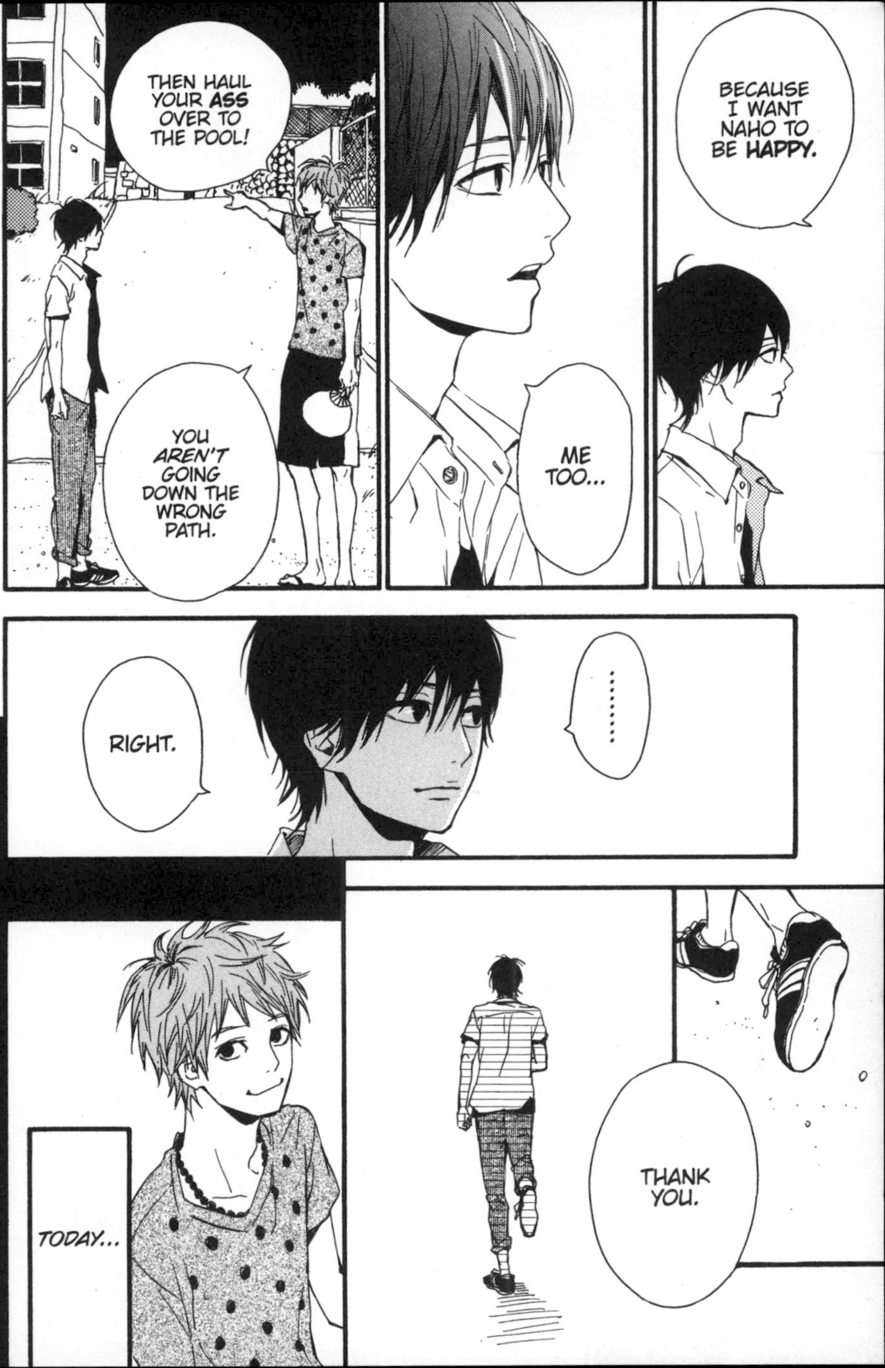
BECAUSE I WANT NAHO TO BE HAPPY.
ME TOO...
THEN HAUL YOUR ASS OVER TO THE POOL!
YOU AREN'T GOING DOWN THE WRONG PATH.
......
RIGHT.
THANK YOU.
TODAY...

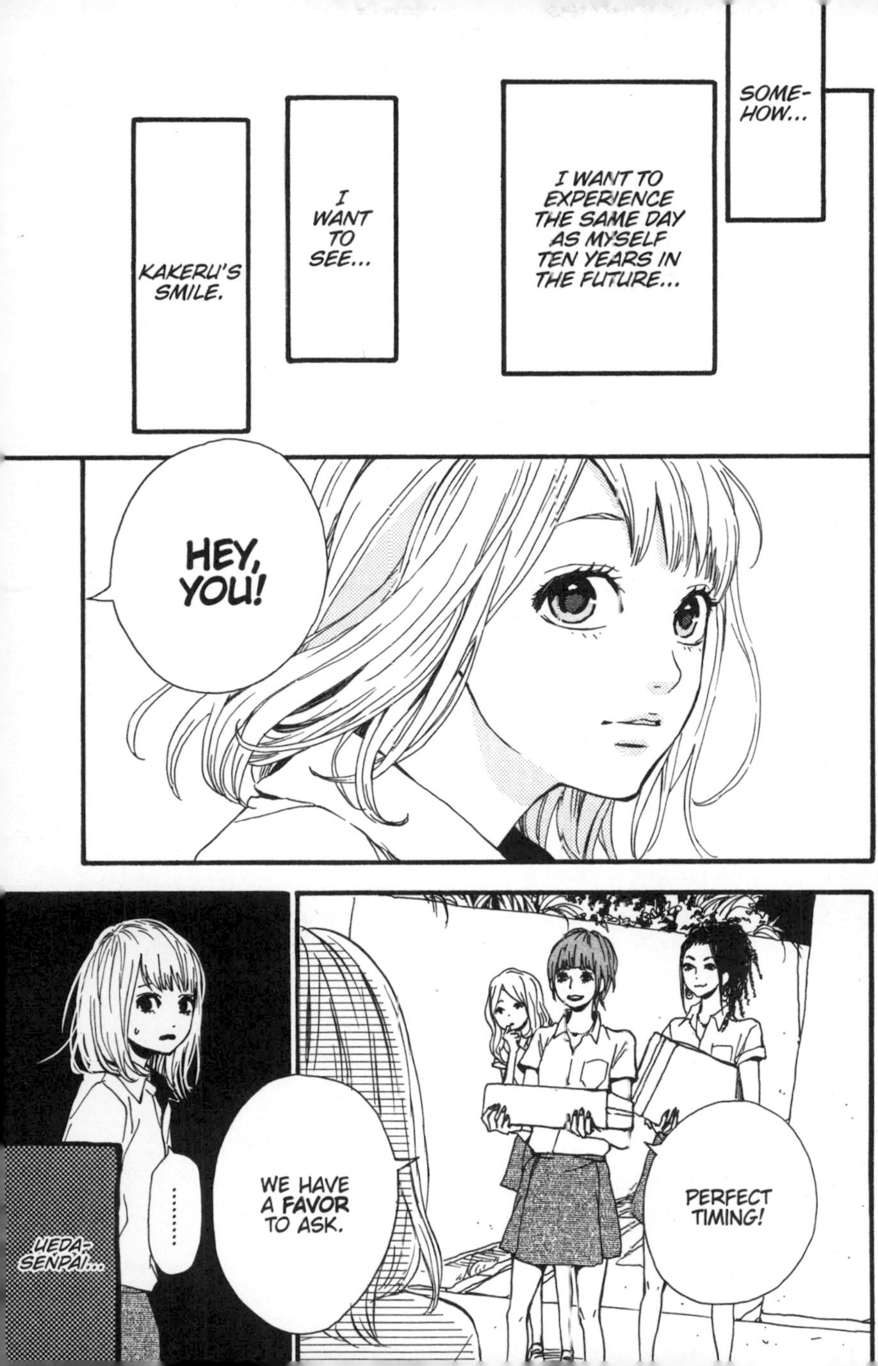
SOME-HOW...
I WANT TO EXPERIENCE THE SAME DAY AS MYSELF TEN YEARS IN THE FUTURE...
I WANT TO SEE...
KAKERU'S SMILE.
HEY, YOU!
PERFECT TIMING!
WE HAVE A FAVOR TO ASK.
......
UEDA-SENPAI...

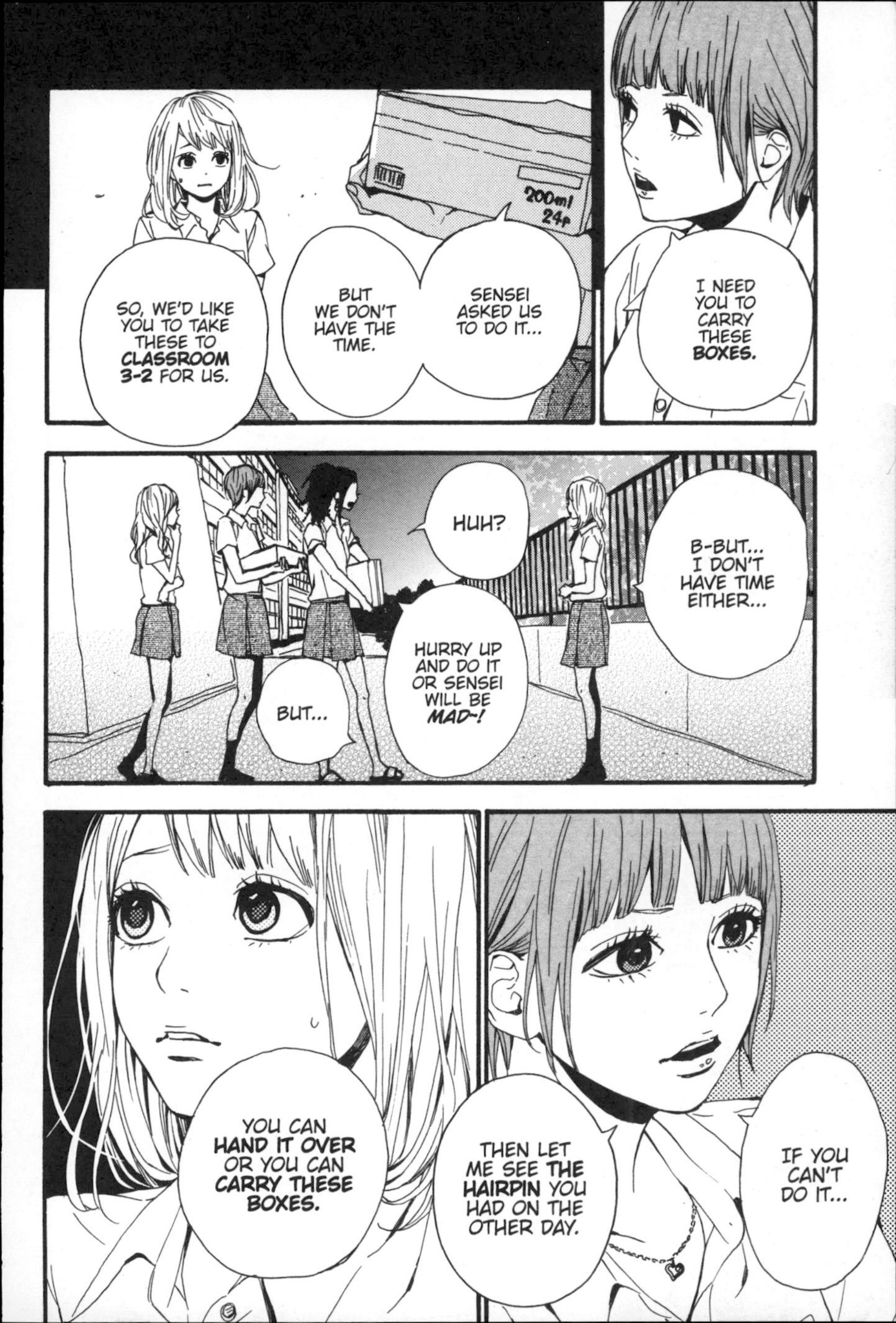
I NEED YOU TO CARRY THESE BOXES.
200ml 24p
SENSEI ASKED US TO DO IT...
BUT WE DON'T HAVE THE TIME.
SO, WE'D LIKE YOU TO TAKE THESE TO CLASSROOM 3-2 FOR US.
B-BUT... I DON'T HAVE TIME EITHER...
HUH?
HURRY UP AND DO IT OR SENSEI WILL BE MAD~!
BUT...
IF YOU CAN'T DO IT...
THEN LET ME SEE THE HAIRPIN YOU HAD ON THE OTHER DAY.
YOU CAN HAND IT OVER OR YOU CAN CARRY THESE BOXES.

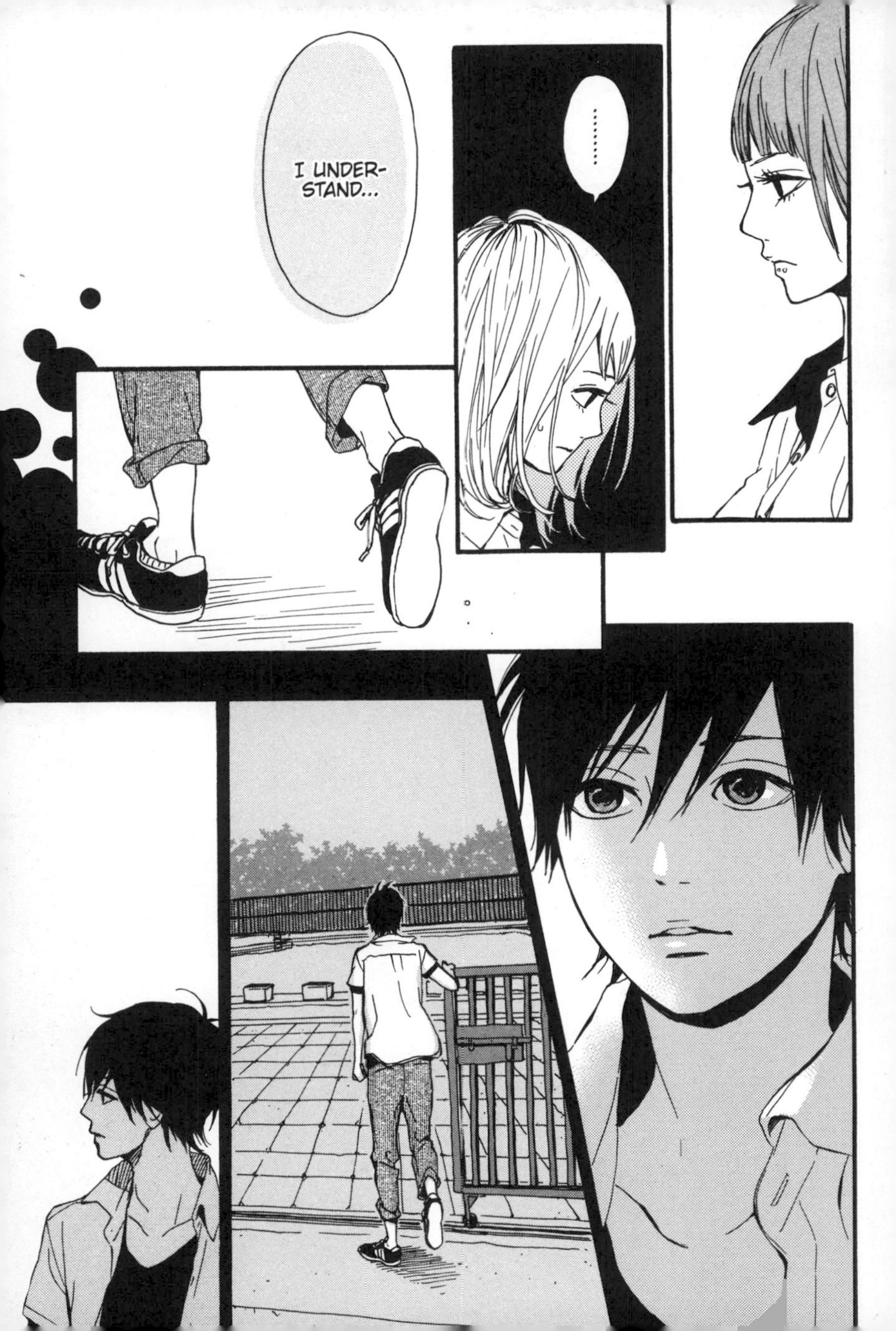
......
I UNDER-STAND...

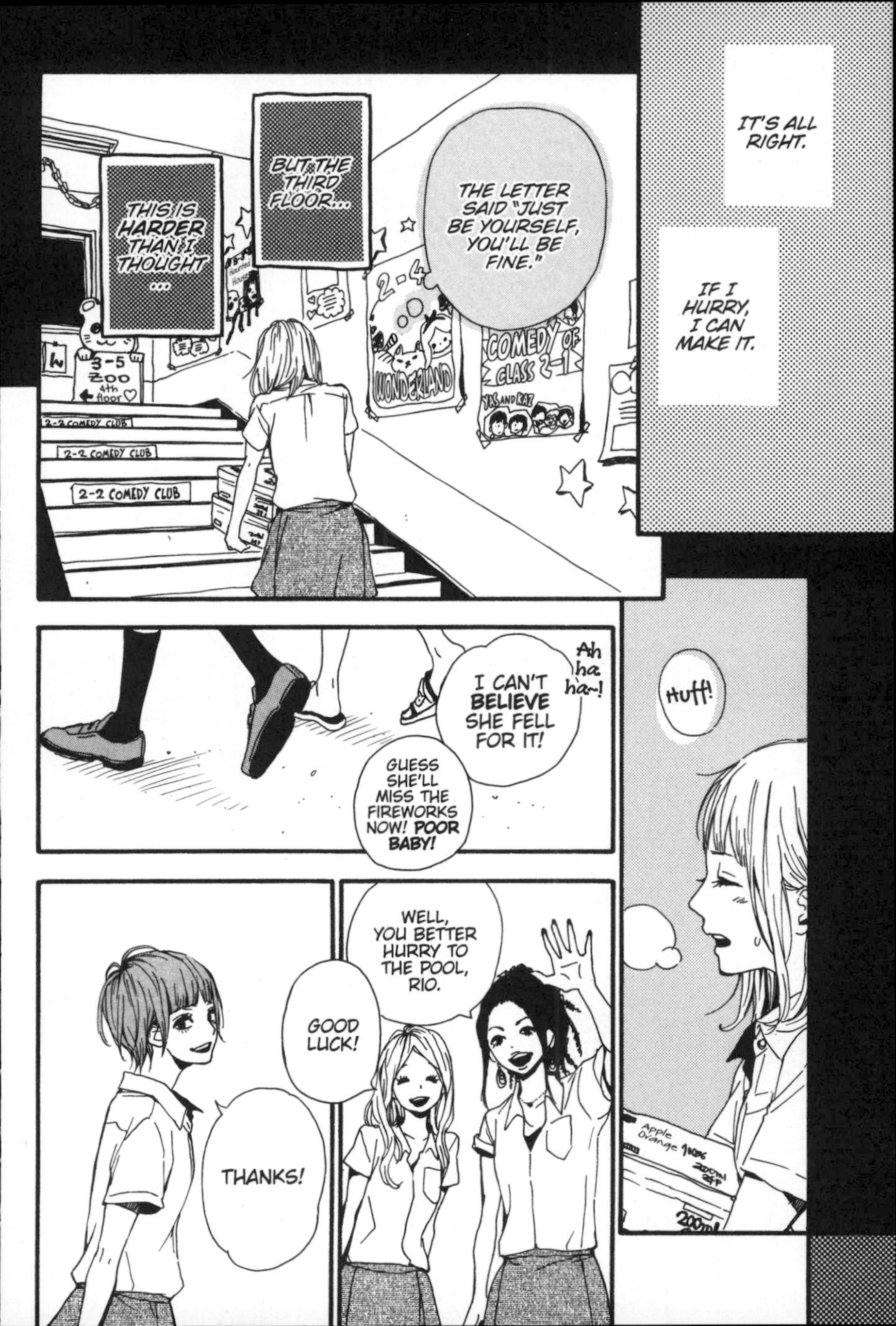

IT'S ALL RIGHT.
IF I HURRY, I CAN MAKE IT.
THE LETTER SAID "JUST BE YOURSELF, YOU'LL BE FINE."
BUT THE THIRD FLOOR...
THIS IS HARDER THAN I THOUGHT...
COMEDY OF CLASS 2-1
YAS AND KAZ
WONDERLAND
Haunted House
3-5 ZOO 4th floor
2-2 COMEDY CLUB
2-2 COMEDY CLUB
2-2 COMEDY CLUB
Huff!
Apple Orange
Ah ha ha~!
I CAN'T BELIEVE SHE FELL FOR IT!
GUESS SHE'LL MISS THE FIREWORKS NOW! POOR BABY!
WELL, YOU BETTER HURRY TO THE POOL, RIO.
GOOD LUCK!
THANKS!

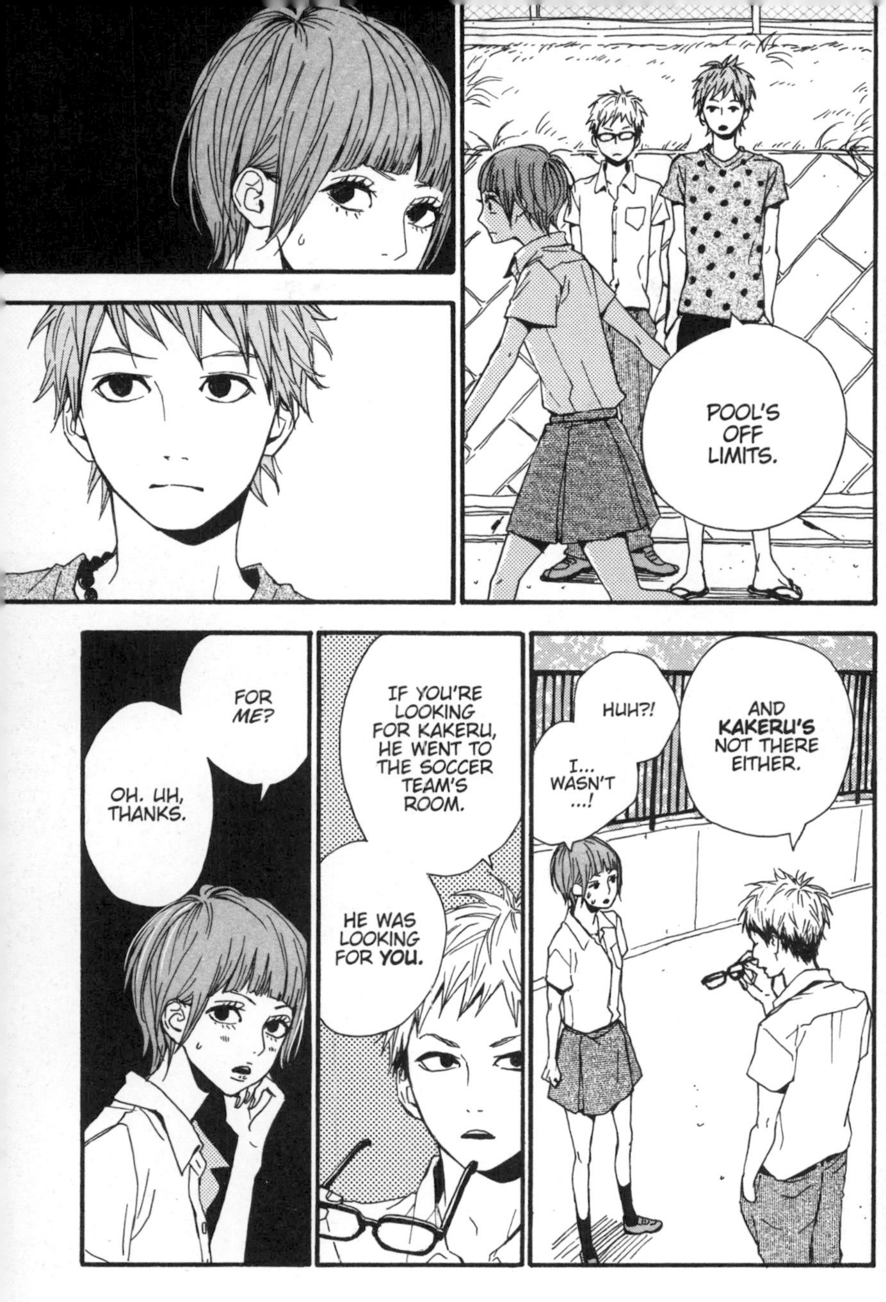
POOL'S OFF LIMITS.
AND **KAKERU'S** NOT THERE EITHER.
HUH?!
I... WASN'T ...!
IF YOU'RE LOOKING FOR KAKERU, HE WENT TO THE SOCCER TEAM'S ROOM.
HE WAS LOOKING FOR **YOU.**
FOR *ME?*
OH. UH, THANKS.

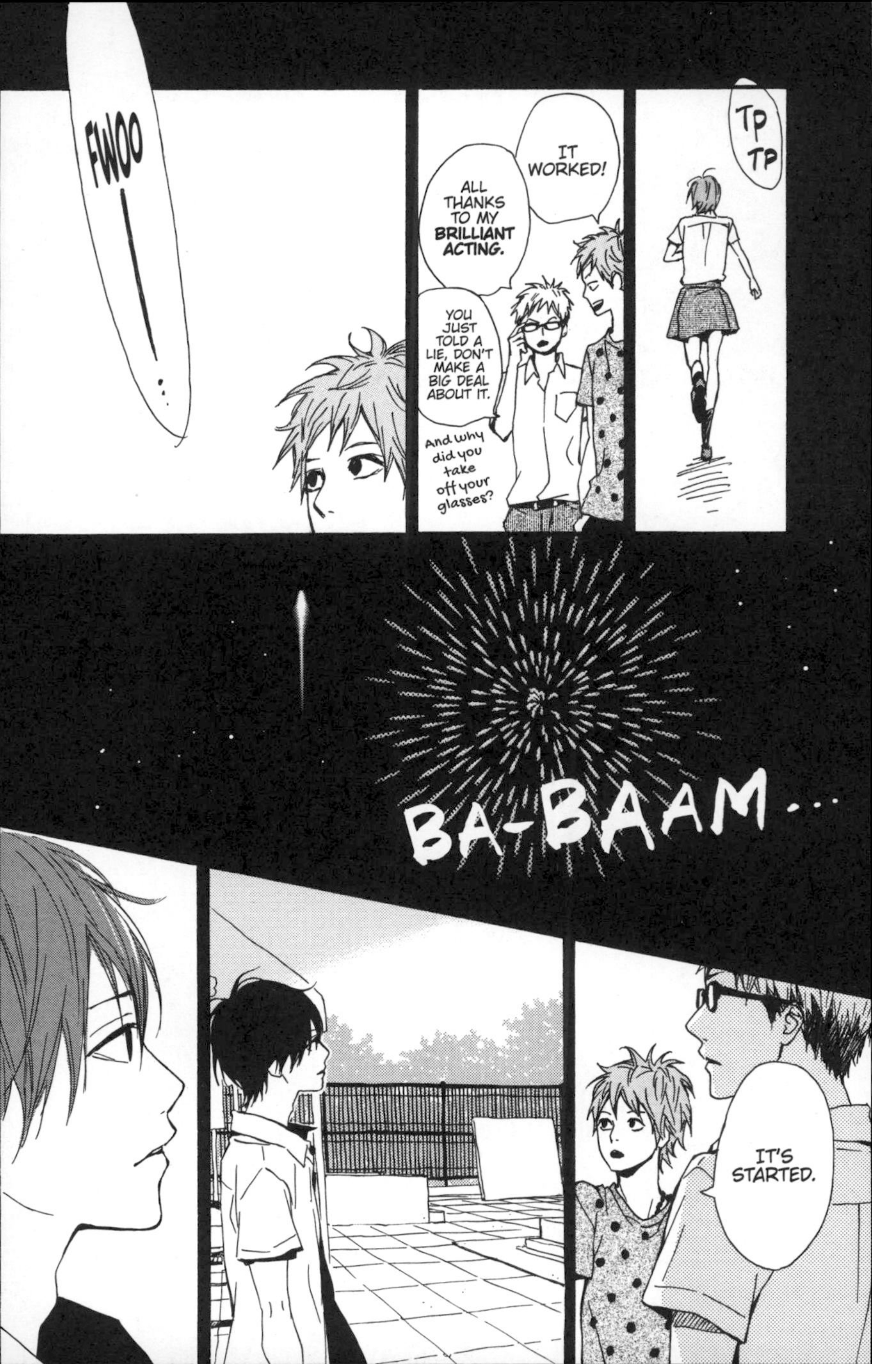
Tp Tp
IT WORKED!
ALL THANKS TO MY **BRILLIANT ACTING.**
YOU JUST TOLD A LIE, DON'T MAKE A BIG DEAL ABOUT IT.
And why did you take off your glasses?
FWOO
BA-BAAM...
IT'S STARTED.

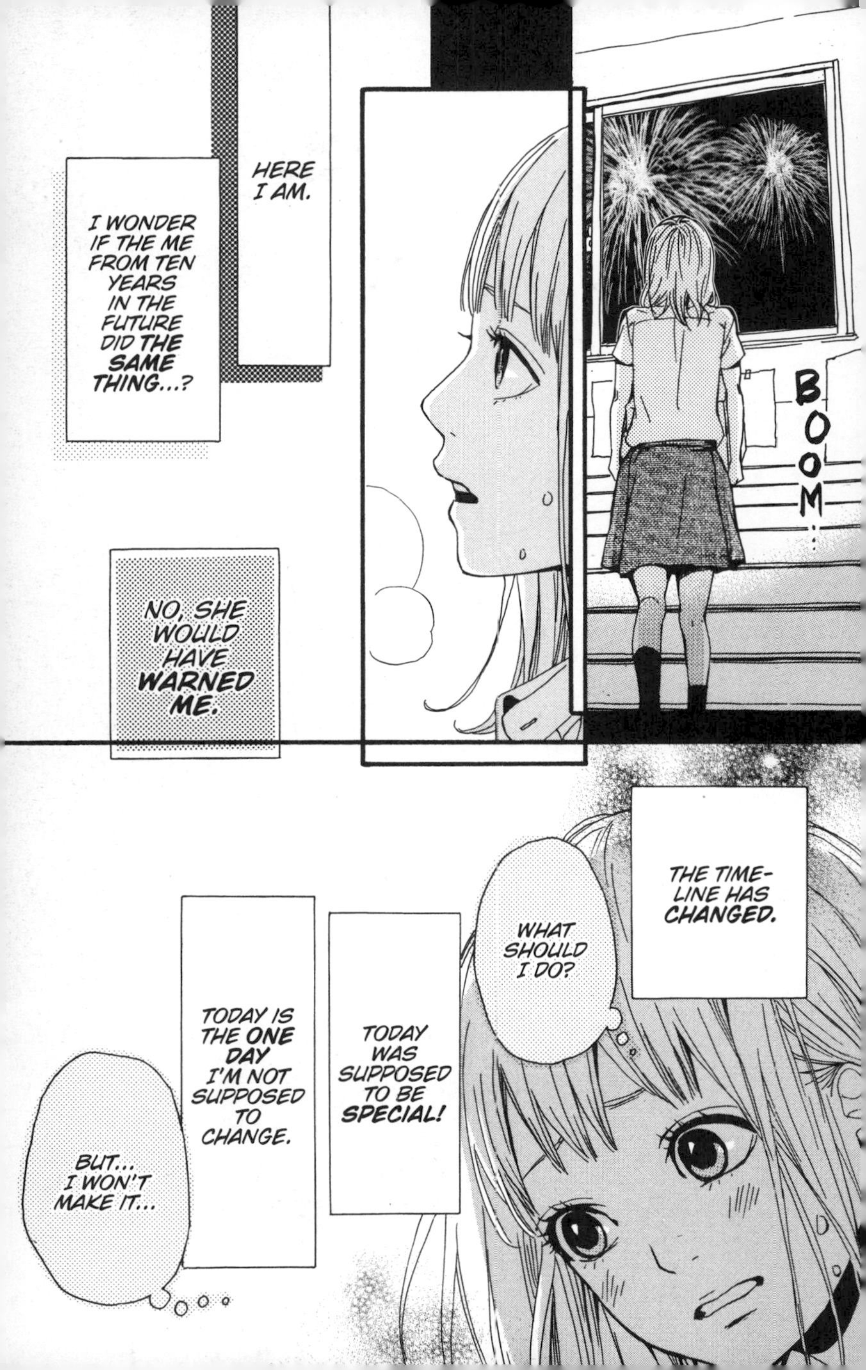
BOOM
HERE I AM.
I WONDER IF THE ME FROM TEN YEARS IN THE FUTURE DID THE SAME THING...?
NO, SHE WOULD HAVE WARNED ME.
THE TIME-LINE HAS CHANGED.
WHAT SHOULD I DO?
TODAY WAS SUPPOSED TO BE SPECIAL!
TODAY IS THE ONE DAY I'M NOT SUPPOSED TO CHANGE.
BUT... I WON'T MAKE IT...

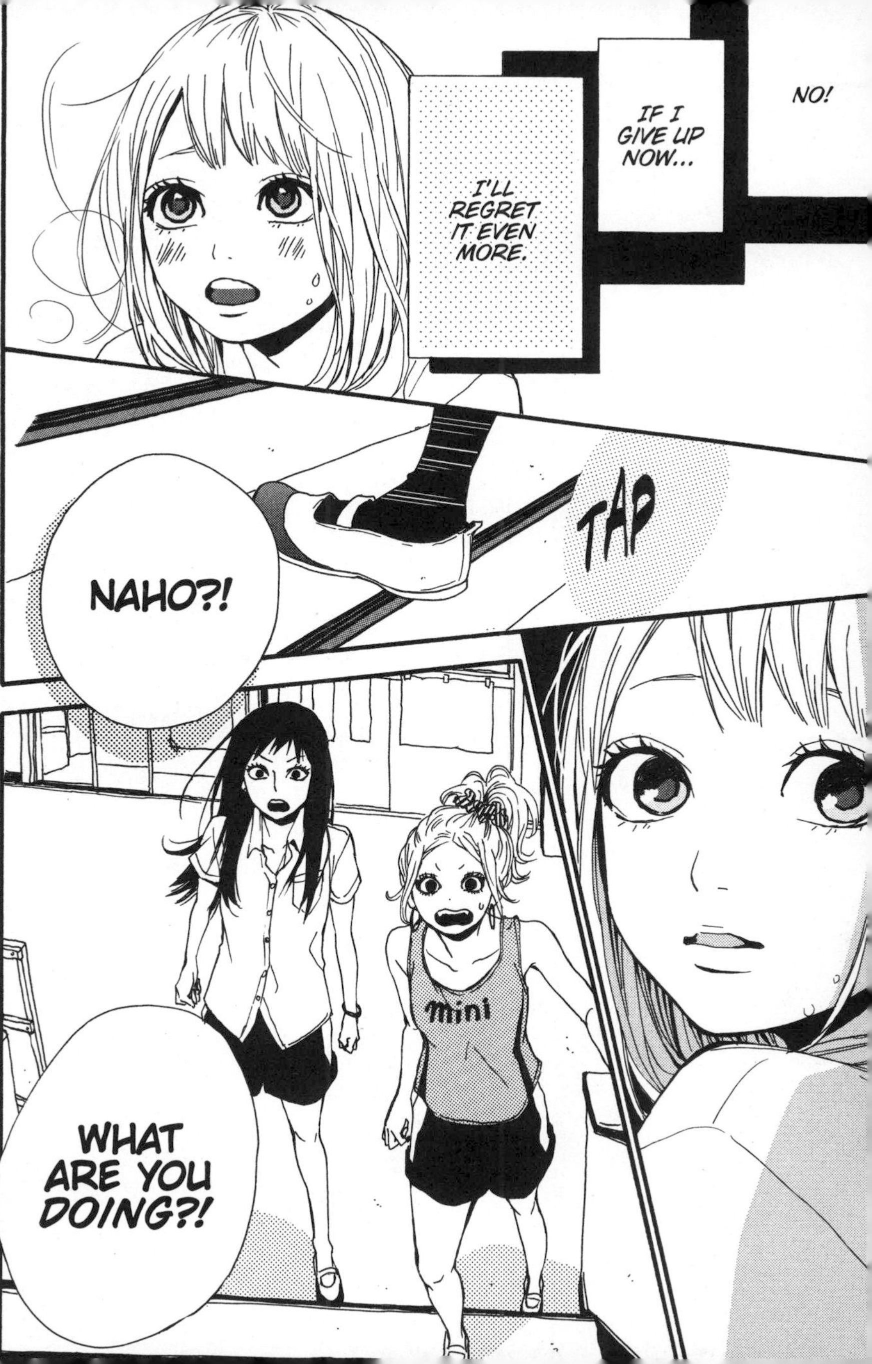
NO!
IF I GIVE UP NOW...
I'LL REGRET IT EVEN MORE.
TAP
NAHO?!
WHAT ARE YOU DOING?!

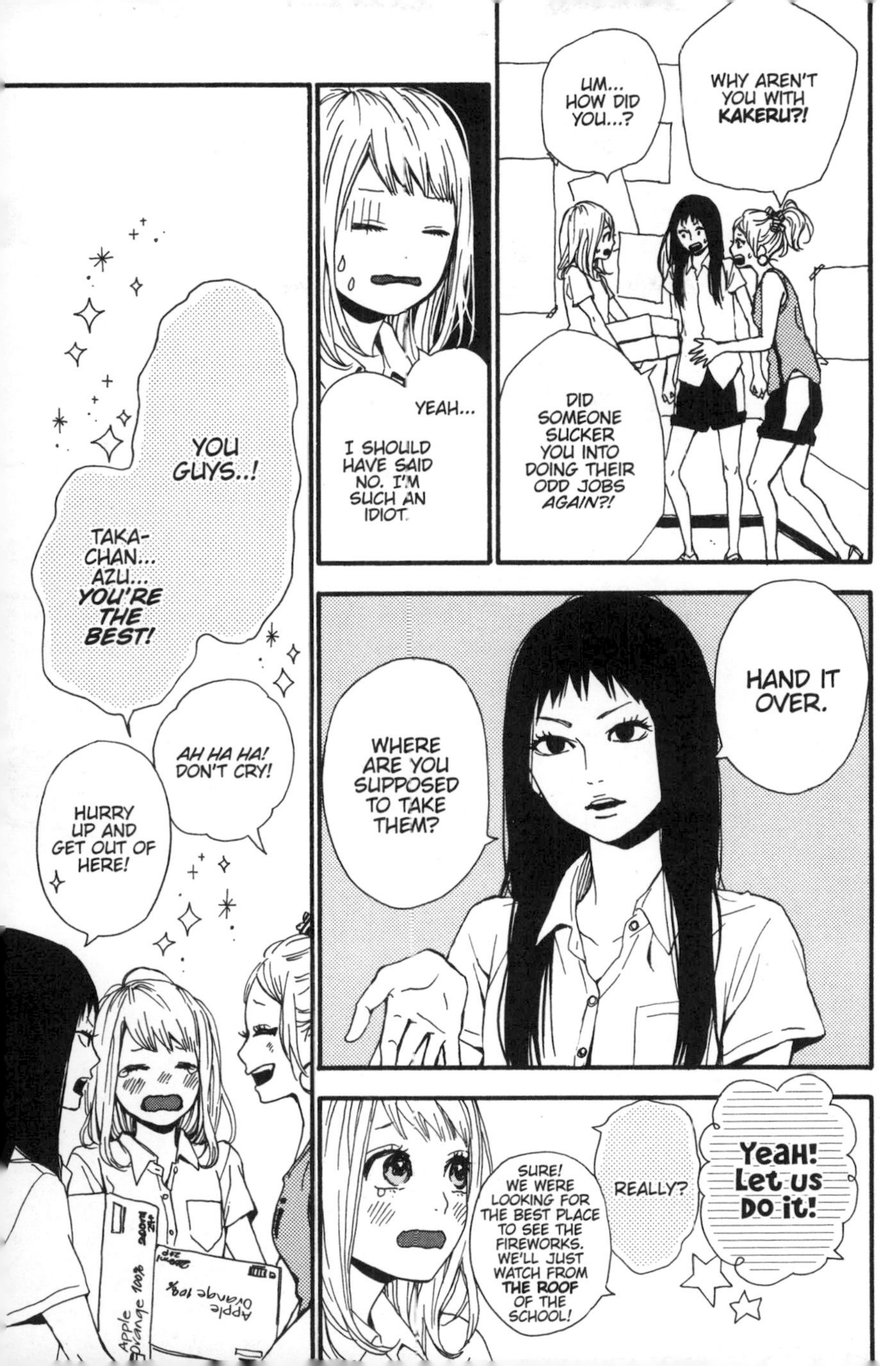
WHY AREN'T YOU WITH **KAKERU?!**
UM... HOW DID YOU...?
DID SOMEONE SUCKER YOU INTO DOING THEIR ODD JOBS *AGAIN?!*
YEAH...
I SHOULD HAVE SAID NO. I'M SUCH AN IDIOT.
HAND IT OVER.
WHERE ARE YOU SUPPOSED TO TAKE THEM?
Yeah! Let us Do it!
REALLY?
SURE! WE WERE LOOKING FOR THE BEST PLACE TO SEE THE FIREWORKS. WE'LL JUST WATCH FROM **THE ROOF** OF THE SCHOOL!
YOU GUYS..!
TAKA-CHAN... AZU... ***YOU'RE THE BEST!***
AH HA HA! DON'T CRY!
HURRY UP AND GET OUT OF HERE!
Apple Orange 100%
Apple Orange 100%

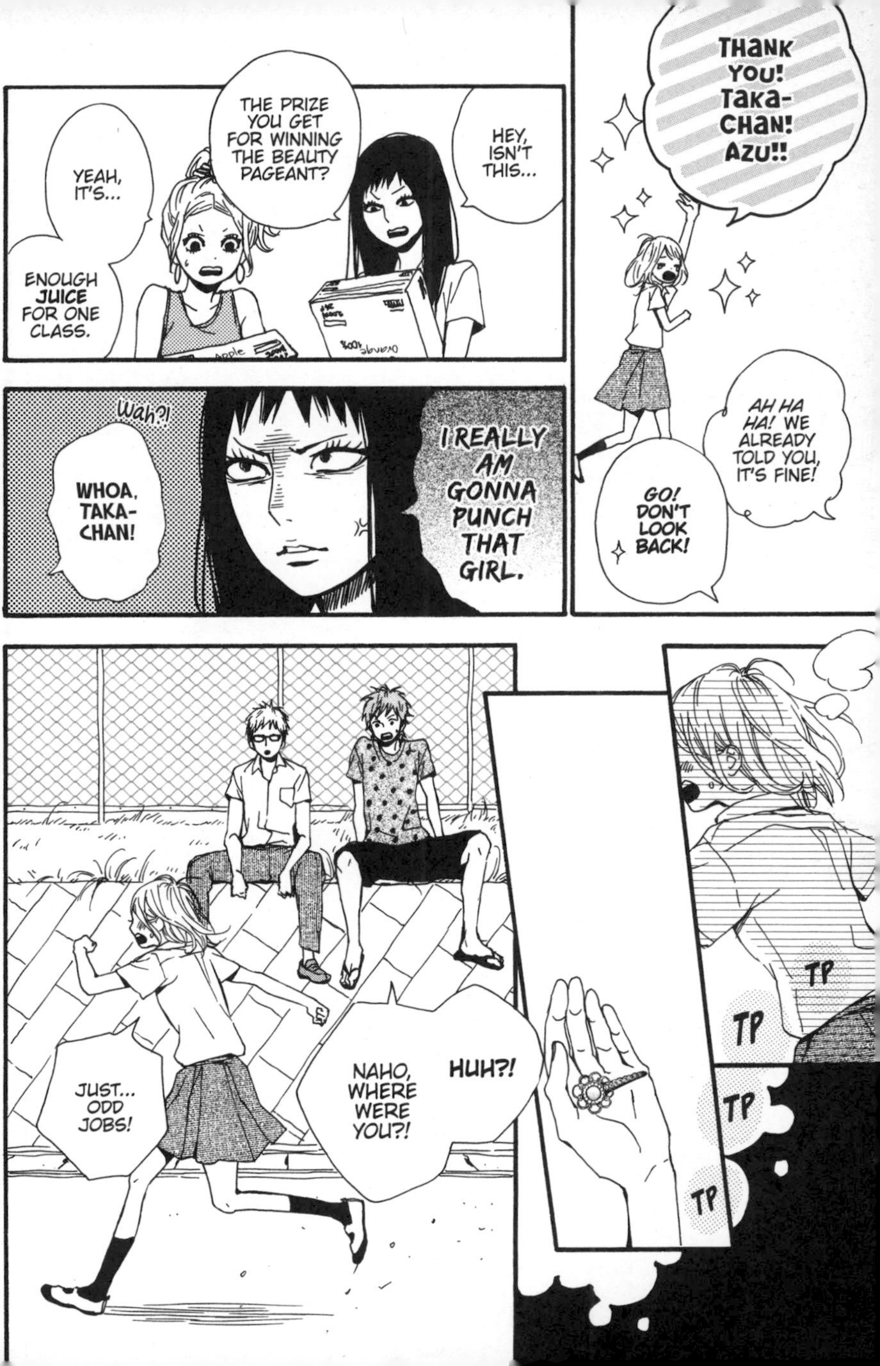

THANK YOU! TAKA-CHAN! AZU!!
AH HA HA! WE ALREADY TOLD YOU, IT'S FINE!
GO! DON'T LOOK BACK!
HEY, ISN'T THIS...
THE PRIZE YOU GET FOR WINNING THE BEAUTY PAGEANT?
YEAH, IT'S...
ENOUGH JUICE FOR ONE CLASS.
I REALLY AM GONNA PUNCH THAT GIRL.
Wah?!
WHOA, TAKA-CHAN!
TP
TP
TP
TP
HUH?!
NAHO, WHERE WERE YOU?!
JUST... ODD JOBS!

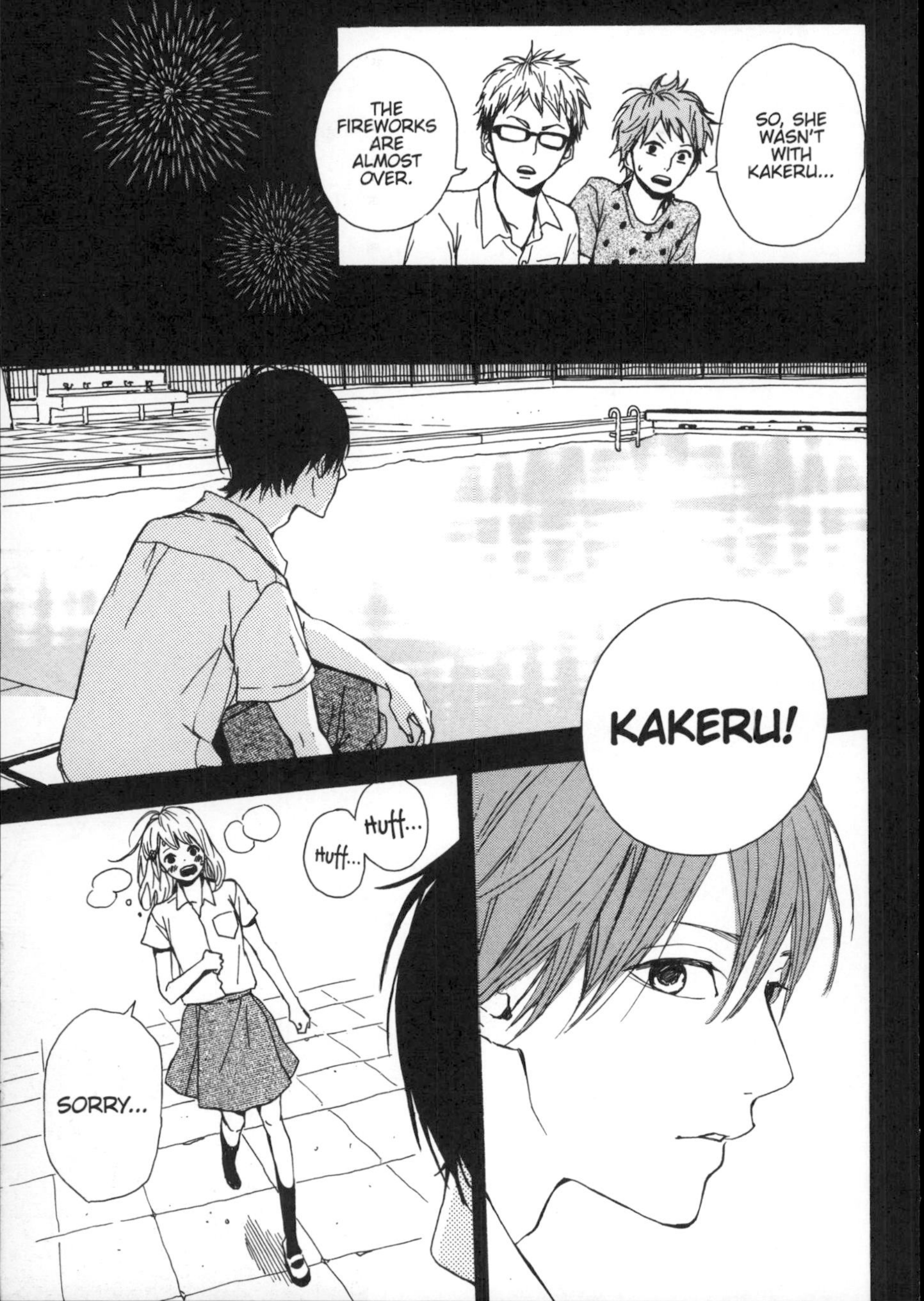
SO, SHE WASN'T WITH KAKERU...
THE FIREWORKS ARE ALMOST OVER.
KAKERU!
Huff...
Huff...
SORRY...

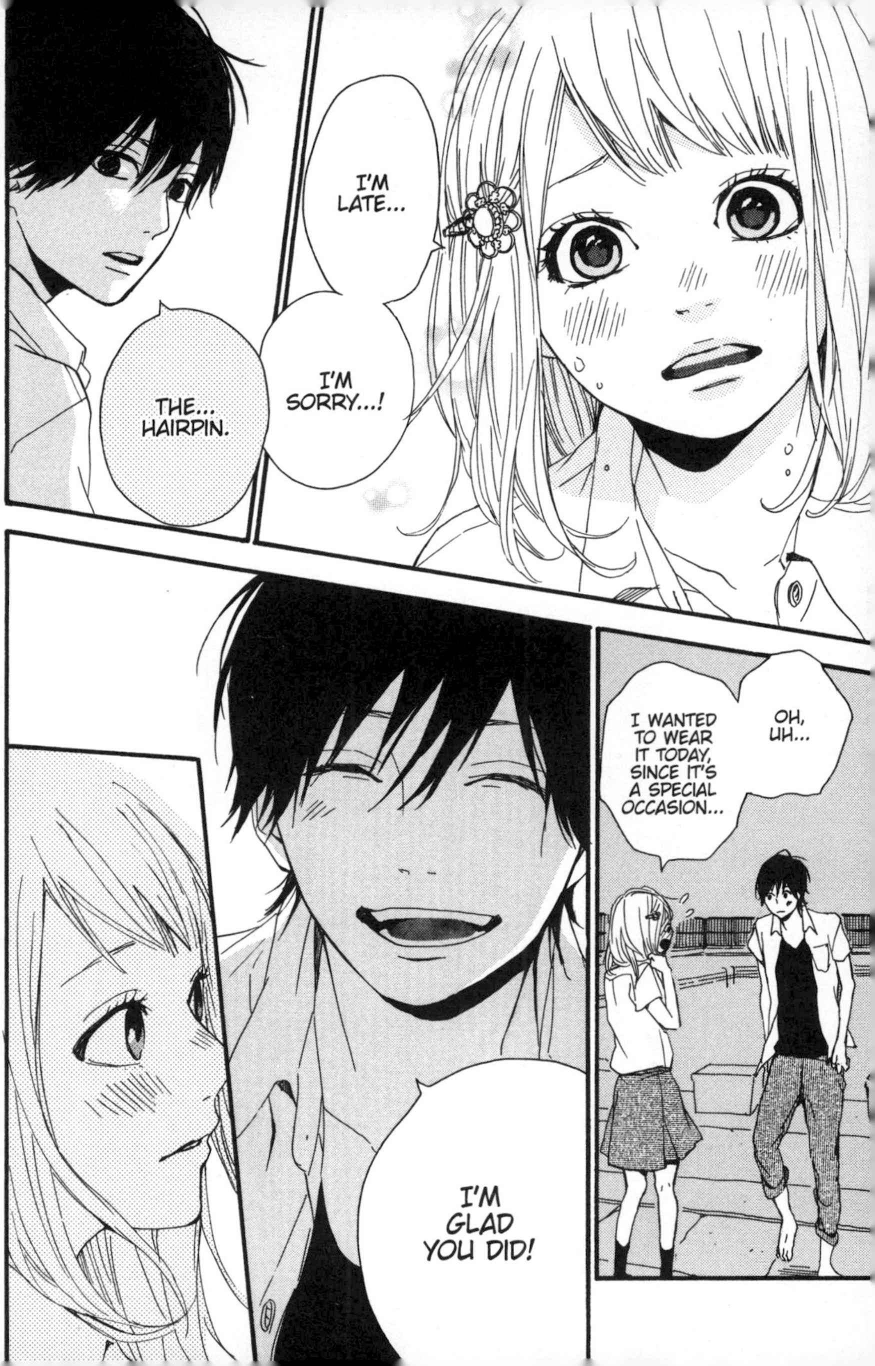
I'M LATE...
I'M SORRY...!
THE... HAIRPIN.
OH, UH...
I WANTED TO WEAR IT TODAY, SINCE IT'S A SPECIAL OCCASION...
I'M GLAD YOU DID!

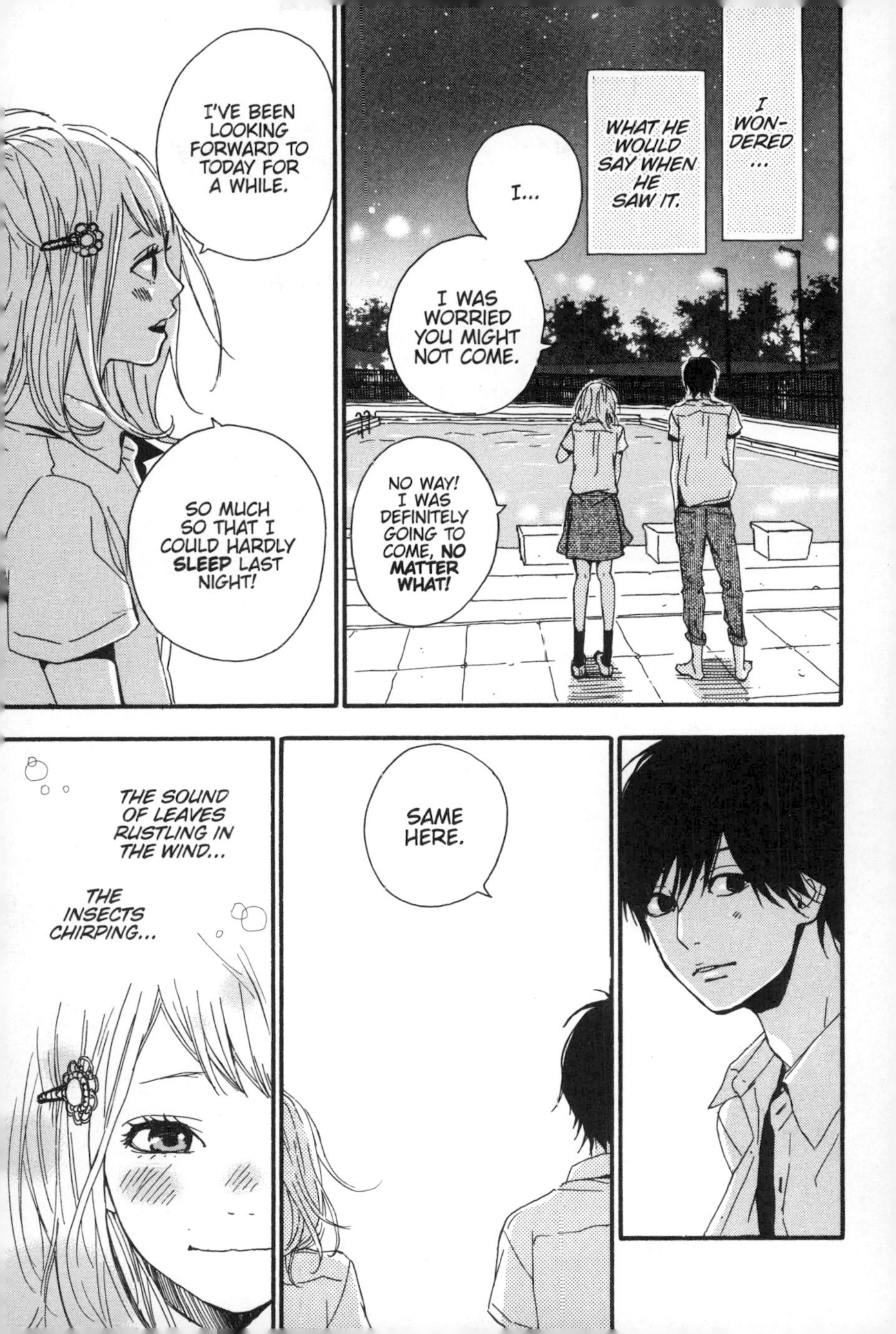
I WONDERED...
WHAT HE WOULD SAY WHEN HE SAW IT.
I...
I WAS WORRIED YOU MIGHT NOT COME.
NO WAY! I WAS DEFINITELY GOING TO COME, **NO MATTER WHAT!**
I'VE BEEN LOOKING FORWARD TO TODAY FOR A WHILE.
SO MUCH SO THAT I COULD HARDLY **SLEEP** LAST NIGHT!
SAME HERE.
THE SOUND OF LEAVES RUSTLING IN THE WIND...
THE INSECTS CHIRPING...

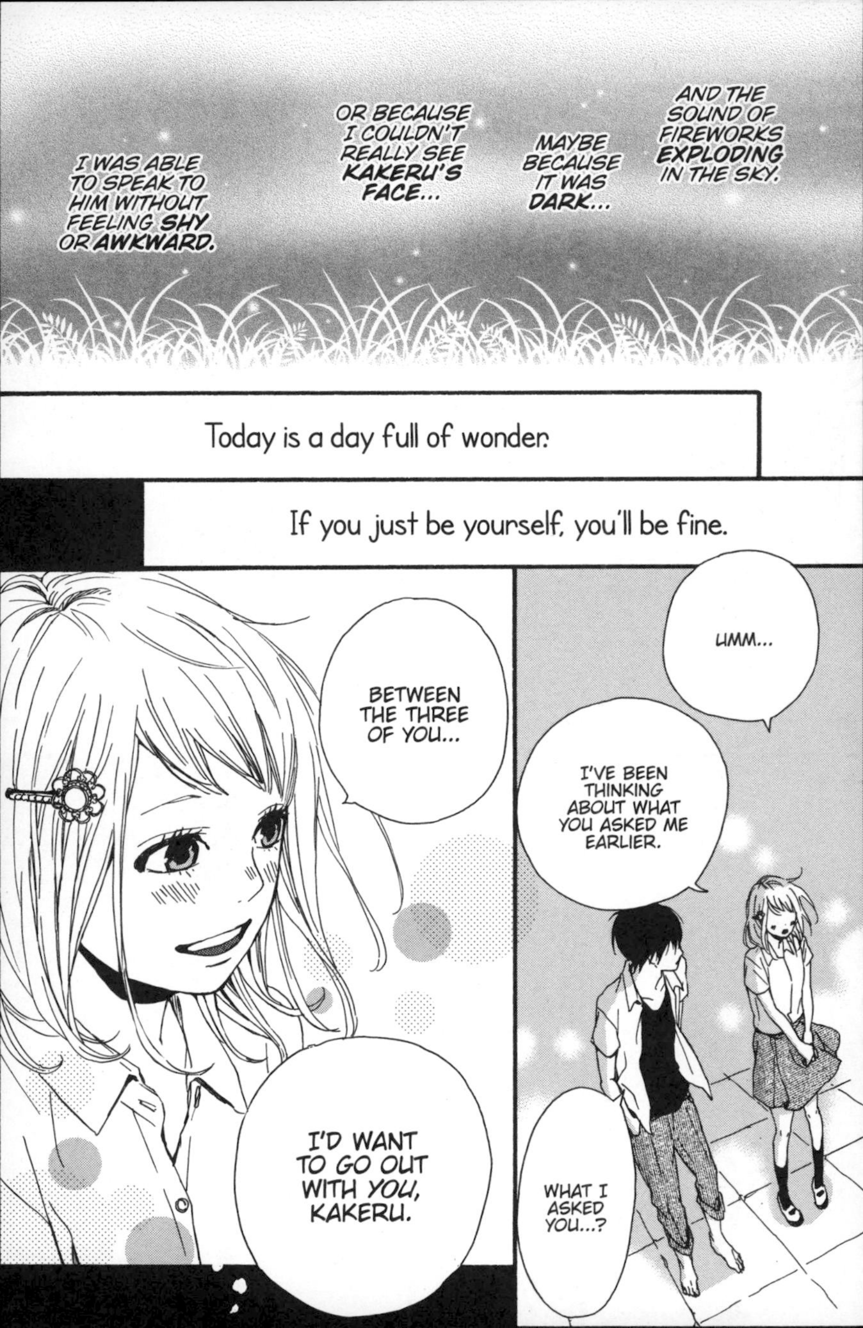
AND THE SOUND OF FIREWORKS EXPLODING IN THE SKY.
MAYBE BECAUSE IT WAS DARK...
OR BECAUSE I COULDN'T REALLY SEE KAKERU'S FACE...
I WAS ABLE TO SPEAK TO HIM WITHOUT FEELING SHY OR AWKWARD.
Today is a day full of wonder.
If you just be yourself, you'll be fine.
UMM...
I'VE BEEN THINKING ABOUT WHAT YOU ASKED ME EARLIER.
WHAT I ASKED YOU...?
BETWEEN THE THREE OF YOU...
I'D WANT TO GO OUT WITH YOU, KAKERU.

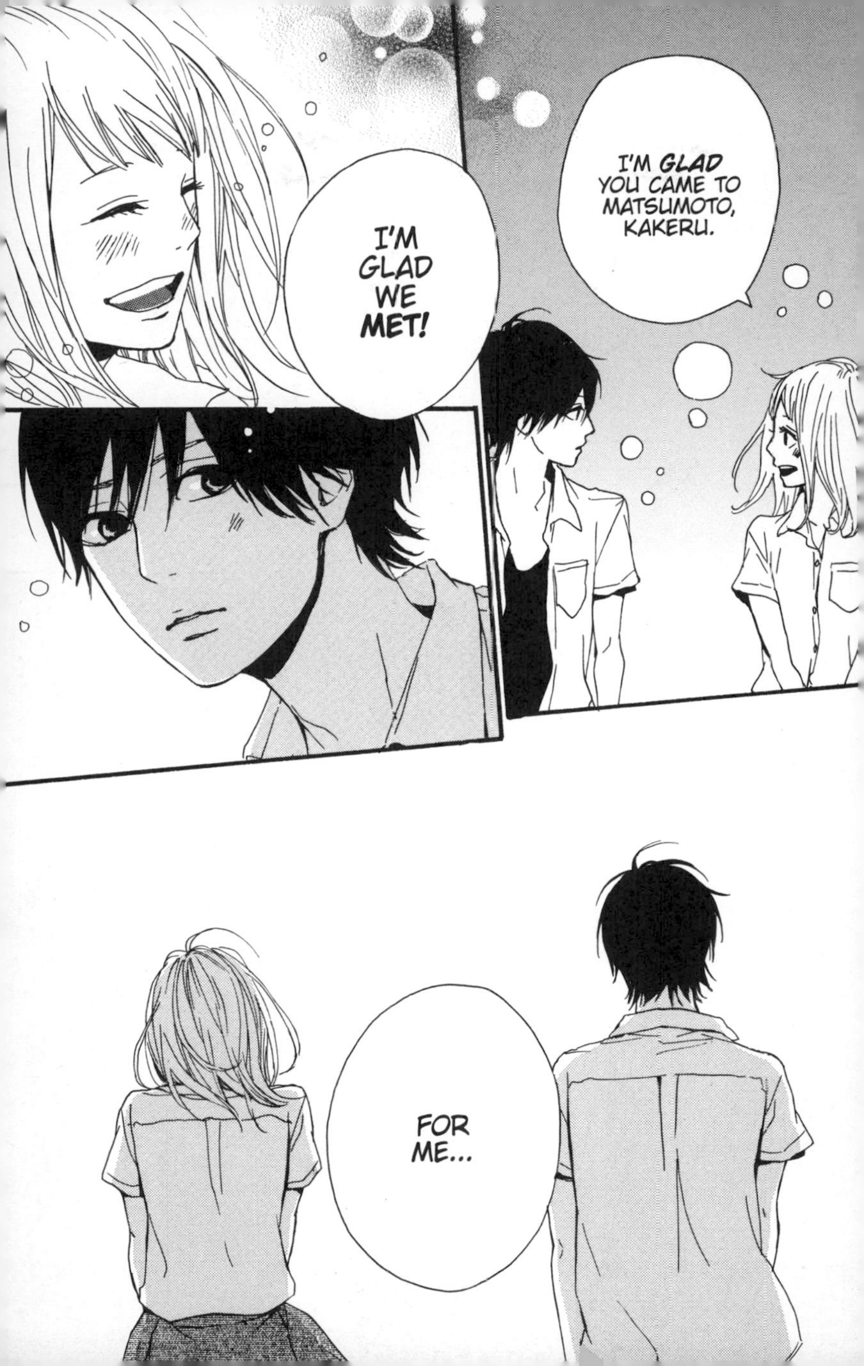
I'M GLAD YOU CAME TO MATSUMOTO, KAKERU.
I'M GLAD WE MET!
FOR ME...

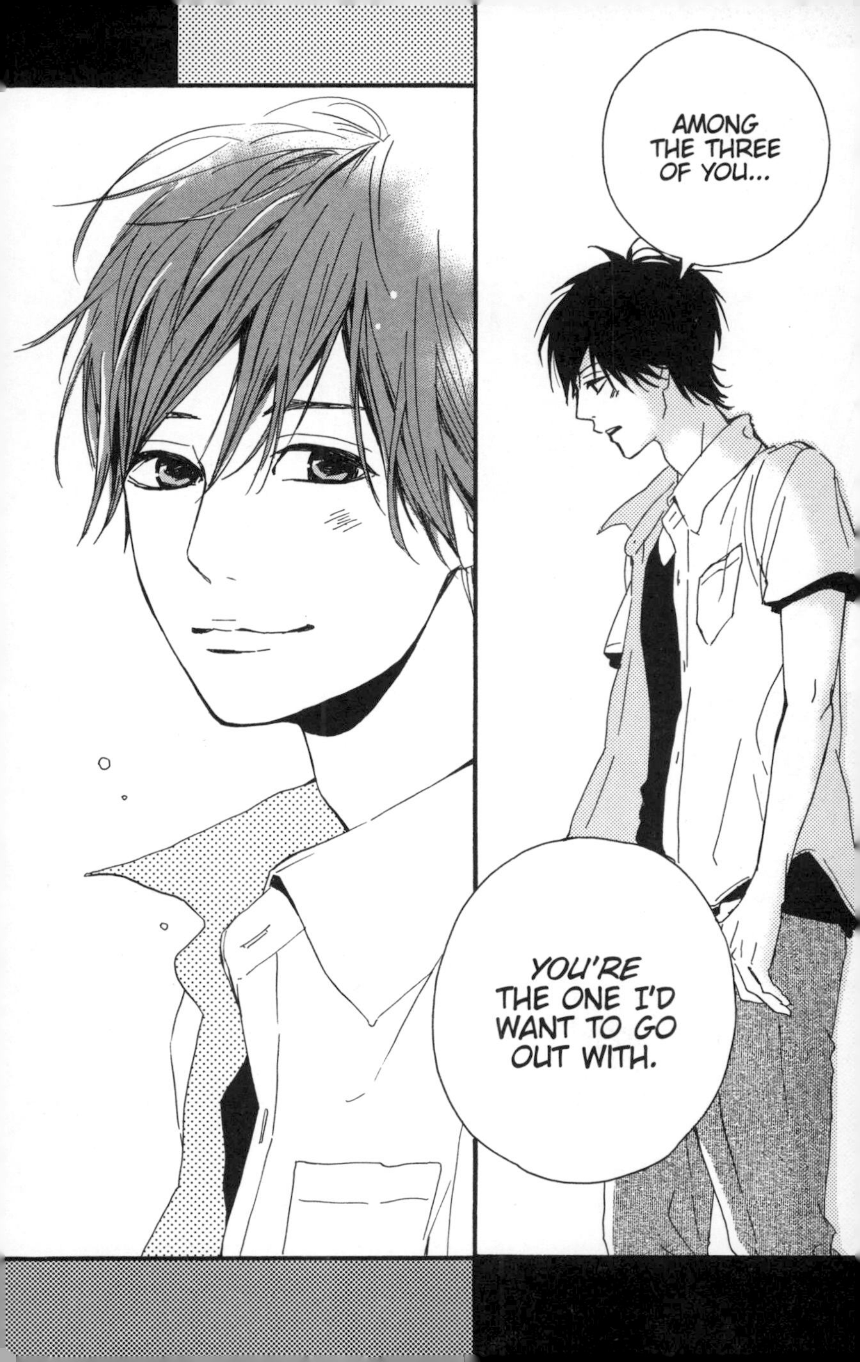
AMONG THE THREE OF YOU...
YOU'RE THE ONE I'D WANT TO GO OUT WITH.

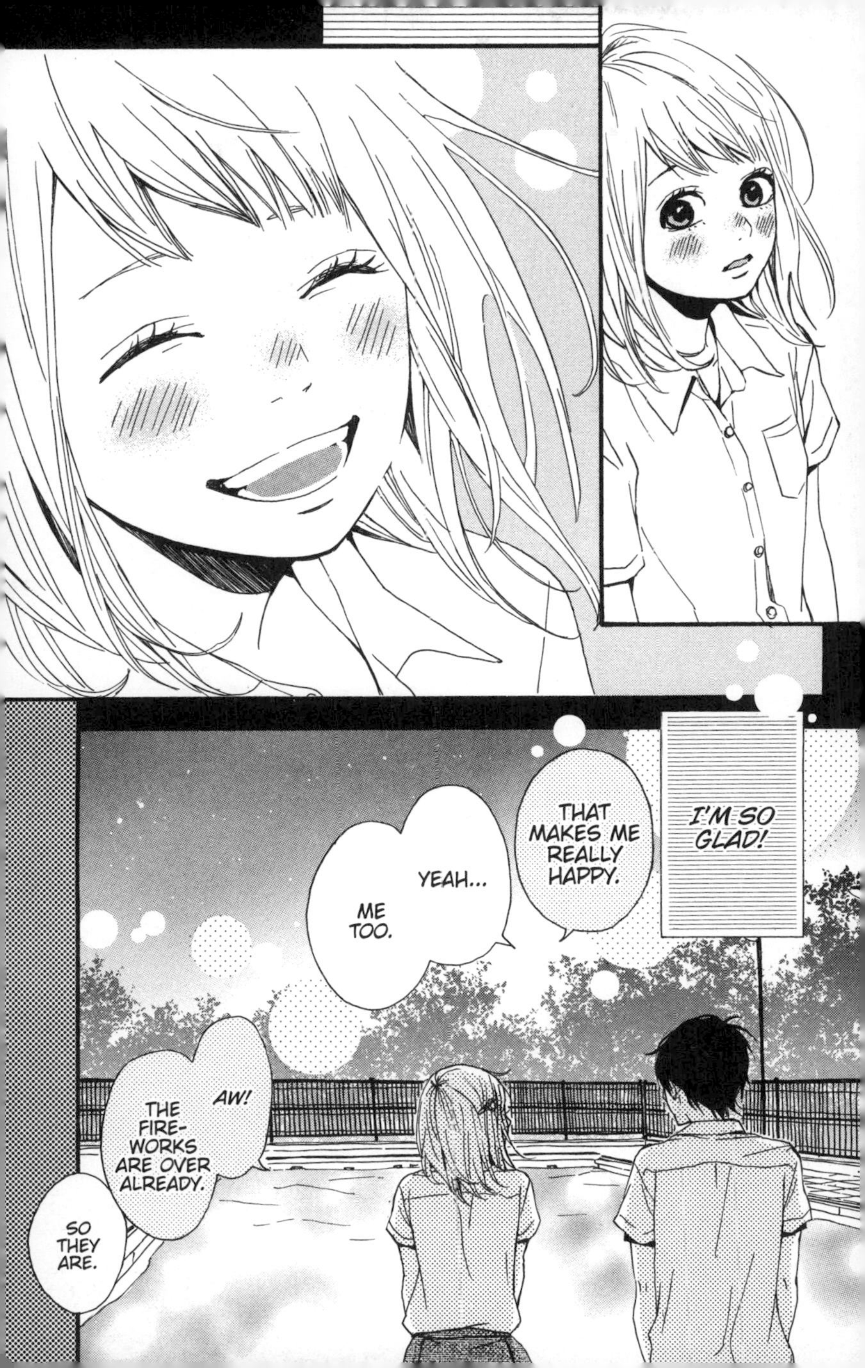
I'M SO GLAD!
THAT MAKES ME REALLY HAPPY.
YEAH... ME TOO.
AW! THE FIRE-WORKS ARE OVER ALREADY.
SO THEY ARE.

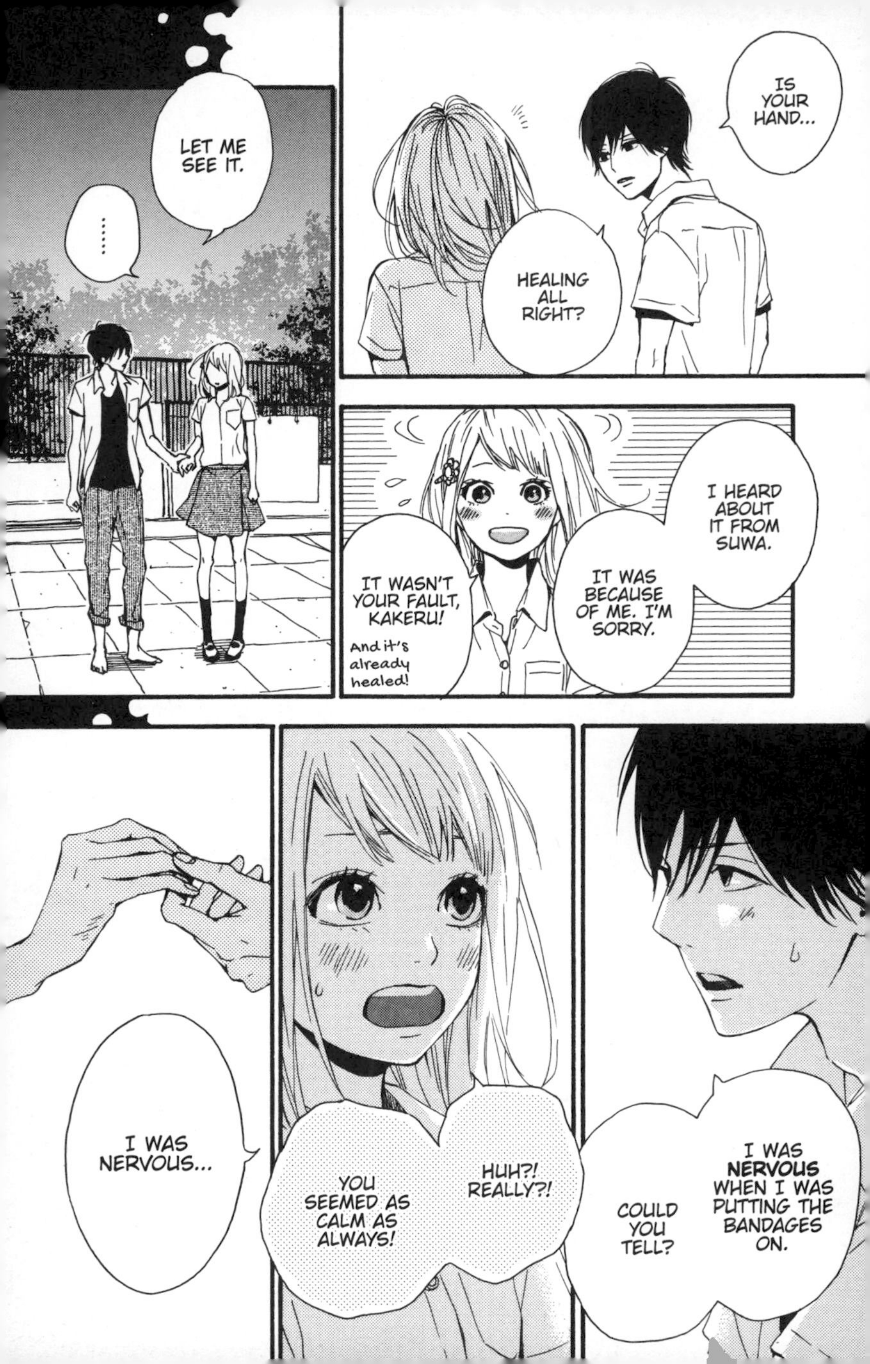
IS YOUR HAND...
HEALING ALL RIGHT?
I HEARD ABOUT IT FROM SUWA.
IT WAS BECAUSE OF ME. I'M SORRY.
IT WASN'T YOUR FAULT, KAKERU!
And it's already healed!
LET ME SEE IT.
......
I WAS **NERVOUS** WHEN I WAS PUTTING THE BANDAGES ON.
COULD YOU TELL?
HUH?! REALLY?!
YOU SEEMED AS CALM AS ALWAYS!
I WAS NERVOUS...

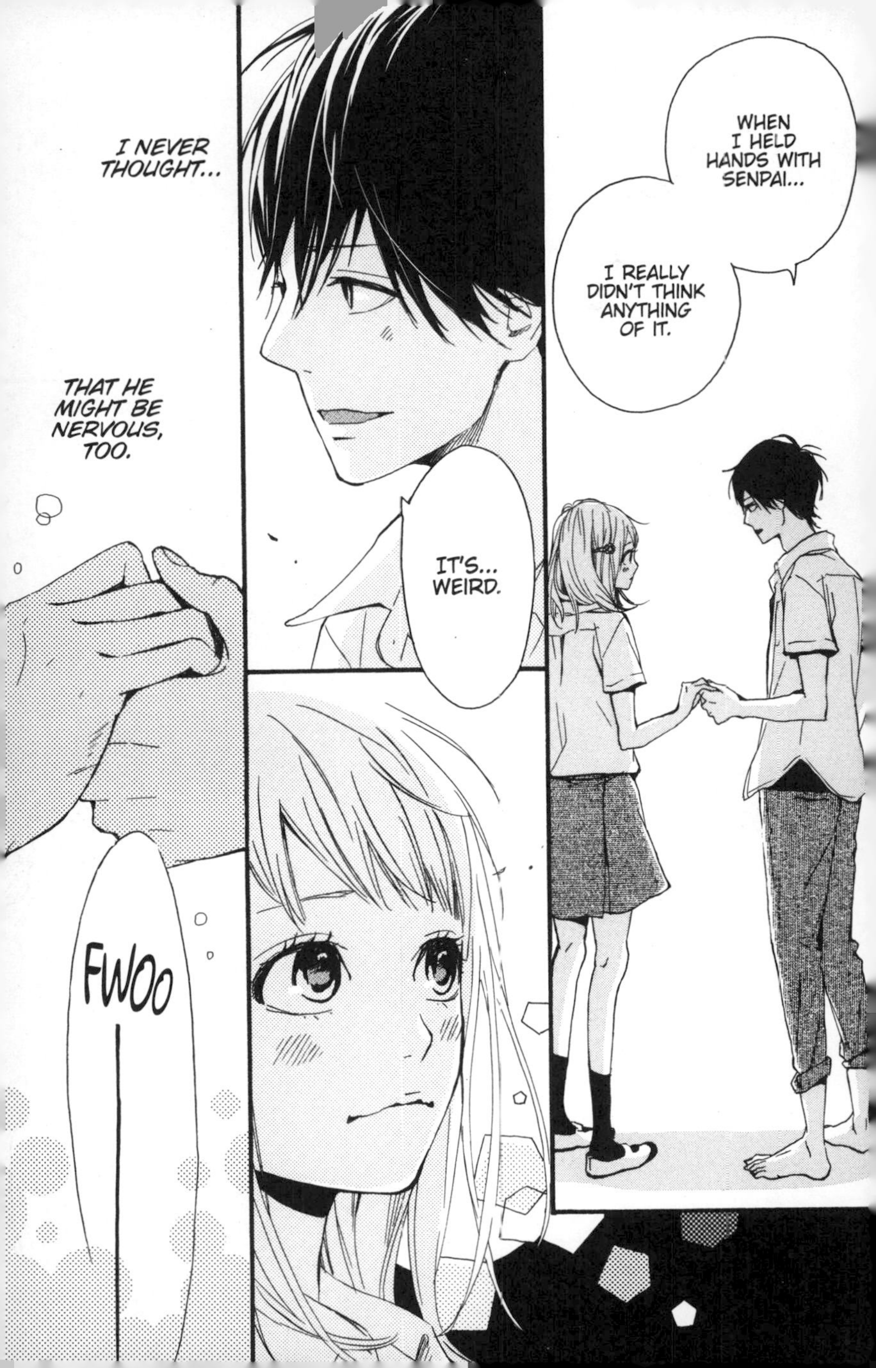
WHEN I HELD HANDS WITH SENPAI...
I REALLY DIDN'T THINK ANYTHING OF IT.
IT'S... WEIRD.
I NEVER THOUGHT...
THAT HE MIGHT BE NERVOUS, TOO.
FWOO

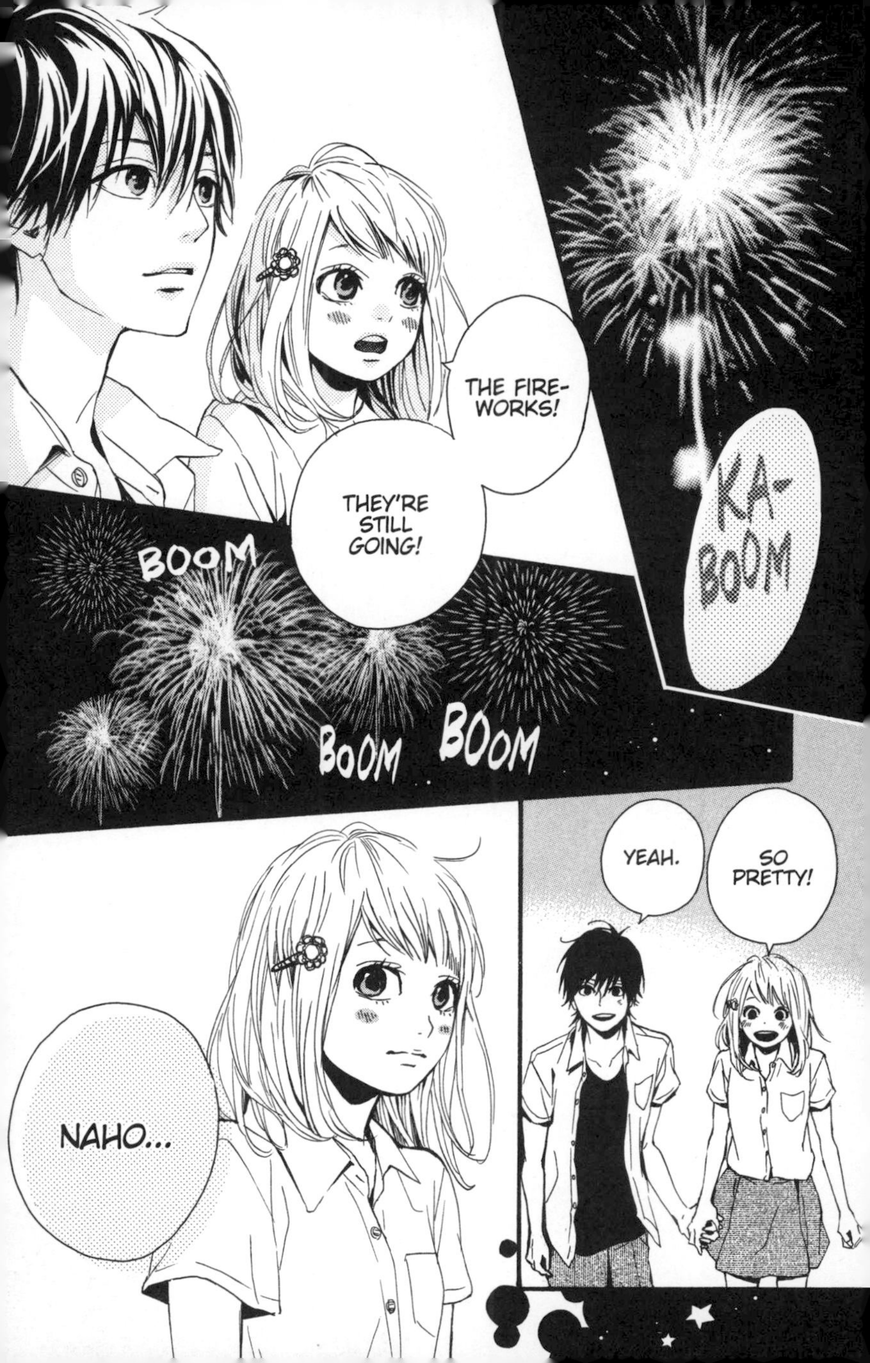
KA-BOOM
THE FIRE-WORKS!
THEY'RE STILL GOING!
BOOM
BOOM BOOM
SO PRETTY!
YEAH.
NAHO...

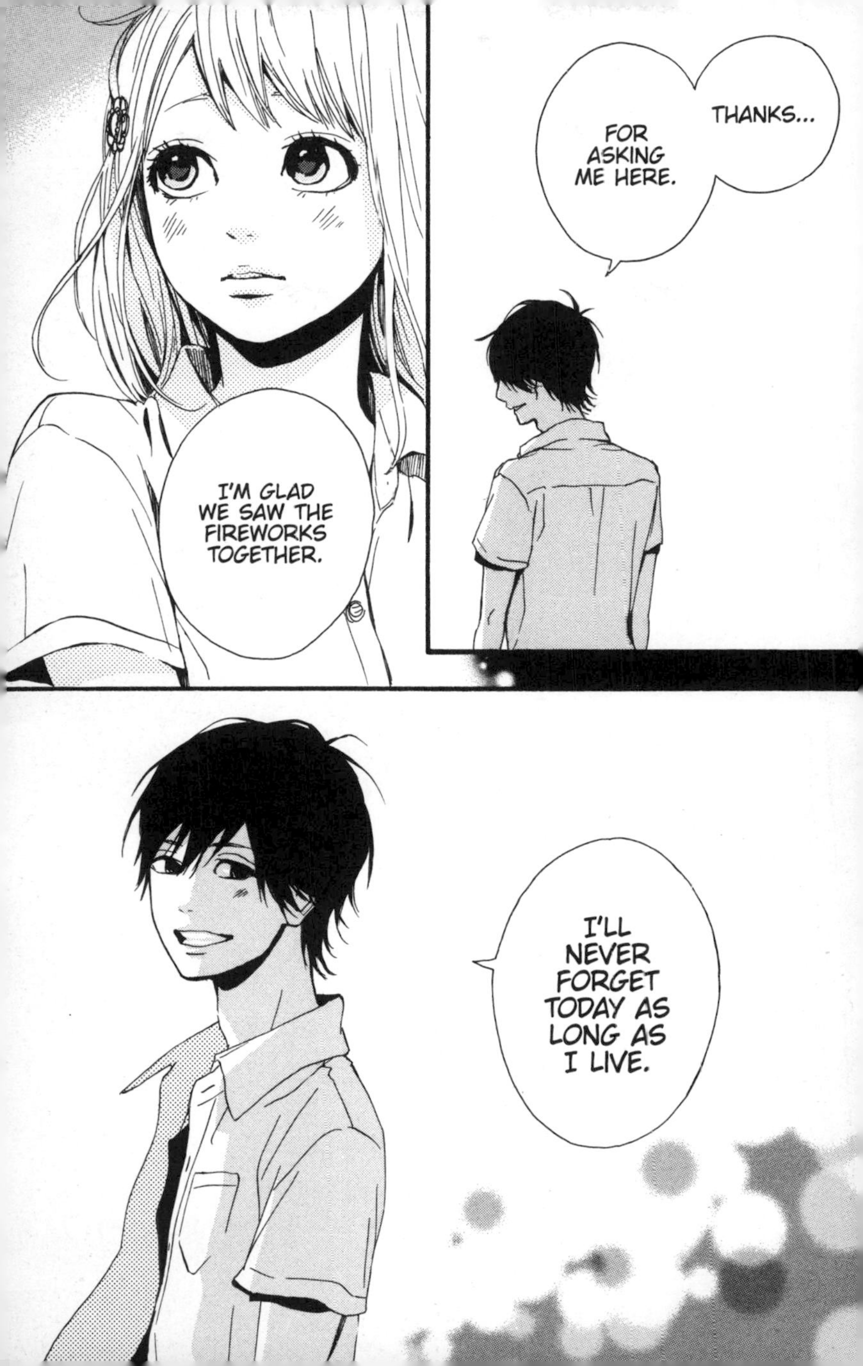
THANKS... FOR ASKING ME HERE.
I'M GLAD WE SAW THE FIREWORKS TOGETHER.
I'LL NEVER FORGET TODAY AS LONG AS I LIVE.

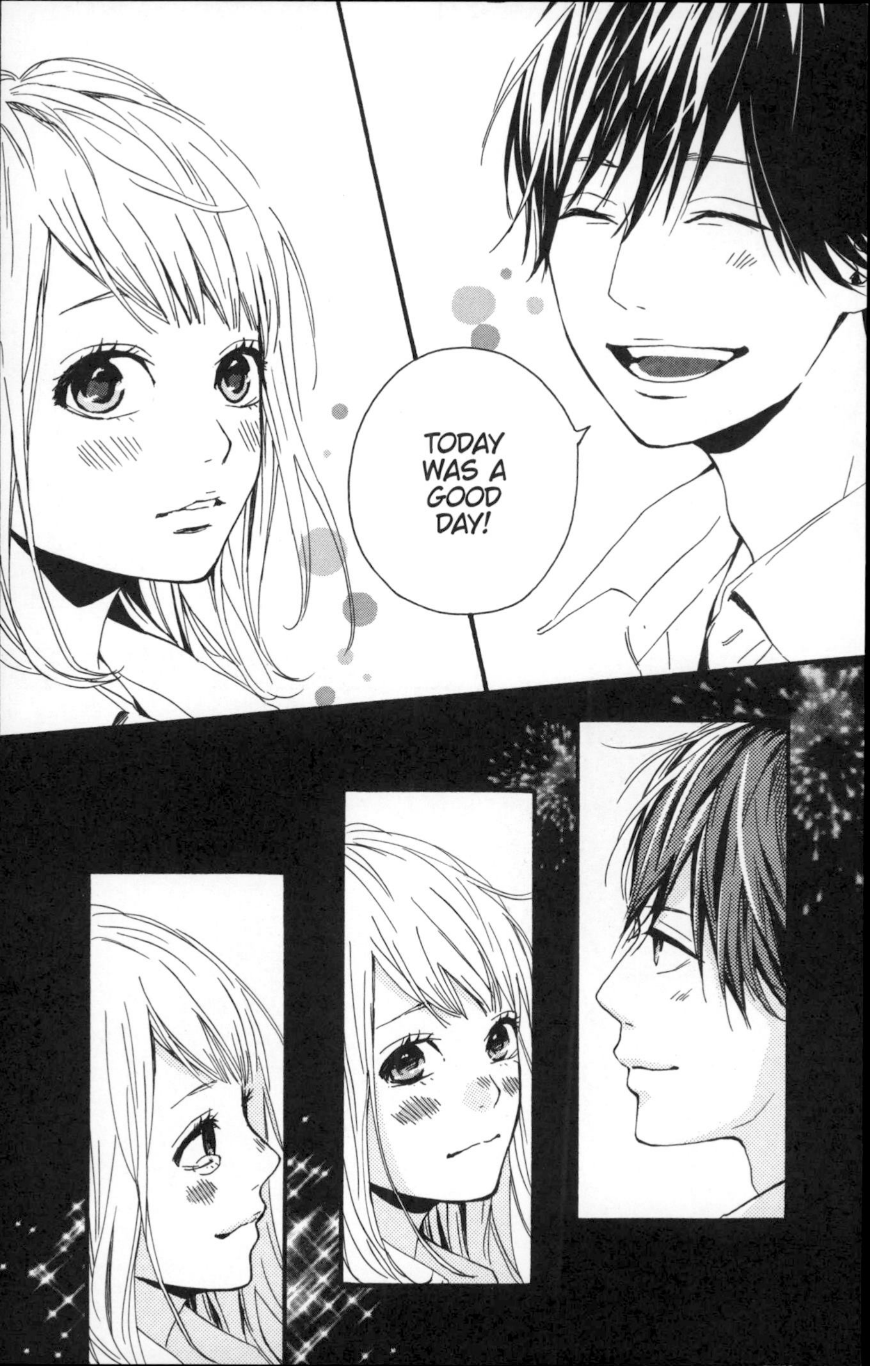
TODAY WAS A GOOD DAY!

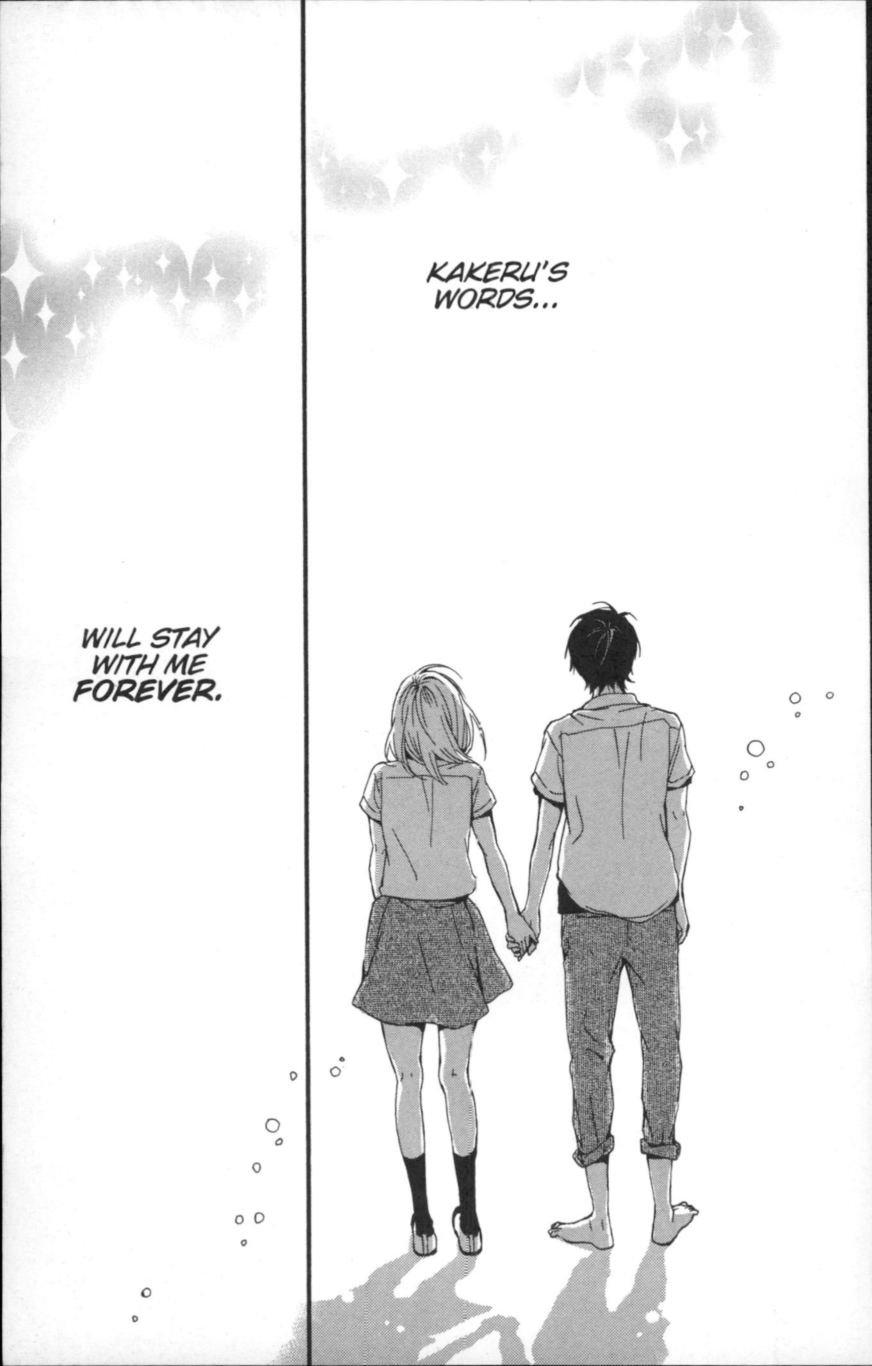
KAKERU'S WORDS...
WILL STAY WITH ME FOREVER.

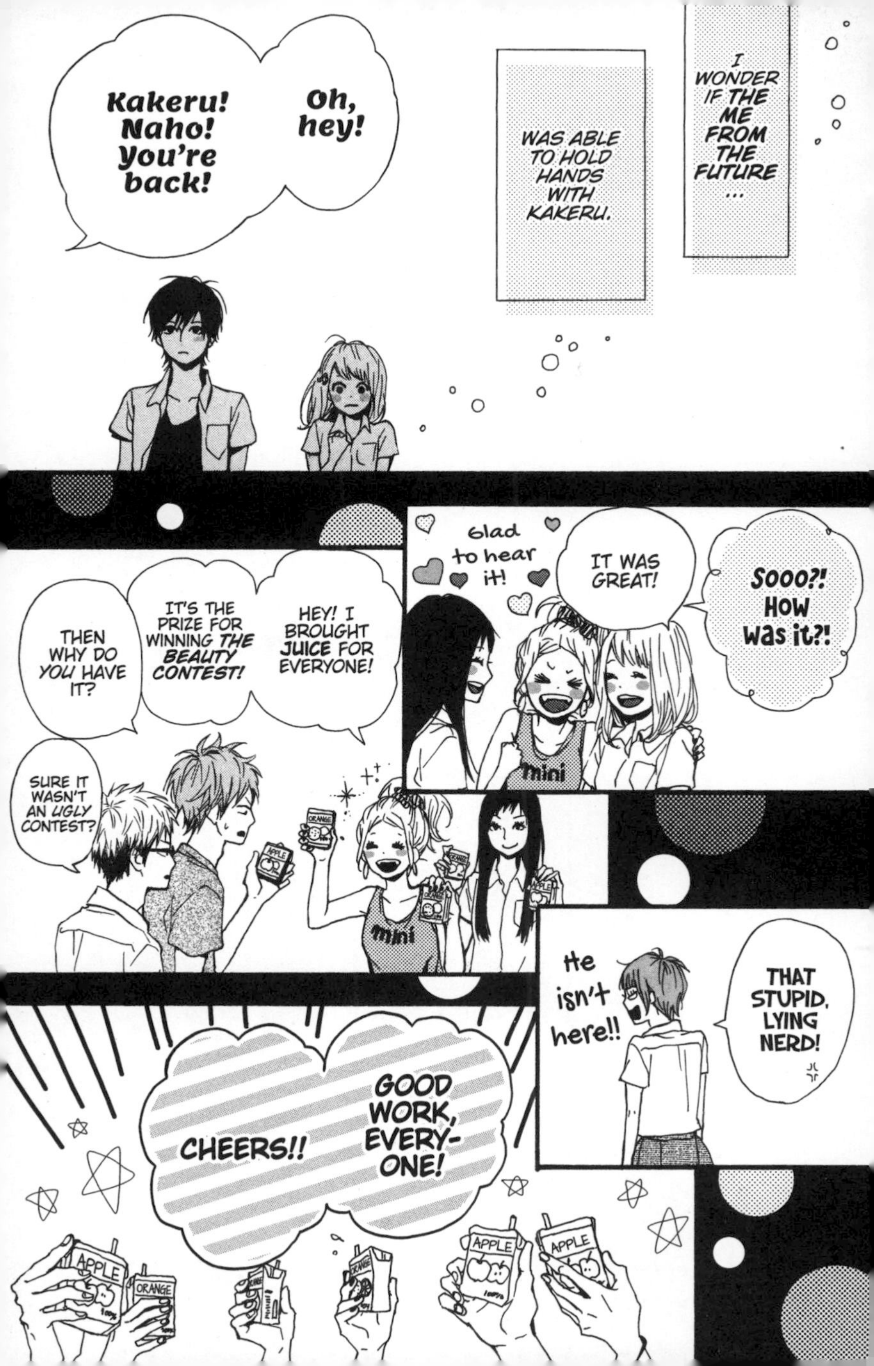

I WONDER IF THE ME FROM THE FUTURE ...
WAS ABLE TO HOLD HANDS WITH KAKERU.
Oh, hey!
Kakeru! Naho! You're back!
Sooo?! How was it?!
IT WAS GREAT!
Glad to hear it!
HEY! I BROUGHT JUICE FOR EVERYONE!
IT'S THE PRIZE FOR WINNING THE BEAUTY CONTEST!
THEN WHY DO YOU HAVE IT?
SURE IT WASN'T AN UGLY CONTEST?
THAT STUPID, LYING NERD!
He isn't here!!
GOOD WORK, EVERY-ONE!
CHEERS!!

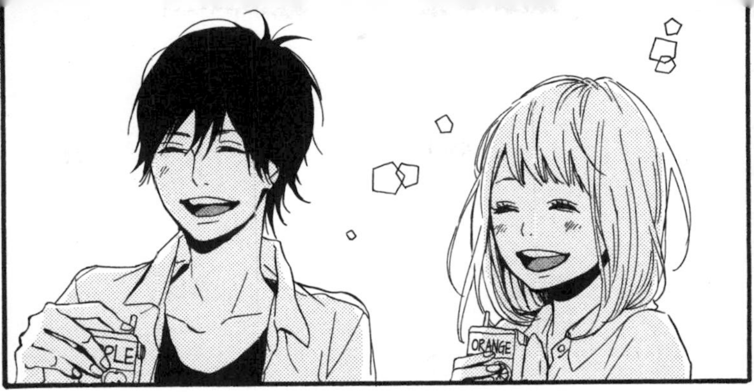
PLE
ORANGE

• Kakeru said it was a good day.

From here on, please watch over Kakeru so that he can have many more happy days.

• That will surely **save him from himself.**

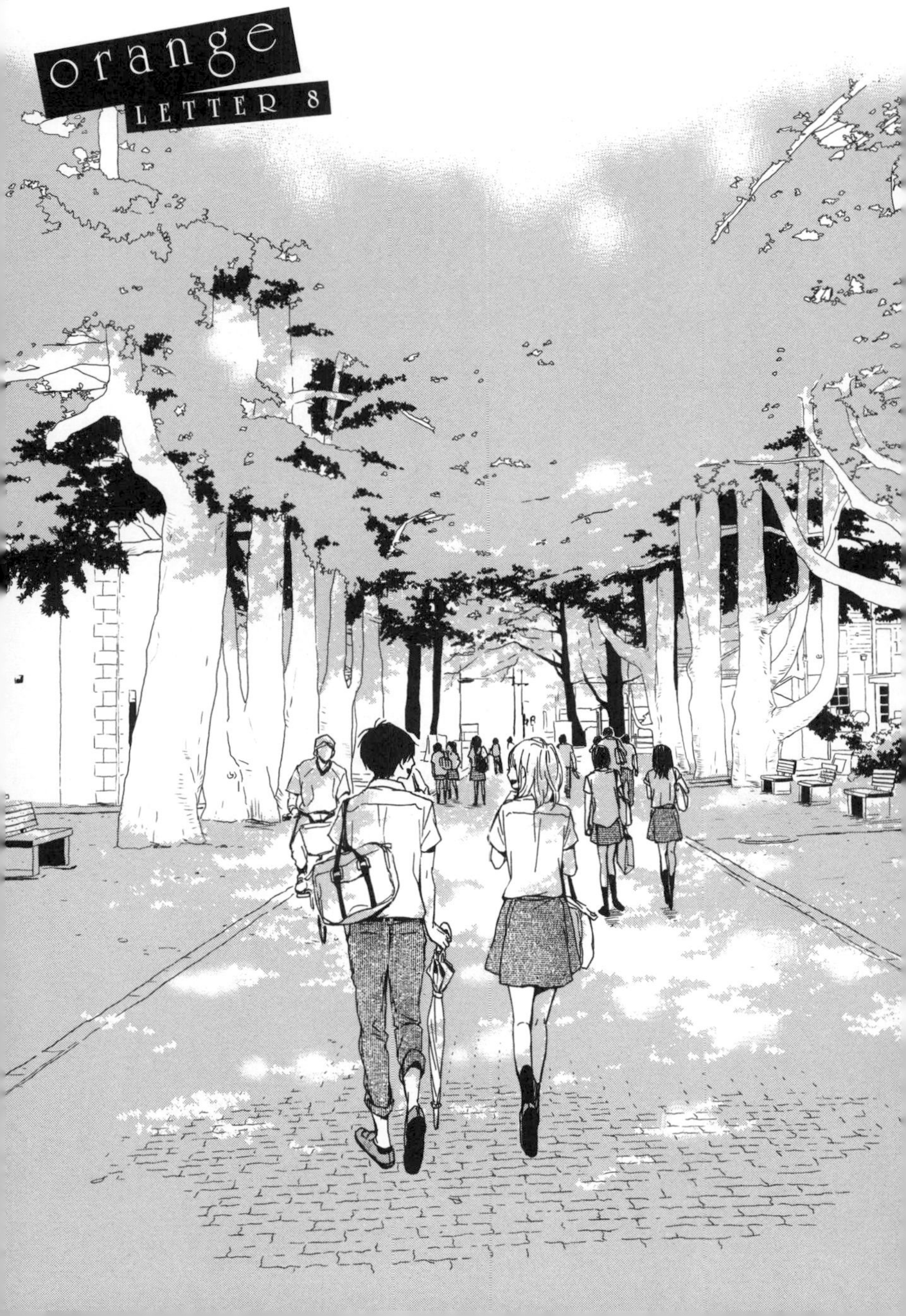
orange
LETTER 8

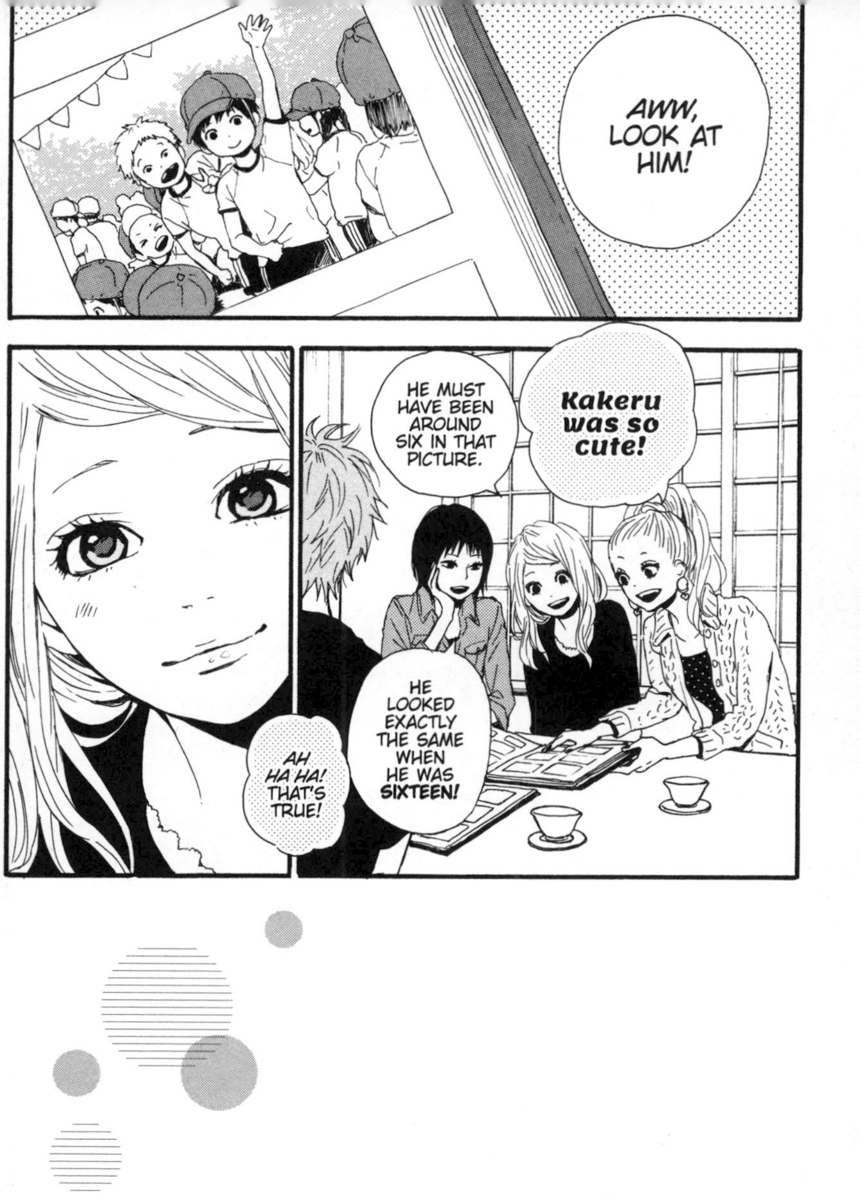
AWW, LOOK AT HIM!
Kakeru was so cute!
HE MUST HAVE BEEN AROUND SIX IN THAT PICTURE.
HE LOOKED EXACTLY THE SAME WHEN HE WAS SIXTEEN!
AH HA HA! THAT'S TRUE!

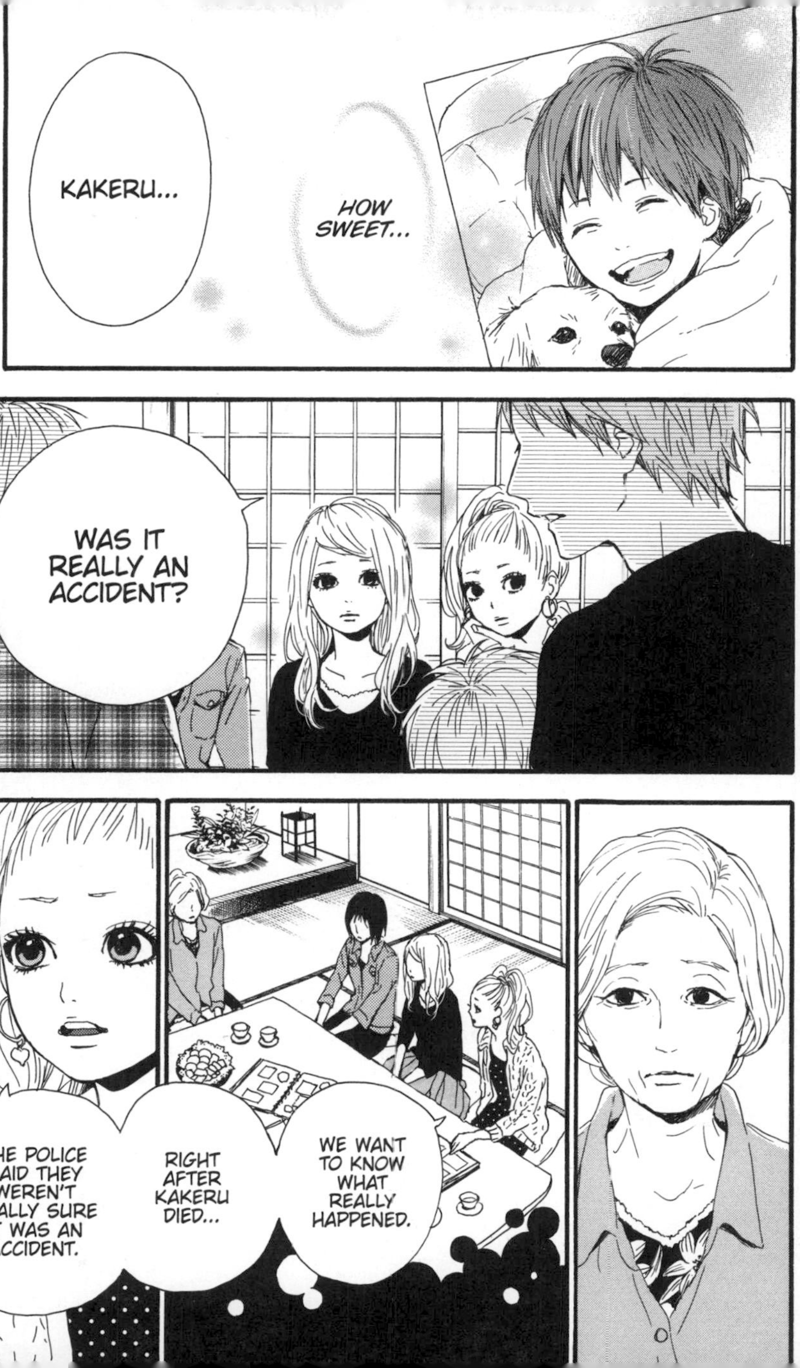
HOW SWEET...
KAKERU...
WAS IT REALLY AN ACCIDENT?
WE WANT TO KNOW WHAT REALLY HAPPENED.
RIGHT AFTER KAKERU DIED...
THE POLICE SAID THEY WEREN'T REALLY SURE IT WAS AN ACCIDENT.

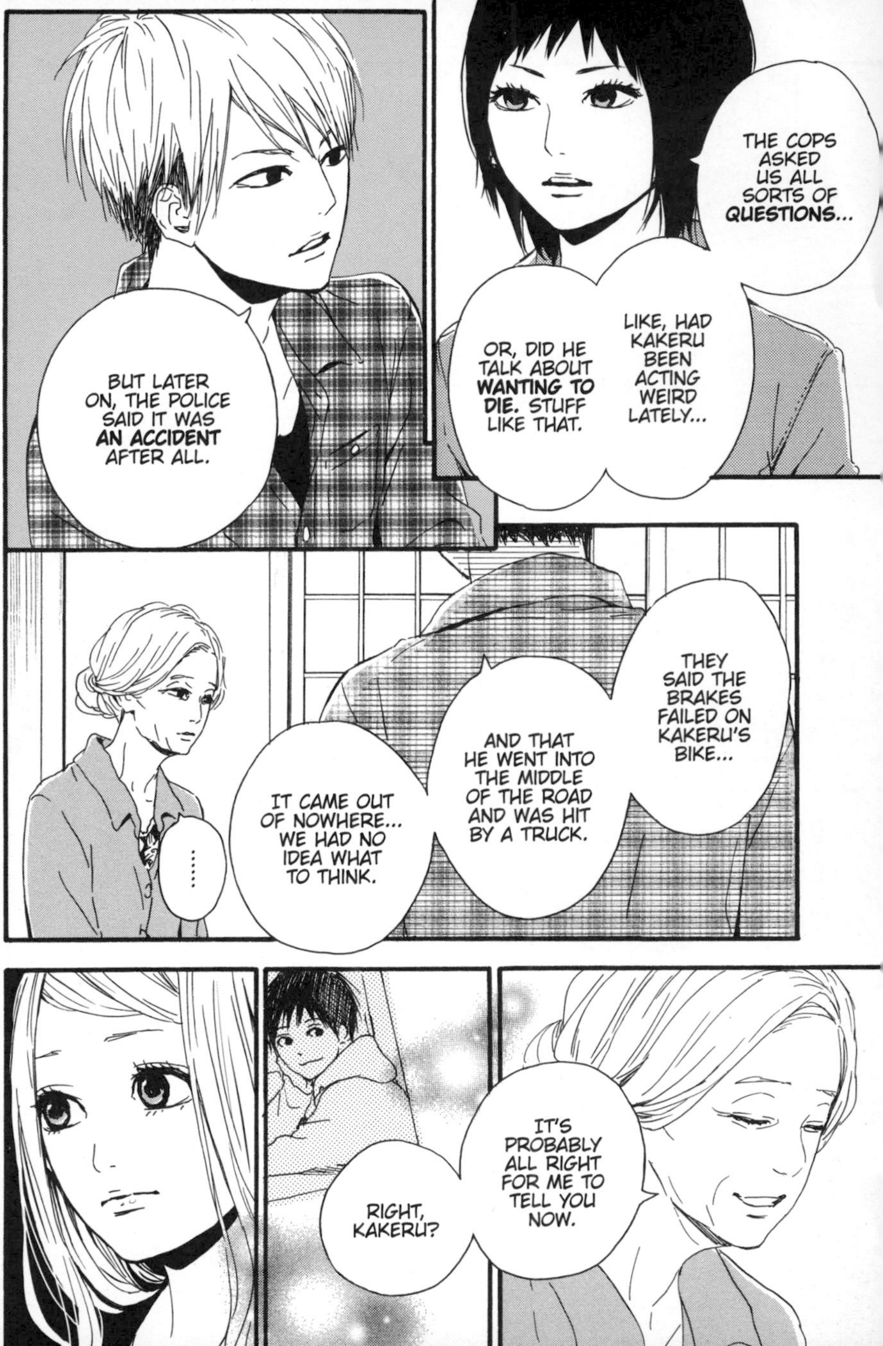
THE COPS ASKED US ALL SORTS OF QUESTIONS...
LIKE, HAD KAKERU BEEN ACTING WEIRD LATELY...
OR, DID HE TALK ABOUT WANTING TO DIE. STUFF LIKE THAT.
BUT LATER ON, THE POLICE SAID IT WAS AN ACCIDENT AFTER ALL.
THEY SAID THE BRAKES FAILED ON KAKERU'S BIKE...
AND THAT HE WENT INTO THE MIDDLE OF THE ROAD AND WAS HIT BY A TRUCK.
IT CAME OUT OF NOWHERE... WE HAD NO IDEA WHAT TO THINK.
......
IT'S PROBABLY ALL RIGHT FOR ME TO TELL YOU NOW.
RIGHT, KAKERU?

Grandmother, I'm so sorry. I know this will hurt you, and I'm really sorry about that. If something should happen to me, please tell everyone it was an accident.

I'm going to apologize to my mother. Thank you for all you've done for me.

Grandmother, I'm so sorry. I know this will hurt you, and I'm really sorry about that. If something should happen to me, please tell everyone it was an accident.

I'm going to apologize to my mother. Thank you for all you've done for me.

Kakeru

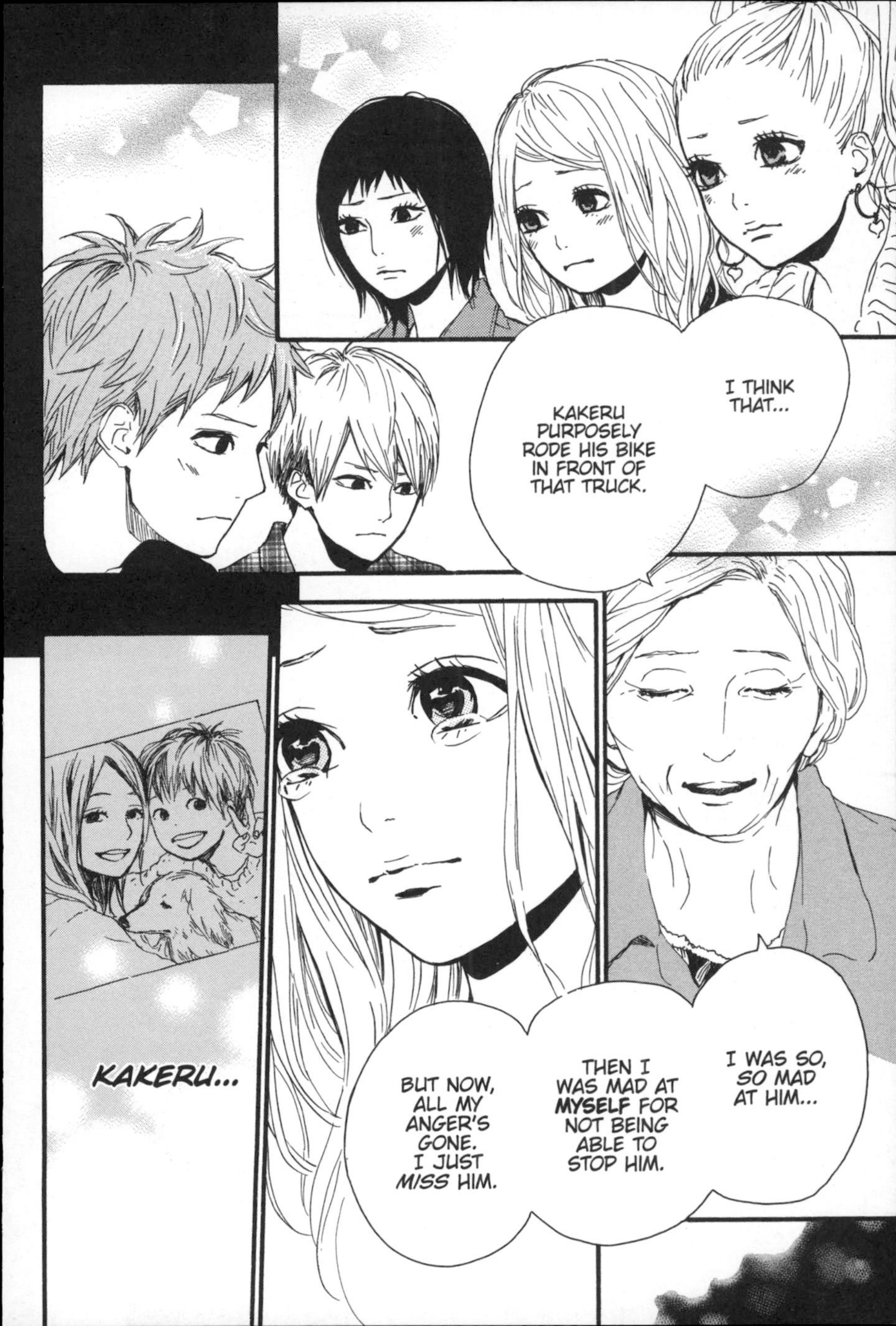
I THINK THAT...
KAKERU PURPOSELY RODE HIS BIKE IN FRONT OF THAT TRUCK.
I WAS SO, SO MAD AT HIM...
THEN I WAS MAD AT MYSELF FOR NOT BEING ABLE TO STOP HIM.
BUT NOW, ALL MY ANGER'S GONE. I JUST MISS HIM.
KAKERU...

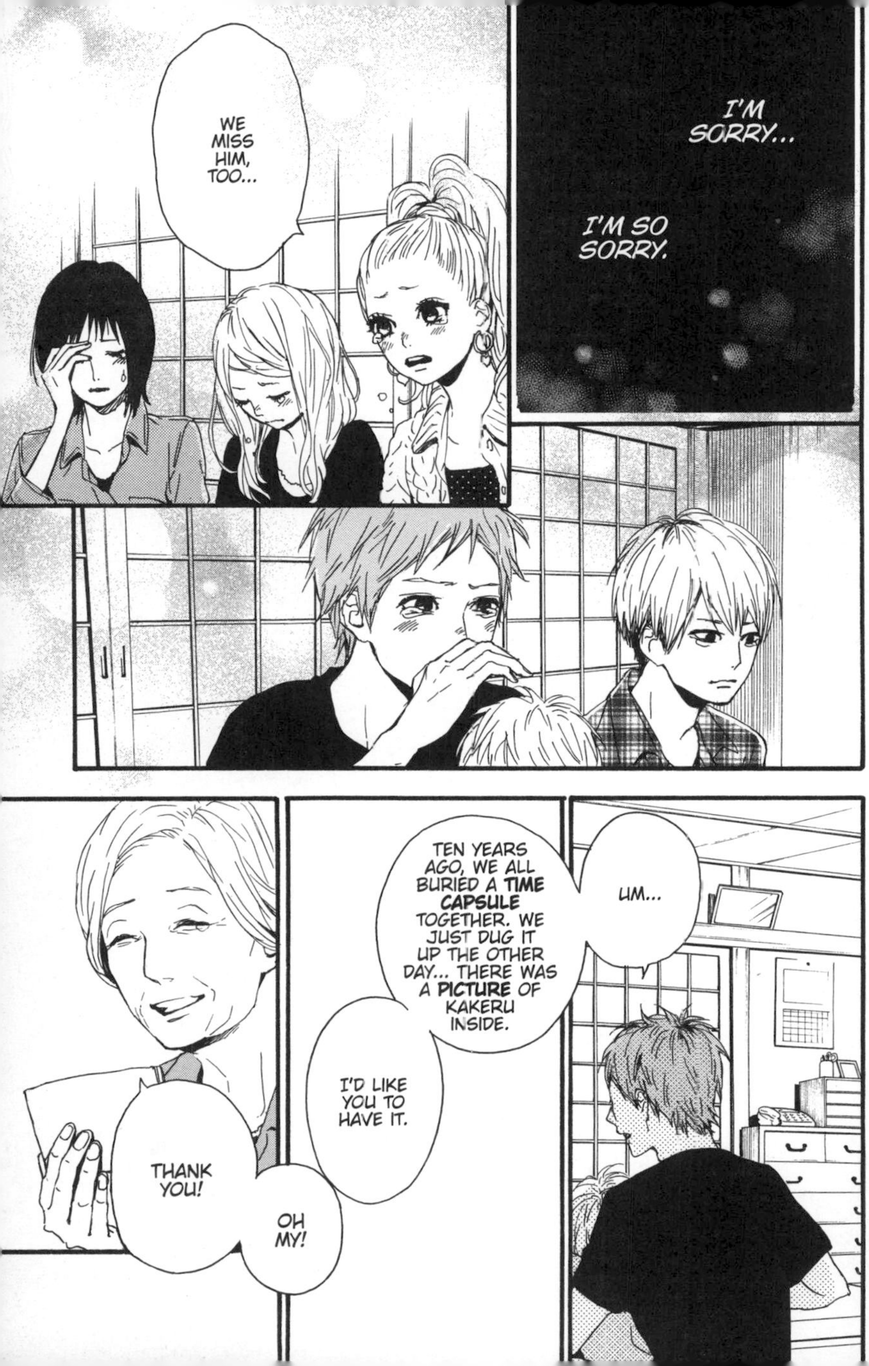
I'M SORRY...
I'M SO SORRY.
WE MISS HIM, TOO...
UM...
TEN YEARS AGO, WE ALL BURIED A **TIME CAPSULE** TOGETHER. WE JUST DUG IT UP THE OTHER DAY... THERE WAS A **PICTURE** OF KAKERU INSIDE.
I'D LIKE YOU TO HAVE IT.
OH MY!
THANK YOU!

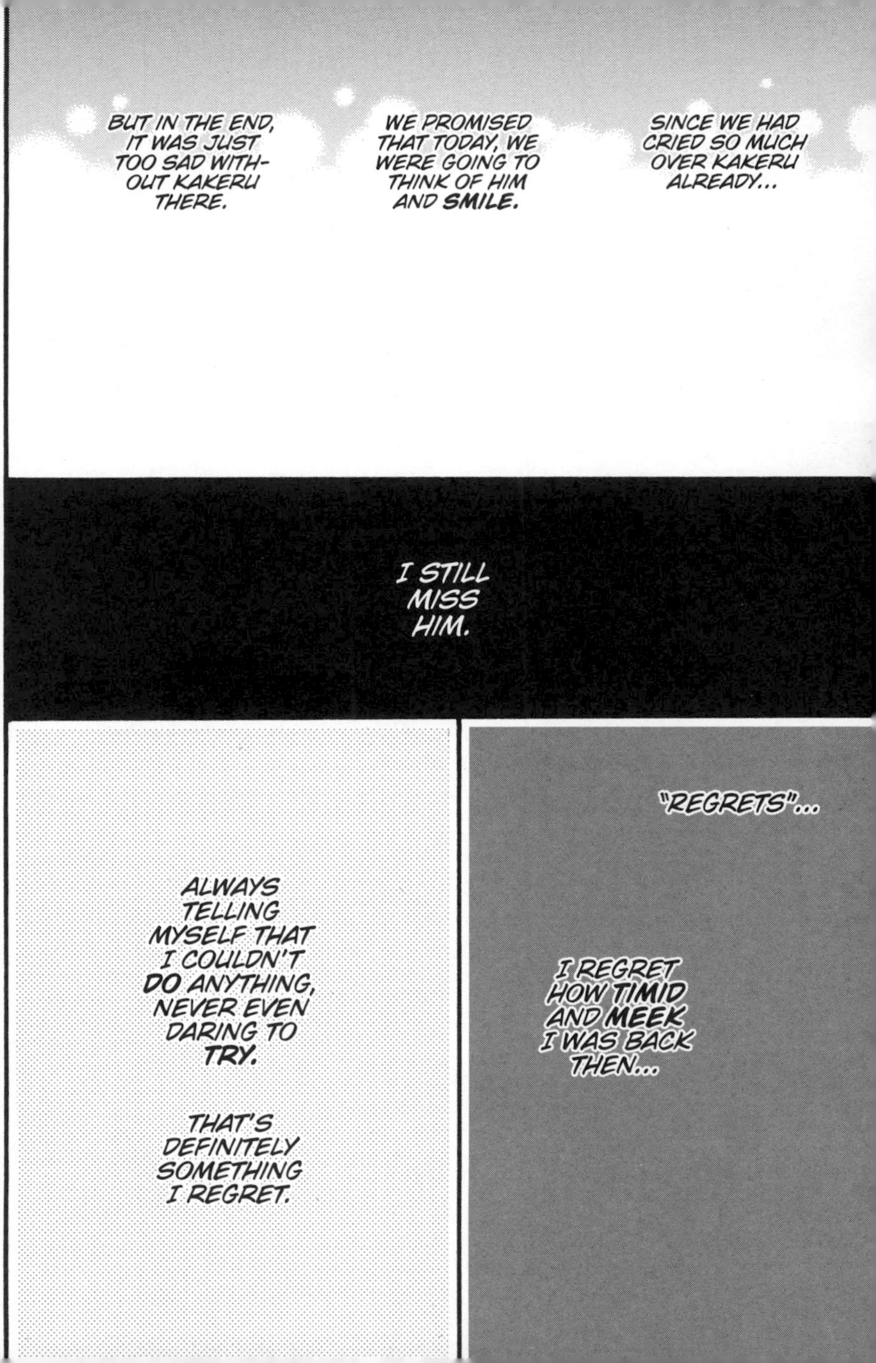
SINCE WE HAD CRIED SO MUCH OVER KAKERU ALREADY...
WE PROMISED THAT TODAY, WE WERE GOING TO THINK OF HIM AND SMILE.
BUT IN THE END, IT WAS JUST TOO SAD WITH-OUT KAKERU THERE.
I STILL MISS HIM.
"REGRETS"...
I REGRET HOW TIMID AND MEEK I WAS BACK THEN...
ALWAYS TELLING MYSELF THAT I COULDN'T DO ANYTHING, NEVER EVEN DARING TO TRY.
THAT'S DEFINITELY SOMETHING I REGRET.

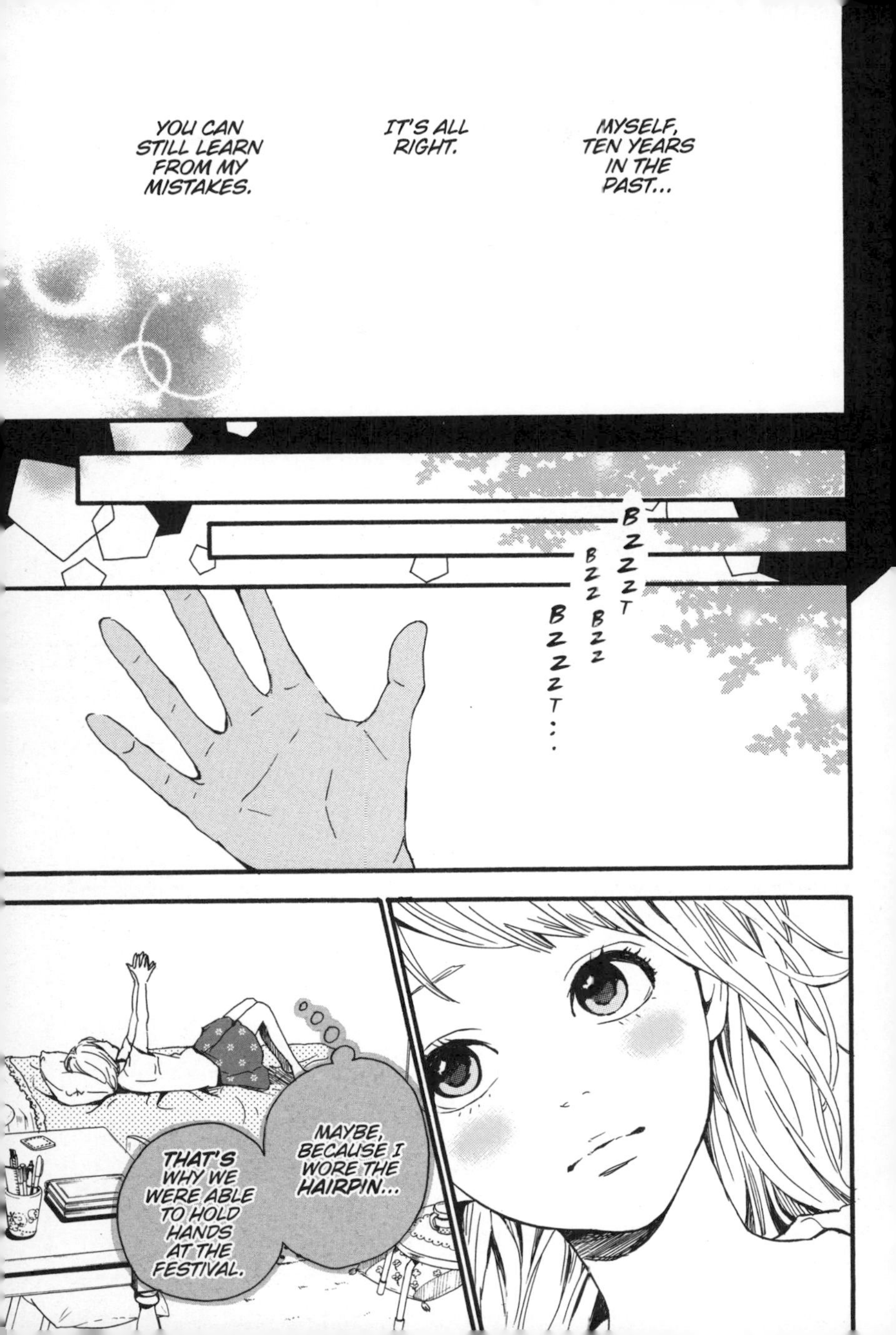
MYSELF, TEN YEARS IN THE PAST...
IT'S ALL RIGHT.
YOU CAN STILL LEARN FROM MY MISTAKES.
BZZZT
BZZ BZZ
BZZZT..
MAYBE, BECAUSE I WORE THE HAIRPIN...
THAT'S WHY WE WERE ABLE TO HOLD HANDS AT THE FESTIVAL.

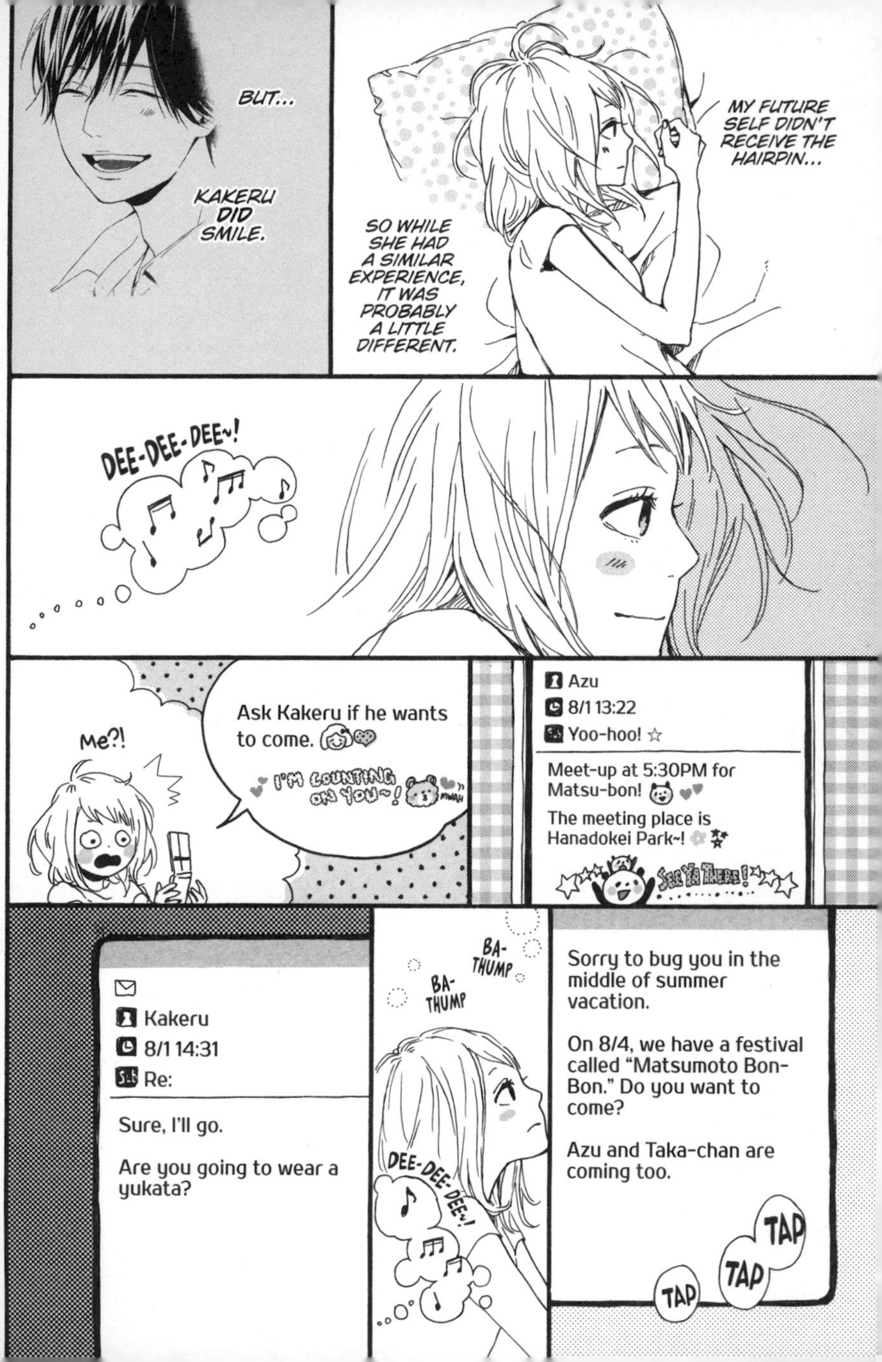
MY FUTURE SELF DIDN'T RECEIVE THE HAIRPIN...
SO WHILE SHE HAD A SIMILAR EXPERIENCE, IT WAS PROBABLY A LITTLE DIFFERENT.
BUT...
KAKERU DID SMILE.
DEE-DEE-DEE~!
Azu
8/1 13:22
Yoo-hoo! ☆
Meet-up at 5:30PM for Matsu-bon!
The meeting place is Hanadokei Park~!
SEE YA THERE!
Ask Kakeru if he wants to come.
I'M COUNTING ON YOU~!
MWAH
Me?!
Sorry to bug you in the middle of summer vacation.
On 8/4, we have a festival called "Matsumoto Bon-Bon." Do you want to come?
Azu and Taka-chan are coming too.
TAP
TAP
TAP
BA-THUMP
BA-THUMP
DEE-DEE-DEE~!
Kakeru
8/1 14:31
Re:
Sure, I'll go.
Are you going to wear a yukata?

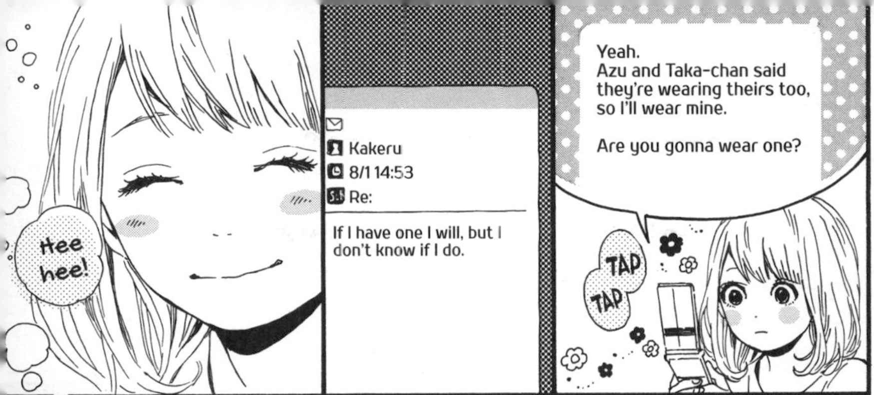
Yeah.
Azu and Taka-chan said they're wearing theirs too, so I'll wear mine.
Are you gonna wear one?
TAP TAP
Kakeru
8/1 14:53
Re:
If I have one I will, but I don't know if I do.
Hee hee!

August 4

- The six of us went to Matsumoto Bon-Bon.
- Even though Kakeru acted like he didn't have a yukata, he wore one after all.
- While we were walking around, we got separated from the others, leaving Kakeru and me alone together.

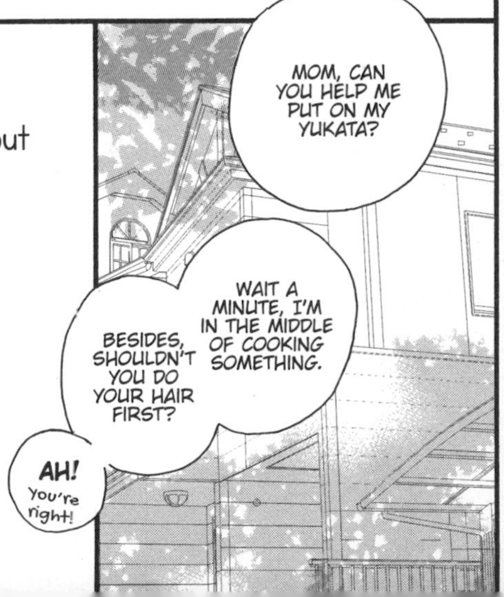
MOM, CAN YOU HELP ME PUT ON MY YUKATA?
WAIT A MINUTE, I'M IN THE MIDDLE OF COOKING SOMETHING.
BESIDES, SHOULDN'T YOU DO YOUR HAIR FIRST?
AH! You're right!

- While the two of us were talking, I asked Kakeru about his mother.

Kakeru just got quiet.

I changed the subject.

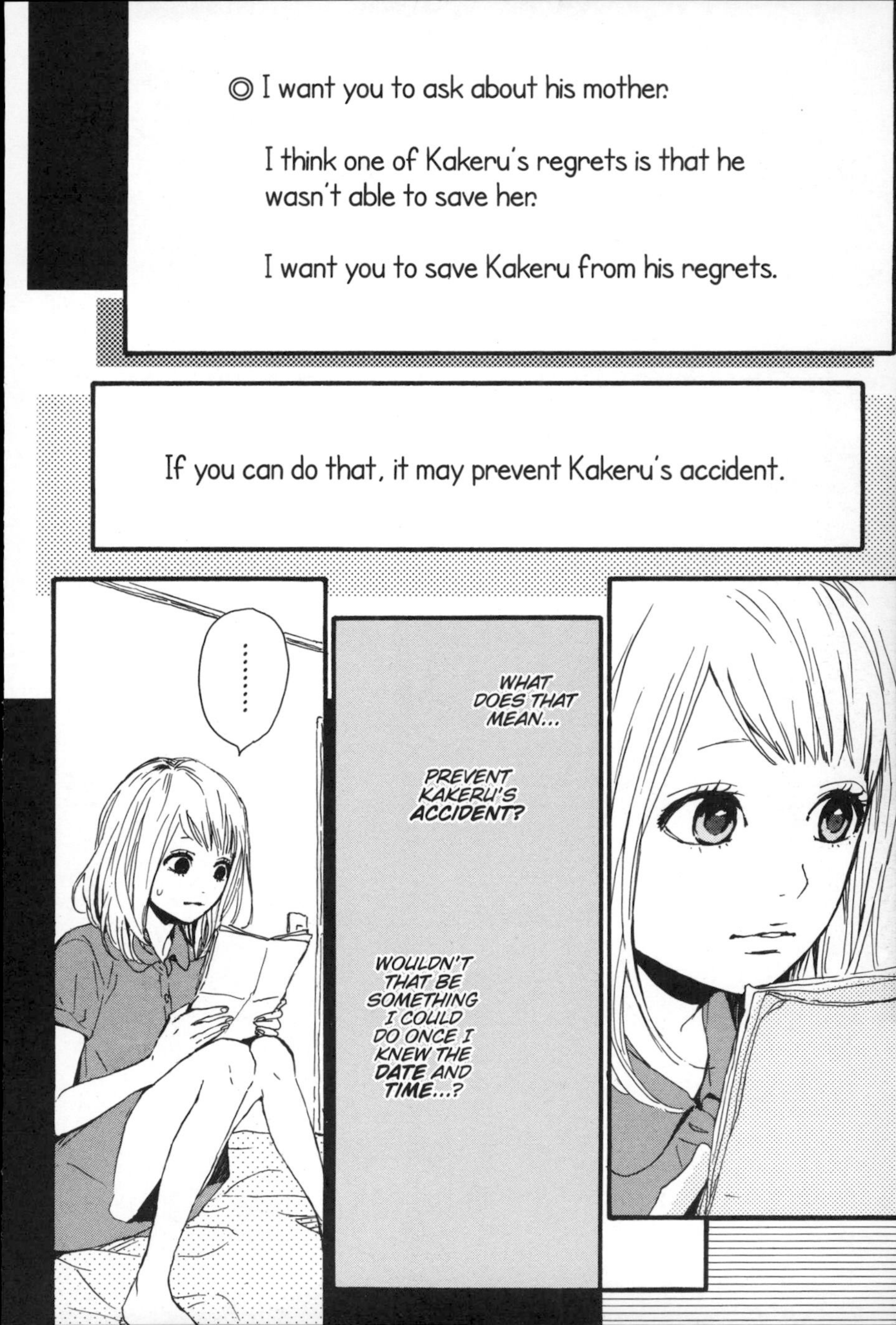
◎ I want you to ask about his mother.
I think one of Kakeru's regrets is that he wasn't able to save her.
I want you to save Kakeru from his regrets.
If you can do that, it may prevent Kakeru's accident.
WHAT DOES THAT MEAN...
PREVENT KAKERU'S ACCIDENT?
WOULDN'T THAT BE SOMETHING I COULD DO ONCE I KNEW THE DATE AND TIME...?
......

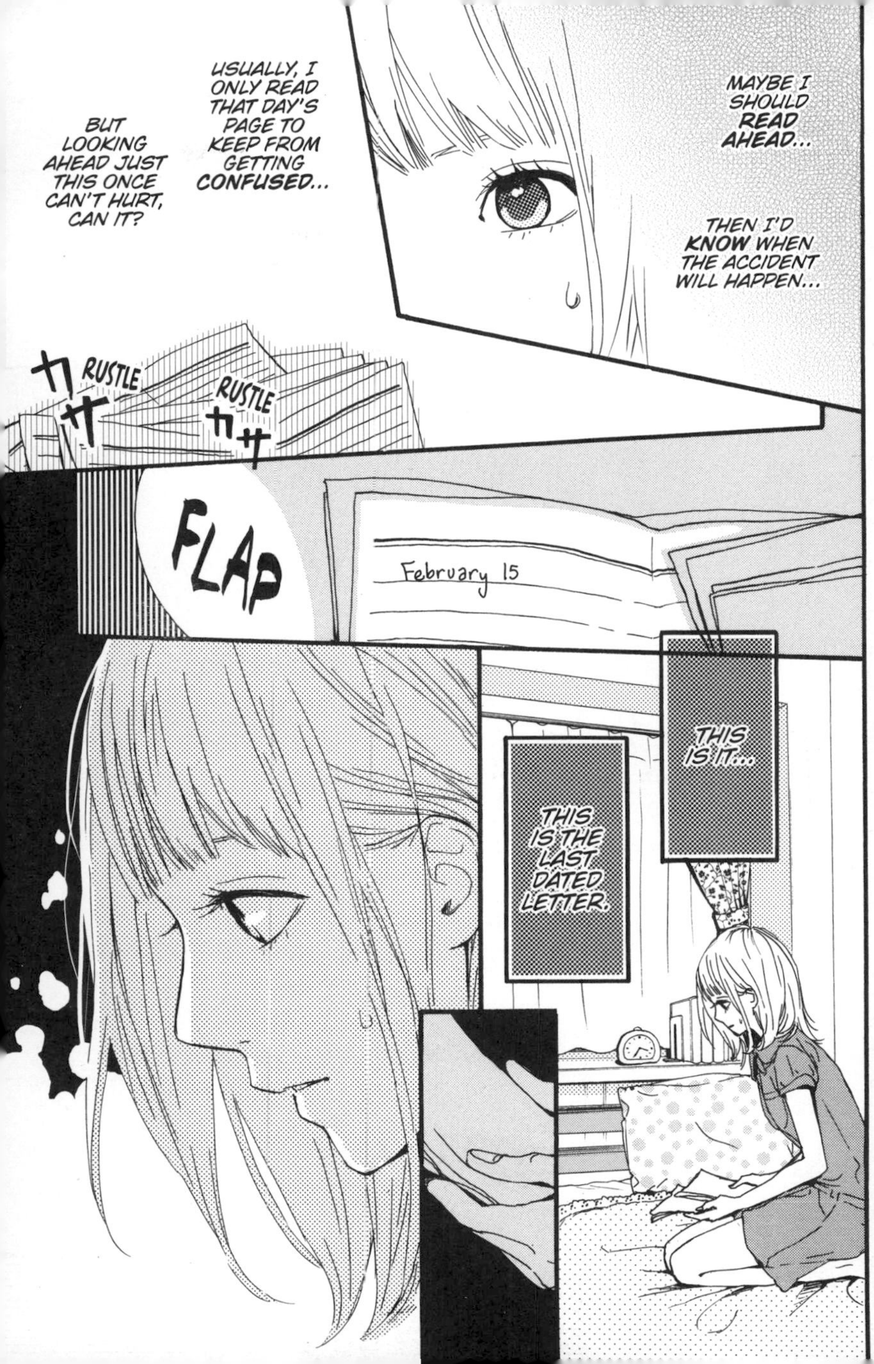
MAYBE I SHOULD READ AHEAD...
THEN I'D KNOW WHEN THE ACCIDENT WILL HAPPEN...
USUALLY, I ONLY READ THAT DAY'S PAGE TO KEEP FROM GETTING CONFUSED...
BUT LOOKING AHEAD JUST THIS ONCE CAN'T HURT, CAN IT?
RUSTLE
カサ
RUSTLE
カサ
February 15
FLAP
THIS IS IT...
THIS IS THE LAST DATED LETTER.

February 15th

- This day started off no different than any other.

- That night, as I was writing in my diary, Suwa called me and said, "Kakeru was in an accident."

Then he told me that Kakeru had died.

- The accident happened sometime after eight at night.
  It happened at an intersection near Kakeru's house.

- While riding his bike, Kakeru rode out in front of an oncoming truck.

- There was nothing that could be done.
  Even if it hadn't been the truck, it would have been something else.

◎ I want you keep Kakeru from choosing death.

◎ I want you to lighten the load that Kakeru is carrying.

◎ I want you to help Kakeru bear his worries.

◎ I don't want you to leave Kakeru alone.

◎ I want you to mend Kakeru's heart.

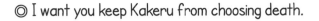

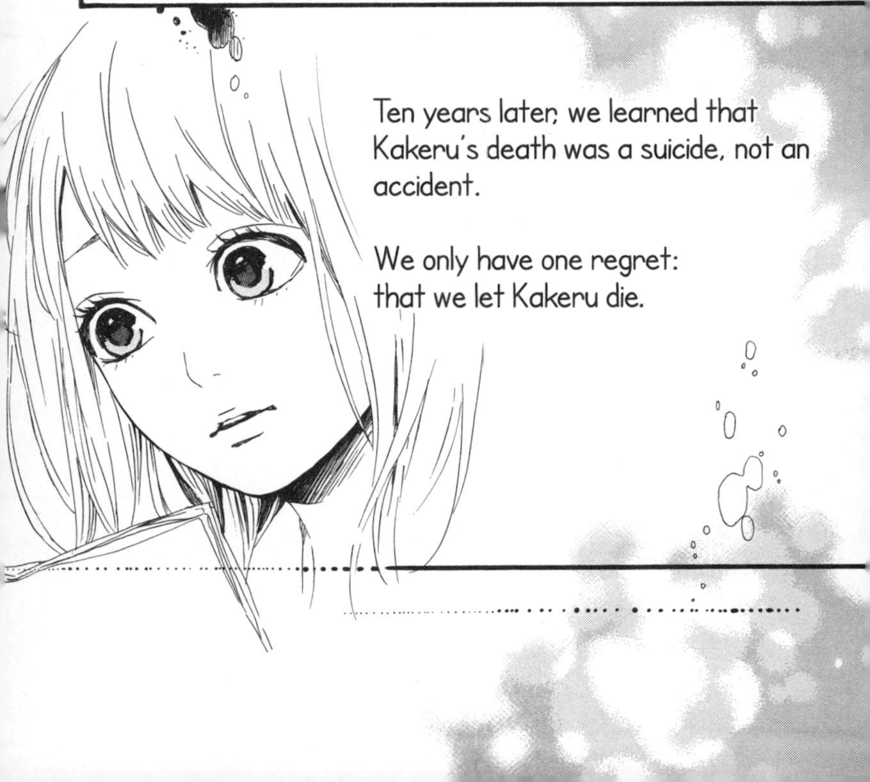
Ten years later, we learned that Kakeru's death was a suicide, not an accident.
We only have one regret: that we let Kakeru die.

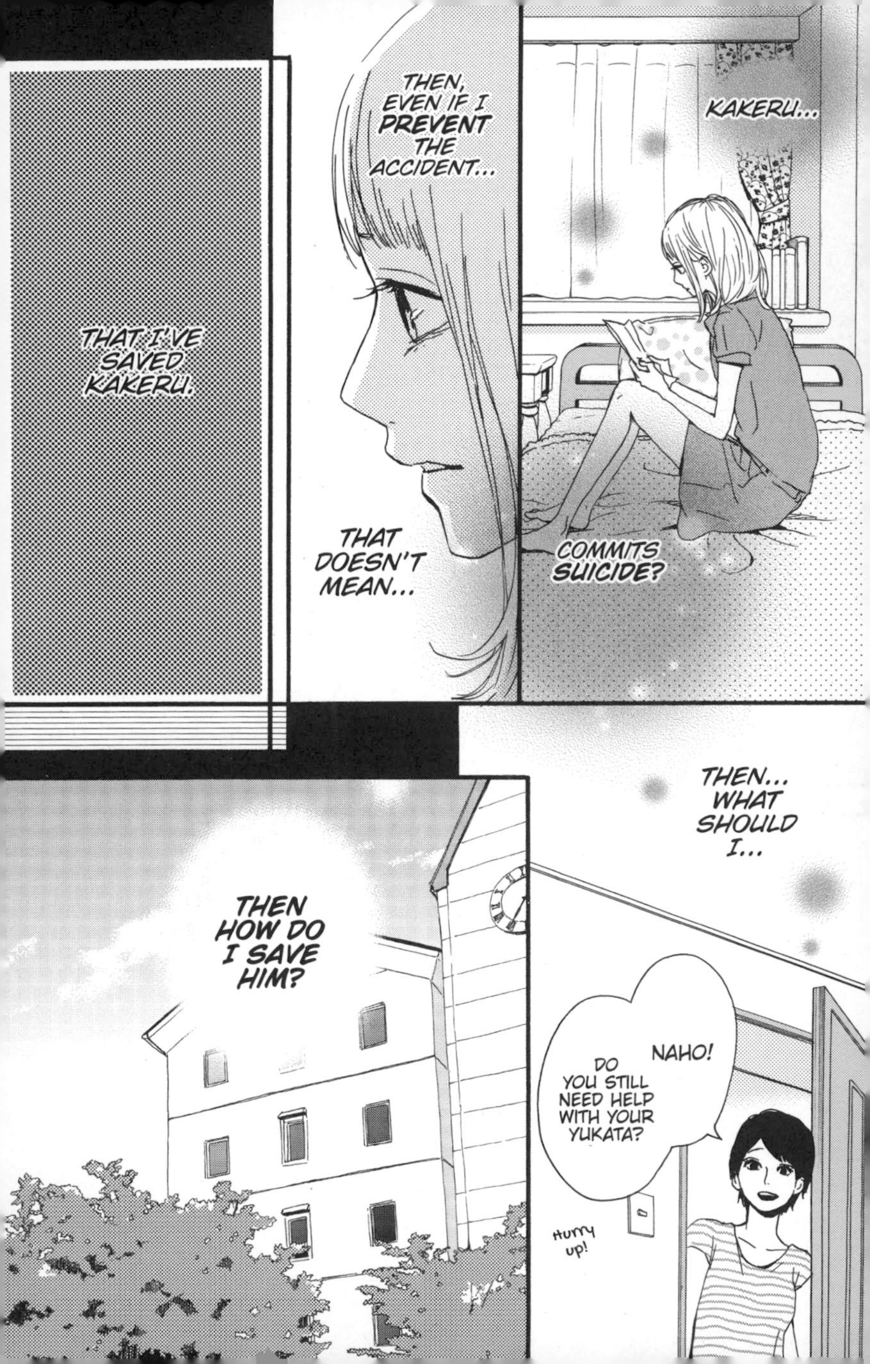
KAKERU...
COMMITS SUICIDE?
THEN, EVEN IF I PREVENT THE ACCIDENT...
THAT DOESN'T MEAN...
THAT I'VE SAVED KAKERU.
THEN... WHAT SHOULD I...
NAHO!
DO YOU STILL NEED HELP WITH YOUR YUKATA?
Hurry up!
THEN HOW DO I SAVE HIM?

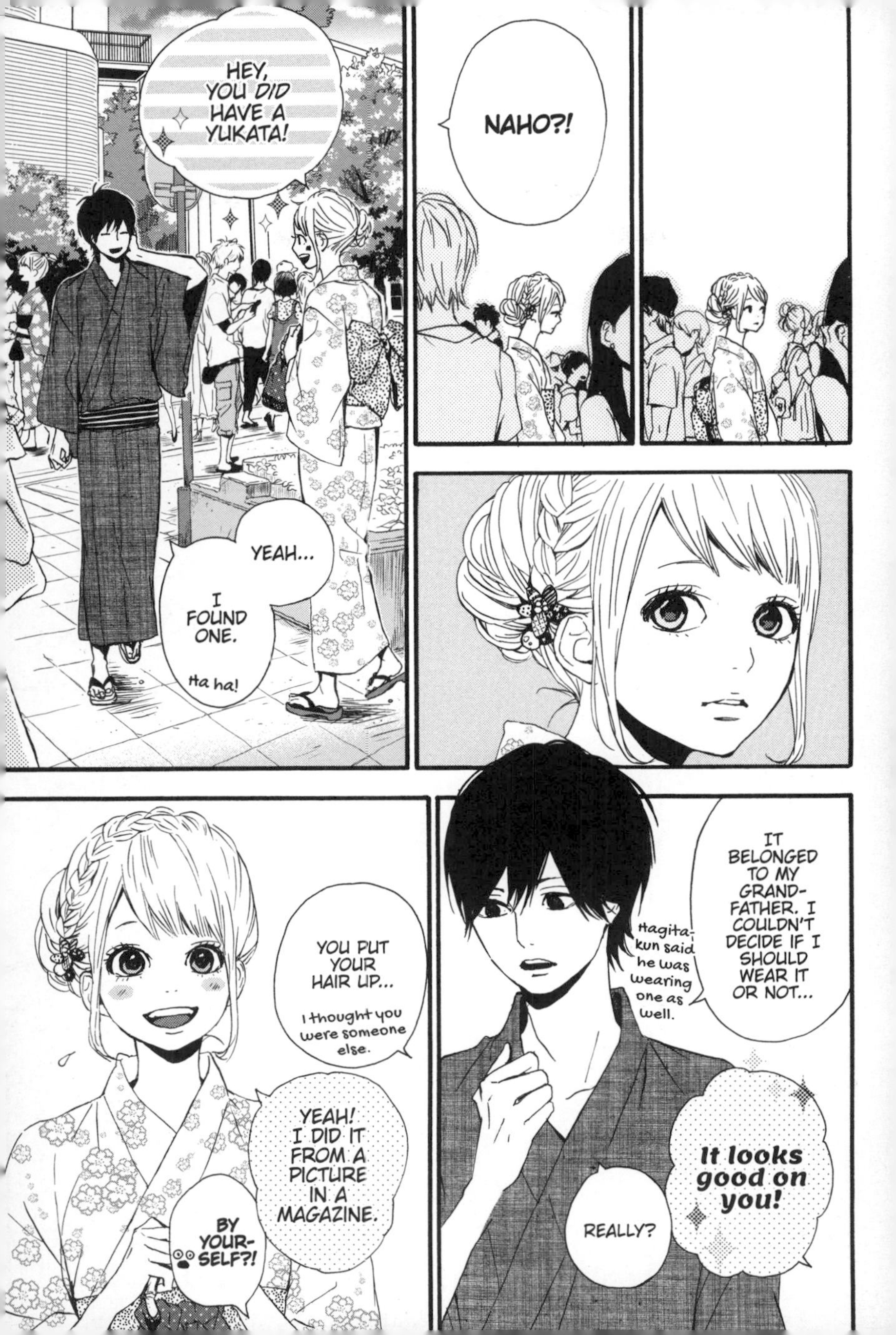
NAHO?!
HEY, YOU DID HAVE A YUKATA!
YEAH... I FOUND ONE.
Ha ha!
IT BELONGED TO MY GRAND-FATHER. I COULDN'T DECIDE IF I SHOULD WEAR IT OR NOT...
Hagita-kun said he was wearing one as well.
It looks good on you!
REALLY?
YOU PUT YOUR HAIR UP...
I thought you were someone else.
YEAH! I DID IT FROM A PICTURE IN A MAGAZINE.
BY YOUR-SELF?!

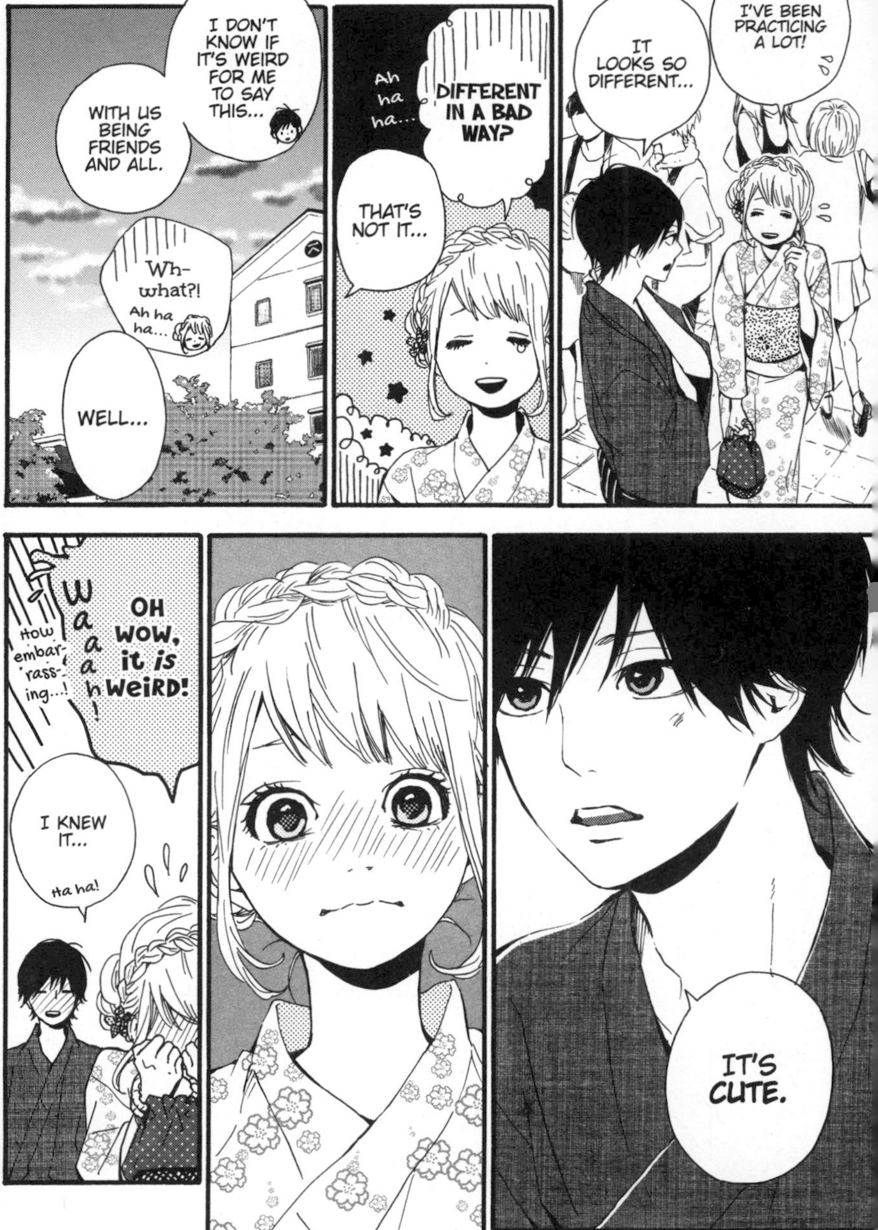
I'VE BEEN PRACTICING A LOT!
IT LOOKS SO DIFFERENT...
DIFFERENT IN A BAD WAY?
Ah ha ha...
THAT'S NOT IT...
I DON'T KNOW IF IT'S WEIRD FOR ME TO SAY THIS...
WITH US BEING FRIENDS AND ALL.
Wh-what?!
Ah ha ha...
WELL...
IT'S CUTE.
OH WOW, it is WEIRD!
Waaaah!
How embar-rass-ing...!
I KNEW IT...
Ha ha!

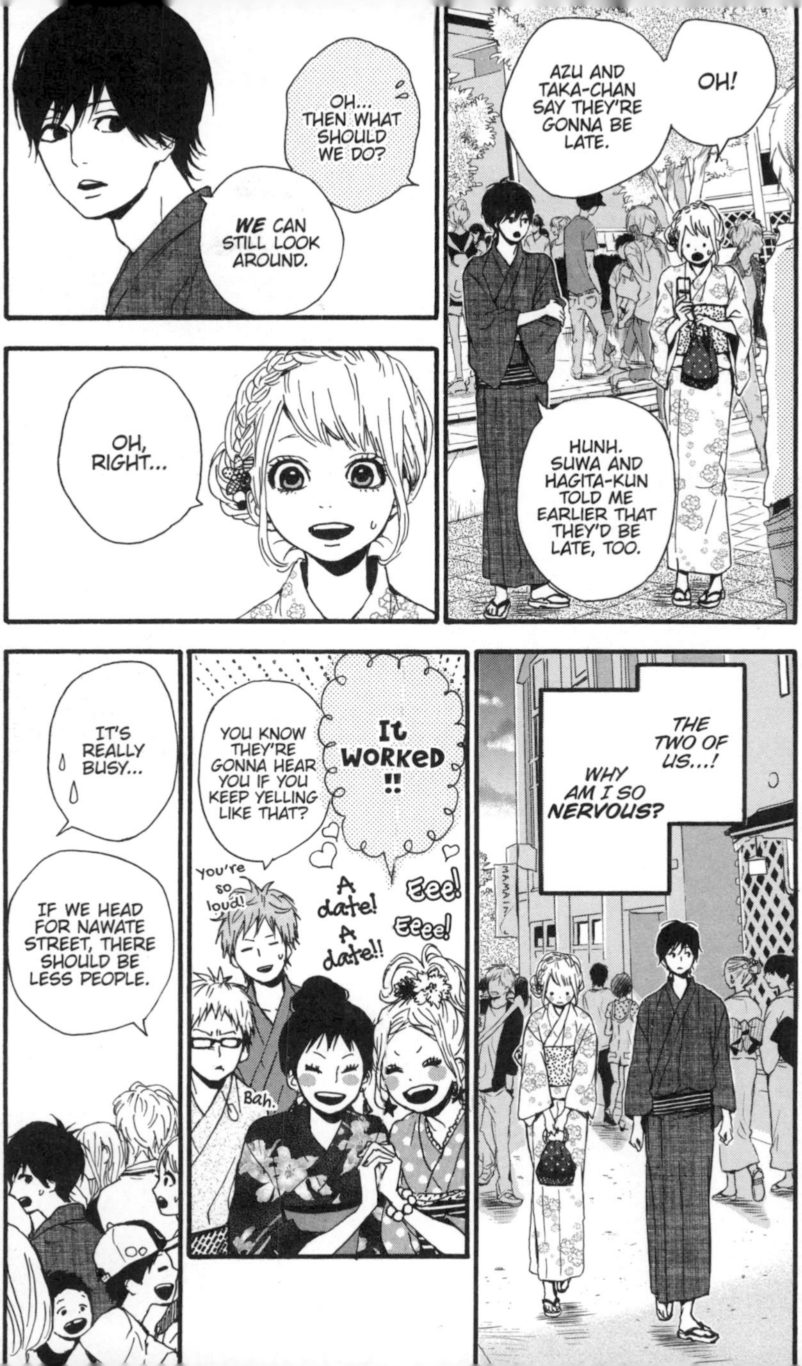
OH!
AZU AND TAKA-CHAN SAY THEY'RE GONNA BE LATE.
HUNH. SUWA AND HAGITA-KUN TOLD ME EARLIER THAT THEY'D BE LATE, TOO.
OH... THEN WHAT SHOULD WE DO?
WE CAN STILL LOOK AROUND.
OH, RIGHT...
THE TWO OF US...!
WHY AM I SO NERVOUS?
It WORKED!!
YOU KNOW THEY'RE GONNA HEAR YOU IF YOU KEEP YELLING LIKE THAT?
Eee!
Eeee!
A date! A date!!
You're so loud!
Bah.
IT'S REALLY BUSY...
IF WE HEAD FOR NAWATE STREET, THERE SHOULD BE LESS PEOPLE.

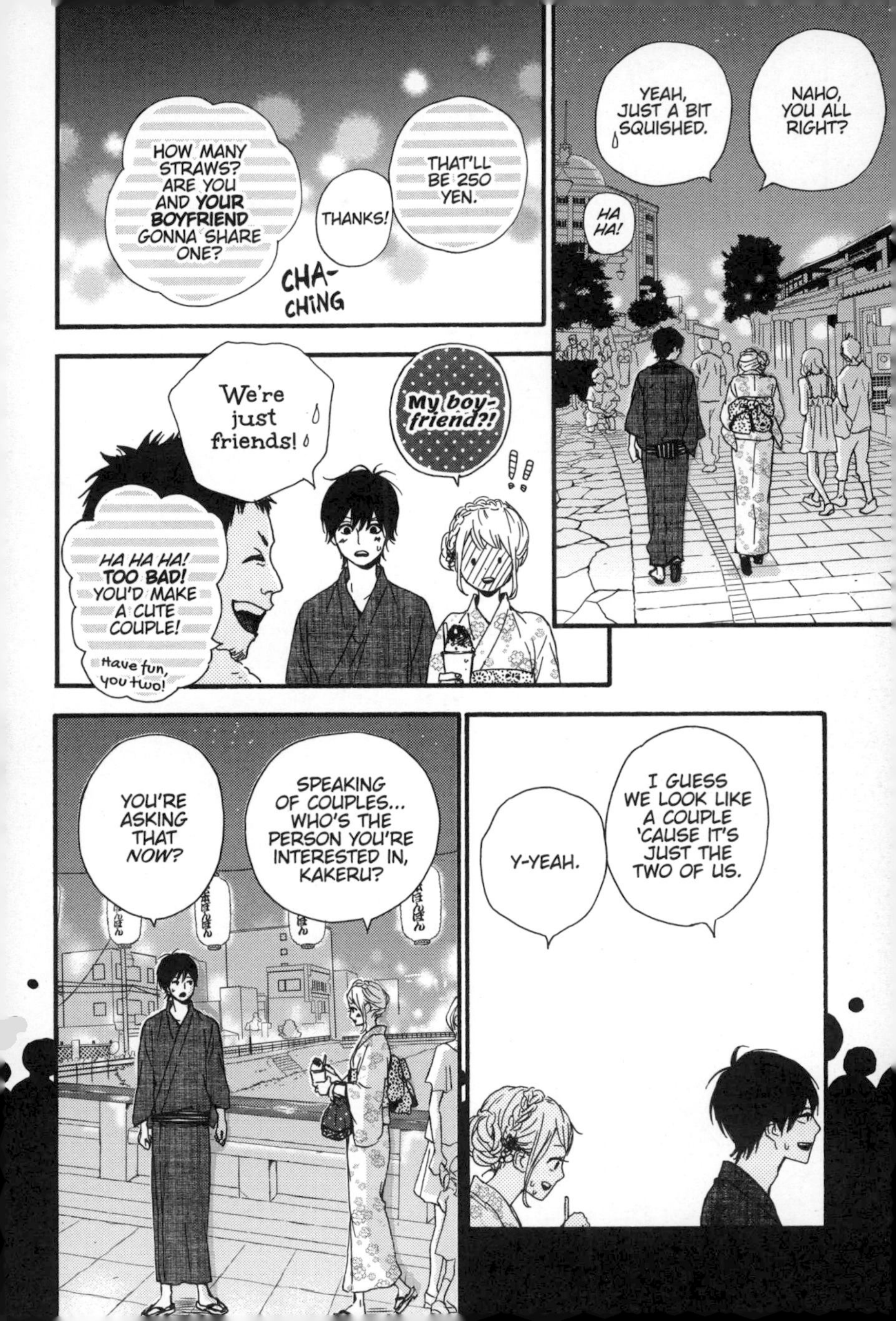
NAHO, YOU ALL RIGHT?
YEAH, JUST A BIT SQUISHED.
HA HA!
THAT'LL BE 250 YEN.
THANKS!
HOW MANY STRAWS? ARE YOU AND YOUR BOYFRIEND GONNA SHARE ONE?
CHA-CHING
My boy-friend?!
We're just friends!
HA HA HA! TOO BAD! YOU'D MAKE A CUTE COUPLE!
Have fun, you two!
I GUESS WE LOOK LIKE A COUPLE 'CAUSE IT'S JUST THE TWO OF US.
Y-YEAH.
SPEAKING OF COUPLES... WHO'S THE PERSON YOU'RE INTERESTED IN, KAKERU?
YOU'RE ASKING THAT NOW?

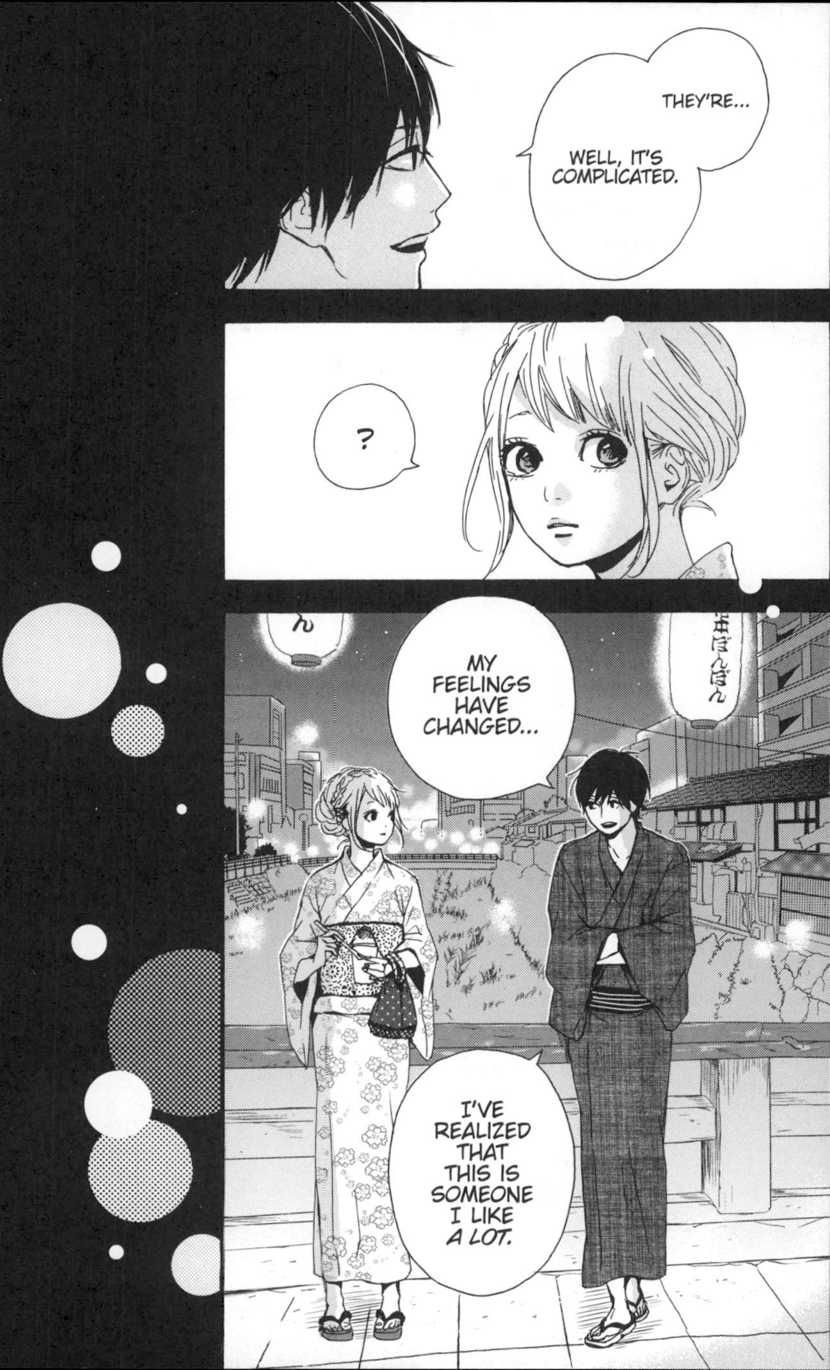
THEY'RE...
WELL, IT'S COMPLICATED.
?
MY FEELINGS HAVE CHANGED...
I'VE REALIZED THAT THIS IS SOMEONE I LIKE A LOT.

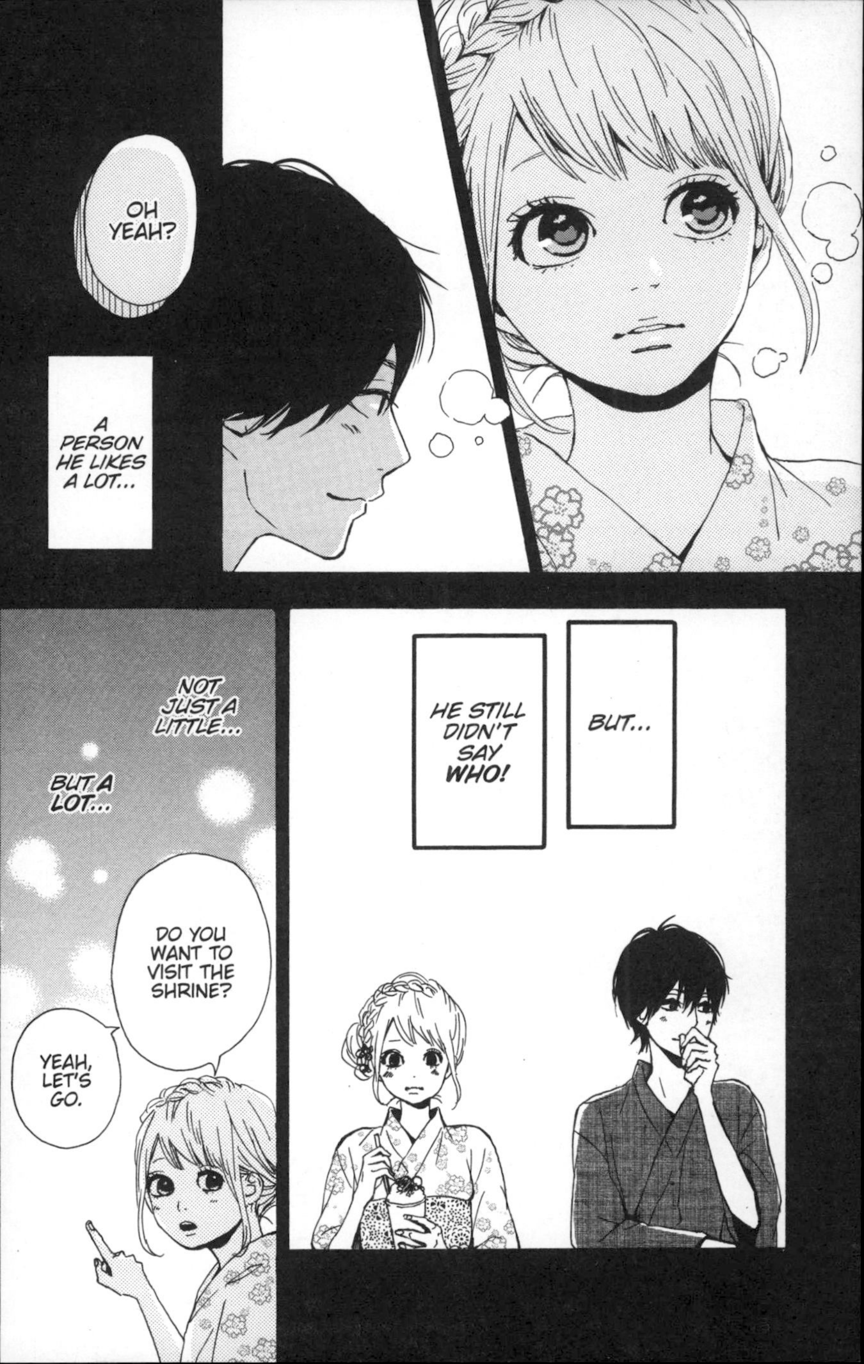
OH YEAH?
A PERSON HE LIKES A LOT...
BUT...
HE STILL DIDN'T SAY WHO!
NOT JUST A LITTLE...
BUT A LOT...
DO YOU WANT TO VISIT THE SHRINE?
YEAH, LET'S GO.

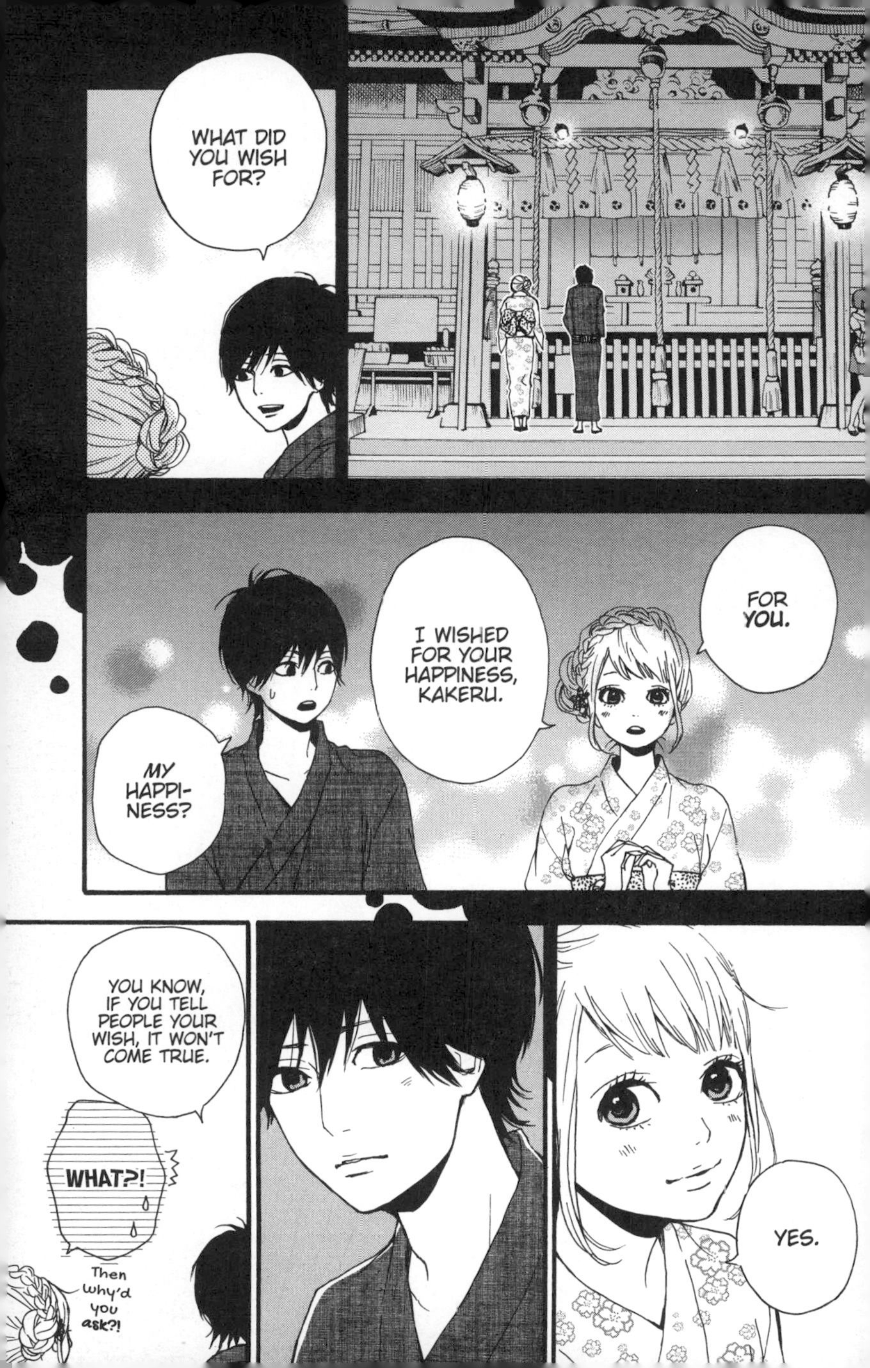
WHAT DID YOU WISH FOR?
FOR YOU.
I WISHED FOR YOUR HAPPINESS, KAKERU.
MY HAPPINESS?
YES.
YOU KNOW, IF YOU TELL PEOPLE YOUR WISH, IT WON'T COME TRUE.
WHAT?!
Then why'd you ask?!

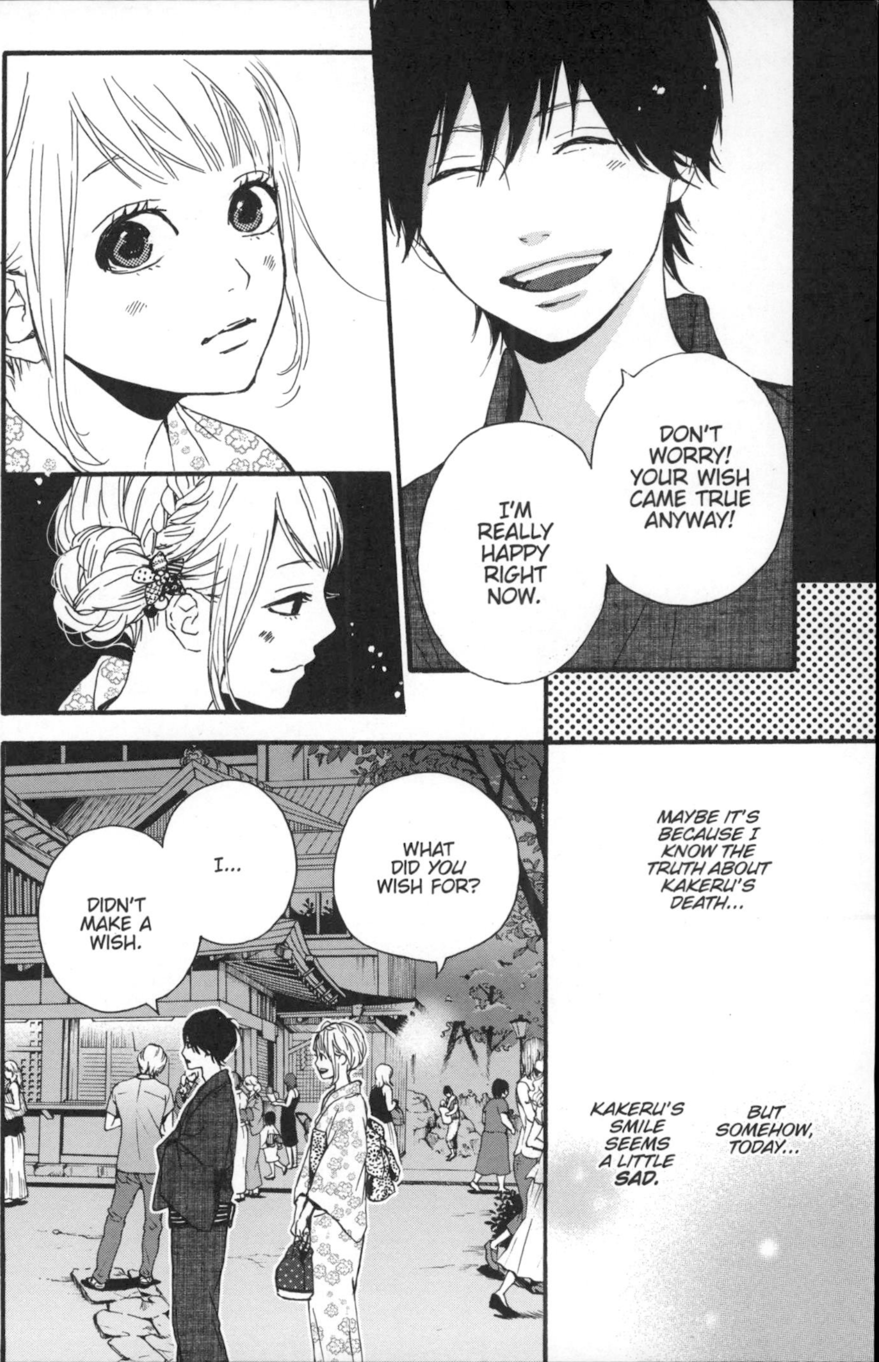
DON'T WORRY! YOUR WISH CAME TRUE ANYWAY!
I'M REALLY HAPPY RIGHT NOW.
MAYBE IT'S BECAUSE I KNOW THE TRUTH ABOUT KAKERU'S DEATH...
BUT SOMEHOW, TODAY...
KAKERU'S SMILE SEEMS A LITTLE SAD.
WHAT DID YOU WISH FOR?
I...
DIDN'T MAKE A WISH.

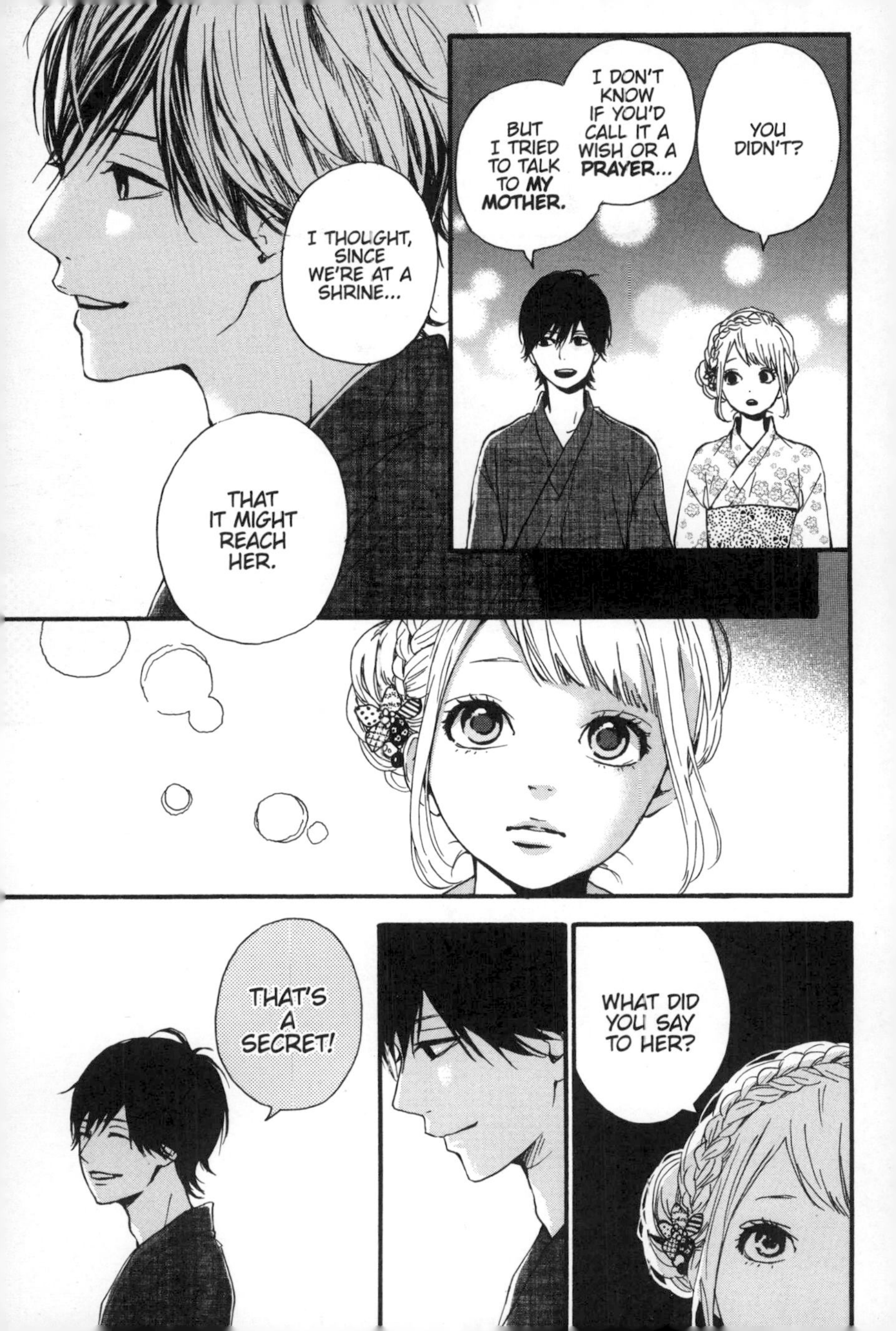
YOU DIDN'T?
I DON'T KNOW IF YOU'D CALL IT A WISH OR A PRAYER...
BUT I TRIED TO TALK TO MY MOTHER.
I THOUGHT, SINCE WE'RE AT A SHRINE...
THAT IT MIGHT REACH HER.
WHAT DID YOU SAY TO HER?
THAT'S A SECRET!

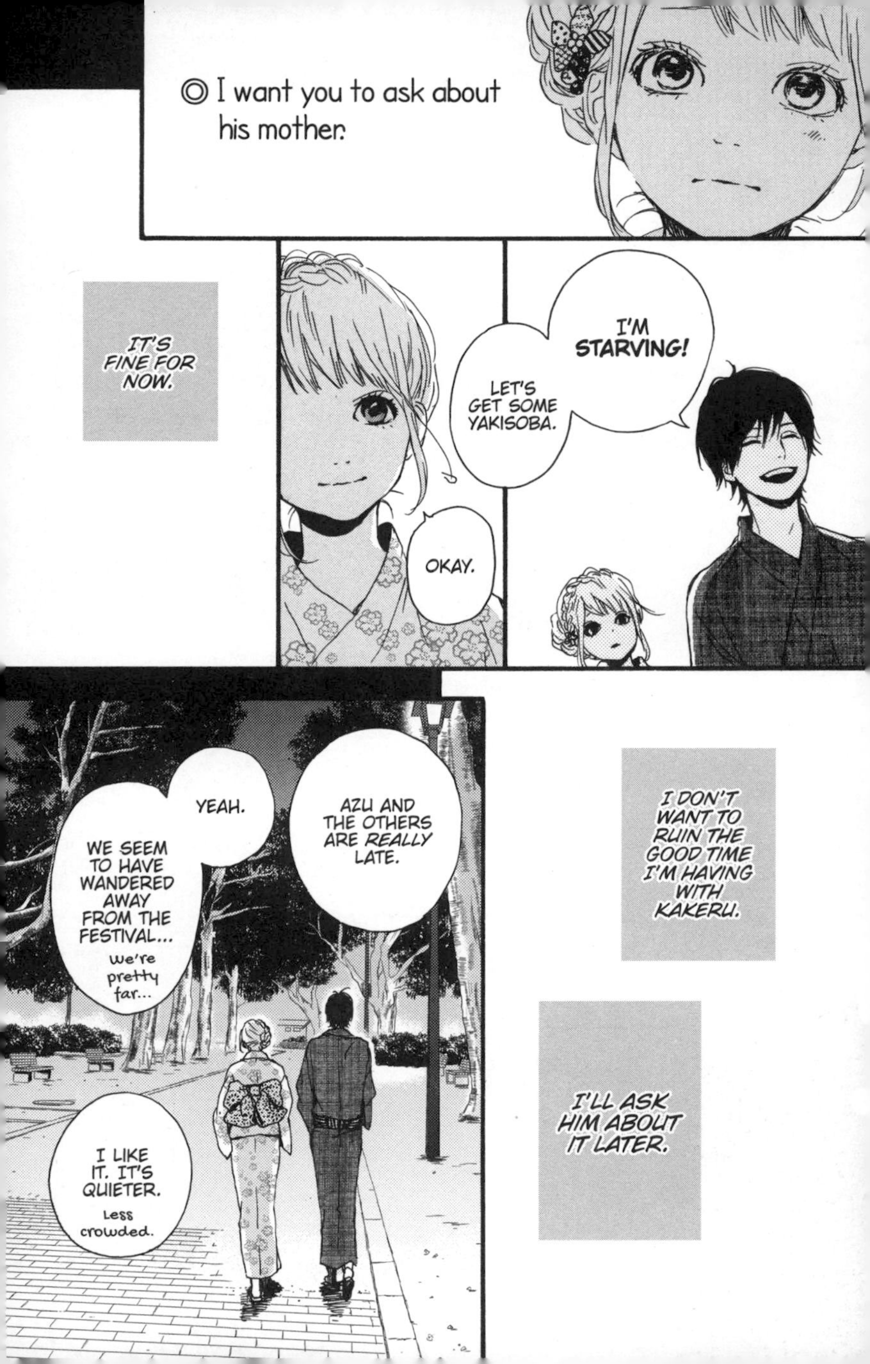
◎ I want you to ask about his mother.
I'M STARVING!
LET'S GET SOME YAKISOBA.
OKAY.
IT'S FINE FOR NOW.
I DON'T WANT TO RUIN THE GOOD TIME I'M HAVING WITH KAKERU.
I'LL ASK HIM ABOUT IT LATER.
AZU AND THE OTHERS ARE REALLY LATE.
YEAH.
WE SEEM TO HAVE WANDERED AWAY FROM THE FESTIVAL... we're pretty far...
I LIKE IT. IT'S QUIETER. Less crowded.

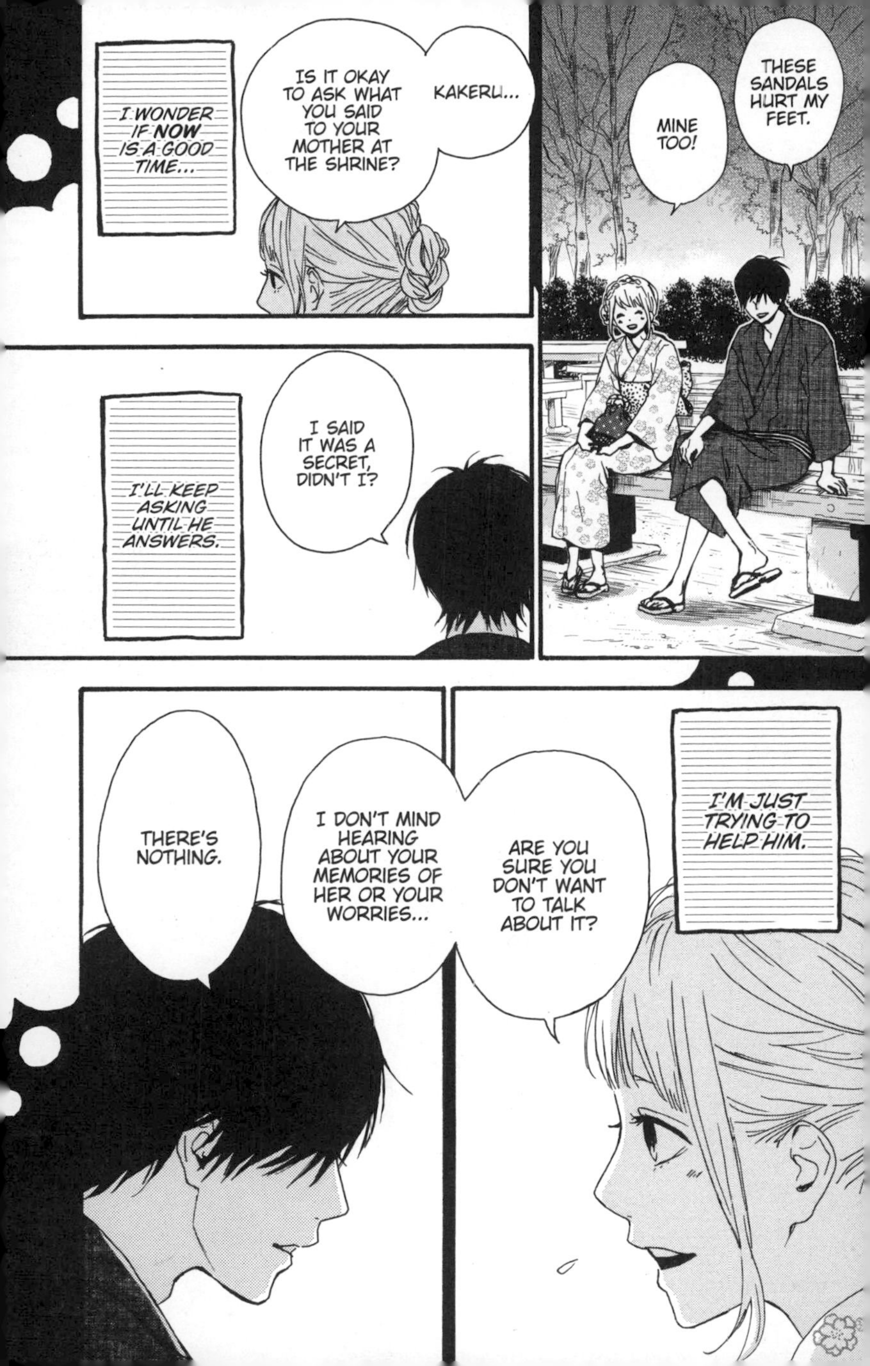
THESE SANDALS HURT MY FEET.
MINE TOO!
KAKERU...
IS IT OKAY TO ASK WHAT YOU SAID TO YOUR MOTHER AT THE SHRINE?
I WONDER IF **NOW** IS A GOOD TIME...
I SAID IT WAS A SECRET, DIDN'T I?
I'LL KEEP ASKING UNTIL HE ANSWERS.
I'M JUST TRYING TO HELP HIM.
ARE YOU SURE YOU DON'T WANT TO TALK ABOUT IT?
I DON'T MIND HEARING ABOUT YOUR MEMORIES OF HER OR YOUR WORRIES...
THERE'S NOTHING.

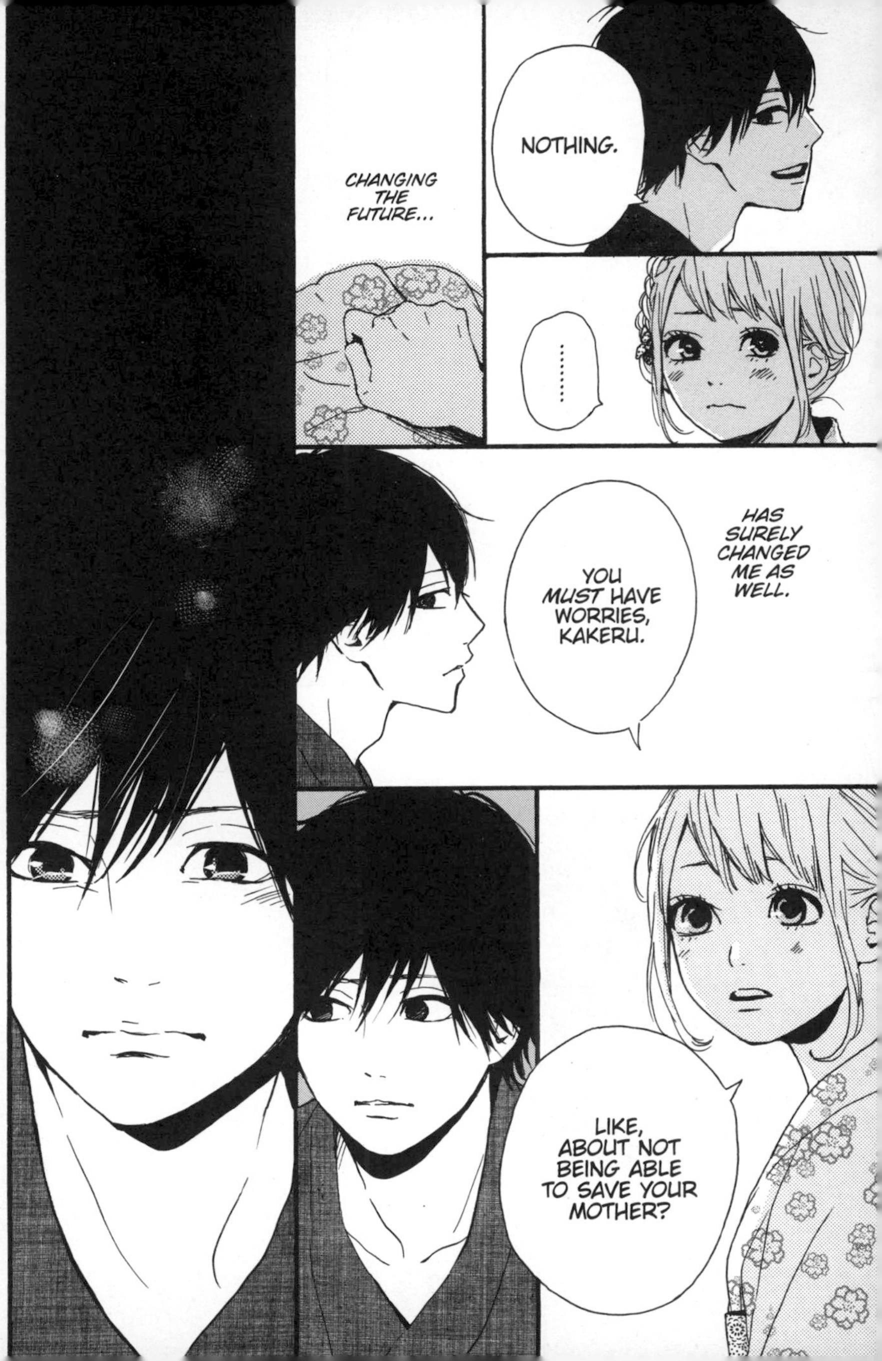
NOTHING.
......
CHANGING THE FUTURE...
HAS SURELY CHANGED ME AS WELL.
YOU MUST HAVE WORRIES, KAKERU.
LIKE, ABOUT NOT BEING ABLE TO SAVE YOUR MOTHER?

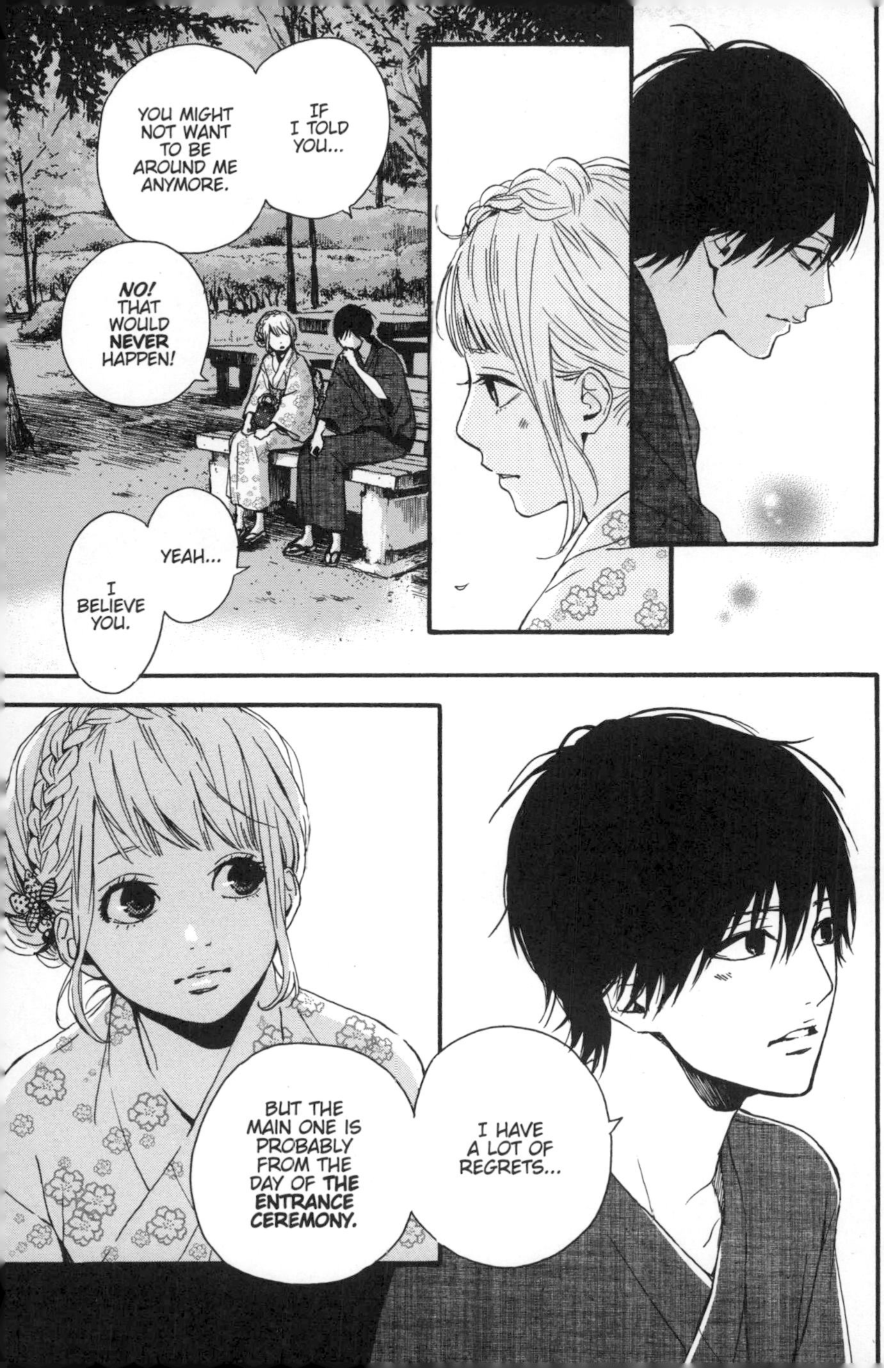
IF I TOLD YOU...
YOU MIGHT NOT WANT TO BE AROUND ME ANYMORE.
NO! THAT WOULD NEVER HAPPEN!
YEAH... I BELIEVE YOU.
I HAVE A LOT OF REGRETS...
BUT THE MAIN ONE IS PROBABLY FROM THE DAY OF THE ENTRANCE CEREMONY.

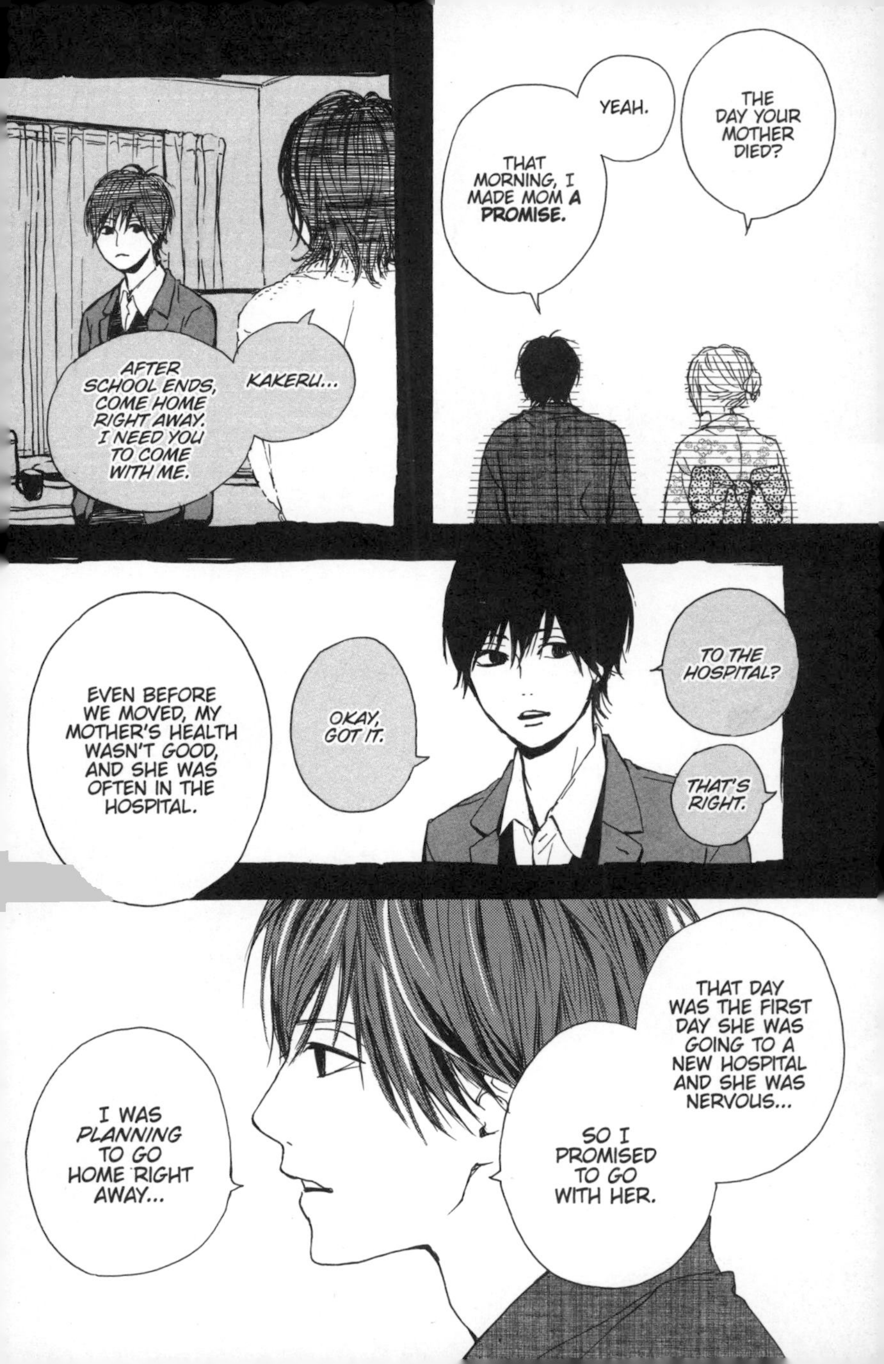
THE DAY YOUR MOTHER DIED?
YEAH.
THAT MORNING, I MADE MOM **A PROMISE.**
KAKERU...
AFTER SCHOOL ENDS, COME HOME RIGHT AWAY. I NEED YOU TO COME WITH ME.
TO THE HOSPITAL?
THAT'S RIGHT.
OKAY, GOT IT.
EVEN BEFORE WE MOVED, MY MOTHER'S HEALTH WASN'T GOOD, AND SHE WAS OFTEN IN THE HOSPITAL.
THAT DAY WAS THE FIRST DAY SHE WAS GOING TO A NEW HOSPITAL AND SHE WAS NERVOUS...
SO I PROMISED TO GO WITH HER.
I WAS *PLANNING* TO GO HOME RIGHT AWAY...

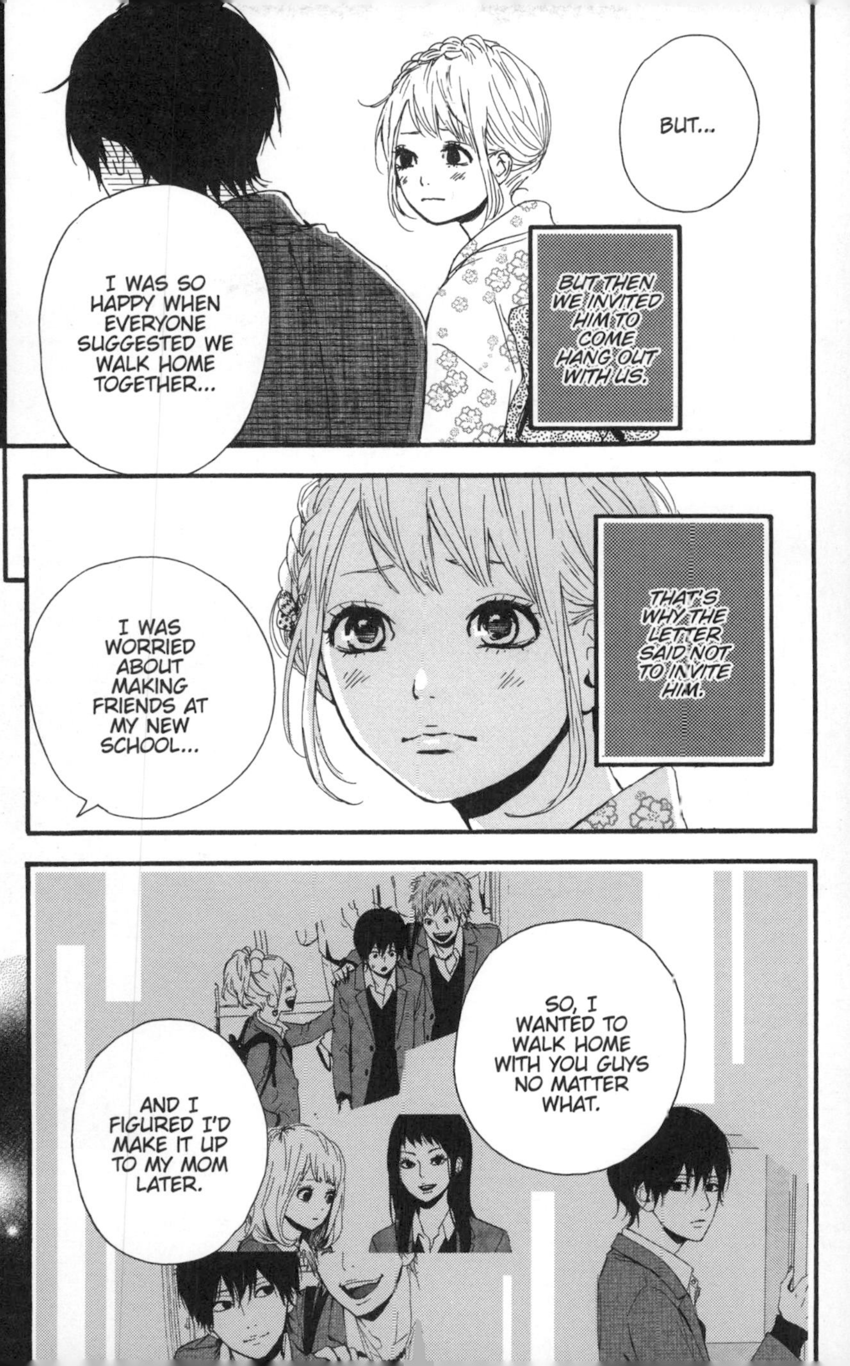
BUT...
BUT THEN WE INVITED HIM TO COME HANG OUT WITH US.
I WAS SO HAPPY WHEN EVERYONE SUGGESTED WE WALK HOME TOGETHER...
THAT'S WHY THE LETTER SAID NOT TO INVITE HIM.
I WAS WORRIED ABOUT MAKING FRIENDS AT MY NEW SCHOOL...
SO, I WANTED TO WALK HOME WITH YOU GUYS NO MATTER WHAT.
AND I FIGURED I'D MAKE IT UP TO MY MOM LATER.

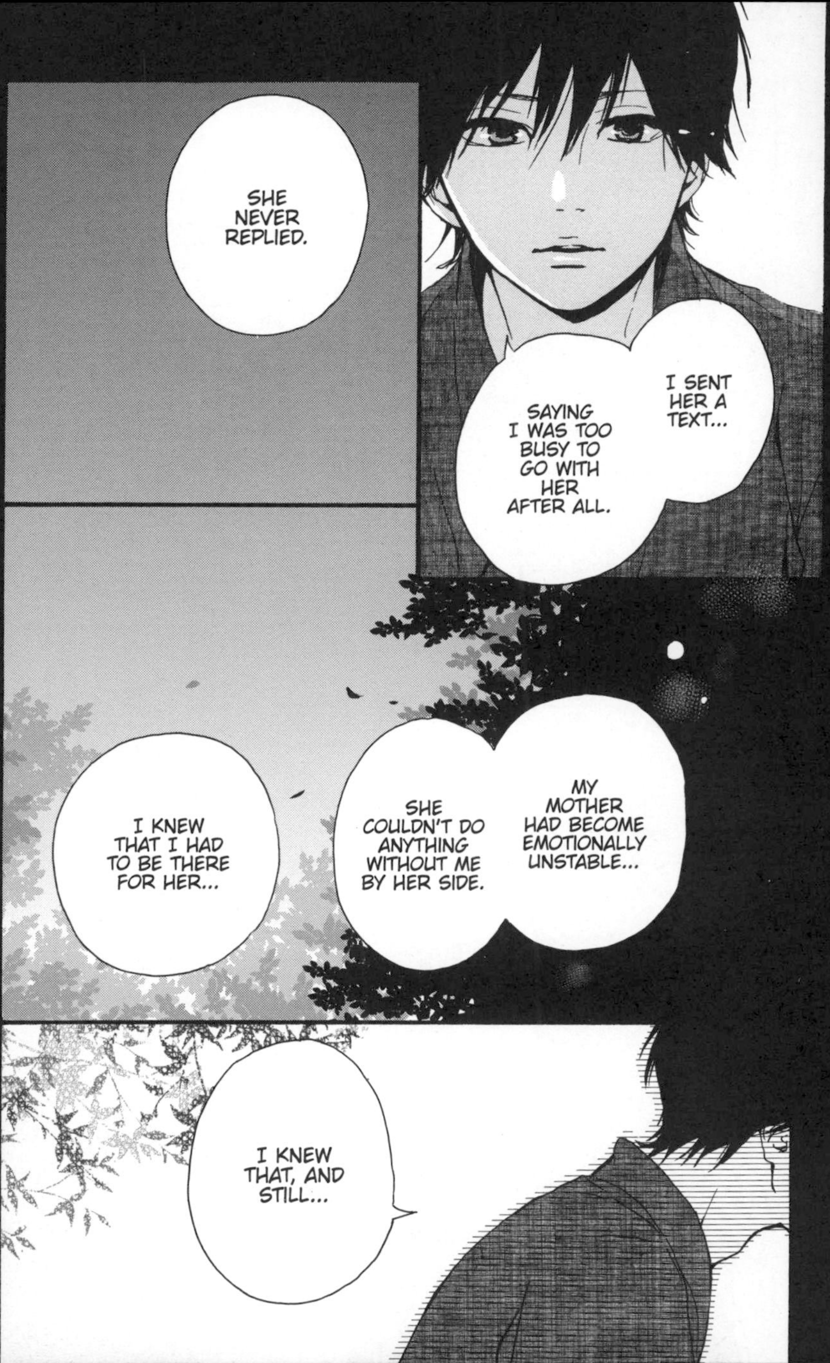
I SENT HER A TEXT...
SAYING I WAS TOO BUSY TO GO WITH HER AFTER ALL.
SHE NEVER REPLIED.
MY MOTHER HAD BECOME EMOTIONALLY UNSTABLE...
SHE COULDN'T DO ANYTHING WITHOUT ME BY HER SIDE.
I KNEW THAT I HAD TO BE THERE FOR HER...
I KNEW THAT, AND STILL...

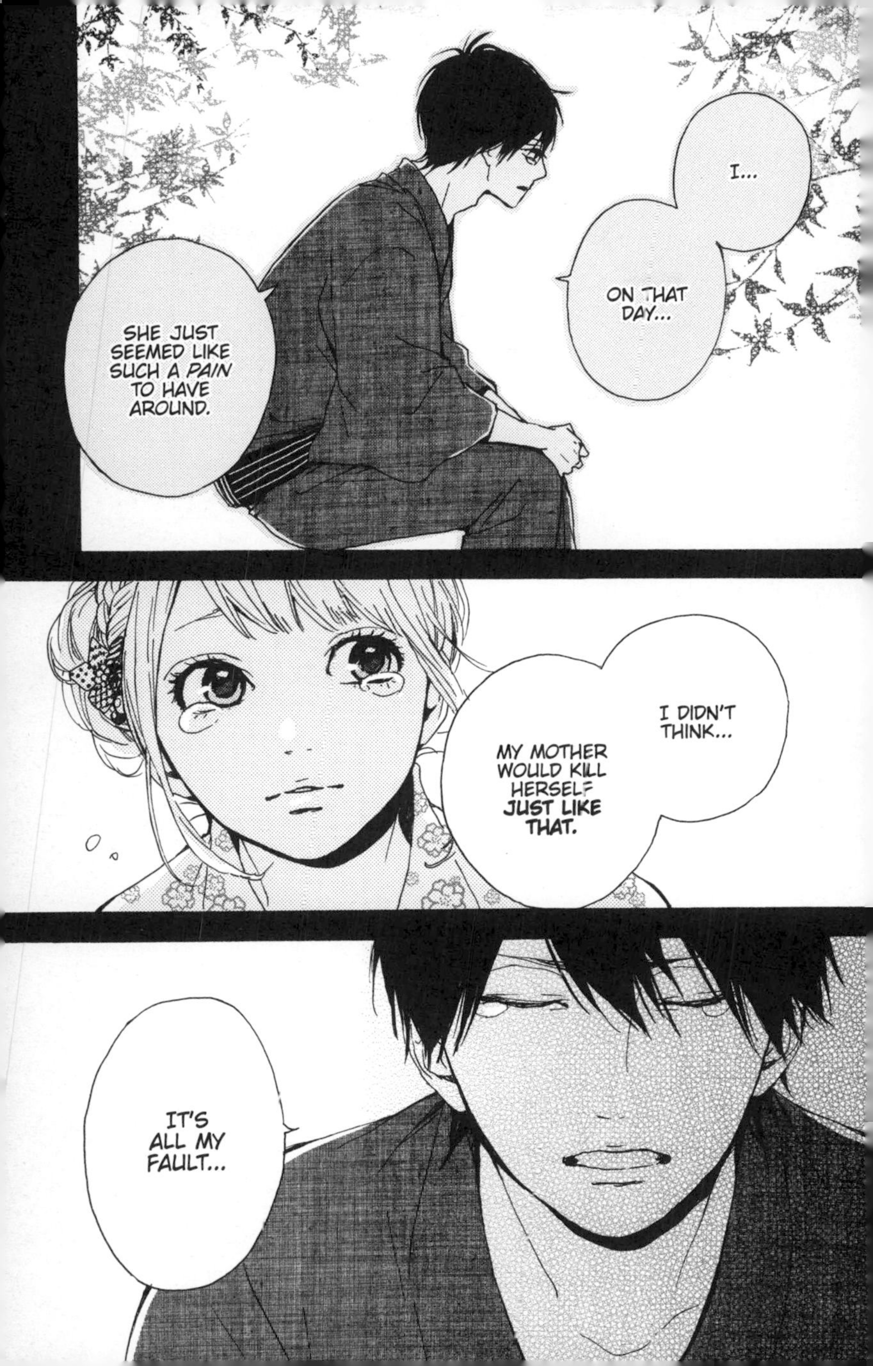
I...
ON THAT DAY...
SHE JUST SEEMED LIKE SUCH A *PAIN* TO HAVE AROUND.
I DIDN'T THINK...
MY MOTHER WOULD KILL HERSELF **JUST LIKE THAT.**
IT'S ALL MY FAULT...

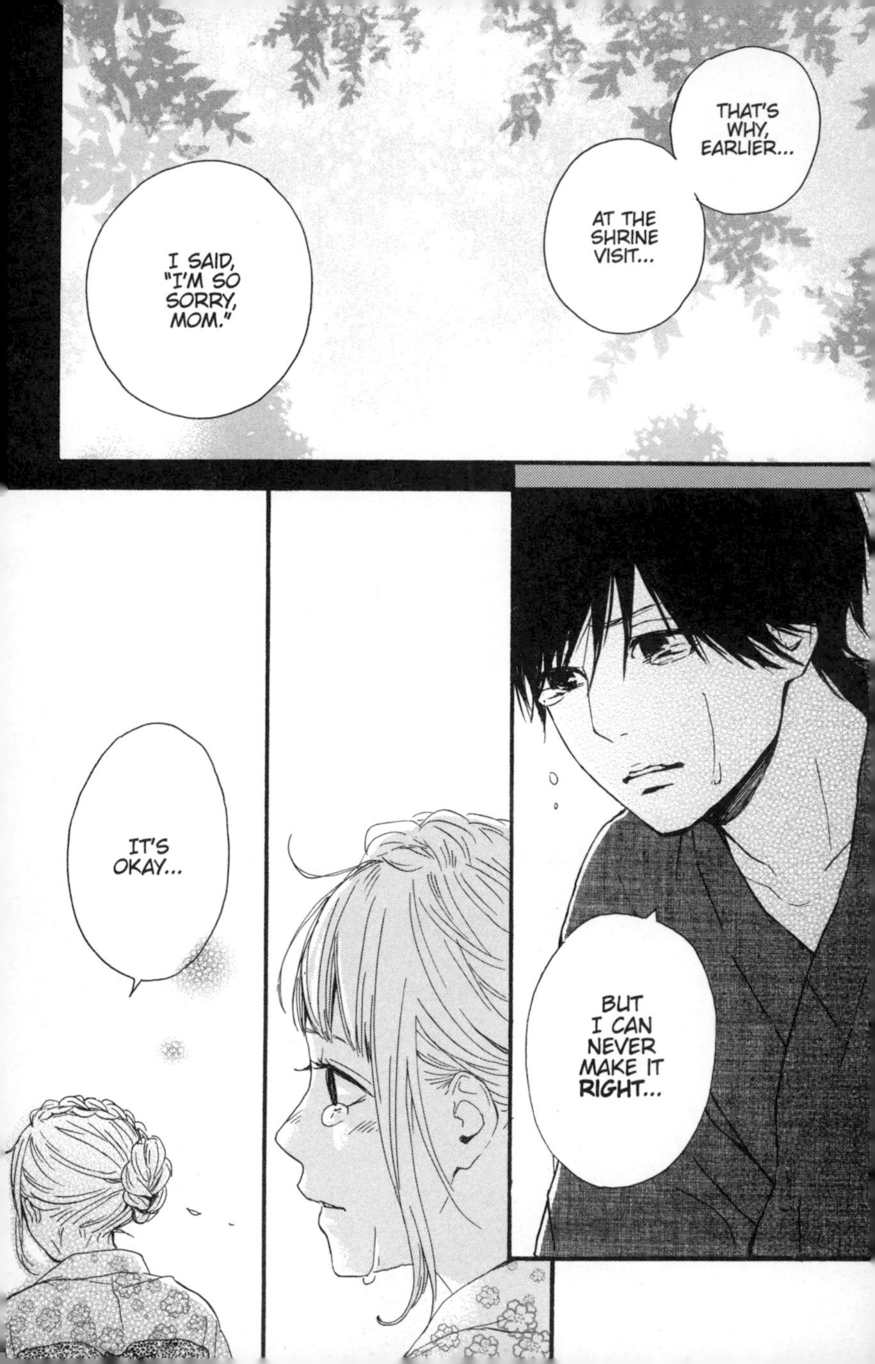
THAT'S WHY, EARLIER...
AT THE SHRINE VISIT...
I SAID, "I'M SO SORRY, MOM."
BUT I CAN NEVER MAKE IT **RIGHT**...
IT'S OKAY...

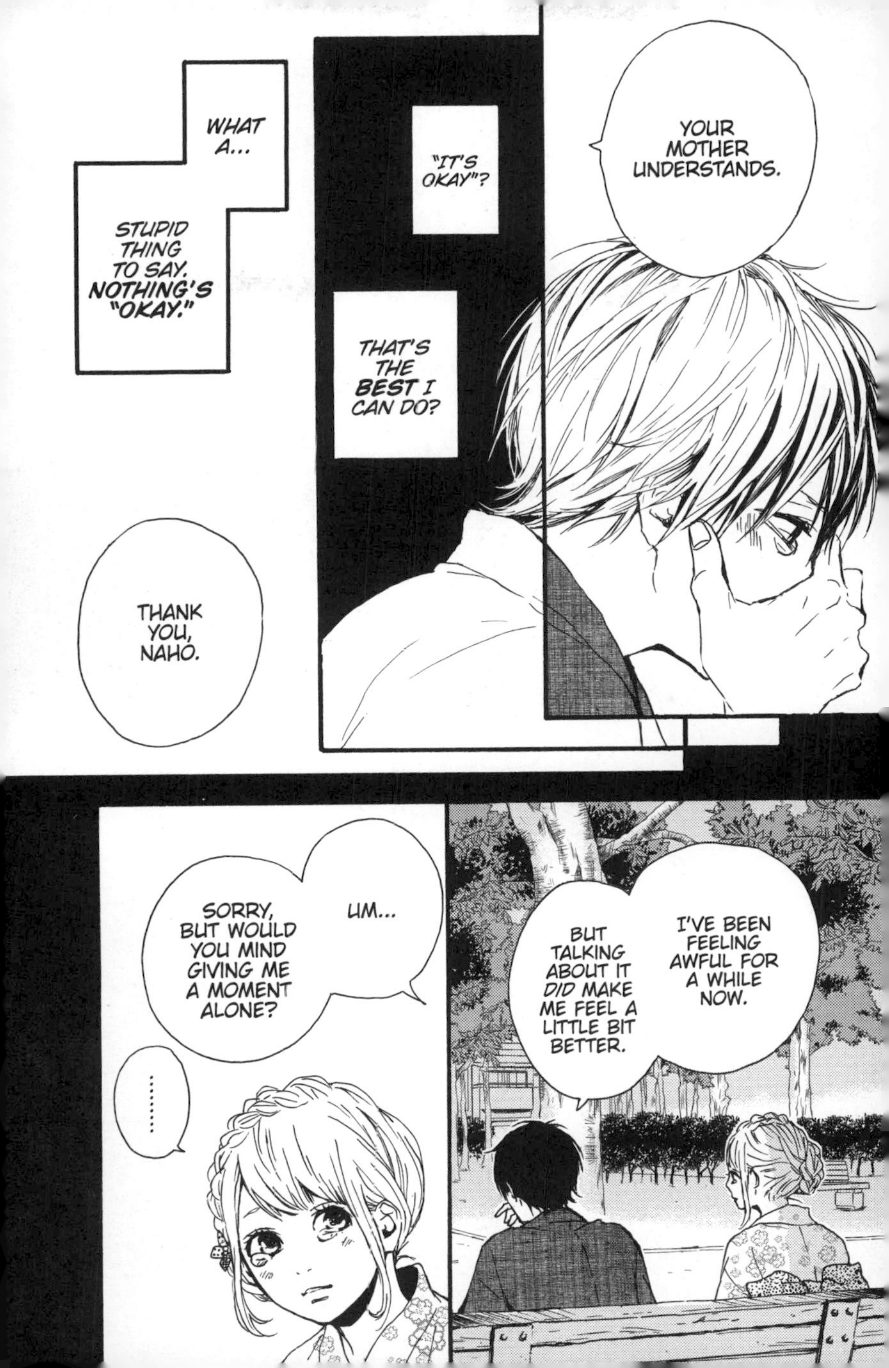
YOUR MOTHER UNDERSTANDS.
"IT'S OKAY"?
THAT'S THE BEST I CAN DO?
WHAT A...
STUPID THING TO SAY. NOTHING'S "OKAY."
THANK YOU, NAHO.
I'VE BEEN FEELING AWFUL FOR A WHILE NOW.
BUT TALKING ABOUT IT DID MAKE ME FEEL A LITTLE BIT BETTER.
UM...
SORRY, BUT WOULD YOU MIND GIVING ME A MOMENT ALONE?
......

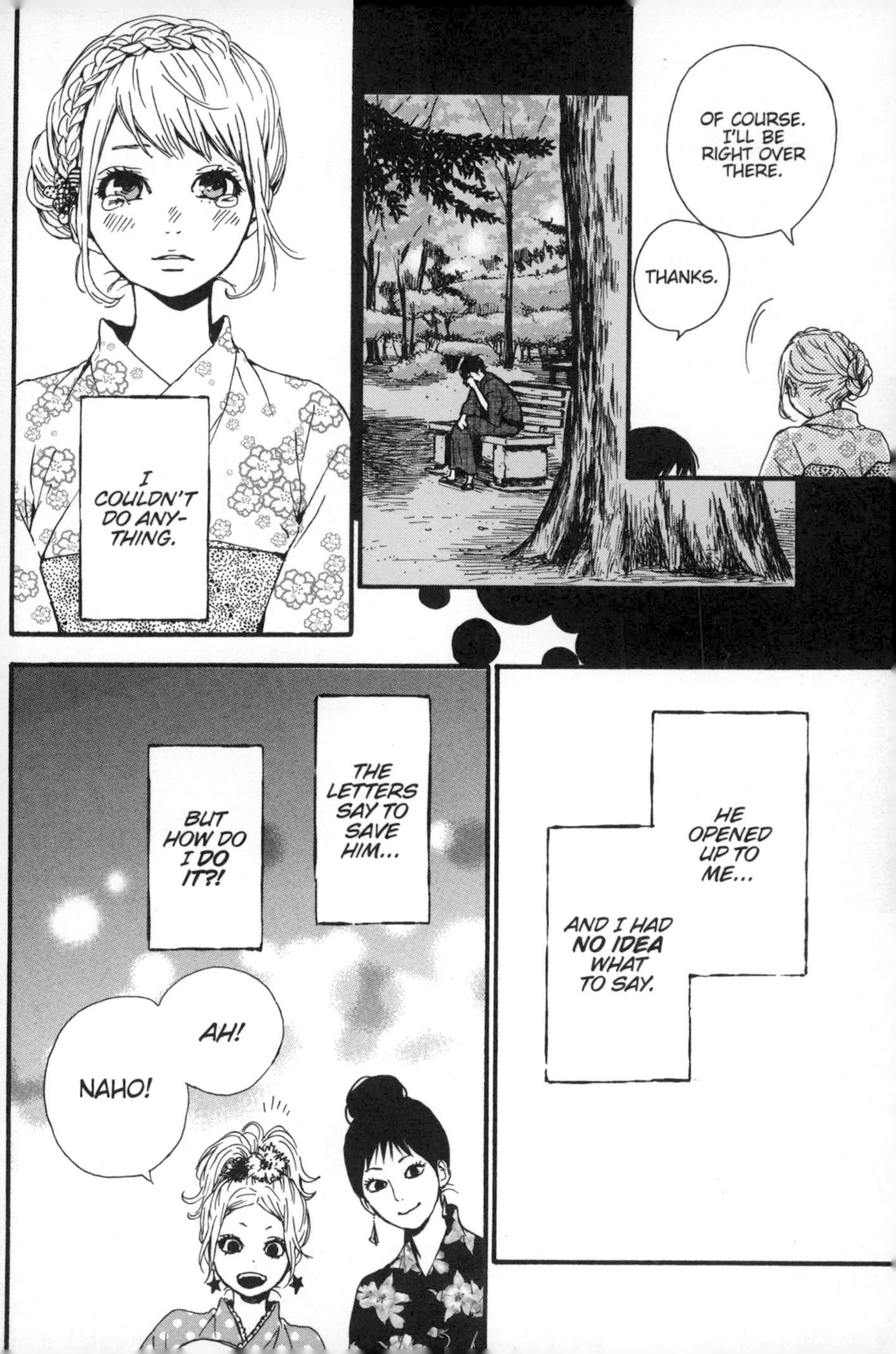
OF COURSE. I'LL BE RIGHT OVER THERE.
THANKS.
I COULDN'T DO ANYTHING.
HE OPENED UP TO ME...
AND I HAD NO IDEA WHAT TO SAY.
THE LETTERS SAY TO SAVE HIM...
BUT HOW DO I DO IT?!
AH!
NAHO!

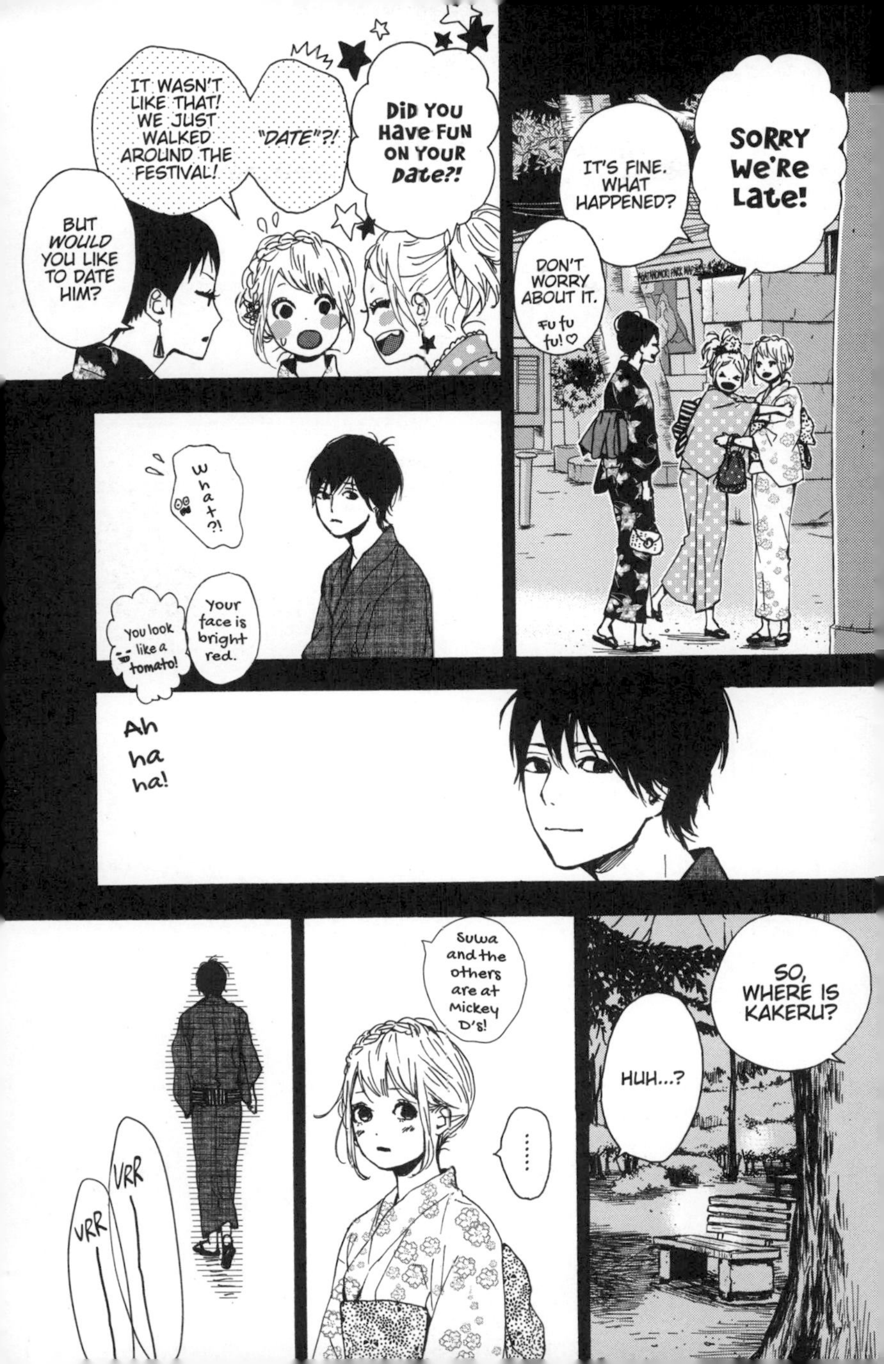
SORRY WE'RE LATE!
IT'S FINE. WHAT HAPPENED?
DON'T WORRY ABOUT IT.
Fu fu fu! ♡
DID YOU HAVE FUN ON YOUR DATE?!
"DATE"?!
IT WASN'T LIKE THAT! WE JUST WALKED AROUND THE FESTIVAL!
BUT WOULD YOU LIKE TO DATE HIM?
What?!
Your face is bright red.
You look like a tomato!
Ah ha ha!
SO, WHERE IS KAKERU?
HUH...?
Suwa and the others are at Mickey D's!
......
VRR
VRR

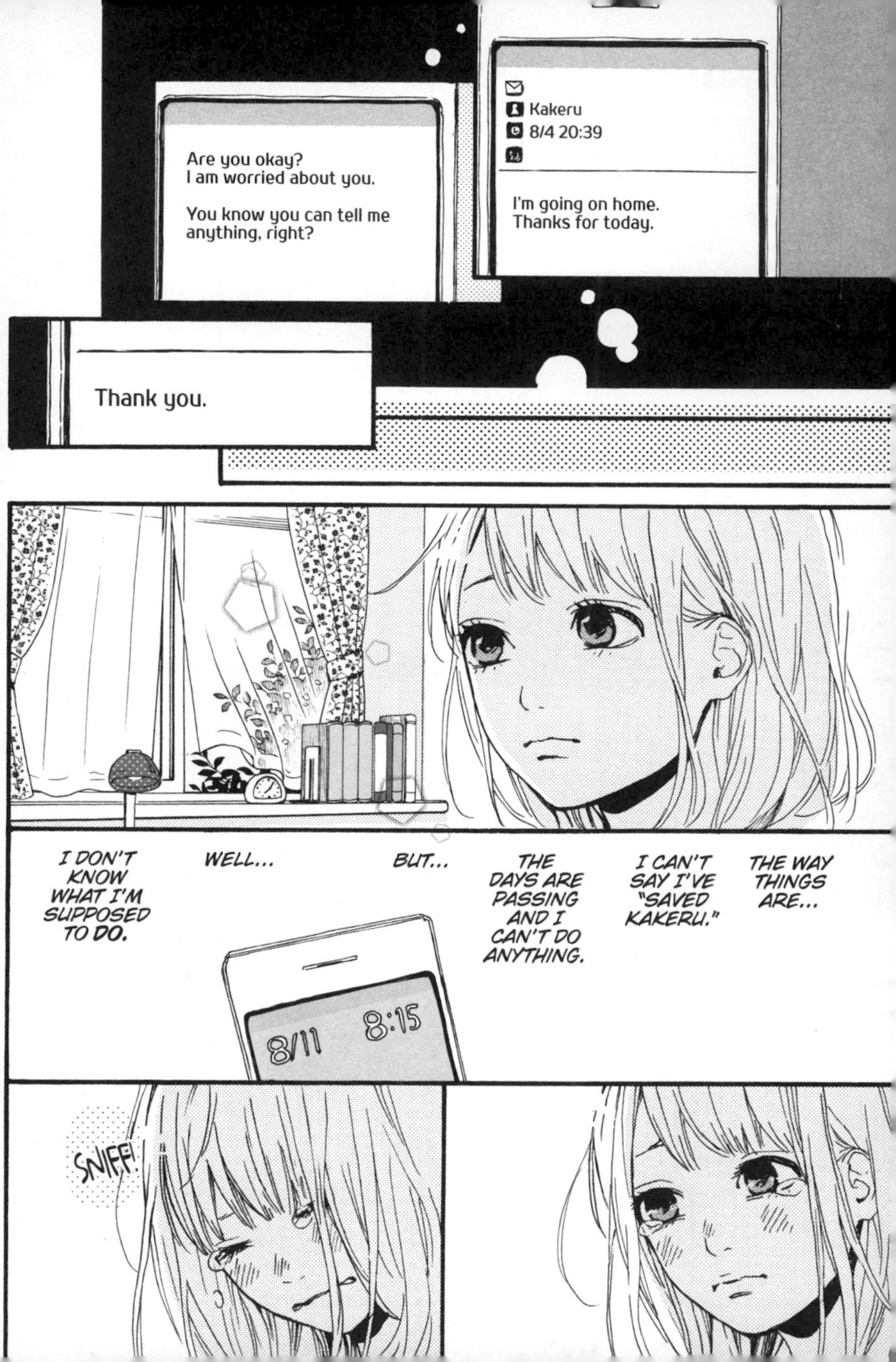
Kakeru
8/4 20:39
I'm going on home. Thanks for today.
Are you okay? I am worried about you.
You know you can tell me anything, right?
Thank you.
THE WAY THINGS ARE...
I CAN'T SAY I'VE "SAVED KAKERU."
THE DAYS ARE PASSING AND I CAN'T DO ANYTHING.
BUT...
WELL...
I DON'T KNOW WHAT I'M SUPPOSED TO DO.
8/11 8:15
SNIFF!

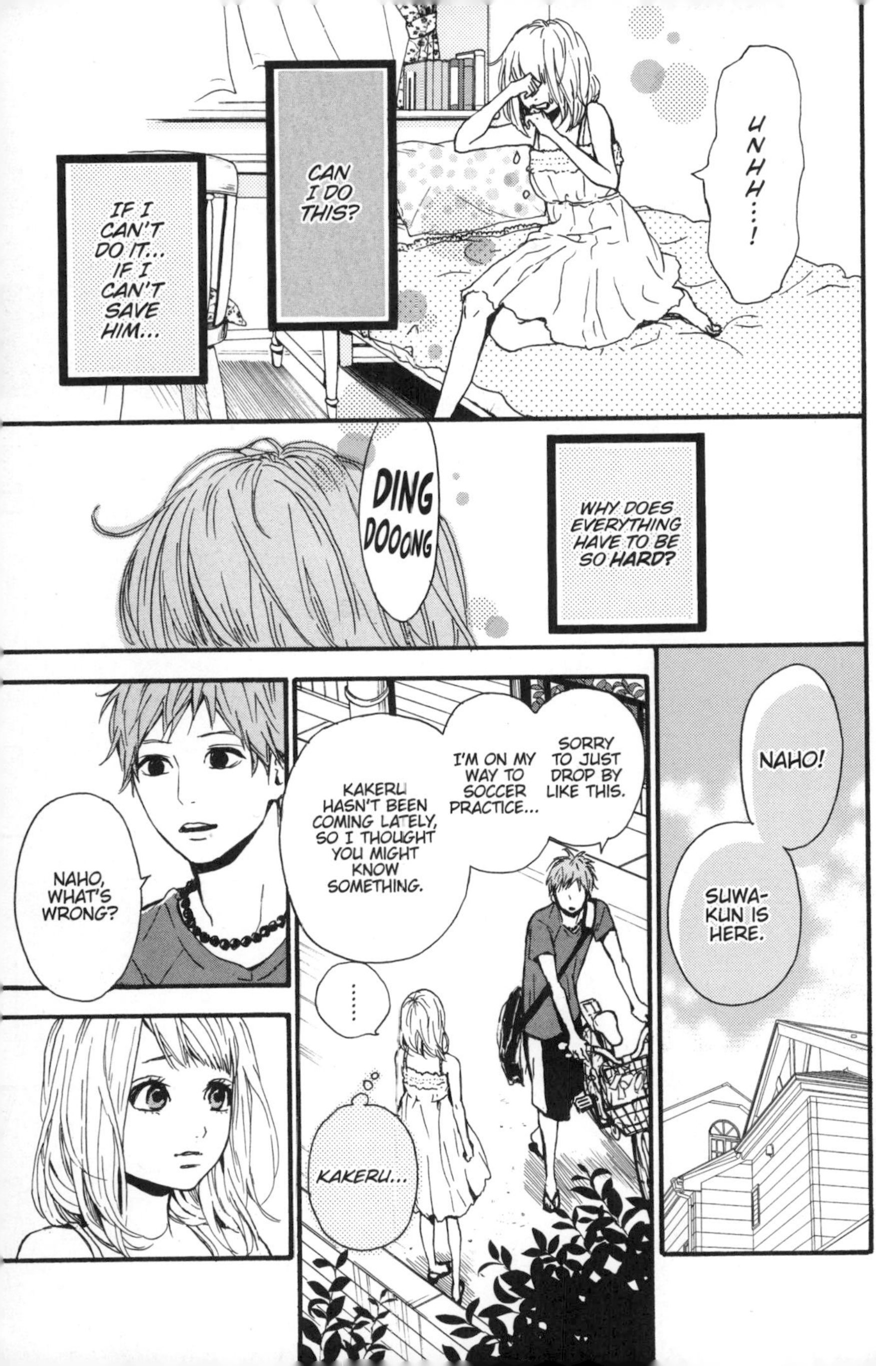
UNHH...!
CAN I DO THIS?
IF I CAN'T DO IT... IF I CAN'T SAVE HIM...
WHY DOES EVERYTHING HAVE TO BE SO HARD?
DING DOOONG
NAHO!
SUWA-KUN IS HERE.
SORRY TO JUST DROP BY LIKE THIS.
I'M ON MY WAY TO SOCCER PRACTICE...
KAKERU HASN'T BEEN COMING LATELY, SO I THOUGHT YOU MIGHT KNOW SOMETHING.
......
KAKERU...
NAHO, WHAT'S WRONG?

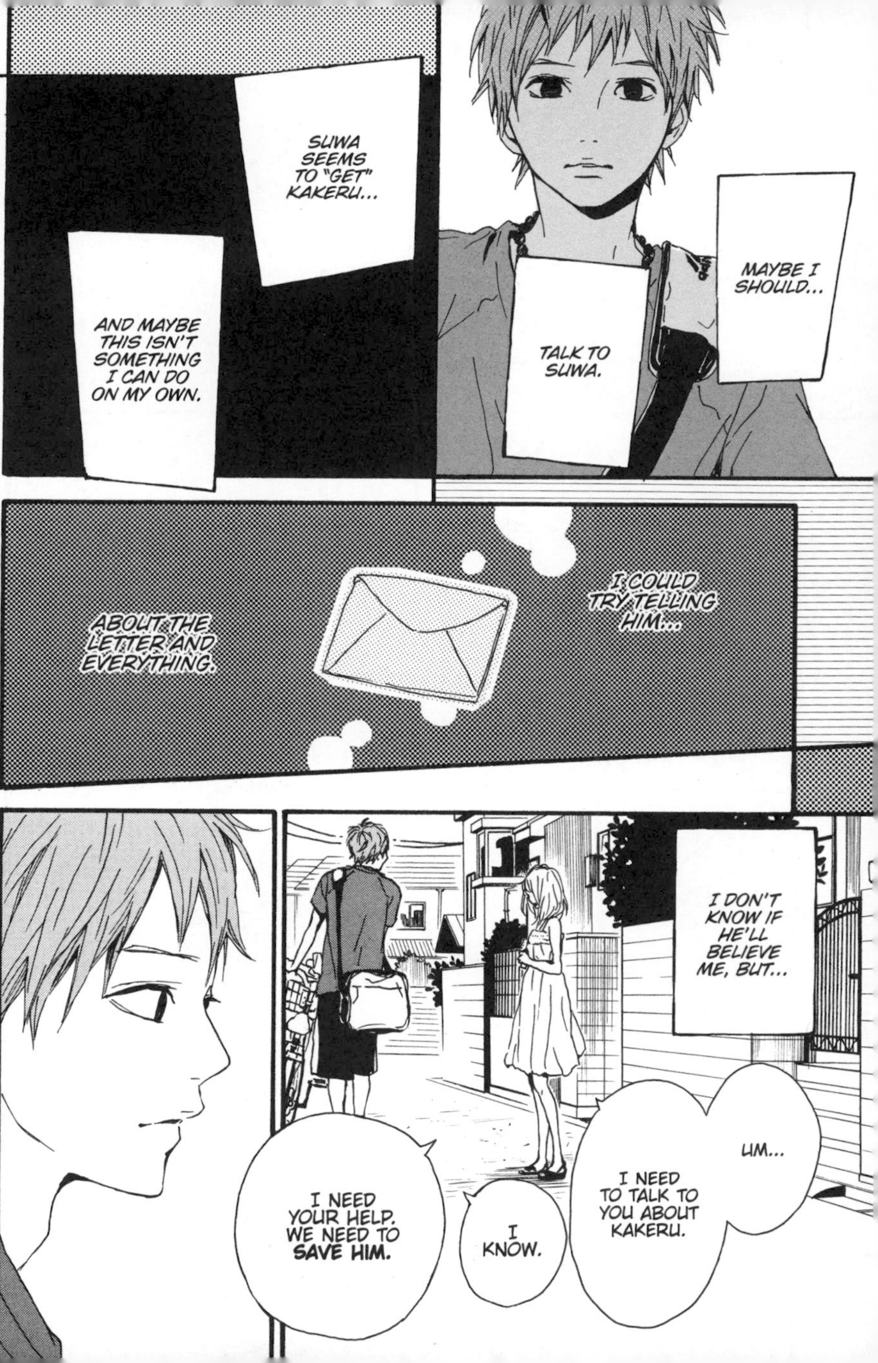
MAYBE I SHOULD...
TALK TO SUWA.
SUWA SEEMS TO "GET" KAKERU...
AND MAYBE THIS ISN'T SOMETHING I CAN DO ON MY OWN.
I COULD TRY TELLING HIM...
ABOUT THE LETTER AND EVERYTHING.
I DON'T KNOW IF HE'LL BELIEVE ME, BUT...
UM...
I NEED TO TALK TO YOU ABOUT KAKERU.
I KNOW.
I NEED YOUR HELP. WE NEED TO **SAVE HIM.**

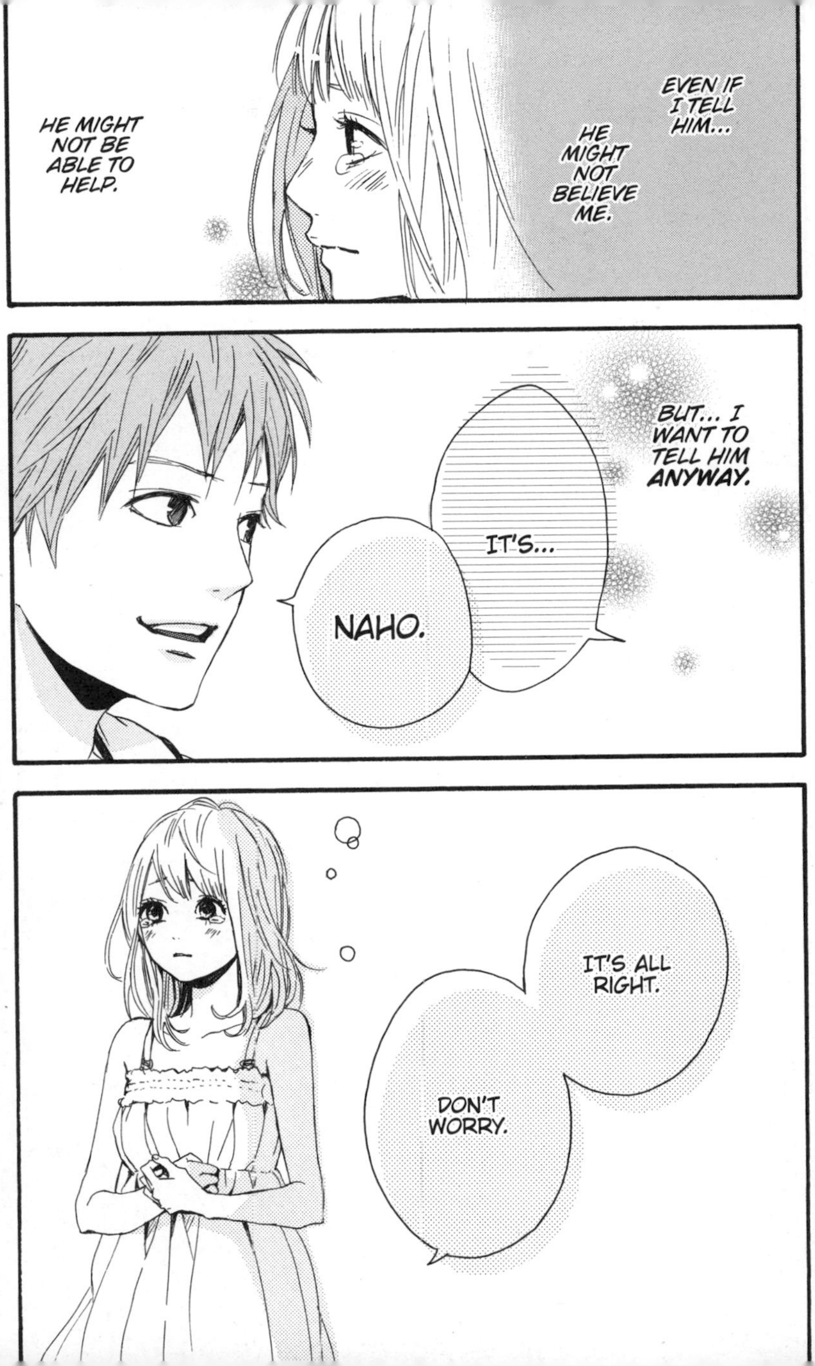
EVEN IF I TELL HIM...
HE MIGHT NOT BELIEVE ME.
HE MIGHT NOT BE ABLE TO HELP.
BUT... I WANT TO TELL HIM ANYWAY.
IT'S...
NAHO.
IT'S ALL RIGHT.
DON'T WORRY.

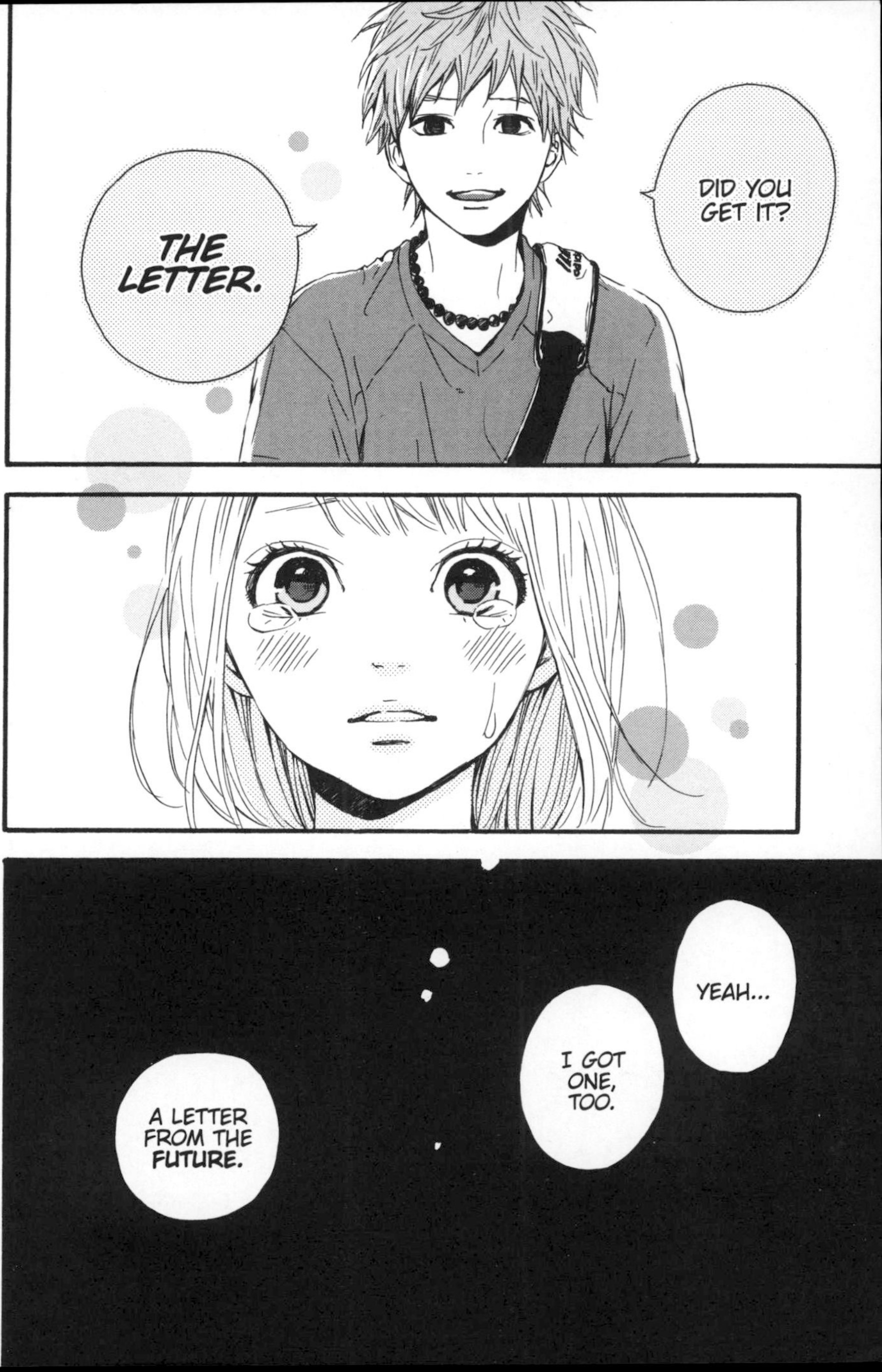
DID YOU GET IT?
THE LETTER.
YEAH...
I GOT ONE, TOO.
A LETTER FROM THE FUTURE.

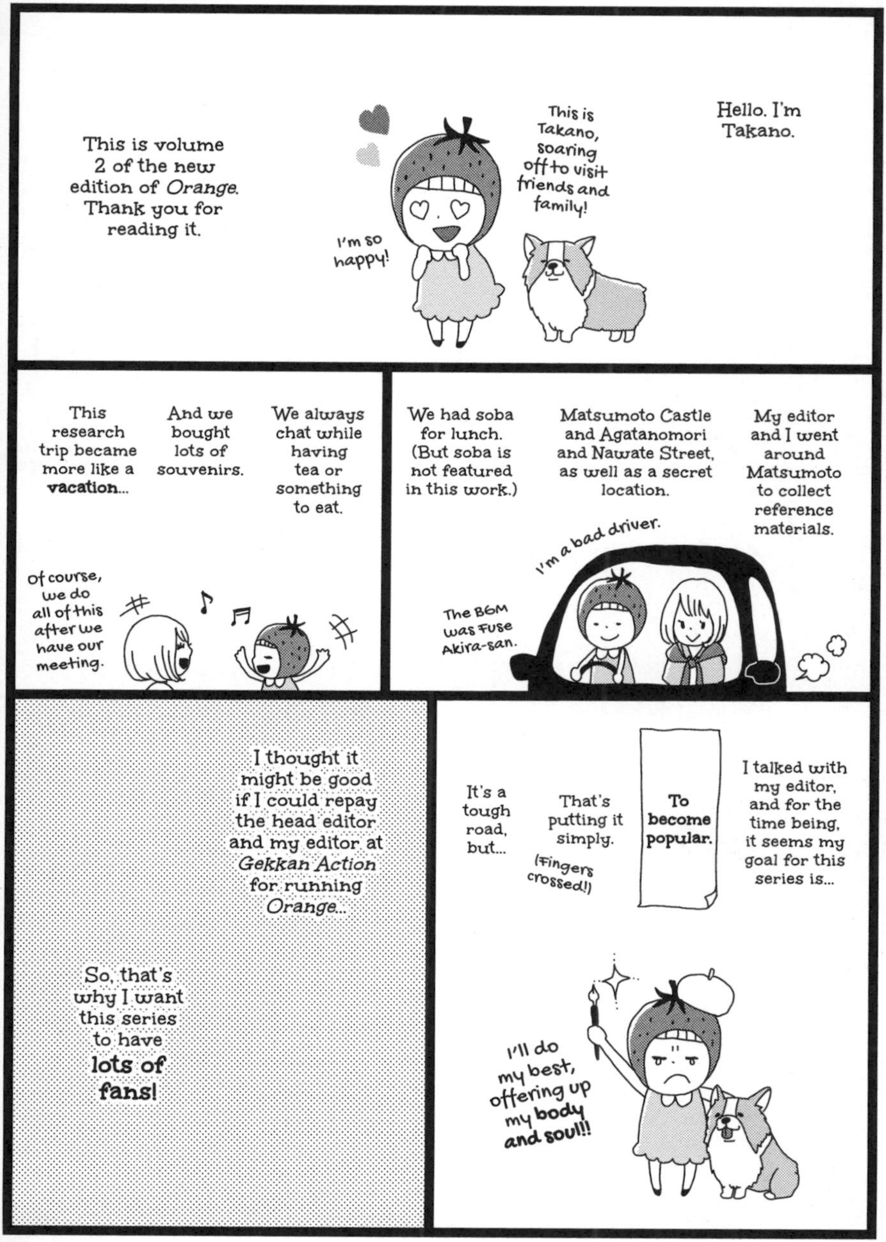
Hello. I'm Takano.
This is Takano, soaring off to visit friends and family!
This is volume 2 of the new edition of *Orange*. Thank you for reading it.
I'm so happy!
My editor and I went around Matsumoto to collect reference materials.
Matsumoto Castle and Agatanomori and Nawate Street, as well as a secret location.
We had soba for lunch. (But soba is not featured in this work.)
I'm a bad driver.
The BGM was Fuse Akira-san.
We always chat while having tea or something to eat.
And we bought lots of souvenirs.
This research trip became more like a **vacation**...
Of course, we do all of this after we have our meeting.
I talked with my editor, and for the time being, it seems my goal for this series is...
To become popular.
That's putting it simply.
(Fingers crossed!)
It's a tough road, but...
I'll do my best, offering up my **body and soul!!**
I thought it might be good if I could repay the head editor and my editor at *Gekkan Action* for running *Orange*...
So, that's why I want this series to have **lots of fans!**

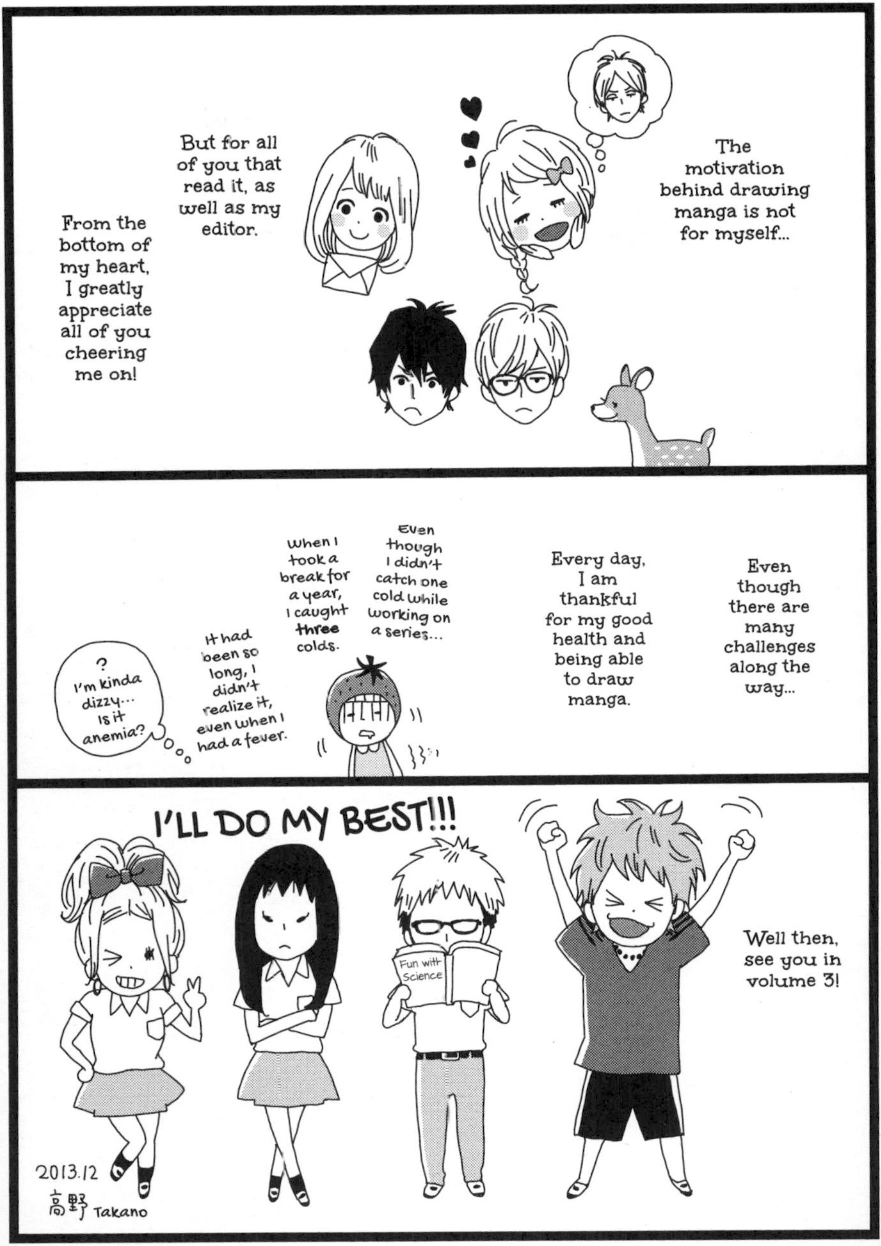

The motivation behind drawing manga is not for myself...
But for all of you that read it, as well as my editor.
From the bottom of my heart, I greatly appreciate all of you cheering me on!
Even though there are many challenges along the way...
Every day, I am thankful for my good health and being able to draw manga.
Even though I didn't catch one cold while working on a series...
When I took a break for a year, I caught three colds.
It had been so long, I didn't realize it, even when I had a fever.
? I'm kinda dizzy... Is it anemia?
I'LL DO MY BEST!!!
Well then, see you in volume 3!
Fun with Science
2013.12
高野 Takano

orange

orange

ICHIGO TAKANO presents

3

the third
volume

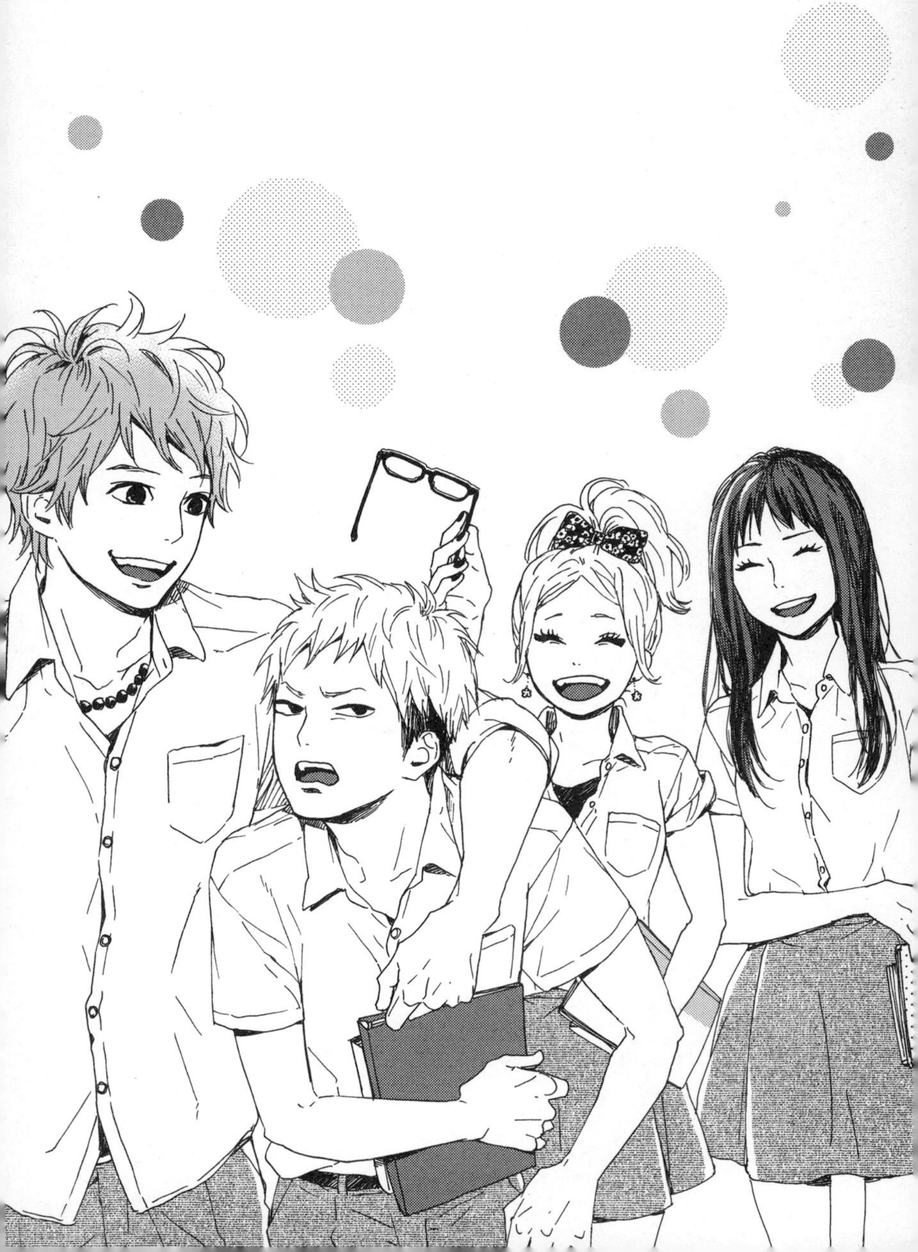

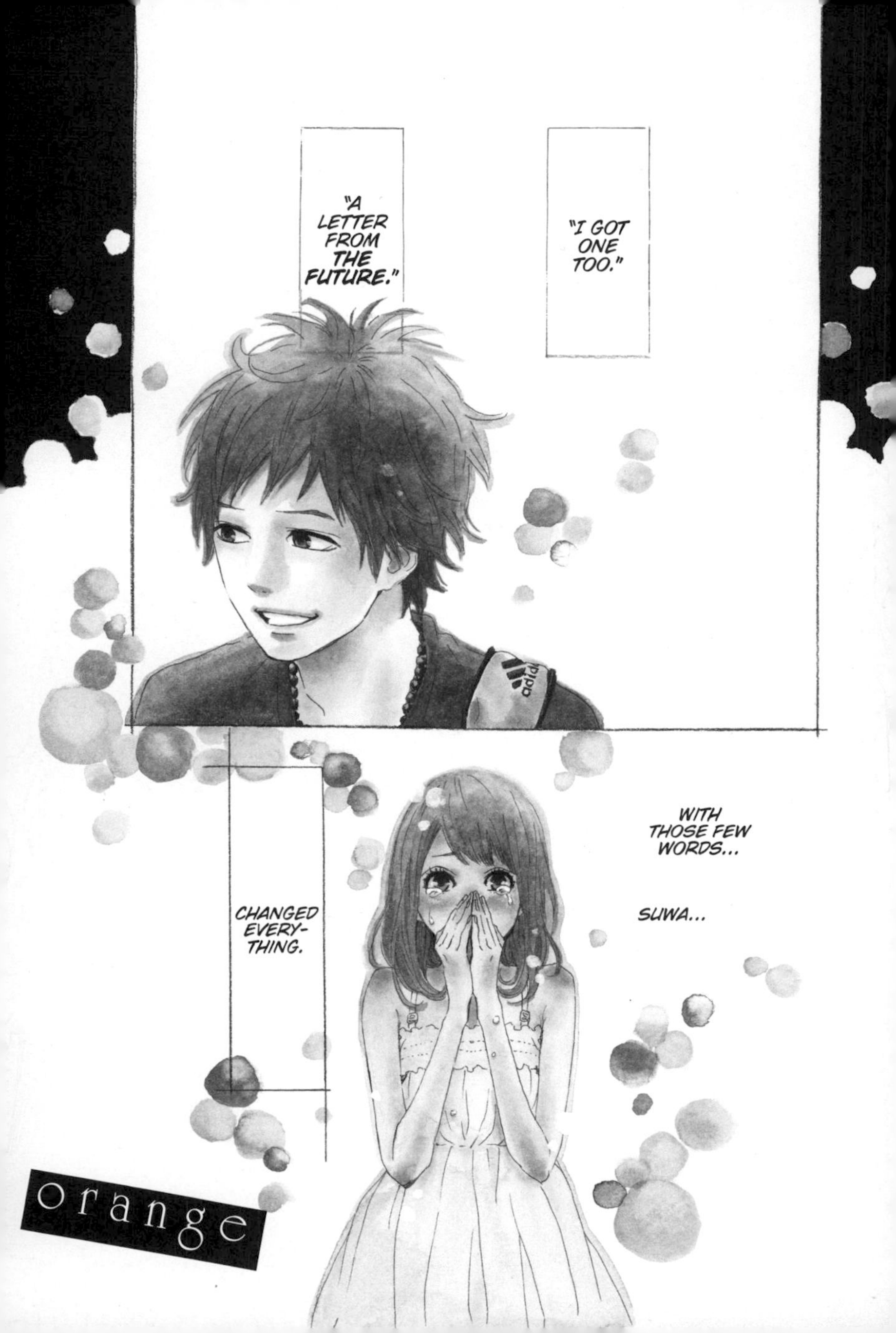
"I GOT ONE TOO."
"A LETTER FROM THE FUTURE."
WITH THOSE FEW WORDS...
SUWA...
CHANGED EVERY-THING.
orange

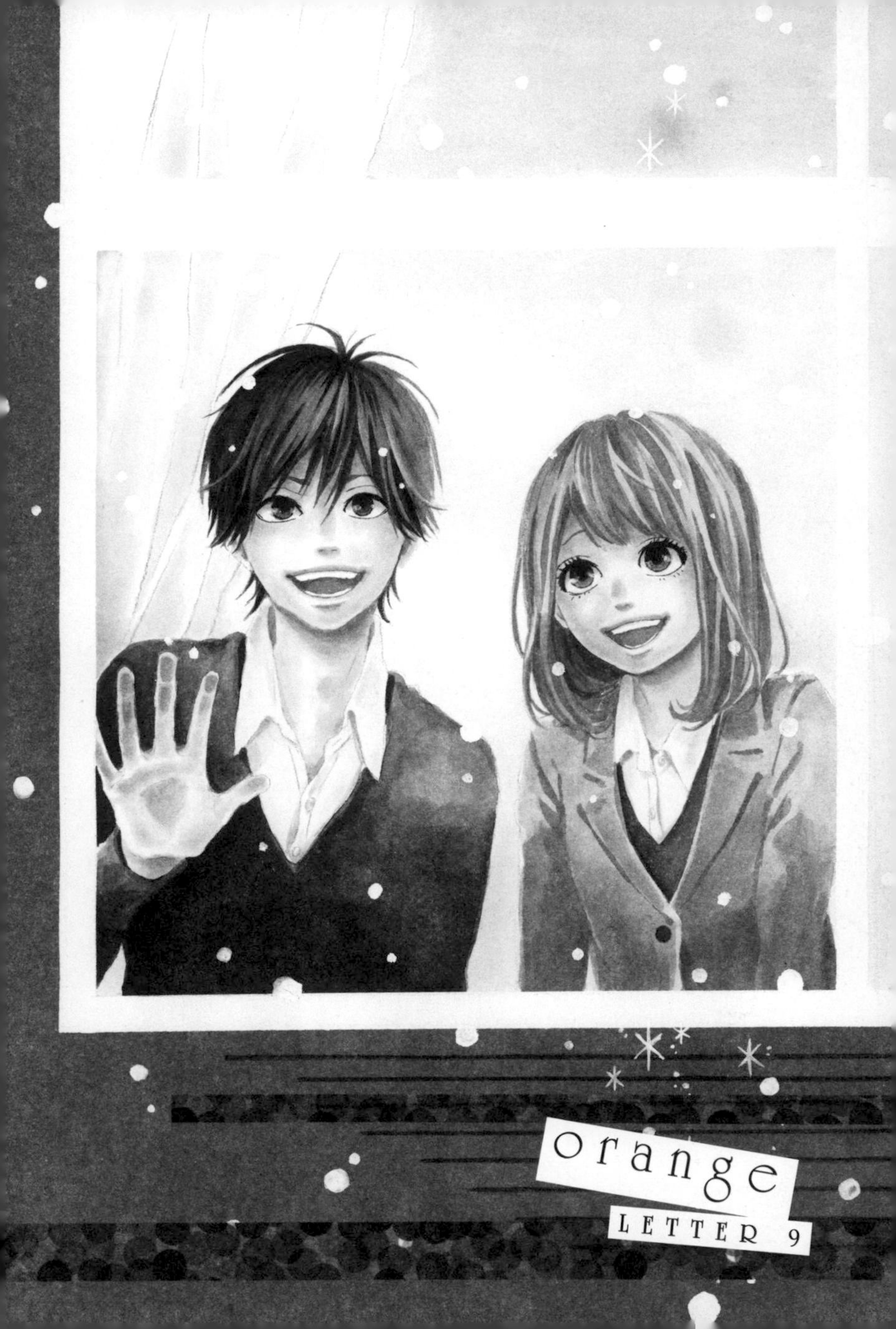
orange
LETTER 9

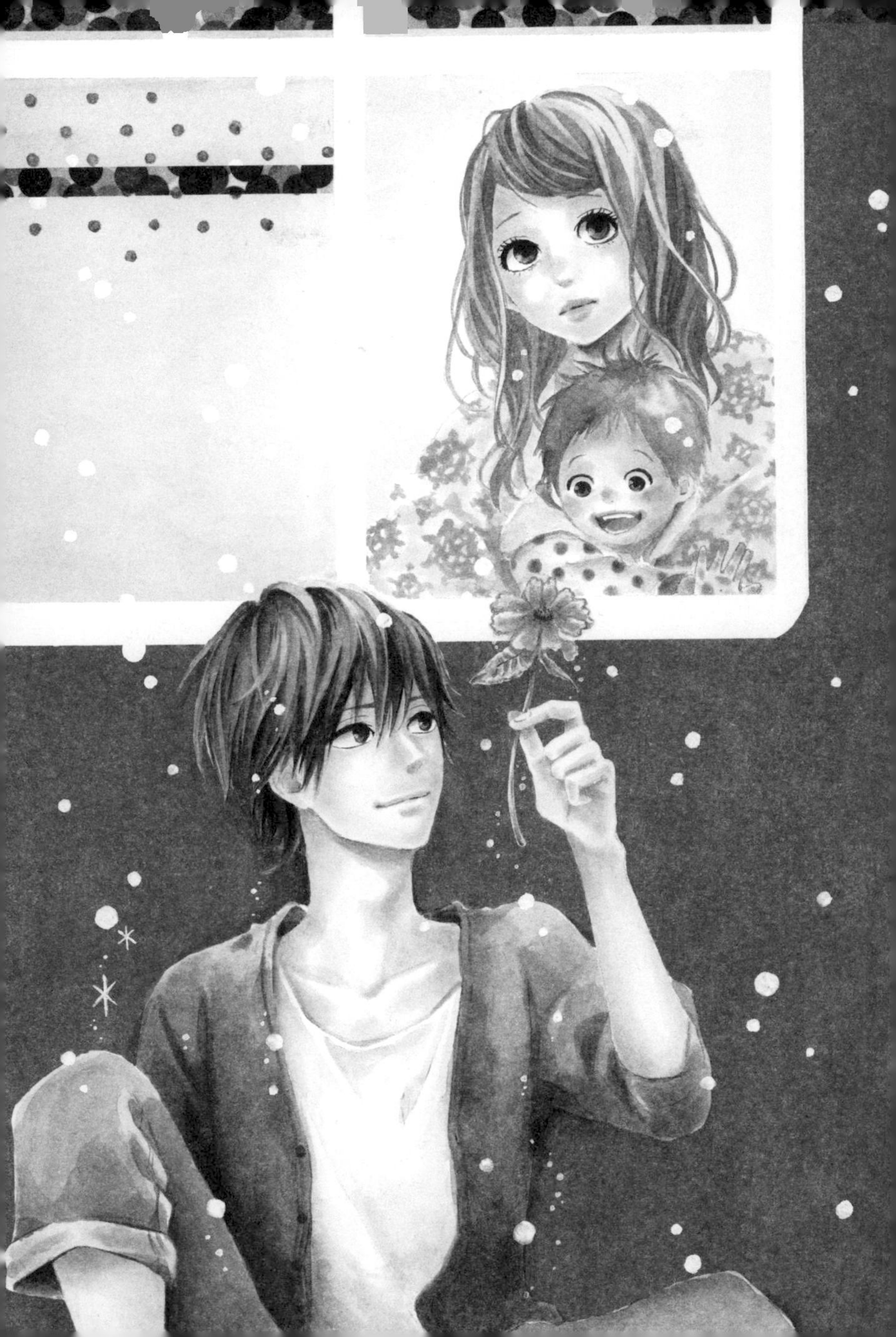

orange

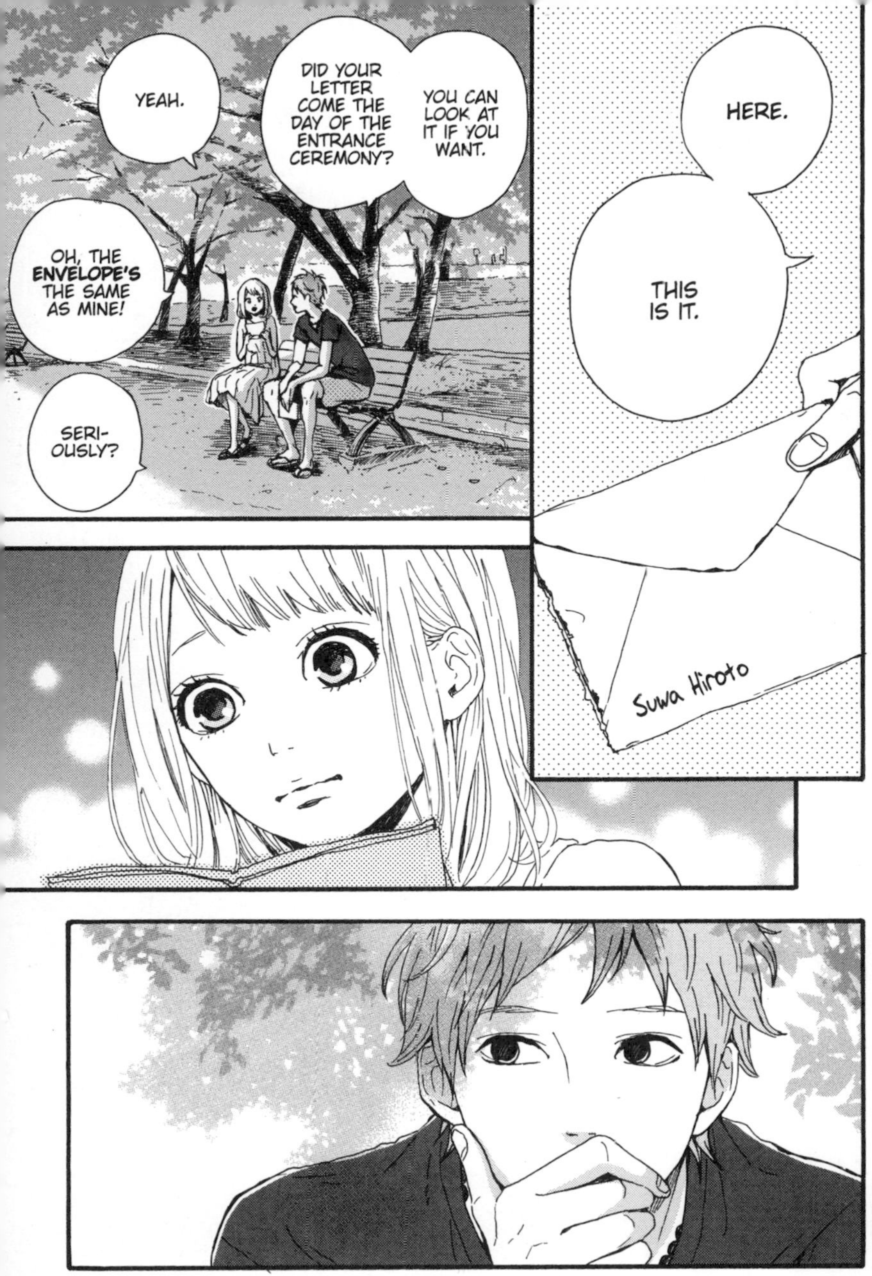
HERE.
THIS IS IT.
Suwa Hiroto
YOU CAN LOOK AT IT IF YOU WANT.
DID YOUR LETTER COME THE DAY OF THE ENTRANCE CEREMONY?
YEAH.
OH, THE **ENVELOPE'S** THE SAME AS MINE!
SERI-OUSLY?

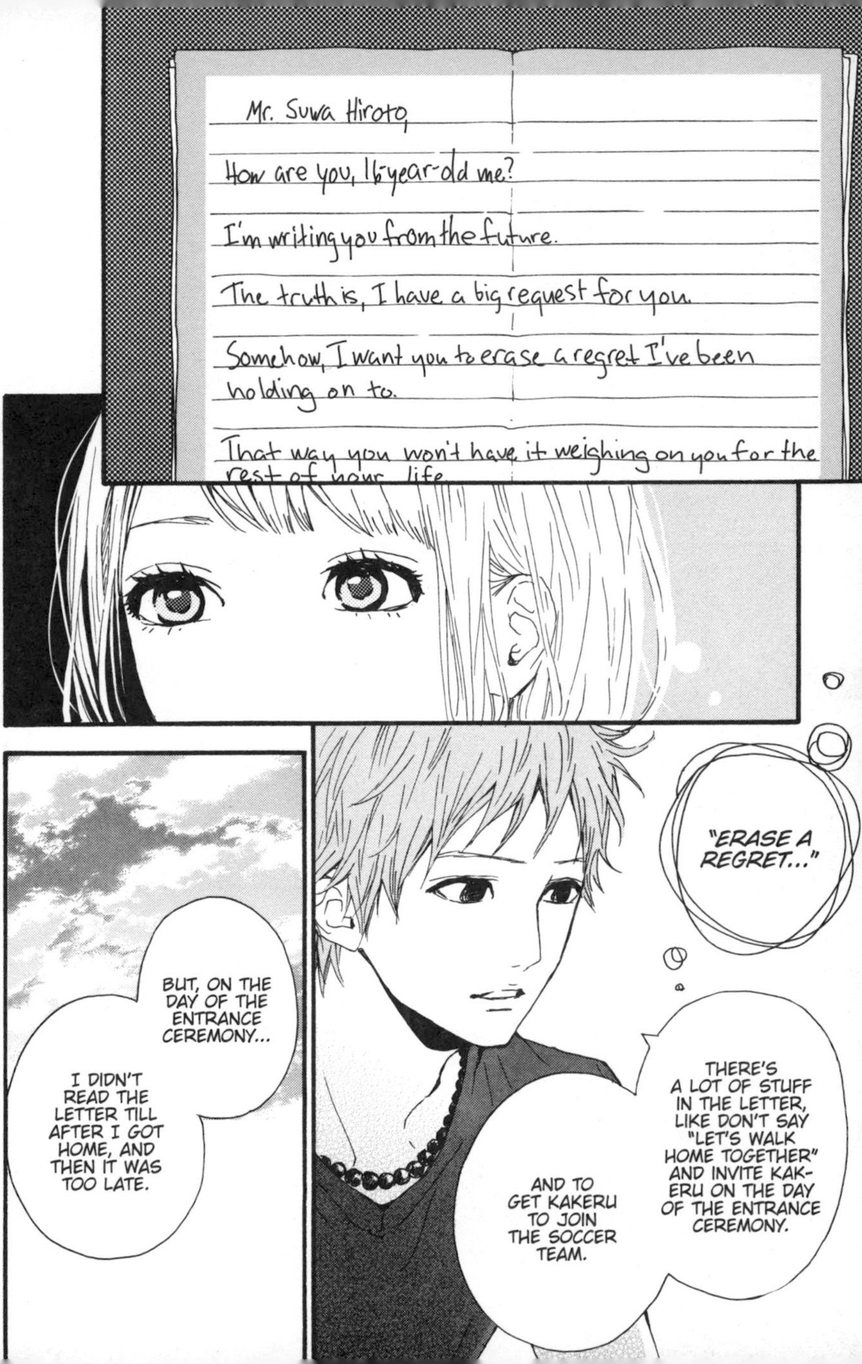
Mr. Suwa Hiroto,
How are you, 16-year-old me?
I'm writing you from the future.
The truth is, I have a big request for you.
Somehow, I want you to erase a regret I've been holding on to.
That way you won't have it weighing on you for the rest of your life.
"ERASE A REGRET..."
THERE'S A LOT OF STUFF IN THE LETTER, LIKE DON'T SAY "LET'S WALK HOME TOGETHER" AND INVITE KAKERU ON THE DAY OF THE ENTRANCE CEREMONY.
AND TO GET KAKERU TO JOIN THE SOCCER TEAM.
BUT, ON THE DAY OF THE ENTRANCE CEREMONY...
I DIDN'T READ THE LETTER TILL AFTER I GOT HOME, AND THEN IT WAS TOO LATE.

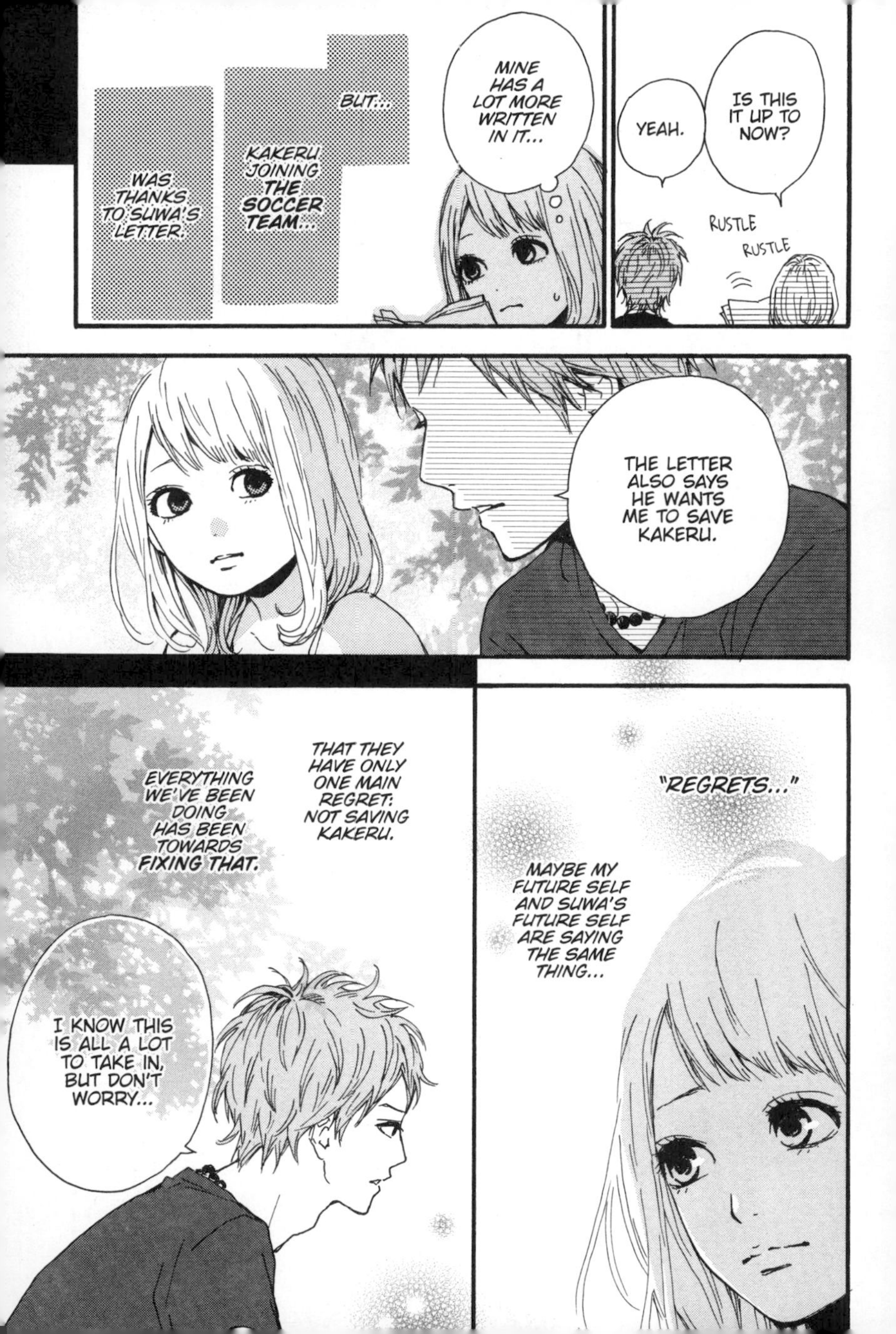
IS THIS IT UP TO NOW?
YEAH.
RUSTLE
RUSTLE
MINE HAS A LOT MORE WRITTEN IN IT...
BUT...
KAKERU JOINING THE SOCCER TEAM...
WAS THANKS TO SUWA'S LETTER.
THE LETTER ALSO SAYS HE WANTS ME TO SAVE KAKERU.
"REGRETS..."
MAYBE MY FUTURE SELF AND SUWA'S FUTURE SELF ARE SAYING THE SAME THING...
THAT THEY HAVE ONLY ONE MAIN REGRET: NOT SAVING KAKERU.
EVERYTHING WE'VE BEEN DOING HAS BEEN TOWARDS FIXING THAT.
I KNOW THIS IS ALL A LOT TO TAKE IN, BUT DON'T WORRY...

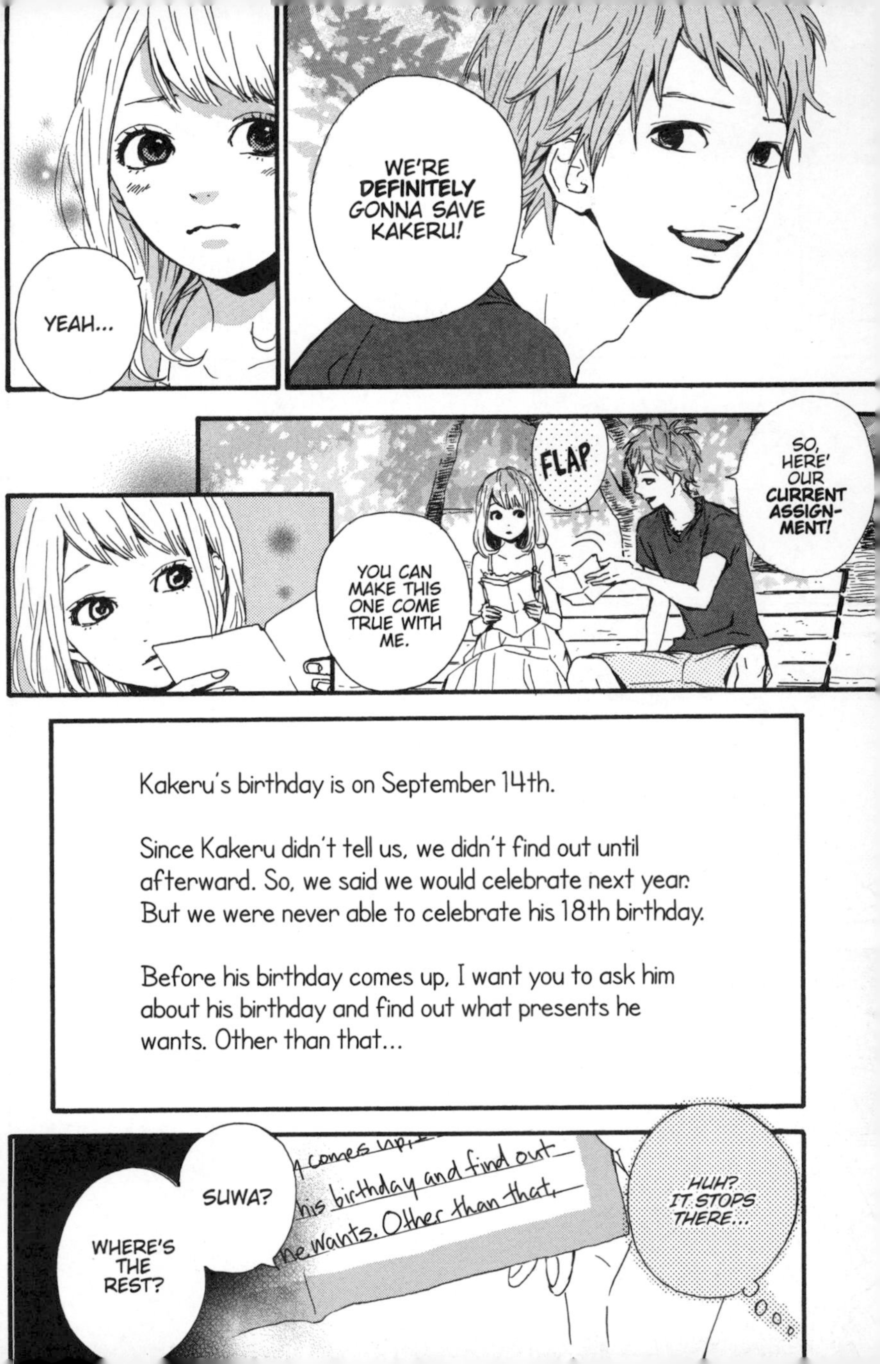
WE'RE DEFINITELY GONNA SAVE KAKERU!
YEAH...
SO, HERE' OUR CURRENT ASSIGNMENT!
FLAP
YOU CAN MAKE THIS ONE COME TRUE WITH ME.
Kakeru's birthday is on September 14th.
Since Kakeru didn't tell us, we didn't find out until afterward. So, we said we would celebrate next year. But we were never able to celebrate his 18th birthday.
Before his birthday comes up, I want you to ask him about his birthday and find out what presents he wants. Other than that...
his birthday and find out
wants. Other than that.
HUH? IT STOPS THERE...
SUWA?
WHERE'S THE REST?

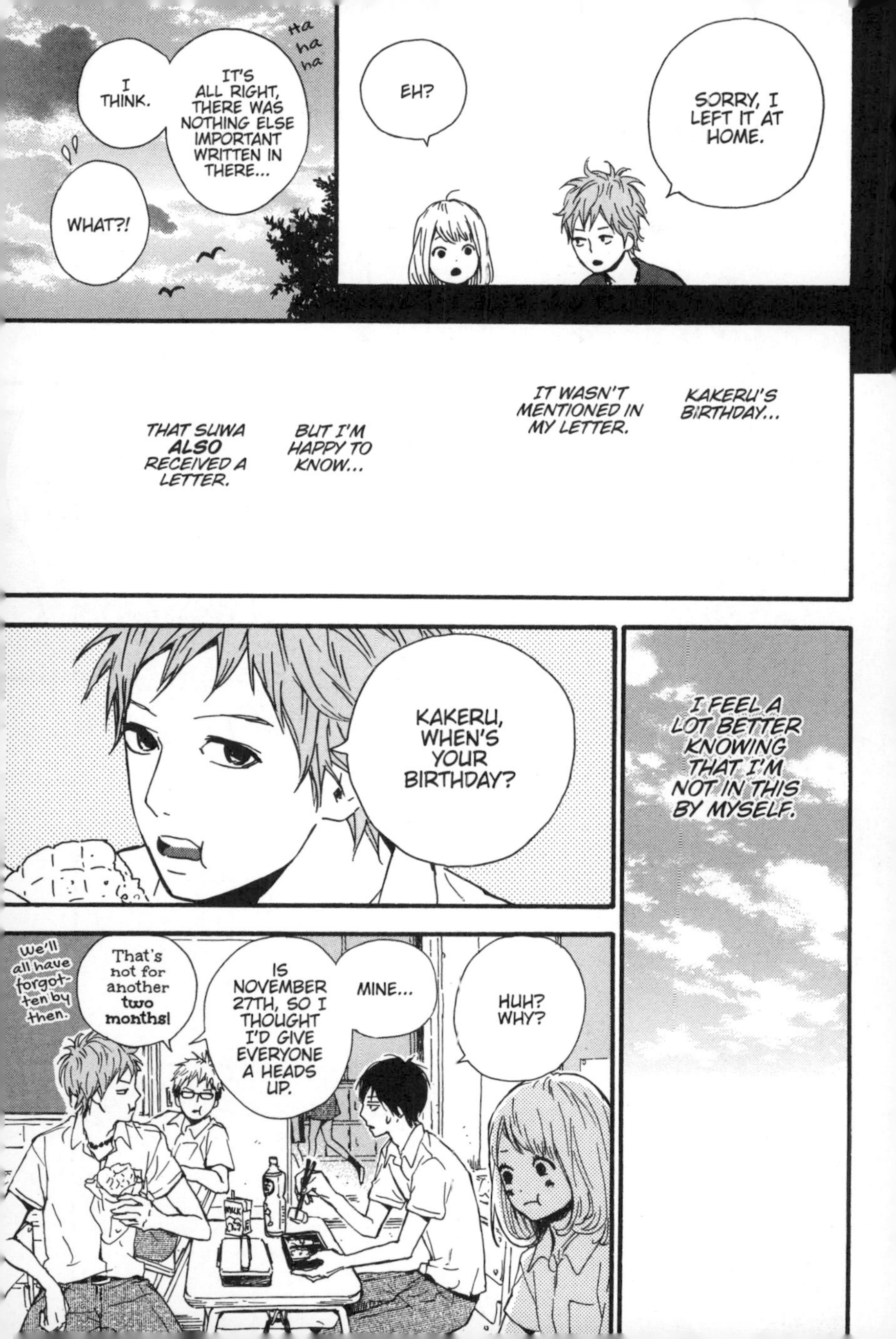
SORRY, I LEFT IT AT HOME.
EH?
IT'S ALL RIGHT, THERE WAS NOTHING ELSE IMPORTANT WRITTEN IN THERE...
Ha ha ha
I THINK.
WHAT?!
KAKERU'S BIRTHDAY...
IT WASN'T MENTIONED IN MY LETTER.
BUT I'M HAPPY TO KNOW...
THAT SUWA **ALSO** RECEIVED A LETTER.
I FEEL A LOT BETTER KNOWING THAT I'M NOT IN THIS BY MYSELF.
KAKERU, WHEN'S YOUR BIRTHDAY?
HUH? WHY?
MINE...
IS NOVEMBER 27TH, SO I THOUGHT I'D GIVE EVERYONE A HEADS UP.
That's not for another **two months!**
We'll all have forgot-ten by then.

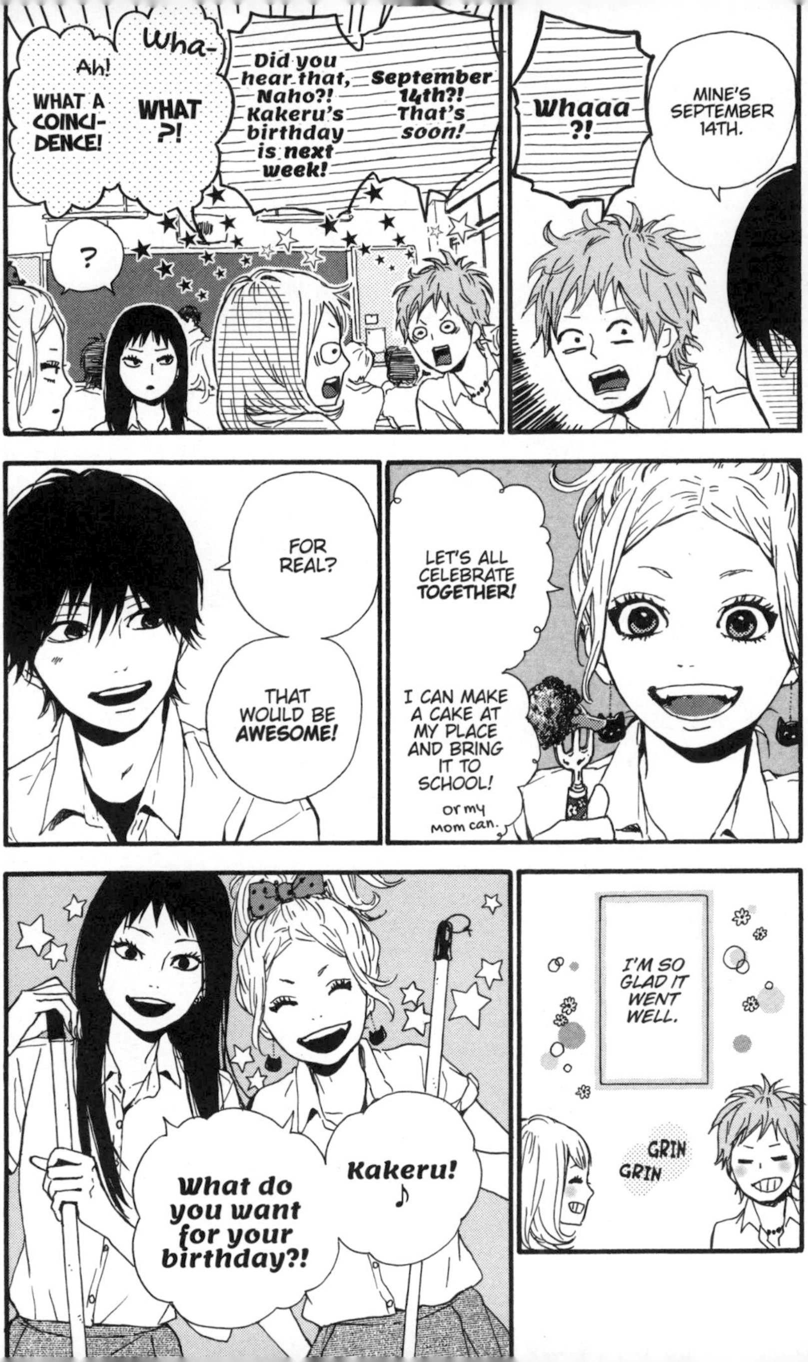
MINE'S SEPTEMBER 14TH.
Whaaa?!
September 14th?! That's soon!
Did you hear that, Naho?! Kakeru's birthday is next week!
Wha-
WHAT?!
Ah! WHAT A COINCIDENCE!
?
LET'S ALL CELEBRATE TOGETHER!
I CAN MAKE A CAKE AT MY PLACE AND BRING IT TO SCHOOL!
Or my Mom can.
FOR REAL?
THAT WOULD BE AWESOME!
I'M SO GLAD IT WENT WELL.
GRIN GRIN
Kakeru! ♪
What do you want for your birthday?!

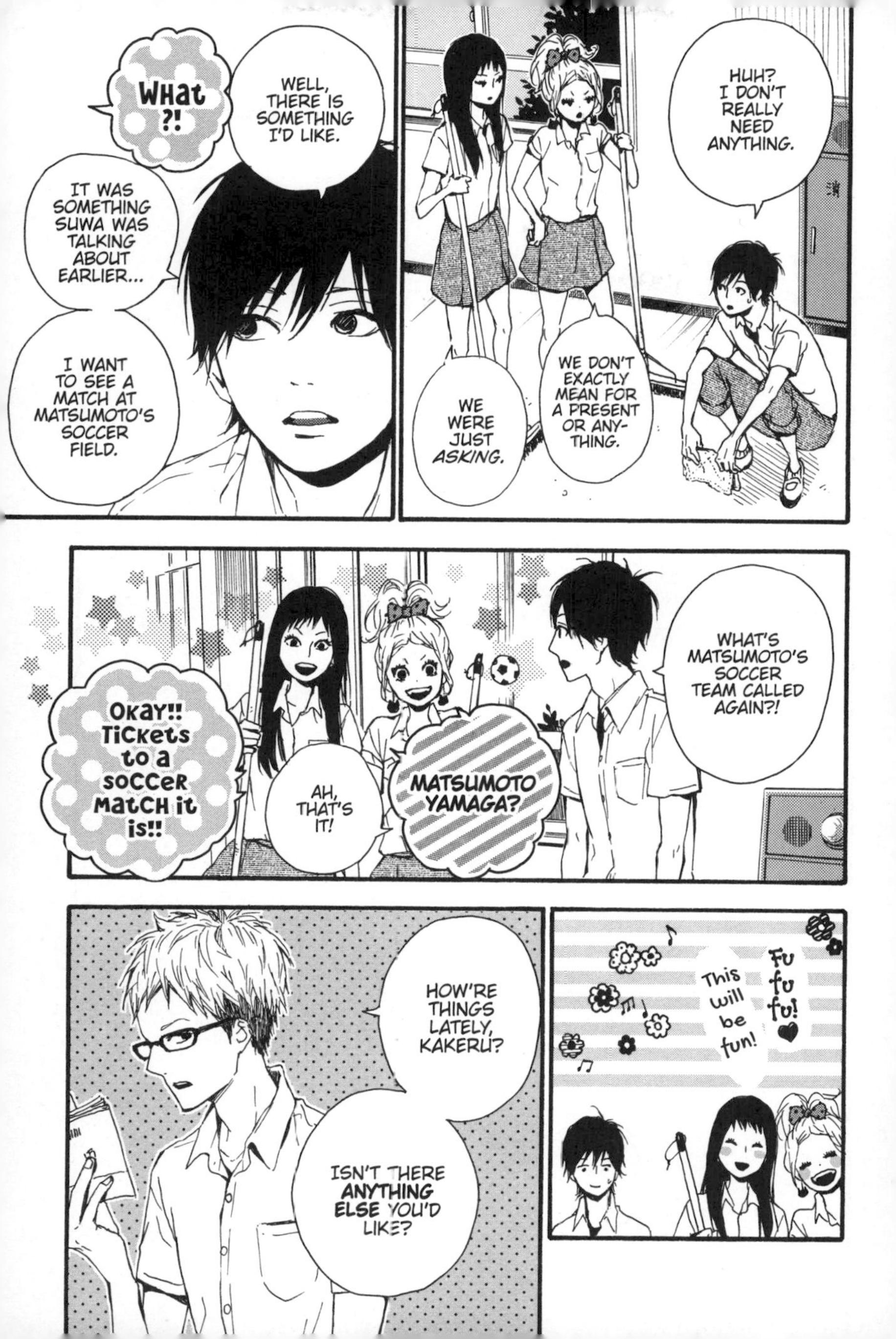
HUH? I DON'T REALLY NEED ANYTHING.
WE DON'T EXACTLY MEAN FOR A PRESENT OR ANYTHING.
WE WERE JUST ASKING.
WELL, THERE IS SOMETHING I'D LIKE.
What?!
IT WAS SOMETHING SUWA WAS TALKING ABOUT EARLIER...
I WANT TO SEE A MATCH AT MATSUMOTO'S SOCCER FIELD.
WHAT'S MATSUMOTO'S SOCCER TEAM CALLED AGAIN?!
MATSUMOTO YAMAGA?
AH, THAT'S IT!
Okay!! Tickets to a soccer match it is!!
Fu fu fu!
This will be fun!
HOW'RE THINGS LATELY, KAKERU?
ISN'T THERE ANYTHING ELSE YOU'D LIKE?

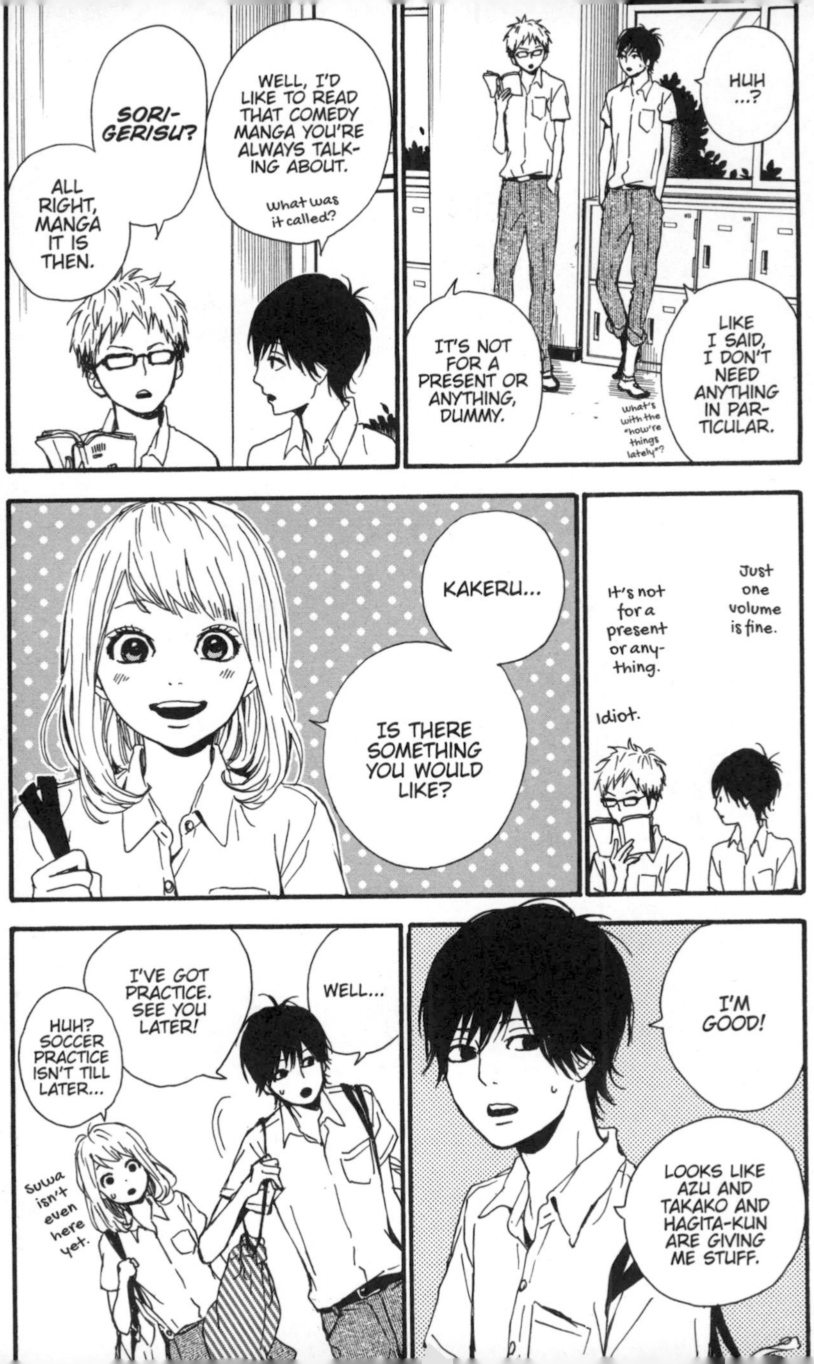
HUH ...?
LIKE I SAID, I DON'T NEED ANYTHING IN PARTICULAR.
What's with the "how're things lately"?
IT'S NOT FOR A PRESENT OR ANYTHING, DUMMY.
WELL, I'D LIKE TO READ THAT COMEDY MANGA YOU'RE ALWAYS TALKING ABOUT.
What was it called?
SORI-GERISU?
ALL RIGHT, MANGA IT IS THEN.
Just one volume is fine.
It's not for a present or anything.
Idiot.
KAKERU...
IS THERE SOMETHING YOU WOULD LIKE?
I'M GOOD!
LOOKS LIKE AZU AND TAKAKO AND HAGITA-KUN ARE GIVING ME STUFF.
WELL...
I'VE GOT PRACTICE. SEE YOU LATER!
HUH? SOCCER PRACTICE ISN'T TILL LATER...
Suwa isn't even here yet.

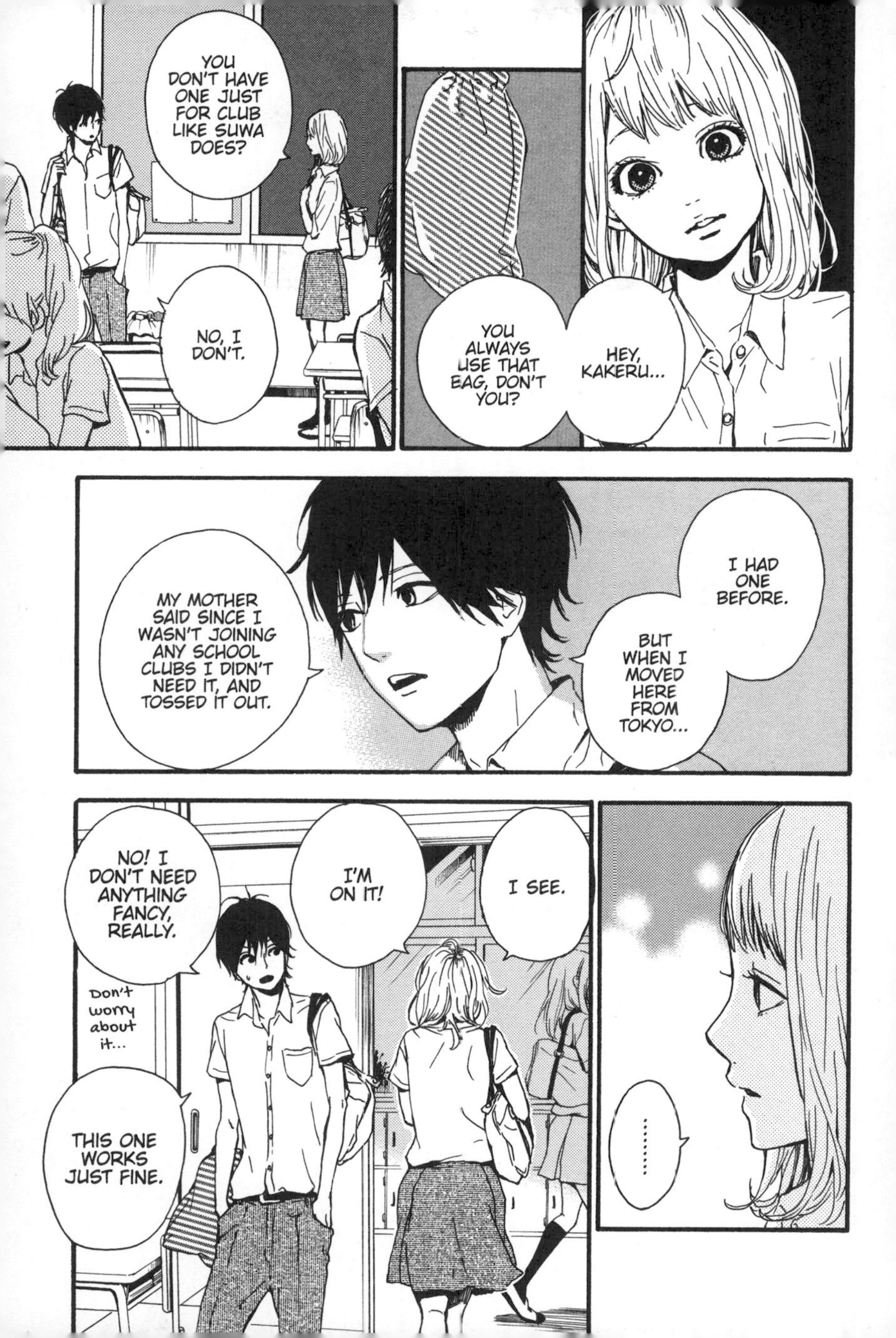
HEY, KAKERU...
YOU ALWAYS USE THAT BAG, DON'T YOU?
YOU DON'T HAVE ONE JUST FOR CLUB LIKE SUWA DOES?
NO, I DON'T.
I HAD ONE BEFORE.
BUT WHEN I MOVED HERE FROM TOKYO...
MY MOTHER SAID SINCE I WASN'T JOINING ANY SCHOOL CLUBS I DIDN'T NEED IT, AND TOSSED IT OUT.
......
I SEE.
I'M ON IT!
NO! I DON'T NEED ANYTHING FANCY, REALLY.
Don't worry about it...
THIS ONE WORKS JUST FINE.

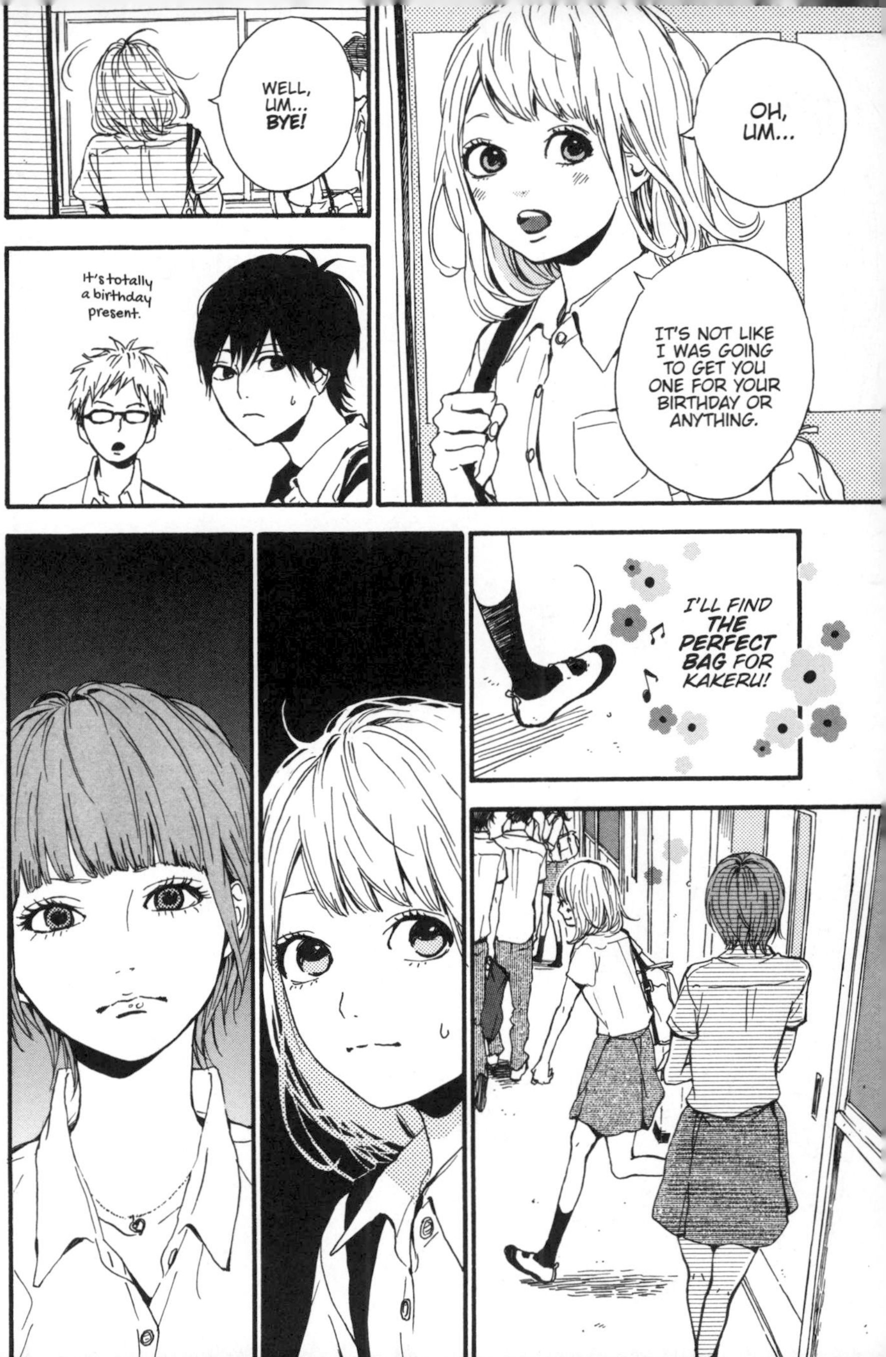
OH, UM...
IT'S NOT LIKE I WAS GOING TO GET YOU ONE FOR YOUR BIRTHDAY OR ANYTHING.
WELL, UM... BYE!
It's totally a birthday present.
I'LL FIND THE PERFECT BAG FOR KAKERU!

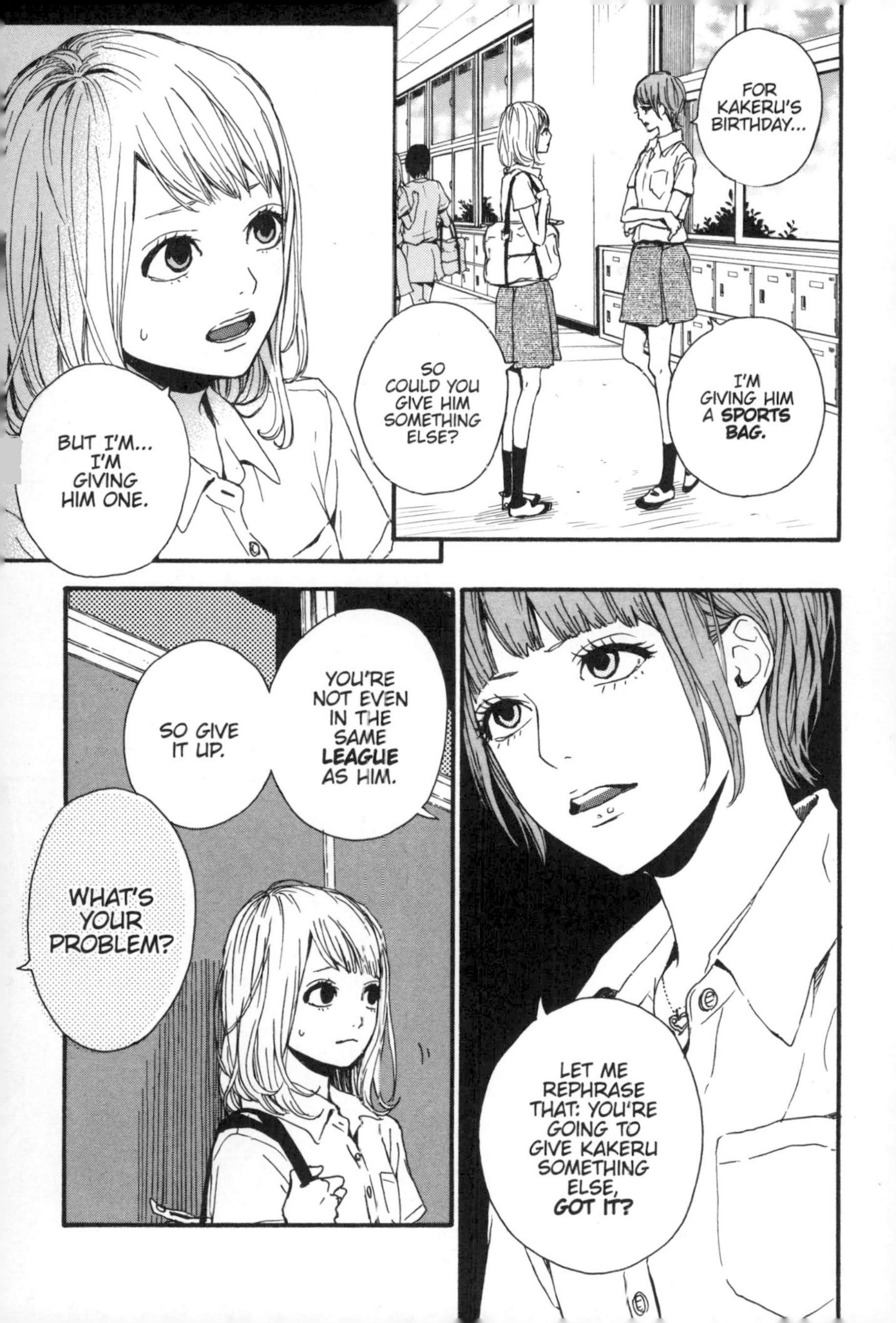
FOR KAKERU'S BIRTHDAY...
I'M GIVING HIM A **SPORTS BAG.**
SO COULD YOU GIVE HIM SOMETHING ELSE?
BUT I'M... I'M GIVING HIM ONE.
LET ME REPHRASE THAT: YOU'RE GOING TO GIVE KAKERU SOMETHING ELSE, **GOT IT?**
YOU'RE NOT EVEN IN THE SAME **LEAGUE** AS HIM.
SO GIVE IT UP.
WHAT'S YOUR PROBLEM?

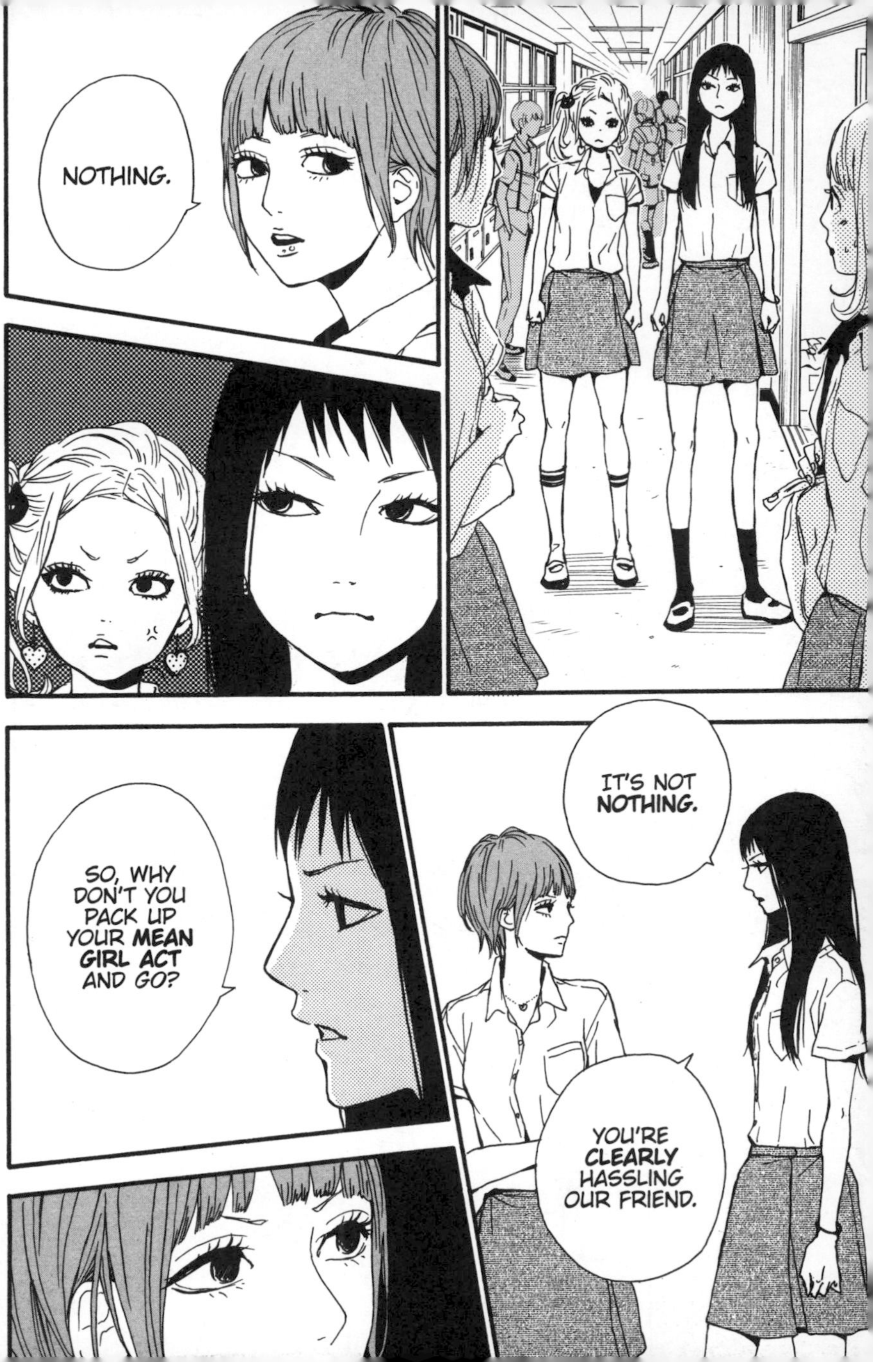
NOTHING.
IT'S NOT NOTHING.
YOU'RE CLEARLY HASSLING OUR FRIEND.
SO, WHY DON'T YOU PACK UP YOUR MEAN GIRL ACT AND GO?

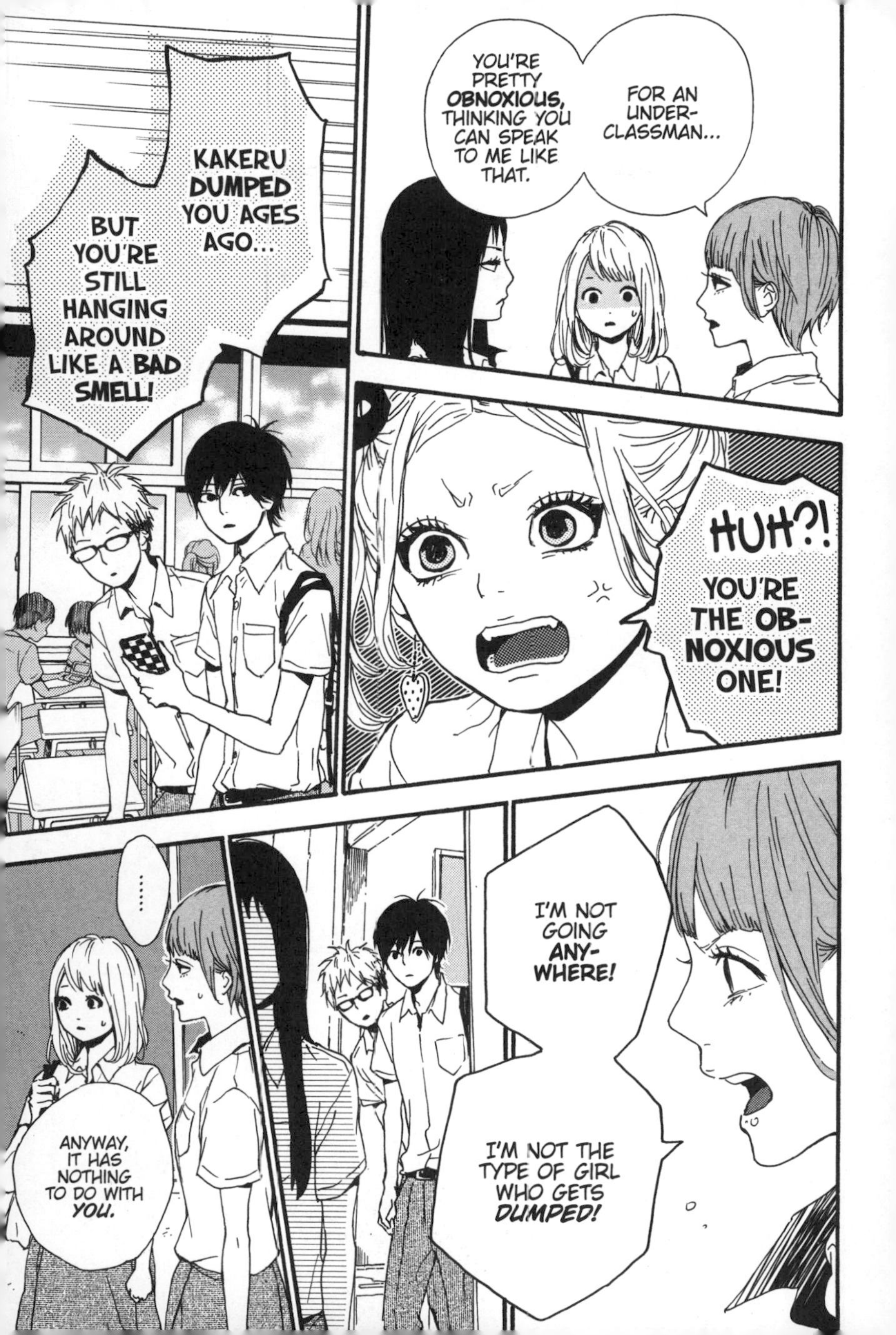

FOR AN UNDER-CLASSMAN...
YOU'RE PRETTY OBNOXIOUS, THINKING YOU CAN SPEAK TO ME LIKE THAT.
HUH?!
YOU'RE THE OB-NOXIOUS ONE!
KAKERU DUMPED YOU AGES AGO...
BUT YOU'RE STILL HANGING AROUND LIKE A BAD SMELL!
I'M NOT GOING ANY-WHERE!
I'M NOT THE TYPE OF GIRL WHO GETS DUMPED!
......
ANYWAY, IT HAS NOTHING TO DO WITH YOU.

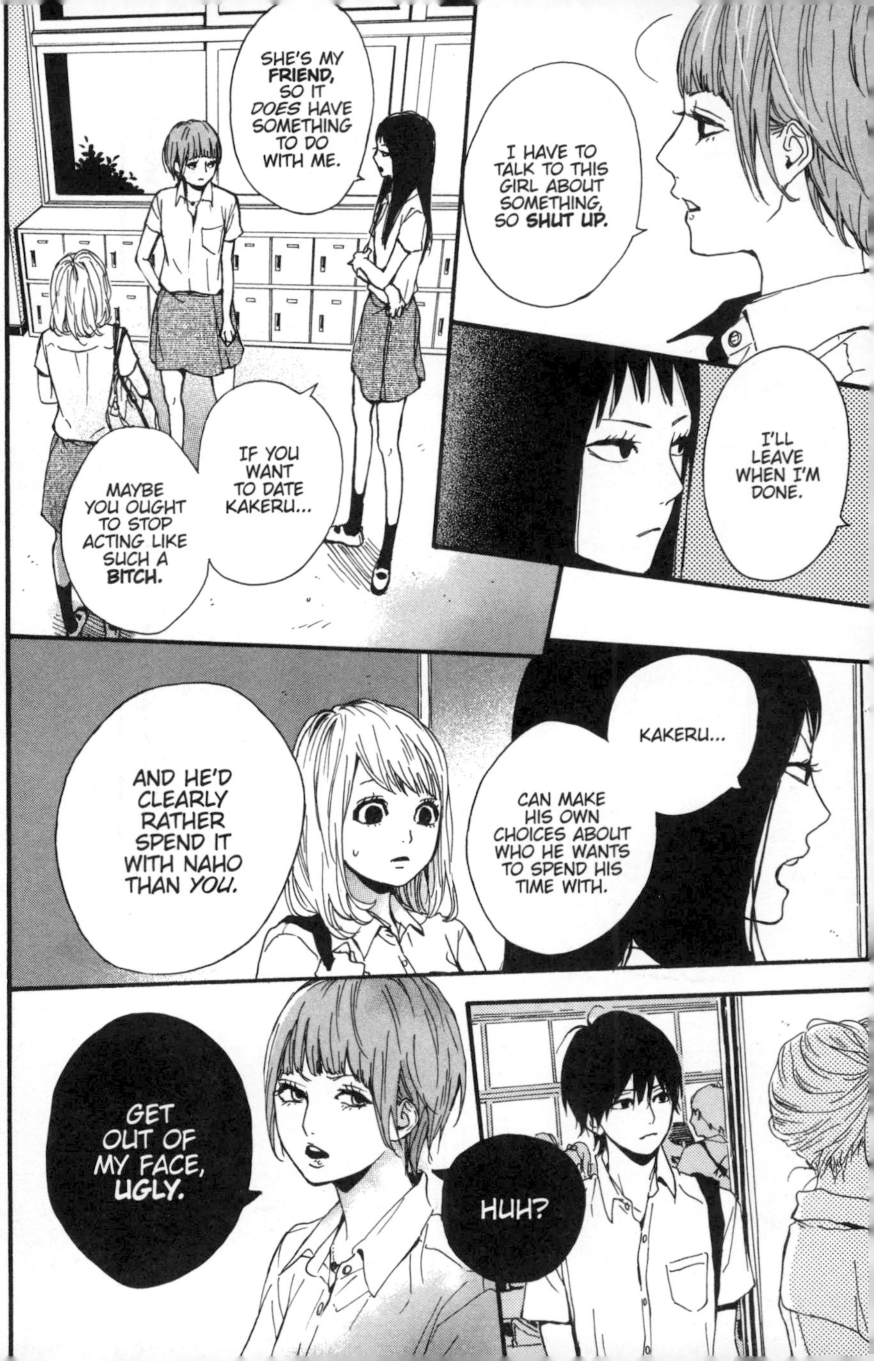
I HAVE TO TALK TO THIS GIRL ABOUT SOMETHING, SO SHUT UP.
I'LL LEAVE WHEN I'M DONE.
SHE'S MY FRIEND, SO IT DOES HAVE SOMETHING TO DO WITH ME.
IF YOU WANT TO DATE KAKERU...
MAYBE YOU OUGHT TO STOP ACTING LIKE SUCH A BITCH.
KAKERU...
CAN MAKE HIS OWN CHOICES ABOUT WHO HE WANTS TO SPEND HIS TIME WITH.
AND HE'D CLEARLY RATHER SPEND IT WITH NAHO THAN YOU.
GET OUT OF MY FACE, UGLY.
HUH?

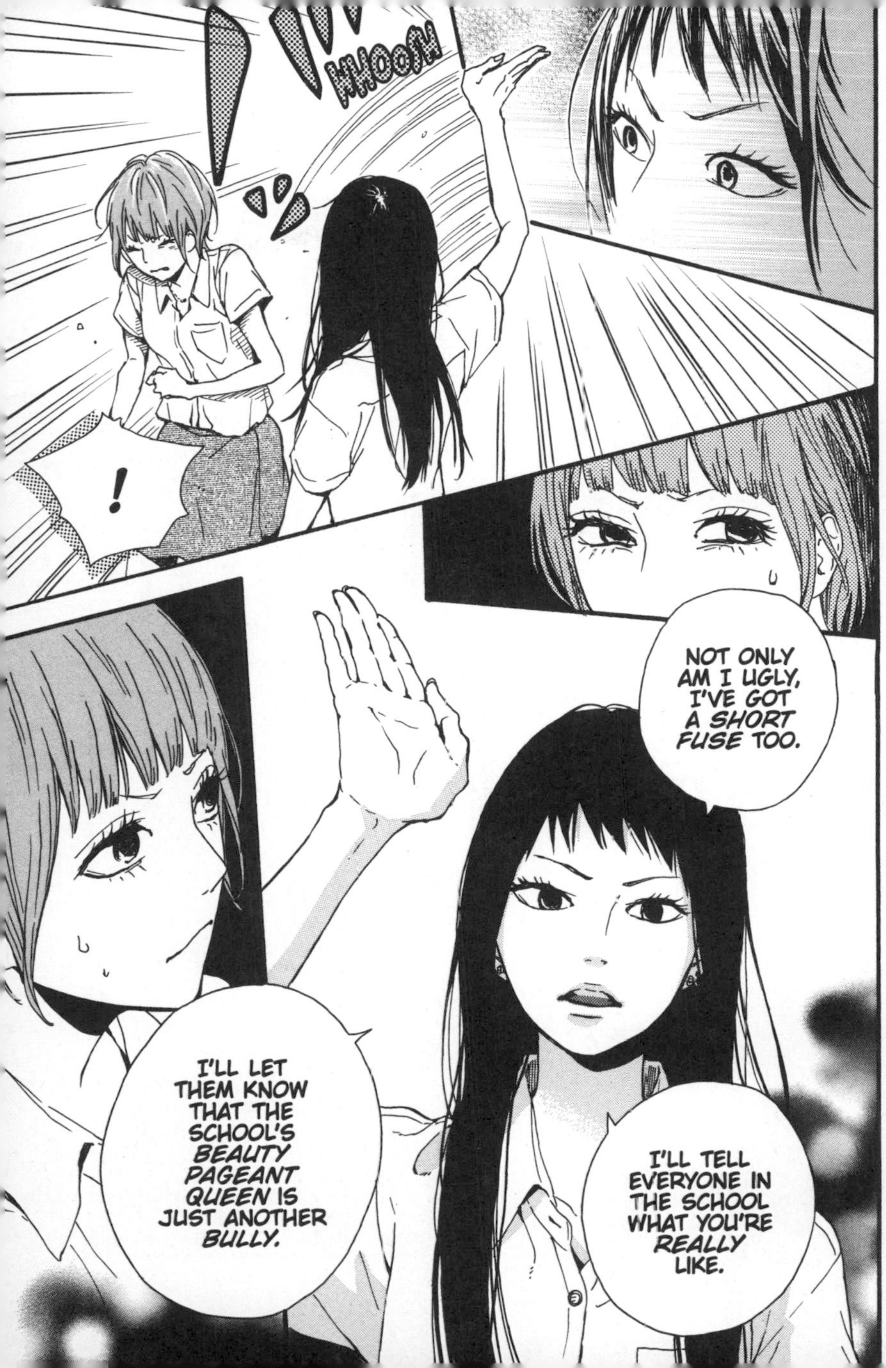
WHOOM
!
NOT ONLY AM I UGLY, I'VE GOT A SHORT FUSE TOO.
I'LL TELL EVERYONE IN THE SCHOOL WHAT YOU'RE REALLY LIKE.
I'LL LET THEM KNOW THAT THE SCHOOL'S BEAUTY PAGEANT QUEEN IS JUST ANOTHER BULLY.

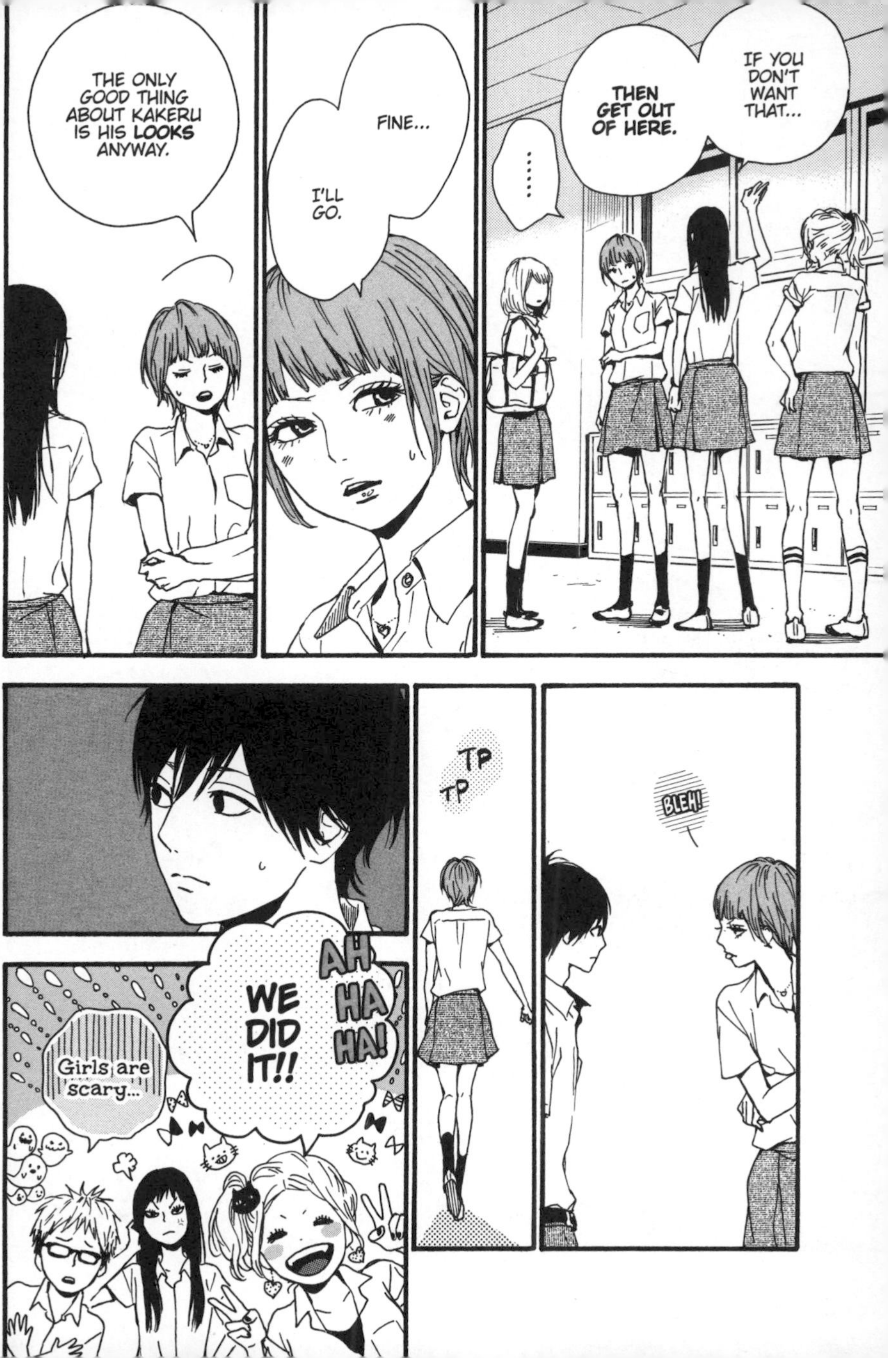
IF YOU DON'T WANT THAT...
THEN GET OUT OF HERE.
......
FINE...
I'LL GO.
THE ONLY GOOD THING ABOUT KAKERU IS HIS LOOKS ANYWAY.
BLEH!
TP TP
AH HA HA!
WE DID IT!!
Girls are scary...

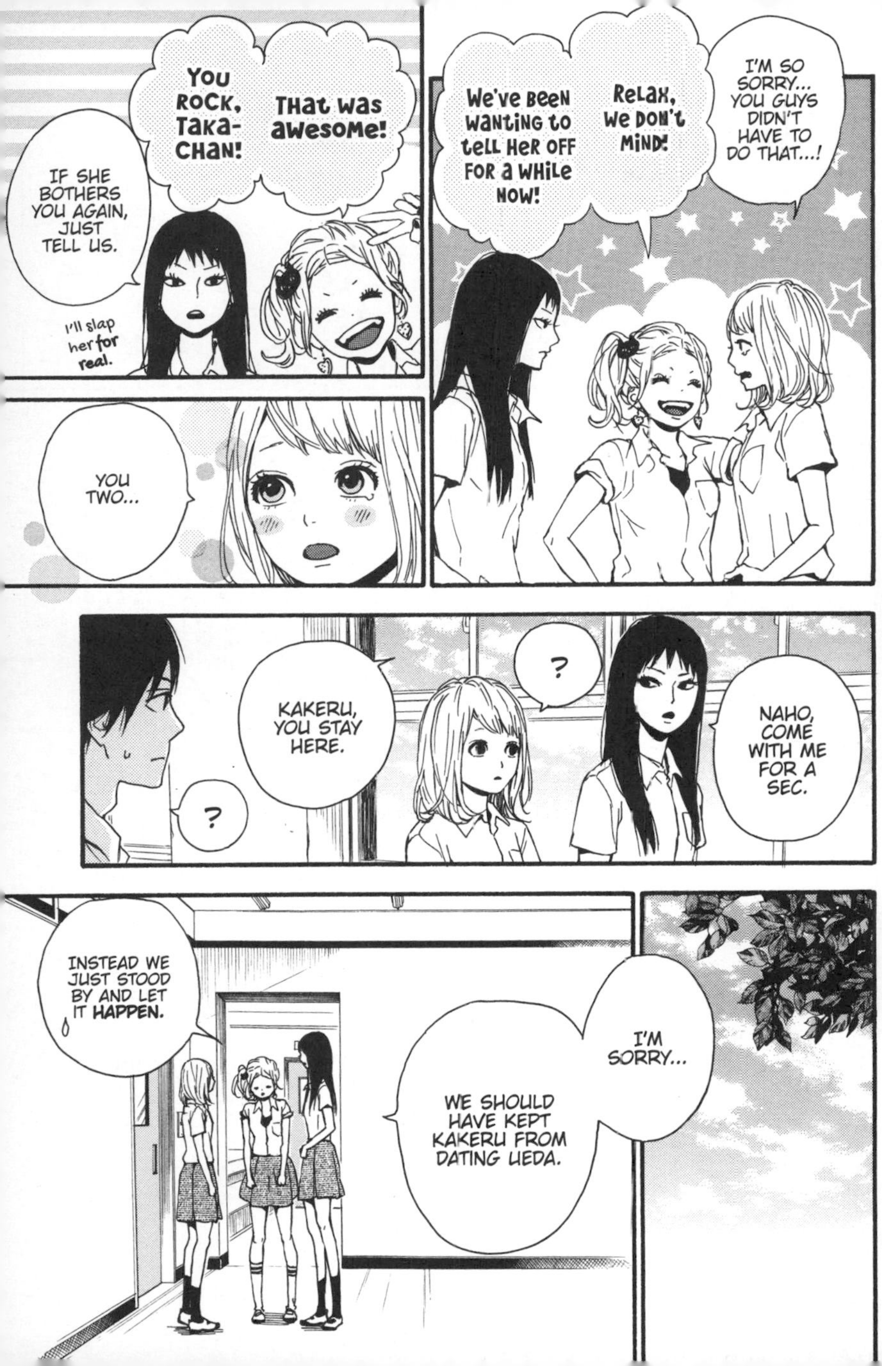
I'M SO SORRY... YOU GUYS DIDN'T HAVE TO DO THAT...!
Relax, we don't mind!
We've been wanting to tell her off for a while now!
That was awesome!
You rock, Taka-chan!
IF SHE BOTHERS YOU AGAIN, JUST TELL US.
I'll slap her for real.
YOU TWO...
NAHO, COME WITH ME FOR A SEC.
?
KAKERU, YOU STAY HERE.
?
I'M SORRY...
WE SHOULD HAVE KEPT KAKERU FROM DATING UEDA.
INSTEAD WE JUST STOOD BY AND LET IT HAPPEN.

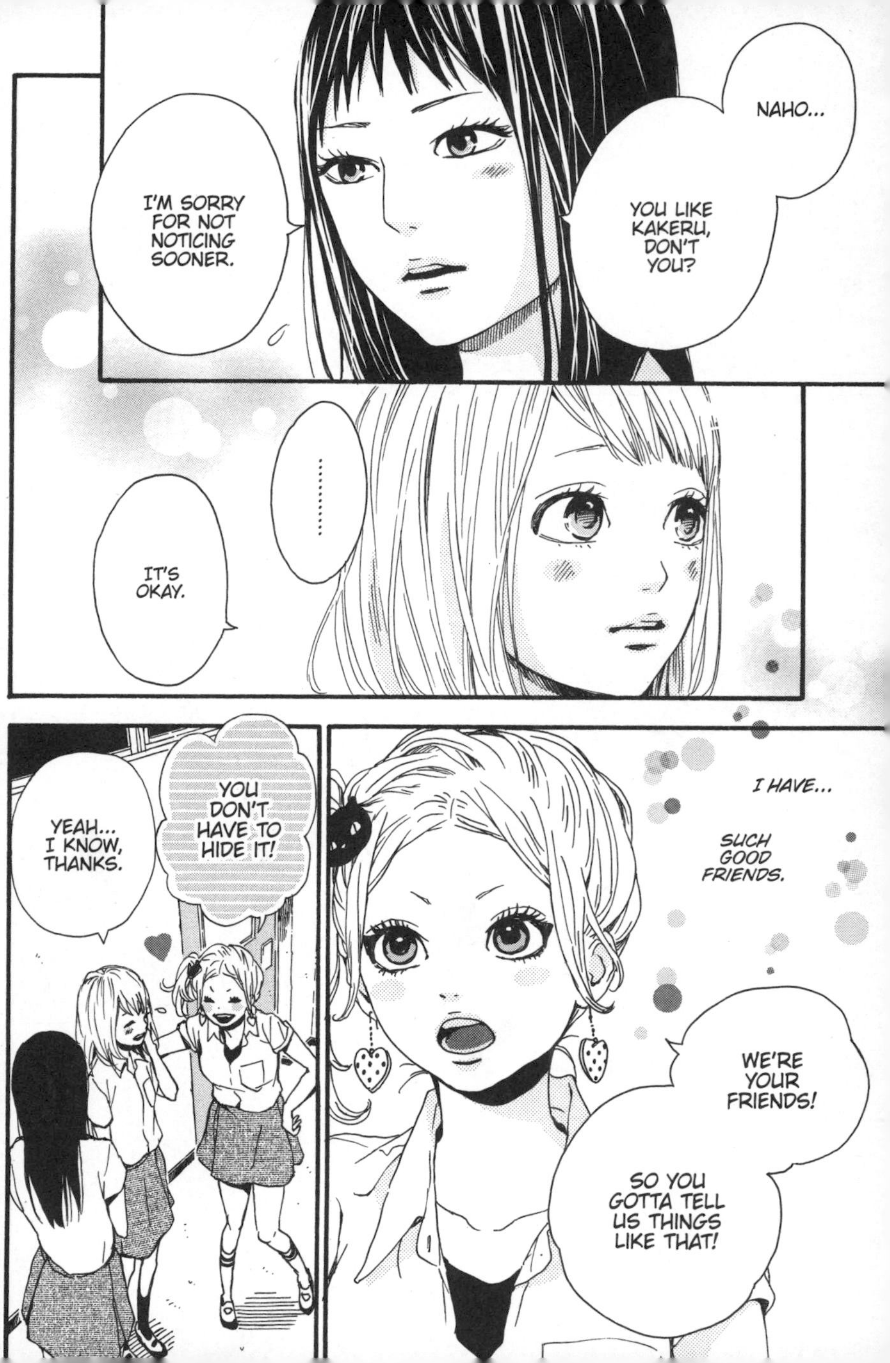
NAHO...
YOU LIKE KAKERU, DON'T YOU?
I'M SORRY FOR NOT NOTICING SOONER.
......
IT'S OKAY.
I HAVE...
SUCH GOOD FRIENDS.
WE'RE YOUR FRIENDS!
SO YOU GOTTA TELL US THINGS LIKE THAT!
YOU DON'T HAVE TO HIDE IT!
YEAH... I KNOW, THANKS.

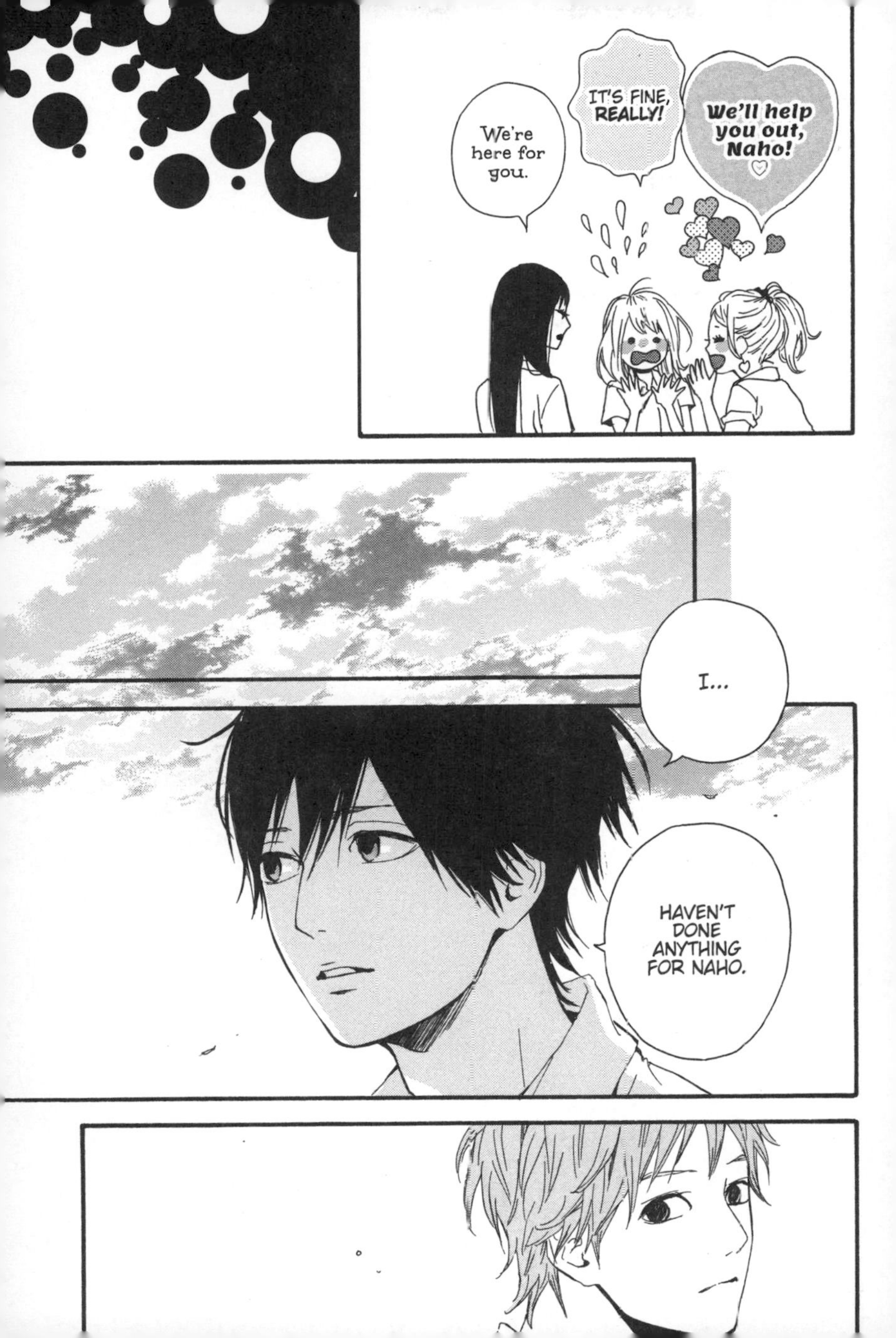
We'll help you out, Naho!
IT'S FINE, REALLY!
We're here for you.
I...
HAVEN'T DONE ANYTHING FOR NAHO.

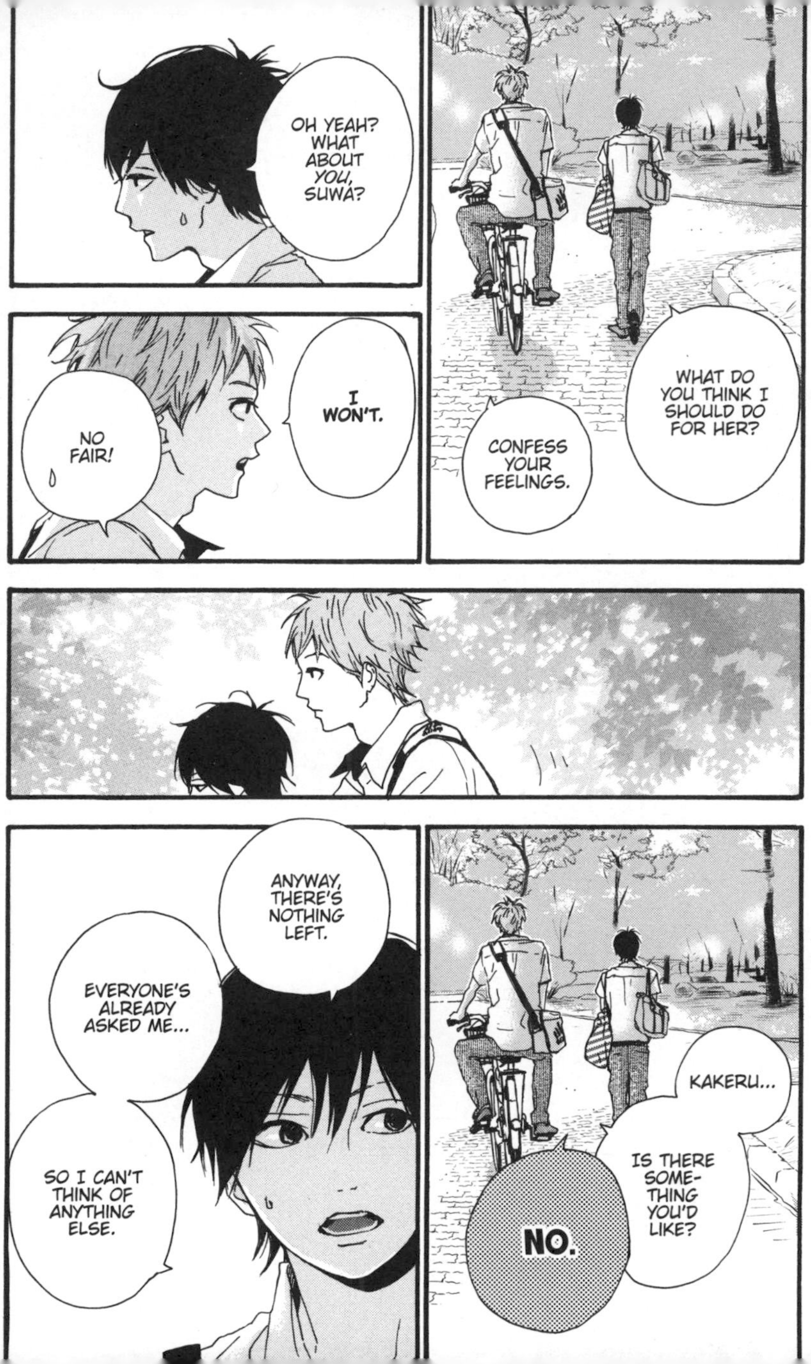
WHAT DO YOU THINK I SHOULD DO FOR HER?
CONFESS YOUR FEELINGS.
OH YEAH? WHAT ABOUT YOU, SUWA?
I WON'T.
NO FAIR!
KAKERU...
IS THERE SOME-THING YOU'D LIKE?
NO.
ANYWAY, THERE'S NOTHING LEFT.
EVERYONE'S ALREADY ASKED ME...
SO I CAN'T THINK OF ANYTHING ELSE.

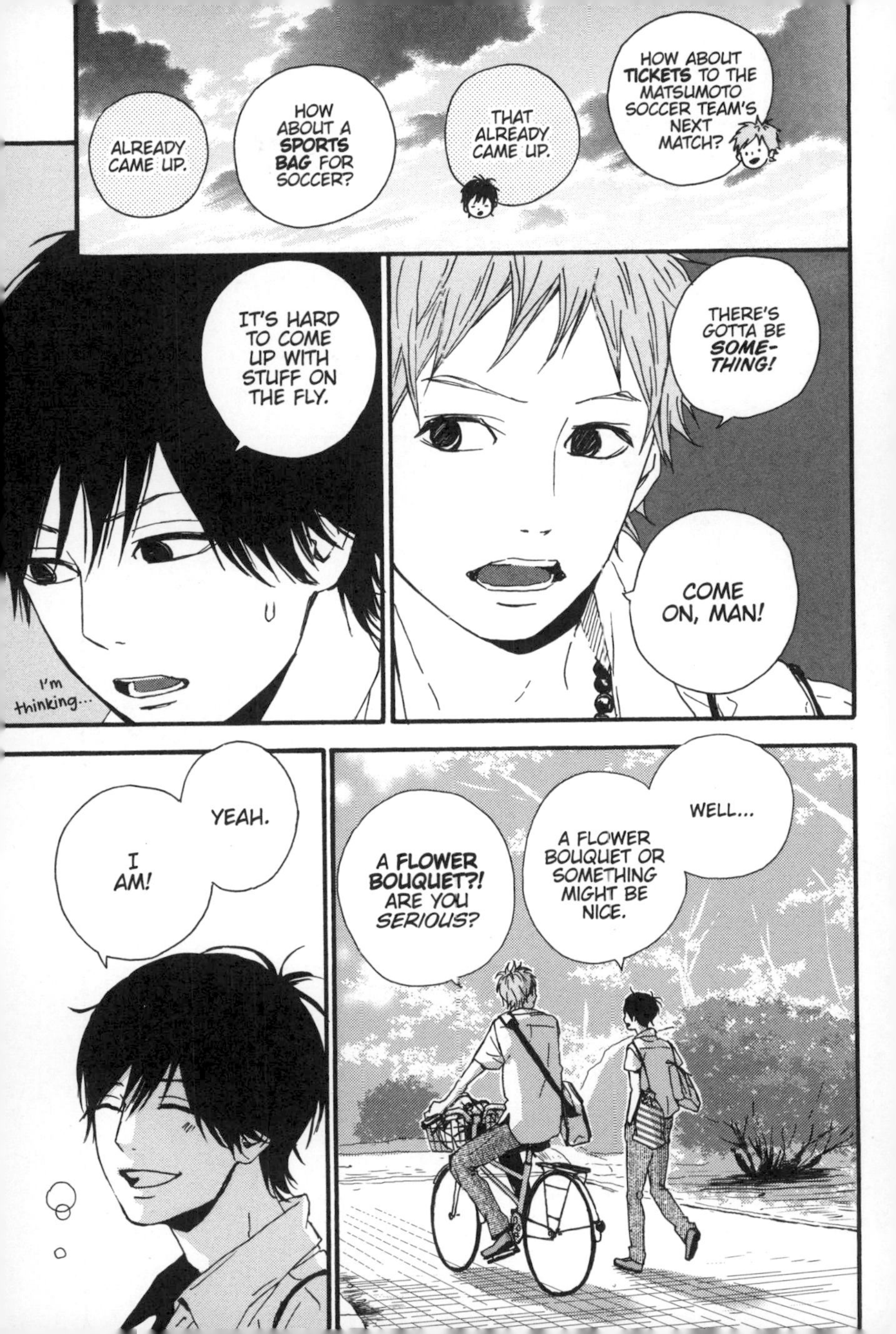
HOW ABOUT TICKETS TO THE MATSUMOTO SOCCER TEAM'S NEXT MATCH?
THAT ALREADY CAME UP.
HOW ABOUT A SPORTS BAG FOR SOCCER?
ALREADY CAME UP.
THERE'S GOTTA BE SOMETHING!
COME ON, MAN!
IT'S HARD TO COME UP WITH STUFF ON THE FLY.
I'm thinking...
WELL...
A FLOWER BOUQUET OR SOMETHING MIGHT BE NICE.
A FLOWER BOUQUET?! ARE YOU SERIOUS?
YEAH.
I AM!

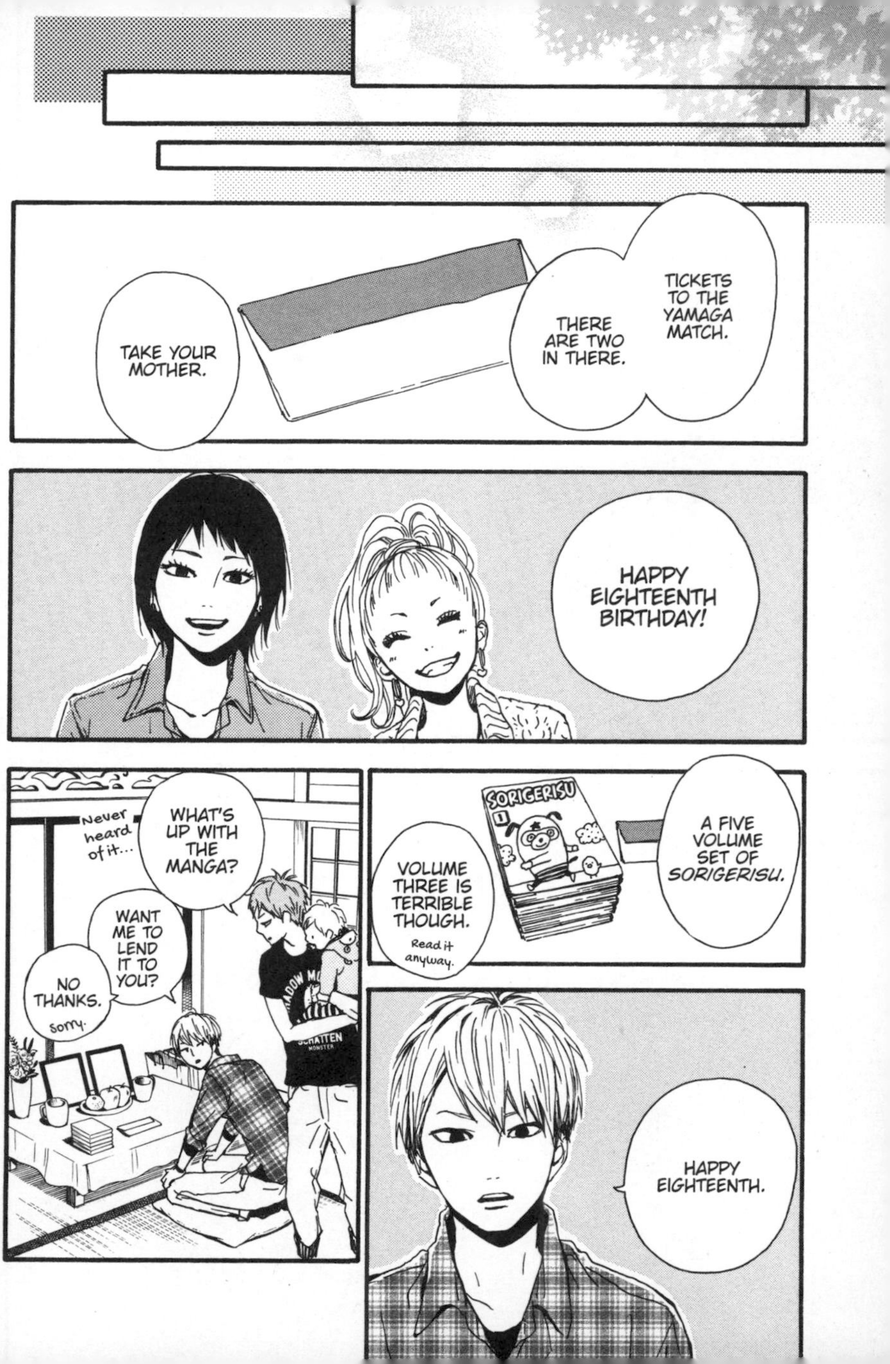
TICKETS TO THE YAMAGA MATCH.
THERE ARE TWO IN THERE.
TAKE YOUR MOTHER.
HAPPY EIGHTEENTH BIRTHDAY!
A FIVE VOLUME SET OF SORIGERISU.
SORIGERISU
VOLUME THREE IS TERRIBLE THOUGH.
Read it anyway.
HAPPY EIGHTEENTH.
WHAT'S UP WITH THE MANGA?
Never heard of it...
WANT ME TO LEND IT TO YOU?
NO THANKS.
sorry.
SCHATTEN
MONSTER

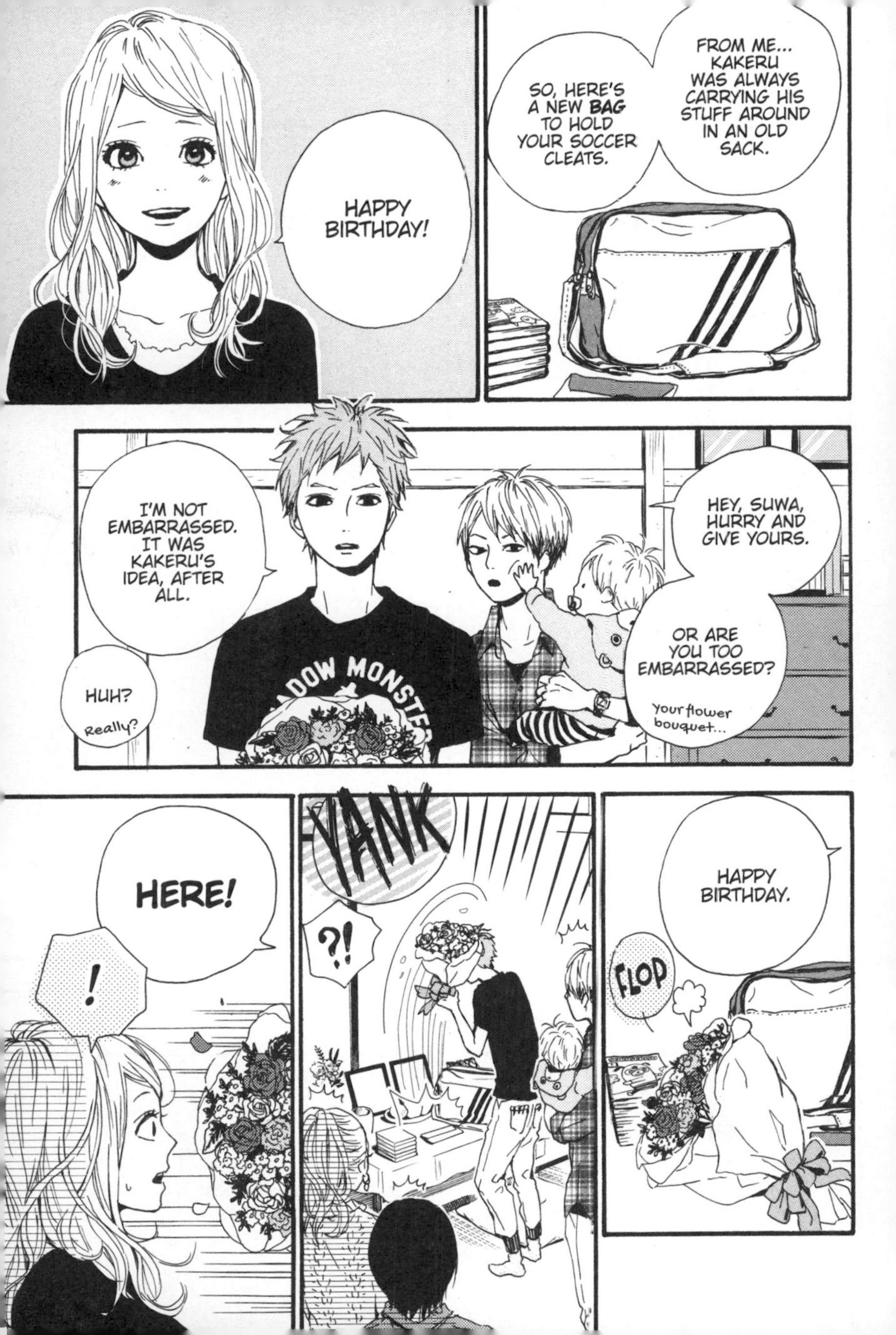
FROM ME... KAKERU WAS ALWAYS CARRYING HIS STUFF AROUND IN AN OLD SACK.
SO, HERE'S A NEW **BAG** TO HOLD YOUR SOCCER CLEATS.
HAPPY BIRTHDAY!
HEY, SUWA, HURRY AND GIVE YOURS.
OR ARE YOU TOO EMBARRASSED?
Your flower bouquet...
I'M NOT EMBARRASSED. IT WAS KAKERU'S IDEA, AFTER ALL.
HUH?
Really?
HAPPY BIRTHDAY.
FLOP
YANK
?!
HERE!
!

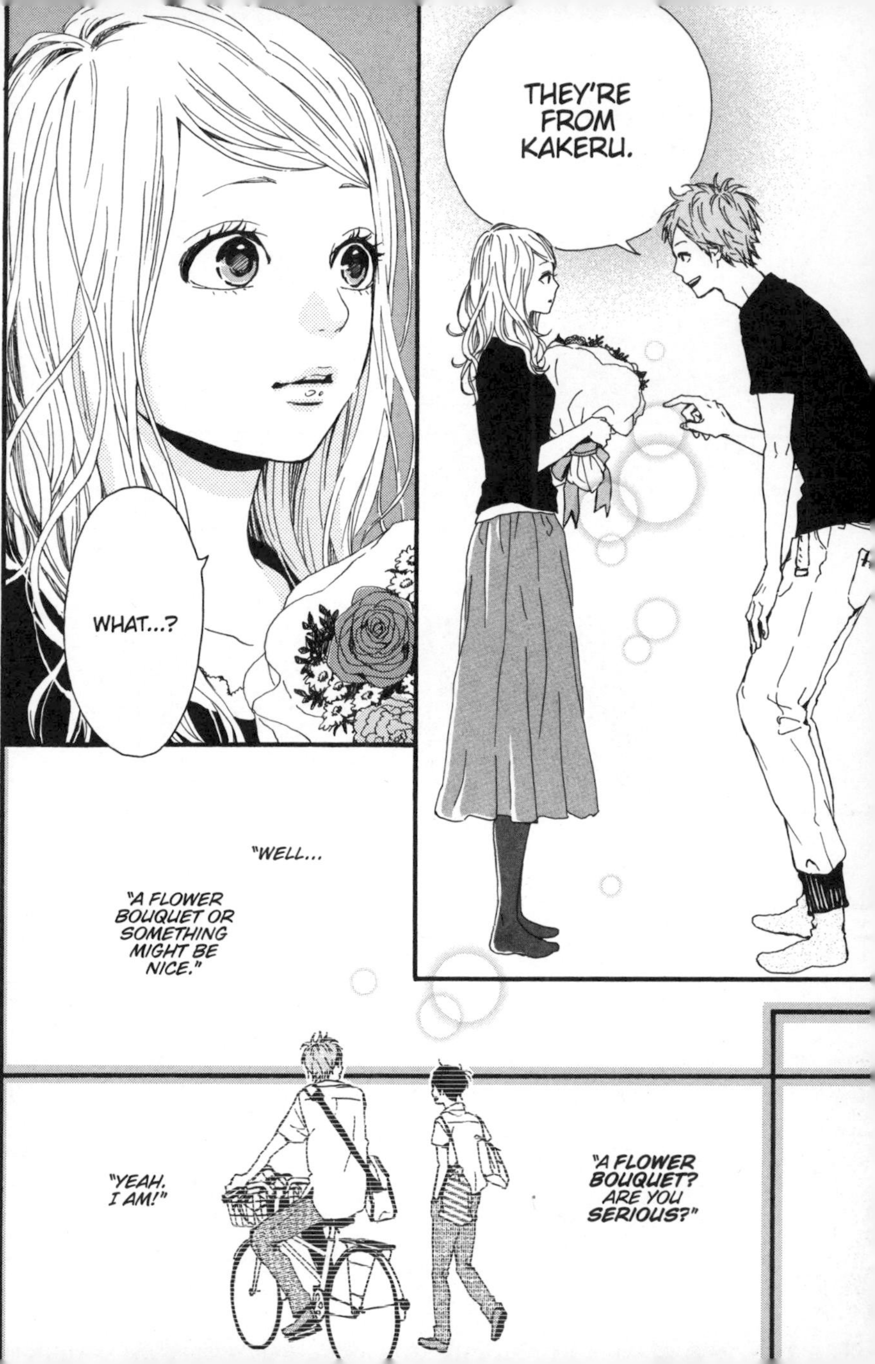
THEY'RE FROM KAKERU.
WHAT...?
"WELL...
"A FLOWER BOUQUET OR SOMETHING MIGHT BE NICE."
"A FLOWER BOUQUET? ARE YOU SERIOUS?"
"YEAH. I AM!"

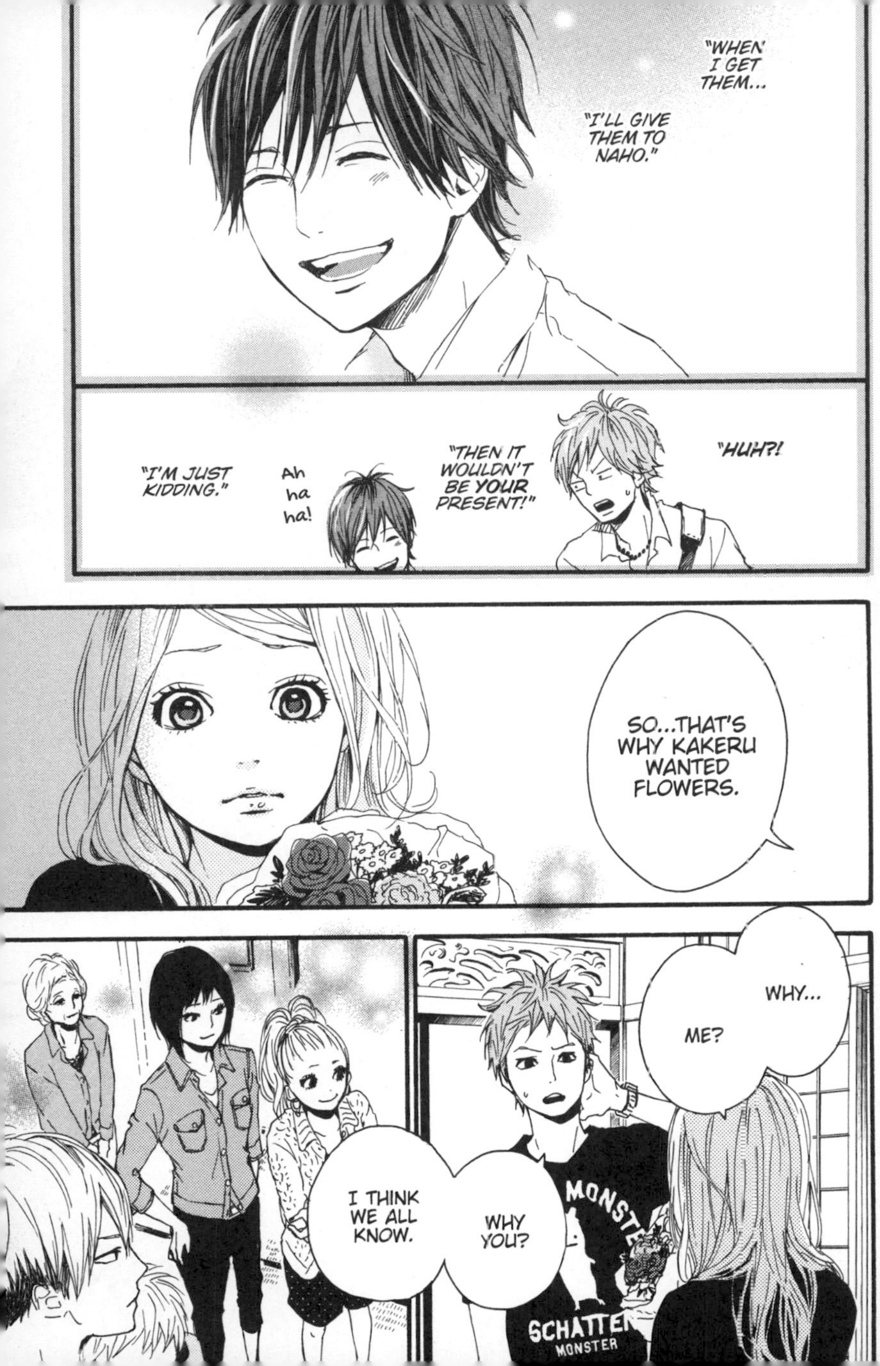
"WHEN I GET THEM...
"I'LL GIVE THEM TO NAHO."
"HUH?!
"THEN IT WOULDN'T BE YOUR PRESENT!"
Ah ha ha!
"I'M JUST KIDDING."
SO...THAT'S WHY KAKERU WANTED FLOWERS.
WHY... ME?
WHY YOU?
I THINK WE ALL KNOW.

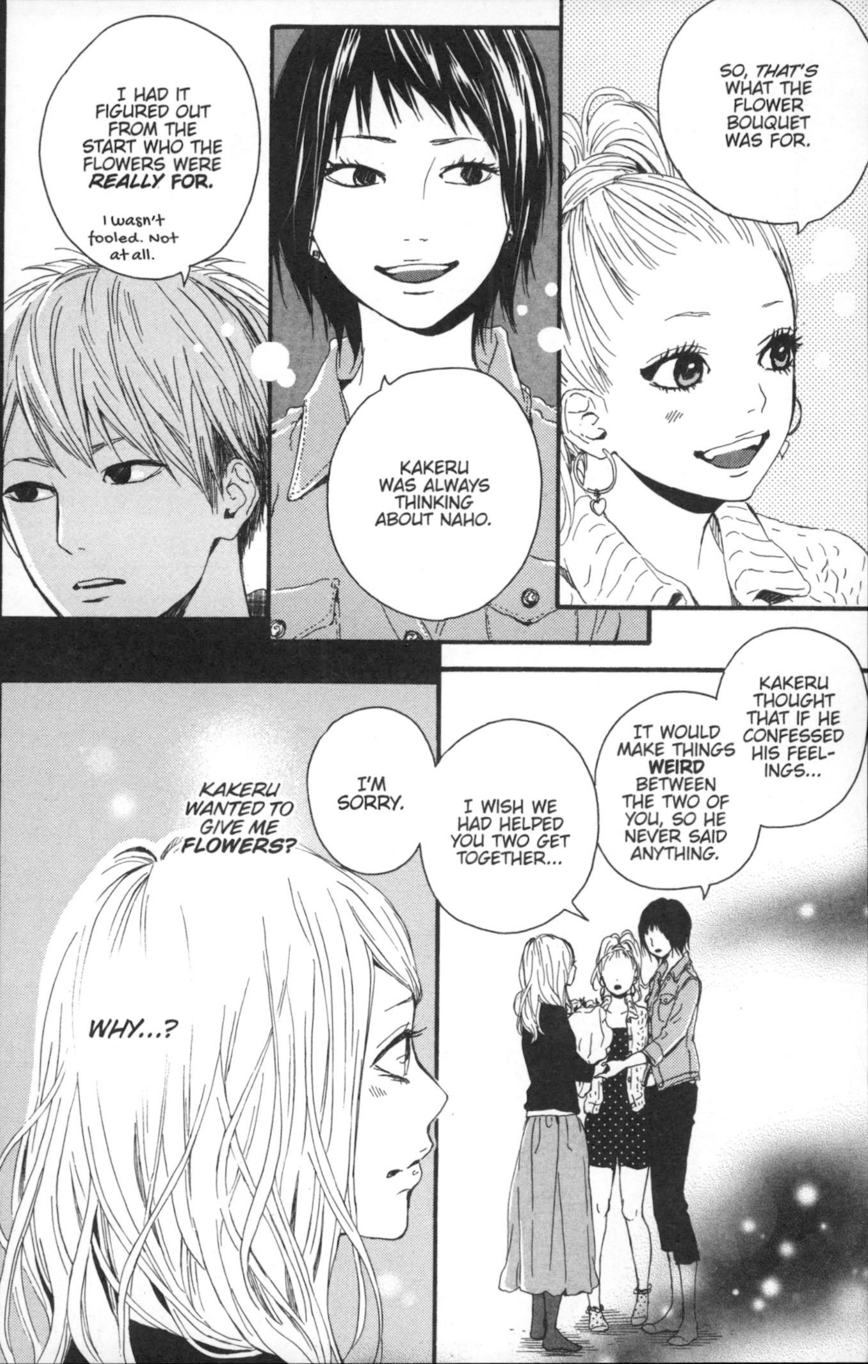
SO, THAT'S WHAT THE FLOWER BOUQUET WAS FOR.
KAKERU WAS ALWAYS THINKING ABOUT NAHO.
I HAD IT FIGURED OUT FROM THE START WHO THE FLOWERS WERE REALLY FOR.
I wasn't fooled. Not at all.
KAKERU THOUGHT THAT IF HE CONFESSED HIS FEEL- INGS...
IT WOULD MAKE THINGS WEIRD BETWEEN THE TWO OF YOU, SO HE NEVER SAID ANYTHING.
I WISH WE HAD HELPED YOU TWO GET TOGETHER...
I'M SORRY.
KAKERU WANTED TO GIVE ME FLOWERS?
WHY...?

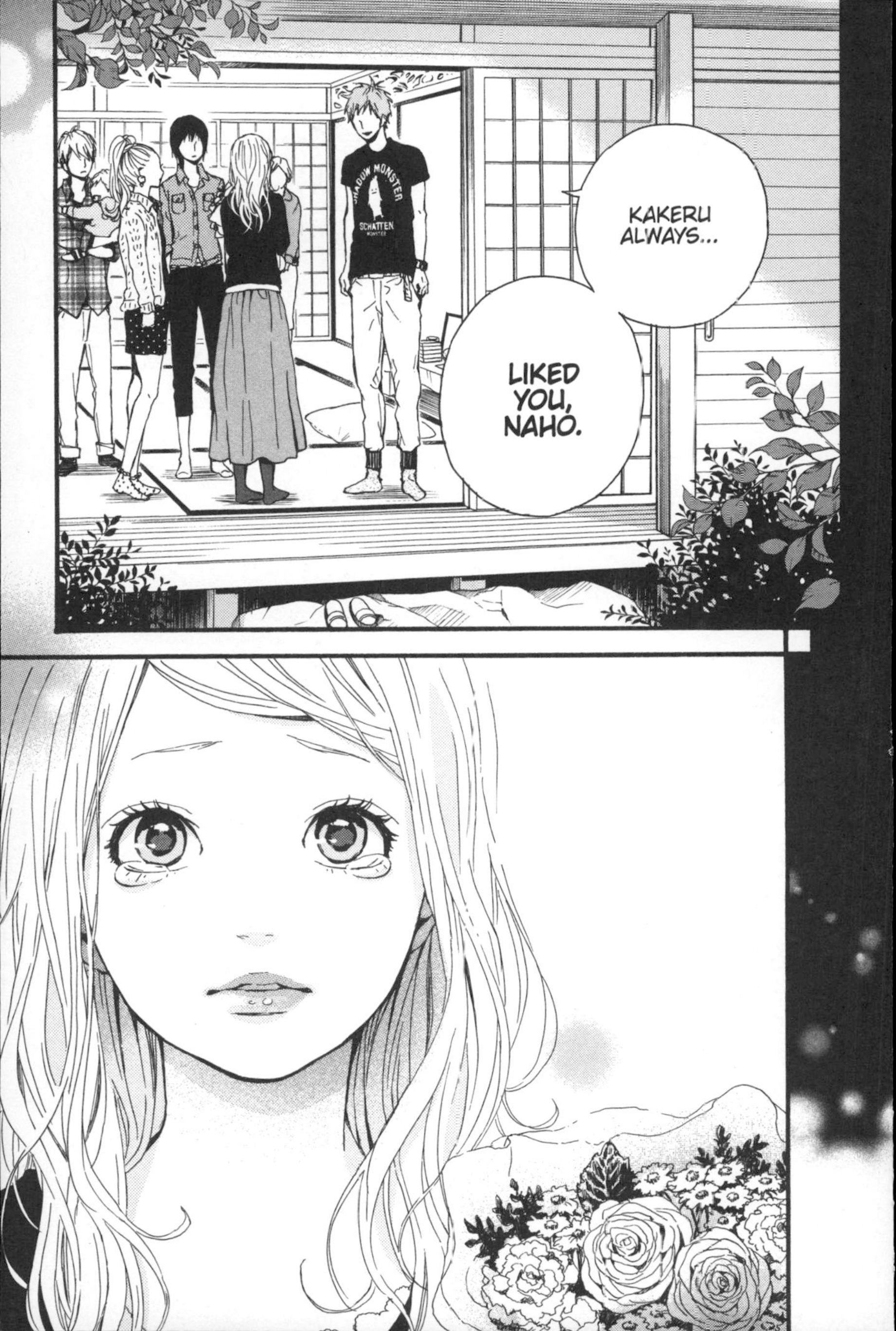
KAKERU ALWAYS...
LIKED YOU, NAHO.
SHADOW MONSTER
SCHATTEN

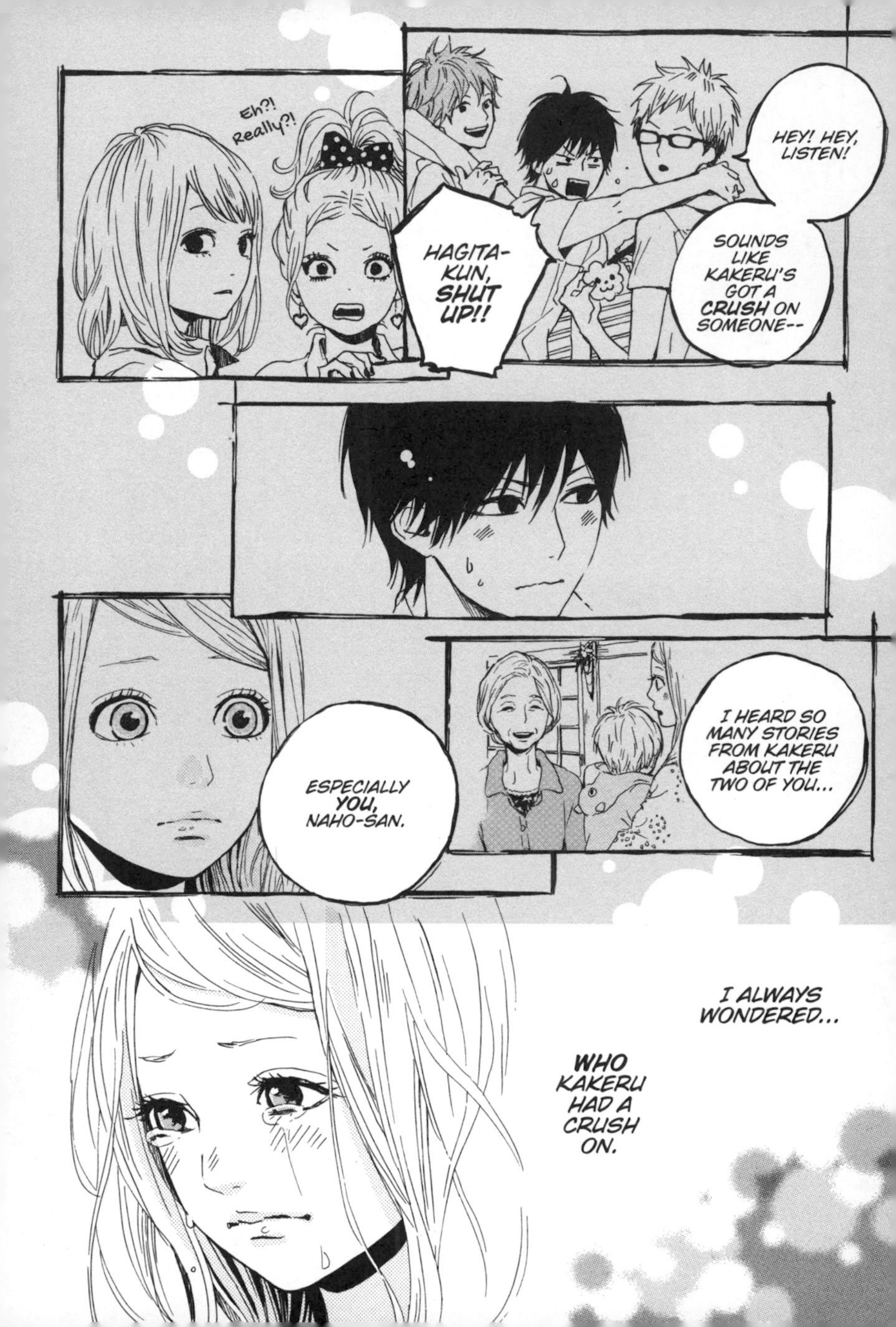
HEY! HEY, LISTEN!
SOUNDS LIKE KAKERU'S GOT A CRUSH ON SOMEONE--
HAGITA-KUN, SHUT UP!!
Eh?! Really?!
I HEARD SO MANY STORIES FROM KAKERU ABOUT THE TWO OF YOU...
ESPECIALLY YOU, NAHO-SAN.
I ALWAYS WONDERED...
WHO KAKERU HAD A CRUSH ON.

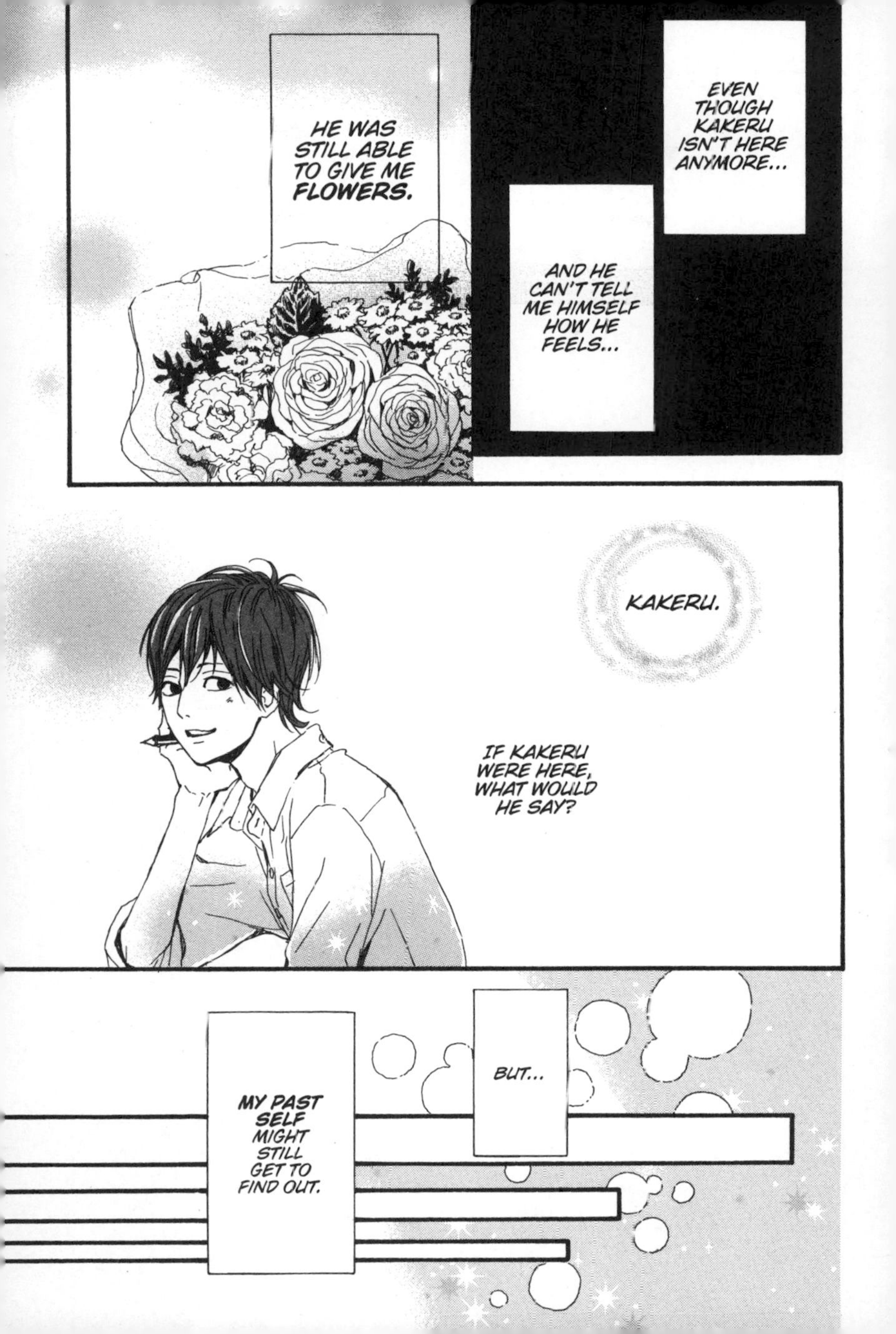
EVEN THOUGH KAKERU ISN'T HERE ANYMORE...
AND HE CAN'T TELL ME HIMSELF HOW HE FEELS...
HE WAS STILL ABLE TO GIVE ME FLOWERS.
KAKERU.
IF KAKERU WERE HERE, WHAT WOULD HE SAY?
BUT...
MY PAST SELF MIGHT STILL GET TO FIND OUT.

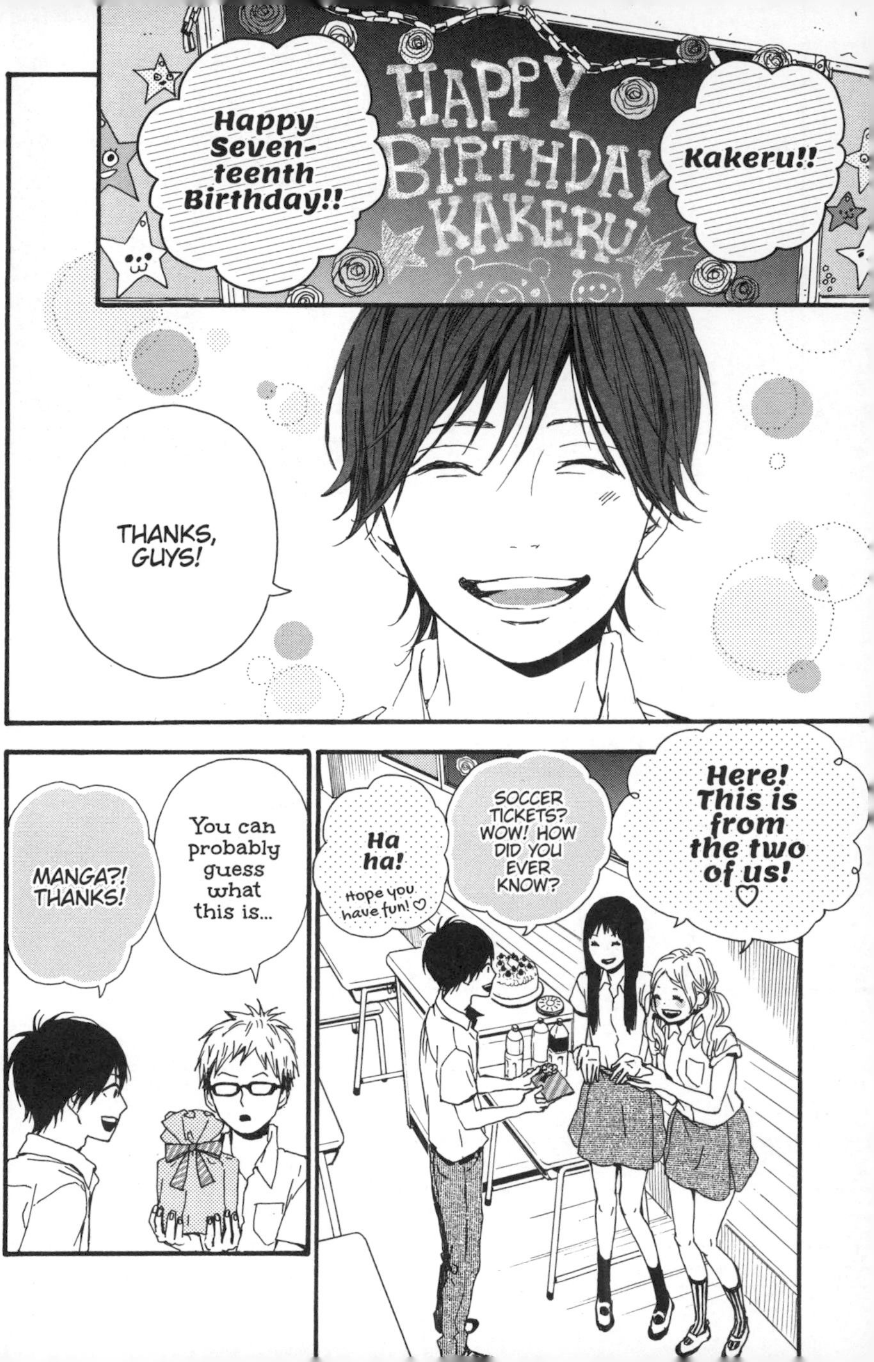
Kakeru!!
HAPPY BIRTHDAY KAKERU
Happy Seventeenth Birthday!!
THANKS, GUYS!
Here! This is from the two of us! ♡
SOCCER TICKETS? WOW! HOW DID YOU EVER KNOW?
Ha ha!
Hope you have fun! ♡
You can probably guess what this is...
MANGA?! THANKS!

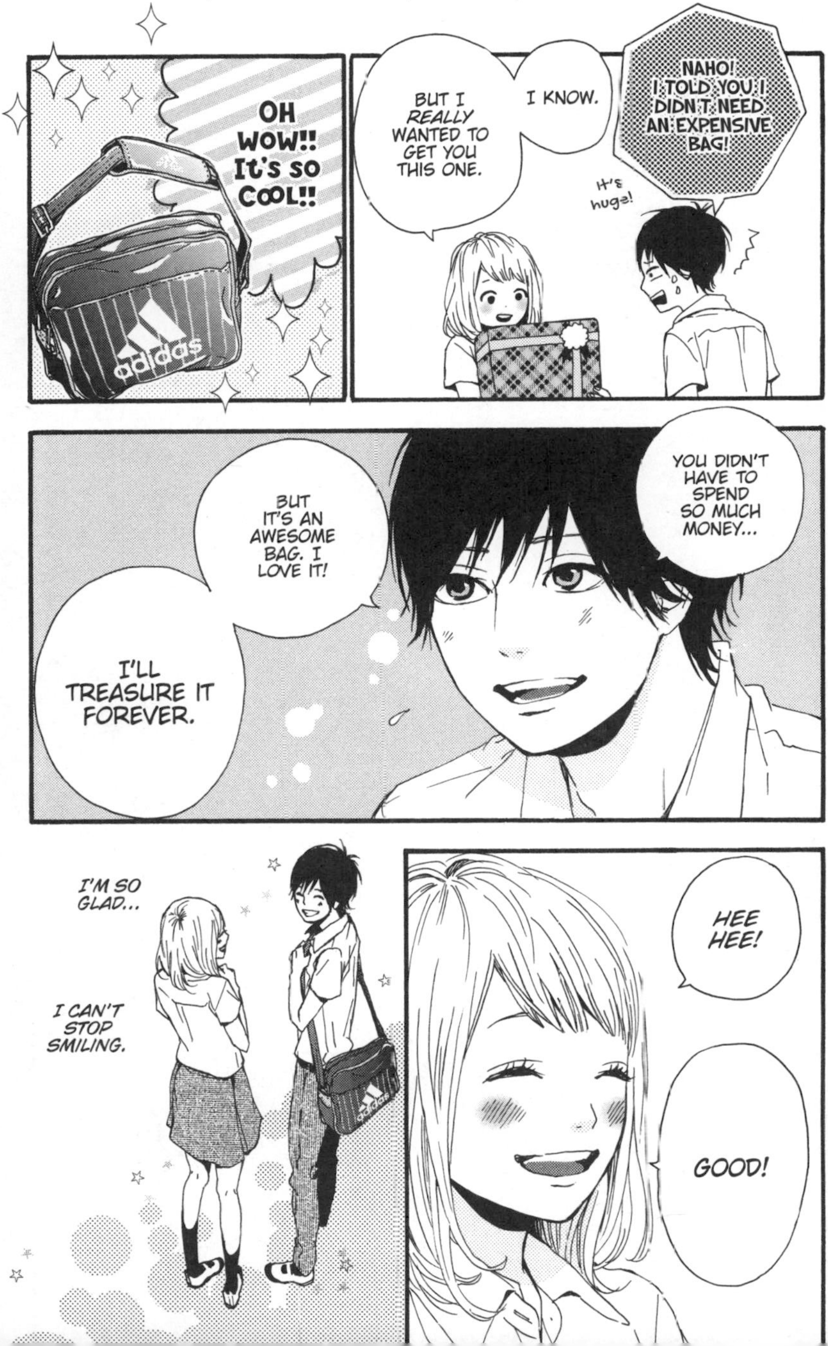
NAHO! I TOLD YOU I DIDN'T NEED AN EXPENSIVE BAG!
It's huge!
I KNOW.
BUT I REALLY WANTED TO GET YOU THIS ONE.
OH WOW!! It's so COOL!!
adidas
YOU DIDN'T HAVE TO SPEND SO MUCH MONEY...
BUT IT'S AN AWESOME BAG. I LOVE IT!
I'LL TREASURE IT FOREVER.
HEE HEE!
GOOD!
I'M SO GLAD...
I CAN'T STOP SMILING.
adidas

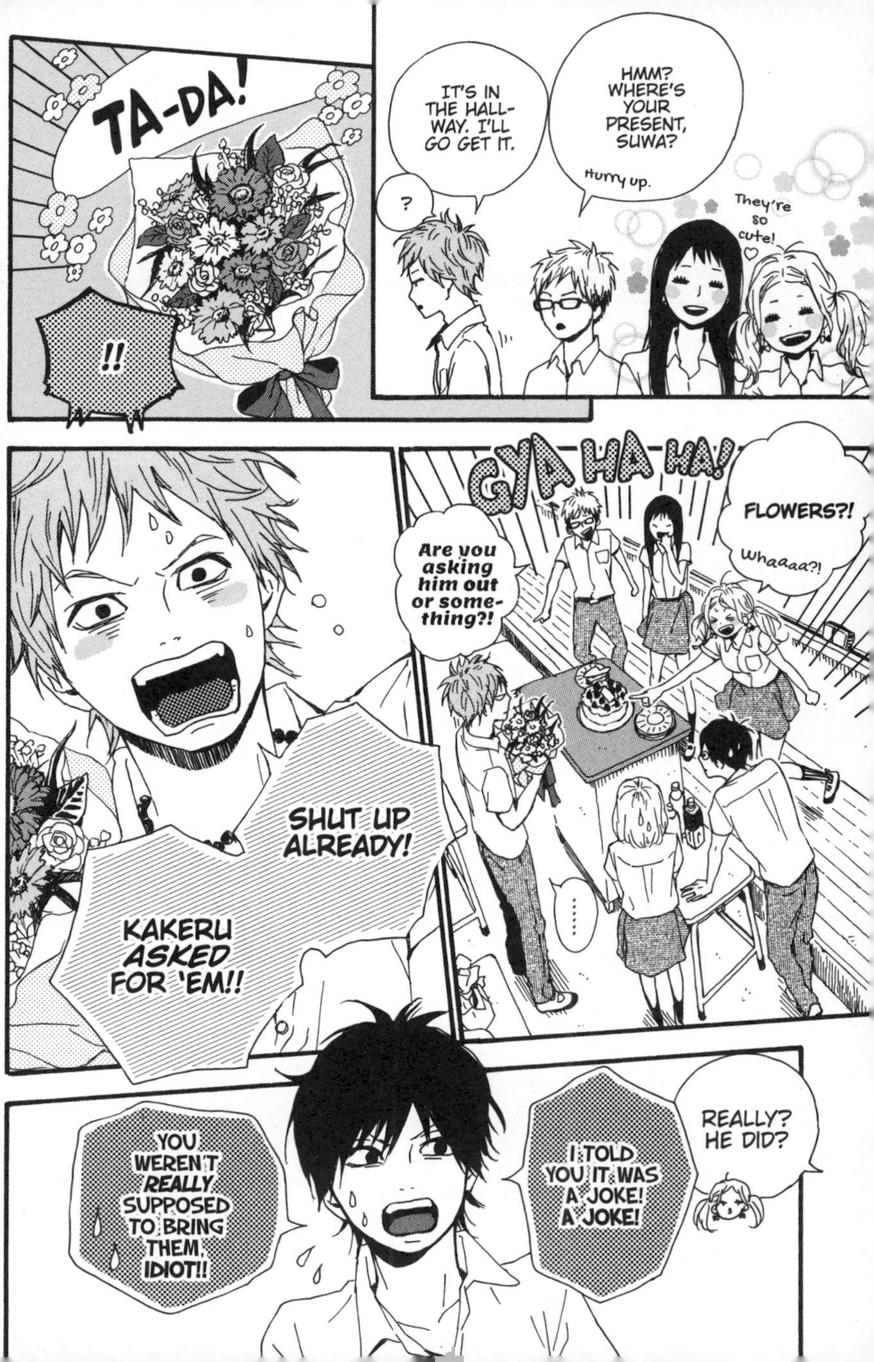
HMM? WHERE'S YOUR PRESENT, SUWA?
Hurry up.
They're so cute!
IT'S IN THE HALL-WAY. I'LL GO GET IT.
?
TA-DA!
!!
GYA HA HA!
FLOWERS?!
Whaaaa?!
Are you asking him out or some-thing?!
......
SHUT UP ALREADY!
KAKERU ASKED FOR 'EM!!
REALLY? HE DID?
I TOLD YOU IT WAS A JOKE! A JOKE!
YOU WEREN'T REALLY SUPPOSED TO BRING THEM, IDIOT!!

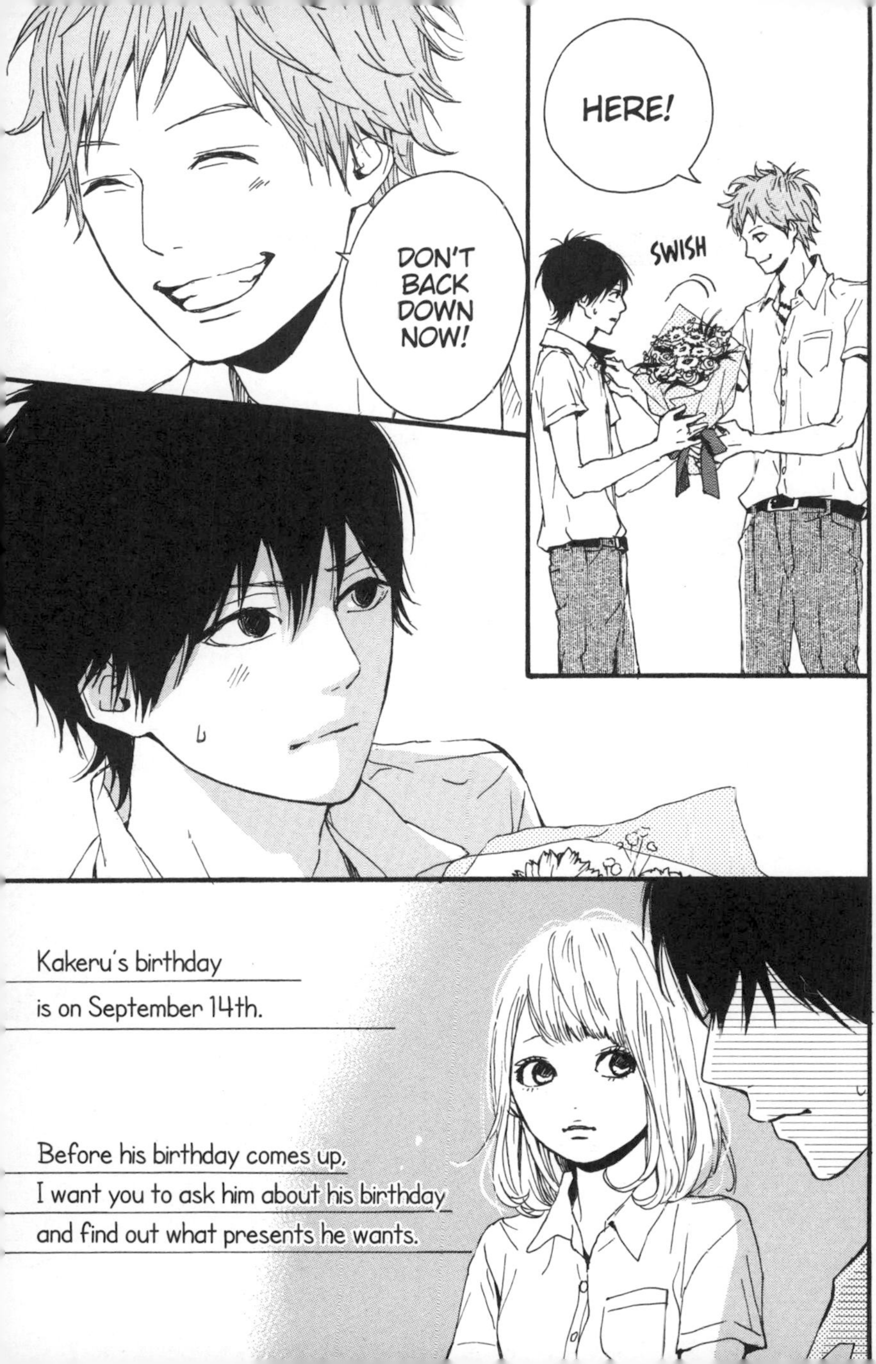
HERE!
SWISH
DON'T BACK DOWN NOW!
Kakeru's birthday
is on September 14th.
Before his birthday comes up,
I want you to ask him about his birthday
and find out what presents he wants.

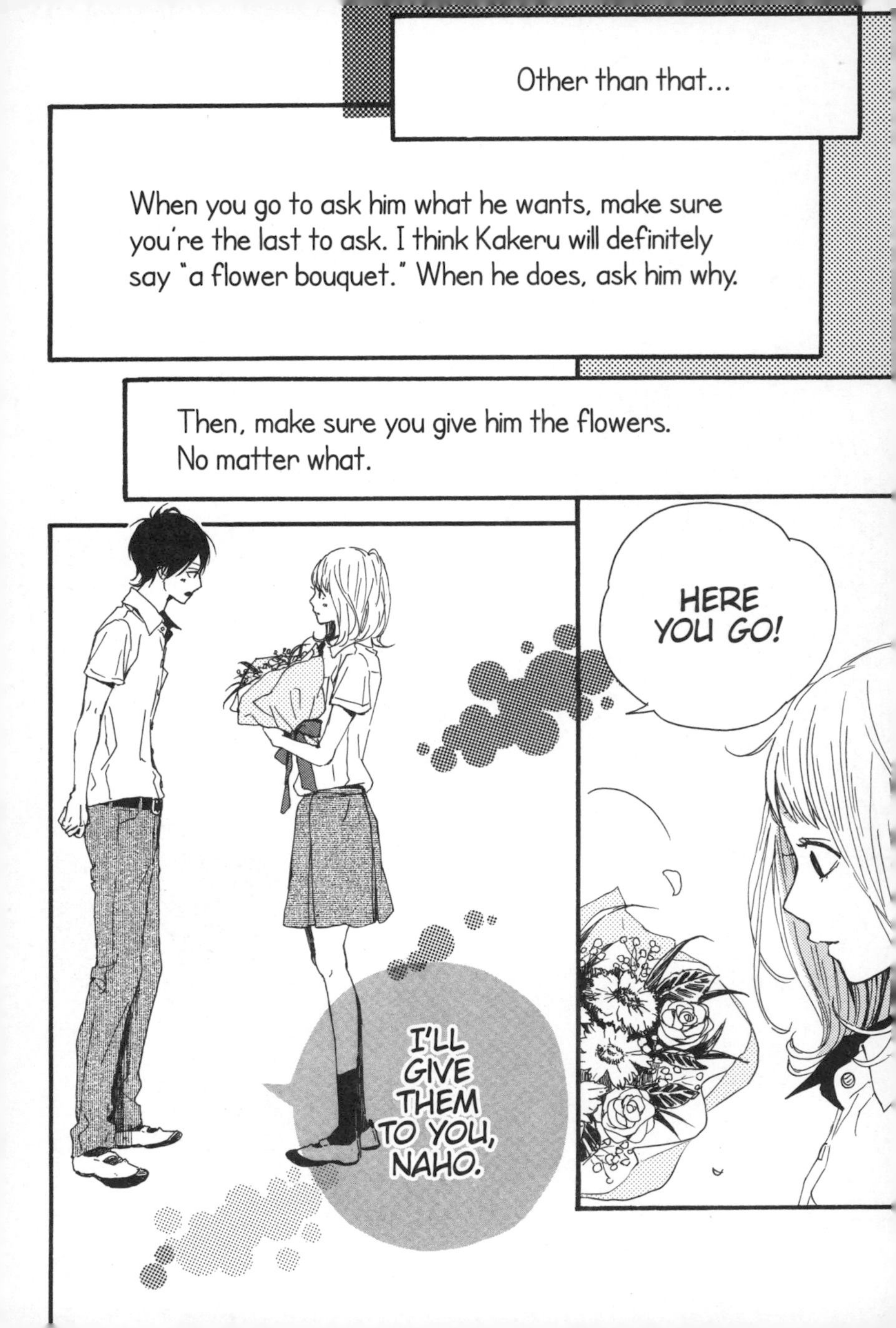
Other than that...
When you go to ask him what he wants, make sure you're the last to ask. I think Kakeru will definitely say "a flower bouquet." When he does, ask him why.
Then, make sure you give him the flowers. No matter what.
HERE YOU GO!
I'LL GIVE THEM TO YOU, NAHO.

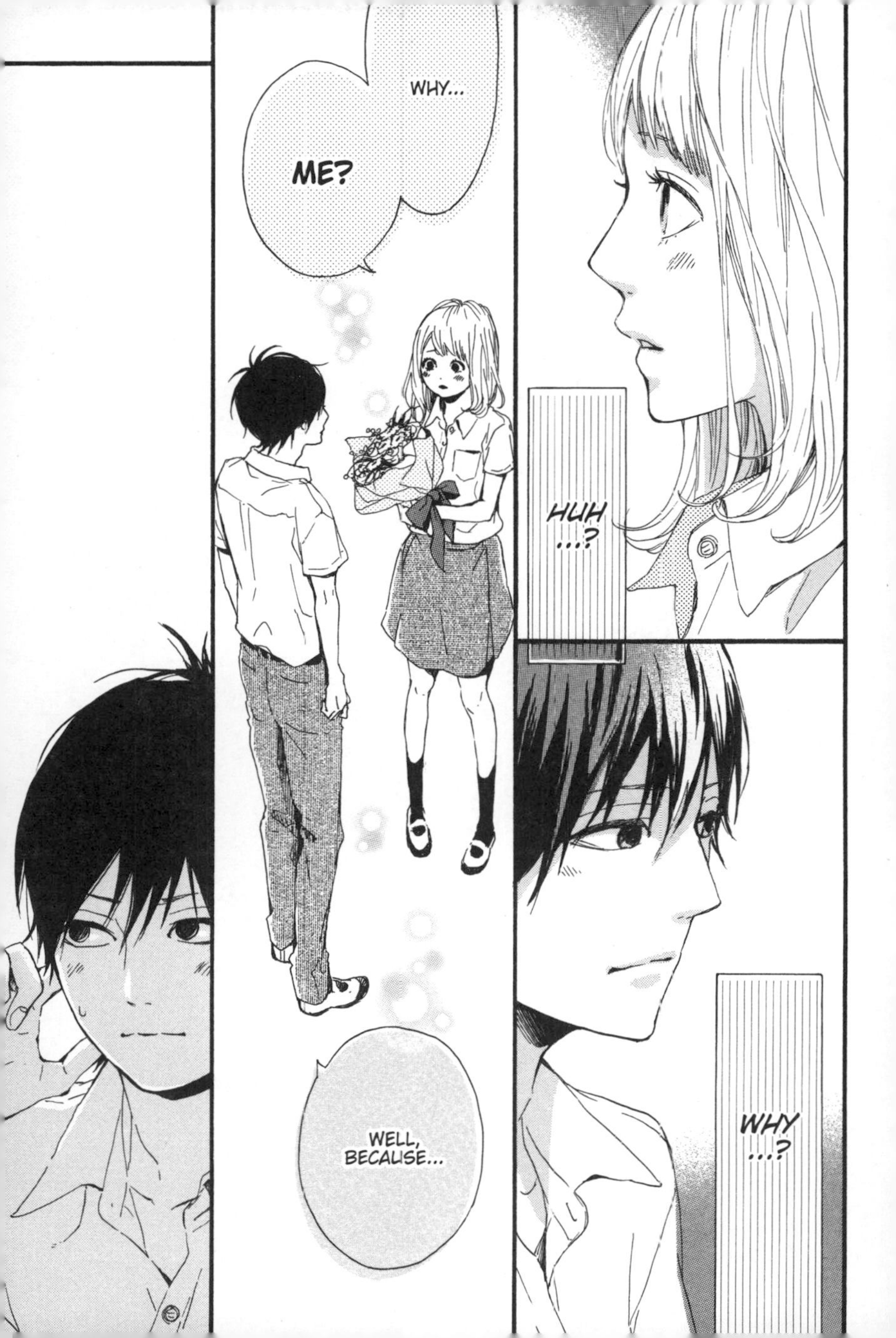
HUH ...?
WHY ...?
WHY... ME?
WELL, BECAUSE...

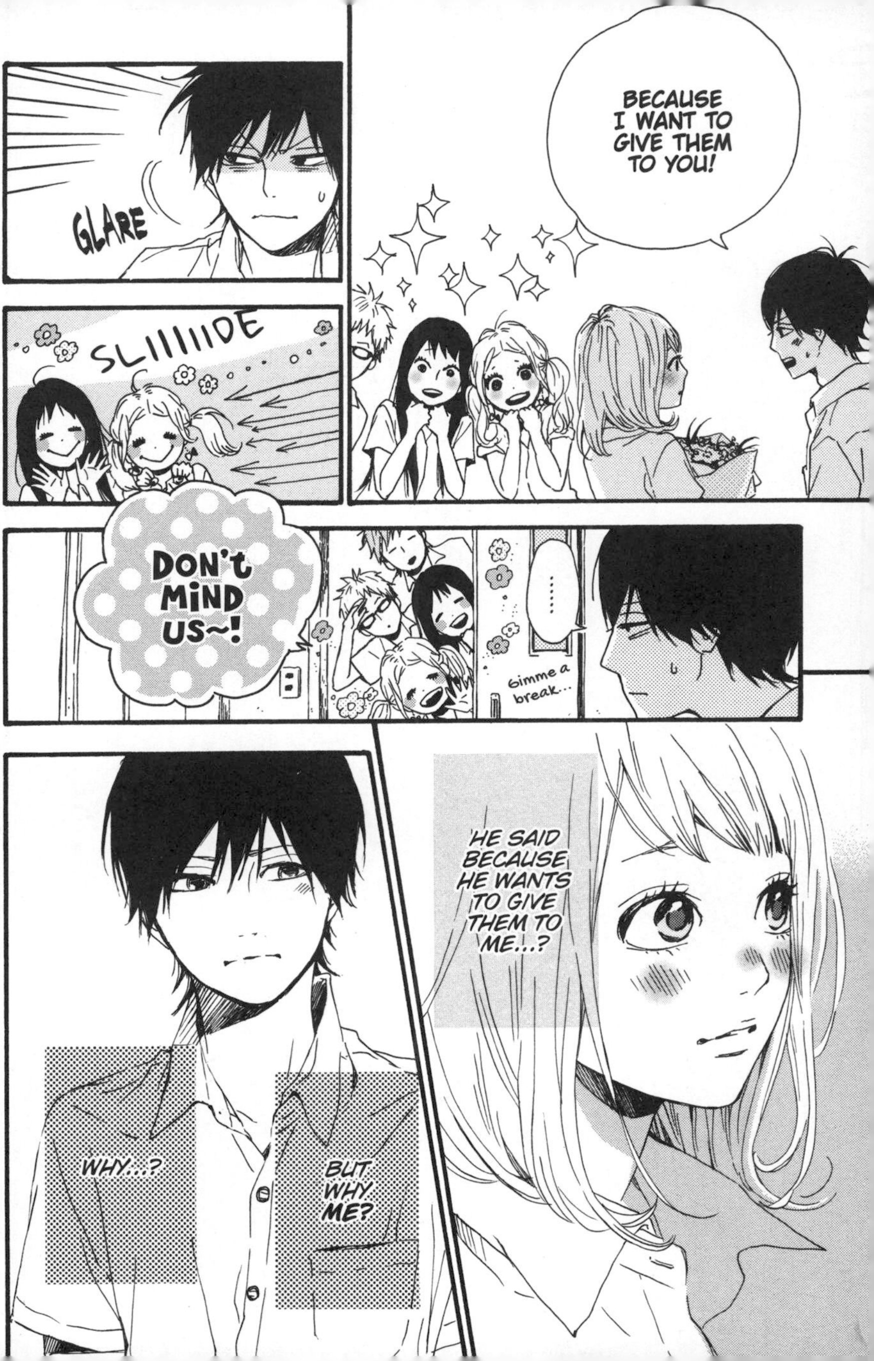
BECAUSE I WANT TO GIVE THEM TO YOU!
GLARE
SLIIIIIDE
......
Gimme a break...
DON'T MIND US~!
HE SAID BECAUSE HE WANTS TO GIVE THEM TO ME...?
WHY...?
BUT WHY ME?

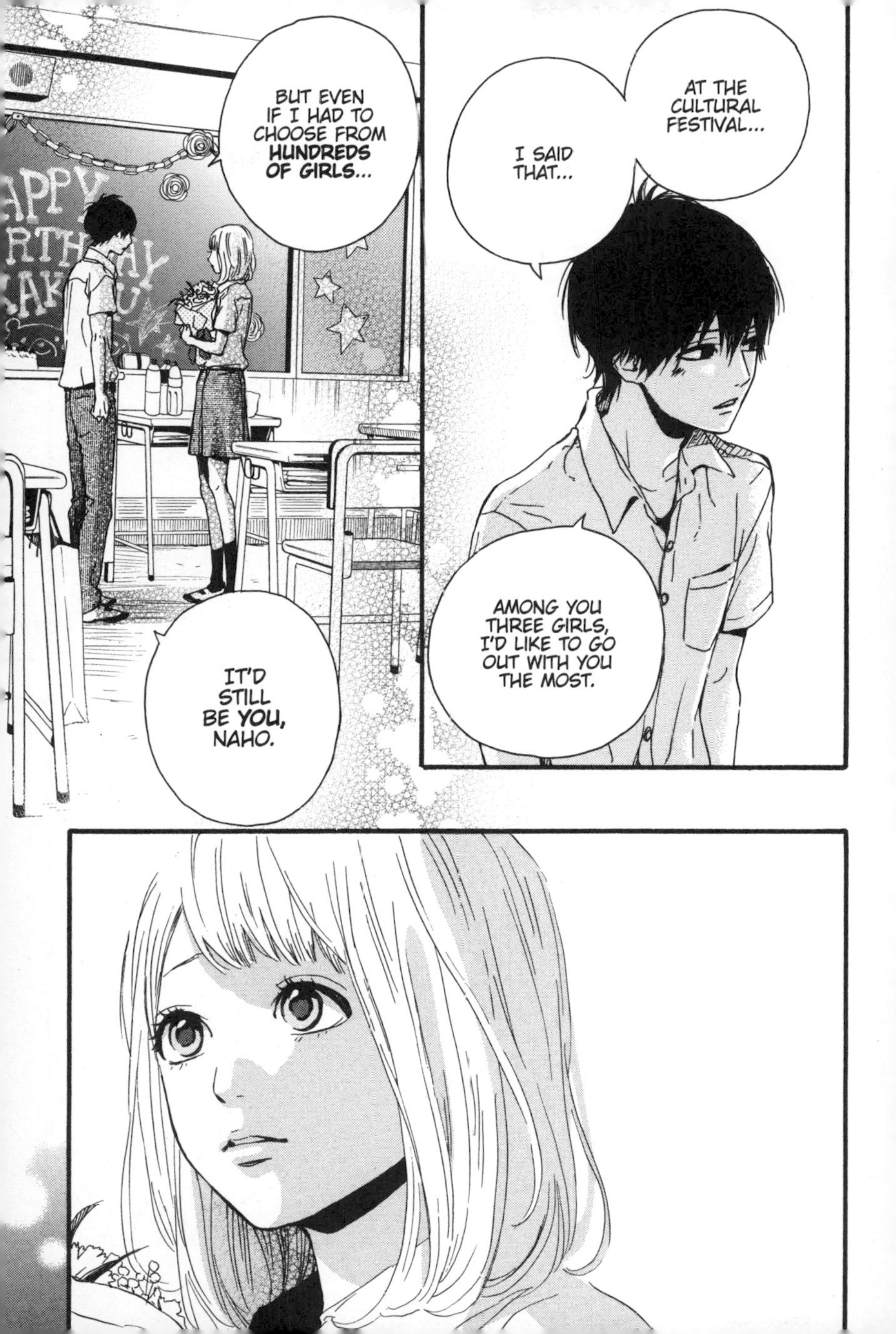
AT THE CULTURAL FESTIVAL...
I SAID THAT...
AMONG YOU THREE GIRLS, I'D LIKE TO GO OUT WITH YOU THE MOST.
BUT EVEN IF I HAD TO CHOOSE FROM **HUNDREDS OF GIRLS...**
IT'D STILL BE **YOU,** NAHO.

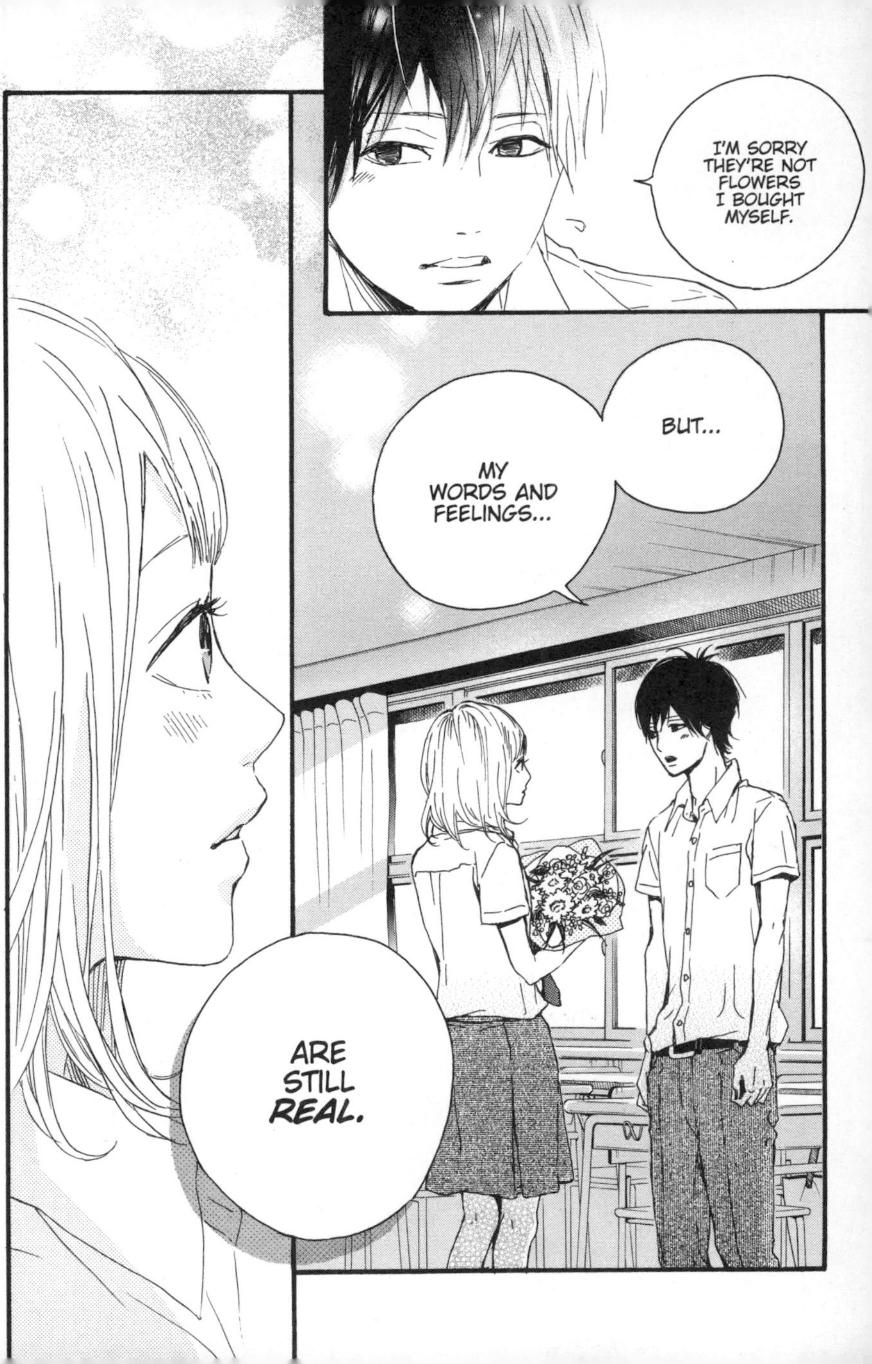
I'M SORRY THEY'RE NOT FLOWERS I BOUGHT MYSELF.
BUT...
MY WORDS AND FEELINGS...
ARE STILL REAL.

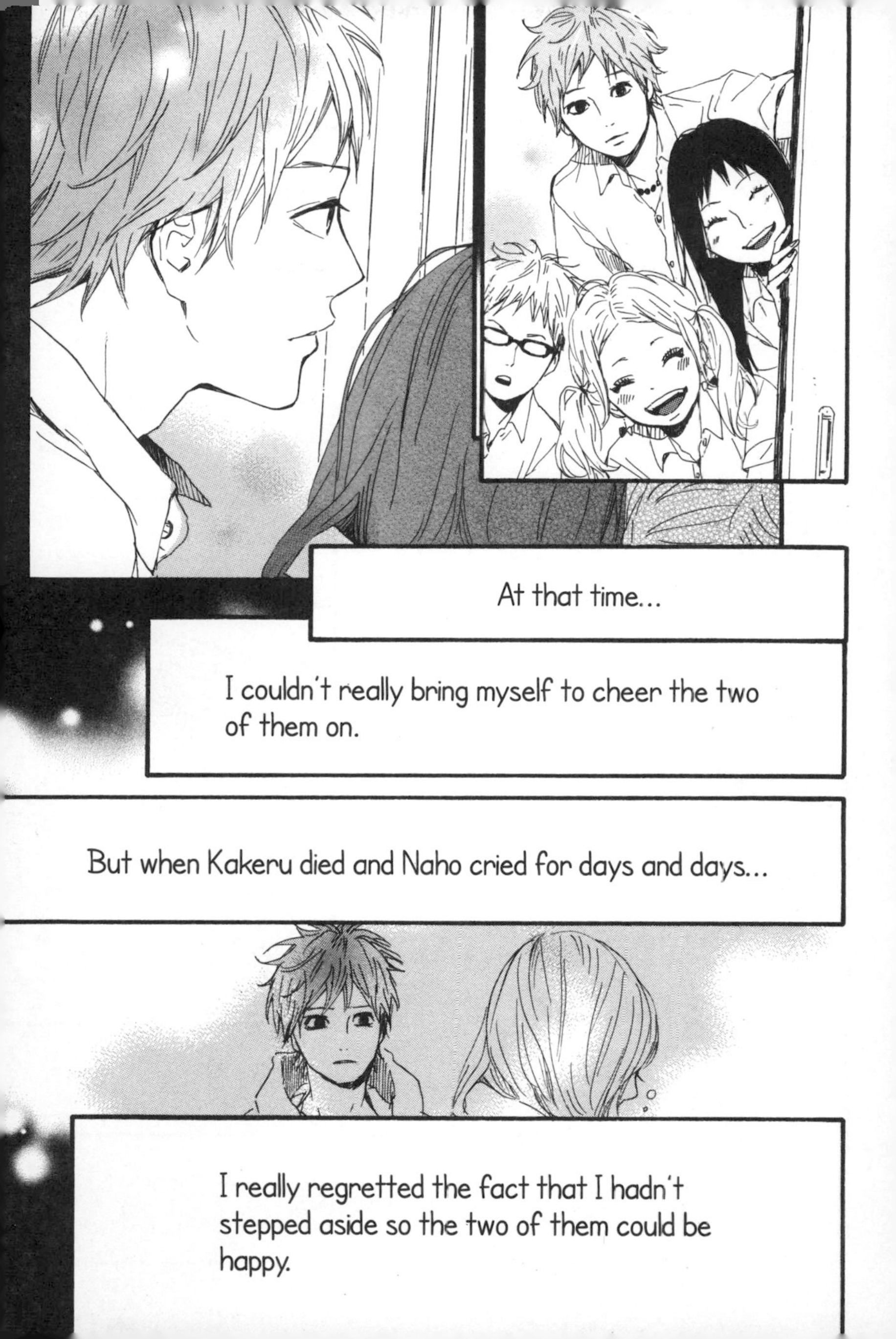
At that time...
I couldn't really bring myself to cheer the two of them on.
But when Kakeru died and Naho cried for days and days...
I really regretted the fact that I hadn't stepped aside so the two of them could be happy.

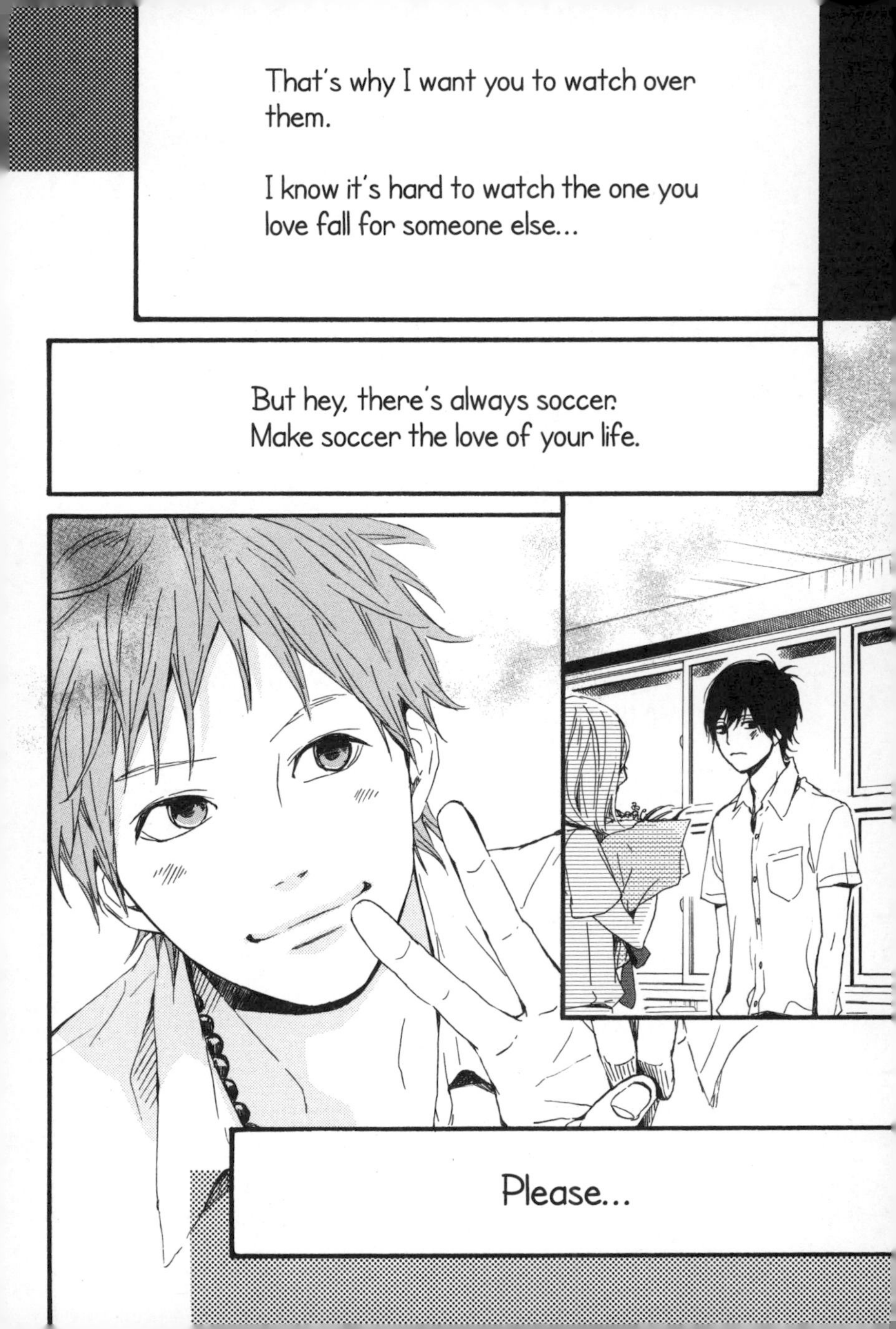
That's why I want you to watch over them.
I know it's hard to watch the one you love fall for someone else...
But hey, there's always soccer. Make soccer the love of your life.
Please...

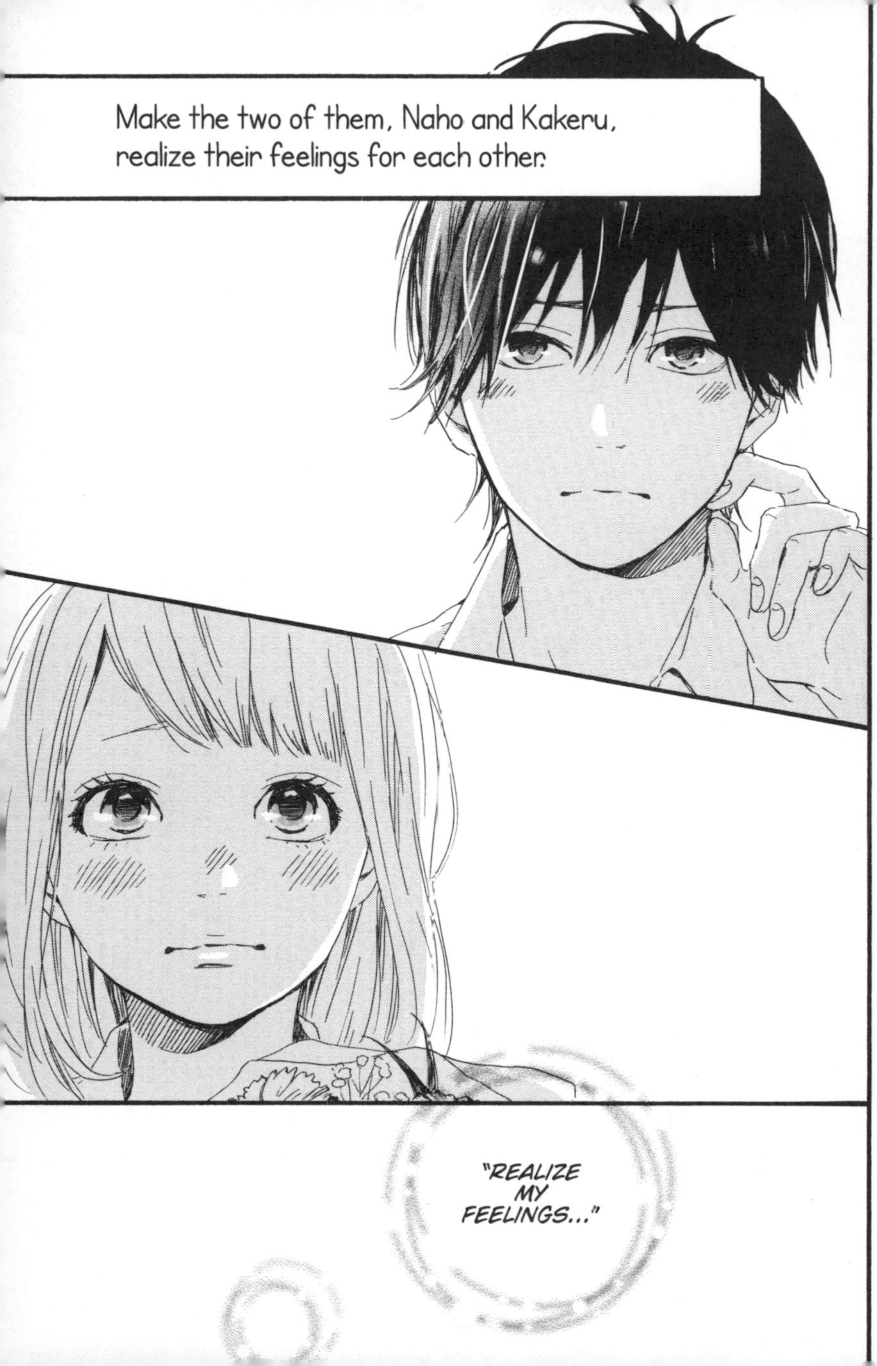
Make the two of them, Naho and Kakeru, realize their feelings for each other.
"REALIZE MY FEELINGS..."

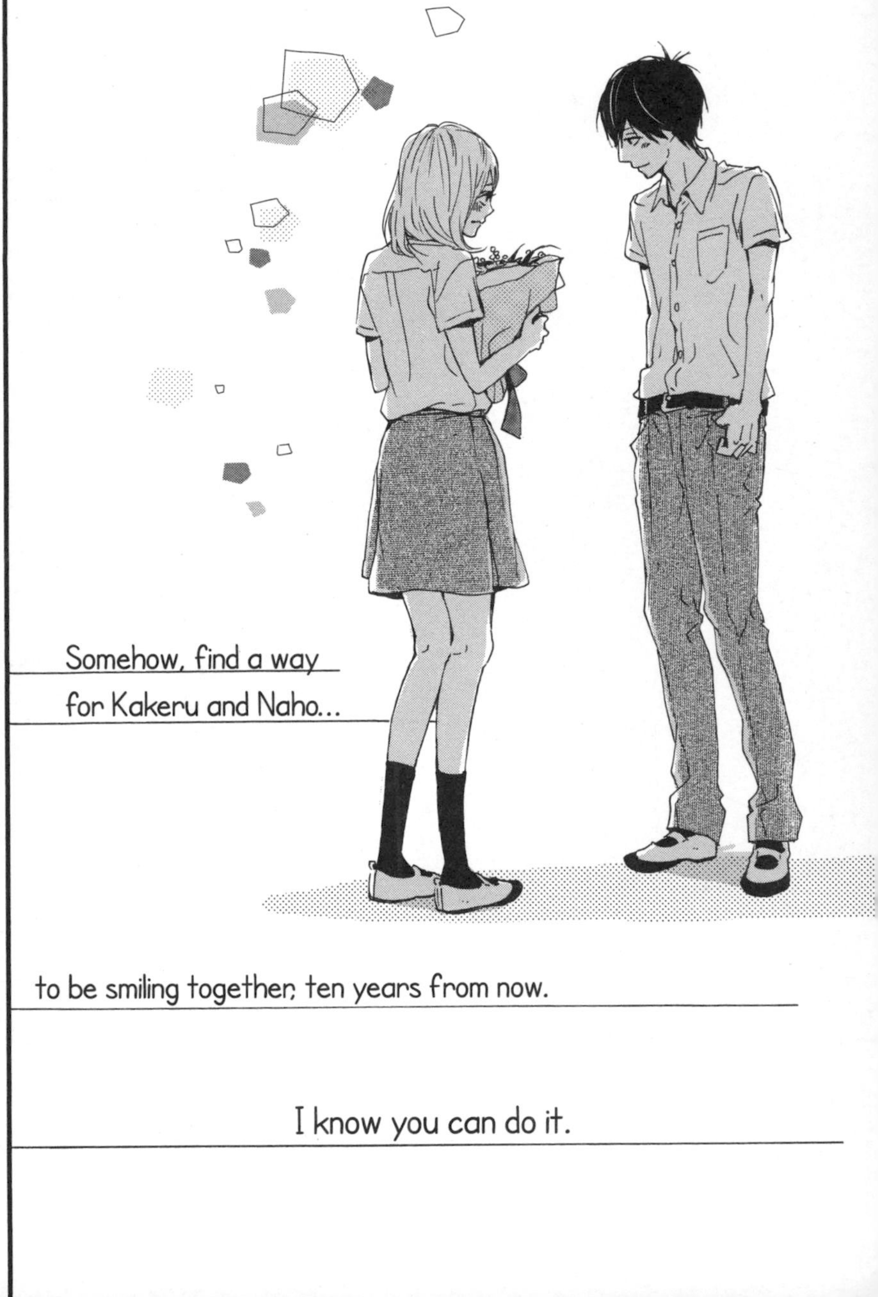
Somehow, find a way
for Kakeru and Naho...
to be smiling together, ten years from now.
I know you can do it.

orange

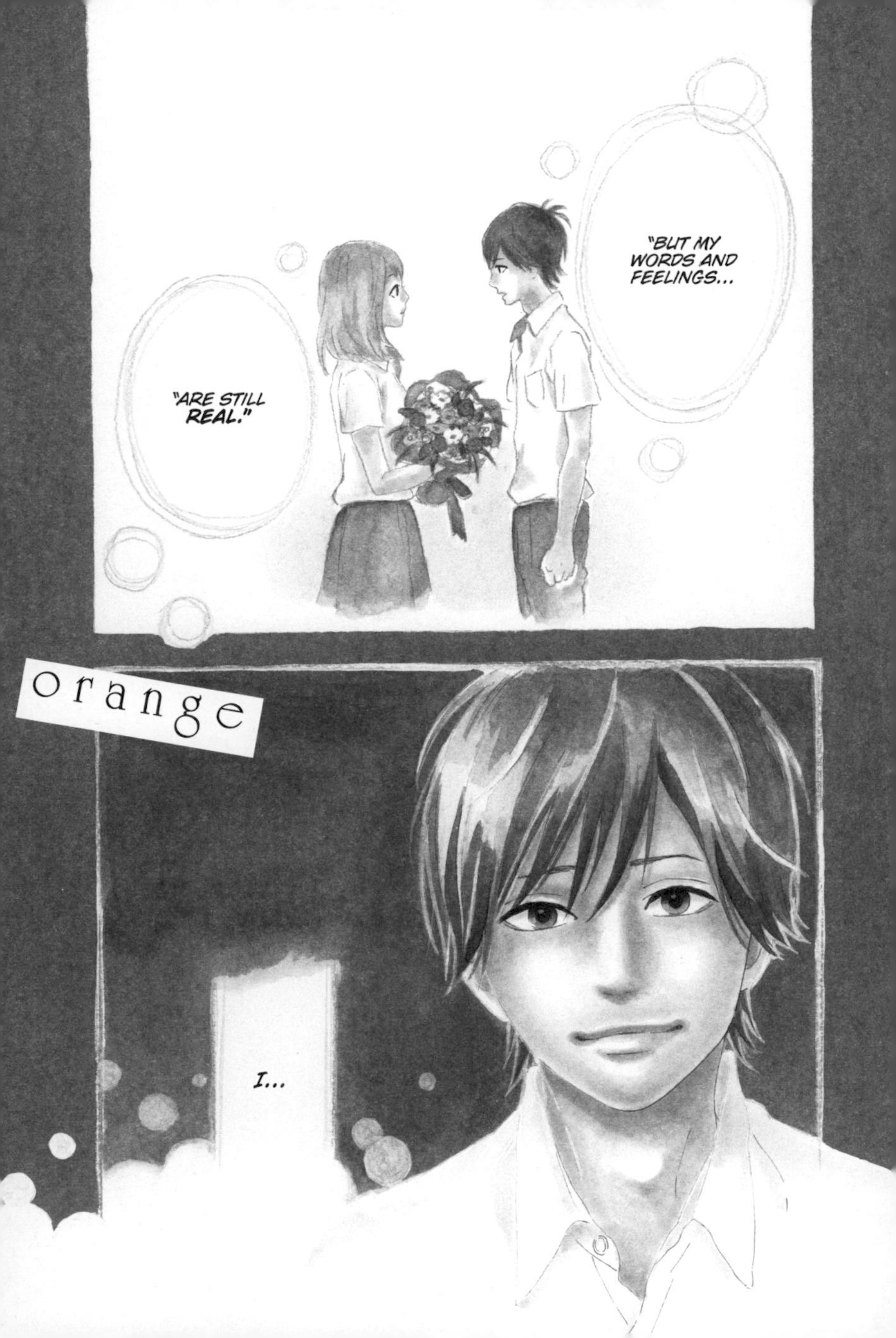
"BUT MY WORDS AND FEELINGS...
"ARE STILL REAL."
orange
I...

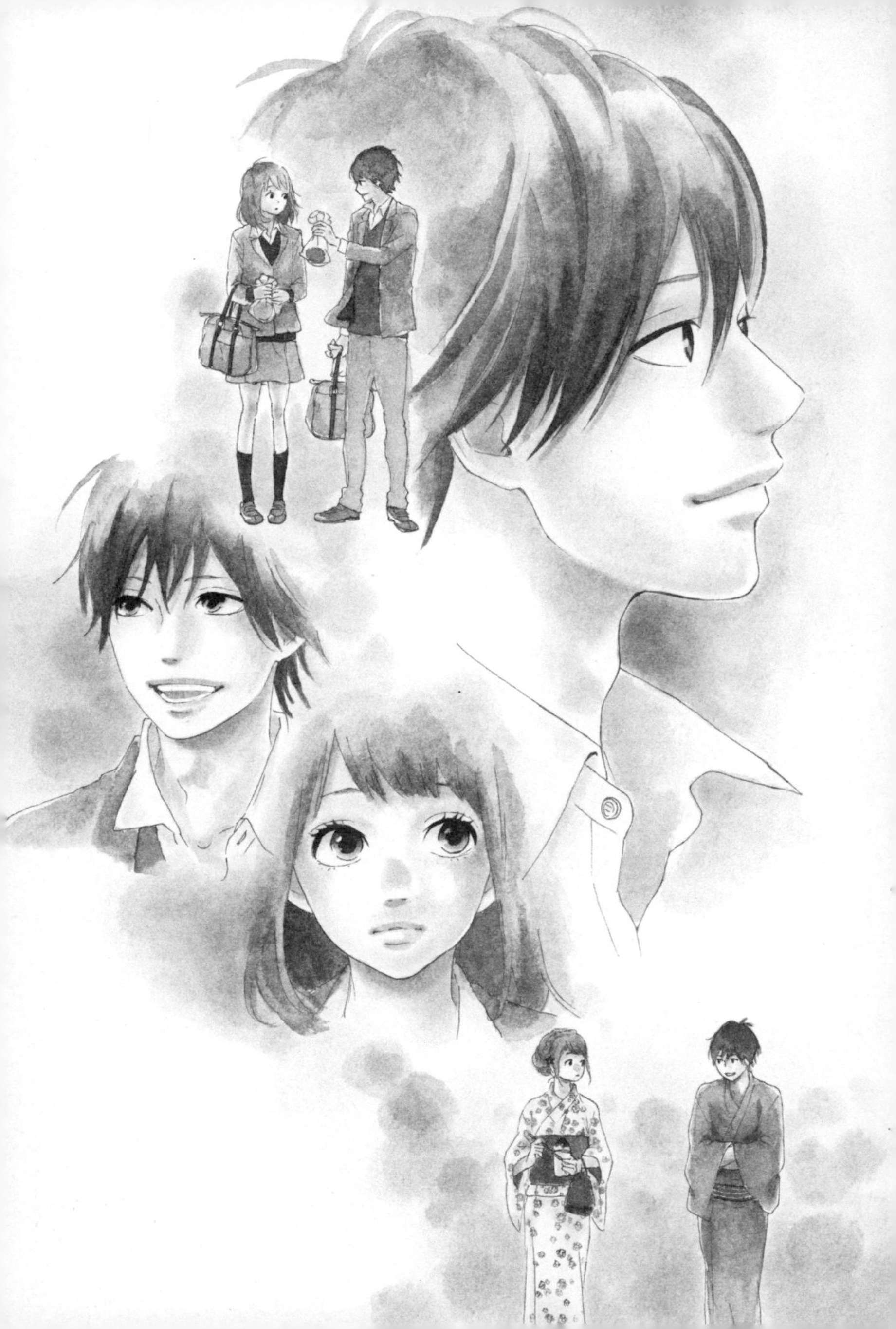

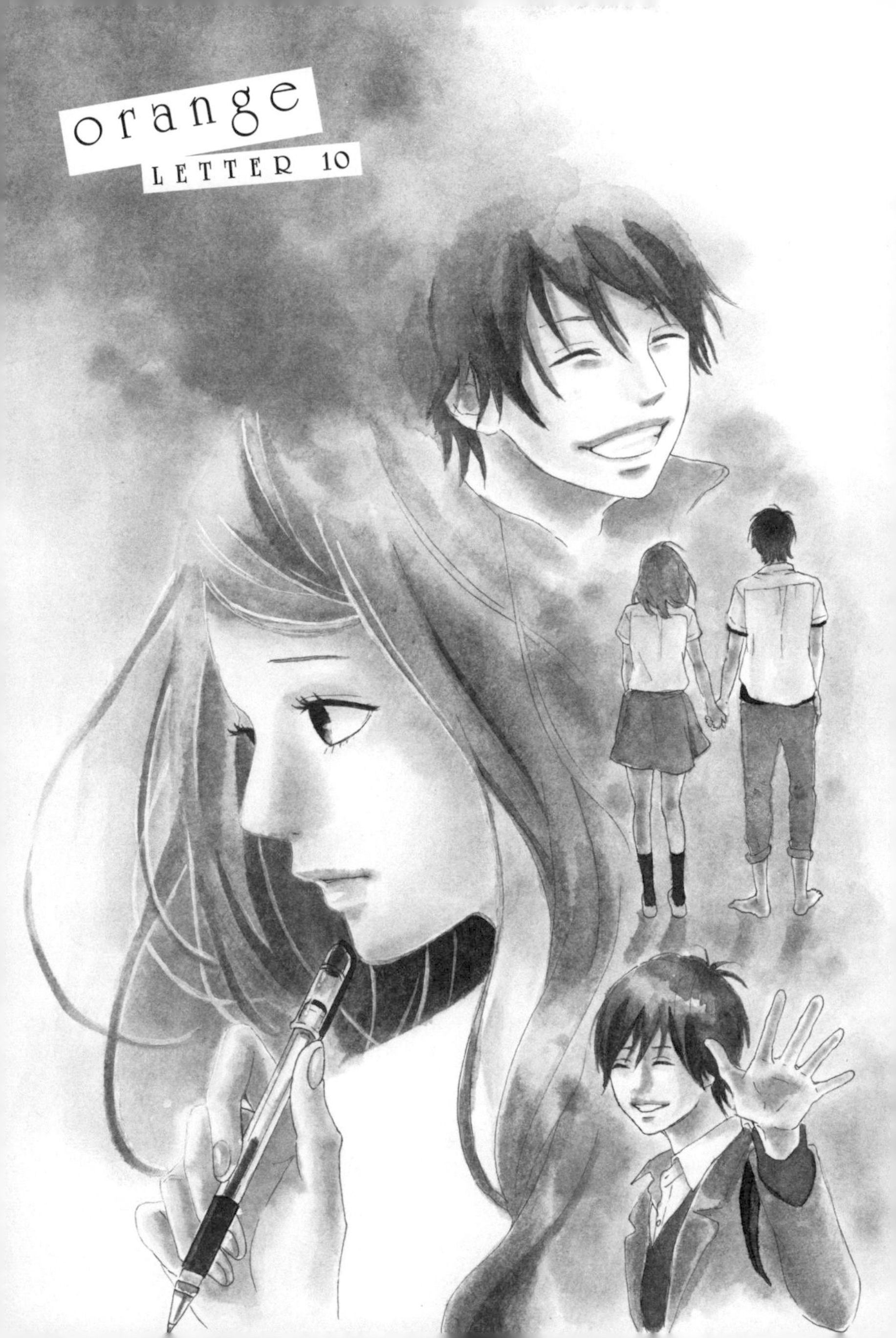
orange
LETTER 10

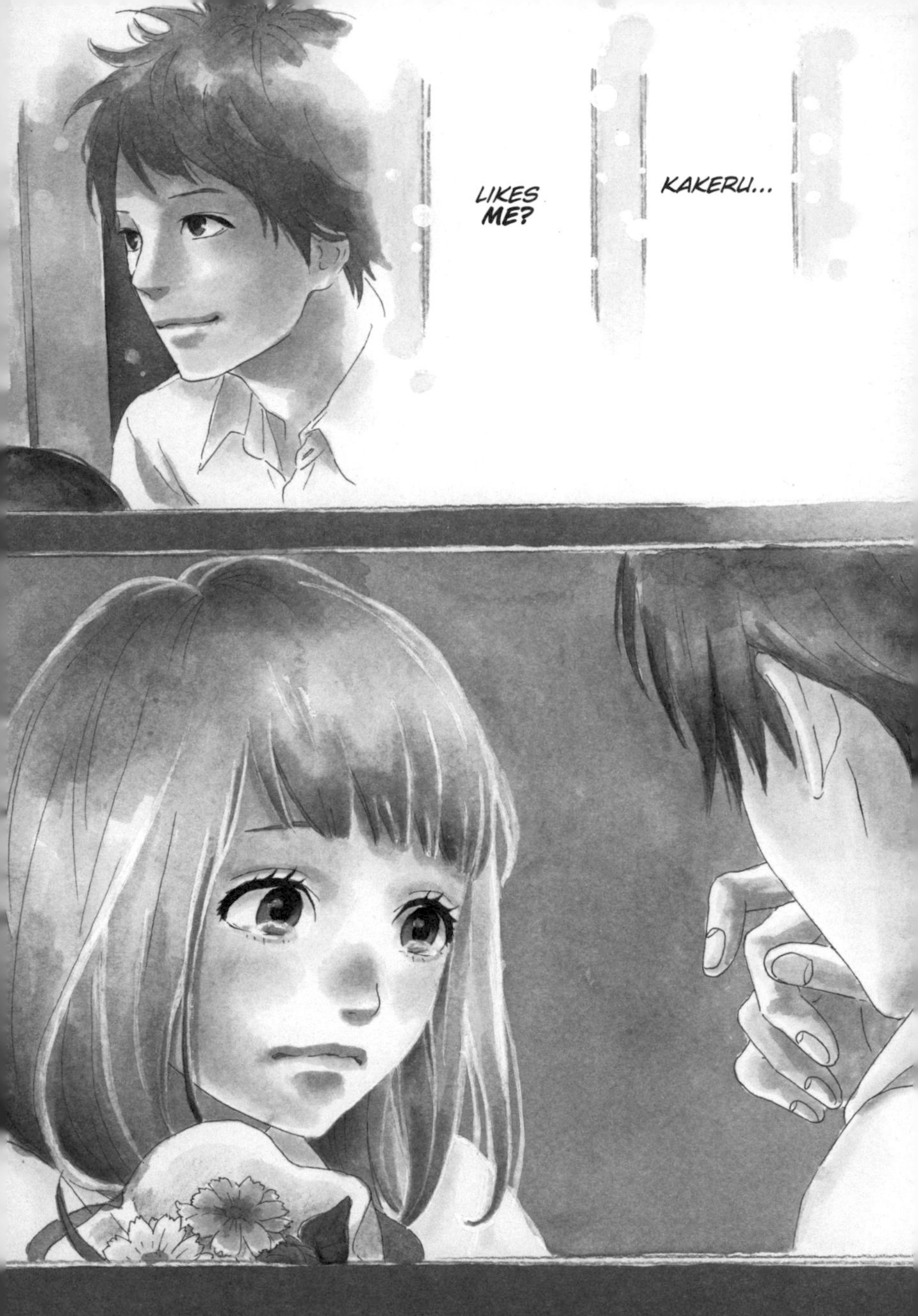
KAKERU...
LIKES ME?

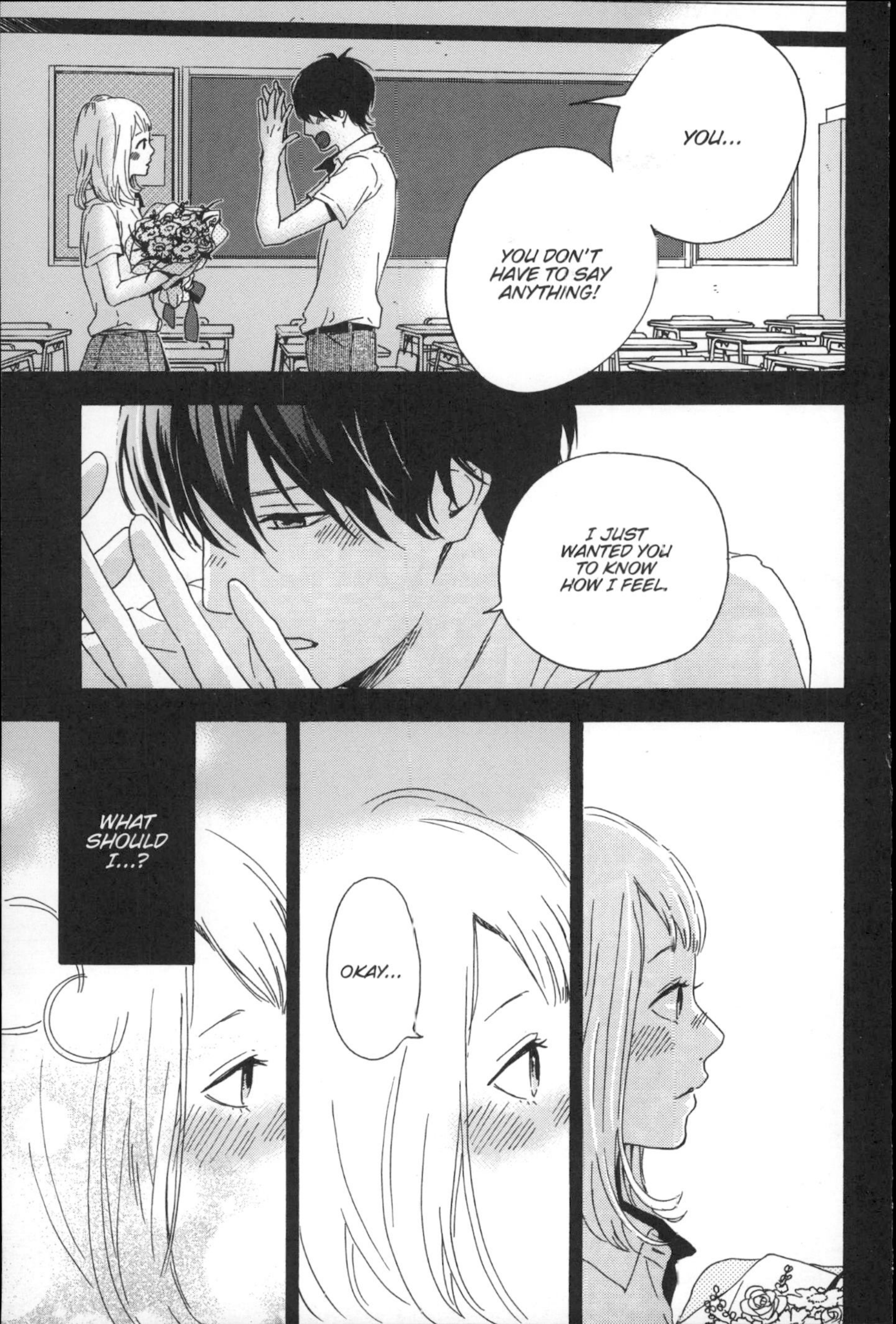
YOU...
YOU DON'T HAVE TO SAY ANYTHING!
I JUST WANTED YOU TO KNOW HOW I FEEL.
OKAY...
WHAT SHOULD I...?

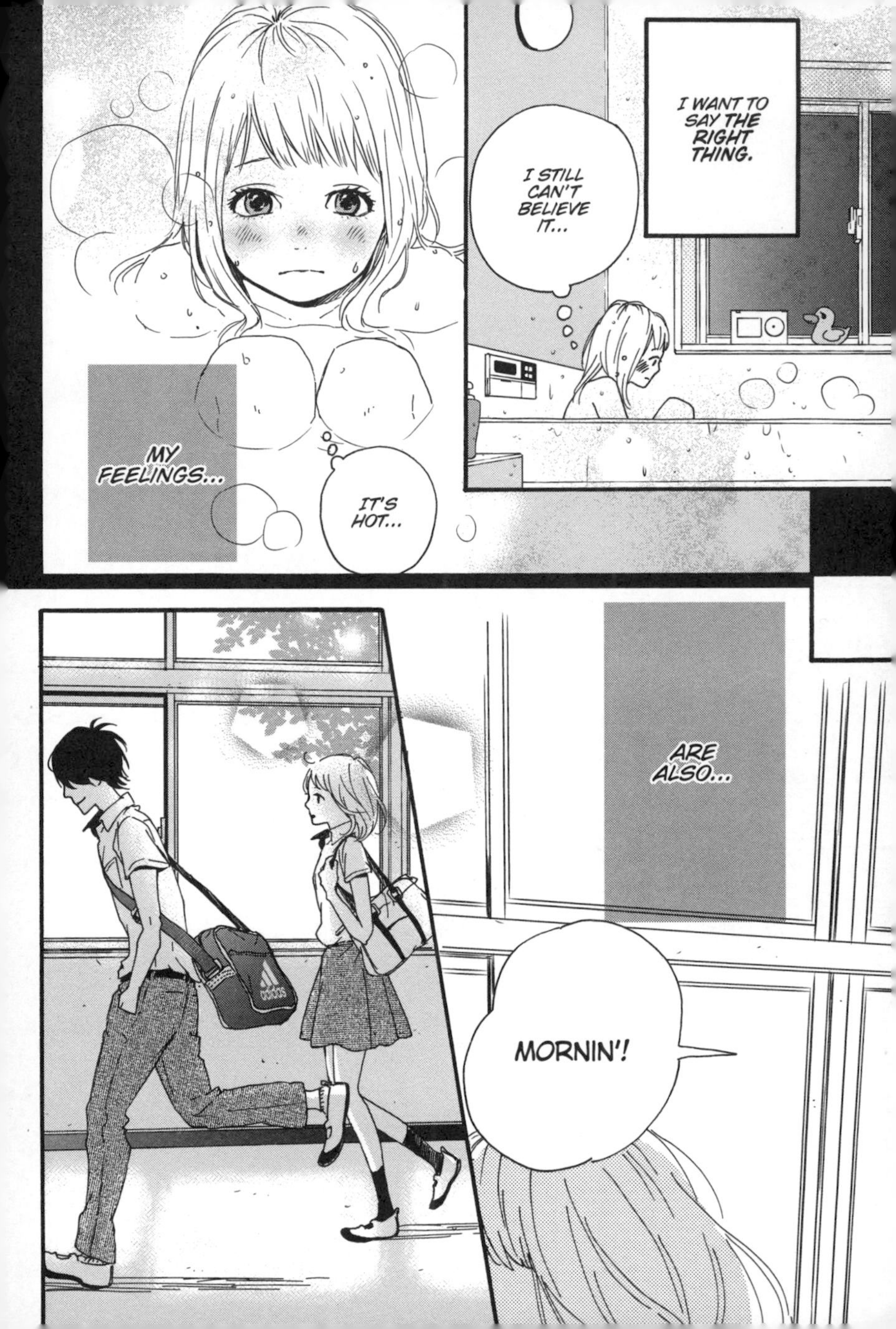
I WANT TO SAY THE RIGHT THING.
I STILL CAN'T BELIEVE IT...
IT'S HOT...
MY FEELINGS...
ARE ALSO...
MORNIN'!

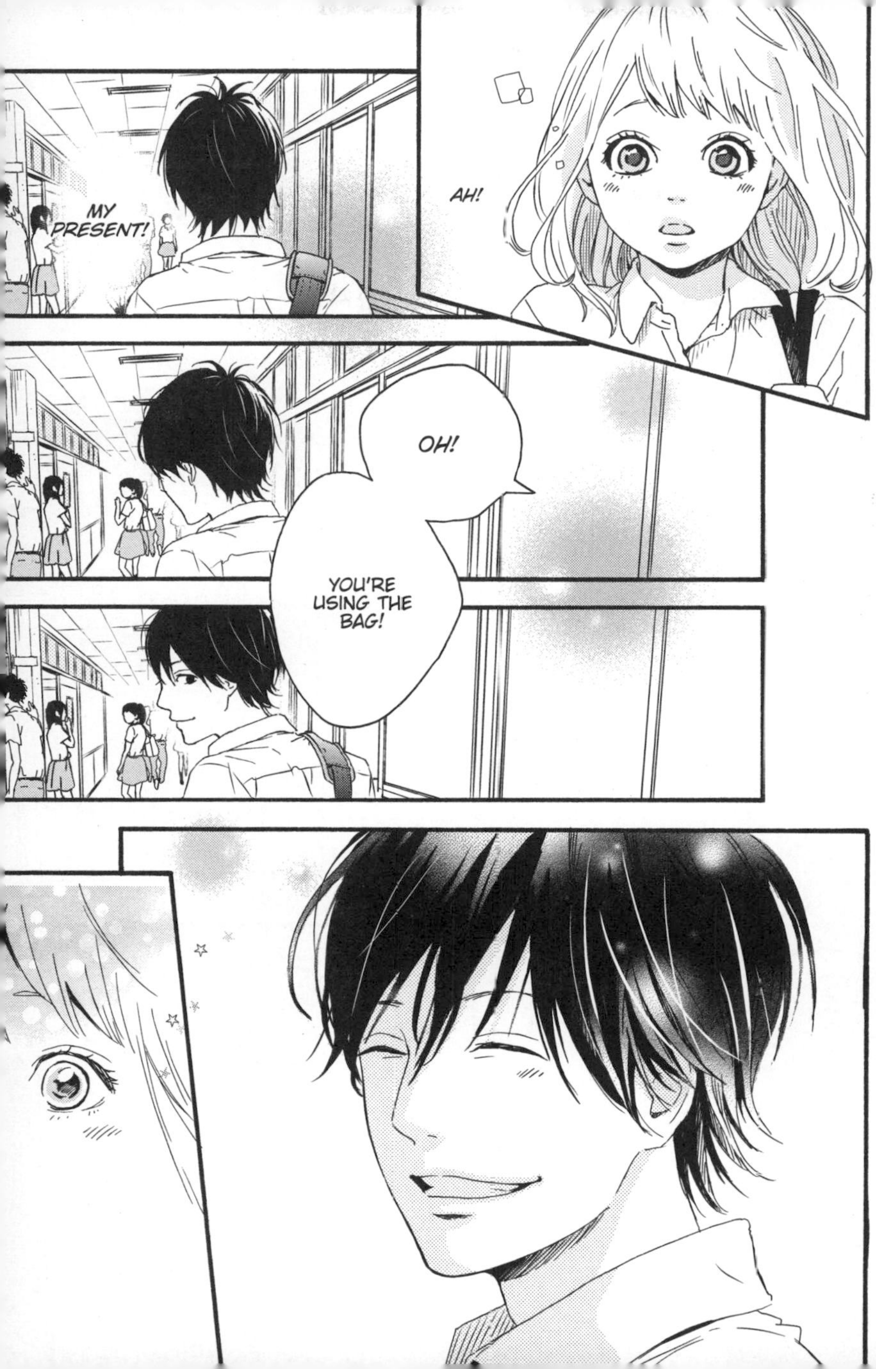
AH!
MY PRESENT!
OH!
YOU'RE USING THE BAG!

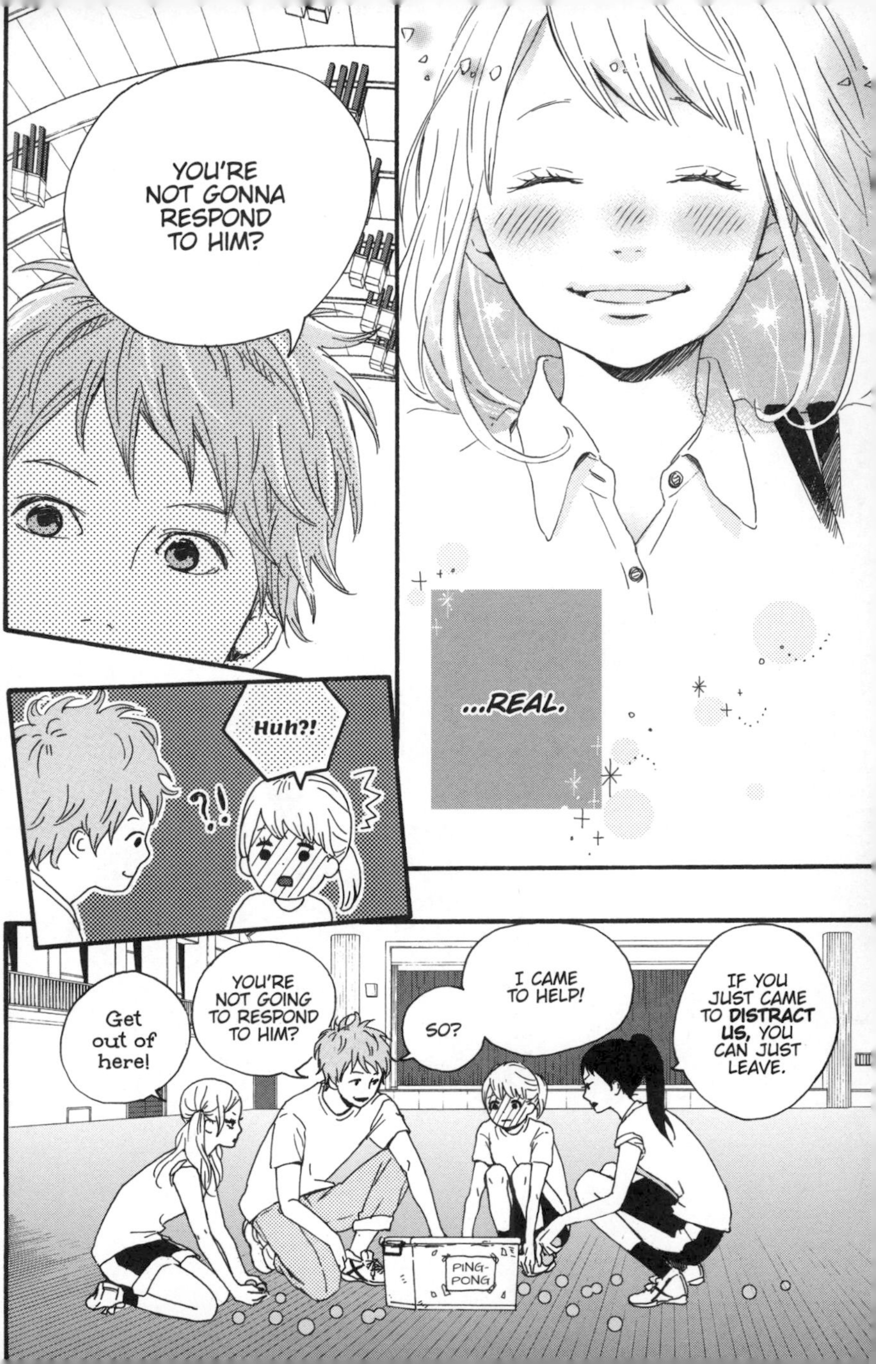
...REAL.
YOU'RE NOT GONNA RESPOND TO HIM?
Huh?!
?!
IF YOU JUST CAME TO **DISTRACT US,** YOU CAN JUST LEAVE.
I CAME TO HELP!
SO?
YOU'RE NOT GOING TO RESPOND TO HIM?
Get out of here!
PING-PONG

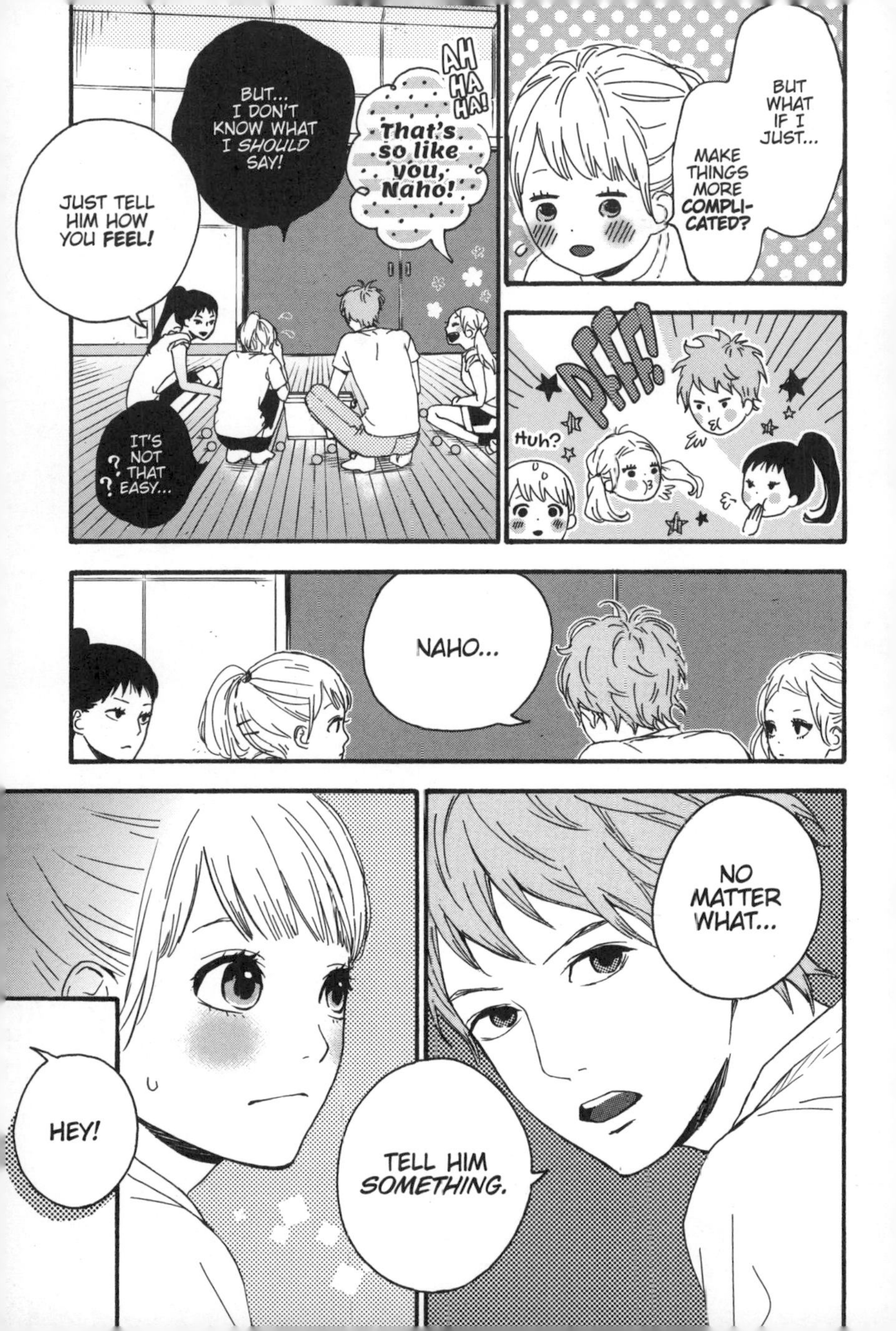
BUT WHAT IF I JUST... MAKE THINGS MORE COMPLICATED?
PFFF!
Huh?
AH HA HA!
That's so like you, Naho!
BUT... I DON'T KNOW WHAT I SHOULD SAY!
JUST TELL HIM HOW YOU FEEL!
IT'S NOT THAT EASY...
NAHO...
NO MATTER WHAT...
TELL HIM SOMETHING.
HEY!

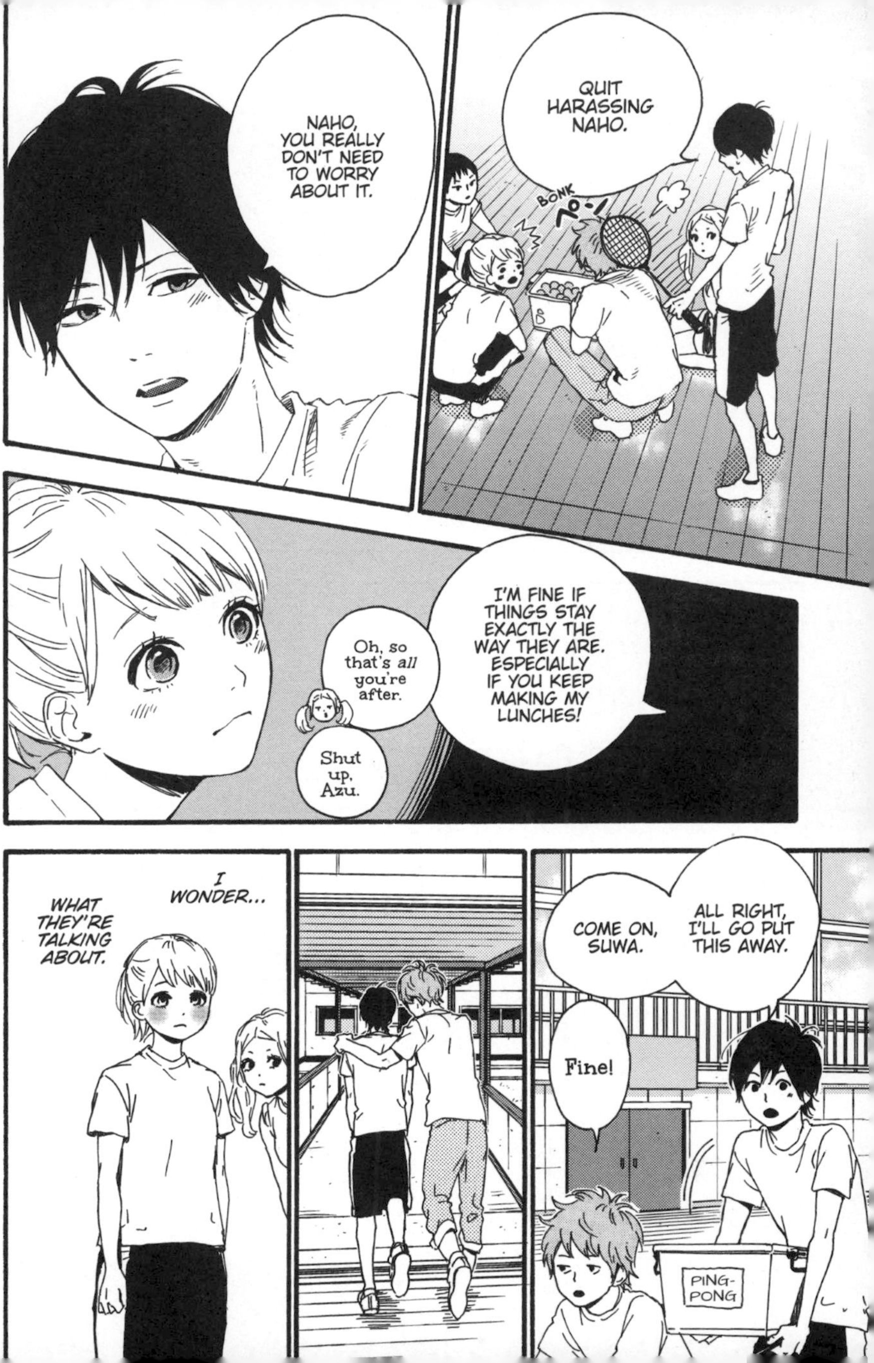
QUIT HARASSING NAHO.
BONK
NAHO, YOU REALLY DON'T NEED TO WORRY ABOUT IT.
I'M FINE IF THINGS STAY EXACTLY THE WAY THEY ARE. ESPECIALLY IF YOU KEEP MAKING MY LUNCHES!
Oh, so that's *all* you're after.
Shut up, Azu.
ALL RIGHT, I'LL GO PUT THIS AWAY.
COME ON, SUWA.
Fine!
PING-PONG
I WONDER...
WHAT THEY'RE TALKING ABOUT.

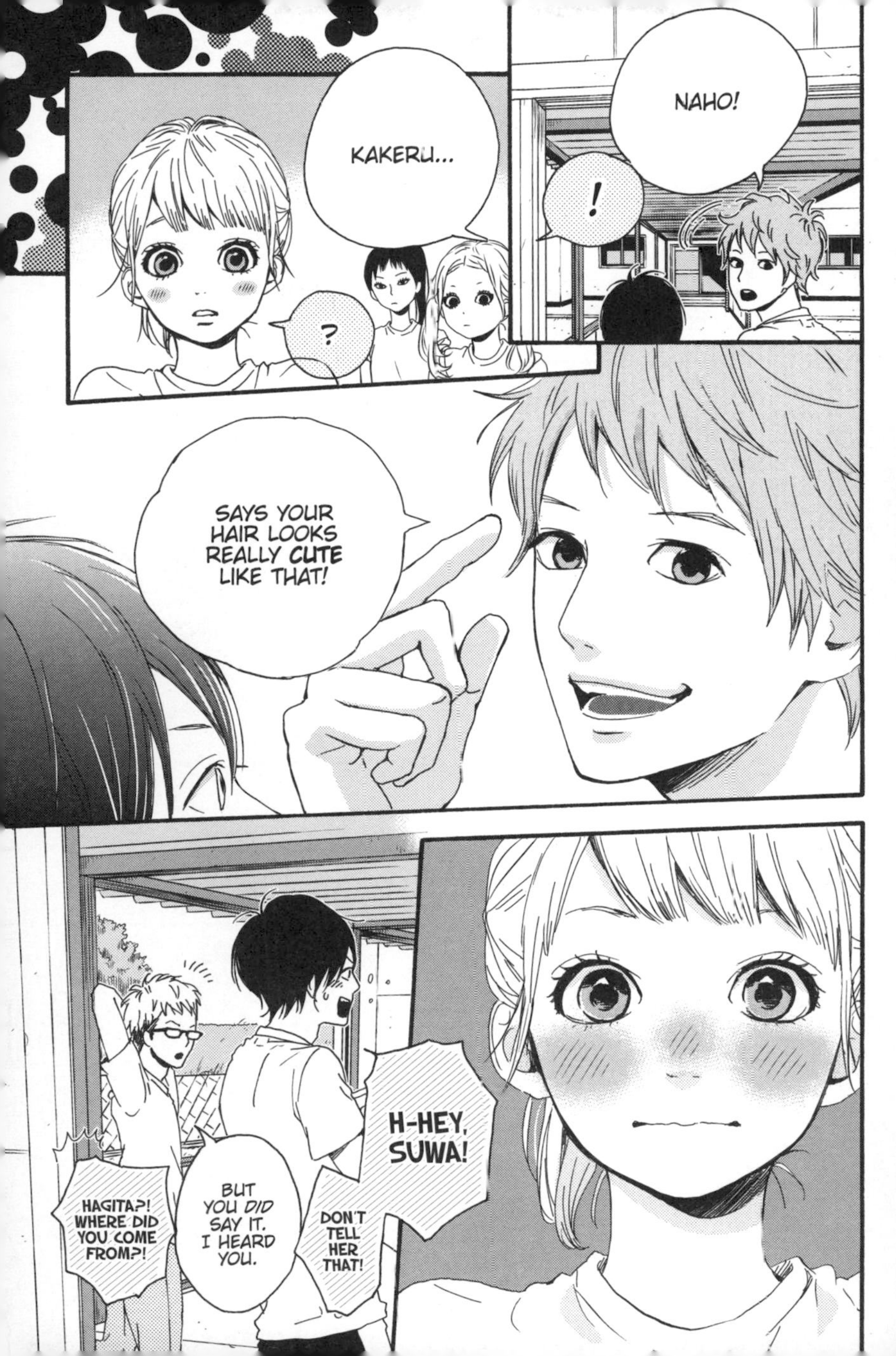
NAHO!
!
KAKERU...
?
SAYS YOUR HAIR LOOKS REALLY CUTE LIKE THAT!
H-HEY, SUWA!
DON'T TELL HER THAT!
BUT YOU DID SAY IT. I HEARD YOU.
HAGITA?! WHERE DID YOU COME FROM?!

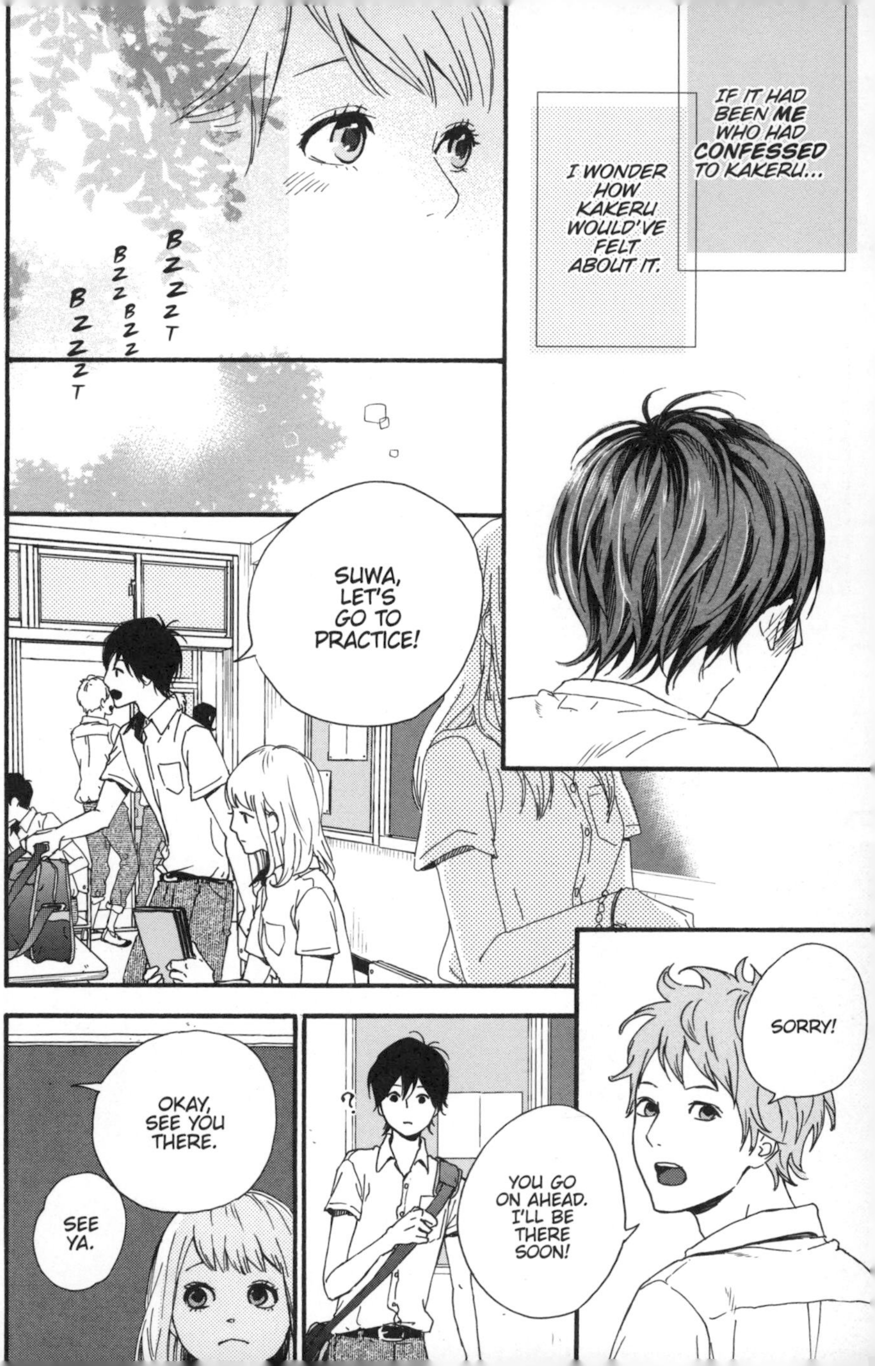
IF IT HAD BEEN ME WHO HAD CONFESSED TO KAKERU...
I WONDER HOW KAKERU WOULD'VE FELT ABOUT IT.
BZZZT
BZZ BZZ
BZZZT
SUWA, LET'S GO TO PRACTICE!
SORRY!
YOU GO ON AHEAD. I'LL BE THERE SOON!
OKAY, SEE YOU THERE.
SEE YA.

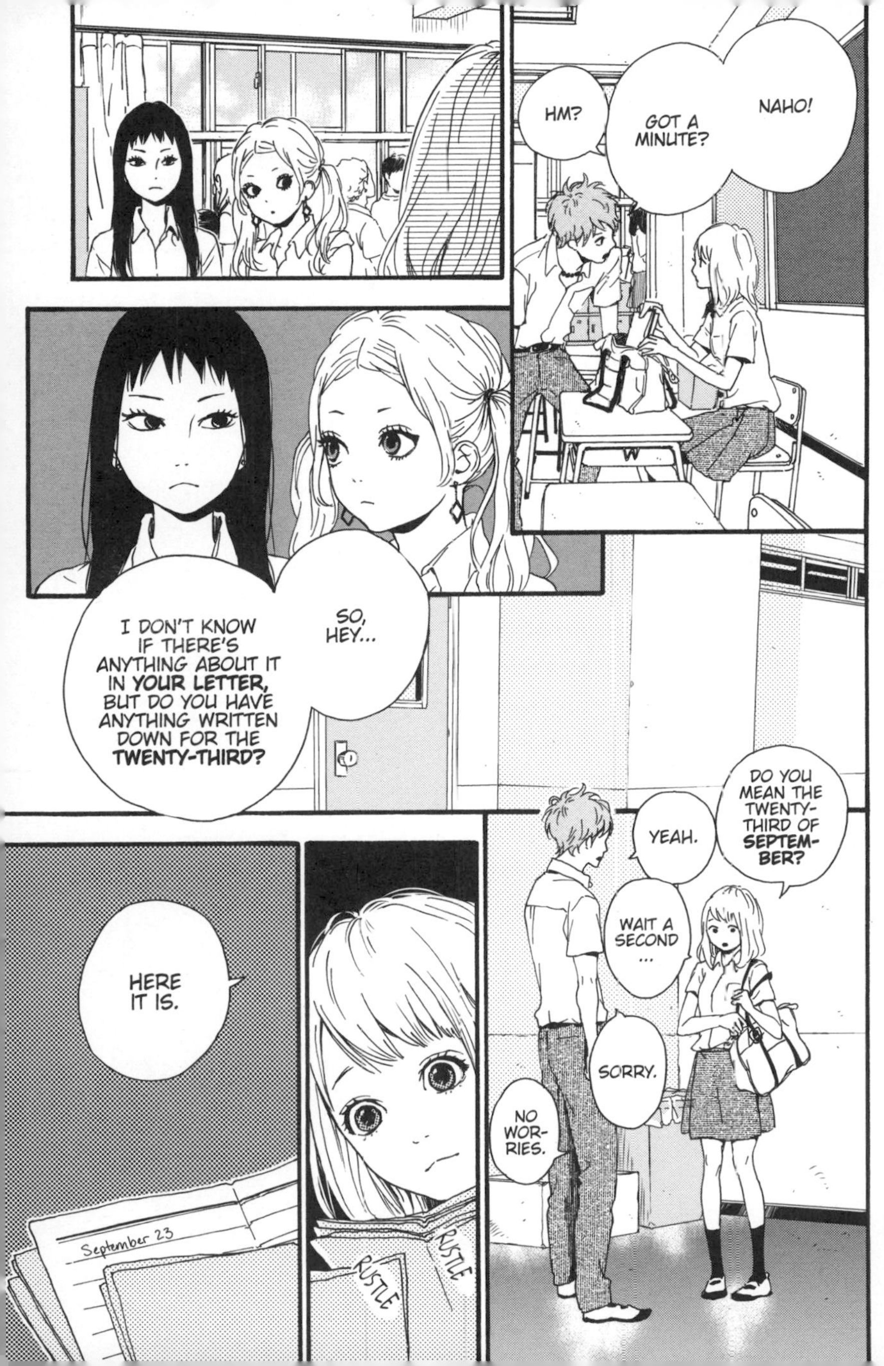
NAHO!
GOT A MINUTE?
HM?
SO, HEY...
I DON'T KNOW IF THERE'S ANYTHING ABOUT IT IN **YOUR LETTER**, BUT DO YOU HAVE ANYTHING WRITTEN DOWN FOR THE **TWENTY-THIRD?**
DO YOU MEAN THE TWENTY-THIRD OF **SEPTEMBER?**
YEAH.
WAIT A SECOND ...
SORRY.
NO WORRIES.
RUSTLE
RUSTLE
HERE IT IS.
September 23

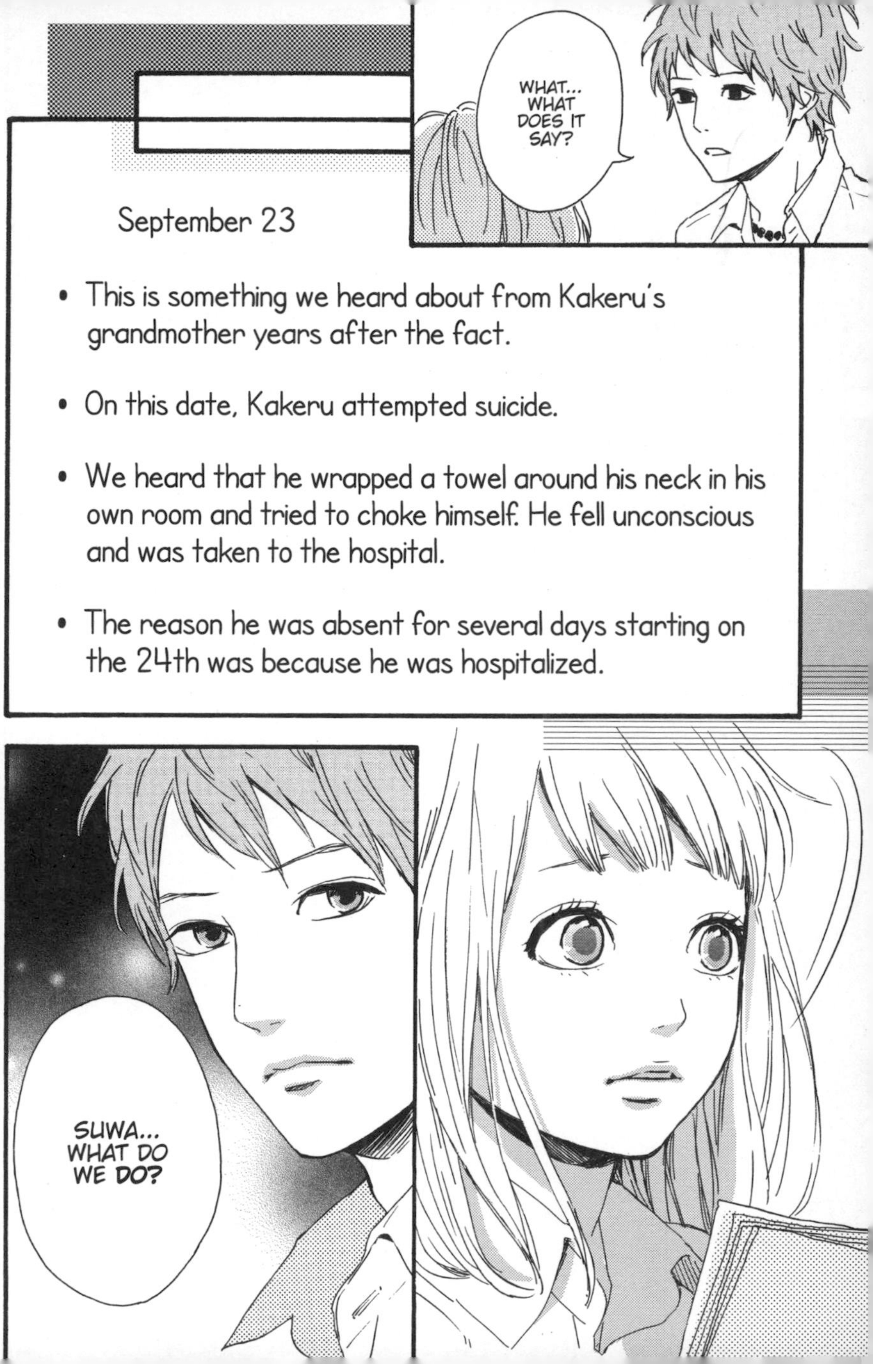
WHAT... WHAT DOES IT SAY?
September 23
• This is something we heard about from Kakeru's grandmother years after the fact.
• On this date, Kakeru attempted suicide.
• We heard that he wrapped a towel around his neck in his own room and tried to choke himself. He fell unconscious and was taken to the hospital.
• The reason he was absent for several days starting on the 24th was because he was hospitalized.
SUWA... WHAT DO WE DO?

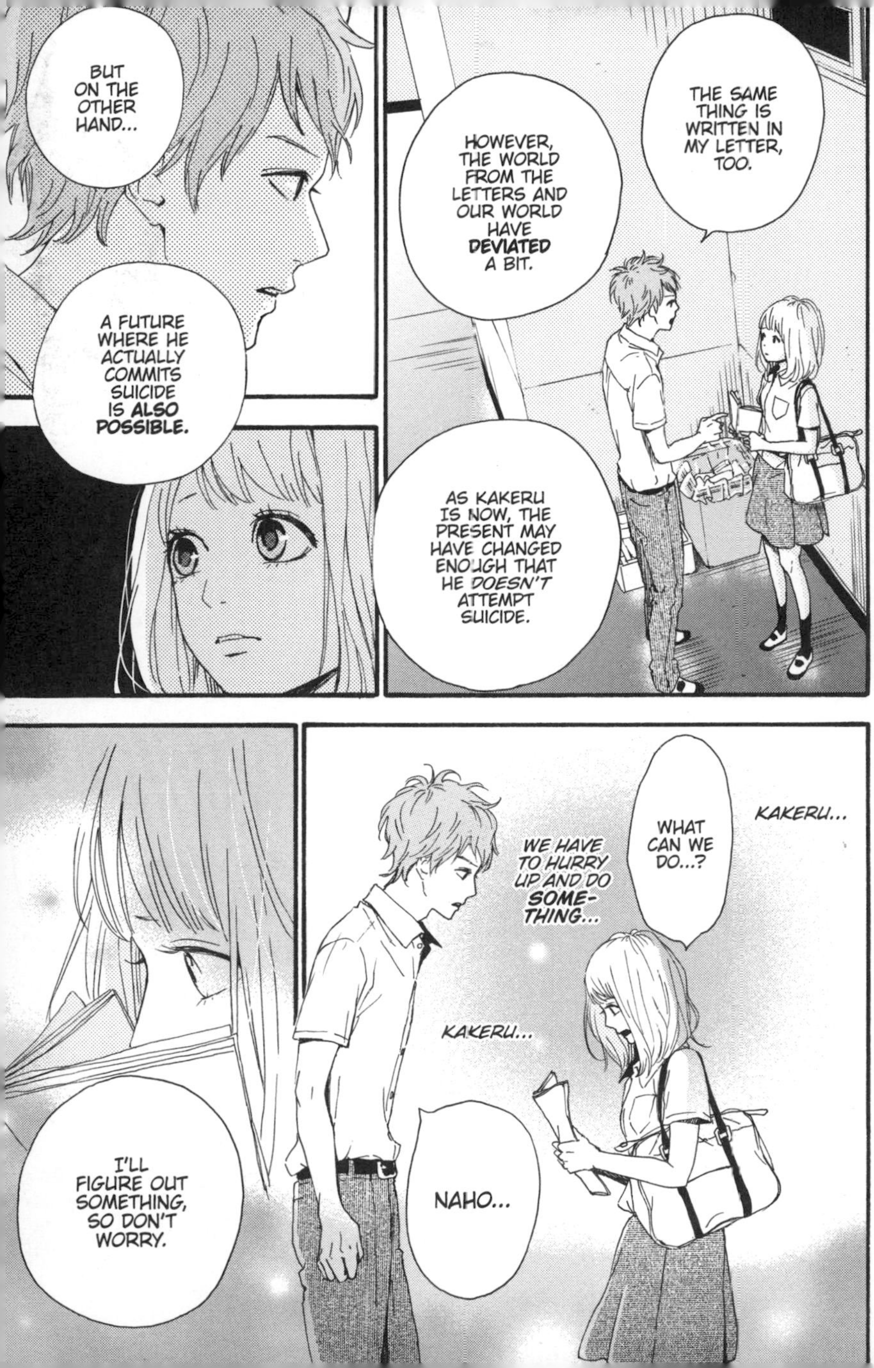
THE SAME THING IS WRITTEN IN MY LETTER, TOO.
HOWEVER, THE WORLD FROM THE LETTERS AND OUR WORLD HAVE **DEVIATED** A BIT.
AS KAKERU IS NOW, THE PRESENT MAY HAVE CHANGED ENOUGH THAT HE *DOESN'T* ATTEMPT SUICIDE.
BUT ON THE OTHER HAND...
A FUTURE WHERE HE ACTUALLY COMMITS SUICIDE IS **ALSO POSSIBLE.**
KAKERU...
WHAT CAN WE DO...?
WE HAVE TO HURRY UP AND DO ***SOME-THING...***
KAKERU...
NAHO...
I'LL FIGURE OUT SOMETHING, SO DON'T WORRY.

- On the day before the 23rd, Kakeru meets up with a friend from his old school.

  At that time, he spoke about his mother's suicide and told his friend that he also wants to die.

  But apparently his friend thought it was a joke and laughed it off.

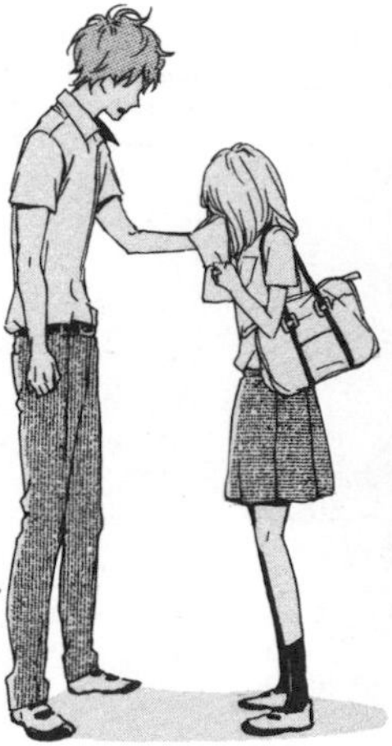

◎ Get Kakeru to confide in your group of friends.

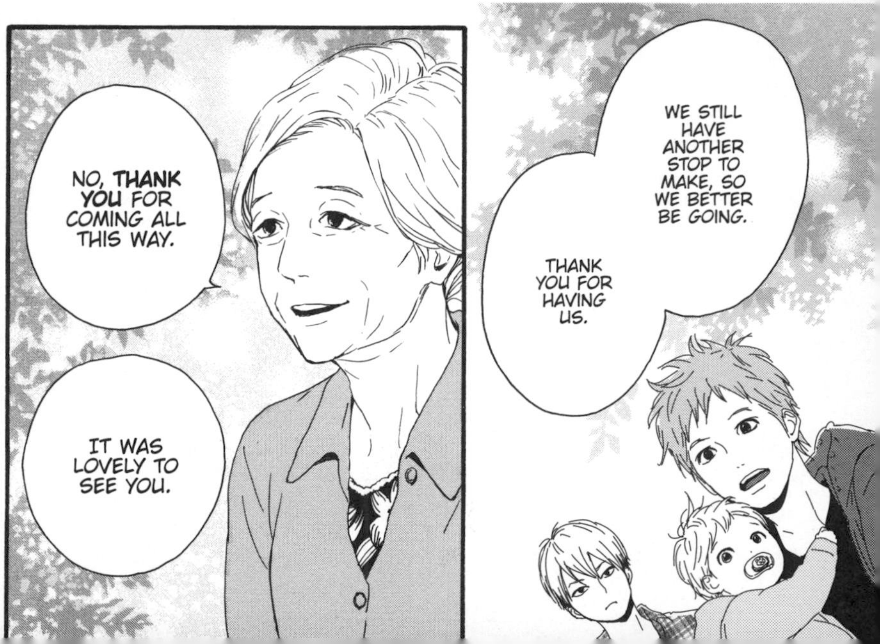
WE STILL HAVE ANOTHER STOP TO MAKE, SO WE BETTER BE GOING.
THANK YOU FOR HAVING US.
NO, **THANK YOU** FOR COMING ALL THIS WAY.
IT WAS LOVELY TO SEE YOU.

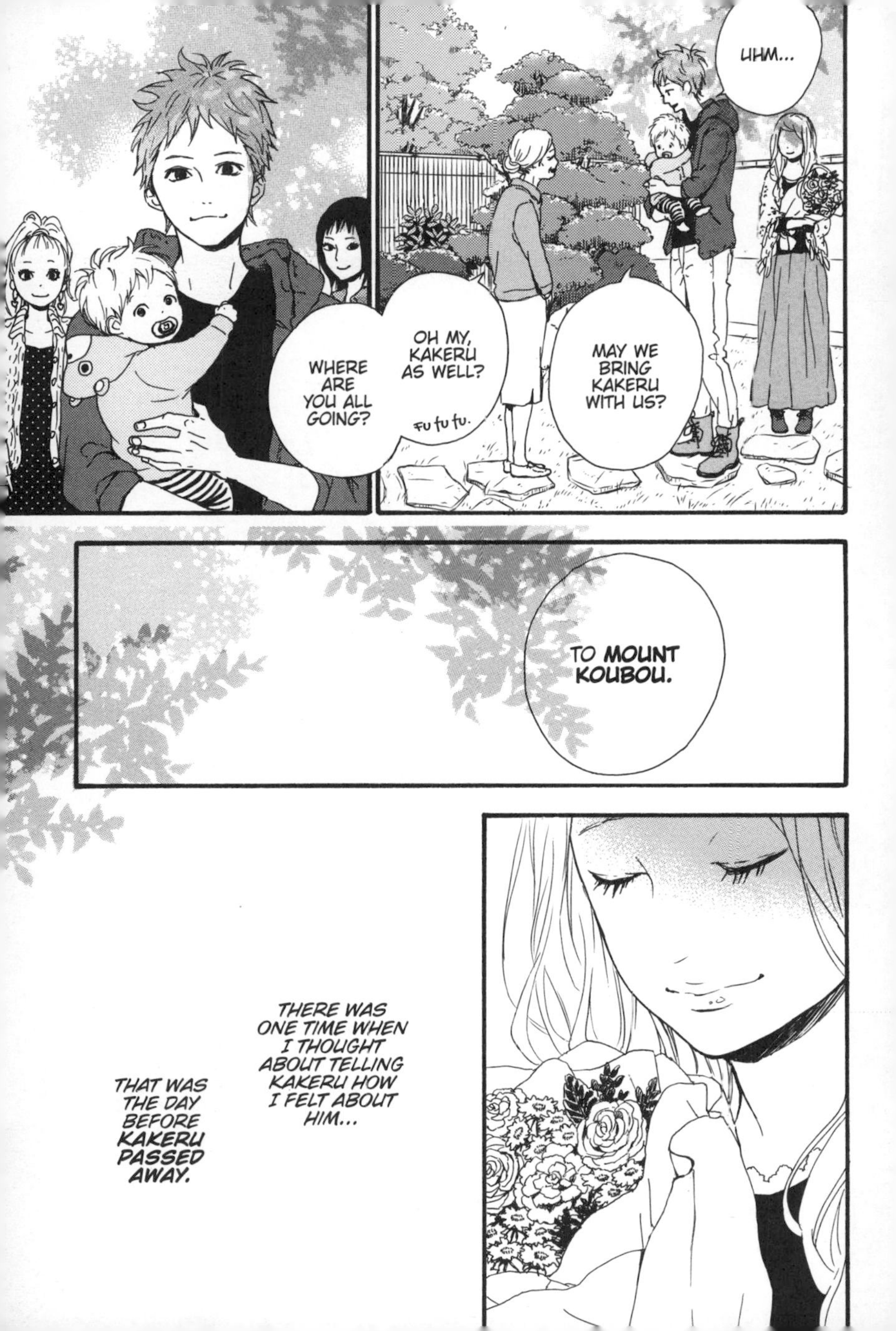
UHM...
MAY WE BRING KAKERU WITH US?
OH MY, KAKERU AS WELL?
FU FU FU.
WHERE ARE YOU ALL GOING?
TO MOUNT KOUBOU.
THERE WAS ONE TIME WHEN I THOUGHT ABOUT TELLING KAKERU HOW I FELT ABOUT HIM...
THAT WAS THE DAY BEFORE KAKERU PASSED AWAY.

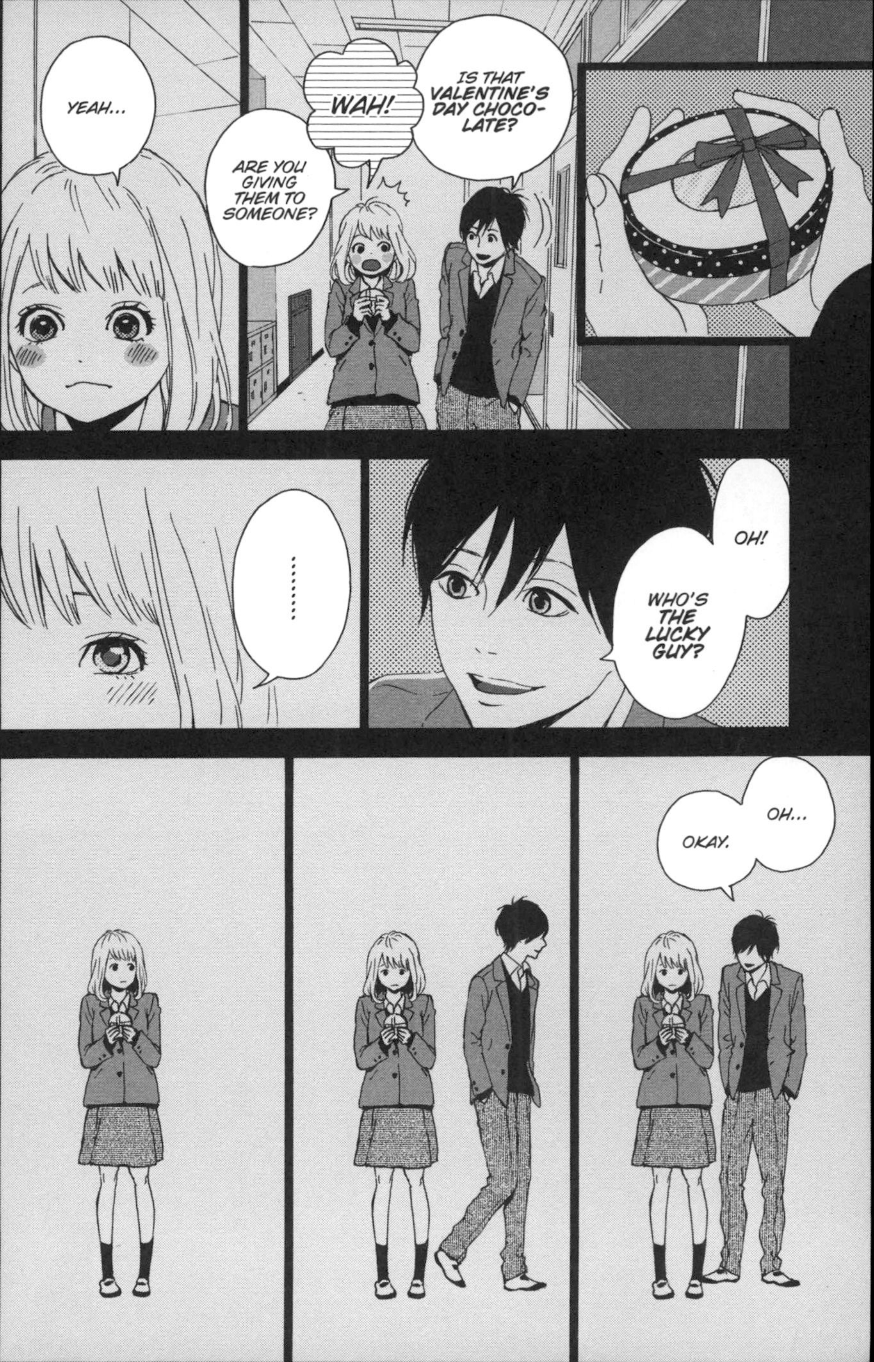
IS THAT VALENTINE'S DAY CHOCOLATE?
WAH!
ARE YOU GIVING THEM TO SOMEONE?
YEAH...
OH!
WHO'S THE LUCKY GUY?
....
OH...
OKAY.

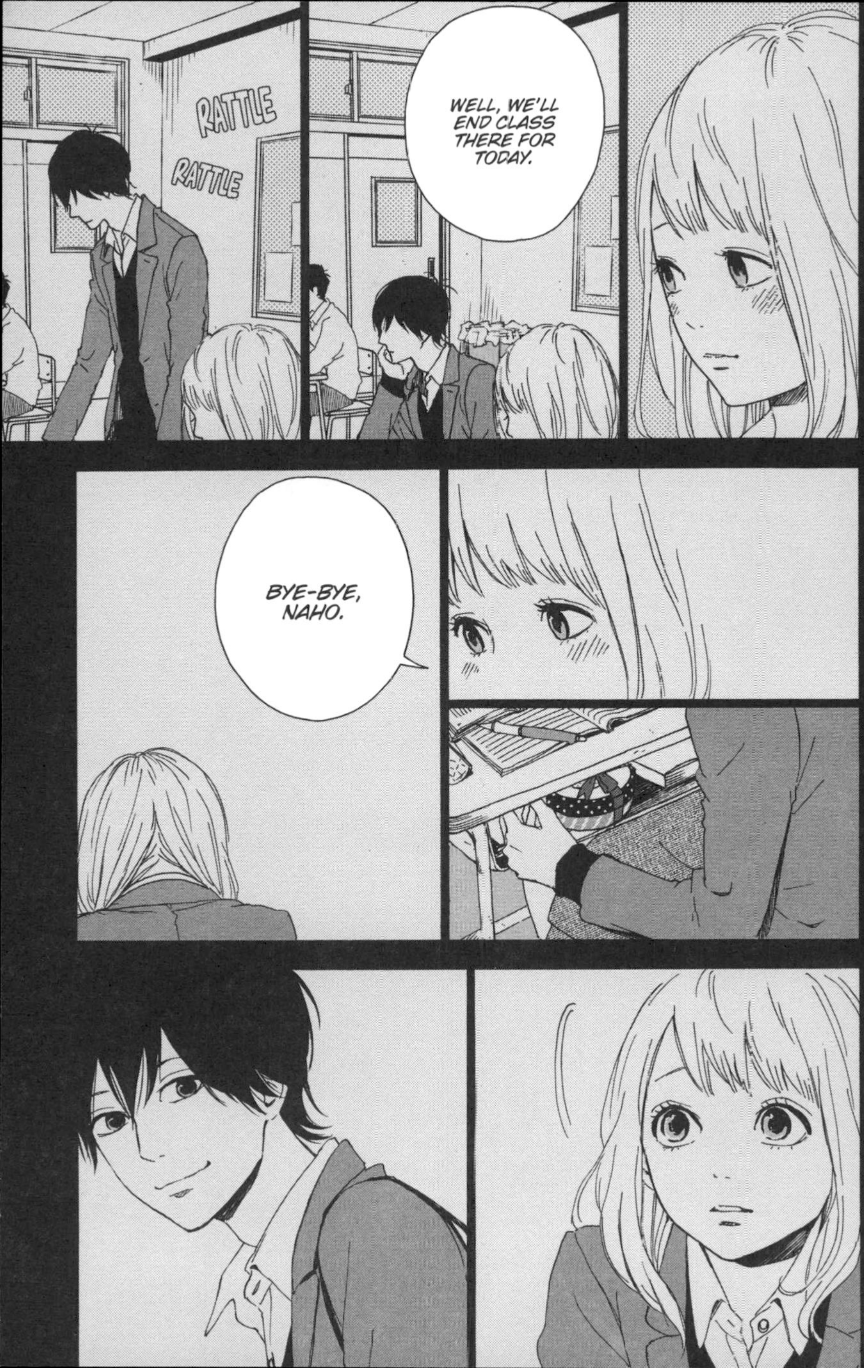
WELL, WE'LL END CLASS THERE FOR TODAY.
RATTLE
RATTLE
BYE-BYE, NAHO.

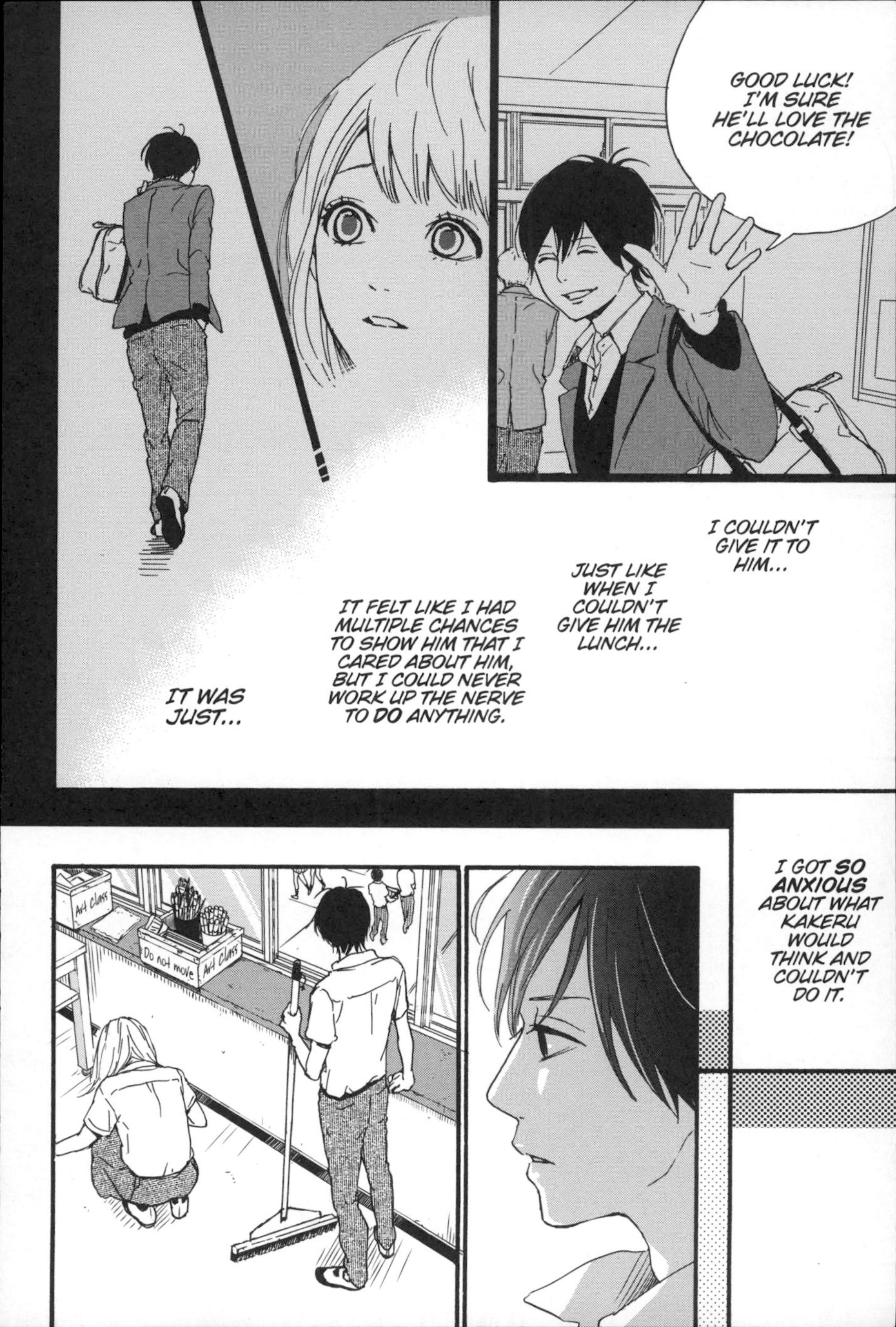
GOOD LUCK! I'M SURE HE'LL LOVE THE CHOCOLATE!
I COULDN'T GIVE IT TO HIM...
JUST LIKE WHEN I COULDN'T GIVE HIM THE LUNCH...
IT FELT LIKE I HAD MULTIPLE CHANCES TO SHOW HIM THAT I CARED ABOUT HIM, BUT I COULD NEVER WORK UP THE NERVE TO DO ANYTHING.
IT WAS JUST...
I GOT SO ANXIOUS ABOUT WHAT KAKERU WOULD THINK AND COULDN'T DO IT.
Art Class
Do not move
Art Class

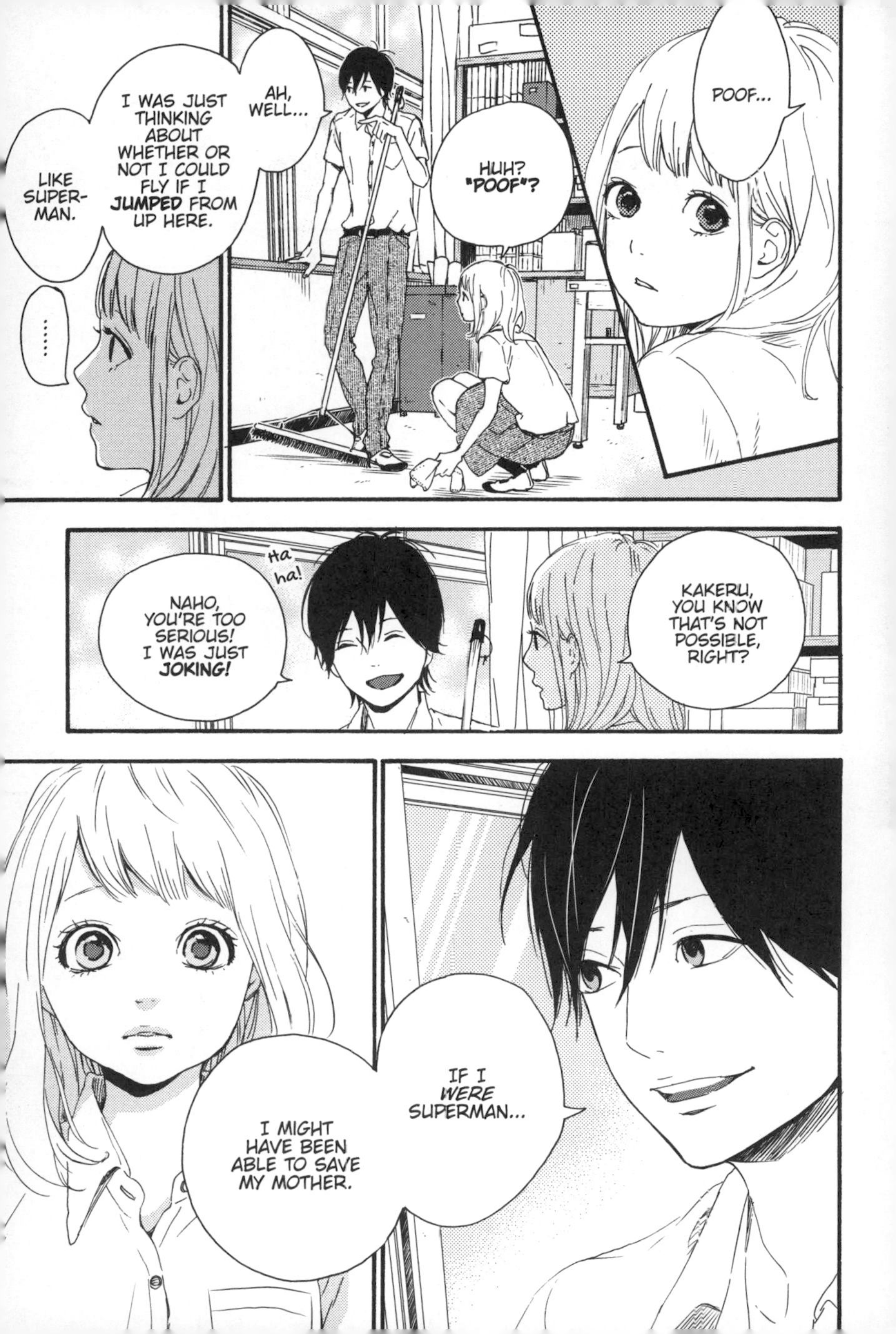

POOF...
HUH? **"POOF"?**
AH, WELL...
I WAS JUST THINKING ABOUT WHETHER OR NOT I COULD FLY IF I **JUMPED** FROM UP HERE.
LIKE SUPER-MAN.
......
KAKERU, YOU KNOW THAT'S NOT POSSIBLE, RIGHT?
Ha ha!
NAHO, YOU'RE TOO SERIOUS! I WAS JUST **JOKING!**
IF I *WERE* SUPERMAN...
I MIGHT HAVE BEEN ABLE TO SAVE MY MOTHER.

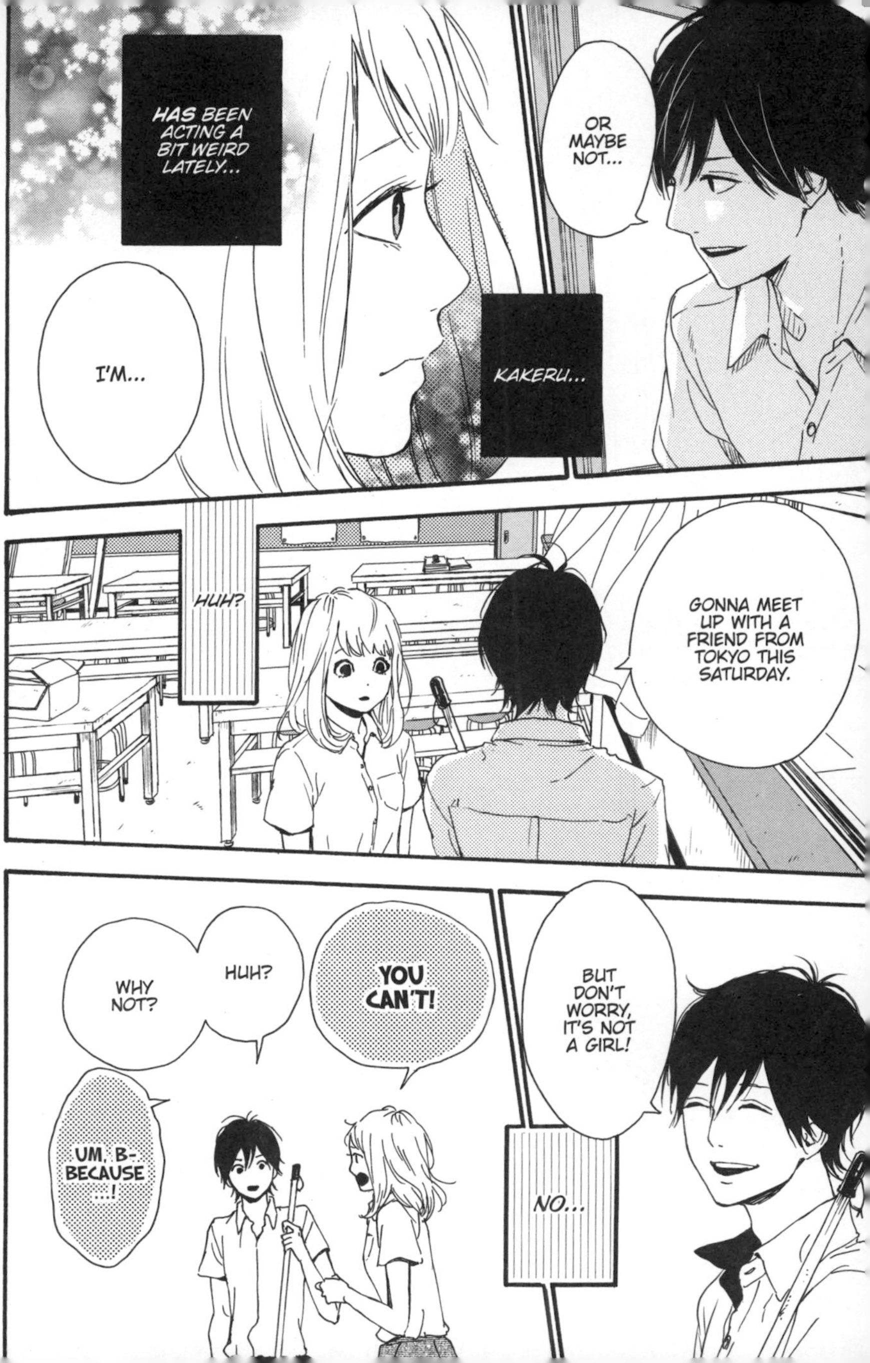
OR MAYBE NOT...
KAKERU...
HAS BEEN ACTING A BIT WEIRD LATELY...
I'M...
GONNA MEET UP WITH A FRIEND FROM TOKYO THIS SATURDAY.
HUH?
BUT DON'T WORRY, IT'S NOT A GIRL!
NO...
YOU CAN'T!
HUH?
WHY NOT?
UM, B-BECAUSE ...!

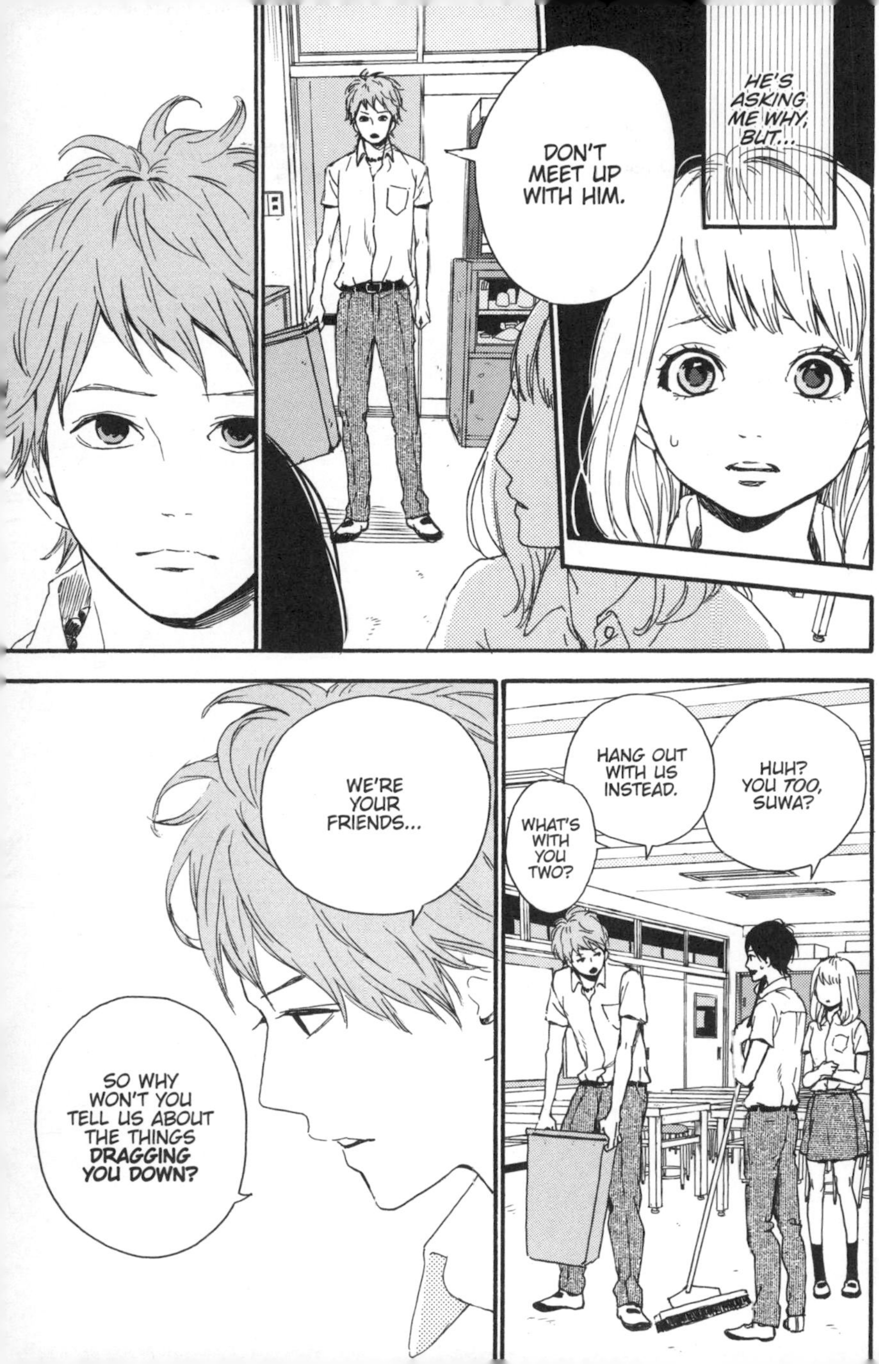
HE'S ASKING ME WHY, BUT...
DON'T MEET UP WITH HIM.
HUH? YOU TOO, SUWA?
HANG OUT WITH US INSTEAD.
WHAT'S WITH YOU TWO?
WE'RE YOUR FRIENDS...
SO WHY WON'T YOU TELL US ABOUT THE THINGS **DRAGGING YOU DOWN?**

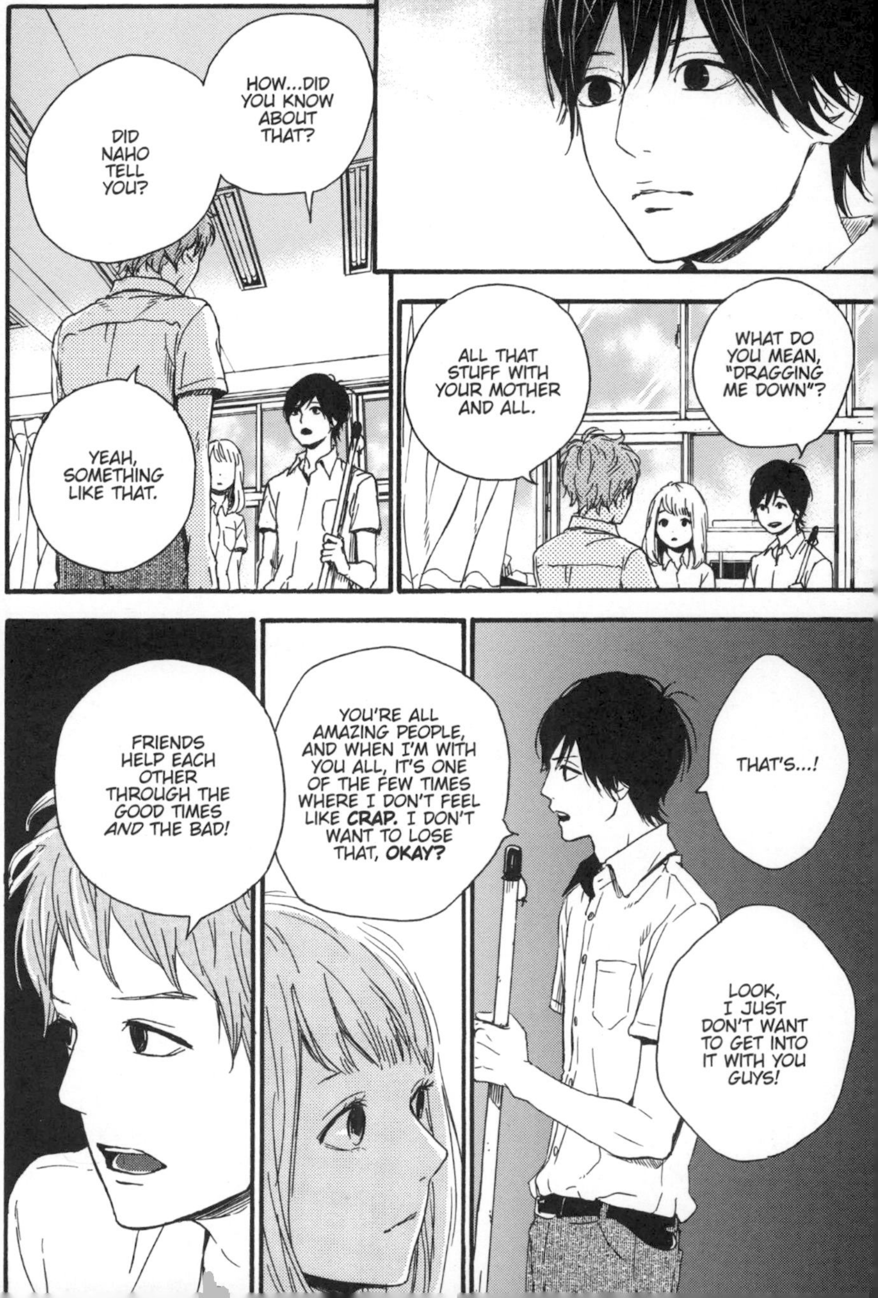
WHAT DO YOU MEAN, "DRAGGING ME DOWN"?
ALL THAT STUFF WITH YOUR MOTHER AND ALL.
HOW...DID YOU KNOW ABOUT THAT?
DID NAHO TELL YOU?
YEAH, SOMETHING LIKE THAT.
THAT'S...!
LOOK, I JUST DON'T WANT TO GET INTO IT WITH YOU GUYS!
YOU'RE ALL AMAZING PEOPLE, AND WHEN I'M WITH YOU ALL, IT'S ONE OF THE FEW TIMES WHERE I DON'T FEEL LIKE CRAP. I DON'T WANT TO LOSE THAT, OKAY?
FRIENDS HELP EACH OTHER THROUGH THE GOOD TIMES AND THE BAD!

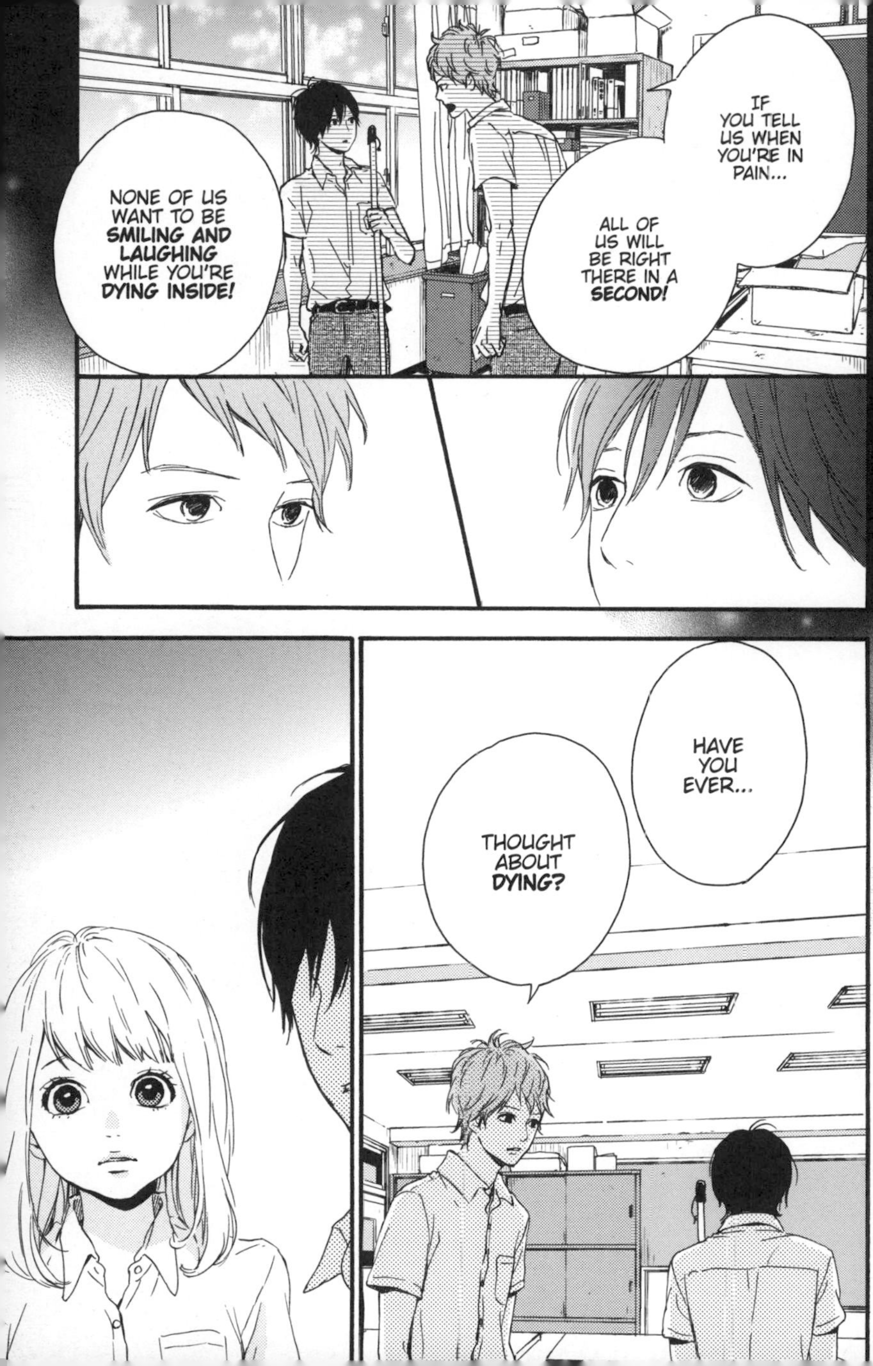
IF YOU TELL US WHEN YOU'RE IN PAIN...
ALL OF US WILL BE RIGHT THERE IN A **SECOND!**
NONE OF US WANT TO BE **SMILING AND LAUGHING** WHILE YOU'RE **DYING INSIDE!**
HAVE YOU EVER...
THOUGHT ABOUT **DYING?**

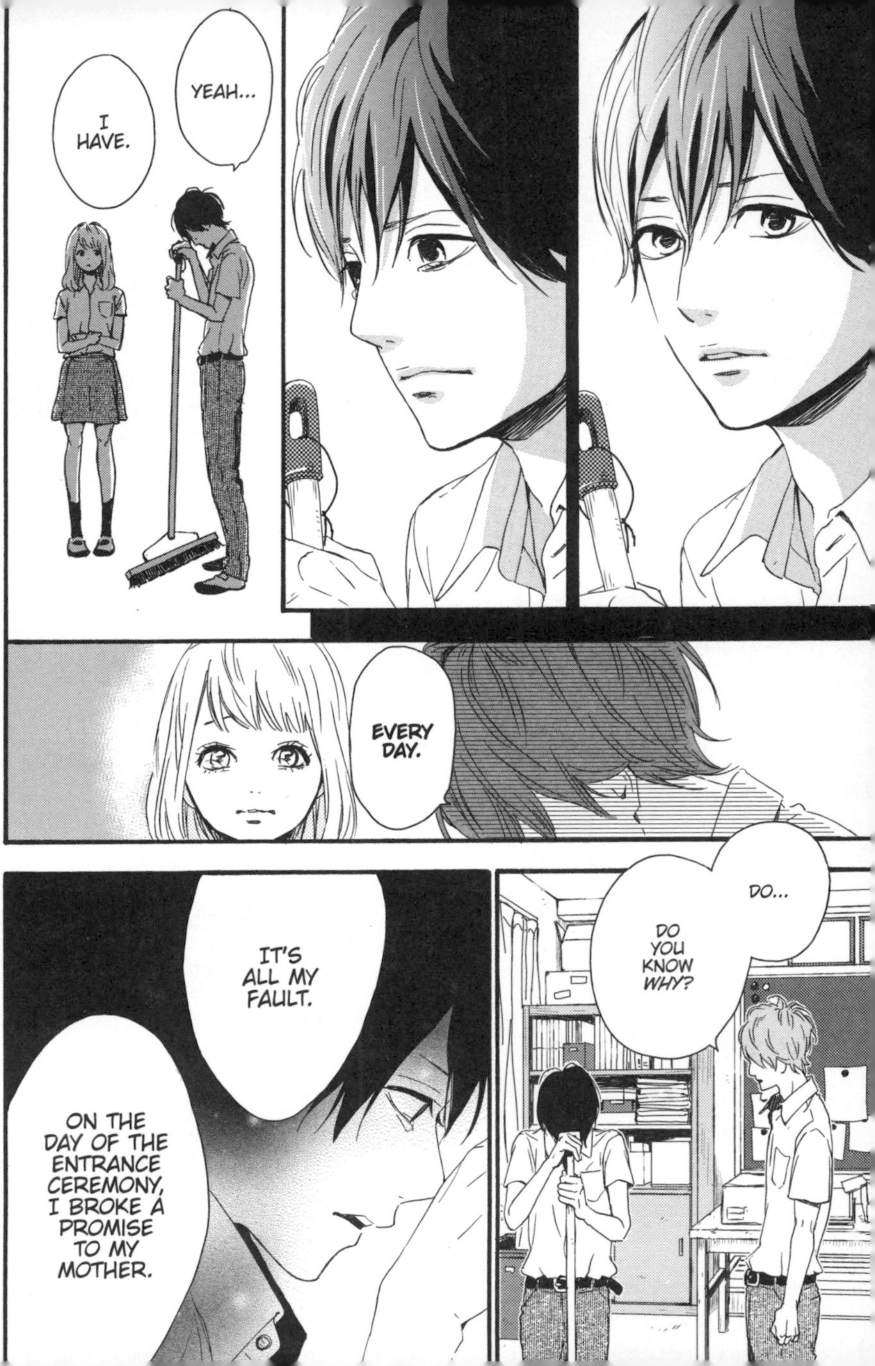
YEAH...
I HAVE.
EVERY DAY.
DO...
DO YOU KNOW WHY?
IT'S ALL MY FAULT.
ON THE DAY OF THE ENTRANCE CEREMONY, I BROKE A PROMISE TO MY MOTHER.

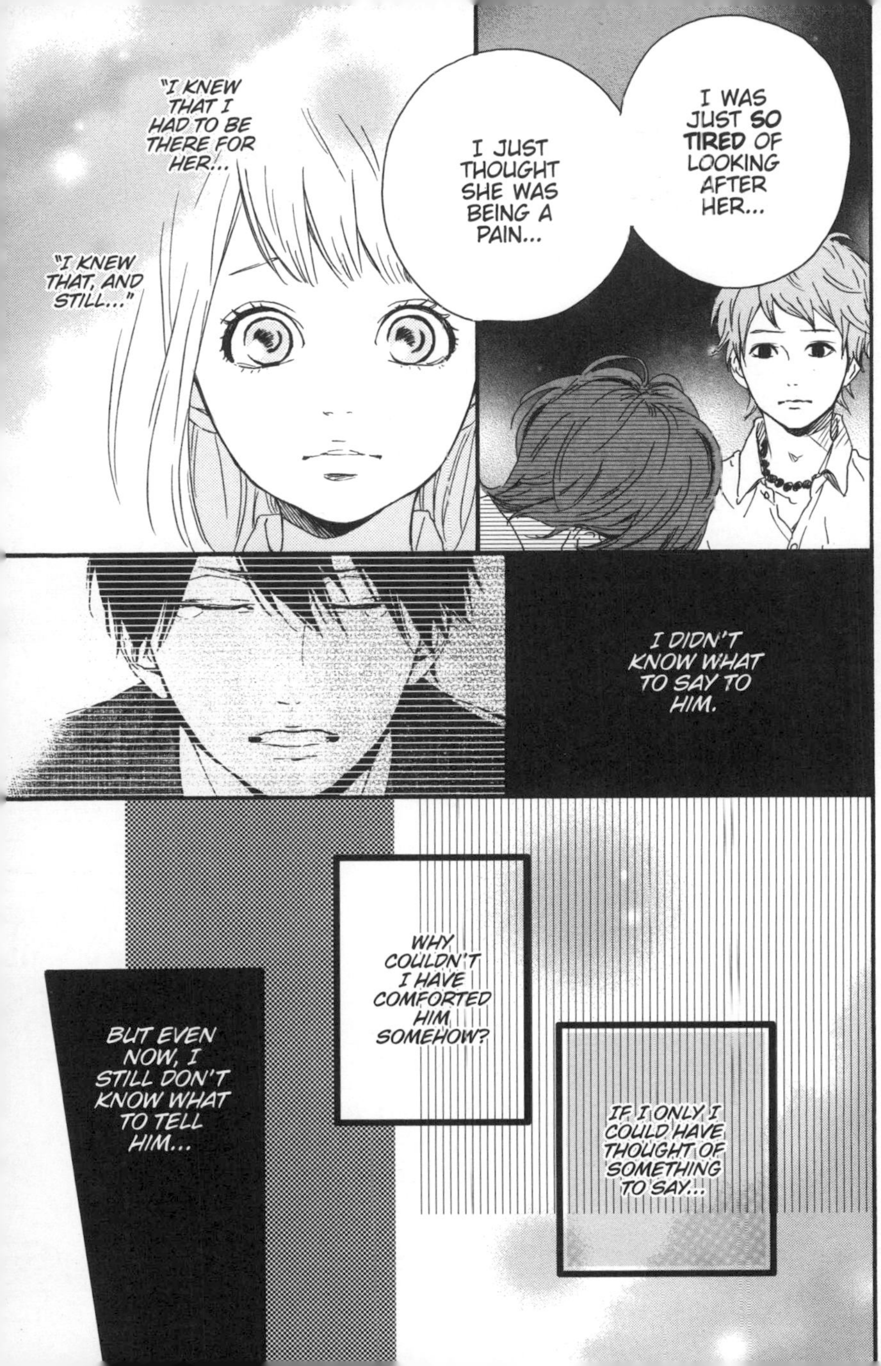
I WAS JUST **SO TIRED** OF LOOKING AFTER HER...
I JUST THOUGHT SHE WAS BEING A PAIN...
"I KNEW THAT I HAD TO BE THERE FOR HER...
"I KNEW THAT, AND STILL..."
I DIDN'T KNOW WHAT TO SAY TO HIM.
WHY COULDN'T I HAVE COMFORTED HIM SOMEHOW?
IF I ONLY I COULD HAVE THOUGHT OF SOMETHING TO SAY...
BUT EVEN NOW, I STILL DON'T KNOW WHAT TO TELL HIM...

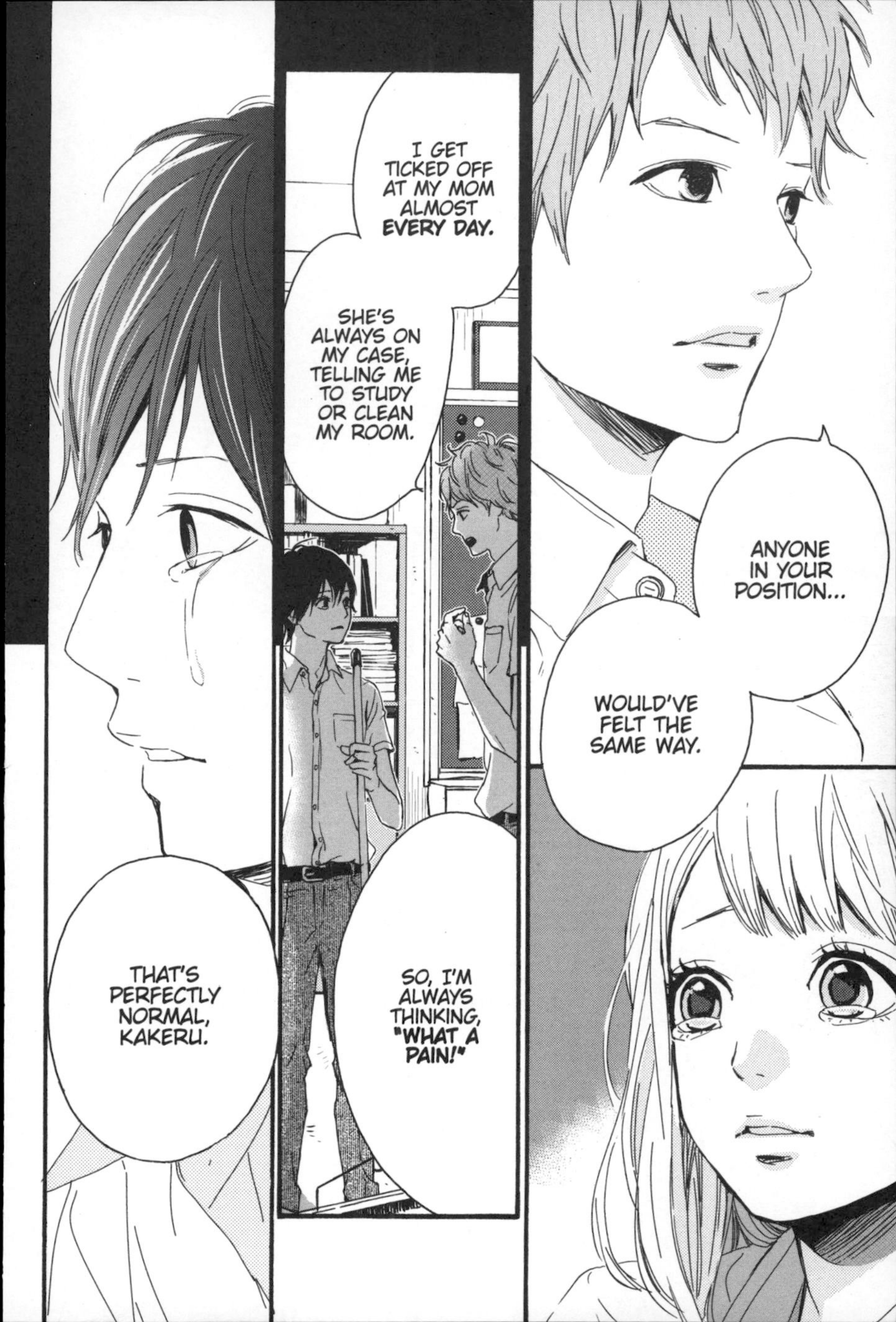
ANYONE IN YOUR POSITION...
WOULD'VE FELT THE SAME WAY.
I GET TICKED OFF AT MY MOM ALMOST EVERY DAY.
SHE'S ALWAYS ON MY CASE, TELLING ME TO STUDY OR CLEAN MY ROOM.
SO, I'M ALWAYS THINKING, "WHAT A PAIN!"
THAT'S PERFECTLY NORMAL, KAKERU.

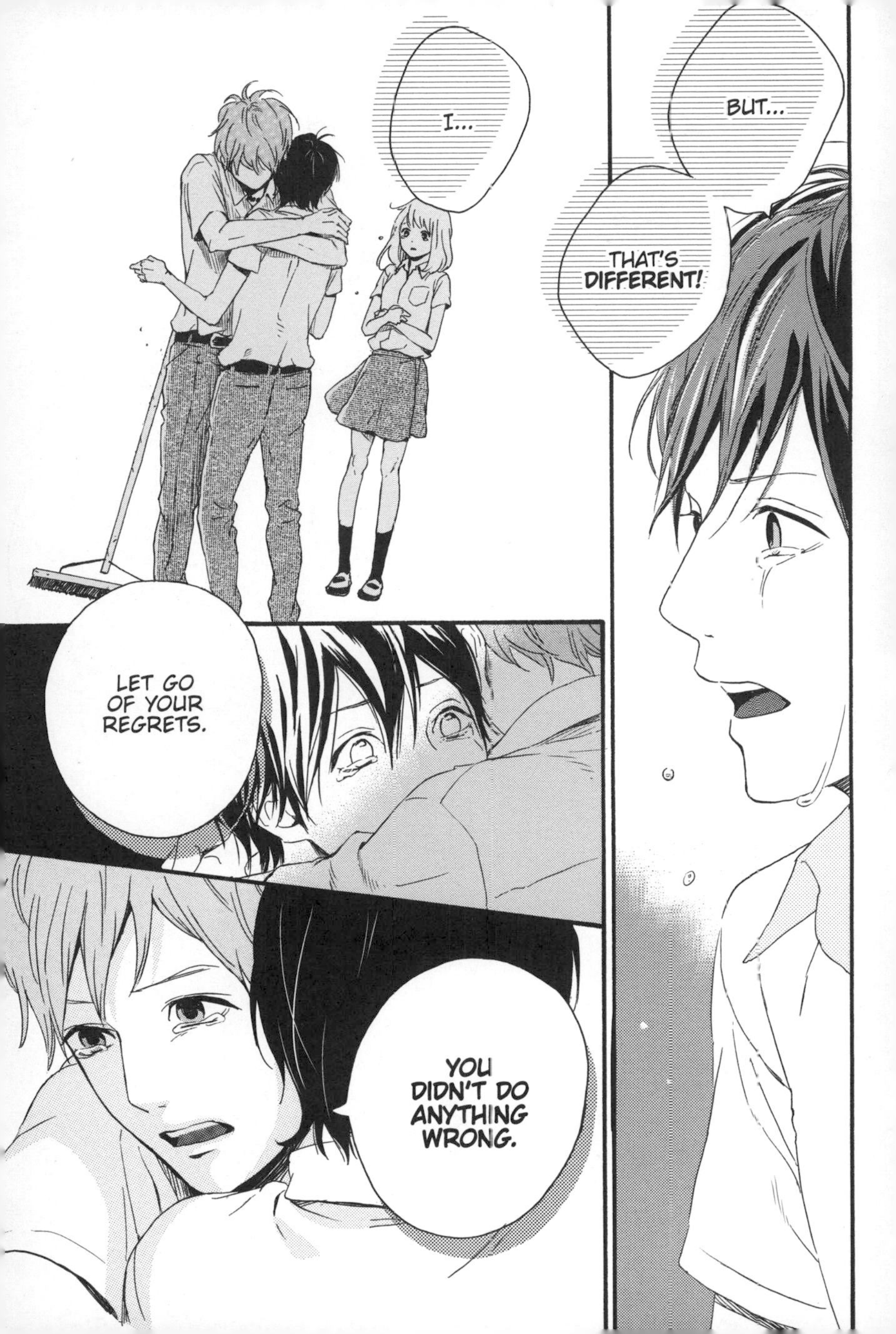
BUT...
THAT'S DIFFERENT!
I...
LET GO OF YOUR REGRETS.
YOU DIDN'T DO ANYTHING WRONG.

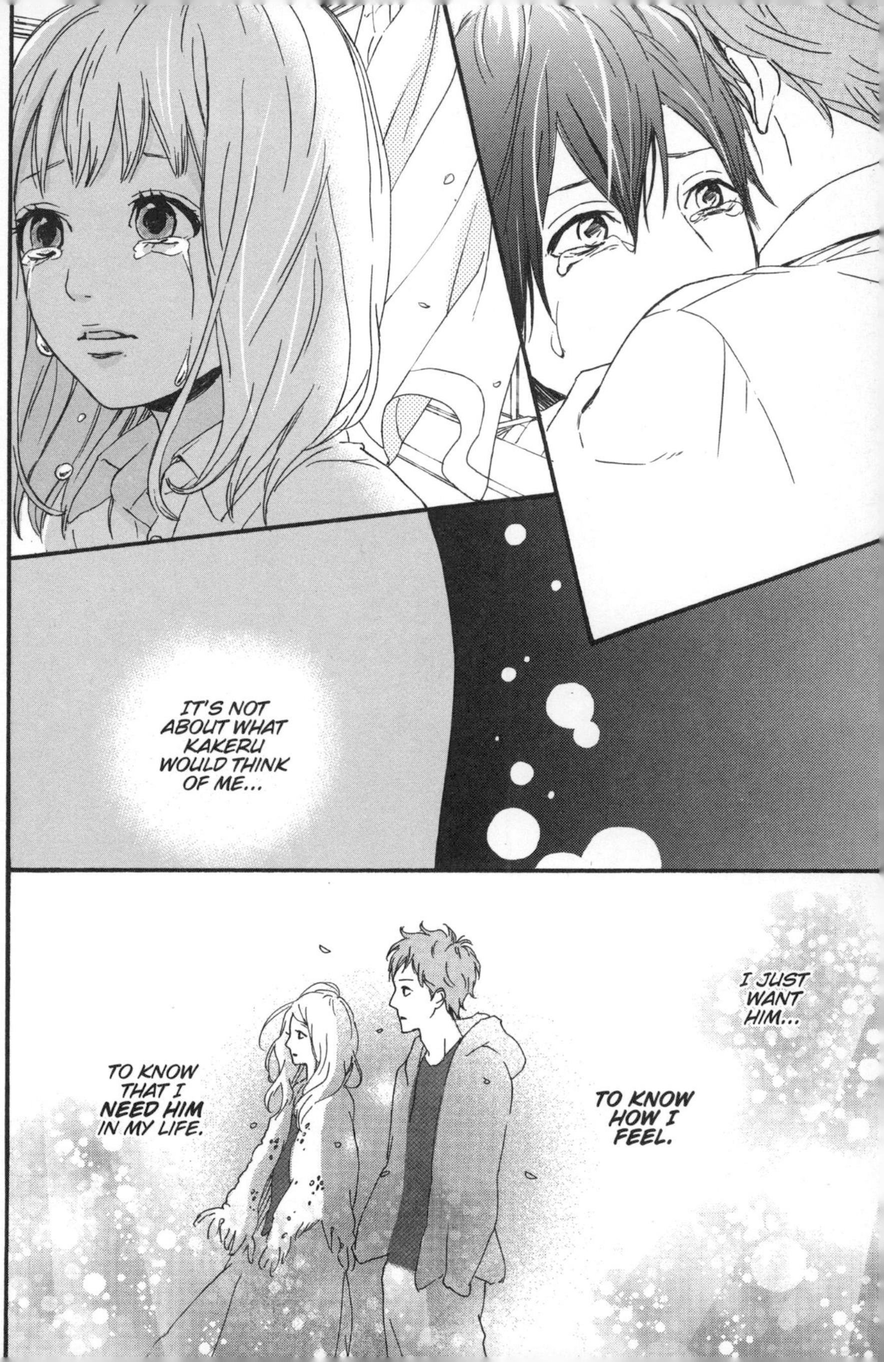
IT'S NOT ABOUT WHAT KAKERU WOULD THINK OF ME...
I JUST WANT HIM...
TO KNOW HOW I FEEL.
TO KNOW THAT I **NEED HIM** IN MY LIFE.

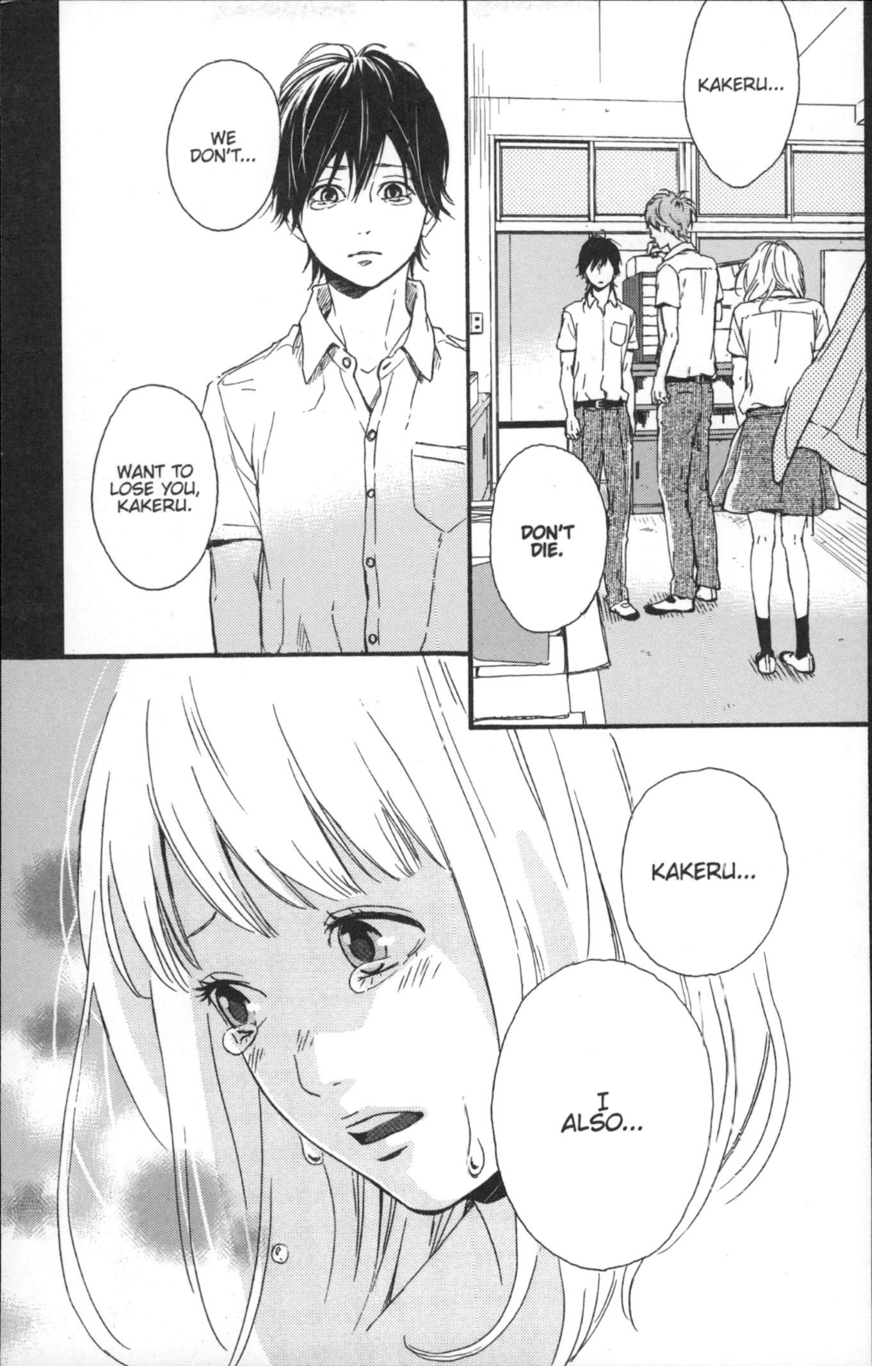
KAKERU...
DON'T DIE.
WE DON'T...
WANT TO LOSE YOU, KAKERU.
KAKERU...
I ALSO...

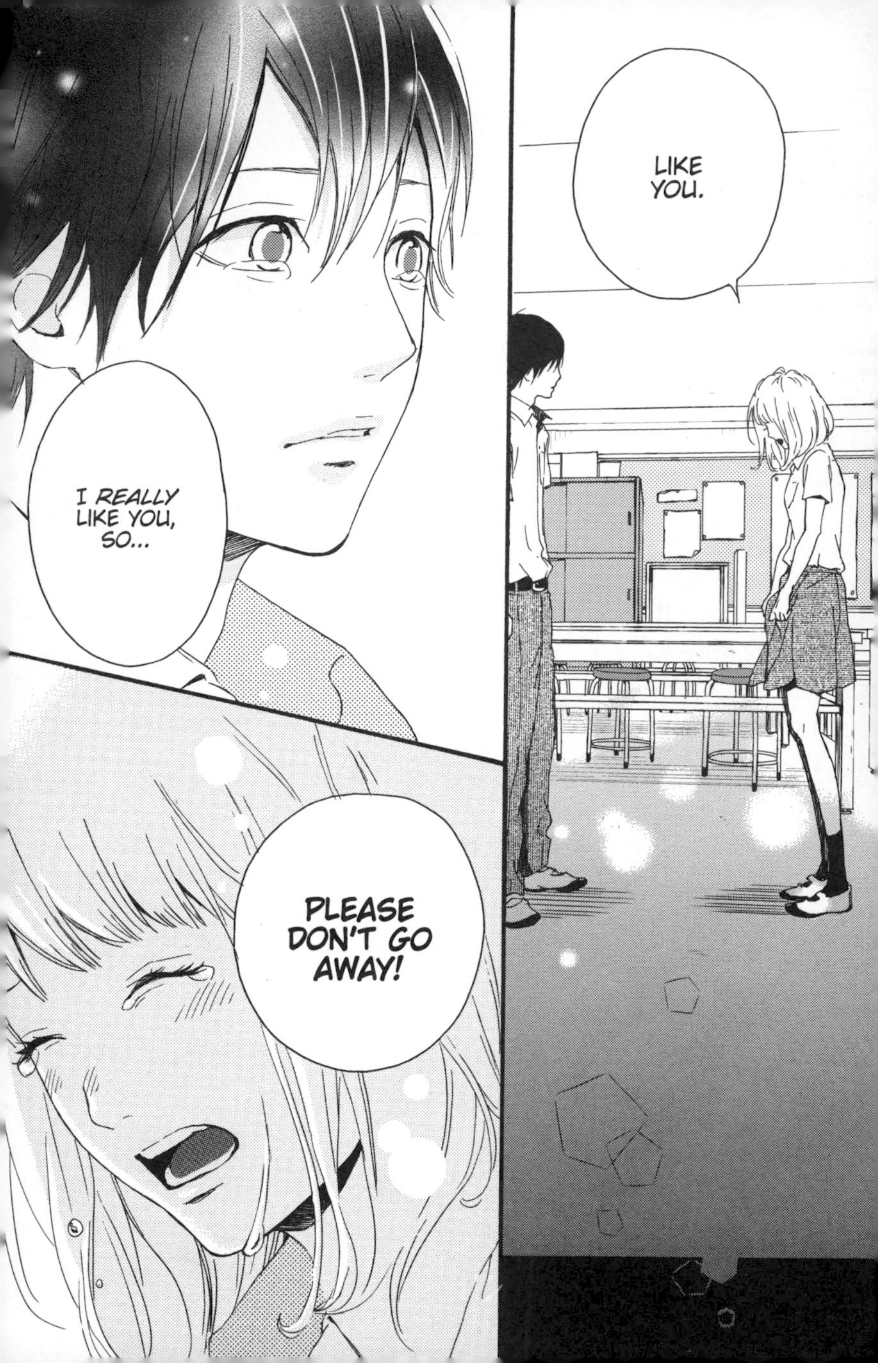
LIKE YOU.
I REALLY LIKE YOU, SO...
PLEASE DON'T GO AWAY!

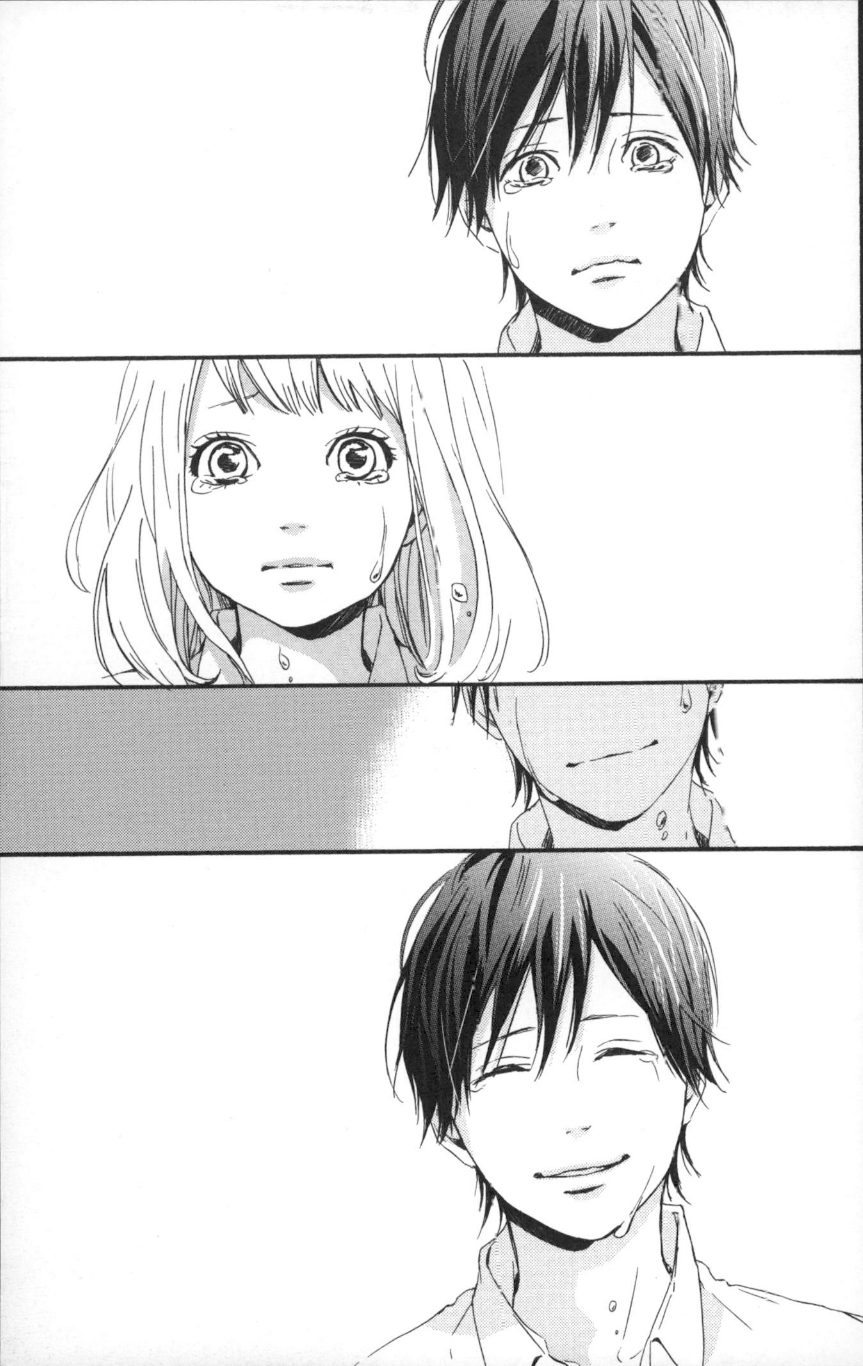

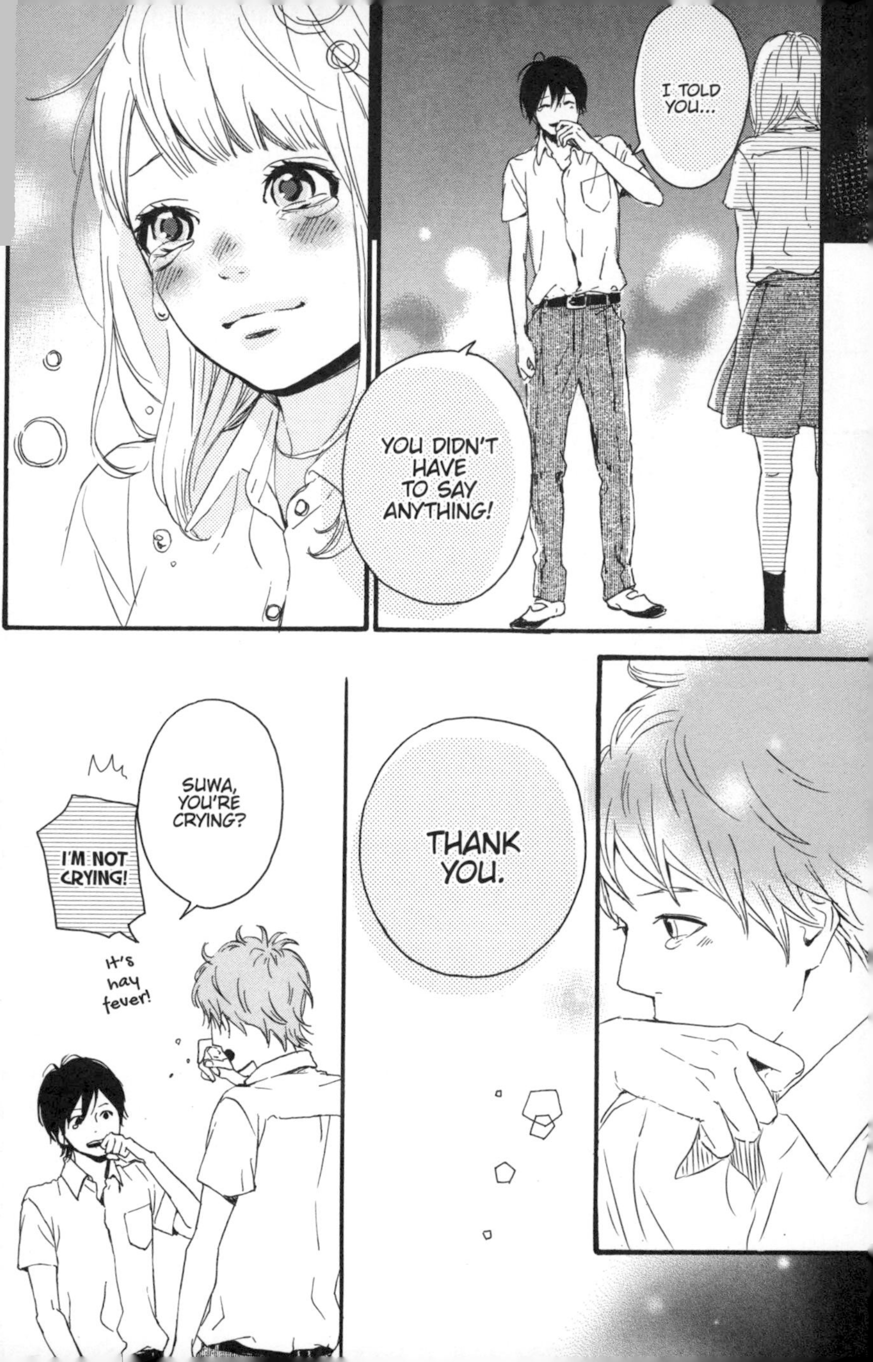
I TOLD YOU...
YOU DIDN'T HAVE TO SAY ANYTHING!
THANK YOU.
SUWA, YOU'RE CRYING?
I'M NOT CRYING!
It's hay fever!

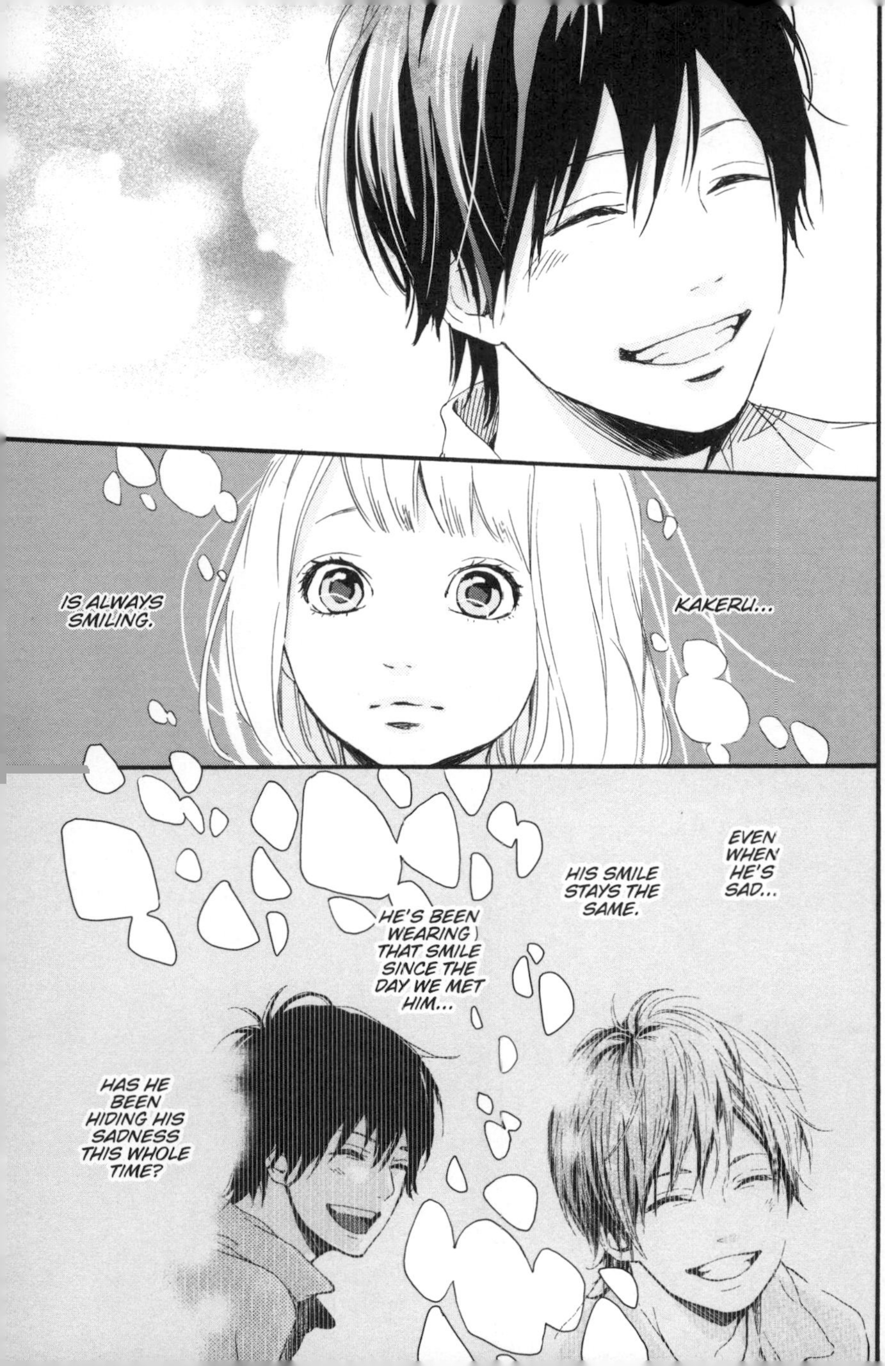
KAKERU...
IS ALWAYS SMILING.
EVEN WHEN HE'S SAD...
HIS SMILE STAYS THE SAME.
HE'S BEEN WEARING THAT SMILE SINCE THE DAY WE MET HIM...
HAS HE BEEN HIDING HIS SADNESS THIS WHOLE TIME?

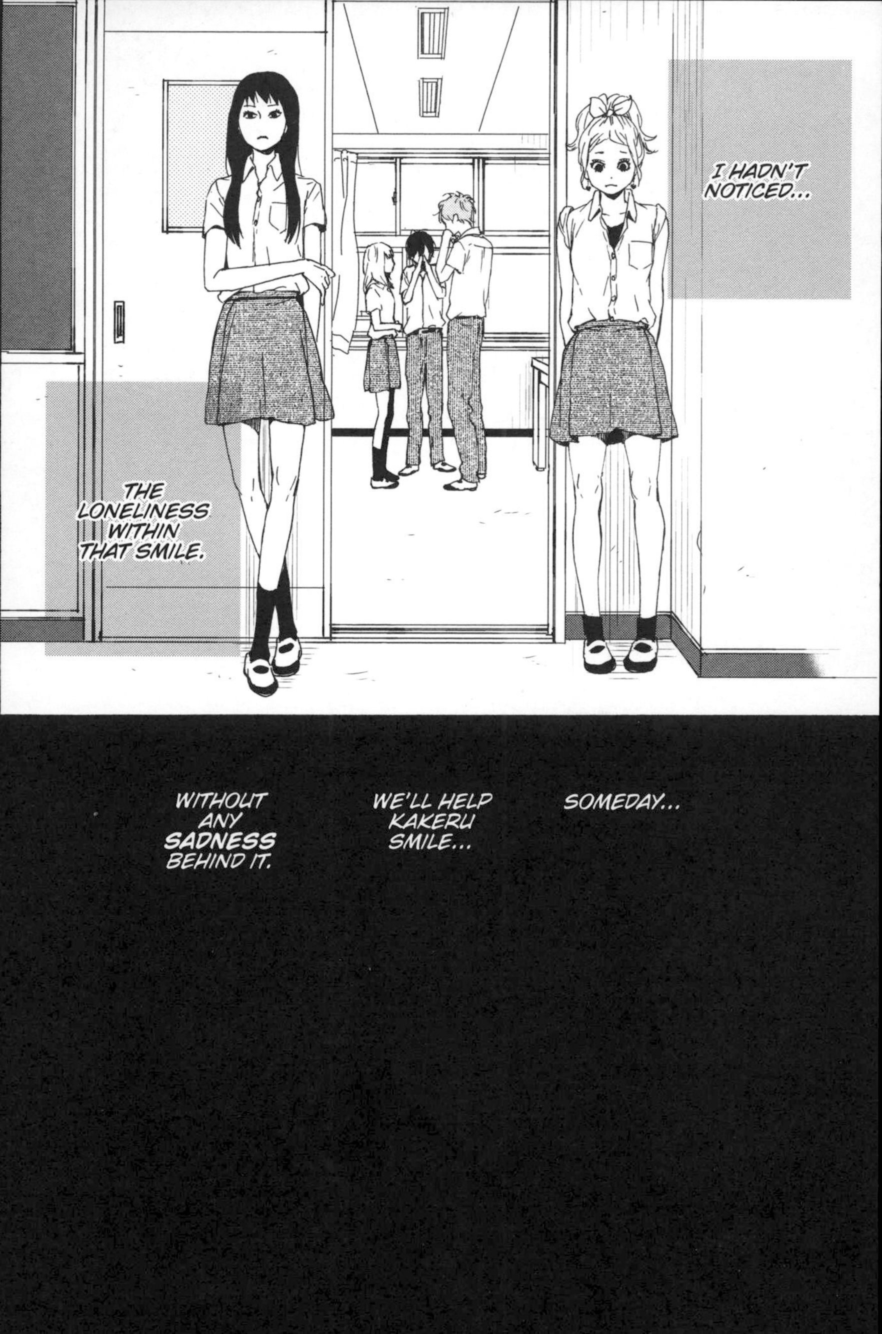
I HADN'T NOTICED...
THE LONELINESS WITHIN THAT SMILE.
SOMEDAY...
WE'LL HELP KAKERU SMILE...
WITHOUT ANY SADNESS BEHIND IT.

orange

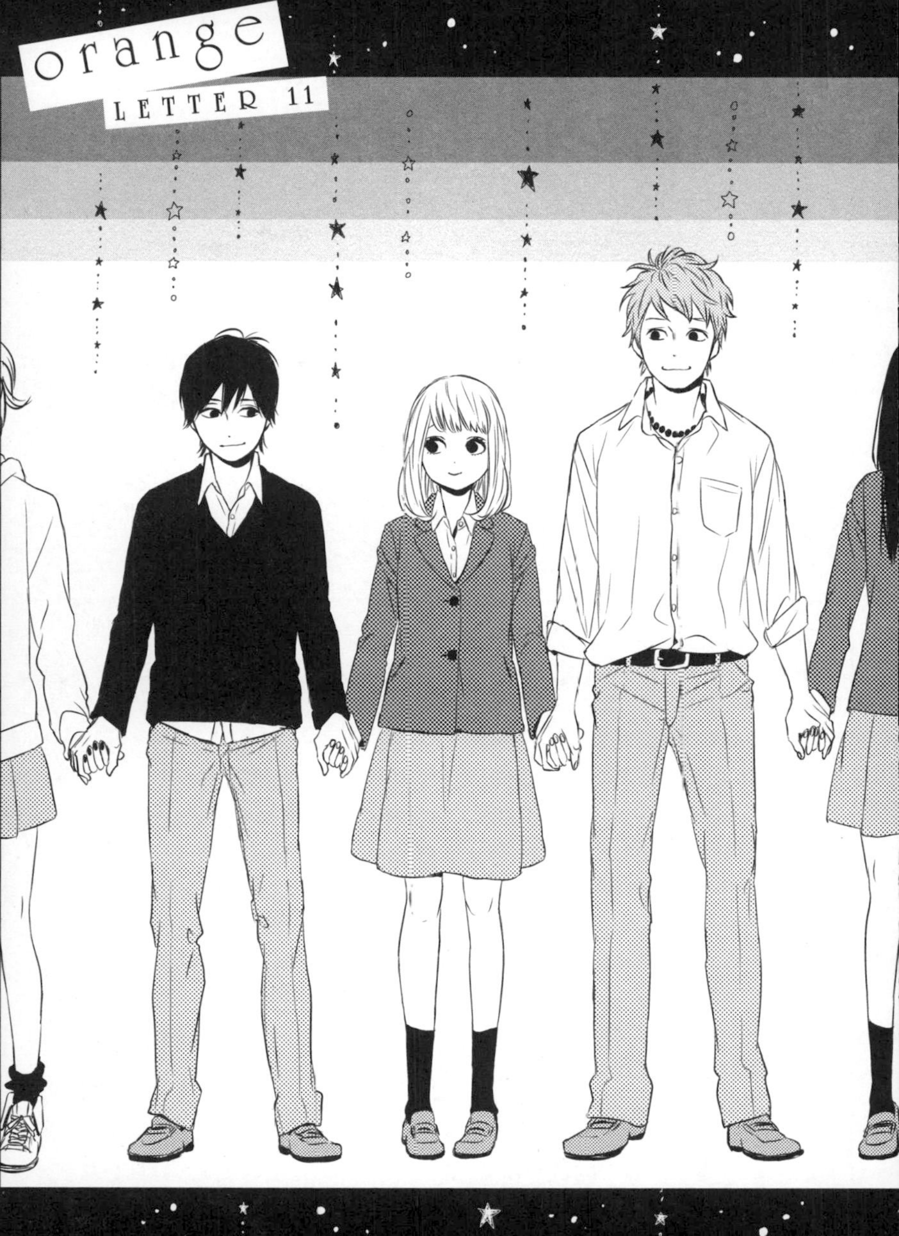
orange
LETTER 11

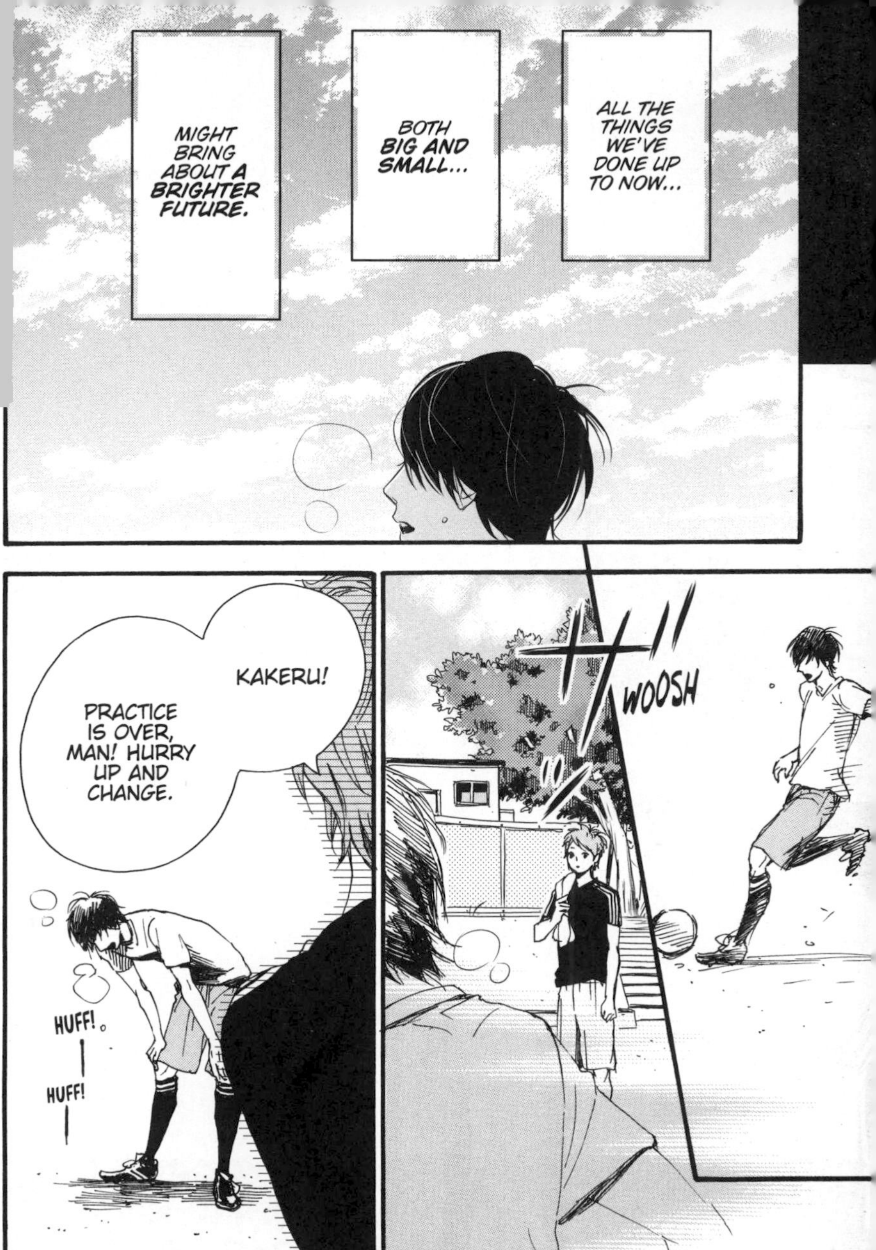
ALL THE THINGS WE'VE DONE UP TO NOW...
BOTH BIG AND SMALL...
MIGHT BRING ABOUT A BRIGHTER FUTURE.
WOOSH
KAKERU!
PRACTICE IS OVER, MAN! HURRY UP AND CHANGE.
HUFF!
HUFF!

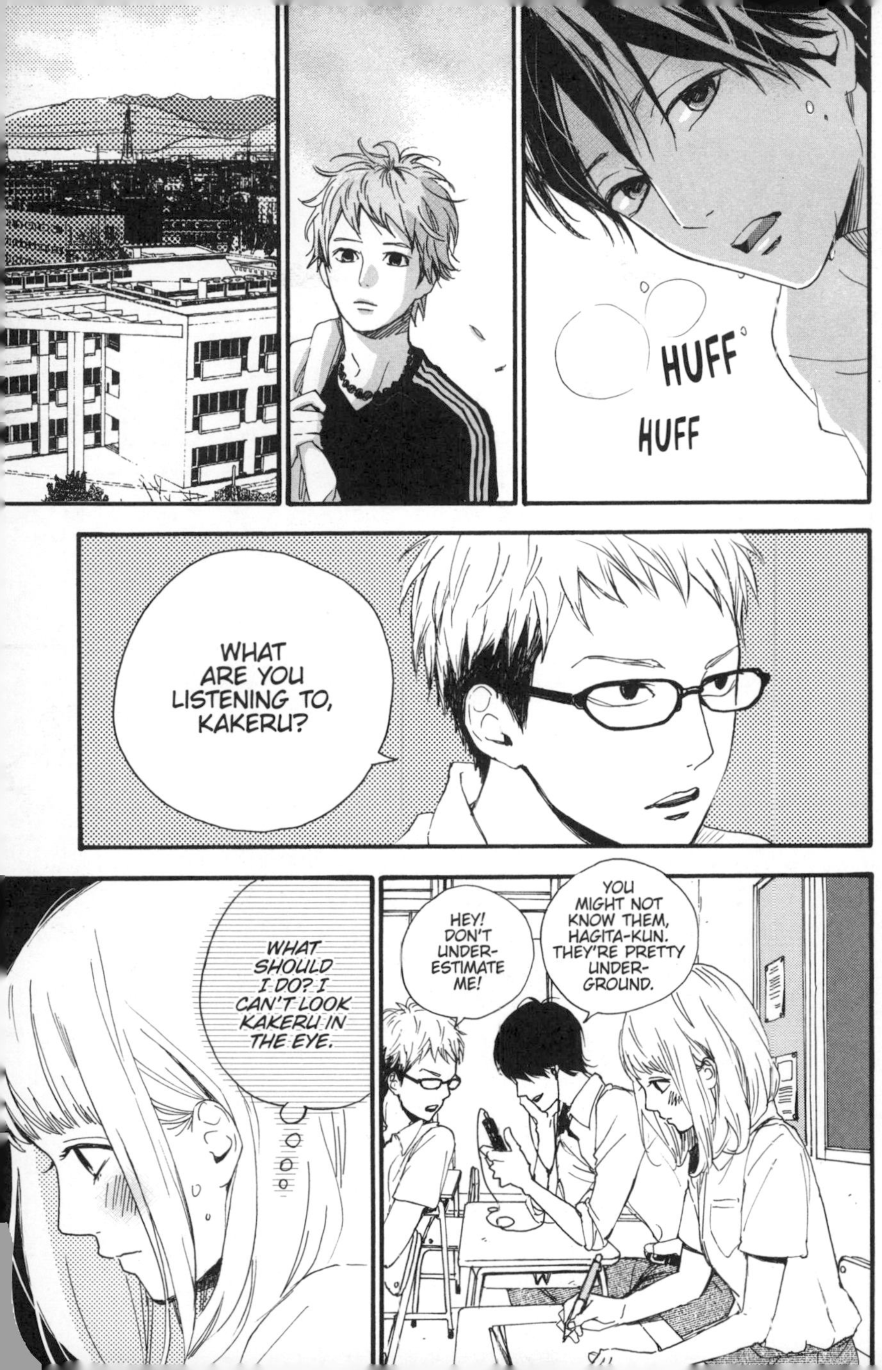
HUFF
HUFF
WHAT ARE YOU LISTENING TO, KAKERU?
YOU MIGHT NOT KNOW THEM, HAGITA-KUN. THEY'RE PRETTY UNDER-GROUND.
HEY! DON'T UNDER-ESTIMATE ME!
WHAT SHOULD I DO? I CAN'T LOOK KAKERU IN THE EYE.

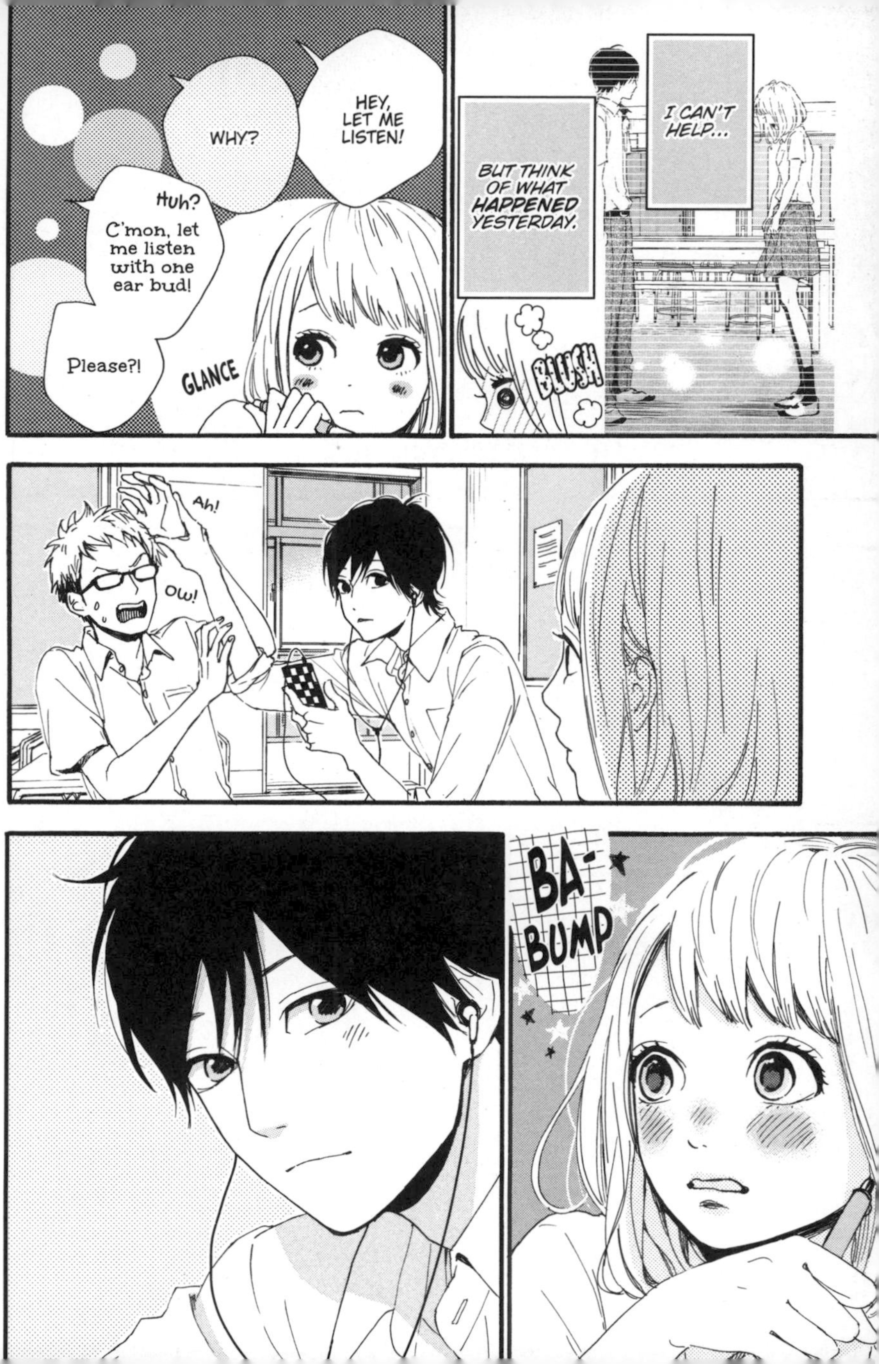
I CAN'T HELP...
BUT THINK OF WHAT HAPPENED YESTERDAY.
BLUSH
HEY, LET ME LISTEN!
WHY?
Huh? C'mon, let me listen with one ear bud!
Please?!
GLANCE
Ah!
OW!
BA-BUMP

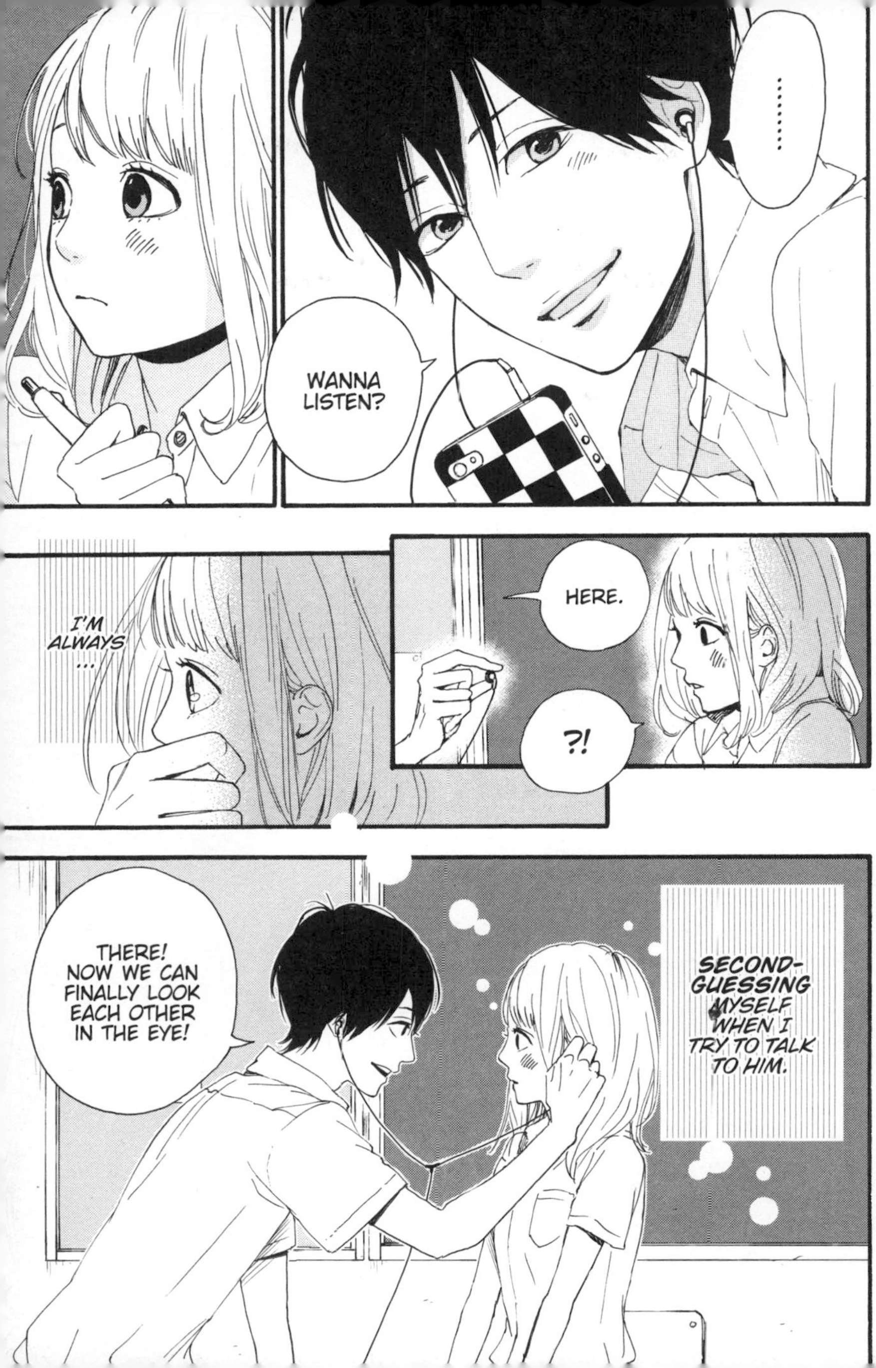
......
WANNA LISTEN?
HERE.
?!
I'M ALWAYS ...
SECOND-GUESSING MYSELF WHEN I TRY TO TALK TO HIM.
THERE! NOW WE CAN FINALLY LOOK EACH OTHER IN THE EYE!

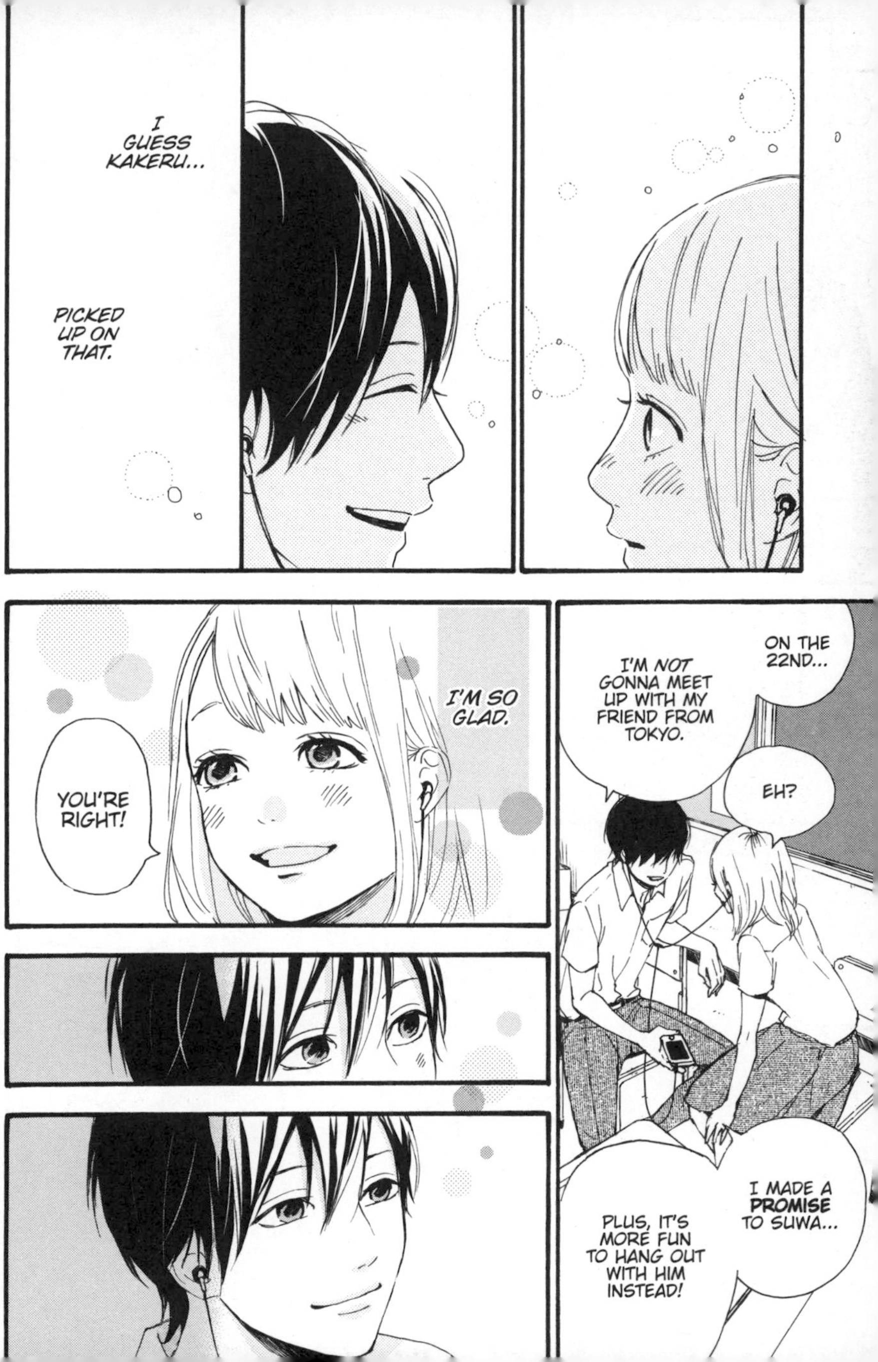
I GUESS KAKERU...
PICKED UP ON THAT.
ON THE 22ND...
I'M *NOT* GONNA MEET UP WITH MY FRIEND FROM TOKYO.
EH?
I MADE A **PROMISE** TO SUWA...
PLUS, IT'S MORE FUN TO HANG OUT WITH HIM INSTEAD!
I'M SO GLAD.
YOU'RE RIGHT!

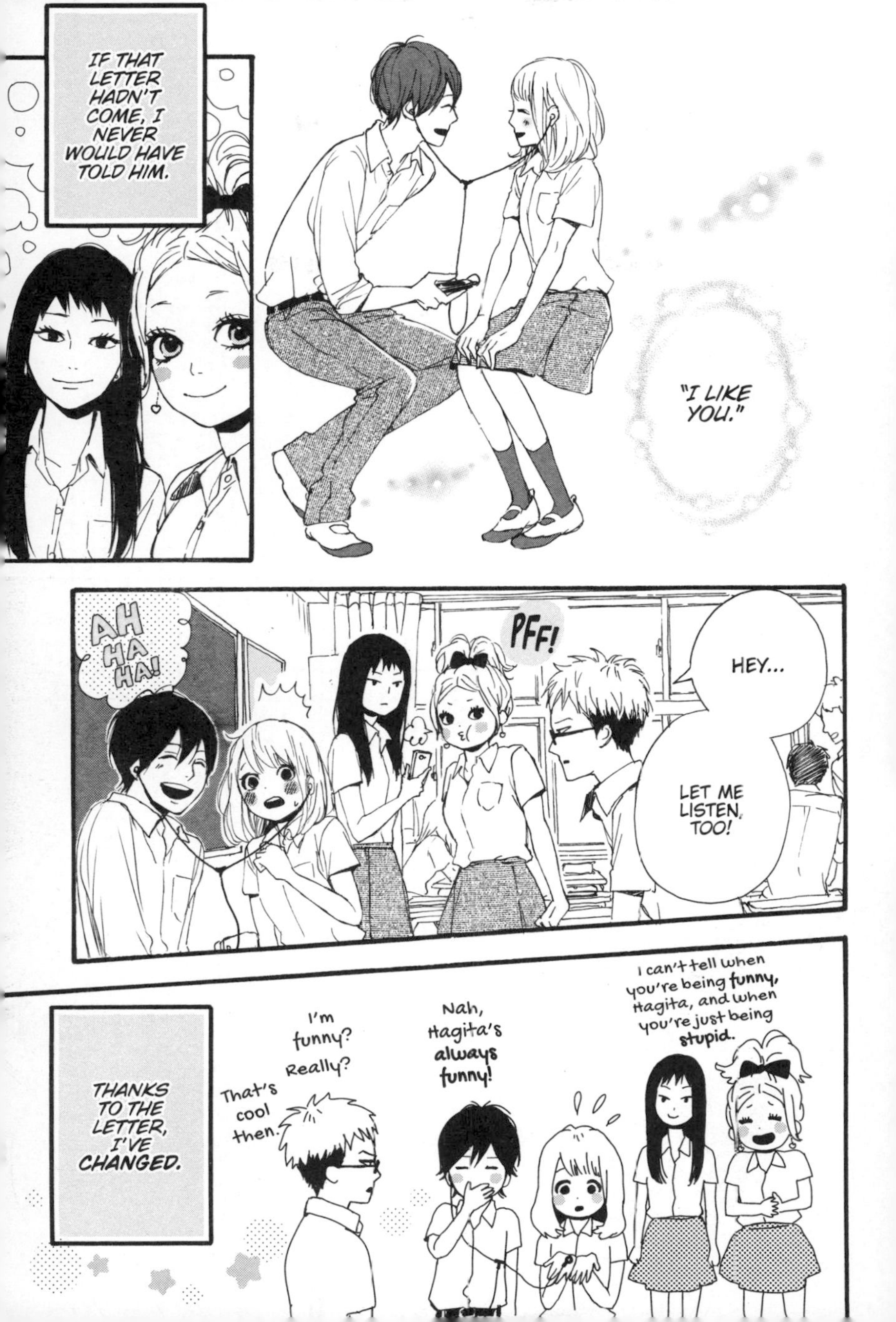
"I LIKE YOU."
IF THAT LETTER HADN'T COME, I NEVER WOULD HAVE TOLD HIM.
HEY...
LET ME LISTEN, TOO!
PFF!
AH HA HA!
I can't tell when you're being funny, Hagita, and when you're just being stupid.
Nah, Hagita's always funny!
I'm funny? Really?
That's cool then.
THANKS TO THE LETTER, I'VE CHANGED.

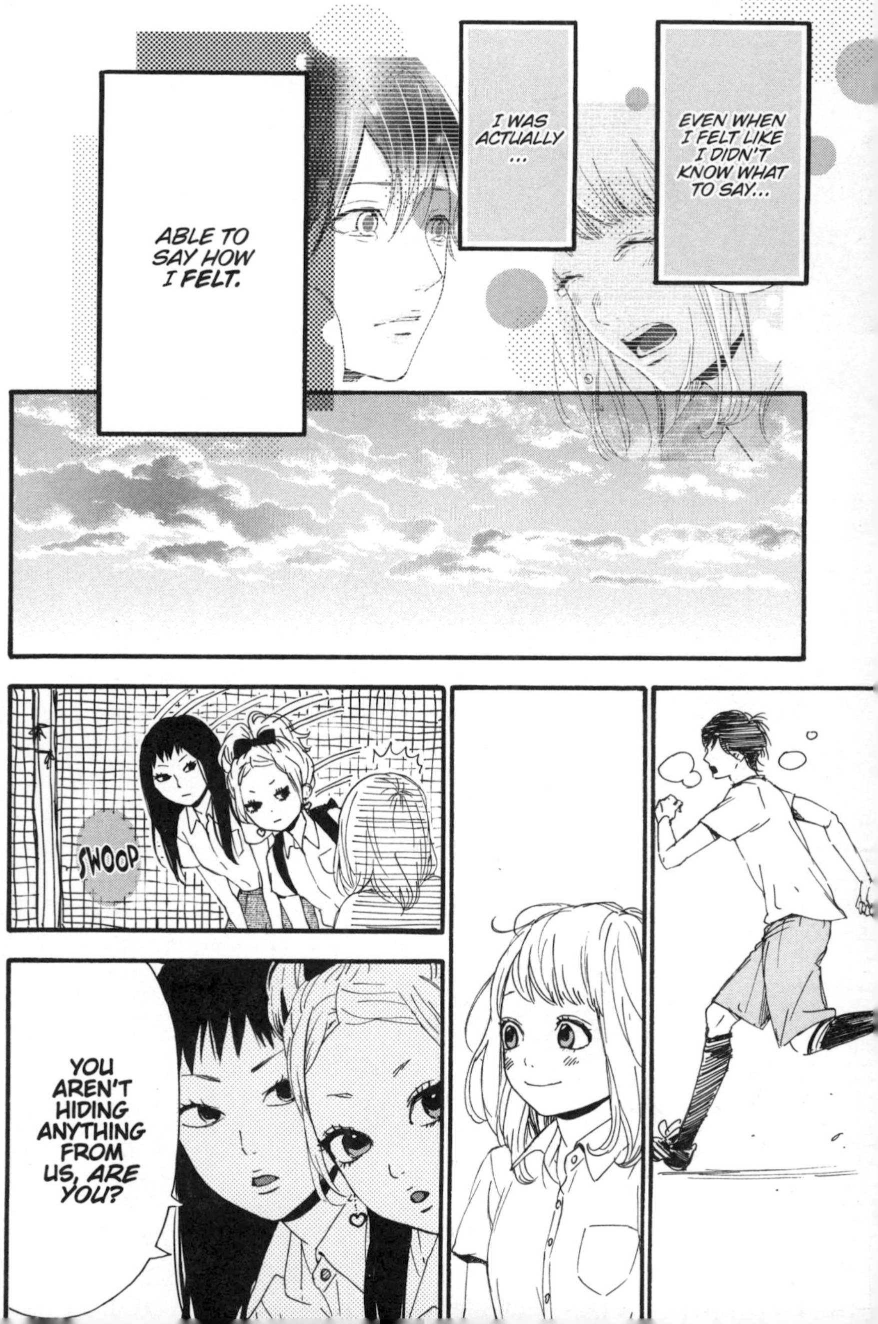
EVEN WHEN I FELT LIKE I DIDN'T KNOW WHAT TO SAY...
I WAS ACTUALLY ...
ABLE TO SAY HOW I FELT.
SWOOP
YOU AREN'T HIDING ANYTHING FROM US, ARE YOU?

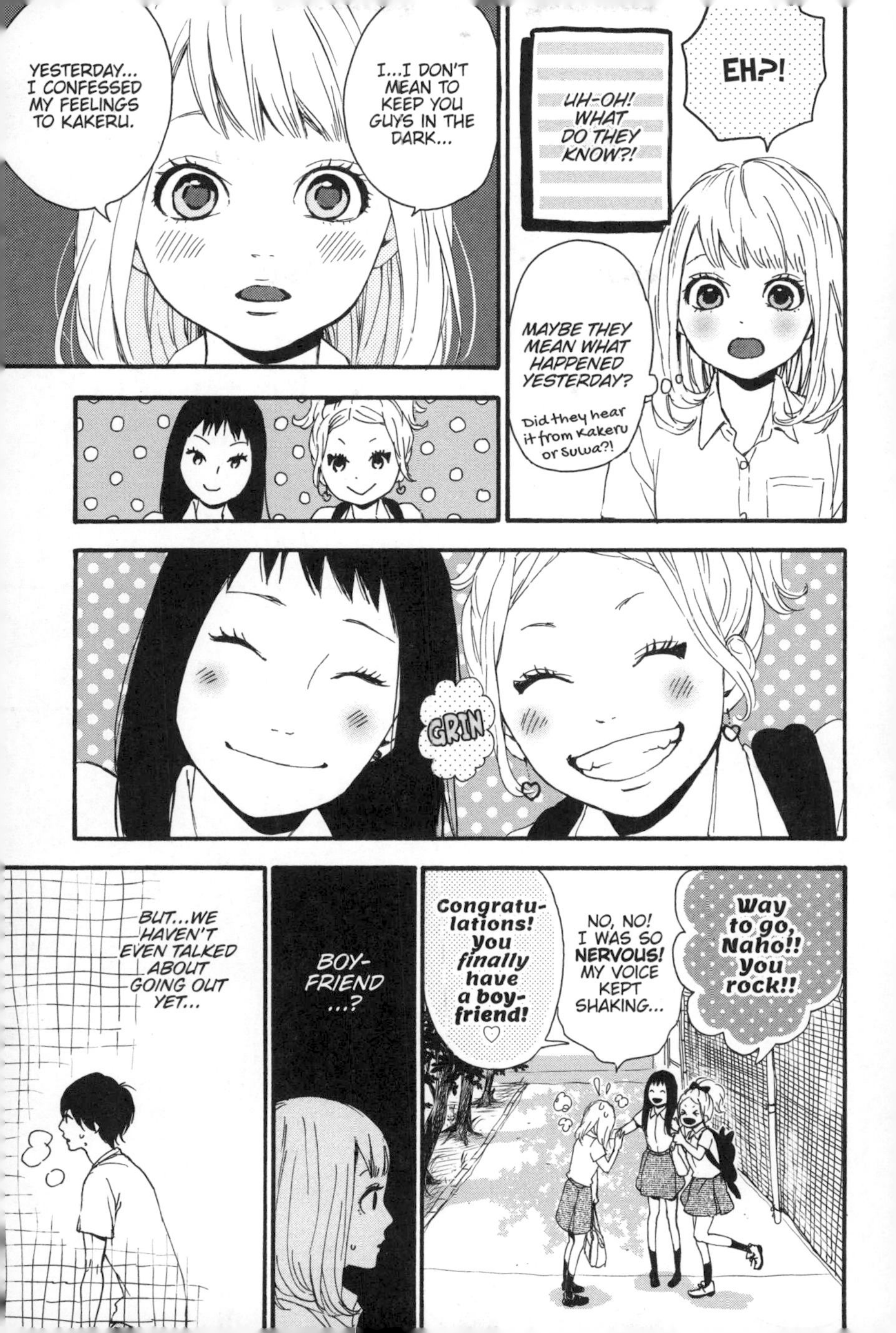
EH?!
UH-OH! WHAT DO THEY KNOW?!
MAYBE THEY MEAN WHAT HAPPENED YESTERDAY?
Did they hear it from Kakeru or Suwa?!
I...I DON'T MEAN TO KEEP YOU GUYS IN THE DARK...
YESTERDAY... I CONFESSED MY FEELINGS TO KAKERU.
GRIN
Way to go, Naho!! You rock!!
NO, NO! I WAS SO NERVOUS! MY VOICE KEPT SHAKING...
Congratulations! You finally have a boyfriend! ♡
BOY-FRIEND ...?
BUT...WE HAVEN'T EVEN TALKED ABOUT GOING OUT YET...

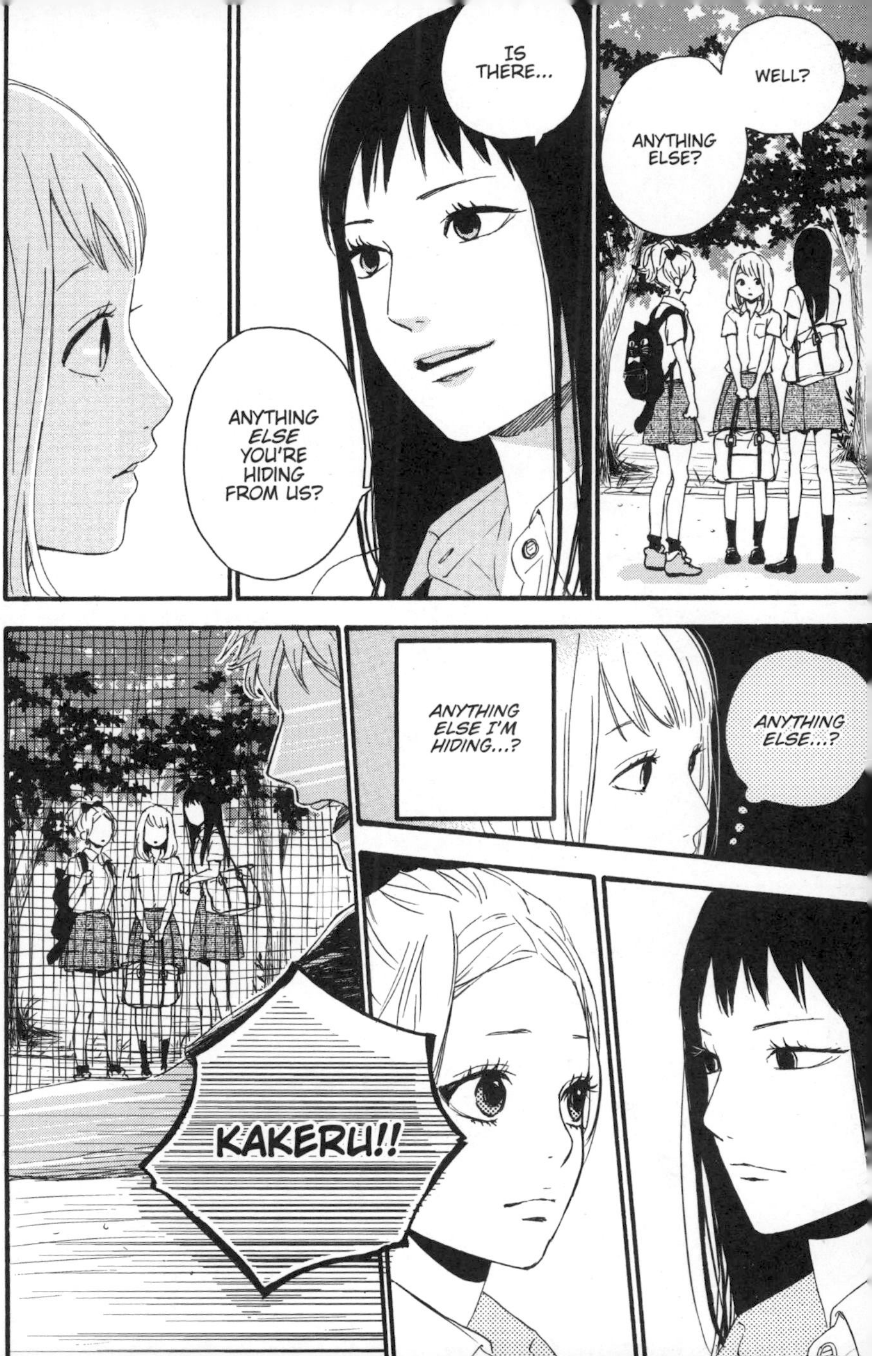
WELL?
ANYTHING ELSE?
IS THERE...
ANYTHING ELSE YOU'RE HIDING FROM US?
ANYTHING ELSE...?
ANYTHING ELSE I'M HIDING...?
KAKERU!!

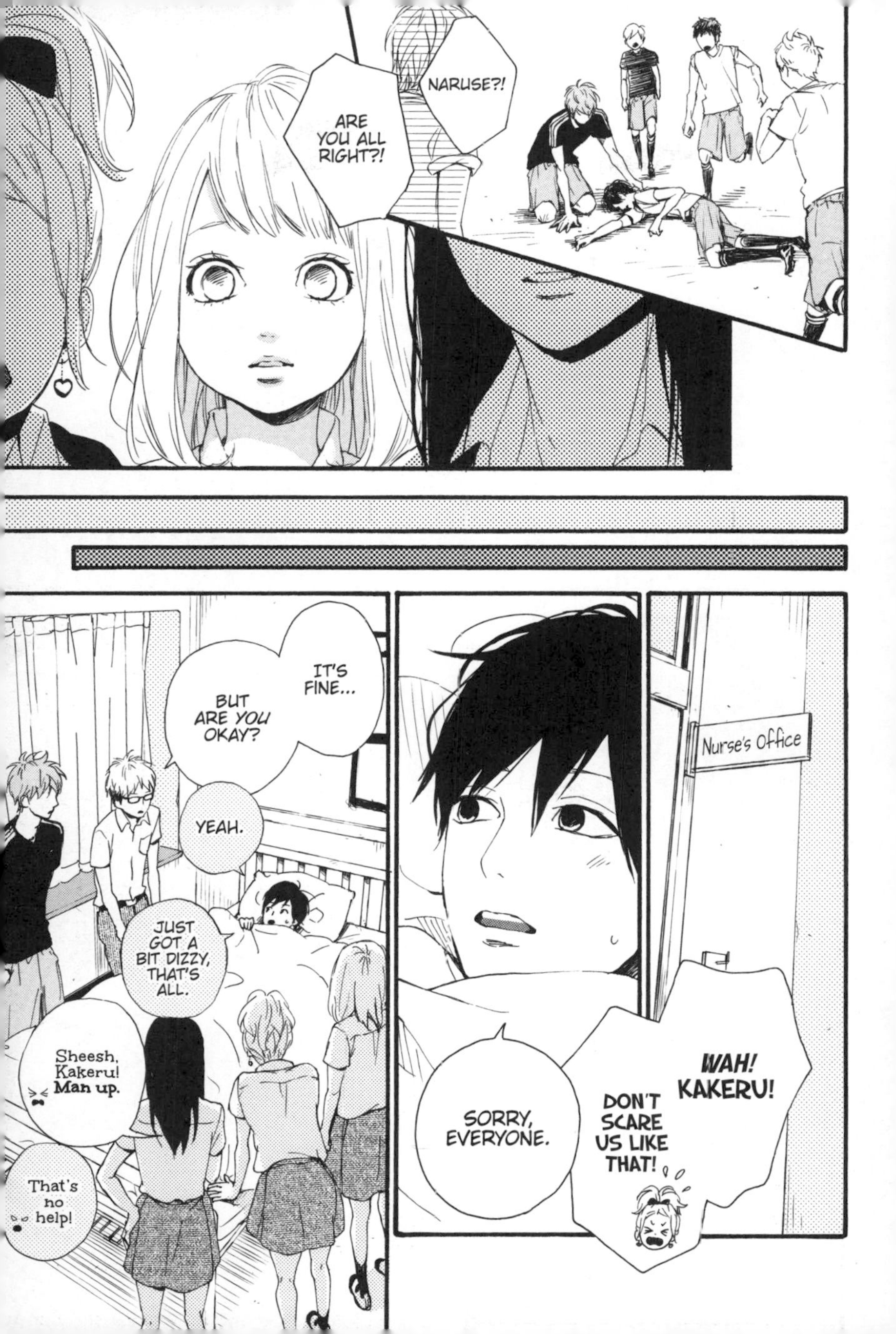
NARUSE?!
ARE YOU ALL RIGHT?!
Nurse's Office
WAH! KAKERU!
DON'T SCARE US LIKE THAT!
SORRY, EVERYONE.
IT'S FINE...
BUT ARE YOU OKAY?
YEAH.
JUST GOT A BIT DIZZY, THAT'S ALL.
Sheesh, Kakeru! Man up.
That's no help!

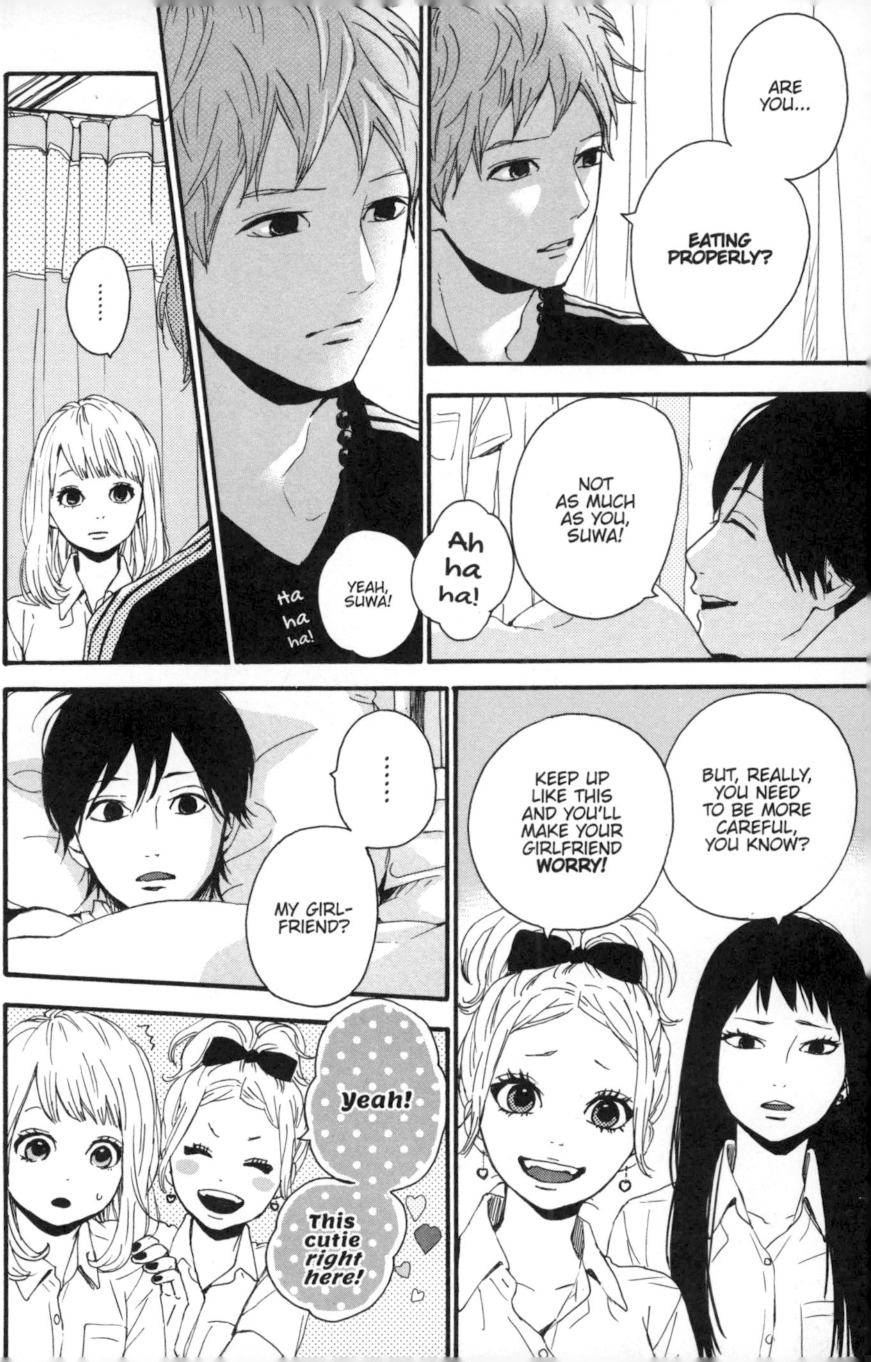
ARE YOU...
EATING PROPERLY?
NOT AS MUCH AS YOU, SUWA!
Ah ha ha!
YEAH, SUWA!
Ha ha ha!
......
BUT, REALLY, YOU NEED TO BE MORE CAREFUL, YOU KNOW?
KEEP UP LIKE THIS AND YOU'LL MAKE YOUR GIRLFRIEND **WORRY!**
......
MY GIRL-FRIEND?
Yeah!
This cutie right here!

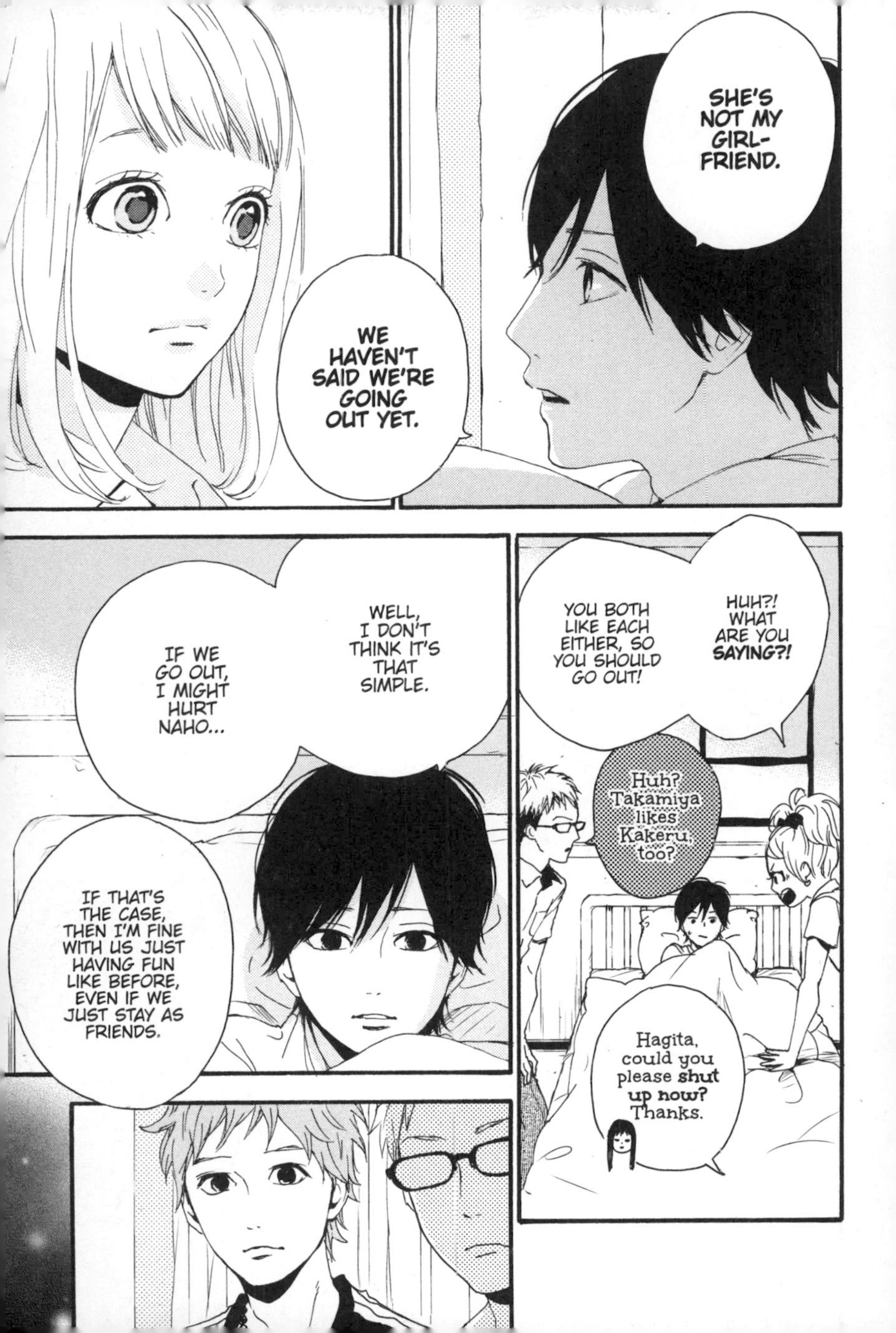
SHE'S NOT MY GIRL-FRIEND.
WE HAVEN'T SAID WE'RE GOING OUT YET.
HUH?! WHAT ARE YOU SAYING?!
YOU BOTH LIKE EACH EITHER, SO YOU SHOULD GO OUT!
Huh? Takamiya likes Kakeru, too?
Hagita, could you please shut up now? Thanks.
WELL, I DON'T THINK IT'S THAT SIMPLE.
IF WE GO OUT, I MIGHT HURT NAHO...
IF THAT'S THE CASE, THEN I'M FINE WITH US JUST HAVING FUN LIKE BEFORE, EVEN IF WE JUST STAY AS FRIENDS.

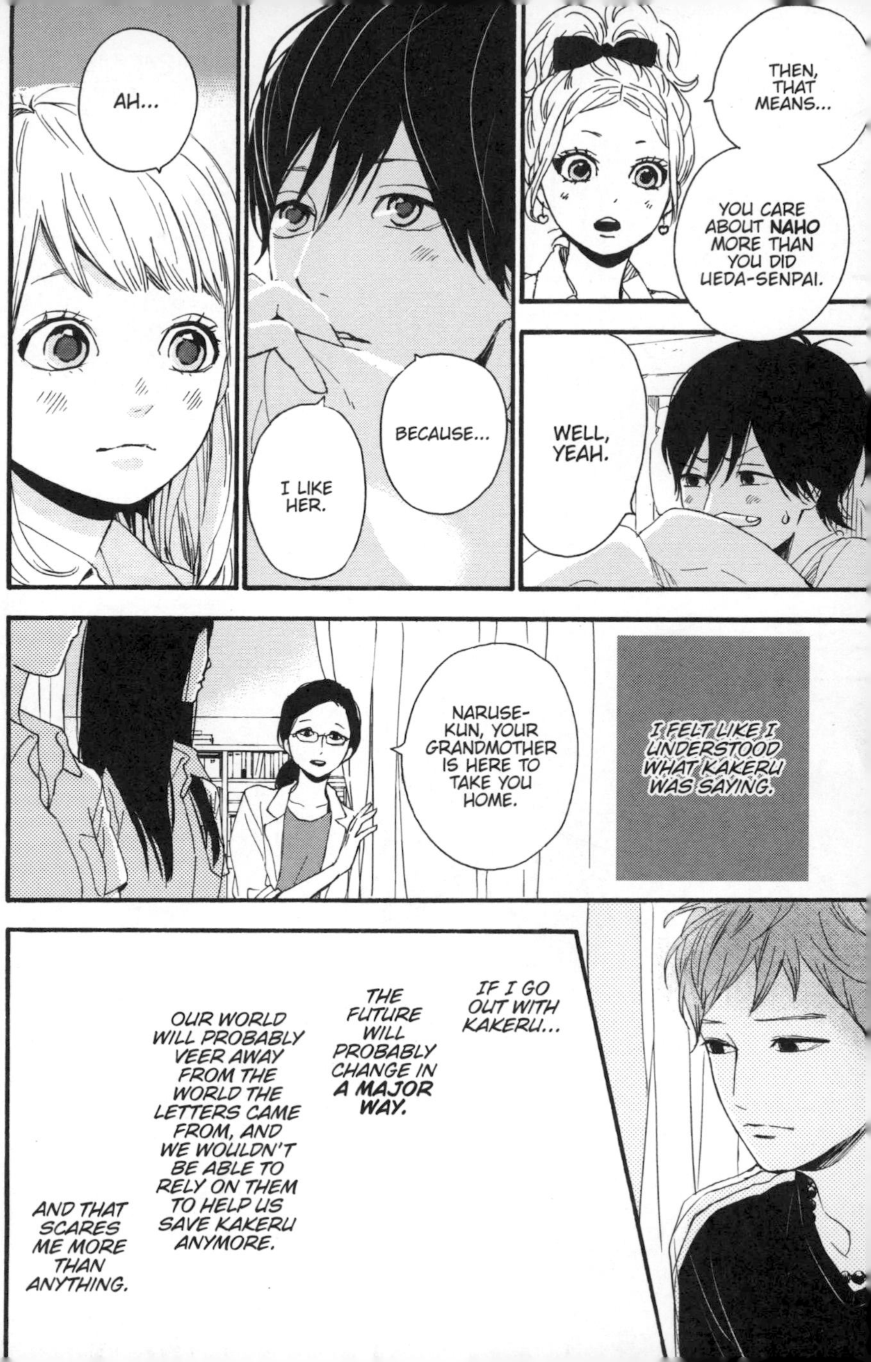
THEN, THAT MEANS...
YOU CARE ABOUT NAHO MORE THAN YOU DID UEDA-SENPAI.
WELL, YEAH.
BECAUSE...
I LIKE HER.
AH...
I FELT LIKE I UNDERSTOOD WHAT KAKERU WAS SAYING.
NARUSE-KUN, YOUR GRANDMOTHER IS HERE TO TAKE YOU HOME.
IF I GO OUT WITH KAKERU...
THE FUTURE WILL PROBABLY CHANGE IN A MAJOR WAY.
OUR WORLD WILL PROBABLY VEER AWAY FROM THE WORLD THE LETTERS CAME FROM, AND WE WOULDN'T BE ABLE TO RELY ON THEM TO HELP US SAVE KAKERU ANYMORE.
AND THAT SCARES ME MORE THAN ANYTHING.

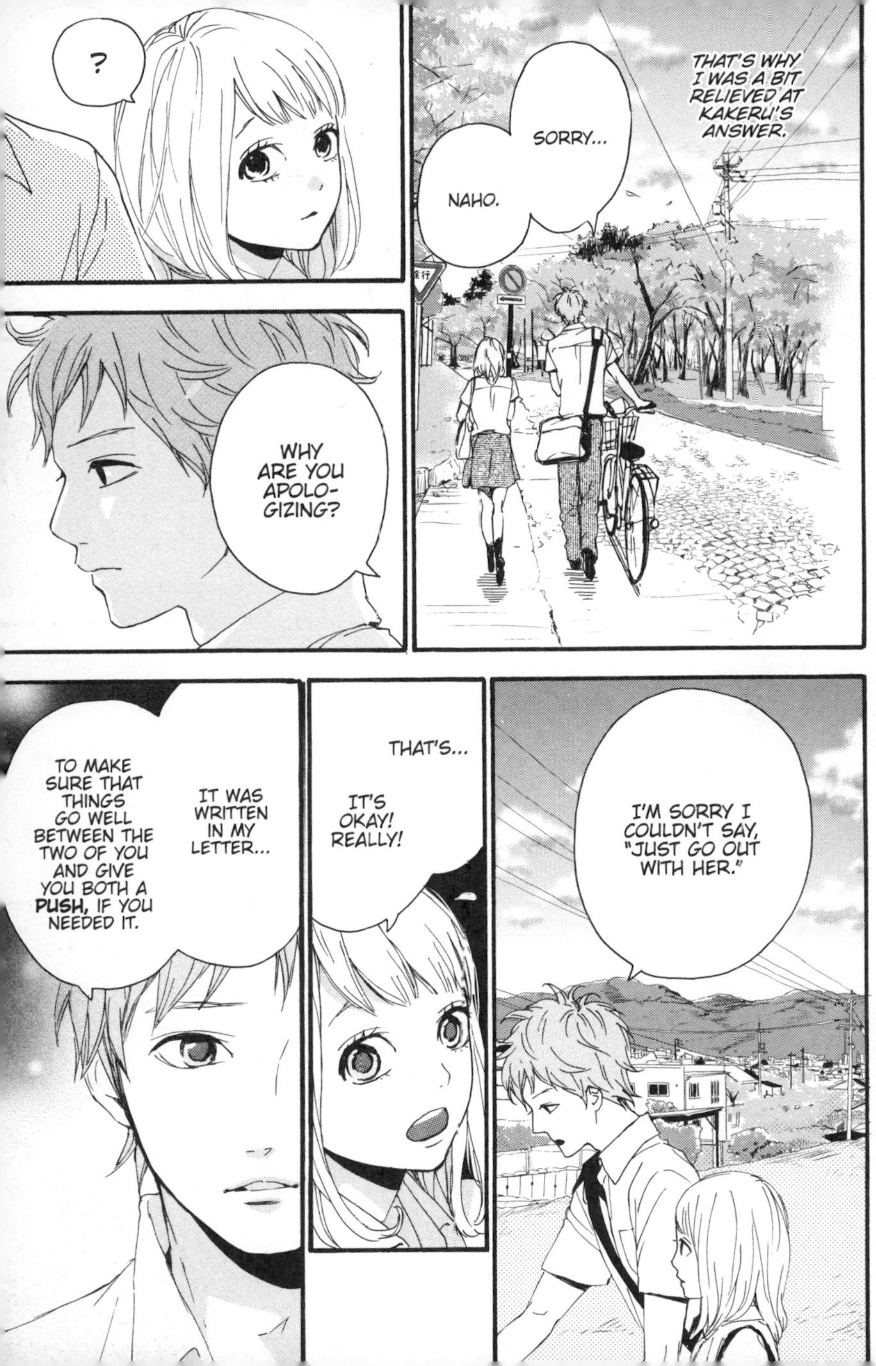
THAT'S WHY I WAS A BIT RELIEVED AT KAKERU'S ANSWER.
SORRY...
NAHO.
?
WHY ARE YOU APOLOGIZING?
I'M SORRY I COULDN'T SAY, "JUST GO OUT WITH HER."
THAT'S...
IT'S OKAY! REALLY!
IT WAS WRITTEN IN MY LETTER...
TO MAKE SURE THAT THINGS GO WELL BETWEEN THE TWO OF YOU AND GIVE YOU BOTH A PUSH, IF YOU NEEDED IT.

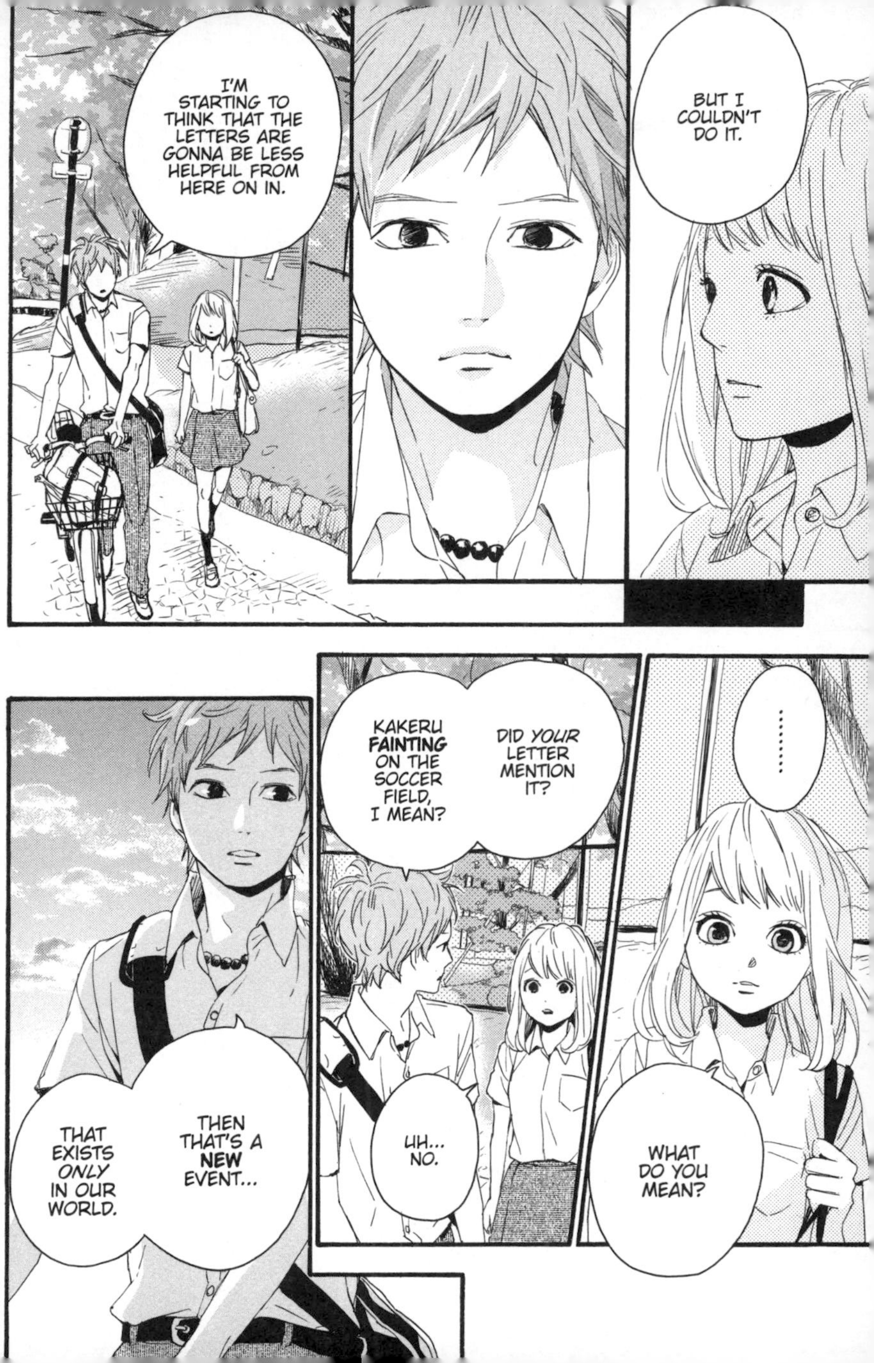
BUT I COULDN'T DO IT.
I'M STARTING TO THINK THAT THE LETTERS ARE GONNA BE LESS HELPFUL FROM HERE ON IN.
......
WHAT DO YOU MEAN?
DID *YOUR* LETTER MENTION IT?
KAKERU **FAINTING** ON THE SOCCER FIELD, I MEAN?
UH... NO.
THEN THAT'S A **NEW** EVENT...
THAT EXISTS *ONLY* IN OUR WORLD.

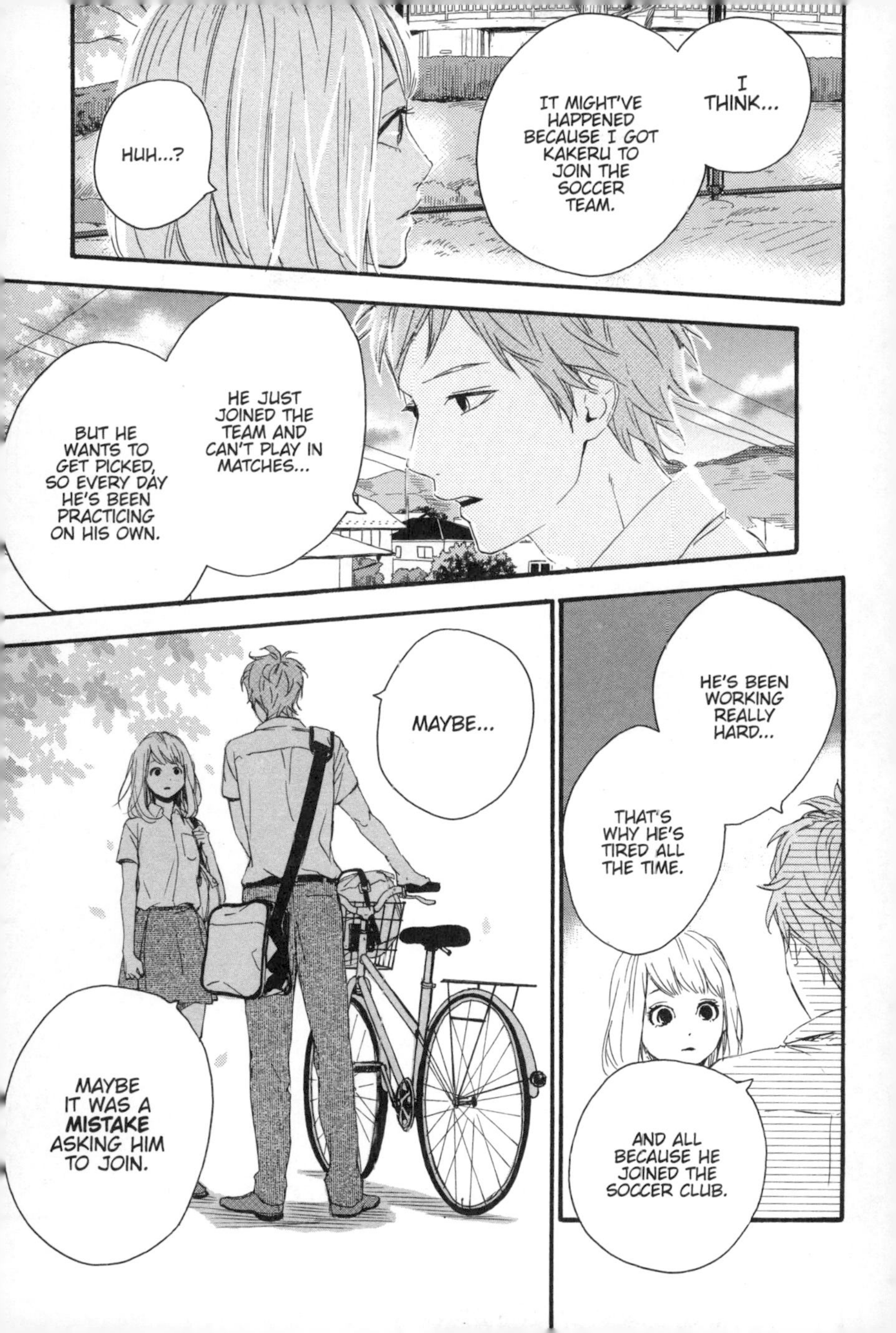
I THINK...
IT MIGHT'VE HAPPENED BECAUSE I GOT KAKERU TO JOIN THE SOCCER TEAM.
HUH...?
HE JUST JOINED THE TEAM AND CAN'T PLAY IN MATCHES...
BUT HE WANTS TO GET PICKED, SO EVERY DAY HE'S BEEN PRACTICING ON HIS OWN.
HE'S BEEN WORKING REALLY HARD...
THAT'S WHY HE'S TIRED ALL THE TIME.
AND ALL BECAUSE HE JOINED THE SOCCER CLUB.
MAYBE...
MAYBE IT WAS A **MISTAKE** ASKING HIM TO JOIN.

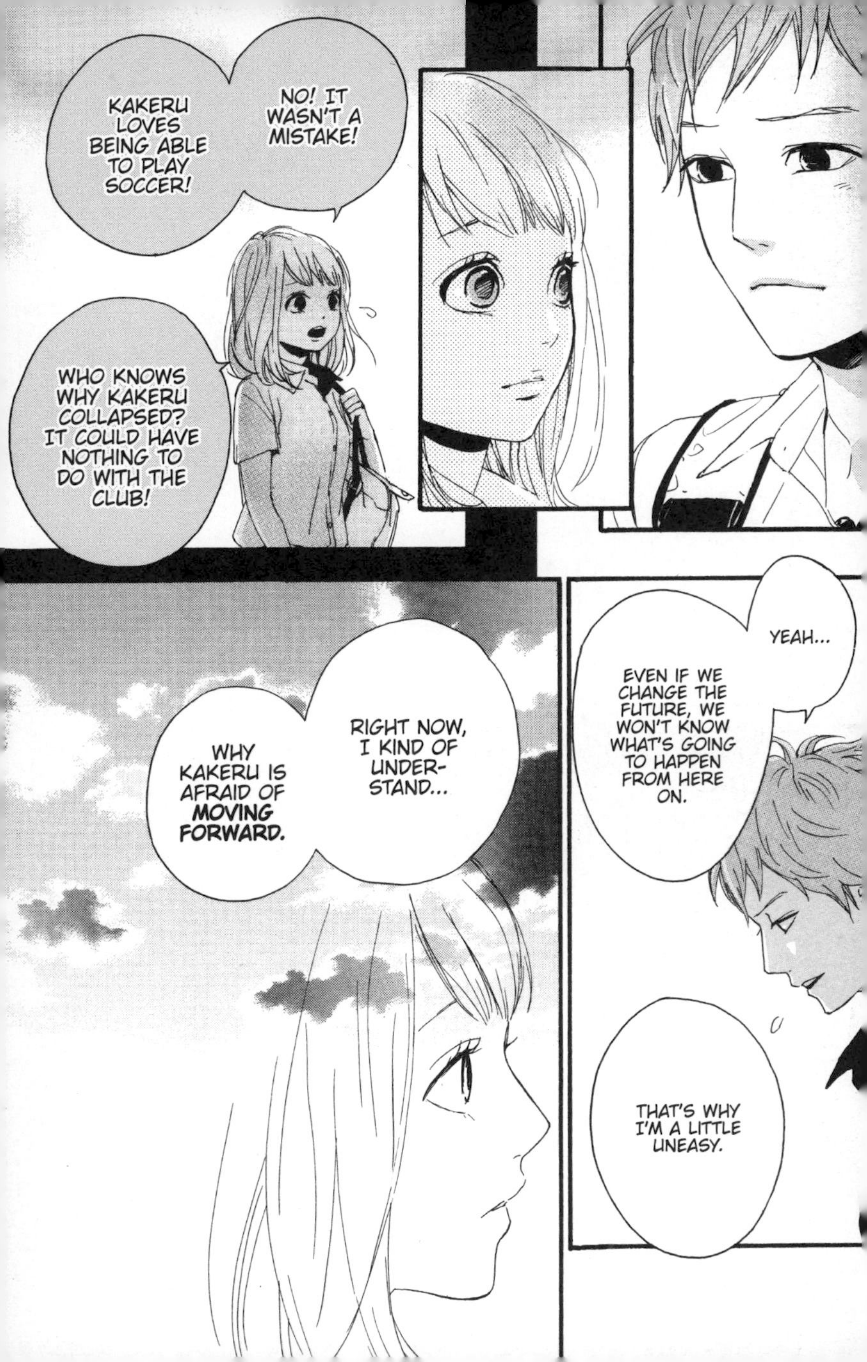
NO! IT WASN'T A MISTAKE!
KAKERU LOVES BEING ABLE TO PLAY SOCCER!
WHO KNOWS WHY KAKERU COLLAPSED? IT COULD HAVE NOTHING TO DO WITH THE CLUB!
YEAH...
EVEN IF WE CHANGE THE FUTURE, WE WON'T KNOW WHAT'S GOING TO HAPPEN FROM HERE ON.
THAT'S WHY I'M A LITTLE UNEASY.
RIGHT NOW, I KIND OF UNDER-STAND...
WHY KAKERU IS AFRAID OF **MOVING FORWARD.**

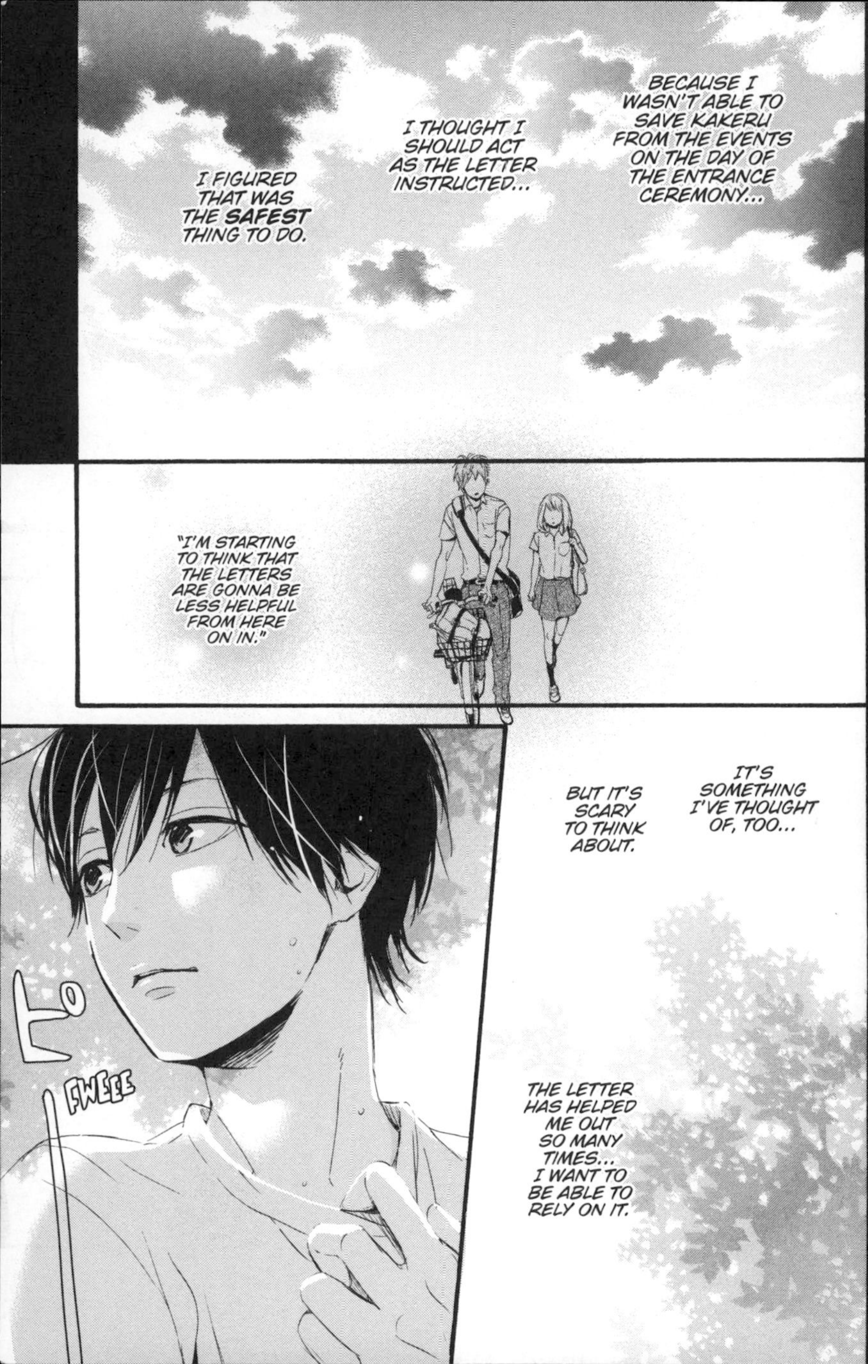
BECAUSE I WASN'T ABLE TO SAVE KAKERU FROM THE EVENTS ON THE DAY OF THE ENTRANCE CEREMONY...
I THOUGHT I SHOULD ACT AS THE LETTER INSTRUCTED...
I FIGURED THAT WAS THE **SAFEST** THING TO DO.
"I'M STARTING TO THINK THAT THE LETTERS ARE GONNA BE LESS HELPFUL FROM HERE ON IN."
IT'S SOMETHING I'VE THOUGHT OF, TOO...
BUT IT'S SCARY TO THINK ABOUT.
THE LETTER HAS HELPED ME OUT SO MANY TIMES... I WANT TO BE ABLE TO RELY ON IT.
ピ
FWEEE

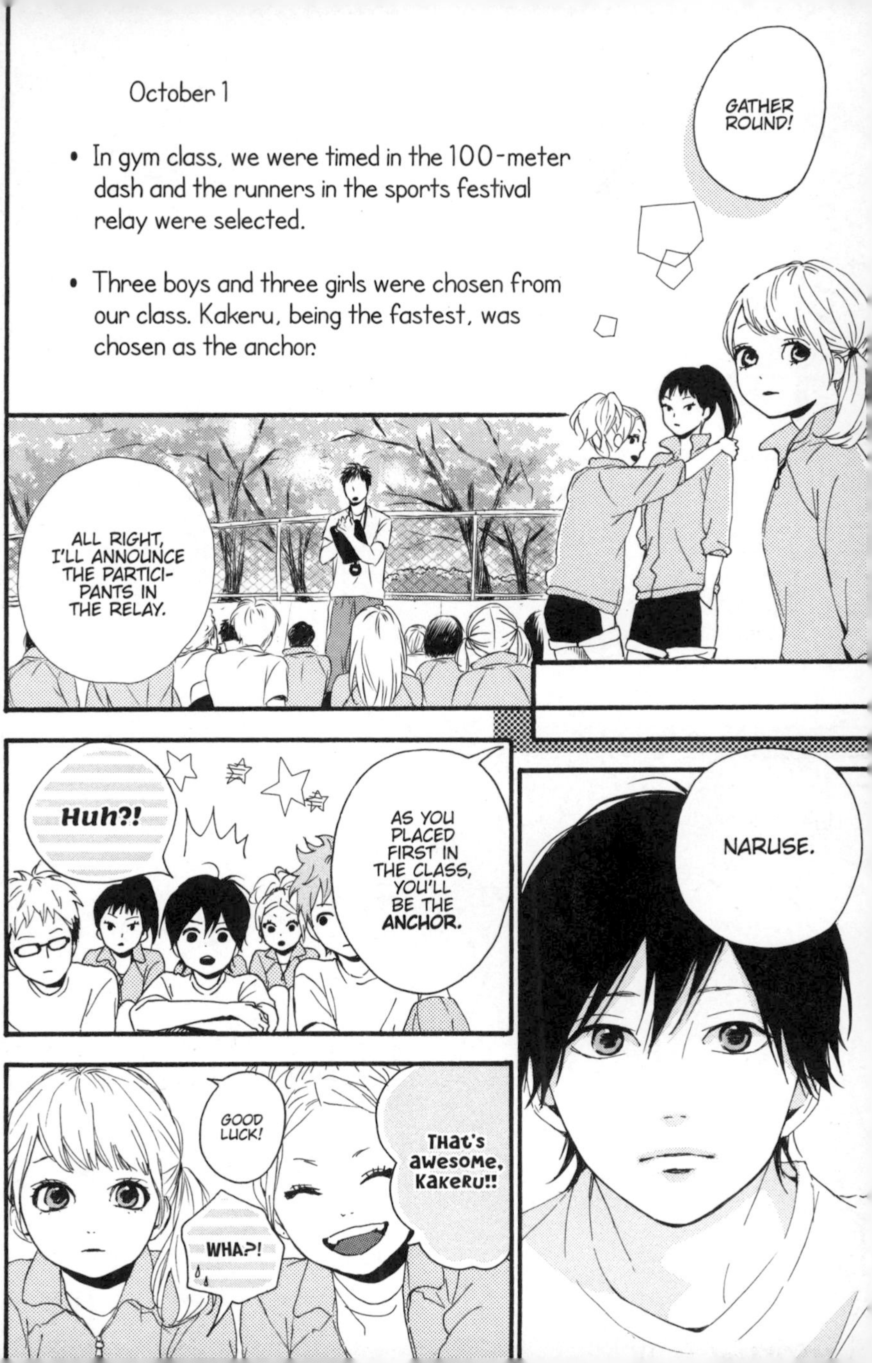
GATHER ROUND!
October 1
• In gym class, we were timed in the 100-meter dash and the runners in the sports festival relay were selected.
• Three boys and three girls were chosen from our class. Kakeru, being the fastest, was chosen as the anchor.
ALL RIGHT, I'LL ANNOUNCE THE PARTICI-PANTS IN THE RELAY.
NARUSE.
AS YOU PLACED FIRST IN THE CLASS, YOU'LL BE THE ANCHOR.
Huh?!
That's awesome, Kakeru!!
GOOD LUCK!
WHA?!

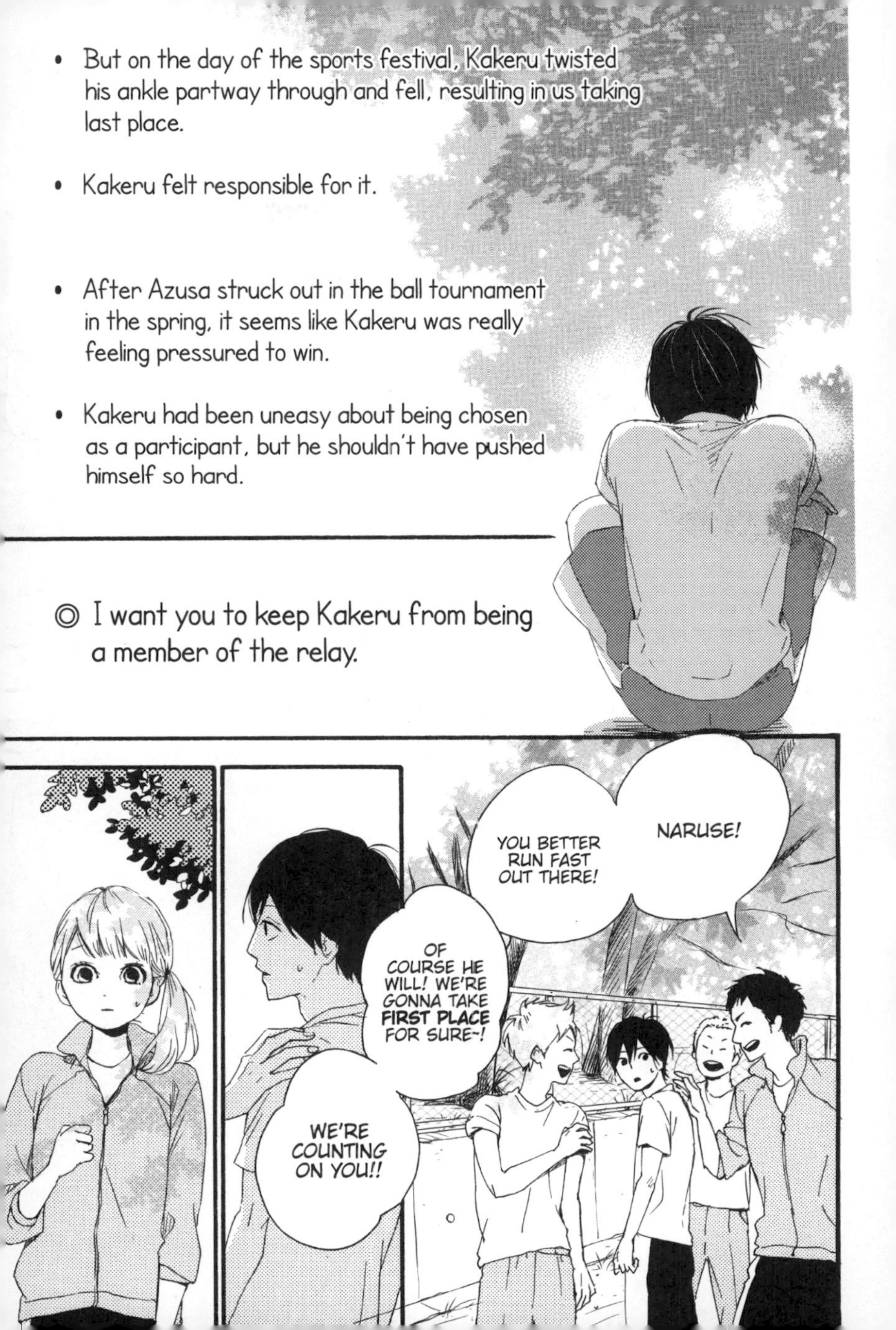
• But on the day of the sports festival, Kakeru twisted his ankle partway through and fell, resulting in us taking last place.
• Kakeru felt responsible for it.
• After Azusa struck out in the ball tournament in the spring, it seems like Kakeru was really feeling pressured to win.
• Kakeru had been uneasy about being chosen as a participant, but he shouldn't have pushed himself so hard.
◎ I want you to keep Kakeru from being a member of the relay.
NARUSE!
YOU BETTER RUN FAST OUT THERE!
OF COURSE HE WILL! WE'RE GONNA TAKE **FIRST PLACE** FOR SURE~!
WE'RE COUNTING ON YOU!!

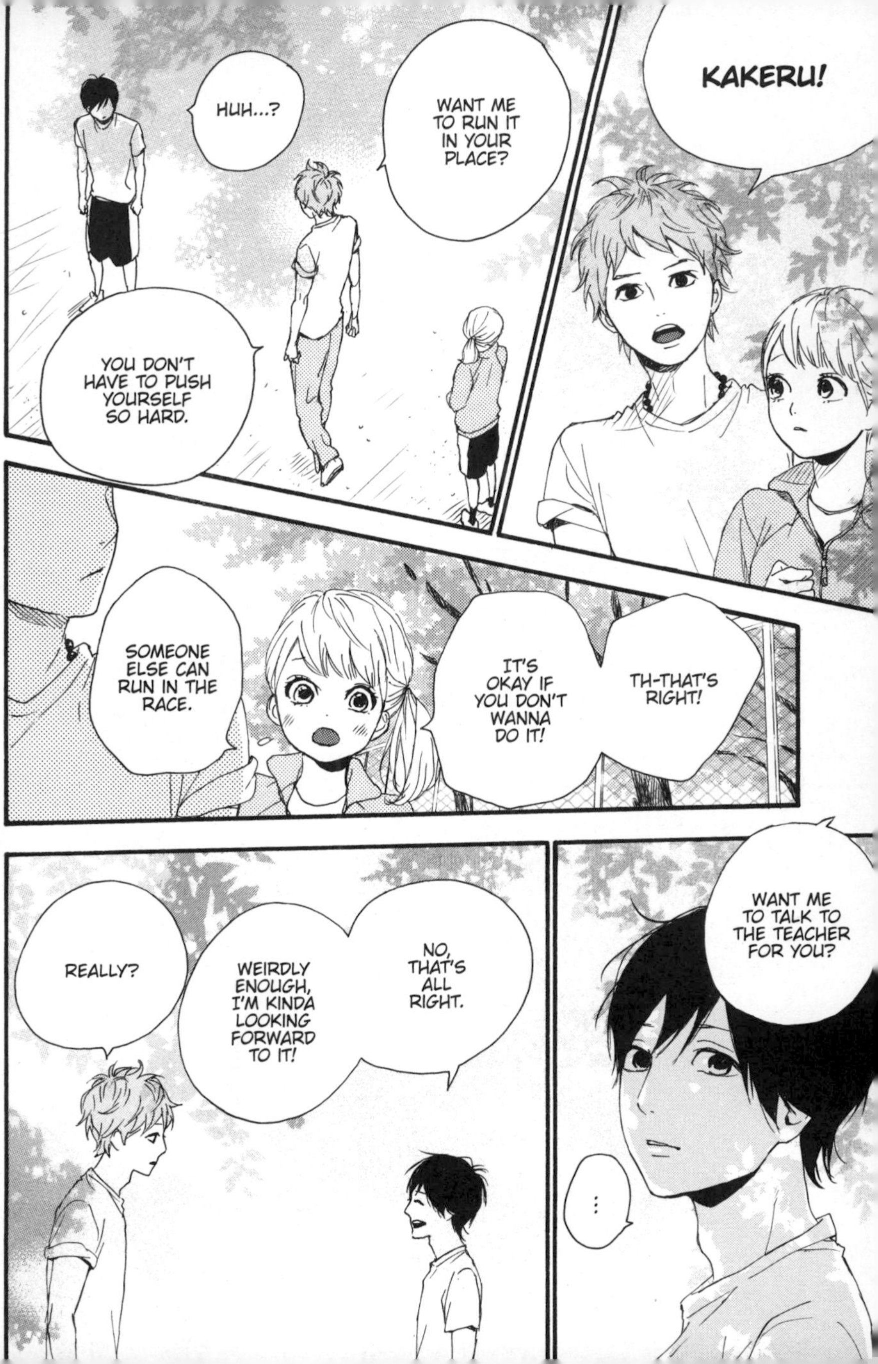
KAKERU!
WANT ME TO RUN IT IN YOUR PLACE?
HUH...?
YOU DON'T HAVE TO PUSH YOURSELF SO HARD.
TH-THAT'S RIGHT!
IT'S OKAY IF YOU DON'T WANNA DO IT!
SOMEONE ELSE CAN RUN IN THE RACE.
WANT ME TO TALK TO THE TEACHER FOR YOU?
...
NO, THAT'S ALL RIGHT.
WEIRDLY ENOUGH, I'M KINDA LOOKING FORWARD TO IT!
REALLY?

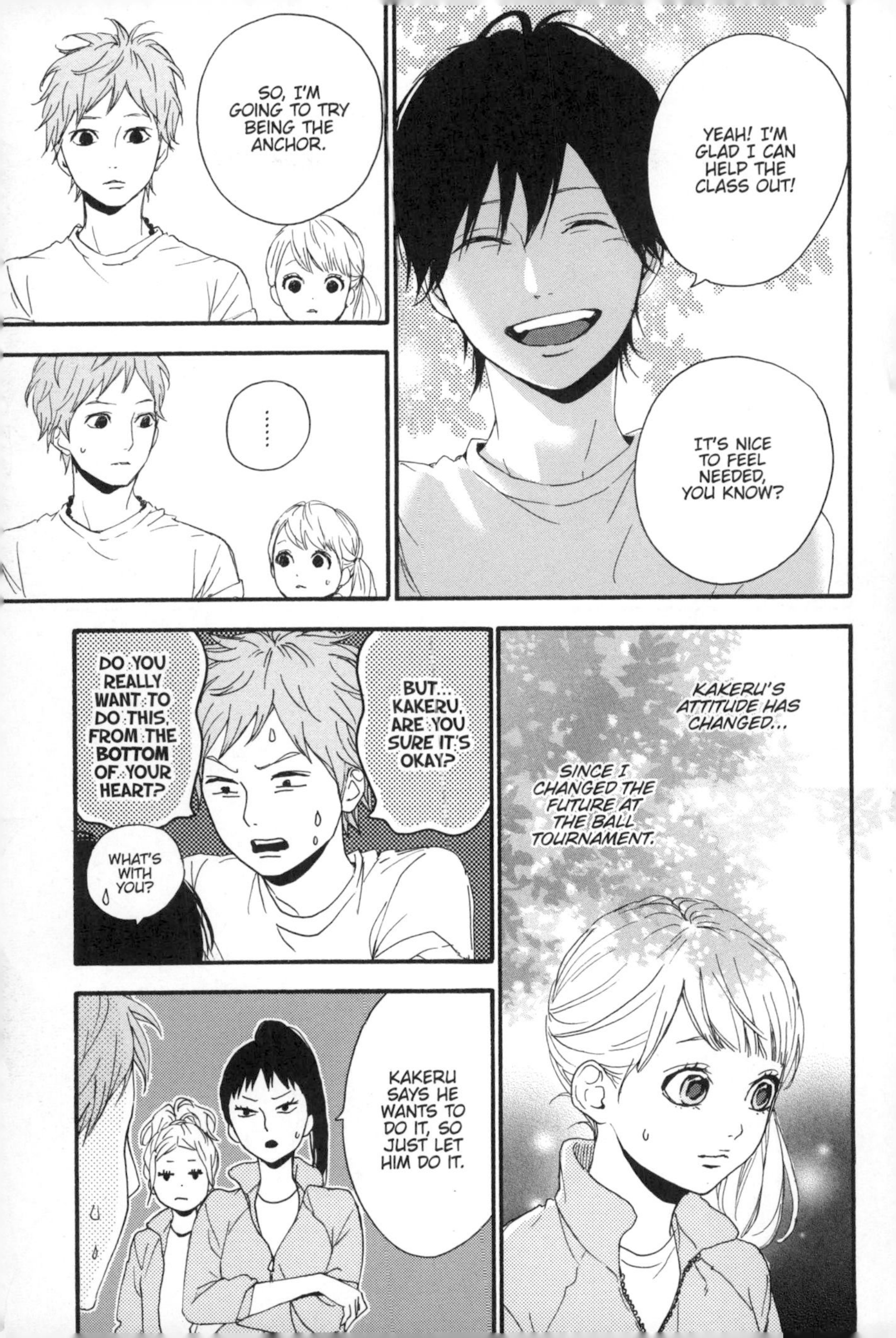
YEAH! I'M GLAD I CAN HELP THE CLASS OUT!
IT'S NICE TO FEEL NEEDED, YOU KNOW?
SO, I'M GOING TO TRY BEING THE ANCHOR.
......
KAKERU'S ATTITUDE HAS CHANGED...
SINCE I CHANGED THE FUTURE AT THE BALL TOURNAMENT.
BUT... KAKERU, ARE YOU SURE IT'S OKAY?
DO YOU REALLY WANT TO DO THIS, FROM THE BOTTOM OF YOUR HEART?
WHAT'S WITH YOU?
KAKERU SAYS HE WANTS TO DO IT, SO JUST LET HIM DO IT.

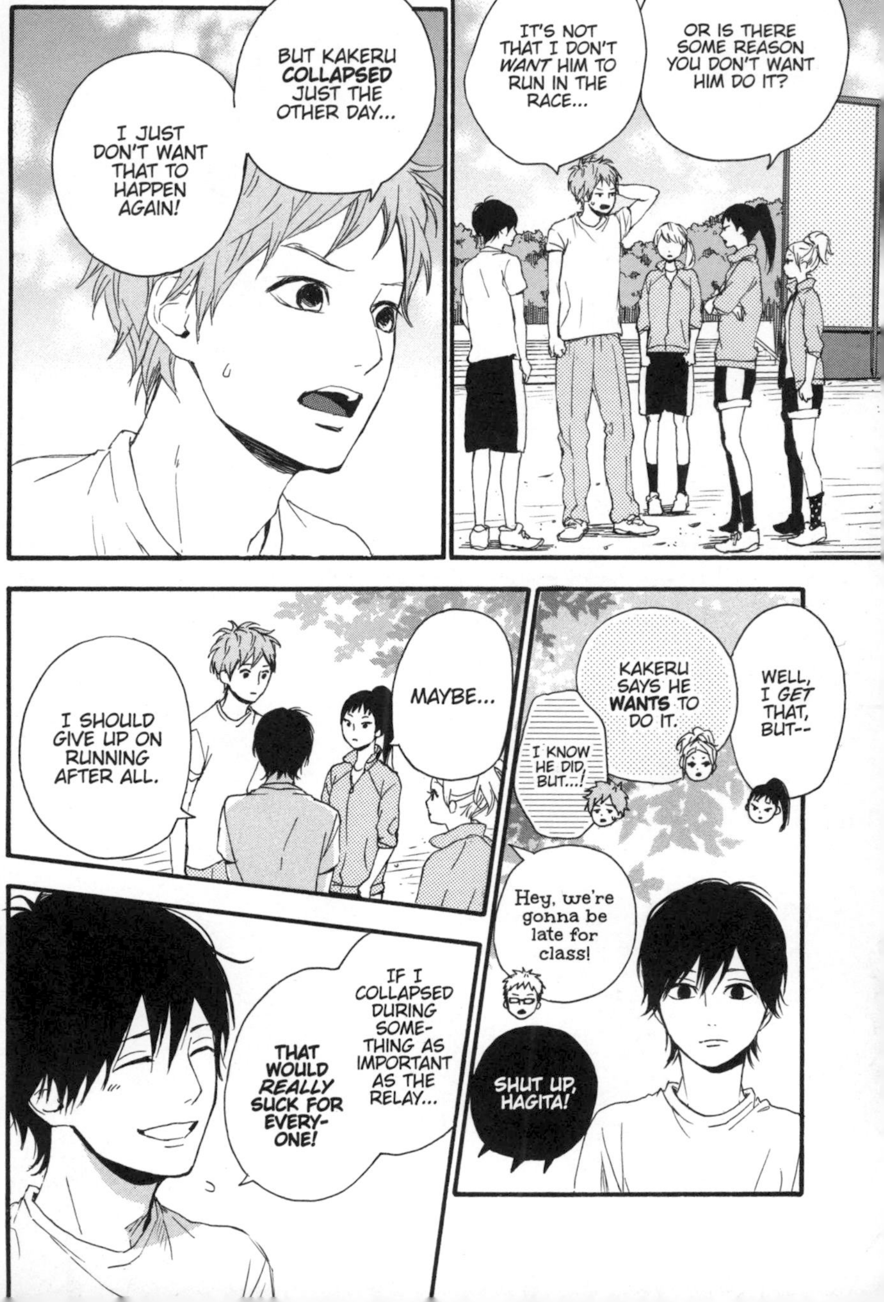
OR IS THERE SOME REASON YOU DON'T WANT HIM DO IT?
IT'S NOT THAT I DON'T *WANT* HIM TO RUN IN THE RACE...
BUT KAKERU **COLLAPSED** JUST THE OTHER DAY...
I JUST DON'T WANT THAT TO HAPPEN AGAIN!
WELL, I *GET* THAT, BUT--
KAKERU SAYS HE **WANTS** TO DO IT.
I KNOW HE DID, BUT...!
Hey, we're gonna be late for class!
SHUT UP, HAGITA!
MAYBE...
I SHOULD GIVE UP ON RUNNING AFTER ALL.
IF I COLLAPSED DURING SOME-THING AS IMPORTANT AS THE RELAY...
THAT WOULD *REALLY* SUCK FOR EVERY-ONE!

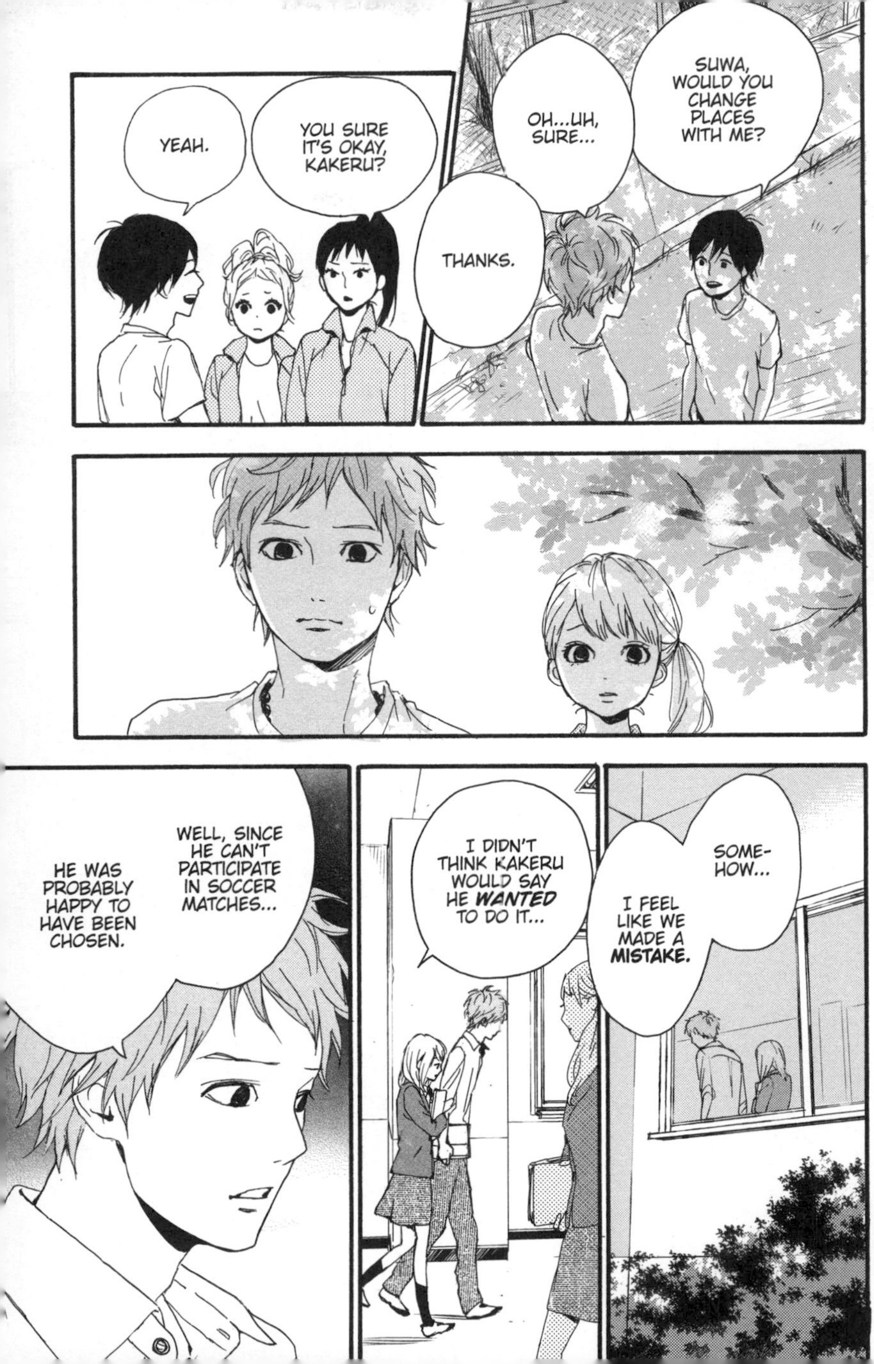
SUWA, WOULD YOU CHANGE PLACES WITH ME?
OH...UH, SURE...
THANKS.
YOU SURE IT'S OKAY, KAKERU?
YEAH.
SOME-HOW...
I FEEL LIKE WE MADE A **MISTAKE.**
I DIDN'T THINK KAKERU WOULD SAY HE ***WANTED*** TO DO IT...
WELL, SINCE HE CAN'T PARTICIPATE IN SOCCER MATCHES...
HE WAS PROBABLY HAPPY TO HAVE BEEN CHOSEN.

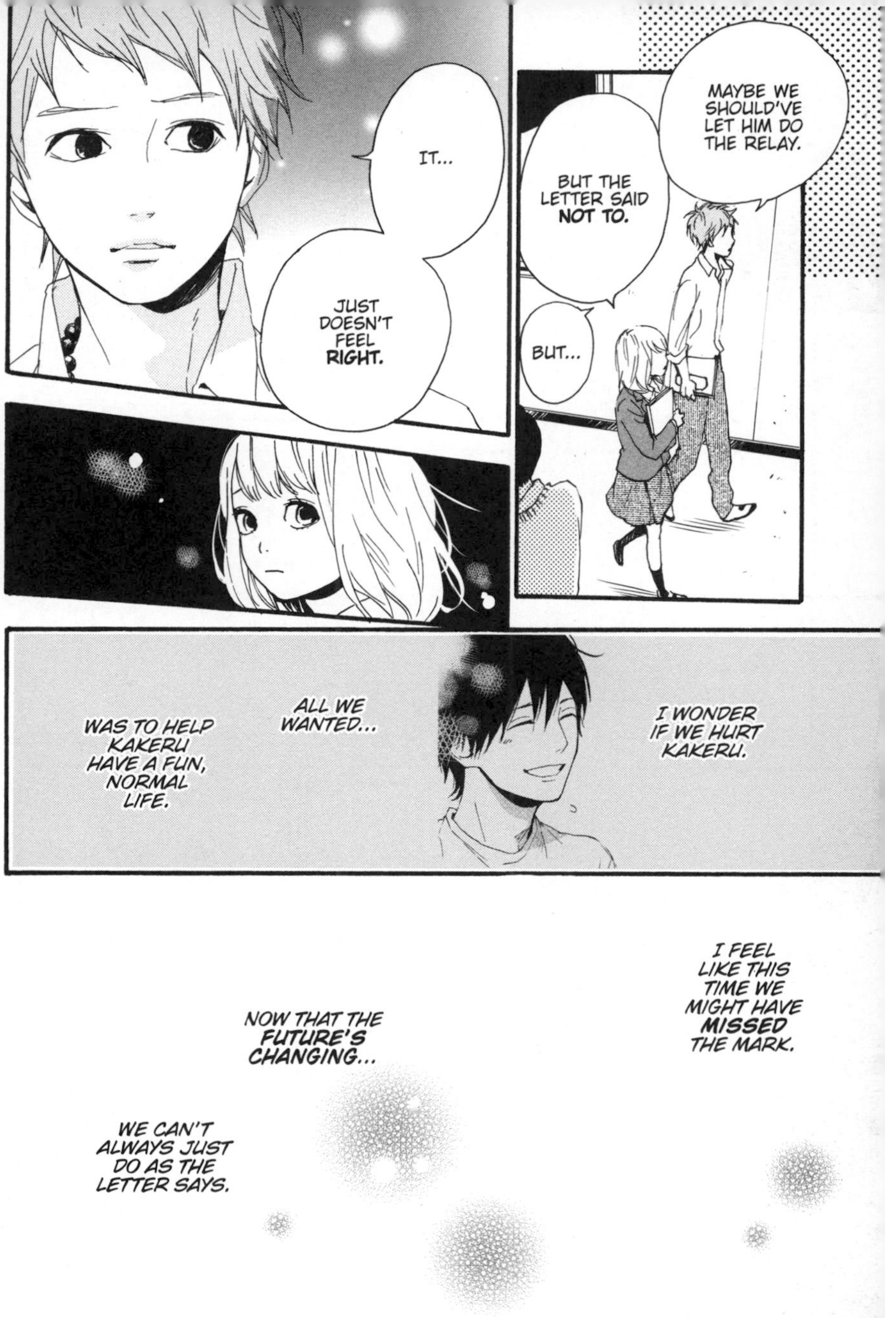
MAYBE WE SHOULD'VE LET HIM DO THE RELAY.
BUT THE LETTER SAID NOT TO.
BUT...
IT...
JUST DOESN'T FEEL RIGHT.
I WONDER IF WE HURT KAKERU.
ALL WE WANTED...
WAS TO HELP KAKERU HAVE A FUN, NORMAL LIFE.
I FEEL LIKE THIS TIME WE MIGHT HAVE MISSED THE MARK.
NOW THAT THE FUTURE'S CHANGING...
WE CAN'T ALWAYS JUST DO AS THE LETTER SAYS.

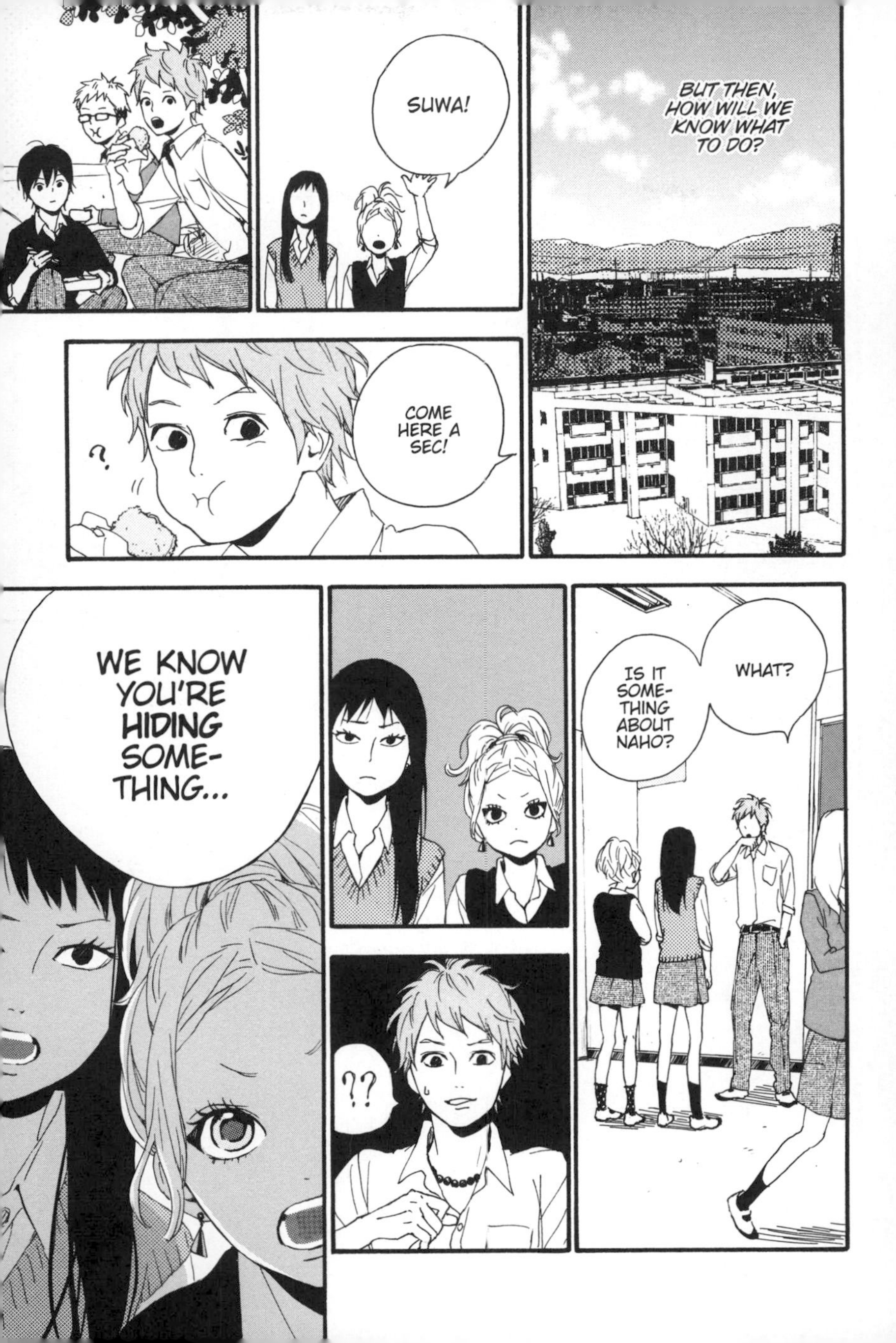
BUT THEN, HOW WILL WE KNOW WHAT TO DO?
SUWA!
COME HERE A SEC!
?
WHAT?
IS IT SOME-THING ABOUT NAHO?
??
WE KNOW YOU'RE HIDING SOME-THING...

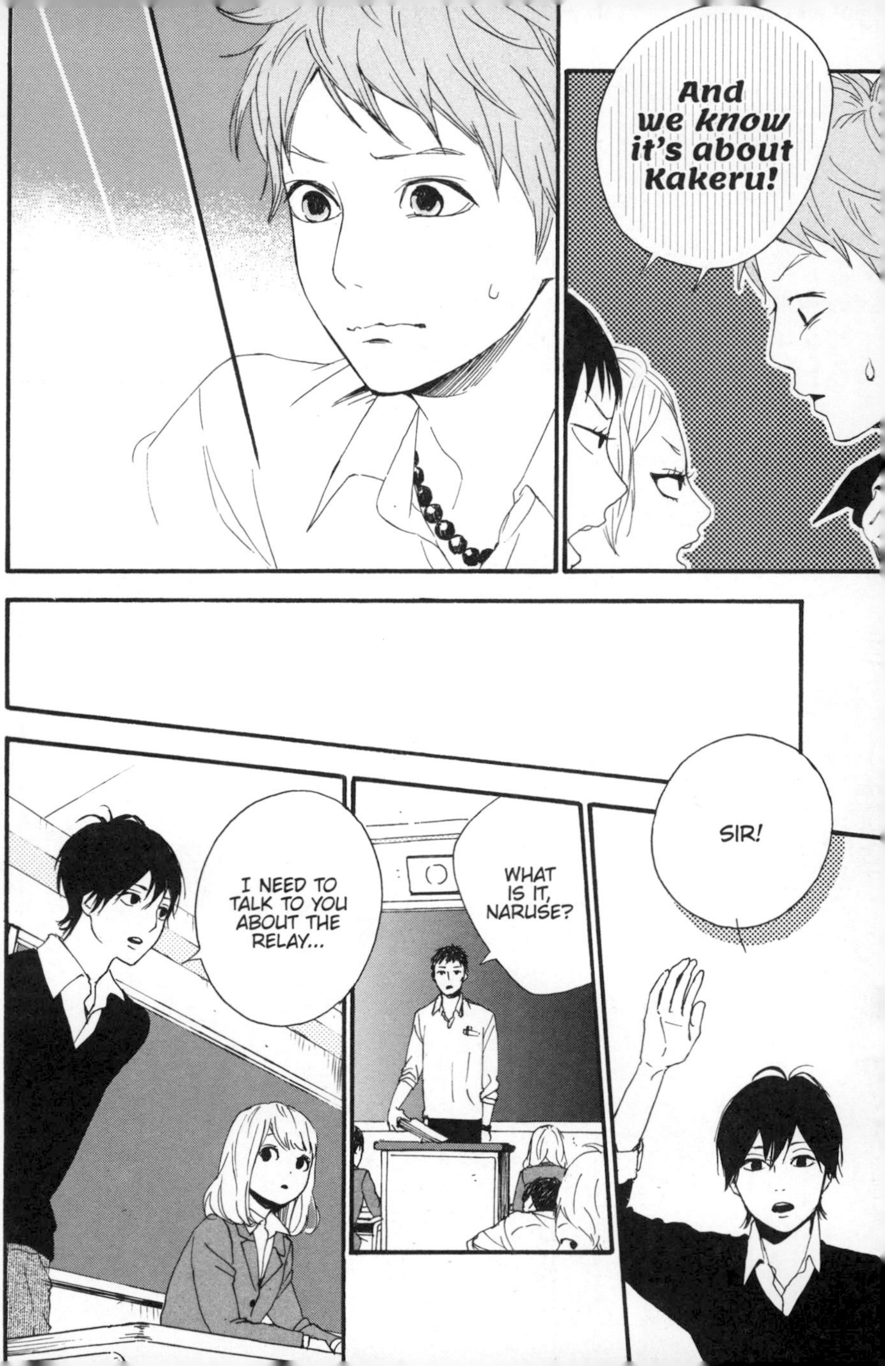
And we know it's about Kakeru!
SIR!
WHAT IS IT, NARUSE?
I NEED TO TALK TO YOU ABOUT THE RELAY...

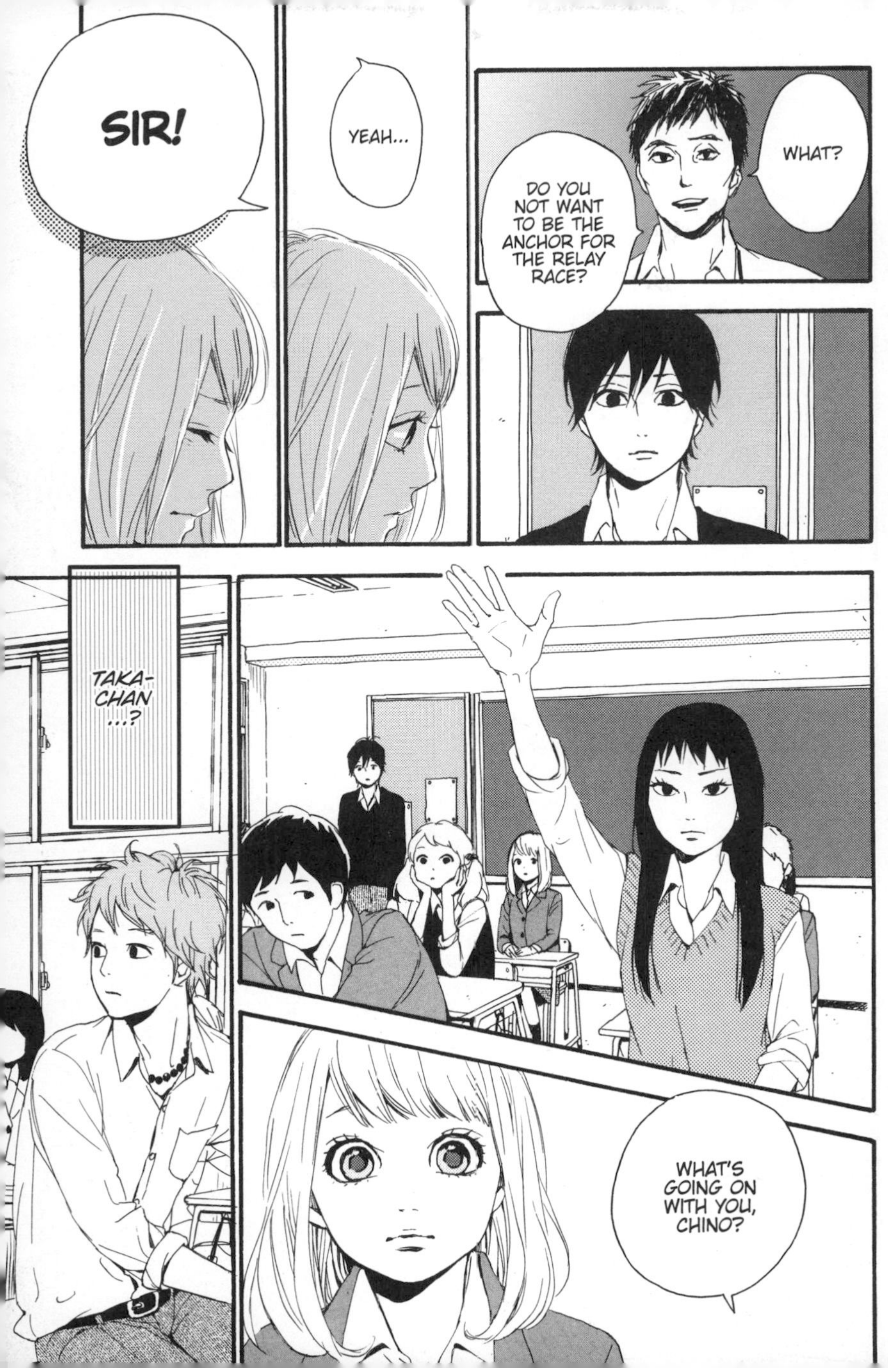
WHAT?
DO YOU NOT WANT TO BE THE ANCHOR FOR THE RELAY RACE?
YEAH...
SIR!
WHAT'S GOING ON WITH YOU, CHINO?
TAKA-CHAN ...?

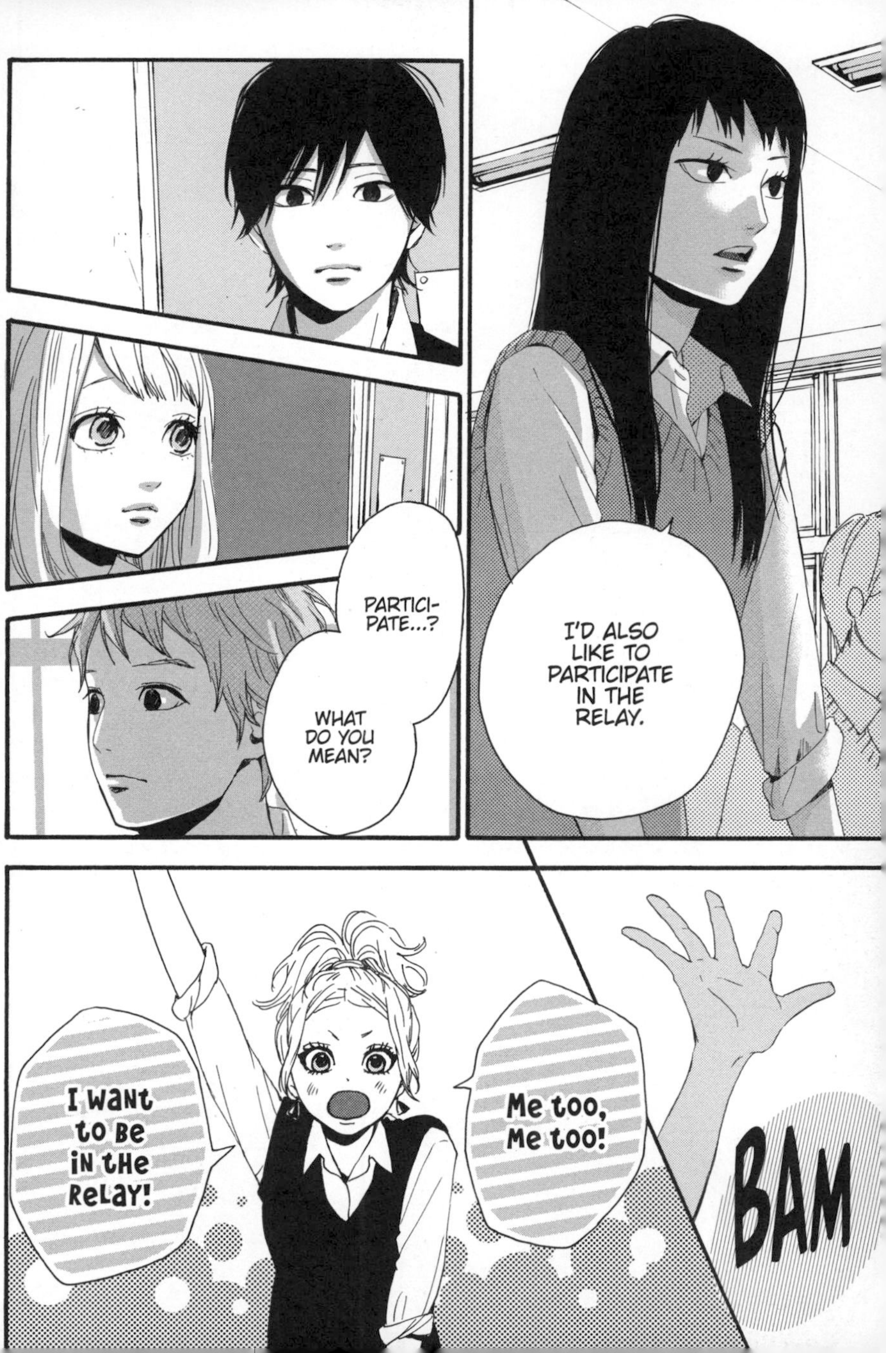
I'D ALSO LIKE TO PARTICIPATE IN THE RELAY.
PARTICI-PATE...?
WHAT DO YOU MEAN?
BAM
Me too, Me too!
I want to be in the relay!

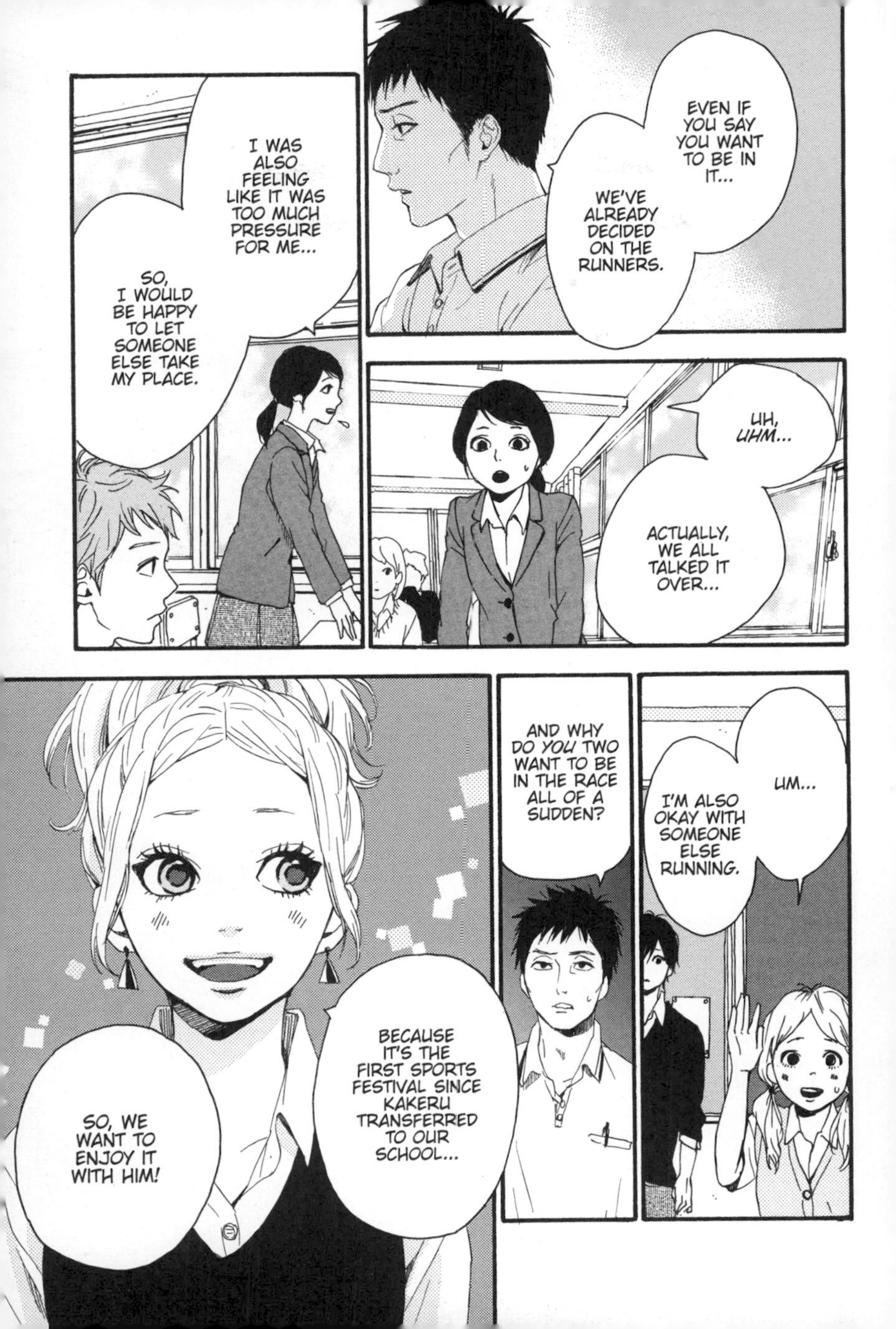
EVEN IF YOU SAY YOU WANT TO BE IN IT...
WE'VE ALREADY DECIDED ON THE RUNNERS.
UH, *UHM*...
ACTUALLY, WE ALL TALKED IT OVER...
I WAS ALSO FEELING LIKE IT WAS TOO MUCH PRESSURE FOR ME...
SO, I WOULD BE HAPPY TO LET SOMEONE ELSE TAKE MY PLACE.
UM...
I'M ALSO OKAY WITH SOMEONE ELSE RUNNING.
AND WHY DO *YOU* TWO WANT TO BE IN THE RACE ALL OF A SUDDEN?
BECAUSE IT'S THE FIRST SPORTS FESTIVAL SINCE KAKERU TRANSFERRED TO OUR SCHOOL...
SO, WE WANT TO ENJOY IT WITH HIM!

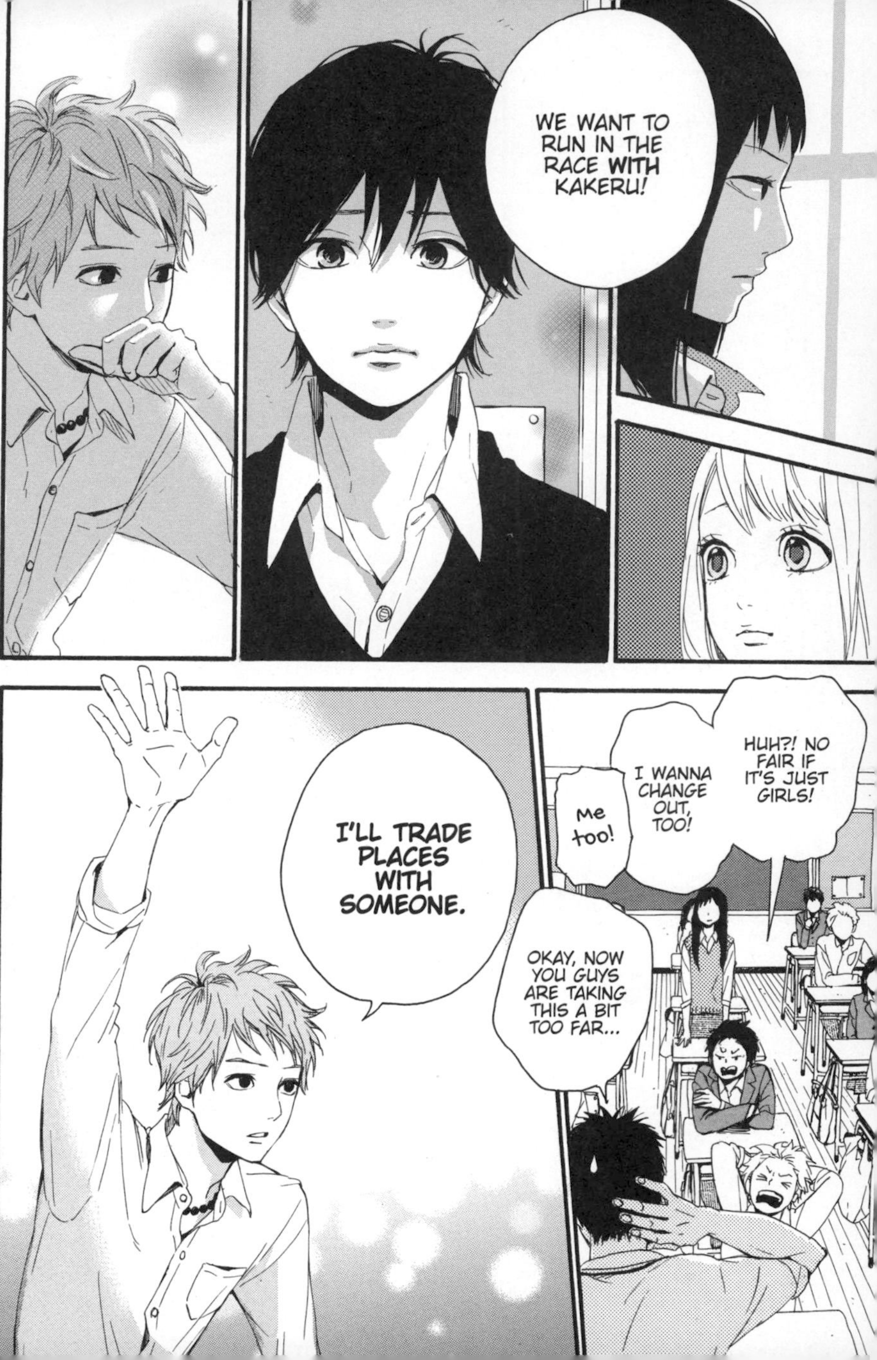
WE WANT TO RUN IN THE RACE WITH KAKERU!
HUH?! NO FAIR IF IT'S JUST GIRLS!
I WANNA CHANGE OUT, TOO!
Me too!
OKAY, NOW YOU GUYS ARE TAKING THIS A BIT TOO FAR...
I'LL TRADE PLACES WITH SOMEONE.

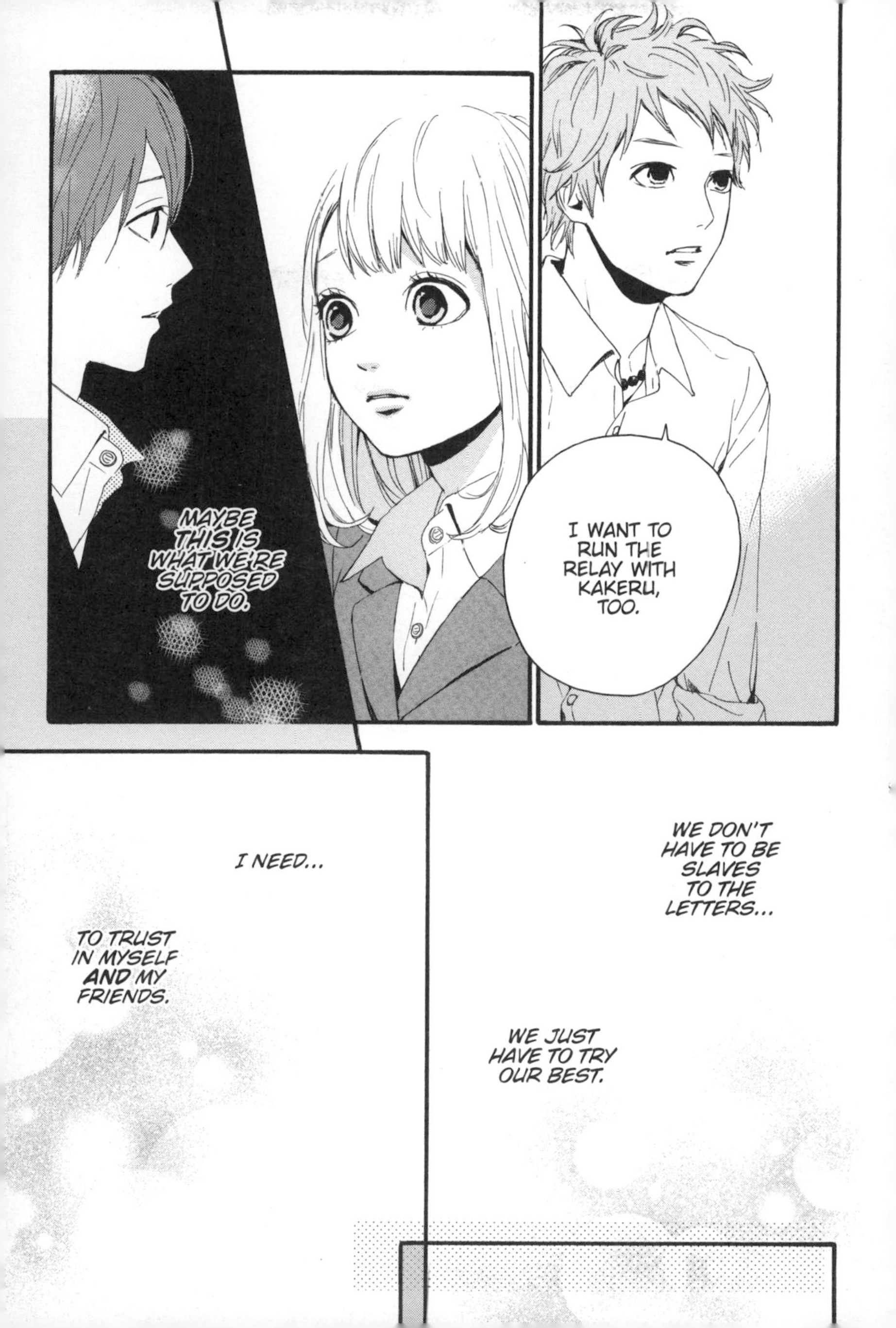
I WANT TO RUN THE RELAY WITH KAKERU, TOO.
MAYBE THIS IS WHAT WE'RE SUPPOSED TO DO.
WE DON'T HAVE TO BE SLAVES TO THE LETTERS...
WE JUST HAVE TO TRY OUR BEST.
I NEED...
TO TRUST IN MYSELF AND MY FRIENDS.

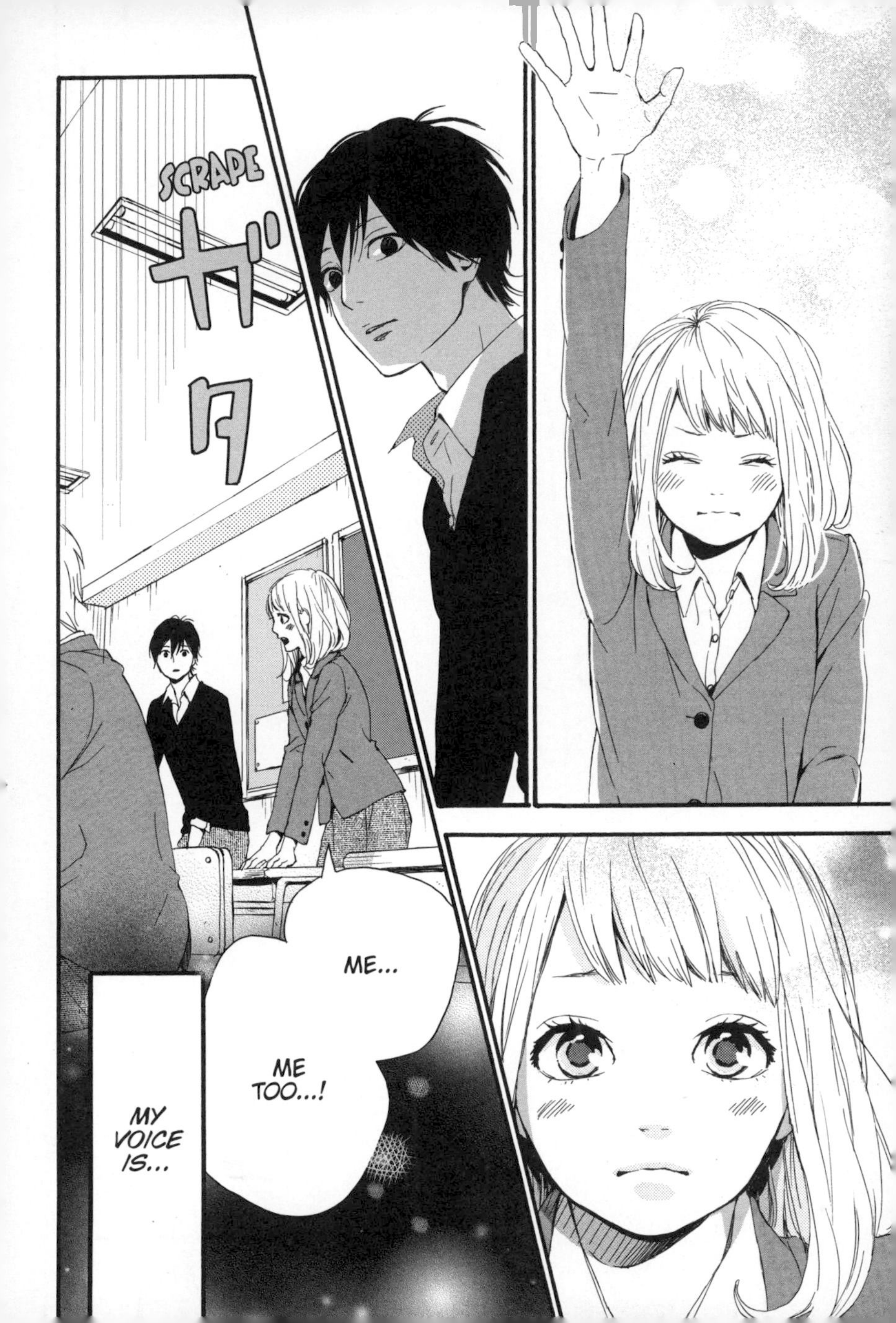
SCRAPE
ガタ
ME...
ME TOO...!
MY VOICE IS...

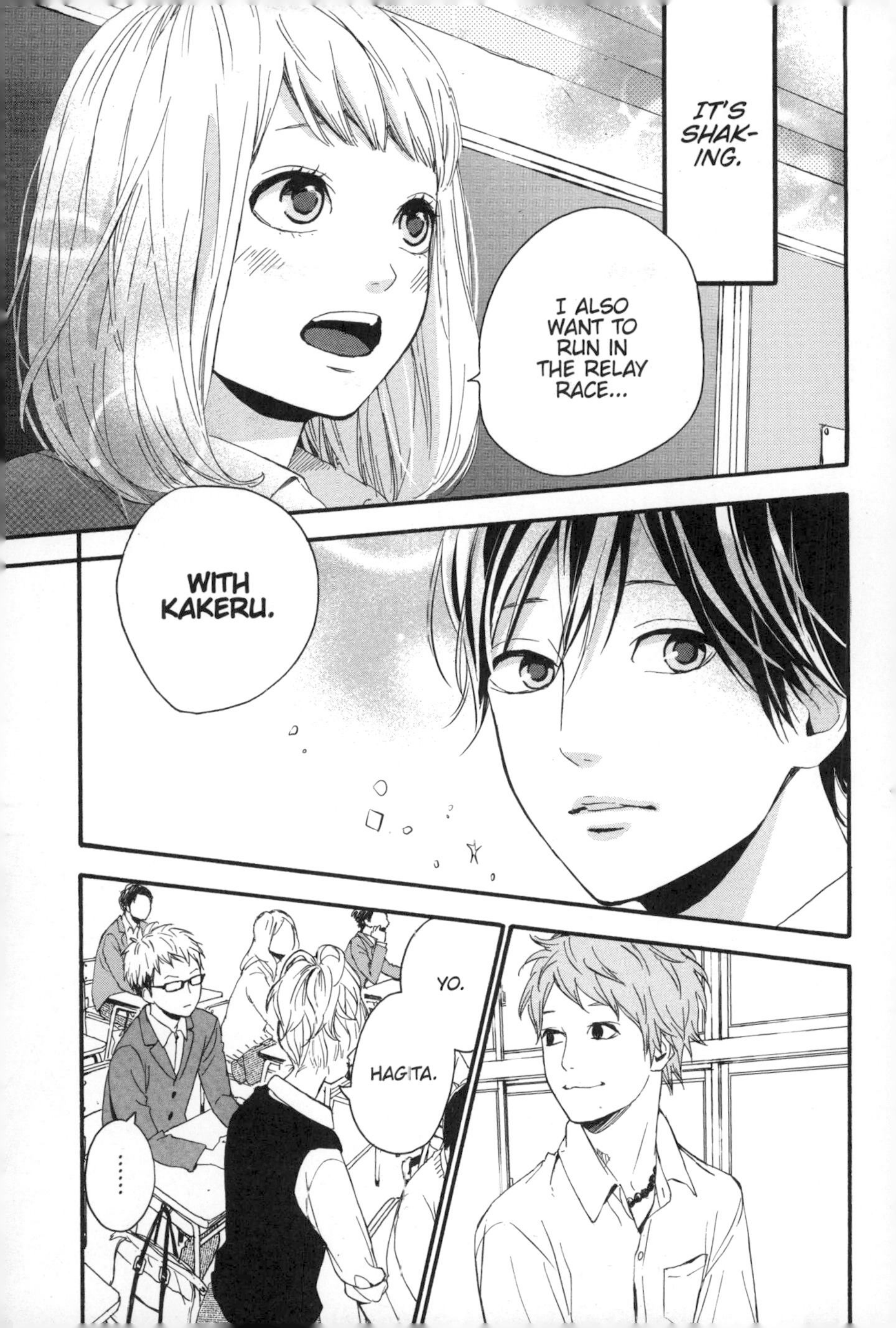
IT'S SHAK- ING.
I ALSO WANT TO RUN IN THE RELAY RACE...
WITH KAKERU.
YO.
HAGITA.
......

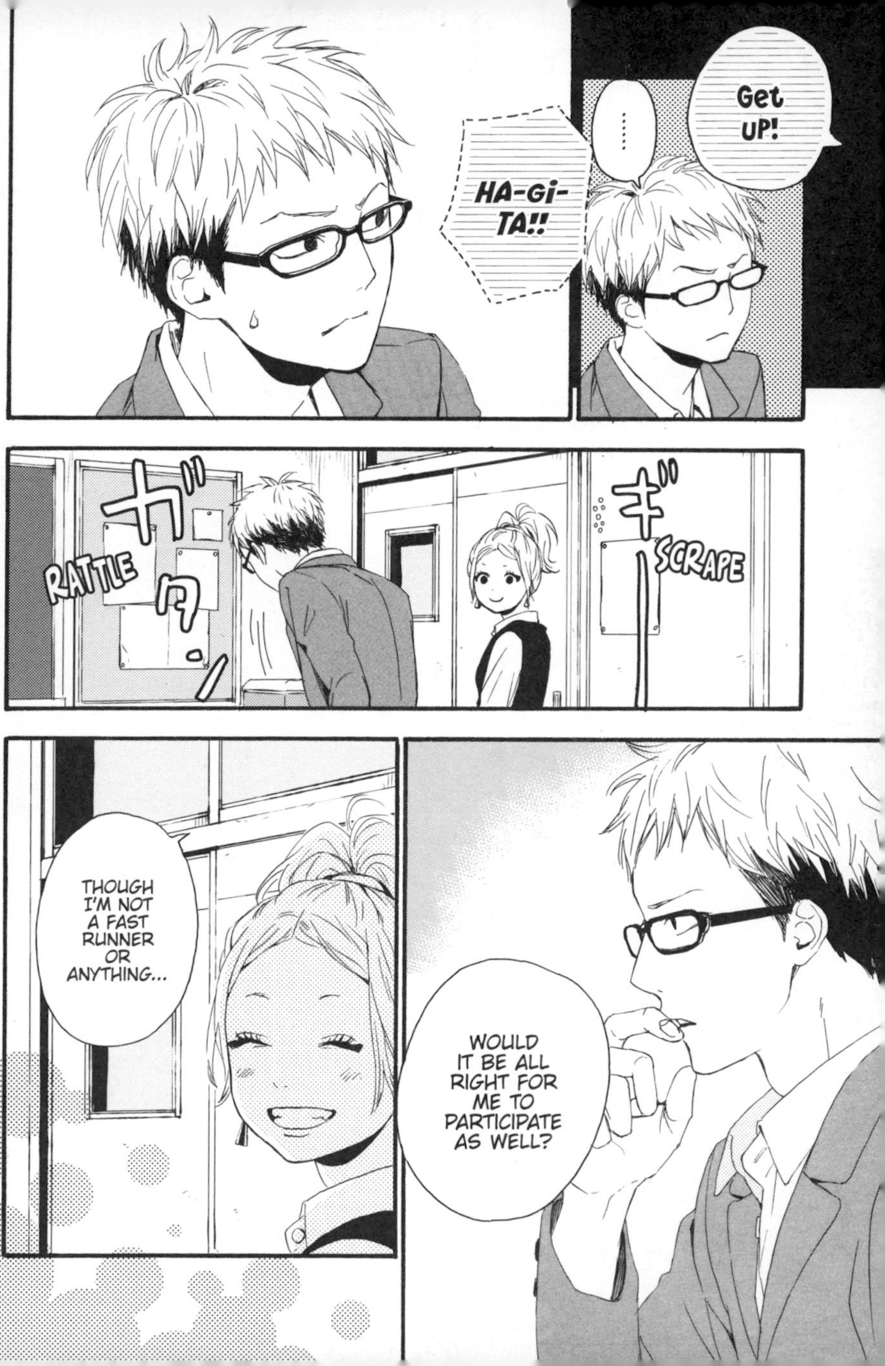
Get UP!
……
HA-GI-TA!!
ギ
SCRAPE
ガタ
RATTLE
WOULD IT BE ALL RIGHT FOR ME TO PARTICIPATE AS WELL?
THOUGH I'M NOT A FAST RUNNER OR ANYTHING...

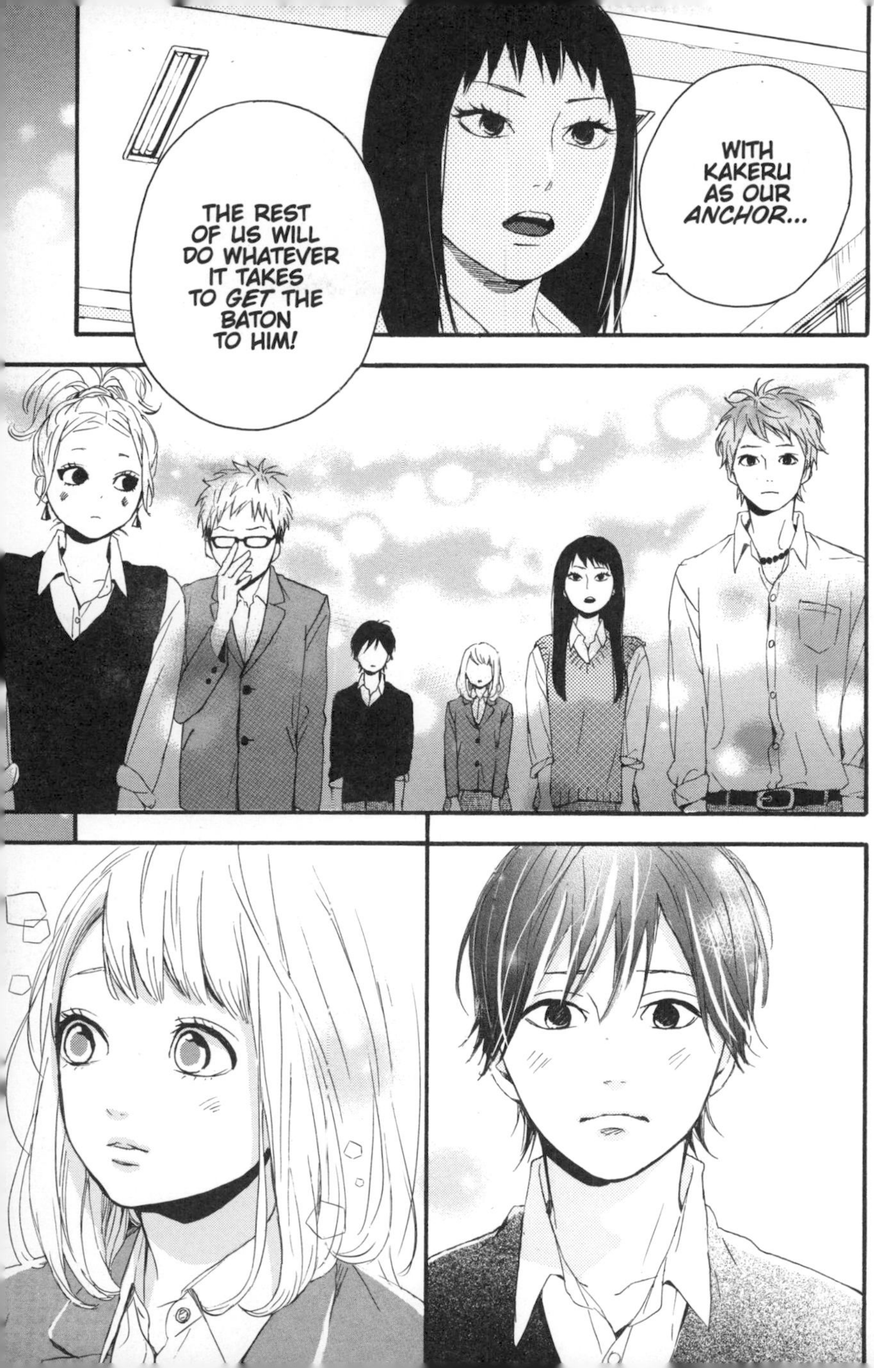
WITH KAKERU AS OUR ANCHOR...
THE REST OF US WILL DO WHATEVER IT TAKES TO GET THE BATON TO HIM!

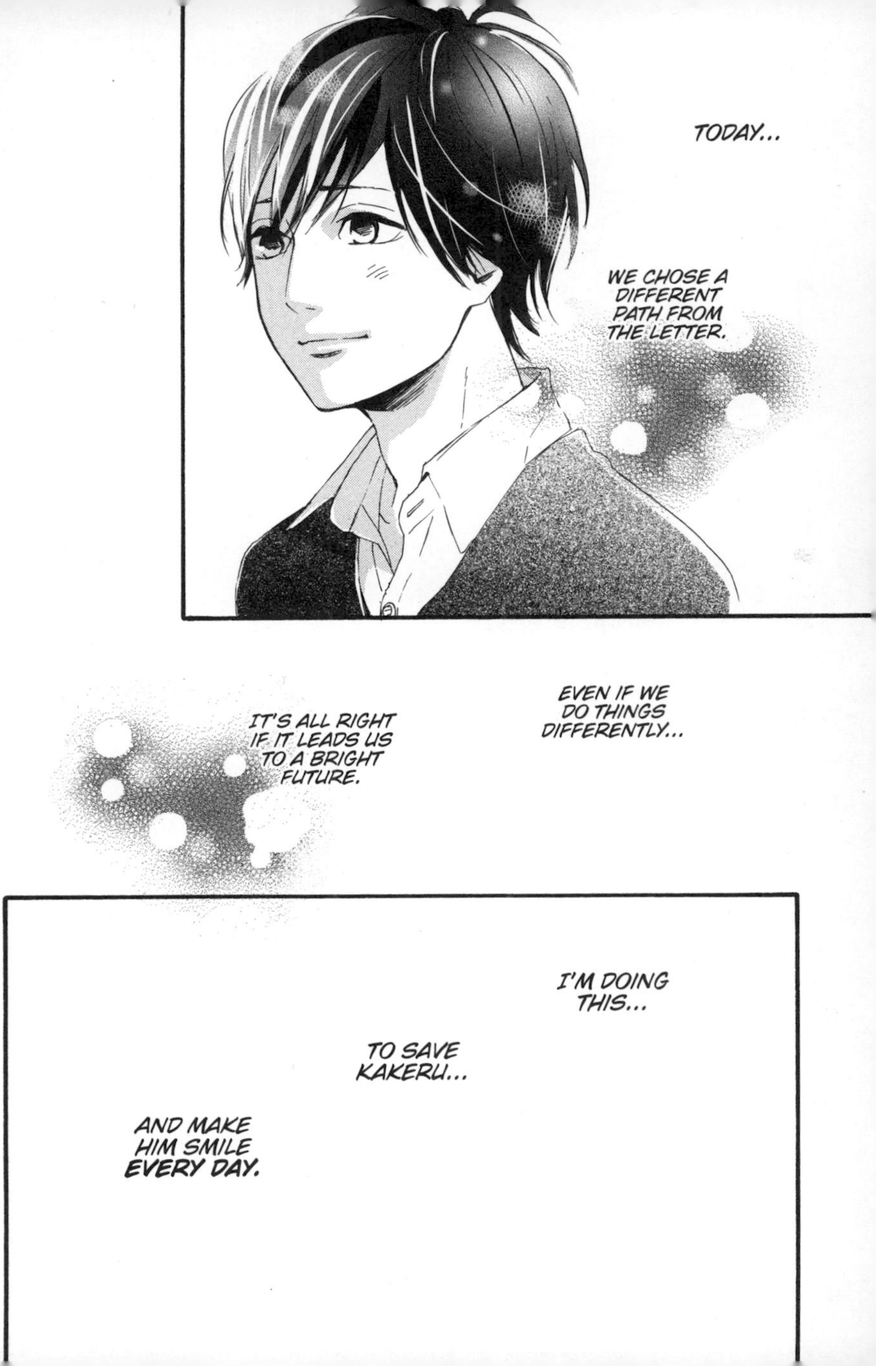
TODAY...
WE CHOSE A DIFFERENT PATH FROM THE LETTER.
EVEN IF WE DO THINGS DIFFERENTLY...
IT'S ALL RIGHT IF IT LEADS US TO A BRIGHT FUTURE.
I'M DOING THIS...
TO SAVE KAKERU...
AND MAKE HIM SMILE EVERY DAY.

orange

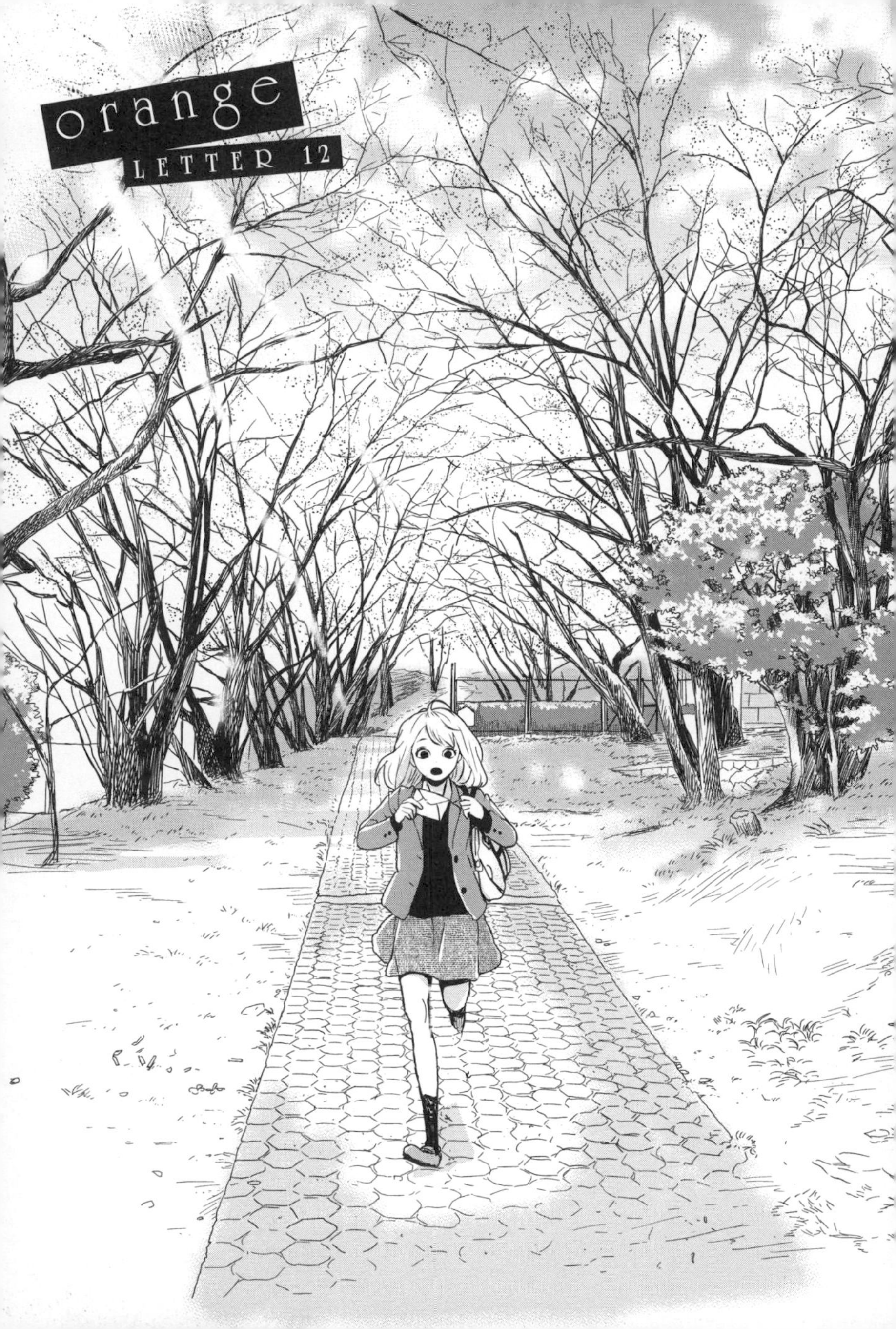
orange
LETTER 12

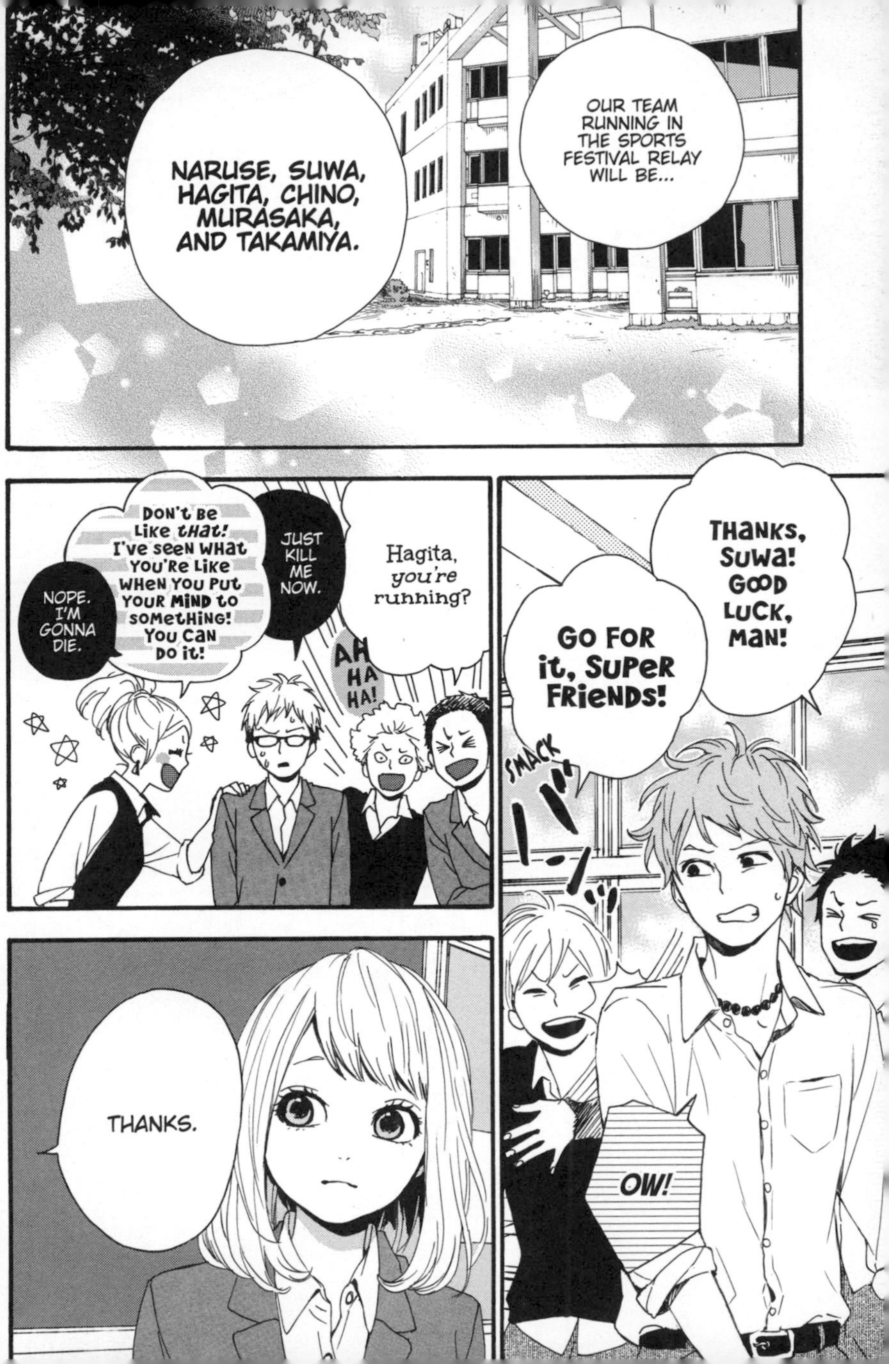
OUR TEAM RUNNING IN THE SPORTS FESTIVAL RELAY WILL BE...
NARUSE, SUWA, HAGITA, CHINO, MURASAKA, AND TAKAMIYA.
THANKS, SUWA! GOOD LUCK, MAN!
GO FOR IT, SUPER FRIENDS!
SMACK
OW!
Hagita, *you're* running?
AH HA HA!
JUST KILL ME NOW.
DON'T BE LIKE *THAT!* I'VE SEEN WHAT YOU'RE LIKE WHEN YOU PUT YOUR MIND TO SOMETHING! YOU CAN DO IT!
NOPE. I'M GONNA DIE.
THANKS.

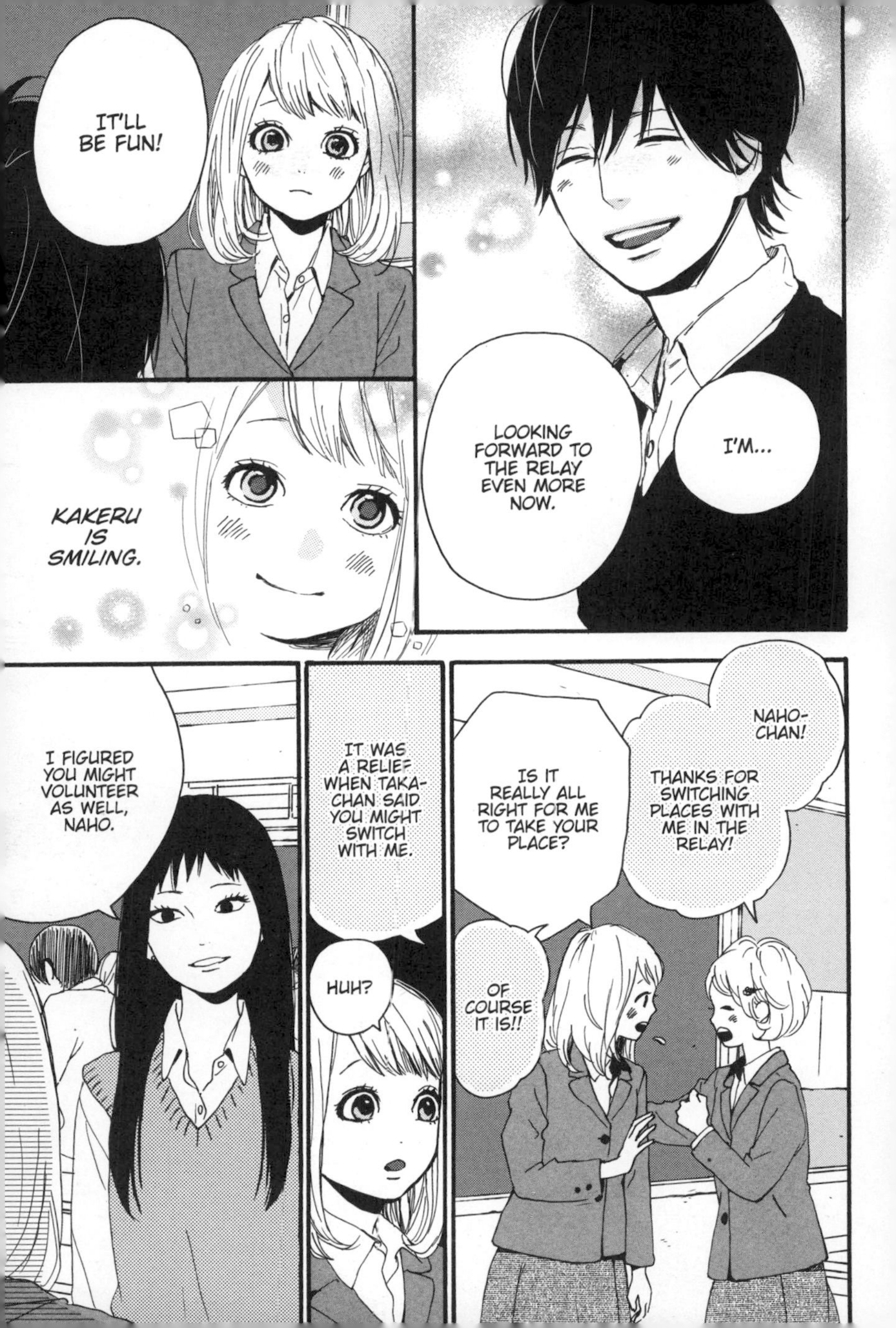
I'M...
LOOKING FORWARD TO THE RELAY EVEN MORE NOW.
IT'LL BE FUN!
KAKERU IS SMILING.
NAHO-CHAN!
THANKS FOR SWITCHING PLACES WITH ME IN THE RELAY!
IS IT REALLY ALL RIGHT FOR ME TO TAKE YOUR PLACE?
OF COURSE IT IS!!
IT WAS A RELIEF WHEN TAKA-CHAN SAID YOU MIGHT SWITCH WITH ME.
HUH?
I FIGURED YOU MIGHT VOLUNTEER AS WELL, NAHO.

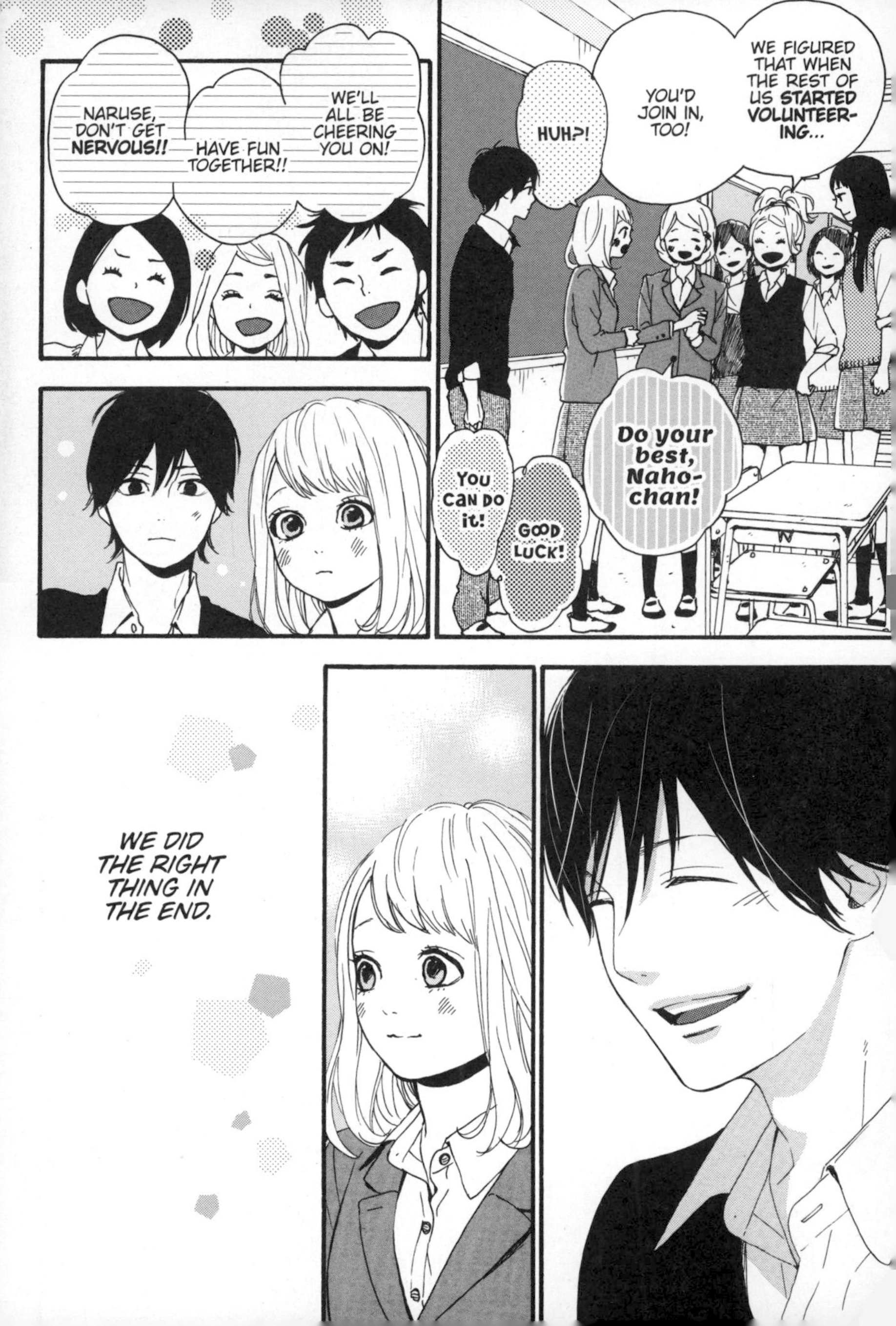
WE FIGURED THAT WHEN THE REST OF US STARTED VOLUNTEERING...
YOU'D JOIN IN, TOO!
HUH?!
Do your best, Naho-chan!
GOOD LUCK!
You CAN DO it!
WE'LL ALL BE CHEERING YOU ON!
HAVE FUN TOGETHER!!
NARUSE, DON'T GET NERVOUS!!
WE DID THE RIGHT THING IN THE END.

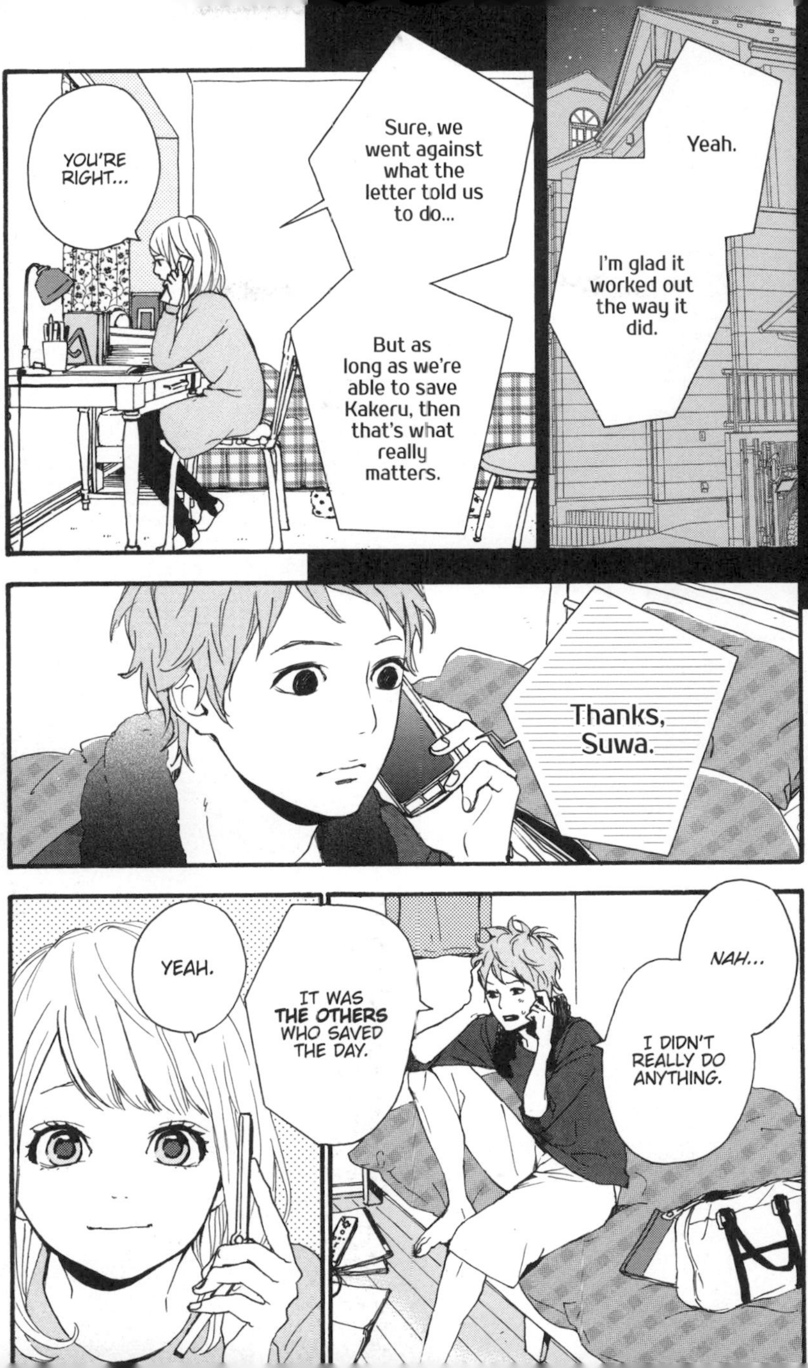
Yeah.
I'm glad it worked out the way it did.
Sure, we went against what the letter told us to do...
YOU'RE RIGHT...
But as long as we're able to save Kakeru, then that's what really matters.
Thanks, Suwa.
NAH...
I DIDN'T REALLY DO ANYTHING.
IT WAS **THE OTHERS** WHO SAVED THE DAY.
YEAH.

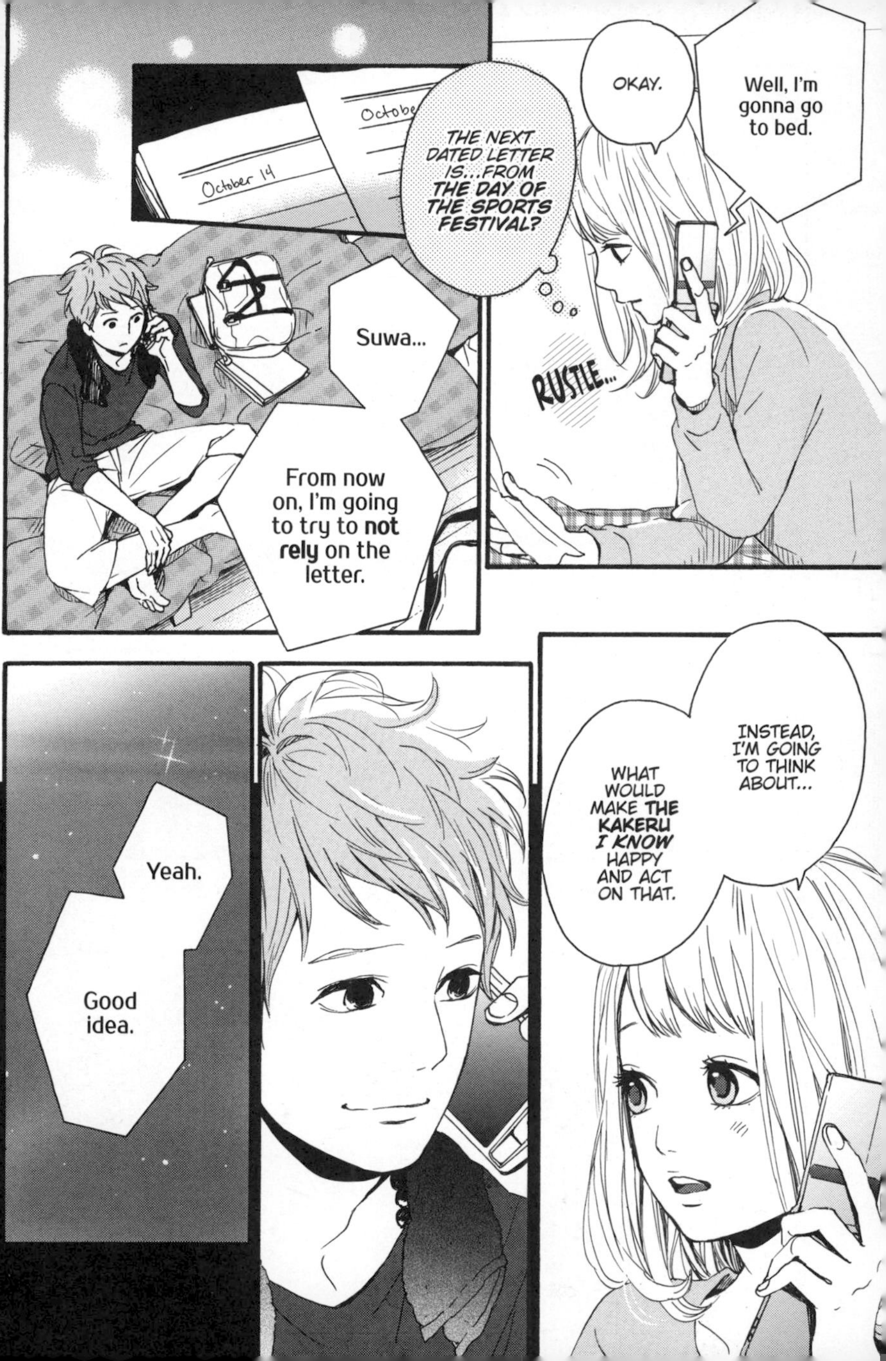
Well, I'm gonna go to bed.
OKAY.
THE NEXT DATED LETTER IS...FROM THE DAY OF THE SPORTS FESTIVAL?
RUSTLE...
October 14
Suwa...
From now on, I'm going to try to not rely on the letter.
INSTEAD, I'M GOING TO THINK ABOUT...
WHAT WOULD MAKE THE KAKERU I KNOW HAPPY AND ACT ON THAT.
Yeah.
Good idea.

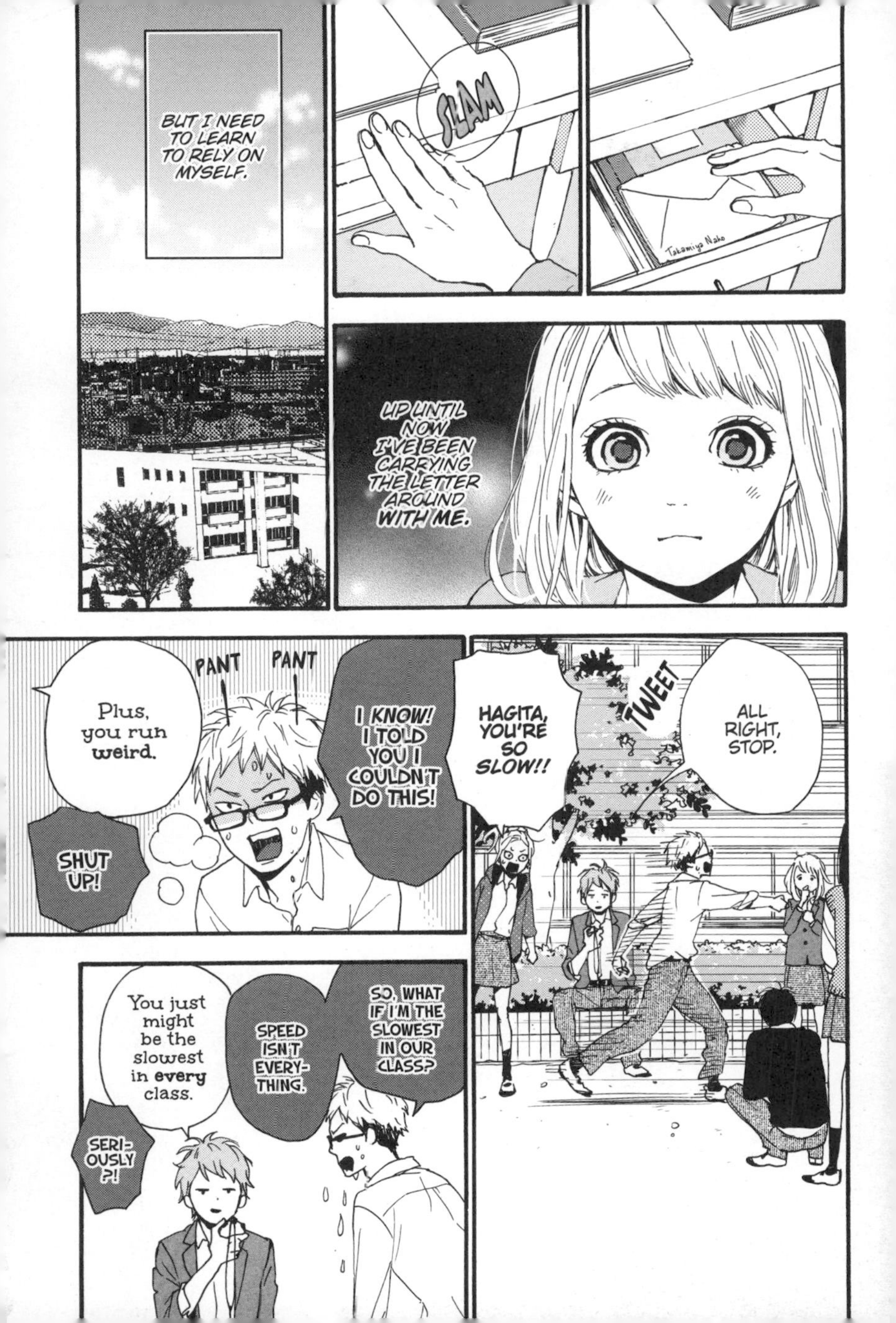
Takamiya Nako
SLAM
UP UNTIL NOW I'VE BEEN CARRYING THE LETTER AROUND WITH ME.
BUT I NEED TO LEARN TO RELY ON MYSELF.
ALL RIGHT, STOP.
TWEET
HAGITA, YOU'RE SO SLOW!!
PANT PANT
I KNOW! I TOLD YOU I COULDN'T DO THIS!
Plus, you run **weird.**
SHUT UP!
SO, WHAT IF I'M THE SLOWEST IN OUR CLASS?
SPEED ISN'T EVERY-THING.
You just might be the slowest in **every** class.
SERI-OUSLY?!

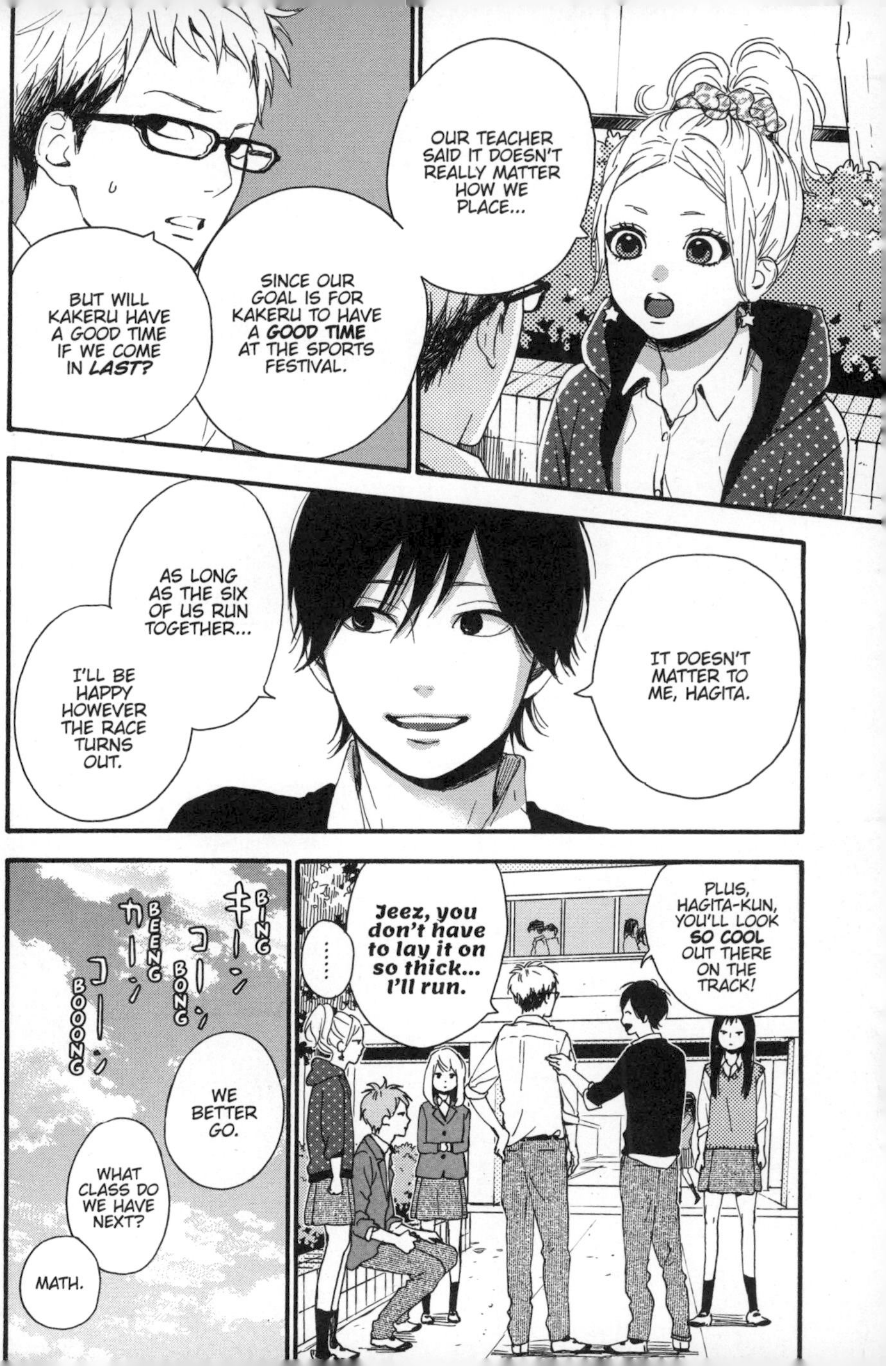
OUR TEACHER SAID IT DOESN'T REALLY MATTER HOW WE PLACE...
SINCE OUR GOAL IS FOR KAKERU TO HAVE A **GOOD TIME** AT THE SPORTS FESTIVAL.
BUT WILL KAKERU HAVE A GOOD TIME IF WE COME IN ***LAST?***
IT DOESN'T MATTER TO ME, HAGITA.
AS LONG AS THE SIX OF US RUN TOGETHER...
I'LL BE HAPPY HOWEVER THE RACE TURNS OUT.
PLUS, HAGITA-KUN, YOU'LL LOOK **SO COOL** OUT THERE ON THE TRACK!
Jeez, you don't have to lay it on so thick... I'll run.
......
キーン、コーン、 BING BONG
カーン、コーン、 BEENG BOOOONG
WE BETTER GO.
WHAT CLASS DO WE HAVE NEXT?
MATH.

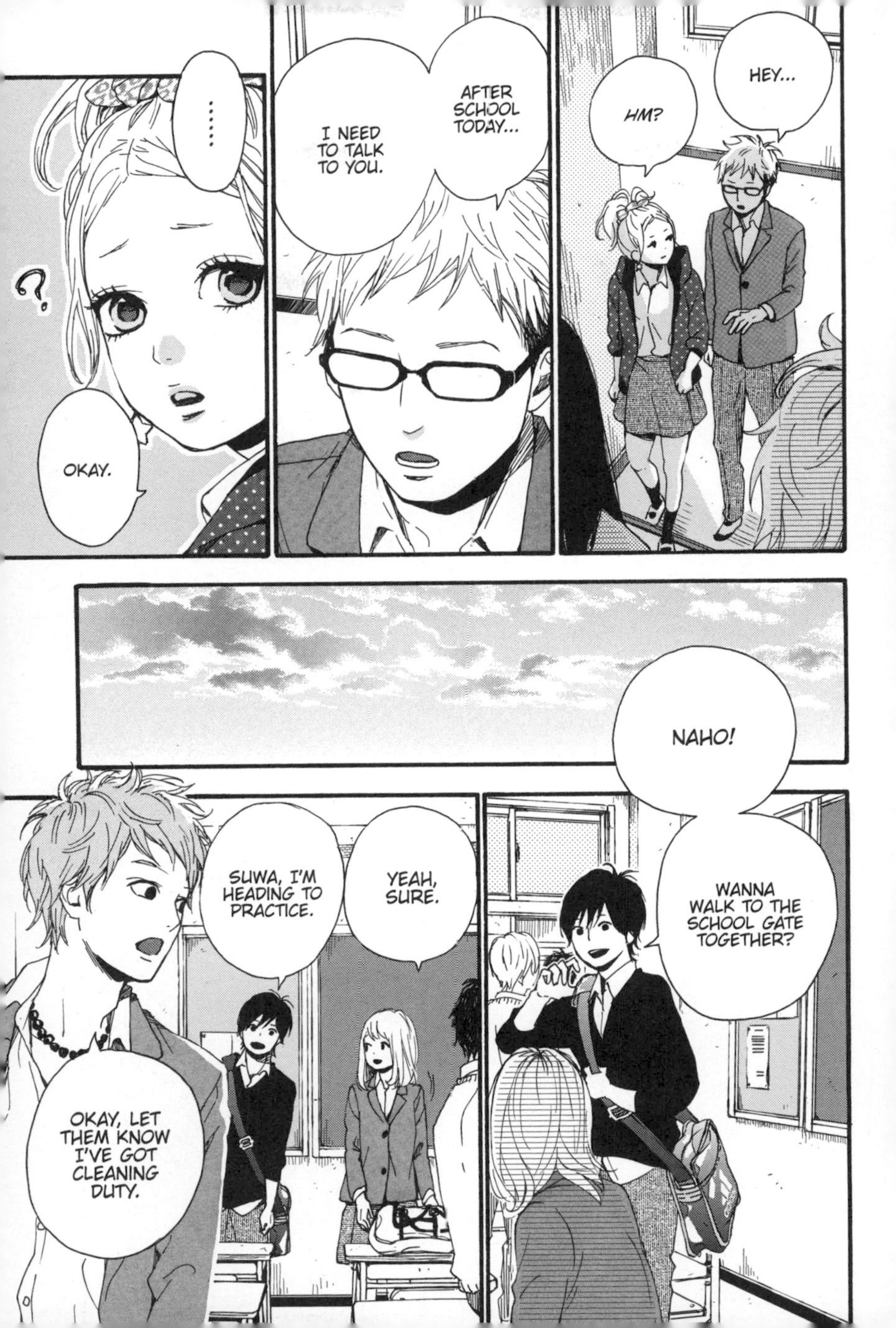
HEY...
HM?
AFTER SCHOOL TODAY...
I NEED TO TALK TO YOU.
......
OKAY.
NAHO!
WANNA WALK TO THE SCHOOL GATE TOGETHER?
YEAH, SURE.
SUWA, I'M HEADING TO PRACTICE.
OKAY, LET THEM KNOW I'VE GOT CLEANING DUTY.

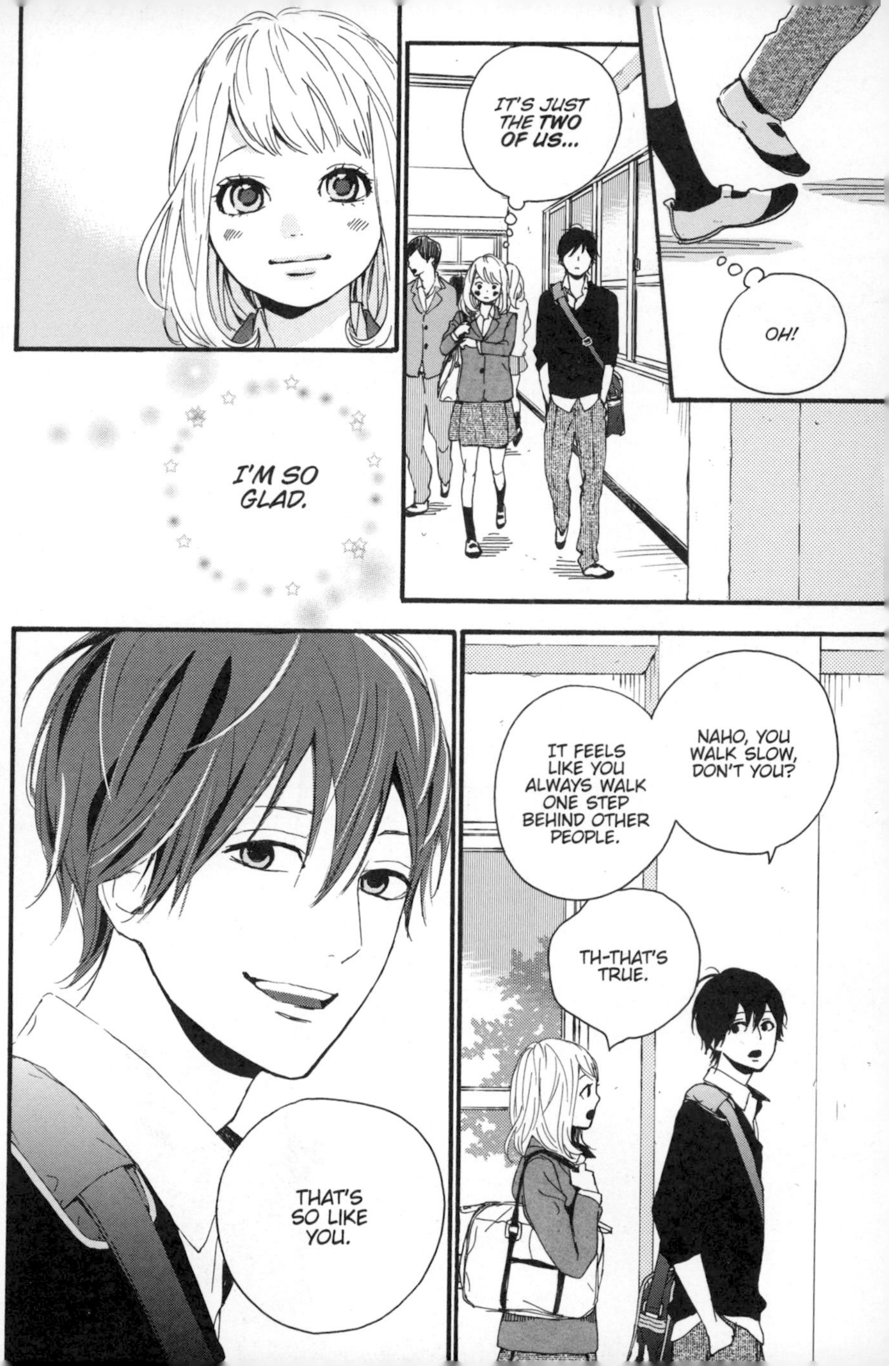
OH!
IT'S JUST THE TWO OF US...
I'M SO GLAD.
NAHO, YOU WALK SLOW, DON'T YOU?
IT FEELS LIKE YOU ALWAYS WALK ONE STEP BEHIND OTHER PEOPLE.
TH-THAT'S TRUE.
THAT'S SO LIKE YOU.

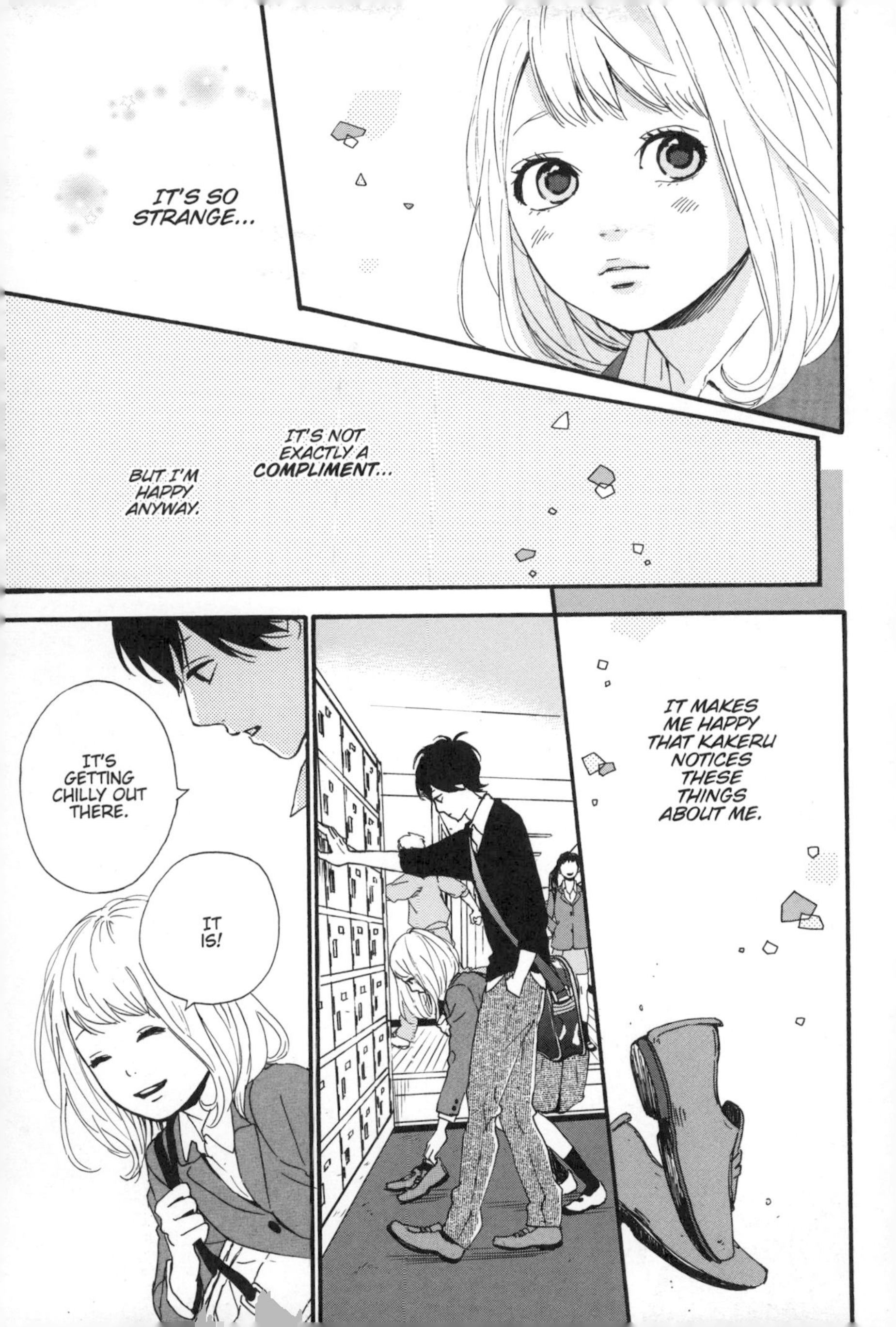
IT'S SO STRANGE...
IT'S NOT EXACTLY A **COMPLIMENT**...
BUT I'M HAPPY ANYWAY.
IT MAKES ME HAPPY THAT KAKERU NOTICES THESE THINGS ABOUT ME.
IT'S GETTING CHILLY OUT THERE.
IT IS!

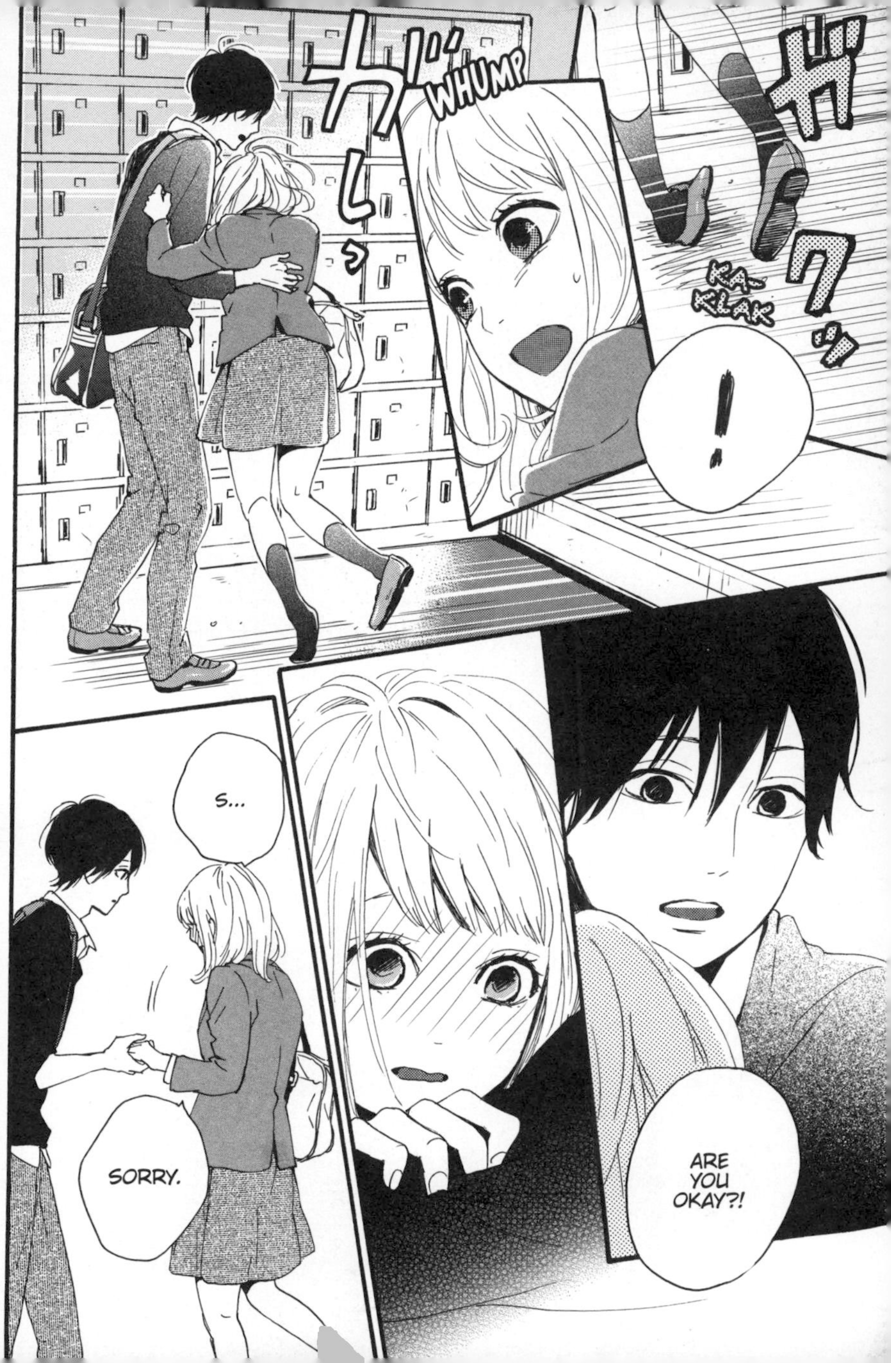

ガタッ
KA-KLAK
!
ガシッ
WHUMP
ARE YOU OKAY?!
S...
SORRY.

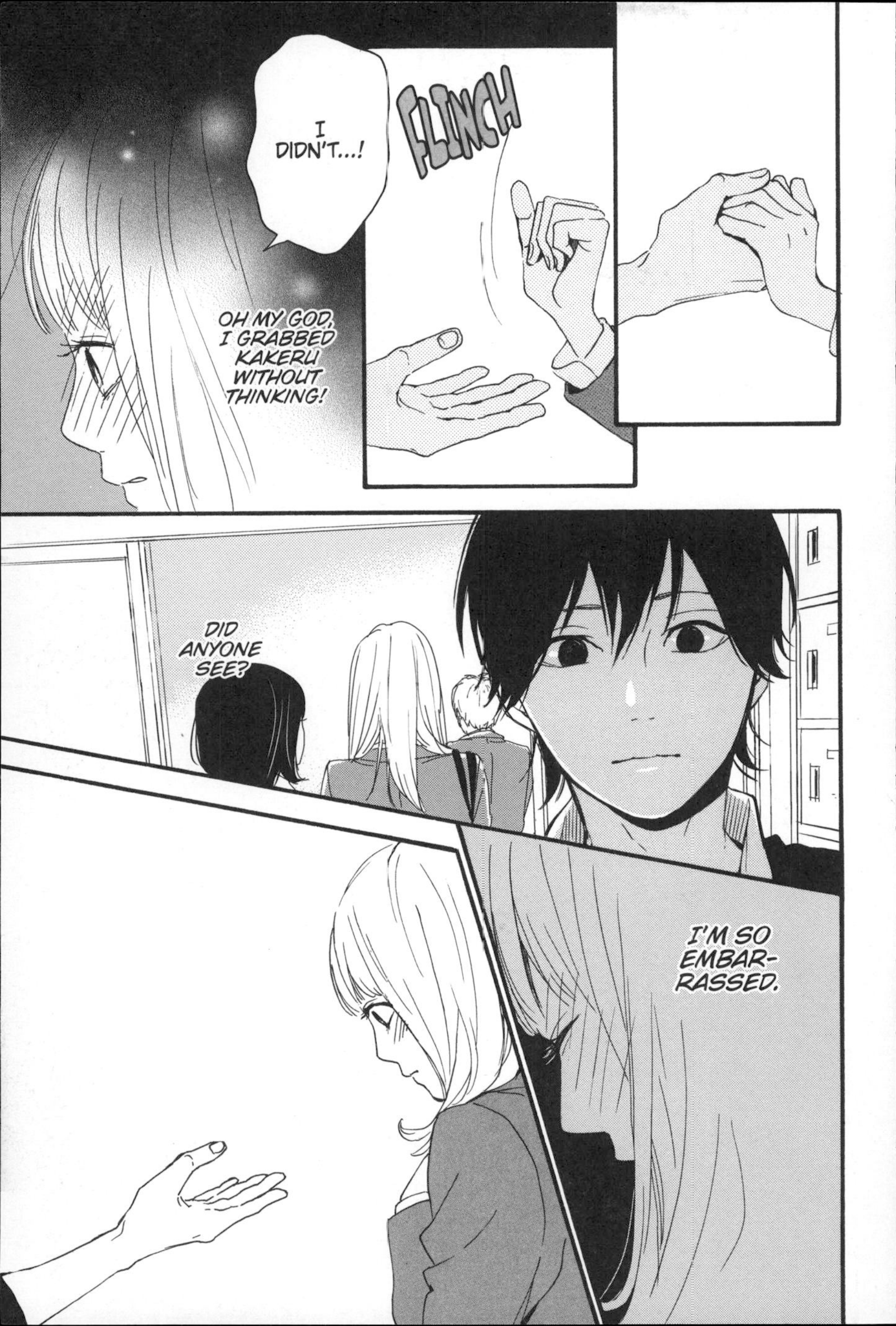
FLINCH
I DIDN'T...!
OH MY GOD, I GRABBED KAKERU WITHOUT THINKING!
DID ANYONE SEE?
I'M SO EMBARRASSED.

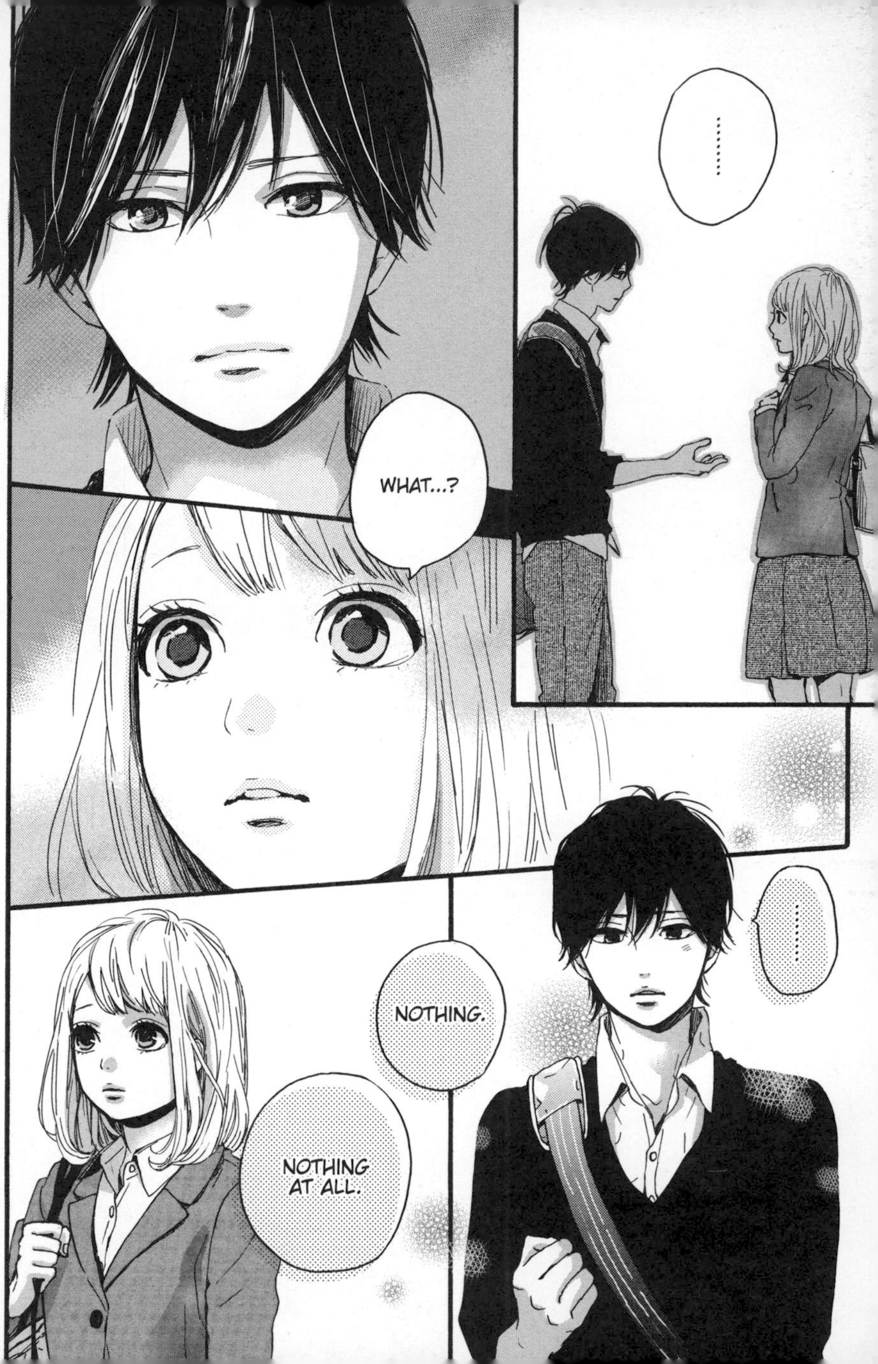
......
WHAT...?
......
NOTHING.
NOTHING AT ALL.

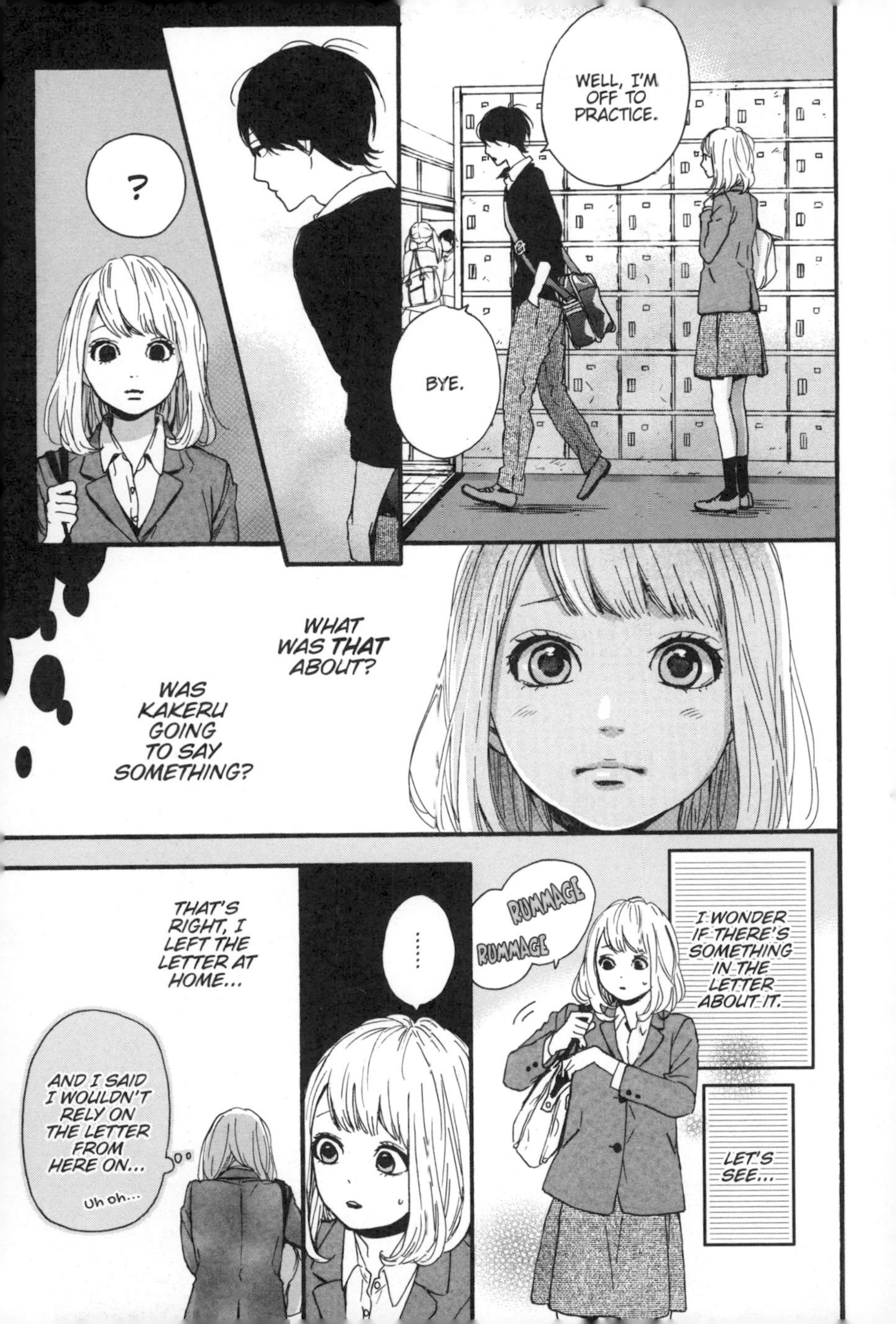
WELL, I'M OFF TO PRACTICE.
BYE.
?
WHAT WAS THAT ABOUT?
WAS KAKERU GOING TO SAY SOMETHING?
RUMMAGE
RUMMAGE
I WONDER IF THERE'S SOMETHING IN THE LETTER ABOUT IT.
LET'S SEE...
......
THAT'S RIGHT, I LEFT THE LETTER AT HOME...
AND I SAID I WOULDN'T RELY ON THE LETTER FROM HERE ON...
Uh oh...

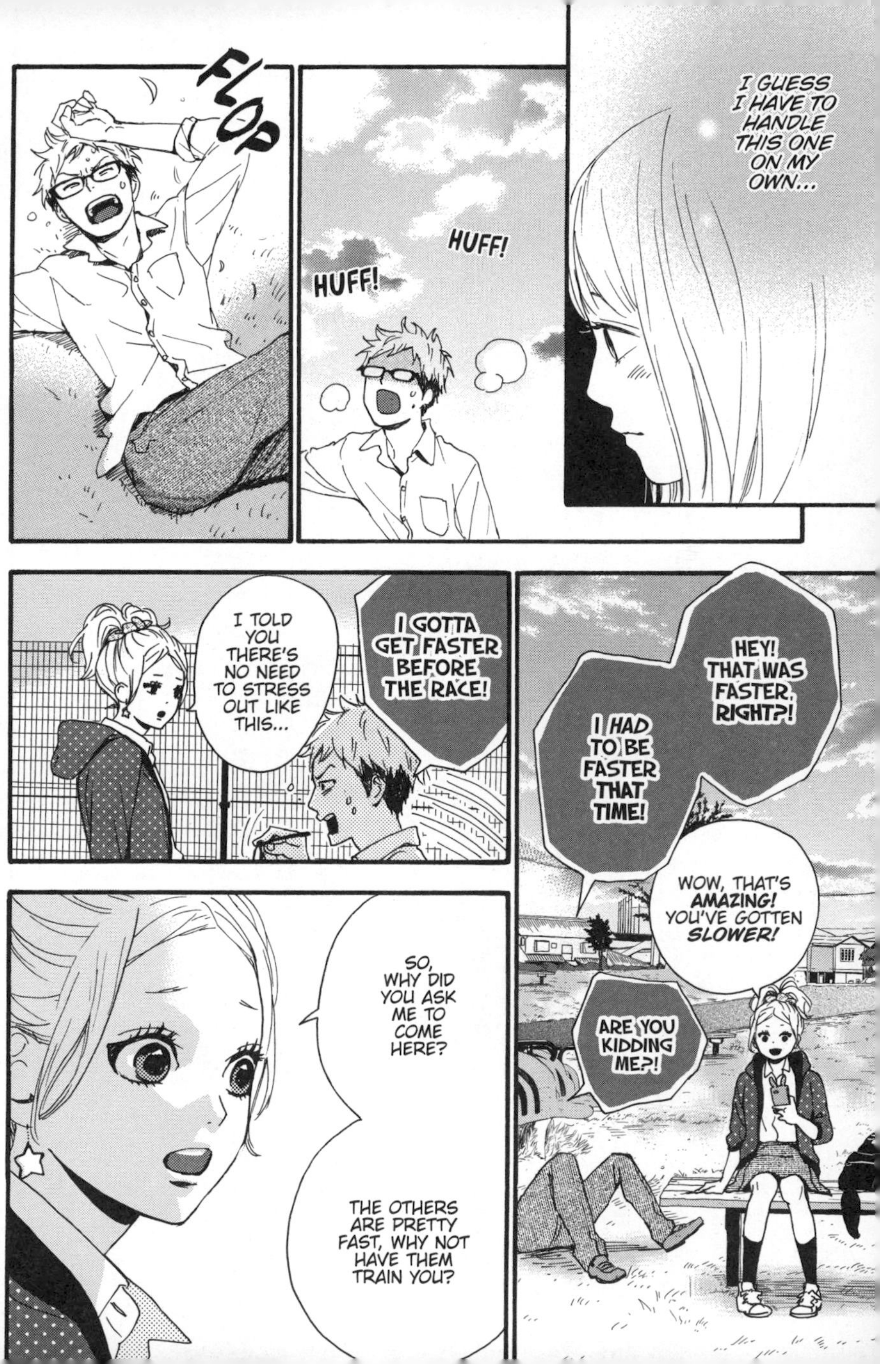
I GUESS I HAVE TO HANDLE THIS ONE ON MY OWN...
HUFF!
HUFF!
FLOP
HEY! THAT WAS FASTER, RIGHT?!
I *HAD* TO BE FASTER THAT TIME!
WOW, THAT'S **AMAZING!** YOU'VE GOTTEN **SLOWER!**
ARE YOU KIDDING ME?!
I GOTTA GET FASTER BEFORE THE RACE!
I TOLD YOU THERE'S NO NEED TO STRESS OUT LIKE THIS...
SO, WHY DID YOU ASK ME TO COME HERE?
THE OTHERS ARE PRETTY FAST, WHY NOT HAVE THEM TRAIN YOU?

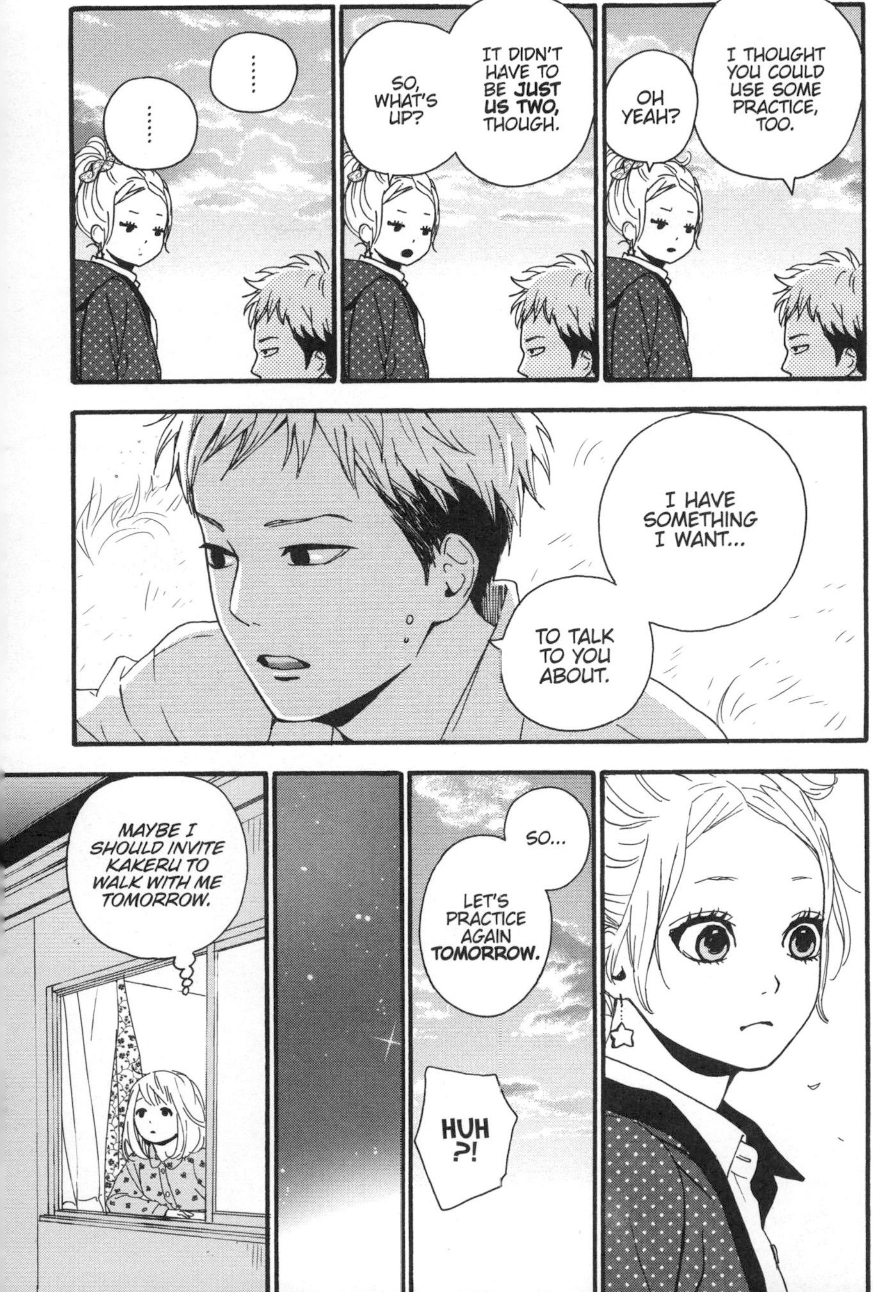
I THOUGHT YOU COULD USE SOME PRACTICE, TOO.
OH YEAH?
IT DIDN'T HAVE TO BE JUST US TWO, THOUGH.
SO, WHAT'S UP?
......
......
I HAVE SOMETHING I WANT...
TO TALK TO YOU ABOUT.
SO...
LET'S PRACTICE AGAIN TOMORROW.
HUH ?!
MAYBE I SHOULD INVITE KAKERU TO WALK WITH ME TOMORROW.

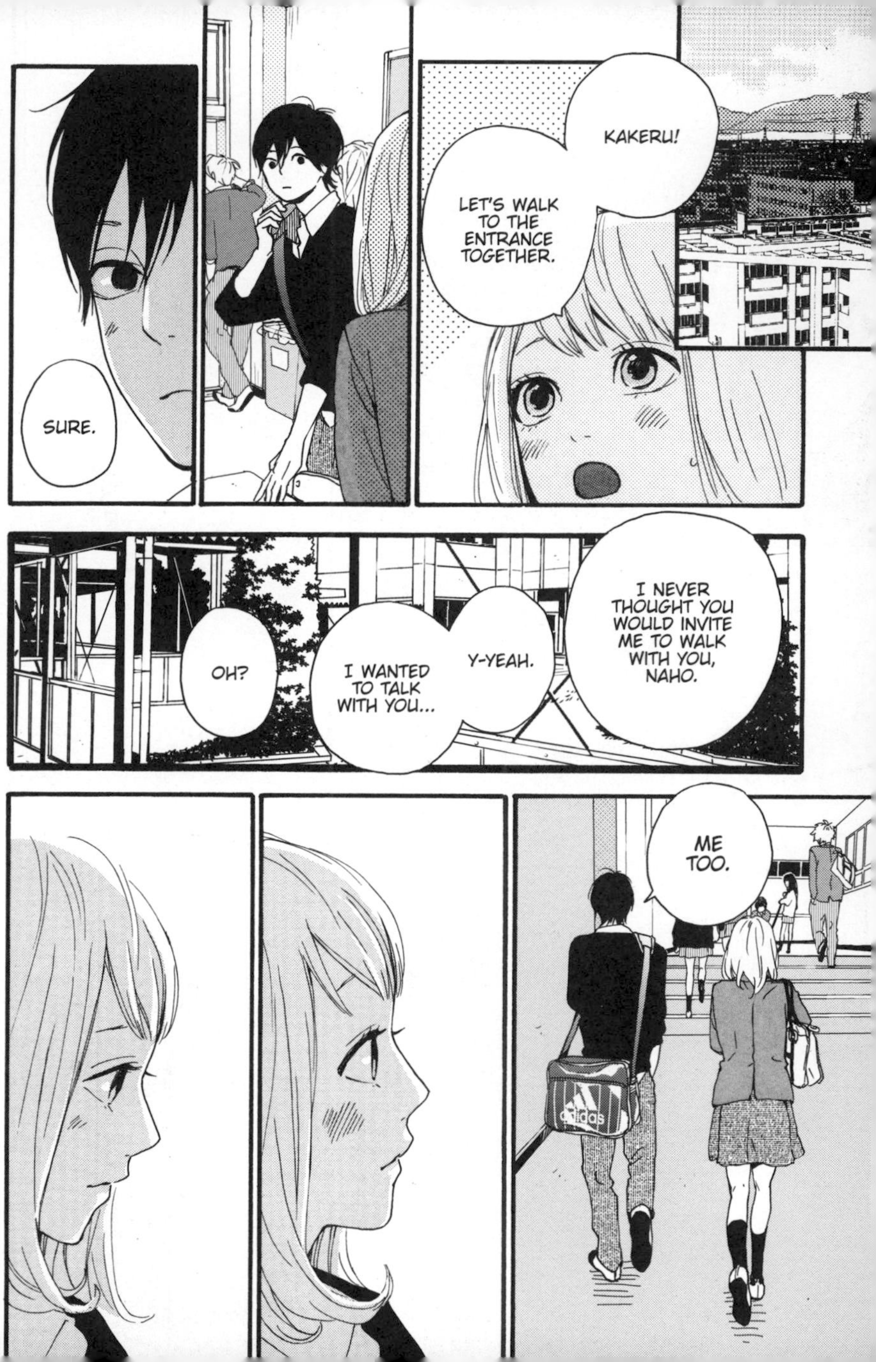
KAKERU!
LET'S WALK TO THE ENTRANCE TOGETHER.
SURE.
I NEVER THOUGHT YOU WOULD INVITE ME TO WALK WITH YOU, NAHO.
Y-YEAH.
I WANTED TO TALK WITH YOU...
OH?
ME TOO.
adidas

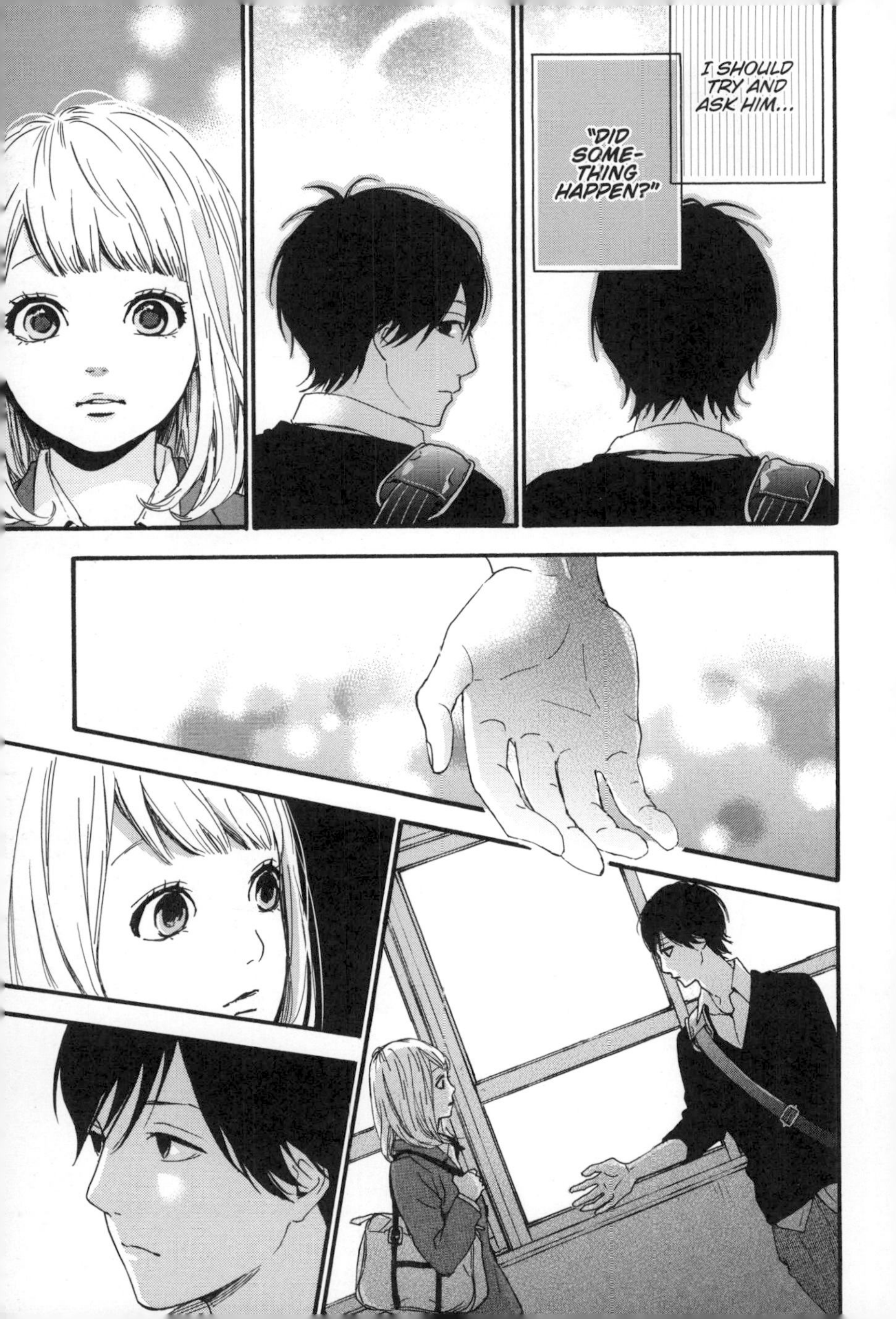
I SHOULD TRY AND ASK HIM...
"DID SOME-THING HAPPEN?"

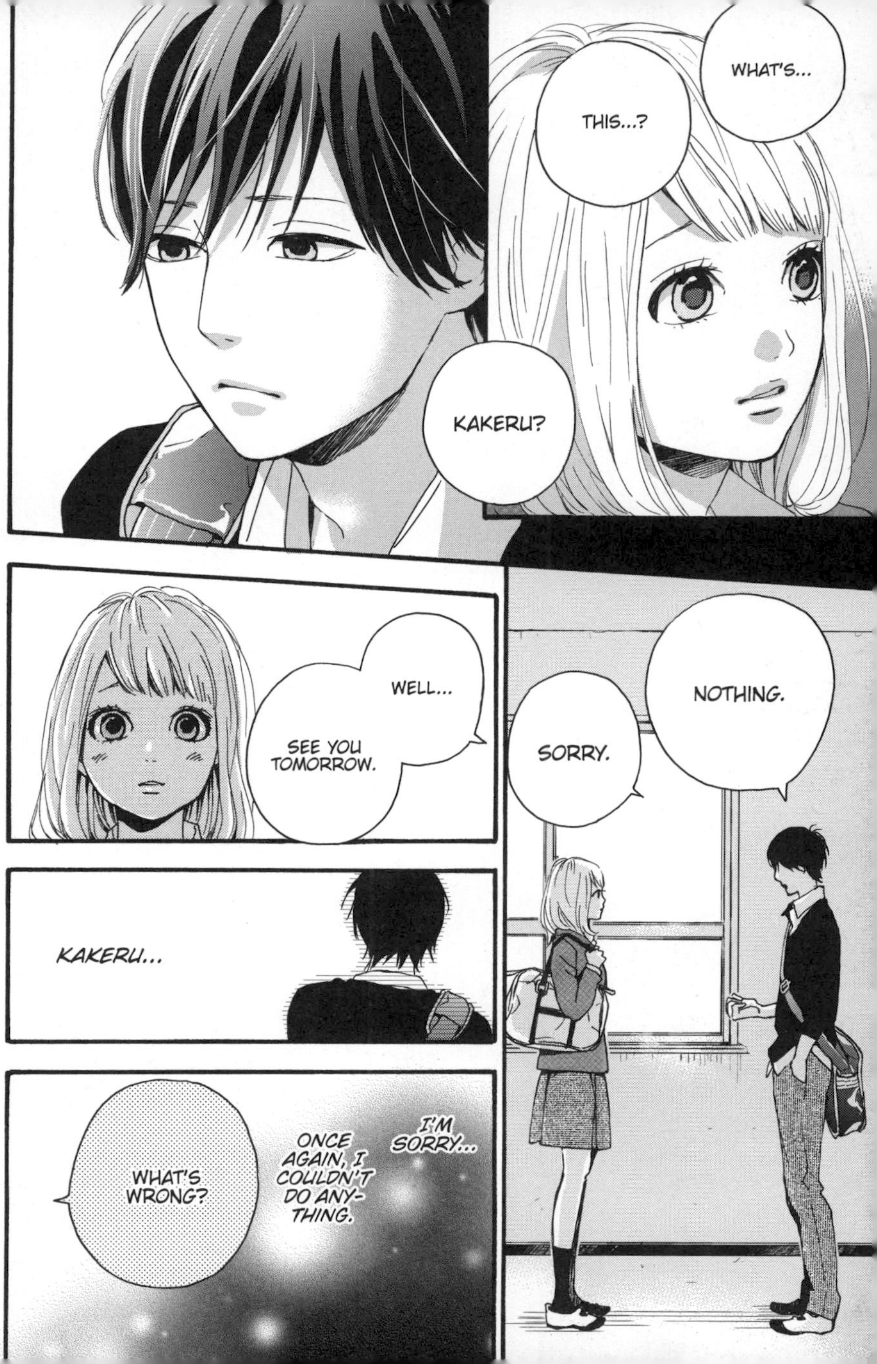
WHAT'S...
THIS...?
KAKERU?
NOTHING.
SORRY.
WELL...
SEE YOU TOMORROW.
KAKERU...
I'M SORRY...
ONCE AGAIN, I COULDN'T DO ANY-THING.
WHAT'S WRONG?

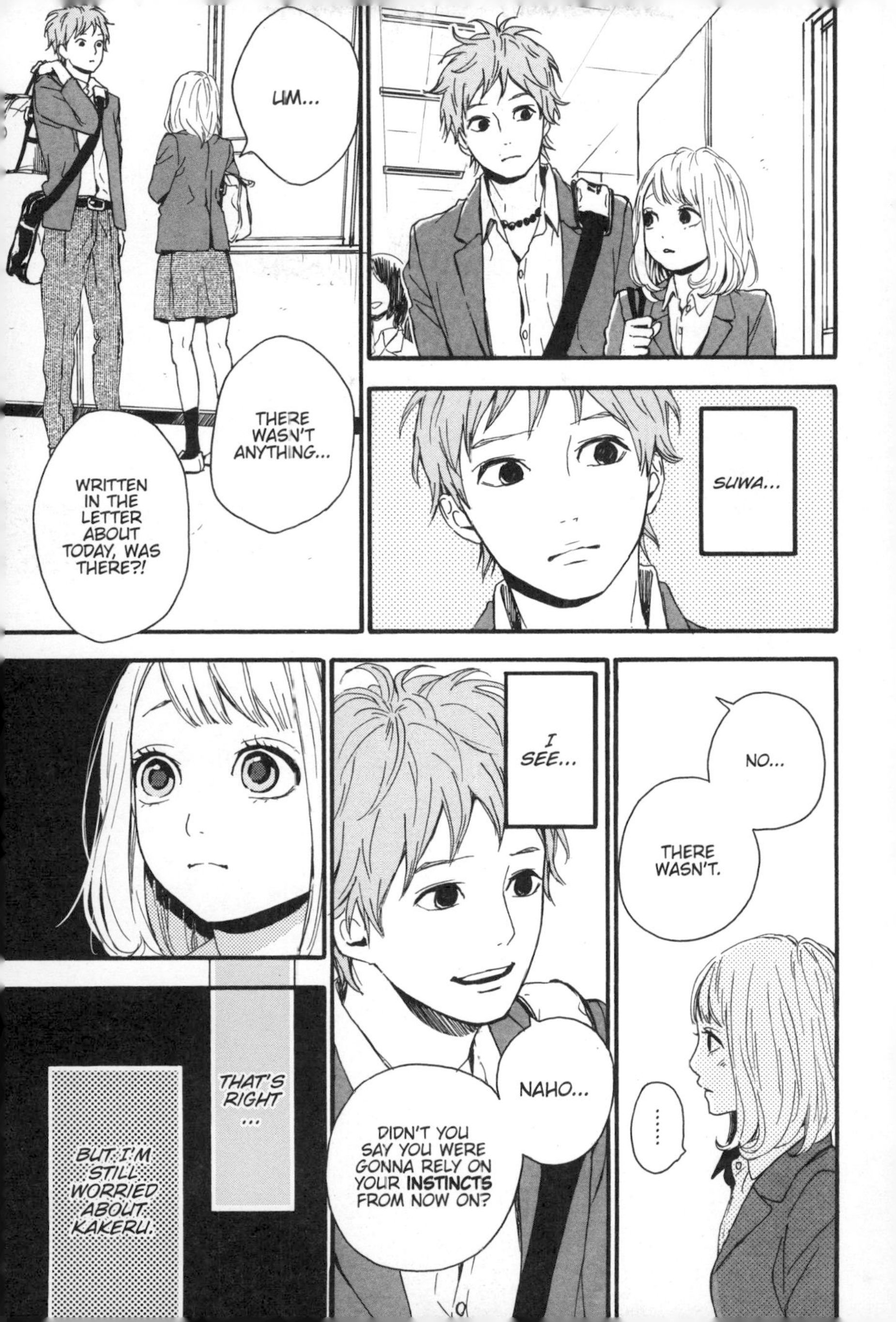
SUWA...
UM...
THERE WASN'T ANYTHING...
WRITTEN IN THE LETTER ABOUT TODAY, WAS THERE?!
NO...
THERE WASN'T.
......
I SEE...
NAHO...
DIDN'T YOU SAY YOU WERE GONNA RELY ON YOUR **INSTINCTS** FROM NOW ON?
THAT'S RIGHT...
BUT I'M STILL WORRIED ABOUT KAKERU.

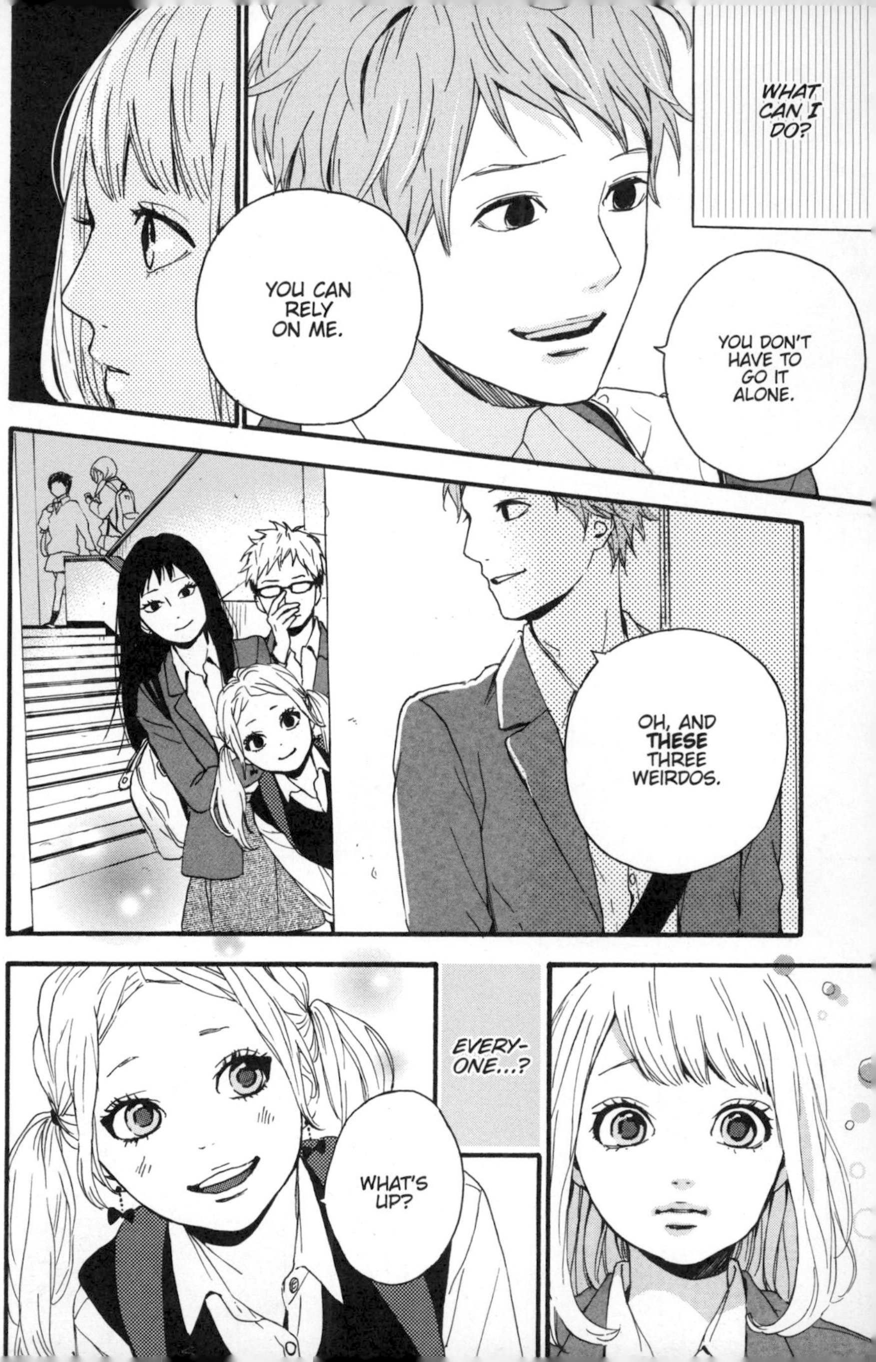
WHAT CAN I DO?
YOU DON'T HAVE TO GO IT ALONE.
YOU CAN RELY ON ME.
OH, AND **THESE** THREE WEIRDOS.
EVERY-ONE...?
WHAT'S UP?

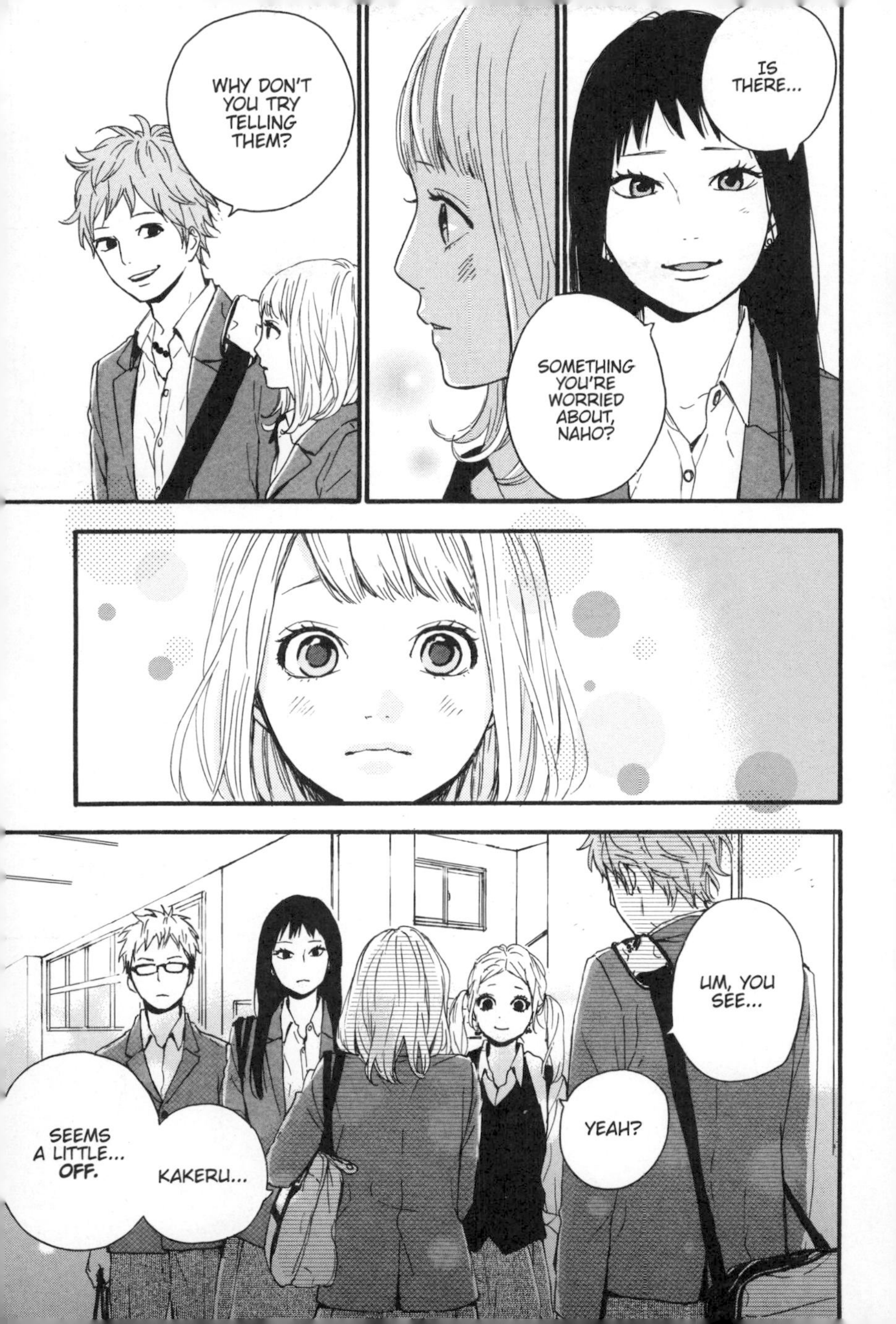
IS THERE...
SOMETHING YOU'RE WORRIED ABOUT, NAHO?
WHY DON'T YOU TRY TELLING THEM?
UM, YOU SEE...
YEAH?
KAKERU...
SEEMS A LITTLE... OFF.

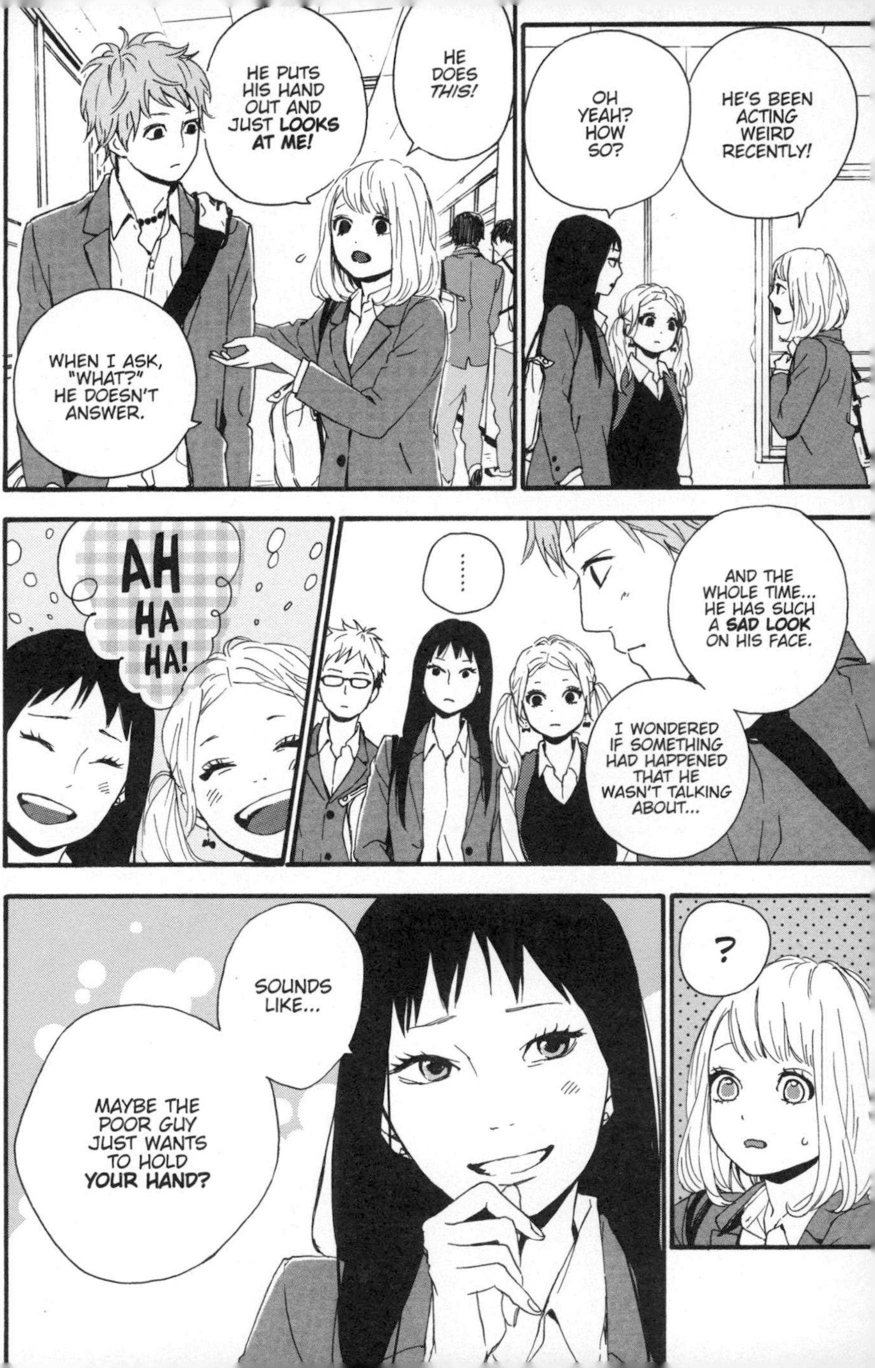
HE'S BEEN ACTING WEIRD RECENTLY!
OH YEAH? HOW SO?
HE DOES THIS!
HE PUTS HIS HAND OUT AND JUST LOOKS AT ME!
WHEN I ASK, "WHAT?" HE DOESN'T ANSWER.
AND THE WHOLE TIME... HE HAS SUCH A SAD LOOK ON HIS FACE.
I WONDERED IF SOMETHING HAD HAPPENED THAT HE WASN'T TALKING ABOUT...
......
AH HA HA!
?
SOUNDS LIKE...
MAYBE THE POOR GUY JUST WANTS TO HOLD YOUR HAND?

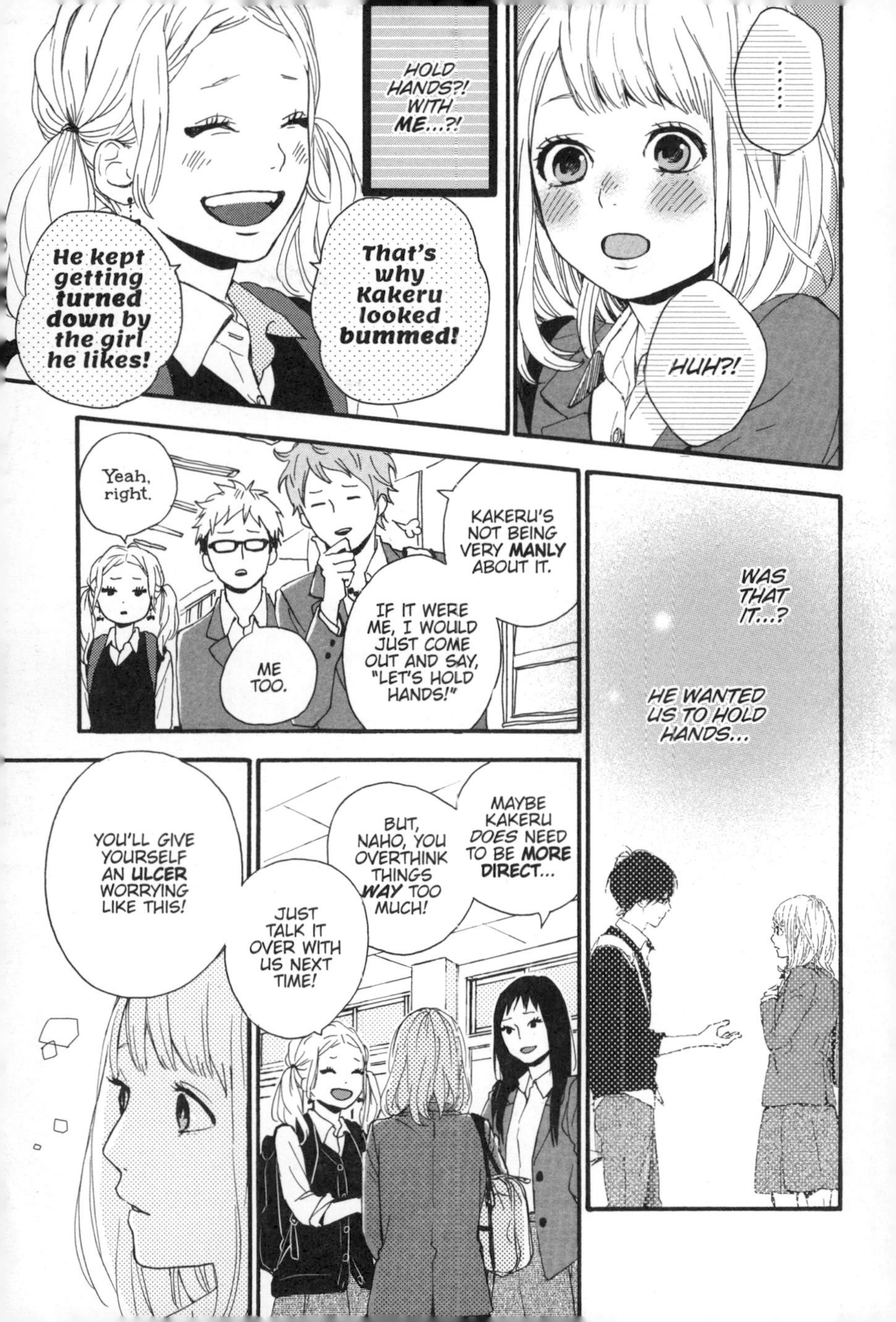
……
HUH?!
HOLD HANDS?! WITH ME…?!
That's why Kakeru looked bummed!
He kept getting turned down by the girl he likes!
WAS THAT IT…?
HE WANTED US TO HOLD HANDS…
KAKERU'S NOT BEING VERY MANLY ABOUT IT.
IF IT WERE ME, I WOULD JUST COME OUT AND SAY, "LET'S HOLD HANDS!"
Yeah, right.
ME TOO.
MAYBE KAKERU DOES NEED TO BE MORE DIRECT…
BUT, NAHO, YOU OVERTHINK THINGS WAY TOO MUCH!
JUST TALK IT OVER WITH US NEXT TIME!
YOU'LL GIVE YOURSELF AN ULCER WORRYING LIKE THIS!

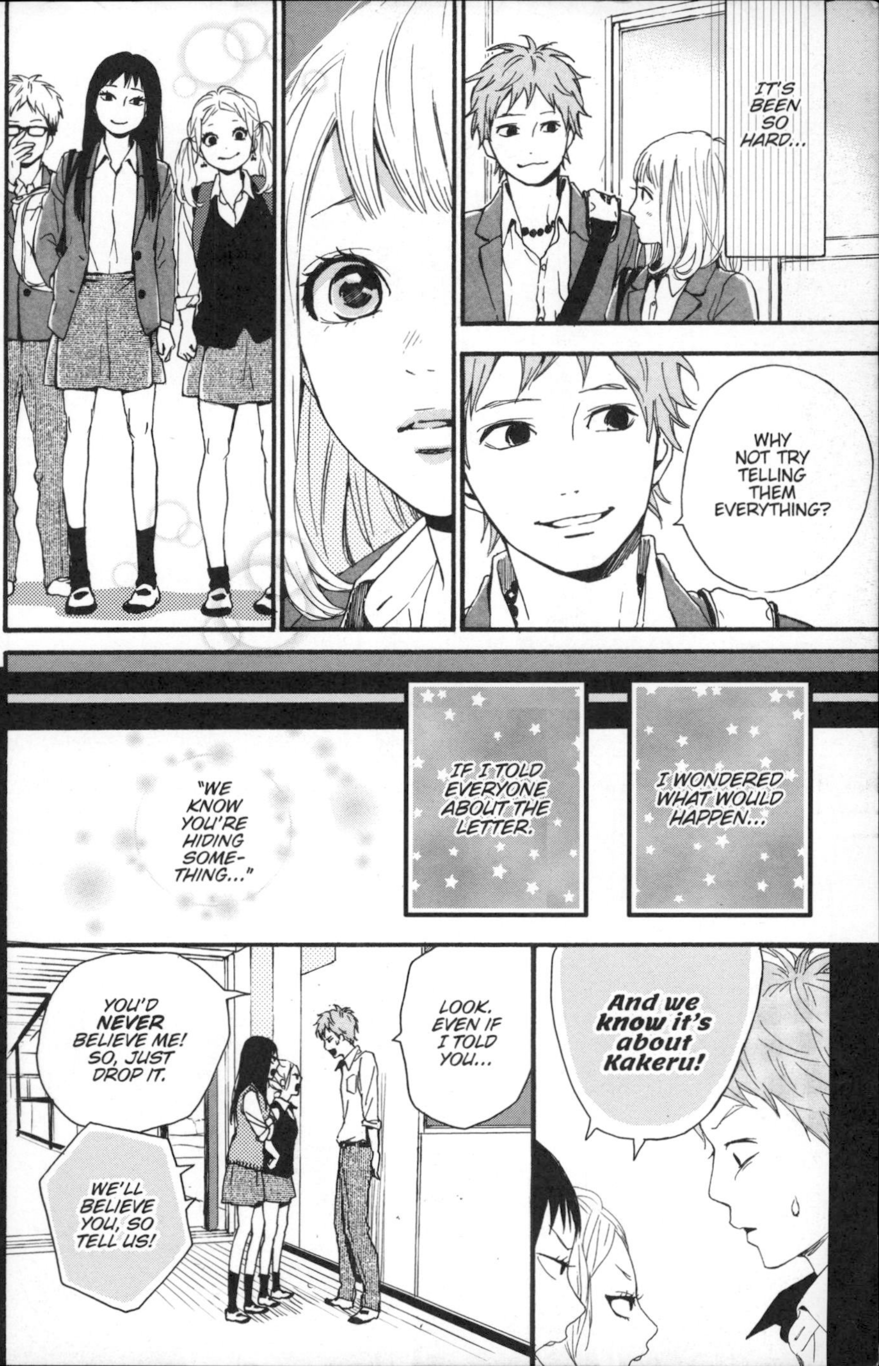
IT'S BEEN SO HARD...
WHY NOT TRY TELLING THEM EVERYTHING?
I WONDERED WHAT WOULD HAPPEN...
IF I TOLD EVERYONE ABOUT THE LETTER.
"WE KNOW YOU'RE HIDING SOME-THING..."
And we know it's about Kakeru!
LOOK. EVEN IF I TOLD YOU...
YOU'D NEVER BELIEVE ME! SO, JUST DROP IT.
WE'LL BELIEVE YOU, SO TELL US!

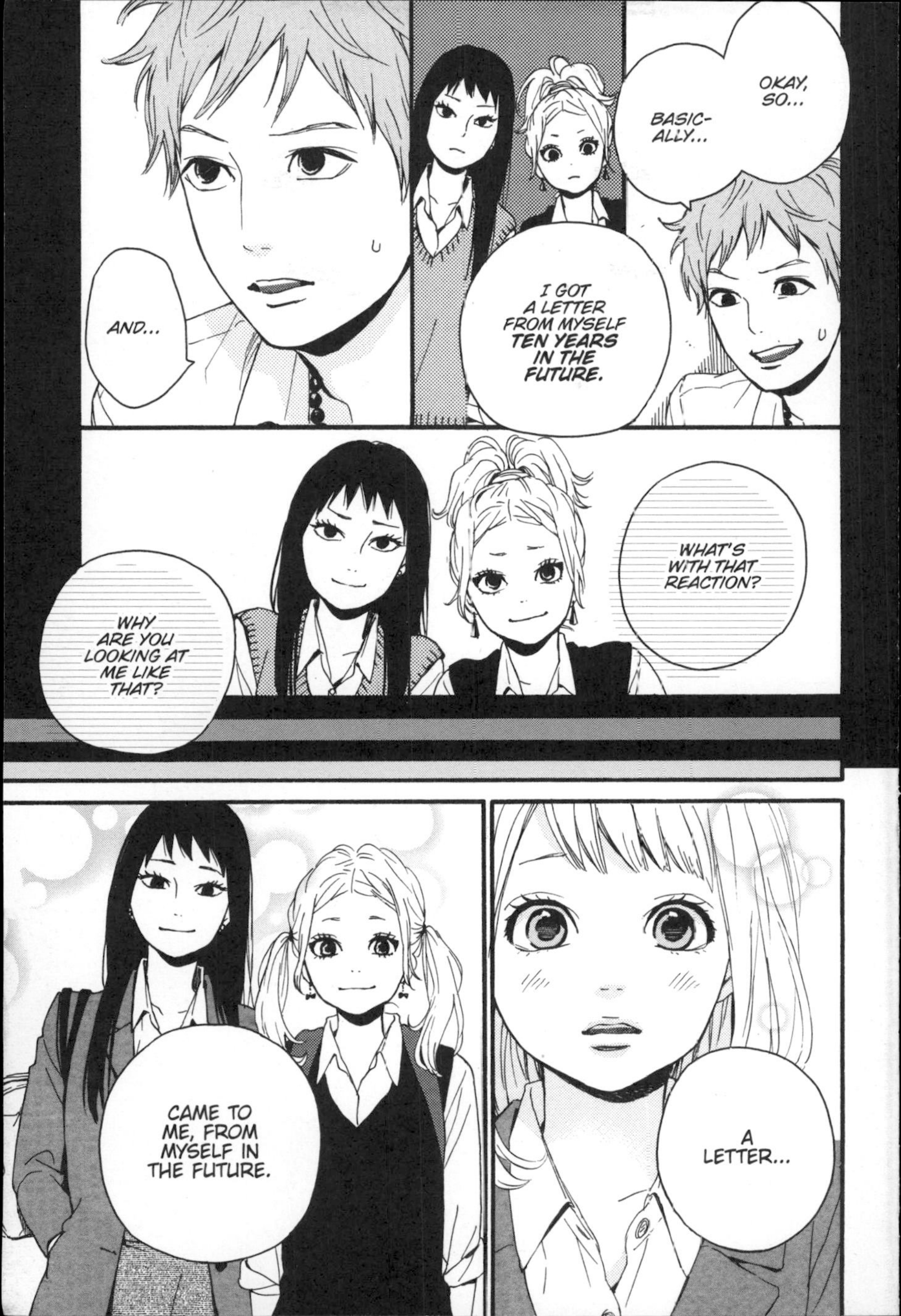
OKAY, SO...
BASIC-ALLY...
I GOT A LETTER FROM MYSELF TEN YEARS IN THE FUTURE.
AND...
WHAT'S WITH THAT REACTION?
WHY ARE YOU LOOKING AT ME LIKE THAT?
A LETTER...
CAME TO ME, FROM MYSELF IN THE FUTURE.

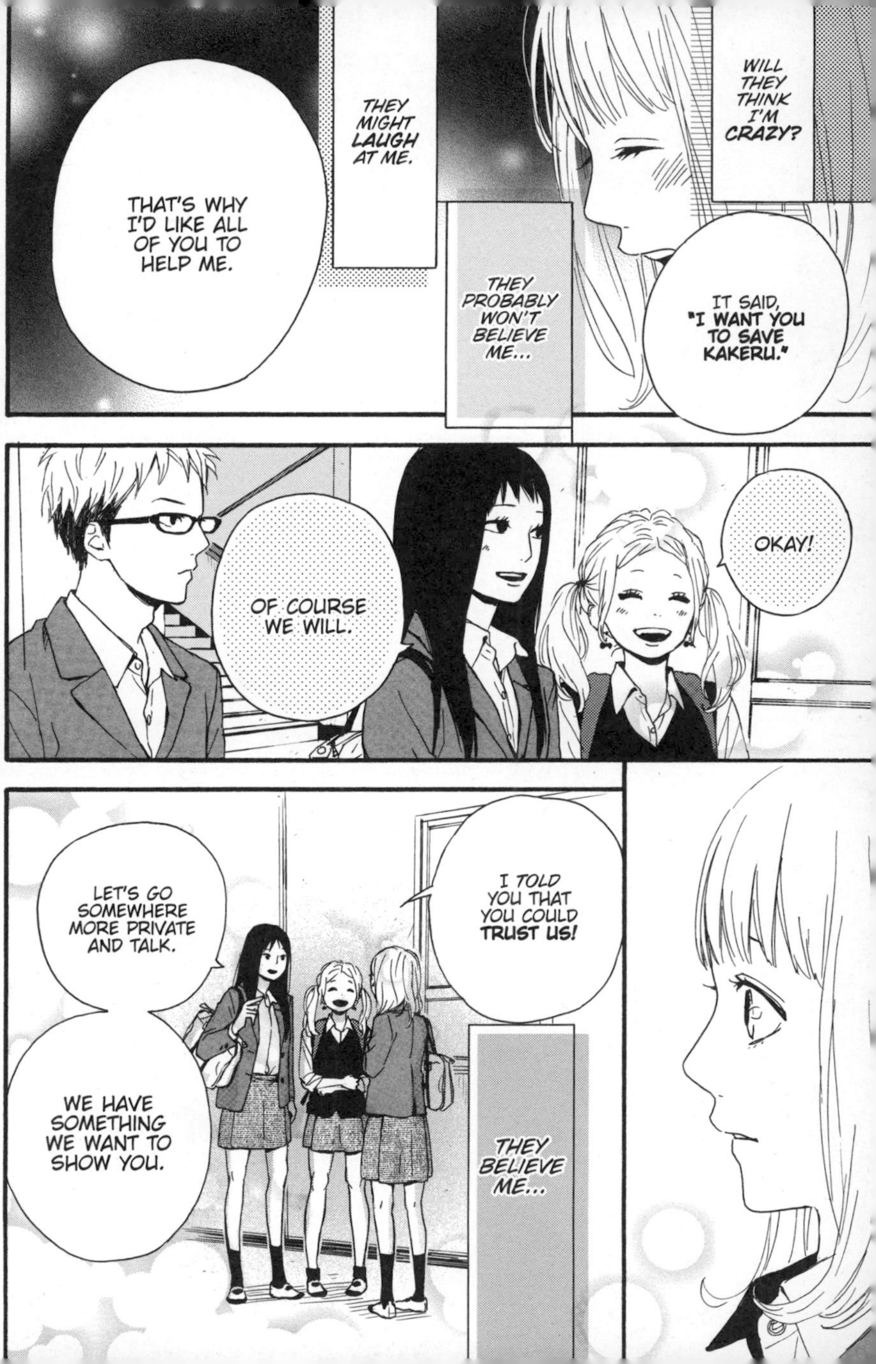

WILL THEY THINK I'M CRAZY?
IT SAID, "I WANT YOU TO SAVE KAKERU."
THEY PROBABLY WON'T BELIEVE ME...
THEY MIGHT LAUGH AT ME.
THAT'S WHY I'D LIKE ALL OF YOU TO HELP ME.
OKAY!
OF COURSE WE WILL.
I TOLD YOU THAT YOU COULD TRUST US!
THEY BELIEVE ME...
LET'S GO SOMEWHERE MORE PRIVATE AND TALK.
WE HAVE SOMETHING WE WANT TO SHOW YOU.

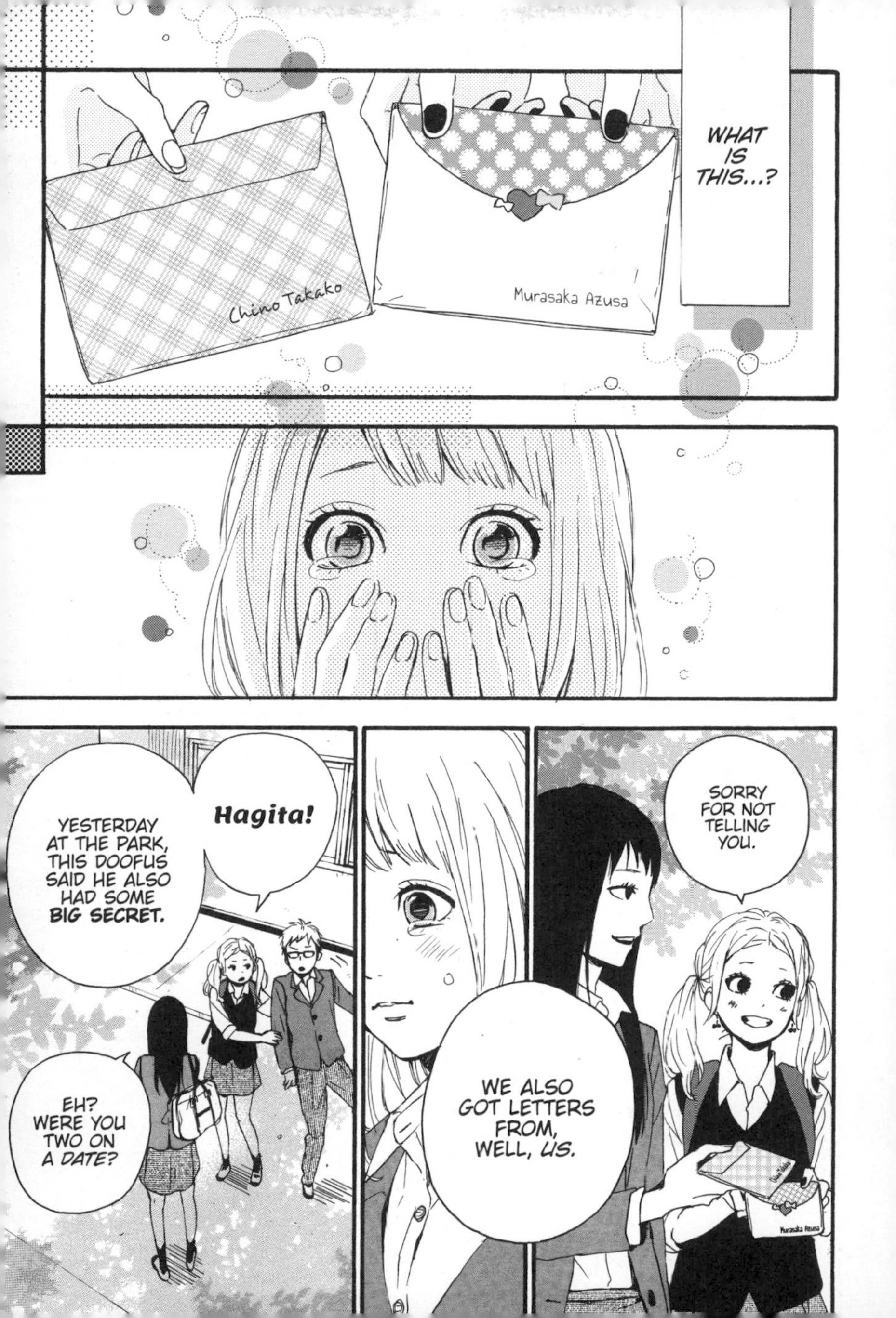
WHAT IS THIS...?
Murasaka Azusa
Chino Takako
SORRY FOR NOT TELLING YOU.
WE ALSO GOT LETTERS FROM, WELL, US.
Murasaka Azusa
Hagita!
YESTERDAY AT THE PARK, THIS DOOFUS SAID HE ALSO HAD SOME BIG SECRET.
EH? WERE YOU TWO ON A DATE?

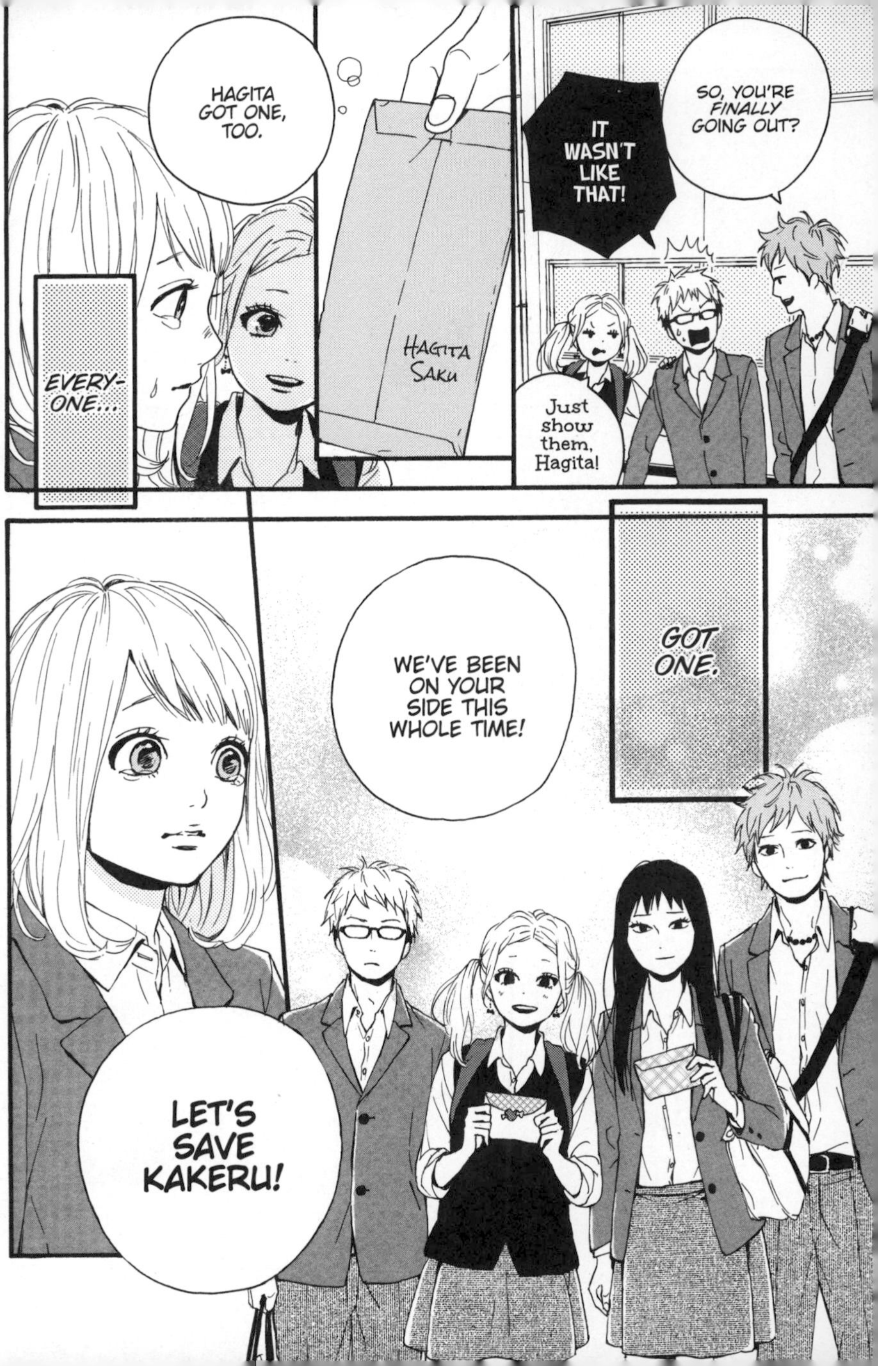
SO, YOU'RE FINALLY GOING OUT?
IT WASN'T LIKE THAT!
Just show them, Hagita!
HAGITA GOT ONE, TOO.
HAGITA SAKU
EVERY-ONE...
GOT ONE.
WE'VE BEEN ON YOUR SIDE THIS WHOLE TIME!
LET'S SAVE KAKERU!

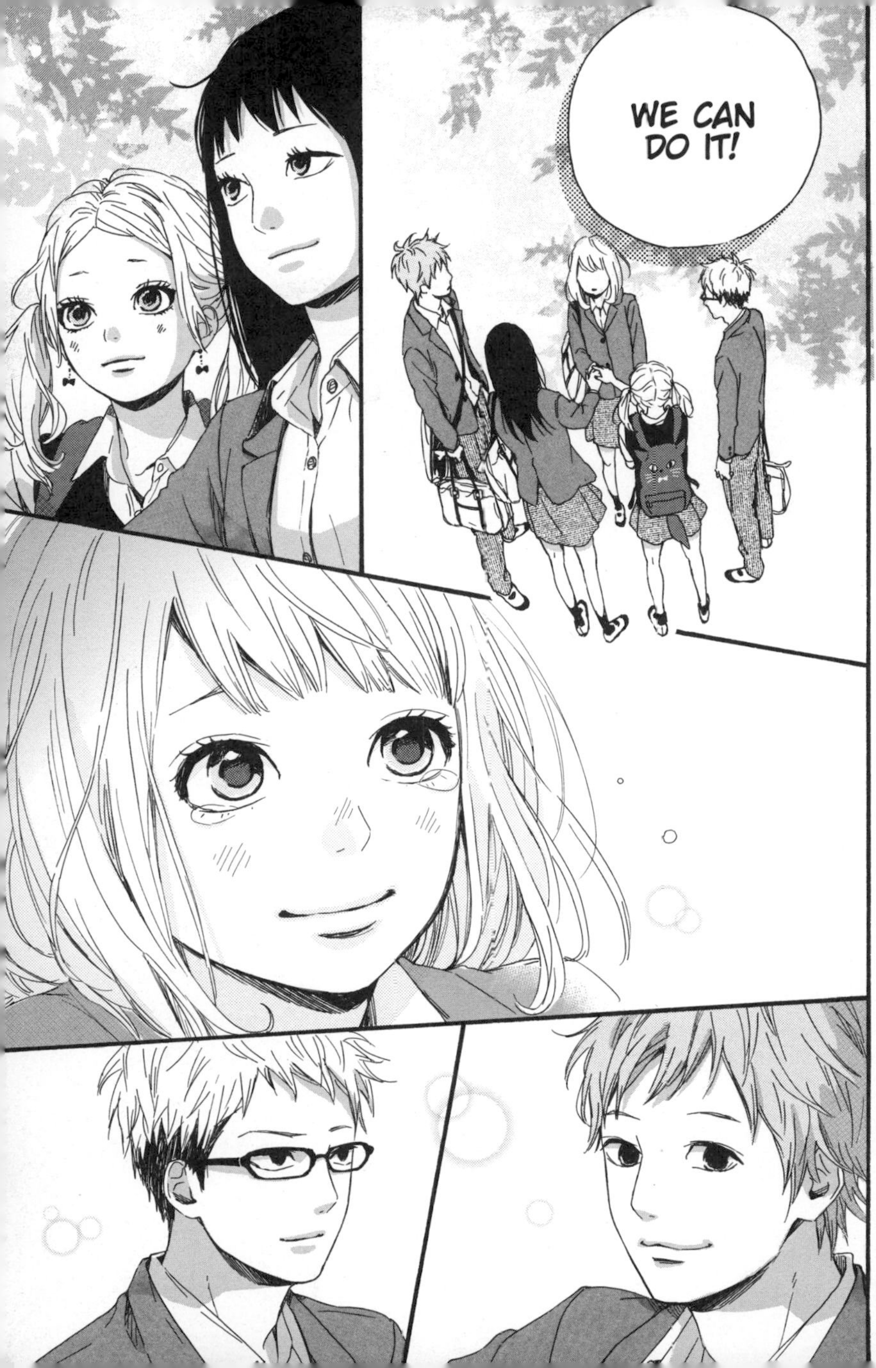
WE CAN DO IT!

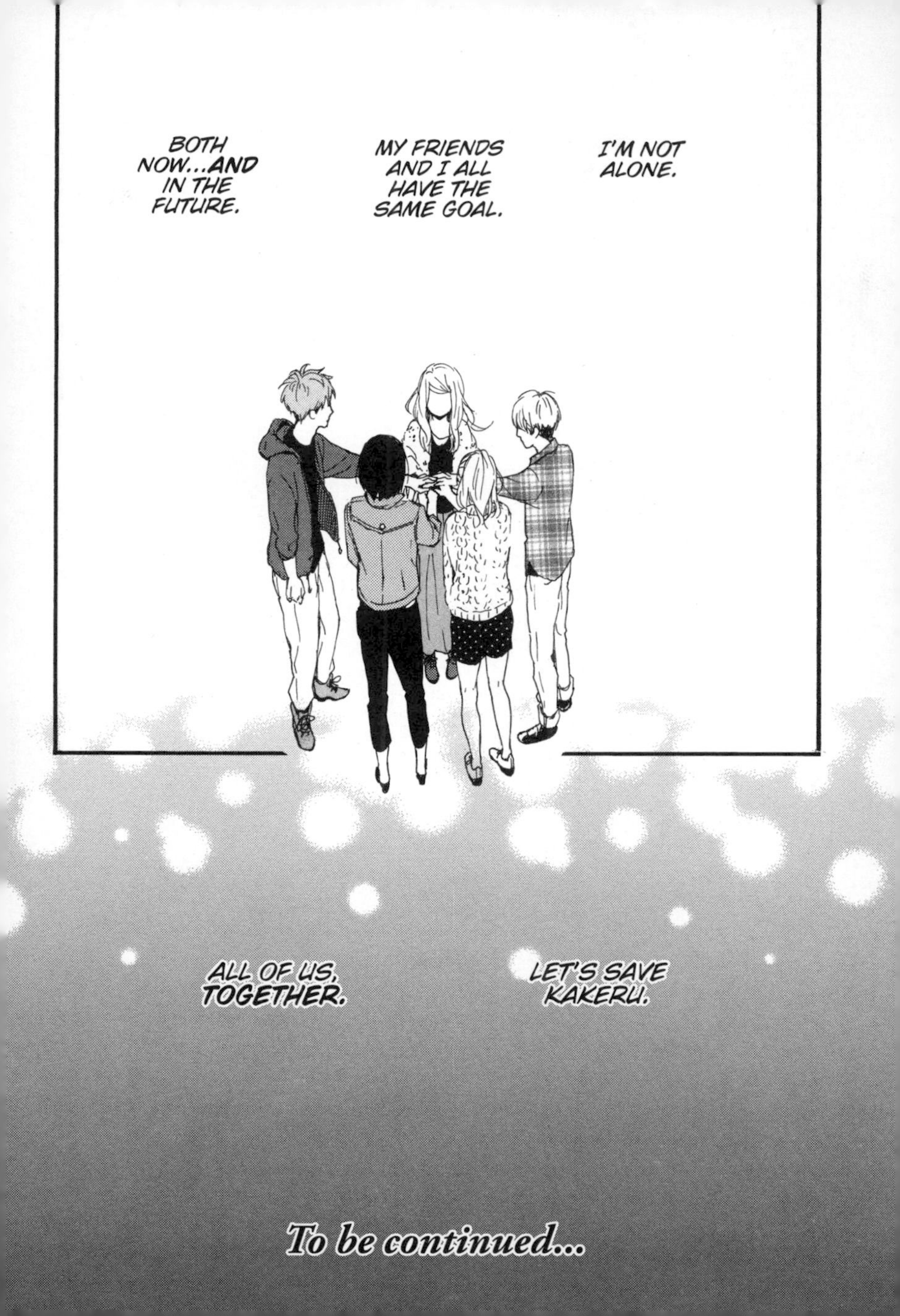
I'M NOT ALONE.
MY FRIENDS AND I ALL HAVE THE SAME GOAL.
BOTH NOW...AND IN THE FUTURE.
LET'S SAVE KAKERU.
ALL OF US, TOGETHER.
To be continued...

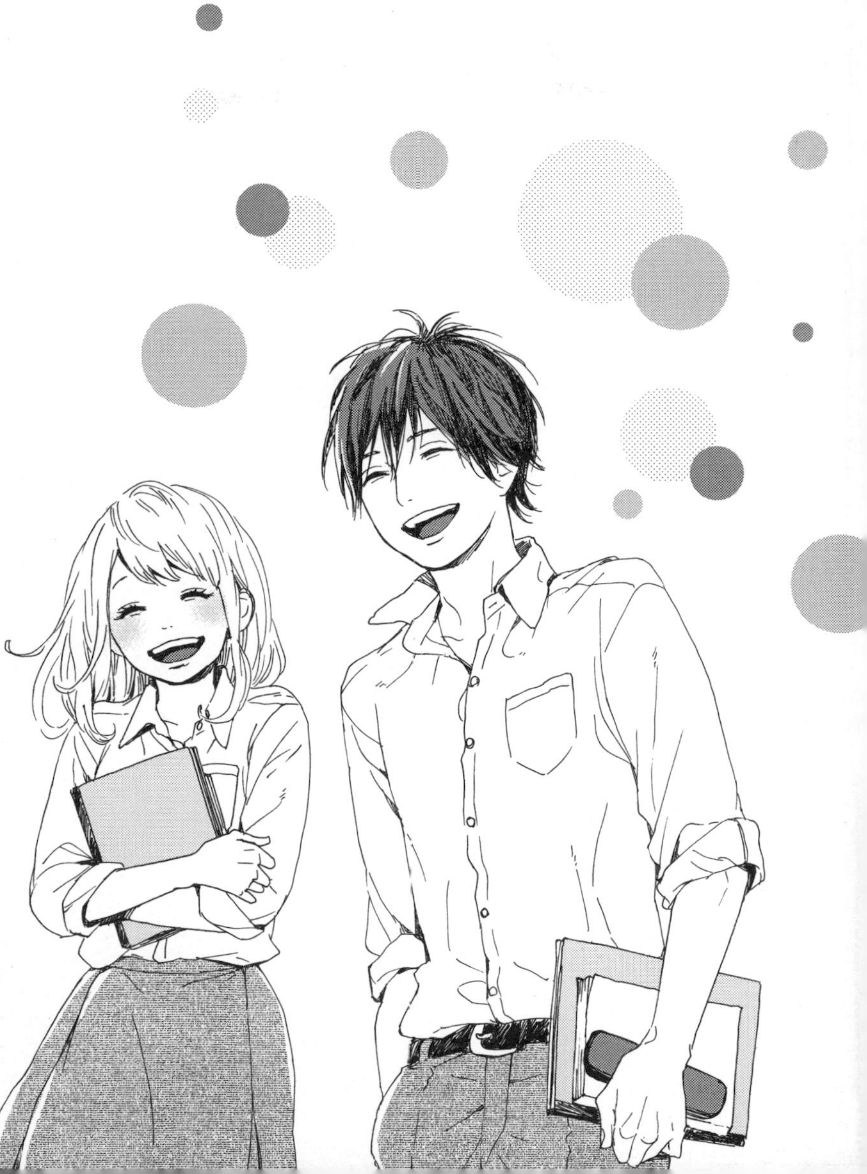

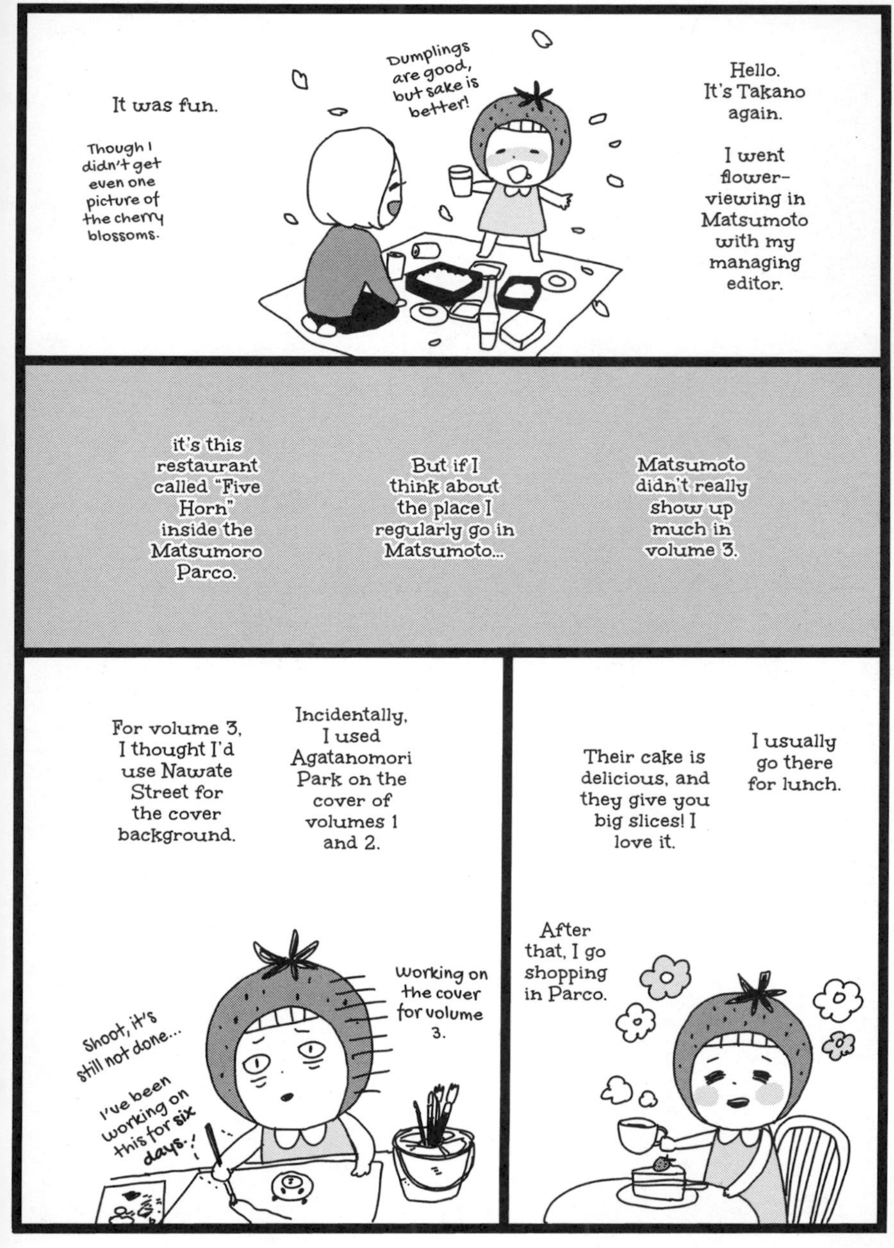
Hello. It's Takano again.
I went flower-viewing in Matsumoto with my managing editor.
Dumplings are good, but sake is better!
It was fun.
Though I didn't get even one picture of the cherry blossoms.
Matsumoto didn't really show up much in volume 3.
But if I think about the place I regularly go in Matsumoto...
it's this restaurant called "Five Horn" inside the Matsumoro Parco.
I usually go there for lunch.
Their cake is delicious, and they give you big slices! I love it.
After that, I go shopping in Parco.
Incidentally, I used Agatanomori Park on the cover of volumes 1 and 2.
For volume 3, I thought I'd use Nawate Street for the cover background.
Working on the cover for volume 3.
Shoot, it's still not done...
I've been working on this for **six days..!**

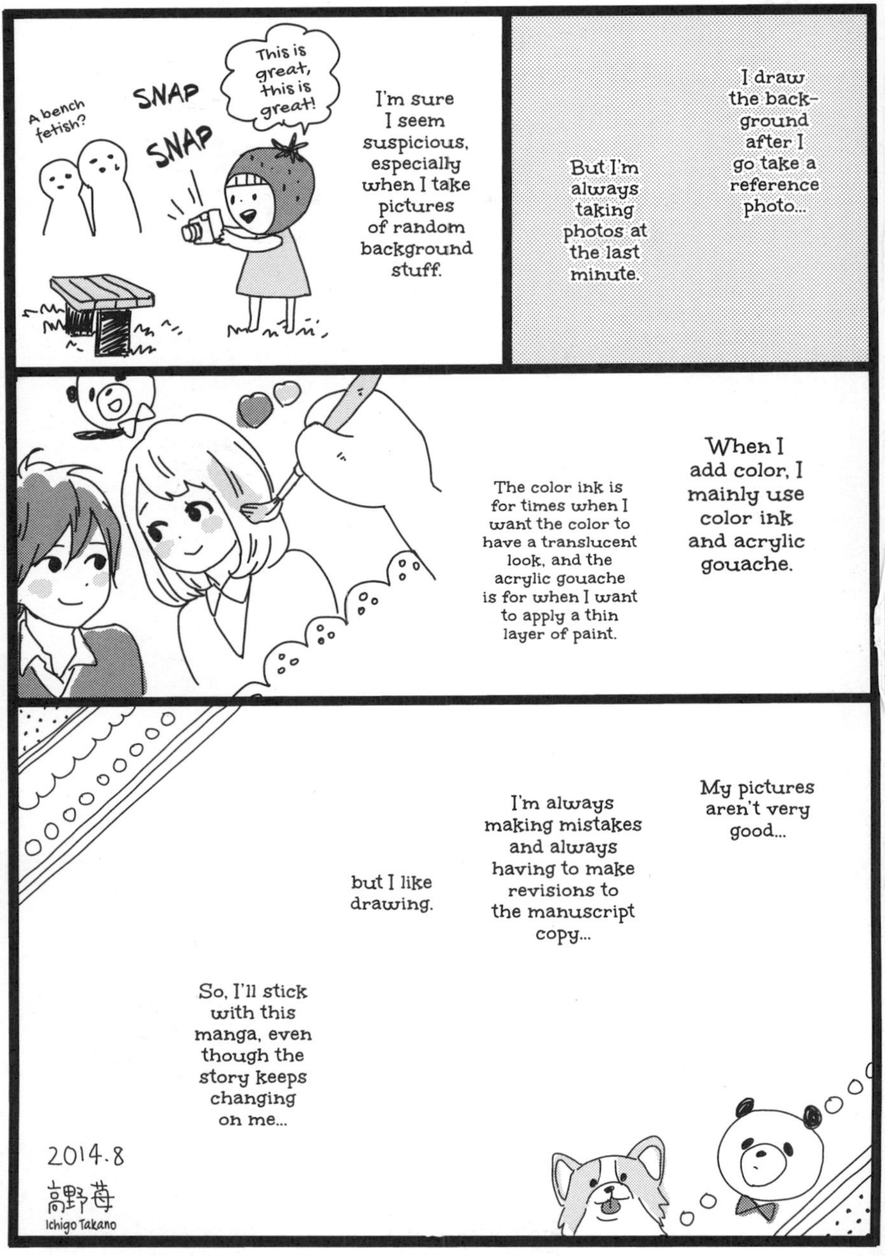
I draw the background after I go take a reference photo...
But I'm always taking photos at the last minute.
I'm sure I seem suspicious, especially when I take pictures of random background stuff.
This is great, this is great!
SNAP
SNAP
A bench fetish?
When I add color, I mainly use color ink and acrylic gouache.
The color ink is for times when I want the color to have a translucent look, and the acrylic gouache is for when I want to apply a thin layer of paint.
My pictures aren't very good...
I'm always making mistakes and always having to make revisions to the manuscript copy...
but I like drawing.
So, I'll stick with this manga, even though the story keeps changing on me...
2014.8
高野苺
Ichigo Takano

SEVEN SEAS ENTERTAINMENT PRESENTS

orange
THE COMPLETE COLLECTION 1

story and art by Ichigo Takano

TRANSLATION
Amber Tamosaitis

ADAPTATION
Shannon Fay

LETTERING AND LAYOUT
Lys Blakeslee

COVER DESIGN
Nicky Lim

PROOFREADER
Shanti Whitesides

PRODUCTION MANAGER
Lissa Pattillo

EDITOR IN CHIEF
Adam Arnold

PUBLISHER
Jason DeAngelis

ORANGE: THE COMPLETE COLLECTION 1 (VOLUMES 1-3)
© Ichigo Takano 2012
All rights reserved.
First published in Japan in 2013 by Futabasha Publishers Ltd., Tokyo.
English version published by Seven Seas Entertainment, LLC.
Under license from Futabasha Publishers Ltd.

Seven Seas books may be purchased in bulk for educational, business, or promotional use. For information on bulk purchases, please contact Macmillan Corporate & Premium Sales Department at 1-800-221-7945 (ext 5442) or write specialmarkets@macmillan.com.

Seven Seas and the Seven Seas logo are trademarks of Seven Seas Entertainment, LLC. All rights reserved.

ISBN: 978-1-626923-02-7

Printed in China

Second Printing: September 2021

10 9 8 7 6 5 4 3

FOLLOW US ONLINE: *www.gomanga.com*

READING DIRECTIONS

This book reads from *right to left*, Japanese style. If this is your first time reading manga, you start reading from the top right panel on each page and take it from there. If you get lost, just follow the numbered diagram here. It may seem backwards at first, but you'll get the hang of it! Have fun!!

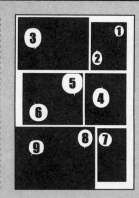